The Writings of Herman Melville

The Northwestern–Newberry Edition

VOLUME NINE

The Piazza Tales

and Other Prose Pieces

1839–1860

This volume edited by
HARRISON HAYFORD
ALMA A. MACDOUGALL
G. THOMAS TANSELLE
and others

Historical Note by
MERTON M. SEALTS, JR.

Associates
RICHARD COLLES JOHNSON
BRIAN HIGGINS
LYNN HORTH
R. D. MADISON
ROBERT C. RYAN
DONALD YANNELLA

Contributing Scholars
MARY K. BERCAW
PATRICIA L. WARD

Editorial Coordinator
ALMA A. MACDOUGALL

The Piazza Tales

and Other Prose Pieces

1839–1860

HERMAN MELVILLE

NORTHWESTERN UNIVERSITY PRESS
and
THE NEWBERRY LIBRARY

Evanston and Chicago
1987

The Research *leading to the establishment of the text printed herein exclusive of "Statues in Rome," "The South Seas," and "Traveling" was undertaken pursuant to a contract with the United States Department of Health, Education, and Welfare, Office of Education, under the provisions of the Coöperative Research Program. The research pertaining to Melville's lectures was previously conducted by Merton M. Sealts, Jr., for the volume* Melville as Lecturer *(Cambridge, Massachusetts: Harvard University Press, 1957), and materials from that publication are incorporated herein with the authorization of Harvard University Press. The Historical Note was prepared independently of the text.*

Publication of the Northwestern-Newberry Edition of The Writings of Herman Melville *has been made possible through the financial support of Northwestern University and its Research Committee, and of The Newberry Library. Northwestern University Press produced and published this edition and reserves all rights.*

Library of Congress Catalog Card Number 87-60937

Printed in the United States of America

First Printing, 1987
Second Printing, 1992
Third Printing, 1995

Textual change in this printing: 418.24 some are killed

Cloth Edition, ISBN 0-8101-0550-0
Paper Edition, ISBN 0-8101-0551-9

Contents

EDITORIAL APPENDIX

The Piazza Tales

The Piazza

"With fairest flowers,
Whilst summer lasts, and I live here, Fidele—"

WHEN I REMOVED into the country, it was to occupy an old-fashioned farm-house, which had no piazza—a deficiency the more regretted, because not only did I like piazzas as somehow combining the coziness of in-doors with the freedom of out-doors, and it is so pleasant to inspect your thermometer there, but the country round about was such a picture, that in berry time no boy climbs hill or crosses vale without coming upon easels planted in every nook, and sun-burnt painters painting there. A very paradise of painters. The circle of the stars cut by the circle of the mountains. At least, so looks it from the house; though, once upon the mountains, no circle of them can you see. Had the site been chosen five rods off, this charmed ring would not have been.

The house is old. Seventy years since, from the heart of the Hearth Stone Hills, they quarried the Kaaba, or Holy Stone, to which, each Thanksgiving, the social pilgrims used to come. So long ago, that, in digging for the foundation, the workmen used both spade and axe, fighting the Troglodytes of those subterranean parts—sturdy roots of a sturdy wood, encamped upon what is now a long land-slide of sleeping meadow, sloping away off from my poppy-bed. Of that knit wood, but one survivor stands—an elm, lonely through steadfastness.

Whoever built the house, he builded better than he knew; or else

Orion in the zenith flashed down his Damocles' sword to him some starry night, and said, "Build there." For how, otherwise, could it have entered the builder's mind, that, upon the clearing being made, such a purple prospect would be his?—nothing less than Greylock, with all his hills about him, like Charlemagne among his peers.

Now, for a house, so situated in such a country, to have no piazza for the convenience of those who might desire to feast upon the view, and take their time and ease about it, seemed as much of an omission as if a picture-gallery should have no bench; for what but picture-galleries are the marble halls of these same limestone hills?—galleries hung, month after month anew, with pictures ever fading into pictures ever fresh. And beauty is like piety—you cannot run and read it; tranquillity and constancy, with, now-a-days, an easy chair, are needed. For though, of old, when reverence was in vogue, and indolence was not, the devotees of Nature, doubtless, used to stand and adore—just as, in the cathedrals of those ages, the worshipers of a higher Power did—yet, in these times of failing faith and feeble knees, we have the piazza and the pew.

During the first year of my residence, the more leisurely to witness the coronation of Charlemagne (weather permitting, they crown him every sunrise and sunset), I chose me, on the hill-side bank near by, a royal lounge of turf—a green velvet lounge, with long, moss-padded back; while at the head, strangely enough, there grew (but, I suppose, for heraldry) three tufts of blue violets in a field-argent of wild strawberries; and a trellis, with honey-suckle, I set for canopy. Very majestical lounge, indeed. So much so, that here, as with the reclining majesty of Denmark in his orchard, a sly ear-ache invaded me. But, if damps abound at times in Westminster Abbey, because it is so old, why not within this monastery of mountains, which is older?

A piazza must be had.

The house was wide—my fortune narrow; so that, to build a panoramic piazza, one round and round, it could not be—although, indeed, considering the matter by rule and square, the carpenters, in the kindest way, were anxious to gratify my furthest wishes, at I've forgotten how much a foot.

Upon but one of the four sides would prudence grant me what I wanted. Now, which side?

To the east, that long camp of the Hearth Stone Hills, fading far away towards Quito; and every fall, a small white flake of something peering suddenly, of a coolish morning, from the topmost cliff—the season's new-dropped lamb, its earliest fleece; and then the Christmas dawn, draping those dun highlands with red-barred plaids and tartans—goodly sight from your piazza, that. Goodly sight; but, to the north is Charlemagne—can't have the Hearth Stone Hills with Charlemagne.

Well, the south side. Apple-trees are there. Pleasant, of a balmy morning, in the month of May, to sit and see that orchard, white-budded, as for a bridal; and, in October, one green arsenal yard; such piles of ruddy shot. Very fine, I grant; but, to the north is Charlemagne.

The west side, look. An upland pasture, alleying away into a maple wood at top. Sweet, in opening spring, to trace upon the hill-side, otherwise gray and bare—to trace, I say, the oldest paths by their streaks of earliest green. Sweet, indeed, I can't deny; but, to the north is Charlemagne.

So Charlemagne, he carried it. It was not long after 1848; and, somehow, about that time, all round the world, these kings, they had the casting vote, and voted for themselves.

No sooner was ground broken, than all the neighborhood, neighbor Dives, in particular, broke, too—into a laugh. Piazza to the north! Winter piazza! Wants, of winter midnights, to watch the Aurora Borealis, I suppose; hope he's laid in good store of Polar muffs and mittens.

That was in the lion month of March. Not forgotten are the blue noses of the carpenters, and how they scouted at the greenness of the cit, who would build his sole piazza to the north. But March don't last forever; patience, and August comes. And then, in the cool elysium of my northern bower, I, Lazarus in Abraham's bosom, cast down the hill a pitying glance on poor old Dives, tormented in the purgatory of his piazza to the south.

But, even in December, this northern piazza does not repel—nipping cold and gusty though it be, and the north wind, like any miller, bolting by the snow, in finest flour—for then, once more, with frosted beard, I pace the sleety deck, weathering Cape Horn.

In summer, too, Canute-like, sitting here, one is often reminded of the sea. For not only do long ground-swells roll the slanting grain, and little wavelets of the grass ripple over upon the low piazza, as their beach, and the blown down of dandelions is wafted like the spray, and the purple of the mountains is just the purple of the billows, and a still August noon broods upon the deep meadows, as a calm upon the Line; but the vastness and the lonesomeness are so oceanic, and the silence and the sameness, too, that the first peep of a strange house, rising beyond the trees, is for all the world like spying, on the Barbary coast, an unknown sail.

And this recalls my inland voyage to fairy-land. A true voyage; but, take it all in all, interesting as if invented.

From the piazza, some uncertain object I had caught, mysteriously snugged away, to all appearance, in a sort of purpled breast-pocket, high up in a hopper-like hollow, or sunken angle, among the northwestern mountains—yet, whether, really, it was on a mountain-side, or a mountain-top, could not be determined; because, though, viewed from favorable points, a blue summit, peering up away behind the rest, will, as it were, talk to you over their heads, and plainly tell you, that, though he (the blue summit) seems among them, he is not of them (God forbid!), and, indeed, would have you know that he considers himself—as, to say truth, he has good right—by several cubits their superior, nevertheless, certain ranges, here and there double-filed, as in platoons, so shoulder and follow up upon one another, with their irregular shapes and heights, that, from the piazza, a nigher and lower mountain will, in most states of the atmosphere, effacingly shade itself away into a higher and further one; that an object, bleak on the former's crest, will, for all that, appear nested in the latter's flank. These mountains, somehow, they play at hide-and-seek, and all before one's eyes.

But, be that as it may, the spot in question was, at all events, so situated as to be only visible, and then but vaguely, under certain witching conditions of light and shadow.

Indeed, for a year or more, I knew not there was such a spot, and might, perhaps, have never known, had it not been for a wizard afternoon in autumn—late in autumn—a mad poet's afternoon; when the turned maple woods in the broad basin below me, having lost their first vermilion tint, dully smoked, like smouldering towns, when flames expire upon their prey; and rumor had it, that this smokiness in the general air was not all Indian summer—which was not used to be so sick a thing, however mild—but, in great part, was blown from far-off forests, for weeks on fire, in Vermont; so that no wonder the sky was ominous as Hecate's cauldron—and two sportsmen, crossing a red stubble buck-wheat field, seemed guilty Macbeth and foreboding Banquo; and the hermit-sun, hutted in an Adullam cave, well towards the south, according to his season, did little else but, by indirect reflection of narrow rays shot down a Simplon pass among the clouds, just steadily paint one small, round, strawberry mole upon the wan cheek of northwestern hills. Signal as a candle. One spot of radiance, where all else was shade.

Fairies there, thought I; some haunted ring where fairies dance.

Time passed; and the following May, after a gentle shower upon the mountains—a little shower islanded in misty seas of sunshine; such a distant shower—and sometimes two, and three, and four of them, all visible together in different parts—as I love to watch from the piazza, instead of thunder storms, as I used to, which wrap old Greylock, like a Sinai, till one thinks swart Moses must be climbing among scathed hemlocks there; after, I say, that gentle shower, I saw a rainbow, resting its further end just where, in autumn, I had marked the mole. Fairies there, thought I; remembering that rainbows bring out the blooms, and that, if one can but get to the rainbow's end, his fortune is made in a bag of gold. Yon rainbow's end, would I were there, thought I. And none the less I wished it, for now first noticing what seemed some sort of glen, or grotto, in the mountain side; at least, whatever it was, viewed through the rainbow's medium, it glowed like the Potosi mine. But a work-a-day neighbor said, no doubt it was but some old barn—an abandoned one, its broadside beaten in, the acclivity its back-ground. But I, though I had never been there, I knew better.

A few days after, a cheery sunrise kindled a golden sparkle in the same spot as before. The sparkle was of that vividness, it seemed as if it could only come from glass. The building, then—if building, after all, it was—could, at least, not be a barn, much less an abandoned one; stale hay ten years musting in it. No; if aught built by mortal, it must be a cottage; perhaps long vacant and dismantled, but this very spring magically fitted up and glazed.

Again, one noon, in the same direction, I marked, over dimmed tops of terraced foliage, a broader gleam, as of a silver buckler, held sunwards over some croucher's head; which gleam, experience in like cases taught, must come from a roof newly shingled. This, to me, made pretty sure the recent occupancy of that far cot in fairy land.

Day after day, now, full of interest in my discovery, what time I could spare from reading the Midsummer Night's Dream, and all about Titania, wishfully I gazed off towards the hills; but in vain. Either troops of shadows, an imperial guard, with slow pace and solemn, defiled along the steeps; or, routed by pursuing light, fled broadcast from east to west—old wars of Lucifer and Michael; or the mountains, though unvexed by these mirrored sham fights in the sky, had an atmosphere otherwise unfavorable for fairy views. I was sorry; the more so, because I had to keep my chamber for some time after—which chamber did not face those hills.

At length, when pretty well again, and sitting out, in the September morning, upon the piazza, and thinking to myself, when, just after a little flock of sheep, the farmers' banded children passed, a-nutting, and said, "How sweet a day"—it was, after all, but what their fathers call a weather-breeder—and, indeed, was become so sensitive through my illness, as that I could not bear to look upon a Chinese creeper of my adoption, and which, to my delight, climbing a post of the piazza, had burst out in starry bloom, but now, if you removed the leaves a little, showed millions of strange, cankerous worms, which, feeding upon those blossoms, so shared their blessed hue, as to make it unblessed evermore—worms, whose germs had doubtless lurked in the very bulb which, so hopefully, I had planted: in this ingrate peevishness of my weary convalescence, was I sitting there; when, suddenly looking off, I saw the golden mountain-window, dazzling like a deep-sea dolphin. Fairies there, thought I, once more; the queen of fairies at her fairy-window; at any rate, some glad mountain-girl; it will do me good, it will cure this weariness, to look on her. No more; I'll launch my yawl—ho, cheerly, heart! and push away for fairy-land—for rainbow's end, in fairy-land.

How to get to fairy-land, by what road, I did not know; nor could any one inform me; not even one Edmund Spenser, who had been there—so he wrote me—further than that to reach fairy-land, it must be voyaged to, and with faith. I took the fairy-mountain's bearings, and the first fine day, when strength permitted, got into my yawl—high-pommeled, leather one—cast off the fast, and away I sailed, free voyager as an autumn leaf. Early dawn; and, sallying westward, I sowed the morning before me.

Some miles brought me nigh the hills; but out of present sight of them. I was not lost; for road-side golden-rods, as guide-posts, pointed, I doubted not, the way to the golden window. Following them, I came to a lone and languid region, where the grass-grown ways were traveled but by drowsy cattle, that, less waked than stirred by day, seemed to walk in sleep. Browse, they did not—the enchanted never eat. At least, so says Don Quixote, that sagest sage that ever lived.

On I went, and gained at last the fairy mountain's base, but saw yet no fairy ring. A pasture rose before me. Letting down five mouldering bars—so moistly green, they seemed fished up from some sunken wreck—a wigged old Aries, long-visaged, and with crumpled horn, came snuffing up; and then, retreating, decorously led on along a milky-way of white-weed, past dim-clustering Pleiades and Hyades, of small forget-me-nots; and would have led me further still his astral path, but for golden flights of yellow-birds—pilots, surely, to the golden window, to one side flying before me, from bush to bush, towards deep woods—which woods themselves were luring—and, somehow, lured, too, by their fence, banning a dark road, which, however dark, led up. I pushed through; when Aries, renouncing me now for some lost soul, wheeled, and went his wiser way. Forbidding and forbidden ground—to him.

A winter wood road, matted all along with winter-green. By the side of pebbly waters—waters the cheerier for their solitude; beneath swaying fir-boughs, petted by no season, but still green in all, on I journeyed—my horse and I; on, by an old saw-mill, bound down and hushed with vines, that his grating voice no more was heard; on, by a deep flume clove through snowy marble, vernal-tinted, where freshet eddies had, on each side, spun out empty chapels in the living rock; on, where Jacks-in-the-pulpit, like their Baptist namesake, preached but to the wilderness; on, where a huge, cross-grain block, fern-bedded, showed where, in forgotten times, man after man had tried to split it, but lost his wedges for his pains—which wedges yet rusted in their holes; on, where, ages past, in step-like ledges of a cascade, skull-hollow pots had been churned out by ceaseless whirling of a flint-stone—ever wearing, but itself unworn; on, by wild rapids pouring into a secret pool, but soothed by circling there awhile, issued forth serenely; on, to less broken ground, and by a little ring, where, truly, fairies must have danced, or else some wheel-tire been heated—for all was bare; still on, and up, and out into a hanging orchard, where maidenly looked down upon me a crescent moon, from morning.

My horse hitched low his head. Red apples rolled before him; Eve's apples; seek-no-furthers. He tasted one, I another; it tasted of the ground. Fairy land not yet, thought I, flinging my bridle to a humped old tree, that crooked out an arm to catch it. For the way now lay where path was none, and none might go but by himself, and only go by daring. Through blackberry brakes that tried to pluck me back, though I but strained towards fruitless growths of mountain-laurel; up slippery steeps to barren heights, where stood none to welcome. Fairy land not yet, thought I, though the morning is here before me.

Foot-sore enough and weary, I gained not then my journey's end, but came ere long to a craggy pass, dipping towards growing regions still beyond. A zigzag road, half overgrown with blueberry bushes, here turned among the cliffs. A rent was in their ragged sides; through it a little track branched off, which, upwards threading that short defile, came breezily out above, to where the mountain-top, part sheltered northward, by a taller brother, sloped gently off a space, ere darkly plunging; and here, among fantastic rocks, reposing in a herd, the foot-track wound, half beaten, up to a little, low-storied, grayish cottage, capped, nun-like, with a peaked roof.

On one slope, the roof was deeply weather-stained, and, nigh the turfy eaves-trough, all velvet-napped; no doubt the snail-monks founded mossy priories there. The other slope was newly shingled. On the north side, doorless and windowless, the clap-boards, innocent of paint, were yet green as the north side of lichened pines, or copperless hulls of Japanese junks, becalmed. The whole base, like those of the neighboring rocks, was rimmed about with shaded streaks of richest sod; for, with hearth-stones in fairy land, the natural rock, though housed, preserves to the last, just as in open fields, its fertilizing charm; only, by necessity, working now at a remove, to the sward without. So, at least, says Oberon, grave authority in fairy lore. Though setting Oberon aside, certain it is, that, even in the common world, the soil, close up to farm-houses, as close up to pasture rocks, is, even though untended, ever richer than it is a few rods off—such gentle, nurturing heat is radiated there.

But with this cottage, the shaded streaks were richest in its front and about its entrance, where the ground-sill, and especially the door-sill had, through long eld, quietly settled down.

No fence was seen, no inclosure. Near by—ferns, ferns, ferns; further—woods, woods, woods; beyond—mountains, mountains, mountains; then—sky, sky, sky. Turned out in ærial commons, pasture for the mountain moon. Nature, and but nature, house and all; even a low cross-pile of silver birch, piled openly, to season; up among whose silvery sticks, as through the fencing of some sequestered grave, sprang vagrant raspberry bushes—willful assertors of their right of way.

The foot-track, so dainty narrow, just like a sheep-track, led through long ferns that lodged. Fairy land at last, thought I; Una and her lamb dwell here. Truly, a small abode—mere palanquin, set down on the summit, in a pass between two worlds, participant of neither.

A sultry hour, and I wore a light hat, of yellow sinnet, with white duck trowsers—both relics of my tropic sea-going. Clogged in the muffling ferns, I softly stumbled, staining the knees a sea-green.

Pausing at the threshold, or rather where threshold once had been, I saw, through the open door-way, a lonely girl, sewing at a lonely window. A pale-cheeked girl, and fly-specked window, with wasps about the mended upper panes. I spoke. She shyly started, like some Tahiti girl, secreted for a sacrifice, first catching sight, through palms, of Captain Cook. Recovering, she bade me enter; with her apron brushed off a stool; then silently resumed her own. With thanks I took the stool; but now, for a space, I, too, was mute. This, then, is the fairy-mountain house, and here, the fairy queen sitting at her fairy window.

I went up to it. Downwards, directed by the tunneled pass, as through a leveled telescope, I caught sight of a far-off, soft, azure world. I hardly knew it, though I came from it.

"You must find this view very pleasant," said I, at last.

"Oh, sir," tears starting in her eyes, "the first time I looked out of this window, I said 'never, never shall I weary of this.'"

"And what wearies you of it now?"

"I don't know," while a tear fell; "but it is not the view, it is Marianna."

Some months back, her brother, only seventeen, had come hither, a long way from the other side, to cut wood and burn coal, and she, elder sister, had accompanied him. Long had they been orphans, and now, sole inhabitants of the sole house upon the mountain. No guest came, no traveler passed. The zigzag, perilous road was only used at seasons by the coal wagons. The brother was absent the entire day, sometimes the entire night. When at evening, fagged out, he did come home, he soon left his bench, poor fellow, for his bed; just as one, at last, wearily quits that, too, for still deeper rest. The bench, the bed, the grave.

Silent I stood by the fairy window, while these things were being told.

"Do you know," said she at last, as stealing from her story, "do you know who lives yonder?—I have never been down into that country—away off there, I mean; that house, that marble one," pointing far across the lower landscape; "have you not caught it? there, on the long hill-side: the field before, the woods behind; the white shines out against their blue; don't you mark it? the only house in sight."

I looked; and after a time, to my surprise, recognized, more by its position than its aspect, or Marianna's description, my own abode, glimmering much like this mountain one from the piazza. The mirage haze made it appear less a farm-house than King Charming's palace.

"I have often wondered who lives there; but it must be some happy one; again this morning was I thinking so."

"Some happy one," returned I, starting; "and why do you think that? You judge some rich one lives there?"

"Rich or not, I never thought; but it looks so happy, I can't tell how;

and it is so far away. Sometimes I think I do but dream it is there. You should see it in a sunset."

"No doubt the sunset gilds it finely; but not more than the sunrise does this house, perhaps."

"This house? The sun is a good sun, but it never gilds this house. Why should it? This old house is rotting. That makes it so mossy. In the morning, the sun comes in at this old window, to be sure—boarded up, when first we came; a window I can't keep clean, do what I may—and half burns, and nearly blinds me at my sewing, besides setting the flies and wasps astir—such flies and wasps as only lone mountain houses know. See, here is the curtain—this apron—I try to shut it out with then. It fades it, you see. Sun gild this house? not that ever Marianna saw."

"Because when this roof is gilded most, then you stay here within."

"The hottest, weariest hour of day, you mean? Sir, the sun gilds not this roof. It leaked so, brother newly shingled all one side. Did you not see it? The north side, where the sun strikes most on what the rain has wetted. The sun is a good sun; but this roof, it first scorches, and then rots. An old house. They went West, and are long dead, they say, who built it. A mountain house. In winter no fox could den in it. That chimney-place has been blocked up with snow, just like a hollow stump."

"Yours are strange fancies, Marianna."

"They but reflect the things."

"Then I should have said, 'These are strange things,' rather than, 'Yours are strange fancies.'"

"As you will;" and took up her sewing.

Something in those quiet words, or in that quiet act, it made me mute again; while, noting, through the fairy window, a broad shadow stealing on, as cast by some gigantic condor, floating at brooding poise on outstretched wings, I marked how, by its deeper and inclusive dusk, it wiped away into itself all lesser shades of rock or fern.

"You watch the cloud," said Marianna.

"No, a shadow; a cloud's, no doubt—though that I cannot see. How did you know it? Your eyes are on your work."

"It dusked my work. There, now the cloud is gone, Tray comes back."

"How?"

"The dog, the shaggy dog. At noon, he steals off, of himself, to change his shape—returns, and lies down awhile, nigh the door. Don't you see him? His head is turned round at you; though, when you came, he looked before him."

"Your eyes rest but on your work; what do you speak of?"

"By the window, crossing."

"You mean this shaggy shadow—the nigh one? And, yes, now that I mark it, it is not unlike a large, black Newfoundland dog. The invading shadow gone, the invaded one returns. But I do not see what casts it."

"For that, you must go without."

"One of those grassy rocks, no doubt."

"You see his head, his face?"

"The shadow's? You speak as if *you* saw it, and all the time your eyes are on your work."

"Tray looks at you," still without glancing up; "this is his hour; I see him."

"Have you, then, so long sat at this mountain-window, where but clouds and vapors pass, that, to you, shadows are as things, though you speak of them as of phantoms; that, by familiar knowledge, working like a second sight, you can, without looking for them, tell just where they are, though, as having mice-like feet, they creep about, and come and go; that, to you, these lifeless shadows are as living friends, who, though out of sight, are not out of mind, even in their faces—is it so?"

"That way I never thought of it. But the friendliest one, that used to soothe my weariness so much, coolly quivering on the ferns, it was taken from me, never to return, as Tray did just now. The shadow of a birch. The tree was struck by lightning, and brother cut it up. You saw the cross-pile out-doors—the buried root lies under it; but not the shadow. That is flown, and never will come back, nor ever anywhere stir again."

Another cloud here stole along, once more blotting out the dog, and blackening all the mountain; while the stillness was so still, deafness might have forgot itself, or else believed that noiseless shadow spoke.

"Birds, Marianna, singing-birds, I hear none; I hear nothing. Boys and bob-o-links, do they never come a-berrying up here?"

"Birds, I seldom hear; boys, never. The berries mostly ripe and fall—few, but me, the wiser."

"But yellow-birds showed me the way—part way, at least."

"And then flew back. I guess they play about the mountain-side, but don't make the top their home. And no doubt you think that, living so lonesome here, knowing nothing, hearing nothing—little, at least, but sound of thunder and the fall of trees—never reading, seldom speaking, yet ever wakeful, this is what gives me my strange thoughts—for so you call them—this weariness and wakefulness together. Brother, who stands and works in open air, would I could rest like him; but mine is mostly but dull woman's work—sitting, sitting, restless sitting."

"But, do you not go walk at times? These woods are wide."

"And lonesome; lonesome, because so wide. Sometimes, 'tis true, of afternoons, I go a little way; but soon come back again. Better feel lone by hearth, than rock. The shadows hereabouts I know—those in the woods are strangers."

"But the night?"

"Just like the day. Thinking, thinking—a wheel I cannot stop; pure want of sleep it is that turns it."

"I have heard that, for this wakeful weariness, to say one's prayers, and then lay one's head upon a fresh hop pillow——"

"Look!"

Through the fairy window, she pointed down the steep to a small garden patch near by—mere pot of rifled loam, half rounded in by sheltering rocks—where, side by side, some feet apart, nipped and puny, two hop-vines climbed two poles, and, gaining their tip-ends, would have then joined over in an upward clasp, but the baffled shoots, groping awhile in empty air, trailed back whence they sprung.

"You have tried the pillow, then?"

"Yes."

"And prayer?"

"Prayer and pillow."

"Is there no other cure, or charm?"

"Oh, if I could but once get to yonder house, and but look upon whoever the happy being is that lives there! A foolish thought: why do I think it? Is it that I live so lonesome, and know nothing?"

"I, too, know nothing; and, therefore, cannot answer; but, for your sake, Marianna, well could wish that I were that happy one of the happy house you dream you see; for then you would behold him now, and, as you say, this weariness might leave you."

—Enough. Launching my yawl no more for fairy-land, I stick to the piazza. It is my box-royal; and this amphitheatre, my theatre of San Carlo. Yes, the scenery is magical—the illusion so complete. And Madam Meadow Lark, my prima donna, plays her grand engagement here; and, drinking in her sunrise note, which, Memnon-like, seems struck from the golden window, how far from me the weary face behind it.

But, every night, when the curtain falls, truth comes in with darkness. No light shows from the mountain. To and fro I walk the piazza deck, haunted by Marianna's face, and many as real a story.

Bartleby, the Scrivener

A Story of Wall-Street

I AM A RATHER ELDERLY MAN. The nature of my avocations for the last thirty years has brought me into more than ordinary contact with what would seem an interesting and somewhat singular set of men, of whom as yet nothing that I know of has ever been written:—I mean the law-copyists or scriveners. I have known very many of them, professionally and privately, and if I pleased, could relate divers histories, at which good-natured gentlemen might smile, and sentimental souls might weep. But I waive the biographies of all other scriveners for a few passages in the life of Bartleby, who was a scrivener the strangest I ever saw or heard of. While of other law-copyists I might write the complete life, of Bartleby nothing of that sort can be done. I believe that no materials exist for a full and satisfactory biography of this man. It is an irreparable loss to literature. Bartleby was one of those beings of whom nothing is ascertainable, except from the original sources, and in his case those are very small. What my own astonished eyes saw of Bartleby, *that* is all I know of him, except, indeed, one vague report which will appear in the sequel.

Ere introducing the scrivener, as he first appeared to me, it is fit I make some mention of myself, my *employés*, my business, my chambers, and general surroundings; because some such description is indispensable to an adequate understanding of the chief character about to be presented.

Imprimis: I am a man who, from his youth upwards, has been filled with a profound conviction that the easiest way of life is the best. Hence, though I belong to a profession proverbially energetic and nervous, even to turbulence, at times, yet nothing of that sort have I ever suffered to invade my peace. I am one of those unambitious lawyers who never addresses a jury, or in any way draws down public applause; but in the cool tranquillity of a snug retreat, do a snug business among rich men's bonds and mortgages and title-deeds. All who know me, consider me an eminently *safe* man. The late John Jacob Astor, a personage little given to poetic enthusiasm, had no hesitation in pronouncing my first grand point to be prudence; my next, method. I do not speak it in vanity, but simply record the fact, that I was not unemployed in my profession by the late John Jacob Astor; a name which, I admit, I love to repeat, for it hath a rounded and orbicular sound to it, and rings like unto bullion. I will freely add, that I was not insensible to the late John Jacob Astor's good opinion.

Some time prior to the period at which this little history begins, my avocations had been largely increased. The good old office, now extinct in the State of New-York, of a Master in Chancery, had been conferred upon me. It was not a very arduous office, but very pleasantly remunerative. I seldom lose my temper; much more seldom indulge in dangerous indignation at wrongs and outrages; but I must be permitted to be rash here and declare, that I consider the sudden and violent abrogation of the office of Master in Chancery, by the new Constitution, as a —— premature act; inasmuch as I had counted upon a life-lease of the profits, whereas I only received those of a few short years. But this is by the way.

My chambers were up stairs at No. — Wall-street. At one end they looked upon the white wall of the interior of a spacious sky-light shaft, penetrating the building from top to bottom. This view might have been considered rather tame than otherwise, deficient in what landscape painters call "life." But if so, the view from the other end of my chambers offered, at least, a contrast, if nothing more. In that direction my windows commanded an unobstructed view of a lofty brick wall, black by age and everlasting shade; which wall required no spy-glass to bring out its lurking beauties, but for the benefit of all near-sighted spectators, was pushed up to within ten feet of my window panes. Owing to the great height of the surrounding buildings, and my chambers being on the second floor, the interval between this wall and mine not a little resembled a huge square cistern.

At the period just preceding the advent of Bartleby, I had two persons as copyists in my employment, and a promising lad as an office-boy. First, Turkey; second, Nippers; third, Ginger Nut. These may seem names, the like of which are not usually found in the Directory. In truth they were nicknames, mutually conferred upon each other by my three clerks, and were deemed expressive of their respective persons or characters. Turkey was a short, pursy Englishman of about my own age, that is, somewhere not far from sixty. In the morning, one might say, his face was of a fine florid hue, but after twelve o'clock, meridian—his dinner hour—it blazed like a grate full of Christmas coals; and continued blazing—but, as it were, with a gradual wane—till 6 o'clock, P.M. or thereabouts, after which I saw no more of the proprietor of the face, which gaining its meridian with the sun, seemed to set with it, to rise, culminate, and decline the following day, with the like regularity and undiminished glory. There are many singular coincidences I have known in the course of my life, not the least among which was the fact, that exactly when Turkey displayed his fullest beams from his red and radiant countenance, just then, too, at that critical moment, began the daily period when I considered his business capacities as seriously disturbed for the remainder of the twenty-four hours. Not that he was absolutely idle, or averse to business then; far from it. The difficulty was, he was apt to be altogether too energetic. There was a strange, inflamed, flurried, flighty recklessness of activity about him. He would be incautious in dipping his pen into his inkstand. All his blots upon my documents, were dropped there after twelve o'clock, meridian. Indeed, not only would he be reckless and sadly given to making blots in the afternoon, but some days he went further, and was rather noisy. At such times, too, his face flamed with augmented blazonry, as if cannel coal had been heaped on anthracite. He made an unpleasant racket with his chair; spilled his sand-box; in mending his pens, impatiently split them all to pieces, and threw them on the floor in a sudden passion; stood up and leaned over his table, boxing his papers about in a most indecorous manner, very sad to behold in an elderly man like him. Nevertheless, as he was in many ways a most valuable person to me, and all the time before twelve o'clock, meridian, was the quickest, steadiest creature too, accomplishing a great deal of work in a style not easy to be matched—for these reasons, I was willing to overlook his eccentricities, though indeed, occasionally, I remonstrated with him. I did this very gently, however, because, though the civilest, nay, the blandest and most reverential of men in the morning, yet in the afternoon he was disposed, upon provocation, to be slightly rash with his tongue, in fact, insolent. Now, valuing his morning services as I did, and resolved not to lose them; yet, at the same time made uncomfortable by his inflamed ways after twelve o'clock; and being a man of peace, unwilling by my admonitions to call forth unseemly retorts from him; I took upon me, one Saturday noon (he was always worse on Saturdays), to hint to him, very kindly, that perhaps now that he was growing old, it might be well to abridge his labors; in short, he need not come to my chambers after twelve o'clock, but, dinner over, had best go home to his lodgings and rest himself till tea-time. But no; he insisted upon his afternoon devotions. His countenance became intolerably fervid, as he oratorically assured me—gesticulating with a long ruler at the other end of the room—that if his services in the morning were useful, how indispensable, then, in the afternoon?

"With submission, sir," said Turkey on this occasion, "I consider myself your right-hand man. In the morning I but marshal and deploy my columns; but in the afternoon I put myself at their head, and gallantly charge the foe, thus!"—and he made a violent thrust with the ruler.

"But the blots, Turkey," intimated I.

"True,—but, with submission, sir, behold these hairs! I am getting old. Surely, sir, a blot or two of a warm afternoon is not to be severely urged against gray hairs. Old age—even if it blot the page—is honorable. With submission, sir, we *both* are getting old."

This appeal to my fellow-feeling was hardly to be resisted. At all events, I saw that go he would not. So I made up my mind to let him stay, resolving, nevertheless, to see to it, that during the afternoon he had to do with my less important papers.

Nippers, the second on my list, was a whiskered, sallow, and, upon the whole, rather piratical-looking young man of about five and twenty. I always deemed him the victim of two evil powers—ambition and indigestion. The ambition was evinced by a certain impatience of the duties of a mere copyist, an unwarrantable usurpation of strictly professional affairs, such as the original drawing up of legal documents. The indigestion seemed betokened in an occasional nervous testiness and grinning irritability, causing the teeth to audibly grind together over mistakes committed in copying; unnecessary maledictions, hissed, rather than spoken, in the heat of business; and especially by a continual discontent with the height of the table where he worked. Though of a very ingenious mechanical turn, Nippers could never get this table to suit him. He put chips under it, blocks of various sorts, bits of pasteboard, and at last went so far as to attempt an exquisite adjustment by final pieces of folded blotting-paper. But no invention would answer. If, for the sake of easing his back, he brought the table lid at a sharp angle well up towards his chin, and wrote there like a man using the steep roof of a Dutch house for his desk:—then he declared that it stopped the circulation in his arms. If now he lowered the table to his waistbands, and stooped over it in writing, then there was a sore aching in his back. In short, the truth of the matter was, Nippers knew not what he wanted. Or, if he wanted any thing, it was to be rid of a scrivener's table altogether. Among the manifestations of his diseased ambition was a fondness he had for receiving visits from certain ambiguous-looking fellows in seedy coats, whom he called his clients. Indeed I was aware that not only was he, at times, considerable of a ward-politician, but he occasionally did a little business at the Justices' courts, and was not unknown on the steps of the Tombs. I have good reason to believe, however, that one individual who called upon him at my chambers, and who, with a grand air, he insisted was his client, was no other than a dun, and the alleged title-deed, a bill. But with all his failings, and the annoyances he caused me, Nippers, like his compatriot Turkey, was a very useful man to me; wrote a neat, swift hand; and, when he chose, was not deficient in a gentlemanly sort of deportment. Added to this, he always dressed in a gentlemanly sort of way; and so, incidentally, reflected credit upon my chambers. Whereas with respect to Turkey, I had much ado to keep him from being a reproach to me. His clothes were apt to look oily and smell of eating-houses. He wore his pantaloons very loose and baggy in summer. His coats were execrable; his hat not to be handled. But while the hat was a thing of indifference to me, inasmuch as his natural civility and deference, as a dependent Englishman, always led him to doff it the moment he entered the room, yet his coat was another matter. Concerning his coats, I reasoned with him; but with no effect. The truth was, I suppose, that a man with so small an income, could not afford to sport such a lustrous face and a lustrous coat at one and the same time. As Nippers once observed, Turkey's money went chiefly for red ink. One winter day I presented Turkey with a highly-respectable looking coat of my own, a padded gray coat, of a most comfortable warmth, and which buttoned straight up from the knee to the neck. I thought Turkey would appreciate the favor, and abate his rashness and obstreperousness of afternoons. But no. I verily believe that buttoning himself up in so downy and blanket-like a coat had a pernicious effect upon him; upon the same principle that too much oats are bad for horses. In fact, precisely as a rash, restive horse is said to feel his oats, so Turkey felt his coat. It made him insolent. He was a man whom prosperity harmed.

Though concerning the self-indulgent habits of Turkey I had my own private surmises, yet touching Nippers I was well persuaded that whatever might be his faults in other respects, he was, at least, a temperate young man. But indeed, nature herself seemed to have been his vintner, and at his birth charged him so thoroughly with an irritable, brandy-like disposition, that all subsequent potations were needless. When I consider how, amid the stillness of my chambers, Nippers would sometimes impatiently rise from his seat, and stooping over his table, spread his arms wide apart, seize the whole desk, and move it, and jerk it, with a grim, grinding motion on the floor, as if the table were a perverse voluntary agent, intent on thwarting and vexing him; I plainly perceive that for Nippers, brandy and water were altogether superfluous.

It was fortunate for me that, owing to its peculiar cause—indigestion—the irritability and consequent nervousness of Nippers, were mainly observable in the morning, while in the afternoon he was comparatively mild. So that Turkey's paroxysms only coming on about twelve o'clock, I never had to do with their eccentricities at one time. Their fits relieved each other like guards. When Nippers' was on, Turkey's was off; and *vice versa*. This was a good natural arrangement under the circumstances.

Ginger Nut, the third on my list, was a lad some twelve years old. His father was a carman, ambitious of seeing his son on the bench instead of a cart, before he died. So he sent him to my office as student at law, errand boy, and cleaner and sweeper, at the rate of one dollar a week. He had a little desk to himself, but he did not use it much. Upon inspection, the drawer exhibited a great array of the shells of various sorts of nuts. Indeed, to this quick-witted youth the whole noble science of the law was contained in a nut-shell. Not the least among the employments of Ginger Nut, as well as one which he discharged with the most alacrity, was his duty as cake and apple purveyor for Turkey and Nippers. Copying law papers being proverbially a dry, husky sort of business, my two scriveners were fain to moisten their mouths very often with Spitzenbergs to be had at the numerous stalls nigh the Custom House and Post Office. Also, they sent Ginger Nut very frequently for that peculiar cake—small, flat, round, and very spicy—after which he had been named by them. Of a cold morning when business was but dull, Turkey would gobble up scores of these cakes, as if they were mere wafers—indeed they sell them at the rate of six or eight for a penny—the scrape of his pen blending with the crunching of the crisp particles in his mouth. Of all the fiery afternoon blunders and flurried rashnesses of Turkey, was his once moistening a ginger-cake between his lips, and clapping it on to a mortgage for a seal. I came within an ace of dismissing him then. But he mollified me by making an oriental bow, and saying—"With submission, sir, it was generous of me to find you in stationery on my own account."

Now my original business—that of a conveyancer and title hunter, and drawer-up of recondite documents of all sorts—was considerably increased by receiving the master's office. There was now great work for scriveners. Not only must I push the clerks already with me, but I must have additional help. In answer to my advertisement, a motionless young man one morning, stood upon my office threshold, the door being open, for it was summer. I can see that figure now—pallidly neat, pitiably respectable, incurably forlorn! It was Bartleby.

After a few words touching his qualifications, I engaged him, glad to have among my corps of copyists a man of so singularly sedate an aspect, which I thought might operate beneficially upon the flighty temper of Turkey, and the fiery one of Nippers.

I should have stated before that ground glass folding-doors divided my premises into two parts, one of which was occupied by my scriveners, the other by myself. According to my humor I threw open these doors, or closed them. I resolved to assign Bartleby a corner by the folding-doors, but on my side of them, so as to have this quiet man within easy call, in case any trifling thing was to be done. I placed his desk close up to a small side-window in that part of the room, a window which originally had afforded a lateral view of certain grimy back-yards and bricks, but which, owing to subsequent erections, commanded at present no view at all, though it gave some light. Within three feet of the panes was a wall, and the light came down from far above, between two lofty buildings, as from a very small opening in a dome. Still further to a satisfactory arrangement, I procured a high green folding screen, which might entirely isolate Bartleby from my sight, though not remove him from my voice. And thus, in a manner, privacy and society were conjoined.

At first Bartleby did an extraordinary quantity of writing. As if long famishing for something to copy, he seemed to gorge himself on my documents. There was no pause for digestion. He ran a day and night line, copying by sun-light and by candle-light. I should have been quite delighted with his application, had he been cheerfully industrious. But he wrote on silently, palely, mechanically.

It is, of course, an indispensable part of a scrivener's business to verify the accuracy of his copy, word by word. Where there are two or more scriveners in an office, they assist each other in this examination, one reading from the copy, the other holding the original. It is a very dull, wearisome, and lethargic affair. I can readily imagine that to some sanguine temperaments it would be altogether intolerable. For example, I cannot credit that the mettlesome poet Byron would have contentedly sat down with Bartleby to examine a law document of, say five hundred pages, closely written in a crimpy hand.

Now and then, in the haste of business, it had been my habit to assist in comparing some brief document myself, calling Turkey or Nippers for this purpose. One object I had in placing Bartleby so handy to me behind the screen, was to avail myself of his services on such trivial occasions. It was on the third day, I think, of his being with me, and before any necessity had arisen for having his own writing examined, that, being much hurried to complete a small affair I had in hand, I abruptly called to Bartleby. In my haste and natural expectancy of instant compliance, I sat with my head bent over the original on my desk, and my right hand sideways, and somewhat nervously extended with the copy, so that immediately upon emerging from his retreat, Bartleby might snatch it and proceed to business without the least delay.

In this very attitude did I sit when I called to him, rapidly stating what it was I wanted him to do—namely, to examine a small paper with me. Imagine my surprise, nay, my consternation, when without moving from his privacy, Bartleby in a singularly mild, firm voice, replied, "I would prefer not to."

I sat awhile in perfect silence, rallying my stunned faculties. Immediately it occurred to me that my ears had deceived me, or Bartleby had entirely misunderstood my meaning. I repeated my request in the clearest tone I could assume. But in quite as clear a one came the previous reply, "I would prefer not to."

"Prefer not to," echoed I, rising in high excitement, and crossing the room with a stride. "What do you mean? Are you moon-struck? I want you to help me compare this sheet here—take it," and I thrust it towards him.

"I would prefer not to," said he.

I looked at him steadfastly. His face was leanly composed; his gray eye dimly calm. Not a wrinkle of agitation rippled him. Had there been the least uneasiness, anger, impatience or impertinence in his manner; in other words, had there been any thing ordinarily human about him, doubtless I should have violently dismissed him from the premises. But as it was, I should have as soon thought of turning my pale plaster-of-paris bust of Cicero out of doors. I stood gazing at him awhile, as he went on with his own writing, and then reseated myself at my desk. This is very strange, thought I. What had one best do? But my business hurried me. I concluded to forget the matter for the present, reserving it for my future leisure. So calling Nippers from the other room, the paper was speedily examined.

A few days after this, Bartleby concluded four lengthy documents, being quadruplicates of a week's testimony taken before me in my High Court of Chancery. It became necessary to examine them. It was an important suit, and great accuracy was imperative. Having all things arranged I called Turkey, Nippers and Ginger Nut from the next room, meaning to place the four copies in the hands of my four clerks, while I should read from the original. Accordingly Turkey, Nippers and Ginger Nut had taken their seats in a row, each with his document in hand, when I called to Bartleby to join this interesting group.

"Bartleby! quick, I am waiting."

I heard a slow scrape of his chair legs on the uncarpeted floor, and soon he appeared standing at the entrance of his hermitage.

"What is wanted?" said he mildly.

"The copies, the copies," said I hurriedly. "We are going to examine them. There"—and I held towards him the fourth quadruplicate.

"I would prefer not to," he said, and gently disappeared behind the screen.

For a few moments I was turned into a pillar of salt, standing at the head of my seated column of clerks. Recovering myself, I advanced towards the screen, and demanded the reason for such extraordinary conduct.

"*Why* do you refuse?"

"I would prefer not to."

With any other man I should have flown outright into a dreadful passion, scorned all further words, and thrust him ignominiously from my presence. But there was something about Bartleby that not only strangely disarmed me, but in a wonderful manner touched and disconcerted me. I began to reason with him.

"These are your own copies we are about to examine. It is labor saving to you, because one examination will answer for your four papers. It is common usage. Every copyist is bound to help examine his copy. Is it not so? Will you not speak? Answer!"

"I prefer not to," he replied in a flute-like tone. It seemed to me that while I had been addressing him, he carefully revolved every statement that I made; fully comprehended the meaning; could not gainsay the irresistible conclusion; but, at the same time, some paramount consideration prevailed with him to reply as he did.

"You are decided, then, not to comply with my request—a request made according to common usage and common sense?"

He briefly gave me to understand that on that point my judgment was sound. Yes: his decision was irreversible.

It is not seldom the case that when a man is browbeaten in some unprecedented and violently unreasonable way, he begins to stagger in his own plainest faith. He begins, as it were, vaguely to surmise that, wonderful as it may be, all the justice and all the reason is on the other side. Accordingly, if any disinterested persons are present, he turns to them for some reinforcement for his own faltering mind.

"Turkey," said I, "what do you think of this? Am I not right?"

"With submission, sir," said Turkey, with his blandest tone, "I think that you are."

"Nippers," said I, "what do *you* think of it?"

"I think I should kick him out of the office."

(The reader of nice perceptions will here perceive that, it being morning, Turkey's answer is couched in polite and tranquil terms, but Nippers replies in ill-tempered ones. Or, to repeat a previous sentence, Nippers's ugly mood was on duty, and Turkey's off.)

"Ginger Nut," said I, willing to enlist the smallest suffrage in my behalf, "what do *you* think of it?"

"I think, sir, he's a little *luny*," replied Ginger Nut, with a grin.

"You hear what they say," said I, turning towards the screen, "come forth and do your duty."

But he vouchsafed no reply. I pondered a moment in sore perplexity. But once more business hurried me. I determined again to postpone the consideration of this dilemma to my future leisure. With a little trouble we made out to examine the papers without Bartleby, though at every page or two, Turkey deferentially dropped his opinion that this proceeding was quite out of the common; while Nippers, twitching in his chair with a dyspeptic nervousness, ground out between his set teeth occasional hissing maledictions against the stubborn oaf behind the screen. And for his (Nippers's) part, this was the first and the last time he would do another man's business without pay.

Meanwhile Bartleby sat in his hermitage, oblivious to every thing but his own peculiar business there.

Some days passed, the scrivener being employed upon another lengthy work. His late remarkable conduct led me to regard his ways narrowly. I observed that he never went to dinner; indeed that he never went any where. As yet I had never of my personal knowledge known him to be outside of my office. He was a perpetual sentry in the corner. At about eleven o'clock though, in the morning, I noticed that Ginger Nut would advance toward the opening in Bartleby's screen, as if silently beckoned thither by a gesture invisible to me where I sat. The boy would then leave the office jingling a few pence, and reappear with a handful of ginger-nuts which he delivered in the hermitage, receiving two of the cakes for his trouble.

He lives, then, on ginger-nuts, thought I; never eats a dinner, properly speaking; he must be a vegetarian then; but no; he never eats even vegetables, he eats nothing but ginger-nuts. My mind then ran on in reveries concerning the probable effects upon the human constitution of living entirely on ginger-nuts. Ginger-nuts are so called because they contain ginger as one of their peculiar constituents, and the final flavoring one. Now what was ginger? A hot, spicy thing. Was Bartleby hot and spicy? Not at all. Ginger, then, had no effect upon Bartleby. Probably he preferred it should have none.

Nothing so aggravates an earnest person as a passive resistance. If the individual so resisted be of a not inhumane temper, and the resisting one perfectly harmless in his passivity; then, in the better moods of the former, he will endeavor charitably to construe to his imagination what proves impossible to be solved by his judgment. Even so, for the most part, I regarded Bartleby and his ways. Poor fellow! thought I, he means no mischief; it is plain he intends no insolence; his aspect sufficiently evinces that his eccentricities are involuntary. He is useful to me. I can get along with him. If I turn him away, the chances are he will fall in with some less indulgent employer, and then he will be rudely treated, and perhaps driven forth miserably to starve. Yes. Here I can cheaply purchase a delicious self-approval. To befriend Bartleby; to humor him in his strange wilfulness, will cost me little or nothing, while I lay up in my soul what will eventually prove a sweet morsel for my conscience. But this mood was not invariable with me. The passiveness of Bartleby sometimes irritated me. I felt strangely goaded on to encounter him in new opposition, to elicit some angry spark from him answerable to my own. But indeed I might as well have essayed to strike fire with my knuckles against a bit of Windsor soap. But one afternoon the evil impulse in me mastered me, and the following little scene ensued:

"Bartleby," said I, "when those papers are all copied, I will compare them with you."

"I would prefer not to."

"How? Surely you do not mean to persist in that mulish vagary?"

No answer.

I threw open the folding-doors near by, and turning upon Turkey and Nippers, exclaimed:

"Bartleby a second time says, he won't examine his papers. What do you think of it, Turkey?"

It was afternoon, be it remembered. Turkey sat glowing like a brass boiler, his bald head steaming, his hands reeling among his blotted papers.

"Think of it?" roared Turkey; "I think I'll just step behind his screen, and black his eyes for him!"

So saying, Turkey rose to his feet and threw his arms into a pugilistic position. He was hurrying away to make good his promise, when I detained him, alarmed at the effect of incautiously rousing Turkey's combativeness after dinner.

"Sit down, Turkey," said I, "and hear what Nippers has to say. What do you think of it, Nippers? Would I not be justified in immediately dismissing Bartleby?"

"Excuse me, that is for you to decide, sir. I think his conduct quite unusual, and indeed unjust, as regards Turkey and myself. But it may only be a passing whim."

"Ah," exclaimed I, "you have strangely changed your mind then—you speak very gently of him now."

"All beer," cried Turkey; "gentleness is effects of beer—Nippers and I dined together to-day. You see how gentle *I* am, sir. Shall I go and black his eyes?"

"You refer to Bartleby, I suppose. No, not to-day, Turkey," I replied; "pray, put up your fists."

I closed the doors, and again advanced towards Bartleby. I felt additional incentives tempting me to my fate. I burned to be rebelled against again. I remembered that Bartleby never left the office.

"Bartleby," said I, "Ginger Nut is away; just step round to the Post Office, won't you? (it was but a three minutes walk,) and see if there is any thing for me."

"I would prefer not to."

"You *will* not?"

"I *prefer* not."

I staggered to my desk, and sat there in a deep study. My blind inveteracy returned. Was there any other thing in which I could procure myself to be ignominiously repulsed by this lean, penniless wight?—my hired clerk? What added thing is there, perfectly reasonable, that he will be sure to refuse to do?

"Bartleby!"

No answer.

"Bartleby," in a louder tone.

No answer.

"Bartleby," I roared.

Like a very ghost, agreeably to the laws of magical invocation, at the third summons, he appeared at the entrance of his hermitage.

"Go to the next room, and tell Nippers to come to me."

"I prefer not to," he respectfully and slowly said, and mildly disappeared.

"Very good, Bartleby," said I, in a quiet sort of serenely severe self-possessed tone, intimating the unalterable purpose of some terrible retribution very close at hand. At the moment I half intended something of the kind. But upon the whole, as it was drawing towards my dinner-hour, I thought it best to put on my hat and walk home for the day, suffering much from perplexity and distress of mind.

Shall I acknowledge it? The conclusion of this whole business was, that it soon became a fixed fact of my chambers, that a pale young scrivener, by the name of Bartleby, had a desk there; that he copied for me at the usual rate of four cents a folio (one hundred words); but he was permanently exempt from examining the work done by him, that duty being transferred to Turkey and Nippers, out of compliment doubtless to their superior acuteness; moreover, said Bartleby was never on any account to be dispatched on the most trivial errand of any sort; and that even if entreated to take upon him such a matter, it was generally understood that he would prefer not to—in other words, that he would refuse point-blank.

As days passed on, I became considerably reconciled to Bartleby. His steadiness, his freedom from all dissipation, his incessant industry (except when he chose to throw himself into a standing revery behind his screen), his great stillness, his unalterableness of demeanor under all circumstances, made him a valuable acquisition. One prime thing was this,—*he was always there;*—first in the morning, continually through the day, and the last at night. I had a singular confidence in his honesty. I felt my most precious papers perfectly safe in his hands. Sometimes to be sure I could not, for the very soul of me, avoid falling into sudden spasmodic passions with him. For it was exceeding difficult to bear in mind all the time those strange peculiarities, privileges, and unheard of exemptions, forming the tacit stipulations on Bartleby's part under which he remained in my office. Now and then, in the eagerness of dispatching pressing business, I would inadvertently summon Bartleby, in a short, rapid tone, to put his finger, say, on the incipient tie of a bit of red tape with which I was about compressing some papers. Of course, from behind the screen the usual answer, "I prefer not to," was sure to come; and then, how could a human creature with the common infirmities of our nature, refrain from bitterly exclaiming upon such perverseness—such unreasonableness. However, every added repulse of this sort which I received only tended to lessen the probability of my repeating the inadvertence.

Here it must be said, that according to the custom of most legal gentlemen occupying chambers in densely-populated law buildings, there were several keys to my door. One was kept by a woman residing in the attic, which person weekly scrubbed and daily swept and dusted my apartments. Another was kept by Turkey for convenience sake. The third I sometimes carried in my own pocket. The fourth I knew not who had.

Now, one Sunday morning I happened to go to Trinity Church, to hear a celebrated preacher, and finding myself rather early on the ground, I thought I would walk round to my chambers for a while. Luckily I had my key with me; but upon applying it to the lock, I found it resisted by something inserted from the inside. Quite surprised, I called out; when to my consternation a key was turned from within; and thrusting his lean visage at me, and holding the door ajar, the apparition of Bartleby appeared, in his shirt sleeves, and otherwise in a strangely tattered dishabille, saying quietly that he was sorry, but he was deeply engaged just then, and—preferred not admitting me at present. In a brief word or two, he moreover added, that perhaps I had better walk round the block two or three times, and by that time he would probably have concluded his affairs.

Now, the utterly unsurmised appearance of Bartleby, tenanting my law-chambers of a Sunday morning, with his cadaverously gentlemanly *nonchalance*, yet withal firm and self-possessed, had such a strange effect upon me, that incontinently I slunk away from my own door, and did as desired. But not without sundry twinges of impotent rebellion against the mild effrontery of this unaccountable scrivener. Indeed, it was his wonderful mildness chiefly, which not only disarmed me, but unmanned me, as it were. For I consider that one, for the time, is a sort of unmanned when he tranquilly permits his hired clerk to dictate to him, and order him away from his own premises. Furthermore, I was full of uneasiness as to what Bartleby could possibly be doing in my office in his shirt sleeves, and in an otherwise dismantled condition of a Sunday morning. Was any thing amiss going on? Nay, that was out of the question. It was not to be thought of for a moment that Bartleby was an immoral person. But what could he be doing there?—copying? Nay again, whatever might be his eccentricities, Bartleby was an eminently decorous person. He would be the last man to sit down to his desk in any state approaching to nudity. Besides, it was Sunday; and there was something about Bartleby that forbade the supposition that he would by any secular occupation violate the proprieties of the day.

Nevertheless, my mind was not pacified; and full of a restless curiosity, at last I returned to the door. Without hindrance I inserted my key, opened it, and entered. Bartleby was not to be seen. I looked round anxiously, peeped behind his screen; but it was very plain that he was gone. Upon more closely examining the place, I surmised that for an indefinite period Bartleby must have ate, dressed, and slept in my office, and that too without plate, mirror, or bed. The cushioned seat of a ricketty old sofa in one corner bore the faint impress of a lean, reclining form. Rolled away under his desk, I found a blanket; under the empty grate, a blacking box and brush; on a chair, a tin basin, with soap and a ragged towel; in a newspaper a few crumbs of ginger-nuts and a morsel of cheese. Yes, thought I, it is evident enough that Bartleby has been making his home here, keeping bachelor's hall all by himself. Immediately then the thought came sweeping across me, What miserable friendlessness and loneliness are here revealed! His poverty is great; but his solitude, how horrible! Think of it. Of a Sunday, Wall-street is deserted as Petra; and every night of every day it is an emptiness. This building too, which of week-days hums with industry and life, at nightfall echoes with sheer vacancy, and all through Sunday is forlorn. And here Bartleby makes his home; sole spectator of a solitude which he has seen all populous—a sort of innocent and transformed Marius brooding among the ruins of Carthage!

For the first time in my life a feeling of overpowering stinging melancholy seized me. Before, I had never experienced aught but a not-unpleasing sadness. The bond of a common humanity now drew me irresistibly to gloom. A fraternal melancholy! For both I and Bartleby were sons of Adam. I remembered the bright silks and sparkling faces I had seen that day, in gala trim, swan-like sailing down the Mississippi of Broadway; and I contrasted them with the pallid copyist, and thought to myself, Ah, happiness courts the light, so we deem the world is gay; but misery hides aloof, so we deem that misery there is none. These sad fancyings—chimeras, doubtless, of a sick and silly brain—led on to other and more special thoughts, concerning the eccentricities of Bartleby. Presentiments of strange discoveries hovered round me. The scrivener's pale form appeared to me laid out, among uncaring strangers, in its shivering winding sheet.

Suddenly I was attracted by Bartleby's closed desk, the key in open sight left in the lock.

I mean no mischief, seek the gratification of no heartless curiosity, thought I; besides, the desk is mine, and its contents too, so I will make bold to look within. Every thing was methodically arranged, the papers smoothly placed. The pigeon holes were deep, and removing the files of documents, I groped into their recesses. Presently I felt something there, and dragged it out. It was an old bandanna handkerchief, heavy and knotted. I opened it, and saw it was a savings' bank.

I now recalled all the quiet mysteries which I had noted in the man. I remembered that he never spoke but to answer; that though at intervals he had considerable time to himself, yet I had never seen him reading—no, not even a newspaper; that for long periods he would stand looking out, at his pale window behind the screen, upon the dead brick wall; I was quite sure he never visited any refectory or eating house; while his pale face clearly indicated that he never drank beer like Turkey, or tea and coffee even, like other men; that he never went any where in particular that I could learn; never went out for a walk, unless indeed that was the case at present; that he had declined telling who he was, or whence he came, or whether he had any relatives in the world; that though so thin and pale, he never complained of ill health. And more than all, I remembered a certain unconscious air of pallid—how shall I call it?—of pallid haughtiness, say, or rather an austere reserve about him, which had positively awed me into my tame compliance with his eccentricities, when I had feared to ask him to do the slightest incidental thing for me, even though I might know, from his long-continued motionlessness, that behind his screen he must be standing in one of those dead-wall reveries of his.

Revolving all these things, and coupling them with the recently discovered fact that he made my office his constant abiding place and home, and not forgetful of his morbid moodiness; revolving all these things, a prudential feeling began to steal over me. My first emotions had been those of pure melancholy and sincerest pity; but just in proportion as the forlornness of Bartleby grew and grew to my imagination, did that same melancholy merge into fear, that pity into repulsion. So true it is, and so terrible too, that up to a certain point the thought or sight of misery enlists our best affections; but, in certain special cases, beyond that point it does not. They err who would assert that invariably this is owing to the inherent selfishness of the human heart. It rather proceeds from a certain hopelessness of remedying excessive and organic ill. To a sensitive being, pity is not seldom pain. And when at last it is perceived that such pity cannot lead to effectual succor, common sense bids the soul be rid of it. What I saw that morning persuaded me that the scrivener was the victim of innate and incurable disorder. I might give alms to his body; but his body did not pain him; it was his soul that suffered, and his soul I could not reach.

I did not accomplish the purpose of going to Trinity Church that morning. Somehow, the things I had seen disqualified me for the time from church-going. I walked homeward, thinking what I would do with Bartleby. Finally, I resolved upon this;—I would put certain calm questions to him the next morning, touching his history, &c., and if he declined to answer them openly and unreservedly (and I supposed he would prefer not), then to give him a twenty dollar bill over and above whatever I might owe him, and tell him his services were no longer required; but that if in any other way I could assist him, I would be happy to do so, especially if he desired to return to his native place, wherever that might be, I would willingly help to defray the expenses. Moreover, if, after reaching home, he found himself at any time in want of aid, a letter from him would be sure of a reply.

The next morning came.

"Bartleby," said I, gently calling to him behind his screen.

No reply.

"Bartleby," said I, in a still gentler tone, "come here; I am not going to ask you to do any thing you would prefer not to do—I simply wish to speak to you."

Upon this he noiselessly slid into view.

"Will you tell me, Bartleby, where you were born?"

"I would prefer not to."

"Will you tell me *any thing* about yourself?"

"I would prefer not to."

"But what reasonable objection can you have to speak to me? I feel friendly towards you."

He did not look at me while I spoke, but kept his glance fixed upon my bust of Cicero, which as I then sat, was directly behind me, some six inches above my head.

"What is your answer, Bartleby?" said I, after waiting a considerable time for a reply, during which his countenance remained immovable, only there was the faintest conceivable tremor of the white attenuated mouth.

"At present I prefer to give no answer," he said, and retired into his hermitage.

It was rather weak in me I confess, but his manner on this occasion nettled me. Not only did there seem to lurk in it a certain calm disdain, but his perverseness seemed ungrateful, considering the undeniable good usage and indulgence he had received from me.

Again I sat ruminating what I should do. Mortified as I was at his behavior, and resolved as I had been to dismiss him when I entered my office, nevertheless I strangely felt something superstitious knocking at my heart, and forbidding me to carry out my purpose, and denouncing me for a villain if I dared to breathe one bitter word against this forlornest of mankind. At last, familiarly drawing my chair behind his screen, I sat down and said: "Bartleby, never mind then about revealing your history; but let me entreat you, as a friend, to comply as far as may be with the usages of this office. Say now you will help to examine papers to-morrow or next day: in short, say now that in a day or two you will begin to be a little reasonable:—say so, Bartleby."

"At present I would prefer not to be a little reasonable," was his mildly cadaverous reply.

Just then the folding-doors opened, and Nippers approached. He seemed suffering from an unusually bad night's rest, induced by severer indigestion than common. He overheard those final words of Bartleby.

"*Prefer not*, eh?" gritted Nippers—"I'd *prefer* him, if I were you, sir," addressing me—"I'd *prefer* him; I'd give him preferences, the stubborn mule! What is it, sir, pray, that he *prefers* not to do now?"

Bartleby moved not a limb.

"Mr. Nippers," said I, "I'd prefer that you would withdraw for the present."

Somehow, of late I had got into the way of involuntarily using this word "prefer" upon all sorts of not exactly suitable occasions. And I trembled to think that my contact with the scrivener had already and seriously affected me in a mental way. And what further and deeper aberration might it not yet produce? This apprehension had not been without efficacy in determining me to summary measures.

As Nippers, looking very sour and sulky, was departing, Turkey blandly and deferentially approached.

"With submission, sir," said he, "yesterday I was thinking about Bartleby here, and I think that if he would but prefer to take a quart of good ale every day, it would do much towards mending him, and enabling him to assist in examining his papers."

"So you have got the word too," said I, slightly excited.

"With submission, what word, sir," asked Turkey, respectfully crowding himself into the contracted space behind the screen, and by so doing, making me jostle the scrivener. "What word, sir?"

"I would prefer to be left alone here," said Bartleby, as if offended at being mobbed in his privacy.

"*That's* the word, Turkey," said I—"*that's* it."

"Oh, *prefer*? oh yes—queer word. I never use it myself. But, sir, as I was saying, if he would but prefer—"

"Turkey," interrupted I, "you will please withdraw."

"Oh certainly, sir, if you prefer that I should."

As he opened the folding-doors to retire, Nippers at his desk caught a glimpse of me, and asked whether I would prefer to have a certain paper copied on blue paper or white. He did not in the least roguishly accent the word prefer. It was plain that it involuntarily rolled from his tongue. I thought to myself, surely I must get rid of a demented man, who already has in some degree turned the tongues, if not the heads of myself and clerks. But I thought it prudent not to break the dismission at once.

The next day I noticed that Bartleby did nothing but stand at his window in his dead-wall revery. Upon asking him why he did not write, he said that he had decided upon doing no more writing.

"Why, how now? what next?" exclaimed I, "do no more writing?"

"No more."

"And what is the reason?"

"Do you not see the reason for yourself," he indifferently replied.

I looked steadfastly at him, and perceived that his eyes looked dull and glazed. Instantly it occurred to me, that his unexampled diligence in copying by his dim window for the first few weeks of his stay with me might have temporarily impaired his vision.

I was touched. I said something in condolence with him. I hinted that of course he did wisely in abstaining from writing for a while; and urged him to embrace that opportunity of taking wholesome exercise in the open air. This, however, he did not do. A few days after this, my other clerks being absent, and being in a great hurry to dispatch certain letters by the mail, I thought that, having nothing else earthly to do, Bartleby would surely be less inflexible than usual, and carry these letters to the post-office. But he blankly declined. So, much to my inconvenience, I went myself.

Still added days went by. Whether Bartleby's eyes improved or not, I could not say. To all appearance, I thought they did. But when I asked him if they did, he vouchsafed no answer. At all events, he would do no copying. At last, in reply to my urgings, he informed me that he had permanently given up copying.

"What!" exclaimed I; "suppose your eyes should get entirely well—better than ever before—would you not copy then?"

"I have given up copying," he answered, and slid aside.

He remained as ever, a fixture in my chamber. Nay—if that were possible—he became still more of a fixture than before. What was to be done? He would do nothing in the office: why should he stay there? In plain fact, he had now become a millstone to me, not only useless as a necklace, but afflictive to bear. Yet I was sorry for him. I speak less than truth when I say that, on his own account, he occasioned me uneasiness. If he would but have named a single relative or friend, I would instantly have written, and urged their taking the poor fellow away to some convenient retreat. But he seemed alone, absolutely alone in the universe. A bit of wreck in the mid Atlantic. At length, necessities connected with my business tyrannized over all other considerations. Decently as I could, I told Bartleby that in six days' time he must unconditionally leave the office. I warned him to take measures, in the interval, for procuring some other abode. I offered to assist him in this endeavor, if he himself would but take the first step towards a removal. "And when you finally quit me, Bartleby," added I, "I shall see that you go not away entirely unprovided. Six days from this hour, remember."

At the expiration of that period, I peeped behind the screen, and lo! Bartleby was there.

I buttoned up my coat, balanced myself; advanced slowly towards him, touched his shoulder, and said, "The time has come; you must quit this place; I am sorry for you; here is money; but you must go."

"I would prefer not," he replied, with his back still towards me.

"You *must.*"

He remained silent.

Now I had an unbounded confidence in this man's common honesty. He had frequently restored to me sixpences and shillings carelessly dropped upon the floor, for I am apt to be very reckless in such shirt-button affairs. The proceeding then which followed will not be deemed extraordinary.

"Bartleby," said I, "I owe you twelve dollars on account; here are thirty-two; the odd twenty are yours.—Will you take it?" and I handed the bills towards him.

But he made no motion.

"I will leave them here then," putting them under a weight on the table. Then taking my hat and cane and going to the door I tranquilly turned and added—"After you have removed your things from these offices, Bartleby, you will of course lock the door—since every one is now gone for the day but you—and if you please, slip your key underneath the mat, so that I may have it in the morning. I shall not see you again; so good-bye to you. If hereafter in your new place of abode I can be of any service to you, do not fail to advise me by letter. Good-bye, Bartleby, and fare you well."

But he answered not a word; like the last column of some ruined temple, he remained standing mute and solitary in the middle of the otherwise deserted room.

As I walked home in a pensive mood, my vanity got the better of my pity. I could not but highly plume myself on my masterly management in getting rid of Bartleby. Masterly I call it, and such it must appear to any dispassionate thinker. The beauty of my procedure seemed to consist in its perfect quietness. There was no vulgar bullying, no bravado of any sort, no choleric hectoring, and striding to and fro across the apartment, jerking out vehement commands for Bartleby to bundle himself off with his beggarly traps. Nothing of the kind. Without loudly bidding Bartleby depart—as an inferior genius might have done—I *assumed* the ground that depart he must; and upon that assumption built all I had to say. The more I thought over my procedure, the more I was charmed with it. Nevertheless, next morning, upon awakening, I had my doubts,—I had somehow slept off the fumes of vanity. One of the coolest and wisest hours a man has, is just after he awakes in the morning. My procedure seemed as sagacious as ever,—but only in theory. How it would prove in practice—there was the rub. It was truly a beautiful thought to have assumed Bartleby's departure; but, after all, that assumption was simply my own, and none of Bartleby's. The great point was, not whether I had assumed that he would quit me, but whether he would prefer so to do. He was more a man of preferences than assumptions.

After breakfast, I walked down town, arguing the probabilities *pro* and *con*. One moment I thought it would prove a miserable failure, and Bartleby would be found all alive at my office as usual; the next moment it seemed certain that I should find his chair empty. And so I kept veering about. At the corner of Broadway and Canal-street, I saw quite an excited group of people standing in earnest conversation.

"I'll take odds he doesn't," said a voice as I passed.

"Doesn't go?—done!" said I, "put up your money."

I was instinctively putting my hand in my pocket to produce my own, when I remembered that this was an election day. The words I had overheard bore no reference to Bartleby, but to the success or non-success of some candidate for the mayoralty. In my intent frame of mind, I had, as it were, imagined that all Broadway shared in my excitement, and were debating the same question with me. I passed on, very thankful that the uproar of the street screened my momentary absent-mindedness.

As I had intended, I was earlier than usual at my office door. I stood listening for a moment. All was still. He must be gone. I tried the knob. The door was locked. Yes, my procedure had worked to a charm; he indeed must be vanished. Yet a certain melancholy mixed with this: I was almost sorry for my brilliant success. I was fumbling under the door mat for the key, which Bartleby was to have left there for me, when accidentally my knee knocked against a panel, producing a summoning sound, and in response a voice came to me from within—"Not yet; I am occupied."

It was Bartleby.

I was thunderstruck. For an instant I stood like the man who, pipe in mouth, was killed one cloudless afternoon long ago in Virginia, by

twelve o'clock came; Turkey began to glow in the face, overturn his inkstand, and become generally obstreperous; Nippers abated down into quietude and courtesy; Ginger Nut munched his noon apple; and Bartleby remained standing at his window in one of his profoundest dead-wall reveries. Will it be credited? Ought I to acknowledge it? That afternoon I left the office without saying one further word to him.

Some days now passed, during which, at leisure intervals I looked a little into "Edwards on the Will," and "Priestley on Necessity." Under the circumstances, those books induced a salutary feeling. Gradually I slid into the persuasion that these troubles of mine touching the scrivener, had been all predestinated from eternity, and Bartleby was billeted upon me for some mysterious purpose of an all-wise Providence, which it was not for a mere mortal like me to fathom. Yes, Bartleby, stay there behind your screen, thought I; I shall persecute you no more; you are harmless and noiseless as any of these old chairs; in short, I never feel so private as when I know you are here. At last I see it, I feel it; I penetrate to the predestinated purpose of my life. I am content. Others may have loftier parts to enact; but my mission in this world, Bartleby, is to furnish you with office-room for such period as you may see fit to remain.

I believe that this wise and blessed frame of mind would have continued with me, had it not been for the unsolicited and uncharitable remarks obtruded upon me by my professional friends who visited the rooms. But thus it often is, that the constant friction of illiberal minds wears out at last the best resolves of the more generous. Though to be sure, when I reflected upon it, it was not strange that people entering my office should be struck by the peculiar aspect of the unaccountable Bartleby, and so be tempted to throw out some sinister observations concerning him. Sometimes an attorney having business with me, and calling at my office, and finding no one but the scrivener there, would undertake to obtain some sort of precise information from him touching my whereabouts; but without heeding his idle talk, Bartleby would remain standing immovable in the middle of the room. So after contemplating him in that position for a time, the attorney would depart, no wiser than he came.

Also, when a Reference was going on, and the room full of lawyers and witnesses and business was driving fast; some deeply occupied legal gentleman present, seeing Bartleby wholly unemployed, would request him to run round to his (the legal gentleman's) office and fetch some papers for him. Thereupon, Bartleby would tranquilly decline, and yet remain idle as before. Then the lawyer would give a great stare, and turn to me. And what could I say? At last I was made aware that all through the circle of my professional acquaintance, a whisper of wonder was running round, having reference to the strange creature I kept at my office. This worried me very much. And as the idea came upon me of his possibly turning out a long-lived man, and keep occupying my chambers, and denying my authority; and perplexing my visitors; and scandalizing my professional reputation; and casting a general gloom over the premises; keeping soul and body together to the last upon his savings (for doubtless he spent but half a dime a day), and in the end perhaps outlive me, and claim possession of my office by right of his perpetual occupancy: as all these dark anticipations crowded upon me more and more, and my friends continually intruded their relentless remarks upon the apparition in my room; a great change was wrought in me. I resolved to gather all my faculties together, and for ever rid me of this intolerable incubus.

Ere revolving any complicated project, however, adapted to this end, I first simply suggested to Bartleby the propriety of his permanent departure. In a calm and serious tone, I commended the idea to his careful and mature consideration. But having taken three days to meditate upon it, he apprised me that his original determination remained the same; in short, that he still preferred to abide with me.

What shall I do? I now said to myself, buttoning up my coat to the last button. What shall I do? what ought I to do? what does conscience say I *should* do with this man, or rather ghost? Rid myself of him, I must; go, he shall. But how? You will not thrust him, the poor, pale, passive mortal,—you will not thrust such a helpless creature out of your door? you will not dishonor yourself by such cruelty? No, I will not, I cannot do that. Rather would I let him live and die here, and then mason up his remains in the wall. What then will you do? For all your coaxing, he will not budge. Bribes he leaves under your own paper-weight on your table; in short, it is quite plain that he prefers to cling to you.

Then something severe, something unusual must be done. What! surely you will not have him collared by a constable, and commit his innocent pallor to the common jail? And upon what ground could you procure such a thing to be done?—a vagrant, is he? What! he a vagrant, a wanderer, who refuses to budge? It is because he will *not* be a vagrant, then, that you seek to count him *as* a vagrant. That is too absurd. No visible means of support: there I have him. Wrong again: for indubitably he *does* support himself, and that is the only unanswerable proof that any man can show of his possessing the means so to do. No more then.

Since he will not quit me, I must quit him. I will change my offices; I will move elsewhere; and give him fair notice, that if I find him on my new premises I will then proceed against him as a common trespasser.

Acting accordingly, next day I thus addressed him: "I find these chambers too far from the City Hall; the air is unwholesome. In a word, I propose to remove my offices next week, and shall no longer require your services. I tell you this now, in order that you may seek another place."

He made no reply, and nothing more was said.

On the appointed day I engaged carts and men, proceeded to my chambers, and having but little furniture, every thing was removed in a few hours. Throughout, the scrivener remained standing behind the screen, which I directed to be removed the last thing. It was withdrawn; and being folded up like a huge folio, left him the motionless occupant of a naked room. I stood in the entry watching him a moment, while something from within me upbraided me.

I re-entered, with my hand in my pocket—and—and my heart in my mouth.

"Good-bye, Bartleby; I am going—good-bye, and God some way bless you; and take that," slipping something in his hand. But it dropped upon the floor, and then,—strange to say—I tore myself from him whom I had so longed to be rid of.

Established in my new quarters, for a day or two I kept the door locked, and started at every footfall in the passages. When I returned to my rooms after any little absence, I would pause at the threshold for an instant, and attentively listen, ere applying my key. But these fears were needless. Bartleby never came nigh me.

I thought all was going well, when a perturbed looking stranger visited me, inquiring whether I was the person who had recently occupied rooms at No. — Wall-street.

Full of forebodings, I replied that I was.

"Then sir," said the stranger, who proved a lawyer, "you are responsible for the man you left there. He refuses to do any copying; he refuses to do any thing; he says he prefers not to; and he refuses to quit the premises."

"I am very sorry, sir," said I, with assumed tranquillity, but an inward tremor, "but, really, the man you allude to is nothing to me—he is no relation or apprentice of mine, that you should hold me responsible for him."

"In mercy's name, who is he?"

"I certainly cannot inform you. I know nothing about him. Formerly I employed him as a copyist; but he has done nothing for me now for some time past."

"I shall settle him then,—good morning, sir."

Several days passed, and I heard nothing more; and though I often felt a charitable prompting to call at the place and see poor Bartleby, yet a certain squeamishness of I know not what withheld me.

All is over with him, by this time, thought I at last, when through another week no further intelligence reached me. But coming to my room the day after, I found several persons waiting at my door in a high state of nervous excitement.

"That's the man—here he comes," cried the foremost one, whom I recognized as the lawyer who had previously called upon me alone.

"You must take him away, sir, at once," cried a portly person among them, advancing upon me, and whom I knew to be the landlord of No. — Wall-street. "These gentlemen, my tenants, cannot stand it any longer; Mr. B——" pointing to the lawyer, "has turned him out of his room, and he now persists in haunting the building generally, sitting upon the banisters of the stairs by day, and sleeping in the entry by night. Every body is concerned; clients are leaving the offices; some fears are entertained of a mob; something you must do, and that without delay."

Aghast at this torrent, I fell back before it, and would fain have locked myself in my new quarters. In vain I persisted that Bartleby was nothing to me—no more than to any one else. In vain:—I was the last person known to have any thing to do with him, and they held me to the terrible account. Fearful then of being exposed in the papers (as one person present obscurely threatened) I considered the matter, and at length said, that if the lawyer would give me a confidential interview with the scrivener, in his (the lawyer's) own room, I would that afternoon strive my best to rid them of the nuisance they complained of.

Going up stairs to my old haunt, there was Bartleby silently sitting upon the banister at the landing.

"What are you doing here, Bartleby?" said I.

"Sitting upon the banister," he mildly replied.

I motioned him into the lawyer's room, who then left us.

"Bartleby," said I, "are you aware that you are the cause of great tribulation to me, by persisting in occupying the entry after being dismissed from the office?"

No answer.

"Now one of two things must take place. Either you must do something, or something must be done to you. Now what sort of business would you like to engage in? Would you like to re-engage in copying for some one?"

"No; I would prefer not to make any change."

"Would you like a clerkship in a dry-goods store?"

"There is too much confinement about that. No, I would not like a clerkship; but I am not particular."

"Too much confinement," I cried, "why you keep yourself confined all the time!"

"I would prefer not to take a clerkship," he rejoined, as if to settle that little item at once.

"How would a bar-tender's business suit you? There is no trying of the eyesight in that."

"I would not like it at all; though, as I said before, I am not particular."

His unwonted wordiness inspirited me. I returned to the charge.

"Well then, would you like to travel through the country collecting bills for the merchants? That would improve your health."

"No, I would prefer to be doing something else."

"How then would going as a companion to Europe, to entertain some young gentleman with your conversation,—how would that suit you?"

"Not at all. It does not strike me that there is any thing definite about that. I like to be stationary. But I am not particular."

"Stationary you shall be then," I cried, now losing all patience, and for the first time in all my exasperating connection with him fairly flying into a passion. "If you do not go away from these premises before night, I shall feel bound—indeed I *am* bound—to—to—to quit the premises myself!" I rather absurdly concluded, knowing not with what possible threat to try to frighten his immobility into compliance. Despairing of all further efforts, I was precipitately leaving him, when a final thought occurred to me—one which had not been wholly unindulged before.

"Bartleby," said I, in the kindest tone I could assume under such exciting circumstances, "will you go home with me now—not to my office, but my dwelling—and remain there till we can conclude upon some convenient arrangement for you at our leisure? Come, let us start now, right away."

"No: at present I would prefer not to make any change at all."

I answered nothing; but effectually dodging every one by the suddenness and rapidity of my flight, rushed from the building, ran up Wall-street towards Broadway, and jumping into the first omnibus was soon removed from pursuit. As soon as tranquillity returned I distinctly perceived that I had now done all that I possibly could, both in respect to the demands of the landlord and his tenants, and with regard to my own desire and sense of duty, to benefit Bartleby, and shield him from rude persecution. I now strove to be entirely care-free and quiescent; and my conscience justified me in the attempt; though indeed it was not so successful as I could have wished. So fearful was I of being again hunted out by the incensed landlord and his exasperated tenants, that, surrendering my business to Nippers, for a few days I drove about the upper part of the town and through the suburbs, in my rockaway; crossed over to Jersey City and Hoboken, and paid fugitive visits to Manhattanville and Astoria. In fact I almost lived in my rockaway for the time.

When again I entered my office, lo, a note from the landlord lay upon the desk. I opened it with trembling hands. It informed me that the writer had sent to the police, and had Bartleby removed to the Tombs as a vagrant. Moreover, since I knew more about him than any one else, he wished me to appear at that place, and make a suitable statement of the facts. These tidings had a conflicting effect upon me. At first I was indignant; but at last almost approved. The landlord's energetic, summary disposition, had led him to adopt a procedure which I do not think I would have decided upon myself; and yet as a last resort, under such peculiar circumstances, it seemed the only plan.

As I afterwards learned, the poor scrivener, when told that he must be conducted to the Tombs, offered not the slightest obstacle, but in his pale unmoving way, silently acquiesced.

Some of the compassionate and curious bystanders joined the party; and headed by one of the constables arm in arm with Bartleby, the silent procession filed its way through all the noise, and heat, and joy of the roaring thoroughfares at noon.

The same day I received the note I went to the Tombs, or to speak more properly, the Halls of Justice. Seeking the right officer, I stated the purpose of my call, and was informed that the individual I described was indeed within. I then assured the functionary that Bartleby was a perfectly honest man, and greatly to be compassionated, however unaccountably eccentric. I narrated all I knew, and closed by suggesting the idea of letting him remain in as indulgent confinement as possible till something less harsh might be done—though indeed I hardly knew what. At all events, if nothing else could be decided upon, the alms-house must receive him. I then begged to have an interview.

Being under no disgraceful charge, and quite serene and harmless in all his ways, they had permitted him freely to wander about the prison, and especially in the inclosed grass-platted yards thereof. And so I found him there, standing all alone in the quietest of the yards, his face towards a high wall, while all around, from the narrow slits of the jail windows, I thought I saw peering out upon him the eyes of murderers and thieves.

"Bartleby!"

"I know you," he said, without looking round,—"and I want nothing to say to you."

"It was not I that brought you here, Bartleby," said I, keenly pained at his implied suspicion. "And to you, this should not be so vile a place. Nothing reproachful attaches to you by being here. And see, it is not so sad a place as one might think. Look, there is the sky, and here is the grass."

"I know where I am," he replied, but would say nothing more, and so I left him.

As I entered the corridor again, a broad meat-like man, in an apron, accosted me, and jerking his thumb over his shoulder said—"Is that your friend?"

"Yes."

"Does he want to starve? If he does, let him live on the prison fare, that's all."

"Who are you?" asked I, not knowing what to make of such an unofficially speaking person in such a place.

"I am the grub-man. Such gentlemen as have friends here, hire me to provide them with something good to eat."

"Is this so?" said I, turning to the turnkey.

He said it was.

"Well then," said I, slipping some silver into the grub-man's hands (for so they called him). "I want you to give particular attention to my friend there; let him have the best dinner you can get. And you must be as polite to him as possible."

"Introduce me, will you?" said the grub-man, looking at me with an expression which seemed to say he was all impatience for an opportunity to give a specimen of his breeding.

Thinking it would prove of benefit to the scrivener, I acquiesced; and asking the grub-man his name, went up with him to Bartleby.

"Bartleby, this is Mr. Cutlets; you will find him very useful to you."

"Your sarvant, sir, your sarvant," said the grub-man, making a low salutation behind his apron. "Hope you find it pleasant here, sir; nice grounds—cool apartments, sir—hope you'll stay with us some time—try to make it agreeable. May Mrs. Cutlets and I have the pleasure of your company to dinner, sir, in Mrs. Cutlets' private room?"

"I prefer not to dine to-day," said Bartleby, turning away. "It would disagree with me; I am unused to dinners." So saying he slowly moved to the other side of the inclosure, and took up a position fronting the dead-wall.

"How's this?" said the grub-man, addressing me with a stare of astonishment. "He's odd, aint he?"

"I think he is a little deranged," said I, sadly.

"Deranged? deranged is it? Well now, upon my word, I thought that friend of yourn was a gentleman forger; they are always pale and genteel-like, them forgers. I can't help pity 'em—can't help it, sir. Did you know Monroe Edwards?" he added touchingly, and paused. Then, laying his hand pityingly on my shoulder, sighed, "he died of consumption at Sing-Sing. So you weren't acquainted with Monroe?"

"No, I was never socially acquainted with any forgers. But I cannot stop longer. Look to my friend yonder. You will not lose by it. I will see you again."

Some few days after this, I again obtained admission to the Tombs, and went through the corridors in quest of Bartleby; but without finding him.

"I saw him coming from his cell not long ago," said a turnkey, "may be he's gone to loiter in the yards."

So I went in that direction.

"Are you looking for the silent man?" said another turnkey passing me. "Yonder he lies—sleeping in the yard there. 'Tis not twenty minutes since I saw him lie down."

The yard was entirely quiet. It was not accessible to the common prisoners. The surrounding walls, of amazing thickness, kept off all sounds behind them. The Egyptian character of the masonry weighed upon me with its gloom. But a soft imprisoned turf grew under foot. The heart of the eternal pyramids, it seemed, wherein, by some strange magic, through the clefts, grass-seed, dropped by birds, had sprung.

Strangely huddled at the base of the wall, his knees drawn up, and lying on his side, his head touching the cold stones, I saw the wasted Bartleby. But nothing stirred. I paused; then went close up to him;

stooped over, and saw that his dim eyes were open; otherwise he seemed profoundly sleeping. Something prompted me to touch him. I felt his hand, when a tingling shiver ran up my arm and down my spine to my feet.

The round face of the grub-man peered upon me now. "His dinner is ready. Won't he dine to-day, either? Or does he live without dining?"

"Lives without dining," said I, and closed the eyes.

"Eh!—He's asleep, aint he?"

"With kings and counsellors," murmured I.

* * * * *

There would seem little need for proceeding further in this history. Imagination will readily supply the meagre recital of poor Bartleby's interment. But ere parting with the reader, let me say, that if this little narrative has sufficiently interested him, to awaken curiosity as to who Bartleby was, and what manner of life he led prior to the present narrator's making his acquaintance, I can only reply, that in such curiosity I fully share, but am wholly unable to gratify it. Yet here I hardly know whether I should divulge one little item of rumor, which came to my ear a few months after the scrivener's decease. Upon what basis it rested, I could never ascertain; and hence, how true it is I cannot now tell. But inasmuch as this vague report has not been without a certain strange suggestive interest to me, however sad, it may prove the same with some others; and so I will briefly mention it. The report was this: that Bartleby had been a subordinate clerk in the Dead Letter Office at Washington, from which he had been suddenly removed by a change in the administration. When I think over this rumor, hardly can I express the emotions which seize me. Dead letters! does it not sound like dead men? Conceive a man by nature and misfortune prone to a pallid hopelessness, can any business seem more fitted to heighten it than that of continually handling these dead letters, and assorting them for the flames? For by the cart-load they are annually burned. Sometimes from out the folded paper the pale clerk takes a ring:—the finger it was meant for, perhaps, moulders in the grave; a bank-note sent in swiftest charity:—he whom it would relieve, nor eats nor hungers any more; pardon for those who died despairing; hope for those who died unhoping; good tidings for those who died stifled by unrelieved calamities. On errands of life, these letters speed to death.

Ah Bartleby! Ah humanity!

Benito Cereno

IN THE YEAR 1799, Captain Amasa Delano, of Duxbury, in Massachusetts, commanding a large sealer and general trader, lay at anchor, with a valuable cargo, in the harbor of St. Maria—a small, desert, uninhabited island toward the southern extremity of the long coast of Chili. There he had touched for water.

On the second day, not long after dawn, while lying in his berth, his mate came below, informing him that a strange sail was coming into the bay. Ships were then not so plenty in those waters as now. He rose, dressed, and went on deck.

The morning was one peculiar to that coast. Everything was mute and calm; everything gray. The sea, though undulated into long roods of swells, seemed fixed, and was sleeked at the surface like waved lead that has cooled and set in the smelter's mould. The sky seemed a gray surtout. Flights of troubled gray fowl, kith and kin with flights of troubled gray vapors among which they were mixed, skimmed low and fitfully over the waters, as swallows over meadows before storms. Shadows present, foreshadowing deeper shadows to come.

To Captain Delano's surprise, the stranger, viewed through the glass, showed no colors; though to do so upon entering a haven, however uninhabited in its shores, where but a single other ship might be lying, was the custom among peaceful seamen of all nations. Considering the lawlessness and loneliness of the spot, and the sort of stories, at that day, associated with those seas, Captain Delano's surprise might have deepened into some uneasiness had he not been a person of a singularly undistrustful good nature, not liable, except on extraordinary and repeated incentives, and hardly then, to indulge in personal alarms, any way involving the imputation of malign evil in man. Whether, in view of what humanity is capable, such a trait implies, along with a benevolent heart, more than ordinary quickness and accuracy of intellectual perception, may be left to the wise to determine.

But whatever misgivings might have obtruded on first seeing the stranger, would almost, in any seaman's mind, have been dissipated by observing that, the ship, in navigating into the harbor, was drawing too near the land, for her own safety's sake, owing to a sunken reef making out off her bow. This seemed to prove her a stranger, indeed, not only to the sealer, but the island; consequently, she could be no wonted free-booter on that ocean. With no small interest, Captain Delano continued to watch her—a proceeding not much facilitated by the vapors partly mantling the hull, through which the far matin light from her cabin streamed equivocally enough; much like the sun—by this time hemi-sphered on the rim of the horizon, and apparently, in company with the strange ship, entering the harbor—which, wimpled by the same low, creeping clouds, showed not unlike a Lima intriguante's one sinister eye peering across the Plaza from the Indian loop-hole of her dusk *saya-y-manta.*

It might have been but a deception of the vapors, but, the longer the stranger was watched, the more singular appeared her maneuvers. Ere long it seemed hard to decide whether she meant to come in or no—what she wanted, or what she was about. The wind, which had breezed up a little during the night, was now extremely light and baffling, which the more increased the apparent uncertainty of her movements.

Surmising, at last, that it might be a ship in distress, Captain Delano ordered his whale-boat to be dropped, and, much to the wary opposition of his mate, prepared to board her, and, at the least, pilot her in. On the night previous, a fishing-party of the seamen had gone a long distance to some detached rocks out of sight from the sealer, and, an hour or two before day-break, had returned, having met with no small success. Presuming that the stranger might have been long off soundings, the good captain put several baskets of the fish, for presents, into his boat, and so pulled away. From her continuing too near the sunken reef, deeming her in danger, calling to his men, he made all haste to apprise those on board of their situation. But, some time ere the boat came up, the wind, light though it was, having shifted, had headed the vessel off, as well as partly broken the vapors from about her.

Upon gaining a less remote view, the ship, when made signally visible on the verge of the leaden-hued swells, with the shreds of fog here and there raggedly furring her, appeared like a white-washed monastery after a thunder-storm, seen perched upon some dun cliff among the Pyrenees. But it was no purely fanciful resemblance which now, for a moment, almost led Captain Delano to think that nothing less than a ship-load of monks was before him. Peering over the bulwarks were what really seemed, in the hazy distance, throngs of dark cowls; while, fitfully revealed through the open port-holes, other dark moving figures were dimly descried, as of Black Friars pacing the cloisters.

Upon a still nigher approach, this appearance was modified, and the true character of the vessel was plain—a Spanish merchantman of the first class; carrying negro slaves, amongst other valuable freight, from one colonial port to another. A very large, and, in its time, a very fine vessel, such as in those days were at intervals encountered along that main; sometimes superseded Acapulco treasure-ships, or retired frigates of the Spanish king's navy, which, like superannuated Italian palaces, still, under a decline of masters, preserved signs of former state.

As the whale-boat drew more and more nigh, the cause of the peculiar pipe-clayed aspect of the stranger was seen in the slovenly neglect pervading her. The spars, ropes, and great part of the bulwarks, looked woolly, from long unacquaintance with the scraper, tar, and the brush. Her keel seemed laid, her ribs put together, and she launched, from Ezekiel's Valley of Dry Bones.

In the present business in which she was engaged, the ship's general model and rig appeared to have undergone no material change from their original war-like and Froissart pattern. However, no guns were seen.

The tops were large, and were railed about with what had once been octagonal net-work, all now in sad disrepair. These tops hung overhead like three ruinous aviaries, in one of which was seen perched, on a ratlin, a white noddy, a strange fowl, so called from its lethargic, somnambulistic character, being frequently caught by hand at sea. Battered and mouldy, the castellated forecastle seemed some ancient turret, long ago taken by assault, and then left to decay. Toward the stern, two high-raised quarter galleries—the balustrades here and there covered with dry, tindery sea-moss—opening out from the unoccupied state-cabin, whose dead lights, for all the mild weather, were hermetically closed and calked—these tenantless balconies hung over the sea as if it were the grand Venetian canal. But the principal relic of faded grandeur was the ample oval of the shield-like stern-piece, intricately carved with the arms of Castile and Leon, medallioned about by groups of mythological or symbolical devices; uppermost and central of which was a dark satyr in a mask, holding his foot on the prostrate neck of a writhing figure, likewise masked.

Whether the ship had a figure-head, or only a plain beak, was not quite certain, owing to canvas wrapped about that part, either to protect it while undergoing a re-furbishing, or else decently to hide its decay. Rudely painted or chalked, as in a sailor freak, along the forward side of a sort of pedestal below the canvas, was the sentence, "*Seguid vuestro jefe,*" (follow your leader); while upon the tarnished head-boards, near by, appeared, in stately capitals, once gilt, the ship's name, "SAN DOMINICK," each letter streakingly corroded with tricklings of copper-spike rust; while, like mourning weeds, dark festoons of sea-grass slimily swept to and fro over the name, with every hearse-like roll of the hull.

As at last the boat was hooked from the bow along toward the gang-way amidship, its keel, while yet some inches separated from the hull, harshly grated as on a sunken coral reef. It proved a huge bunch of conglobated barnacles adhering below the water to the side like a wen; a token of baffling airs and long calms passed somewhere in those seas.

Climbing the side, the visitor was at once surrounded by a clamorous throng of whites and blacks, but the latter outnumbering the former more than could have been expected, negro transportation-ship as the stranger in port was. But, in one language, and as with one voice, all poured out a common tale of suffering; in which the negresses, of whom there were not a few, exceeded the others in their dolorous vehemence. The scurvy, together with a fever, had swept off a great part of their number, more especially the Spaniards. Off Cape Horn, they had narrowly escaped shipwreck; then, for days together, they had lain tranced without wind; their provisions were low; their water next to none; their lips that moment were baked.

While Captain Delano was thus made the mark of all eager tongues, his one eager glance took in all the faces, with every other object about him.

Always upon first boarding a large and populous ship at sea, especially a foreign one, with a nondescript crew such as Lascars or Manilla men, the impression varies in a peculiar way from that produced by first entering a strange house with strange inmates in a strange land. Both house and ship, the one by its walls and blinds, the other by its high bulwarks like ramparts, hoard from view their interiors till the last moment; but in the case of the ship there is this addition; that the living spectacle it contains, upon its sudden and complete disclosure, has, in contrast with the blank ocean which zones it, something of the effect of enchantment. The ship seems unreal; these strange costumes, gestures, and faces, but a shadowy tableau just emerged from the deep, which directly must receive back what it gave.

Perhaps it was some such influence as above is attempted to be described, which, in Captain Delano's mind, heightened whatever, upon a staid scrutiny, might have seemed unusual; especially the conspicuous figures of four elderly grizzled negroes, their heads like black, doddered willow tops, who, in venerable contrast to the tumult below them, were couched sphynx-like, one on the starboard cat-head, another on the larboard, and the remaining pair face to face on the opposite bulwarks above the main-chains. They each had bits of unstranded old junk in their hands, and, with a sort of stoical self-content, were picking the junk into oakum, a small heap of which lay by their sides. They accompanied the task with a continuous, low, monotonous chant; droning and druling away like so many gray-headed bag-pipers playing a funeral march.

The quarter-deck rose into an ample elevated poop, upon the forward verge of which, lifted, like the oakum-pickers, some eight feet above the general throng, sat along in a row, separated by regular spaces, the cross-legged figures of six other blacks; each with a rusty hatchet in his hand, which, with a bit of brick and a rag, he was engaged like a scullion in scouring; while between each two was a small stack of hatchets, their rusted edges turned forward awaiting a like operation. Though occasionally the four oakum-pickers would briefly address some person or persons in the crowd below, yet the six hatchet-polishers neither spoke to others, nor breathed a whisper among themselves, but sat intent upon their task, except at intervals, when, with the peculiar love in negroes of uniting industry with pastime, two and two they sideways clashed their hatchets together, like cymbals, with a barbarous din. All six, unlike the generality, had the raw aspect of unsophisticated Africans.

But that first comprehensive glance which took in those ten figures, with scores less conspicuous, rested but an instant upon them, as, impatient of the hubbub of voices, the visitor turned in quest of whomsoever it might be that commanded the ship.

But as if not unwilling to let nature make known her own case among his suffering charge, or else in despair of restraining it for the time, the Spanish captain, a gentlemanly, reserved-looking, and rather young man to a stranger's eye, dressed with singular richness, but bearing plain traces of recent sleepless cares and disquietudes, stood passively by, leaning against the main-mast, at one moment casting a dreary, spiritless look upon his excited people, at the next an unhappy glance toward his visitor. By his side stood a black of small stature, in whose rude face, as occasionally, like a shepherd's dog, he mutely turned it up into the Spaniard's, sorrow and affection were equally blended.

Struggling through the throng, the American advanced to the Spaniard, assuring him of his sympathies, and offering to render whatever assistance might be in his power. To which the Spaniard returned, for the present, but grave and ceremonious acknowledgments, his national formality dusked by the saturnine mood of ill health.

But losing no time in mere compliments, Captain Delano returning to the gangway, had his baskets of fish brought up; and as the wind still continued light, so that some hours at least must elapse ere the ship could be brought to the anchorage, he bade his men return to the sealer, and fetch back as much water as the whale-boat could carry, with whatever soft bread the steward might have, all the remaining pumpkins on board, with a box of sugar, and a dozen of his private bottles of cider.

Not many minutes after the boat's pushing off, to the vexation of all, the wind entirely died away, and the tide turning, began drifting back the ship helplessly seaward. But trusting this would not long last, Captain Delano sought with good hopes to cheer up the strangers, feeling no small satisfaction that, with persons in their condition he could—thanks to his frequent voyages along the Spanish main—converse with some freedom in their native tongue.

While left alone with them, he was not long in observing some things tending to heighten his first impressions; but surprise was lost in pity, both for the Spaniards and blacks, alike evidently reduced from scarcity of water and provisions; while long-continued suffering seemed to have brought out the less good-natured qualities of the negroes, besides, at the same time, impairing the Spaniard's authority over them. But, under the circumstances, precisely this condition of things was to have been anticipated. In armies, navies, cities, or families, in nature herself, nothing more relaxes good order than misery. Still, Captain Delano was not without the idea, that had Benito Cereno been a man of greater energy, misrule would hardly have come to the present pass. But the debility, constitutional or induced by the hardships, bodily and mental, of the Spanish captain, was too obvious to be overlooked. A prey to settled dejection, as if long mocked with hope he would not now indulge it, even when it had ceased to be a mock, the prospect of that day or evening at furthest, lying at anchor, with plenty of water for his people, and a brother captain to counsel and befriend, seemed in no perceptible degree to encourage him. His mind appeared unstrung, if not still more seriously affected. Shut up in these oaken walls, chained to one dull round of command, whose unconditionality cloyed him, like some hypochondriac abbot he moved slowly about, at times suddenly pausing, starting, or staring, biting his lip, biting his finger-nail, flushing, paling, twitching his beard, with other symptoms of an absent or moody mind. This distempered spirit was lodged, as before hinted, in as distempered a frame. He was rather tall, but seemed never to have been robust, and now with nervous suffering was almost worn to a skeleton. A tendency to some pulmonary complaint appeared to have been lately confirmed. His voice was like that of one with lungs half gone, hoarsely suppressed, a husky whisper. No wonder that, as in this state he tottered about, his private servant apprehensively followed him. Sometimes the negro gave his master his arm, or took his handkerchief out of his pocket for him; performing these and similar offices with that affectionate zeal which transmutes into something filial or fraternal acts in themselves but menial; and which has gained for the negro the repute of making the most pleasing body servant in the world; one, too, whom a master need be on no stiffly superior terms with, but may treat with familiar trust; less a servant than a devoted companion.

Marking the noisy indocility of the blacks in general, as well as what seemed the sullen inefficiency of the whites, it was not without humane satisfaction that Captain Delano witnessed the steady good conduct of Babo.

But the good conduct of Babo, hardly more than the ill-behavior of others, seemed to withdraw the half-lunatic Don Benito from his cloudy languor. Not that such precisely was the impression made by the Spaniard on the mind of his visitor. The Spaniard's individual unrest was, for the present, but noted as a conspicuous feature in the ship's general affliction. Still, Captain Delano was not a little concerned at what he could not help taking for the time to be Don Benito's unfriendly indifference towards himself. The Spaniard's manner, too, conveyed a sort of sour and gloomy disdain, which he seemed at no pains to disguise. But this the American in charity ascribed to the harassing effects of sickness, since, in former instances, he had noted that there are peculiar natures on whom prolonged physical suffering seems to cancel every social instinct of kindness; as if forced to black bread themselves, they deemed it but equity that each person coming nigh them should, indirectly, by some slight or affront, be made to partake of their fare.

But ere long Captain Delano bethought him that, indulgent as he was at the first, in judging the Spaniard, he might not, after all, have exercised charity enough. At bottom it was Don Benito's reserve which displeased him; but the same reserve was shown towards all but his faithful personal attendant. Even the formal reports which, according to sea-usage, were, at stated times, made to him by some petty underling, either a white, mulatto or black, he hardly had patience enough to listen to, without betraying contemptuous aversion. His manner upon such occasions was, in its degree, not unlike that which might be supposed to have been his imperial countryman's, Charles V., just previous to the anchoritish retirement of that monarch from the throne.

This splenetic disrelish of his place was evinced in almost every function pertaining to it. Proud as he was moody, he condescended to no personal mandate. Whatever special orders were necessary, their delivery was delegated to his body-servant, who in turn transferred them to their ultimate destination, through runners, alert Spanish boys or slave boys, like pages or pilot-fish within easy call continually hovering round Don Benito. So that to have beheld this undemonstrative invalid gliding about, apathetic and mute, no landsman could have dreamed that in him was lodged a dictatorship beyond which, while at sea, there was no earthly appeal.

Thus, the Spaniard, regarded in his reserve, seemed as the involuntary victim of mental disorder. But, in fact, his reserve might, in some degree, have proceeded from design. If so, then here was evinced the unhealthy climax of that icy though conscientious policy, more or less adopted by all commanders of large ships, which, except in signal emergencies, obliterates alike the manifestation of sway with every trace of sociality; transforming the man into a block, or rather into a loaded cannon, which, until there is call for thunder, has nothing to say.

Viewing him in this light, it seemed but a natural token of the perverse habit induced by a long course of such hard self-restraint, that, notwithstanding the present condition of his ship, the Spaniard should still persist in a demeanor, which, however harmless, or, it may be, appropriate, in a well appointed vessel, such as the San Dominick might have been at the outset of the voyage, was anything but judicious now. But the Spaniard perhaps thought that it was with captains as with gods: reserve, under all events, must still be their cue. But more probably this appearance of slumbering dominion might have been but an attempted disguise to conscious imbecility—not deep policy, but shallow device. But be all this as it might, whether Don Benito's manner was designed or not, the more Captain Delano noted its pervading reserve, the less he felt uneasiness at any particular manifestation of that reserve towards himself.

Neither were his thoughts taken up by the captain alone. Wonted to the quiet orderliness of the sealer's comfortable family of a crew, the noisy confusion of the San Dominick's suffering host repeatedly challenged his eye. Some prominent breaches not only of discipline but of decency were observed. These Captain Delano could not but ascribe, in the main, to the absence of those subordinate deck-officers to whom, along with higher duties, is entrusted what may be styled the police department of a populous ship. True, the old oakum-pickers appeared at times to act the part of monitorial constables to their countrymen, the blacks; but though occasionally succeeding in allaying trifling outbreaks now and then between man and man, they could do little or nothing toward establishing general quiet. The San Dominick was in the condition of a transatlantic emigrant ship, among whose multitude of living freight are some individuals, doubtless, as little troublesome as crates and bales; but the friendly remonstrances of such with their ruder companions are of not so much avail as the unfriendly arm of the mate. What the San Dominick wanted was, what the emigrant ship has, stern superior officers. But on these decks not so much as a fourth mate was to be seen.

The visitor's curiosity was roused to learn the particulars of those mishaps which had brought about such absenteeism, with its consequences; because, though deriving some inkling of the voyage from the wails which at the first moment had greeted him, yet of the details no clear understanding had been had. The best account would, doubtless, be given by the captain. Yet at first the visitor was loth to ask it, unwilling to provoke some distant rebuff. But plucking up courage, he at last accosted Don Benito, renewing the expression of his benevolent interest, adding, that did he (Captain Delano) but know the particulars of the ship's misfortunes, he would, perhaps, be better able in the end to relieve them. Would Don Benito favor him with the whole story?

Don Benito faltered; then, like some somnambulist suddenly interfered with, vacantly stared at his visitor, and ended by looking down on the deck. He maintained this posture so long, that Captain Delano, almost equally disconcerted, and involuntarily almost as rude, turned suddenly from him, walking forward to accost one of the Spanish seamen for the desired information. But he had hardly gone five paces, when with a sort of eagerness Don Benito invited him back, regretting his momentary absence of mind, and professing readiness to gratify him.

While most part of the story was being given, the two captains stood on the after part of the main-deck, a privileged spot, no one being near but the servant.

"It is now a hundred and ninety days," began the Spaniard, in his husky whisper, "that this ship, well officered and well manned, with several cabin passengers—some fifty Spaniards in all—sailed from Buenos Ayres bound to Lima, with a general cargo, hardware, Paraguay tea and the like—and," pointing forward, "that parcel of negroes, now not more than a hundred and fifty, as you see, but then numbering over three hundred souls. Off Cape Horn we had heavy gales. In one moment, by night, three of my best officers, with fifteen sailors, were lost, with the main-yard; the spar snapping under them in the slings, as they sought, with heavers, to beat down the icy sail. To lighten the hull, the heavier sacks of mate were thrown into the sea, with most of the water-pipes lashed on deck at the time. And this last necessity it was, combined with the prolonged detentions afterwards experienced, which eventually brought about our chief causes of suffering. When——"

Here there was a sudden fainting attack of his cough, brought on, no doubt, by his mental distress. His servant sustained him, and drawing a cordial from his pocket placed it to his lips. He a little revived. But unwilling to leave him unsupported while yet imperfectly restored, the black with one arm still encircled his master, at the same time keeping his eye fixed on his face, as if to watch for the first sign of complete restoration, or relapse, as the event might prove.

The Spaniard proceeded, but brokenly and obscurely, as one in a dream.

—"Oh, my God! rather than pass through what I have, with joy I would have hailed the most terrible gales; but——"

His cough returned and with increased violence; this subsiding, with reddened lips and closed eyes he fell heavily against his supporter.

"His mind wanders. He was thinking of the plague that followed the gales," plaintively sighed the servant; "my poor, poor master!" wringing one hand, and with the other wiping the mouth. "But be patient, Señor," again turning to Captain Delano, "these fits do not last long; master will soon be himself."

Don Benito reviving, went on; but as this portion of the story was very brokenly delivered, the substance only will here be set down.

It appeared that after the ship had been many days tossed in storms off the Cape, the scurvy broke out, carrying off numbers of the whites and blacks. When at last they had worked round into the Pacific, their spars and sails were so damaged, and so inadequately handled by the surviving mariners, most of whom were become invalids, that, unable to lay her northerly course by the wind, which was powerful, the unmanageable ship for successive days and nights was blown northwestward, where the breeze suddenly deserted her, in unknown waters, to sultry calms. The absence of the water-pipes now proved as fatal to life as before their presence had menaced it. Induced, or at least aggravated, by the more than scanty allowance of water, a malignant fever followed the scurvy; with the excessive heat of the lengthened calm, making such short work of it as to sweep away, as by billows, whole families of the Africans, and a yet larger number, proportionably, of the Spaniards, including, by a luckless fatality, every remaining officer on board. Consequently, in the smart west winds eventually following the calm, the already rent sails having to be simply dropped, not furled, at need, had been gradually reduced to the beggar's rags they were now. To procure substitutes for his lost sailors, as well as supplies of water and sails, the captain at the earliest opportunity had made for Baldivia, the southermost civilized port of Chili and South America; but upon nearing the coast the thick weather had prevented him from so much as sighting that harbor. Since which period, almost without a crew, and almost without canvas and almost without water, and at intervals giving its added dead to the sea, the San Dominick had been battle-dored about by contrary winds, inveigled by currents, or grown weedy in calms. Like a man lost in woods, more than once she had doubled upon her own track.

"But throughout these calamities," huskily continued Don Benito, painfully turning in the half embrace of his servant, "I have to thank those negroes you see, who, though to your inexperienced eyes appearing unruly, have, indeed, conducted themselves with less of restlessness than even their owner could have thought possible under such circumstances."

Here he again fell faintly back. Again his mind wandered: but he rallied, and less obscurely proceeded.

"Yes, their owner was quite right in assuring me that no fetters would be needed with his blacks; so that while, as is wont in this transportation, those negroes have always remained upon deck—not thrust below, as in the Guinea-men—they have, also, from the beginning, been freely permitted to range within given bounds at their pleasure."

Once more the faintness returned—his mind roved—but, recovering, he resumed:

"But it is Babo here to whom, under God, I owe not only my own preservation, but likewise to him, chiefly, the merit is due, of pacifying his more ignorant brethren, when at intervals tempted to murmurings."

"Ah, master," sighed the black, bowing his face, "don't speak of me; Babo is nothing; what Babo has done was but duty."

"Faithful fellow!" cried Capt. Delano. "Don Benito, I envy you such a friend; slave I cannot call him."

As master and man stood before him, the black upholding the white, Captain Delano could not but bethink him of the beauty of that relationship which could present such a spectacle of fidelity on the one hand and confidence on the other. The scene was heightened by the contrast in dress, denoting their relative positions. The Spaniard wore a loose Chili jacket of dark velvet; white small clothes and stockings, with silver buckles at the knee and instep; a high-crowned sombrero, of fine grass; a slender sword, silver mounted, hung from a knot in his sash; the last being an almost invariable adjunct, more for utility than ornament, of a South American gentleman's dress to this hour. Excepting when his occasional nervous contortions brought about disarray, there was a certain precision in his attire, curiously at variance with the unsightly disorder around; especially in the belittered Ghetto, forward of the main-mast, wholly occupied by the blacks.

The servant wore nothing but wide trowsers, apparently, from their coarseness and patches, made out of some old topsail; they were clean, and confined at the waist by a bit of unstranded rope, which, with his composed, deprecatory air at times, made him look something like a begging friar of St. Francis.

However unsuitable for the time and place, at least in the blunt-thinking American's eyes, and however strangely surviving in the midst of all his afflictions, the toilette of Don Benito might not, in fashion at least, have gone beyond the style of the day among South Americans of his class. Though on the present voyage sailing from Buenos Ayres, he had avowed himself a native and resident of Chili, whose inhabitants had not so generally adopted the plain coat and once plebeian pantaloons;

but, with a becoming modification, adhered to their provincial costume, picturesque as any in the world. Still, relatively to the pale history of the voyage, and his own pale face, there seemed something so incongruous in the Spaniard's apparel, as almost to suggest the image of an invalid courtier tottering about London streets in the time of the plague.

The portion of the narrative which, perhaps, most excited interest, as well as some surprise, considering the latitudes in question, was the long calms spoken of, and more particularly the ship's so long drifting about. Without communicating the opinion, of course, the American could not but impute at least part of the detentions both to clumsy seamanship and faulty navigation. Eying Don Benito's small, yellow hands, he easily inferred that the young captain had not got into command at the hawse-hole, but the cabin-window; and if so, why wonder at incompetence, in youth, sickness, and gentility united?

But drowning criticism in compassion, after a fresh repetition of his sympathies, Captain Delano having heard out his story, not only engaged, as in the first place, to see Don Benito and his people supplied in their immediate bodily needs, but, also, now further promised to assist him in procuring a large permanent supply of water, as well as some sails and rigging; and, though it would involve no small embarrassment to himself, yet he would spare three of his best seamen for temporary deck officers; so that without delay the ship might proceed to Conception, there fully to refit for Lima, her destined port.

Such generosity was not without its effect, even upon the invalid. His face lighted up; eager and hectic, he met the honest glance of his visitor. With gratitude he seemed overcome.

"This excitement is bad for master," whispered the servant, taking his arm, and with soothing words gently drawing him aside.

When Don Benito returned, the American was pained to observe that his hopefulness, like the sudden kindling in his cheek, was but febrile and transient.

Ere long, with a joyless mien, looking up towards the poop, the host invited his guest to accompany him there, for the benefit of what little breath of wind might be stirring.

As during the telling of the story, Captain Delano had once or twice started at the occasional cymballing of the hatchet-polishers, wondering why such an interruption should be allowed, especially in that part of the ship, and in the ears of an invalid; and moreover, as the hatchets had anything but an attractive look, and the handlers of them still less so, it was, therefore, to tell the truth, not without some lurking reluctance, or even shrinking, it may be, that Captain Delano, with apparent complaisance, acquiesced in his host's invitation. The more so, since with an untimely caprice of punctilio, rendered distressing by his cadaverous aspect, Don Benito, with Castilian bows, solemnly insisted upon his guest's preceding him up the ladder leading to the elevation; where, one on each side of the last step, sat for armorial supporters and sentries two of the ominous file. Gingerly enough stepped good Captain Delano between them, and in the instant of leaving them behind, like one running the gauntlet, he felt an apprehensive twitch in the calves of his legs.

But when, facing about, he saw the whole file, like so many organ-grinders, still stupidly intent on their work, unmindful of everything beside, he could not but smile at his late fidgeting panic.

Presently, while standing with his host, looking forward upon the decks below, he was struck by one of those instances of insubordination previously alluded to. Three black boys, with two Spanish boys, were sitting together on the hatches, scraping a rude wooden platter, in which some scanty mess had recently been cooked. Suddenly, one of the black boys, enraged at a word dropped by one of his white companions, seized a knife, and though called to forbear by one of the oakum-pickers, struck the lad over the head, inflicting a gash from which blood flowed.

In amazement, Captain Delano inquired what this meant. To which the pale Don Benito dully muttered, that it was merely the sport of the lad.

"Pretty serious sport, truly," rejoined Captain Delano. "Had such a thing happened on board the Bachelor's Delight, instant punishment would have followed."

At these words the Spaniard turned upon the American one of his sudden, staring, half-lunatic looks; then relapsing into his torpor, answered, "Doubtless, doubtless, Señor."

Is it, thought Captain Delano, that this hapless man is one of those paper captains I've known, who by policy wink at what by power they cannot put down? I know no sadder sight than a commander who has little of command but the name.

"I should think, Don Benito," he now said, glancing towards the oakum-picker who had sought to interfere with the boys, "that you would find it advantageous to keep all your blacks employed, especially the younger ones, no matter at what useless task, and no matter what happens to the ship. Why, even with my little band, I find such a course indispensable. I once kept a crew on my quarter-deck thrumming mats for my cabin, when, for three days, I had given up my ship—mats, men, and all—for a speedy loss, owing to the violence of a gale, in which we could do nothing but helplessly drive before it."

"Doubtless, doubtless," muttered Don Benito.

"But," continued Captain Delano, again glancing upon the oakum-pickers and then at the hatchet-polishers, near by, "I see you keep some at least of your host employed."

"Yes," was again the vacant response.

"Those old men there, shaking their pows from their pulpits," continued Captain Delano, pointing to the oakum-pickers, "seem to act the part of old dominies to the rest, little heeded as their admonitions are at times. Is this voluntary on their part, Don Benito, or have you appointed them shepherds to your flock of black sheep?"

"What posts they fill, I appointed them," rejoined the Spaniard, in an acrid tone, as if resenting some supposed satiric reflection.

"And these others, these Ashantee conjurors here," continued Captain Delano, rather uneasily eying the brandished steel of the hatchet-polishers, where in spots it had been brought to a shine, "this seems a curious business they are at, Don Benito?"

"In the gales we met," answered the Spaniard, "what of our general cargo was not thrown overboard was much damaged by the brine. Since coming into calm weather, I have had several cases of knives and hatchets daily brought up for overhauling and cleaning."

"A prudent idea, Don Benito. You are part owner of ship and cargo, I presume; but not of the slaves, perhaps?"

"I am owner of all you see," impatiently returned Don Benito, "except the main company of blacks, who belonged to my late friend, Alexandro Aranda."

As he mentioned this name, his air was heart-broken; his knees shook: his servant supported him.

Thinking he divined the cause of such unusual emotion, to confirm his surmise, Captain Delano, after a pause, said, "And may I ask, Don Benito, whether—since awhile ago you spoke of some cabin passengers—the friend, whose loss so afflicts you at the outset of the voyage accompanied his blacks?"

"Yes."

"But died of the fever?"

"Died of the fever.—Oh, could I but——"

Again quivering, the Spaniard paused.

"Pardon me," said Captain Delano lowly, "but I think that, by a sympathetic experience, I conjecture, Don Benito, what it is that gives the keener edge to your grief. It was once my hard fortune to lose at sea a dear friend, my own brother, then supercargo. Assured of the welfare of his spirit, its departure I could have borne like a man; but that honest eye, that honest hand—both of which had so often met mine—and that warm heart; all, all—like scraps to the dogs—to throw all to the sharks! It was then I vowed never to have for fellow-voyager a man I loved, unless, unbeknown to him, I had provided every requisite, in case of a fatality, for embalming his mortal part for interment on shore. Were your friend's remains now on board this ship, Don Benito, not thus strangely would the mention of his name affect you."

"On board this ship?" echoed the Spaniard. Then, with horrified gestures, as directed against some specter, he unconsciously fell into the ready arms of his attendant, who, with a silent appeal toward Captain Delano, seemed beseeching him not again to broach a theme so unspeakably distressing to his master.

This poor fellow now, thought the pained American, is the victim of that sad superstition which associates goblins with the deserted body of man, as ghosts with an abandoned house. How unlike are we made! What to me, in like case, would have been a solemn satisfaction, the bare suggestion, even, terrifies the Spaniard into this trance. Poor Alexandro Aranda! what would you say could you here see your friend—who, on former voyages, when you for months were left behind, has, I dare say, often longed, and longed, for one peep at you—now transported with terror at the least thought of having you anyway nigh him.

At this moment, with a dreary grave-yard toll, betokening a flaw, the ship's forecastle bell, smote by one of the grizzled oakum-pickers, proclaimed ten o'clock through the leaden calm; when Captain Delano's attention was caught by the moving figure of a gigantic black, emerging from the general crowd below, and slowly advancing towards the elevated poop. An iron collar was about his neck, from which depended a chain, thrice wound round his body; the terminating links padlocked together at a broad band of iron, his girdle.

"How like a mute Atufal moves," murmured the servant.

The black mounted the steps of the poop, and, like a brave prisoner, brought up to receive sentence, stood in unquailing muteness before Don Benito, now recovered from his attack.

At the first glimpse of his approach, Don Benito had started, a resentful shadow swept over his face; and, as with the sudden memory of bootless rage, his white lips glued together.

This is some mulish mutineer, thought Captain Delano, surveying, not without a mixture of admiration, the colossal form of the negro.

"See, he waits your question, master," said the servant.

Thus reminded, Don Benito, nervously averting his glance, as if shunning, by anticipation, some rebellious response, in a disconcerted voice, thus spoke:—

"Atufal, will you ask my pardon now?"

The black was silent.

"Again, master," murmured the servant, with bitter upbraiding eying his countryman, "Again, master; he will bend to master yet."

"Answer," said Don Benito, still averting his glance, "say but the one word *pardon*, and your chains shall be off."

Upon this, the black, slowly raising both arms, let them lifelessly fall, his links clanking, his head bowed; as much as to say, "no, I am content."

"Go," said Don Benito, with inkept and unknown emotion.

Deliberately as he had come, the black obeyed.

"Excuse me, Don Benito," said Captain Delano, "but this scene surprises me; what means it, pray?"

"It means that that negro alone, of all the band, has given me peculiar cause of offense. I have put him in chains; I——"

Here he paused; his hand to his head, as if there were a swimming there, or a sudden bewilderment of memory had come over him; but meeting his servant's kindly glance seemed reassured, and proceeded:—

"I could not scourge such a form. But I told him he must ask my pardon. As yet he has not. At my command, every two hours he stands before me."

"And how long has this been?"

"Some sixty days."

"And obedient in all else? And respectful?"

"Yes."

"Upon my conscience, then," exclaimed Captain Delano, impulsively, "he has a royal spirit in him, this fellow."

"He may have some right to it," bitterly returned Don Benito, "he says he was king in his own land."

"Yes," said the servant, entering a word, "those slits in Atufal's ears once held wedges of gold; but poor Babo here, in his own land, was only a poor slave; a black man's slave was Babo, who now is the white's."

Somewhat annoyed by these conversational familiarities, Captain Delano turned curiously upon the attendant, then glanced inquiringly at his master; but, as if long wonted to these little informalities, neither master nor man seemed to understand him.

"What, pray, was Atufal's offense, Don Benito?" asked Captain Delano; "if it was not something very serious, take a fool's advice, and, in view of his general docility, as well as in some natural respect for his spirit, remit him his penalty."

"No, no, master never will do that," here murmured the servant to himself, "proud Atufal must first ask master's pardon. The slave there carries the padlock, but master here carries the key."

His attention thus directed, Captain Delano now noticed for the first time that, suspended by a slender silken cord, from Don Benito's neck hung a key. At once, from the servant's muttered syllables divining the key's purpose, he smiled and said:—"So, Don Benito—padlock and key—significant symbols, truly."

Biting his lip, Don Benito faltered.

Though the remark of Captain Delano, a man of such native simplicity as to be incapable of satire or irony, had been dropped in playful allusion to the Spaniard's singularly evidenced lordship over the black; yet the hypochondriac seemed in some way to have taken it as a malicious reflection upon his confessed inability thus far to break down, at least, on a verbal summons, the entrenched will of the slave. Deploring this supposed misconception, yet despairing of correcting it, Captain Delano shifted the subject; but finding his companion more than ever withdrawn, as if still sourly digesting the lees of the presumed affront above-mentioned, by-and-by Captain Delano likewise became less talkative, oppressed, against his own will, by what seemed the secret vindictiveness of the morbidly sensitive Spaniard. But the good sailor himself, of a quite contrary disposition, refrained, on his part, alike from the appearance as from the feeling of resentment, and if silent, was only so from contagion.

Presently the Spaniard, assisted by his servant, somewhat discourteously crossed over from his guest; a procedure which, sensibly enough, might have been allowed to pass for idle caprice of ill-humor, had not master and man, lingering round the corner of the elevated skylight, began whispering together in low voices. This was unpleasing. And more: the moody air of the Spaniard, which at times had not been without a sort of valetudinarian stateliness, now seemed anything but dignified; while the menial familiarity of the servant lost its original charm of simple-hearted attachment.

In his embarrassment, the visitor turned his face to the other side of the ship. By so doing, his glance accidentally fell on a young Spanish sailor, a coil of rope in his hand, just stepped from the deck to the first round of the mizzen-rigging. Perhaps the man would not have been particularly noticed, were it not that, during his ascent to one of the yards, he, with a sort of covert intentness, kept his eye fixed on Captain Delano, from whom, presently, it passed, as if by a natural sequence, to the two whisperers.

His own attention thus redirected to that quarter, Captain Delano gave a slight start. From something in Don Benito's manner just then, it seemed as if the visitor had, at least partly, been the subject of the withdrawn consultation going on—a conjecture as little agreeable to the guest as it was little flattering to the host.

The singular alternations of courtesy and ill-breeding in the Spanish captain were unaccountable, except on one of two suppositions—innocent lunacy, or wicked imposture.

But the first idea, though it might naturally have occurred to an indifferent observer, and, in some respect, had not hitherto been wholly a stranger to Captain Delano's mind, yet, now that, in an incipient way, he began to regard the stranger's conduct something in the light of an intentional affront, of course the idea of lunacy was virtually vacated. But if not a lunatic, what then? Under the circumstances, would a gentleman, nay, any honest boor, act the part now acted by his host? The man was an impostor. Some low-born adventurer, masquerading as an oceanic grandee; yet so ignorant of the first requisites of mere gentlemanhood as to be betrayed into the present remarkable indecorum. That strange ceremoniousness, too, at other times evinced, seemed not uncharacteristic of one playing a part above his real level. Benito Cereno—Don Benito Cereno—a sounding name. One, too, at that period, not unknown, in the surname, to supercargoes and sea captains trading along the Spanish Main, as belonging to one of the most enterprising and extensive mercantile families in all those provinces; several members of it having titles; a sort of Castilian Rothschild, with a noble brother, or cousin, in every great trading town of South America. The alleged Don Benito was in early manhood, about twenty-nine or thirty. To assume a sort of roving cadetship in the maritime affairs of such a house, what more likely scheme for a young knave of talent and spirit? But the Spaniard was a pale invalid. Never mind. For even to the degree of simulating mortal disease, the craft of some tricksters had been known to attain. To think that, under the aspect of infantile weakness, the most savage energies might be couched—those velvets of the Spaniard but the silky paw to his fangs.

From no train of thought did these fancies come; not from within, but from without; suddenly, too, and in one throng, like hoar frost; yet as soon to vanish as the mild sun of Captain Delano's good-nature regained its meridian.

Glancing over once more towards his host—whose side-face, revealed above the skylight, was now turned towards him—he was struck by the profile, whose clearness of cut was refined by the thinness incident to ill-health, as well as ennobled about the chin by the beard. Away with suspicion. He was a true off-shoot of a true hidalgo Cereno.

Relieved by these and other better thoughts, the visitor, lightly humming a tune, now began indifferently pacing the poop, so as not to betray to Don Benito that he had at all mistrusted incivility, much less duplicity; for such mistrust would yet be proved illusory, and by the event; though, for the present, the circumstance which had provoked that distrust remained unexplained. But when that little mystery should have been cleared up, Captain Delano thought he might extremely regret it, did he allow Don Benito to become aware that he had indulged in ungenerous surmises. In short, to the Spaniard's black-letter text, it was best, for awhile, to leave open margin.

Presently, his pale face twitching and overcast, the Spaniard, still supported by his attendant, moved over towards his guest, when, with even more than his usual embarrassment, and a strange sort of intriguing intonation in his husky whisper, the following conversation began:—

"Señor, may I ask how long you have lain at this isle?"

"Oh, but a day or two, Don Benito."

"And from what port are you last?"

"Canton."

"And there, Señor, you exchanged your seal-skins for teas and silks, I think you said?"

"Yes. Silks, mostly."

"And the balance you took in specie, perhaps?"

Captain Delano, fidgeting a little, answered—

"Yes; some silver; not a very great deal, though."

"Ah—well. May I ask how many men have you, Señor?"

Captain Delano slightly started, but answered—

"About five-and-twenty, all told."

"And at present, Señor, all on board, I suppose?"

"All on board, Don Benito," replied the Captain, now with satisfaction.

"And will be to-night, Señor?"

At this last question, following so many pertinacious ones, for the soul of him Captain Delano could not but look very earnestly at the questioner, who, instead of meeting the glance, with every token of craven discomposure dropped his eyes to the deck; presenting an unworthy contrast to his servant, who, just then, was kneeling at his feet, adjusting a loose shoe-buckle; his disengaged face meantime, with humble curiosity, turned openly up into his master's downcast one.

The Spaniard, still with a guilty shuffle, repeated his question:—

"And—and will be to-night, Señor?"

"Yes, for aught I know," returned Captain Delano,—"but nay," rallying himself into fearless truth, "some of them talked of going off on another fishing party about midnight."

"Your ships generally go—go more or less armed, I believe, Señor?"

"Oh, a six-pounder or two, in case of emergency," was the intrepidly indifferent reply, "with a small stock of muskets, sealing-spears, and cutlasses, you know."

As he thus responded, Captain Delano again glanced at Don Benito, but the latter's eyes were averted; while abruptly and awkwardly shifting the subject, he made some peevish allusion to the calm, and then, without apology, once more, with his attendant, withdrew to the opposite bulwarks, where the whispering was resumed.

At this moment, and ere Captain Delano could cast a cool thought upon what had just passed, the young Spanish sailor before mentioned was seen descending from the rigging. In act of stooping over to spring inboard to the deck, his voluminous, unconfined frock, or shirt, of coarse woollen, much spotted with tar, opened out far down the chest, revealing a soiled under garment of what seemed the finest linen, edged, about the neck, with a narrow blue ribbon, sadly faded and worn. At this moment the young sailor's eye was again fixed on the whisperers, and Captain Delano thought he observed a lurking significance in it, as if silent signs of some Freemason sort had that instant been interchanged.

This once more impelled his own glance in the direction of Don Benito, and, as before, he could not but infer that himself formed the subject of the conference. He paused. The sound of the hatchet-polishing fell on his ears. He cast another swift side-look at the two. They had the air of conspirators. In connection with the late questionings and the incident of the young sailor, these things now begat such return of involuntary suspicion, that the singular guilelessness of the American could not endure it. Plucking up a gay and humorous expression, he crossed over to the two rapidly, saying:—"Ha, Don Benito, your black here seems high in your trust; a sort of privy-counselor, in fact."

Upon this, the servant looked up with a good-natured grin, but the master started as from a venomous bite. It was a moment or two before the Spaniard sufficiently recovered himself to reply; which he did, at last, with cold constraint:—"Yes, Señor, I have trust in Babo."

Here Babo, changing his previous grin of mere animal humor into an intelligent smile, not ungratefully eyed his master.

Finding that the Spaniard now stood silent and reserved, as if involuntarily, or purposely giving hint that his guest's proximity was inconvenient just then, Captain Delano, unwilling to appear uncivil even to incivility itself, made some trivial remark and moved off; again and again turning over in his mind the mysterious demeanor of Don Benito Cereno.

He had descended from the poop, and, wrapped in thought, was passing near a dark hatchway, leading down into the steerage, when, perceiving motion there, he looked to see what moved. The same instant there was a sparkle in the shadowy hatchway, and he saw one of the Spanish sailors prowling there hurriedly placing his hand in the bosom of his frock, as if hiding something. Before the man could have been certain who it was that was passing, he slunk below out of sight. But enough was seen of him to make it sure that he was the same young sailor before noticed in the rigging.

What was that which so sparkled? thought Captain Delano. It was no lamp—no match—no live coal. Could it have been a jewel? But how come sailors with jewels?—or with silk-trimmed under-shirts either? Has he been robbing the trunks of the dead cabin passengers? But if so, he would hardly wear one of the stolen articles on board ship here. Ah, ah—if now that was, indeed, a secret sign I saw passing between this suspicious fellow and his captain awhile since; if I could only be certain that in my uneasiness my senses did not deceive me, then——

Here, passing from one suspicious thing to another, his mind revolved the point of the strange questions put to him concerning his ship.

By a curious coincidence, as each point was recalled, the black wizards of Ashantee would strike up with their hatchets, as in ominous comment on the white stranger's thoughts. Pressed by such enigmas and portents, it would have been almost against nature, had not, even into the least distrustful heart, some ugly misgivings obtruded.

Observing the ship now helplessly fallen into a current, with enchanted sails, drifting with increased rapidity seaward; and noting that, from a lately intercepted projection of the land, the sealer was hidden, the stout mariner began to quake at thoughts which he barely durst confess to himself. Above all, he began to feel a ghostly dread of Don Benito. And yet when he roused himself, dilated his chest, felt himself strong on his legs, and coolly considered it—what did all these phantoms amount to?

Had the Spaniard any sinister scheme, it must have reference not so much to him (Captain Delano) as to his ship (the Bachelor's Delight). Hence the present drifting away of the one ship from the other, instead of favoring any such possible scheme, was, for the time at least, opposed to it. Clearly any suspicion, combining such contradictions, must need be delusive. Beside, was it not absurd to think of a vessel in distress—a vessel by sickness almost dismanned of her crew—a vessel whose inmates were parched for water—was it not a thousand times absurd that such a craft should, at present, be of a piratical character; or her commander, either for himself or those under him, cherish any desire but for speedy relief and refreshment? But then, might not general distress, and thirst in particular, be affected? And might not that same undiminished Spanish crew, alleged to have perished off to a remnant, be at that very moment lurking in the hold? On heart-broken pretense of entreating a cup of cold water, fiends in human form had got into lonely dwellings, nor retired until a dark deed had been done. And among the Malay pirates, it was no unusual thing to lure ships after them into their treacherous harbors, or entice boarders from a declared enemy at sea, by the spectacle of thinly manned or vacant decks, beneath which prowled a hundred spears with yellow arms ready to upthrust them through the mats. Not that Captain Delano had entirely credited such things. He had heard of them—and now, as stories, they recurred. The present destination of the ship was the anchorage. There she would be near his own vessel. Upon gaining that vicinity, might not the San Dominick, like a slumbering volcano, suddenly let loose energies now hid?

He recalled the Spaniard's manner while telling his story. There was a gloomy hesitancy and subterfuge about it. It was just the manner of one making up his tale for evil purposes, as he goes. But if that story was not true, what was the truth? That the ship had unlawfully come into the Spaniard's possession? But in many of its details, especially in reference to the more calamitous parts, such as the fatalities among the seamen, the consequent prolonged beating about, the past sufferings from obstinate calms, and still continued suffering from thirst; in all these points, as well as others, Don Benito's story had been corroborated not only by the wailing ejaculations of the indiscriminate multitude, white and black, but likewise—what seemed impossible to be counterfeit—by the very expression and play of every human feature, which Captain Delano saw. If Don Benito's story was throughout an invention, then every soul on board, down to the youngest negress, was his carefully drilled recruit in the plot: an incredible inference. And yet, if there was ground for mistrusting his veracity, that inference was a legitimate one.

But those questions of the Spaniard. There, indeed, one might pause. Did they not seem put with much the same object with which the burglar or assassin, by day-time, reconnoitres the walls of a house? But, with ill purposes, to solicit such information openly of the chief person endangered, and so, in effect, setting him on his guard; how unlikely a procedure was that? Absurd, then, to suppose that those questions had been prompted by evil designs. Thus, the same conduct, which, in this instance, had raised the alarm, served to dispel it. In short, scarce any suspicion or uneasiness, however apparently reasonable at the time, which was not now, with equal apparent reason, dismissed.

At last he began to laugh at his former forebodings; and laugh at the strange ship for, in its aspect someway siding with them, as it were; and laugh, too, at the odd-looking blacks, particularly those old scissors-grinders, the Ashantees; and those bed-ridden old knitting-women, the oakum-pickers; and almost at the dark Spaniard himself, the central hobgoblin of all.

For the rest, whatever in a serious way seemed enigmatical, was now good-naturedly explained away by the thought that, for the most part, the poor invalid scarcely knew what he was about; either sulking in black vapors, or putting idle questions without sense or object. Evidently, for the present, the man was not fit to be entrusted with the ship. On some benevolent plea withdrawing the command from him, Captain Delano would yet have to send her to Conception, in charge of his second mate, a worthy person and good navigator—a plan not more convenient for the San Dominick than for Don Benito; for, relieved from all anxiety, keeping wholly to his cabin, the sick man, under the good nursing of his servant, would probably, by the end of the passage, be in a measure restored to health, and with that he should also be restored to authority.

Such were the American's thoughts. They were tranquilizing. There was a difference between the idea of Don Benito's darkly pre-ordaining Captain Delano's fate, and Captain Delano's lightly arranging Don Benito's. Nevertheless, it was not without something of relief that the good seaman presently perceived his whale-boat in the distance. Its absence had been prolonged by unexpected detention at the sealer's side, as well as its returning trip lengthened by the continual recession of the goal.

The advancing speck was observed by the blacks. Their shouts attracted the attention of Don Benito, who, with a return of courtesy, approaching Captain Delano, expressed satisfaction at the coming of some supplies, slight and temporary as they must necessarily prove.

Captain Delano responded; but while doing so, his attention was drawn to something passing on the deck below: among the crowd climbing the landward bulwarks, anxiously watching the coming boat, two blacks, to all appearances accidentally incommoded by one of the sailors, flew out against him with horrible curses, which the sailor someway resenting, the two blacks dashed him to the deck and jumped upon him, despite the earnest cries of the oakum-pickers.

"Don Benito," said Captain Delano quickly, "do you see what is going on there? Look!"

But, seized by his cough, the Spaniard staggered, with both hands to his face, on the point of falling. Captain Delano would have supported him, but the servant was more alert, who, with one hand sustaining his master, with the other applied the cordial. Don Benito restored, the black withdrew his support, slipping aside a little, but dutifully remaining within call of a whisper. Such discretion was here evinced as quite wiped away, in the visitor's eyes, any blemish of impropriety which might have attached to the attendant, from the indecorous conferences before mentioned; showing, too, that if the servant were to blame, it might be more the master's fault than his own, since when left to himself he could conduct thus well.

His glance thus called away from the spectacle of disorder to the more pleasing one before him, Captain Delano could not avoid again congratulating his host upon possessing such a servant, who, though perhaps a little too forward now and then, must upon the whole be invaluable to one in the invalid's situation.

"Tell me, Don Benito," he added, with a smile—"I should like to have your man here myself—what will you take for him? Would fifty doubloons be any object?"

"Master wouldn't part with Babo for a thousand doubloons," murmured the black, overhearing the offer, and taking it in earnest, and, with the strange vanity of a faithful slave appreciated by his master, scorning to hear so paltry a valuation put upon him by a stranger. But Don Benito, apparently hardly yet completely restored, and again interrupted by his cough, made but some broken reply.

Soon his physical distress became so great, affecting his mind, too, apparently, that, as if to screen the sad spectacle, the servant gently conducted his master below.

Left to himself, the American, to while away the time till his boat should arrive, would have pleasantly accosted some one of the few Spanish seamen he saw; but recalling something that Don Benito had said touching their ill conduct, he refrained, as a ship-master indisposed to countenance cowardice or unfaithfulness in seamen.

While, with these thoughts, standing with eye directed forward towards that handful of sailors, suddenly he thought that one or two of them returned the glance and with a sort of meaning. He rubbed his eyes, and looked again; but again seemed to see the same thing. Under a new form, but more obscure than any previous one, the old suspicions recurred, but, in the absence of Don Benito, with less of panic than before. Despite the bad account given of the sailors, Captain Delano resolved forthwith to accost one of them. Descending the poop, he made his way through the blacks, his movement drawing a queer cry from the oakum-pickers, prompted by whom, the negroes, twitching each other aside, divided before him; but, as if curious to see what was the object of this deliberate visit to their Ghetto, closing in behind, in tolerable order, followed the white stranger up. His progress thus proclaimed as by mounted kings-at-arms, and escorted as by a Caffre guard of honor, Captain Delano, assuming a good humored, off-handed air, continued to advance; now and then saying a blithe word to the negroes, and his eye curiously surveying the white faces, here and there sparsely mixed in with the blacks, like stray white pawns venturously involved in the ranks of the chess-men opposed.

While thinking which of them to select for his purpose, he chanced to observe a sailor seated on the deck engaged in tarring the strap of a large block, with a circle of blacks squatted round him inquisitively eying the process.

The mean employment of the man was in contrast with something superior in his figure. His hand, black with continually thrusting it into the tar-pot held for him by a negro, seemed not naturally allied to his face, a face which would have been a very fine one but for its haggardness. Whether this haggardness had aught to do with criminality, could not be determined; since, as intense heat and cold, though unlike, produce like sensations, so innocence and guilt, when, through casual association with mental pain, stamping any visible impress, use one seal—a hacked one.

Not again that this reflection occurred to Captain Delano at the time, charitable man as he was. Rather another idea. Because observing so singular a haggardness combined with a dark eye, averted as in trouble and shame, and then again recalling Don Benito's confessed ill opinion of his crew, insensibly he was operated upon by certain general notions, which, while disconnecting pain and abashment from virtue, invariably link them with vice.

If, indeed, there be any wickedness on board this ship, thought Captain Delano, be sure that man there has fouled his hand in it, even as now he fouls it in the pitch. I don't like to accost him. I will speak to this other, this old Jack here on the windlass.

He advanced to an old Barcelona tar, in ragged red breeches and dirty night-cap, cheeks trenched and bronzed, whiskers dense as thorn hedges. Seated between two sleepy-looking Africans, this mariner, like his younger shipmate, was employed upon some rigging—splicing a cable—the sleepy-looking blacks performing the inferior function of holding the outer parts of the ropes for him.

Upon Captain Delano's approach, the man at once hung his head below its previous level; the one necessary for business. It appeared as if he desired to be thought absorbed, with more than common fidelity, in his task. Being addressed, he glanced up, but with what seemed a furtive, diffident air, which sat strangely enough on his weather-beaten visage, much as if a grizzly bear, instead of growling and biting, should simper and cast sheep's eyes. He was asked several questions concerning the voyage, questions purposely referring to several particulars in Don Benito's narrative, not previously corroborated by those impulsive cries greeting the visitor on first coming on board. The questions were briefly answered, confirming all that remained to be confirmed of the story. The negroes about the windlass joined in with the old sailor, but, as they became talkative, he by degrees became mute, and at length quite glum, seemed morosely unwilling to answer more questions, and yet, all the while, this ursine air was somehow mixed with his sheepish one.

Despairing of getting into unembarrassed talk with such a centaur, Captain Delano, after glancing round for a more promising countenance, but seeing none, spoke pleasantly to the blacks to make way for him; and so, amid various grins and grimaces, returned to the poop, feeling a little strange at first, he could hardly tell why, but upon the whole with regained confidence in Benito Cereno.

How plainly, thought he, did that old whiskerando yonder betray a consciousness of ill-desert. No doubt, when he saw me coming, he dreaded lest I, apprised by his Captain of the crew's general misbehavior, came with sharp words for him, and so down with his head. And yet—and yet, now that I think of it, that very old fellow, if I err not, was one of those who seemed so earnestly eying me here awhile since. Ah, these currents spin one's head round almost as much as they do the ship. Ha, there now's a pleasant sort of sunny sight; quite sociable, too.

His attention had been drawn to a slumbering negress, partly disclosed through the lace-work of some rigging, lying, with youthful limbs carelessly disposed, under the lee of the bulwarks, like a doe in the shade of a woodland rock. Sprawling at her lapped breasts was her wide-awake fawn, stark naked, its black little body half lifted from the deck, crosswise with its dam's; its hands, like two paws, clambering upon her; its mouth and nose ineffectually rooting to get at the mark; and meantime giving a vexatious half-grunt, blending with the composed snore of the negress.

The uncommon vigor of the child at length roused the mother. She started up, at distance facing Captain Delano. But as if not at all concerned at the attitude in which she had been caught, delightedly she caught the child up, with maternal transports, covering it with kisses.

There's naked nature, now; pure tenderness and love, thought Captain Delano, well pleased.

This incident prompted him to remark the other negresses more particularly than before. He was gratified with their manners; like most uncivilized women, they seemed at once tender of heart and tough of constitution; equally ready to die for their infants or fight for them. Unsophisticated as leopardesses; loving as doves. Ah! thought Captain Delano, these perhaps are some of the very women whom Mungo Park saw in Africa, and gave such a noble account of.

These natural sights somehow insensibly deepened his confidence and ease. At last he looked to see how his boat was getting on; but it was still pretty remote. He turned to see if Don Benito had returned; but he had not.

To change the scene, as well as to please himself with a leisurely observation of the coming boat, stepping over into the mizzen-chains he clambered his way into the starboard quarter-gallery; one of those abandoned Venetian-looking water-balconies previously mentioned; retreats cut off from the deck. As his foot pressed the half-damp, half-dry sea-mosses matting the place, and a chance phantom cats-paw—an islet of breeze, unheralded, unfollowed—as this ghostly cats-paw came fanning his cheek, as his glance fell upon the row of small, round dead-lights, all closed like coppered eyes of the coffined, and the state-cabin door, once connecting with the gallery, even as the dead-lights had once looked out upon it, but now calked fast like a sarcophagus lid, to a purple-black, tarred-over panel, threshold, and post; and he bethought him of the time, when that state-cabin and this state-balcony had heard the voices of the Spanish king's officers, and the forms of the Lima viceroy's daughters had perhaps leaned where he stood—as these and other images flitted through his mind, as the cats-paw through the calm, gradually he felt rising a dreamy inquietude, like that of one who alone on the prairie feels unrest from the repose of the noon.

He leaned against the carved balustrade, again looking off toward his boat; but found his eye falling upon the ribbon grass, trailing along the ship's water-line, straight as a border of green box; and parterres of sea-weed, broad ovals and crescents, floating nigh and far, with what seemed long formal alleys between, crossing the terraces of swells, and sweeping round as if leading to the grottoes below. And overhanging all was the balustrade by his arm, which, partly stained with pitch and partly embossed with moss, seemed the charred ruin of some summer-house in a grand garden long running to waste.

Trying to break one charm, he was but becharmed anew. Though upon the wide sea, he seemed in some far inland country; prisoner in some deserted château, left to stare at empty grounds, and peer out at vague roads, where never wagon or wayfarer passed.

But these enchantments were a little disenchanted as his eye fell on the corroded main-chains. Of an ancient style, massy and rusty in link, shackle and bolt, they seemed even more fit for the ship's present business than the one for which probably she had been built.

Presently he thought something moved nigh the chains. He rubbed his eyes, and looked hard. Groves of rigging were about the chains; and there, peering from behind a great stay, like an Indian from behind a hemlock, a Spanish sailor, a marlingspike in his hand, was seen, who made what seemed an imperfect gesture towards the balcony, but immediately, as if alarmed by some advancing step along the deck within, vanished into the recesses of the hempen forest, like a poacher.

What meant this? Something the man had sought to communicate, unbeknown to any one, even to his captain. Did the secret involve aught unfavorable to his captain? Were those previous misgivings of Captain Delano's about to be verified? Or, in his haunted mood at the moment, had some random, unintentional motion of the man, while busy with the stay, as if repairing it, been mistaken for a significant beckoning?

Not unbewildered, again he gazed off for his boat. But it was temporarily hidden by a rocky spur of the isle. As with some eagerness he bent forward, watching for the first shooting view of its beak, the balustrade gave way before him like charcoal. Had he not clutched an outreaching rope he would have fallen into the sea. The crash, though feeble, and the fall, though hollow, of the rotten fragments, must have been overheard. He glanced up. With sober curiosity peering down upon him was one of the old oakum-pickers, slipped from his perch to an outside boom; while below the old negro, and, invisible to him, reconnoitering from a porthole like a fox from the mouth of its den, crouched the Spanish sailor again. From something suddenly suggested by the man's air, the mad idea now darted into Captain Delano's mind, that Don Benito's plea of indisposition, in withdrawing below, was but a pretense: that he was engaged there maturing some plot, of which the sailor, by some means gaining an inkling, had a mind to warn the stranger against; incited, it may be, by gratitude for a kind word on first boarding the ship. Was it from foreseeing some possible interference like this, that Don Benito had, beforehand, given such a bad character of his sailors, while praising the negroes; though, indeed, the former seemed as docile as the latter the contrary? The whites, too, by nature, were the shrewder race. A man with some evil design, would he not be likely to speak well of that stupidity which was blind to his depravity, and malign that intelligence from which it might not be hidden? Not unlikely, perhaps. But if the whites had dark secrets concerning Don Benito, could then Don Benito be any way in complicity with the blacks? But they were too stupid. Besides, who ever heard of a white so far a renegade as to apostatize from his very species almost, by leaguing in against it with negroes? These difficulties recalled former ones. Lost in their mazes, Captain Delano, who had now regained the deck, was uneasily advancing along it, when he observed a new face; an aged sailor seated cross-legged near the main hatchway. His skin was shrunk up with wrinkles like a pelican's empty pouch; his hair frosted; his countenance grave and composed. His hands were full of ropes, which he was working into a large knot. Some blacks were about him obligingly dipping the strands for him, here and there, as the exigencies of the operation demanded.

Captain Delano crossed over to him, and stood in silence surveying the knot; his mind, by a not uncongenial transition, passing from its own entanglements to those of the hemp. For intricacy such a knot he had never seen in an American ship, or indeed any other. The old man looked like an Egyptian priest, making gordian knots for the temple of Ammon. The knot seemed a combination of double-bowline-knot, treble-crown-knot, back-handed-well-knot, knot-in-and-out-knot, and jamming-knot.

At last, puzzled to comprehend the meaning of such a knot, Captain Delano addressed the knotter:—

"What are you knotting there, my man?"

"The knot," was the brief reply, without looking up.

"So it seems; but what is it for?"

"For some one else to undo," muttered back the old man, plying his fingers harder than ever, the knot being now nearly completed.

While Captain Delano stood watching him, suddenly the old man threw the knot towards him, saying in broken English,—the first heard in the ship,—something to this effect—"Undo it, cut it, quick." It was said lowly, but with such condensation of rapidity, that the long, slow words in Spanish, which had preceded and followed, almost operated as covers to the brief English between.

For a moment, knot in hand, and knot in head, Captain Delano stood mute; while, without further heeding him, the old man was now intent upon other ropes. Presently there was a slight stir behind Captain Delano. Turning, he saw the chained negro, Atufal, standing quietly there. The next moment the old sailor rose, muttering, and, followed by his subordinate negroes, removed to the forward part of the ship, where in the crowd he disappeared.

An elderly negro, in a clout like an infant's, and with a pepper and salt head, and a kind of attorney air, now approached Captain Delano. In tolerable Spanish, and with a good-natured, knowing wink, he informed him that the old knotter was simple-witted, but harmless; often playing his old tricks. The negro concluded by begging the knot, for of course the stranger would not care to be troubled with it. Unconsciously, it was handed to him. With a sort of congé, the negro received it, and turning his back, ferreted into it like a detective Custom House officer after smuggled laces. Soon, with some African word, equivalent to pshaw, he tossed the knot overboard.

All this is very queer now, thought Captain Delano, with a qualmish sort of emotion; but as one feeling incipient sea-sickness, he strove, by ignoring the symptoms, to get rid of the malady. Once more he looked off for his boat. To his delight, it was now again in view, leaving the rocky spur astern.

The sensation here experienced, after at first relieving his uneasiness, with unforeseen efficacy, soon began to remove it. The less distant sight of that well-known boat—showing it, not as before, half blended with the haze, but with outline defined, so that its individuality, like a man's, was manifest; that boat, Rover by name, which, though now in strange seas, had often pressed the beach of Captain Delano's home, and, brought to its threshold for repairs, had familiarly lain there, as a Newfoundland dog; the sight of that household boat evoked a thousand trustful associations, which, contrasted with previous suspicions, filled him not only with lightsome confidence, but somehow with half humorous self-reproaches at his former lack of it.

"What, I, Amasa Delano—Jack of the Beach, as they called me when a lad—I, Amasa; the same that, duck-satchel in hand, used to paddle along the waterside to the school-house made from the old hulk;—I, little Jack of the Beach, that used to go berrying with cousin Nat and the rest; I to be murdered here at the ends of the earth, on board a haunted pirate-ship by a horrible Spaniard?—Too nonsensical to think of! Who would murder Amasa Delano? His conscience is clean. There is some one above. Fie, fie, Jack of the Beach! you are a child indeed; a child of the second childhood, old boy; you are beginning to dote and drule, I'm afraid."

Light of heart and foot, he stepped aft, and there was met by Don Benito's servant, who, with a pleasing expression, responsive to his own present feelings, informed him that his master had recovered from the effects of his coughing fit, and had just ordered him to go present his compliments to his good guest, Don Amasa, and say that he (Don Benito) would soon have the happiness to rejoin him.

There now, do you mark that? again thought Captain Delano, walking the poop. What a donkey I was. This kind gentleman who here sends me his kind compliments, he, but ten minutes ago, dark-lantern in hand, was dodging round some old grind-stone in the hold, sharpening a hatchet for me, I thought. Well, well; these long calms have a morbid effect on the mind, I've often heard, though I never believed it before. Ha! glancing towards the boat; there's Rover; good dog; a white bone in her mouth. A pretty big bone though, seems to me.—What? Yes, she has fallen afoul of the bubbling tide-rip there. It sets her the other way, too, for the time. Patience.

It was now about noon, though, from the grayness of everything, it seemed to be getting towards dusk.

The calm was confirmed. In the far distance, away from the influence of land, the leaden ocean seemed laid out and leaded up, its course finished, soul gone, defunct. But the current from landward, where the ship was, increased; silently sweeping her further and further towards the tranced waters beyond.

Still, from his knowledge of those latitudes, cherishing hopes of a breeze, and a fair and fresh one, at any moment, Captain Delano, despite present prospects, buoyantly counted upon bringing the San Dominick safely to anchor ere night. The distance swept over was nothing; since, with a good wind, ten minutes' sailing would retrace more than sixty minutes' drifting. Meantime, one moment turning to mark "Rover" fighting the tide-rip, and the next to see Don Benito approaching, he continued walking the poop.

Gradually he felt a vexation arising from the delay of his boat; this soon merged into uneasiness; and at last, his eye falling continually, as from a stage-box into the pit, upon the strange crowd before and below him, and by and by recognising there the face—now composed to indifference—of the Spanish sailor who had seemed to beckon from the main chains, something of his old trepidations returned.

Ah, thought he—gravely enough—this is like the ague: because it went off, it follows not that it won't come back.

Though ashamed of the relapse, he could not altogether subdue it; and so, exerting his good nature to the utmost, insensibly he came to a compromise.

Yes, this is a strange craft; a strange history, too, and strange folks on board. But—nothing more.

By way of keeping his mind out of mischief till the boat should arrive, he tried to occupy it with turning over and over, in a purely speculative sort of way, some lesser peculiarities of the captain and crew. Among others, four curious points recurred.

First, the affair of the Spanish lad assailed with a knife by the slave boy; an act winked at by Don Benito. Second, the tyranny in Don Benito's treatment of Atufal, the black; as if a child should lead a bull of the Nile by the ring in his nose. Third, the trampling of the sailor by the two negroes; a piece of insolence passed over without so much as a reprimand. Fourth, the cringing submission to their master of all the ship's underlings, mostly blacks; as if by the least inadvertence they feared to draw down his despotic displeasure.

Coupling these points, they seemed somewhat contradictory. But what then, thought Captain Delano, glancing towards his now nearing boat,—what then? Why, Don Benito is a very capricious commander. But he is not the first of the sort I have seen; though it's true he rather exceeds any other. But as a nation—continued he in his reveries—these Spaniards are all an odd set; the very word Spaniard has a curious, conspirator, Guy-Fawkish twang to it. And yet, I dare say, Spaniards in the main are as good folks as any in Duxbury, Massachusetts. Ah good! At last "Rover" has come.

As, with its welcome freight, the boat touched the side, the oakum-pickers, with venerable gestures, sought to restrain the blacks, who, at the sight of three gurried water-casks in its bottom, and a pile of wilted pumpkins in its bow, hung over the bulwarks in disorderly raptures.

Don Benito with his servant now appeared; his coming, perhaps, hastened by hearing the noise. Of him Captain Delano sought permission to serve out the water, so that all might share alike, and none injure themselves by unfair excess. But sensible, and, on Don Benito's account, kind as this offer was, it was received with what seemed impatience; as if aware that he lacked energy as a commander, Don Benito, with the true jealousy of weakness, resented as an affront any interference. So, at least, Captain Delano inferred.

In another moment the casks were being hoisted in, when some of the eager negroes accidentally jostled Captain Delano, where he stood by the gangway; so that, unmindful of Don Benito, yielding to the impulse of the moment, with good-natured authority he bade the blacks stand back; to enforce his words making use of a half-mirthful, half-menacing gesture. Instantly the blacks paused, just where they were, each negro and negress suspended in his or her posture, exactly as the word had found them—for a few seconds continuing so—while, as between the responsive posts of a telegraph, an unknown syllable ran from man to man among the perched oakum-pickers. While the visitor's attention was fixed by this scene, suddenly the hatchet-polishers half rose, and a rapid cry came from Don Benito.

Thinking that at the signal of the Spaniard he was about to be massacred, Captain Delano would have sprung for his boat, but paused, as the oakum-pickers, dropping down into the crowd with earnest exclamations, forced every white and every negro back, at the same moment, with gestures friendly and familiar, almost jocose, bidding him, in substance, not be a fool. Simultaneously the hatchet-polishers resumed their seats, quietly as so many tailors, and at once, as if nothing had happened, the work of hoisting in the casks was resumed, whites and blacks singing at the tackle.

Captain Delano glanced towards Don Benito. As he saw his meager form in the act of recovering itself from reclining in the servant's arms, into which the agitated invalid had fallen, he could not but marvel at the panic by which himself had been surprised on the darting supposition that such a commander, who upon a legitimate occasion, so trivial, too, as it now appeared, could lose all self-command, was, with energetic iniquity, going to bring about his murder.

The casks being on deck, Captain Delano was handed a number of jars and cups by one of the steward's aids, who, in the name of his captain, entreated him to do as he had proposed: dole out the water. He complied, with republican impartiality as to this republican element, which always seeks one level, serving the oldest white no better than the youngest black; excepting, indeed, poor Don Benito, whose condition, if not rank, demanded an extra allowance. To him, in the first place, Captain Delano presented a fair pitcher of the fluid; but, thirsting as he was for it, the Spaniard quaffed not a drop until after several grave bows and salutes. A reciprocation of courtesies which the sight-loving Africans hailed with clapping of hands.

Two of the less wilted pumpkins being reserved for the cabin table, the residue were minced up on the spot for the general regalement. But the soft bread, sugar, and bottled cider, Captain Delano would have given the whites alone, and in chief Don Benito; but the latter objected; which disinterestedness, on his part, not a little pleased the American; and so mouthfuls all around were given alike to whites and blacks; excepting one bottle of cider, which Babo insisted upon setting aside for his master.

Here it may be observed that as, on the first visit of the boat, the American had not permitted his men to board the ship, neither did he now; being unwilling to add to the confusion of the decks.

Not uninfluenced by the peculiar good humor at present prevailing, and for the time oblivious of any but benevolent thoughts, Captain Delano, who from recent indications counted upon a breeze within an hour or two at furthest, dispatched the boat back to the sealer with orders for all the hands that could be spared immediately to set about rafting casks to the watering-place and filling them. Likewise he bade word be carried to his chief officer, that if against present expectation the ship was not brought to anchor by sunset, he need be under no concern, for as there was to be a full moon that night, he (Captain Delano) would remain on board ready to play the pilot, come the wind soon or late.

As the two Captains stood together, observing the departing boat—the servant as it happened having just spied a spot on his master's velvet sleeve, and silently engaged rubbing it out—the American expressed his regrets that the San Dominick had no boats; none, at least, but the unseaworthy old hulk of the long-boat, which, warped as a camel's skeleton in the desert, and almost as bleached, lay pot-wise inverted amidships, one side a little tipped, furnishing a subterraneous sort of den for family groups of the blacks, mostly women and small children; who, squatting on old mats below, or perched above in the dark dome, on the elevated seats, were descried, some distance within, like a social circle of bats, sheltering in some friendly cave; at intervals, ebon flights of naked boys and girls, three or four years old, darting in and out of the den's mouth.

"Had you three or four boats now, Don Benito," said Captain Delano, "I think that, by tugging at the oars, your negroes here might help along matters some.—Did you sail from port without boats, Don Benito?"

"They were stove in the gales, Señor."

"That was bad. Many men, too, you lost then. Boats and men.—Those must have been hard gales, Don Benito."

"Past all speech," cringed the Spaniard.

"Tell me, Don Benito," continued his companion with increased interest, "tell me, were these gales immediately off the pitch of Cape Horn?"

"Cape Horn?—who spoke of Cape Horn?"

"Yourself did, when giving me an account of your voyage," answered Captain Delano with almost equal astonishment at this eating of his own words, even as he ever seemed eating his own heart, on the part of the Spaniard. "You yourself, Don Benito, spoke of Cape Horn," he emphatically repeated.

The Spaniard turned, in a sort of stooping posture, pausing an instant, as one about to make a plunging exchange of elements, as from air to water.

At this moment a messenger-boy, a white, hurried by, in the regular performance of his function carrying the last expired half hour forward to the forecastle, from the cabin time-piece, to have it struck at the ship's large bell.

"Master," said the servant, discontinuing his work on the coat sleeve, and addressing the rapt Spaniard with a sort of timid apprehensiveness, as one charged with a duty, the discharge of which, it was foreseen, would prove irksome to the very person who had imposed it, and for whose benefit it was intended, "master told me never mind where he was, or how engaged, always to remind him, to a minute, when shaving-time comes. Miguel has gone to strike the half-hour afternoon. It is *now*, master. Will master go into the cuddy?"

"Ah—yes," answered the Spaniard, starting, somewhat as from dreams into realities; then turning upon Captain Delano, he said that ere long he would resume the conversation.

"Then if master means to talk more to Don Amasa," said the servant, "why not let Don Amasa sit by master in the cuddy, and master can talk, and Don Amasa can listen, while Babo here lathers and strops."

"Yes," said Captain Delano, not unpleased with this sociable plan, "yes, Don Benito, unless you had rather not, I will go with you."

"Be it so, Señor."

As the three passed aft, the American could not but think it another strange instance of his host's capriciousness, this being shaved with such uncommon punctuality in the middle of the day. But he deemed it more than likely that the servant's anxious fidelity had something to do with the matter; inasmuch as the timely interruption served to rally his master from the mood which had evidently been coming upon him.

The place called the cuddy was a light deck-cabin formed by the poop, a sort of attic to the large cabin below. Part of it had formerly been the quarters of the officers; but since their death all the partitionings had been thrown down, and the whole interior converted into one spacious and airy marine hall; for absence of fine furniture and picturesque disarray, of odd appurtenances, somewhat answering to the wide, cluttered hall of some eccentric bachelor-squire in the country, who hangs his shooting-jacket and tobacco-pouch on deer antlers, and keeps his fishing-rod, tongs, and walking-stick in the same corner.

The similitude was heightened, if not originally suggested, by glimpses of the surrounding sea; since, in one aspect, the country and the ocean seem cousins-german.

The floor of the cuddy was matted. Overhead, four or five old muskets were stuck into horizontal holes along the beams. On one side was a claw-footed old table lashed to the deck; a thumbed missal on it, and over it a small, meager crucifix attached to the bulk-head. Under the table lay a dented cutlass or two, with a hacked harpoon, among some melancholy old rigging, like a heap of poor friar's girdles. There were also two long, sharp-ribbed settees of malacca cane, black with age, and uncomfortable to look at as inquisitors' racks, with a large, misshapen arm-chair, which, furnished with a rude barber's crutch at the back, working with a screw, seemed some grotesque, middle-age engine of torment. A flag locker was in one corner, open, exposing various colored bunting, some rolled up, others half unrolled, still others tumbled. Opposite was a cumbrous washstand, of black mahogany, all of one block, with a pedestal, like a font, and over it a railed shelf, containing combs, brushes, and other implements of the toilet. A torn hammock of stained grass swung near; the sheets tossed, and the pillow wrinkled up like a brow, as if whoever slept here slept but illy, with alternate visitations of sad thoughts and bad dreams.

The further extremity of the cuddy, overhanging the ship's stern, was pierced with three openings, windows or port holes, according as men or cannon might peer, socially or unsocially, out of them. At present neither men nor cannon were seen, though huge ring-bolts and other rusty iron fixtures of the wood-work hinted of twenty-four-pounders.

Glancing towards the hammock as he entered, Captain Delano said, "You sleep here, Don Benito?"

"Yes, Señor, since we got into mild weather."

"This seems a sort of dormitory, sitting-room, sail-loft, chapel, armory, and private closet all together, Don Benito," added Captain Delano, looking round.

"Yes, Señor; events have not been favorable to much order in my arrangements."

Here the servant, napkin on arm, made a motion as if waiting his master's good pleasure. Don Benito signified his readiness, when, seating him in the malacca arm-chair, and for the guest's convenience drawing opposite it one of the settees, the servant commenced operations by throwing back his master's collar and loosening his cravat.

There is something in the negro which, in a peculiar way, fits him for avocations about one's person. Most negroes are natural valets and hair-dressers; taking to the comb and brush congenially as to the castinets, and flourishing them apparently with almost equal satisfaction. There is, too, a smooth tact about them in this employment, with a marvelous, noiseless, gliding briskness, not ungraceful in its way, singularly pleasing to behold, and still more so to be the manipulated subject of. And above all is the great gift of good humor. Not the mere grin or laugh is here meant. Those were unsuitable. But a certain easy cheerfulness, harmonious in every glance and gesture; as though God had set the whole negro to some pleasant tune.

When to all this is added the docility arising from the unaspiring contentment of a limited mind, and that susceptibility of blind attachment sometimes inhering in indisputable inferiors, one readily perceives why those hypochondriacs, Johnson and Byron—it may be something like the hypochondriac, Benito Cereno—took to their hearts, almost to the exclusion of the entire white race, their serving men, the negroes, Barber and Fletcher. But if there be that in the negro which exempts him from the inflicted sourness of the morbid or cynical mind, how, in his most prepossessing aspects, must he appear to a benevolent one? When at ease with respect to exterior things, Captain Delano's nature was not only benign, but familiarly and humorously so. At home, he had often taken rare satisfaction in sitting in his door, watching some free man of color at his work or play. If on a voyage he chanced to have a black sailor, invariably he was on chatty, and half-gamesome terms with him. In fact, like most men of a good, blithe heart, Captain Delano took to negroes, not philanthropically, but genially, just as other men to Newfoundland dogs.

Hitherto the circumstances in which he found the San Dominick had repressed the tendency. But in the cuddy, relieved from his former uneasiness, and, for various reasons, more sociably inclined than at any previous period of the day, and seeing the colored servant, napkin on arm, so debonair about his master, in a business so familiar as that of shaving, too, all his old weakness for negroes returned.

Among other things, he was amused with an odd instance of the African love of bright colors and fine shows, in the black's informally taking from the flag-locker a great piece of bunting of all hues, and lavishly tucking it under his master's chin for an apron.

The mode of shaving among the Spaniards is a little different from what it is with other nations. They have a basin, specifically called a barber's basin, which on one side is scooped out, so as accurately to receive the chin, against which it is closely held in lathering; which is done, not with a brush, but with soap dipped in the water of the basin and rubbed on the face.

In the present instance salt-water was used for lack of better; and the parts lathered were only the upper lip, and low down under the throat, all the rest being cultivated beard.

The preliminaries being somewhat novel to Captain Delano, he sat curiously eying them, so that no conversation took place, nor for the present did Don Benito appear disposed to renew any.

Setting down his basin, the negro searched among the razors, as for the sharpest, and having found it, gave it an additional edge by expertly strapping it on the firm, smooth, oily skin of his open palm; he then made a gesture as if to begin, but midway stood suspended for an instant, one hand elevating the razor, the other professionally dabbling among the bubbling suds on the Spaniard's lank neck. Not unaffected by the close sight of the gleaming steel, Don Benito nervously shuddered; his usual ghastliness was heightened by the lather, which lather, again, was intensified in its hue by the contrasting sootiness of the negro's body. Altogether the scene was somewhat peculiar, at least to Captain Delano, nor, as he saw the two thus postured, could he resist the vagary, that in the black he saw a headsman, and in the white, a man at the block. But this was one of those antic conceits, appearing and vanishing in a breath, from which, perhaps, the best regulated mind is not always free.

Meantime the agitation of the Spaniard had a little loosened the bunting from around him, so that one broad fold swept curtain-like over the chair-arm to the floor, revealing, amid a profusion of armorial bars and ground-colors—black, blue, and yellow—a closed castle in a blood-red field diagonal with a lion rampant in a white.

"The castle and the lion," exclaimed Captain Delano—"why, Don Benito, this is the flag of Spain you use here. It's well it's only I, and not the King, that sees this," he added with a smile, "but"—turning towards the black,—"it's all one, I suppose, so the colors be gay;" which playful remark did not fail somewhat to tickle the negro.

"Now, master," he said, readjusting the flag, and pressing the head gently further back into the crotch of the chair; "now master," and the steel glanced nigh the throat.

Again Don Benito faintly shuddered.

"You must not shake so, master.—See, Don Amasa, master always shakes when I shave him. And yet master knows I never yet have drawn blood, though it's true, if master will shake so, I may some of these times. Now master," he continued. "And now, Don Amasa, please go on with your talk about the gale, and all that, master can hear, and between times master can answer."

"Ah yes, these gales," said Captain Delano; "but the more I think of your voyage, Don Benito, the more I wonder, not at the gales, terrible as they must have been, but at the disastrous interval following them. For here, by your account, have you been these two months and more getting from Cape Horn to St. Maria, a distance which I myself, with a good wind, have sailed in a few days. True, you had calms, and long ones, but to be becalmed for two months, that is, at least, unusual. Why, Don Benito, had almost any other gentleman told me such a story, I should have been half disposed to a little incredulity."

Here an involuntary expression came over the Spaniard, similar to that just before on the deck, and whether it was the start he gave, or a sudden gawky roll of the hull in the calm, or a momentary unsteadiness of the servant's hand; however it was, just then the razor drew blood, spots of which stained the creamy lather under the throat; immediately the black barber drew back his steel, and remaining in his professional attitude, back to Captain Delano, and face to Don Benito, held up the trickling razor, saying, with a sort of half humorous sorrow, "See, master,—you shook so—here's Babo's first blood."

No sword drawn before James the First of England, no assassination in that timid King's presence, could have produced a more terrified aspect than was now presented by Don Benito.

Poor fellow, thought Captain Delano, so nervous he can't even bear the sight of barber's blood; and this unstrung, sick man, is it credible that I should have imagined he meant to spill all my blood, who can't endure the sight of one little drop of his own? Surely, Amasa Delano, you have been beside yourself this day. Tell it not when you get home, sappy Amasa. Well, well, he looks like a murderer, doesn't he? More like as if himself were to be done for. Well, well, this day's experience shall be a good lesson.

Meantime, while these things were running through the honest seaman's mind, the servant had taken the napkin from his arm, and to Don Benito had said—"But answer Don Amasa, please, master, while I wipe this ugly stuff off the razor, and strop it again."

As he said the words, his face was turned half round, so as to be alike visible to the Spaniard and the American, and seemed by its expression to hint, that he was desirous, by getting his master to go on with the conversation, considerately to withdraw his attention from the recent annoying accident. As if glad to snatch the offered relief, Don Benito resumed, rehearsing to Captain Delano, that not only were the calms of unusual duration, but the ship had fallen in with obstinate currents; and other things he added, some of which were but repetitions of former statements, to explain how it came to pass that the passage from Cape Horn to St. Maria had been so exceedingly long, now and then mingling with his words, incidental praises, less qualified than before, to the blacks, for their general good conduct.

These particulars were not given consecutively, the servant, at convenient times, using his razor, and so, between the intervals of shaving, the story and panegyric went on with more than usual huskiness.

To Captain Delano's imagination, now again not wholly at rest, there was something so hollow in the Spaniard's manner, with apparently some reciprocal hollowness in the servant's dusky comment of silence, that the idea flashed across him, that possibly master and man, for some unknown purpose, were acting out, both in word and deed, nay, to the very tremor of Don Benito's limbs, some juggling play before him. Neither did the suspicion of collusion lack apparent support, from the fact of those whispered conferences before mentioned. But then, what could be the object of enacting this play of the barber before him? At last, regarding the notion as a whimsy, insensibly suggested, perhaps, by the theatrical aspect of Don Benito in his harlequin ensign, Captain Delano speedily banished it.

The shaving over, the servant bestirred himself with a small bottle of scented waters, pouring a few drops on the head, and then diligently rubbing; the vehemence of the exercise causing the muscles of his face to twitch rather strangely.

His next operation was with comb, scissors and brush; going round and round, smoothing a curl here, clipping an unruly whisker-hair there, giving a graceful sweep to the temple-lock, with other impromptu touches evincing the hand of a master; while, like any resigned gentleman in barber's hands, Don Benito bore all, much less uneasily, at least, than he had done the razoring; indeed, he sat so pale and rigid now, that the negro seemed a Nubian sculptor finishing off a white statue-head.

All being over at last, the standard of Spain removed, tumbled up, and tossed back into the flag-locker, the negro's warm breath blowing away any stray hair which might have lodged down his master's neck; collar and cravat readjusted; a speck of lint whisked off the velvet lapel; all this being done; backing off a little space, and pausing with an expression of subdued self-complacency, the servant for a moment surveyed his master, as, in toilet at least, the creature of his own tasteful hands.

Captain Delano playfully complimented him upon his achievement; at the same time congratulating Don Benito.

But neither sweet waters, nor shampooing, nor fidelity, nor sociality, delighted the Spaniard. Seeing him relapsing into forbidding gloom, and still remaining seated, Captain Delano, thinking that his presence was undesired just then, withdrew, on pretense of seeing whether, as he had prophecied, any signs of a breeze were visible.

Walking forward to the mainmast, he stood awhile thinking over the scene, and not without some undefined misgivings, when he heard a noise near the cuddy, and turning, saw the negro, his hand to his cheek. Advancing, Captain Delano perceived that the cheek was bleeding. He was about to ask the cause, when the negro's wailing soliloquy enlightened him.

"Ah, when will master get better from his sickness; only the sour heart that sour sickness breeds made him serve Babo so; cutting Babo with the razor, because, only by accident, Babo had given master one little scratch; and for the first time in so many a day, too. Ah, ah, ah," holding his hand to his face.

Is it possible, thought Captain Delano; was it to wreak in private his Spanish spite against this poor friend of his, that Don Benito, by his sullen manner, impelled me to withdraw? Ah, this slavery breeds ugly passions in man.—Poor fellow!

He was about to speak in sympathy to the negro, but with a timid reluctance he now reëntered the cuddy.

Presently master and man came forth; Don Benito leaning on his servant as if nothing had happened.

But a sort of love-quarrel, after all, thought Captain Delano.

He accosted Don Benito, and they slowly walked together. They had gone but a few paces, when the steward—a tall, rajah-looking mulatto, orientally set off with a pagoda turban formed by three or four Madras handkerchiefs wound about his head, tier on tier—approaching with a salaam, announced lunch in the cabin.

On their way thither, the two Captains were preceded by the mulatto, who, turning round as he advanced, with continual smiles and bows, ushered them on, a display of elegance which quite completed the insignificance of the small bare-headed Babo, who, as if not unconscious of inferiority, eyed askance the graceful steward. But in part, Captain Delano imputed his jealous watchfulness to that peculiar feeling which the full-blooded African entertains for the adulterated one. As for the steward, his manner, if not bespeaking much dignity of self-respect, yet evidenced his extreme desire to please; which is doubly meritorious, as at once Christian and Chesterfieldian.

Captain Delano observed with interest that while the complexion of the mulatto was hybrid, his physiognomy was European; classically so.

"Don Benito," whispered he, "I am glad to see this usher-of-the-golden-rod of yours; the sight refutes an ugly remark once made to me by a Barbadoes planter; that when a mulatto has a regular European face, look out for him; he is a devil. But see, your steward here has features more regular than King George's of England; and yet there he nods, and bows, and smiles; a king, indeed—the king of kind hearts and polite fellows. What a pleasant voice he has, too!"

"He has, Señor."

"But, tell me, has he not, so far as you have known him, always proved a good, worthy fellow?" said Captain Delano, pausing, while with a final genuflexion the steward disappeared into the cabin; "come, for the reason just mentioned, I am curious to know."

"Francesco is a good man," a sort of sluggishly responded Don Benito, like a phlegmatic appreciator, who would neither find fault nor flatter.

"Ah, I thought so. For it were strange indeed, and not very creditable to us white-skins, if a little of our blood mixed with the African's, should, far from improving the latter's quality, have the sad effect of pouring vitriolic acid into black broth; improving the hue, perhaps, but not the wholesomeness."

"Doubtless, doubtless, Señor, but"—glancing at Babo—"not to speak of negroes, your planter's remark I have heard applied to the Spanish and Indian intermixtures in our provinces. But I know nothing about the matter," he listlessly added.

And here they entered the cabin.

The lunch was a frugal one. Some of Captain Delano's fresh fish and pumpkins, biscuit and salt beef, the reserved bottle of cider, and the San Dominick's last bottle of Canary.

As they entered, Francesco, with two or three colored aids, was hovering over the table giving the last adjustments. Upon perceiving their master they withdrew, Francesco making a smiling congé, and the Spaniard, without condescending to notice it, fastidiously remarking to his companion that he relished not superfluous attendance.

Without companions, host and guest sat down, like a childless married couple, at opposite ends of the table, Don Benito waving Captain Delano to his place, and, weak as he was, insisting upon that gentleman being seated before himself.

The negro placed a rug under Don Benito's feet, and a cushion behind his back, and then stood behind, not his master's chair, but Captain Delano's. At first, this a little surprised the latter. But it was soon evident that, in taking his position, the black was still true to his master; since by facing him he could the more readily anticipate his slightest want.

"This is an uncommonly intelligent fellow of yours, Don Benito," whispered Captain Delano across the table.

"You say true, Señor."

During the repast, the guest again reverted to parts of Don Benito's story, begging further particulars here and there. He inquired how it was that the scurvy and fever should have committed such wholesale havoc upon the whites, while destroying less than half of the blacks. As if this question reproduced the whole scene of plague before the Spaniard's eyes, miserably reminding him of his solitude in a cabin where before he had had so many friends and officers round him, his hand shook, his face became hueless, broken words escaped; but directly the sane memory of the past seemed replaced by insane terrors of the present. With starting eyes he stared before him at vacancy. For nothing was to be seen but the hand of his servant pushing the Canary over towards him. At length a few sips served partially to restore him. He made random reference to the different constitution of races, enabling one to offer more resistance to certain maladies than another. The thought was new to his companion.

Presently Captain Delano, intending to say something to his host concerning the pecuniary part of the business he had undertaken for him, especially—since he was strictly accountable to his owners—with reference to the new suit of sails, and other things of that sort; and naturally preferring to conduct such affairs in private, was desirous that the servant should withdraw; imagining that Don Benito for a few minutes could dispense with his attendance. He, however, waited awhile; thinking that, as the conversation proceeded, Don Benito, without being prompted, would perceive the propriety of the step.

But it was otherwise. At last catching his host's eye, Captain Delano, with a slight backward gesture of his thumb, whispered, "Don Benito, pardon me, but there is an interference with the full expression of what I have to say to you."

Upon this the Spaniard changed countenance; which was imputed to his resenting the hint, as in some way a reflection upon his servant. After a moment's pause, he assured his guest that the black's remaining with them could be of no disservice; because since losing his officers he had made Babo (whose original office, it now appeared, had been captain of the slaves) not only his constant attendant and companion, but in all things his confidant.

After this, nothing more could be said; though, indeed, Captain Delano could hardly avoid some little tinge of irritation upon being left ungratified in so inconsiderable a wish, by one, too, for whom he intended such solid services. But it is only his querulousness, thought he; and so filling his glass he proceeded to business.

The price of the sails and other matters was fixed upon. But while this was being done, the American observed that, though his original offer of assistance had been hailed with hectic animation, yet now when it was reduced to a business transaction, indifference and apathy were betrayed. Don Benito, in fact, appeared to submit to hearing the details more out of regard to common propriety, than from any impression that weighty benefit to himself and his voyage was involved.

Soon, this manner became still more reserved. The effort was vain to seek to draw him into social talk. Gnawed by his splenetic mood, he sat twitching his beard, while to little purpose the hand of his servant, mute as that on the wall, slowly pushed over the Canary.

Lunch being over, they sat down on the cushioned transom; the servant placing a pillow behind his master. The long continuance of the calm had now affected the atmosphere. Don Benito sighed heavily, as if for breath.

"Why not adjourn to the cuddy," said Captain Delano; "there is more air there." But the host sat silent and motionless.

Meantime his servant knelt before him, with a large fan of feathers. And Francesco coming in on tiptoes, handed the negro a little cup of aromatic waters, with which at intervals he chafed his master's brow; smoothing the hair along the temples as a nurse does a child's. He spoke no word. He only rested his eye on his master's, as if, amid all Don Benito's distress, a little to refresh his spirit by the silent sight of fidelity.

Presently the ship's bell sounded two o'clock; and through the cabin-windows a slight rippling of the sea was discerned; and from the desired direction.

"There," exclaimed Captain Delano, "I told you so, Don Benito, look!"

He had risen to his feet, speaking in a very animated tone, with a view the more to rouse his companion. But though the crimson curtain of the stern-window near him that moment fluttered against his pale cheek, Don Benito seemed to have even less welcome for the breeze than the calm.

Poor fellow, thought Captain Delano, bitter experience has taught him that one ripple does not make a wind, any more than one swallow a summer. But he is mistaken for once. I will get his ship in for him, and prove it.

Briefly alluding to his weak condition, he urged his host to remain quietly where he was, since he (Captain Delano) would with pleasure take upon himself the responsibility of making the best use of the wind.

Upon gaining the deck, Captain Delano started at the unexpected figure of Atufal, monumentally fixed at the threshold, like one of those sculptured porters of black marble guarding the porches of Egyptian tombs.

But this time the start was, perhaps, purely physical. Atufal's presence, singularly attesting docility even in sullenness, was contrasted with that of the hatchet-polishers, who in patience evinced their industry; while both spectacles showed, that lax as Don Benito's general authority might be, still, whenever he chose to exert it, no man so savage or colossal but must, more or less, bow.

Snatching a trumpet which hung from the bulwarks, with a free step Captain Delano advanced to the forward edge of the poop, issuing his orders in his best Spanish. The few sailors and many negroes, all equally pleased, obediently set about heading the ship towards the harbor.

While giving some directions about setting a lower stu'n'-sail, suddenly Captain Delano heard a voice faithfully repeating his orders. Turning, he saw Babo, now for the time acting, under the pilot, his original part of captain of the slaves. This assistance proved valuable. Tattered sails and warped yards were soon brought into some trim. And no brace or halyard was pulled but to the blithe songs of the inspirited negroes.

Good fellows, thought Captain Delano, a little training would make fine sailors of them. Why see, the very women pull and sing too. These must be some of those Ashantee negresses that make such capital soldiers, I've heard. But who's at the helm. I must have a good hand there.

He went to see.

The San Dominick steered with a cumbrous tiller, with large horizontal pullies attached. At each pully-end stood a subordinate black, and between them, at the tiller-head, the responsible post, a Spanish seaman, whose countenance evinced his due share in the general hopefulness and confidence at the coming of the breeze.

He proved the same man who had behaved with so shame-faced an air on the windlass.

"Ah,—it is you, my man," exclaimed Captain Delano—"well, no more sheep's-eyes now;—look straight forward and keep the ship so. Good hand, I trust? And want to get into the harbor, don't you?"

The man assented with an inward chuckle, grasping the tiller-head firmly. Upon this, unperceived by the American, the two blacks eyed the sailor intently.

Finding all right at the helm, the pilot went forward to the forecastle, to see how matters stood there.

The ship now had way enough to breast the current. With the approach of evening, the breeze would be sure to freshen.

Having done all that was needed for the present, Captain Delano, giving his last orders to the sailors, turned aft to report affairs to Don Benito in the cabin; perhaps additionally incited to rejoin him by the hope of snatching a moment's private chat while his servant was engaged upon deck.

From opposite sides, there were, beneath the poop, two approaches to the cabin; one further forward than the other, and consequently communicating with a longer passage. Marking the servant still above, Captain Delano, taking the nighest entrance—the one last named, and at whose porch Atufal still stood—hurried on his way, till, arrived at the cabin threshold, he paused an instant, a little to recover from his eagerness. Then, with the words of his intended business upon his lips, he entered. As he advanced toward the seated Spaniard, he heard another footstep, keeping time with his. From the opposite door, a salver in hand, the servant was likewise advancing.

"Confound the faithful fellow," thought Captain Delano; "what a vexatious coincidence."

Possibly, the vexation might have been something different, were it not for the brisk confidence inspired by the breeze. But even as it was, he felt a slight twinge, from a sudden indefinite association in his mind of Babo with Atufal.

"Don Benito," said he, "I give you joy; the breeze will hold, and will increase. By the way, your tall man and time-piece, Atufal, stands without. By your order, of course?"

Don Benito recoiled, as if at some bland satirical touch, delivered with such adroit garnish of apparent good-breeding as to present no handle for retort.

He is like one flayed alive, thought Captain Delano; where may one touch him without causing a shrink?

The servant moved before his master, adjusting a cushion; recalled to civility, the Spaniard stiffly replied: "you are right. The slave appears where you saw him, according to my command; which is, that if at the given hour I am below, he must take his stand and abide my coming."

"Ah now, pardon me, but that is treating the poor fellow like an ex-king indeed. Ah, Don Benito," smiling, "for all the license you permit in some things, I fear lest, at bottom, you are a bitter hard master."

Again Don Benito shrank; and this time, as the good sailor thought, from a genuine twinge of his conscience.

Again conversation became constrained. In vain Captain Delano called attention to the now perceptible motion of the keel gently cleaving the sea; with lack-lustre eye, Don Benito returned words few and reserved.

By-and-by, the wind having steadily risen, and still blowing right into the harbor, bore the San Dominick swiftly on. Rounding a point of land, the sealer at distance came into open view.

Meantime Captain Delano had again repaired to the deck, remaining there some time. Having at last altered the ship's course, so as to give the reef a wide berth, he returned for a few moments below.

I will cheer up my poor friend, this time, thought he.

"Better and better, Don Benito," he cried as he blithely reëntered; "there will soon be an end to your cares, at least for awhile. For when, after a long, sad voyage, you know, the anchor drops into the haven, all its vast weight seems lifted from the captain's heart. We are getting on famously, Don Benito. My ship is in sight. Look through this side-light here; there she is; all a-taunt-o! The Bachelor's Delight, my good friend. Ah, how this wind braces one up. Come, you must take a cup of coffee with me this evening. My old steward will give you as fine a cup as ever any sultan tasted. What say you, Don Benito, will you?"

At first, the Spaniard glanced feverishly up, casting a longing look towards the sealer, while with mute concern his servant gazed into his face. Suddenly the old ague of coldness returned, and dropping back to his cushions he was silent.

"You do not answer. Come, all day you have been my host; would you have hospitality all on one side?"

"I cannot go," was the response.

"What? it will not fatigue you. The ships will lie together as near as they can, without swinging foul. It will be little more than stepping from deck to deck; which is but as from room to room. Come, come, you must not refuse me."

"I cannot go," decisively and repulsively repeated Don Benito.

Renouncing all but the last appearance of courtesy, with a sort of cadaverous sullenness, and biting his thin nails to the quick, he glanced, almost glared, at his guest; as if impatient that a stranger's presence should interfere with the full indulgence of his morbid hour. Meantime the sound of the parted waters came more and more gurglingly and merrily in at the windows; as reproaching him for his dark spleen; as telling him that, sulk as he might, and go mad with it, nature cared not a jot; since, whose fault was it, pray?

But the foul mood was now at its depth, as the fair wind at its height.

There was something in the man so far beyond any mere unsociality or sourness previously evinced, that even the forbearing good-nature of his guest could no longer endure it. Wholly at a loss to account for such demeanor, and deeming sickness with eccentricity, however extreme, no adequate excuse, well satisfied, too, that nothing in his own conduct could justify it, Captain Delano's pride began to be roused. Himself became reserved. But all seemed one to the Spaniard. Quitting him, therefore, Captain Delano once more went to the deck.

The ship was now within less than two miles of the sealer. The whale-boat was seen darting over the interval.

To be brief, the two vessels, thanks to the pilot's skill, ere long in neighborly style lay anchored together.

Before returning to his own vessel, Captain Delano had intended communicating to Don Benito the smaller details of the proposed services to be rendered. But, as it was, unwilling anew to subject himself to rebuffs, he resolved, now that he had seen the San Dominick safely moored, immediately to quit her, without further allusion to hospitality or business. Indefinitely postponing his ulterior plans, he would regulate his future actions according to future circumstances. His boat was ready to receive him; but his host still tarried below. Well, thought Captain Delano, if he has little breeding, the more need to show mine. He descended to the cabin to bid a ceremonious, and, it may be, tacitly rebukeful adieu. But to his great satisfaction, Don Benito, as if he began to feel the weight of that treatment with which his slighted guest had, not indecorously, retaliated upon him, now supported by his servant, rose to his feet, and grasping Captain Delano's hand, stood tremulous; too much agitated to speak. But the good augury hence drawn was suddenly dashed, by his resuming all his previous reserve, with augmented gloom, as, with half-averted eyes, he silently reseated himself on his cushions. With a corresponding return of his own chilled feelings, Captain Delano bowed and withdrew.

He was hardly midway in the narrow corridor, dim as a tunnel, leading from the cabin to the stairs, when a sound, as of the tolling for execution in some jail-yard, fell on his ears. It was the echo of the ship's flawed bell, striking the hour, drearily reverberated in this subterranean vault. Instantly, by a fatality not to be withstood, his mind, responsive to the portent, swarmed with superstitious suspicions. He paused. In images far swifter than these sentences, the minutest details of all his former distrusts swept through him.

Hitherto, credulous good-nature had been too ready to furnish excuses for reasonable fears. Why was the Spaniard, so superfluously punctilious at times, now heedless of common propriety in not accompanying to the side his departing guest? Did indisposition forbid? Indisposition had not forbidden more irksome exertion that day. His last equivocal demeanor recurred. He had risen to his feet, grasped his guest's hand, motioned toward his hat; then, in an instant, all was eclipsed in sinister muteness and gloom. Did this imply one brief, repentent relenting at the final moment, from some iniquitous plot, followed by remorseless return to it? His last glance seemed to express a calamitous, yet acquiescent farewell to Captain Delano forever. Why decline the invitation to visit the sealer that evening? Or was the Spaniard less hardened than the Jew, who refrained not from supping at the board of him whom the same night he meant to betray? What imported all those day-long enigmas and contradictions, except they were intended to mystify, preliminary to some stealthy blow? Atufal, the pretended rebel, but punctual shadow, that moment lurked by the threshold without. He seemed a sentry, and more. Who, by his own confession, had stationed him there? Was the negro now lying in wait?

The Spaniard behind—his creature before: to rush from darkness to light was the involuntary choice.

The next moment, with clenched jaw and hand, he passed Atufal, and stood unharmed in the light. As he saw his trim ship lying peacefully at her anchor, and almost within ordinary call; as he saw his household boat, with familiar faces in it, patiently rising and falling on the short waves by the San Dominick's side; and then, glancing about the decks where he stood, saw the oakum-pickers still gravely plying their fingers; and heard the low, buzzing whistle and industrious hum of the hatchet-polishers, still bestirring themselves over their endless occupation; and more than all, as he saw the benign aspect of nature, taking her innocent repose in the evening; the screened sun in the quiet camp of the west shining out like the mild light from Abraham's tent; as charmed eye and ear took in all these, with the chained figure of the black, clenched jaw and hand relaxed. Once again he smiled at the phantoms which had mocked him, and felt something like a tinge of remorse, that, by harboring them even for a moment, he should, by implication, have betrayed an almost atheist doubt of the ever-watchful Providence above.

There was a few minutes' delay, while, in obedience to his orders, the boat was being hooked along to the gangway. During this interval, a sort of saddened satisfaction stole over Captain Delano, at thinking of the kindly offices he had that day discharged for a stranger. Ah, thought he, after good actions one's conscience is never ungrateful, however much so the benefited party may be.

Presently, his foot, in the first act of descent into the boat, pressed the first round of the side-ladder, his face presented inward upon the deck. In the same moment, he heard his name courteously sounded; and, to his pleased surprise, saw Don Benito advancing—an unwonted energy in his air, as if, at the last moment, intent upon making amends for his recent discourtesy. With instinctive good feeling, Captain Delano, withdrawing his foot, turned and reciprocally advanced. As he did so, the Spaniard's nervous eagerness increased, but his vital energy failed; so that, the better to support him, the servant, placing his master's hand on his naked shoulder, and gently holding it there, formed himself into a sort of crutch.

When the two captains met, the Spaniard again fervently took the hand of the American, at the same time casting an earnest glance into his eyes, but, as before, too much overcome to speak.

I have done him wrong, self-reproachfully thought Captain Delano; his apparent coldness has deceived me; in no instance has he meant to offend.

Meantime, as if fearful that the continuance of the scene might too much unstring his master, the servant seemed anxious to terminate it. And so, still presenting himself as a crutch, and walking between the two captains, he advanced with them towards the gangway; while still, as if full of kindly contrition, Don Benito would not let go the hand of Captain Delano, but retained it in his, across the black's body.

Soon they were standing by the side, looking over into the boat, whose crew turned up their curious eyes. Waiting a moment for the Spaniard to relinquish his hold, the now embarrassed Captain Delano lifted his foot, to overstep the threshold of the open gangway; but still Don Benito would not let go his hand. And yet, with an agitated tone, he said, "I can go no further; here I must bid you adieu. Adieu, my dear, dear Don Amasa. Go—go!" suddenly tearing his hand loose, "go, and God guard you better than me, my best friend."

Not unaffected, Captain Delano would now have lingered; but catching the meekly admonitory eye of the servant, with a hasty farewell he descended into his boat, followed by the continual adieus of Don Benito, standing rooted in the gangway.

Seating himself in the stern, Captain Delano, making a last salute, ordered the boat shoved off. The crew had their oars on end. The bowsman pushed the boat a sufficient distance for the oars to be lengthwise dropped. The instant that was done, Don Benito sprang over the bulwarks, falling at the feet of Captain Delano; at the same time, calling towards his ship, but in tones so frenzied, that none in the boat could understand him. But, as if not equally obtuse, three sailors, from three different and distant parts of the ship, splashed into the sea, swimming after their captain, as if intent upon his rescue.

The dismayed officer of the boat eagerly asked what this meant. To which, Captain Delano, turning a disdainful smile upon the unaccountable Spaniard, answered that, for his part, he neither knew nor cared; but it seemed as if Don Benito had taken it into his head to produce the impression among his people that the boat wanted to kidnap him. "Or else—give way for your lives," he wildly added, starting at a clattering hubbub in the ship, above which rang the tocsin of the hatchet-polishers; and seizing Don Benito by the throat he added, "this plotting pirate means murder!" Here, in apparent verification of the words, the servant, a dagger in his hand, was seen on the rail overhead, poised, in the act of leaping, as if with desperate fidelity to befriend his master to the last; while, seemingly to aid the black, the three white sailors were trying to clamber into the hampered bow. Meantime, the whole host of negroes, as if inflamed at the sight of their jeopardized captain, impended in one sooty avalanche over the bulwarks.

All this, with what preceded, and what followed, occurred with such involutions of rapidity, that past, present, and future seemed one.

Seeing the negro coming, Captain Delano had flung the Spaniard aside, almost in the very act of clutching him, and, by the unconscious recoil, shifting his place, with arms thrown up, so promptly grappled the servant in his descent, that with dagger presented at Captain Delano's heart, the black seemed of purpose to have leaped there as to his mark. But the weapon was wrenched away, and the assailant dashed down into the bottom of the boat, which now, with disentangled oars, began to speed through the sea.

At this juncture, the left hand of Captain Delano, on one side, again clutched the half-reclined Don Benito, heedless that he was in a speechless faint, while his right foot, on the other side, ground the prostrate negro; and his right arm pressed for added speed on the after oar, his eye bent forward, encouraging his men to their utmost.

But here, the officer of the boat, who had at last succeeded in beating off the towing sailors, and was now, with face turned aft, assisting the bowsman at his oar, suddenly called to Captain Delano, to see what the black was about; while a Portuguese oarsman shouted to him to give heed to what the Spaniard was saying.

Glancing down at his feet, Captain Delano saw the freed hand of the servant aiming with a second dagger—a small one, before concealed in his wool—with this he was snakishly writhing up from the boat's bottom, at the heart of his master, his countenance lividly vindictive, expressing the centred purpose of his soul; while the Spaniard, half-choked, was vainly shrinking away, with husky words, incoherent to all but the Portuguese.

That moment, across the long-benighted mind of Captain Delano, a flash of revelation swept, illuminating in unanticipated clearness his host's whole mysterious demeanor, with every enigmatic event of the day, as well as the entire past voyage of the San Dominick. He smote Babo's hand down, but his own heart smote him harder. With infinite pity he withdrew his hold from Don Benito. Not Captain Delano, but Don Benito, the black, in leaping into the boat, had intended to stab.

Both the black's hands were held, as, glancing up towards the San Dominick, Captain Delano, now with the scales dropped from his eyes, saw the negroes, not in misrule, not in tumult, not as if frantically concerned for Don Benito, but with mask torn away, flourishing hatchets and knives, in ferocious piratical revolt. Like delirious black dervishes, the six Ashantees danced on the poop. Prevented by their foes from springing into the water, the Spanish boys were hurrying up to the topmost spars, while such of the few Spanish sailors, not already in the sea, less alert, were descried, helplessly mixed in, on deck, with the blacks.

Meantime Captain Delano hailed his own vessel, ordering the ports up, and the guns run out. But by this time the cable of the San Dominick had been cut; and the fag-end, in lashing out, whipped away the canvas shroud about the beak, suddenly revealing, as the bleached hull swung round towards the open ocean, death for the figure-head, in a human skeleton; chalky comment on the chalked words below, "*Follow your leader.*"

At the sight, Don Benito, covering his face, wailed out: "'Tis he, Aranda! my murdered, unburied friend!"

Upon reaching the sealer, calling for ropes, Captain Delano bound the negro, who made no resistance, and had him hoisted to the deck. He would then have assisted the now almost helpless Don Benito up the side; but Don Benito, wan as he was, refused to move, or be moved, until the negro should have been first put below out of view. When, presently assured that it was done, he no more shrank from the ascent.

The boat was immediately dispatched back to pick up the three swimming sailors. Meantime, the guns were in readiness, though, owing to the San Dominick having glided somewhat astern of the sealer, only the aftermost one could be brought to bear. With this, they fired six times; thinking to cripple the fugitive ship by bringing down her spars. But only a few inconsiderable ropes were shot away. Soon the ship was beyond the gun's range, steering broad out of the bay; the blacks thickly clustering round the bowsprit, one moment with taunting cries towards the whites, the next with upthrown gestures hailing the now dusky moors of ocean—cawing crows escaped from the hand of the fowler.

The first impulse was to slip the cables and give chase. But, upon second thoughts, to pursue with whale-boat and yawl seemed more promising.

Upon inquiring of Don Benito what fire arms they had on board the San Dominick, Captain Delano was answered that they had none that could be used; because, in the earlier stages of the mutiny, a cabin-passenger, since dead, had secretly put out of order the locks of what few muskets there were. But with all his remaining strength, Don Benito entreated the American not to give chase, either with ship or boat; for the negroes had already proved themselves such desperadoes, that, in case of a present assault, nothing but a total massacre of the whites could be looked for. But, regarding this warning as coming from one whose spirit had been crushed by misery, the American did not give up his design.

The boats were got ready and armed. Captain Delano ordered his men into them. He was going himself when Don Benito grasped his arm.

"What! have you saved my life, señor, and are you now going to throw away your own?"

The officers also, for reasons connected with their interests and those of the voyage, and a duty owing to the owners, strongly objected against their commander's going. Weighing their remonstrances a moment, Captain Delano felt bound to remain; appointing his chief mate—an athletic and resolute man, who had been a privateer's-man, and, as his enemies whispered, a pirate—to head the party. The more to encourage the sailors, they were told, that the Spanish captain considered his ship as good as lost; that she and her cargo, including some gold and silver, were worth more than a thousand doubloons. Take her, and no small part should be theirs. The sailors replied with a shout.

The fugitives had now almost gained an offing. It was nearly night; but the moon was rising. After hard, prolonged pulling, the boats came up on the ship's quarters, at a suitable distance laying upon their oars to discharge their muskets. Having no bullets to return, the negroes sent their yells. But, upon the second volley, Indian-like, they hurtled their hatchets. One took off a sailor's fingers. Another struck the whale-boat's bow, cutting off the rope there, and remaining stuck in the gunwale like a woodman's axe. Snatching it, quivering from its lodgment, the mate hurled it back. The returned gauntlet now stuck in the ship's broken quarter-gallery, and so remained.

The negroes giving too hot a reception, the whites kept a more respectful distance. Hovering now just out of reach of the hurtling hatchets, they, with a view to the close encounter which must soon come, sought to decoy the blacks into entirely disarming themselves of their most murderous weapons in a hand-to-hand fight, by foolishly flinging them, as missiles, short of the mark, into the sea. But ere long perceiving the stratagem, the negroes desisted, though not before many of them had to replace their lost hatchets with handspikes; an exchange which, as counted upon, proved in the end favorable to the assailants.

Meantime, with a strong wind, the ship still clove the water; the boats alternately falling behind, and pulling up, to discharge fresh volleys.

The fire was mostly directed towards the stern, since there, chiefly, the negroes, at present, were clustering. But to kill or maim the negroes was not the object. To take them, with the ship, was the object. To do it, the ship must be boarded; which could not be done by boats while she was sailing so fast.

A thought now struck the mate. Observing the Spanish boys still aloft, high as they could get, he called to them to descend to the yards, and cut adrift the sails. It was done. About this time, owing to causes hereafter to be shown, two Spaniards, in the dress of sailors and conspicuously showing themselves, were killed; not by volleys, but by deliberate marksman's shots; while, as it afterwards appeared, by one of the general discharges, Atufal, the black, and the Spaniard at the helm likewise were killed. What now, with the loss of the sails, and loss of leaders, the ship became unmanageable to the negroes.

With creaking masts, she came heavily round to the wind; the prow slowly swinging, into view of the boats, its skeleton gleaming in the horizontal moonlight, and casting a gigantic ribbed shadow upon the water. One extended arm of the ghost seemed beckoning the whites to avenge it.

"Follow your leader!" cried the mate; and, one on each bow, the boats boarded. Sealing-spears and cutlasses crossed hatchets and hand-spikes. Huddled upon the long-boat amidships, the negresses raised a wailing chant, whose chorus was the clash of the steel.

For a time, the attack wavered; the negroes wedging themselves to beat it back; the half-repelled sailors, as yet unable to gain a footing, fighting as troopers in the saddle, one leg sideways flung over the bulwarks, and one without, plying their cutlasses like carters' whips. But in vain. They were almost overborne, when, rallying themselves into a squad as one man, with a huzza, they sprang inboard; where, entangled, they involuntarily separated again. For a few breaths' space, there was a vague, muffled, inner sound, as of submerged sword-fish rushing hither and thither through shoals of black-fish. Soon, in a reunited band, and joined by the Spanish seamen, the whites came to the surface, irresistibly driving the negroes toward the stern. But a barricade of casks and sacks, from side to side, had been thrown up by the mainmast. Here the negroes faced about, and though scorning peace or truce, yet fain would have had a respite. But, without pause, overleaping the barrier, the unflagging sailors again closed. Exhausted, the blacks now fought in despair. Their red tongues lolled, wolf-like, from their black mouths. But the pale sailors' teeth were set; not a word was spoken; and, in five minutes more, the ship was won.

Nearly a score of the negroes were killed. Exclusive of those by the balls, many were mangled; their wounds—mostly inflicted by the long-edged sealing-spears—resembling those shaven ones of the English at Preston Pans, made by the poled scythes of the Highlanders. On the other side, none were killed, though several were wounded; some severely, including the mate. The surviving negroes were temporarily secured, and the ship, towed back into the harbor at midnight, once more lay anchored.

Omitting the incidents and arrangements ensuing, suffice it that, after two days spent in refitting, the two ships sailed in company for Concepcion, in Chili, and thence for Lima, in Peru; where, before the vice-regal courts, the whole affair, from the beginning, underwent investigation.

Though, midway on the passage, the ill-fated Spaniard, relaxed from constraint, showed some signs of regaining health with free-will; yet, agreeably to his own foreboding, shortly before arriving at Lima, he relapsed, finally becoming so reduced as to be carried ashore in arms. Hearing of his story and plight, one of the many religious institutions of the City of Kings opened an hospitable refuge to him, where both physician and priest were his nurses, and a member of the order volunteered to be his one special guardian and consoler, by night and by day.

The following extracts, translated from one of the official Spanish documents, will it is hoped, shed light on the preceding narrative, as well as, in the first place, reveal the true port of departure and true history of the San Dominick's voyage, down to the time of her touching at the island of St. Maria.

But, ere the extracts come, it may be well to preface them with a remark.

The document selected, from among many others, for partial translation, contains the deposition of Benito Cereno; the first taken in the case. Some disclosures therein were, at the time, held dubious for both learned and natural reasons. The tribunal inclined to the opinion that the deponent, not undisturbed in his mind by recent events, raved of some things which could never have happened. But subsequent depositions of the surviving sailors, bearing out the revelations of their captain in several of the strangest particulars, gave credence to the rest. So that the tribunal, in its final decision, rested its capital sentences upon statements which, had they lacked confirmation, it would have deemed it but duty to reject.

I, DON JOSE DE ABOS AND PADILLA, His Majesty's Notary for the Royal Revenue, and Register of this Province, and Notary Public of the Holy Crusade of this Bishopric, etc.

Do certify and declare, as much as is requisite in law, that, in the criminal cause commenced the twenty-fourth of the month of September, in the year seventeen hundred and ninety-nine, against the negroes of the ship San Dominick, the following declaration before me was made.

Declaration of the first witness, DON BENITO CERENO.

The same day, and month, and year, His Honor, Doctor Juan Martinez de Rozas, Councilor of the Royal Audience of this Kingdom, and learned in the law of this Intendency, ordered the captain of the ship San Dominick, Don Benito Cereno, to appear; which he did in his litter, attended by the monk Infelez; of whom he received the oath, which he took by God, our Lord, and a sign of the Cross; under which he promised to tell the truth of whatever he should know and should be asked;—and being interrogated agreeably to the tenor of the act commencing the process, he said, that on the twentieth of May last, he set sail with his ship from the port of Valparaiso, bound to that of Callao; loaded with the produce of the country beside thirty cases of hardware and one hundred and sixty blacks, of both sexes, mostly belonging to Don Alexandro Aranda, gentleman, of the city of Mendoza; that the crew of the ship consisted of thirty-six men, beside the persons who went as passengers; that the negroes were in part as follows:

[Here, in the original, follows a list of some fifty names, descriptions, and ages, compiled from certain recovered documents of Aranda's, and also from recollections of the deponent, from which portions only are extracted.]

—One, from about eighteen to nineteen years, named José, and this was the man that waited upon his master, Don Alexandro, and who speaks well the Spanish, having served him four or five years; * * * a mulatto, named Francesco, the cabin steward, of a good person and voice, having sung in the Valparaiso churches, native of the province of Buenos Ayres, aged about thirty-five years. * * * A smart negro, named Dago, who had been for many years a grave-digger among the Spaniards, aged forty-six years. * * * Four old negroes, born in Africa, from sixty to seventy, but sound, calkers by trade, whose names are as follows:—the first was named Mure, and he was killed (as was also his son named Diamelo); the second, Natu; the third, Yola, likewise killed; the fourth, Ghofan; and six full-grown negroes, aged from thirty to forty-five, all raw, and born among the Ashantees—Matiluqui, Yau, Lecbe, Mapenda, Yambaio, Akim; four of whom were killed; * * * a powerful negro named Atufal, who, being supposed to have been a chief in Africa, his owners set great store by him. * * * And a small negro of Senegal, but some years among the Spaniards, aged about thirty, which negro's name was Babo; * * * that he does not remember the names of the others, but that still expecting the residue of Don Alexandro's papers will be found, will then take due account of them all, and remit to the court; * * * and thirty-nine women and children of all ages.

[The catalogue over, the deposition goes on:]

* * * That all the negroes slept upon deck, as is customary in this navigation, and none wore fetters, because the owner, his friend Aranda, told him that they were all tractable; * * * that on the seventh day after

leaving port, at three o'clock in the morning, all the Spaniards being asleep except the two officers on the watch, who were the boatswain, Juan Robles, and the carpenter, Juan Bautista Gayete, and the helmsman and his boy, the negroes revolted suddenly, wounded dangerously the boatswain and the carpenter, and successively killed eighteen men of those who were sleeping upon deck, some with hand-spikes and hatchets, and others by throwing them alive overboard, after tying them; that of the Spaniards upon deck, they left about seven, as he thinks, alive and tied, to manœuvre the ship, and three or four more, who hid themselves, remained also alive. Although in the act of revolt the negroes made themselves masters of the hatchway, six or seven wounded went through it to the cockpit, without any hindrance on their part; that during the act of revolt, the mate and another person, whose name he does not recollect, attempted to come up through the hatchway, but being quickly wounded, they were obliged to return to the cabin; that the deponent resolved at break of day to come up the companion-way, where the negro Babo was, being the ringleader, and Atufal, who assisted him, and having spoken to them, exhorted them to cease committing such atrocities, asking them, at the same time, what they wanted and intended to do, offering, himself, to obey their commands; that, notwithstanding this, they threw, in his presence, three men, alive and tied, overboard; that they told the deponent to come up, and that they would not kill him; which having done, the negro Babo asked him whether there were in those seas any negro countries where they might be carried, and he answered them, No; that the negro Babo afterwards told him to carry them to Senegal, or to the neighboring islands of St. Nicolas; and he answered, that this was impossible, on account of the great distance, the necessity involved of rounding Cape Horn, the bad condition of the vessel, the want of provisions, sails, and water; but that the negro Babo replied to him he must carry them in any way; that they would do and conform themselves to everything the deponent should require as to eating and drinking; that after a long conference, being absolutely compelled to please them, for they threatened him to kill all the whites if they were not, at all events, carried to Senegal, he told them that what was most wanting for the voyage was water; that they would go near the coast to take it, and thence they would proceed on their course; that the negro Babo agreed to it; and the deponent steered towards the intermediate ports, hoping to meet some Spanish or foreign vessel that would save them; that within ten or eleven days they saw the land, and continued their course by it in the vicinity of Nasca; that the deponent observed that the negroes were now restless and mutinous, because he did not effect the taking in of water, the negro Babo having required, with threats, that it should be done, without fail, the following day; he told him they saw plainly that the coast was steep, and the rivers designated in the maps were not to be found, with other reasons suitable to the circumstances; that the best way would be to go to the island of Santa Maria, where they might water and victual easily, it being a solitary island, as the foreigners did; that the deponent did not go to Pisco, that was near, nor make any other port of the coast, because the negro Babo had intimated to him several times, that he would kill all the whites the very moment he should perceive any city, town, or settlement of any kind on the shores to which they should be carried: that having determined to go to the island of Santa Maria, as the deponent had planned, for the purpose of trying whether, on the passage or near the island itself, they could find any vessel that should favor them, or whether he could escape from it in a boat to the neighboring coast of Arauco; to adopt the necessary means he immediately changed his course, steering for the island; that the negroes Babo and Atufal held daily conferences, in which they discussed what was necessary for their design of returning to Senegal, whether they were to kill all the Spaniards, and particularly the deponent; that eight days after parting from the coast of Nasca, the deponent being on the watch a little after day-break, and soon after the negroes had their meeting, the negro Babo came to the place where the deponent was, and told him that he had determined to kill his master, Don Alexandro Aranda, both because he and his companions could not otherwise be sure of their liberty, and that, to keep the seamen in subjection, he wanted to prepare a warning of what road they should be made to take did they or any of them oppose him; and that, by means of the death of Don Alexandro, that warning would best be given; but, that what this last meant, the deponent did not at the time comprehend, nor could not, further than that the death of Don Alexandro was intended; and moreover, the negro Babo proposed to the deponent to call the mate Raneds, who was sleeping in the cabin, before the thing was done, for fear, as the deponent understood it, that the mate, who was a good navigator, should be killed with Don Alexandro and the rest; that the deponent, who was the friend, from youth, of Don Alexandro, prayed and conjured, but all was useless; for the negro Babo answered him that the thing could not be prevented, and that all the Spaniards risked their death if they should attempt to frustrate his will in this matter, or any other; that, in this conflict, the deponent called the mate, Raneds, who was forced to go apart, and immediately the negro Babo commanded the Ashantee Matiluqui and the Ashantee Lecbe to go and commit the murder; that those two went down with hatchets to the berth of Don Alexandro; that, yet half alive and mangled, they dragged him on deck; that they were going to throw him overboard in that state, but the negro Babo stopped them, bidding the murder be completed on the deck before him, which was done, when, by his orders, the body was carried below, forward; that nothing more was seen of it by the deponent for three days; * * * that Don Alonzo Sidonia, an old man, long resident at Valparaiso, and lately appointed to a civil office in Peru, whither he had taken passage, was at the time sleeping in the berth opposite Don Alexandro's; that, awakening at his cries, surprised by them, and at the sight of the negroes with their bloody hatchets in their hands, he threw himself into the sea through a window which was near him, and was drowned, without it being in the power of the deponent to assist or take him up; * * * that, a short time after killing Aranda, they brought upon deck his german-cousin, of middle-age, Don Francisco Masa, of Mendoza, and the young Don Joaquin, Marques de Arambaolaza, then lately from Spain, with his Spanish servant Ponce, and the three young clerks of Aranda, José Morairi, Lorenzo Bargas, and Hermenegildo Gandix, all of Cadiz; that Don Joaquin and Hermenegildo Gandix, the negro Babo for purposes hereafter to appear, preserved alive; but Don Francisco Masa, José Morairi, and Lorenzo Bargas, with Ponce the servant, beside the boatswain, Juan Robles, the boatswain's mates, Manuel Viscaya and Roderigo Hurta, and four of the sailors, the negro Babo ordered to be thrown alive into the sea, although they made no resistance, nor begged for anything else but mercy; that the boatswain, Juan Robles, who knew how to swim, kept the longest above water, making acts of contrition, and, in the last words he uttered, charged this deponent to cause mass to be said for his soul to our Lady of Succor; * * * that, during the three days which followed, the deponent, uncertain what fate had befallen the remains of Don Alexandro, frequently asked the negro Babo where they were, and, if still on board, whether they were to be preserved for interment ashore, entreating him so to order it; that the negro Babo answered nothing till the fourth day, when at sunrise, the deponent coming on deck, the negro Babo showed him a skeleton, which had been substituted for the ship's proper figure-head, the image of Christopher Colon, the discoverer of the New World; that the negro Babo asked him whose skeleton that was, and whether, from its whiteness, he should not think it a white's; that, upon his covering his face, the negro Babo, coming close, said words to this effect: "Keep faith with the blacks from here to Senegal, or you shall in spirit, as now in body, follow your leader," pointing to the prow; * * * that the same morning the negro Babo took by succession each Spaniard forward, and asked him whose skeleton that was, and whether, from its whiteness, he should not think it a white's; that each Spaniard covered his face; that then to each the negro Babo repeated the words in the first place said to the deponent; * * * that they (the Spaniards), being then assembled aft, the negro Babo harangued them, saying that he had now done all; that the deponent (as navigator for the negroes) might pursue his course, warning him and all of them that they should, soul and body, go the way of Don Alexandro if he saw them (the Spaniards) speak or plot anything against them (the negroes)—a threat which was repeated every day; that, before the events last mentioned, they had tied the cook to throw him overboard, for it is not known what thing they heard him speak, but finally the negro Babo spared his life, at the request of the deponent; that a few days after, the deponent, endeavoring not to omit any means to preserve the lives of the remaining whites, spoke to the negroes peace and tranquillity, and agreed to draw up a paper, signed by the deponent and the sailors who could write, as also by the negro Babo, for himself and all the blacks, in which the deponent obliged himself to carry them to Senegal, and they not to kill any more, and he formally to make over to them the ship, with the cargo, with which they were for that time satisfied and quieted. * * * But the next day, the more surely to guard against the sailors' escape, the negro Babo commanded all the boats to be destroyed but the long-boat, which was unseaworthy, and another, a cutter in good condition, which, knowing it would yet be wanted for towing the water casks, he had it lowered down into the hold.

* * * * *

[Various particulars of the prolonged and perplexed navigation ensuing here follow, with incidents of a calamitous calm, from which portion one passage is extracted, to wit:]

—That on the fifth day of the calm, all on board suffering much from the heat, and want of water, and five having died in fits, and mad, the negroes became irritable, and for a chance gesture, which they deemed suspicious—though it was harmless—made by the mate, Raneds, to the deponent, in the act of handing a quadrant, they killed him; but that for this they afterwards were sorry, the mate being the only remaining navigator on board, except the deponent.

* * * * *

—That omitting other events, which daily happened, and which can only serve uselessly to recall past misfortunes and conflicts, after seventy-three days' navigation, reckoned from the time they sailed from Nasca, during which they navigated under a scanty allowance of water, and were afflicted with the calms before mentioned, they at last arrived at the island of Santa Maria, on the seventeenth of the month of August, at about six o'clock in the afternoon, at which hour they cast anchor very near the American ship, Bachelor's Delight, which lay in the same bay, commanded by the generous Captain Amasa Delano; but at six o'clock in the morning, they had already descried the port, and the negroes became uneasy, as soon as at distance they saw the ship, not having expected to see one there; that the negro Babo pacified them, assuring them that no fear need be had; that straightway he ordered the figure on the bow to be covered with canvas, as for repairs, and had the decks a little set in order; that for a time the negro Babo and the negro Atufal conferred; that the negro Atufal was for sailing away, but the negro Babo would not, and, by himself, cast about what to do; that at last he came to the deponent, proposing to him to say and do all that the deponent declares to have said and done to the American captain; * * * * * * that the negro Babo warned him that if he varied in the least, or uttered any word, or gave any look that should give the least intimation of the past events or present state, he would instantly kill him, with all his companions, showing a dagger, which he carried hid, saying something which, as he understood it, meant that that dagger would be alert as his eye; that the negro Babo then announced the plan to all his companions, which pleased them; that he then, the better to disguise the truth, devised many expedients, in some of them uniting deceit and defense; that of this sort was the device of the six Ashantees before named, who were his bravoes; that them he stationed on the break of the poop, as if to clean certain hatchets (in cases, which were part of the cargo), but in reality to use them, and distribute them at need, and at a given word he told them; that, among other devices, was the device of presenting Atufal, his right-hand man, as chained, though in a moment the chains could be dropped; that in every particular he informed the deponent what part he was expected to enact in every device, and what story he was to tell on every occasion, always threatening him with instant death if he varied in the least: that, conscious that many of the negroes would be turbulent, the negro Babo appointed the four aged negroes, who were calkers, to keep what domestic order they could on the decks; that again and again he harangued the Spaniards and his companions, informing them of his intent, and of his devices, and of the invented story that this deponent was to tell, charging them lest any of them varied from that story; that these arrangements were made and matured during the interval of two or three hours, between their first sighting the ship and the arrival on board of Captain Amasa Delano; that this happened about half-past seven o'clock in the morning, Captain Amasa Delano coming in his boat, and all gladly receiving him; that the deponent, as well as he could force himself, acting then the part of principal owner, and a free captain of the ship, told Captain Amasa Delano, when called upon, that he came from Buenos Ayres, bound to Lima, with three hundred negroes; that off Cape Horn, and in a subsequent fever, many negroes had died; that also, by similar casualties, all the sea officers and the greatest part of the crew had died.

* * * * *

[And so the deposition goes on, circumstantially recounting the fictitious story dictated to the deponent by Babo, and through the deponent imposed upon Captain Delano; and also recounting the friendly offers of Captain Delano, with other things, but all of which is here omitted. After the fictitious, strange story, etc., the deposition proceeds:]

—that the generous Captain Amasa Delano remained on board all the day, till he left the ship anchored at six o'clock in the evening, deponent speaking to him always of his pretended misfortunes, under the forementioned principles, without having had it in his power to tell a single word, or give him the least hint, that he might know the truth and state of things; because the negro Babo, performing the office of an officious servant with all the appearance of submission of the humble slave, did not leave the deponent one moment; that this was in order to observe the deponent's actions and words, for the negro Babo understands well the Spanish; and besides, there were thereabout some others who were constantly on the watch, and likewise understood the Spanish; * * * that upon one occasion, while deponent was standing on the deck conversing with Amasa Delano, by a secret sign the negro Babo drew him (the deponent) aside, the act appearing as if originating with the deponent; that then, he being drawn aside, the negro Babo proposed to him to gain from Amasa Delano full particulars about his ship, and crew, and arms; that the deponent asked "For what?" that the negro Babo answered he might conceive; that, grieved at the prospect of what might overtake the generous Captain Amasa Delano, the deponent at first refused to ask the desired questions, and used every argument to induce the negro Babo to give up this new design; that the negro Babo showed the point of his dagger; that, after the information had been obtained, the negro Babo again drew him aside, telling him that that very night he (the deponent) would be captain of two ships, instead of one, for that, great part of the American's ship's crew being to be absent fishing, the six Ashantees, without any one else, would easily take it; that at this time he said other things to the same purpose; that no entreaties availed; that, before Amasa Delano's coming on board, no hint had been given touching the capture of the American ship: that to prevent this project the deponent was powerless; * * *—that in some things his memory is confused, he cannot distinctly recall every event; * * *—that as soon as they had cast anchor at six of the clock in the evening, as has before been stated, the American Captain took leave to return to his vessel; that upon a sudden impulse, which the deponent believes to have come from God and his angels, he, after the farewell had been said, followed the generous Captain Amasa Delano as far as the gunwale, where he stayed, under pretense of taking leave, until Amasa Delano should have been seated in his boat; that on shoving off, the deponent sprang from the gunwale into the boat, and fell into it, he knows not how, God guarding him; that—

* * * * *

[Here, in the original, follows the account of what further happened at the escape, and how the San Dominick was retaken, and of the passage to the coast; including in the recital many expressions of "eternal gratitude" to the "generous Captain Amasa Delano." The deposition then proceeds with recapitulatory remarks, and a partial renumeration of the negroes, making record of their individual part in the past events, with a view to furnishing, according to command of the court, the data whereon to found the criminal sentences to be pronounced. From this portion is the following:]

—That he believes that all the negroes, though not in the first place knowing to the design of revolt, when it was accomplished, approved it. * * * That the negro, José, eighteen years old, and in the personal service of Don Alexandro, was the one who communicated the information to the negro Babo, about the state of things in the cabin, before the revolt; that this is known, because, in the preceding midnights, he used to come from his berth, which was under his master's, in the cabin, to the deck where the ringleader and his associates were, and had secret conversations with the negro Babo, in which he was several times seen by the mate; that, one night, the mate drove him away twice; * * that this same negro José, was the one who, without being commanded to do so by the negro Babo, as Lecbe and Matiluqui were, stabbed his master, Don Alexandro, after he had been dragged half-lifeless to the deck; * * that the mulatto steward, Francesco, was of the first band of revolters, that he was, in all things, the creature and tool of the negro Babo; that, to make his court, he, just before a repast in the cabin, proposed, to the negro Babo, poisoning a dish for the generous Captain Amasa Delano; this is known and believed, because the negroes have said it; but that the negro Babo, having another design, forbade Francesco; * * that the Ashantee Lecbe was one of the worst of them; for that, on the day the ship was retaken, he assisted in the defense of her, with a hatchet in each hand, with one of which he wounded, in the breast, the chief mate of Amasa Delano, in the first act of boarding; this all knew; that, in sight of the deponent, Lecbe struck, with a hatchet, Don Francisco Masa when, by the negro Babo's orders, he was carrying him to throw him overboard, alive; beside participating in the murder, before mentioned, of Don Alexandro Aranda, and others of the cabin-passengers; that, owing to the fury with which the Ashantees fought in the engagement with the boats, but this Lecbe and Yau survived; that Yau was bad as Lecbe; that Yau was the man who, by Babo's command, willingly prepared the skeleton of Don Alexandro, in a way the negroes afterwards told the deponent, but which he, so long as reason is left him, can never divulge; that Yau and Lecbe were the two who, in a calm by night, riveted the skeleton to the bow; this also the negroes told him; that the negro Babo was he who traced the inscription below it; that the negro Babo was the plotter from first to last; he ordered every murder, and was the helm and keel of the revolt; that Atufal was his lieutenant in all; but Atufal, with his own hand, committed no murder; nor did the negro Babo; * * that Atufal was shot, being killed in the fight with the boats, ere boarding; * * that the negresses, of age, were knowing to the revolt, and testified themselves satisfied at the death of their master, Don Alexandro; that, had the negroes not restrained them, they would have tortured to death, instead of simply killing, the Spaniards slain by command of the negro Babo; that the negresses used their utmost influence to have the deponent made away with; that, in the various acts of murder, they sang songs and danced—not gaily, but solemnly; and before the engagement with the boats, as well as during the action, they sang melancholy songs to the negroes, and that this melancholy tone was more inflaming than a different one would have been, and was so intended; that all this is believed, because the negroes have said it.

—that of the thirty-six men of the crew exclusive of the passengers, (all of whom are now dead), which the deponent had knowledge of, six only remained alive, with four cabin-boys and ship-boys, not included with the crew; * * —that the negroes broke an arm of one of the cabin-boys and gave him strokes with hatchets.

[Then follow various random disclosures referring to various periods of time. The following are extracted:]

—That during the presence of Captain Amasa Delano on board, some attempts were made by the sailors, and one by Hermenegildo Gandix, to convey hints to him of the true state of affairs; but that these attempts were ineffectual, owing to fear of incurring death, and furthermore owing to the devices which offered contradictions to the true state of affairs; as well as owing to the generosity and piety of Amasa Delano incapable of sounding such wickedness; * * * that Luys Galgo, a sailor about sixty years of age, and formerly of the king's navy, was one of those who sought to convey tokens to Captain Amasa Delano; but his intent, though undiscovered, being suspected, he was, on a pretense, made to retire out of sight, and at last into the hold, and there was made away with. This the negroes have since said; * * * that one of the ship-boys feeling, from Captain Amasa Delano's presence, some hopes of release, and not having enough prudence, dropped some chance-word respecting his expectations, which being overheard and understood by a slave-boy with whom he was eating at the time, the latter struck him on the head with a knife, inflicting a bad wound, but of which the boy is now healing; that likewise, not long before the ship was brought to anchor, one of the seamen, steering at the time, endangered himself by letting the blacks remark some expression in his countenance, arising from a cause similar to the above; but this sailor, by his heedful after conduct, escaped; * * * that these statements are made to show the court that from the beginning to the end of the revolt, it was impossible for the deponent and his men to act otherwise than they did; * * * —that the third clerk, Hermenegildo Gandix, who before had been forced to live among the seamen, wearing a seaman's habit, and in all respects appearing to be one for the time; he, Gandix, was killed by a musket-ball fired through a mistake from the American boats before boarding; having in his fright ran up the mizzen-rigging, calling to the boats—"don't board," lest upon their boarding the negroes should kill him; that this inducing the Americans to believe he some way favored the cause of the negroes, they fired two balls at him, so that he fell wounded from the rigging, and was drowned in the sea; * * * —that the young Don Joaquin, Marques de Arambaolaza, like Hermenegildo Gandix, the third clerk, was degraded to the office and appearance of a common seaman; that upon one occasion when Don Joaquin shrank, the negro Babo commanded the Ashantee Lecbe to take tar and heat it, and pour it upon Don Joaquin's hands; * * * —that Don Joaquin was killed owing to another mistake of the Americans, but one impossible to be avoided, as upon the approach of the boats, Don Joaquin, with a hatchet tied edge out and upright to his hand, was made by the negroes to appear on the bulwarks; whereupon, seen with arms in his hands and in a questionable attitude, he was shot for a renegade seaman; * * * —that on the person of Don Joaquin was found secreted a jewel, which, by papers that were discovered, proved to have been meant for the shrine of our Lady of Mercy in Lima; a votive offering, beforehand prepared and guarded, to attest his gratitude, when he should have landed in Peru, his last destination, for the safe conclusion of his entire voyage from Spain; * * * —that the jewel, with the other effects of the late Don Joaquin, is in the custody of the brethren of the Hospital de Sacerdotes, awaiting the disposition of the honorable court; * * * —that, owing to the condition of the deponent, as well as the haste in which the boats departed for the attack, the Americans were not forewarned that there were, among the apparent crew, a passenger and one of the clerks disguised by the negro Babo; * * * —that, beside the negroes killed in the action, some were killed after the capture and re-anchoring at night, when shackled to the ring-bolts on deck; that these deaths were committed by the sailors, ere they could be prevented. That so soon as informed of it, Captain Amasa Delano used all his authority, and, in particular with his own hand, struck down Martinez Gola, who, having found a razor in the pocket of an old jacket of his, which one of the shackled negroes had on, was aiming it at the negro's throat; that the noble Captain Amasa Delano also wrenched from the hand of Bartholomew Barlo, a dagger secreted at the time of the massacre of the whites, with which he was in the act of stabbing a shackled negro, who, the same day, with another negro, had thrown him down and jumped upon him; * * * —that, for all the events, befalling through so long a time, during which the ship was in the hands of the negro Babo, he cannot here give account; but that, what he has said is the most substantial of what occurs to him at present, and is the truth under the oath which he has taken; which declaration he affirmed and ratified, after hearing it read to him.

He said that he is twenty-nine years of age, and broken in body and mind; that when finally dismissed by the court, he shall not return home to Chili, but betake himself to the monastery on Mount Agonia without; and signed with his honor, and crossed himself, and, for the time, departed as he came, in his litter, with the monk Infelez, to the Hospital de Sacerdotes. BENITO CERENO.

DOCTOR ROZAS.

If the Deposition have served as the key to fit into the lock of the complications which precede it, then, as a vault whose door has been flung back, the San Dominick's hull lies open to-day.

Hitherto the nature of this narrative, besides rendering the intricacies in the beginning unavoidable, has more or less required that many things, instead of being set down in the order of occurrence, should be retrospectively, or irregularly given; this last is the case with the following passages, which will conclude the account:

During the long, mild voyage to Lima, there was, as before hinted, a period during which the sufferer a little recovered his health, or, at least in some degree, his tranquillity. Ere the decided relapse which came, the two captains had many cordial conversations—their fraternal unreserve in singular contrast with former withdrawments.

Again and again, it was repeated, how hard it had been to enact the part forced on the Spaniard by Babo.

"Ah, my dear friend," Don Benito once said, "at those very times when you thought me so morose and ungrateful, nay, when, as you now admit, you half thought me plotting your murder, at those very times my heart was frozen; I could not look at you, thinking of what, both on board this ship and your own, hung, from other hands, over my kind benefactor. And as God lives, Don Amasa, I know not whether desire for my own safety alone could have nerved me to that leap into your boat, had it not been for the thought that, did you, unenlightened, return to your ship, you, my best friend, with all who might be with you, stolen upon, that night, in your hammocks, would never in this world have wakened again. Do but think how you walked this deck, how you sat in this cabin, every inch of ground mined into honey-combs under you. Had I dropped the least hint, made the least advance towards an understanding between us, death, explosive death—yours as mine—would have ended the scene."

"True, true," cried Captain Delano, starting, "you have saved my life, Don Benito, more than I yours; saved it, too, against my knowledge and will."

"Nay, my friend," rejoined the Spaniard, courteous even to the point of religion, "God charmed your life, but you saved mine. To think of some things you did—those smilings and chattings, rash pointings and gesturings. For less than these, they slew my mate, Raneds; but you had the Prince of Heaven's safe conduct through all ambuscades."

"Yes, all is owing to Providence, I know; but the temper of my mind that morning was more than commonly pleasant, while the sight of so much suffering, more apparent than real, added to my good nature, compassion, and charity, happily interweaving the three. Had it been otherwise, doubtless, as you hint, some of my interferences might have ended unhappily enough. Besides that, those feelings I spoke of enabled me to get the better of momentary distrust, at times when acuteness might have cost me my life, without saving another's. Only at the end did my suspicions get the better of me, and you know how wide of the mark they then proved."

"Wide, indeed," said Don Benito, sadly; "you were with me all day; stood with me, sat with me, talked with me, looked at me, ate with me, drank with me; and yet, your last act was to clutch for a monster, not only an innocent man, but the most pitiable of all men. To such degree may malign machinations and deceptions impose. So far may even the best man err, in judging the conduct of one with the recesses of whose condition he is not acquainted. But you were forced to it; and you were in time undeceived. Would that, in both respects, it was so ever, and with all men."

"You generalize, Don Benito; and mournfully enough. But the past is passed; why moralize upon it? Forget it. See, yon bright sun has forgotten it all, and the blue sea, and the blue sky; these have turned over new leaves."

"Because they have no memory," he dejectedly replied; "because they are not human."

"But these mild trades that now fan your cheek, do they not come with a human-like healing to you? Warm friends, steadfast friends are the trades."

"With their steadfastness they but waft me to my tomb, señor," was the foreboding response.

"You are saved," cried Captain Delano, more and more astonished and pained; "you are saved; what has cast such a shadow upon you?"

"The negro."

There was silence, while the moody man sat, slowly and unconsciously gathering his mantle about him, as if it were a pall.

There was no more conversation that day.

But if the Spaniard's melancholy sometimes ended in muteness upon topics like the above, there were others upon which he never spoke at all; on which, indeed, all his old reserves were piled. Pass over the worst, and, only to elucidate, let an item or two of these be cited. The dress so precise and costly, worn by him on the day whose events have been narrated, had not willingly been put on. And that silver-mounted sword, apparent symbol of despotic command, was not, indeed, a sword, but the ghost of one. The scabbard, artificially stiffened, was empty.

As for the black—whose brain, not body, had schemed and led the revolt, with the plot—his slight frame, inadequate to that which it held, had at once yielded to the superior muscular strength of his captor, in the boat. Seeing all was over, he uttered no sound, and could not be forced to. His aspect seemed to say, since I cannot do deeds, I will not speak words. Put in irons in the hold, with the rest, he was carried to Lima. During the passage Don Benito did not visit him. Nor then, nor at any time after, would he look at him. Before the tribunal he refused. When pressed by the judges he fainted. On the testimony of the sailors alone rested the legal identity of Babo.

Some months after, dragged to the gibbet at the tail of a mule, the black met his voiceless end. The body was burned to ashes; but for many days, the head, that hive of subtlety, fixed on a pole in the Plaza, met, unabashed, the gaze of the whites; and across the Plaza looked towards

St. Bartholomew's church, in whose vaults slept then, as now, the recovered bones of Aranda; and across the Rimac bridge looked towards the monastery, on Mount Agonia without; where, three months after being dismissed by the court, Benito Cereno, borne on the bier, did, indeed, follow his leader.

The Lightning-Rod Man

WHAT GRAND IRREGULAR THUNDER, thought I, standing on my hearthstone among the Acroceraunian hills, as the scattered bolts boomed overhead and crashed down among the valleys, every bolt followed by zig-zag irradiations, and swift slants of sharp rain, which audibly rang, like a charge of spear-points, on my low shingled roof. I suppose, though, that the mountains hereabouts break and churn up the thunder, so that it is far more glorious here than on the plain. Hark!—some one at the door. Who is this that chooses a time of thunder for making calls? And why don't he, man-fashion, use the knocker, instead of making that doleful undertaker's clatter with his fist against the hollow panel? But let him in. Ah, here he comes. "Good day, sir:" an entire stranger. "Pray be seated." What is that strange-looking walking-stick he carries:—"A fine thunder-storm, sir."

"Fine?—Awful!"

"You are wet. Stand here on the hearth before the fire."

"Not for worlds!"

The stranger still stood in the exact middle of the cottage, where he had first planted himself. His singularity impelled a closer scrutiny. A lean, gloomy figure. Hair dark and lank, mattedly streaked over his brow. His sunken pitfalls of eyes were ringed by indigo halos, and played with an innocuous sort of lightning: the gleam without the bolt. The whole man was dripping. He stood in a puddle on the bare oak floor; his strange walking-stick vertically resting at his side.

It was a polished copper rod, four feet long, lengthwise attached to a neat wooden staff, by insertion into two balls of greenish glass, ringed with copper bands. The metal rod terminated at the top tripodwise, in three keen tines, brightly gilt. He held the thing by the wooden part alone.

"Sir," said I, bowing politely, "have I the honor of a visit from that illustrious god, Jupiter Tonans? So stood he in the Greek statue of old, grasping the lightning-bolt. If you be he, or his viceroy, I have to thank you for this noble storm you have brewed among our mountains. Listen: That was a glorious peal. Ah, to a lover of the majestic, it is a good thing to have the Thunderer himself in one's cottage. The thunder grows finer for that. But pray be seated. This old rush-bottomed arm-chair, I grant, is a poor substitute for your evergreen throne on Olympus; but, condescend to be seated."

While I thus pleasantly spoke, the stranger eyed me, half in wonder and half in a strange sort of horror; but did not move a foot.

"Do, sir, be seated; you need to be dried ere going forth again."

I planted the chair invitingly on the broad hearth, where a little fire had been kindled that afternoon to dissipate the dampness, not the cold; for it was early in the month of September.

But without heeding my solicitation, and still standing in the middle of the floor, the stranger gazed at me portentously and spoke.

"Sir," said he, "excuse me, but instead of my accepting your invitation to be seated on the hearth there, I solemnly warn *you*, that you had best accept *mine*, and stand with me in the middle of the room. Good heavens!" he cried, starting—"there's another of those awful crashes. I warn you, sir, quit the hearth."

"Mr. Jupiter Tonans," said I, quietly rolling my body on the stone, "I stand very well here."

"Are you so horridly ignorant, then," he cried, "as not to know, that by far the most dangerous part of a house during such a terrific tempest as this, is the fire-place?"

"Nay, I did not know that," involuntarily stepping upon the first board next to the stone.

The stranger now assumed such an unpleasant air of successful admonition, that—quite involuntarily again—I stepped back upon the hearth, and threw myself into the erectest, proudest posture I could command. But I said nothing.

"For Heaven's sake," he cried, with a strange mixture of alarm and intimidation—"for Heaven's sake, get off of the hearth! Know you not, that the heated air and soot are conductors;—to say nothing of those immense iron fire-dogs? Quit the spot,—I conjure,—I command you."

"Mr. Jupiter Tonans, I am not accustomed to be commanded in my own house."

"Call me not by that pagan name. You are profane in this time of terror."

"Sir, will you be so good as to tell me your business? If you seek shelter from the storm, you are welcome, so long as you be civil; but if you come on business, open it forthwith. Who are you?"

"I am a dealer in lightning-rods," said the stranger, softening his tone; "my special business is——— Merciful heaven! what a crash!—Have you ever been struck—your premises, I mean? No? It's best to be provided;"—significantly rattling his metallic staff on the floor;—"by nature, there are no castles in thunder-storms; yet, say but the word, and of this cottage I can make a Gibraltar by a few waves of this wand. Hark, what Himmalayas of concussions!"

"You interrupted yourself; your special business you were about to speak of."

"My special business is to travel the country for orders for lightning-rods. This is my specimen-rod;" tapping his staff; "I have the best of references"—fumbling in his pockets. "In Criggan last month, I put up three-and-twenty rods on only five buildings."

"Let me see. Was it not at Criggan last week, about midnight on Saturday, that the steeple, the big elm and the Assembly-room cupola were struck? Any of your rods there?"

"Not on the tree and cupola, but the steeple."

"Of what use is your rod then?"

"Of life-and-death use. But my workman was heedless. In fitting the rod at top to the steeple, he allowed a part of the metal to graze the tin sheeting. Hence the accident. Not my fault, but his. Hark!"

"Never mind. That clap burst quite loud enough to be heard without finger-pointing. Did you hear of the event at Montreal last year? A servant girl struck at her bed-side with a rosary in her hand; the beads being metal. Does your beat extend into the Canadas?"

"No. And I hear that there, iron rods only are in use. They should have *mine*, which are copper. Iron is easily fused. Then they draw out the rod so slender, that it has not body enough to conduct the full electric current. The metal melts; the building is destroyed. My copper rods never act so. Those Canadians are fools. Some of them knob the rod at the top, which risks a deadly explosion, instead of imperceptibly carrying down the current into the earth, as this sort of rod does. *Mine* is the only true rod. Look at it. Only one dollar a foot."

"This abuse of your own calling in another might make one distrustful with respect to yourself."

"Hark! The thunder becomes less muttering. It is nearing us, and nearing the earth, too. Hark! One crammed crash! All the vibrations made one by nearness. Another flash. Hold!"

"What do you?" I said, seeing him now, instantaneously relinquishing his staff, lean intently forward towards the window, with his right fore and middle fingers on his left wrist.

But ere the words had well escaped me, another exclamation escaped him.

"Crash! only three pulses—less than a third of a mile off—yonder, somewhere in that wood. I passed three stricken oaks there, ripped out new and glittering. The oak draws lightning more than other timber, having iron in solution in its sap. Your floor here seems oak."

"Heart-of-oak. From the peculiar time of your call upon me, I suppose you purposely select stormy weather for your journeys. When the thunder is roaring, you deem it an hour peculiarly favorable for producing impressions favorable to your trade."

"Hark!—Awful!"

"For one who would arm others with fearlessness, you seem unbeseemingly timorous yourself. Common men choose fair weather for their travels: you choose thunder-storms; and yet———"

"That I travel in thunder-storms, I grant; but not without particular precautions, such as only a lightning-rod man may know. Hark! Quick—look at my specimen rod. Only one dollar a foot."

"A very fine rod, I dare say. But what are these particular precautions of yours? Yet first let me close yonder shutters; the slanting rain is beating through the sash. I will bar up."

"Are you mad? Know you not that yon iron bar is a swift conductor? Desist."

"I will simply close the shutters then, and call my boy to bring me a wooden bar. Pray, touch the bell-pull there."

"Are you frantic? That bell-wire might blast you. Never touch bell-wire in a thunder-storm, nor ring a bell of any sort."

"Nor those in belfries? Pray, will you tell me where and how one may be safe in a time like this? Is there any part of my house I may touch with hopes of my life?"

"There is; but not where you now stand. Come away from the wall. The current will sometimes run down a wall, and—a man being a better conductor than a wall—it would leave the wall and run into him. Swoop! *That* must have fallen very nigh. That must have been globular lightning."

"Very probably. Tell me at once, which is, in your opinion, the safest part of this house?"

"This room, and this one spot in it where I stand. Come hither."

"The reasons first."

"Hark!—after the flash the gust—the sashes shiver—the house, the house!—Come hither to me!"

"The reasons, if you please."

"Come hither to me!"

"Thank you again, I think I will try my old stand,—the hearth. And now Mr. Lightning-rod-man, in the pauses of the thunder, be so good as to tell me your reasons for esteeming this one room of the house the safest, and your own one stand-point there the safest spot in it."

There was now a little cessation of the storm for a while. The Lightning-rod man seemed relieved, and replied:—

"Your house is a one-storied house, with an attic and a cellar; this room is between. Hence its comparative safety. Because lightning sometimes passes from the clouds to the earth, and sometimes from the earth to the clouds. Do you comprehend?—and I choose the middle of the room, because, if the lightning should strike the house at all, it would come down the chimney or walls; so, obviously, the further you are from them, the better. Come hither to me, now."

"Presently. Something you just said, instead of alarming me, has strangely inspired confidence."

"What have I said?"

"You said that sometimes lightning flashes from the earth to the clouds."

"Aye, the returning-stroke, as it is called; when the earth, being overcharged with the fluid, flashes its surplus upward."

"The returning-stroke; that is, from earth to sky. Better and better. But come here on the hearth and dry yourself."

"I am better here, and better wet."

"How?"

"It is the safest thing you can do—Hark, again!—to get yourself thoroughly drenched in a thunder-storm. Wet clothes are better conductors than the body; and so, if the lightning strike, it might pass down the wet clothes without touching the body. The storm deepens again. Have you a rug in the house? Rugs are non-conductors. Get one, that I may stand on it here, and you too. The skies blacken—it is dusk at noon. Hark!—the rug, the rug!"

I gave him one; while the hooded mountains seemed closing and tumbling into the cottage.

"And now, since our being dumb will not help us," said I, resuming my place, "let me hear your precautions in travelling during thunder-storms."

"Wait till this one is passed."

"Nay, proceed with the precautions. You stand in the safest possible place according to your own account. Go on."

"Briefly then. I avoid pine-trees, high houses, lonely barns, upland pastures, running water, flocks of cattle and sheep, a crowd of men. If I travel on foot,—as to-day—I do not walk fast; if in my buggy, I touch not its back or sides; if on horseback, I dismount and lead the horse. But of all things, I avoid tall men."

"Do I dream? Man avoid man? and in danger-time too?"

"Tall men in a thunder-storm I avoid. Are you so grossly ignorant as not to know, that the height of a six-footer is sufficient to discharge an electric cloud upon him? Are not lonely Kentuckians, ploughing, smit in the unfinished furrow? Nay, if the six-footer stand by running water, the cloud will sometimes *select* him as its conductor to that running water. Hark! Sure, yon black pinnacle is split. Yes, a man is a good conductor. The lightning goes through and through a man, but only peels a tree. But sir, you have kept me so long answering your questions, that I have not yet come to business. Will you order one of my rods? Look at this specimen one? See: it is of the best of copper. Copper 's the best conductor. Your house is low; but being upon the mountains, that lowness does not one whit depress it. You mountaineers are most exposed. In mountainous countries the lightning-rod man should have most business. Look at the specimen, sir. One rod will answer for a house so small as this. Look over these recommendations. Only one rod, sir; cost, only twenty dollars. Hark! There go all the granite Taconics and Hoosics dashed together like pebbles. By the sound, that must have struck something. An elevation of five feet above the house, will protect twenty feet radius all about the rod. Only twenty dollars, sir—a dollar a foot. Hark!—Dreadful!—Will you order? Will you buy? Shall I put down your name? Think of being a heap of charred offal, like a haltered horse burnt in his stall;—and all in one flash!"

"You pretended envoy extraordinary and minister plenipotentiary to and from Jupiter Tonans," laughed I; "you mere man who come here to put you and your pipestem between clay and sky, do you think that because you can strike a bit of green light from the Leyden jar, that you can thoroughly avert the supernal bolt? Your rod rusts, or breaks, and where are you? Who has empowered you, you Tetzel, to peddle round your indulgences from divine ordinations? The hairs of our heads are numbered, and the days of our lives. In thunder as in sunshine, I stand at ease in the hands of my God. False negotiator, away! See, the scroll of the storm is rolled back; the house is unharmed; and in the blue heavens I read in the rainbow, that the Deity will not, of purpose, make war on man's earth."

"Impious wretch!" foamed the stranger, blackening in the face as the rainbow beamed, "I will publish your infidel notions."

"Begone! move quickly! if quickly you can, you that shine forth into sight in moist times like the worm."

The scowl grew blacker on his face; the indigo-circles enlarged round his eyes as the storm rings round the midnight moon. He sprang upon me; his tri-forked thing at my heart.

I seized it; I snapped it; I dashed it; I trod it; and dragging the dark lightning-king out of my door, flung his elbowed, copper sceptre after him.

But spite of my treatment, and spite of my dissuasive talk of him to my neighbors, the Lightning-rod man still dwells in the land; still travels in storm-time, and drives a brave trade with the fears of man.

The Encantadas, or Enchanted Isles

By Salvator R. Tarnmoor

Sketch First

The Isles at Large

—"*That may not be, said then the ferryman,*
Least we unweeting hap to be fordonne;
For those same islands seeming now and than,
Are not firme land, nor any certein wonne,
But stragling plots which to and fro do ronne
In the wide waters; therefore are they hight
The Wandering Islands; therefore do them shonne;
For they have oft drawne many a wandring wight
Into most deadly daunger and distressed plight;
For whosoever once hath fastened
His foot thereon may never it recure
But wandreth evermore uncertein and unsure."

*   *   *   *   *

"Darke, dolefull, dreary, like a greedy grave,
That still for carrion carcasses doth crave;
On top whereof ay dwelt the ghastly owl,
Shrieking his balefull note, which ever drave
Far from that haunt all other cheerful fowl,
And all about it wandring ghosts did wayle and howl."

Take five-and-twenty heaps of cinders dumped here and there in an outside city lot; imagine some of them magnified into mountains, and the vacant lot the sea; and you will have a fit idea of the general aspect of the Encantadas, or Enchanted Isles. A group rather of extinct volcanoes than of isles; looking much as the world at large might, after a penal conflagration.

It is to be doubted whether any spot of earth can, in desolateness, furnish a parallel to this group. Abandoned cemeteries of long ago, old cities by piecemeal tumbling to their ruin, these are melancholy enough; but, like all else which has but once been associated with humanity they still awaken in us some thoughts of sympathy, however sad. Hence, even the Dead Sea, along with whatever other emotions it may at times inspire, does not fail to touch in the pilgrim some of his less unpleasurable feelings.

And as for solitariness; the great forests of the north, the expanses of unnavigated waters, the Greenland ice-fields, are the profoundest of solitudes to a human observer; still the magic of their changeable tides and seasons mitigates their terror; because, though unvisited by men, those forests are visited by the May; the remotest seas reflect familiar stars even as Lake Erie does; and in the clear air of a fine Polar day, the irradiated, azure ice shows beautifully as malachite.

But the special curse, as one may call it, of the Encantadas, that which exalts them in desolation above Idumea and the Pole, is that to them change never comes; neither the change of seasons nor of sorrows. Cut by the Equator, they know not autumn and they know not spring; while already reduced to the lees of fire, ruin itself can work little more upon them. The showers refresh the deserts, but in these isles, rain never falls. Like split Syrian gourds left withering in the sun, they are cracked by an everlasting drought beneath a torrid sky. "Have mercy upon me," the wailing spirit of the Encantadas seems to cry, "and send Lazarus that he may dip the tip of his finger in water and cool my tongue, for I am tormented in this flame."

Another feature in these isles is their emphatic uninhabitableness. It is deemed a fit type of all-forsaken overthrow, that the jackal should den in the wastes of weedy Babylon; but the Encantadas refuse to harbor even the outcasts of the beasts. Man and wolf alike disown them. Little but reptile life is here found:—tortoises, lizards, immense spiders, snakes, and that strangest anomaly of outlandish nature, the *iguana*. No voice, no low, no howl is heard; the chief sound of life here is a hiss.

On most of the isles where vegetation is found at all, it is more ungrateful than the blankness of Atacama. Tangled thickets of wiry bushes, without fruit and without a name, springing up among deep fissures of calcined rock, and treacherously masking them; or a parched growth of distorted cactus trees.

In many places the coast is rock-bound, or more properly, clinker-bound; tumbled masses of blackish or greenish stuff like the dross of an iron-furnace, forming dark clefts and caves here and there, into which a ceaseless sea pours a fury of foam; overhanging them with a swirl of gray, haggard mist, amidst which sail screaming flights of unearthly birds heightening the dismal din. However calm the sea without, there is no rest for these swells and those rocks; they lash and are lashed, even when the outer ocean is most at peace with itself. On the oppressive, clouded days, such as are peculiar to this part of the watery Equator, the dark, vitrified masses, many of which raise themselves among white whirlpools and breakers in detached and perilous places off the shore, present a most Plutonian sight. In no world but a fallen one could such lands exist.

Those parts of the strand free from the marks of fire, stretch away in wide level beaches of multitudinous dead shells, with here and there decayed bits of sugar-cane, bamboos, and cocoanuts, washed upon this other and darker world from the charming palm isles to the westward and southward; all the way from Paradise to Tartarus; while mixed with the relics of distant beauty you will sometimes see fragments of charred wood and mouldering ribs of wrecks. Neither will any one be surprised at meeting these last, after observing the conflicting currents which eddy throughout nearly all the wide channels of the entire group. The capriciousness of the tides of air sympathizes with those of the sea. Nowhere is the wind so light, baffling, and every way unreliable, and so given to perplexing calms, as at the Encantadas. Nigh a month has been spent by a ship going from one isle to another, though but ninety miles between; for owing to the force of the current, the boats employed to tow barely suffice to keep the craft from sweeping upon the cliffs, but do nothing towards accelerating her voyage. Sometimes it is impossible for a vessel from afar to fetch up with the group itself, unless large allowances for prospective lee-way have been made ere its coming in sight. And yet, at other times, there is a mysterious indraft, which irresistibly draws a passing vessel among the isles, though not bound to them.

True, at one period, as to some extent at the present day, large fleets of whalemen cruised for Spermaceti upon what some seamen call the Enchanted Ground. But this, as in due place will be described, was off the great outer isle of Albemarle, away from the intricacies of the smaller isles, where there is plenty of sea-room; and hence, to that vicinity, the above remarks do not altogether apply; though even there the current runs at times with singular force, shifting, too, with as singular a caprice. Indeed, there are seasons when currents quite unaccountable prevail for a great distance round about the total group, and are so strong and irregular as to change a vessel's course against the helm, though sailing at the rate of four or five miles the hour. The difference in the reckonings of navigators produced by these causes, along with the light and variable winds, long nourished a persuasion that there existed two distinct clusters of isles in the parallel of the Encantadas, about a hundred leagues apart. Such was the idea of their earlier visitors, the Buccaneers; and as late as 1750, the charts of that part of the Pacific accorded with the strange delusion. And this apparent fleetingness and unreality of the locality of the isles was most probably one reason for the Spaniards calling them the Encantada, or Enchanted Group.

But not uninfluenced by their character, as they now confessedly exist, the modern voyager will be inclined to fancy that the bestowal of this name might have in part originated in that air of spell-bound desertness which so significantly invests the isles. Nothing can better suggest the aspect of once living things malignly crumbled from ruddiness into ashes. Apples of Sodom, after touching, seem these isles.

However wavering their place may seem by reason of the currents, they themselves, at least to one upon the shore, appear invariably the same: fixed, cast, glued into the very body of cadaverous death.

Nor would the appellation, enchanted, seem misapplied in still another sense. For concerning the peculiar reptile inhabitant of these wilds—whose presence gives the group its second Spanish name, Gallipagos—concerning the tortoises found here, most mariners have long cherished a superstition, not more frightful than grotesque. They earnestly believe that all wicked sea-officers, more especially commodores and captains, are at death (and in some cases, before death) transformed into tortoises;

thenceforth dwelling upon these hot aridities, sole solitary Lords of Asphaltum.

Doubtless so quaintly dolorous a thought was originally inspired by the woe-begone landscape itself, but more particularly, perhaps, by the tortoises. For apart from their strictly physical features, there is something strangely self-condemned in the appearance of these creatures. Lasting sorrow and penal hopelessness are in no animal form so suppliantly expressed as in theirs; while the thought of their wonderful longevity does not fail to enhance the impression.

Nor even at the risk of meriting the charge of absurdly believing in enchantments, can I restrain the admission that sometimes, even now, when leaving the crowded city to wander out July and August among the Adirondack Mountains, far from the influences of towns and proportionally nigh to the mysterious ones of nature; when at such times I sit me down in the mossy head of some deep-wooded gorge, surrounded by prostrate trunks of blasted pines, and recall, as in a dream, my other and far-distant rovings in the baked heart of the charmed isles; and remember the sudden glimpses of dusky shells, and long languid necks protruded from the leafless thickets; and again have beheld the vitreous inland rocks worn down and grooved into deep ruts by ages and ages of the slow draggings of tortoises in quest of pools of scanty water; I can hardly resist the feeling that in my time I have indeed slept upon evilly enchanted ground.

Nay, such is the vividness of my memory, or the magic of my fancy, that I know not whether I am not the occasional victim of optical delusion concerning the Gallipagos. For often in scenes of social merriment, and especially at revels held by candle-light in old-fashioned mansions, so that shadows are thrown into the further recesses of an angular and spacious room, making them put on a look of haunted undergrowth of lonely woods, I have drawn the attention of my comrades by my fixed gaze and sudden change of air, as I have seemed to see, slowly emerging from those imagined solitudes, and heavily crawling along the floor, the ghost of a gigantic tortoise, with "Memento ****" burning in live letters upon his back.

Sketch Second

Two Sides to a Tortoise

"Most ugly shapes and horrible aspects,
Such as Dame Nature selfe mote feare to see,
Or shame, that ever should so fowle defects
From her most cunning hand escaped bee;
All dreadfull pourtraicts of deformitee.
Ne wonder if these do a man appall;
For all that here at home we dreadfull hold
Be but as bugs to fearen babes withall
Compared to the creatures in these isles' entrall.

* * * * *

Fear naught, then said the palmer, well avized,
For these same monsters are not these indeed,
But are into these fearful shapes disguized.

* * * * *

And lifting up his vertuous staffe on high,
Then all that dreadful armie fast gan flye
Into great Tethys' bosom, where they hidden lye."

In view of the description given, may one be gay upon the Encantadas? Yes: that is, find one the gayety, and he will be gay. And indeed, sackcloth and ashes as they are, the isles are not perhaps unmitigated gloom. For while no spectator can deny their claims to a most solemn and superstitious consideration, no more than my firmest resolutions can decline to behold the spectre-tortoise when emerging from its shadowy recess; yet even the tortoise, dark and melancholy as it is upon the back, still possesses a bright side; its calapee or breast-plate being sometimes of a faint yellowish or golden tinge. Moreover, every one knows that tortoises as well as turtle are of such a make, that if you but put them on their backs you thereby expose their bright sides without the possibility of their recovering themselves, and turning into view the other. But after you have done this, and because you have done this, you should not swear that the tortoise has no dark side. Enjoy the bright, keep it turned up perpetually if you can, but be honest and don't deny the black. Neither should he who cannot turn the tortoise from its natural position so as to hide the darker and expose his livelier aspect, like a great October pumpkin in the sun, for that cause declare the creature to be one total inky blot. The tortoise is both black and bright. But let us to particulars.

Some months before my first stepping ashore upon the group, my ship was cruising in its close vicinity. One noon we found ourselves off the South Head of Albemarle, and not very far from the land. Partly by way of freak, and partly by way of spying out so strange a country, a boat's crew was sent ashore, with orders to see all they could, and besides, bring back whatever tortoises they could conveniently transport.

It was after sunset when the adventurers returned. I looked down over the ship's high side as if looking down over the curb of a well, and dimly saw the damp boat deep in the sea with some unwonted weight. Ropes were dropt over, and presently three huge antediluvian-looking tortoises after much straining were landed on deck. They seemed hardly of the seed of earth. We had been broad upon the waters for five long months, a period amply sufficient to make all things of the land wear a fabulous hue to the dreamy mind. Had three Spanish custom-house officers boarded us then, it is not unlikely that I should have curiously stared at them, felt of them, and stroked them much as savages serve civilized guests. But instead of three custom-house officers, behold these really wondrous tortoises—none of your schoolboy mud-turtles—but black as widower's weeds, heavy as chests of plate, with vast shells medallioned and orbed like shields, and dented and blistered like shields that have breasted a battle, shaggy too, here and there, with dark green moss, and slimy with the spray of the sea. These mystic creatures suddenly translated by night from unutterable solitudes to our peopled deck, affected me in a manner not easy to unfold. They seemed newly crawled forth from beneath the foundations of the world. Yea, they seemed the identical tortoises whereon the Hindoo plants this total sphere. With a lantern I inspected them more closely. Such worshipful venerableness of aspect! Such furry greenness mantling the rude peelings and healing the fissures of their shattered shells. I no more saw three tortoises. They expanded—became transfigured. I seemed to see three Roman Coliseums in magnificent decay.

Ye oldest inhabitants of this, or any other isle, said I, pray, give me the freedom of your three walled towns.

The great feeling inspired by these creatures was that of age:—dateless, indefinite endurance. And in fact that any other creature can live and breathe as long as the tortoise of the Encantadas, I will not readily believe. Not to hint of their known capacity of sustaining life, while going without food for an entire year, consider that impregnable armor of their living mail. What other bodily being possesses such a citadel wherein to resist the assaults of Time?

As, lantern in hand, I scraped among the moss and beheld the ancient scars of bruises received in many a sullen fall among the marly mountains of the isle—scars strangely widened, swollen, half obliterate, and yet distorted like those sometimes found in the bark of very hoary trees, I seemed an antiquary of a geologist, studying the bird-tracks and ciphers upon the exhumed slates trod by incredible creatures whose very ghosts are now defunct.

As I lay in my hammock that night, overhead I heard the slow weary draggings of the three ponderous strangers along the encumbered deck. Their stupidity or their resolution was so great, that they never went aside for any impediment. One ceased his movements altogether just before the mid-watch. At sunrise I found him butted like a battering-ram against the immovable foot of the foremast, and still striving, tooth and nail, to force the impossible passage. That these tortoises are the victims of a penal, or malignant, or perhaps a downright diabolical enchanter, seems in nothing more likely than in that strange infatuation of hopeless toil which so often possesses them. I have known them in their journeyings ram themselves heroically against rocks, and long abide there, nudging, wriggling, wedging, in order to displace them, and so hold on their inflexible path. Their crowning curse is their drudging impulse to straightforwardness in a belittered world.

Meeting with no such hinderance as their companion did, the other tortoises merely fell foul of small stumbling-blocks; buckets, blocks, and coils of rigging; and at times in the act of crawling over them would slip with an astounding rattle to the deck. Listening to these draggings and concussions, I thought me of the haunt from which they came; an isle full of metallic ravines and gulches, sunk bottomlessly into the hearts of splintered mountains, and covered for many miles with inextricable thickets. I then pictured these three straightforward monsters, century after century, writhing through the shades, grim as blacksmiths; crawling so slowly and ponderously, that not only did toadstools and all fungous things grow beneath their feet, but a sooty moss sprouted upon their backs. With them I lost myself in volcanic mazes; brushed away endless boughs of rotting thickets; till finally in a dream I found myself sitting crosslegged upon the foremost, a Brahmin similarly mounted upon either side, forming a tripod of foreheads which upheld the universal cope.

Such was the wild nightmare begot by my first impression of the Encantadas tortoise. But next evening, strange to say, I sat down with my shipmates, and made a merry repast from tortoise steaks and tortoise stews; and supper over, out knife, and helped convert the three mighty concave shells into three fanciful soup-tureens, and polished the three flat yellowish calapees into three gorgeous salvers.

Sketch Third

Rock Rodondo

"Forthy this hight the Rock of vile Reproach,
A dangerous and dreadful place,
To which nor fish nor fowl did once approach,
But yelling meaws with sea-gulls hoars and bace
And cormoyrants with birds of ravenous race,
Which still sit waiting on that dreadful clift."

* * * * *

"With that the rolling sea resounding soft
In his big base them fitly answered,
And on the Rock, the waves breaking aloft,
A solemn meane unto them measured."

* * * * *

"Then he the boteman bad row easily,
And let him heare some part of that rare melody."

* * * * *

"Suddeinly an innumerable flight
Of harmefull fowles about them fluttering cride,
And with their wicked wings them oft did smight
And sore annoyed, groping in that griesly night."

* * * * *

"Even all the nation of unfortunate
And fatal birds about them flocked were."

To go up into a high stone tower is not only a very fine thing in itself, but the very best mode of gaining a comprehensive view of the region round about. It is all the better if this tower stand solitary and alone, like that mysterious Newport one, or else be sole survivor of some perished castle.

Now, with reference to the Enchanted Isles, we are fortunately supplied with just such a noble point of observation in a remarkable rock, from its peculiar figure called of old by the Spaniards, Rock Rodondo, or Round Rock. Some two hundred and fifty feet high, rising straight from the sea ten miles from land, with the whole mountainous group to the south and east, Rock Rodondo occupies, on a large scale, very much the position which the famous Campanile or detached Bell Tower of St. Mark does with respect to the tangled group of hoary edifices around it.

Ere ascending, however, to gaze abroad upon the Encantadas, this sea-tower itself claims attention. It is visible at the distance of thirty miles; and, fully participating in that enchantment which pervades the group, when first seen afar invariably is mistaken for a sail. Four leagues away, of a golden, hazy noon, it seems some Spanish Admiral's ship, stacked up with glittering canvas. Sail ho! Sail ho! Sail ho! from all three masts. But coming nigh, the enchanted frigate is transformed apace into a craggy keep.

My first visit to the spot was made in the gray of the morning. With a view of fishing, we had lowered three boats, and pulling some two miles from our vessel, found ourselves just before dawn of day close under the moon-shadow of Rodondo. Its aspect was heightened, and yet softened, by the strange double twilight of the hour. The great full moon burnt in the low west like a half-spent beacon, casting a soft mellow tinge upon the sea like that cast by a waning fire of embers upon a midnight hearth; while along the entire east the invisible sun sent pallid intimations of his coming. The wind was light; the waves languid; the stars twinkled with a faint effulgence; all nature seemed supine with the long night watch, and half-suspended in jaded expectation of the sun. This was the critical hour to catch Rodondo in his perfect mood. The twilight was just enough to reveal every striking point, without tearing away the dim investiture of wonder.

From a broken, stair-like base, washed, as the steps of a water-palace, by the waves, the tower rose in entablatures of strata to a shaven summit. These uniform layers which compose the mass form its most peculiar feature. For at their lines of junction they project flatly into encircling shelves, from top to bottom, rising one above another in graduated series. And as the eaves of any old barn or abbey are alive with swallows, so were all these rocky ledges with unnumbered sea-fowl. Eaves upon eaves, and nests upon nests. Here and there were long birdlime streaks of a ghostly white staining the tower from sea to air, readily accounting for its sail-like look afar. All would have been bewitchingly quiescent, were it not for the demoniac din created by the birds. Not only were the eaves rustling with them, but they flew densely overhead, spreading themselves into a winged and continually shifting canopy. The tower is the resort of aquatic birds for hundreds of leagues around. To the north, to the east, to the west, stretches nothing but eternal ocean; so that the man-of-war hawk coming from the coasts of North America, Polynesia, or Peru, makes his first land at Rodondo. And yet though Rodondo be terra-firma, no land-bird ever lighted on it. Fancy a red-robbin or a canary there! What a falling into the hands of the Philistines, when the poor warbler should be surrounded by such locust-flights of strong bandit birds, with long bills cruel as daggers.

I know not where one can better study the Natural History of strange sea-fowl than at Rodondo. It is the aviary of Ocean. Birds light here which never touched mast or tree; hermit-birds, which ever fly alone, cloud-birds, familiar with unpierced zones of air.

Let us first glance low down to the lowermost shelf of all, which is the widest too, and but a little space from high-water mark. What outlandish beings are these? Erect as men, but hardly as symmetrical, they stand all round the rock like sculptured caryatides, supporting the next range of eaves above. Their bodies are grotesquely misshapen; their bills short; their feet seemingly legless; while the members at their sides are neither fin, wing, nor arm. And truly neither fish, flesh, nor fowl is the penguin; as an edible, pertaining neither to Carnival nor Lent; without exception the most ambiguous and least lovely creature yet discovered by man. Though dabbling in all three elements, and indeed possessing some rudimental claims to all, the penguin is at home in none. On land it stumps; afloat it sculls; in the air it flops. As if ashamed of her failure, Nature keeps this ungainly child hidden away at the ends of the earth, in the Straits of Magellan, and on the abased sea-story of Rodondo.

But look, what are yon wobegone regiments drawn up on the next shelf above? what rank and file of large strange fowl? what sea Friars of Orders Gray? Pelicans. Their elongated bills, and heavy leathern pouches suspended thereto, give them the most lugubrious expression. A pensive race, they stand for hours together without motion. Their dull, ashy plumage imparts an aspect as if they had been powdered over with cinders. A penitential bird indeed, fitly haunting the shores of the clinkered Encantadas, whereon tormented Job himself might have well sat down and scraped himself with potsherds.

Higher up now we mark the gony, or gray albatross, anomalously so called, an unsightly unpoetic bird, unlike its storied kinsman, which is the snow-white ghost of the haunted Capes of Hope and Horn.

As we still ascend from shelf to shelf, we find the tenants of the tower serially disposed in order of their magnitude:—gannets, black and speckled haglets, jays, sea-hens, sperm-whale-birds, gulls of all varieties:—thrones, princedoms, powers, dominating one above another in senatorial array; while sprinkled over all, like an ever-repeated fly in a great piece of broidery, the stormy petrel or Mother Cary's chicken sounds his continual challenge and alarm. That this mysterious humming-bird of ocean, which had it but brilliancy of hue might from its evanescent liveliness be almost called its butterfly, yet whose chirrup under the stern is ominous to mariners as to the peasant the death-tick sounding from behind the chimney jam—should have its special haunt at the Encantadas, contributes in the seaman's mind, not a little to their dreary spell.

As day advances the dissonant din augments. With ear-splitting cries the wild birds celebrate their matins. Each moment, flights push from the tower, and join the aerial choir hovering overhead, while their places below are supplied by darting myriads. But down through all this discord of commotion, I hear clear silver bugle-like notes unbrokenly falling, like oblique lines of swift slanting rain in a cascading shower. I gaze far up, and behold a snow-white angelic thing, with one long lance-like feather thrust out behind. It is the bright inspiriting chanticleer of ocean, the beauteous bird, from its bestirring whistle of musical invocation, fitly styled the "Boatswain's Mate."

The winged life clouding Rodondo on that well-remembered morning, I saw had its full counterpart in the finny hosts which peopled the waters at its base. Below the water-line, the rock seemed one honeycomb of grottoes, affording labyrinthine lurking places for swarms of fairy fish. All were strange; many exceedingly beautiful; and would have well graced the costliest glass globes in which gold-fish are kept for a show. Nothing was more striking than the complete novelty of many individuals of this multitude. Here hues were seen as yet unpainted, and figures which are unengraved.

To show the multitude, avidity, and nameless fearlessness and tameness of these fish, let me say, that often, marking through clear spaces of water—temporarily made so by the concentric dartings of the fish above the surface—certain larger and less unwary wights, which swam slow and deep; our anglers would cautiously essay to drop their lines down to these last. But in vain; there was no passing the uppermost zone. No sooner did the hook touch the sea, than a hundred infatuates contended for the honor of capture. Poor fish of Rodondo! in your victimized confidence, you are of the number of those who inconsiderately trust, while they do not understand, human nature.

But the dawn is now fairly day. Band after band, the sea-fowl sail away to forage the deep for their food. The tower is left solitary, save the fish caves at its base. Its birdlime gleams in the golden rays like the whitewash of a tall light-house, or the lofty sails of a cruiser. This moment, doubtless, while we know it to be a dead desert rock, other voyagers are taking oaths it is a glad populous ship.

But ropes now, and let us ascend. Yet soft, this is not so easy.

Sketch Fourth

A Pisgah View from the Rock

—"That done, he leads him to the highest mount,
From whence, far off he unto him did show:"——

If you seek to ascend Rock Rodondo, take the following prescription. Go three voyages round the world as a main-royal-man of the tallest frigate that floats; then serve a year or two apprenticeship to the guides who conduct strangers up the Peak of Teneriffe; and as many more, respectively, to a rope-dancer, an Indian Juggler, and a chamois. This done, come and be rewarded by the view from our tower. How we get there, we alone know. If we sought to tell others, what the wiser were they? Suffice it, that here at the summit you and I stand. Does any balloonist, does the outlooking man in the moon, take a broader view of space? Much thus, one fancies, looks the universe from Milton's celestial battlements. A boundless watery Kentucky. Here Daniel Boone would have dwelt content.

Never heed for the present yonder Burnt District of the Enchanted Isles. Look edgeways, as it were, past them, to the south. You see nothing; but permit me to point out the direction, if not the place, of certain interesting objects in the vast sea, which kissing this tower's base, we behold unscrolling itself towards the Antarctic Pole.

We stand now ten miles from the Equator. Yonder, to the East, some six hundred miles, lies the continent; this Rock being just about on the parallel of Quito.

Observe another thing here. We are at one of three uninhabited clusters, which, at pretty nearly uniform distances from the main, sentinel, at long intervals from each other, the entire coast of South America. In a peculiar manner, also, they terminate the South American character of country. Of the unnumbered Polynesian chains to the westward, not one partakes of the qualities of the Encantadas or Gallipagos, the isles St. Felix and St. Ambrose, the isles Juan Fernandes and Massafuero. Of the first it needs not here to speak. The second lie a little above the Southern

Tropic; lofty, inhospitable, and uninhabitable rocks, one of which, presenting two round hummocks connected by a low reef, exactly resembles a huge double-headed shot. The last lie in the latitude of 33°; high, wild and cloven. Juan Fernandes is sufficiently famous without further description. Massafuero is a Spanish name, expressive of the fact, that the isle so called lies *more without*, that is, further off the main than its neighbor Juan. This isle Massafuero has a very imposing aspect at a distance of eight or ten miles. Approached in one direction, in cloudy weather, its great overhanging height and rugged contour, and more especially a peculiar slope of its broad summits, give it much the air of a vast iceberg drifting in tremendous poise. Its sides are split with dark cavernous recesses, as an old cathedral with its gloomy lateral chapels. Drawing nigh one of these gorges from sea after a long voyage, and beholding some tatterdemallion outlaw, staff in hand, descending its steep rocks toward you, conveys a very queer emotion to a lover of the picturesque.

On fishing parties from ships, at various times, I have chanced to visit each of these groups. The impression they give to the stranger pulling close up in his boat under their grim cliffs is, that surely he must be their first discoverer, such for the most part is the unimpaired . . . . . silence and solitude. And here, by the way, the mode in which these isles were really first lighted upon by Europeans is not unworthy mention, especially as what is about to be said, likewise applies to the original discovery of our Encantadas.

Prior to the year 1563, the voyages made by Spanish ships from Peru to Chili, were full of difficulty. Along this coast the winds from the South most generally prevail; and it had been an invariable custom to keep close in with the land, from a superstitious conceit on the part of the Spaniards, that were they to lose sight of it, the eternal trade wind would waft them into unending waters, from whence would be no return. Here, involved among tortuous capes and headlands, shoals and reefs, beating too against a continual head wind, often light, and sometimes for days and weeks sunk into utter calm, the provincial vessels, in many cases, suffered the extremest hardships, in passages, which at the present day seem to have been incredibly protracted. There is on record in some collections of nautical disasters, an account of one of these ships, which starting on a voyage whose duration was estimated at ten days, spent four months at sea, and indeed never again entered harbor, for in the end she was cast away. Singular to tell, this craft never encountered a gale, but was the vexed sport of malicious calms and currents. Thrice, out of provisions, she put back to an intermediate port, and started afresh, but only yet again to return. Frequent fogs enveloped her; so that no observation could be had of her place, and once, when all hands were joyously anticipating sight of their destination, lo! the vapors lifted and disclosed the mountains from which they had taken their first departure. In the like deceptive vapors she at last struck upon a reef, whence ensued a long series of calamities too sad to detail.

It was the famous pilot, Juan Fernandes, immortalized by the island named after him, who put an end to these coasting tribulations, by boldly venturing the experiment—as Da Gama did before him with respect to Europe—of standing broad out from land. Here he found the winds favorable for getting to the south, and by running westward till beyond the influence of the trades, he regained the coast without difficulty; making the passage which, though in a high degree circuitous, proved far more expeditious than the nominally direct one. Now it was upon these new tracks, and about the year 1670 or thereabouts, that the Enchanted Isles and the rest of the sentinel groups, as they may be called, were discovered. Though I know of no account as to whether any of them were found inhabited or no, it may be reasonably concluded that they have been immemorial solitudes. But let us return to Rodondo.

Southwest from our tower lies all Polynesia, hundreds of leagues away; but straight west, on the precise line of his parallel, no land rises till your keel is beached upon the Kingsmills, a nice little sail of say 5,000 miles.

Having thus by such distant references—with Rodondo the only possible ones—settled our relative place on the sea, let us consider objects not quite so remote. Behold the grim and charred Enchanted Isles. This nearest crater-shaped headland is part of Albemarle, the largest of the group, being some sixty miles or more long, and fifteen broad. Did you ever lay eye on the real genuine Equator? Have you ever, in the largest sense, toed the Line? Well, that identical crater-shaped headland there, all yellow lava, is cut by the Equator exactly as a knife cuts straight through the centre of a pumpkin pie. If you could only see so far, just to one side of that same headland, across yon low dykey ground, you would catch sight of the isle of Narborough, the loftiest land of the cluster; no soil whatever; one seamed clinker from top to bottom; abounding in black caves like smithies; its metallic shore ringing under foot like plates of iron; its central volcanoes standing grouped like a gigantic chimney-stack.

Narborough and Albemarle are neighbors after a quite curious fashion. A familiar diagram will illustrate this strange neighborhood:

Ǝ

Cut a channel at the above letter joint, and the middle transverse limb is Narborough, and all the rest is Albemarle. Volcanic Narborough lies in the black jaws of Albemarle like a wolf's red tongue in his open mouth.

If now you desire the population of Albemarle, I will give you, in round numbers, the statistics, according to the most reliable estimates made upon the spot:

Men,	none.
Ant-eaters,	unknown.
Man-haters,	unknown.
Lizards,	500,000.
Snakes,	500,000.
Spiders,	10,000,000.
Salamanders,	unknown.
Devils,	do.
Making a clean total of	11,000,000.

exclusive of an incomputable host of fiends, ant-eaters, man-haters, and salamanders.

Albemarle opens his mouth towards the setting sun. His distended jaws form a great bay, which Narborough, his tongue, divides into halves, one whereof is called Weather Bay, the other Lee Bay; while the volcanic promontories terminating his coasts are styled South Head and North Head. I note this, because these Bays are famous in the annals of the Sperm Whale Fishery. The whales come here at certain seasons to calve. When ships first cruised hereabouts, I am told, they used to blockade the entrance of Lee Bay, when their boats going round by Weather Bay, passed through Narborough channel, and so had the Leviathans very neatly in a pen.

The day after we took fish at the base of this Round Tower, we had a fine wind, and shooting round the north headland, suddenly descried a fleet of full thirty sail, all beating to windward like a squadron in line. A brave sight as ever man saw. A most harmonious concord of rushing keels. Their thirty kelsons hummed like thirty harp-strings, and looked as straight whilst they left their parallel traces on the sea. But there proved too many hunters for the game. The fleet broke up, and went their separate ways out of sight, leaving my own ship and two trim gentlemen of

London. These last, finding no luck either, likewise vanished; and Lee Bay, with all its appurtenances, and without a rival, devolved to us.

The way of cruising here is this. You keep hovering about the entrance of the bay, in one beat and out the next. But at times—not always, as in other parts of the group—a race-horse of a current sweeps right across its mouth. So, with all sails set, you carefully ply your tacks. How often, standing at the foremast head at sunrise, with our patient prow pointed in between these isles, did I gaze upon that land, not of cakes but of clinkers, not of streams of sparkling water, but arrested torrents of tormented lava.

As the ship runs in from the open sea, Narborough presents its side in one dark craggy mass, soaring up some five or six thousand feet, at which point it hoods itself in heavy clouds, whose lowest level fold is as clearly defined against the rocks, as the snow-line against the Andes. There is dire mischief going on in that upper dark. There toil the demons of fire, who at intervals irradiate the nights with a strange spectral illumination for miles and miles around, but unaccompanied by any further demonstration; or else, suddenly announce themselves by terrific concussions, and the full drama of a volcanic eruption. The blacker that cloud by day, the more may you look for light by night. Often whalemen have found themselves cruising nigh that burning mountain when all aglow with a ball-room blaze. Or, rather, glass-works, you may call this same vitreous isle of Narborough, with its tall chimney-stacks.

Where we still stand, here on Rodondo, we cannot see all the other isles, but it is a good place from which to point out where they lie. Yonder, though, to the E.N.E., I mark a distant dusky ridge. It is Abington Isle, one of the most northerly of the group; so solitary, remote, and blank, it looks like No-Man's Land seen off our northern shore. I doubt whether two human beings ever touched upon that spot. So far as yon Abington Isle is concerned, Adam and his billions of posterity remain uncreated.

Ranging south of Abington, and quite out of sight behind the long spine of Albemarle, lies James's Isle, so called by the early Buccaneers after the luckless Stuart, Duke of York. Observe here, by the way, that, excepting the isles particularized in comparatively recent times, and which mostly received the names of famous Admirals, the Encantadas were first christened by the Spaniards; but these Spanish names were generally effaced on English charts by the subsequent christenings of the Buccaneers, who, in the middle of the seventeenth century, called them after English noblemen and kings. Of these loyal freebooters and the things which associate their name with the Encantadas, we shall hear anon. Nay, for one little item, immediately; for between James's Isle and Albemarle, lies a fantastic islet, strangely known as "Cowley's Enchanted Isle." But as all the group is deemed enchanted, the reason must be given for the spell within a spell involved by this particular designation. The name was bestowed by that excellent Buccaneer himself, on his first visit here. Speaking in his published voyages of this spot, he says—"My fancy led me to call it Cowley's Enchanted Isle, for we having had a sight of it upon several points of the compass, it appeared always in so many different forms; sometimes like a ruined fortification; upon another point like a great city," &c. No wonder though, that among the Encantadas all sorts of ocular deceptions and mirages should be met.

That Cowley linked his name with this self-transforming and bemocking isle, suggests the possibility that it conveyed to him some meditative image of himself. At least, as is not impossible, if he were any relative of the mildly thoughtful, and self-upbraiding poet Cowley, who lived about his time, the conceit might seem not unwarranted; for that sort of thing evinced in the naming of this isle runs in the blood, and may be seen in pirates as in poets.

Still south of James's Isle lie Jervis Isle, Duncan Isle, Crossman's Isle, Brattle Isle, Wood's Isle, Chatham Isle, and various lesser isles, for the most part an archipelago of aridities, without inhabitant, history, or hope of either in all time to come. But not far from these are rather notable isles —Barrington, Charles's, Norfolk, and Hood's. Succeeding chapters will reveal some ground for their notability.

Sketch Fifth

The Frigate, and Ship Flyaway

"Looking far forth into the ocean wide,
A goodly ship with banners bravely dight,
And flag in her top-gallant I espide,
Through the main sea making her merry flight."

Ere quitting Rodondo, it must not be omitted that here, in 1813, the U.S. frigate Essex, Captain David Porter, came near leaving her bones. Lying becalmed one morning with a strong current setting her rapidly towards the rock, a strange sail was descried, which—not out of keeping with alleged enchantments of the neighborhood—seemed to be staggering under a violent wind, while the frigate lay lifeless as if spell-bound. But a light air springing up, all sail was made by the frigate in chase of the enemy, as supposed—he being deemed an English whale-ship—but the rapidity of the current was so great, that soon all sight was lost of him; and at meridian the Essex, spite of her drags, was driven so close under the foam-lashed cliffs of Rodondo that for a time all hands gave her up. A smart breeze, however, at last helped her off, though the escape was so critical as to seem almost miraculous.

Thus saved from destruction herself, she now made use of that salvation to destroy the other vessel, if possible. Renewing the chase in the direction in which the stranger had disappeared, sight was caught of him the following morning. Upon being descried he hoisted American colors and stood away from the Essex. A calm ensued; when, still confident that the stranger was an Englishman, Porter despatched a cutter, not to board the enemy, but drive back his boats engaged in towing him. The cutter succeeded. Cutters were subsequently sent to capture him; the stranger now showing English colors in place of American. But when the frigate's boats were within a short distance of their hoped-for prize, another sudden breeze sprang up; the stranger under all sail bore off to the northward, and ere night was hull down ahead of the Essex, which all this time lay perfectly becalmed.

This enigmatic craft—American in the morning, and English in the evening—her sails full of wind in a calm—was never again beheld. An enchanted ship no doubt. So at least the sailors swore.

This cruise of the Essex in the Pacific during the war of 1812, is perhaps the strangest and most stirring to be found in the history of the American navy. She captured the furthest wandering vessels; visited the remotest seas and isles; long hovered in the charmed vicinity of the enchanted group; and finally valiantly gave up the ghost fighting two English frigates in the harbor of Valparaiso. Mention is made of her here for the same reason that the buccaneers will likewise receive record; because, like them, by long cruising among the isles, tortoise-hunting upon their shores, and generally exploring them; for these and other reasons, the Essex is peculiarly associated with the Encantadas.

Here be it said that you have but three eye-witness authorities worth mentioning touching the Enchanted Isles:—Cowley, the buccaneer (1684); Colnett, the whaling-ground explorer (1793); Porter, the post captain (1813). Other than these you have but barren, bootless allusions from some few passing voyagers or compilers.

Sketch Sixth

Barrington Isle and the Buccaneers

"Let us all servile base subjection scorn,
And as we be sons of the earth so wide,
Let us our father's heritage divide,
And challenge to ourselves our portions dew
Of all the patrimony, which a few
Now hold in hugger-mugger in their hand."

* * * * *

"Lords of the world, and so will wander free,
Where-so us listeth, uncontroll'd of any."

* * * * *

"How bravely now we live, how jocund, how near the first inheritance, without fears, how free from little troubles!"

Near two centuries ago Barrington Isle was the resort of that famous wing of the West Indian buccaneers, which, upon their repulse from the Cuban waters, crossing the Isthmus of Darien, ravaged the Pacific side of the Spanish colonies, and, with the regularity and timing of a modern mail, waylaid the royal treasure ships plying between Manilla and Acapulco. After the toils of piratic war, here they came to say their prayers, enjoy their free-and-easies, count their crackers from the cask, their doubloons from the keg, and measure their silks of Asia with long Toledos for their yard-sticks.

As a secure retreat, an undiscoverable hiding place, no spot in those days could have been better fitted. In the centre of a vast and silent sea, but very little traversed; surrounded by islands, whose inhospitable aspect might well drive away the chance navigator; and yet within a few days' sail of the opulent countries which they made their prey; the unmolested buccaneers found here that tranquillity which they fiercely denied to every civilized harbor in that part of the world. Here, after stress of weather, or a temporary drubbing at the hands of their vindictive foes, or in swift flight with golden booty, those old marauders came, and lay snugly out of all harm's reach. But not only was the place a harbor of safety, and a bower of ease, but for utility in other things it was most admirable.

Barrington Isle is in many respects singularly adapted to careening, refitting, refreshing, and other seamen's purposes. Not only has it good water, and good anchorage, well sheltered from all winds by the high land of Albemarle, but it is the least unproductive isle of the group. Tortoises good for food, trees good for fuel, and long grass good for bedding, abound here, and there are pretty natural walks, and several landscapes to be seen. Indeed, though in its locality belonging to the Enchanted group, Barrington Isle is so unlike most of its neighbors, that it would hardly seem of kin to them.

"I once landed on its western side," says a sentimental voyager long ago, "where it faces the black buttress of Albemarle. I walked beneath groves of trees; not very lofty, and not palm trees, or orange trees, or peach trees, to be sure; but for all that, after long sea-faring very beautiful to walk under, even though they supplied no fruit. And here, in calm spaces at the heads of glades, and on the shaded tops of slopes commanding the most quiet scenery—what do you think I saw? Seats which might have served Brahmins and presidents of peace societies. Fine old ruins of what had once been symmetric lounges of stone and turf; they bore every mark both of artificialness and age, and were undoubtedly made by the buccaneers. One had been a long sofa, with back and arms, just such a sofa as the poet Gray might have loved to throw himself upon, his Crebillon in hand.

"Though they sometimes tarried here for months at a time, and used the spot for a storing-place for spare spars, sails, and casks; yet it is highly improbable that the buccaneers ever erected dwelling-houses upon the isle. They never were here except their ships remained, and they would most likely have slept on board. I mention this, because I cannot avoid the thought, that it is hard to impute the construction of these romantic seats to any other motive than one of pure peacefulness and kindly fellowship with nature. That the buccaneers perpetrated the greatest outrages is very true; that some of them were mere cut-throats is not to be denied; but we know that here and there among their host was a Dampier, a Wafer, and a Cowley, and likewise other men, whose worst reproach was their desperate fortunes; whom persecution, or adversity, or secret and unavengeable wrongs, had driven from Christian society to seek the melancholy solitude or the guilty adventures of the sea. At any rate, long as those ruins of seats on Barrington remain, the most singular monuments are furnished to the fact, that all of the buccaneers were not unmitigated monsters.

"But during my ramble on the isle I was not long in discovering other tokens, of things quite in accordance with those wild traits, popularly, and no doubt truly enough imputed to the freebooters at large. Had I picked up old nails and rusty hoops I would only have thought of the ship's carpenter and cooper. But I found old cutlasses and daggers reduced to mere threads of rust, which doubtless had stuck between Spanish ribs ere now. These were signs of the murderer and robber; the reveller likewise had left his trace. Mixed with shells, fragments of broken jars were lying here and there, high up upon the beach. They were precisely like the jars now used upon the Spanish coast for the wine and Pisco spirits of that country.

"With a rusty dagger-fragment in one hand, and a bit of a wine-jar in another, I sat me down on the ruinous green sofa I have spoken of, and bethought me long and deeply of these same buccaneers. Could it be possible, that they robbed and murdered one day, revelled the next, and rested themselves by turning meditative philosophers, rural poets, and seat-builders on the third? Not very improbable, after all. For consider the vacillations of a man. Still, strange as it may seem, I must also abide by the more charitable thought; namely, that among these adventurers were some gentlemanly, companionable souls, capable of genuine tranquillity and virtue."

Sketch Seventh

Charles' Isle and the Dog-King

——————So with outragious cry,
A thousand villeins round about him swarmed
Out of the rocks and caves adjoining nye;
Vile caitive wretches, ragged, rude, deformed;
All threatning death, all in straunge manner armed;
Some with unweldy clubs, some with long speares,
Some rusty knives, some staves in fier warmd.

* * * * *

We will not be of any occupation,
Let such vile vassals, born to base vocation,
Drudge in the world, and for their living droyle,
Which have no wit to live withouten toyle.

Southwest of Barrington lies Charles' Isle. And hereby hangs a history which I gathered long ago from a shipmate learned in all the lore of outlandish life.

During the successful revolt of the Spanish provinces from Old Spain, there fought on behalf of Peru a certain Creole adventurer from Cuba, who by his bravery and good fortune at length advanced himself to high rank in the patriot army. The war being ended, Peru found itself like many valorous gentlemen, free and independent enough, but with few shot in the locker. In other words, Peru had not wherewithal to pay off its troops. But the Creole—I forget his name—volunteered to take his pay in lands. So they told him he might have his pick of the Enchanted Isles, which were then, as they still remain, the nominal appanage of Peru. The soldier straightway embarks thither, explores the group, returns to Callao, and says he will take a deed of Charles' Isle. Moreover, this deed must stipulate that thenceforth Charles' Isle is not only the sole property of the Creole, but is for ever free of Peru, even as Peru of Spain. To be short, this adventurer procures himself to be made in effect Supreme Lord of the Island, one of the princes of the powers of the earth.*

He now sends forth a proclamation inviting subjects to his as yet unpopulated kingdom. Some eighty souls, men and women, respond; and being provided by their leader with necessaries, and tools of various sorts, together with a few cattle and goats, take ship for the promised land; the last arrival on board, prior to sailing, being the Creole himself, accompanied, strange to say, by a disciplined cavalry company of large grim dogs. These, it was observed on the passage, refusing to consort with the emigrants, remained aristocratically grouped around their master on the elevated quarter-deck, casting disdainful glances forward upon the inferior rabble there; much as from the ramparts, the soldiers of a garrison thrown into a conquered town, eye the inglorious citizen-mob over which they are set to watch.

Now Charles' Isle not only resembles Barrington Isle in being much more inhabitable than other parts of the group; but it is double the size of Barrington; say forty or fifty miles in circuit.

Safely debarked at last, the company under direction of their lord and patron, forthwith proceeded to build their capital city. They make considerable advance in the way of walls of clinkers, and lava floors, nicely sanded with cinders. On the least barren hills they pasture their cattle, while the goats, adventurers by nature, explore the far inland solitudes for a scanty livelihood of lofty herbage. Meantime, abundance of fish and

* The American Spaniards have long been in the habit of making presents of islands to deserving individuals. The pilot Juan Fernandez procured a deed of the isle named after him, and for some years resided there before Selkirk came. It is supposed, however, that he eventually contracted the blues upon his princely property, for after a time he returned to the main, and as report goes, became a very garrulous barber in the city of Lima.

tortoises supply their other wants.

The disorders incident to settling all primitive regions, in the present case were heightened by the peculiarly untoward character of many of the pilgrims. His Majesty was forced at last to proclaim martial law, and actually hunted and shot with his own hand several of his rebellious subjects, who, with most questionable intentions, had clandestinely encamped in the interior; whence they stole by night, to prowl barefooted on tiptoe round the precincts of the lava-palace. It is to be remarked, however, that prior to such stern proceedings, the more reliable men had been judiciously picked out for an infantry body-guard, subordinate to the cavalry body-guard of dogs. But the state of politics in this unhappy nation may be somewhat imagined from the circumstance, that all who were not of the body-guard were downright plotters and malignant traitors. At length the death penalty was tacitly abolished, owing to the timely thought, that were strict sportsman's justice to be dispensed among such subjects, ere long the Nimrod King would have little or no remaining game to shoot. The human part of the life-guard was now disbanded, and set to work cultivating the soil, and raising potatoes; the regular army now solely consisting of the dog-regiment. These, as I have heard, were of a singularly ferocious character, though by severe training rendered docile to their master. Armed to the teeth, the Creole now goes in state, surrounded by his canine janizaries, whose terrific bayings prove quite as serviceable as bayonets in keeping down the surgings of revolt.

But the census of the isle, sadly lessened by the dispensation of justice, and not materially recruited by matrimony, began to fill his mind with sad mistrust. Some way the population must be increased. Now, from its possessing a little water, and its comparative pleasantness of aspect, Charles' Isle at this period was occasionally visited by foreign whalers. These His Majesty had always levied upon for port charges, thereby contributing to his revenue. But now he had additional designs. By insidious arts he from time to time cajoles certain sailors to desert their ships and enlist beneath his banner. Soon as missed, their captains crave permission to go and hunt them up. Whereupon His Majesty first hides them very carefully away, and then freely permits the search. In consequence, the delinquents are never found, and the ships retire without them.

Thus, by a two-edged policy of this crafty monarch, foreign nations were crippled in the number of their subjects, and his own were greatly multiplied. He particularly petted these renegado strangers. But alas for the deep-laid schemes of ambitious princes, and alas for the vanity of glory. As the foreign-born Pretorians, unwisely introduced into the Roman state, and still more unwisely made favorites of the Emperors, at last insulted and overturned the throne, even so these lawless mariners, with all the rest of the body-guard and all the populace, broke out into a terrible mutiny, and defied their master. He marched against them with all his dogs. A deadly battle ensued upon the beach. It raged for three hours, the dogs fighting with determined valor, and the sailors reckless of every thing but victory. Three men and thirteen dogs were left dead upon the field, many on both sides were wounded, and the king was forced to fly with the remainder of his canine regiment. The enemy pursued, stoning the dogs with their master into the wilderness of the interior. Discontinuing the pursuit, the victors returned to the village on the shore, stove the spirit-casks, and proclaimed a Republic. The dead men were interred with the honors of war, and the dead dogs ignominiously thrown into the sea. At last, forced by stress of suffering, the fugitive Creole came down from the hills and offered to treat for peace. But the rebels refused it on any other terms than his unconditional banishment. Accordingly, the next ship that arrived carried away the ex-king to Peru.

The history of the king of Charles' Island furnishes another illustration of the difficulty of colonizing barren islands with unprincipled pilgrims.

Doubtless for a long time the exiled monarch, pensively ruralizing in Peru, which afforded him a safe asylum in his calamity, watched every arrival from the Encantadas, to hear news of the failure of the Republic, the consequent penitence of the rebels, and his own recall to royalty. Doubtless he deemed the Republic but a miserable experiment which would soon explode. But no, the insurgents had confederated themselves into a democracy neither Grecian, Roman, nor American. Nay, it was no democracy at all, but a permanent *Riotocracy*, which gloried in having no law but lawlessness. Great inducements being offered to deserters, their ranks were swelled by accessions of scamps from every ship which touched their shores. Charles' Island was proclaimed the asylum of the oppressed of all navies. Each runaway tar was hailed as a martyr in the cause of freedom, and became immediately installed a ragged citizen of this universal nation. In vain the captains of absconding seamen strove to regain them. Their new compatriots were ready to give any number of ornamental eyes in their behalf. They had few cannon, but their fists were not to be trifled with. So at last it came to pass that no vessels acquainted with the character of that country durst touch there, however sorely in want of refreshment. It became Anathema—a sea Alsatia—the unassailed lurking-place of all sorts of desperadoes, who in the name of liberty did just what they pleased. They continually fluctuated in their numbers. Sailors deserting ships at other islands, or in boats at sea any where in that vicinity, steered for Charles' Isle, as to their sure home of refuge; while sated with the life of the isle, numbers from time to time crossed the water to the neighboring ones, and there presenting themselves to strange captains as shipwrecked seamen, often succeeded in getting on board vessels bound to the Spanish coast; and having a compassionate purse made up for them on landing there.

One warm night during my first visit to the group, our ship was floating along in languid stillness, when some one on the forecastle shouted "Light ho!" We looked and saw a beacon burning on some obscure land off the beam. Our third mate was not intimate with this part of the world. Going to the captain he said, "Sir, shall I put off in a boat? These must be shipwrecked men."

The captain laughed rather grimly, as, shaking his fist towards the beacon, he rapped out an oath, and said—"No, no, you precious rascals, you don't juggle one of my boats ashore this blessed night. You do well, you thieves—you do benevolently to hoist a light yonder as on a dangerous shoal. It tempts no wise man to pull off and see what's the matter, but bids him steer small and keep off shore—that is Charles' Island; brace up, Mr. Mate, and keep the light astern."

SKETCH EIGHTH

NORFOLK ISLE AND THE CHOLA WIDOW

"At last they in an island did espy
A seemly woman sitting by the shore,
That with great sorrow and sad agony
Seemed some great misfortune to deplore,
And loud to them for succor called evermore."

"Black his eye as the midnight sky,
White his neck as the driven snow,
Red his cheek as the morning light;—
Cold he lies in the ground below.
My love is dead,
Gone to his death-bed,
All under the cactus tree."

"Each lonely scene shall thee restore,
For thee the tear be duly shed;
Belov'd till life can charm no more,
And mourned till Pity's self be dead."

Far to the northeast of Charles' Isle, sequestered from the rest, lies Norfolk Isle; and, however insignificant to most voyagers, to me, through sympathy, that lone island has become a spot made sacred by the strongest trials of humanity.

It was my first visit to the Encantadas. Two days had been spent ashore in hunting tortoises. There was not time to capture many; so on the third afternoon we loosed our sails. We were just in the act of getting under way, the uprooted anchor yet suspended and invisibly swaying beneath the wave, as the good ship gradually turned on her heel to leave the isle behind, when the seaman who heaved with me at the windlass paused suddenly, and directed my attention to something moving on the land, not along the beach, but somewhat back, fluttering from a height.

In view of the sequel of this little story, be it here narrated how it came to pass, that an object which partly from its being so small was quite lost to every other man on board, still caught the eye of my handspike companion. The rest of the crew, myself included, merely stood up to our spikes in heaving; whereas, unwontedly exhilarated at every turn of the ponderous windlass, my belted comrade leaped atop of it, with might and main giving a downward, thewey, perpendicular heave, his raised eye bent in cheery animation upon the slowly receding shore. Being high lifted above all others was the reason he perceived the object, otherwise unperceivable: and this elevation of his eye was owing to the elevation of his spirits; and this again—for truth must out—to a dram of Peruvian pisco, in guerdon for some kindness done, secretly administered to him that morning by our mulatto steward. Now, certainly, pisco does a deal of mischief in the world; yet seeing that, in the present case, it was the means, though indirect, of rescuing a human being from the most dreadful fate, must we not also needs admit that sometimes pisco does a deal of good?

Glancing across the water in the direction pointed out, I saw some white thing hanging from an inland rock, perhaps half a mile from the sea.

"It is a bird; a white-winged bird; perhaps a——no; it is——it is a handkerchief!"

"Aye, a handkerchief!" echoed my comrade, and with a louder shout apprised the captain.

Quickly now—like the running out and training of a great gun—the long cabin spy-glass was thrust through the mizzen rigging from the high platform of the poop; whereupon a human figure was plainly seen upon the inland rock, eagerly waving towards us what seemed to be the handkerchief.

Our captain was a prompt, good fellow. Dropping the glass, he lustily ran forward, ordering the anchor to be dropped again; hands to stand by a boat, and lower away.

In a half-hour's time the swift boat returned. It went with six and came with seven; and the seventh was a woman.

It is not artistic heartlessness, but I wish I could but draw in crayons; for this woman was a most touching sight; and crayons, tracing softly melancholy lines, would best depict the mournful image of the dark-damasked Chola widow.

Her story was soon told, and though given in her own strange language was as quickly understood, for our captain from long trading on the Chilian coast was well versed in the Spanish. A Chola, or half-breed Indian woman of Payta in Peru, three years gone by, with her young new-wedded husband Felipe, of pure Castilian blood, and her one only Indian brother, Truxill, Hunilla had taken passage on the main in a French whaler, commanded by a joyous man; which vessel, bound to the cruising grounds beyond the Enchanted Isles, proposed passing close by their vicinity. The object of the little party was to procure tortoise oil, a fluid which for its great purity and delicacy is held in high estimation wherever known; and it is well known all along this part of the Pacific coast. With a chest of clothes, tools, cooking utensils, a rude apparatus for trying out the oil, some casks of biscuit, and other things, not omitting two favorite dogs, of which faithful animal all the Cholos are very fond, Hunilla and her companions were safely landed at their chosen place; the Frenchman, according to the contract made ere sailing, engaged to take them off upon returning from a four months' cruise in the westward seas; which interval the three adventurers deemed quite sufficient for their purposes.

On the isle's lone beach they paid him in silver for their passage out, the stranger having declined to carry them at all except upon that condition; though willing to take every means to insure the due fulfilment of his promise. Felipe had striven hard to have this payment put off to the period of the ship's return. But in vain. Still, they thought they had, in another way, ample pledge of the good faith of the Frenchman. It was arranged that the expenses of the passage home should not be payable in silver, but in tortoises; one hundred tortoises ready captured to the returning captain's hand. These the Cholos meant to secure after their own work was done, against the probable time of the Frenchman's coming back; and no doubt in prospect already felt, that in those hundred tortoises—now somewhere ranging the isle's interior—they possessed one hundred hostages. Enough: the vessel sailed; the gazing three on shore answered the loud glee of the singing crew; and ere evening, the French craft was hull down in the distant sea, its masts three faintest lines which quickly faded from Hunilla's eye.

The stranger had given a blithesome promise, and anchored it with oaths; but oaths and anchors equally will drag; nought else abides on fickle earth but unkept promises of joy. Contrary winds from out unstable skies, or contrary moods of his more varying mind, or shipwreck and sudden death in solitary waves; whatever was the cause, the blithe stranger never was seen again.

Yet, however dire a calamity was here in store, misgivings of it ere due time never disturbed the Cholos' busy mind, now all intent upon the toilsome matter which had brought them hither. Nay, by swift doom coming like the thief at night, ere seven weeks went by, two of the little party were removed from all anxieties of land or sea. No more they sought to gaze with feverish fear, or still more feverish hope, beyond the present's horizon line; but into the furthest future their own silent spirits sailed. By persevering labor beneath that burning sun, Felipe and Truxill had brought down to their hut many scores of tortoises, and tried out the oil, when, elated with their good success, and to reward themselves for such hard work, they, too hastily, made a catamaran, or Indian raft, much used on the Spanish main, and merrily started on a fishing trip, just without a long reef with many jagged gaps, running parallel with the shore, about half a mile from it. By some bad tide or hap, or natural negligence of joyfulness (for though they could not be heard, yet by their gestures they seemed singing at the time), forced in deep water against that iron bar, the ill-made catamaran was overset, and came all to pieces; when, dashed by broad-chested swells between their broken logs and the sharp teeth of the reef, both adventurers perished before Hunilla's eyes.

Before Hunilla's eyes they sank. The real woe of this event passed before her sight as some sham tragedy on the stage. She was seated on a rude bower among the withered thickets, crowning a lofty cliff, a little back from the beach. The thickets were so disposed, that in looking upon the sea at large she peered out from among the branches as from the lattice of a high balcony. But upon the day we speak of here, the better to watch the adventure of those two hearts she loved, Hunilla had withdrawn the branches to one side, and held them so. They formed an oval frame, through which the bluely boundless sea rolled like a painted one. And there, the invisible painter painted to her view the wave-tossed and disjointed raft, its once level logs slantingly upheaved, as raking masts, and the four struggling arms undistinguishable among them; and then all subsided into smooth-flowing creamy waters, slowly drifting the splintered wreck; while first and last, no sound of any sort was heard. Death in a silent picture; a dream of the eye; such vanishing shapes as the mirage shows.

So instant was the scene, so trance-like its mild pictorial effect, so distant from her blasted bower and her common sense of things, that Hunilla gazed and gazed, nor raised a finger or a wail. But as good to sit thus dumb, in stupor staring on that dumb show, for all that otherwise might be done. With half a mile of sea between, how could her two enchanted arms aid those four fated ones? The distance long, the time one sand. After the lightning is beheld, what fool shall stay the thunderbolt? Felipe's body was washed ashore, but Truxill's never came; only his gay, braided hat of golden straw—that same sunflower thing he waved to her, pushing from the strand—and now, to the last gallant, it still saluted her. But Felipe's body floated to the marge, with one arm encirclingly outstretched. Lock-jawed in grim death, the lover-husband, softly clasped his bride, true to her even in death's dream. Ah, Heaven, when man thus keeps his faith, wilt thou be faithless who created the faithful one? But they cannot break faith who never plighted it.

It needs not to be said what nameless misery now wrapped the lonely widow. In telling her own story she passed this almost entirely over, simply recounting the event. Construe the comment of her features, as you might; from her mere words little would you have weened that Hunilla was herself the heroine of her tale. But not thus did she defraud us of our tears. All hearts bled that grief could be so brave.

She but showed us her soul's lid, and the strange ciphers thereon engraved; all within, with pride's timidity, was withheld. Yet was there one exception. Holding out her small olive hand before our captain, she said in mild and slowest Spanish, "Señor, I buried him;" then paused, struggled as against the writhed coilings of a snake, and cringing suddenly, leaped up, repeating in impassioned pain, "I buried him, my life, my soul!"

Doubtless it was by half-unconscious, automatic motions of her hands, that this heavy-hearted one performed the final offices for Felipe, and planted a rude cross of withered sticks—no green ones might be had—at the head of that lonely grave, where rested now in lasting uncomplaint and quiet haven he whom untranquil seas had overthrown.

But some dull sense of another body that should be interred, of another cross that should hallow another grave—unmade as yet;—some dull anxiety and pain touching her undiscovered brother now haunted the oppressed Hunilla. Her hands fresh from the burial earth, she slowly went back to the beach, with unshaped purposes wandered there, her spell-bound eye bent upon the incessant waves. But they bore nothing to her but a dirge, which maddened her to think that murderers should mourn. As time went by, and these things came less dreamingly to her mind, the strong persuasions of her Romish faith, which sets peculiar store by consecrated urns, prompted her to resume in waking earnest that pious search which had but been begun as in somnambulism. Day after day, week after week, she trod the cindery beach, till at length a double motive edged every eager glance. With equal longing she now looked for the living and the dead; the brother and the captain; alike vanished, never to return. Little accurate note of time had Hunilla taken under such emotions as were hers, and little, outside herself, served for calendar or dial. As to poor Crusoe in the self-same sea, no saint's bell pealed forth the lapse of week or month; each day went by unchallenged; no chanticleer announced those sultry dawns, no lowing herds those poisonous nights. All wonted and steadily recurring sounds, human, or humanized by sweet fellowship with man, but one stirred that torrid trance,—the cry of dogs;

save which nought but the rolling sea invaded it, an all pervading monotone; and to the widow that was the least loved voice she could have heard.

No wonder that as her thoughts now wandered to the unreturning ship, and were beaten back again, the hope against hope so struggled in her soul, that at length she desperately said, "Not yet, not yet; my foolish heart runs on too fast." So she forced patience for some further weeks. But to those whom earth's sure indraft draws, patience or impatience is still the same.

Hunilla now sought to settle precisely in her mind, to an hour, how long it was since the ship had sailed; and then, with the same precision, how long a space remained to pass. But this proved impossible. What present day or month it was she could not say. Time was her labyrinth, in which Hunilla was entirely lost.

And now follows——

Against my own purposes a pause descends upon me here. One knows not whether nature doth not impose some secrecy upon him who has been privy to certain things. At least, it is to be doubted whether it be good to blazon such. If some books are deemed most baneful and their sale forbid, how then with deadlier facts, not dreams of doting men? Those whom books will hurt will not be proof against events. Events, not books, should be forbid. But in all things man sows upon the wind, which bloweth just there whither it listeth; for ill or good man cannot know. Often ill comes from the good, as good from ill.

When Hunilla——

Dire sight it is to see some silken beast long dally with a golden lizard ere she devour. More terrible, to see how feline Fate will sometimes dally with a human soul, and by a nameless magic make it repulse a sane despair with a hope which is but mad. Unwittingly I imp this cat-like thing, sporting with the heart of him who reads; for if he feel not, he reads in vain.

—"The ship sails this day, to-day," at last said Hunilla to herself; "this gives me certain time to stand on; without certainty I go mad. In loose ignorance I have hoped and hoped; now in firm knowledge I will but wait. Now I live and no longer perish in bewilderings. Holy Virgin, aid me! Thou wilt waft back the ship. Oh, past length of weary weeks—all to be dragged over—to buy the certainty of to-day, I freely give ye, though I tear ye from me!"

As mariners tossed in tempest on some desolate ledge patch them a boat out of the remnants of their vessel's wreck, and launch it in the self-same waves, see here Hunilla, this lone shipwrecked soul, out of treachery invoking trust. Humanity, thou strong thing, I worship thee, not in the laurelled victor, but in this vanquished one.

Truly Hunilla leaned upon a reed, a real one; no metaphor; a real Eastern reed. A piece of hollow cane, drifted from unknown isles, and found upon the beach, its once jagged ends rubbed smoothly even as by sand-paper; its golden glazing gone. Long ground between the sea and land, upper and nether stone, the unvarnished substance was filed bare, and wore another polish now, one with itself, the polish of its agony. Circular lines at intervals cut all round this surface, divided it into six panels of unequal length. In the first were scored the days, each tenth one marked by a longer and deeper notch; the second was scored for the number of sea-fowl eggs for sustenance, picked out from the rocky nests; the third, how many fish had been caught from the shore; the fourth, how many small tortoises found inland; the fifth, how many days of sun; the sixth, of clouds; which last, of the two, was the greater one. Long night of busy numbering, misery's mathematics, to weary her too-wakeful soul to sleep; yet sleep for that was none.

The panel of the days was deeply worn, the long tenth notches half effaced, as alphabets of the blind. Ten thousand times the longing widow had traced her finger over the bamboo; dull flute, which played on, gave no sound; as if counting birds flown by in air, would hasten tortoises creeping through the woods.

After the one hundred and eightieth day no further mark was seen; that last one was the faintest, as the first the deepest.

"There were more days," said our Captain; "many, many more; why did you not go on and notch them too, Hunilla?"

"Señor, ask me not."

"And meantime, did no other vessel pass the isle?"

"Nay, Señor;—but——"

"You do not speak; but *what,* Hunilla?"

"Ask me not, Señor."

"You saw ships pass, far away; you waved to them; they passed on;—was that it, Hunilla?"

"Señor, be it as you say."

Braced against her woe, Hunilla would not, durst not trust the weakness of her tongue. Then when our Captain asked whether any whale-boats had———

But no, I will not file this thing complete for scoffing souls to quote, and call it firm proof upon their side. The half shall here remain untold.

Those two unnamed events which befell Hunilla on this isle, let them abide between her and her God. In nature, as in law, it may be libellous to speak some truths.

Still, how it was that although our vessel had lain three days anchored nigh the isle, its one human tenant should not have discovered us till just upon the point of sailing, never to revisit so lone and far a spot; this needs explaining ere the sequel come.

The place where the French captain had landed the little party was on the farther and opposite end of the isle. There too it was that they had afterwards built their hut. Nor did the widow in her solitude desert the spot where her loved ones had dwelt with her, and where the dearest of the twain now slept his last long sleep, and all her plaints awaked him not, and he of husbands the most faithful during life.

Now, high broken land rises between the opposite extremities of the isle. A ship anchored at one side is invisible from the other. Neither is the isle so small, but a considerable company might wander for days through the wilderness of one side, and never be seen, or their halloos heard, by any stranger holding aloof on the other. Hence Hunilla, who naturally associated the possible coming of ships with her own part of the isle, might to the end have remained quite ignorant of the presence of our vessel, were it not for a mysterious presentiment, borne to her, so our mariners averred, by this isle's enchanted air. Nor did the widow's answer undo the thought.

"How did you come to cross the isle this morning then, Hunilla?" said our Captain.

"Señor, something came flitting by me. It touched my cheek, my heart, Señor."

"What do you say, Hunilla?"

"I have said, Señor; something came through the air."

It was a narrow chance. For when in crossing the isle Hunilla gained the high land in the centre, she must then for the first have perceived our masts, and also marked that their sails were being loosed, perhaps even heard the echoing chorus of the windlass song. The strange ship was about to sail, and she behind. With all haste she now descends the height on the hither side, but soon loses sight of the ship among the sunken jungles at the mountain's base. She struggles on through the withered branches, which seek at every step to bar her path, till she comes to the isolated rock, still some way from the water. This she climbs, to reassure herself. The ship is still in plainest sight. But now worn out with over tension, Hunilla all but faints; she fears to step down from her giddy perch; she is feign to pause, there where she is, and as a last resort catches the turban from her head, unfurls and waves it over the jungles towards us.

During the telling of her story the mariners formed a voiceless circle round Hunilla and the Captain; and when at length the word was given to man the fastest boat, and pull round to the isle's thither side, to bring away Hunilla's chest and the tortoise-oil; such alacrity of both cheery and sad obedience seldom before was seen. Little ado was made. Already the anchor had been recommitted to the bottom, and the ship swung calmly to it.

But Hunilla insisted upon accompanying the boat as indispensable pilot to her hidden hut. So being refreshed with the best the steward could supply, she started with us. Nor did ever any wife of the most famous admiral in her husband's barge receive more silent reverence of respect, than poor Hunilla from this boat's crew.

Rounding many a vitreous cape and bluff, in two hours' time we shot inside the fatal reef; wound into a secret cove, looked up along a green many-gabled lava wall, and saw the island's solitary dwelling.

It hung upon an impending cliff, sheltered on two sides by tangled thickets, and half-screened from view in front by juttings of the rude stairway, which climbed the precipice from the sea. Built of canes, it was thatched with long, mildewed grass. It seemed an abandoned hay-rick whose haymakers were now no more. The roof inclined but one way; the eaves coming to within two feet of the ground. And here was a simple apparatus to collect the dews, or rather doubly-distilled and finest winnowed rains, which, in mercy or in mockery, the night-skies sometimes drop upon these blighted Encantadas. All along beneath the eaves, a spotted sheet, quite weather-stained, was spread, pinned to short, upright stakes, set in the shallow sand. A small clinker, thrown into the cloth, weighed its middle down, thereby straining all moisture into a calabash placed below. This vessel supplied each drop of water ever drunk upon the isle by the Cholos. Hunilla told us the calabash would sometimes, but not often, be half filled over-night. It held six quarts, perhaps. "But," said she, "we were used to thirst. At sandy Payta, where I live, no shower from heaven ever fell; all the water there is brought on mules from the inland vales."

Tied among the thickets were some twenty moaning tortoises, supplying Hunilla's lonely larder; while hundreds of vast tableted black bucklers, like displaced, shattered tomb-stones of dark slate, were also scattered round. These were the skeleton backs of those great tortoises from which Felipe and Truxill had made their precious oil. Several large calabashes and two goodly kegs were filled with it. In a pot near by were the caked crusts of a quantity which had been permitted to evaporate. "They meant to have strained it off next day," said Hunilla, as she turned aside.

I forgot to mention the most singular sight of all, though the first that greeted us after landing.

Some ten small, soft-haired, ringleted dogs, of a beautiful breed, peculiar to Peru, set up a concert of glad welcomings when we gained the beach, which was responded to by Hunilla. Some of these dogs had, since her widowhood, been born upon the isle, the progeny of the two brought from Payta. Owing to the jagged steeps and pitfalls, tortuous thickets, sunken clefts and perilous intricacies of all sorts in the interior; Hunilla, admonished by the loss of one favorite among them, never allowed these delicate creatures to follow her in her occasional birds'-nests climbs and other wanderings; so that, through long habituation, they offered not to follow, when that morning she crossed the land; and her own soul was then too full of other things to heed their lingering behind. Yet, all along she had so clung to them, that, besides what moisture they lapped up at early daybreak from the small scoop-holes among the adjacent rocks, she had shared the dew of her calabash among them; never laying by any considerable store against those prolonged and utter droughts, which in some disastrous seasons warp these isles.

Having pointed out, at our desire, what few things she would like transported to the ship—her chest, the oil, not omitting the live tortoises which she intended for a grateful present to our Captain—we immediately set to work, carrying them to the boat down the long, sloping stair of deeply-shadowed rock. While my comrades were thus employed, I looked, and Hunilla had disappeared.

It was not curiosity alone, but, it seems to me, something different mingled with it, which prompted me to drop my tortoise, and once more gaze slowly around. I remembered the husband buried by Hunilla's hands. A narrow pathway led into a dense part of the thickets. Following it through many mazes, I came out upon a small, round, open space, deeply chambered there.

The mound rose in the middle; a bare heap of finest sand, like that unverdured heap found at the bottom of an hour-glass run out. At its head stood the cross of withered sticks; the dry, peeled bark still fraying from it; its transverse limb tied up with rope, and forlornly adroop in the silent air.

Hunilla was partly prostrate upon the grave; her dark head bowed, and lost in her long, loosened Indian hair; her hands extended to the cross-foot, with a little brass crucifix clasped between; a crucifix worn featureless, like an ancient graven knocker long plied in vain. She did not see me, and I made no noise, but slid aside, and left the spot.

A few moments ere all was ready for our going, she reappeared among us. I looked into her eyes, but saw no tear. There was something which seemed strangely haughty in her air, and yet it was the air of woe. A Spanish and an Indian grief, which would not visibly lament. Pride's height in vain abased to proneness on the rack; nature's pride subduing nature's torture.

Like pages the small and silken dogs surrounded her, as she slowly descended towards the beach. She caught the two most eager creatures in her arms:—"Mia Teeta! Mia Tomoteeta!" and fondling them, inquired how many could we take on board.

The mate commanded the boat's crew; not a hard-hearted man, but his way of life had been such that in most things, even in the smallest, simple utility was his leading motive.

"We cannot take them all, Hunilla; our supplies are short; the winds are unreliable; we may be a good many days going to Tombez. So take those you have, Hunilla; but no more."

She was in the boat; the oarsmen too were seated; all save one, who stood ready to push off and then spring himself. With the sagacity of their race, the dogs now seemed aware that they were in the very instant of being deserted upon a barren strand. The gunwales of the boat were high; its prow—presented inland—was lifted; so owing to the water, which they seemed instinctively to shun, the dogs could not well leap into the little craft. But their busy paws hard scraped the prow, as it had been some farmer's door shutting them out from shelter in a winter storm. A clamorous agony of alarm. They did not howl, or whine; they all but spoke.

"Push off! Give way!" cried the mate. The boat gave one heavy drag and lurch, and next moment shot swiftly from the beach, turned on her heel, and sped. The dogs ran howling along the water's marge; now pausing to gaze at the flying boat, then motioning as if to leap in chase, but mysteriously withheld themselves; and again ran howling along the beach. Had they been human beings hardly would they have more vividly inspired the sense of desolation. The oars were plied as confederate feathers of two wings. No one spoke. I looked back upon the beach, and then upon Hunilla, but her face was set in a stern dusky calm. The dogs crouching in her lap vainly licked her rigid hands. She never looked behind her; but sat motionless, till we turned a promontory of the coast and lost all sights and sounds astern. She seemed as one, who having experienced the sharpest of mortal pangs, was henceforth content to have all lesser heart-strings riven, one by one. To Hunilla, pain seemed so necessary, that pain in other beings, though by love and sympathy made her own, was unrepiningly to be borne. A heart of yearning in a frame of steel. A heart of earthly yearning, frozen by the frost which falleth from the sky.

The sequel is soon told. After a long passage, vexed by calms and baffling winds, we made the little port of Tombez in Peru, there to recruit the ship. Payta was not very distant. Our captain sold the tortoise oil to a Tombez merchant; and adding to the silver a contribution from all hands, gave it to our silent passenger, who knew not what the mariners had done.

The last seen of lone Hunilla she was passing into Payta town, riding upon a small gray ass; and before her on the ass's shoulders, she eyed the jointed workings of the beast's armorial cross.

Sketch Ninth

Hood's Isle and the Hermit Oberlus

"That darkesome glen they enter, where they find
That cursed man low sitting on the ground,
Musing full sadly in his sullein mind;
His griesly lockes long growen and unbound,
Disordered hong about his shoulders round,
And hid his face, through which his hollow eyne
Lookt deadly dull, and stared as astound;
His raw-bone cheekes, through penurie and pine,
Were shronke into the jawes, as he did never dine.
His garments nought but many ragged clouts,
With thornes together pind and patched was,
The which his naked sides he wrapt abouts."

Southeast of Crossman's Isle lies Hood's Isle, or McCain's Beclouded Isle; and upon its south side is a vitreous cove with a wide strand of dark pounded black lava, called Black Beach, or Oberlus's Landing. It might fitly have been styled Charon's.

It received its name from a wild white creature who spent many years here; in the person of a European bringing into this savage region qualities more diabolical than are to be found among any of the surrounding cannibals.

About half a century ago, Oberlus deserted at the above-named island, then, as now, a solitude. He built himself a den of lava and clinkers, about a mile from the Landing, subsequently called after him, in a vale, or expanded gulch, containing here and there among the rocks about two acres of soil capable of rude cultivation; the only place on the isle not too blasted for that purpose. Here he succeeded in raising a sort of degenerate potatoes and pumpkins, which from time to time he exchanged with needy whalemen passing, for spirits or dollars.

His appearance, from all accounts, was that of the victim of some malignant sorceress; he seemed to have drunk of Circe's cup; beast-like; rags insufficient to hide his nakedness; his befreckled skin blistered by continual exposure to the sun; nose flat; countenance contorted, heavy, earthy; hair and beard unshorn, profuse, and of a fiery red. He struck strangers much as if he were a volcanic creature thrown up by the same convulsion which exploded into sight the isle. All bepatched and coiled asleep in his lonely lava den among the mountains, he looked, they say, as a heaped drift of withered leaves, torn from autumn trees, and so left in some hidden nook by the whirling halt for an instant of a fierce night-wind, which then ruthlessly sweeps on, somewhere else to repeat the capricious act. It is also reported to have been the strangest sight, this same Oberlus, of a sultry, cloudy morning, hidden under his shocking old black tarpaulin hat, hoeing potatoes among the lava. So warped and crooked was his strange nature, that the very handle of his hoe seemed gradually to have shrunk and twisted in his grasp, being a wretched bent stick, elbowed more like a savage's war-sickle than a civilized hoe-handle. It was his mysterious custom upon a first encounter with a stranger ever to present his back; possibly, because that was his better side, since it revealed the least. If the encounter chanced in his garden, as it sometimes did—the new-landed strangers going from the sea-side straight through the gorge, to hunt up the queer green-grocer reported doing business here—Oberlus for a time hoed on, unmindful of all greeting, jovial or bland; as the curious stranger would turn to face him, the recluse, hoe in hand, as diligently would avert himself; bowed over, and sullenly revolving round his murphy hill. Thus far for hoeing. When planting, his whole aspect and all his gestures were so malevolently and uselessly sinister and secret, that he seemed rather in act of dropping poison into wells than potatoes into soil. But among his lesser and more harmless marvels was an idea he ever had, that his visitors came equally as well led by longings to behold the mighty hermit Oberlus in his royal state of solitude, as simply to obtain potatoes, or find whatever company might be upon a barren isle. It seems incredible that such a being should possess such vanity; a misanthrope be conceited; but he really had his notion; and upon the strength of it, often gave himself amusing airs to captains. But after all, this is somewhat of a piece with the well-known eccentricity of some convicts, proud of that very hatefulness which makes them notorious. At other times, another unaccountable whim would seize him, and he would long dodge advancing strangers round the clinkered corners of his hut; sometimes like a stealthy bear, he would slink through the withered thickets up the mountains, and refuse to see the human face.

Except his occasional visitors from the sea, for a long period, the only companions of Oberlus were the crawling tortoises; and he seemed more than degraded to their level, having no desires for a time beyond theirs, unless it were for the stupor brought on by drunkenness. But sufficiently debased as he appeared, there yet lurked in him, only awaiting occasion for discovery, a still further proneness. Indeed the sole superiority of Oberlus over the tortoises was his possession of a larger capacity of degradation; and along with that, something like an intelligent will to it. Moreover, what is about to be revealed, perhaps will show, that selfish ambition, or the love of rule for its own sake, far from being the peculiar infirmity of noble minds, is shared by beings which have no mind at all. No creatures are so selfishly tyrannical as some brutes; as any one who has observed the tenants of the pasture must occasionally have observed.

"This island's mine by Sycorax my mother;" said Oberlus to himself, glaring round upon his haggard solitude. By some means, barter or theft—for in those days ships at intervals still kept touching at his Landing—he obtained an old musket, with a few charges of powder and ball. Possessed of arms, he was stimulated to enterprise, as a tiger that first feels the coming of its claws. The long habit of sole dominion over every object round him, his almost unbroken solitude, his never encountering humanity except on terms of misanthropic independence, or mercantile craftiness, and even such encounters being comparatively but rare; all this must have gradually nourished in him a vast idea of his own importance, together with a pure animal sort of scorn for all the rest of the universe.

The unfortunate Creole, who enjoyed his brief term of royalty at Charles's Isle was perhaps in some degree influenced by not unworthy motives; such as prompt other adventurous spirits to lead colonists into distant regions and assume political pre-eminence over them. His summary execution of many of his Peruvians is quite pardonable, considering the desperate characters he had to deal with; while his offering canine battle to the banded rebels seems under the circumstances altogether just. But for this King Oberlus and what shortly follows, no shade of palliation can be given. He acted out of mere delight in tyranny and cruelty, by virtue of a quality in him inherited from Sycorax his mother. Armed now with that shocking blunderbuss, strong in the thought of being master of that horrid isle, he panted for a chance to prove his potency upon the first specimen of humanity which should fall unbefriended into his hands.

Nor was he long without it. One day he spied a boat upon the beach, with one man, a negro, standing by it. Some distance off was a ship, and Oberlus immediately knew how matters stood. The vessel had put in for wood, and the boat's crew had gone into the thickets for it. From a convenient spot he kept watch of the boat, till presently a straggling company appeared loaded with billets. Throwing these on the beach, they again went into the thickets, while the negro proceeded to load the boat.

Oberlus now makes all haste and accosts the negro, who aghast at seeing any living being inhabiting such a solitude, and especially so horrific a one, immediately falls into a panic, not at all lessened by the ursine suavity of Oberlus, who begs the favor of assisting him in his labors. The negro stands with several billets on his shoulder, in act of shouldering others; and Oberlus, with a short cord concealed in his bosom, kindly proceeds to lift those other billets to their place. In so doing he persists in keeping behind the negro, who rightly suspicious of this, in vain dodges about to gain the front of Oberlus; but Oberlus dodges also; till at last, weary of this bootless attempt at treachery, or fearful of being surprised by the remainder of the party, Oberlus runs off a little space to a bush, and fetching his blunderbuss, savagely commands the negro to desist work and follow him. He refuses. Whereupon, presenting his piece, Oberlus snaps at him. Luckily the blunderbuss misses fire; but by this time, frightened out of his wits, the negro, upon a second intrepid summons drops his billets, surrenders at discretion, and follows on. By a narrow defile familiar to him, Oberlus speedily removes out of sight of the water.

On their way up the mountains, he exultingly informs the negro, that henceforth he is to work for him, and be his slave, and that his treatment would entirely depend on his future conduct. But Oberlus, deceived by the first impulsive cowardice of the black, in an evil moment slackens his vigilance. Passing through a narrow way, and perceiving his leader quite off his guard, the negro, a powerful fellow, suddenly grasps him in his arms, throws him down, wrests his musketoon from him, ties his hands with the monster's own cord, shoulders him, and returns with him down to the boat. When the rest of the party arrive, Oberlus is carried on board the ship. This proved an Englishman, and a smuggler; a sort of craft not apt to be over-charitable. Oberlus is severely whipped, then handcuffed, taken ashore, and compelled to make known his habitation and produce his property. His potatoes, pumpkins, and tortoises, with a pile of dollars he had hoarded from his mercantile operations were secured on the spot. But while the too vindictive smugglers were busy destroying his hut and garden, Oberlus makes his escape into the mountains, and conceals himself there in impenetrable recesses, only known to himself, till the ship sails, when he ventures back, and by means of an old file which he sticks into a tree, contrives to free himself from his handcuffs.

Brooding among the ruins of his hut, and the desolate clinkers and extinct volcanoes of this outcast isle, the insulted misanthrope now meditates a signal revenge upon humanity, but conceals his purposes. Vessels still touch the Landing at times; and by and by Oberlus is enabled to supply them with some vegetables.

Warned by his former failure in kidnapping strangers, he now pursues a quite different plan. When seamen come ashore, he makes up to them like a free-and-easy comrade, invites them to his hut, and with whatever affability his red-haired grimness may assume, entreats them to drink his liquor and be merry. But his guests need little pressing; and so, soon as rendered insensible, are tied hand and foot, and pitched among the clinkers, are there concealed till the ship departs, when finding themselves entirely dependent upon Oberlus, alarmed at his changed demeanor, his savage threats, and above all, that shocking blunderbuss, they willingly enlist under him, becoming his humble slaves, and Oberlus the most incredible of tyrants. So much so, that two or three perish beneath his initiating process. He sets the remainder—four of them—to breaking the caked soil; transporting upon their backs loads of loamy earth, scooped up in moist clefts among the mountains; keeps them on the roughest fare; presents his piece at the slightest hint of insurrection; and in all respects converts them into reptiles at his feet; plebeian garter-snakes to this Lord Anaconda.

At last, Oberlus contrives to stock his arsenal with four rusty cutlasses, and an added supply of powder and ball intended for his blunderbuss. Remitting in good part the labor of his slaves, he now approves himself a man, or rather devil, of great abilities in the way of cajoling or coercing others into acquiescence with his own ulterior designs, however at first abhorrent to them. But indeed, prepared for almost any eventual evil by their previous lawless life, as a sort of ranging Cow-Boys of the sea, which had dissolved within them the whole moral man, so that they were ready to concrete in the first offered mould of baseness now; rotted down from manhood by their hopeless misery on the isle; wonted to cringe in all things to their lord, himself the worst of slaves; these wretches were now become wholly corrupted to his hands. He used them as creatures of an inferior race; in short, he gaffles his four animals, and makes murderers of them; out of cowards fitly manufacturing bravos.

Now, sword or dagger, human arms are but artificial claws and fangs, tied on like false spurs to the fighting cock. So, we repeat, Oberlus, czar of the isle, gaffles his four subjects; that is, with intent of glory, puts four rusty cutlasses into their hands. Like any other autocrat, he had a noble army now.

It might be thought a servile war would hereupon ensue. Arms in the hands of trodden slaves? how indiscreet of Emperor Oberlus! Nay, they had but cutlasses—sad old scythes enough—he a blunderbuss, which by its blind scatterings of all sorts of boulders, clinkers and other scoria would annihilate all four mutineers, like four pigeons at one shot. Besides, at first he did not sleep in his accustomed hut; every lurid sunset, for a time, he might have been seen wending his way among the riven mountains, there to secret himself till dawn in some sulphurous pitfall, undiscoverable to his gang; but finding this at last too troublesome, he now each evening tied his slaves hand and foot, hid the cutlasses, and thrusting them into his barracks, shut to the door, and lying down before it, beneath a rude shed lately added, slept out the night, blunderbuss in hand.

It is supposed that not content with daily parading over a cindery solitude at the head of his fine army, Oberlus now meditated the most active mischief; his probable object being to surprise some passing ship touching at his dominions, massacre the crew, and run away with her to parts unknown. While these plans were simmering in his head, two ships touch in company at the isle, on the opposite side to his; when his designs undergo a sudden change.

The ships are in want of vegetables, which Oberlus promises in great abundance, provided they send their boats round to his landing, so that the crews may bring the vegetables from his garden; informing the two captains, at the same time, that his rascals—slaves and soldiers—had become so abominably lazy and good-for-nothing of late, that he could not make them work by ordinary inducements, and did not have the heart to be severe with them.

The arrangement was agreed to, and the boats were sent and hauled upon the beach. The crews went to the lava hut; but to their surprise nobody was there. After waiting till their patience was exhausted, they returned to the shore, when lo, some stranger—not the Good Samaritan either—seems to have very recently passed that way. Three of the boats were broken in a thousand pieces, and the fourth was missing. By hard toil over the mountains and through the clinkers, some of the strangers succeeded in returning to that side of the isle where the ships lay, when fresh boats are sent to the relief of the rest of the hapless party.

However amazed at the treachery of Oberlus, the two captains afraid of new and still more mysterious atrocities,—and indeed, half imputing such strange events to the enchantments associated with these isles,—perceive no security but in instant flight; leaving Oberlus and his army in quiet possession of the stolen boat.

On the eve of sailing they put a letter in a keg, giving the Pacific Ocean intelligence of the affair, and moored the keg in the bay. Some time subsequent, the keg was opened by another captain chancing to anchor there, but not until after he had dispatched a boat round to Oberlus's Landing. As may be readily surmised, he felt no little inquietude till the boat's return; when another letter was handed him, giving Oberlus's version of the affair. This precious document had been found pinned half-mildewed to the clinker wall of the sulphurous and deserted hut. It ran as follows; showing that Oberlus was at least an accomplished writer, and no mere boor; and what is more, was capable of the most tristful eloquence.

> "Sir: I am the most unfortunate ill-treated gentleman that lives. I am a patriot, exiled from my country by the cruel hand of tyranny.
>
> "Banished to these Enchanted Isles, I have again and again besought captains of ships to sell me a boat, but always have been refused, though I offered the handsomest prices in Mexican dollars. At length an opportunity presented of possessing myself of one, and I did not let it slip.
>
> "I have been long endeavoring by hard labor and much solitary suffering to accumulate something to make myself comfortable in a virtuous though unhappy old age; but at various times have been robbed and beaten by men professing to be Christians.
>
> "To-day I sail from the Enchanted group in the good boat Charity bound to the Feejee Isles. "FATHERLESS OBERLUS.
>
> "*P.S.*—Behind the clinkers, nigh the oven, you will find the old fowl. Do not kill it; be patient; I leave it setting; if it shall have any chicks, I hereby bequeathe them to you, whoever you may be. But don't count your chicks before they are hatched."

The fowl proved a starveling rooster, reduced to a sitting posture by sheer debility.

Oberlus declares that he was bound to the Feejee Isles; but this was only to throw pursuers on a false scent. For after a long time he arrived, alone in his open boat, at Guayaquil. As his miscreants were never again beheld on Hood's Isle, it is supposed, either that they perished for want of water on the passage to Guayaquil, or, what is quite as probable, were thrown overboard by Oberlus, when he found the water growing scarce.

From Guayaquil Oberlus proceeded to Payta; and there, with that nameless witchery peculiar to some of the ugliest animals, wound himself into the affections of a tawny damsel; prevailing upon her to accompany him back to his Enchanted Isle; which doubtless he painted as a Paradise of flowers, not a Tartarus of clinkers.

But unfortunately for the colonization of Hood's Isle with a choice variety of animated nature, the extraordinary and devilish aspect of Oberlus made him to be regarded in Payta as a highly suspicious character. So that being found concealed one night, with matches in his pocket, under the hull of a small vessel just ready to be launched, he was seized and thrown into jail.

The jails in most South American towns are generally of the least wholesome sort. Built of huge cakes of sun-burnt brick, and containing but one room, without windows or yard, and but one door heavily grated with wooden bars, they present both within and without the grimmest aspect. As public edifices they conspicuously stand upon the hot and dusty Plaza, offering to view, through the gratings, their villanous and hopeless inmates, burrowing in all sorts of tragic squalor. And here, for a long time Oberlus was seen; the central figure of a mongrel and assassin band; a creature whom it is religion to detest, since it is philanthropy to hate a misanthrope.

Note.—They who may be disposed to question the possibility of the character above depicted, are referred to the 1st vol. of Porter's Voyage into the Pacific, where they will recognize many sentences, for expedition's sake derived verbatim from thence, and incorporated here; the main difference—save a few passing reflections—between the two accounts being, that the present writer has added to Porter's facts accessory ones picked up in the Pacific from reliable sources; and where facts conflict, has naturally preferred his own authorities to Porter's. As, for instance, *his* authorities place Oberlus on Hood's Isle: Porter's, on Charles's Isle. The letter found in the hut is also somewhat different, for while at the Encantadas he was informed that not only did it evince a certain clerkliness, but was full of the strangest satiric effrontery which does not adequately appear in Porter's version. I accordingly altered it to suit the general character of its author.

SKETCH TENTH

RUNAWAYS, CASTAWAYS, SOLITARIES, GRAVE-STONES, ETC.

"*And all about old stocks and stubs of trees,*
Whereon nor fruit nor leaf was ever seen,
Did hang upon the ragged knotty knees,
On which had many wretches hanged been."

Some relics of the hut of Oberlus partially remain to this day at the head of the clinkered valley. Nor does the stranger wandering among other of the Enchanted Isles fail to stumble upon still other solitary abodes, long abandoned to the tortoise and the lizard. Probably few parts of earth have in modern times sheltered so many solitaries. The reason is, that these isles are situated in a distant sea, and the vessels which occasionally visit them are mostly all whalers, or ships bound on dreary and protracted voyages, exempting them in a good degree from both the oversight and the memory of human law. Such is the character of some commanders and some seamen, that under these untoward circumstances, it is quite impossible but that scenes of unpleasantness and discord should occur between them. A sullen hatred of the tyrannic ship will seize the sailor, and he gladly exchanges it for isles, which though blighted as by a continual sirocco and burning breeze, still offer him in their labyrinthine interior, a retreat beyond the possibility of capture. To flee the ship in any Peruvian or Chilian port, even the smallest and most rustical, is not unattended with great risk of apprehension, not to speak of jaguars. A reward of five pesos sends fifty dastardly Spaniards into the woods, who with long knives scour them day and night in eager hopes of securing their prey. Neither is it, in general, much easier to escape pursuit at the isles of Polynesia. Those of them which have felt a civilizing influence present the same difficulty to the runaway with the Peruvian ports, the advanced natives being quite as mercenary and keen of knife and scent, as the retrograde Spaniards; while, owing to the bad odor in which all Europeans lie in the minds of aboriginal savages who have chanced to hear aught of them, to desert the ship among primitive Polynesians, is, in most cases, a hope not unforlorn. Hence the Enchanted Isles become the voluntary tarrying places of all sorts of refugees; some of whom too sadly experience the fact that flight from tyranny does not of itself insure a safe asylum, far less a happy home.

Moreover, it has not seldom happened that hermits have been made upon the isles by the accidents incident to tortoise-hunting. The interior of most of them is tangled and difficult of passage beyond description; the air is sultry and stifling; an intolerable thirst is provoked, for which no running stream offers its kind relief. In a few hours, under an equatorial sun, reduced by these causes to entire exhaustion, woe betide the straggler at the Enchanted Isles! Their extent is such as to forbid an adequate search unless weeks are devoted to it. The impatient ship waits a day or two; when the missing man remaining undiscovered, up goes a stake on the beach, with a letter of regret, and a keg of crackers and another of water tied to it, and away sails the craft.

Nor have there been wanting instances where the inhumanity of some captains has led them to wreak a secure revenge upon seamen who have given their caprice or pride some singular offence. Thrust ashore upon the scorching marl, such mariners are abandoned to perish outright, unless by solitary labors they succeed in discovering some precious dribblets of moisture oozing from a rock or stagnant in a mountain pool.

I was well acquainted with a man, who, lost upon the Isle of Narborough, was brought to such extremes by thirst, that at last he only saved his life by taking that of another being. A large hair-seal came upon the beach. He rushed upon it, stabbed it in the neck, and then throwing himself upon the panting body quaffed at the living wound; the palpitations of the creature's dying heart injecting life into the drinker.

Another seaman thrust ashore in a boat upon an isle at which no ship ever touched, owing to its peculiar sterility and the shoals about it, and from which all other parts of the group were hidden; this man feeling that it was sure death to remain there, and that nothing worse than death menaced him in quitting it, killed two seals, and inflating their skins, made a float, upon which he transported himself to Charles's Island, and joined the republic there.

But men not endowed with courage equal to such desperate attempts, find their only resource in forthwith seeking for some watering-place, however precarious or scanty; building a hut; catching tortoises and birds; and in all respects preparing for hermit life, till tide or time, or a passing ship arrives to float them off.

At the foot of precipices on many of the isles, small rude basins in the rocks are found, partly filled with rotted rubbish or vegetable decay, or overgrown with thickets, and sometimes a little moist; which, upon examination, reveal plain tokens of artificial instruments employed in hollowing them out, by some poor castaway or still more miserable runaway. These basins are made in places where it was supposed some scanty drops of dew might exude into them from the upper crevices.

The relics of hermitages and stone basins, are not the only signs of vanishing humanity to be found upon the isles. And curious to say, that spot which of all others in settled communities is most animated, at the Enchanted Isles presents the most dreary of aspects. And though it may seem very strange to talk of post-offices in this barren region, yet post-offices are occasionally to be found there. They consist of a stake and bottle. The letters being not only sealed, but corked. They are generally deposited by captains of Nantucketers for the benefit of passing fishermen; and contain statements as to what luck they had in whaling or tortoise-hunting. Frequently, however, long months and months, whole years glide by and no applicant appears. The stake rots and falls, presenting no very exhilarating object.

If now it be added that grave-stones, or rather grave-boards, are also discovered upon some of the isles, the picture will be complete.

Upon the beach of James's Isle for many years, was to be seen a rude finger-post pointing inland. And perhaps taking it for some signal of possible hospitality in this otherwise desolate spot—some good hermit living there with his maple dish—the stranger would follow on in the path thus indicated, till at last he would come out in a noiseless nook, and find his only welcome, a dead man; his sole greeting the inscription over a grave: "Here, in 1813, fell in a daybreak duel, a Lieutenant of the U.S. frigate Essex, aged twenty-one: attaining his majority in death."

It is but fit that like those old monastic institutions of Europe, whose inmates go not out of their own walls to be inurned, but are entombed there where they die; the Encantadas too should bury their own dead, even as the great general monastery of earth does hers.

It is known that burial in the ocean is a pure necessity of sea-faring life, and that it is only done when land is far astern, and not clearly visible from the bow. Hence to vessels cruising in the vicinity of the Enchanted Isles, they afford a convenient Potter's Field. The interment over, some good-natured forecastle poet and artist seizes his paint-brush, and inscribes a doggerel epitaph. When after a long lapse of time, other good-natured seamen chance to come upon the spot, they usually make a table of the mound, and quaff a friendly can to the poor soul's repose.

As a specimen of these epitaphs, take the following, found in a bleak gorge of Chatham Isle:—

"Oh Brother Jack, as you pass by,
As you are now, so once was I.
Just so game and just so gay,
But now, alack, they've stopped my pay.
No more I peep out of my blinkers,
Here I be—tucked in with clinkers!"

The Bell-Tower

"Like negroes, these powers own man sullenly; mindful of their higher master; while serving, plot revenge."

"The world is apoplectic with high-living of ambition; and apoplexy has its fall."

"Seeking to conquer a larger liberty, man but extends the empire of necessity."

From a Private MS.

IN THE SOUTH of Europe, nigh a once-frescoed capital, now with dank mould cankering its bloom, central in a plain, stands what, at distance, seems the black mossed stump of some immeasurable pine, fallen, in forgotten days, with Anak and the Titan.

As all along where the pine tree falls, its dissolution leaves a mossy mound—last-flung shadow of the perished trunk; never lengthening, never lessening; unsubject to the fleet falsities of the sun; shade immutable and true gauge which cometh by prostration—so westward from what seems the stump, one steadfast spear of lichened ruin veins the plain.

From that tree-top, what birded chimes of silver throats had rung. A stone pine; a metallic aviary in its crown: the Bell-Tower, built by the great mechanician, the unblest foundling, Bannadonna.

Like Babel's, its base was laid in a high hour of renovated earth, following the second deluge, when the waters of the Dark Ages had dried up, and once more the green appeared. No wonder that, after so long and deep submersion, the jubilant expectation of the race should, as with Noah's sons, soar into Shinar aspiration.

In firm resolve, no man in Europe at that period went beyond Bannadonna. Enriched through commerce with the Levant, the state in which he lived voted to have the noblest Bell-Tower in Italy. His repute assigned him to be architect.

Stone by stone, month by month, the tower rose. Higher, higher; snail-like in pace, but torch or rocket in its pride.

After the masons would depart, the builder, standing alone upon its ever-ascending summit, at close of every day saw that he overtopped still higher walls and trees. He would tarry till a late hour there, wrapped in schemes of other and still loftier piles. Those who of saints' days thronged the spot—hanging to the rude poles of scaffolding, like sailors on yards, or bees on boughs, unmindful of lime and dust, and falling chips of stone—their homage not the less inspirited him to self-esteem.

At length the holiday of the Tower came. To the sound of viols, the climax-stone slowly rose in air, and, amid the firing of ordnance, was laid by Bannadonna's hands upon the final course. Then mounting it, he stood erect, alone, with folded arms; gazing upon the white summits of blue inland Alps, and whiter crests of bluer Alps off-shore—sights invisible from the plain. Invisible, too, from thence was that eye he turned below, when, like the cannon booms, came up to him the people's combustions of applause.

That which stirred them so was, seeing with what serenity the builder stood three hundred feet in air, upon an unrailed perch. This none but he durst do. But his periodic standing upon the pile, in each stage of its growth—such discipline had its last result.

Little remained now but the bells. These, in all respects, must correspond with their receptacle.

The minor ones were prosperously cast. A highly enriched one followed, of a singular make, intended for suspension in a manner before unknown. The purpose of this bell, its rotary motion, and connection with the clock-work, also executed at the time, will, in the sequel, receive mention.

In the one erection, bell-tower and clock-tower were united, though, before that period, such structures had commonly been built distinct; as the Campanile and Torre dell' Orologio of St. Mark to this day attest.

But it was upon the great state-bell that the founder lavished his more daring skill. In vain did some of the less elated magistrates here caution him; saying that though truly the tower was Titanic, yet limit should be set to the dependent weight of its swaying masses. But undeterred, he prepared his mammouth mould, dented with mythological devices; kindled his fires of balsamic firs; melted his tin and copper; and throwing in much plate, contributed by the public spirit of the nobles, let loose the tide.

The unleashed metals bayed like hounds. The workmen shrunk. Through their fright, fatal harm to the bell was dreaded. Fearless as Shadrach, Bannadonna, rushing through the glow, smote the chief culprit with his ponderous ladle. From the smitten part, a splinter was dashed into the seething mass, and at once was melted in.

Next day a portion of the work was heedfully uncovered. All seemed right. Upon the third morning, with equal satisfaction, it was bared still lower. At length, like some old Theban king, the whole cooled casting was disinterred. All was fair except in one strange spot. But as he suffered no one to attend him in these inspections, he concealed the blemish by some preparation which none knew better to devise.

The casting of such a mass was deemed no small triumph for the caster; one, too, in which the state might not scorn to share. The homicide was overlooked. By the charitable that deed was but imputed to sudden transports of esthetic passion, not to any flagitious quality. A kick from an Arabian charger: not sign of vice, but blood.

His felony remitted by the judge, absolution given him by the priest, what more could even a sickly conscience have desired!

Honoring the tower and its builder with another holiday, the republic witnessed the hoisting of the bells and clock-work amid shows and pomps superior to the former.

Some months of more than usual solitude on Bannadonna's part ensued. It was not unknown that he was engaged upon something for the belfry, intended to complete it, and surpass all that had gone before. Most people imagined that the design would involve a casting like the bells. But those who thought they had some further insight, would shake their heads, with hints, that not for nothing did the mechanician keep so secret. Meantime, his seclusion failed not to invest his work with more or less of that sort of mystery pertaining to the forbidden.

Ere long he had a heavy object hoisted to the belfry, wrapped in a dark sack or cloak; a procedure sometimes had in the case of an elaborate piece of sculpture, or statue, which, being intended to grace the front of a new edifice, the architect does not desire exposed to critical eyes, till set up, finished, in its appointed place. Such was the impression now. But, as the object rose, a statuary present observed, or thought he did, that it was not entirely rigid, but was, in a manner, pliant. At last, when the hidden thing had attained its final height, and, obscurely seen from below, seemed almost of itself to step into the belfry, as if with little assistance from the crane, a shrewd old blacksmith present ventured the suspicion that it was but a living man. This surmise was thought a foolish one, while the general interest failed not to augment.

Not without demur from Bannadonna, the chief-magistrate of the town, with an associate—both elderly men—followed what seemed the image up the tower. But, arrived at the belfry, they had little recompense. Plausibly entrenching himself behind the conceded mysteries of his art, the mechanician withheld present explanation. The magistrates glanced toward the cloaked object, which, to their surprise, seemed now to have changed its attitude, or else had before been more perplexingly concealed by the violent muffling action of the wind without. It seemed now seated upon some sort of frame, or chair, contained within the domino. They observed that nigh the top, in a sort of square, the web of the cloth, either from accident or design, had its warp partly withdrawn, and the cross-threads plucked out here and there, so as to form a sort of woven grating. Whether it were the low wind or no, stealing through the stone lattice-work, or only their own perturbed imaginations, is uncertain, but they thought they discerned a slight sort of fitful, spring-like motion, in the domino. Nothing, however incidental or insignificant, escaped their uneasy eyes. Among other things, they pried out, in a corner, an earthen cup, partly corroded and partly encrusted, and one whispered to the other, that this cup was just such a one as might, in mockery, be offered to the lips of some brazen statue, or, perhaps, still worse.

But, being questioned, the mechanician said, that the cup was simply used in his founder's business, and described the purpose; in short, a cup to test the condition of metals in fusion. He added, that it had got into the belfry by the merest chance.

Again, and again, they gazed at the domino, as at some suspicious incognito—at a Venetian mask. All sorts of vague apprehensions stirred them. They even dreaded lest, when they should descend, the mechanician, though without a flesh and blood companion, for all that, would not be left alone.

Affecting some merriment at their disquietude, he begged to relieve them, by extending a coarse sheet of workman's canvas between them and the object.

Meantime he sought to interest them in his other work; nor, now that the domino was out of sight, did they long remain insensible to the artistic wonders lying round them; wonders hitherto beheld but in their unfinished state; because, since hoisting the bells, none but the caster had entered within the belfry. It was one trait of his, that, even in details, he would not let another do what he could, without too great loss of time, accomplish for himself. So, for several preceding weeks, whatever hours were unemployed in his secret design, had been devoted to elaborating the figures on the bells.

The clock-bell, in particular, now drew attention. Under a patient chisel, the latent beauty of its enrichments, before obscured by the cloudings incident to casting that beauty in its shyest grace, was now revealed. Round and round the bell, twelve figures of gay girls, garlanded, hand-in-hand, danced in a choral ring—the embodied hours.

"Bannadonna," said the chief, "this bell excels all else. No added touch could here improve. Hark!" hearing a sound, "was that the wind?"

"The wind, Eccellenza," was the light response. "But the figures, they are not yet without their faults. They need some touches yet. When those are given, and the——block yonder," pointing towards the canvas screen, "when Haman there, as I merrily call him,—him? *it*, I mean——when Haman is fixed on this, his lofty tree, then, gentlemen, will I be most happy to receive you here again."

The equivocal reference to the object caused some return of restlessness. However, on their part, the visitors forbore further allusion to it, unwilling, perhaps, to let the foundling see how easily it lay within his plebeian art to stir the placid dignity of nobles.

"Well, Bannadonna," said the chief, "how long ere you are ready to set the clock going, so that the hour shall be sounded? Our interest in you, not less than in the work itself, makes us anxious to be assured of your success. The people, too,—why, they are shouting now. Say the exact hour when you will be ready."

"To-morrow, Eccellenza, if you listen for it,—or should you not, all the same—strange music will be heard. The stroke of one shall be the first from yonder bell," pointing to the bell adorned with girls and garlands, "that stroke shall fall there, where the hand of Una clasps Dua's. The stroke of one shall sever that loved clasp. To-morrow, then, at one o'clock, as struck here, precisely here," advancing and placing his finger upon the clasp, "the poor mechanic will be most happy once more to give you liege audience, in this his littered shop. Farewell till then, illustrious magnificoes, and hark ye for your vassal's stroke."

His still, Vulcanic face hiding its burning brightness like a forge, he moved with ostentatious deference towards the scuttle, as if so far to escort their exit. But the junior magistrate, a kind hearted man, troubled at what seemed to him a certain sardonical disdain, lurking beneath the foundling's humble mien, and in Christian sympathy more distressed at it on his account than on his own, dimly surmising what might be the final fate of such a cynic solitaire, nor perhaps uninfluenced by the general strangeness of surrounding things, this good magistrate had glanced sadly, sideways from the speaker, and thereupon his foreboding eye had started at the expression of the unchanging face of the Hour Una.

"How is this, Bannadonna?" he lowly asked, "Una looks unlike her sisters."

"In Christ's name, Bannadonna," impulsively broke in the chief, his attention, for the first time, attracted to the figure, by his associate's remark, "Una's face looks just like that of Deborah, the prophetess, as painted by the Florentine, Del Fonca."

"Surely, Bannadonna," lowly resumed the milder magistrate, "you meant the twelve should wear the same jocundly abandoned air. But see, the smile of Una seems but a fatal one. 'Tis different."

While his mild associate was speaking, the chief glanced, inquiringly, from him to the caster, as if anxious to mark how the discrepancy would be accounted for. As the chief stood, his advanced foot was on the scuttle's curb.

Bannadonna spoke.

"Eccellenza, now that, following your keener eye, I glance upon the face of Una, I do, indeed, perceive some little variance. But look all round the bell, and you will find no two faces entirely correspond. Because there is a law in art——but the cold wind is rising more; these lattices are but a poor defense. Suffer me, magnificoes, to conduct you, at least, partly on your way. Those in whose well-being there is a public stake, should be heedfully attended."

"Touching the look of Una, you were saying, Bannadonna, that there was a certain law in art," observed the chief, as the three now descended the stone shaft, "pray, tell me, then——."

"Pardon; another time, Eccellenza;—the tower is damp."

"Nay, I must rest, and hear it now. Here,—here is a wide landing, and through this leeward slit, no wind, but ample light. Tell us of your law; and at large."

"Since, Eccellenza, you insist, know that there is a law in art, which bars the possibility of duplicates. Some years ago, you may remember, I graved a small seal for your republic, bearing, for its chief device, the head of your own ancestor, its illustrious founder. It becoming necessary, for the customs' use, to have innumerable impressions for bales and boxes, I graved an entire plate, containing one hundred of the seals. Now, though, indeed, my object was to have those hundred heads identical, and though, I dare say, people think them so, yet, upon closely scanning an uncut impression from the plate, no two of those five-score faces, side by side, will be found alike. Gravity is the air of all; but, diversified in all. In some, benevolent; in some, ambiguous; in two or three, to a close scrutiny, all but incipiently malign, the variation of less than a hair's breadth in the linear shadings round the mouth sufficing to all this. Now, Eccellenza, transmute that general gravity into joyousness, and subject it to twelve of those variations I have described, and tell me, will you not have my hours here, and Una one of them? But I like——."

"Hark! is that——a footfall above?"

"Mortar, Eccellenza; sometimes it drops to the belfry-floor from the arch where the stone-work was left undressed. I must have it seen to. As I was about to say: for one, I like this law forbidding duplicates. It evokes fine personalities. Yes, Eccellenza, that strange, and—to you—uncertain smile, and those fore-looking eyes of Una, suit Bannadonna very well."

"Hark!—sure we left no soul above?"

"No soul, Eccellenza; rest assured, no *soul*.—Again the mortar."

"It fell not while we were there."

"Ah, in your presence, it better knew its place, Eccellenza," blandly bowed Bannadonna.

"But, Una," said the milder magistrate, "she seemed intently gazing on you; one would have almost sworn that she picked you out from among us three."

"If she did, possibly, it might have been her finer apprehension, Eccellenza."

"How, Bannadonna? I do not understand you."

"No consequence, no consequence, Eccellenza—but the shifted wind is blowing through the slit. Suffer me to escort you on; and then, pardon, but the toiler must to his tools."

"It may be foolish, Signore," said the milder magistrate, as, from the third landing, the two now went down unescorted, "but, somehow, our great mechanician moves me strangely. Why, just now, when he so superciliously replied, his look seemed Sisera's, God's vain foe, in Del Fonca's painting.—And that young, sculptured Deborah, too. Aye, and that——."

"Tush, tush, Signore!" returned the chief. "A passing whim. Deborah? —Where's Jael, pray?"

"Ah," said the other, as they now stepped upon the sod, "Ah, Signore, I see you leave your fears behind you with the chill and gloom; but mine, even in this sunny air, remain. Hark!"

It was a sound from just within the tower door, whence they had emerged. Turning, they saw it closed.

"He has slipped down and barred us out," smiled the chief; "but it is his custom."

Proclamation was now made, that the next day, at one hour after meridian, the clock would strike, and—thanks to the mechanician's powerful art—with unusual accompaniments. But what those should be, none as yet could say. The announcement was received with cheers.

By the looser sort, who encamped about the tower all night, lights were seen gleaming through the topmost blind-work, only disappearing with the morning sun. Strange sounds, too, were heard, or were thought to be, by those whom anxious watching might not have left mentally undisturbed, sounds, not only of some ringing implement, but also—so they said—half-suppressed screams and plainings, such as might have issued from some ghostly engine, overplied.

Slowly the day drew on; part of the concourse chasing the weary time with songs and games, till, at last, the great blurred sun rolled, like a football, against the plain.

At noon, the nobility and principal citizens came from the town in cavalcade; a guard of soldiers, also, with music, the more to honor the occasion.

Only one hour more. Impatience grew. Watches were held in hands of feverish men, who stood, now scrutinizing their small dial-plates, and then, with neck thrown back, gazing toward the belfry, as if the eye might foretell that which could only be made sensible to the ear, for, as yet, there was no dial to the tower-clock.

The hour-hands of a thousand watches now verged within a hair's breadth of the figure I. A silence, as of the expectation of some Shiloh, pervaded the swarming plain. Suddenly a dull, mangled sound—naught ringing in it; scarcely audible, indeed, to the outer circles of the people—that dull sound dropped heavily from the belfry. At the same moment, each man stared at his neighbor blankly. All watches were upheld. All hour-hands were at—had passed—the figure I. No bell-stroke from the tower. The multitude became tumultuous.

Waiting a few moments, the chief magistrate, commanding silence, hailed the belfry, to know what thing unforeseen had happened there.

No response.

He hailed again and yet again.

All continued hushed.

By his order the soldiers burst in the tower-door; when, stationing guards to defend it from the now surging mob, the chief, accompanied by his former associate, climbed the winding stairs. Half-way up, they stopped to listen. No sound. Mounting faster, they reached the belfry; but, at the threshold, startled at the spectacle disclosed. A spaniel which, unbeknown to them, had followed them thus far, stood shivering as before some unknown monster in a brake: or, rather, as if it snuffed footsteps leading to some other world.

Bannadonna lay prostrate and bleeding at the base of the bell which was adorned with girls and garlands. He lay at the feet of the hour Una; his head coinciding, in a vertical line, with her left hand, clasped by the hour Dua. With downcast face impending over him, like Jael over nailed Sisera in the tent, was the domino; now no more becloaked.

It had limbs, and seemed clad in a scaly mail, lustrous as a dragon-beetle's. It was manacled, and its clubbed arms were uplifted, as if, with its manacles, once more to smite its already smitten victim. One advanced foot of it was inserted beneath the dead body, as if in the act of spurning it.

Uncertainty falls on what now followed.

It were but natural to suppose that the magistrates would at first shrink from immediate personal contact with what they saw. At the least, for a time, they would stand in involuntary doubt; it may be, in more or less of horrified alarm. Certain it is, that an arquebuss was called for from below. And some add, that its report, followed by a fierce whiz, as of the sudden snapping of a main-spring, with a steely din, as if a stack of sword blades should be dashed upon a pavement, these blended sounds came ringing to the plain, attracting every eye far upward to the belfry, whence, through the lattice-work, thin wreaths of smoke were curling.

Some averred that it was the spaniel, gone mad by fear, which was shot. This, others denied. True it was, the spaniel never more was seen; and, probably, for some unknown reason, it shared the burial now to be related of the domino. For, whatever the preceding circumstances may have been, the first instinctive panic over, or else all ground of reasonable fear removed, the two magistrates, by themselves, quickly rehooded the figure in the dropped cloak wherein it had been hoisted. The same night, it was secretly lowered to the ground, smuggled to the beach, pulled far out to sea, and sunk. Nor to any after urgency, even in free convivial hours, would the twain ever disclose the full secrets of the belfry.

From the mystery unavoidably investing it, the popular solution of the foundling's fate involved more or less of supernatural agency. But some few less unscientific minds pretended to find little difficulty in otherwise accounting for it. In the chain of circumstantial inferences drawn, there may, or may not, have been some absent or defective links. But, as the explanation in question is the only one which tradition has explicitly preserved, in dearth of better, it will here be given. But, in the first place, it is requisite to present the supposition entertained as to the entire motive and mode, with their origin, of the secret design of Bannadonna; the minds above-mentioned assuming to penetrate as well into his soul as into the event. The disclosure will indirectly involve reference to peculiar matters, none of the clearest, beyond the immediate subject.

At that period, no large bell was made to sound otherwise than as at present, by agitation of a tongue within, by means of ropes, or percussion from without, either from cumbrous machinery, or stalwart watchmen, armed with heavy hammers, stationed in the belfry, or in sentry-boxes on the open roof, according as the bell was sheltered or exposed.

It was from observing these exposed bells, with their watchmen, that the foundling, as was opined, derived the first suggestion of his scheme. Perched on a great mast or spire, the human figure, viewed from below, undergoes such a reduction in its apparent size, as to obliterate its intelligent features. It evinces no personality. Instead of bespeaking volition, its gestures rather resemble the automatic ones of the arms of a telegraph.

Musing, therefore, upon the purely Punchinello aspect of the human figure thus beheld, it had indirectly occurred to Bannadonna to devise some metallic agent, which should strike the hour with its mechanic hand, with even greater precision than the vital one. And, moreover, as the vital watchman on the roof, sallying from his retreat at the given periods, walked to the bell with uplifted mace, to smite it, Bannadonna had resolved that his invention should likewise possess the power of locomotion, and, along with that, the appearance, at least, of intelligence and will.

If the conjectures of those who claimed acquaintance with the intent of Bannadonna be thus far correct, no unenterprising spirit could have been his. But they stopped not here; intimating that though, indeed, his design had, in the first place, been prompted by the sight of the watchman, and confined to the devising of a subtle substitute for him; yet, as is not seldom the case with projectors, by insensible gradations, proceeding from comparatively pigmy aims to Titanic ones, the original scheme had, in its anticipated eventualities, at last, attained to an unheard of degree of daring. He still bent his efforts upon the locomotive figure for the belfry, but only as a partial type of an ulterior creature, a sort of elephantine Helot, adapted to further, in a degree scarcely to be imagined, the universal conveniences and glories of humanity; supplying nothing less than a supplement to the Six Days' Work; stocking the earth with a new serf, more useful than the ox, swifter than the dolphin, stronger than the lion, more cunning than the ape, for industry an ant, more fiery than serpents, and yet, in patience, another ass. All excellences of all God-made creatures, which served man, were here to receive advancement, and then to be combined in one. Talus was to have been the all-accomplished Helot's name. Talus, iron slave to Bannadonna, and, through him, to man.

Here, it might well be thought that, were these last conjectures as to the foundling's secrets not erroneous, then must he have been hopelessly infected with the craziest chimeras of his age; far outgoing Albert Magnus and Cornelius Agrippa. But the contrary was averred. However marvelous his design, however apparently transcending not alone the bounds of human invention, but those of divine creation, yet the proposed means to be employed were alleged to have been confined within the sober forms of sober reason. It was affirmed that, to a degree of more than sceptic scorn, Bannadonna had been without sympathy for any of the vainglorious irrationalities of his time. For example, he had not concluded, with the visionaries among the metaphysicians, that between the finer mechanic forces and the ruder animal vitality, some germ of correspondence might prove discoverable. As little did his scheme partake of the enthusiasm of some natural philosophers, who hoped, by physiological and chemical inductions, to arrive at a knowledge of the source of life, and so qualify themselves to manufacture and improve upon it. Much less had he aught in common with the tribe of alchemists, who sought, by a species of incantations, to evoke some surprising vitality from the laboratory. Neither had he imagined with certain sanguine theosophists, that, by faithful adoration of the Highest, unheard-of powers would be vouchsafed to man. A practical materialist, what Bannadonna had aimed at was to have been reached, not by logic, not by crucible, not by conjuration, not by altars; but by plain vice-bench and hammer. In short, to solve nature, to steal into her, to intrigue beyond her, to procure some one else to bind her to his hand;—these, one and all, had not been his objects; but, asking no favors from any element or any being, of himself, to rival her, outstrip her, and rule her. He stooped to conquer. With him, common sense was theurgy; machinery, miracle; Prometheus, the heroic name for machinist; man, the true God.

Nevertheless, in his initial step, so far as the experimental automaton for the belfry was concerned, he allowed fancy some little play; or, perhaps, what seemed his fancifulness was but his utilitarian ambition collaterally extended. In figure, the creature for the belfry should not be likened after the human pattern, nor any animal one, nor after the ideals, however wild, of ancient fable, but equally in aspect as in organism be an original production; the more terrible to behold, the better.

Such, then, were the suppositions as to the present scheme, and the reserved intent. How, at the very threshold, so unlooked for a catastrophe overturned all, or, rather, what was the conjecture here, is now to be set forth.

It was thought that on the day preceding the fatality, his visitors having left him, Bannadonna had unpacked the belfry image, adjusted it, and placed it in the retreat provided,—a sort of sentry-box in one corner of the belfry; in short, throughout the night, and for some part of the ensuing morning, he had been engaged in arranging every thing connected with the domino: the issuing from the sentry-box each sixty minutes; sliding along a grooved way, like a railway; advancing to the clock-bell, with uplifted manacles; striking it at one of the twelve junctions of the four-and-twenty hands: then wheeling, circling the bell, and retiring to its post, there to bide for another sixty minutes, when the same process was to be repeated; the bell, by a cunning mechanism, meantime turning on its vertical axis, so as to present, to the descending mace, the clasped hands of the next two figures, when it would strike two, three, and so on, to the end. The musical metal in this time-bell being so managed in the fusion, by some art perishing with its originator, that each of the clasps of the four-and-twenty hands should give forth its own peculiar resonance when parted.

But on the magic metal, the magic and metallic stranger never struck but that one stroke, drove but that one nail, severed but that one clasp, by which Bannadonna clung to his ambitious life. For, after winding up the creature in the sentry-box, so that, for the present, skipping the intervening hours, it should not emerge till the hour of one, but should then infallibly emerge, and, after deftly oiling the grooves whereon it was to slide, it was surmised that the mechanician must then have hurried to the bell, to give his final touches to its sculpture. True artist, he here became absorbed; an absorption still further intensified, it may be, by his striving to abate that strange look of Una; which, though, before others, he had treated with such unconcern, might not, in secret, have been without its thorn.

And so, for the interval, he was oblivious of his creature; which, not oblivious of him, and true to its creation, and true to its heedful winding up, left its post precisely at the given moment; along its well-oiled route, slid noiselessly towards its mark; and aiming at the hand of Una, to ring one clangorous note, dully smote the intervening brain of Bannadonna, turned backwards to it; the manacled arms then instantly upspringing to their hovering poise. The falling body clogged the thing's return; so there it stood, still impending over Bannadonna, as if whispering some post-mortem terror. The chisel lay dropped from the hand, but beside the hand; the oil-flask spilled across the iron track.

In his unhappy end, not unmindful of the rare genius of the mechanician, the republic decreed him a stately funeral. It was resolved that the great bell—the one whose casting had been jeopardized through the timidity of the ill-starred workman—should be rung upon the entrance of the bier into the cathedral. The most robust man of the country round was assigned the office of bell-ringer.

But as the pall-bearers entered the cathedral porch, nought but a broken and disastrous sound, like that of some lone Alpine land-slide, fell from the tower upon their ears. And then, all was hushed.

Glancing backwards, they saw the groined belfry crashed sideways in. It afterwards appeared that the powerful peasant who had the bell-rope in charge, wishing to test at once the full glory of the bell, had swayed down upon the rope with one concentrate jerk. The mass of quaking metal, too ponderous for its frame, and strangely feeble somewhere at its top, loosed from its fastening, tore sideways down, and tumbling in one sheer fall, three hundred feet to the soft sward below, buried itself inverted and half out of sight.

Upon its disinterment, the main fracture was found to have started from a small spot in the ear; which, being scraped, revealed a defect, deceptively minute, in the casting; which defect must subsequently have been pasted over with some unknown compound.

The remolten metal soon reässumed its place in the tower's repaired superstructure. For one year the metallic choir of birds sang musically in its belfry-bough-work of sculptured blinds and traceries. But on the first anniversary of the tower's completion—at early dawn, before the concourse had surrounded it—an earthquake came; one loud crash was heard. The stone-pine, with all its bower of songsters, lay overthrown upon the plain.

So the blind slave obeyed its blinder lord; but, in obedience, slew him.

So the creator was killed by the creature. So the bell was too heavy for the tower. So that bell's main weakness was where man's blood had flawed it. And so pride went before the fall.*

*It was not deemed necessary to adhere to the peculiar notation of Italian time. Adherence to it would have impaired the familiar comprehension of the story. Kindred remarks might be offered touching an anachronism or two that occur.

Other Prose Pieces

UNCOLLECTED PIECES

Fragments from a Writing Desk

No. 1

MY DEAR M——, I can imagine you seated on that dear, delightful, old fashioned sofa; your head supported by its luxurious padding, and with feet perched aloft on the aspiring back of that straight limbed, stiff-necked, quaint old chair, which, as our facetious W—— assured me, was the identical seat in which old Burton composed his Anatomy of Melancholy. I see you reluctantly raise your optics from the huge-clasped quarto which encumbers your lap, to receive the package which the servant hands you, and can almost imagine that I see those beloved features illumined for a moment with an expression of joy, as you read the superscription of your gentle protege. Lay down I beseech you that odious black-lettered volume and let not its musty and withered leaves sully the virgin purity and whiteness of the sheet which is the vehicle of so much good sense, sterling thought, and chaste and elegant sentiment.

You remember how you used to rate me for my hang-dog modesty, my *mauvaise honte*, as my Lord Chesterfield would style it. Well! I have determined that hereafter you shall not have occasion again to inflict upon me those flattering appellations, of "Fool!" "Dolt!" "Sheep!" which in your indignation you used to shower upon me, with a vigor and a facility which excited my wonder, while it provoked my resentment.

And how do you imagine that I rid myself of this annoying hindrance? Why, truly, by coming to the conclusion that in this pretty corpus of mine was lodged every manly grace; that my limbs were modeled in the symmetry of the Phidian Jupiter; my countenance radiant with the beams of wit and intelligence, and my whole person, the envy of the beaux, the idol of the women and the admiration of the tailor. And then my mind! why, sir, I have discovered it to be endowed with the most rare and extraordinary powers, stored with universal knowledge, and embellished with every polite accomplishment.

Pollux! what a comfortable thing is a good opinion of one's self! Why, I walk the Broadway of our village with a certain air, that puts me down at once in the estimation of any intelligent stranger who may chance to meet me, as a *distingue* of the purest water, a blade of the true temper, a blood of the first quality! Lord! how I despise the little sneaking vermin who dodge along the street as though they were so many footmen or errand-boys; who, have never learned to carry the head erect in conscious importance, but hang that noblest of the human members as though it had been boxed by some virago of an Amazon; who shuffle along the walk, with a quick uneasy step, a hasty clownish motion, which by the magnitude of the contrast, set off to advantage my own slow and magisterial gait, which I can at pleasure vary to an easy, abandoned sort of carriage, or, to the more engaging alert and lively walk, to suit the varieties of time, occasion, and company.

And in society, too—how often have I commiserated the poor wretches who stood aloof, in a corner, like a flock of scared sheep; while myself, beautiful as Apollo, dressed in a style which would extort admiration from a Brummell, and belted round with self-esteem as with a girdle, sallied up to the ladies—complimenting one, exchanging a repartee with another; tapping this one under the chin, and clasping this one round the waist; and finally, winding up the operation by kissing round the whole circle to the great edification of the fair, and to the unbounded horror, amazement and ill-suppressed chagrin of the aforesaid sheepish multitude; who with eyes wide open and mouths distended, afforded good subjects on whom to exercise my polished wit, which like the glittering edge of a Damascus sabre "dazzled all it shone upon."

And then, when the folding doors are thrown open, as the lacquey announces supper to be ready, how often have I stepped forward and with a profound obeisance to the ladies, vowing by the bow of Cupid, and appealing to Venus for my sincerity, when I wished I had an hundred arms at their service, escorted them right gallantly and merrily to the banquet; while those poor bashful creatures, like a drove of dumb cattle, strayed into the apartment, stumbling, blushing, stammering and alone.

Verily! by my elegant accomplishments and superior parts; by my graceful address, and above all by my easy self-possession, I have unwittingly provoked to an irreconcilable degree, the resentment of half a score of these village beaux; whom, although I had rather have their esteem, I value too little to dread their malice.

By my halidome! sir, this same village of Lansingburgh contains within its pretty limits as fair a set of blushing damsels, as one would wish to look upon on a dreamy summer-day!—When I traverse the broad pavements of my own metropolis, my eyes are arrested by beautiful forms flitting hither and thither; and I pause to admire the elegance of their attire, the taste displayed in their embellishments; the richness of the material; and sometimes, it may be, at the loveliness of the features, which no art can heighten and no negligence conceal.

But here, sir, here—where woman seems to have erected her throne, and established her empire; here, where all feel and acknowledge her sway, she blooms in unborrowed charms; and the eye undazzled by the profusion of extraneous ornament, settles at once upon the loveliest faces, which our clayey natures can assume. The poet has sung:

> "When first the Rhodian's mimic art arrayed
> The queen of Beauty in her Cyprian shade,
> The happy master mingled on his piece
> Each look that charm'd him in the fair of Greece.
> To faultless nature true, he stole a grace
> From every finer form and sweeter face;
> And, as he sojourned on the Ægean isles,
> Woo'd all their love and treasur'd all their smiles;
> Then glowed the tints, pure, precious, and refined,
> And mortal charms seemed heavenly when combined."

Now, had this same Apelles flourished in our own enlightened day, and more particularly, had he taken up his domicile in this goodly village, I could with ease have presented him with many a Hebe, in whom were united all the requisite graces which make up the beau-ideal of female loveliness. Nor, my dear M., does there reign in all this bright display, that same monotony of feature, form, complexion, which elsewhere is beheld; no, here are all varieties, all the orders of Beauty's architecture; the Doric, the Ionic, the Corinthian, all are here.

I have in "my mind's eye, Horatio," three (the number of the Graces, you remember) who may stand, each at the head of their respective orders. The one, were she arrayed in sylvan garb, and did she in her hand carry her bow, might with equal justice and propriety stand the picture of Diana herself. Her figure is bold, her stature erect and tall, her presence queenly and commanding, and her complexion is clear and fair as the face of Heaven on a May day, through which sparkles an eye of that indefinable hue, which is beyond comparison the most striking that can garnish the human countenance. The vermillion in her cheeks perpetually wears that ruddy healthful tint, which one is accustomed to behold illumine, but for a moment alas! the face of a city belle when she takes her annual ramble in the country, to revel for a period in the retreats of rustic life.

If to these qualities you superadd, that majesty of carriage, and dignity of mien, which we would fancy the royal mistress of Antony to have possessed; together with that heroic and Grecian cast of countenance which the imagination unconsciously ascribes to the Jewess, Rebecca, when resisting the vile arts of the Templar,—you have in my poor opinion the portraiture of ———.

When I venture to describe the second of this beautiful trinity, I feel my powers of delineation inadequate to the task; but, nevertheless I will try my hand at the matter, although like an unskilful limner, I am fearful I shall but scandalize the charms I endeavor to copy.

Come to my aid, ye guardian spirits of the Fair! Guide my awkward hand, and preserve from mutilation the features ye hover over and protect! Pour down whole floods of sparkling champaigne, my dear M———, until your brain grows giddy with emotion; con over the latter portion of the 1st Canto of Childe Harold, and ransack your intellectual repository for the liveliest visions of the Fairy Land, and you will be in a measure prepared to relish the epicurian banquet *I* shall spread.

The stature of this beautiful mortal (if she be indeed of earth) is of that perfect heighth, which while it is freed from the charge of being low, cannot with propriety be denominated tall. Her figure is slender almost to fragility but strikingly modeled in spiritual elegance, and is the only form I ever saw, which could bear the trial of a rigid criticism.

Every man who is gifted with the least particle of imagination, must in some of his reveries have conjured up from the realms of fancy, a being bright and beautiful beyond every thing he had ever before apprehended, whose main and distinguishing attribute invariably proves to be a form the indiscribable loveliness of which seems to,

——"Sail in liquid light,
And float on seas of bliss."

The realization of these seraphic visions is seldom permitted us; but I can truly say that when my eyes for the first time fell upon this lovely creature, I thought myself transported to the land of Dreams, where lay embodied, the most brilliant conceptions of the wildest fancy. Indeed, could the Promethean spark throw life and animation into the Venus de' Medici, it would but present the counterpart of ——.

Her complexion has the delicate tinge of the Brunett, with a little of the roseate hue of the Circassian; and one would swear that none but the sunny skies of Spain had shone upon the infancy of the being, who looks so like her own "dark-glancing daughters."

The outline of her head, together with the profile of her countenance are sketched in classick purity, and while the one indicates refined and elegant sentiment; the other is not more chaste and regular than the mind which beams from every feature of the face. Her hair is black as the wing of the raven, and is parted a la Madonna over a forehead where sits, girt round with her sister graces the very genius of poetic beauty, hope and love.

And then her eyes! they open their dark, rich orbs upon you like the full noon of heaven, and blaze into your very soul the fires of day! Like the offerings laid upon the sacrificial altars of the Hebrew, when in an instant the divine spark falling from the propitiated God kindled them in flames; so, a single glance from that oriental eye as quickly fires your soul, and leaves your bosom in a perfect conflagration! Odds Cupids and Darts! with one broad sweep of vision in a crowded ball-room, that splendid creature would lay around her like the two-handed sword of Minotti, hearts on hearts, piled round in semicircles! But it is well for the more rugged sex that this glorious being can vary her proud dominion, and give to the expression of her eye a melting tenderness which dissolves the most frigid heart and heals the wounds she gave before.

If the devout and exemplary Mussulman who dying fast in the faith of his Prophet, anticipates reclining on beds of roses, gloriously drunk through all the ages of eternity, is to be waited on by Houris such as these: waft me ye gentle gales beyond this lower world and,

"Lap me in soft Lydian airs"!

But I am falling into I know not what extravagances, so I will briefly give you a portrait of the last of these three divinities, and will then terminate my tiresome lucubrations.

This last is a Lilliputian beauty; diminutive in stature, fair haired, and with a foot for which Cinderella's slipper would be too large; a countenance sweet and interesting and in her manners eminently refined and engaging. The cast of her physiognomy is singularly mild and amiable, and her whole person is replete with every feminine grace. Her eyes,

"Effuse the mildness of their azure beam;"

and to her, above all her sex, are applicable the lines of our gentle Coleridge:

"Maid of my Love, sweet ———!
In beauty's light you glide along:
Your eye is like the star of eve,
And sweet your voice as seraph's song.
Yet not your heavenly beauty gives
This heart with passion soft to glow:
Within your soul a voice there lives!
It bids you hear the tale of woe.
When sinking low the sufferer wan
Beholds no hand outstretched to save,
Fair as the bosom of the swan
That rises graceful o'er the wave,
I've seen your breast with pity heave,
And therefore love I you sweet ———."

Here my dear M———, closes this catalogue of the Graces, this chapter of Beauties, and I should implore your pardon for trespassing so long on your attention. If you, yourself, in whose breast may possibly be extinguished the amatory flame, should not feel an interest in these three "counterfeit presentments," do not fail to show them to ——— and solicit her opinion as to their respective merits.

Tender my best acknowledgments to the Major for his prompt attention to my request, and, for yourself, accept the assurance of my undiminished regard; and hoping that the smiles of heaven may continue to illumine your way,

I remain, ever yours,

L. A. V.

No. 2

"Confusion seize the Greek!" exclaimed I, as wrathfully rising from my chair, I flung my ancient Lexicon across the room, and seizing my hat and cane, and throwing on my cloak, I sallied out into the clear air of heaven. The bracing coolness of an April evening calmed my aching temples, and I slowly wended my way to the river side. I had promenaded the bank for about half an hour, when flinging myself upon the grassy turf, I was soon lost in revery, and up to the lips in sentiment.

I had not lain more than five minutes, when a figure effectually concealed in the ample folds of a cloak, glided past me, and hastily dropping something at my feet, disappeared behind the angle of an adjoining house, ere I could recover from my astonishment at so singular an occurrence.—"Certes!" cried I, springing up, "here is a spice of the marvelous!" and stooping down, I picked up an elegant little, rose-coloured, lavender-scented billet-doux, and hurriedly breaking the seal (a heart, transfixed with an arrow) I read by the light of the moon, the following:

"Gentle Sir—

If my fancy has painted you in genuine colours, you will on the receipt of this, incontinently follow the bearer where she will lead you.

INAMORATA."

"The deuce I will!" exclaimed I,—"But soft!"—And I reperused this singular document, turned over the billet in my fingers, and examined the hand-writing; which was femininely delicate, and I could have sworn was a woman's. Is it possible, thought I, that the days of romance are revived?—No, "The days of chivalry are over!" says Burke.

As I made this reflection, I looked up, and beheld the same figure which had handed me this questionable missive, beckoning me forward. I started towards her; but, as I approached, she receded from me, and fled swiftly along the margin of the river at a pace, which, encumbered as I was with my heavy cloak and boots, I was unable to follow; and which filled me with sundry misgivings, as to the nature of the being, who could travel with such amazing celerity. At last perfectly breathless, I fell into a walk; which, my mysterious fugitive perceiving, she likewise lessened her pace, so as to keep herself still in sight, although at too great a distance to permit me to address her.

Having recovered from my fatigue and regained my breath: I loosened the clasp of my cloak, and inwardly resolving that I would come at the bottom of the mystery, I desperately flung the mantle from my shoulders, and dashing my beaver to the ground, gave chase in good earnest to the tantalizing stranger. No sooner did I from my extravagant actions announce my intention to overtake her, than with a light laugh of derision, she sprang forward at a rate, which in attempting to outstrip, soon left me far in the rear, heartily disconcerted and crest-fallen, and inly cursing the ignus fatuus, that danced so provokingly before me.

At length, like every one else, learning wisdom from experience; I thought my policy lay in silently following the footsteps of my eccentric guide, and quietly waiting the denouement of this extraordinary adventure. So soon as I relaxed my speed, and gave evidence of having renounced my more summary mode of procedure; the stranger, regulating her movements by mine, proceeded at a pace which preserved between us a uniform distance, ever and anon, looking back like a wary general to see if I were again inclined to try the mettle of her limbs.

After pursuing our way in this monotonous style for some time; I observed that my conductress rather abated in her precautions, and had not for the last ten or fifteen minutes taken her periodical survey over her shoulder; whereat, plucking up my spirits, which I can assure you courteous reader, had fallen considerably below zero by the ill-success of my previous efforts,—I again rushed madly forward at the summit of my speed, and having advanced ten or twelve rods unperceived, was flattering myself that I should this time make good my purpose; when, turning suddenly round, as though reminded of her late omission, and descrying me plunging ahead like an infuriated steed, she gave a slightly audible scream of surprise, and once more fled, as though helped forward by invisible wings.

This last failure was too much. I stopped short, and stamping the ground in ungovernable rage, gave vent to my chagrin in a volley of exclamations: in which, perhaps, if narrowly inspected, might have been detected two or three expressions which savored somewhat of the jolly days of the jolly cavaliers. But if a man was ever excusable for swearing; surely, the circumstances of the case were palliative of the crime. What! to be thwarted by a woman? Peradventure, baffled by a girl? Confusion! It was too bad! To be outgeneraled, routed, defeated, by a mere rib of the earth? It was not to be borne! I thought I should never survive the inexpressible mortification of the moment; and in the heighth of my despair, I bethought me of putting a romantic end to my existence upon the very spot which had witnessed my discomfiture.

But when the first transports of my wrath had passed away, and perceiving that the waters of the river, instead of presenting an unruffled calm, as they are wont to do on so interesting an occasion, were discomposed and turbid; and remembering, that beside this, I had no other means of accomplishing my heroic purpose, except the vulgar and inelegant one, of braining myself against the stone wall which traversed the road; I sensibly determined after taking into consideration the aforementioned particulars, together with the fact that I had an unfinished game of chess to win, on which depended no inconsiderable wager, that to commit suicide under such circumstances would be highly inexpedient, and probably be attended with many inconveniencies.—During the time I had consumed in arriving at this most wise and discreet conclusion, my mind had time to recover its former tone, and had become comparatively calm and collected; and I saw my folly in endeavoring to trifle with one, apparently so mysterious and inexplicable.

I now resolved, that whatever might betide, I would patiently await the issue of the affair: and advancing forward in the direction of my guide, who all this time had maintained her ground, stedfastly watching my actions,—we both simultaneously strode forward, and were soon on the same footing as before.

We walked on at an increased pace, and were just passed the suburbs of the town, when my conductress plunging into a neighboring grove, pursued her way with augmented speed, till we arrived at a spot, whose singular and grotesque beauty, even amidst the agitating occurrences of the evening I could not refrain from observing. A circular space of about a dozen acres in extent had been cleared in the very heart of the grove: leaving, however, two parallel rows of lofty trees, which at the distance of about twenty paces, and intersected in the centre by two similar ranges, traversed the whole diameter of the circle. These noble plants shooting their enormous trunks to an amazing heighth, bore their verdant honors far aloft, throwing their gigantic limbs abroad and embracing each other with their rugged arms. This fanciful union of their sturdy boughs formed a magnificent arch, whose grand proportions, swelling upward in proud preeminence, presented to the eye a vaulted roof, which to my perturbed imagination at the time, seemed to have canopied the triumphal feasts of the sylvan god.—This singular prospect burst upon me in all its beauty, as we emerged from the surrounding thicket, and I had unconsciously lingered on the borders of the wood, the better to enjoy so unrivalled a view; when as my eye was following the dusky outline of the grove, I caught the diminutive figure of my guide, who standing at the entrance of the arched-way I have been endeavoring to describe, was making the most extravagant gestures of impatience at my delay.—Reminded at once of the situation, which put me for a time under the control of this capricious mortal, I replied to her summons by immediately throwing myself forward, and we soon entered the Atlantean arbor, in whose umbrageous shades we were completely hid.

Lost in conjecture, during the whole of this eccentric ramble, as to its probable termination—the sombre gloom of these ancestral trees, gave a darkning hue to my imaginings, and I began to repent the inconsiderate haste which had hurried me on, in an expedition, so peculiar and suspicious. In spite of all my efforts to exclude them, the fictions of the nursery poured in upon my recollection, and I felt with Bob Acres in the "Rivals," that "my valor was certainly going." Once, I am almost ashamed to own it to thee, gentle reader, my mind was so haunted with ghostly images, that in an agony of apprehension, I was about to turn and flee, and had actually made some preliminary movements to that effect, when my hand, accidentally straying into my bosom, griped the billet, whose romantic summons had caused this nocturnal adventure. I felt my soul regain her fortitude, and smiling at the absurd conceits which infested my brain, I once more stalked proudly forward, under the overhanging branches of these ancient trees.

Emergent from the shades of this romantic region, we soon beheld an edifice, which seated on a gentle eminence, and embowered amidst surrounding trees, bore the appearance of a country villa; although its plain exterior showed none of those fantastic devices which usually adorn the elegant chateaux. My conductress as we neared this unpretending mansion seemed to redouble her precautions; and although she evinced no positive alarm, yet her quick and startled glances bespoke no small degree of apprehension. Motioning me to conceal myself behind an adjacent tree, she approached the house with rapid but cautious steps; my eyes followed her until she disappeared behind the shadow of the garden wall, and I remained waiting her reappearance with the utmost anxiety.—An interval of several moments had elapsed, when I descried her, swinging open a small postern, and beckoning me to advance. I obeyed the summons, and was soon by her side, not a little amazed at the complacency, which after what had transpired, brooked my immediate vicinity. Dissembling my astonishment, however, and rallying all my powers, I followed with noiseless strides the footsteps of my guide, fully persuaded that this mysterious affair was now about to be brought to an eclaircissement.

The appearance of this spacious habitation was any thing but inviting; it seemed to have been built with a jealous eye to concealment; and its few, but well-defended windows were sufficiently high from the ground, as effectually to baffle the prying curiosity of the inquisitive stranger. Not a single light shone from the narrow casement; but all was harsh, gloomy and forbidding. As my imagination, ever alert on such an occasion, was busily occupied in assigning some fearful motive for such unusual precautions; my leader suddenly halted beneath a lofty window, and making a low call, I perceived slowly descending therefrom, a thick silken chord, attached to an ample basket, which was silently deposited at our feet. Amazed at this apparition, I was about soliciting an explanation: when laying her fingers impressively upon her lips, and placing herself in the basket, my guide motioned me to seat myself beside her. I obeyed; but not without considerable trepidation: and in obedience to the same low call which had procured its descent our curious vehicle, with sundry creakings, rose in air.

To attempt an analysis of my feelings at this moment were impossible. The solemnity of the hour—the romantic nature of my present situation—the singularity of my whole adventure—the profound stillness which prevailed—the solitude of the place, were enough of themselves to strike a panic into the stoutest heart, and to unsettle the strongest nerves. But when to these, was added the thought,—that at the dead of night, and in the company of a being so perfectly inexplicable, I was effecting a clandestine entrance into so remarkable an abode: the kind and sympathising reader will not wonder, when I wished myself safely bestowed in my own snug quarters in ——— street.

Such were the reflections which passed through my mind, during our aerial voyage, throughout which my guide maintained the most rigid silence, only broken at intervals by the occasional creakings of our machine, as it rubbed against the side of the house in its ascent. No sooner had we gained the window, than two brawny arms were extended circling me in their embrace, and ere I was aware of the change of locality, I found myself standing upright in an apartment, dimly illuminated by a solitary taper. My fellow voyager was quickly beside me, and again enjoining silence with her finger, she seized the lamp and bidding me follow, conducted me through a long corridor, till we reached a low door concealed behind some old tapestry, which opening to the touch, disclosed a spectacle as beautiful and enchanting as any described in the Arabian Nights.

The apartment we now entered, was filled up in a style of Eastern splendor, and its atmosphere was redolent of the most delicious perfumes. The walls were hung round with the most elegant draperies, waving in graceful folds, on which were delineated scenes of Arcadian beauty. The floor was covered with a carpet of the finest texture, in which were wrought with exquisite skill, the most striking events in ancient mythology. Attached to the wall by chords composed of alternate threads of crimson silk and gold, were several magnificent pictures illustrative of the loves of Jupiter and Semele,—Psyche before the tribunal of Venus, and a variety of other scenes, limned all with felicitous grace. Disposed around the room, were luxurious couches, covered with the finest damask, on which were likewise executed after the Italian fashion the early fables of Greece and Rome. Tripods, designed to represent the Graces bearing aloft vases, richly chiseled in the classic taste, were distributed in the angles of the room, and exhaled an intoxicating fragrance.

Chandeliers of the most fanciful description, suspended from the lofty ceiling by rods of silver, shed over this voluptuous scene a soft and tempered light, and imparted to the whole, that dreamy beauty, which must be seen in order to be duly appreciated. Mirrors of unusual magnitude, multiplying in all directions the gorgeous objects, deceived the eye by their reflections, and mocked the vision with long perspective.

But overwhelming as was the display of opulence, it yielded in attraction to the being for whom all this splendour glistened; and the grandeur of the room served only to show to advantage the matchless beauty of its inmate. These superb decorations, though lavished in boundless profusion, were the mere accessories of a creature, whose loveliness was of that spiritual cast that depended upon no adventitious aid, and which as no obscurity could diminish, so, no art could heighten.

When I first obtained a glimpse of this lovely being, she lay reclining upon an ottoman; in one hand holding a lute, and with the other lost in the profusion of her silken tresses, she supported her head.—I could not refrain from recalling the passionate exclamation of Romeo:

> "See how she leans her cheek upon her hand;
> Oh! that I were a glove upon that hand,
> That I might kiss that cheek!"

She was habited in a flowing robe of the purest white, and her hair, escaping from the fillet of roses which had bound it, spread its negligent graces over neck and bosom and shoulder, as though unwilling to reveal the extent of such transcendant charms.—Her zone was of pink satin, on which were broidered figures of Cupid in the act of drawing his bow; while the ample folds of her Turkish sleeve were gathered at the wrist by a bracelet of immense rubies, each of which represented a heart pierced thro' by a golden shaft. Her fingers were decorated with a variety of rings, which as she waved her hand to me as I entered, darted forth a thousand coruscations, and gleamed their brilliant splendors to the sight. Peeping from beneath the envious skirts of her mantle, and almost buried in the downy quishion on which it reposed, lay revealed the prettiest little foot you can imagine; cased in a satin slipper, which clung to the fairy-like member by means of a diamond clasp.

As I entered the apartment, her eyes were downcast, and the expression of her face was mournfully interesting; she had apparently been lost in some melancholy revery. Upon my entrance, however, her countenance brightened, as with a queenly wave of the hand, she motioned my conductress from the room, and left me standing, mute, admiring and bewildered in her presence.

For a moment my brain spun round, and I had not at command a single one of my faculties. Recovering my self possession however, and with that, my good-breeding, I advanced en cavalier, and gracefully sinking on one knee, I bowed my head and exclaimed—"Here do I prostrate myself, thou sweet Divinity, and kneel at the shrine of thy peerless charms!"—I hesitated,—blushed, looked up, and beheld bent upon me a pair of Andalusian eyes, whose melting earnestness of expression pierced me to the soul, and I felt my heart dissolving away like ice before the equinoctial heats.

Alas! For all the vows of eternal constancy I had sworn to another!—The silken threads were snapped asunder; the golden chords had parted! A new dominion was creeping o'er my soul, and I fell, bound at the feet of my fair enchantress. A moment of unutterable interest passed, while I met the gaze of this glorious being with a look as ardent, as burning, as steadfast as her own.—But it was not in mortal woman to stand the glance of an eye which had never quailed before a foe; and whose fierce lightnings were now playing in the wild expression of a love, that rent my bosom like a whirlwind, and tore up my past attachments as though they were but of the growth of yesterday.—The long dark lashes fell!

smothered were the fires, whose brightness had kindled my soul in flames! I seized the passive hand, I lifted it to my lips and covered it with burning kisses! "Fair mortal!" I exclaimed, "I feel my passion is requited: but, seal it with thy own sweet voice, or I shall expire in uncertainty!"

Those lustrous orbs again opened on me all their fires; and maddened at her silence, I caught her in my arms, and imprinting one long, long kiss upon her hot and glowing lips, I cried "Speak! Tell me, thou cruel! Does thy heart send forth vital fluid like my own? Am I loved,—even wildly, madly as I love?" She was silent; gracious God! what horrible apprehension crossed my soul?—Frantic with the thought, I held her from me, and looking in her face, I met the same impassioned gaze; her lips moved—my senses ached with the intensity with which I listened,—all was still,—they uttered no sound; I flung her from me, even though she clung to my vesture, and with a wild cry of agony I burst from the apartment!—She was dumb! Great God, she was dumb! DUMB AND DEAF!

L. A. V.

Etchings of a Whaling Cruise

Etchings of a Whaling Cruise, with Notes of a Sojourn on the Island of Zanzibar. To which is appended, a Brief History of the Whale Fishery; its Past and Present Condition. By J. Ross Browne. Illustrated with numerous Engravings on Steel and Wood. Harper & Brothers: 1846. 8vo.

Sailors' Life and Sailors' Yarns. By Captain Ringbolt. New York: C. S. Francis & Co. 1847. 12mo.

FROM TIME IMMEMORIAL many fine things have been said and sung of the sea. And the days have been, when sailors were considered veritable mermen; and the ocean itself, as the peculiar theatre of the romantic and wonderful. But of late years there have been revealed so many plain, matter-of-fact details connected with nautical life that at the present day the poetry of salt water is very much on the wane. The perusal of Dana's Two Years Before The Mast, for instance, somewhat impairs the relish with which we read Byron's spiritual address to the ocean. And when the noble poet raves about laying his hands upon the ocean's mane (in other words manipulating the crest of a wave) the most vivid image suggested is that of a valetudinarian bather at Rockaway, spluttering and choaking in the surf, with his mouth full of brine.

Mr J. Ross Browne's narrative tends still further to impair the charm with which poesy and fiction have invested the sea. It is a book of unvarnished facts; and with some allowances for the general application of an individual example unquestionably presents a faithful picture of the life led by the 20 thousand seamen employed in the 700 whaling vessels which pursue their game under the American flag. Indeed, what Mr Dana has so admirably done in describing the vicissitudes of the merchant sailor's life, Mr Browne has very creditably achieved with respect to that of the hardy whaleman's. And the book which possesses this merit deserves much in the way of commendation. The personal narrative interwoven with it, also, can not fail to enlist our sympathies for the adventurous author himself. The scenes presented are always graphicly and truthfully sketched, and hence fastidious objections may be made to some of them, on the score of their being too coarsly or harshly drawn. But we take it, that as true unreserved descriptions they are in no respect faulty—and doubtless the author never dreamed of softening down or withholding anything with a view of rendering his sketches the more attractive and pretty. The book is eminently a practical one; and written with the set purpose of accomplishing good by revealing the simple truth. When the brutal tyranny of the Captain of the "Styx" is painted without apology or palliation, it holds up the outrageous abuse to which seamen in our whaling marine are actually subjected, a matter which demands legislation. Mr Browne himself—it seems, was to some extent, the victim of the tyranny of which he complains, and, upon this ground, the personal bitterness in which he at times indulges may be deemed excusable, though it is rather out of place.

As the book professes to embrace a detailed account of all that is interesting in the business of whaling, and, essentially, possesses this merit, one or two curious errors into which the author has unaccountably fallen may, without captiousness, be pointed out.—We are told, for example, of a whale's *roaring* when wounded by the harpoon. We can imagine the veteran Coffins and Colemans and Maceys of old Nantucket elevating their brows at the bare announcement of such a thing. Now the creature in question is as dumb as a shad, or any other of the finny tribes. And no doubt, if Jonah himself could be summoned to the stand, he would cheerfully testify to his not having heard a single syllable, growl, grunt, or bellow engendered in the ventricle cells of the leviathan, during the irksome period of his incarceration therein.

That in some encounters with the sperm whale a low indistinct sound *apparently* issues from the monster is true enough. But all Nantucket and New Bedford are divided as to the causes which produce the phenomenon. Many suppose, however, that it is produced—not by the creature itself—but by the peculiar motion in the water of the line which is attached to the harpoon. For, if upon being struck, the whale "sounds" (descends) as is usually the case, and remains below the surface for any length of time, the rope frequently becomes as stiff as the cord of a harp and the struggles of the animal keep it continually vibrating.

Considering the disenchanting nature of the revelations of sea life with which we are presented in Mr Browne's book we are inclined to believe that the shipping agents employed in our various cities by the merchants of New Bedford will have to present additional inducements to "enterprising and industrious young Americans of good moral character" in order to persuade them to embark in the fishery. In particular the benevolent old gentleman in Front Street (one of the shipping agents of whom our author discourseth) who so politely accosted Browne and his comrade, upon their entering his office for the purpose of seeking further information touching the rate of promotion in the whaling service—this old gentleman, we say, must hereafter infuse into his address still more of the *suaviter in modo.*

As unaffectedly described by Browne the scene alluded to is irresistably comic. The agent's business, be it understood, consists in decoying "green hands" to send on to the different whaling ports. A conspicuous placard without the office announces to the anxious world, that a few choice vacancies remain to be filled in certain crews of whalemen about to sail upon the most delightful voyages imaginable (only four years long)— To secure a place, of course, instant application should be made.

Our author and his friend attracted by the placard, hurry up a ladder to a dark loft above, where the old man lurks like a spider in the midst of his toils.—But a single glance at the gentlemanly dress and white hands of his visitors impresses the wily agent with the idea that notwithstanding their calling upon him, they may very possibly have heard disagreeable accounts of the nature of whaling. So, after making a bow, and offering a few legs of a chair, he proceeds to disabuse their minds of any unfavorable impressions.—Succeeding in this, he then becomes charmingly facetious and complimentary; assuring the youths that they need not be concerned because of their slender waists and silken muscles; for those who employed him were not so particular about weight as beauty. In short the captains of whaling vessels preferred handsome young fellows who dressed well and conversed genteelly—in short, those who would reflect credit upon the business of tarring down rigging and cutting up blubber. Delighted with the agreeable address of the old gentleman and with many pleasant anticipations of sea-life the visitors listen with increased attention. Whereupon the agent waxes eloquent, and enlarges upon his animating theme in the style parliamentary. "A whaler, gentlemen" he observes "is the home of the unfortunate—the asylum of the oppressed &c &c &c"

Duped Browne! Hapless H———! In the end, they enter into an engagement with the old gentleman, who subsequently sends them on to New Bedford consigned to a mercantile house there. From New Bedford the adventurers at length sail in a small whaling barque bound to the Indian ocean. While yet half dead with sea sickness the unfortunate H——— is sent by the brutal captain to the mast-head, to stand there his allotted two hours on the look out for whale-spouts. He receives a stroke of the sun, which, for a time, takes away his reason and endangers his life. He raves of home and friends, and poor Browne watching by his side, upbraids himself for having been concerned in bringing his companion to such a state.—Ere long the vessel touches at the Azores, where H——— being altogether unfit for duty is left to be sent home by the American consul.

He never recovered from the effects of his hardships; for in the sequel Browne relates that after reaching home himself, he visited his old friend in Ohio, and found him still liable to temporary prostrations directly referable to his sufferings at sea.

With a heavy heart our author after leaving the Azores weathers the Cape of Good Hope and enters upon the Indian ocean. The ship's company—composed mostly of ignorant, half-civilized Portuguese from the Western Islands—are incessantly quarrelling and fighting; the provisions are of the most wretched kind;—their success in the fishery is small; and to crown all, the captain himself is the very incarnation of all that is dastardly, mean, and heartless.

We can not follow Browne through all his adventures. Suffice it to say, that heartily disgusted with his situation he at length, with great difficulty, succeeds in leaving the vessel on the coast of Zanzibar. Here he tarries for some months, and his residence in this remote region (the Eastern coast of Africa, near Madagascar) enables him to make sundry curious observations upon men and things, of which the reader of his work has the benefit. From Zanzibar he ultimately sails for home in a merchant brig; and at last arrives in Boston thoroughly out of conceit of the ocean.

Give ear, now, all ye shore-disdaining, ocean-enamored youths, who labor under the lamentable delusion, that the sea—the "glorious sea" is always and in reality "the blue, the fresh, the ever free!" Give ear to Mr J. Ross Browne, and hearken unto what that experienced young gentleman has to say about the manner in which Barry Cornwall has been humbugging the rising generation on this subject.—Alas! Hereafter we shall never look upon an unsophisticated stripling in flowing "duck" trowsers and a bright blue jacket, loitering away the interval which elapses before sailing on his maiden cruise, without mourning over the hard fate in store for him.—In a ship's forecastle, alas, he will find no Psyche glass in which to survey his picturesque attire. And the business of making his toilet will be comprised in trying to keep as dry and comfortable as the utter absence of umbrellas, wet decks, and leaky forecastles will admit of.—We shudder at all realities of the career they will be entering upon. The long, dark, cold night-watches, which, month after month, they must battle out the best way they can,—the ship pitching and thumping against the bullying waves—every plank dripping—every jacket soaked—and the Captain not at all bland in issuing his order for the poor fellows to mount aloft in the icy sleet and howling tempest.—"Bless me, Captain, go way up there this excessively disagreeable night?"—"Aye up with you, you lubber—*bare*, I say, or look out for squalls"—a figurative expression, conveying a remote allusion to the hasty application of a sea-bludgeon to the head.

Then the whaling part of the business.—My young friends, just fancy yourselves, for the first time in an open boat (so slight that three men might walk off with it) some 12 or 15 miles from your ship and about a hundred times as far from the nearest land, giving chase to one of the oleaginous monsters. "Pull, Pull, you lubberly *hay-makers!*" cries the boat-header jumping up and down in the stern-sheets in a frenzy of professional excitement, while the gasping admirers of Captain Marryat and the sea, tug with might and main at the buckling oars—"Pull, Pull, I say; Break your lazy backs!" Presently the whale is within "darting distance" and you hear the roar of the waters in his wake.—How palpitating the hearts of the frightened oarsmen at this interesting juncture! My young friends, just turn round and snatch a look at that whale—. There he goes, surging through the brine, which ripples about his vast head as if it were the bow of a ship. Believe me, it's quite as terrible as going into battle to a raw recruit.

"Stand up and give it to him!" shrieks the boat-header at the steering-oar to the harpooneer in the bow. The latter drops his oar and snatches his "iron". It flies from his hands—and where are we then, my lovelies?—It's all a mist, a crash,—a horrible blending of sounds and sights, as the agonized whale lashes the water around him into suds and vapor—dashes the boat aside, and at last rushes, madly, through the water towing after him the half-filled craft which rocks from side to side while the disordered crew, clutch at the gunwale to avoid being tossed out. Meanwhile all sorts of horrific edged tools—lances, harpoons and spades—are slipping about; and the imminent line itself—smoking round the logger-head and passing along the entire length of the boat—is almost death to handle, though it grazes your person.

But all this is nothing to what follows. As yet you have but simply *fastened* to the whale: he must be fought and killed. But let imagination supply the rest:—the monster staving the boat with a single sweep of his ponderous flukes;—taking its bows between his jaws (as is frequently the case) and playing with it, as a cat with a mouse. Sometimes he bites it in twain; sometimes crunches it into chips, and strews the sea with them. —But we forbear. Enough has been said to convince the uninitiated what sort of a vocation whaling in truth is. If further information is desired, Mr Browne's book is purchasable in which they will find the whole matter described in all its interesting details.

After reading the "Etchings of a Whaling Cruise" a perusal of "Sailors' Life and Sailors' Yarns" is in one respect at least like hearing "the other side of the question". For, while Browne's is a "Voice from the Forecastle" Captain Ringbolt hails us from the quarter deck, the other end of the ship. Browne gives us a sailor's version of sailors' wrongs, and is not altogether free from prejudices acquired during his little experience on ship board; Captain Ringbolt almost denies that the sailor has any wrongs and more than insinuates that sea-captains are not only the best natured fellows in the world but that they have been sorely maligned. Indeed he explicitly charges Mr Dana and Mr Browne with having presented a decidedly one sided view of the matter. And he mournfully exclaims that the Captain of the Pilgrim—poor fellow!—died too soon to vindicate his character from unjust aspersions.

—Now as a class ship owners are seldom disposed partially to judge the captains in their employ. And yet we know of a verity that at least one of the owners of the Pilgrim,—an esteemed citizen of the good old town of Boston—will never venture to dispute that to the extent of his knowledge at least Mr Dana's captain was a most "strict and harsh disciplinarian", which words so applied by a ship owner, mean that the man in question was nothing less than what Mr Dana describes him to have been.—But where is Browne's captain? He is alive and hearty we presume. Let him come forward then and show why he ought not to be regarded in the decidedly unfavorable light in which he is held up to us in the narrative we have noticed? Now for ought we know to the contrary this same Captain of the Styx—who was such a heartless domineering tyrant at sea—may be quite a different character ashore. In truth we think this very probable. For the god Janus never had two more decidedly different faces than your sea captain. Ashore his Nautical

Highness has nothing to ruffle him—friends grasp him by the hand and are overjoyed to see him after his long absence—he is invited out and relates his adventures pleasantly and everybody thinks what lucky dogs his sailors must have been to have sailed with such a capital fellow.

—But let poor Jack have a word to say—Why Sir, he will tell you that when they embarked His Nautical Highness left behind him all his "quips and cranks and wanton smiles". Very far indeed is the Captain from cracking any of his jokes with his crew—that would be altogether too condescending. But then there is no reason why he should bestow a curse every time he gives an order—there is no reason why he should never say a word of kindness or sympathy to his men. True; in this respect all sea captains are not alike but still there is enough truth in both Mr Dana's and Mr Browne's statements to justify nearly to the full, the general conclusions to be drawn from what they have said on this subject.—

But Captain Ringbolt's book is very far from being a mere plea for the class to which he belongs.—What he has to say upon the matter is chiefly contained in one brief sketch under the head of Sailors' Rights and Sailors' Wrongs.—The rest of the book is made up of little stories of the sea, simply and pleasantly told and withall entertaining.

Authentic Anecdotes of "Old Zack"

[Reported for YANKEE DOODLE by his special correspondent at the seat of War]

AT THE PRESENT TIME when everything connected with the homespun old hero is perused with unusual interest, and unprincipled paragraphists daily perpetrate the most absurd stories wherewith to titilate public curiosity concerning him, YANKEE DOODLE has thought that a few authentic anecdotes may not be unacceptable to his numerous readers.

They have been collected on the ground from the most reliable and respectable sources, (of course we refer to the anecdotes and not our readers, who every one knows are both respectable and reliable;) and we have the very best reason to believe have never before appeared in print.

Since we are determined to have all the credit of first circulating these anecdotes, be it here known, that YANKEE DOODLE, with his customary enterprise and utter recklessness of all expense where the diversion of his readers is concerned, has sent on a correspondent to the seat of war for the express purpose of getting together and transmitting to us all reliable *on dits* connected with old ZACK: And here we cannot refrain from noticing the flattering reception which our esteemed correspondent received from the venerable hero himself. No sooner did the valiant General hear of his arrival and the object of his visit, than he forthwith bestrided his historic nag and galloped through the camp to meet him, and conduct him to his quarters, where our aforesaid esteemed correspondent is now permanently domiciled as one of the General's family.

Our correspondent moreover informs us that the General was exceedingly delighted at the object of the visit, inasmuch as the fabular anecdotes which he had seen in the papers had greatly scandalized him. "Sir," said he, striking his longitudinal posterior with his clenched hand (a habit of his when greatly excited) "they are making a downright ass of me there at the North—those infernal editors deserve a sound thrashing for hatching such a pack of lies—they do, indeed." Nor was this all that the choleric old hero observed. But as we do not desire further to expose a little weakness of his which the papers have occasionally hinted at, and which he has in common with Gen. JACKSON and other military heroes—namely, that of profane swearing when in a violent passion—we will disclose nothing more on this head. Suffice it to say, that after venting his ire upon the anecdote-making editors of the North the old hero expressed his unbounded satisfaction at the prospect of henceforth having his most trifling actions and sayings faithfully chronicled by a man of purity. He also expressed his intention to further our laudable object in every possible way—immediately gave our correspondent the privilege of his shot box (upon which the General's famous dispatches are written) and agreed to frank all his communications to YANKEE DOODLE.

So eager was the old hero to prevent for the future the circulation of any but authentic anecdotes concerning him, that without solicitation on the part of our esteemed correspondent, he furnished him with a written certificate, to be published in YANKEE DOODLE, asserting our columns to be the only true source where an anxious public can procure a correct insight into his private life and little personal peculiarities.

The certificate, we have caused to be placed in a brass frame cast from a captured Mexican forty-two brass shot. It occupies a conspicuous place in our office, where it may be seen from 9 A.M. till 3 1-2 P.M. every day, Sundays excepted.

The certificate runs thus:

> This is to certify that the undersigned hereby authorises Mr. YANKEE DOODLE to publish and circulate such illustrative stories and anecdotes of the undersigned, as may be transmitted to Mr. YANKEE DOODLE by the highly respectable correspondent who has recently been sent into the camp for that purpose.
>
> And the undersigned hereby declares that all other stories and anecdotes which may be hereafter published in any other columns than

YANKEE DOODLE's, are base and malignant publications, mostly of no credence, and strongly suspected to be a covert attempt on the part of the enemies of the undersigned to injure his reputation with the people of the United States with a view of defeating his election to the presidency should he run for that office.

MAJOR GENERAL Z. TAYLOR.

CAMP NEAR ——— *June 3d*, 1847.

This much by way of introducing the anecdotes, which here follow regularly numbered, and in the order in which they are sent us.

ANECDOTE I

It is well known that upon the battle field the hero of Palo Alto is as cool as a Roman Punch. His surprising self-collectedness and imperturbability in times of the greatest peril, was never more forcibly shown than in a little circumstance at Buena Vista.

A Mexican mortar being in full play upon the front of the American columns, a large shell with the burning fusee fizzing at the aperture weighing hard on 200 cwt: fell directly at the feet of old Zack, who, with his characteristic contempt of danger, was sitting on his horse upon a conspicuous knoll and was surrounded by several of his staff. Thinking it altogether fool-hardy and supererogatory to stand still and be blown to pieces, the officers betrayed no delicacy in instantly galloping out of harm's way. But old ZACK moved not a peg. "Don't be alarmed, gentlemen," he observed quietly, shifting his attitude by throwing the other leg on the neck of his horse—"don't be alarmed—them 'are chaps don't bust always. What will you wager now, Major BLISS, that the fusee doesn't go out afore harm's done?"* While the Major at a good distance leveled his long spy glass at the globular apparition, the old hero calmly took out his spectacles, polished their glasses by rubbing them gently against his thigh—clapped them on his nose—descended, and approaching the shell, bent over and closely scrutinized the fusee. It had just burnt to within a

* In all cases we give the old man's very words. If they show a want of early attendance at the Grammar School, it must be borne in mind that old ZACK never took a college diploma—was cradled in the backwood camp—and rather glories in the simplicity and unostentation of his speech. "Describe me, Sir," said he to our correspondent,—"describe me, Sir, as I am—no polysyllables—no stuff—it's time they should know me in my true light."

hair's breadth of the inflammable bowels of the shell—and old ZACK taking it between his fore finger and thumb, drew forth the fusee and waving it towards his aghast officers, quietly observed that if any of them had a cigar to smoke he could supply them with a light.

P. S. to *Anecdote, No.* 1.—Mr. BARNUM happening to drop in when we opened our communications from our correspondent, we read him the above. He immediately seized pen and ink and wrote to a military acquaintance of his in the army, to institute a diligent search after the above mentioned shell—pack up carefully in cotton and send it on for his Museum with all possible despatch. Thinking, however, that the search might not prove effectual, Mr. BARNUM has given orders for a shell of the proper dimensions to be cast at one of the foundries up town. We feel confident, however, in stating that the latter will not be exhibited for the genuine article, unless the genuine article fails to come to hand.

ANECDOTE II

The Cincinnatus-like simplicity and unaffectedness of old ZACK's habits have frequently been celebrated. But it is not commonly known, perhaps, that he generally does his own washing. Of a pleasant evening, after the war-like toils of the day are closed, the old hero may be seen at the opening of his tent, sitting plump on the ground with a camp-kettle between his legs—and with shirt sleeves rolled up, creating a loud splashing of his garments in the suds. The old General by the way, wholly excludes hard soap as an unsoldier-like luxury, and uses nothing but the soft; a barrel of which furnishes part of his tent furniture.

The old hero, however, on account of his eye sight, is not very nimble with the needle. Nevertheless, he insists upon doing his own mending, and particularly prides himself upon the neatness and expedition with which he puts a new seat in his ample pants. These nether garments, of course, require frequent repairs, owing to the constant practice, and the habit the old hero has of violently slapping his person when excited. At Buena Vista his being a long time in the saddle, united to the ire-provoking and dastardly conduct of the Illinois regiments, came near entirely rending them in pieces and it was late that night before the General retired, as he always makes it a principle not to permit his basket of new clothes to accumulate.

SIMPLICITY OF OLD ZACK'S HABITS.

From *Yankee Doodle*, II, No. 43 (July 31, 1847), [165].

At Monterey, when the deputies from Gen. Ampudia first ushered the old hero at his quarters, they found him sitting cross-legged upon a gun carriage and earnestly engaged in letting out the seams of his coat—a proceeding necessitated by his increasing bulkiness.

Anecdote III

Old Zack's insensibility to bodily pain is almost equal to his utter indifference to danger. The following little incident will illustrate what we mean. The morning preceding one of his battles, a mischievous young drummer boy came up to the orderly, who, just without the tent, was holding the General's horse ready accoutred for mounting, and offered to relieve him a few moments at the duty. The offer was accepted, and off went the orderly leaving the lad in his place. What now does the young rascal do, but cunningly insert a sharp iron tack, point upwards, into the august saddle of the hero of Palo Alto. Shortly after, the orderly returned to his post, and the General sprang into his saddle and galloped off. He did not dismount for several hours, during all of which time, according to the experience of school boys, the tack must have been within the closest possible vicinity of a rather sensitive part. But, wonderful to relate, the illustrious Zack never betrayed the slightest consciousness of the presence of what an ordinary man would have deemed no small annoyance. But at evening when he dismounted at the door of his tent, he was most unexpectedly made aware of what must have seemed to him, at the time, a base and pitiful trick of the enemy. The tack caught in the seat of his inexpressibles, and as he sprang to the ground, would not let go, but left the greater part of the garment upon the saddle. Though valiant as Cid, the old hero is as modest as any miss. Instantly muffling up with his coat tails the exposed part, he hurried into his tent, violently and most perfectly enraged at the occurrence.

The outrage was at once imputed to some lurking Mexican spy, concealed in the camp, and as soon as Major Bliss could prepare it, the following proclamation was forthwith made by sound of trumpet:

PROCLAMATION

"The abominable insult offered to the American nation in the diabolical outrage upon the person of the Commanding General calls for the most active measures to discover and condignly punish the author. He is strongly suspected to be one of the Mexican rancheros, observed prowling in the vicinity of the camp yesterday. Any one, whether officer or private, who will apprehend the offender and bring the scoundrel to the General's quarters shall have his name honorably mentioned in the next dispatch to the War Department."

The drummer-boy, however, never was found out. But no sooner did Secretary MARCY receive the dispatch announcing the circumstance to Government, than a generous sympathy prompted him at once to address an unofficial and very friendly letter to the old hero, condoling with him upon the occurrence. He suggested, as a piece of friendly advice, also, that the General had better keep dark about the matter, since he (Secretary MARCY) knew by experience that any thing touching one's inexpressibles was calculated to provoke vulgar mirth. With his customary straightforwardness, however, Old ZACK announced his resolution not to disguise or suppress the fact—and to the utter consternation of his military family, BARNUM's letter audaciously begging the torn garment for exhibition at his Museum here, was promptly and favorably answered. The public may therefore rely upon soon having a peep at the inexpressibles in which Old ZACK has *so often cased his valiant legs!*

Note.—Yesterday YANKEE DOODLE forwarded to BARNUM the following draught of a placard for the occasion:

"PRODIGIOUS EXCITEMENT!!!!!!

OLD ZACK'S PANTS!!!

GREAT SIGHTS AT THE AMERICAN MUSEUM!!!

OLD ROUGH AND READY!

UP TOWN EMPTIED OF ITS INHABITANTS!

TOM THUMB FLOORED!

The Proprietor of the American Museum has the honor to announce to the American public that at vast expense and trouble he has succeeded in regulating an arrangement whereby the identical sheep-greys worn by Old Rough and Ready at the celebrated engagement of Resaca de la Palma, will be exhibited for three days in a glass case. Also, in a sealed vial, the poisoned Mexican tack taken from the old hero's saddle, and which came near being his death.

Certificates from Major BLISS, GEN. BRAGG, and other distinguished officers of the army will be shown proving the articles genuine.

Take notice: The exhibition will certainly close upon the third day.

Admittance twenty-five cents, &c. &c. &c."

[In lieu of anything of his own our correspondent has furnished us this week the following vivid and powerful description of the personal appearance of Old ZACK, which, from his private note to us, he appears to have procured from a friend in the army, with no little difficulty. We call the attention of our readers to its bold and massive English.]

"GEN. TAYLOR'S PERSONAL APPEARANCE,"

OR OLD ZACK PHYSIOLOGICALLY AND OTHERWISE CONSIDERED

BY A SURGEON OF THE ARMY IN MEXICO

The hero of Buena Vista, upon the crown of whose caput have descended so many interleaved chaplets of fame, presents in his general exterior personal appearance many of those extraordinary characteristics distinctive of the noble spirit tabernacled within. Of about the common length of ordinary mortals—say about five feet, nine inches, and two barley corns, Long Measure—he rather leans to a squat colossalness of frame and universal spread of figure, particularly on the lower part of the abdominal regions. To counteract a bulging forth of the latter parts, he is said to wear a truss of peculiar conformation. This circumstance, however, is not as yet fully established. Of a thick set and quadratular build, he now inclines to tenuity in the parts lying round about the calf. Originally of great agility of the locomotive apparatus, he now betrays on his partially denuded head a want of energy in the capillary tubes of the hair, as his digestive machinery is liable to frequent suspensions of activity.

His broad and expanded chest shows the hero fully capable of encountering the prodigious fatigues of war, whether in the interminably interlocked everglades of the Floridian southerly terminus of the Republic, or upon the wide-spreading and generally level table-land savannahs of Mexico. His face is a physiognomical phenomenon, which Lavater would have crossed the Atlantic to contemplate. Of soul-awing determination of expression and significant of inflexible and immovable ironness of purpose, it (the external features of the countenance) are softened down and melted into a kindly benevolence which would prepossess a perfect stranger in his favor. His head is large, extremely well developed in the frontal quarter, but not classically elegant in the anterior portion. To employ an expressive, though somewhat rude comparison, it appears as if *squashed* between his shoulders. By close observers, the lobe of the right ear is thought to be depressed more than the corresponding auricular organ, on the opposite lateral part of the caput.

In early adolescence of a beautiful amber or brown color, the hair, through the gradual ravages of time, has assumed a speckled, pepper and salt external appearance. In a most touching manner the thin and scattered locks are parted picturesquely on one side and combed slickly over the brows. The latter are Jupiternian in their awful bushiness—the hairy appendage curling over upon the optic orbits. His frown is Olympian and strikes terror and confusion into the overwhelmed soul of the spectator. The muscular energy of the brows is truly extraordinary. When ever their pupular is under mental excitation, they frequently become knit together in wrinkular pleats like unto the foldular developments under the lateral shoulder of the rhinoceros species of animated nature. His eye is Websternian, though grey. The left organ somewhat affects the dexter side of the socket, while examined by a powerful telescope several minute specks are observable in the pupil of the sinister orbit. But this detracts not from the majesty of its expression: the sun even has its spots. When the hero's soul is lashed into intellectual agitation by the external occurrence of irritating and stimulating circumstance, the eye assumes an inflamed and fiery appearance. The scantiness of the lashes and their short and singed appearance are ascribable, perhaps, to their vicinity to the pupil when thus kindled into fury. When a mental calm, however, pervades the serene soul of the hero, a Saucernian placidity is diffused over the entire visionary orb.

The nostrilian organ, or proboscis, is straight, but neither inclining to the Roman, or Grecian, or, indeed, the Doric or Composite order of nasal architecture. The labial appendages (suspended just under the proboscis) are attenuated—the upper tightly and firmly spread upon the dental parts beneath; and the lower pendant and projecting as represented in the prints. The outline of the caput, generally, is an ovalular ellipsis inclining to the rotund, but having no predisposition to the quadrangular. The obvious cuticle or scarf-skin is wrinkled, freckled, and embrowned—doubtless through age and constant exposure to the ardent rays of the Floridian and Mexicanian sun combined.

The manner of the hero is frank and companionable—and never did mortal leave his society without being constantly impressed with the unavoidable conviction that he had been conversing with a good fellow and a gentleman.

At times he is seen in deep and earnest meditation—the left auricular organ with the head attached thereto, deposited upon the open palm and outspread digits of the manual termination of the arm. At other times he assumes when meditating quite a different posture; the fore finger of the left hand being placed on the dexter side of the proboscis.

In his military discipline, he is firm and unyielding to the last degree of military inflexibility—but is, nevertheless, remarkably lenient to those under him, officers and privates included. Particularly to the youthful portion of his command, whom he treats with all the indulgence of a paternal relative or guardian—often permitting them to lay a-bed late in the morning, when the battle is raging at the fiercest.

In his general toilet he is far from imitating a Brummellian precision and starchedness of cravat. He has no violent predilection for his regimentals and seldom appears in them, which, in fact, is the case with most of his officers, of whom it is even observed, that "*they seldom appear in externals on duty*,"—a habit indicative of superiority to foppish adornments, but might be construed by the fastidious into a want of good taste and decorousness.

Their custom in this respect, however, is defensible upon the ground, that called by Divine Providence to perform their martial functions in the genial and delightful regions of the sunny south, the cumbersome military costume, or, indeed, any dress at all, "*is disagreeable to the physical feelings.*"

The hero himself may be usually seen by an ordinary spectator arrayed in a pair of sheep's grey pants, shapeless and inclined to bagging—the latter predisposition being imputed, by a reflecting observer, to the singular fact that the hero never wears the common-place articles called suspenders. His coat is generally of a brownish tinge which in some cases is to be imputed to the original color imparted to the cloth when in the vat of the dyer, and in other cases to an heroic disregard of dust and oleaginous spots on the part of the ungent wearer. His vest usually, though not invariably, is of a darksome hue—resembling the ordinary sable. He wears a long crumpled black silk neck-handkerchief, much knotted and super-twisted, and evidently not put on with any great degree of care. But the carelessness with which it is tied in no respect approaches to the studied artlessness of the Byronic bow. The shirt collar is open, revealing considerable superfluous hair just above the region of the thorax and windpipe, and betokening a disdain of Gouraud's Depillatory. Several individual hairs partake of the greyish tinge of the sparse covering of the head.

The hero sometimes wears a white wool hat, much marked by indentation and irregular depressions and prominences upon the crown. It resembles in most respects the castor of a Mississippi flat-boatman.—His shoes are the common cow-hide sandals served out by the Commissary Department to the free use of the army. They are usually stringless and not much polished.

Anecdote IV

In the words of the gallant Count Hamilton, "War is but one half the glory of heroes." So with the valiant Zack. Years ago, ere 'rose the sun at Palo Alto, or fled the Mexican host at Buena Vista, Old Rough and Ready was every bit as good and true a man, and every whit the hero he is now acknowledged to be. What has he done, but stepped forward to the foot-lights, to receive the applause he deserves? And here let Yankee Doodle slip in a sentence, and swear that no lungs are louder, no hands clapped so heartily, and no stick thumped more vehemently than his. Aye! thrice three times three for old Zack, and, "Damned be he that says Hold, enough." Never mind denting your hats, my lads; toss them into the air!—hurrah! And the ladies, God bless their sweet hearts, how their cambric waves!

It is not our purpose, however, merely to sit perched upon the old hero's shoulder and crow his triumphs; as faithful chroniclers we have something else in view—the circulation of authentic anecdotes, tending to elucidate his character.

And now for something good—nothing less, my countrymen, than the private letters of condolement, hitherto unpublished and unheard of, addressed by old Zack to Santa Anna and other Mexican Generals, upon their successive defeats on the field.

P.S. by Yankee Doodle.—It was never intended by their illustrious author that these letters of his should be published. They were written from the dictates of pure and unostentatious benevolence, and solely for the tearful eyes of those to whom they were addressed.

"D—— me, Sir," exclaimed old ZACK, upon our correspondent begging him for copies of the documents in question;—"D—— me, Sir, you can't have 'em! I'll not consent to it—why, you are worse than BARNUM himself, who, yesterday, Major BLISS tells me, wrote on for my private tobacco box, sending a tortoise-shell one as a substitute. No, Sir, those letters can't be published."

"But, my dear Sir, consider the duty you owe to history—to the world—to your own reputation—"

"Well, well—let him have 'em, Major."

And so here they are:

PRIVATE LETTER

ADDRESSED BY MAJOR GENERAL ZACHARY TAYLOR TO GENERAL SANTA ANNA ON THE EVENING SUCCEEDING THE BATTLE OF BUENA VISTA.

NOTE.—The autograph letter presents a remarkable appearance. The characters are almost illegible, and, from certain indications, were most probably traced with the point of a ram-rod on a drum head.

MY DEAR AND MOST AFFLICTED SIR:

Tho' at the call of my country I am your enemy on the field—and tho', as a private gentleman, I have no very elevated notions of your merits, I still consider it my bounden duty, as a fellow creature, to offer you my honest condolence upon this melancholy occasion. You have been beaten, my dear Sir, and tho' I rejoice for my country, I am sincerely sorry for you. But I am most concerned at your inglorious retreat, and at the ridiculous figure you will eventually cut in history.—My dear Sir, I beseech you, for your own sake, as well as mine, that the next time you come to sup on cannon balls, that you will stand up to it like a man, and not bolt two or three and then precipitately leave the table.

I would also respectfully suggest, that a little additional drilling of yourself and troops would not be altogether unprofitable. I would advise, indeed, daily practice at facing bayonets and great guns—so that the next time, you will be able to tell what it is that hurts you.

I regret exceedingly that you should have mistaken our musketry fire for a horizontal falling of hail-stones.

For the future, I am grieved to say that I cannot promise you anything different from what you have already received at my hands. It is my fixed determination to drub you soundly whenever I can, and until you cry *enough*. As for the chance of your ever beating *me*, that, Sir, I cannot hear of. It is out of the question; and I have repeatedly given positive orders to all the troops whom I have the honor to command, not to permit it on any account. My own friendly suggestion to you is, that you had better give up at once and go home and keep quiet. If you do not, but persist in presenting yourself as an object to be repeatedly "*wolloped*," all that I can say is, that "*wolloped*" you shall be to your heart's desire. I wash my hands of all the blood shed at Buena Vista, and remain,

Dear Sir, very respectfully,

And with assurance of high commiseration,

Yours, in the bonds of compassion,

Z. TAYLOR.

The above is the only letter of the batch that has yet come to hand. If the remainder are forwarded to us in time, we shall give them in our next number.

Anecdote V

Just before the capitulation of Monterey, Old Zack had called a council of a few of his chief officers to meet at his quarters, about the time when his dinner is usually served after the deliberations; the old hero with characteristic hospitality invited his fellow soldiers to stay to dinner, which invitation (their quarters not being at that particular time at the Astor House, and a nice smell of hot pie, made out of chickens presented by one desirous of the General's favor, further inducing) was accepted. Just as the hot pie was placed by the General's confidential black servant Sambo, on the table, a round shot struck the table and tin pan, knocking it so as to fall directly on the venerable white head of the brave old hero; in the midst of the confusion caused by this uninvited guest, the hoarse and convulsive laugh of Sambo was heard echoing through the tent, "I 'spect you go now, Massa, lick the Mexicans, you armed *cap a pie*—cause aint you got the hot pie for a cap, ha ha!" On this the General, who hates a pun worse than a Mexican, told Sambo if he dared to make another joke, as bad as that, for the remainder of the campaign, he would send him back to Louisiana.

It is perhaps needless to add that the agent of the individual who is so anxious to secure every relic of General Taylor, immediately bought up the damaged tin pan, in which the hot pie had been baked, giving one dozen perfectly new tin pans for the same.

Anecdote VI

INFAMOUS PLOT TO OBTAIN POSSESSION OF THE GENERAL

It appears that Sambo who has sold to some sort of agent various articles of dress and furniture belonging to General Taylor; the other day while talking to the old hero, was informed that his principal, who is no other than PETER TAMERLANE B———M, had already possession of one General and hoped soon to get another, and that he need not wonder if he saw his master grinning through the bars of a cage. The next day the General received the following impertinent letter:

DEAR GENERAL:—In case you should resign that post in the armies of your country, which you have filled so nobly, and retire from the fields of warlike powers you have adorned, remember this letter. You have already done enough for your country and for fame; Republics are proverbially ungrateful, and BAJAZET the famous conqueror was exhibited in a cage, remember this. You have been ill-treated by the administration, and every press opposed to that administration would justify your resignation. I, then, in the name and behalf of Peter Tamerlane B———, offer you an engagement in a different and highly honorable service. Your salary will be five times the pay of a Major-General in the service of the United States; your rations will be provided for by my principal, you will be associated with all that is curious in nature and art, you will enjoy the society of a General almost as famous as yourself, and more than all you will gratify the lawful desires and advance the happiness of myriads of your countrymen and countrywomen. Can a philanthropist doubt? No, my dear General! I wait with confidence your determination. The easy and only condition will be to surrender yourself entirely to the control and direction of the said Peter Tamerlane B———m, who will treat you no worse than he has the venerable nurse of our beloved Washington and the illustrious General Tom Thumb. Think General, of yourself reclining on the poop of the Chinese Junk, receiving the visits of your friends; adopt this course and you must be elected President; reject it and perhaps—but I forbear to press this matter. I have already sounded Sambo and he appears to have no objection.

Your's on behalf of

P. T. B.

P.S.—We are in treaty for General Antonio Lopez De Santa Anna, and do not know but he will be the better speculation.

It is needless to add that the above insulting missive was torn to a thousand pieces by the indignant old hero, who cautioned Sambo to have no communication with the fellow, who had been so anxious to buy his old clothes, old knives, old forks, old cups, old kettles and old pans, and also to suggest the solemn procession of a ceremonious ride on a Mexican rail, accompanied by the music of the drum solo.

Anecdote VII

Nothing has lately occurred to rouse the indignation of old Zack to such a pitch, as the false and lying version of the celebrated Steamboat story, which has been sent to him in various newspapers from the States. You have of course seen it, and will recollect it describes the General, in the scarcity of births, yielding his own to a sick soldier, and taking his place before the fire in the engine-room, where he was regarded for a long time by the stoker and firemen as some vagabond interloper. He is represented as having passed the better part of the night dozing in the comfortable warmth of its blaze. Now nothing could be more entirely foreign to the restless temper and active habits of the old war horse. The idea of *his* snoozing away a night in front of a Steamboat fire is perfectly ludicrous, nothing could be more grossly absurd. The true state of the case as I have had it from persons who received it directly from the old General's lips, was simply this. There was a sick soldier in the case (one of the Illinoisians, who had caught a severe shot in his neck, on the hard-fought field of Buena Vista,) and to him the General did certainly and most willingly yield up his own comfortable bed. The only embarrassment it occasioned was in the shape of the question, what was he to do with himself for the rest of the night? His first thought was to withdraw to the light of the lamp on the forward deck and spreading himself according to custom on the ground, 'do up' a little mending and patching which his garments at that time happened to require. He found the river air and the fresh breeze from up stream, rather colder than his increasing breadth and fleshiness of constitution would cheerfully endure, and his next thought was of course of the fire. Thither he accordingly repaired, and, always bent on distinguishing himself, the old hero, with the utmost imaginable *sang froid* drew back the door of the oven, with a light spring (surprising in one of his bulkiness) leaped in, and spent the rest of the night in walking about in the flame, and cracking jokes with the firemen or stoker outside, every time his circuit about the oven brought him to the door. At first the stoker was alarmed at what seemed this perilous exposure of the brave old General's person; but when he saw how coolly *he* took it, he entered into the thing—although he kept outside of the fire—with as much spirit as the general himself.

Anecdote VIII

I have procured for you, after many applications and great difficulty, the following communication addressed to yourself, which the General says must be taken as a reply to all letters on the subject, once for all.

Dear Yankee Doodle:—Major Bliss handed to me just now a letter from you. He told me it was upon the Presidency question! I threw it aside at first, with disgust, but the Major told me it was from yourself; I looked at it! I saw that you wish to know my principles! I don't like to commit myself positively; but as a printer, and I'm a sort of a printer myself, having often made a strong impression—you will understand what I say. I shall always endeavor to support the——

* * * * * * ————————

* * * * * * ————————

* * * * * * ————————

* * * * * * ————————

* * * * * * ————————

————————————————

————————————————

————————————————

D'you understand?

Your's, &c.,

Z. TAYLOR.

Anecdote IX

The greatest curiosity is expressed to learn the habits of the old General at table. Constant false reports are flying about the Camp, misrepresenting most grossly his conduct in this respect; when one would think in so plain a matter there could be no opportunity for mistake or malinformation. The errors which are spread about are the more to be wondered at, as witnesses are assuredly not wanting as to the exact state of things: the General's tent being, almost as a matter of course, regularly beset during his meals with lookers on, and the door fairly obstructed with letter-writers note-book in hand, making a minute of every motion of the old hero. What motive these can have for deceiving the public, I cannot imagine unless it be that they are deceived in the first place themselves, mis-apprehending what happens, by reason of the steam, which rises from every dish set before the General, who insists that every thing shall be brought in piping hot. To rectify these deceptions and give you what I have promised from the beginning, authentic and reliable particulars, I have been at some pains for several days past to watch the old General closely, before, at, and immediately after meals. It may be stated as a general truth applicable to the three meals, that the General begins by laying aside his *chapeau* and depositing himself on some sort of settle or other; his present bulk rendering it discomforting and inconvenient to him to partake standing or from on horseback as he used to in the younger and less fleshy period of his life. Seated, he grasps with a firm hold the fork in his left hand and the knife in the right; and in an inappreciably short space of time begins striking right and left in the nearest dish. If the dish should happen (but this is rather a rare chance in camp) to be green peas, the old hero makes indiscriminate play with either hand, tossing the vegetables down his grand old throat pitch-fork fashion at one time, and the next minute sending them home to their destination with shovel-like profusion. His habit is perhaps most marked and striking, and most characteristic of the great strategist he is, when the dish to be disposed of is the common or apple-dumpling. Here he brings into play all the resources of his long experience and practised military skill. It may be premised that the General hates a hot dumpling as he hates the devil; and it is in consequence of this settled feeling that he eyes the smoking pile for several minutes after they are set upon the table before he will touch one of them. His proceedings, even after he has made up his mind to a venture, are extremely cautious and reserved. At first he selects one from the smoking platter, the smallest to start with, and begins tossing it gently, something in the manner of a conjuror with a ball, into the air. Presently he selects a second and sends it up after the first, a third joins it and a fourth, and these he keeps in motion juggler-like, for some minutes, when he allows them to descend one by one to the plate, to the last; this he takes upon his fork as it descends, and contemplates in that exposed position with great gravity and steadiness for several minutes; what his object may be in this survey no human being has been able to conjecture. Some suppose that he sees in the spherical piece of pastry, a microcosm or miniature world, and that he is revolving great political events and the possible future destiny of our globe, from the universal spread of republican principles during his coming Presidency. Others have thought that nearer personal considerations affected him, and that at such moments he must be calling to mind his friend, the editor of the New York *Mirror*. It should be observed that he always selects the softest of the dumplings as the subject of these singular contemplations.

With regard to the old General's course after meal, there could be no fouler slander than that which asserts he is accustomed to wipe his mouth on his coat-tail. It is simply untrue, and for a plain reason, he has no coat-tail about him on such occasions, but uniformly and invariably breakfasts, dines and sups in a camp-roundabout or bob. False as are all the other stories in reference to OLD ZACK's private habits, this latter fact is so well known, that I have had innumerable applications during the last three months, from all parts of the Union, for one of the General's old roundabouts. Mr. BARNUM has one which he will exhibit early in September, at his museum, for the satisfaction of the curious. I have also been able to forward one to Secretary MARCY, who, I am told, does the old General the honor to wear it when writing all his official dispatches to him, particularly when he is disposed to put the old hero on a short allowance of troops, the brevity of the garment seeming to harmonize with the nature and character of the communication. From these constant appropriations which require to be replenished, I am sure nothing would be more gratifying to the feelings of old ZACK, than if you would go to BROOKS & SON, corner of Catharine and Cherry Streets, N. Y., and order down to the Camp, a box of their most substantial brown roundabouts, large over the back and free in the arms. Please address Z. TAYLOR, United States Camp, MEXICO.

Mr Parkman's Tour

The California and Oregon Trail; being Sketches of Prairie and Rocky Mountain Life. By Francis Parkman, Jr. With Illustrations by Darley. Putnam.

MR Parkman's book is the record of some months' adventures in the year 1846 among the Indian tribes scattered between the Western boundary of Missouri and the Rocky Mountains. Though without literary pretension, it is a very entertaining work, straightforward and simple throughout, and obviously truthful.

The title will be apt to mislead. There is nothing about California or Oregon in the book; but though we like it the better for this, the title is not the less ill-chosen. And here we must remind all authors of a fact, which sometimes seems to slip their memory. The christening of books is very different from the christening of men. Among men, the object of a name is to individualize; hence, that object is gained whatever name you bestow, though it be wholly irrespective of the character of the person named. Not thus with books; whose names or titles are presumed to express the contents. And, although during this present gold fever, patriotic fathers have a perfect right to christen their offspring "Sacramento," or "California"; we deny this privilege to authors, with respect to their books. For example, a work on Botany published to day, should not be entitled "California, or Buds and Flowers"; on the contrary, the "California" should be dropped. For the correctness of our judgement in this matter we are willing to appeal to any sensible man in the community (provided he has no thought of emigrating to the gold region); nay, we will leave the matter to Mr Parkman himself.—

Possibly, however, it may be urged that the title is correct after all—"California and the Oregon Trail"—inasmuch, as the route or "trail" pursued by Mr Parkman towards the Rocky Mountains would be the one pursued by a traveller bound overland to the Pacific. Very true. And it would also be part of the route followed by a traveller bound due West from Missouri to Pekin or Bombay. But we again appeal to any sensible man whether the "Pekin and Bombay Trail" would be a correct title for a book of travels in a region lying East of the Rocky Mountains.

In a brief and appropriate preface Mr Parkman adverts to the representations of the Indian character given by poets and novelists, which he asserts are for the most part mere creations of fancy. He adds that "the Indian is certainly entitled to a high rank among savages, but his good qualities are not those of an Uncas or Outalissi." Now, this is not to be gainsaid. But when in the body of the book we are informed that it is difficult for any white man, after a domestication among the Indians, to hold them much better than brutes; when we are told too, that to such a person, the slaughter of an Indian is indifferent as the slaughter of a buffalo; with all deference, we beg leave to dissent.

It is too often the case, that civilized beings sojourning among savages soon come to regard them with disdain and contempt. But though in many cases this feeling is almost natural, it is not defensible; and it is wholly wrong. Why should we contemn them?—Because we are better than they? Assuredly not; for herein we are rebuked by the story of the Publican and the Pharisee.—Because, then, that in many things we are happier?—But this should be ground for commiseration, not disdain. Xavier and Eliot despised not the savages; and had Newton or Milton dwelt among them, they would not have done so.—When we affect to contemn savages, we should remember that by so doing we asperse our own progenitors; for they were savages also. Who can swear that among the naked British barbarians sent to Rome to be stared at more than 1500 years ago, the ancestor of Bacon might not have been found?—Why, among the very Thugs of India, or the bloody Dyaks of Borneo, exists the germ of all that is intellectually elevated and grand. We are all of us—Anglo-Saxons, Dyaks and Indians—sprung from one head and made in one image. And if we reject this brotherhood now, we shall be forced to join hands hereafter.—A misfortune is not a fault; and good luck is not meritorious. The savage is born a savage; and the civilized being but inherits his civilization, nothing more. Let us not disdain then, but pity. And wherever we recognize the image of God let us reverence it; though it swing from the gallows.

We have found one fault with the title, and another with the matter of the book; this done, the unpleasantness of fault-finding is done; and gladly we turn.

Mr Parkman's sole object, he tells us, in penetrating into the Land of Moccasons, was to gratify a curiosity he had felt from boyhood:—to inform himself accurately of Indian life. And it may well be expected that with such an object in view, the travels of an educated man, should, when published, impart to others the knowledge he himself sought to attain. And this holds true concerning the book before us. As a record of gentlemanly adventure among our Indian tribes it is by far the most pleasant book which has ever fallen in our way. The style is easy and free, quite flowingly correct. There are no undue sallies of fancy, and no attempts at wit which flash in the pan.

Accompanied by his friend Mr Quincy A. Shaw, our young author sets forth from St Louis, that city of outward-bound caravans for the West, and which is to the praries, what Cairo is to the Desert. At St Louis the friends engaged the services of Delorier, a gay cheerful Canadian and Henry Chatillon a hunter, who as guides went out and returned with them.—

In a steamer, crammed with all sorts of adventurers, Spaniards and Indians, Santa-Fe traders and trappers, gamblers and Mormons, the party ascend the Mississippi and Missouri, and at last debark on the banks of the latter stream at a point on the verge of the wilderness. Here they tarry awhile, amused with the strange aspect of things. They visit a man in whose house is a shelf for books, and where they observe a curious illustration of life: they find a holster-pistol standing guard over a copy of Paradise Lost. We presume, then, that on our Western frontier, when a man desires to soar with Milton, he does so with his book in one hand, and a pistol in the other; which last, indeed, might help him in sustaining an "armed neutrality" during the terrible but bloodless battles between Captain Beelzebub and that gallant warrior Michael.

From the banks of the Missouri the adventurers push straight out into the praries; and when they cast off their horses' halters from the post before the log-cabin door, they do as sailors, when they unmoor their cables, and set sail for sea.—They start well provided with horses and mules, rifles and powder, food and medicine, good will and stout hearts.

After encountering certain caravans of Oregon emigrants, the first place of note they arrive at is Fort Laramie, a fortified trading post near a stream tributary to the Platte river.—Here for some days they lounge upon Buffalo robes and eat Buffalo meat, and smoke Indian pipes among mongrel swarms of Canadians and Indians.

We cannot attempt to follow the friends through all their wild rovings. But he who desires to throw himself unreservedly into all the perilous charms of prarie life; to camp out by night in the wilderness, standing guard against prowling Indians and wolves; to ford rivers and creeks; to hunt buffalo, and kill them at full gallop in the saddle, and afterwards banquet on delectable roasted "hump-ribs"; to lodge with Indian warriors in their villages and receive the hospitalities of polite squaws in brass and vermillion; to hear of wars and rumors of wars among the hostile tribes of savages; to listen to the wildest and most romantic little tales of border and wilderness life; in short, he who desires to quit Broadway and the Bowery—though only in fancy—for the region of wampum and calumet, the land of beavers and buffalo—birch canoes and "smoked buckskin shirts" will do well to read Mr Parkman's book. There he will fall in with the veritable grandsons of Daniel Boon; with the Mormons; with war-parties; with Santa Fe traders; with General Kearney; with runaway United States troops; and all manner of outlandish and interesting characters.

There, too, he will make the acquaintance of Henry Chatillon Esq., as gallant a gentleman and hunter-and-trapper as ever shot buffalo. For this Henry Chatillon we feel a fresh and unbounded love. He belongs to a class of men, of whom Kit Carson is the model; a class, unique and not to be transcended in interest by any personages introduced to us by Scott. Long live and hunt Henry Chatillon! May his good rifle never miss fire; and where he roves through the praries, may the buffalo forever abound!

The Reader too will make the acquaintance of Mr Quincy A. Shaw, a high-spirited young gentleman, who always hunted his buffalo, somewhat like Murat charging at the head of cavalry—in wild and ornate attire. He sported richly worked Indian leggins, a red tunic and sash; and let loose among a herd of bison, did execution like our fierce friend Alp in Byron's "Siege of Corinth"—piling the dead round him in semicircles.—Returned from his hunting tour across the Western hemisphere, Mr Shaw, we learn, is now among the wild Bedouins of Arabia.

The book, in brief, is excellent, and has the true wild-game flavor. And amazingly tickled will all their palates be, who are so lucky as to read it.

It has two pictorial illustrations by the well-known and talented artist Darley, one of which is exceedingly good.

In conclusion we can not omit mentioning that the book was put together under a most sad and serious disadvantage. Owing to the remote effects of a sickness contracted through the wild experiences of prarie life, the author was obliged to compose his work, throughout, by dictation.

Among numerous fine and dashing descriptive chapters we have only room for the following.

[The long passage Melville selected was printed with his review and is given on pp. 641–44.]

Cooper's New Novel

The Sea Lions; or, The Lost Sealers: a Tale of the Antarctic Ocean. By J. Fenimore Cooper. 2 vols. 12mo. Stringer & Townsend.

The Sea Lions, or The Lost Sealers! An attractive title truly. Nor does this last of Cooper's novels disappoint the promise held forth on the title page.

The story opens on the sea coast of Suffolk County, Long Island; and turns mainly upon the mysterious existence of certain wild islands within the Antarctic Circle, whose precise whereabouts is known but to a choice few, and whose latitude and longitude even the author declares he is not at liberty to make known. For this region, impelled by adverse, if not hostile motives, the two vessels—the Sea Lions—in due time sail, under circumstances full of romance.

After encountering a violent gale, described with a force peculiarly Cooper's, they at last reach the Antarctic seas, finding themselves walled in by "thrilling regions of rock-ribbed ice". Few descriptions of the lonely and the terrible, we imagine, can surpass the grandeur of many of the scenes here depicted. The reader is reminded of the appalling adventures of the United States Exploring Ship in the same part of the world as narrated by Wilkes, and of Scoresby's Greenland narrative.—In these inhospitable regions the hardy crews of the Sea Lions winter,—not snugly at anchor under the lee of a Dutch stove, nor baking and browning over the ovens by which the Muscovite warms himself—but jammed in, masoned up, bolted and barred, and almost hermetically sealed by the ice.—To keep from freezing into chrystal they are fain to turn part of their vessels into fuel.—All this, and much more of the like nature are told in a style singularly plain, downright and truthful.

At length, after many narrow escapes from ice-bergs, ice-isles, fields and floes of ice, the mariners, at least most of them, make good their return to the North, where the action of the book is crowned by the nuptials of Roswell Gardiner the hero and Mary Pratt the heroine. Roswell we admire for a noble fellow; and Mary we love for a fine example of womanly affection, earnestness, and constancy.—Deacon Pratt, her respected father is a hard-handed, hard-hearted, psalm-singing old man, with a very stretchy conscience; intent upon getting to heaven, and getting money by the same course of conduct, in defiance of the scriptural maxim to the contrary. There is a good deal of wisdom to be gathered from the story of the Deacon.

Then we have one Stimson, an old Kennebunk boatsteerer, and Professor of Theology, who, wintering on an ice-berg, discourses most unctuously upon various dogmas. This honest old worthy may possibly be recognized for an old acquaintance by the readers of Cooper's novels.—But who would have dreampt of his turning up at the South Pole?—One of the subordinate parts of the book is the timely conversion of Roswell the hero from a too latitudinarian view of Christianity to a more orthodox, and hence a better belief. And as the reader will perceive, the moist rosy hand of our Mary is the reward of his orthodoxy. Somewhat in the pleasant spirit of the Mahometan, this; who rewards all true believers with a houri.

Upon the whole, we warmly recommend The Sea Lions. And even those who more for fashion's sake than any thing else, have of late joined in decrying our National Novelist, will in this last work perhaps recognize one of his happiest.

A Thought on Book-Binding

The Red Rover. By J. Fenimore Cooper. Revised edition. Putnam.

THE SIGHT of the far-famed Red Rover sailing under the sober hued muslin wherewith Mr Putnam equips his lighter sort of craft begets in us a fastidious feeling touching the propriety of such a binding for such a book. Not that we ostentatiously pretend to any elevated degree of artistic taste in this matter;—our remarks are but limited to our egotistical fancies. Egotistically, then, we would have preferred for the "Red Rover" a flaming suit of flame-colored morrocco, as evanescently thin and gauze-like as possible, so that the binding might happily correspond with the sanguinary fugitive title of the book. Still better, perhaps, were it bound in jet black, with a red streak round the borders (pirate fashion)—or, upon third thoughts, omit the streak, and substitute a square of blood-colored bunting on the back, imprinted with the title, so that the flag of the "Red Rover" might be congenially flung to the popular breeze after the buccaneer fashion of Morgan, Black-Beard, and other free and easy, dare-devil, accomplished gentlemen of the sea.

While throwing out these cursory suggestions, we gladly acknowledge that the tasteful publisher has attached to the volume, a very felicitous touch of the sea superstitions of pirates. In the mysterious cyphers in book-binders' relievo stamped upon the covers we joyfully recognize a poetical signification and pictorial shadowing forth of the horse-shoe, which in all honest and God-fearing piratical vessels is invariably found nailed to the mast.—By force of contrast this clever device reminds us of the sad lack of invention in most of our bookbinders. Books, gentlemen, are a species of men, and introduced to them you circulate in the "very best society" that this world can furnish, without the intolerable infliction of "dressing" to go into it. In your shabbiest coat and cosiest slippers you may socially chat even with the fastidious Earl of Chesterfield, and lounging under a tree enjoy the divinest intimacy with my late lord of Verulam. Men, then, that they are—living, without vulgarly breathing—never speaking unless spoken to—books should be appropriately apparelled. Their bindings should indicate and distinguish their various characters. A crowd of illustrations press upon us, but we must dismiss them at present with the simple expression of the hope that our suggestion may not entirely be thrown away.

That we have said thus much concerning the mere outside of the book whose title prefaces this notice, is sufficient evidence of the fact that at the present day we deem any elaborate criticism of Cooper's Red Rover quite unnecessary and uncalled-for. Long ago, and far inland, we read it in our uncritical days, and enjoyed it as much as thousands of the rising generation will when supplied with such an entertaining volume in such agreeable type.

Hawthorne and His Mosses

By a Virginian Spending July in Vermont

A PAPERED CHAMBER in a fine old farm-house—a mile from any other dwelling, and dipped to the eaves in foliage—surrounded by mountains, old woods, and Indian ponds,—this, surely, is the place to write of Hawthorne. Some charm is in this northern air, for love and duty seem both impelling to the task. A man of a deep and noble nature has seized me in this seclusion. His wild, witch voice rings through me; or, in softer cadences, I seem to hear it in the songs of the hill-side birds, that sing in the larch trees at my window.

Would that all excellent books were foundlings, without father or mother, that so it might be, we could glorify them, without including their ostensible authors. Nor would any true man take exception to this;—least of all, he who writes,—"When the Artist rises high enough to achieve the Beautiful, the symbol by which he makes it perceptible to mortal senses becomes of little value in his eyes, while his spirit possesses itself in the enjoyment of the reality."

But more than this. I know not what would be the right name to put on the title-page of an excellent book, but this I feel, that the names of all fine authors are fictitious ones, far more so than that of Junius,—simply standing, as they do, for the mystical, ever-eluding Spirit of all Beauty, which ubiquitously possesses men of genius. Purely imaginative as this fancy may appear, it nevertheless seems to receive some warranty from the fact, that on a personal interview no great author has ever come up to the idea of his reader. But that dust of which our bodies are composed, how can it fitly express the nobler intelligences among us? With reverence be it spoken, that not even in the case of one deemed more than man, not even in our Saviour, did his visible frame betoken anything of the augustness of the nature within. Else, how could those Jewish eyewitnesses fail to see heaven in his glance.

It is curious, how a man may travel along a country road, and yet miss the grandest, or sweetest of prospects, by reason of an intervening hedge, so like all other hedges, as in no way to hint of the wide landscape beyond. So has it been with me concerning the enchanting landscape in the soul of this Hawthorne, this most excellent Man of Mosses. His "Old Manse" has been written now four years, but I never read it till a day or two since. I had seen it in the book-stores—heard of it often—even had it recommended to me by a tasteful friend, as a rare, quiet book, perhaps too deserving of popularity to be popular. But there are so many books called "excellent", and so much unpopular merit, that amid the thick stir of other things, the hint of my tasteful friend was disregarded; and for four years the Mosses on the old Manse never refreshed me with their perennial green. It may be, however, that all this while, the book, like wine, was only improving in flavor and body. At any rate, it so chanced that this long procrastination eventuated in a happy result. At breakfast the other day, a mountain girl, a cousin of mine, who for the last two weeks has every morning helped me to strawberries and raspberries,—which, like the roses and pearls in the fairy-tale, seemed to fall into the saucer from those strawberry-beds her cheeks,—this delightful creature, this charming Cherry says to me—"I see you spend your mornings in the hay-mow; and yesterday I found there 'Dwight's Travels in New England'. Now I have something far better than that,—something more congenial to our summer on these hills. Take these raspberries, and then I will give you some moss."—"Moss!" said I.—"Yes, and you must take it to the barn with you, and good-bye to 'Dwight' ".

With that she left me, and soon returned with a volume, verdantly bound, and garnished with a curious frontispiece in green,—nothing less, than a fragment of real moss cunningly pressed to a fly-leaf.—"Why this," said I spilling my raspberries, "this is the 'Mosses from an Old Manse' ". "Yes" said cousin Cherry "yes, it is that flowery Hawthorne."—"Hawthorne and Mosses" said I "no more: it is morning: it is July in the country: and I am off for the barn".

Stretched on that new mown clover, the hill-side breeze blowing over me through the wide barn door, and soothed by the hum of the bees in the meadows around, how magically stole over me this Mossy Man! and how amply, how bountifully, did he redeem that delicious promise to his guests in the Old Manse, of whom it is written—"Others could give them pleasure, or amusement, or instruction—these could be picked up anywhere—but it was for me to give them rest. Rest, in a life of trouble! What better could be done for weary and world-worn spirits? what better could be done for anybody, who came within our magic circle, than to throw the spell of a magic spirit over him?"—So all that day, half-buried in the new clover, I watched this Hawthorne's "Assyrian dawn, and Paphian sunset and moonrise, from the summit of our Eastern Hill."

The soft ravishments of the man spun me round about in a web of dreams, and when the book was closed, when the spell was over, this wizard "dismissed me with but misty reminiscences, as if I had been dreaming of him".

What a mild moonlight of contemplative humor bathes that Old Manse!—the rich and rare distilment of a spicy and slowly-oozing heart. No rollicking rudeness, no gross fun fed on fat dinners, and bred in the lees of wine,—but a humor so spiritually gentle, so high, so deep, and yet so richly relishable, that it were hardly inappropriate in an angel. It is the very religion of mirth; for nothing so human but it may be advanced to that. The orchard of the Old Manse seems the visible type of the fine mind that has described it. Those twisted, and contorted old trees, "that stretch out their crooked branches, and take such hold of the imagination, that we remember them as humorists, and odd-fellows." And then, as surrounded by these grotesque forms, and hushed in the noon-day repose of this Hawthorne's spell, how aptly might the still fall of his ruddy thoughts into your soul be symbolized by "the thump of a great apple, in the stillest afternoon, falling without a breath of wind, from the mere necessity of perfect ripeness"! For no less ripe than ruddy are the apples of the thoughts and fancies in this sweet Man of Mosses.

"Buds and Bird-voices"—What a delicious thing is that!—"Will the world ever be so decayed, that Spring may not renew its greenness?"—And the "Fire-Worship". Was ever the hearth so glorified into an altar before? The mere title of that piece is better than any common work in fifty folio volumes. How exquisite is this:—"Nor did it lessen the charm of his soft, familiar courtesy and helpfulness, that the mighty spirit, were opportunity offered him, would run riot through the peaceful house, wrap its inmates in his terrible embrace, and leave nothing of them save their whitened bones. This possibility of mad destruction only made his domestic kindness the more beautiful and touching. It was so sweet of him, being endowed with such power, to dwell, day after day, and one long, lonesome night after another, on the dusky hearth, only now and then betraying his wild nature, by thrusting his red tongue out of the chimney-top! True, he had done much mischief in the world, and was pretty certain to do more, but his warm heart atoned for all. He was kindly to the race of man."

But he has still other apples, not quite so ruddy, though full as ripe;—apples, that have been left to wither on the tree, after the pleasant autumn gathering is past. The sketch of "The Old Apple Dealer" is conceived in the subtlest spirit of sadness; he whose "subdued and nerveless boyhood prefigured his abortive prime, which, likewise, contained within itself the prophecy and image of his lean and torpid age". Such touches as are in this piece can not proceed from any common heart. They argue such a depth of tenderness, such a boundless sympathy with all forms of being, such an omnipresent love, that we must needs say, that this Hawthorne is here almost alone in his generation,—at least, in the artistic manifestation of these things. Still more. Such touches as these,—and many, very many similar ones, all through his chapters—furnish clews, whereby we enter a little way into the intricate, profound heart where they originated. And we see, that suffering, some time or other and in some shape or other,—this only can enable any man to depict it in others. All over him, Hawthorne's melancholy rests like an Indian Summer, which though bathing a whole country in one softness, still reveals the distinctive hue of every towering hill, and each far-winding vale.

But it is the least part of genius that attracts admiration. Where Hawthorne is known, he seems to be deemed a pleasant writer, with a pleasant style,—a sequestered, harmless man, from whom any deep and weighty thing would hardly be anticipated:—a man who means no meanings. But there is no man, in whom humor and love, like mountain peaks, soar to such a rapt height, as to receive the irradiations of the upper skies;—there is no man in whom humor and love are developed in that high form called genius; no such man can exist without also possessing, as the indispensable complement of these, a great, deep intellect, which drops down into the universe like a plummet. Or, love and humor are only the eyes, through which such an intellect views this world. The great beauty in such a mind is but the product of its strength. What, to all readers, can be more charming than the piece entitled "Monsieur du

Miroir"; and to a reader at all capable of fully fathoming it, what, at the same time, can possess more mystical depth of meaning?—Yes, there he sits, and looks at me,—this "shape of mystery", this "identical Monsieur du Miroir".—"Methinks I should tremble now, were his wizard power of gliding through all impediments in search of me, to place him suddenly before my eyes".

How profound, nay appalling, is the moral evolved by the "Earth's Holocaust"; where—beginning with the hollow follies and affectations of the world,—all vanities and empty theories and forms, are, one after another, and by an admirably graduated, growing comprehensiveness, thrown into the allegorical fire, till, at length, nothing is left but the all-engendering heart of man; which remaining still unconsumed, the great conflagration is nought.

Of a piece with this, is the "Intelligence Office", a wondrous symbolizing of the secret workings in men's souls. There are other sketches, still more charged with ponderous import.

"The Christmas Banquet", and "The Bosom Serpent" would be fine subjects for a curious and elaborate analysis, touching the conjectural parts of the mind that produced them. For spite of all the Indian-summer sunlight on the hither side of Hawthorne's soul, the other side—like the dark half of the physical sphere—is shrouded in a blackness, ten times black. But this darkness but gives more effect to the ever-moving dawn, that forever advances through it, and circumnavigates his world. Whether Hawthorne has simply availed himself of this mystical blackness as a means to the wondrous effects he makes it to produce in his lights and shades; or whether there really lurks in him, perhaps unknown to himself, a touch of Puritanic gloom,—this, I cannot altogether tell. Certain it is, however, that this great power of blackness in him derives its force from its appeals to that Calvinistic sense of Innate Depravity and Original Sin, from whose visitations, in some shape or other, no deeply thinking mind is always and wholly free. For, in certain moods, no man can weigh this world, without throwing in something, somehow like Original Sin, to strike the uneven balance. At all events, perhaps no writer has ever wielded this terrific thought with greater terror than this same harmless Hawthorne. Still more: this black conceit pervades him, through and through. You may be witched by his sunlight,—transported by the bright gildings in the skies he builds over you;—but there is the blackness of darkness beyond; and even his bright gildings but fringe, and play upon the edges of thunder-clouds.—In one word, the world is mistaken in this

Nathaniel Hawthorne. He himself must often have smiled at its absurd misconception of him. He is immeasurably deeper than the plummet of the mere critic. For it is not the brain that can test such a man; it is only the heart. You cannot come to know greatness by inspecting it; there is no glimpse to be caught of it, except by intuition; you need not ring it, you but touch it, and you find it is gold.

Now it is that blackness in Hawthorne, of which I have spoken, that so fixes and fascinates me. It may be, nevertheless, that it is too largely developed in him. Perhaps he does not give us a ray of his light for every shade of his dark. But however this may be, this blackness it is that furnishes the infinite obscure of his back-ground,—that back-ground, against which Shakespeare plays his grandest conceits, the things that have made for Shakespeare his loftiest, but most circumscribed renown, as the profoundest of thinkers. For by philosophers Shakespeare is not adored as the great man of tragedy and comedy.—"Off with his head! so much for Buckingham!" this sort of rant, interlined by another hand, brings down the house,—those mistaken souls, who dream of Shakespeare as a mere man of Richard-the-Third humps, and Macbeth daggers. But it is those deep far-away things in him; those occasional flashings-forth of the intuitive Truth in him; those short, quick probings at the very axis of reality;—these are the things that make Shakespeare, Shakespeare. Through the mouths of the dark characters of Hamlet, Timon, Lear, and Iago, he craftily says, or sometimes insinuates the things, which we feel to be so terrifically true, that it were all but madness for any good man, in his own proper character, to utter, or even hint of them. Tormented into desperation, Lear the frantic King tears off the mask, and speaks the sane madness of vital truth. But, as I before said, it is the least part of genius that attracts admiration. And so, much of the blind, unbridled admiration that has been heaped upon Shakespeare, has been lavished upon the least part of him. And few of his endless commentators and critics seem to have remembered, or even perceived, that the immediate products of a great mind are not so great, as that undeveloped, (and sometimes undevelopable) yet dimly-discernable greatness, to which these immediate products are but the infallible indices. In Shakespeare's tomb lies infinitely more than Shakspeare ever wrote. And if I magnify Shakespeare, it is not so much for what he did do, as for what he did not do, or refrained from doing. For in this world of lies, Truth is forced to fly like a scared white doe in the woodlands; and only by cunning glimpses will she reveal herself, as in Shakespeare and other masters of the great Art of Telling the Truth,—even though it be covertly, and by snatches.

But if this view of the all-popular Shakespeare be seldom taken by his readers, and if very few who extol him, have ever read him deeply, or, perhaps, only have seen him on the tricky stage, (which alone made, and is still making him his mere mob renown)—if few men have time, or patience, or palate, for the spiritual truth as it is in that great genius;—it is, then, no matter of surprise that in a contemporaneous age, Nathaniel Hawthorne is a man, as yet, almost utterly mistaken among men. Here and there, in some quiet arm-chair in the noisy town, or some deep nook among the noiseless mountains, he may be appreciated for something of what he is. But unlike Shakespeare, who was forced to the contrary course by circumstances, Hawthorne (either from simple disinclination, or else from inaptitude) refrains from all the popularizing noise and show of broad farce, and blood-besmeared tragedy; content with the still, rich utterances of a great intellect in repose, and which sends few thoughts into circulation, except they be arterialized at his large warm lungs, and expanded in his honest heart.

Nor need you fix upon that blackness in him, if it suit you not. Nor, indeed, will all readers discern it, for it is, mostly, insinuated to those who may best understand it, and account for it; it is not obtruded upon every one alike.

Some may start to read of Shakespeare and Hawthorne on the same page. They may say, that if an illustration were needed, a lesser light might have sufficed to elucidate this Hawthorne, this small man of yesterday. But I am not, willingly, one of those, who, as touching Shakespeare at least, exemplify the maxim of Rochefoucault, that "we exalt the reputation of some, in order to depress that of others";—who, to teach all noble-souled aspirants that there is no hope for them, pronounce Shakespeare absolutely unapproachable. But Shakespeare has been approached. There are minds that have gone as far as Shakespeare into the universe. And hardly a mortal man, who, at some time or other, has not felt as great thoughts in him as any you will find in Hamlet. We must not inferentially malign mankind for the sake of any one man, whoever he may be. This is too cheap a purchase of contentment for conscious mediocrity to make. Besides, this absolute and unconditional adoration of Shakespeare has grown to be a part of our Anglo Saxon superstitions. The Thirty Nine articles are now Forty. Intolerance has come to exist in this matter. You must believe in Shakespeare's unapproachability, or quit the country. But what sort of a belief is this for an American, a man who is bound to carry republican progressiveness into Literature, as well as into Life? Believe me, my friends, that Shakespeares are this day being born on the banks of the Ohio. And the day will come, when you shall say who reads a book by an Englishman that is a modern? The great mistake seems to be, that even with those Americans who look forward to the coming of a great literary genius among us, they somehow fancy he will come in the costume of Queen Elizabeth's day,—be a writer of dramas founded upon old English history, or the tales of Boccaccio. Whereas, great geniuses are parts of the times; they themselves are the times; and possess a correspondent coloring. It is of a piece with the Jews, who while their Shiloh was meekly walking in their streets, were still praying for his magnificent coming; looking for him in a chariot, who was already among them on an ass. Nor must we forget, that, in his own life-time, Shakespeare was not Shakespeare, but only Master William Shakespeare of the shrewd, thriving, business firm of Condell, Shakespeare & Co., proprietors of the Globe Theatre in London; and by a courtly author, of the name of Greene, was hooted at, as an "upstart crow" beautified "with other birds' feathers". For, mark it well, imitation is often the first charge brought against real originality. Why this is so, there is not space to set forth here. You must have plenty of sea-room to tell the Truth in; especially, when it seems to have an aspect of newness, as America did in 1492, though it was then just as old, and perhaps older than Asia, only those sagacious philosophers, the common sailors, had never seen it before; swearing it was all water and moonshine there.

Now, I do not say that Nathaniel of Salem is a greater than William of Avon, or as great. But the difference between the two men is by no means immeasurable. Not a very great deal more, and Nathaniel were verily William.

This, too, I mean, that if Shakespeare has not been equalled, he is sure to be surpassed, and surpassed by an American born now or yet to be born. For it will never do for us who in most other things out-do as well as out-brag the world, it will not do for us to fold our hands and say, In the highest department advance there is none. Nor will it at all do to say, that the world is getting grey and grizzled now, and has lost that fresh charm which she wore of old, and by virtue of which the great poets of past times made themselves what we esteem them to be. Not so. The world is as young today, as when it was created; and this Vermont morning dew is as wet to my feet, as Eden's dew to Adam's. Nor has Nature been all over ransacked by our progenitors, so that no new charms and mysteries remain for this latter generation to find. Far from it. The trillionth part has not yet been said; and all that has been said, but multiplies the avenues to what remains to be said. It is not so much paucity, as superabundance of material that seems to incapacitate modern authors.

Let America then prize and cherish her writers; yea, let her glorify them. They are not so many in number, as to exhaust her good-will. And while she has good kith and kin of her own, to take to her bosom, let her not lavish her embraces upon the household of an alien. For believe it or not England, after all, is, in many things, an alien to us. China has more bowels of real love for us than she. But even were there no Hawthorne, no Emerson, no Whittier, no Irving, no Bryant, no Dana, no Cooper, no Willis (not the author of the "Dashes", but the author of the "Belfry Pigeon")—were there none of these, and others of like calibre among us, nevertheless, let America first praise mediocrity even, in her own children, before she praises (for everywhere, merit demands acknowledgment from every one) the best excellence in the children of any other land. Let her own authors, I say, have the priority of appreciation. I was much pleased with a hot-headed Carolina cousin of mine, who once said,—"If there were no other American to stand by, in Literature,—why, then, I would stand by Pop Emmons and his 'Fredoniad,' and till a better epic came along, swear it was not very far behind the Iliad." Take away the words, and in spirit he was sound.

Not that American genius needs patronage in order to expand. For that explosive sort of stuff will expand though screwed up in a vice, and burst it, though it were triple steel. It is for the nation's sake, and not for her authors' sake, that I would have America be heedful of the increasing greatness among her writers. For how great the shame, if other nations should be before her, in crowning her heroes of the pen. But this is almost the case now. American authors have received more just and discriminating praise (however loftily and ridiculously given, in certain cases) even from some Englishmen, than from their own countrymen. There are hardly five critics in America; and several of them are asleep. As for patronage, it is the American author who now patronizes his country, and not his country him. And if at times some among them appeal to the people for more recognition, it is not always with selfish motives, but patriotic ones.

It is true, that but few of them as yet have evinced that decided originality which merits great praise. But that graceful writer, who perhaps of all Americans has received the most plaudits from his own country for his productions,—that very popular and amiable writer, however good, and self-reliant in many things, perhaps owes his chief reputation to the self-acknowledged imitation of a foreign model, and to the studied avoidance of all topics but smooth ones. But it is better to fail in originality, than to succeed in imitation. He who has never failed somewhere, that man can not be great. Failure is the true test of greatness. And if it be said, that continual success is a proof that a man wisely knows his powers,—it is only to be added, that, in that case, he knows them to be small. Let us believe it, then, once for all, that there is no hope for us in these smooth pleasing writers that know their powers. Without malice, but to speak the plain fact, they but furnish an appendix to Goldsmith, and other English authors. And we want no American Goldsmiths; nay, we want no American Miltons. It were the vilest thing you could say of a true American author, that he were an American Tompkins. Call him an American, and have done; for you can not say a nobler thing of him.—But it is not meant that all American writers should studiously cleave to nationality in their writings; only this, no American writer should write like an Englishman, or a Frenchman; let him write like a man, for then he will be sure to write like an American. Let us away with this Bostonian leaven of literary flunkeyism towards England. If either must play the flunkey in this thing, let England do it, not us. And the time is not far off when circumstances may force her to it. While we are rapidly preparing for that political supremacy among the nations, which prophetically awaits us at the close of the present century; in a literary point of view, we are deplorably unprepared for it; and we seem studious to remain so. Hitherto, reasons might have existed why this should be; but no good reason exists now. And all that is requisite to amendment in this matter, is simply this: that, while freely acknowledging all excellence, everywhere, we should refrain from unduly lauding foreign writers and, at the same time, duly recognize the meritorious writers that are our own;—those writers, who breathe that unshackled, democratic spirit of Christianity in all things, which now takes the practical lead in this world, though at the same time led by ourselves—us Americans. Let us boldly contemn all imitation, though it comes to us graceful and fragrant as the morning; and foster all originality, though, at first, it be crabbed and ugly as our own pine knots. And if any of our authors fail, or seem to fail, then, in the words of my enthusiastic Carolina cousin, let us clap him on the shoulder, and back him against all Europe for his second round. The truth is, that in our point of view, this matter of a national literature has come to such a pass with us, that in some sense we must turn bullies, else the day is lost, or superiority so far beyond us, that we can hardly say it will ever be ours.

And now, my countrymen, as an excellent author, of your own flesh and blood,—an unimitating, and, perhaps, in his way, an inimitable man—whom better can I commend to you, in the first place, than Nathaniel

Hawthorne. He is one of the new, and far better generation of your writers. The smell of your beeches and hemlocks is upon him; your own broad praries are in his soul; and if you travel away inland into his deep and noble nature, you will hear the far roar of his Niagara. Give not over to future generations the glad duty of acknowledging him for what he is. Take that joy to your self, in your own generation; and so shall he feel those grateful impulses in him, that may possibly prompt him to the full flower of some still greater achievement in your eyes. And by confessing him, you thereby confess others; you brace the whole brotherhood. For genius, all over the world, stands hand in hand, and one shock of recognition runs the whole circle round.

In treating of Hawthorne, or rather of Hawthorne in his writings (for I never saw the man; and in the chances of a quiet plantation life, remote from his haunts, perhaps never shall) in treating of his works, I say, I have thus far omitted all mention of his "Twice Told Tales", and "Scarlet Letter". Both are excellent; but full of such manifold, strange and diffusive beauties, that time would all but fail me, to point the half of them out. But there are things in those two books, which, had they been written in England a century ago, Nathaniel Hawthorne had utterly displaced many of the bright names we now revere on authority. But I am content to leave Hawthorne to himself, and to the infallible finding of posterity; and however great may be the praise I have bestowed upon him, I feel, that in so doing, I have more served and honored myself, than him. For, at bottom, great excellence is praise enough to itself; but the feeling of a sincere and appreciative love and admiration towards it, this is relieved by utterance; and warm, honest praise ever leaves a pleasant flavor in the mouth; and it is an honorable thing to confess to what is honorable in others.

But I cannot leave my subject yet. No man can read a fine author, and relish him to his very bones, while he reads, without subsequently fancying to himself some ideal image of the man and his mind. And if you rightly look for it, you will almost always find that the author himself has somewhere furnished you with his own picture.—For poets (whether in prose or verse), being painters of Nature, are like their brethren of the pencil, the true portrait-painters, who, in the multitude of likenesses to be sketched, do not invariably omit their own; and in all high instances, they paint them without any vanity, though, at times, with a lurking something, that would take several pages to properly define.

I submit it, then, to those best acquainted with the man personally, whether the following is not Nathaniel Hawthorne;—and to himself, whether something involved in it does not express the temper of his mind,—that lasting temper of all true, candid men—a seeker, not a finder yet:—

> "A man now entered, in neglected attire, with the aspect of a thinker, but somewhat too rough-hewn and brawny for a scholar. His face was full of sturdy vigor, with some finer and keener attribute beneath; though harsh at first, it was tempered with the glow of a large, warm heart, which had force enough to heat his powerful intellect through and through. He advanced to the Intelligencer, and looked at him with a glance of such stern sincerity, that perhaps few secrets were beyond its scope.
>
> "'I seek for Truth', said he."

* * * * *

Twenty four hours have elapsed since writing the foregoing. I have just returned from the hay mow, charged more and more with love and admiration of Hawthorne. For I have just been gleaning through the Mosses, picking up many things here and there that had previously escaped me. And I found that but to glean after this man, is better than to be in at the harvest of others. To be frank (though, perhaps, rather foolish) notwithstanding what I wrote yesterday of these Mosses, I had not then culled them all; but had, nevertheless, been sufficiently sensible of the subtle essence, in them, as to write as I did. To what infinite height of loving wonder and admiration I may yet be borne, when by repeatedly banquetting on these Mosses, I shall have thoroughly incorporated their whole stuff into my being,—that, I can-not tell. But already I feel that this Hawthorne has dropped germinous seeds into my soul. He expands and deepens down, the more I contemplate him; and further, and further, shoots his strong New-England roots into the hot soil of my Southern soul.

By careful reference to the "Table of Contents", I now find, that I have gone through all the sketches; but that when I yesterday wrote, I had not at all read two particular pieces, to which I now desire to call special attention,—"A Select Party", and "Young Goodman Brown". Here, be it said to all those whom this poor fugitive scrawl of mine may tempt to the perusal of the "Mosses," that they must on no account suffer themselves to be trifled with, disappointed, or deceived by the triviality of many of the titles to these Sketches. For in more than one instance, the title utterly belies the piece. It is as if rustic demijohns containing the very best and costliest of Falernian and Tokay, were labelled "Cider", "Perry," and "Elderberry wine". The truth seems to be, that like many other geniuses, this Man of Mosses takes great delight in hoodwinking the world,—at least, with respect to himself. Personally, I doubt not, that he rather prefers to be generally esteemed but a so-so sort of author; being willing to reserve the thorough and acute appreciation of what he is, to that party most qualified to judge—that is, to himself. Besides, at the bottom of their natures, men like Hawthorne, in many things, deem the plaudits of the public such strong presumptive evidence of mediocrity in the object of them, that it would in some degree render them doubtful of their own powers, did they hear much and vociferous braying concerning them in the public pastures. True, I have been braying myself (if you please to be witty enough, to have it so) but then I claim to be the first that has so brayed in this particular matter; and therefore, while pleading guilty to the charge still claim all the merit due to originality.

But with whatever motive, playful or profound, Nathaniel Hawthorne has chosen to entitle his pieces in the manner he has, it is certain, that some of them are directly calculated to deceive—egregiously deceive, the superficial skimmer of pages. To be downright and candid once more, let me cheerfully say, that two of these titles did dolefully dupe no less an eagle-eyed reader than myself; and that, too, after I had been impressed with a sense of the great depth and breadth of this American man. "Who in the name of thunder" (as the country-people say in this neighborhood) "who in the name of thunder", would anticipate any marvel in a piece entitled "Young Goodman Brown"? You would of course suppose that it was a simple little tale, intended as a supplement to "Goody Two Shoes". Whereas, it is deep as Dante; nor can you finish it, without addressing the author in his own words—"It is yours to penetrate, in every bosom, the deep mystery of sin". And with Young Goodman, too, in allegorical pursuit of his Puritan wife, you cry out in your anguish,—

> "'Faith!' shouted Goodman Brown, in a voice of agony and desperation; and the echoes of the forest mocked him, crying—'Faith! Faith!' as if bewildered wretches were seeking her all through the wilderness."

Now this same piece, entitled "Young Goodman Brown", is one of the two that I had not all read yesterday; and I allude to it now, because it is, in itself, such a strong positive illustration of that blackness in Hawthorne, which I had assumed from the mere occasional shadows of it, as revealed in several of the other sketches. But had I previously perused "Young Goodman Brown", I should have been at no pains to draw the conclusion, which I came to, at a time, when I was ignorant that the book contained one such direct and unqualified manifestation of it.

The other piece of the two referred to, is entitled "A Select Party", which, in my first simplicity upon originally taking hold of the book, I fancied must treat of some pumpkin-pie party in Old Salem, or some chowder party on Cape Cod. Whereas, by all the gods of Peedee! it is the sweetest and sublimest thing that has been written since Spencer wrote. Nay, there is nothing in Spencer that surpasses it, perhaps, nothing that equals it. And the test is this: read any canto in "The Faery Queen", and then read "A Select Party", and decide which pleases you the most,—that is, if you are qualified to judge. Do not be frightened at this; for when Spencer was alive, he was thought of very much as Hawthorne is now,—was generally accounted just such a "gentle" harmless man. It may be, that to common eyes, the sublimity of Hawthorne seems lost in his sweetness,—as perhaps in this same "Select Party" of his; for whom, he has builded so august a dome of sunset clouds, and served them on richer plate, than Belshazzar's when he banquetted his lords in Babylon.

But my chief business now, is to point out a particular page in this piece, having reference to an honored guest, who under the name of "The Master Genius" but in the guise of "a young man of poor attire, with no insignia of rank or acknowledged eminence", is introduced to the Man of Fancy, who is the giver of the feast. Now the page having reference to this "Master Genius", so happily expresses much of what I yesterday wrote, touching the coming of the literary Shiloh of America, that I cannot but be charmed by the coincidence; especially, when it shows such a parity of ideas, at least in this one point, between a man like Hawthorne and a man like me.

And here, let me throw out another conceit of mine touching this American Shiloh, or "Master Genius", as Hawthorne calls him. May it not be, that this commanding mind has not been, is not, and never will be, individually developed in any one man? And would it, indeed, appear so unreasonable to suppose, that this great fullness and overflowing may be, or may be destined to be, shared by a plurality of men of genius? Surely, to take the very greatest example on record, Shakespeare cannot be regarded as in himself the concretion of all the genius of his time; nor as so immeasurably beyond Marlow, Webster, Ford, Beaumont, Jonson, that those great men can be said to share none of his power? For one, I conceive that there were dramatists in Elizabeth's day, between whom and Shakespeare the distance was by no means great. Let anyone, hitherto little acquainted with those neglected old authors, for the first time read them thoroughly, or even read Charles Lamb's Specimens of them, and he will be amazed at the wondrous ability of those Anaks of men, and shocked at this renewed example of the fact, that Fortune has more to do with fame than merit,—though, without merit, lasting fame there can be none.

Nevertheless, it would argue too illy of my country were this maxim to hold good concerning Nathaniel Hawthorne, a man, who already, in some few minds, has shed "such a light, as never illuminates the earth, save when a great heart burns as the household fire of a grand intellect."

The words are his,—in the "Select Party"; and they are a magnificent setting to a coincident sentiment of my own, but ramblingly expressed yesterday, in reference to himself. Gainsay it who will, as I now write, I am Posterity speaking by proxy—and after times will make it more than good, when I declare—that the American, who up to the present day, has evinced, in Literature, the largest brain with the largest heart, that man is Nathaniel Hawthorne. Moreover, that whatever Nathaniel Hawthorne may hereafter write, "The Mosses from an Old Manse" will be ultimately accounted his masterpiece. For there is a sure, though a secret sign in some works which prove the culmination of the powers (only the developable ones, however) that produced them. But I am by no means desirous of the glory of a prophet. I pray Heaven that Hawthorne may *yet* prove me an impostor in this prediction. Especially, as I somehow cling to the strange fancy, that, in all men, hiddenly reside certain wondrous, occult properties—as in some plants and minerals—which by some happy but very rare accident (as bronze was discovered by the melting of the iron and brass in the burning of Corinth) may chance to be called forth here on earth; not entirely waiting for their better discovery in the more congenial, blessed atmosphere of heaven.

Once more—for it is hard to be finite upon an infinite subject, and all subjects are infinite. By some people, this entire scrawl of mine may be esteemed altogether unnecessary, inasmuch, "as years ago" (they may say) "we found out the rich and rare stuff in this Hawthorne, whom you now parade forth, as if only *yourself* were the discoverer of this Portuguese diamond in our Literature".—But even granting all this; and adding to it, the assumption that the books of Hawthorne have sold by the five-thousand,—what does that signify?—They should be sold by the hundred-thousand; and read by the million; and admired by every one who is capable of admiration.

The Happy Failure

A Story of the River Hudson

THE APPOINTMENT was that I should meet my elderly uncle at the river-side, precisely at nine in the morning. The skiff was to be ready, and the apparatus to be brought down by his grizzled old black man. As yet, the nature of the wonderful experiment remained a mystery to all but the projector.

I was first on the spot. The village was high up the river, and the inland summer sun was already oppressively warm. Presently I saw my uncle advancing beneath the trees, hat off, and wiping his brow; while far behind staggered poor old Yorpy, with what seemed one of the gates of Gaza on his back.

"Come, hurrah, stump along, Yorpy!" cried my uncle, impatiently turning round every now and then.

Upon the black's staggering up to the skiff, I perceived that the great gate of Gaza was transformed into a huge, shabby, oblong box, hermetically sealed. The sphinx-like blankness of the box quadrupled the mystery in my mind.

"Is *this* the wonderful apparatus?" said I, in amazement. "Why, it's nothing but a battered old dry-goods box, nailed up. And is *this* the thing, uncle, that is to make you a million of dollars ere the year be out? What a forlorn-looking, lack-lustre, old ash-box it is."

"Put it into the skiff!" roared my uncle to Yorpy, without heeding my boyish disdain. "Put it in, you grizzled-headed cherub—put it in carefully, carefully! If that box bursts, my everlasting fortune collapses."

"Bursts?—collapses?" cried I, in alarm. "It ain't full of combustibles? Quick! let me go to the further end of the boat!"

"Sit still, you simpleton!" cried my uncle again. "Jump in, Yorpy, and hold on to the box like grim death while I shove off. Carefully! carefully! you dunderheaded black! Mind t'other side of the box, I say! Do you mean to destroy the box?"

"Duyvel take te pox!" muttered old Yorpy, who was a sort of Dutch African. "De pox has been my cuss for de ten long 'ear."

"Now, then, we're off—take an oar, youngster; you, Yorpy, clinch the box fast. Here we go now. Carefully! carefully! You, Yorpy, stop shaking the box! Easy! easy! there's a big snag. Pull now. Hurrah! deep water at last! Now give way, youngster, and away to the island."

"The island!" said I. "There's no island hereabouts."

"There is ten miles above the bridge, though," said my uncle, determinately.

"Ten miles off! Pull that old dry-goods box ten miles up the river in this blazing sun!"

"All that I have to say," said my uncle, firmly, "is that we are bound to Quash Island."

"Mercy, uncle! if I had known of this great long pull of ten mortal miles in this fiery sun, you wouldn't have juggled *me* into the skiff so easy. What's *in* that box?—paving-stones? See how the skiff settles down under it. I won't help pull a box of paving-stones ten miles. What's the use of pulling 'em?"

"Look you, simpleton," quoth my uncle, pausing upon his suspended oar. "Stop rowing, will ye! Now then, if you don't want to share in the glory of my experiment; if you are wholly indifferent to halving its immortal renown; I say, sir, if you care not to be present at the first trial of my Great Hydraulic-Hydrostatic Apparatus for draining swamps and marshes, and converting them, at the rate of one acre the hour, into fields more fertile than those of the Genessee; if you care not, I repeat, to have this proud thing to tell—in far future days, when poor old I shall have been long dead and gone, boy—to your children, and your children's children; in that case, sir, you are free to land forthwith."

"Oh, uncle! I did not mean—"

"No words, sir! Yorpy, take his oar, and help pull him ashore."

"But, my dear uncle; I declare to you that—"

"Not a syllable, sir: you have cast open scorn upon the Great Hydraulic-Hydrostatic Apparatus. Yorpy, put him ashore, Yorpy. It's shallow here again. Jump out, Yorpy, and wade with him ashore."

"Now, my dear, good, kind uncle, do but pardon me this one time, and I will say just nothing about the apparatus."

"Say nothing about it! when it is my express end and aim it shall be famous! Put him ashore, Yorpy."

"Nay uncle, I *will* not give up my oar. I have an oar in this matter, and I mean to keep it. You shall not cheat me out of my share of your glory."

"Ah, now there—that's sensible. You may stay, youngster. Pull again now."

We were all silent for a time, steadily plying our way. At last I ventured to break water once more.

"I am glad, dear uncle, you have revealed to me at last the nature and end of your great experiment. It is the effectual draining of swamps; an attempt, dear uncle, in which, if you do but succeed (as I know you will), you will earn the glory denied to a Roman emperor. He tried to drain the Pontine marsh, but failed."

"The world has shot ahead the length of its own diameter since then," quoth my uncle, proudly. "If that Roman emperor were here, *I*'d show him what can be done in the present enlightened age."

Seeing my good uncle so far mollified now as to be quite self-complacent, I ventured another remark.

"This is a rather severe, hot pull, dear uncle."

"Glory is not to be gained, youngster, without pulling hard for it—against the stream, too, as we do now. The natural tendency of man, in the mass, is to go down with the universal current into oblivion."

"But why pull so far, dear uncle, upon the present occasion? Why pull ten miles for it? You do but propose, as I understand it, to put to the actual test this admirable invention of yours. And could it not be tested almost any where?"

"Simple boy," quoth my uncle, "would you have some malignant spy steal from me the fruits of ten long years of high-hearted, persevering endeavor? Solitary in my scheme, I go to a solitary place to test it. If I fail—for all things are possible—no one out of the family will know it. If I succeed, secure in the secrecy of my invention, I can boldly demand any price for its publication."

"Pardon me, dear uncle; you are wiser than I."

"'One would think years and gray hairs should bring wisdom, boy."

"Yorpy there, dear uncle; think you his grizzled locks thatch a brain improved by long life?"

"Am I Yorpy, boy? Keep to your oar!"

Thus padlocked again, I said no further word till the skiff grounded on the shallows, some twenty yards from the deep-wooded isle.

"Hush!" whispered my uncle, intensely; "not a word now!" and he sat perfectly still, slowly sweeping with his glance the whole country around, even to both banks of the here wide-expanded stream.

"Wait till that horseman, yonder, passes!" he whispered again, pointing to a speck moving along a lofty, river-side road, which perilously wound on midway up a long line of broken bluffs and cliffs. "There—he's out of sight now, behind the copse. Quick! Yorpy! Carefully, though! Jump overboard, and shoulder the box, and—Hold!"

We were all mute and motionless again.

"Ain't that a boy, sitting like Zaccheus in yonder tree of the orchard on the other bank? Look, youngster—young eyes are better than old—don't you see him?"

"Dear uncle, I see the orchard, but I can't see any boy."

"He's a spy—I know he is," suddenly said my uncle, disregardful of my answer, and intently gazing, shading his eyes with his flattened hand. "Don't touch the box, Yorpy. Crouch! crouch down, all of ye!"

"Why, uncle—there—see—the boy is only a withered white bough. I see it very plainly now."

"You don't see the tree I mean," quoth my uncle, with a decided air of relief, "but never mind; I defy the boy. Yorpy, jump out, and shoulder the box. And now then, youngster, off with your shoes and stockings, roll up your trowsers legs, and follow me. Carefully, Yorpy, carefully. That's more precious than a box of gold, mind."

"Heavy as de gelt anyhow," growled Yorpy, staggering and splashing in the shallows beneath it.

"There, stop under the bushes there—in among the flags—so—gently, gently—there, put it down just there. Now, youngster, are you ready? Follow—tiptoes, tiptoes!"

"I can't wade in this mud and water on my tiptoes, uncle; and I don't see the need of it either."

"Go ashore, sir—instantly!"

"Why, uncle, I *am* ashore."

"Peace! follow me, and no more."

Crouching in the water in complete secrecy, beneath the bushes and among the tall flags, my uncle now stealthily produced a hammer and wrench from one of his enormous pockets, and presently tapped the box. But the sound alarmed him.

"Yorpy," he whispered, "go you off to the right, behind the bushes, and keep watch. If you see any one coming, whistle softly. Youngster, you do the same to the left."

We obeyed; and presently, after considerable hammering and supplemental tinkering, my uncle's voice was heard in the utter solitude, loudly commanding our return.

Again we obeyed, and now found the cover of the box removed. All eagerness, I peeped in, and saw a surprising multiplicity of convoluted metal pipes and syringes of all sorts and varieties, all sizes and calibres, inextricably interwreathed together in one gigantic coil. It looked like a huge nest of anacondas and adders.

"Now then, Yorpy," said my uncle, all animation, and flushed with the foretaste of glory, "do you stand this side, and be ready to tip when I give the word. And do you, youngster, stand ready to do as much for the other side. Mind, don't budge it the fraction of a barley-corn till I say the word. All depends on a proper adjustment."

"No fear, uncle. I will be careful as a lady's tweezers."

"I s'ant lift de heavy pox," growled old Yorpy, "till de wort pe given; no fear o' dat."

"Oh boy," said my uncle now, upturning his face devotionally, while a really noble gleam irradiated his gray eyes, locks, and wrinkles; "oh boy! this, *this* is the hour which for ten long years has, in the prospect, sustained me through all my pains-taking obscurity. Fame will be the sweeter because it comes at the last; the truer, because it comes to an old man like me, not to a boy like you. Sustainer! I glorify Thee."

He bowed over his venerable head, and—as I live—something like a shower-drop somehow fell from my face into the shallows.

"Tip!"

We tipped.

"A little more!"

We tipped a little more.

"A *leetle* more!"

We tipped a *leetle* more.

"Just a *leetle*, very *leetle* bit more."

With great difficulty we tipped just a *leetle*, very *leetle* more.

All this time my uncle was diligently stooping over, and striving to peep in, up, and under the box where the coiled anacondas and adders lay; but the machine being now fairly immersed, the attempt was wholly vain.

He rose erect, and waded slowly all round the box; his countenance firm and reliant, but not a little troubled and vexed.

It was plain something or other was going wrong. But as I was left in utter ignorance as to the mystery of the contrivance, I could not tell where the difficulty lay, or what was the proper remedy.

Once more, still more slowly, still more vexedly, my uncle waded round the box, the dissatisfaction gradually deepening, but still controlled, and still with hope at the bottom of it.

Nothing could be more sure than that some anticipated effect had, as yet, failed to develop itself. Certain I was, too, that the water-line did not lower about my legs.

"Tip it a *leetle* bit—very *leetle* now."

"Dear uncle, it is tipped already as far as it can be. Don't you see it rests now square on its bottom?"

"You, Yorpy, take your black hoof from under the box!"

This gust of passion on the part of my uncle made the matter seem still more dubious and dark. It was a bad symptom, I thought.

"Surely you *can* tip it just a *leetle* more!"

"Not a hair, uncle."

"Blast and blister the cursed box then!" roared my uncle, in a terrific voice, sudden as a squall. Running at the box, he dashed his bare foot into it, and with astonishing power all but crushed in the side. Then seizing the whole box, he disemboweled it of all its anacondas and adders, and, tearing and wrenching them, flung them right and left over the water.

"Hold, hold, my dear, dear uncle!—do for heaven's sake desist. Don't destroy so, in one frantic moment, all your long calm years of devotion to one darling scheme. Hold, I conjure!"

Moved by my vehement voice and uncontrollable tears, he paused in his work of destruction, and stood steadfastly eying me, or rather blankly staring at me, like one demented.

"It is not yet wholly ruined, dear uncle; come put it together now. You have hammer and wrench; put it together again, and try it once more. While there is life there is hope."

"While there is life hereafter there is *despair*," he howled.

"Do, do now, dear uncle—here, here, put these pieces together; or, if that can't be done without more tools, try a *section* of it—that will do just as well. Try it once; try, uncle."

My persistent persuasiveness told upon him. The stubborn stump of hope, plowed at and uprooted in vain, put forth one last miraculous green sprout.

Steadily and carefully culling out of the wreck some of the more curious-looking fragments, he mysteriously involved them together, and then, clearing out the box, slowly inserted them there, and ranging Yorpy and me as before, bade us tip the box once again.

We did so; and as no perceptible effect yet followed, I was each moment looking for the previous command to tip the box over yet more, when, glancing into my uncle's face, I started aghast. It seemed pinched, shriveled into mouldy whiteness, like a mildewed grape. I dropped the box, and sprang toward him just in time to prevent his fall.

Leaving the woeful box where we had dropped it, Yorpy and I helped the old man into the skiff, and silently pulled from Quash Isle.

How swiftly the current now swept us down! How hardly before had we striven to stem it! I thought of my poor uncle's saying, not an hour gone by, about the universal drift of the mass of humanity toward utter oblivion.

"Boy!" said my uncle at last, lifting his head.

I looked at him earnestly, and was gladdened to see that the terrible blight of his face had almost departed.

"Boy, there's not much left in an old world for an old man to invent."

I said nothing.

"Boy, take my advice, and never try to invent any thing but—happiness."

I said nothing.

"Boy, about ship, and pull back for the box."

"Dear uncle!"

"It will make a good wood-box, boy. And faithful old Yorpy can sell the old iron for tobacco-money."

"Dear massa! dear old massa! dat be very fust time in de ten long 'ear yoo hab mention kindly old Yorpy. I tank yoo, dear old massa; I tank yoo so kindly. Yoo is yourself agin in de ten long 'ear."

"Ay, long ears enough," sighed my uncle; "Esopian ears. But it's all over now. Boy, I'm glad I've failed. I say, boy, failure has made a good old man of me. It was horrible at first, but I'm glad I've failed. Praise be to God for the failure!"

His face kindled with a strange, rapt earnestness. I have never forgotten that look. If the event made my uncle a good old man, as he called it, it made me a wise young one. Example did for me the work of experience.

When some years had gone by, and my dear old uncle began to fail, and, after peaceful days of autumnal content, was gathered gently to his fathers—faithful old Yorpy closing his eyes—as I took my last look at his venerable face, the pale resigned lips seemed to move. I seemed to hear again his deep, fervent cry—"Praise be to God for the failure!"

The Fiddler

SO MY POEM IS DAMNED, and immortal fame is not for me! I am nobody forever and ever. Intolerable fate!

Snatching my hat, I dashed down the criticism, and rushed out into Broadway, where enthusiastic throngs were crowding to a circus in a side-street near by, very recently started, and famous for a capital clown.

Presently my old friend Standard rather boisterously accosted me.

"Well met, Helmstone, my boy! Ah! what's the matter? Haven't been committing murder? Ain't flying justice? You look wild!"

"You have seen it, then?" said I, of course referring to the criticism.

"Oh yes; I was there at the morning performance. Great clown, I assure you. But here comes Hautboy. Hautboy—Helmstone."

Without having time or inclination to resent so mortifying a mistake, I was instantly soothed as I gazed on the face of the new acquaintance so unceremoniously introduced. His person was short and full, with a juvenile, animated cast to it. His complexion rurally ruddy; his eye sincere, cheery, and gray. His hair alone betrayed that he was not an overgrown boy. From his hair I set him down as forty or more.

"Come, Standard," he gleefully cried to my friend, "are you not going to the circus? The clown is inimitable, they say. Come; Mr. Helmstone, too—come both; and circus over, we'll take a nice stew and punch at Taylor's."

The sterling content, good-humor, and extraordinary ruddy, sincere expression of this most singular new acquaintance acted upon me like magic. It seemed mere loyalty to human nature to accept an invitation from so unmistakably kind and honest a heart.

During the circus performance I kept my eye more on Hautboy than on the celebrated clown. Hautboy was the sight for me. Such genuine enjoyment as his struck me to the soul with a sense of the reality of the thing called happiness. The jokes of the clown he seemed to roll under his tongue as ripe magnum-bonums. Now the foot, now the hand, was employed to attest his grateful applause. At any hit more than ordinary, he turned upon Standard and me to see if his rare pleasure was shared. In a man of forty I saw a boy of twelve; and this too without the slightest abatement of my respect. Because all was so honest and natural, every expression and attitude so graceful with genuine good-nature, that the marvelous juvenility of Hautboy assumed a sort of divine and immortal air, like that of some forever youthful god of Greece.

But much as I gazed upon Hautboy, and much as I admired his air, yet that desperate mood in which I had first rushed from the house had not so entirely departed as not to molest me with momentary returns. But from these relapses I would rouse myself, and swiftly glance round the broad amphitheatre of eagerly interested and all-applauding human faces. Hark! claps, thumps, deafening huzzas; the vast assembly seemed frantic with acclamation; and what, mused I, has caused all this? Why, the clown only comically grinned with one of his extra grins.

Then I repeated in my mind that sublime passage in my poem, in which Cleothemes the Argive vindicates the justice of the war. Ay, ay, thought I to myself, did I now leap into the ring there, and repeat that identical passage, nay, enact the whole tragic poem before them, would they applaud the poet as they applaud the clown? No! They would hoot me, and call me doting or mad. Then what does this prove? Your infatuation or their insensibility? Perhaps both; but indubitably the first. But why wail? Do you seek admiration from the admirers of a buffoon? Call to mind the saying of the Athenian, who, when the people vociferously applauded in the forum, asked his friend in a whisper, what foolish thing had he said?

Again my eye swept the circus, and fell on the ruddy radiance of the countenance of Hautboy. But its clear honest cheeriness disdained my disdain. My intolerant pride was rebuked. And yet Hautboy dreamed not what magic reproof to a soul like mine sat on his laughing brow. At the very instant I felt the dart of the censure, his eye twinkled, his hand waved, his voice was lifted in jubilant delight at another joke of the inexhaustible clown.

Circus over, we went to Taylor's. Among crowds of others, we sat down to our stews and punches at one of the small marble tables. Hautboy sat opposite to me. Though greatly subdued from its former hilarity, his face still shone with gladness. But added to this was a quality not so prominent before; a certain serene expression of leisurely, deep good sense. Good sense and good humor in him joined hands. As the conversation proceeded between the brisk Standard and him—for I said little or nothing—I was more and more struck with the excellent judgment he evinced. In most of his remarks upon a variety of topics Hautboy seemed intuitively to hit the exact line between enthusiasm and apathy. It was plain that while Hautboy saw the world pretty much as it was, yet he did not theoretically espouse its bright side nor its dark side. Rejecting all solutions, he but acknowledged facts. What was sad in the world he did not superficially gainsay; what was glad in it he did not cynically slur; and all which was to him personally enjoyable, he gratefully took to his heart. It was plain, then—so it seemed at that moment, at least—that his extraordinary cheerfulness did not arise either from deficiency of feeling or thought.

Suddenly remembering an engagement, he took up his hat, bowed pleasantly, and left us.

"Well, Helmstone," said Standard, inaudibly drumming on the slab, "what do you think of your new acquaintance?"

The two last words tingled with a peculiar and novel significance.

"New acquaintance indeed," echoed I. "Standard, I owe you a thousand thanks for introducing me to one of the most singular men I have ever seen. It needed the optical sight of such a man to believe in the possibility of his existence."

"You rather like him, then," said Standard, with ironical dryness.

"I hugely love and admire him, Standard. I wish I were Hautboy."

"Ah? That's a pity now. There's only one Hautboy in the world."

This last remark set me to pondering again, and somehow it revived my dark mood.

"His wonderful cheerfulness, I suppose," said I, sneering with spleen, "originates not less in a felicitous fortune than in a felicitous temper. His great good sense is apparent; but great good sense may exist without sublime endowments. Nay, I take it, in certain cases, that good sense is simply owing to the absence of those. Much more, cheerfulness. Unpossessed of genius, Hautboy is eternally blessed."

"Ah? You would not think him an extraordinary genius then?"

"Genius? What! such a short, fat fellow a genius! Genius, like Cassius, is lank."

"Ah? But could you not fancy that Hautboy might formerly have had genius, but luckily getting rid of it, at last fatted up?"

"For a genius to get rid of his genius is as impossible as for a man in the galloping consumption to get rid of that."

"Ah? You speak very decidedly."

"Yes, Standard," cried I, increasing in spleen, "your cheery Hautboy, after all, is no pattern, no lesson for you and me. With average abilities; opinions clear, because circumscribed; passions docile, because they are feeble; a temper hilarious, because he was born to it—how can your Hautboy be made a reasonable example to a heady fellow like you, or an ambitious dreamer like me? Nothing tempts him beyond common limit; in himself he has nothing to restrain. By constitution he is exempted from all moral harm. Could ambition but prick him; had he but once heard applause, or endured contempt, a very different man would your Hautboy be. Acquiescent and calm from the cradle to the grave, he obviously slides through the crowd."

"Ah?"

"Why do you say *ah* to me so strangely whenever I speak?"

"Did you ever hear of Master Betty?"

"The great English prodigy, who long ago ousted the Siddons and the Kembles from Drury Lane, and made the whole town run mad with acclamation?"

"The same," said Standard, once more inaudibly drumming on the slab.

I looked at him perplexed. He seemed to be holding the master-key of our theme in mysterious reserve; seemed to be throwing out his Master Betty too, to puzzle me only the more.

"What under heaven can Master Betty, the great genius and prodigy, an English boy twelve years old, have to do with the poor common-place plodder Hautboy, an American of forty?"

"Oh, nothing in the least. I don't imagine that they ever saw each other. Besides, Master Betty must be dead and buried long ere this."

"Then why cross the ocean, and rifle the grave to drag his remains into this living discussion?"

"Absent-mindedness, I suppose. I humbly beg pardon. Proceed with your observations on Hautboy. You think he never had genius, quite too contented and happy, and fat for that—ah? You think him no pattern for men in general? affording no lesson of value to neglected merit, genius ignored, or impotent presumption rebuked?—all of which three amount to much the same thing. You admire his cheerfulness, while scorning his common-place soul. Poor Hautboy, how sad that your very cheerfulness should, by a by-blow, bring you despite!"

"I don't say I scorn him; you are unjust. I simply declare that he is no pattern for me."

A sudden noise at my side attracted my ear. Turning, I saw Hautboy again, who very blithely reseated himself on the chair he had left.

"I was behind time with my engagement," said Hautboy, "so thought I would run back and rejoin you. But come, you have sat long enough here. Let us go to my rooms. It is only a five minutes' walk."

"If you will promise to fiddle for us, we will," said Standard.

Fiddle! thought I—he's a jigembob *fiddler* then? No wonder genius declines to measure its pace to a fiddler's bow. My spleen was very strong on me now.

"I will gladly fiddle you your fill," replied Hautboy to Standard. "Come on."

In a few minutes we found ourselves in the fifth story of a sort of storehouse, in a lateral street to Broadway. It was curiously furnished with all sorts of odd furniture which seemed to have been obtained, piece by piece, at auctions of old-fashioned household stuff. But all was charmingly clean and cosy.

Pressed by Standard, Hautboy forthwith got out his dented old fiddle, and sitting down on a tall rickety stool, played away right merrily at Yankee Doodle and other off-handed, dashing, and disdainfully care-free airs. But common as were the tunes, I was transfixed by something miraculously superior in the style. Sitting there on the old stool, his rusty hat sideways cocked on his head, one foot dangling adrift, he plied the bow of an enchanter. All my moody discontent, every vestige of peevishness fled. My whole splenetic soul capitulated to the magical fiddle.

"Something of an Orpheus, ah?" said Standard, archly nudging me beneath the left rib.

"And I, the charmed Bruin," murmured I.

The fiddle ceased. Once more, with redoubled curiosity, I gazed upon the easy, indifferent Hautboy. But he entirely baffled inquisition.

When, leaving him, Standard and I were in the street once more, I earnestly conjured him to tell me who, in sober truth, this marvelous Hautboy was.

"Why, haven't you seen him? And didn't you yourself lay his whole anatomy open on the marble slab at Taylor's? What more can you possibly learn? Doubtless your own masterly insight has already put you in possession of all."

"You mock me, Standard. There is some mystery here. Tell me, I entreat you, who is Hautboy?"

"An extraordinary genius, Helmstone," said Standard, with sudden ardor, "who in boyhood drained the whole flagon of glory; whose going from city to city was a going from triumph to triumph. One who has been an object of wonder to the wisest, been caressed by the loveliest, received the open homage of thousands on thousands of the rabble. But to-day he walks Broadway and no man knows him. With you and me, the elbow of the hurrying clerk, and the pole of the remorseless omnibus, shove him. He who has a hundred times been crowned with laurels, now wears, as you see, a bunged beaver. Once fortune poured showers of gold into his lap, as showers of laurel leaves upon his brow. To-day, from house to house he hies, teaching fiddling for a living. Crammed once with fame, he is now hilarious without it. *With* genius and *without* fame, he is happier than a king. More a prodigy now than ever."

"His true name?"

"Let me whisper it in your ear."

"What! Oh Standard, myself, as a child, have shouted myself hoarse applauding that very name in the theatre."

"I have heard your poem was not very handsomely received," said Standard, now suddenly shifting the subject.

"Not a word of that, for heaven's sake!" cried I. "If Cicero, traveling in the East, found sympathetic solace for his grief in beholding the arid overthrow of a once gorgeous city, shall not my petty affair be as nothing, when I behold in Hautboy the vine and the rose climbing the shattered shafts of his tumbled temple of Fame?"

Next day I tore all my manuscripts, bought me a fiddle, and went to take regular lessons of Hautboy.

Cock-A-Doodle-Doo!

Or, The Crowing of the Noble Cock Beneventano

IN ALL PARTS OF THE WORLD many high-spirited revolts from rascally despotisms had of late been knocked on the head; many dreadful casualties, by locomotive and steamer, had likewise knocked hundreds of high-spirited travelers on the head (I lost a dear friend in one of them); my own private affairs were also full of despotisms, casualties, and knockings on the head, when early one morning in Spring, being too full of hypoes to sleep, I sallied out to walk on my hill-side pasture.

It was a cool and misty, damp, disagreeable air. The country looked underdone, its raw juices squirting out all round. I buttoned out this squitchy air as well as I could with my lean, double-breasted dress-coat—my over-coat being so long-skirted I only used it in my wagon—and spitefully thrusting my crab-stick into the oozy sod, bent my blue form to the steep ascent of the hill. This toiling posture brought my head pretty well earthward, as if I were in the act of butting it against the world. I marked the fact, but only grinned at it with a ghastly grin.

All round me were tokens of a divided empire. The old grass and the new grass were striving together. In the low wet swales the verdure peeped out in vivid green; beyond, on the mountains, lay light patches of snow, strangely relieved against their russet sides; all the humped hills looked like brindled kine in the shivers. The woods were strewn with dry dead boughs, snapped off by the riotous winds of March, while the young trees skirting the woods were just beginning to show the first yellowish tinge of the nascent spray.

I sat down for a moment on a great rotting log nigh the top of the hill, my back to a heavy grove, my face presented toward a wide sweeping circuit of mountains enclosing a rolling, diversified country. Along the base of one long range of heights ran a lagging, fever-and-agueish river, over which was a duplicate stream of dripping mist, exactly corresponding in every meander with its parent water below. Low down, here and there, shreds of vapor listlessly wandered in the air, like abandoned or helmless nations or ships—or very soaky towels hung on criss-cross clothes-lines to dry. Afar, over a distant village lying in a bay of the plain formed by the mountains, there rested a great flat canopy of haze, like a pall. It was the condensed smoke of the chimneys, with the condensed, exhaled breath of the villagers, prevented from dispersion by the imprisoning hills. It was too heavy and lifeless to mount of itself; so there it lay, between the village and the sky, doubtless hiding many a man with the mumps, and many a queasy child.

My eye ranged over the capacious rolling country, and over the mountains, and over the village, and over a farm-house here and there, and over woods, groves, streams, rocks, fells—and I thought to myself, what a slight mark, after all, does man make on this huge great earth. Yet the earth makes a mark on him. What a horrid accident was that on the Ohio, where my good friend and thirty other good fellows were sloped into eternity at the bidding of a thick-headed engineer, who knew not a valve from a flue. And that crash on the railroad just over yon mountains there, where two infatuate trains ran pell-mell into each other, and climbed and clawed each other's backs; and one locomotive was found fairly shelled, like a chick, inside of a passenger car in the antagonist train; and near a score of noble hearts, a bride and her groom, and an innocent little infant, were all disembarked into the grim hulk of Charon, who ferried them over, all baggageless, to some clinkered iron-foundry country or other. Yet what's the use of complaining? What justice of the peace will right this matter? Yea, what's the use of bothering the very heavens about it? Don't the heavens themselves ordain these things—else they could not happen?

A miserable world! Who would take the trouble to make a fortune in it, when he knows not how long he can keep it, for the thousand villains and asses who have the management of railroads and steamboats, and innumerable other vital things in the world. If they would make me Dictator in North America a while, I'd string them up! and hang, draw, and quarter; fry, roast, and boil; stew, grill, and devil them, like so many turkey-legs—the rascally numskulls of stokers; I'd set them to stokering in Tartarus—I would.

Great improvements of the age! What! to call the facilitation of death and murder an improvement! Who wants to travel so fast? My grandfather did not, and he was no fool. Hark! here comes that old dragon again—that gigantic gad-fly of a Moloch—snort! puff! scream!—here he comes straight-bent through these vernal woods, like the Asiatic cholera cantering on a camel. Stand aside! here he comes, the chartered murderer! the death monopolizer! judge, jury, and hangman all together, whose victims die always without benefit of clergy. For two hundred and fifty miles that iron fiend goes yelling through the land, crying "More! more! more!" Would fifty conspiring mountains would fall atop of him! And, while they were about it, would they would also fall atop of that smaller dunning fiend, my creditor, who frightens the life out of me more than any locomotive—a lantern-jawed rascal, who seems to run on a railroad track too, and duns me even on Sunday, all the way to church and back, and comes and sits in the same pew with me, and pretending to be polite and hand me the prayer-book opened at the proper place, pokes his pesky bill under my nose in the very midst of my devotions, and so shoves himself between me and salvation; for how can one keep his temper on such occasions?

I can't pay this horrid man; and yet they say money was never so plentiful—a drug in the market; but blame me if I can get any of the drug, though there never was a sick man more in need of that particular sort of medicine. It's a lie; money ain't plenty—feel of my pocket. Ha! here's a powder I was going to send to the sick baby in yonder hovel, where the Irish ditcher lives. That baby has the scarlet fever. They say the measles are rife in the country too, and the varioloid, and the chicken-pox, and it's bad for teething children. And after all, I suppose many of the poor little ones, after going through all this trouble, snap off short; and so they had the measles, mumps, croup, scarlet-fever, chicken-pox, cholera-morbus, summer-complaint, and all else, in vain! Ah! there's that twinge of the rheumatics in my right shoulder. I got it one night on the North River, when, in a crowded boat, I gave up my berth to a sick lady, and staid on deck till morning in drizzling weather. There's the thanks one gets for charity! Twinge! Shoot away, ye rheumatics! Ye couldn't lay on worse if I were some villain who had murdered the lady instead of befriending her. Dyspepsia too—I am troubled with that.

Hallo! here come the calves, the two-year-olds, just turned out of the barn into the pasture, after six months of cold victuals. What a miserable-looking set, to be sure! A breaking up of a hard winter, that's certain: sharp bones sticking out like elbows; all quilted with a strange stuff dried on their flanks like layers of pancakes. Hair worn quite off too, here and there; and where it ain't pancaked, or worn off, looks like the rubbed sides of mangy old hair-trunks. In fact, they are not six two-year-olds, but six abominable old hair-trunks wandering about here in this pasture.

Hark! By Jove, what's that? See! the very hair-trunks prick their ears at it, and stand and gaze away down into the rolling country yonder. Hark again! How clear! how musical! how prolonged! What a triumphant thanksgiving of a cock-crow! "*Glory be to God in the highest!*" It says those very words as plain as ever cock did in this world. Why, why, I begin to feel a little in sorts again. It ain't so very misty, after all. The sun yonder is beginning to show himself: I feel warmer.

Hark! There again! Did ever such a blessed cock-crow so ring out over the earth before! Clear, shrill, full of pluck, full of fire, full of fun, full of glee. It plainly says—"*Never say die!*" My friends, it is extraordinary is it not?

Unwittingly, I found that I had been addressing the two-year-olds—the calves—in my enthusiasm; which shows how one's true nature will betray itself at times in the most unconscious way. For what a very two-year-old, and calf, I had been to fall into the sulks, on a hill-top too, when a cock down in the lowlands there, without discourse of reason, and quite penniless in the world, and with death hanging over him at any moment from his hungry master, sends up a cry like a very laureate celebrating the glorious victory of New Orleans.

Hark! there it goes again! My friends, that must be a Shanghai; no domestic-born cock could crow in such prodigious exulting strains. Plainly, my friends, a Shanghai of the Emperor of China's breed.

But my friends the hair-trunks, fairly alarmed at last by such clamorously-victorious tones, were now scampering off, with their tails flirting in the air, and capering with their legs in clumsy enough sort of style, sufficiently evincing that they had not freely flourished them for the six months last past.

Hark! there again! Whose cock is that? Who in this region can afford to buy such an extraordinary Shanghai? Bless me—it makes my blood bound—I feel wild. What? jumping on this rotten old log here, to flap my elbows and crow too? And just now in the doleful dumps. And all this from the simple crow of a cock. Marvelous cock! But soft—this fellow now crows most lustily; but it's only morning; let's see how he'll crow about noon, and toward night-fall. Come to think of it, cocks crow mostly in the beginning of the day. Their pluck ain't lasting, after all. Yes, yes; even cocks have to succumb to the universal spell of tribulation: jubilant in the beginning, but down in the mouth at the end.

> . . . . "Of fine mornings,
> We fine lusty cocks begin our crows in gladness;
> But when eve does come we don't crow quite so much,
> For then cometh despondency and madness."

The poet had this very Shanghai in his mind when he wrote that. But stop. There he rings out again, ten times richer, fuller, longer, more obstreperously exulting than before! Why this is equal to hearing the great bell of St. Paul's rung at a coronation! In fact, that bell ought to be taken down, and this Shanghai put in its place. Such a crow would jollify all London, from Mile-End (which is no end) to Primrose Hill (where there ain't any primroses), and scatter the fog.

Well, I have an appetite for my breakfast this morning, if I have not had it for a week before. I meant to have only tea and toast; but I'll have coffee and eggs—no, brown-stout and a beef-steak. I want something hearty. Ah, here comes the down-train: white cars, flashing through the trees like a vein of silver. How cheerfully the steam-pipe chirps! Gay are the passengers. There waves a handkerchief—going down to the city to eat oysters, and see their friends, and drop in at the circus. Look at the mist yonder; what soft curls and undulations round the hills, and the sun weaving his rays among them. See the azure smoke of the village, like the azure tester over a bridal-bed. How bright the country looks there where the river overflowed the meadows. The old grass has to knock under to the new. Well, I feel the better for this walk. Home now, and walk into that steak and crack that bottle of brown-stout; and by the time that's drank—a quart of stout—by that time, I shall feel about as stout as Samson. Come to think of it, that dun may call, though. I'll just visit the woods and cut a club. I'll club him, by Jove, if he duns me this day.

Hark! there goes Shanghai again. Shanghai says, "Bravo!" Shanghai says, "Club him!"

Oh, brave cock!

I felt in rare spirits the whole morning. The dun called about eleven. I had the boy Jake send the dun up. I was reading Tristram Shandy, and could not go down under the circumstances. The lean rascal (a lean farmer, too—think of that!) entered, and found me seated in an arm-chair, with my feet on the table, and the second bottle of brown-stout handy, and the book under eye.

"Sit down," said I; "I'll finish this chapter, and then attend to you. Fine morning. Ha! ha!—this is a fine joke about my Uncle Toby and the Widow Wadman! Ha! ha! ha! let me read this to you."

"I have no time; I've got my noon *chores* to do."

"To the deuce with your *chores!*" said I. "Don't drop your old tobacco about here, or I'll turn you out."

"Sir!"

"Let me read you this about the Widow Wadman. 'Said the Widow Wadman—' "

"There's my bill, sir."

"Very good. Just twist it up, will you;—it's about my smoking-time; and hand a coal, will you, from the hearth yonder!"

"My bill, sir!" said the rascal, turning pale with rage and amazement at my unwonted air (formerly I had always dodged him with a pale face), but too prudent as yet to betray the extremity of his astonishment. "My bill, sir!"—and he stiffly poked it at me.

"My friend," said I, "what a charming morning! How sweet the country looks! Pray, did you hear that extraordinary cock-crow this morning? Take a glass of my stout!"

"*Yours?* First pay your debts before you offer folks *your* stout!"

"You think, then, that, properly speaking, I have no *stout*," said I, deliberately rising. "I'll undeceive you. I'll show you stout of a superior brand to Barclay and Perkins."

Without more ado, I seized that insolent dun by the slack of his coat—(and, being a lean, shad-bellied wretch, there was plenty of slack to it)—I seized him that way, tied him with a sailor-knot, and, thrusting his bill between his teeth, introduced him to the open country lying round about my place of abode.

"Jake," said I, "you'll find a sack of blue-nosed potatoes lying under the shed. Drag it here, and pelt this pauper away: he's been begging pence of me, and I know he can work, but he's lazy. Pelt him away, Jake!"

Bless my stars, what a crow! Shanghai sent up such a perfect pæan and *laudamus*—such a trumpet-blast of triumph, that my soul fairly snorted in me. Duns!—I could have fought an army of them! Plainly, Shanghai was of the opinion that duns only came into the world to be kicked, hanged, bruised, battered, choked, walloped, hammered, drowned, clubbed!

Returning in-doors, when the exultation of my victory over the dun had a little subsided, I fell to musing over the mysterious Shanghai. I had no idea I would hear him so nigh my house. I wondered from what rich gentleman's yard he crowed. Nor had he cut short his crows so easily as I had supposed he would. This Shanghai crowed till mid-day, at least. Would he keep a-crowing all day? I resolved to learn. Again I ascended the hill. The whole country was now bathed in a rejoicing sunlight. The warm verdure was bursting all round me. Teams were a-field. Birds, newly arrived from the South, were blithely singing in the air. Even the crows cawed with a certain unction, and seemed a shade or two less black than usual.

Hark! there goes the cock! How shall I describe the crow of the Shanghai at noon-tide? His sun-rise crow was a whisper to it. It was the loudest, longest, and most strangely-musical crow that ever amazed mortal man. I had heard plenty of cock-crows before, and many fine ones; —but this one! so smooth and flute-like in its very clamor—so self-possessed in its very rapture of exultation—so vast, mounting, swelling, soaring, as if spurted out from a golden throat, thrown far back. Nor did it sound like the foolish, vain-glorious crow of some young sophomorean cock, who knew not the world, and was beginning life in audacious gay spirits, because in wretched ignorance of what might be to come. It was the crow of a cock who crowed not without advice; the crow of a cock who knew a thing or two; the crow of a cock who had fought the world and got the better of it, and was now resolved to crow, though the earth should heave and the heavens should fall. It was a wise crow; an invincible crow; a philosophic crow; a crow of all crows.

I returned home once more full of reinvigorated spirits, with a dauntless sort of feeling. I thought over my debts and other troubles, and over the unlucky risings of the poor oppressed *peoples* abroad, and over the railroad and steamboat accidents, and over even the loss of my dear friend, with a calm, good-natured rapture of defiance, which astounded myself. I felt as though I could meet Death, and invite him to dinner, and toast the Catacombs with him, in pure overflow of self-reliance and a sense of universal security.

Toward evening I went up to the hill once more to find whether, indeed, the glorious cock would prove game even from the rising of the sun unto the going down thereof. Talk of Vespers or Curfew!—the evening crow of the cock went out of his mighty throat all over the land and inhabited it, like Xerxes from the East with his double-winged host. It was miraculous. Bless me, what a crow! The cock went game to roost that night, depend upon it, victorious over the entire day, and bequeathing the echoes of his thousand crows to night.

After an unwontedly sound, refreshing sleep I rose early, feeling like a carriage-spring—light—elliptical—airy—buoyant as sturgeon-nose—and, like a foot-ball, bounded up the hill. Hark! Shanghai was up before me. The early bird that caught the worm—crowing like a bugle worked by an engine—lusty, loud, all jubilation. From the scattered farm-houses a multitude of other cocks were crowing, and replying to each other's crows. But they were as flageolets to a trombone. Shanghai would suddenly break in, and overwhelm all their crows with his one domineering blast. He seemed to have nothing to do with any other concern. He replied to no other crow, but crowed solely by himself, on his own account, in solitary scorn and independence.

Oh, brave cock!—oh, noble Shanghai!—oh, bird rightly offered up by the invincible Socrates, in testimony of his final victory over life.

As I live, thought I, this blessed day will I go and seek out the Shanghai, and buy him, if I have to clap another mortgage on my land.

I listened attentively now, striving to mark from what direction the crow came. But it so charged and replenished, and made bountiful and overflowing all the air, that it was impossible to say from what precise point the exultation came. All that I could decide upon was this: the crow came from out of the East, and not from out of the West. I then considered with myself how far a cock-crow might be heard. In this still country, shut in, too, by mountains, sounds were audible at great distances. Besides, the undulations of the land, the abuttings of the mountains into the rolling hill and valley below, produced strange echoes, and reverberations, and multiplications, and accumulations of resonance, very remarkable to hear, and very puzzling to think of. Where lurked this valiant Shanghai—this bird of cheerful Socrates—the game-fowl Greek who died unappalled? Where lurked he? Oh, noble cock, where are you? Crow once more, my Bantam! my princely, my imperial Shanghai! my bird of the Emperor of China! Brother of the Sun! Cousin of great Jove! where are you?—one crow more, and tell me your master!

Hark! like a full orchestra of the cocks of all nations, forth burst the crow. But where from? There it is; but where? There was no telling, further than it came from out the East.

After breakfast I took my stick and sallied down the road. There were many gentlemen's seats dotting the neighboring country, and I made no doubt that some of these opulent gentlemen had invested a hundred dollar bill in some royal Shanghai recently imported in the ship Trade Wind, or the ship White Squall, or the ship Sovereign of the Seas; for it must needs have been a brave ship with a brave name which bore the fortunes of so brave a cock. I resolved to walk the entire country, and find this noble foreigner out; but thought it would not be amiss to inquire on the way at the humblest homesteads, whether, peradventure, they had heard of a lately-imported Shanghai belonging to any of the gentlemen settlers from the city; for it was plain that no poor farmer, no poor man of any sort, could own such an Oriental trophy—such a Great Bell of St. Paul's swung in a cock's throat.

I met an old man, plowing, in a field nigh the road-side fence.

"My friend, have you heard an extraordinary cock-crow of late?"

"Well, well," he drawled, "I don't know—the Widow Crowfoot has a cock—and Squire Squaretoes has a cock—and I have a cock, and they all crow. But I don't know of any on 'em with 'strordinary crows."

"Good-morning to you," said I, shortly; "it's plain that you have not heard the crow of the Emperor of China's chanticleer."

Presently I met another old man mending a tumble-down old rail-fence. The rails were rotten, and at every move of the old man's hand they crumbled into yellow ochre. He had much better let the fence alone, or else get him new rails. And here I must say, that one cause of the sad fact why idiocy more prevails among farmers than any other class of people, is owing to their undertaking the mending of rotten rail-fences in warm, relaxing spring weather. The enterprise is a hopeless one. It is a laborious one; it is a bootless one. It is an enterprise to make the heart break. Vast pains squandered upon a vanity. For how can one make rotten rail-fences stand up on their rotten pins? By what magic put pith into sticks which have lain freezing and baking through sixty consecutive winters and summers? This it is, this wretched endeavor to mend rotten rail-fences with their own rotten rails, which drives many farmers into the asylum.

On the face of the old man in question incipient idiocy was plainly marked. For, about sixty rods before him extended one of the most unhappy and desponding broken-hearted Virginia rail-fences I ever saw in my life. While in a field behind, were a set of young steers, possessed as by devils, continually butting at this forlorn old fence, and breaking through it here and there, causing the old man to drop his work and chase them back within bounds. He would chase them with a piece of rail huge as Goliath's beam, but as light as cork. At the first flourish, it crumbled into powder.

"My friend," said I, addressing this woeful mortal, "have you heard an extraordinary cock-crow of late?"

I might as well have asked him if he had heard the death-tick. He stared at me with a long, bewildered, doleful, and unutterable stare, and without reply resumed his unhappy labors.

What a fool, thought I, to have asked such an uncheerful and uncheerable creature about a cheerful cock!

I walked on. I had now descended the high land where my house stood, and being in a low tract could not hear the crow of the Shanghai, which doubtless overshot me there. Besides, the Shanghai might be at lunch of corn and oats, or taking a nap, and so interrupted his jubilations for a while.

At length, I encountered riding along the road, a portly gentleman—nay, a *pursy* one—of great wealth, who had recently purchased him some noble acres, and built him a noble mansion, with a goodly fowl-house attached, the fame whereof spread through all that country. Thought I, Here now is the owner of the Shanghai.

"Sir," said I, "excuse me, but I am a countryman of yours, and would ask, if so be you own any Shanghais?"

"Oh, yes; I have ten Shanghais."

"Ten!" exclaimed I, in wonder; "and do they all crow?"

"Most lustily; every soul of them; I wouldn't own a cock that wouldn't crow."

"Will you turn back, and show me those Shanghais?"

"With pleasure: I am proud of them. They cost me, in the lump, six hundred dollars."

As I walked by the side of his horse, I was thinking to myself whether possibly I had not mistaken the harmoniously combined crowings of ten Shanghais in a squad, for the supernatural crow of a single Shanghai by himself.

"Sir," said I, "is there one of your Shanghais which far exceeds all the others in the lustiness, musicalness, and inspiring effects of his crow?"

"They crow pretty much alike, I believe," he courteously replied; "I really don't know that I could tell their crow apart."

I began to think that after all my noble chanticleer might not be in the possession of this wealthy gentleman. However, we went into his fowl-yard, and I saw his Shanghais. Let me say that hitherto I had never clapped eye on this species of imported fowl. I had heard what enormous prices were paid for them, and also that they were of an enormous size, and had somehow fancied they must be of a beauty and brilliancy proportioned both to size and price. What was my surprise, then, to see ten carrot-colored monsters, without the smallest pretension to effulgence of plumage. Immediately, I determined that my royal cock was neither among these, nor could possibly be a Shanghai at all; if these gigantic gallows-bird fowl were fair specimens of the true Shanghai.

I walked all day, dining and resting at a farm-house, inspecting various fowl-yards, interrogating various owners of fowls, hearkening to various crows, but discovered not the mysterious chanticleer. Indeed, I had wandered so far and deviously, that I could not hear his crow. I began to suspect that this cock was a mere visitor in the country, who had taken his departure by the eleven o'clock train for the South, and was now crowing and jubilating somewhere on the verdant banks of Long Island Sound.

But next morning, again I heard the inspiring blast, again felt my blood bound in me, again felt superior to all the ills of life, again felt like turning my dun out of doors. But displeased with the reception given him at his last visit, the dun staid away. Doubtless being in a huff; silly fellow that he was to take a harmless joke in earnest.

Several days passed, during which I made sundry excursions in the regions roundabout, but in vain sought the cock. Still, I heard him from the hill, and sometimes from the house, and sometimes in the stillness of the night. If at times I would relapse into my doleful dumps, straightway at the sound of the exultant and defiant crow, my soul, too, would turn chanticleer, and clap her wings, and throw back her throat, and breathe forth a cheerful challenge to all the world of woes.

At last, after some weeks I was necessitated to clap another mortgage on my estate, in order to pay certain debts, and among others the one I owed the dun, who of late had commenced a civil-process against me. The way the process was served was a most insulting one. In a private room I had been enjoying myself in the village-tavern over a bottle of Philadelphia porter, and some Herkimer cheese, and a roll, and having apprised the landlord, who was a friend of mine, that I would settle with him when I received my next remittances, stepped to the peg where I had hung my hat in the bar-room, to get a choice cigar I had left in the hall, when lo! I found the civil-process enveloping the cigar. When I unrolled the cigar, I unrolled the civil-process, and the constable standing by rolled out, with a thick tongue, "Take notice!" and added, in a whisper, "Put that in your pipe and smoke it!"

I turned short round upon the gentlemen then and there present in that bar-room. Said I, "Gentlemen, is this an honorable—nay, is this a lawful way of serving a civil-process? Behold!"

One and all they were of opinion, that it was a highly inelegant act in the constable to take advantage of a gentleman's lunching on cheese and porter, to be so uncivil as to slip a civil-process into his hat. It was ungenerous; it was cruel; for the sudden shock of the thing coming instanter upon the lunch, would impair the proper digestion of the cheese, which is proverbially not so easy of digestion as *blanc-mange*.

Arrived home, I read the process, and felt a twinge of melancholy. Hard world! hard world! Here I am, as good a fellow as ever lived—hospitable—open-hearted—generous to a fault: and the Fates forbid that I should possess the fortune to bless the country with my bounteousness. Nay, while many a stingy curmudgeon rolls in idle gold, I, heart of nobleness as I am, I have civil-processes served on me! I bowed my head, and felt forlorn—unjustly used—abused—unappreciated—in short, miserable.

Hark! like a clarion! yea, like a jolly bolt of thunder with bells to it—came the all-glorious and defiant crow! Ye gods, how it set me up again! Right on my pins! Yea, verily on stilts!

Oh, noble cock!

Plain as cock could speak, it said, "Let the world and all aboard of it go to pot. Do you be jolly, and never say die. What's the world compared to you? What is it, any how, but a lump of loam? Do you be jolly!"

Oh, noble cock!

"But my dear and glorious cock," mused I, upon second thought, "one can't so easily send this world to pot; one can't so easily be jolly with civil processes in his hat or hand."

Hark! the crow again. Plain as cock could speak, it said: "Hang the process, and hang the fellow that sent it! If you have not land or cash, go and thrash the fellow, and tell him you never mean to pay him. Be jolly!"

Now this was the way—through the imperative intimations of the cock—that I came to clap the added mortgage on my estate; paid all my debts by fusing them into this one added bond and mortgage. Thus made at ease again, I renewed my search for the noble cock. But in vain, though I heard him every day. I began to think there was some sort of deception in this mysterious thing: some wonderful ventriloquist prowled around my barns, or in my cellar, or on my roof, and was minded to be gayly mischievous. But no—what ventriloquist could so crow with such an heroic and celestial crow?

At last, one morning there came to me a certain singular man, who had sawed and split my wood in March—some five-and-thirty cords of it—and now he came for his pay. He was a singular man, I say. He was tall and spare, with a long saddish face, yet somehow a latently joyous eye, which offered the strangest contrast. His air seemed staid, but undepressed. He wore a long, gray, shabby coat, and a big battered hat. This man had sawed my wood at so much a cord. He would stand and saw all day long in a driving snow-storm, and never wink at it. He never spoke unless spoken to. He only sawed. Saw, saw, saw—snow, snow, snow. The saw and the snow went together like two natural things. The first day this man came, he brought his dinner with him, and volunteered to eat it sitting on his buck in the snow-storm. From my window, where I was reading Burton's Anatomy of Melancholy, I saw him in the act. I burst out of doors bare-headed. "Good heavens!" cried I; "what are you doing? Come in. *This* your dinner!"

He had a hunk of stale bread and another hunk of salt beef, wrapped in a wet newspaper, and washed his morsels down by melting a handful of fresh snow in his mouth. I took this rash man indoors, planted him by the fire, gave him a dish of hot pork and beans, and a mug of cider.

"Now," said I, "don't you bring any of your damp dinners here. You work by the job, to be sure; but I'll dine you for all that."

He expressed his acknowledgments in a calm, proud, but not ungrateful way, and dispatched his meal with satisfaction to himself, and me also. It afforded me pleasure to perceive that he quaffed down his mug of cider like a man. I honored him. When I addressed him in the way of business at his buck, I did so in a guardedly respectful and deferential manner. Interested in his singular aspect, struck by his wondrous intensity of application at his saw—a most wearisome and disgustful occupation to most people—I often sought to gather from him who he was, what sort of a life he led, where he was born, and so on. But he was mum. He came to saw my wood, and eat my dinners—if I chose to offer them—but not to gabble. At first, I somewhat resented his sullen silence under the circumstances. But better considering it, I honored him the more. I increased the respectfulness and deferentialness of my address toward him. I concluded within myself that this man had experienced hard times; that he had had many sore rubs in the world; that he was of a solemn disposition; that he was of the mind of Solomon; that he lived calmly, decorously, temperately; and though a very poor man, was, nevertheless, a highly respectable one. At times I imagined that he might even be an elder or deacon of some small country church. I thought it would not be a bad plan to run this excellent man for President of the United States. He would prove a great reformer of abuses.

His name was Merrymusk. I had often thought how jolly a name for so unjolly a wight. I inquired of people whether they knew Merrymusk. But it was some time before I learned much about him. He was by birth a Marylander, it appeared, who had long lived in the country round about; a wandering man; until within some ten years ago, a thriftless man, though perfectly innocent of crime; a man who would work hard a month with surprising soberness, and then spend all his wages in one riotous night. In youth he had been a sailor, and run away from his ship at Batavia, where he caught the fever, and came nigh dying. But he rallied, reshipped, landed home, found all his friends dead, and struck for the Northern interior, where he had since tarried. Nine years back he had married a wife, and now had four children. His wife was become a perfect invalid; one child had the white-swelling, and the rest were rickety. He and his family lived in a shanty on a lonely barren patch nigh the railroad-track, where it passed close to the base of a mountain. He had bought a fine cow to have plenty of wholesome milk for his children; but the cow died during an accouchement, and he could not afford to buy another. Still, his family never suffered for lack of food. He worked hard and brought it to them.

Now, as I said before, having long previously sawed my wood, this Merrymusk came for his pay.

"My friend," said I, "do you know of any gentleman hereabouts who owns an extraordinary cock?"

The twinkle glittered quite plain in the wood-sawyer's eye.

"I know of no *gentleman*," he replied, "who has what might well be called an extraordinary cock."

Oh, thought I, this Merrymusk is not the man to enlighten me. I am afraid I shall never discover this extraordinary cock.

Not having the full change to pay Merrymusk, I gave him his due, as nigh as I could make it, and told him that in a day or two I would take a walk and visit his place, and hand him the remainder. Accordingly one fine morning I sallied forth upon the errand. I had much ado finding the best road to the shanty. No one seemed to know where it was exactly. It lay in a very lonely part of the country, a densely-wooded mountain on one side (which I call October Mountain, on account of its bannered aspect in that month), and a thicketed swamp on the other, the railroad cutting the swamp. Straight as a die the railroad cut it; many times a day tantalizing the wretched shanty with the sight of all the beauty, rank, fashion, health, trunks, silver and gold, dry-goods and groceries, brides and grooms, happy wives and husbands, flying by the lonely door—no time to stop—flash! here they are—and there they go!—out of sight at both ends—as if that part of the world were only made to fly over, and not to settle upon. And this was about all the shanty saw of what people call "life."

Though puzzled somewhat, yet I knew the general direction where the shanty lay, and on I trudged. As I advanced, I was surprised to hear the mysterious cock-crow with more and more distinctness. Is it possible, thought I, that any gentleman owning a Shanghai can dwell in such a lonesome, dreary region? Louder and louder, nigher and nigher, sounded the glorious and defiant clarion. Though somehow I may be out of the track to my wood-sawyer's, I said to myself, yet, thank heaven, I seem to be on the way toward that extraordinary cock. I was delighted with this auspicious accident. On I journeyed; while at intervals the crow sounded most invitingly, and jocundly, and superbly; and the last crow was ever nigher than the former one. At last, emerging from a thicket of alders, straight before me I saw the most resplendent creature that ever blessed the sight of man.

A cock, more like a golden eagle than a cock. A cock, more like a Field-Marshal than a cock. A cock, more like Lord Nelson with all his glittering arms on, standing on the Vanguard's quarter-deck going into battle, than a cock. A cock, more like the Emperor Charlemagne in his robes at Aix la Chapelle, than a cock.

Such a cock!

He was of a haughty size, stood haughtily on his haughty legs. His colors were red, gold, and white. The red was on his crest alone, which was a mighty and symmetric crest, like unto Hector's helmet, as delineated on antique shields. His plumage was snowy, traced with gold. He walked in front of the shanty, like a peer of the realm; his crest lifted, his chest heaved out, his embroidered trappings flashing in the light. His pace was wonderful. He looked like some noble foreigner. He looked like some Oriental king in some magnificent Italian Opera.

Merrymusk advanced from the door.

"Pray is not that the Signor Beneventano?"

"Sir?"

"That's the cock," said I, a little embarrassed. The truth was, my enthusiasm had betrayed me into a rather silly inadvertence. I had made a somewhat learned sort of allusion in the presence of an unlearned man.

Consequently, upon discovering it by his honest stare, I felt foolish; but carried it off by declaring that *this was the cock.*

Now, during the preceding autumn I had been to the city, and had chanced to be present at a performance of the Italian Opera. In that Opera figured in some royal character a certain Signor Beneventano—a man of a tall, imposing person, clad in rich raiment, like to plumage, and with a most remarkable, majestic, scornful stride. The Signor Beneventano seemed on the point of tumbling over backward with exceeding haughtiness. And, for all the world, the proud pace of the cock seemed the very stage-pace of the Signor Beneventano.

Hark! Suddenly the cock paused, lifted his head still higher, ruffled his plumes, seemed inspired, and sent forth a lusty crow. October Mountain echoed it; other mountains sent it back; still others rebounded it; it overran the country round. Now I plainly perceived how it was I had chanced to hear the gladdening sound on my distant hill.

"Good Heavens! do you own the cock? Is that cock yours?"

"Is it my cock!" said Merrymusk, looking slyly gleeful out of the corner of his long, solemn face.

"Where did you get it?"

"It chipped the shell here. I raised it."

"You?"

Hark! Another crow. It might have raised the ghosts of all the pines and hemlocks ever cut down in that country. Marvelous cock! Having crowed, he strode on again, surrounded by a bevy of admiring hens.

"What will you take for Signor Beneventano?"

"Sir?"

"That magic cock!—what will you take for him?"

"I won't sell him."

"I will give you fifty dollars."

"Pooh!"

"One hundred!"

"Pish!"

"Five hundred!"

"Bah!"

"And you a poor man?"

"No; don't I own that cock, and haven't I refused five hundred dollars for him?"

"True," said I, in profound thought; "that's a fact. You won't sell him, then?"

"No."

"Will you give him?"

"No."

"Will you *keep* him, then!" I shouted, in a rage.

"Yes."

I stood awhile admiring the cock, and wondering at the man. At last I felt a redoubled admiration of the one, and a redoubled deference for the other.

"Won't you step in?" said Merrymusk.

"But won't the cock be prevailed upon to join us?" said I.

"Yes. Trumpet! hither, boy! hither!"

The cock turned round, and strode up to Merrymusk.

"Come!"

The cock followed us into the shanty.

"Crow!"

The roof jarred.

Oh, noble cock!

I turned in silence upon my entertainer. There he sat on an old battered chest, in his old battered gray coat, with patches at his knees and elbows, and a deplorably bunged hat. I glanced round the room. Bare rafters overhead, but solid junks of jerked beef hanging from them. Earth floor, but a heap of potatoes in one corner, and a sack of Indian meal in another. A blanket was strung across the apartment at the further end, from which came a woman's ailing voice and the voices of ailing children. But somehow in the ailing of these voices there seemed no complaint.

"Mrs. Merrymusk and children?"

"Yes."

I looked at the cock. There he stood majestically in the middle of the room. He looked like a Spanish grandee caught in a shower, and standing under some peasant's shed. There was a strange supernatural look of contrast about him. He irradiated the shanty; he glorified its meanness. He glorified the battered chest, and tattered gray coat, and the bunged hat. He glorified the very voices which came in ailing tones from behind the screen.

"Oh, father," cried a little sickly voice, "let Trumpet sound again."

"Crow," cried Merrymusk.

The cock threw himself into a posture.

The roof jarred.

"Does not this disturb Mrs. Merrymusk and the sick children?"

"Crow again, Trumpet."

The roof jarred.

"It does not disturb them, then?"

"Didn't you hear 'em *ask* for it?"

"How is it, that your sick family like this crowing?" said I. "The cock is a glorious cock, with a glorious voice, but not exactly the sort of thing for a sick chamber, one would suppose. Do they really like it?"

"Don't *you* like it? Don't it do *you* good? Ain't it inspiring? don't it impart pluck? give stuff against despair?"

"All true," said I, removing my hat with profound humility before the brave spirit disguised in the base coat.

"But then," said I still, with some misgivings, "so loud, so wonderfully clamorous a crow, methinks might be amiss to invalids, and retard their convalescence."

"Crow your best now, Trumpet!"

I leaped from my chair. The cock frightened me, like some overpowering angel in the Apocalypse. He seemed crowing over the fall of wicked Babylon, or crowing over the triumph of righteous Joshua in the vale of Ajalon. When I regained my composure somewhat, an inquisitive thought occurred to me. I resolved to gratify it.

"Merrymusk, will you present me to your wife and children?"

"Yes. Wife, the gentleman wants to step in."

"He is very welcome," replied a weak voice.

Going behind the curtain, there lay a wasted, but strangely cheerful human face; and that was pretty much all; the body, hid by the counterpane and an old coat, seemed too shrunken to reveal itself through such impediments. At the bedside, sat a pale girl, ministering. In another bed lay three children, side by side: three more pale faces.

"Oh, father, we don't mislike the gentleman, but let us see Trumpet too."

At a word, the cock strode behind the screen, and perched himself on the children's bed. All their wasted eyes gazed at him with a wild and spiritual delight. They seemed to sun themselves in the radiant plumage of the cock.

"Better than a 'pothecary, eh?" said Merrymusk. "This is Dr. Cock himself."

We retired from the sick ones, and I reseated myself again, lost in thought, over this strange household.

"You seem a glorious independent fellow!" said I.

"And I don't think you a fool, and never did. Sir, you are a trump."

"Is there any hope of your wife's recovery?" said I, modestly seeking to turn the conversation.

"Not the least."

"The children?"

"Very little."

"It must be a doleful life, then, for all concerned. This lonely solitude—this shanty—hard work—hard times."

"Haven't I Trumpet? He's the cheerer. He crows through all; crows at the darkest; 'Glory to God in the highest!' continually he crows it."

"Just the import I first ascribed to his crow, Merrymusk, when first I heard it from my hill. I thought some rich nabob owned some costly Shanghai; little weening any such poor man as you owned this lusty cock of a domestic breed."

"*Poor* man like *me?* Why call *me* poor? Don't the cock *I* own glorify this otherwise inglorious, lean, lantern-jawed land? Didn't *my* cock encourage *you?* And *I* give you all this glorification away gratis. I am a great philanthropist. I am a rich man—a very rich man, and a very happy one. Crow, Trumpet."

The roof jarred.

I returned home in a deep mood. I was not wholly at rest concerning the soundness of Merrymusk's views of things, though full of admiration for him. I was thinking on the matter before my door, when I heard the cock crow again. Enough. Merrymusk is right.

Oh, noble cock! oh, noble man!

I did not see Merrymusk for some weeks after this; but hearing the glorious and rejoicing crow, I supposed that all went as usual with him. My own frame of mind remained a rejoicing one. The cock still inspired me. I saw another mortgage piled on my plantation; but only bought another dozen of stout, and a dozen-dozen of Philadelphia porter. Some of my relatives died; I wore no mourning, but for three days drank stout in preference to porter, stout being of the darker color. I heard the cock crow the instant I received the unwelcome tidings.

"Your health in this stout, oh noble cock!"

I thought I would call on Merrymusk again, not having seen or heard of him for some time now. Approaching the place, there were no signs of motion about the shanty. I felt a strange misgiving. But the cock crew from within doors, and the boding vanished. I knocked at the door. A feeble voice bade me enter. The curtain was no longer drawn; the whole house was a hospital now. Merrymusk lay on a heap of old clothes; wife and children were all in their beds. The cock was perched on an old hogshead hoop, swung from the ridge-pole in the middle of the shanty.

"You are sick, Merrymusk," said I, mournfully.

"No, I am well," he feebly answered.—"Crow, Trumpet."

I shrunk. The strong soul in the feeble body appalled me.

But the cock crew.

The roof jarred.

"How is Mrs. Merrymusk?"

"Well."

"And the children?"

"Well. All well."

The last two words he shouted forth in a kind of wild ecstasy of triumph over ill. It was too much. His head fell back. A white napkin seemed dropped upon his face. Merrymusk was dead.

An awful fear seized me.

But the cock crew.

The cock shook his plumage as if each feather were a banner. The cock hung from the shanty roof as erewhile the trophied flags from the dome of St. Paul's. The cock terrified me with exceeding wonder.

I drew nigh the bedsides of the woman and children. They marked my look of strange affright; they knew what had happened.

"My good man is just dead," breathed the woman lowly. "Tell me true?"

"Dead," said I.

The cock crew.

She fell back, without a sigh, and through long-loving sympathy was dead.

The cock crew.

The cock shook sparkles from his golden plumage. The cock seemed in a rapture of benevolent delight. Leaping from the hoop, he strode up majestically to the pile of old clothes, where the wood-sawyer lay, and planted himself, like an armorial supporter, at his side. Then raised one long, musical, triumphant, and final sort of crow, with throat heaved far back, as if he meant the blast to waft the wood-sawyer's soul sheer up to the seventh heavens. Then he strode, king-like, to the woman's bed. Another upturned and exultant crow, mated to the former.

The pallor of the children was changed to radiance. Their faces shone celestially through grime and dirt. They seemed children of emperors and kings, disguised. The cock sprang upon their bed, shook himself, and crowed, and crowed again, and still and still again. He seemed bent upon crowing the souls of the children out of their wasted bodies. He seemed bent upon rejoining instanter this whole family in the upper air. The children seemed to second his endeavors. Far, deep, intense longings for release transfigured them into spirits before my eyes. I saw angels where they lay.

They were dead.

The cock shook his plumage over them. The cock crew. It was now like a Bravo! like a Hurrah! like a Three-times-three! hip! hip! He strode out of the shanty. I followed. He flew upon the apex of the dwelling, spread wide his wings, sounded one supernatural note, and dropped at my feet.

The cock was dead.

If now you visit that hilly region, you will see, nigh the railroad track, just beneath October Mountain, on the other side of the swamp—there you will see a grave-stone, not with skull and cross-bones, but with a lusty cock in act of crowing, chiseled on it, with the words beneath:

—"Oh! death, where is thy sting?
Oh! grave, where is thy victory?"

The wood-sawyer and his family, with the Signor Beneventano, lie in that spot; and I buried them, and planted the stone, which was a stone made to order; and never since then have I felt the doleful dumps, but under all circumstances crow late and early with a continual crow.

Cock-a-doodle-doo!—oo!—oo!—oo!—oo!

Poor Man's Pudding and Rich Man's Crumbs

Picture First

Poor Man's Pudding

"YOU SEE," said poet Blandmour, enthusiastically—as some forty years ago we walked along the road in a soft, moist snow-fall, toward the end of March—"you see, my friend, that the blessed almoner, Nature, is in all things beneficent; and not only so, but considerate in her charities, as any discreet human philanthropist might be. This snow, now, which seems so unseasonable, is in fact just what a poor husbandman needs. Rightly is this soft March snow, falling just before seed-time, rightly is it called 'Poor Man's Manure.' Distilling from kind heaven upon the soil, by a gentle penetration it nourishes every clod, ridge, and furrow. To the poor farmer it is as good as the rich farmer's farm-yard enrichments. And the poor man has no trouble to spread it, while the rich man has to spread his."

"Perhaps so," said I, without equal enthusiasm, brushing some of the damp flakes from my chest. "It may be as you say, dear Blandmour. But tell me, how is it that the wind drives yonder drifts of 'Poor Man's Manure' off poor Coulter's two-acre patch here, and piles it up yonder on rich Squire Teamster's twenty-acre field?"

"Ah! to be sure—yes—well; Coulter's field, I suppose, is sufficiently moist without further moistenings. Enough is as good as a feast, you know."

"Yes," replied I, "of this sort of damp fare," shaking another shower of the damp flakes from my person. "But tell me, this warm spring-snow may answer very well, as you say; but how is it with the cold snows of the long, long winters here?"

"Why, do you not remember the words of the Psalmist?—'The Lord giveth snow like wool;' meaning not only that snow is white as wool, but warm, too, as wool. For the only reason, as I take it, that wool is comfortable, is because air is entangled, and therefore warmed among its fibres. Just so, then, take the temperature of a December field when covered with this snow-fleece, and you will no doubt find it several degrees above that of the air. So, you see, the winter's snow *itself* is beneficent; under the pretense of frost—a sort of gruff philanthropist—actually warming the earth, which afterward is to be fertilizingly moistened by these gentle flakes of March."

"I like to hear you talk, dear Blandmour; and, guided by your benevolent heart, can only wish to poor Coulter plenty of this 'Poor Man's Manure.'"

"But that is not all," said Blandmour, eagerly. "Did you never hear of the 'Poor Man's Eye-water?'"

"Never."

"Take this soft March snow, melt it, and bottle it. It keeps pure as alcohol. The very best thing in the world for weak eyes. I have a whole demijohn of it myself. But the poorest man, afflicted in his eyes, can freely help himself to this same all-bountiful remedy. Now, what a kind provision is that!"

"Then 'Poor Man's Manure' is 'Poor Man's Eye-water' too?"

"Exactly. And what could be more economically contrived? One thing answering two ends—ends so very distinct."

"Very distinct, indeed."

"Ah! that is your way. Making sport of earnest. But never mind. We have been talking of snow; but common rain-water—such as falls all the year round—is still more kindly. Not to speak of its known fertilizing quality as to fields, consider it in one of its minor lights. Pray, did you ever hear of a 'Poor Man's Egg?'"

"Never. What is that, now?"

"Why, in making some culinary preparations of meal and flour, where eggs are recommended in the receipt-book, a substitute for the eggs may be had in a cup of cold rain-water, which acts as leaven. And so a cup of cold rain-water thus used is called by housewives a 'Poor Man's Egg.' And many rich men's housekeepers sometimes use it."

"But only when they are out of hen's eggs, I presume, dear Blandmour. But your talk is—I sincerely say it—most agreeable to me. Talk on."

"Then there's 'Poor Man's Plaster' for wounds and other bodily harms; an alleviative and curative, compounded of simple, natural things; and so, being very cheap, is accessible to the poorest of sufferers. Rich men often use 'Poor Man's Plaster.'"

"But not without the judicious advice of a fee'd physician, dear Blandmour."

"Doubtless, they first consult the physician; but that may be an unnecessary precaution."

"Perhaps so. I do not gainsay it. Go on."

"Well, then, did you ever eat of a 'Poor Man's Pudding?'"

"I never so much as heard of it before."

"Indeed! Well, now you shall eat of one; and you shall eat it, too, as made, unprompted, by a poor man's wife, and you shall eat it at a poor man's table, and in a poor man's house. Come now, and if after this eating, you do not say that a 'Poor Man's Pudding' is as relishable as a rich man's, I will give up the point altogether; which briefly is: that, through kind Nature, the poor, out of their very poverty, extract comfort."

Not to narrate any more of our conversations upon this subject (for we had several—I being at that time the guest of Blandmour in the country, for the benefit of my health), suffice it that, acting upon Blandmour's hint, I introduced myself into Coulter's house on a wet Monday noon (for the snow had thawed), under the innocent pretense of craving a pedestrian's rest and refreshment for an hour or two.

I was greeted, not without much embarrassment—owing, I suppose, to my dress—but still with unaffected and honest kindness. Dame Coulter was just leaving the wash-tub to get ready her one o'clock meal against her good man's return from a deep wood about a mile distant among the hills, where he was chopping by day's-work—seventy-five cents per day and found himself. The washing being done outside the main building, under an infirm-looking old shed, the dame stood upon a half-rotten, soaked board to protect her feet, as well as might be, from the penetrating damp of the bare ground; hence she looked pale and chill. But her paleness had still another and more secret cause—the paleness of a mother to be. A quiet, fathomless heart-trouble, too, couched beneath the mild, resigned blue of her soft and wife-like eye. But she smiled upon me, as apologizing for the unavoidable disorder of a Monday and a washing-day, and, conducting me into the kitchen, set me down in the best seat it had—an old-fashioned chair of an enfeebled constitution.

I thanked her; and sat rubbing my hands before the ineffectual low fire, and—unobservedly as I could—glancing now and then about the room, while the good woman, throwing on more sticks, said she was sorry the room was no warmer. Something more she said, too—not repiningly, however—of the fuel, as old and damp; picked-up sticks in Squire Teamster's forest, where her husband was chopping the sappy logs of the living tree for the Squire's fires. It needed not her remark, whatever it was, to convince me of the inferior quality of the sticks; some being quite mossy and toad-stooled with long lying bedded among the accumulated dead leaves of many autumns. They made a sad hissing, and vain spluttering enough.

"You must rest yourself here till dinner-time, at least," said the dame; "what I have you are heartily welcome to."

I thanked her again, and begged her not to heed my presence in the least, but go on with her usual affairs.

I was struck by the aspect of the room. The house was old, and constitutionally damp. The window-sills had beads of exuded dampness upon them. The shriveled sashes shook in their frames, and the green panes of glass were clouded with the long thaw. On some little errand the dame passed into an adjoining chamber, leaving the door partly open. The floor of that room was carpetless, as the kitchen's was. Nothing but bare necessaries were about me; and those not of the best sort. Not a print on the wall; but an old volume of Doddridge lay on the smoked chimney-shelf.

"You must have walked a long way, sir; you sigh so with weariness."

"No, I am not nigh so weary as yourself, I dare say."

"Oh, but *I* am accustomed to that; *you* are not, I should think," and her soft, sad blue eye ran over my dress. "But I must sweep these shavings away; husband made him a new ax-helve this morning before sunrise, and I have been so busy washing, that I have had no time to clear up. But now they are just the thing I want for the fire. They'd be much better though, were they not so green."

Now if Blandmour were here, thought I to myself, he would call those green shavings "Poor Man's Matches," or "Poor Man's Tinder," or some pleasant name of that sort.

"I do not know," said the good woman, turning round to me again—as she stirred among her pots on the smoky fire—"I do not know how you will like our pudding. It is only rice, milk, and salt boiled together."

"Ah, what they call 'Poor Man's Pudding,' I suppose you mean."

A quick flush, half resentful, passed over her face.

"*We* do not call it so, sir," she said, and was silent.

Upbraiding myself for my inadvertence, I could not but again think to myself what Blandmour would have said, had he heard those words and seen that flush.

At last a slow, heavy footfall was heard; then a scraping at the door, and another voice said, "Come, wife; come, come—I must be back again in a jif—if you say I *must* take all my meals at home, you must be speedy; because the Squire—Good-day, sir," he exclaimed, now first catching sight of me as he entered the room. He turned toward his wife, inquiringly, and stood stock-still, while the moisture oozed from his patched boots to the floor.

"This gentleman stops here awhile to rest and refresh: he will take dinner with us, too. All will be ready now in a trice: so sit down on the bench, husband, and be patient, I pray. You see, sir," she continued, turning to me, "William there wants, of mornings, to carry a cold meal into the woods with him, to save the long one-o'clock walk across the fields to and fro. But I won't let him. A warm dinner is more than pay for the long walk."

"I don't know about that," said William, shaking his head. "I have often debated in my mind whether it really paid. There's not much odds, either way, between a wet walk after hard work, and a wet dinner before it. But I like to oblige a good wife like Martha. And you know, sir, that women will have their whimseys."

"I wish they all had as kind whimseys as your wife has," said I.

"Well, I've heard that some women ain't all maple-sugar; but, content with dear Martha, I don't know much about others."

"You find rare wisdom in the woods," mused I.

"Now, husband, if you ain't too tired, just lend a hand to draw the table out."

"Nay," said I; "let him rest, and let me help."

"No," said William, rising.

"Sit still," said his wife to me.

The table set, in due time we all found ourselves with plates before us.

"You see what we have," said Coulter—"salt pork, rye-bread, and pudding. Let me help you. I got this pork of the Squire; some of his last year's pork, which he let me have on account. It isn't quite so sweet as this year's would be; but I find it hearty enough to work on, and that's all I eat for. Only let the rheumatiz and other sicknesses keep clear of me, and I ask no flavors or favors from any. But you don't eat of the pork!"

"I see," said the wife, gently and gravely, "that the gentleman knows the difference between this year's and last year's pork. But perhaps he will like the pudding."

I summoned up all my self-control, and smilingly assented to the proposition of the pudding, without by my looks casting any reflections upon the pork. But, to tell the truth, it was quite impossible for me (not being ravenous, but only a little hungry at the time) to eat of the latter. It had a yellowish crust all round it, and was rather rankish, I thought, to the taste. I observed, too, that the dame did not eat of it, though she suffered some to be put on her plate, and pretended to be busy with it when Coulter looked that way. But she ate of the rye-bread, and so did I.

"Now, then, for the pudding," said Coulter. "Quick, wife; the Squire sits in his sitting-room window, looking far out across the fields. His time-piece is true."

"He don't play the spy on you, does he?" said I.

"Oh, no!—I don't say that. He's a good-enough man. He gives me work. But he's particular. Wife, help the gentleman. You see, sir, if I lose the Squire's work, what will become of—" and, with a look for which I honored humanity, with sly significance he glanced toward his wife; then, a little changing his voice, instantly continued—"that fine horse I am going to buy."

"I guess," said the dame, with a strange, subdued sort of inefficient pleasantry—"I guess that fine horse you sometimes so merrily dream of will long stay in the Squire's stall. But sometimes his man gives me a Sunday ride."

"A Sunday ride!" said I.

"You see," resumed Coulter, "wife loves to go to church; but the nighest is four miles off, over yon snowy hills. So she can't walk it; and I can't carry her in my arms, though I have carried her up-stairs before now. But, as she says, the Squire's man sometimes gives her a lift on the road; and for this cause it is that I speak of a horse I am going to have one of these fine sunny days. And already, before having it, I have christened it 'Martha.' But what am I about? Come, come, wife! the pudding! Help the gentleman, do! The Squire! the Squire!—think of the Squire! and help round the pudding. There, one—two—three mouthfuls must do me. Good-by, wife. Good-by, sir. I'm off."

And, snatching his soaked hat, the noble Poor Man hurriedly went out into the soak and the mire.

I suppose now, thinks I to myself, that Blandmour would poetically say, He goes to take a Poor Man's saunter.

"You have a fine husband," said I to the woman, as we were now left together.

"William loves me this day as on the wedding-day, sir. Some hasty words, but never a harsh one. I wish I were better and stronger for his sake. And, oh! sir, both for his sake and mine" (and the soft, blue, beautiful eyes turned into two well-springs), "how I wish little William and Martha lived—it is so lonely-like now. William named after him, and Martha for me."

When a companion's heart of itself overflows, the best one can do is to do nothing. I sat looking down on my as yet untasted pudding.

"You should have seen little William, sir. Such a bright, manly boy, only six years old—cold, cold now!"

Plunging my spoon into the pudding, I forced some into my mouth to stop it.

"And little Martha—Oh! sir, she was the beauty! Bitter, bitter! but needs must be borne."

The mouthful of pudding now touched my palate, and touched it with a mouldy, briny taste. The rice, I knew, was of that damaged sort sold cheap; and the salt from the last year's pork barrel.

"Ah, sir, if those little ones yet to enter the world were the same little ones which so sadly have left it; returning friends, not strangers, strangers, always strangers! Yet does a mother soon learn to love them; for certain, sir, they come from where the others have gone. Don't you believe that, sir? Yes, I know all good people must. But, still, still—and I fear it is wicked, and very black-hearted, too—still, strive how I may to cheer me with thinking of little William and Martha in heaven, and with reading Dr. Doddridge there—still, still does dark grief leak in, just like the rain through our roof. I am left so lonesome now; day after day, all the day long, dear William is gone; and all the damp day long grief drizzles and drizzles down on my soul. But I pray to God to forgive me for this; and for the rest, manage it as well as I may."

Bitter and mouldy is the "Poor Man's Pudding," groaned I to myself, half choked with but one little mouthful of it, which would hardly go down.

I could stay no longer to hear of sorrows for which the sincerest sympathies could give no adequate relief; of a fond persuasion, to which there could be furnished no further proof than already was had—a persuasion, too, of that sort which much speaking is sure more or less to mar; of causeless self-upbraidings, which no expostulations could have dispelled. I offered no pay for hospitalities gratuitous and honorable as those of a prince. I knew that such offerings would have been more than declined; charity resented.

The native American poor never lose their delicacy or pride; hence, though unreduced to the physical degradation of the European pauper, they yet suffer more in mind than the poor of any other people in the world. Those peculiar social sensibilities nourished by our own peculiar political principles, while they enhance the true dignity of a prosperous American, do but minister to the added wretchedness of the unfortunate; first, by prohibiting their acceptance of what little random relief charity may offer; and, second, by furnishing them with the keenest appreciation of the smarting distinction between their ideal of universal equality and their grind-stone experience of the practical misery and infamy of poverty—a misery and infamy which is, ever has been, and ever will be, precisely the same in India, England, and America.

Under pretense that my journey called me forthwith, I bade the dame good-by; shook her cold hand; looked my last into her blue, resigned eye, and went out into the wet. But cheerless as it was, and damp, damp, damp—the heavy atmosphere charged with all sorts of incipiencies—I yet became conscious, by the suddenness of the contrast, that the house air I had quitted was laden down with that peculiar deleterious quality, the height of which—insufferable to some visitants—will be found in a poor-house ward.

This ill-ventilation in winter of the rooms of the poor—a thing, too, so stubbornly persisted in—is usually charged upon them as their disgraceful neglect of the most simple means to health. But the instinct of the poor is wiser than we think. The air which ventilates, likewise *cools*. And to any shiverer, ill-ventilated warmth is better than well-ventilated cold. Of all the preposterous assumptions of humanity over humanity, nothing exceeds most of the criticisms made on the habits of the poor by the well-housed, well-warmed, and well-fed.

* * * * *

"Blandmour," said I that evening, as after tea I sat on his comfortable sofa, before a blazing fire, with one of his two ruddy little children on my knee, "you are not what may rightly be called a rich man; you have a fair competence; no more. Is it not so? Well then, I do not include *you*, when I say, that if ever a Rich Man speaks prosperously to me of a Poor Man, I shall set it down as— I won't mention the word."

Picture Second

Rich Man's Crumbs

In the year 1814, during the summer following my first taste of the "Poor Man's Pudding," a sea-voyage was recommended to me by my physician. The Battle of Waterloo having closed the long drama of Napoleon's wars, many strangers were visiting Europe. I arrived in London at the time the victorious princes were there assembled enjoying the Arabian Nights' hospitalities of a grateful and gorgeous aristocracy, and the courtliest of gentlemen and kings—George the Prince Regent.

I had declined all letters but one to my banker. I wandered about for the best reception an adventurous traveler can have—the reception, I mean, which unsolicited chance and accident throw in his venturous way.

But I omit all else to recount one hour's hap under the lead of a very friendly man, whose acquaintance I made in the open street of Cheapside. He wore a uniform, and was some sort of a civic subordinate; I forget exactly what. He was off duty that day. His discourse was chiefly of the noble charities of London. He took me to two or three, and made admiring mention of many more.

"But," said he, as we turned into Cheapside again, "if you are at all curious about such things, let me take you—if it be not too late—to one of the most interesting of all—our Lord Mayor's Charities, sir; nay, the charities not only of a Lord Mayor, but, I may truly say, in this one instance, of emperors, regents, and kings. You remember the event of yesterday?"

"That sad fire on the river-side, you mean, unhousing so many of the poor?"

"No. The grand Guildhall Banquet to the princes. Who can forget it? Sir, the dinner was served on nothing but solid silver and gold plate, worth at the least £200,000—that is, 1,000,000 of your dollars; while the mere expenditure of meats, wines, attendance and upholstery, &c., can not be footed under £25,000—125,000 dollars of your hard cash."

"But, surely, my friend, you do not call that charity—feeding kings at that rate?"

"No. The feast came first—yesterday; and the charity after—to-day. How else would you have it, where princes are concerned? But I think we shall be quite in time—come; here we are at King Street, and down there is Guildhall. Will you go?"

"Gladly, my good friend. Take me where you will. I come but to roam and see."

Avoiding the main entrance of the hall, which was barred, he took me through some private way, and we found ourselves in a rear blind-walled place in the open air. I looked round amazed. The spot was grimy as a back-yard in the Five Points. It was packed with a mass of lean, famished, ferocious creatures, struggling and fighting for some mysterious precedency, and all holding soiled blue tickets in their hands.

"There is no other way," said my guide; "we can only get in with the crowd. Will you try it? I hope you have not on your drawing-room suit? What do you say? It will be well worth your sight. So noble a charity does not often offer. The one following the annual banquet of Lord Mayor's day—fine a charity as that certainly is—is not to be mentioned with what will be seen to-day. Is it, ay?"

As he spoke, a basement door in the distance was thrown open, and the squalid mass made a rush for the dark vault beyond.

I nodded to my guide, and sideways we joined in with the rest. Ere long we found our retreat cut off by the yelping crowd behind, and I could not but congratulate myself on having a civic, as well as civil guide; one, too, whose uniform made evident his authority.

It was just the same as if I were pressed by a mob of cannibals on some pagan beach. The beings round me roared with famine. For in this mighty London misery but maddens. In the country it softens. As I gazed on the meagre, murderous pack, I thought of the blue eye of the gentle wife of poor Coulter. Some sort of curved, glittering steel thing (not a sword; I know not what it was), before worn in his belt, was now flourished overhead by my guide, menacing the creatures to forbear offering the stranger violence.

As we drove, slow and wedge-like, into the gloomy vault, the howls of the mass reverberated. I seemed seething in the Pit with the Lost. On and on, through the dark and the damp, and then up a stone stairway to a wide portal; when, diffusing, the pestiferous mob poured in bright day between painted walls and beneath a painted dome. I thought of the anarchic sack of Versailles.

A few moments more and I stood bewildered among the beggars in the famous Guildhall.

Where I stood—where the thronged rabble stood, less than twelve hours before sat His Imperial Majesty, Alexander of Russia; His Royal Majesty, Frederic William, King of Prussia; His Royal Highness, George,

Prince Regent of England; His world-renowned Grace, the Duke of Wellington; with a mob of magnificoes, made up of conquering field-marshals, earls, counts, and innumerable other nobles of mark.

The walls swept to and fro, like the foliage of a forest with blazonings of conquerors' flags. Naught outside the hall was visible. No windows were within four-and-twenty feet of the floor. Cut off from all other sights, I was hemmed in by one splendid spectacle—splendid, I mean, every where, but as the eye fell toward the floor. *That* was foul as a hovel's—as a kennel's; the naked boards being strewed with the smaller and more wasteful fragments of the feast, while the two long parallel lines, up and down the hall, of now unrobed, shabby, dirty pine-tables were piled with less trampled wrecks. The dyed banners were in keeping with the last night's kings; the floor suited the beggars of to-day. The banners looked down upon the floor as from his balcony Dives upon Lazarus. A line of liveried men kept back with their staves the impatient jam of the mob, who, otherwise, might have instantaneously converted the Charity into a Pillage. Another body of gowned and gilded officials distributed the broken meats—the cold victuals and crumbs of kings. One after another the beggars held up their dirty blue tickets, and were served with the plundered wreck of a pheasant, or the rim of a pasty—like the detached crown of an old hat—the solids and meats stolen out.

"What a noble charity!" whispered my guide. "See that pasty now, snatched by that pale girl; I dare say the Emperor of Russia ate of that last night."

"Very probably," murmured I; "it looks as though some omnivorous Emperor or other had had a finger in that pie."

"And see yon pheasant too—there—*that* one—the boy in the torn shirt has it now—look! The Prince Regent might have dined off that."

The two breasts were gouged ruthlessly out, exposing the bare bones, embellished with the untouched pinions and legs.

"Yes, who knows!" said my guide, "his Royal Highness the Prince Regent might have eaten of that identical pheasant."

"I don't doubt it," murmured I, "he is said to be uncommonly fond of the breast. But where is Napoleon's head in a charger? I should fancy *that* ought to have been the principal dish."

"You are merry. Sir, even Cossacks are charitable here in Guildhall. Look! the famous Platoff, the Hetman himself—(he was here last night with the rest)—no doubt he thrust a lance into yon fat pork-pie there. Look! the old shirtless man has it now. How he licks his chops over it, little thinking of or thanking the good, kind Cossack that left it him! Ah! another—a stouter has grabbed it. It falls; bless my soul!—the dish is quite empty—only a bit of the hacked crust."

"The Cossacks, my friend, are said to be immoderately fond of fat," observed I. "The Hetman was hardly so charitable as you thought."

"A noble charity, upon the whole, for all that. See, even Gog and Magog yonder, at the other end of the hall, fairly laugh out their delight at the scene."

"But don't you think, though," hinted I, "that the sculptor, whoever he was, carved the laugh too much into a grin—a sort of sardonical grin?"

"Well, that's as you take it, sir. But see—now I'd wager a guinea the Lord Mayor's lady dipped her golden spoon into yonder golden-hued jelly. See, the jelly-eyed old body has slipped it, in one broad gulp, down his throat."

"Peace to that jelly!" breathed I.

"What a generous, noble, magnanimous charity this is! unheard of in any country but England, which feeds her very beggars with golden-hued jellies."

"But not three times every day, my friend. And do you really think that jellies are the best sort of relief you can furnish to beggars? Would not plain beef and bread, with something to do, and be paid for, be better?"

"But plain beef and bread were not eaten here. Emperors, and prince-regents, and kings, and field marshals don't often dine on plain beef and bread. So the leavings are according. Tell me, can you expect that the crumbs of kings can be like the crumbs of squirrels?"

"*You!* I mean *you!* stand aside, or else be served and away! Here, take this pasty, and be thankful that you taste of the same dish with her Grace the Duchess of Devonshire. Graceless ragamuffin, do you hear?"

These words were bellowed at me through the din by a red-gowned official nigh the board.

"Surely he does not mean *me*," said I to my guide; "he has not confounded *me* with the rest."

"One is known by the company he keeps," smiled my guide. "See! not only stands your hat awry and bunged on your head, but your coat is fouled and torn. Nay," he cried to the red-gown, "this is an unfortunate friend; a simple spectator, I assure you."

"Ah! is that you, old lad?" responded the red-gown, in familiar recognition of my guide—a personal friend as it seemed; "well, convey your friend out forthwith. Mind the grand crash; it will soon be coming; hark! now! away with him!"

Too late. The last dish had been seized. The yet unglutted mob raised a fierce yell, which wafted the banners like a strong gust, and filled the air with a reek as from sewers. They surged against the tables, broke through all barriers, and billowed over the hall—their bare tossed arms like the dashed ribs of a wreck. It seemed to me as if a sudden impotent fury of fell envy possessed them. That one half-hour's peep at the mere remnants of the glories of the Banquets of Kings; the unsatisfying mouthfuls of disembowelled pasties, plundered pheasants, and half-sacked jellies, served to remind them of the intrinsic contempt of the alms. In this sudden mood, or whatever mysterious thing it was that now seized them, these Lazaruses seemed ready to spew up in repentant scorn the contumelious crumbs of Dives.

"This way, this way! stick like a bee to my back," intensely whispered my guide. "My friend there has answered my beck, and thrown open yon private door for us two. Wedge—wedge in—quick—there goes your bunged hat—never stop for your coat-tail—hit that man—strike him down! hold! jam! now! now! wrench along for your life! ha! here we breathe freely; thank God! You faint. Ho!"

"Never mind. This fresh air revives me."

I inhaled a few more breaths of it, and felt ready to proceed.

"And now conduct me, my good friend, by some front passage into Cheapside, forthwith. I must home."

"Not by the side-walk though. Look at your dress. I must get a hack for you."

"Yes, I suppose so," said I, ruefully eying my tatters, and then glancing in envy at the close-bodied coat and flat cap of my guide, which defied all tumblings and tearings.

"There, now, sir," said the honest fellow, as he put me into the hack, and tucked in me and my rags, "when you get back to your own country, you can say you have witnessed the greatest of all England's noble charities. Of course, you will make reasonable allowances for the unavoidable jam. Good-by. Mind, Jehu"—addressing the driver on the box—"this is a *gentleman* you carry. He is just from the Guildhall Charity, which accounts for his appearance. Go on now. London Tavern, Fleet Street, remember, is the place."

*   *   *   *   *

"Now, Heaven in its kind mercy save me from the noble charities of London," sighed I, as that night I lay bruised and battered on my bed; "and Heaven save me equally from the 'Poor Man's Pudding' and the 'Rich Man's Crumbs.'"

The Two Temples

(Dedicated to Sheridan Knowles)

Temple First

THIS IS TOO BAD," said I, "here have I tramped this blessed Sunday morning, all the way from the Battery, three long miles, for this express purpose, prayer-book under arm; here I am, I say, and, after all, I can't get in.

"Too bad. And how disdainful the great, fat-paunched, beadle-faced man looked, when in answer to my humble petition, he said they had no galleries. Just the same as if he'd said, they did n't entertain poor folks. But I'll wager something that had my new coat been done last night, as the false tailor promised, and had I, arrayed therein this bright morning, tickled the fat-paunched, beadle-faced man's palm with a bank-note, then, gallery or no gallery, I would have had a fine seat in this marble-buttressed, stained-glassed, spic-and-span new temple.

"Well, here I am in the porch, very politely bowed out of the nave. I suppose I'm excommunicated; excluded, anyway.—That's a noble string of flashing carriages drawn up along the curb; those champing horses too have a haughty curve to their foam-flaked necks. Property of those 'miserable sinners' inside, I presume. I dont a bit wonder they unreservedly confess to such misery as *that.*—See the gold hat-bands too, and other gorgeous trimmings, on those glossy groups of low-voiced gossippers near by. If I were in England now, I should think those chaps a company of royal dukes, right honorable barons &c. As it is, though, I guess they are only lackeys.—By the way, here I dodge about, as if I wanted to get into their aristocratic circle. In fact, it looks a sort of lackey-ish to be idly standing outside a fine temple, cooling your heels, during service.—I had best move back to the Battery again, peeping into my prayer-book as I go.—But hold; dont I see a small door? Just in there, to one side, if I dont mistake, is a very low and very narrow vaulted door. None seem to go that way. Ten to one, that identical door leads up into the tower. And now that I think of it, there is usually in these splendid, new-fashioned Gothic Temples, a curious little window high over the orchestra and everything else, away up among the gilded clouds of the ceiling's frescoes; and that little window, seems to me, if one could but get there, ought to command a glorious bird's-eye view of the entire field of operations below.—I guess I'll try it. No one in the porch now. The beadle-faced man is smoothing down some ladies' cushions, far up the broad aisle, I dare say. Softly now. If the small door ain't locked, I shall have stolen a march upon the beadle-faced man, and secured a humble seat in the sanctuary, in spite of him.—Good! Thanks for this! The door is not locked. Bell-ringer forgot to lock it, no doubt. Now, like any felt-footed grimalkin, up I steal among the leads."

Ascending some fifty stone steps along a very narrow curving stair-way, I found myself on a blank platform forming the second story of the huge square tower.

I seemed inside some magic-lantern. On three sides, three gigantic Gothic windows of richly dyed glass, filled the otherwise meagre place with all sorts of sun-rises and sun-sets, lunar and solar rainbows, falling stars, and other flaming fire-works and pyrotechnics. But after all, it was but a gorgeous dungeon; for I could n't look out, any more than if I had been the occupant of a basement cell in "the Tombs." With some pains, and care not to do any serious harm, I contrived to scratch a minute opening in a great purple star forming the center of the chief compartment of the middle window; when peeping through, as through goggles, I ducked my head in dismay. The beadle-faced man, with no hat on his head, was just in act of driving three ragged little boys into the middle of the street; and how could I help trembling at the apprehension of his discovering a rebellious caitiff like me peering down on him from the tower? For in stealing up here, I had set at nought his high authority. He whom he thought effectually ejected, had burglariously returned. For a moment I was almost ready to bide my chance, and get to the side walk again with all dispatch. But another Jacob's ladder of lofty steps,—wooden ones, this time—allured me to another and still higher flight,—in sole hopes of gaining that one secret window where I might, at distance, take part in the proceedings.

Presently I noticed something which owing to the first marvellous effulgence of the place, had remained unseen till now. Two strong ropes, dropping through holes in the rude ceiling high overhead, fell a sheer length of sixty feet, right through the center of the space, and dropped in coils upon the floor of the huge magic-lantern. Bell-ropes these, thought I, and quaked. For if the beadle-faced man should learn that a grimalkin was somewhere prowling about the edifice, how easy for him to ring the alarm. Hark!—ah, that's only the organ—yes—it's the "Venite, exultemus Domine". Though an insider in one respect, yet am I but an outsider in another. But for all that, I will not be defrauded of my natural rights. Uncovering my head, and taking out my book, I stood erect, midway up the tall Jacob's ladder, as if standing among the congregation; and in spirit, if not in place, participated in those devout exultings. That over, I continued my upward path; and after crossing sundry minor platforms and irregular landings, all the while on a general ascent, at last I was delighted by catching sight of a small round window in the otherwise dead-wall side of the tower, where the tower attached itself to the main building. In front of the window was a rude narrow gallery, used as a bridge to cross from the lower stairs on one side to the upper stairs on the opposite.

As I drew nigh the spot, I well knew from the added clearness with which the sound of worship came to me, that the window did indeed look down upon the entire interior. But I was hardly prepared to find that no pane of glass, stained or unstained, was to stand between me and the far-under aisles and altar. For the purpose of ventilation, doubtless, the opening had been left unsupplied with sash of any sort. But a sheet of fine-woven, gauzy wire-work was in place of that. When, all eagerness, and open book in hand, I first advanced to stand before the window, I involuntarily shrank, as from before the mouth of a furnace, upon suddenly feeling a forceful puff of strange, heated air, blown, as by a blacksmith's bellows, full into my face and lungs. Yes, thought I, this window is doubtless for ventilation. Nor is it quite so comfortable as I fancied it might be. But beggars must not be choosers. The furnace which makes the people below there feel so snug and cosy in their padded pews, is to me, who stand here upon the naked gallery, cause of grievous trouble.

Besides, though my face is scorched, my back is frozen. But I wont complain. Thanks for this much, any way,—that by hollowing one hand to my ear, and standing a little sideways out of the more violent rush of the torrid current, I can at least hear the priest sufficiently to make my responses in the proper place. Little dream the good congregation away down there, that they have a faithful clerk away up here. Here too is a fitter place for sincere devotions, where, though I see, I remain unseen. Depend upon it, no Pharisee would have my pew. I like it, and admire it too, because it is so very high. Height, somehow, hath devotion in it. The archangelic anthems are raised in a lofty place. All the good shall go to such an one. Yes, Heaven is high.

As thus I mused, the glorious organ burst, like an earthquake, almost beneath my feet; and I heard the invoking cry—"Govern them and *lift* them up forever!" Then down I gazed upon the standing human mass, far, far below, whose heads, gleaming in the many-colored window-stains, showed like beds of spangled pebbles flashing in a Cuban sun. So at least, I knew they needs would look, if but the wire-woven screen were drawn aside. That wire-woven screen had the effect of casting crape upon all I saw. Only by making allowances for the crape, could I gain a right idea of the scene disclosed.

Surprising, most surprising, too, it was. As said before, the window was a circular one; the part of the tower where I stood was dusky-dark; its height above the congregation-floor could not have been less than ninety or a hundred feet; the whole interior temple was lit by nought but glass dimmed, yet glorified with all imaginable rich and russet hues; the approach to my strange look-out, through perfect solitude, and along rude and dusty ways, enhanced the theatric wonder of the populous spectacle of this sumptuous sanctuary. Book in hand, responses on my tongue, standing in the very posture of devotion, I could not rid my soul of the intrusive thought, that, through some necromancer's glass, I looked down upon some sly enchanter's show.

At length the lessons being read, the chants chanted, the white-robed priest, a noble-looking man, with a form like the incomparable Talma's, gave out from the reading-desk the hymn before the sermon, and then through a side door vanished from the scene. In good time I saw the same Talma-like and noble-looking man re-appear through the same side door, his white apparel wholly changed for black.

By the melodious tone and persuasive gesture of the speaker, and the all-approving attention of the throng, I knew the sermon must be eloquent, and well adapted to an opulent auditory; but owing to the priest's changed position from the reading-desk, to the pulpit, I could not so distinctly hear him now as in the previous rites. The text however,—repeated at the outset, and often after quoted,—I could not but plainly catch:—"Ye are the salt of the earth."

At length the benediction was pronounced over the mass of low-inclining foreheads; hushed silence, intense motionlessness followed for a moment, as if the congregation were one of buried, not of living men; when, suddenly, miraculously, like the general rising at the Resurrection, the whole host came to their feet, amid a simultaneous roll, like a great drum-beat from the enrapturing, overpowering organ. Then, in three freshets,—all gay sprightly nods and becks—the gilded brooks poured down the gilded aisles.

Time for me too to go, thought I, as snatching one last look upon the imposing scene, I clasped my book and put it in my pocket. The best thing I can do just now, is to slide out unperceived amid the general crowd. Hurrying down the great length of ladder, I soon found myself at the base of the last stone step of the final flight; but started aghast—the door was locked! The bell-ringer, or more probably that forever-prying suspicious-looking beadle-faced man has done this. He would not let me in at all at first, and now, with the greatest inconsistency, he will not let me out. But what is to be done? Shall I knock on the door? That will never do. It will only frighten the crowd streaming by, and no one can adequately respond to my summons, except the beadle-faced man; and if he see me, he will recognise me, and perhaps roundly rate me—poor, humble worshiper—before the entire public. No, I wont knock. But what then?

Long time I thought, and thought, till at last all was hushed again. Presently a clicking sound admonished me that the church was being closed. In sudden desperation, I gave a rap on the door. But too late. It was not heard. I was left alone and solitary in a temple which but a moment before was more populous than many villages.

A strange trepidation of gloom and loneliness gradually stole over me. Hardly conscious of what I did, I reascended the stone steps; higher and higher still, and only paused, when once more I felt the hot-air blast from the wire-woven screen. Snatching another peep down into the vast arena, I started at its hushed desertness. The long ranges of grouped columns down the nave, and clusterings of them into copses about the corners of the transept; together with the subdued, dim-streaming light from the autumnal glasses; all assumed a secluded and deep-wooded air. I seemed gazing from Pisgah into the forests of old Canaan. A Puseyitish painting of a Madonna and child, adorning a lower window, seemed showing to me the sole tenants of this painted wilderness—the true Hagar and her Ishmael.—

With added trepidation I stole softly back to the magic-lantern platform; and revived myself a little by peeping through the scratch, upon the unstained light of open day.—But what is to be done, thought I, again.

I descended to the door; listened there; heard nothing. A third time climbing the stone steps, once more I stood in the magic-lantern, while the full nature of the more than awkwardness of my position came over me.

The first persons who will reënter the temple, mused I, will doubtless be the beadle-faced man, and the bell-ringer. And the first man to come up here, where I am, will be the latter. Now what will be his natural impressions upon first descrying an unknown prowler here? Rather disadvantageous to said prowler's moral character. Explanations will be vain. Circumstances are against me. True, I may hide, till he retires again. But how do I know, that he will then leave the door unlocked? Besides, in a position of affairs like this, it is generally best, I think, to anticipate discovery, and by magnanimously announcing yourself, forestall an inglorious detection. But how announce myself? Already have I knocked, and no response. That moment, my eye, impatiently ranging roundabout, fell upon the bell-ropes. They suggested the usual signal made at dwelling-houses to convey tidings of a stranger's presence. But I was not an outside caller; alas, I was an inside prowler.—But one little touch of that bell-rope, would be sure to bring relief. I have an appointment at three o'clock. The beadle-faced man must naturally reside very close by the church. He well knows the peculiar ring of his own bell. The slightest possible hum would bring him flying to the rescue. Shall I, or shall I not?—But I may alarm the neighborhood. Oh no; the merest tingle, not by any means a loud vociferous peal. Shall I? Better voluntarily bring the beadle-faced man to me, than be involuntarily dragged out from this most suspicious hiding-place. I have to face him, first or last. Better now than later.—Shall I?—

No more. Creeping to the rope, I gave it a cautious twitch. No sound. A little less warily. All was dumb. Still more strongly. Horrors! my hands, instinctively clapped to my ears, only served to condense the appalling din. Some undreamed-of mechanism seemed to have been touched. The bell must have thrice revolved on its thunderous axis, multiplying the astounding reverberation.

My business is effectually done, this time, thought I, all in a tremble. Nothing will serve me now but the reckless confidence of innocence reduced to desperation.

In less than five minutes, I heard a running noise beneath me; the lock of the door clicked, and up rushed the beadle-faced man, the perspiration starting from his cheeks.

"You! Is it *you?* The man I turned away this very morning, skulking here? *You* dare to touch that bell? Scoundrel!"

And ere I could defend myself, seizing me irresistably in his powerful grasp, he tore me along by the collar, and dragging me down the stairs, thrust me into the arms of three policemen, who, attracted by the sudden toll of the bell, had gathered curiously about the porch.

All remonstrances were vain. The beadle-faced man was bigoted against me. Represented as a lawless violator, and a remorseless disturber of the Sunday peace, I was conducted to the Halls of Justice. Next morning, my rather gentlemany appearance procured me a private hearing from the judge. But the beadle-faced man must have made a Sunday night call on him. Spite of my coolest explanations, the circumstances of the case were deemed so exceedingly suspicious, that only after paying a round fine, and receiving a stinging reprimand, was I permitted to go at large, and pardoned for having humbly indulged myself in the luxury of public worship.

Temple Second

A stranger in London on Saturday night, and without a copper! What hospitalities may such an one expect? What shall I do with myself this weary night? My landlady wont receive me in her parlor. I owe her money. She looks like flint on me. So in this monstrous rabblement must I crawl about till, say ten o'clock, and then slink home to my unlighted bed.

The case was this: The week following my inglorious expulsion from the transatlantic temple, I had packed up my trunks and damaged character, and repaired to the fraternal, loving town of Philadelphia. There chance threw into my way an interesting young orphan lady and her aunt-duenna; the lady rich as Cleopatra, but not as beautiful; the duenna lovely as Charmian, but not so young. For the lady's health, prolonged travel had been prescribed. Maternally connected in old England, the lady chose London for her primal port. But ere securing their passage, the two were looking round for some young physician, whose disengagement from pressing business, might induce him to accept, on a moderate salary, the post of private Esculapius and knightly companion to the otherwise unprotected fair. The more necessary was this, as not only the voyage to England was intended, but an extensive European tour, to follow.

Enough. I came; I saw; I was made the happy man. We sailed. We landed on the other side; when after two weeks of agonized attendance on the vacillations of the lady, I was very cavalierly dismissed, on the score, that the lady's maternal relations had persuaded her to try, through the winter, the salubrious climate of the foggy Isle of Wight, in preference to the fabulous blue atmosphere of the Ionian Isles. So much for national prejudice.

Nota Bene.—The lady was in a sad decline.—

Having ere sailing been obliged to anticipate nearly a quarter's pay to foot my outfit bills, I was dismally cut adrift in Fleet Street without a solitary shilling. By disposing, at certain pawnbrokers, of some of my less indispensable apparel, I had managed to stave off the more slaughterous onsets of my landlady, while diligently looking about for any business that might providentially appear.

So on I drifted amid those indescribable crowds which every seventh night pour and roar through each main artery and block the bye-veins of great London, the Leviathan. Saturday Night it was; and the markets and the shops, and every stall and counter were crushed with the one unceasing tide. A whole Sunday's victualling for three millions of human bodies, was going on. Few of them equally hungry with my own, as through my spent lassitude, the unscrupulous human whirlpools eddied me aside at corners, as any straw is eddied in the Norway Maelstrom. What dire suckings into oblivion must such swirling billows know. Better perish mid myriad sharks in mid Atlantic, than die a penniless stranger in Babylonian London. Forlorn, outcast, without a friend, I staggered on through three millions of my own human kind. The fiendish gas-lights shooting their Tartarean rays across the muddy sticky streets, lit up the pitiless and pitiable scene.

Well, well, if this were but Sunday now, I might conciliate some kind female pew-opener, and rest me in some inn-like chapel, upon some stranger's outside bench. But it is Saturday night. The end of the weary week, and all but the end of weary me.

Disentangling myself at last from those skeins of Pandemonian lanes which snarl one part of the metropolis between Fleet street and Holborn, I found myself at last in a wide and far less noisy street, a short and shopless one, leading up from the Strand, and terminating at its junction with a crosswise avenue. The comparative quietude of the place was inexpressively soothing. It was like emerging upon the green enclosure surrounding some Cathedral church, where sanctity makes all things still. Two lofty brilliant lights attracted me in this tranquil street. Thinking it might prove some moral or religious meeting, I hurried towards the spot; but was surprised to see two tall placards announcing the appearance that night, of the stately Macready in the part of Cardinal Richelieu. Very few loiterers hung about the place, the hour being rather late, and the play-bill hawkers mostly departed, or keeping entirely quiet. This theatre indeed, as I afterwards discovered, was not only one of the best in point of acting, but likewise one of the most decorous in its general management, inside and out. In truth the whole neighborhood, as it seemed to me—issuing from the jam and uproar of those turbulent tides against which, or borne on irresistably by which, I had so long been swimming—the whole neighborhood, I say, of this pleasing street seemed in good keeping with the character imputed to its theatre.

Glad to find one blessed oasis of tranquility, I stood leaning against a column of the porch, and striving to lose my sadness in running over one of the huge placards. No one molested me. A tattered little girl, to be sure, approached, with a hand-bill extended, but marking me more narrowly, retreated; her strange skill in physiognomy at once enabling her to determine that I was penniless. As I read, and read—for the placard, of enormous dimensions, contained minute particulars of each successive scene in the enacted play—gradually a strong desire to witness this celebrated Macready in this his celebrated part stole over me. By one act, I might rest my jaded limbs, and more than jaded spirits. Where else could I go for rest, unless I crawled into my cold and lonely bed far up in an attic of Craven Street, looking down upon the muddy Phlegethon of the Thames. Besides, what I wanted was not merely rest, but cheer; the making one of many pleased and pleasing human faces; the getting into a genial humane assembly of my kind; such as, at its best and highest, is to be found in the unified multitude of a devout congregation. But no such assemblies were accessible that night, even if my unbefriended and rather shabby air would overcome the scruples of those fastidious gentry with red gowns and long gilded staves, who guard the portals of the first-class London tabernacles from all profanation of a poor forlorn and fainting wanderer like me. Not inns, but ecclesiastical hotels, where the pews are the rented chambers.

No use to ponder, thought I, at last; it is Saturday night, not Sunday; and so, a Theatre only can receive me. So powerfully in the end did the longing to get into the edifice come over me, that I almost began to think of pawning my overcoat for admittance. But from this last infatuation I was providentially with-held by a sudden cheery summons, in a voice unmistakably benevolent. I turned, and saw a man who seemed to be some sort of a working-man.

"Take it," said he, holding a plain red ticket towards me, full in the gas-light. "You want to go in; I know you do. Take it. I am suddenly called home. There—hope you'll enjoy yourself. Good-bye."

Blankly, and mechanically, I had suffered the ticket to be thrust into my hand, and now stood quite astonished, bewildered, and for the time, ashamed. The plain fact was, I had received charity; and for the first time in my life. Often in the course of my strange wanderings I had needed charity, but never had asked it, and certainly never, ere this blessed night, had been offered it. And a stranger; and in the very maw of the roaring London too! Next moment my sense of foolish shame departed, and I felt a queer feeling in my left eye, which, as sometimes is the case with people, was the weaker one; probably from being on the same side with the heart.

I glanced round eagerly. But the kind giver was no longer in sight. I looked upon the ticket. I understood. It was one of those checks given to persons inside a theatre when for any cause they desire to step out a moment. Its presentation ensures unquestioned readmittance.

Shall I use it? mused I.—What? It's charity.—But if it be gloriously right to do a charitable deed, can it be ingloriously wrong to receive its benefit?—No one knows you; go boldly in.—Charity.—Why these unvanquishable scruples? All your life, nought but charity sustains you, and all others in the world. Maternal charity nursed you as a babe; paternal charity fed you as a child; friendly charity got you your profession; and to the charity of every man you meet this night in London, are you indebted for your unattempted life. Any knife, any hand of all the millions of knives and hands in London, has you this night at its mercy. You, and all mortals, live but by sufferance of your charitable kind; charitable by omission, not performance.—Stush for your self-upbraidings, and pitiful, poor, shabby pride, you friendless man without a purse.—Go in.

Debate was over. Marking the direction from which the stranger had accosted me, I stepped that way; and soon saw a low-vaulted, inferior-looking door on one side of the edifice. Entering, I wandered on and up, and up and on again, through various doubling stairs and wedge-like, ill-lit passages, whose bare boards much reminded me of my ascent of the Gothic tower on the ocean's far other side. At last I gained a lofty platform, and saw a fixed human countenance facing me from a mysterious window of a sort of sentry-box or closet. Like some saint in a shrine, the countenance was illuminated by two smoky candles. I divined the man. I exhibited my diploma, and he nodded me to a little door beyond; while a sudden burst of orchestral music, admonished me I was now very near my destination, and also revived the memory of the organ-anthems I had heard while on the ladder of the tower at home.

Next moment, the wire-woven gauzy screen of the ventilating window in that same tower, seemed enchantedly reproduced before me. The same hot blast of stifling air once more rushed into my lungs. From the same dizzy altitude, through the same fine-spun, vapory crapey air; far, far down upon just such a packed mass of silent human beings; listening to just such grand harmonies; I stood within the topmost gallery of the temple. But hardly alone and silently as before. This time I had company. Not of the first circles, and certainly not of the dress-circle; but most acceptable, right welcome, cheery company, to otherwise uncompanioned me. Quiet, well-pleased working men, and their glad wives and sisters, with here and there an aproned urchin, with all-absorbed, bright face, vermillioned by the excitement and the heated air, hovering like a painted cherub over the vast human firmament below. The height of the gallery was in truth appalling. The rail was low. I thought of deep-sea-leads, and the mariner in the vessel's chains, drawing up the line, with his long-drawn musical accompaniment. And like beds of glittering coral, through the deep sea of azure smoke, there, far down, I saw the jewelled necks and white sparkling arms of crowds of ladies in the semicirque. But, in the interval of two acts, again the orchestra was heard; some inspiring national anthem now was played. As the volumed sound came undulating up, and broke in showery spray and foam of melody against our gallery rail, my head involuntarily was bowed, my hand instinctively sought my pocket. Only by a second thought, did I check my momentary lunacy and remind myself that this time I had no small morocco book with me, and that this was not the house of prayer.

Quickly was my wandering mind—preternaturally affected by the sudden translation from the desolate street, to this bewildering and blazing spectacle—arrested in its wanderings, by feeling at my elbow a meaning nudge; when turning suddenly, I saw a sort of coffee-pot, and pewter mug hospitably presented to me by a ragged, but good-natured looking boy.

"Thank you", said I, "I wont take any coffee, I guess."

"Coffee?—I guess?—Aint you a Yankee?"

"Aye, boy; true blue."

"Well dad's gone to Yankee-land, a seekin' of his fortin'; so take a penny mug of ale, do Yankee, for poor dad's sake."

Out from the tilted coffee-pot-looking can, came a coffee-colored stream, and a small mug of humming ale was in my hand.

"I dont want it, boy. The fact is, my boy, I have no penny by me. I happened to leave my purse at my lodgings."

"Never do you mind, Yankee; drink to honest dad."

"With all my heart, you generous boy; here's immortal life to him!"

He stared at my strange burst, smiled merrily, and left me, offering his coffee-pot in all directions, and not in vain.

'Tis not always poverty to be poor, mused I; one may fare well without a penny. A ragged boy may be a prince-like benefactor.

Because that unpurchased penny-worth of ale revived my drooping spirits strangely. Stuff was in that barley-malt; a most sweet bitterness in those blessed hops. God bless the glorious boy!

The more I looked about me in this lofty gallery, the more was I delighted with its occupants. It was not spacious. It was, if anything, rather contracted, being the very cheapest portion of the house, where very limited attendance was expected; embracing merely the very crown of the topmost semicircle; and so, commanding, with a sovereign outlook, and imperial downlook, the whole theatre, with the expanded stage directly opposite, though some hundred feet below. As at the tower, peeping into the transatlantic temple, so stood I here, at the very main-mast-head of all the interior edifice.

Such was the decorum of this special theatre, that nothing objectionable was admitted within its walls. With an unhurt eye of perfect love, I sat serenely in the gallery, gazing upon the pleasing scene, around me and below. Neither did it abate from my satisfaction, to remember, that Mr Macready, the chief actor of the night, was an amiable gentleman, combining the finest qualities of social and Christian respectability, with the highest excellence in his particular profession; for which last he had conscientiously done much, in many ways, to refine, elevate, and chasten.

But now the curtain rises, and the robed Cardinal advances. How marvellous this personal resemblance! He looks every inch to be the self-same, stately priest I saw irradiated by the glow-worm dies of the pictured windows from my high tower-pew. And shining as he does, in the rosy reflexes of these stained walls and gorgeous galleries, the mimic priest down there; he too seems lit by Gothic blazonings.—Hark! The same measured, courtly, noble tone. See! the same imposing attitude. Excellent actor is this Richelieu!

He disappears behind the scenes. He slips, no doubt, into the Green Room. He reappears somewhat changed in his habilaments. Do I dream, or is it genuine memory that recalls some similar thing seen through the woven wires?

The curtain falls. Starting to their feet, the enraptured thousands sound their responses, deafeningly; unmistakably sincere. Right from the undoubted heart. I have no duplicate in my memory of this. In earnestness of response, this second temple stands unmatched. And hath mere mimicry done this? What is it then to act a part?

But now the music surges up again, and borne by that rolling billow, I, and all the gladdened crowd, are harmoniously attended to the street.

I went home to my lonely lodging, and slept not much that night, for thinking of the First Temple and the Second Temple; and how that, a stranger in a strange land, I found sterling charity in the one; and at home, in my own land, was thrust out from the other.

The Paradise of Bachelors and the Tartarus of Maids

I. The Paradise of Bachelors

IT LIES not far from Temple-Bar.

Going to it, by the usual way, is like stealing from a heated plain into some cool, deep glen, shady among harboring hills.

Sick with the din and soiled with the mud of Fleet Street—where the Benedick tradesmen are hurrying by, with ledger-lines ruled along their brows, thinking upon rise of bread and fall of babies—you adroitly turn a mystic corner—not a street—glide down a dim, monastic way, flanked by dark, sedate, and solemn piles, and still wending on, give the whole care-worn world the slip, and, disentangled, stand beneath the quiet cloisters of the Paradise of Bachelors.

Sweet are the oases in Sahara; charming the isle-groves of August prairies; delectable pure faith amidst a thousand perfidies: but sweeter, still more charming, most delectable, the dreamy Paradise of Bachelors, found in the stony heart of stunning London.

In mild meditation pace the cloisters; take your pleasure, sip your leisure, in the garden waterward; go linger in the ancient library; go worship in the sculptured chapel: but little have you seen, just nothing do you know, not the sweet kernel have you tasted, till you dine among the banded Bachelors, and see their convivial eyes and glasses sparkle. Not dine in bustling commons, during term-time, in the hall; but tranquilly, by private hint, at a private table; some fine Templar's hospitably invited guest.

Templar? That's a romantic name. Let me see. Brian de Bois Guilbert was a Templar, I believe. Do we understand you to insinuate that those famous Templars still survive in modern London? May the ring of their armed heels be heard, and the rattle of their shields, as in mailed prayer the monk-knights kneel before the consecrated Host? Surely a monk-knight were a curious sight picking his way along the Strand, his gleaming corselet and snowy surcoat spattered by an omnibus. Long-bearded, too, according to his order's rule; his face fuzzy as a pard's; how would the grim ghost look among the crop-haired, close-shaven citizens? We know indeed—sad history recounts it—that a moral blight tainted at last this sacred Brotherhood. Though no sworded foe might outskill them in the fence, yet the worm of luxury crawled beneath their guard, gnawing the core of knightly troth, nibbling the monastic vow, till at last the monk's austerity relaxed to wassailing, and the sworn knights-bachelors grew to be but hypocrites and rakes.

But for all this, quite unprepared were we to learn that Knights-Templars (if at all in being) were so entirely secularized as to be reduced from carving out immortal fame in glorious battling for the Holy Land, to the carving of roast-mutton at a dinner-board. Like Anacreon, do these degenerate Templars now think it sweeter far to fall in banquet than in war? Or, indeed, how can there be any survival of that famous order? Templars in modern London! Templars in their red-cross mantles smoking cigars at the Divan! Templars crowded in a railway train, till, stacked with steel helmet, spear, and shield, the whole train looks like one elongated locomotive!

No. The genuine Templar is long since departed. Go view the wondrous tombs in the Temple Church; see there the rigidly-haughty forms stretched out, with crossed arms upon their stilly hearts, in everlasting and undreaming rest. Like the years before the flood, the bold Knights-Templars are no more. Nevertheless, the name remains, and the nominal society, and the ancient grounds, and some of the ancient edifices. But the iron heel is changed to a boot of patent-leather; the long two-handed sword to a one-handed quill; the monk-giver of gratuitous ghostly counsel now counsels for a fee; the defender of the sarcophagus (if in good practice with his weapon) now has more than one case to defend; the vowed opener and clearer of all highways leading to the Holy Sepulchre, now has it in particular charge to check, to clog, to hinder, and embarrass all the courts and avenues of Law; the knight-combatant of the Saracen, breasting spear-points at Acre, now fights law-points in Westminster Hall. The helmet is a wig. Struck by Time's enchanter's wand, the Templar is to-day a Lawyer.

But, like many others tumbled from proud glory's height—like the apple, hard on the bough but mellow on the ground—the Templar's fall has but made him all the finer fellow.

I dare say those old warrior-priests were but gruff and grouty at the best; cased in Birmingham hardware, how could their crimped arms give yours or mine a hearty shake? Their proud, ambitious, monkish souls clasped shut, like horn-book missals; their very faces clapped in bomb-shells; what sort of genial men were these? But best of comrades, most affable of hosts, capital diner is the modern Templar. His wit and wine are both of sparkling brands.

The church and cloisters, courts and vaults, lanes and passages, banquet-halls, refectories, libraries, terraces, gardens, broad walks, domicils, and dessert-rooms, covering a very large space of ground, and all grouped in central neighborhood, and quite sequestered from the old city's surrounding din; and every thing about the place being kept in most bachelor-like particularity, no part of London offers to a quiet wight so agreeable a refuge.

The Temple is, indeed, a city by itself. A city with all the best appurtenances, as the above enumeration shows. A city with a park to it, and flower-beds, and a river-side—the Thames flowing by as openly, in one part, as by Eden's primal garden flowed the mild Euphrates. In what is now the Temple Garden the old Crusaders used to exercise their steeds and lances; the modern Templars now lounge on the benches beneath the trees, and, switching their patent-leather boots, in gay discourse exercise at repartee.

Long lines of stately portraits in the banquet-halls, show what great men of mark—famous nobles, judges, and Lord Chancellors—have in their time been Templars. But all Templars are not known to universal fame; though, if the having warm hearts and warmer welcomes, full minds and fuller cellars, and giving good advice and glorious dinners, spiced with rare divertisements of fun and fancy, merit immortal mention, set down, ye muses, the names of R. F. C. and his imperial brother.

Though to be a Templar, in the one true sense, you must needs be a lawyer, or a student at the law, and be ceremoniously enrolled as member of the order, yet as many such, though Templars, do not reside within the

Temple's precincts, though they may have their offices there, just so, on the other hand, there are many residents of the hoary old domicils who are not admitted Templars. If being, say, a lounging gentleman and bachelor, or a quiet, unmarried, literary man, charmed with the soft seclusion of the spot, you much desire to pitch your shady tent among the rest in this serene encampment, then you must make some special friend among the order, and procure him to rent, in his name but at your charge, whatever vacant chamber you may find to suit.

Thus, I suppose, did Dr. Johnson, that nominal Benedick and widower but virtual bachelor, when for a space he resided here. So, too, did that undoubted bachelor and rare good soul, Charles Lamb. And hundreds more, of sterling spirits, Brethren of the Order of Celibacy, from time to time have dined, and slept, and tabernacled here. Indeed, the place is all a honeycomb of offices and domicils. Like any cheese, it is quite perforated through and through in all directions with the snug cells of bachelors. Dear, delightful spot! Ah! when I bethink me of the sweet hours there passed, enjoying such genial hospitalities beneath those time-honored roofs, my heart only finds due utterance through poetry; and, with a sigh, I softly sing, "Carry me back to old Virginny!"

Such then, at large, is the Paradise of Bachelors. And such I found it one pleasant afternoon in the smiling month of May, when, sallying from my hotel in Trafalgar Square, I went to keep my dinner-appointment with that fine Barrister, Bachelor, and Bencher, R. F. C. (he *is* the first and second, and *should be* the third; I hereby nominate him), whose card I kept fast pinched between my gloved forefinger and thumb, and every now and then snatched still another look at the pleasant address inscribed beneath the name, "No. —, Elm Court, Temple."

At the core he was a right bluff, care-free, right comfortable, and most companionable Englishman. If on a first acquaintance he seemed reserved, quite icy in his air—patience; this Champagne will thaw. And if it never do, better frozen Champagne than liquid vinegar.

There were nine gentlemen, all bachelors, at the dinner. One was from "No. —, King's Bench Walk, Temple;" a second, third, and fourth, and fifth, from various courts or passages christened with some similarly rich resounding syllables. It was indeed a sort of Senate of the Bachelors, sent to this dinner from widely-scattered districts, to represent the general celibacy of the Temple. Nay it was, by representation, a Grand Parliament of the best Bachelors in universal London; several of those present being from distant quarters of the town, noted immemorial seats of lawyers and unmarried men—Lincoln's Inn, Furnival's Inn; and one gentleman, upon whom I looked with a sort of collateral awe, hailed from the spot where Lord Verulam once abode a bachelor—Gray's Inn.

The apartment was well up toward heaven. I know not how many strange old stairs I climbed to get to it. But a good dinner, with famous company, should be well earned. No doubt our host had his dining-room so high with a view to secure the prior exercise necessary to the due relishing and digesting of it.

The furniture was wonderfully unpretending, old, and snug. No new shining mahogany, sticky with undried varnish; no uncomfortably luxurious ottomans, and sofas too fine to use, vexed you in this sedate apartment. It is a thing which every sensible American should learn from every sensible Englishman, that glare and glitter, gimcracks and gewgaws, are not indispensable to domestic solacement. The American Benedick snatches, down-town, a tough chop in a gilded show-box; the English bachelor leisurely dines at home on that incomparable South Down of his, off a plain deal board.

The ceiling of the room was low. Who wants to dine under the dome of St. Peter's? High ceilings! If that is your demand, and the higher the better, and you be so very tall, then go dine out with the topping giraffe in the open air.

In good time the nine gentlemen sat down to nine covers, and soon were fairly under way.

If I remember right, ox-tail soup inaugurated the affair. Of a rich russet hue, its agreeable flavor dissipated my first confounding of its main ingredient with teamster's gads and the raw-hides of ushers. (By way of interlude, we here drank a little claret.) Neptune's was the next tribute rendered—turbot coming second; snow-white, flaky, and just gelatinous enough, not too turtleish in its unctuousness.

(At this point we refreshed ourselves with a glass of sherry.) After these light skirmishers had vanished, the heavy artillery of the feast marched in, led by that well-known English generalissimo, roast beef. For aids-de-camp we had a saddle of mutton, a fat turkey, a chicken-pie, and endless other savory things; while for avant-couriers came nine silver flagons of humming ale. This heavy ordnance having departed on the track of the light skirmishers, a picked brigade of game-fowl encamped upon the board, their camp-fires lit by the ruddiest of decanters.

Tarts and puddings followed, with innumerable niceties; then cheese and crackers. (By way of ceremony, simply, only to keep up good old fashions, we here each drank a glass of good old port.)

The cloth was now removed; and like Blucher's army coming in at the death on the field of Waterloo, in marched a fresh detachment of bottles, dusty with their hurried march.

All these manœuvrings of the forces were superintended by a surprising old field-marshal (I can not school myself to call him by the inglorious name of waiter), with snowy hair and napkin, and a head like Socrates. Amidst all the hilarity of the feast, intent on important business, he disdained to smile. Venerable man!

I have above endeavored to give some slight schedule of the general plan of operations. But any one knows that a good, genial dinner is a sort of pell-mell, indiscriminate affair, quite baffling to detail in all particulars. Thus, I spoke of taking a glass of claret, and a glass of sherry, and a glass of port, and a mug of ale—all at certain specific periods and times. But those were merely the state bumpers, so to speak. Innumerable impromptu glasses were drained between the periods of those grand imposing ones.

The nine bachelors seemed to have the most tender concern for each other's health. All the time, in flowing wine, they most earnestly expressed their sincerest wishes for the entire well-being and lasting hygiene of the gentlemen on the right and on the left. I noticed that when one of these kind bachelors desired a little more wine (just for his stomach's sake, like Timothy), he would not help himself to it unless some other bachelor would join him. It seemed held something indelicate, selfish, and unfraternal, to be seen taking a lonely, unparticipated glass. Meantime, as the wine ran apace, the spirits of the company grew more and more to perfect genialness and unconstraint. They related all sorts of pleasant stories. Choice experiences in their private lives were now brought out, like choice brands of Moselle or Rhenish, only kept for particular company. One told us how mellowly he lived when a student at Oxford; with various spicy anecdotes of most frank-hearted noble lords, his liberal companions. Another bachelor, a gray-headed man, with a sunny face, who, by his own account, embraced every opportunity of leisure to cross over into the Low Countries, on sudden tours of inspection of the fine old Flemish architecture there—this learned, white-haired, sunny-faced old bachelor, excelled in his descriptions of the elaborate splendors of those old guild-halls, town-halls, and stadthold-houses, to be seen in the land of the ancient Flemings. A third was a great frequenter of the British Museum, and knew all about scores of wonderful antiquities, of Oriental manuscripts, and costly books without a duplicate. A fourth had lately returned from a trip to Old Granada, and, of course, was full of Saracenic scenery. A fifth had a funny case in law to tell. A sixth was erudite in wines. A seventh had a strange characteristic anecdote of the private life of the Iron Duke, never printed, and never before announced in any public or private company. An eighth had lately been amusing his evenings, now and then, with translating a comic poem of Pulci's. He quoted for us the more amusing passages.

And so the evening slipped along, the hours told, not by a water-clock, like King Alfred's, but a wine-chronometer. Meantime the table seemed a sort of Epsom Heath; a regular ring, where the decanters galloped round. For fear one decanter should not with sufficient speed reach his destination, another was sent express after him to hurry him; and then a third to hurry the second; and so on with a fourth and fifth. And throughout all this nothing loud, nothing unmannerly, nothing turbulent. I am quite sure, from the scrupulous gravity and austerity of his air, that had Socrates, the field-marshal, perceived aught of indecorum in the company he served, he would have forthwith departed without giving warning. I afterward learned that, during the repast, an invalid bachelor in an adjoining chamber enjoyed his first sound refreshing slumber in three long, weary weeks.

It was the very perfection of quiet absorption of good living, good drinking, good feeling, and good talk. We were a band of brothers. Comfort—fraternal, household comfort, was the grand trait of the affair. Also, you could plainly see that these easy-hearted men had no wives or children to give an anxious thought. Almost all of them were travelers, too; for bachelors alone can travel freely, and without any twinges of their consciences touching desertion of the fire-side.

The thing called pain, the bugbear styled trouble—those two legends seemed preposterous to their bachelor imaginations. How could men of liberal sense, ripe scholarship in the world, and capacious philosophical and convivial understandings—how could they suffer themselves to be imposed upon by such monkish fables? Pain! Trouble! As well talk of Catholic miracles. No such thing.—Pass the sherry, Sir.—Pooh, pooh! Can't be!—The port, Sir, if you please. Nonsense; don't tell me so.—The decanter stops with you, Sir, I believe.

And so it went.

Not long after the cloth was drawn our host glanced significantly upon Socrates, who, solemnly stepping to a stand, returned with an immense convolved horn, a regular Jericho horn, mounted with polished silver, and otherwise chased and curiously enriched; not omitting two life-like goat's heads, with four more horns of solid silver, projecting from opposite sides of the mouth of the noble main horn.

Not having heard that our host was a performer on the bugle, I was surprised to see him lift this horn from the table, as if he were about to blow an inspiring blast. But I was relieved from this, and set quite right as touching the purposes of the horn, by his now inserting his thumb and forefinger into its mouth; whereupon a slight aroma was stirred up, and my nostrils were greeted with the smell of some choice Rappee. It was a mull of snuff. It went the rounds. Capital idea this, thought I, of taking snuff about this juncture. This goodly fashion must be introduced among my countrymen at home, further ruminated I.

The remarkable decorum of the nine bachelors—a decorum not to be affected by any quantity of wine—a decorum unassailable by any degree of mirthfulness—this was again set in a forcible light to me, by now observing that, though they took snuff very freely, yet not a man so far violated the proprieties, or so far molested the invalid bachelor in the adjoining room as to indulge himself in a sneeze. The snuff was snuffed silently, as if it had been some fine innoxious powder brushed off the wings of butterflies.

But fine though they be, bachelors' dinners, like bachelors' lives, can not endure forever. The time came for breaking up. One by one the bachelors took their hats, and two by two, and arm-in-arm they descended, still conversing, to the flagging of the court; some going to their neighboring chambers to turn over the Decameron ere retiring for the night; some to smoke a cigar, promenading in the garden on the cool river-side; some to make for the street, call a hack, and be driven snugly to their distant lodgings.

I was the last lingerer.

"Well," said my smiling host, "what do you think of the Temple here, and the sort of life we bachelors make out to live in it?"

"Sir," said I, with a burst of admiring candor—"Sir, this is the very Paradise of Bachelors!"

II. The Tartarus of Maids

It lies not far from Woedolor Mountain in New England. Turning to the east, right out from among bright farms and sunny meadows, nodding in early June with odorous grasses, you enter ascendingly among bleak hills. These gradually close in upon a dusky pass, which, from the violent Gulf Stream of air unceasingly driving between its cloven walls of haggard rock, as well as from the tradition of a crazy spinster's hut having long ago stood somewhere hereabouts, is called the Mad Maid's Bellows'-pipe.

Winding along at the bottom of the gorge is a dangerously narrow wheel-road, occupying the bed of a former torrent. Following this road to its highest point, you stand as within a Dantean gateway. From the steepness of the walls here, their strangely ebon hue, and the sudden contraction of the gorge, this particular point is called the Black Notch. The ravine now expandingly descends into a great, purple, hopper-shaped hollow, far sunk among many Plutonian, shaggy-wooded mountains. By the country people this hollow is called the Devil's Dungeon. Sounds of torrents fall on all sides upon the ear. These rapid waters unite at last in one turbid brick-colored stream, boiling through a flume among enormous boulders. They call this strange-colored torrent Blood River. Gaining a dark precipice it wheels suddenly to the west, and makes one maniac spring of sixty feet into the arms of a stunted wood of gray-haired pines, between which it thence eddies on its further way down to the invisible lowlands.

Conspicuously crowning a rocky bluff high to one side, at the cataract's verge, is the ruin of an old saw-mill, built in those primitive times when vast pines and hemlocks superabounded throughout the neighboring region. The black-mossed bulk of those immense, rough-hewn, and spike-knotted logs, here and there tumbled all together, in long abandonment and decay, or left in solitary, perilous projection over the cataract's gloomy brink, impart to this rude wooden ruin not only much of the aspect of one of rough-quarried stone, but also a sort of feudal, Rhineland, and Thurmberg look, derived from the pinnacled wildness of the neighboring scenery.

Not far from the bottom of the Dungeon stands a large white-washed building, relieved, like some great whited sepulchre, against the sullen background of mountain-side firs, and other hardy evergreens, inaccessibly rising in grim terraces for some two thousand feet.

The building is a paper-mill.

Having embarked on a large scale in the seedsman's business (so extensively and broadcast, indeed, that at length my seeds were distributed through all the Eastern and Northern States, and even fell into the far soil of Missouri and the Carolinas), the demand for paper at my place became so great, that the expenditure soon amounted to a most important item in the general account. It need hardly be hinted how paper comes into use with seedsmen, as envelopes. These are mostly made of yellowish paper, folded square; and when filled, are all but flat, and being stamped, and superscribed with the nature of the seeds contained, assume not a little the appearance of business-letters ready for the mail. Of these small envelopes I used an incredible quantity—several hundreds of thousands in a year. For a time I had purchased my paper from the wholesale dealers in a neighboring town. For economy's sake, and partly for the adventure of the trip, I now resolved to cross the mountains, some sixty miles, and order my future paper at the Devil's Dungeon paper-mill.

The sleighing being uncommonly fine toward the end of January, and promising to hold so for no small period, in spite of the bitter cold I started one gray Friday noon in my pung, well fitted with buffalo and wolf robes; and, spending one night on the road, next noon came in sight of Woedolor Mountain.

The far summit fairly smoked with frost; white vapors curled up from its white-wooded top, as from a chimney. The intense congelation made the whole country look like one petrifaction. The steel shoes of my pung craunched and gritted over the vitreous, chippy snow, as if it had been broken glass. The forests here and there skirting the route, feeling the same all-stiffening influence, their inmost fibres penetrated with the cold, strangely groaned—not in the swaying branches merely, but likewise in the vertical trunk—as the fitful gusts remorselessly swept through them. Brittle with excessive frost, many colossal tough-grained maples, snapped in twain like pipe-stems, cumbered the unfeeling earth.

Flaked all over with frozen sweat, white as a milky ram, his nostrils at each breath sending forth two horn-shaped shoots of heated respiration, Black, my good horse, but six years old, started at a sudden turn, where, right across the track—not ten minutes fallen—an old distorted hemlock lay, darkly undulatory as an anaconda.

Gaining the Bellows'-pipe, the violent blast, dead from behind, all but shoved my high-backed pung up-hill. The gust shrieked through the shivered pass, as if laden with lost spirits bound to the unhappy world. Ere gaining the summit, Black, my horse, as if exasperated by the cutting wind, slung out with his strong hind legs, tore the light pung straight up-hill, and sweeping grazingly through the narrow notch, sped downward madly past the ruined saw-mill. Into the Devil's Dungeon horse and cataract rushed together.

With might and main, quitting my seat and robes, and standing backward, with one foot braced against the dash-board, I rasped and churned the bit, and stopped him just in time to avoid collision, at a turn, with the bleak nozzle of a rock, couchant like a lion in the way—a road-side rock.

At first I could not discover the paper-mill.

The whole hollow gleamed with the white, except, here and there, where a pinnacle of granite showed one wind-swept angle bare. The mountains stood pinned in shrouds—a pass of Alpine corpses. Where stands the mill? Suddenly a whirling, humming sound broke upon my ear. I looked, and there, like an arrested avalanche, lay the large white-washed factory. It was subordinately surrounded by a cluster of other and smaller buildings, some of which, from their cheap, blank air, great length, gregarious windows, and comfortless expression, no doubt were boarding-houses of the operatives. A snow-white hamlet amidst the snows. Various rude, irregular squares and courts resulted from the somewhat picturesque clusterings of these buildings, owing to the broken, rocky nature of the ground, which forbade all method in their relative arrangement. Several narrow lanes and alleys, too, partly blocked with snow fallen from the roof, cut up the hamlet in all directions.

When, turning from the traveled highway, jingling with bells of numerous farmers—who, availing themselves of the fine sleighing, were dragging their wood to market—and frequently diversified with swift cutters dashing from inn to inn of the scattered villages—when, I say, turning from that bustling main-road, I by degrees wound into the Mad Maid's Bellows'-pipe, and saw the grim Black Notch beyond, then something latent, as well as something obvious in the time and scene, strangely brought back to my mind my first sight of dark and grimy Temple-Bar. And when Black, my horse, went darting through the Notch, perilously grazing its rocky wall, I remembered being in a runaway London omnibus, which in much the same sort of style, though by no means at an equal rate, dashed through the ancient arch of Wren. Though the two objects did by no means completely correspond, yet this partial inadequacy but served to tinge the similitude not less with the vividness than the disorder of a dream. So that, when upon reining up at the protruding rock I at last caught sight of the quaint groupings of the factory-buildings, and with the traveled highway and the Notch behind, found myself all alone, silently and privily stealing through deep-cloven passages into this sequestered spot, and saw the long, high-gabled main factory edifice, with a rude tower—for hoisting heavy boxes—at one end, standing among its crowded outbuildings and boarding-houses, as the Temple Church amidst the surrounding offices and dormitories, and when the marvelous retirement of this mysterious mountain nook fastened its whole spell upon me, then, what memory lacked, all tributary imagination furnished, and I said to myself, "This is the very counterpart of the Paradise of Bachelors, but snowed upon, and frost-painted to a sepulchre."

Dismounting, and warily picking my way down the dangerous declivity—horse and man both sliding now and then upon the icy ledges—at length I drove, or the blast drove me, into the largest square, before one side of the main edifice. Piercingly and shrilly the shotted blast blew by the corner; and redly and demoniacally boiled Blood River at one side. A long wood-pile, of many scores of cords, all glittering in mail of crusted ice, stood crosswise in the square. A row of horse-posts, their north sides plastered with adhesive snow, flanked the factory wall. The bleak frost packed and paved the square as with some ringing metal.

The inverted similitude recurred—"The sweet, tranquil Temple garden, with the Thames bordering its green beds," strangely meditated I.

But where are the gay bachelors?

Then, as I and my horse stood shivering in the wind-spray, a girl ran from a neighboring dormitory door, and throwing her thin apron over her bare head, made for the opposite building.

"One moment, my girl; is there no shed hereabouts which I may drive into?"

Pausing, she turned upon me a face pale with work, and blue with cold; an eye supernatural with unrelated misery.

"Nay," faltered I, "I mistook you. Go on; I want nothing."

Leading my horse close to the door from which she had come, I knocked. Another pale, blue girl appeared, shivering in the doorway as, to prevent the blast, she jealously held the door ajar.

"Nay, I mistake again. In God's name shut the door. But hold, is there no man about?"

That moment a dark-complexioned well-wrapped personage passed, making for the factory door, and spying him coming, the girl rapidly closed the other one.

"Is there no horse-shed here, Sir?"

"Yonder, to the wood-shed," he replied, and disappeared inside the factory.

With much ado I managed to wedge in horse and pung between the scattered piles of wood all sawn and split. Then, blanketing my horse, and piling my buffalo on the blanket's top, and tucking in its edges well around the breast-band and breeching, so that the wind might not strip him bare, I tied him fast, and ran lamely for the factory door, stiff with frost, and cumbered with my driver's dread-naught.

Immediately I found myself standing in a spacious place, intolerably lighted by long rows of windows, focusing inward the snowy scene without.

At rows of blank-looking counters sat rows of blank-looking girls, with blank, white folders in their blank hands, all blankly folding blank paper.

In one corner stood some huge frame of ponderous iron, with a vertical thing like a piston periodically rising and falling upon a heavy wooden block. Before it—its tame minister—stood a tall girl, feeding the iron animal with half-quires of rose-hued note paper, which, at every downward dab of the piston-like machine, received in the corner the impress of a wreath of roses. I looked from the rosy paper to the pallid cheek, but said nothing.

Seated before a long apparatus, strung with long, slender strings like any harp, another girl was feeding it with foolscap sheets, which, so soon as they curiously traveled from her on the cords, were withdrawn at the opposite end of the machine by a second girl. They came to the first girl blank; they went to the second girl ruled.

I looked upon the first girl's brow, and saw it was young and fair; I looked upon the second girl's brow, and saw it was ruled and wrinkled. Then, as I still looked, the two—for some small variety to the monotony—changed places; and where had stood the young, fair brow, now stood the ruled and wrinkled one.

Perched high upon a narrow platform, and still higher upon a high stool crowning it, sat another figure serving some other iron animal; while below the platform sat her mate in some sort of reciprocal attendance.

Not a syllable was breathed. Nothing was heard but the low, steady, overruling hum of the iron animals. The human voice was banished from the spot. Machinery—that vaunted slave of humanity—here stood menially served by human beings, who served mutely and cringingly as the slave serves the Sultan. The girls did not so much seem accessory wheels to the general machinery as mere cogs to the wheels.

All this scene around me was instantaneously taken in at one sweeping glance—even before I had proceeded to unwind the heavy fur tippet from around my neck. But as soon as this fell from me the dark-complexioned man, standing close by, raised a sudden cry, and seizing my arm, dragged me out into the open air, and without pausing for a word instantly caught up some congealed snow and began rubbing both my cheeks.

"Two white spots like the whites of your eyes," he said; "man, your cheeks are frozen."

"That may well be," muttered I; "'tis some wonder the frost of the Devil's Dungeon strikes in no deeper. Rub away."

Soon a horrible, tearing pain caught at my reviving cheeks. Two gaunt blood-hounds, one on each side, seemed mumbling them. I seemed Actæon.

Presently, when all was over, I re-entered the factory, made known my business, concluded it satisfactorily, and then begged to be conducted throughout the place to view it.

"Cupid is the boy for that," said the dark-complexioned man. "Cupid!" and by this odd fancy-name calling a dimpled, red-cheeked, spirited-looking, forward little fellow, who was rather impudently, I thought, gliding about among the passive-looking girls—like a gold fish through hueless waves—yet doing nothing in particular that I could see,. the man bade him lead the stranger through the edifice.

"Come first and see the water-wheel," said this lively lad, with the air of boyishly-brisk importance.

Quitting the folding-room, we crossed some damp, cold boards, and stood beneath a great wet shed, incessantly showering with foam, like the green barnacled bow of some East Indiaman in a gale. Round and round here went the enormous revolutions of the dark colossal water-wheel, grim with its one immutable purpose.

"This sets our whole machinery a-going, Sir; in every part of all these buildings; where the girls work and all."

I looked, and saw that the turbid waters of Blood River had not changed their hue by coming under the use of man.

"You make only blank paper; no printing of any sort, I suppose? All blank paper, don't you?"

"Certainly; what else should a paper-factory make?"

The lad here looked at me as if suspicious of my common-sense.

"Oh, to be sure!" said I, confused and stammering; "it only struck me as so strange that red waters should turn out pale chee—paper, I mean."

He took me up a wet and rickety stair to a great light room, furnished with no visible thing but rude, manger-like receptacles running all round its sides; and up to these mangers, like so many mares haltered to the rack, stood rows of girls. Before each was vertically thrust up a long, glittering scythe, immovably fixed at bottom to the manger-edge. The curve of the scythe, and its having no snath to it, made it look exactly like a sword. To and fro, across the sharp edge, the girls forever dragged long strips of rags, washed white, picked from baskets at one side; thus ripping asunder every seam, and converting the tatters almost into lint. The air swam with the fine, poisonous particles, which from all sides darted, subtilely, as motes in sun-beams, into the lungs.

"This is the rag-room," coughed the boy.

"You find it rather stifling here," coughed I, in answer; "but the girls don't cough."

"Oh, they are used to it."

"Where do you get such hosts of rags?" picking up a handful from a basket.

"Some from the country round about; some from far over sea—Leghorn and London."

"'Tis not unlikely, then," murmured I, "that among these heaps of rags there may be some old shirts, gathered from the dormitories of the Paradise of Bachelors. But the buttons are all dropped off. Pray, my lad, do you ever find any bachelor's buttons hereabouts?"

"None grow in this part of the country. The Devil's Dungeon is no place for flowers."

"Oh! you mean the *flowers* so called—the Bachelor's Buttons?"

"And was not that what you asked about? Or did you mean the gold bosom-buttons of our boss, Old Bach, as our whispering girls all call him?"

"The man, then, I saw below is a bachelor, is he?"

"Oh, yes, he's a Bach."

"The edges of those swords, they are turned outward from the girls, if I see right; but their rags and fingers fly so, I can not distinctly see."

"Turned outward."

Yes, murmured I to myself; I see it now; turned outward; and each erected sword is so borne, edge-outward, before each girl. If my reading fails me not, just so, of old, condemned state-prisoners went from the hall of judgment to their doom: an officer before, bearing a sword, its edge turned outward, in significance of their fatal sentence. So, through consumptive pallors of this blank, raggy life, go these white girls to death.

"Those scythes look very sharp," again turning toward the boy.

"Yes; they have to keep them so. Look!"

That moment two of the girls, dropping their rags, plied each a whet-stone up and down the sword-blade. My unaccustomed blood curdled at the sharp shriek of the tormented steel.

Their own executioners; themselves whetting the very swords that slay them; meditated I.

"What makes those girls so sheet-white, my lad?"

"Why"—with a roguish twinkle, pure ignorant drollery, not knowing heartlessness—"I suppose the handling of such white bits of sheets all the time makes them so sheety."

"Let us leave the rag-room now, my lad."

More tragical and more inscrutably mysterious than any mystic sight, human or machine, throughout the factory, was the strange innocence of cruel-heartedness in this usage-hardened boy.

"And now," said he, cheerily, "I suppose you want to see our great machine, which cost us twelve thousand dollars only last autumn. That's the machine that makes the paper, too. This way, Sir."

Following him, I crossed a large, bespattered place, with two great round vats in it, full of a white, wet, woolly-looking stuff, not unlike the albuminous part of an egg, soft-boiled.

"There," said Cupid, tapping the vats carelessly, "these are the first beginnings of the paper; this white pulp you see. Look how it swims bubbling round and round, moved by the paddle here. From hence it pours from both vats into that one common channel yonder; and so goes, mixed up and leisurely, to the great machine. And now for that."

He led me into a room, stifling with a strange, blood-like, abdominal heat, as if here, true enough, were being finally developed the germinous particles lately seen.

Before me, rolled out like some long Eastern manuscript, lay stretched one continuous length of iron frame-work—multitudinous and mystical, with all sorts of rollers, wheels, and cylinders, in slowly-measured and unceasing motion.

"Here first comes the pulp now," said Cupid, pointing to the nighest end of the machine. "See; first it pours out and spreads itself upon this wide, sloping board; and then—look—slides, thin and quivering, beneath the first roller there. Follow on now, and see it as it slides from under that to the next cylinder. There; see how it has become just a very little less pulpy now. One step more, and it grows still more to some slight consistence. Still another cylinder, and it is so knitted—though as yet mere dragon-fly wing—that it forms an air-bridge here, like a suspended cobweb, between two more separated rollers; and flowing over the last one, and under again, and doubling about there out of sight for a minute among all those mixed cylinders you indistinctly see, it reappears here, looking now at last a little less like pulp and more like paper, but still quite delicate and defective yet awhile. But—a little further onward, Sir, if you please—here now, at this further point, it puts on something of a real look, as if it might turn out to be something you might possibly handle in the end. But it's not yet done, Sir. Good way to travel yet, and plenty more of cylinders must roll it."

"Bless my soul!" said I, amazed at the elongation, interminable convolutions, and deliberate slowness of the machine; "it must take a long time for the pulp to pass from end to end, and come out paper."

"Oh! not so long," smiled the precocious lad, with a superior and patronizing air; "only nine minutes. But look; you may try it for yourself. Have you a bit of paper? Ah! here's a bit on the floor. Now mark that with any word you please, and let me dab it on here, and we'll see how long before it comes out at the other end."

"Well, let me see," said I, taking out my pencil; "come, I'll mark it with your name."

Bidding me take out my watch, Cupid adroitly dropped the inscribed slip on an exposed part of the incipient mass.

Instantly my eye marked the second-hand on my dial-plate.

Slowly I followed the slip, inch by inch; sometimes pausing for full half a minute as it disappeared beneath inscrutable groups of the lower cylinders, but only gradually to emerge again; and so, on, and on, and on—inch by inch; now in open sight, sliding along like a freckle on the quivering sheet; and then again wholly vanished; and so, on, and on, and on—inch by inch; all the time the main sheet growing more and more to final firmness—when, suddenly, I saw a sort of paper-fall, not wholly unlike a water-fall; a scissory sound smote my ear, as of some cord being snapped; and down dropped an unfolded sheet of perfect foolscap, with my "Cupid" half faded out of it, and still moist and warm.

My travels were at an end, for here was the end of the machine.

"Well, how long was it?" said Cupid.

"Nine minutes to a second," replied I, watch in hand.

"I told you so."

For a moment a curious emotion filled me, not wholly unlike that which one might experience at the fulfillment of some mysterious prophecy. But how absurd, thought I again; the thing is a mere machine, the essence of which is unvarying punctuality and precision.

Previously absorbed by the wheels and cylinders, my attention was now directed to a sad-looking woman standing by.

"That is rather an elderly person so silently tending the machine-end here. She would not seem wholly used to it either."

"Oh," knowingly whispered Cupid, through the din, "she only came last week. She was a nurse formerly. But the business is poor in these parts, and she's left it. But look at the paper she is piling there."

"Ay, foolscap," handling the piles of moist, warm sheets, which continually were being delivered into the woman's waiting hands. "Don't you turn out any thing but foolscap at this machine?"

"Oh, sometimes, but not often, we turn out finer work—cream-laid and royal sheets, we call them. But foolscap being in chief demand, we turn out foolscap most."

It was very curious. Looking at that blank paper continually dropping, dropping, dropping, my mind ran on in wonderings of those strange uses to which those thousand sheets eventually would be put. All sorts of writings would be writ on those now vacant things—sermons, lawyers' briefs, physicians' prescriptions, love-letters, marriage certificates, bills of divorce, registers of births, death-warrants, and so on, without end. Then, recurring back to them as they here lay all blank, I could not but bethink me of that celebrated comparison of John Locke, who, in demonstration of his theory that man had no innate ideas, compared the human mind at birth to a sheet of blank paper; something destined to be scribbled on, but what sort of characters no soul might tell.

Pacing slowly to and fro along the involved machine, still humming with its play, I was struck as well by the inevitability as the evolvement-power in all its motions.

"Does that thin cobweb there," said I, pointing to the sheet in its more imperfect stage, "does that never tear or break? It is marvelous fragile, and yet this machine it passes through is so mighty."

"It never is known to tear a hair's point."

"Does it never stop—get clogged?"

"No. It *must* go. The machinery makes it go just *so;* just that very way, and at that very pace you there plainly *see* it go. The pulp can't help going."

Something of awe now stole over me, as I gazed upon this inflexible iron animal. Always, more or less, machinery of this ponderous, elaborate sort strikes, in some moods, strange dread into the human heart, as some living, panting Behemoth might. But what made the thing I saw so specially terrible to me was the metallic necessity, the unbudging fatality which governed it. Though, here and there, I could not follow the thin, gauzy vail of pulp in the course of its more mysterious or entirely invisible advance, yet it was indubitable that, at those points where it eluded me, it still marched on in unvarying docility to the autocratic cunning of the machine. A fascination fastened on me. I stood spell-bound and wandering in my soul. Before my eyes—there, passing in slow procession along the wheeling cylinders, I seemed to see, glued to the pallid incipience of the pulp, the yet more pallid faces of all the pallid girls I had eyed that heavy day. Slowly, mournfully, beseechingly, yet unresistingly, they gleamed along, their agony dimly outlined on the imperfect paper, like the print of the tormented face on the handkerchief of Saint Veronica.

"Halloa! the heat of the room is too much for you," cried Cupid, staring at me.

"No—I am rather chill, if any thing."

"Come out, Sir—out—out," and, with the protecting air of a careful father, the precocious lad hurried me outside.

In a few moments, feeling revived a little, I went into the folding-room—the first room I had entered, and where the desk for transacting business stood, surrounded by the blank counters and blank girls engaged at them.

"Cupid here has led me a strange tour," said I to the dark-complexioned man before mentioned, whom I had ere this discovered not only to be an old bachelor, but also the principal proprietor. "Yours is a most wonderful factory. Your great machine is a miracle of inscrutable intricacy."

"Yes, all our visitors think it so. But we don't have many. We are in a very out-of-the-way corner here. Few inhabitants, too. Most of our girls come from far-off villages."

"The girls," echoed I, glancing round at their silent forms. "Why is it, Sir, that in most factories, female operatives, of whatever age, are indiscriminately called girls, never women?"

"Oh! as to that—why, I suppose, the fact of their being generally unmarried—that's the reason, I should think. But it never struck me before. For our factory here, we will not have married women; they are apt to be off-and-on too much. We want none but steady workers: twelve hours to the day, day after day, through the three hundred and sixty-five days, excepting Sundays, Thanksgiving, and Fast-days. That's our rule. And so, having no married women, what females we have are rightly enough called girls."

"Then these are all maids," said I, while some pained homage to their pale virginity made me involuntarily bow.

"All maids."

Again the strange emotion filled me.

"Your cheeks look whitish yet, Sir," said the man, gazing at me narrowly. "You must be careful going home. Do they pain you at all now? It's a bad sign, if they do."

"No doubt, Sir," answered I, "when once I have got out of the Devil's Dungeon, I shall feel them mending."

"Ah, yes; the winter air in valleys, or gorges, or any sunken place, is far colder and more bitter than elsewhere. You would hardly believe it now, but it is colder here than at the top of Woedolor Mountain."

"I dare say it is, Sir. But time presses me; I must depart."

With that, remuffling myself in dread-naught and tippet, thrusting my hands into my huge seal-skin mittens, I sallied out into the nipping air, and found poor Black, my horse, all cringing and doubled up with the cold.

Soon, wrapped in furs and meditations, I ascended from the Devil's Dungeon.

At the Black Notch I paused, and once more bethought me of Temple-Bar. Then, shooting through the pass, all alone with inscrutable nature, I exclaimed—Oh! Paradise of Bachelors! and oh! Tartarus of Maids!

Jimmy Rose

A TIME AGO, no matter how long precisely, I, an old man, removed from the country to the city, having become unexpected heir to a great old house in a narrow street of one of the lower wards, once the haunt of style and fashion, full of gay parlors and bridal chambers; but now, for the most part, transformed into counting-rooms and warehouses. There bales and boxes usurp the place of sofas; day-books and ledgers are spread where once the delicious breakfast toast was buttered. In those old wards the glorious old soft-warfle days are over.

Nevertheless, in this old house of mine, so strangely spared, some monument of departed days survived. Nor was this the only one. Amidst the warehouse ranges some few other dwellings likewise stood. The street's transmutation was not yet complete. Like those old English friars and nuns, long haunting the ruins of their retreats after they had been despoiled, so some few strange old gentlemen and ladies still lingered in the neighborhood, and would not, could not, might not quit it. And I thought that when, one spring, emerging from my white-blossoming orchard, my own white hairs and white ivory-headed cane were added to their loitering census, that those poor old souls insanely fancied the ward was looking up—the tide of fashion setting back again.

For many years the old house had been unoccupied by an owner; those into whose hands it from time to time had passed having let it out to various shifting tenants; decayed old towns-people, mysterious recluses, or transient, ambiguous-looking foreigners.

While from certain cheap furbishings to which the exterior had been subjected, such as removing a fine old pulpit-like porch crowning the summit of six lofty steps, and set off with a broad-brimmed sounding-board overshadowing the whole, as well as replacing the original heavy window-shutters (each pierced with a crescent in the upper panel to admit an Oriental and moony light into the otherwise shut-up rooms of a sultry morning in July) with frippery Venetian blinds; while, I repeat, the front of the house hereby presented an incongruous aspect, as if the graft of modernness had not taken in its ancient stock; still, however it might fare without, within little or nothing had been altered. The cellars were full of great grim, arched bins of blackened brick, looking like the ancient tombs of Templars, while overhead were shown the first-floor timbers, huge, square, and massive, all red oak, and through long eld, of a rich and Indian color. So large were those timbers, and so thickly ranked, that to walk in those capacious cellars was much like walking along a line-of-battle ship's gun-deck.

All the rooms in each story remained just as they stood ninety years ago, with all their heavy-moulded, wooden cornices, paneled wainscots, and carved and inaccessible mantles of queer horticultural and zoological devices. Dim with longevity, the very covering of the walls still preserved the patterns of the times of Louis XVI. In the largest parlor (the drawing-room, my daughters called it, in distinction from two smaller parlors, though I did not think the distinction indispensable) the paper hangings were in the most gaudy style. Instantly we knew such paper could only have come from Paris—genuine Versailles paper—the sort of paper that might have hung in Marie Antoinette's boudoir. It was of great diamond lozenges, divided by massive festoons of roses (onions, Biddy the girl said they were, but my wife soon changed Biddy's mind on that head); and in those lozenges, one and all, as in an overarbored garden-cage, sat a grand series of gorgeous illustrations of the natural history of the most imposing Parisian-looking birds; parrots, macaws, and peacocks, but mostly peacocks. Real Prince Esterhazies of birds; all rubies, diamonds, and Orders of the Golden Fleece. But, alas! the north side of this old apartment presented a strange look; half mossy and half mildew; something as ancient forest trees on their north sides, to which particular side the moss most clings, and where, they say, internal decay first strikes. In short, the original resplendence of the peacocks had been sadly dimmed on that north side of the room, owing to a small leak in the eaves, from which the rain had slowly trickled its way down the wall, clean down to the first floor. This leak the irreverent tenants, at that period occupying the premises, did not see fit to stop, or rather, did not think it worth their while, seeing that they only kept their fuel and dried their clothes in the parlor of the peacocks. Hence many of the once glowing birds seemed as if they had their princely plumage bedraggled in a dusty shower. Most mournfully their starry trains were blurred. Yet so patiently and so pleasantly, nay, here and there so ruddily did they seem to bide their bitter doom, so much of real elegance still lingered in their shapes, and so full, too, seemed they of a sweet engaging pensiveness, meditating all day long, for years and years, among their faded bowers, that though my family repeatedly adjured me (especially my wife, who, I fear, was too young for me) to destroy the whole hen-roost, as Biddy called it, and cover the walls with a beautiful, nice, genteel, cream-colored paper, despite all entreaties, I could not be prevailed upon, however submissive in other things.

But chiefly would I permit no violation of the old parlor of the peacocks or room of roses (I call it by both names), on account of its long association in my mind with one of the original proprietors of the mansion—the gentle Jimmy Rose.

Poor Jimmy Rose!

He was among my earliest acquaintances. It is not many years since he died; and I and two other tottering old fellows took hack, and in sole procession followed him to his grave.

Jimmy was born a man of moderate fortune. In his prime he had an uncommonly handsome person; large and manly, with bright eyes of blue, brown curling hair, and cheeks that seemed painted with carmine; but it was health's genuine bloom, deepened by the joy of life. He was by nature a great ladies' man, and like most deep adorers of the sex, never tied up his freedom of general worship by making one willful sacrifice of himself at the altar.

Adding to his fortune by a large and princely business, something like that of the great Florentine trader, Cosmo the Magnificent, he was enabled to entertain on a grand scale. For a long time his dinners, suppers, and balls, were not to be surpassed by any given in the party-giving city of New York. His uncommon cheeriness; the splendor of his dress; his sparkling wit; radiant chandeliers; infinite fund of small-talk; French furniture; glowing welcomes to his guests; his bounteous heart and board; his noble graces and his glorious wine; what wonder if all these drew crowds to Jimmy's hospitable abode? In the winter assemblies he figured first on the manager's list. James Rose, Esq., too, was the man to be found foremost in all presentations of plate to highly successful actors at the Park, or of swords and guns to highly successful generals in the field. Often, also, was he chosen to present the gift on account of his fine gift of finely saying fine things.

"Sir," said he, in a great drawing-room in Broadway, as he extended toward General G——— a brace of pistols set with turquois. "Sir," said Jimmy with a Castilian flourish and a rosy smile, "there would have been more turquois here set, had the names of your glorious victories left room."

Ah, Jimmy, Jimmy! Thou didst excel in compliments. But it was inwrought with thy inmost texture to be affluent in all things which give pleasure. And who shall reproach thee with borrowed wit on this occasion, though borrowed indeed it was? Plagiarize otherwise as they may, not often are the men of this world plagiarists in praise.

But times changed. Time, true plagiarist of the seasons.

Sudden and terrible reverses in business were made mortal by mad prodigality on all hands. When his affairs came to be scrutinized, it was found that Jimmy could not pay more than fifteen shillings in the pound. And yet in time the deficiency might have been made up—of course, leaving Jimmy penniless—had it not been that in one winter gale two vessels of his from China perished off Sandy Hook; perished at the threshold of their port.

Jimmy was a ruined man.

It was years ago. At that period I resided in the country, but happened to be in the city on one of my annual visits. It was but four or five days since seeing Jimmy at his house the centre of all eyes, and hearing him at the close of the entertainment toasted by a brocaded lady, in these well-remembered words: "Our noble host; the bloom on his cheek, may it last long as the bloom in his heart!" And they, the sweet ladies and gentlemen there, they drank that toast so gayly and frankly off; and Jimmy, such a kind, proud, grateful tear stood in his honest eye, angelically glancing round at the sparkling faces, and equally sparkling, and equally feeling, decanters.

Ah! poor, poor Jimmy—God guard us all—poor Jimmy Rose!

Well, it was but four or five days after this that I heard a clap of thunder—no, a clap of bad news. I was crossing the Bowling Green in a snow-storm not far from Jimmy's house on the Battery, when I saw a gentleman come sauntering along, whom I remembered at Jimmy's table as having been the first to spring to his feet in eager response to the lady's toast. Not more brimming the wine in his lifted glass than the moisture in his eye on that happy occasion.

Well, this good gentleman came sailing across the Bowling Green, swinging a silver-headed ratan; seeing me, he paused, "Ah, lad, that was rare wine Jimmy gave us the other night. Sha'n't get any more, though. Heard the news? Jimmy's burst. Clean smash, I assure you. Come along down to the Coffee-house and I'll tell you more. And if you say so, we'll arrange over a bottle of claret for a sleighing party to Cato's to-night. Come along."

"Thank you," said I, "I—I—I am engaged."

Straight as an arrow I went to Jimmy's. Upon inquiring for him, the man at the door told me that his master was not in; nor did he know where he was; nor had his master been in the house for forty-eight hours.

Walking up Broadway again, I questioned passing acquaintances; but though each man verified the report, no man could tell where Jimmy was, and no one seemed to care, until I encountered a merchant, who hinted that probably Jimmy, having scraped up from the wreck a snug lump of coin, had prudently betaken himself off to parts unknown. The next man I saw, a great nabob he was too, foamed at the mouth when I mentioned Jimmy's name. "Rascal; regular scamp, Sir, is Jimmy Rose! But there are keen fellows after him." I afterward heard that this indignant gentleman had lost the sum of seventy-five dollars and seventy-five cents indirectly through Jimmy's failure. And yet I dare say the share of the dinners he had eaten at Jimmy's might more than have balanced that sum, considering that he was something of a wine-bibber, and such wines as Jimmy imported cost a plum or two. Indeed, now that I bethink me, I recall how I had more than once observed this same middle-aged gentleman, and how that toward the close of one of Jimmy's dinners he would sit at the table pretending to be earnestly talking with beaming Jimmy, but all the while, with a half furtive sort of tremulous eagerness and hastiness, pour down glass after glass of noble wine, as if now, while Jimmy's bounteous sun was at meridian, was the time to make his selfish hay.

At last I met a person famed for his peculiar knowledge of whatever was secret or withdrawn in the histories and habits of noted people. When I inquired of this person where Jimmy could possibly be, he took me close to Trinity Church rail, out of the jostling of the crowd, and whispered me, that Jimmy had the evening before entered an old house of his (Jimmy's), in C—— Street, which old house had been for a time untenanted. The inference seemed to be that perhaps Jimmy might be lurking there now. So getting the precise locality, I bent my steps in that direction, and at last halted before the house containing the room of roses. The shutters were closed, and cobwebs were spun in their crescents. The whole place had a dreary, deserted air. The snow lay unswept, drifted in one billowy heap against the porch, no footprint tracking it. Whoever was within, surely that lonely man was an abandoned one. Few or no people were in the street; for even at that period the fashion of the street had departed from it, while trade had not as yet occupied what its rival had renounced.

Looking up and down the sidewalk a moment, I softly knocked at the door. No response. I knocked again, and louder. No one came. I knocked and rung both; still without effect. In despair I was going to quit the spot, when, as a last resource, I gave a prolonged summons, with my utmost strength, upon the heavy knocker, and then again stood still; while from various strange old windows up and down the street, various strange old heads were thrust out in wonder at so clamorous a stranger. As if now frightened from its silence, a hollow, husky voice addressed me through the keyhole.

"Who are you?" it said.

"A friend."

"Then shall you not come in," replied the voice, more hollowly than before.

"Great Heaven! this is not Jimmy Rose?" thought I, starting. This is the wrong house. I have been misdirected. But still, to make all sure, I spoke again.

"Is James Rose within there?"

No reply.

Once more I spoke:

"I am William Ford; let me in."

"Oh, I can not, I can not! I am afraid of every one."

It *was* Jimmy Rose!

"Let me in, Rose; let me in, man. I am your friend."

"I will not. I can trust no man now."

"Let me in, Rose; trust at least one, in me."

"Quit the spot, or—"

With that I heard a rattling against the huge lock, not made by any key, as if some small tube were being thrust into the keyhole. Horrified, I fled fast as feet could carry me.

I was a young man then, and Jimmy was not more than forty. It was five-and-twenty years ere I saw him again. And what a change. He whom I expected to behold—if behold at all—dry, shrunken, meagre, cadaverously fierce with misery and misanthropy—amazement! the old Parisian roses bloomed in his cheeks. And yet poor as any rat; poor in the last dregs of poverty; a pauper beyond alms-house pauperism; a promenading pauper in a thin, thread-bare, careful coat; a pauper with wealth of polished words; a courteous, smiling, shivering gentleman.

Ah, poor, poor Jimmy—God guard us all—poor Jimmy Rose!

Though at the first onset of his calamity, when creditors, once fast friends, pursued him as carrion for jails; though then, to avoid their hunt, as well as the human eye, he had gone and denned in the old abandoned house; and there, in his loneliness, had been driven half mad, yet time and tide had soothed him down to sanity. Perhaps at bottom Jimmy was too thoroughly good and kind to be made from any cause a man-hater. And doubtless it at last seemed irreligious to Jimmy even to shun mankind.

Sometimes sweet sense of duty will entice one to bitter doom. For what could be more bitter than now, in abject need, to be seen of those—nay, crawl and visit them in an humble sort, and be tolerated as an old eccentric, wandering in their parlors—who once had known him richest of the rich, and gayest of the gay? Yet this Jimmy did. Without rudely breaking him right down to it, fate slowly bent him more and more to the lowest deep. From an unknown quarter he received an income of some seventy dollars, more or less. The principal he would never touch, but, by various modes of eking it out, managed to live on the interest. He lived in an attic, where he supplied himself with food. He took but one regular repast a day—meal and milk—and nothing more, unless procured at others' tables. Often about the tea-hour he would drop in upon some old acquaintance, clad in his neat, forlorn frock coat, with worn velvet sewed upon the edges of the cuffs, and a similar device upon the hems of his pantaloons, to hide that dire look of having been grated off by rats. On Sunday he made a point of always dining at some fine house or other.

It is evident that no man could with impunity be allowed to lead this life unless regarded as one who, free from vice, was by fortune brought so low that the plummet of pity alone could reach him. Not much merit redounded to his entertainers because they did not thrust the starving gentleman forth when he came for his poor alms of tea and toast. Some merit had been theirs had they clubbed together and provided him, at small cost enough, with a sufficient income to make him, in point of necessaries, independent of the daily dole of charity; charity not sent to him either, but charity for which he had to trudge round to their doors.

But the most touching thing of all were those roses in his cheeks; those ruddy roses in his nipping winter. How they bloomed; whether meal and milk, and tea and toast could keep them flourishing; whether now he painted them; by what strange magic they were made to blossom so; no son of man might tell. But there they bloomed. And besides the roses, Jimmy was rich in smiles. He smiled ever. The lordly door which received him to his eleemosynary teas, knew no such smiling guest as Jimmy. In his prosperous days the smile of Jimmy was famous far and wide. It should have been trebly famous now.

Wherever he went to tea, he had all of the news of the town to tell. By frequenting the reading-rooms, as one privileged through harmlessness, he kept himself informed of European affairs and the last literature, foreign and domestic. And of this, when encouragement was given, he would largely talk. But encouragement was not always given. At certain houses, and not a few, Jimmy would drop in about ten minutes before the tea-hour, and drop out again about ten minutes after it; well knowing that his further presence was not indispensable to the contentment or felicity of his host.

How forlorn it was to see him so heartily drinking the generous tea, cup after cup, and eating the flavorous bread and butter, piece after piece, when, owing to the lateness of the dinner hour with the rest, and the abundance of that one grand meal with them, no one besides Jimmy touched the bread and butter, or exceeded a single cup of Souchong. And knowing all this very well, poor Jimmy would try to hide his hunger, and yet gratify it too, by striving hard to carry on a sprightly conversation with his hostess, and throwing in the eagerest mouthfuls with a sort of absent-minded air, as if he ate merely for custom's sake, and not starvation's.

Poor, poor Jimmy—God guard us all—poor Jimmy Rose!

Neither did Jimmy give up his courtly ways. Whenever there were ladies at the table, sure were they of some fine word; though, indeed, toward the close of Jimmy's life, the young ladies rather thought his compliments somewhat musty, smacking of cocked hats and small clothes —nay, of old pawnbrokers' shoulder-lace and sword belts. For there still lingered in Jimmy's address a subdued sort of martial air; he having in his palmy days been, among other things, a general of the State militia. There seems a fatality in these militia generalships. Alas! I can recall more than two or three gentlemen who from militia generals became paupers. I am afraid to think why this is so. Is it that this military leaning in a man of an unmilitary heart—that is, a gentle, peaceable heart—is an indication of some weak love of vain display? But ten to one it is not so. At any rate, it is unhandsome, if not unchristian, in the happy, too much to moralize on those who are not so.

So numerous were the houses that Jimmy visited, or so cautious was he in timing his less welcome calls, that at certain mansions he only dropped in about once a year or so. And annually upon seeing at that house the blooming Miss Frances or Miss Arabella, he would profoundly bow in his forlorn old coat, and with his soft, white hand take hers in gallant wise, saying, "Ah, Miss Arabella, these jewels here are bright upon these fingers; but brighter would they look were it not for those still brighter diamonds of your eyes!"

Though in thy own need thou hadst no pence to give the poor, thou, Jimmy, still hadst alms to give the rich. For not the beggar chattering at the corner pines more after bread than the vain heart after compliment. The rich in their craving glut, as the poor in their craving want, we have with us always. So, I suppose, thought Jimmy Rose.

But all women are not vain, or if a little grain that way inclined, more than redeem it all with goodness. Such was the sweet girl that closed poor Jimmy's eyes. The only daughter of an opulent alderman, she knew Jimmy well, and saw to him in his declining days. During his last sickness, with her own hands she carried him jellies and blanc-mange; made tea for him in his attic, and turned the poor old gentleman in his bed. And well hadst thou deserved it, Jimmy, at that fair creature's hands; well merited to have thy old eyes closed by woman's fairy fingers, who through life, in riches and in poverty, was still woman's sworn champion and devotee.

I hardly know that I should mention here one little incident connected with this young lady's ministrations, and poor Jimmy's reception of them. But it is harm to neither; I will tell it.

Chancing to be in town, and hearing of Jimmy's illness, I went to see him. And there in his lone attic I found the lovely ministrant. Withdrawing upon seeing another visitor, she left me alone with him. She had brought some little delicacies, and also several books, of such a sort as are sent by serious-minded well-wishers to invalids in a serious crisis. Now whether it was repugnance at being considered next door to death, or whether it was but the natural peevishness brought on by the general misery of his state; however it was, as the gentle girl withdrew, Jimmy, with what small remains of strength were his, pitched the books into the furthest corner, murmuring, "Why will she bring me this sad old stuff? Does she take me for a pauper? Thinks she to salve a gentleman's heart with Poor Man's Plaster?"

Poor, poor Jimmy—God guard us all—poor Jimmy Rose!

Well, well, I am an old man, and I suppose these tears I drop are dribblets from my dotage. But Heaven be praised, Jimmy needs no man's pity now.

Jimmy Rose is dead!

Meantime, as I sit within the parlor of the peacocks—that chamber from which his husky voice had come ere threatening me with the pistol—I still must meditate upon his strange example, whereof the marvel is, how after that gay, dashing, nobleman's career, he could be content to crawl through life, and peep about among the marbles and mahoganies for contumelious tea and toast, where once like a very Warwick he had feasted the huzzaing world with Burgundy and venison.

And every time I look at the wilted resplendence of those proud peacocks on the wall, I bethink me of the withering change in Jimmy's once resplendent pride of state. But still again, every time I gaze upon those festoons of perpetual roses, mid which the faded peacocks hang, I bethink me of those undying roses which bloomed in ruined Jimmy's cheek.

Transplanted to another soil, all the unkind past forgot, God grant that Jimmy's roses may immortally survive!

The 'Gees

IN RELATING TO MY FRIENDS various passages of my sea-goings, I have at times had occasion to allude to that singular people the 'Gees, sometimes as casual acquaintances, sometimes as shipmates. Such allusions have been quite natural and easy. For instance, I have said *The two 'Gees*, just as another would say *The two Dutchmen*, or *The two Indians*. In fact, being myself so familiar with 'Gees, it seemed as if all the rest of the world must be. But not so. My auditors have opened their eyes as much as to say, "What under the sun is a 'Gee?" To enlighten them I have repeatedly had to interrupt myself, and not without detriment to my stories. To remedy which inconvenience, a friend hinted the advisability of writing out some account of the 'Gees, and having it published. Such as they are, the following memoranda spring from that happy suggestion:

The word '*Gee* (*g* hard) is an abbreviation, by seamen, of *Portuguee*, the corrupt form of *Portuguese*. As the name is a curtailment, so the race is a residuum. Some three centuries ago certain Portuguese convicts were sent as a colony to Fogo, one of the Cape de Verds, off the northwest coast of Africa, an island previously stocked with an aboriginal race of negroes, ranking pretty high in incivility, but rather low in stature and morals. In course of time, from the amalgamated generation all the likelier sort were drafted off as food for powder, and the ancestors of the since called 'Gees were left as the *caput mortuum*, or melancholy remainder.

Of all men seamen have strong prejudices, particularly in the matter of race. They are bigots here. But when a creature of inferior race lives among them, an inferior tar, there seems no bound to their disdain. Now, as ere long will be hinted, the 'Gee, though of an aquatic nature, does not, as regards higher qualifications, make the best of sailors. In short, by seamen the abbreviation 'Gee was hit upon in pure contumely; the degree of which may be partially inferred from this, that with them the primitive word Portuguee itself is a reproach; so that 'Gee, being a subtle distillation from that word, stands, in point of relative intensity to it, as attar of roses does to rose-water. At times, when some crusty old sea-dog has his spleen more than usually excited against some luckless blunderer of Fogo his shipmate, it is marvelous the prolongation of taunt into which he will spin out the one little exclamatory monosyllable Ge-e-e-e-e!

The Isle of Fogo, that is, "Fire Isle," was so called from its volcano, which, after throwing up an infinite deal of stones and ashes, finally threw up business altogether, from its broadcast bounteousness having become bankrupt. But thanks to the volcano's prodigality in its time, the soil of Fogo is such as may be found of a dusty day on a road newly Macadamized. Cut off from farms and gardens, the staple food of the inhabitants is fish, at catching which they are expert. But none the less do they relish ship-biscuit, which, indeed, by most islanders, barbarous or semi-barbarous, is held a sort of lozenge.

In his best estate the 'Gee is rather small (he admits it), but, with some exceptions, hardy; capable of enduring extreme hard work, hard fare, or hard usage, as the case may be. In fact, upon a scientific view, there would seem a natural adaptability in the 'Gee to hard times generally. A theory not uncorroborated by his experiences; and furthermore, that kindly care of Nature in fitting him for them, something as for his hard rubs with a hardened world Fox the Quaker fitted himself, namely, in a tough leather suit from top to toe. In other words, the 'Gee is by no means of that exquisitely delicate sensibility expressed by the figurative adjective thin-skinned. His physicals and spirituals are in singular contrast. The 'Gee has a great appetite, but little imagination; a large eyeball, but small insight. Biscuit he crunches, but sentiment he eschews.

His complexion is hybrid; his hair ditto; his mouth disproportionally large, as compared with his stomach; his neck short; but his head round, compact, and betokening a solid understanding.

Like the negro, the 'Gee has a peculiar savor, but a different one—a sort of wild, marine, gamy savor, as in the sea-bird called haglet. Like venison, his flesh is firm but lean.

His teeth are what are called butter-teeth, strong, durable, square, and yellow. Among captains at a loss for better discourse during dull, rainy weather in the horse-latitudes, much debate has been had whether his teeth are intended for carnivorous or herbivorous purposes, or both conjoined. But as on his isle the 'Gee eats neither flesh nor grass, this inquiry would seem superfluous.

The native dress of the 'Gee is, like his name, compendious. His head being by nature well thatched, he wears no hat. Wont to wade much in the surf, he wears no shoes. He has a serviceably hard heel, a kick from which is by the judicious held almost as dangerous as one from a wild zebra.

Though for a long time back no stranger to the seafaring people of Portugal, the 'Gee, until a comparatively recent period, remained almost undreamed of by seafaring Americans. It is now some forty years since he first became known to certain masters of our Nantucket ships, who commenced the practice of touching at Fogo, on the outward passage, there to fill up vacancies among their crews arising from the short supply of men at home. By degrees the custom became pretty general, till now the 'Gee is found aboard of almost one whaler out of three. One reason why they are in request is this: An unsophisticated 'Gee coming on board a foreign ship never asks for wages. He comes for biscuit. He does not know what other wages mean, unless cuffs and buffets be wages, of which sort he receives a liberal allowance, paid with great punctuality, besides perquisites of punches thrown in now and then. But for all this, some persons there are, and not unduly biassed by partiality to him either, who still insist that the 'Gee never gets his due.

His docile services being thus cheaply to be had, some captains will go the length of maintaining that 'Gee sailors are preferable, indeed every way, physically and intellectually, superior to American sailors—such captains complaining, and justly, that American sailors, if not decently treated, are apt to give serious trouble.

But even by their most ardent admirers it is not deemed prudent to sail a ship with none but 'Gees, at least if they chance to be all green hands, a green 'Gee being of all green things the greenest. Besides, owing to the clumsiness of their feet ere improved by practice in the rigging, green 'Gees are wont, in no inconsiderable numbers, to fall overboard the first dark, squally night; insomuch that when unreasonable owners insist with a captain against his will upon a green 'Gee crew fore and aft, he will ship twice as many 'Gees as he would have shipped of Americans, so as to provide for all contingencies.

The 'Gees are always ready to be shipped. Any day one may go to their isle, and on the showing of a coin of biscuit over the rail, may load down to the water's edge with them.

But though any number of 'Gees are ever ready to be shipped, still it is by no means well to take them as they come. There is a choice even in 'Gees.

Of course the 'Gee has his private nature as well as his public coat. To know 'Gees—to be a sound judge of 'Gees—one must study them, just as to know and be a judge of horses one must study horses. Simple as for the most part are both horse and 'Gee, in neither case can knowledge of the creature come by intuition. How unwise, then, in those ignorant young captains who, on their first voyage, will go and ship their 'Gees at Fogo without any preparatory information, or even so much as taking convenient advice from a 'Gee jockey. By a 'Gee jockey is meant a man well versed in 'Gees. Many a young captain has been thrown and badly hurt by a 'Gee of his own choosing. For notwithstanding the general docility of the 'Gee when green, it may be otherwise with him when ripe. Discreet captains won't have such a 'Gee. "Away with that ripe 'Gee!" they cry; "that smart 'Gee; that knowing 'Gee! Green 'Gees for me!"

For the benefit of inexperienced captains about to visit Fogo, the following may be given as the best way to test a 'Gee: Get square before him, at, say three paces, so that the eye, like a shot, may rake the 'Gee fore and aft, at one glance taking in his whole make and build—how he looks about the head, whether he carry it well; his ears, are they over-lengthy? How fares it in the withers? His legs, does the 'Gee stand strongly on them? His knees, any Belshazzar symptoms there? How stands it in the region of the brisket? etc., etc.

Thus far for bone and bottom. For the rest, draw close to, and put the centre of the pupil of your eye—put it, as it were, right into the 'Gee's eye; even as an eye-stone, gently, but firmly slip it in there, and then note what speck or beam of viciousness, if any, will be floated out.

All this and much more must be done; and yet after all, the best judge may be deceived. But on no account should the skipper negotiate for his 'Gee with any middle-man, himself a 'Gee. Because such an one must be a knowing 'Gee, who will be sure to advise the green 'Gee what things to hide and what to display, to hit the skipper's fancy; which, of course, the knowing 'Gee supposes to lean toward as much physical and moral excellence as possible. The rashness of trusting to one of these middle-men was forcibly shown in the case of the 'Gee who by his countrymen was recommended to a New Bedford captain as one of the most agile 'Gees in Fogo. There he stood straight and stout, in a flowing pair of man-of-war's-man's trowsers, uncommonly well filled out. True, he did not step around much at the time. But that was diffidence. Good. They shipped him. But at the first taking in of sail the 'Gee hung fire. Come to look, both trowser-legs were full of elephantiasis. It was a long sperm-whaling voyage. Useless as so much lumber, at every port prohibited from being dumped ashore, that elephantine 'Gee, ever crunching biscuit, for three weary years was trundled round the globe.

Grown wise by several similar experiences, old Captain Hosea Kean, of Nantucket, in shipping a 'Gee, at present manages matters thus: He lands at Fogo in the night; by secret means gains information where the likeliest 'Gee wanting to ship lodges; whereupon with a strong party he surprises all the friends and acquaintances of that 'Gee; putting them under guard with pistols at their heads; then creeps cautiously toward the 'Gee, now lying wholly at unawares in his hut, quite relaxed from all possibility of displaying aught deceptive in his appearance. Thus silently, thus suddenly, thus unannounced, Captain Kean bursts upon his 'Gee, so to speak, in the very bosom of his family. By this means, more than once, unexpected revelations have been made. A 'Gee, noised abroad for a Hercules in strength and an Apollo Belvidere for beauty, of a sudden is discovered all in a wretched heap; forlornly adroop as upon crutches, his legs looking as if broken at the cart-wheel. Solitude is the house of candor, according to Captain Kean. In the stall, not the street, he says, resides the real nag.

The innate disdain of regularly bred seamen toward 'Gees receives an added edge from this. The 'Gees undersell them, working for biscuit where the sailors demand dollars. Hence, any thing said by sailors to the prejudice of 'Gees should be received with caution. Especially that jeer of theirs, that the monkey-jacket was originally so called from the circumstance that that rude sort of shaggy garment was first known in Fogo. They often call a monkey-jacket a 'Gee-jacket. However this may be, there is no call to which the 'Gee will with more alacrity respond than the word "Man!"

Is there any hard work to be done, and the 'Gees stand round in sulks? "Here, my men!" cries the mate. How they jump. But ten to one when the work is done, it is plain 'Gee again. "Here, 'Gee! you 'Ge-e-e-e!" In fact, it is not unsurmised, that only when extraordinary stimulus is needed, only when an extra strain is to be got out of them, are these hapless 'Gees ennobled with the human name.

As yet, the intellect of the 'Gee has been little cultivated. No well-attested educational experiment has been tried upon him. It is said, however, that in the last century a young 'Gee was by a visionary Portuguese naval officer sent to Salamanca University. Also, among the Quakers of Nantucket, there has been talk of sending five comely 'Gees, aged sixteen, to Dartmouth College; that venerable institution, as is well known, having been originally founded partly with the object of finishing off wild Indians in the classics and higher mathematics. Two qualities of the 'Gee which, with his docility, may be justly regarded as furnishing a hopeful basis for his intellectual training, are his excellent memory, and still more excellent credulity.

The above account may, perhaps, among the ethnologists, raise some curiosity to see a 'Gee. But to see a 'Gee there is no need to go all the way to Fogo, no more than to see a Chinaman to go all the way to China. 'Gees are occasionally to be encountered in our sea-ports, but more particularly in Nantucket and New Bedford. But these 'Gees are not the 'Gees of Fogo. That is, they are no longer green 'Gees. They are sophisticated 'Gees, and hence liable to be taken for naturalized citizens badly sunburnt. Many a Chinaman, in new coat and pantaloons, his long queue coiled out of sight in one of Genin's hats, has promenaded Broadway, and been taken merely for an eccentric Georgia planter. The same with 'Gees; a stranger need have a sharp eye to know a 'Gee, even if he see him.

Thus much for a general sketchy view of the 'Gee. For further and fuller information apply to any sharp-witted American whaling captain, but more especially to the before-mentioned old Captain Hosea Kean, of Nantucket, whose address at present is "Pacific Ocean."

I and My Chimney

I AND MY CHIMNEY, two grey-headed old smokers, reside in the country. We are, I may say, old settlers here; particularly my old chimney, which settles more and more every day.

Though I always say, *I and my chimney*, as Cardinal Wolsey used to say, *I and my King*, yet this egotistic way of speaking, wherein I take precedence of my chimney, is hardly borne out by the facts; in everything, except the above phrase, my chimney taking precedence of me.

Within thirty feet of the turf-sided road, my chimney—a huge, corpulent old Harry VIII. of a chimney—rises full in front of me and all my possessions. Standing well up a hill-side, my chimney, like Lord Rosse's monster telescope, swung vertical to hit the meridian moon, is the first object to greet the approaching traveler's eye, nor is it the last which the sun salutes. My chimney, too, is before me in receiving the first-fruits of the seasons. The snow is on its head ere on my hat; and every spring, as in a hollow beech tree, the first swallows build their nests in it.

But it is within doors that the preëminence of my chimney is most manifest. When in the rear room, set apart for that object, I stand to receive my guests (who, by the way call more, I suspect, to see my chimney than me), I then stand, not so much before, as, strictly speaking, behind my chimney, which is, indeed, the true host. Not that I demur. In the presence of my betters, I hope I know my place.

From this habitual precedence of my chimney over me, some even think that I have got into a sad rearward way altogether; in short, from standing behind my old-fashioned chimney so much, I have got to be quite behind the age too, as well as running behind-hand in everything else. But to tell the truth, I never was a very forward old fellow, nor what my farming neighbors call a forehanded one. Indeed, those rumors about my behindhandedness are so far correct, that I have an odd sauntering way with me sometimes of going about with my hands behind my back. As for my belonging to the rear-guard in general, certain it is, I bring up the rear of my chimney—which, by the way, is this moment before me—and that, too, both in fancy and fact. In brief, my chimney is my superior; my superior by I know not how many heads and shoulders; my superior, too, in that humbly bowing over with shovel and tongs, I much minister to it; yet never does it minister, or incline over to me; but, if any thing, in its settlings, rather leans the other way.

My chimney is grand seignior here—the one great domineering object, not more of the landscape, than of the house; all the rest of which house, in each architectural arrangement, as may shortly appear, is, in the most marked manner, accommodated, not to my wants, but to my chimney's, which, among other things, has the centre of the house to himself, leaving but the odd holes and corners to me.

But I and my chimney must explain; and as we are both rather obese, we may have to expatiate.

In those houses which are strictly double houses—that is, where the hall is in the middle—the fire-places usually are on opposite sides; so that while one member of the household is warming himself at a fire built into a recess of the north wall, say another member, the former's own brother, perhaps, may be holding his feet to the blaze before a hearth in the south wall—the two thus fairly sitting back to back. Is this well? Be it put to any man who has a proper fraternal feeling. Has it not a sort of sulky appearance? But very probably this style of chimney building originated with some architect afflicted with a quarrelsome family.

Then again, almost every modern fire-place has its separate flue—separate throughout, from hearth to chimney-top. At least such an arrangement is deemed desirable. Does not this look egotistical, selfish? But still more, all these separate flues, instead of having independent masonry establishments of their own, or instead of being grouped together in one federal stock in the middle of the house—instead of this, I say, each flue is surreptitiously honeycombed into the walls; so that these last are here and there, or indeed almost anywhere, treacherously hollow, and, in consequence, more or less weak. Of course, the main reason of this style of chimney building is to economize room. In cities, where lots are sold by the inch, small space is to spare for a chimney constructed on magnanimous principles; and, as with most thin men, who are generally tall, so with such houses, what is lacking in breadth must be made up in height. This remark holds true even with regard to many very stylish abodes, built by the most stylish of gentlemen. And yet, when that stylish gentleman, Louis le Grand of France, would build a palace for his lady friend, Madame de Maintenon, he built it but one story high—in fact in the cottage style. But then how uncommonly quadrangular, spacious, and broad—horizontal acres, not vertical ones. Such is the palace, which, in all its one-storied magnificence of Languedoc marble, in the garden of Versailles, still remains to this day. Any man can buy a square foot of land and plant a liberty-pole on it; but it takes a king to set apart whole acres for a grand Trianon.

But nowadays it is different; and furthermore, what originated in a necessity has been mounted into a vaunt. In towns there is large rivalry in building tall houses. If one gentleman builds his house four stories high, and another gentleman comes next door and builds five stories high, then the former, not to be looked down upon that way, immediately sends for his architect and claps a fifth and a sixth story on top of his previous four. And, not till the gentleman has achieved his aspiration, not till he has stolen over the way by twilight and observed how his sixth story soars beyond his neighbor's fifth—not till then does he retire to his rest with satisfaction.

Such folks, it seems to me, need mountains for neighbors, to take this emulous conceit of soaring out of them.

If, considering that mine is a very wide house, and by no means lofty, aught in the above may appear like interested pleading, as if I did but fold myself about in the cloak of a general proposition, cunningly to tickle my individual vanity beneath it, such misconception must vanish upon my frankly conceding, that land adjoining my alder swamp was sold last month for ten dollars an acre, and thought a rash purchase at that; so that for wide houses hereabouts there is plenty of room, and cheap. Indeed so cheap—dirt cheap—is the soil, that our elms thrust out their roots in it, and hang their great boughs over it, in the most lavish and reckless way. Almost all our crops, too, are sown broadcast, even peas and turnips. A farmer among us, who should go about his twenty-acre field, poking his finger into it here and there, and dropping down a mustard seed, would be thought a penurious, narrow-minded husbandman. The dandelions in the river-meadows, and the forget-me-nots along the mountain roads, you see at once they are put to no economy in space. Some seasons, too, our rye comes up, here and there a spear, sole and single like a church-spire. It doesn't care to crowd itself where it knows there is such a deal of room. The world is wide, the world is all before us, says the rye. Weeds, too, it is amazing how they spread. No such thing as arresting them—some of our pastures being a sort of Alsatia for the weeds. As for the grass, every spring it is like Kossuth's rising of what he calls the peoples. Mountains, too, a regular camp-meeting of them. For the same reason, the same all-sufficiency of room, our shadows march and countermarch, going through their various drills and masterly evolutions, like the old imperial guard on the Champs de Mars. As for the hills, especially where the roads cross them, the supervisors of our various towns have given notice to all concerned, that they can come and dig them down and cart them off, and never a cent to pay, no more than for the privilege of picking blackberries. The stranger who is buried here, what liberal-hearted landed proprietor among us grudges him his six feet of rocky pasture?

Nevertheless, cheap, after all, as our land is, and much as it is trodden under foot, I, for one, am proud of it for what it bears; and chiefly for its three great lions—the Great Oak, Ogg Mountain, and my chimney.

Most houses, here, are but one and a half stories high; few exceed two. That in which I and my chimney dwell, is in width nearly twice its height, from sill to eaves—which accounts for the magnitude of its main content—besides, showing that in this house, as in this country at large, there is abundance of space, and to spare, for both of us.

The frame of the old house is of wood—which but the more sets forth the solidity of the chimney, which is of brick. And as the great wrought nails, binding the clapboards, are unknown in these degenerate days, so are the huge bricks in the chimney walls. The architect of the chimney must have had the pyramid of Cheops before him; for, after that famous structure, it seems modeled, only its rate of decrease towards the summit is considerably less, and it is truncated. From the exact middle of the mansion it soars from the cellar, right up through each successive floor, till, four feet square, it breaks water from the ridge-pole of the roof, like an anvil-headed whale, through the crest of a billow. Most people, though, liken it, in that part, to a razeed observatory, masoned up.

The reason for its peculiar appearance above the roof touches upon rather delicate ground. How shall I reveal that, forasmuch as many years ago the original gable roof of the old house had become very leaky, a temporary proprietor hired a band of woodmen, with their huge, cross-cut saws, and went to sawing the old gable roof clean off. Off it went, with all its birds' nests, and dormer windows. It was replaced with a modern roof, more fit for a railway wood-house than an old country gentleman's abode. This operation—razeeing the structure some fifteen feet—was, in effect upon the chimney, something like the falling of the great spring tides. It left uncommon low water all about the chimney—to abate which appearance, the same person now proceeds to slice fifteen feet off the chimney itself, actually beheading my royal old chimney—a regicidal act, which, were it not for the palliating fact, that he was a poulterer by trade, and, therefore, hardened to such neck-wringings, should send that former proprietor down to posterity in the same cart with Cromwell.

Owing to its pyramidal shape, the reduction of the chimney inordinately widened its razeed summit. Inordinately, I say, but only in the estimation of such as have no eye to the picturesque. What care I, if, unaware that my chimney, as a free citizen of this free land, stands upon an independent basis of its own, people passing it, wonder how such a brick-kiln, as they call it, is supported upon mere joists and rafters? What care I? I will give a traveler a cup of switchel, if he want it; but am I bound to supply him with a sweet taste? Men of cultivated minds see, in my old house and chimney, a goodly old elephant-and-castle.

All feeling hearts will sympathize with me in what I am now about to add. The surgical operation, above referred to, necessarily brought into the open air a part of the chimney previously under cover, and intended to remain so, and, therefore, not built of what are called weather-bricks. In consequence, the chimney, though of a vigorous constitution, suffered not a little, from so naked an exposure; and, unable to acclimate itself, ere long began to fail—showing blotchy symptoms akin to those in measles. Whereupon travelers, passing my way, would wag their heads, laughing: "See that wax nose—how it melts off!" But what cared I? The same travelers would travel across the sea to view Kenilworth peeling away, and for a very good reason; that of all artists of the picturesque, decay wears the palm—I would say, the ivy. In fact, I've often thought that the proper place for my old chimney is ivied old England.

In vain my wife—with what probable ulterior intent will, ere long, appear—solemnly warned me, that unless something were done, and speedily, we should be burnt to the ground, owing to the holes crumbling through the aforesaid blotchy parts, where the chimney joined the roof. "Wife," said I, "far better that my house should burn down, than that my chimney should be pulled down, though but a few feet. They call it a wax nose; very good; not for me to tweak the nose of my superior." But at last the man who has a mortgage on the house dropped me a note, reminding me that, if my chimney was allowed to stand in that invalid condition, my policy of insurance would be void. This was a sort of hint not to be neglected. All the world over, the picturesque yields to the pocketesque. The mortgagor cared not, but the mortgagee did.

So another operation was performed. The wax nose was taken off, and a new one fitted on. Unfortunately for the expression—being put up by a squint-eyed mason, who, at the time, had a bad stitch in the same side—the new nose stands a little awry, in the same direction.

Of one thing, however, I am proud. The horizontal dimensions of the new part are unreduced.

Large as the chimney appears upon the roof, that is nothing to its spaciousness below. At its base in the cellar, it is precisely twelve feet square; and hence covers precisely one hundred and forty-four superficial feet. What an appropriation of terra firma for a chimney, and what a huge load for this earth! In fact, it was only because I and my chimney formed no part of his ancient burden, that that stout peddler, Atlas of old, was enabled to stand up so bravely under his pack. The dimensions given may, perhaps, seem fabulous. But, like those stones at Gilgal, which Joshua set up for a memorial of having passed over Jordan, does not my chimney remain, even unto this day?

Very often I go down into my cellar, and attentively survey that vast square of masonry. I stand long, and ponder over, and wonder at it. It has a druidical look, away down in the umbrageous cellar there, whose numerous vaulted passages, and far glens of gloom, resemble the dark, damp depths of primeval woods. So strongly did this conceit steal over me, so deeply was I penetrated with wonder at the chimney, that one day—when I was a little out of my mind, I now think—getting a spade from the garden, I set to work, digging round the foundation, especially at the corners thereof, obscurely prompted by dreams of striking upon some old, earthen-worn memorial of that by-gone day, when, into all this gloom, the light of heaven entered, as the masons laid the foundation-stones, peradventure sweltering under an August sun, or pelted by a March storm. Plying my blunted spade, how vexed was I by that ungracious interruption of a neighbor, who, calling to see me upon some business, and being informed that I was below, said I need not be troubled to come up, but he would go down to me; and so, without ceremony, and without my having been forewarned, suddenly discovered me, digging in my cellar.

"Gold digging, sir?"

"Nay, sir," answered I, starting, "I was merely—ahem!—merely—I say I was merely digging—round my chimney."

"Ah, loosening the soil, to make it grow. Your chimney, sir, you regard as too small, I suppose; needing further development, especially at the top?"

"Sir!" said I, throwing down the spade, "do not be personal. I and my chimney—"

"Personal?"

"Sir, I look upon this chimney less as a pile of masonry than as a personage. It is the king of the house. I am but a suffered and inferior subject."

In fact, I would permit no gibes to be cast at either myself or my chimney; and never again did my visitor refer to it in my hearing, without coupling some compliment with the mention. It well deserves a respectful consideration. There it stands, solitary and alone—not a council of ten flues, but, like his sacred majesty of Russia, a unit of an autocrat.

Even to me, its dimensions, at times, seem incredible. It does not look so big—no, not even in the cellar. By the mere eye, its magnitude can be but imperfectly comprehended, because only one side can be received at one time; and said side can only present twelve feet, linear measure. But then, each other side also is twelve feet long; and the whole obviously forms a square; and twelve times twelve is one hundred and forty-four. And so, an adequate conception of the magnitude of this chimney is only to be got at by a sort of process in the higher mathematics, by a method somewhat akin to those whereby the surprising distances of fixed stars are computed.

It need hardly be said, that the walls of my house are entirely free from fire-places. These all congregate in the middle—in the one grand central chimney, upon all four sides of which are hearths—two tiers of hearths—so that when, in the various chambers, my family and guests are warming themselves of a cold winter's night, just before retiring, then, though at the time they may not be thinking so, all their faces mutually look towards each other, yea, all their feet point to one centre; and, when they go to sleep in their beds, they all sleep round one warm chimney, like so many Iroquois Indians, in the woods, round their one heap of embers. And just as the Indians' fire serves, not only to keep them comfortable, but also to keep off wolves, and other savage monsters, so my chimney, by its obvious smoke at top, keeps off prowling burglars from the towns—for what burglar or murderer would dare break into an abode from whose chimney issues such a continual smoke—betokening that if the inmates are not stirring, at least fires are, and in case of an alarm, candles may readily be lighted, to say nothing of muskets.

But stately as is the chimney—yea, grand high altar as it is, right worthy for the celebration of high mass before the Pope of Rome, and all his cardinals—yet what is there perfect in this world? Caius Julius Cæsar, had he not been so inordinately great, they say that Brutus, Cassius, Antony, and the rest, had been greater. My chimney, were it not so mighty in its magnitude, my chambers had been larger. How often has my wife ruefully told me, that my chimney, like the English aristocracy, casts a contracting shade all round it. She avers that endless domestic inconveniences arise—more particularly from the chimney's stubborn central locality. The grand objection with her is, that it stands midway in the place where a fine entrance-hall ought to be. In truth, there is no hall whatever to the house—nothing but a sort of square landing-place, as you enter from the wide front door. A roomy enough landing-place, I admit, but not attaining to the dignity of a hall. Now, as the front door is precisely in the middle of the front of the house, inwards it faces the chimney. In fact, the opposite wall of the landing-place is formed solely by the chimney; and hence—owing to the gradual tapering of the chimney—is a little less than twelve feet in width. Climbing the chimney in this part, is the principal stair-case—which, by three abrupt turns, and three minor landing-places, mounts to the second floor, where, over the front door, runs a sort of narrow gallery, something less than twelve feet long, leading to chambers on either hand. This gallery, of course, is railed; and so, looking down upon the stairs, and all those landing-places together, with the main one at bottom, resembles not a little a balcony for musicians, in some jolly old abode, in times Elizabethan. Shall I tell a weakness? I cherish the cobwebs there, and many a time arrest Biddy in the act of brushing them with her broom, and have many a quarrel with my wife and daughters about it.

Now the ceiling, so to speak, of the place where you enter the house, that ceiling is, in fact, the ceiling of the second floor, not the first. The two floors are made one here; so that ascending this turning stairs, you seem going up into a kind of soaring tower, or light-house. At the second landing, midway up the chimney, is a mysterious door, entering to a mysterious closet; and here I keep mysterious cordials, of a choice, mysterious flavor, made so by the constant nurturing and subtle ripening of the chimney's gentle heat, distilled through that warm mass of masonry. Better for wines is it than voyages to the Indies; my chimney itself a tropic. A chair by my chimney in a November day is as good for an invalid as a long season spent in Cuba. Often I think how grapes might ripen against my chimney. How my wife's geraniums bud there! Bud in December. Her eggs, too—can't keep them near the chimney, on account of hatching. Ah, a warm heart has my chimney.

How often my wife was at me about that projected grand entrance-hall of hers, which was to be knocked clean through the chimney, from one end of the house to the other, and astonish all guests by its generous amplitude. "But, wife," said I, "the chimney—consider the chimney: if you demolish the foundation, what is to support the superstructure?" "Oh, that will rest on the second floor." The truth is, women know next to nothing about the realities of architecture. However, my wife still talked of running her entries and partitions. She spent many long nights elaborating her plans; in imagination building her boasted hall through the chimney, as though its high mightiness were a mere spear of sorrel-top. At last, I gently reminded her that, little as she might fancy it, the chimney was a fact—a sober, substantial fact, which, in all her plannings, it would be well to take into full consideration. But this was not of much avail.

And here, respectfully craving her permission, I must say a few words about this enterprising wife of mine. Though in years nearly old as myself, in spirit she is young as my little sorrel mare, Trigger, that threw me last fall. What is extraordinary, though she comes of a rheumatic family, she is straight as a pine, never has any aches; while for me with the sciatica, I am sometimes as crippled up as any old apple tree. But she has not so much as a toothache. As for her hearing—let me enter the house in my dusty boots, and she away up in the attic. And for her sight—Biddy, the housemaid, tells other people's housemaids, that her mistress will spy a spot on the dresser straight through the pewter platter, put up on purpose to hide it. Her faculties are alert as her limbs and her senses. No danger of my spouse dying of torpor. The longest night in the year I've known her lie awake, planning her campaign for the morrow. She is a natural projector. The maxim, "Whatever is, is right," is not hers. Her maxim is, Whatever is, is wrong; and what is more, must be altered; and what is still more, must be altered right away. Dreadful maxim for the wife of a dozy old dreamer like me, who dote on seventh days as days of rest, and out of a sabbatical horror of industry, will, on a week day, go out of my road a quarter of a mile, to avoid the sight of a man at work.

That matches are made in heaven, may be, but my wife would have been just the wife for Peter the Great, or Peter the Piper. How she would have set in order that huge littered empire of the one, and with indefatigable painstaking picked the peck of pickled peppers for the other.

But the most wonderful thing is, my wife never thinks of her end. Her youthful incredulity, as to the plain theory, and still plainer fact of death, hardly seems Christian. Advanced in years, as she knows she must be, my wife seems to think that she is to teem on, and be inexhaustible forever. She doesn't believe in old age. At that strange promise in the plain of Mamre, my old wife, unlike old Abraham's, would not have jeeringly laughed within herself.

Judge how to me, who, sitting in the comfortable shadow of my chimney, smoking my comfortable pipe, with ashes not unwelcome at my feet, and ashes not unwelcome all but in my mouth; and who am thus in a comfortable sort of not unwelcome, though, indeed, ashy enough way, reminded of the ultimate exhaustion even of the most fiery life; judge how to me this unwarrantable vitality in my wife must come, sometimes, it is true, with a moral and a calm, but oftener with a breeze and a ruffle.

If the doctrine be true, that in wedlock contraries attract, by how cogent a fatality must I have been drawn to my wife! While spicily impatient of present and past, like a glass of ginger-beer she overflows with her schemes; and, with like energy as she puts down her foot, puts down her preserves and her pickles, and lives with them in a continual future; or ever full of expectations both from time and space, is ever restless for newspapers, and ravenous for letters. Content with the years that are gone, taking no thought for the morrow, and looking for no new thing from any person or quarter whatever, I have not a single scheme or expectation on earth, save in unequal resistance of the undue encroachment of hers.

Old myself, I take to oldness in things; for that cause mainly loving old Montaigne, and old cheese, and old wine; and eschewing young people, hot rolls, new books, and early potatoes, and very fond of my old claw-footed chair, and old club-footed Deacon White, my neighbor, and that still nigher old neighbor, my betwisted old grape-vine, that of a summer evening leans in his elbow for cosy company at my window-sill, while I, within doors, lean over mine to meet his; and above all, high above all, am fond of my high-mantled old chimney. But she, out of that infatuate juvenility of hers, takes to nothing but newness; for that cause mainly, loving new cider in autumn, and in spring, as if she were own daughter of Nebuchadnezzar, fairly raving after all sorts of salads and spinages, and more particularly green cucumbers (though all the time nature rebukes such unsuitable young hankerings in so elderly a person, by never permitting such things to agree with her), and has an itch after recently-discovered fine prospects (so no grave-yard be in the background), and also after Swedenborgianism, and the Spirit Rapping philosophy, with other new views, alike in things natural and unnatural; and immortally hopeful, is forever making new flower-beds even on the north side of the house, where the bleak mountain wind would scarce allow the wiry weed called hard-hack to gain a thorough footing; and on the road-side sets out mere pipe-stems of young elms; though there is no hope of any shade from them, except over the ruins of her great granddaughters' grave-stones; and won't wear caps, but plaits her gray hair; and takes the Ladies' Magazine for the fashions; and always buys her new almanac a month before the new year; and rises at dawn; and to the warmest sunset turns a cold shoulder; and still goes on at odd hours with her new course of history, and her French, and her music; and likes young company; and offers to ride young colts; and sets out young suckers in the orchard; and has a spite against my elbowed old grape-vine, and my club-footed old neighbor, and my claw-footed old chair, and above all, high above all, would fain persecute, unto death, my high-mantled old chimney. By what perverse magic, I a thousand times think, does such a very autumnal old lady have such a very vernal young soul? When I would remonstrate at times, she spins round on me with, "Oh, don't you grumble, old man (she always calls me old man), it's I, young I, that keep you from stagnating." Well, I suppose it is so. Yea, after all, these things are well ordered. My wife, as one of her poor relations, good soul, intimates, is the salt of the earth, and none the less the salt of my sea, which otherwise were unwholesome. She is its monsoon, too, blowing a brisk gale over it, in the one steady direction of my chimney.

Not insensible of her superior energies, my wife has frequently made me propositions to take upon herself all the responsibilities of my affairs. She is desirous that, domestically, I should abdicate; that, renouncing further rule, like the venerable Charles V., I should retire into some sort of monastery. But indeed, the chimney excepted, I have little authority to lay down. By my wife's ingenious application of the principle that certain things belong of right to female jurisdiction, I find myself, through my easy compliances, insensibly stripped by degrees of one masculine prerogative after another. In a dream I go about my fields, a sort of lazy, happy-go-lucky, good-for-nothing, loafing, old Lear. Only by some sudden revelation am I reminded who is over me; as year before last, one day seeing in one corner of the premises fresh deposits of mysterious boards and timbers, the oddity of the incident at length begat serious meditation. "Wife," said I, "whose boards and timbers are those I see near the orchard there? Do you know any thing about them, wife? Who put them there? You know I do not like the neighbors to use my land that way; they should ask permission first."

She regarded me with a pitying smile.

"Why, old man, don't you know I am building a new barn? Didn't you know that, old man?"

This is the poor old lady that was accusing me of tyrannizing over her.

To return now to the chimney. Upon being assured of the futility of her proposed hall, so long as the obstacle remained, for a time my wife was for a modified project. But I could never exactly comprehend it. As far as I could see through it, it seemed to involve the general idea of a sort of irregular archway, or elbowed tunnel, which was to penetrate the chimney at some convenient point under the staircase, and carefully avoiding dangerous contact with the fire-places, and particularly steering clear of the great interior flue, was to conduct the enterprising traveler from the front door all the way into the dining-room in the remote rear of the mansion. Doubtless it was a bold stroke of genius, that plan of hers, and so was Nero's when he schemed his grand canal through the Isthmus of Corinth. Nor will I take oath, that, had her project been accomplished, then, by help of lights hung at judicious intervals through the tunnel, some Belzoni or other might not have succeeded in future ages in penetrating through the masonry, and actually emerging into the dining-room, and once there, it would have been inhospitable treatment of such a traveler to have denied him a recruiting meal.

But my bustling wife did not restrict her objections, nor in the end confine her proposed alterations to the first floor. Her ambition was of the mounting order. She ascended with her schemes to the second floor, and so to the attic. Perhaps there was some small ground for her discontent with things as they were. The truth is, there was no regular passage-way up stairs or down, unless we again except that little orchestra-gallery before mentioned. And all this was owing to the chimney, which my gamesome spouse seemed despitefully to regard as the bully of the house. On all its four sides, nearly all the chambers sidled up to the chimney for the benefit of a fire-place. The chimney would not go to them; they must needs go to it. The consequence was, almost every room, like a philosophical system, was in itself an entry, or passage-way to other rooms, and systems of rooms—a whole suite of entries, in fact. Going through the house, you seem to be forever going somewhere, and getting nowhere. It is like losing one's self in the woods; round and round the chimney you go, and if you arrive at all, it is just where you started, and so you begin again, and again get nowhere. Indeed—though I say it not in the way of fault-finding at all—never was there so labyrinthine an abode. Guests will tarry with me several weeks and every now and then, be anew astonished at some unforeseen apartment.

The puzzling nature of the mansion, resulting from the chimney, is peculiarly noticeable in the dining-room, which has no less than nine doors, opening in all directions, and into all sorts of places. A stranger for the first time entering this dining-room, and naturally taking no special heed at what door he entered, will, upon rising to depart, commit the strangest blunders. Such, for instance, as opening the first door that comes handy, and finding himself stealing up stairs by the back passage. Shutting that door, he will proceed to another, and be aghast at the cellar yawning at his feet. Trying a third, he surprises the housemaid at her work. In the end, no more relying on his own unaided efforts, he procures a trusty guide in some passing person, and in good time successfully emerges. Perhaps as curious a blunder as any, was that of a certain stylish young gentleman, a great exquisite, in whose judicious eyes my daughter Anna had found especial favor. He called upon the young lady one evening, and found her alone in the dining-room at her needle-work. He stayed rather late; and after abundance of superfine discourse, all the while retaining his hat and cane, made his profuse adieus, and with repeated graceful bows proceeded to depart, after the fashion of courtiers from the Queen, and by so doing, opening a door at random, with one hand placed behind, very effectually succeeded in backing himself into a dark pantry, where he carefully shut himself up, wondering there was no light in the entry. After several strange noises as of a cat among the crockery, he reappeared through the same door, looking uncommonly crest-fallen, and, with a deeply embarrassed air, requested my daughter to designate at which of the nine he should find exit. When the mischievous Anna told me the story, she said it was surprising how unaffected and matter-of-fact the young gentleman's manner was after his reappearance. He was more candid than ever, to be sure; having inadvertently thrust his white kids into an open drawer of Havana sugar, under the impression, probably, that being what they call "a sweet fellow," his route might possibly lie in that direction.

Another inconvenience resulting from the chimney is, the bewilderment of a guest in gaining his chamber, many strange doors lying between him and it. To direct him by finger-posts would look rather queer; and just as queer in him to be knocking at every door on his route, like London's city guest, the king, at Temple Bar.

Now, of all these things and many, many more, my family continually complained. At last my wife came out with her sweeping proposition—in toto to abolish the chimney.

"What!" said I, "abolish the chimney? To take out the back-bone of anything, wife, is a hazardous affair. Spines out of backs, and chimneys out of houses, are not to be taken like frosted lead-pipes from the ground. Besides," added I, "the chimney is the one grand permanence of this abode. If undisturbed by innovators, then in future ages, when all the house shall have crumbled from it, this chimney will still survive—a Bunker Hill monument. No, no, wife, I can't abolish my back-bone."

So said I then. But who is sure of himself, especially an old man, with both wife and daughters ever at his elbow and ear? In time, I was persuaded to think a little better of it; in short, to take the matter into preliminary consideration. At length it came to pass that a master-mason—a rough sort of architect—one Mr. Scribe, was summoned to a conference. I formally introduced him to my chimney. A previous introduction from my wife had introduced him to myself. He had been not a little employed by that lady, in preparing plans and estimates for some of her extensive operations in drainage. Having, with much ado, extorted from my spouse the promise that she would leave us to an unmolested survey, I began by leading Mr. Scribe down to the root of the matter, in the cellar. Lamp in hand, I descended; for though up stairs it was noon, below it was night.

We seemed in the pyramids; and I, with one hand holding my lamp over head, and with the other pointing out, in the obscurity, the hoar mass of the chimney, seemed some Arab guide, showing the cobwebbed mausoleum of the great god Apis.

"This is a most remarkable structure, sir," said the master-mason, after long contemplating it in silence, "a most remarkable structure, sir."

"Yes," said I complacently, "every one says so."

"But large as it appears above the roof, I would not have inferred the magnitude of this foundation, sir," eyeing it critically.

Then taking out his rule, he measured it.

"Twelve feet square; one hundred and forty-four square feet! sir, this house would appear to have been built simply for the accommodation of your chimney."

"Yes, my chimney and me. Tell me candidly, now," I added, "would you have such a famous chimney abolished?"

"I wouldn't have it in a house of mine, sir, for a gift," was the reply. "It's a losing affair altogether, sir. Do you know, sir, that in retaining this chimney, you are losing, not only one hundred and forty-four square feet of good ground, but likewise a considerable interest upon a considerable principal?"

"How?"

"Look, sir," said he, taking a bit of red chalk from his pocket, and figuring against a whitewashed wall, "twenty times eight is so and so; then forty-two times thirty-nine is so and so—aint it, sir? Well, add those together, and subtract this here, then that makes so and so," still chalking away.

To be brief, after no small ciphering, Mr. Scribe informed me that my chimney contained, I am ashamed to say how many thousand and odd valuable bricks.

"No more," said I fidgeting. "Pray now, let us have a look above."

In that upper zone we made two more circumnavigations for the first and second floors. That done, we stood together at the foot of the stairway by the front door; my hand upon the knob, and Mr. Scribe hat in hand.

"Well, sir," said he, a sort of feeling his way, and, to help himself, fumbling with his hat, "well, sir, I think it can be done."

"What, pray, Mr. Scribe; *what* can be done?"

"Your chimney, sir; it can without rashness be removed, I think."

"*I* will think of it, too, Mr. Scribe," said I, turning the knob, and bowing him towards the open space without, "I will *think* of it, sir; it demands consideration; much obliged to ye; good morning, Mr. Scribe."

"It is all arranged, then," cried my wife with great glee, bursting from the nighest room.

"When will they begin?" demanded my daughter Julia.

"To-morrow?" asked Anna.

"Patience, patience, my dears," said I, "such a big chimney is not to be abolished in a minute."

Next morning it began again.

"You remember the chimney," said my wife.

"Wife," said I, "it is never out of my house, and never out of my mind."

"But when is Mr. Scribe to begin to pull it down?" asked Anna.

"Not to-day, Anna," said I.

"*When*, then?" demanded Julia, in alarm.

Now, if this chimney of mine was, for size, a sort of belfry, for ding-donging at me about it, my wife and daughters were a sort of bells, always chiming together, or taking up each other's melodies at every pause, my wife the key-clapper of all. A very sweet ringing, and pealing, and chiming, I confess; but then, the most silvery of bells may, sometimes, dismally toll, as well as merrily play. And as touching the subject in question, it became so now. Perceiving a strange relapse of opposition in me, wife and daughters began a soft and dirge-like, melancholy tolling over it.

At length my wife, getting much excited, declared to me, with pointed finger, that so long as that chimney stood, she should regard it as the monument of what she called my broken pledge. But finding this did not answer, the next day, she gave me to understand that either she or the chimney must quit the house.

Finding matters coming to such a pass, I and my pipe philosophized over them awhile, and finally concluded between us, that little as our hearts went with the plan, yet for peace' sake, I might write out the chimney's death-warrant, and, while my hand was in, scratch a note to Mr. Scribe.

Considering that I, and my chimney, and my pipe, from having been so much together, were three great cronies, the facility with which my pipe consented to a project so fatal to the goodliest of our trio; or rather, the way in which I and my pipe, in secret, conspired together, as it were, against our unsuspicious old comrade—this may seem rather strange, if not suggestive of sad reflections upon us two. But, indeed, we, sons of clay, that is my pipe and I, are no whit better than the rest. Far from us, indeed, to have volunteered the betrayal of our crony. We are of a peaceable nature, too. But that love of peace it was which made us false to a mutual friend, as soon as his cause demanded a vigorous vindication. But I rejoice to add, that better and braver thoughts soon returned, as will now briefly be set forth.

To my note, Mr. Scribe replied in person.

Once more we made a survey, mainly now with a view to a pecuniary estimate.

"I will do it for five hundred dollars," said Mr. Scribe at last, again hat in hand.

"Very well, Mr. Scribe, I will think of it," replied I, again bowing him to the door.

Not unvexed by this, for the second time, unexpected response, again he withdrew, and from my wife and daughters again burst the old exclamations.

The truth is, resolve how I would, at the last pinch I and my chimney could not be parted.

"So Holofernes will have his way, never mind whose heart breaks for it," said my wife next morning, at breakfast, in that half-didactic, half-reproachful way of hers, which is harder to bear than her most energetic assault. Holofernes, too, is with her a pet name for any fell domestic despot. So, whenever, against her most ambitious innovations, those which saw me quite across the grain, I, as in the present instance, stand with however little steadfastness on the defence, she is sure to call me Holofernes, and ten to one takes the first opportunity to read aloud, with a suppressed emphasis, of an evening, the first newspaper paragraph about some tyrannic day-laborer, who, after being for many years the Caligula of his family, ends by beating his long-suffering spouse to death, with a garret door wrenched off its hinges, and then, pitching his little innocents out of the window, suicidally turns inward towards the broken wall scored with the butcher's and baker's bills, and so rushes headlong to his dreadful account.

Nevertheless, for a few days, not a little to my surprise, I heard no further reproaches. An intense calm pervaded my wife, but beneath which, as in the sea, there was no knowing what portentous movements might be going on. She frequently went abroad, and in a direction which I thought not unsuspicious; namely, in the direction of New Petra, a griffin-like house of wood and stucco, in the highest style of ornamental art, graced with four chimneys in the form of erect dragons spouting smoke from their nostrils; the elegant modern residence of Mr. Scribe, which he had built for the purpose of a standing advertisement, not more of his taste as an architect, than his solidity as a master-mason.

At last, smoking my pipe one morning, I heard a rap at the door, and my wife, with an air unusually quiet for her, brought me a note. As I have no correspondents except Solomon, with whom, in his sentiments, at least, I entirely correspond, the note occasioned me some little surprise, which was not diminished upon reading the following:—

"NEW PETRA, April 1st.

"SIR:—During my last examination of your chimney, possibly you may have noted that I frequently applied my rule to it in a manner apparently unnecessary. Possibly also, at the same time, you might have observed in me more or less of perplexity, to which, however, I refrained from giving any verbal expression.

"I now feel it obligatory upon me to inform you of what was then but a dim suspicion, and as such would have been unwise to give utterance to, but which now, from various subsequent calculations assuming no little probability, it may be important that you should not remain in further ignorance of.

"It is my solemn duty to warn you, sir, that there is architectural cause to conjecture that somewhere concealed in your chimney is a reserved space, hermetically closed, in short, a secret chamber, or rather closet. How long it has been there, it is for me impossible to say. What it contains is hid, with itself, in darkness. But probably a secret closet would not have been contrived except for some extraordinary object, whether for the concealment of treasure, or what other purpose, may be left to those better acquainted with the history of the house to guess.

"But enough: in making this disclosure, sir, my conscience is eased. Whatever step you choose to take upon it, is of course a matter of indifference to me; though, I confess, as respects the character of the closet, I cannot but share in a natural curiosity.

"Trusting that you may be guided aright, in determining whether it is Christian-like knowingly to reside in a house, hidden in which is a secret closet,

"I remain,
"With much respect,
"Yours very humbly,
"HIRAM SCRIBE."

My first thought upon reading this note was, not of the alleged mystery of manner to which, at the outset, it alluded—for none such had I at all observed in the master mason during his surveys—but of my late kinsman, Captain Julian Dacres, long a ship-master and merchant in the Indian trade, who, about thirty years ago, and at the ripe age of ninety, died a bachelor, and in this very house, which he had built. He was supposed to have retired into this country with a large fortune. But to the general surprise, after being at great cost in building himself this mansion, he settled down into a sedate, reserved, and inexpensive old age, which by the neighbors was thought all the better for his heirs: but lo! upon opening the will, his property was found to consist but of the house and grounds, and some ten thousand dollars in stocks; but the place, being found heavily mortgaged, was in consequence sold. Gossip had its day, and left the grass quietly to creep over the captain's grave, where he still slumbers in a privacy as unmolested as if the billows of the Indian Ocean, instead of the billows of inland verdure, rolled over him. Still, I remembered long ago, hearing strange solutions whispered by the country people for the mystery involving his will, and, by reflex, himself; and that, too, as well in conscience as purse. But people who could circulate the report (which they did), that Captain Julian Dacres had, in his day, been a Borneo pirate, surely were not worthy of credence in their collateral notions. It is queer what wild whimsies of rumors will, like toadstools, spring up about any eccentric stranger, who, settling down among a rustic population, keeps quietly to himself. With some, inoffensiveness would seem a prime cause of offense. But what chiefly had led me to scout at these rumors, particularly as referring to concealed treasure, was the circumstance, that the stranger (the same who razeed the roof and the chimney) into whose hands the estate had passed on my kinsman's death, was of that sort of character, that had there been the least ground for those reports, he would speedily have tested them, by tearing down and rummaging the walls.

Nevertheless, the note of Mr. Scribe, so strangely recalling the memory of my kinsman, very naturally chimed in with what had been mysterious, or at least unexplained, about him; vague flashings of ingots united in my mind with vague gleamings of skulls. But the first cool thought soon dismissed such chimeras; and, with a calm smile, I turned towards my wife, who, meantime, had been sitting near by, impatient enough, I dare say, to know who could have taken it into his head to write me a letter.

"Well, old man," said she, "who is it from, and what is it about?"

"Read it, wife," said I, handing it.

Read it she did, and then—such an explosion! I will not pretend to describe her emotions, or repeat her expressions. Enough that my daughters were quickly called in to share the excitement. Although they had never before dreamed of such a revelation as Mr. Scribe's; yet upon the first suggestion they instinctively saw the extreme likelihood of it. In corroboration, they cited first my kinsman, and second, my chimney; alleging that the profound mystery involving the former, and the equally profound masonry involving the latter, though both acknowledged facts, were alike preposterous on any other supposition than the secret closet.

But all this time I was quietly thinking to myself: Could it be hidden from me that my credulity in this instance would operate very favorably to a certain plan of theirs? How to get to the secret closet, or how to have any certainty about it at all, without making such fell work with the chimney as to render its set destruction superfluous? That my wife wished to get rid of the chimney, it needed no reflection to show; and that Mr. Scribe, for all his pretended disinterestedness, was not opposed to pocketing five hundred dollars by the operation, seemed equally evident. That my wife had, in secret, laid heads together with Mr. Scribe, I at present refrain from affirming. But when I consider her enmity against my chimney, and the steadiness with which at the last she is wont to carry out her schemes, if by hook or by crook she can, especially after having been once baffled, why, I scarcely knew at what step of hers to be surprised.

Of one thing only was I resolved, that I and my chimney should not budge.

In vain all protests. Next morning I went out into the road, where I had noticed a diabolical-looking old gander, that, for its doughty exploits in the way of scratching into forbidden inclosures, had been rewarded by its master with a portentous, four-pronged, wooden decoration, in the shape of a collar of the Order of the Garotte. This gander I cornered, and rummaging out its stiffest quill, plucked it, took it home, and making a stiff pen, inscribed the following stiff note:

"Chimney Side, April 2.

"Mr. Scribe.

"Sir:—For your conjecture, we return you our joint thanks and compliments, and beg leave to assure you, that

"We shall remain,
"Very faithfully,
"The same,
"I and my Chimney."

Of course, for this epistle we had to endure some pretty sharp raps. But having at last explicitly understood from me that Mr. Scribe's note had not altered my mind one jot, my wife, to move me, among other things said, that if she remembered aright, there was a statute placing the keeping in private houses of secret closets on the same unlawful footing with the keeping of gunpowder. But it had no effect.

A few days after, my spouse changed her key.

It was nearly midnight, and all were in bed but ourselves, who sat up, one in each chimney-corner; she, needles in hand, indefatigably knitting a sock; I, pipe in mouth, indolently weaving my vapors.

It was one of the first of the chill nights in autumn. There was a fire on the hearth, burning low. The air without was torpid and heavy; the wood, by an oversight, of the sort called soggy.

"Do look at the chimney," she began; "can't you see that something must be in it?"

"Yes, wife. Truly there is smoke in the chimney, as in Mr. Scribe's note."

"Smoke? Yes, indeed, and in my eyes, too. How you two wicked old sinners do smoke!—this wicked old chimney and you."

"Wife," said I, "I and my chimney like to have a quiet smoke together, it is true, but we don't like to be called names."

"Now, dear old man," said she, softening down, and a little shifting the subject, "when you think of that old kinsman of yours, you *know* there must be a secret closet in this chimney."

"Secret ash-hole, wife, why don't you have it? Yes, I dare say there is a secret ash-hole in the chimney; for where do all the ashes go to that we drop down the queer hole yonder?"

"I know where they go to; I've been there almost as many times as the cat."

"What devil, wife, prompted you to crawl into the ash-hole! Don't you know that St. Dunstan's devil emerged from the ash-hole? You will get your death one of these days, exploring all about as you do. But supposing there be a secret closet, what then?"

"What, then? why what should be in a secret closet but ——"

"Dry bones, wife," broke in I with a puff, while the sociable old chimney broke in with another.

"There again! Oh, how this wretched old chimney smokes," wiping her eyes with her handkerchief. "I've no doubt the reason it smokes so is, because that secret closet interferes with the flue. Do see, too, how the jams here keep settling; and it's down hill all the way from the door to this hearth. This horrid old chimney will fall on our heads yet; depend upon it, old man."

"Yes, wife, I do depend on it; yes, indeed, I place every dependence on my chimney. As for its settling, I like it. I, too, am settling, you know, in my gait. I and my chimney are settling together, and shall keep settling, too, till, as in a great feather-bed, we shall both have settled away clean out of sight. But this secret oven; I mean, secret closet of yours, wife; where exactly do you suppose that secret closet is?"

"That is for Mr. Scribe to say."

"But suppose he cannot say exactly; what, then?"

"Why then he can prove, I am sure, that it must be somewhere or other in this horrid old chimney."

"And if he can't prove that; what, then?"

"Why then, old man," with a stately air, "I shall say little more about it."

"Agreed, wife," returned I, knocking my pipe-bowl against the jam, "and now, to-morrow, I will a third time send for Mr. Scribe. Wife, the sciatica takes me; be so good as to put this pipe on the mantel."

"If you get the step-ladder for me, I will. This shocking old chimney, this abominable old-fashioned old chimney's mantels are so high, I can't reach them."

No opportunity, however trivial, was overlooked for a subordinate fling at the pile.

Here, by way of introduction, it should be mentioned, that besides the fire-places all round it, the chimney was, in the most hap-hazard way, excavated on each floor for certain curious out-of-the-way cupboards and closets, of all sorts and sizes, clinging here and there, like nests in the crotches of some old oak. On the second floor these closets were by far the most irregular and numerous. And yet this should hardly have been so, since the theory of the chimney was, that it pyramidically diminished as it ascended. The abridgment of its square on the roof was obvious enough; and it was supposed that the reduction must be methodically graduated from bottom to top.

"Mr. Scribe," said I when, the next day, with an eager aspect, that individual again came, "my object in sending for you this morning is, not to arrange for the demolition of my chimney, nor to have any particular conversation about it, but simply to allow you every reasonable facility for verifying, if you can, the conjecture communicated in your note."

Though in secret not a little crestfallen, it may be, by my phlegmatic reception, so different from what he had looked for; with much apparent alacrity he commenced the survey; throwing open the cupboards on the first floor, and peering into the closets on the second; measuring one within, and then comparing that measurement with the measurement without. Removing the fire-boards, he would gaze up the flues. But no sign of the hidden work yet.

Now, on the second floor the rooms were the most rambling conceivable. They, as it were, dovetailed into each other. They were of all shapes; not one mathematically square room among them all—a peculiarity which by the master-mason had not been unobserved. With a significant, not to say portentous expression, he took a circuit of the chimney, measuring the area of each room around it; then going down stairs, and out of doors, he measured the entire ground area; then compared the sum total of all the areas of all the rooms on the second floor with the ground area; then, returning to me in no small excitement, announced that there was a difference of no less than two hundred and odd square feet—room enough, in all conscience, for a secret closet.

"But, Mr. Scribe," said I stroking my chin, "have you allowed for the walls, both main and sectional? They take up some space, you know."

"Ah, I had forgotten that," tapping his forehead; "but," still ciphering on his paper, "that will not make up the deficiency."

"But, Mr. Scribe, have you allowed for the recesses of so many fireplaces on a floor, and for the fire-walls, and the flues; in short, Mr. Scribe, have you allowed for the legitimate chimney itself—some one hundred and forty-four square feet or thereabouts, Mr. Scribe?"

"How unaccountable. That slipped my mind, too."

"Did it, indeed, Mr. Scribe?"

He faltered a little, and burst forth with, "But we must not allow one hundred and forty-four square feet for the legitimate chimney. My position is, that within those undue limits the secret closet is contained."

I eyed him in silence a moment; then spoke:

"Your survey is concluded, Mr. Scribe; be so good now as to lay your finger upon the exact part of the chimney wall where you believe this secret closet to be; or would a witch-hazel wand assist you, Mr. Scribe?"

"No, sir, but a crow-bar would," he, with temper, rejoined.

Here, now, thought I to myself, the cat leaps out of the bag. I looked at him with a calm glance, under which he seemed somewhat uneasy. More than ever now I suspected a plot. I remembered what my wife had said about abiding by the decision of Mr. Scribe. In a bland way, I resolved to buy up the decision of Mr. Scribe.

"Sir," said I, "really, I am much obliged to you for this survey. It has quite set my mind at rest. And no doubt you, too, Mr. Scribe, must feel much relieved. Sir," I added, "you have made three visits to the chimney. With a business man, time is money. Here are fifty dollars, Mr. Scribe.

Nay, take it. You have earned it. Your opinion is worth it. And by the way,"—as he modestly received the money—"have you any objections to give me a—a—little certificate—something, say, like a steam-boat certificate, certifying that you, a competent surveyor, have surveyed my chimney, and found no reason to believe any unsoundness; in short, any—any secret closet in it. Would you be so kind, Mr. Scribe?"

"But, but, sir," stammered he with honest hesitation.

"Here, here are pen and paper," said I, with entire assurance.

Enough.

That evening I had the certificate framed and hung over the dining-room fire-place, trusting that the continual sight of it would forever put at rest at once the dreams and stratagems of my household.

But, no. Inveterately bent upon the extirpation of that noble old chimney, still to this day my wife goes about it, with my daughter Anna's geological hammer, tapping the wall all over, and then holding her ear against it, as I have seen the physicians of life insurance companies tap a man's chest, and then incline over for the echo. Sometimes of nights she almost frightens one, going about on this phantom errand, and still following the sepulchral response of the chimney, round and round, as if it were leading her to the threshold of the secret closet.

"How hollow it sounds," she will hollowly cry. "Yes, I declare," with an emphatic tap, "there is a secret closet here. Here, in this very spot. Hark! How hollow!"

"Psha! wife, of course it is hollow. Who ever heard of a solid chimney?"

But nothing avails. And my daughters take after, not me, but their mother.

Sometimes all three abandon the theory of the secret closet, and return to the genuine ground of attack—the unsightliness of so cumbrous a pile, with comments upon the great addition of room to be gained by its demolition, and the fine effect of the projected grand hall, and the convenience resulting from the collateral running in one direction and another of their various partitions. Not more ruthlessly did the Three Powers partition away poor Poland, than my wife and daughters would fain partition away my chimney.

But seeing that, despite all, I and my chimney still smoke our pipes, my wife reoccupies the ground of the secret closet, enlarging upon what wonders are there, and what a shame it is, not to seek it out and explore it.

"Wife," said I, upon one of these occasions, "why speak more of that secret closet, when there before you hangs contrary testimony of a master mason, elected by yourself to decide. Besides, even if there were a secret closet, secret it should remain, and secret it shall. Yes, wife, here for once I must say my say. Infinite sad mischief has resulted from the profane bursting open of secret recesses. Though standing in the heart of this house, though hitherto we have all nestled about it, unsuspicious of aught hidden within, this chimney may or may not have a secret closet. But if it have, it is my kinsman's. To break into that wall, would be to break into his breast. And that wall-breaking wish of Momus I account the wish of a church-robbing gossip and knave. Yes, wife, a vile eaves-dropping varlet was Momus."

"Moses?—Mumps? Stuff with your mumps and your Moses!"

The truth is, my wife, like all the rest of the world, cares not a fig for my philosophical jabber. In dearth of other philosophical companionship, I and my chimney have to smoke and philosophize together. And sitting up so late as we do at it, a mighty smoke it is that we two smoky old philosophers make.

But my spouse, who likes the smoke of my tobacco as little as she does that of the soot, carries on her war against both. I live in continual dread lest, like the golden bowl, the pipes of me and my chimney shall yet be broken. To stay that mad project of my wife's, naught answers. Or, rather, she herself is incessantly answering, incessantly besetting me with her terrible alacrity for improvement, which is a softer name for destruction. Scarce a day I do not find her with her tape-measure, measuring for her grand hall, while Anna holds a yard-stick on one side, and Julia looks approvingly on from the other. Mysterious intimations appear in the nearest village paper, signed "Claude," to the effect that a certain structure, standing on a certain hill, is a sad blemish to an otherwise lovely landscape. Anonymous letters arrive, threatening me with I know not what, unless I remove my chimney. Is it my wife, too, or who, that sets up the neighbors to badgering me on the same subject, and hinting to me that my chimney, like a huge elm, absorbs all moisture from my garden? At night, also, my wife will start from sleep, professing to hear ghostly noises from the secret closet. Assailed on all sides, and in all ways, small peace have I and my chimney.

Were it not for the baggage, we would together pack up, and remove from the country.

What narrow escapes have been ours! Once I found in a drawer a whole portfolio of plans and estimates. Another time, upon returning after a day's absence, I discovered my wife standing before the chimney in earnest conversation with a person whom I at once recognized as a meddlesome architectural reformer, who, because he had no gift for putting up anything, was ever intent upon pulling down; in various parts of the country having prevailed upon half-witted old folks to destroy their old-fashioned houses, particularly the chimneys.

But worst of all was, that time I unexpectedly returned at early morning from a visit to the city, and upon approaching the house, narrowly escaped three brickbats which fell, from high aloft, at my feet. Glancing up, what was my horror to see three savages, in blue jean overalls, in the very act of commencing the long-threatened attack. Aye, indeed, thinking of those three brickbats, I and my chimney have had narrow escapes.

It is now some seven years since I have stirred from home. My city friends all wonder why I don't come to see them, as in former times. They think I am getting sour and unsocial. Some say that I have become a sort of mossy old misanthrope, while all the time the fact is, I am simply standing guard over my mossy old chimney; for it is resolved between me and my chimney, that I and my chimney will never surrender.

The Apple-Tree Table

Or, Original Spiritual Manifestations

WHEN I FIRST SAW THE TABLE, dingy and dusty, in the furthest corner of the old hopper-shaped garret, and set out with broken, be-crusted old purple vials and flasks, and a ghostly, dismantled old quarto, it seemed just such a necromantic little old table as might have belonged to Friar Bacon. Two plain features it had, significant of conjurations and charms—the circle and tripod; the slab being round, supported by a twisted little pillar, which, about a foot from the bottom, sprawled out into three crooked legs, terminating in three cloven feet. A very satanic-looking little old table, indeed.

In order to convey a better idea of it, some account may as well be given of the place it came from. A very old garret of a very old house in an old-fashioned quarter of one of the oldest towns in America. This garret had been closed for years. It was thought to be haunted; a rumor, I confess, which, however absurd (in my opinion), I did not, at the time of purchasing, very vehemently contradict; since, not improbably, it tended to place the property the more conveniently within my means.

It was, therefore, from no dread of the reputed goblins aloft, that, for five years after first taking up my residence in the house, I never entered the garret. There was no special inducement. The roof was well slated, and thoroughly tight. The company that insured the house, waived all visitation of the garret; why, then, should the owner be over-anxious about it?—particularly, as he had no use for it, the house having ample room below. Then the key of the stair-door leading to it was lost. The lock was a huge, old-fashioned one. To open it, a smith would have to be called; an unnecessary trouble, I thought. Besides, though I had taken some care to keep my two daughters in ignorance of the rumor above-mentioned, still, they had, by some means, got an inkling of it, and were well enough pleased to see the entrance to the haunted ground closed. It might have remained so for a still longer time, had it not been for my accidentally discovering, in a corner of our glen-like, old, terraced garden, a large and curious key, very old and rusty, which I, at once, concluded must belong to the garret-door—a supposition which, upon trial, proved correct. Now, the possession of a key to anything, at once provokes a desire to unlock and explore; and this, too, from a mere instinct of gratification, irrespective of any particular benefit to accrue.

Behold me, then, turning the rusty old key, and going up, alone, into the haunted garret.

It embraced the entire area of the mansion. Its ceiling was formed by the roof, showing the rafters and boards on which the slates were laid. The roof shedding the water four ways from a high point in the centre, the space beneath was much like that of a general's marquee—only midway broken by a labyrinth of timbers, for braces, from which waved innumerable cobwebs, that, of a summer's noon, shone like Bagdad tissues and gauzes. On every hand, some strange insect was seen, flying, or running, or creeping, on rafter and floor.

Under the apex of the roof was a rude, narrow, decrepit step-ladder, something like a Gothic pulpit-stairway, leading to a pulpit-like platform, from which a still narrower ladder—a sort of Jacob's ladder—led some ways higher to the lofty scuttle. The slide of this scuttle was about two feet square, all in one piece, furnishing a massive frame for a single small pane of glass, inserted into it like a bull's-eye. The light of the garret came from this sole source, filtrated through a dense curtain of cobwebs. Indeed, the whole stairs, and platform, and ladder, were festooned, and carpeted, and canopied with cobwebs; which, in funereal accumulations, hung, too, from the groined, murky ceiling, like the Carolina moss in the cypress forest. In these cobwebs, swung, as in aerial catacombs, myriads of all tribes of mummied insects.

Climbing the stairs to the platform, and pausing there, to recover my breath, a curious scene was presented. The sun was about half-way up.

Piercing the little sky-light, it slopingly bored a rainbowed tunnel clear across the darkness of the garret. Here, millions of butterfly moles were swarming. Against the sky-light itself, with a cymbal-like buzzing, thousands of insects clustered in a golden mob.

Wishing to shed a clearer light through the place, I sought to withdraw the scuttle-slide. But no sign of latch or hasp was visible. Only after long peering, did I discover a little padlock, imbedded, like an oyster at the bottom of the sea, amid matted masses of weedy webs, chrysalides, and insectivorous eggs. Brushing these away, I found it locked. With a crooked nail, I tried to pick the lock, when scores of small ants and flies, half-torpid, crawled forth from the key-hole, and, feeling the warmth of the sun in the pane, began frisking around me. Others appeared. Presently, I was overrun by them. As if incensed at this invasion of their retreat, countless bands darted up from below, beating about my head, like hornets. At last, with a sudden jerk, I burst open the scuttle. And ah! what a change. As from the gloom of the grave and the companionship of worms, man shall at last rapturously rise into the living greenness and glory immortal, so, from my cobwebbed old garret, I thrust forth my head into the balmy air, and found myself hailed by the verdant tops of great trees, growing in the little garden below—trees, whose leaves soared high above my topmost slate.

Refreshed by this outlook, I turned inward to behold the garret, now unwontedly lit up. Such humped masses of obsolete furniture. An old escritoir, from whose pigeon-holes sprang mice, and from whose secret drawers came subterranean squeakings, as from chipmuncks' holes in the woods; and broken-down old chairs, with strange carvings, which seemed fit to seat a conclave of conjurors. And a rusty, iron-bound chest, lidless, and packed full of mildewed old documents; one of which, with a faded red ink-blot at the end, looked as if it might have been the original bond that Doctor Faust gave to Mephistopheles. And, finally, in the least lighted corner of all, where was a profuse litter of indescribable old rubbish—among which was a broken telescope, and a celestial globe staved in—stood the little old table, one hoofed foot, like that of the Evil One, dimly revealed through the cobwebs. What a thick dust, half paste, had settled upon the old vials and flasks; how their once liquid contents had caked, and how strangely looked the mouldy old book in the middle—Cotton Mather's "Magnalia."

Table and book I removed below, and had the dislocations of the one and the tatters of the other repaired. I resolved to surround this sad little hermit of a table, so long banished from genial neighborhood, with all the kindly influences of warm urns, warm fires, and warm hearts; little dreaming what all this warm nursing would hatch.

I was pleased by the discovery, that the table was not of the ordinary mahogany, but of apple-tree wood, which age had darkened nearly to walnut. It struck me as being quite an appropriate piece of furniture for our cedar-parlor—so called, from its being, after the old fashion, wainscoted with that wood. The table's round slab, or *orb*, was so contrived as to be readily changed from a horizontal to a perpendicular position; so that, when not in use, it could be snugly placed in a corner. For myself, wife, and two daughters, I thought it would make a nice little breakfast and tea-table. It was just the thing for a whist table, too. And I also pleased myself with the idea, that it would make a famous reading-table.

In these fancies, my wife, for one, took little interest. She disrelished the idea of so unfashionable and indigent-looking a stranger as the table intruding into the polished society of more prosperous furniture. But when, after seeking its fortune at the cabinet-maker's, the table came home, varnished over, bright as a guinea, no one exceeded my wife in a gracious reception of it. It was advanced to an honorable position in the cedar-parlor.

But, as for my daughter Julia, she never got over her strange emotions upon first accidentally encountering the table. Unfortunately, it was just as I was in the act of bringing it down from the garret. Holding it by the slab, I was carrying it before me, one cobwebbed hoof thrust out, which weird object, at a turn of the stairs, suddenly touched my girl, as she was ascending; whereupon, turning, and seeing no living creature—for I was quite hidden behind my shield—seeing nothing, indeed, but the apparition of the Evil One's foot, as it seemed, she cried out, and there is no knowing what might have followed, had I not immediately spoken.

From the impression thus produced, my poor girl, of a very nervous temperament, was long recovering. Superstitiously grieved at my violating the forbidden solitude above, she associated in her mind the cloven-footed table with the reputed goblins there. She besought me to give up the idea of domesticating the table. Nor did her sister fail to add her entreaties. Between my girls there was a constitutional sympathy. But my matter-of-fact wife had now declared in the table's favor. She was not wanting in firmness and energy. To her, the prejudices of Julia and Anna were simply ridiculous. It was her maternal duty, she thought, to drive such weakness away. By degrees, the girls, at breakfast and tea, were induced to sit down with us at the table. Continual proximity was not without effect. By and by, they would sit pretty tranquilly, though Julia, as much as possible, avoided glancing at the hoofed feet, and, when at this I smiled, she would look at me seriously—as much as to say, Ah, papa, you, too, may yet do the same. She prophecied that, in connection with the table, something strange would yet happen. But I would only smile the more, while my wife indignantly chided.

Meantime, I took particular satisfaction in my table, as a night reading-table. At a ladies' fair, I bought me a beautifully worked reading-cushion, and, with elbow leaning thereon, and hand shading my eyes from the light, spent many a long hour—nobody by, but the queer old book I had brought down from the garret.

All went well, till the incident now about to be given—an incident, be it remembered, which, like every other in this narration, happened long before the time of the "Fox girls."

It was late on a Saturday night in December. In the little old cedar-parlor, before the little old apple-tree table, I was sitting up, as usual, alone. I had made more than one effort to get up and go to bed; but I could not. I was, in fact, under a sort of fascination. Somehow, too, certain reasonable opinions of mine seemed not so reasonable as before. I felt nervous. The truth was, that though, in my previous night-readings, Cotton Mather had but amused me, upon this particular night he terrified me. A thousand times I had laughed at such stories. Old wives' fables, I thought, however entertaining. But now, how different. They began to put on the aspect of reality. Now, for the first time it struck me that this was no romantic Mrs. Radcliffe, who had written the "Magnalia;" but a practical, hard-working, earnest, upright man, a learned doctor, too, as well as a good Christian and orthodox clergyman. What possible motive could such a man have to deceive? His style had all the plainness and unpoetic boldness of truth. In the most straightforward way, he laid before me detailed accounts of New England witchcraft, each important item corroborated by respectable townsfolk, and, of not a few of the most surprising, he himself had been eye-witness. Cotton Mather testified whereof he had seen. But, is it possible? I asked myself. Then I remembered that Dr. Johnson, the matter-of-fact compiler of a dictionary, had been a believer in ghosts, besides many other sound, worthy men. Yielding to the fascination, I read deeper and deeper into the night. At last, I found myself starting at the least chance sound, and yet wishing that it were not so very still.

A tumbler of warm punch stood by my side, with which beverage, in a moderate way, I was accustomed to treat myself every Saturday night; a habit, however, against which my good wife had long remonstrated; predicting that, unless I gave it up, I would yet die a miserable sot. Indeed, I may here mention that, on the Sunday mornings following my Saturday nights, I had to be exceedingly cautious how I gave way to the slightest impatience at any accidental annoyance; because such impatience was sure to be quoted against me as evidence of the melancholy consequences of over-night indulgence. As for my wife, she, never sipping punch, could yield to any little passing peevishness as much as she pleased.

But, upon the night in question, I found myself wishing that, instead of my usual mild mixture, I had concocted some potent draught. I felt the need of stimulus. I wanted something to hearten me against Cotton Mather—doleful, ghostly, ghastly Cotton Mather. I grew more and more nervous. Nothing but fascination kept me from fleeing the room. The candles burnt low, with long snuffs, and huge winding-sheets. But I durst not raise the snuffers to them. It would make too much noise. And yet, previously, I had been wishing for noise. I read on and on. My hair began to have a sensation. My eyes felt strained; they pained me. I was conscious of it. I knew I was injuring them. I knew I should rue this abuse of them next day; but I read on and on. I could not help it. The skinny hand was on me.

All at once———Hark!

My hair felt like growing grass.

A faint sort of inward rapping or rasping—a strange, inexplicable sound, mixed with a slight kind of wood-pecking or ticking.

Tick! Tick!

Yes, it was a faint sort of ticking.

I looked up at my great Strasbourg clock in one corner. It was not that. The clock had stopped.

Tick! Tick!

Was it my watch?

According to her usual practice at night, my wife had, upon retiring, carried my watch off to our chamber to hang it up on its nail.

I listened with all my ears.

Tick! Tick!

Was it a death-tick in the wainscot?

With a tremulous step I went all round the room, holding my ear to the wainscot.

No; it came not from the wainscot.

Tick! Tick!

I shook myself. I was ashamed of my fright.

Tick! Tick!

It grew in precision and audibleness. I retreated from the wainscot. It seemed advancing to meet me.

I looked round and round, but saw nothing, only one cloven foot of the little apple-tree table.

Bless me, said I to myself, with a sudden revulsion, it must be very late; ain't that my wife calling me? Yes, yes; I must to bed. I suppose all is locked up. No need to go the rounds.

The fascination had departed, though the fear had increased. With trembling hands, putting Cotton Mather out of sight, I soon found myself, candle-stick in hand, in my chamber, with a peculiar rearward feeling, such as some truant dog may feel. In my eagerness to get well into the chamber, I stumbled against a chair.

"Do try and make less noise, my dear," said my wife from the bed. "You have been taking too much of that punch, I fear. That sad habit grows on you. Ah, that I should ever see you thus staggering at night into your chamber."

"Wife, wife," hoarsely whispered I, "there is—is something tick—ticking in the cedar-parlor."

"Poor old man—quite out of his mind—I knew it would be so. Come to bed; come and sleep it off."

"Wife, wife!"

"Do, do come to bed. I forgive you..I won't remind you of it to-morrow. But you must give up the punch-drinking, my dear. It quite gets the better of you."

"Don't exasperate me," I cried now, truly beside myself; "I will quit the house!"

"No, no! not in that state. Come to bed, my dear. I won't say another word."

The next morning, upon waking, my wife said nothing about the past night's affair, and, feeling no little embarrassment myself, especially at having been thrown into such a panic, I also was silent. Consequently, my wife must still have ascribed my singular conduct to a mind disordered, not by ghosts, but by punch. For my own part, as I lay in bed watching the sun in the panes, I began to think that much midnight reading of Cotton Mather was not good for man; that it had a morbid influence upon the nerves, and gave rise to hallucinations. I resolved to put Cotton Mather permanently aside. That done, I had no fear of any return of the ticking. Indeed, I began to think that what seemed the ticking in the room, was nothing but a sort of buzzing in my ear.

As is her wont, my wife having preceded me in rising, I made a deliberate and agreeable toilet. Aware that most disorders of the mind have their origin in the state of the body, I made vigorous use of the flesh-brush, and bathed my head with New England rum, a specific once recommended to me as good for buzzing in the ear. Wrapped in my dressing gown, with cravat nicely adjusted, and finger-nails neatly trimmed, I complacently descended to the little cedar-parlor to breakfast.

What was my amazement to find my wife on her knees, rummaging about the carpet nigh the little apple-tree table, on which the morning meal was laid, while my daughters, Julia and Anna, were running about the apartment distracted.

"Oh, papa, papa!" cried Julia, hurrying up to me, "I knew it would be so. The table, the table!"

"Spirits! spirits!" cried Anna, standing far away from it, with pointed finger.

"Silence!" cried my wife. "How can I hear it, if you make such a noise? Be still. Come here, husband; was this the ticking you spoke of? Why don't you move? Was this it? Here, kneel down and listen to it. Tick, tick, tick!—don't you hear it now?"

"I do, I do," cried I, while my daughters besought us both to come away from the spot.

Tick, tick, tick!

Right from under the snowy cloth, and the cheerful urn, and the smoking milk-toast, the unaccountable ticking was heard.

"Ain't there a fire in the next room, Julia," said I, "let us breakfast there, my dear," turning to my wife—"let us go—leave the table—tell Biddy to remove the things."

And so saying I was moving towards the door in high self-possession, when my wife interrupted me.

"Before I quit this room, I will see into this ticking," she said with energy. "It is something that can be found out, depend upon it. I don't believe in spirits, especially at breakfast-time. Biddy! Biddy! Here, carry these things back to the kitchen," handing the urn. Then, sweeping off the cloth, the little table lay bare to the eye.

"It's the table, the table!" cried Julia.

"Nonsense," said my wife. "Who ever heard of a ticking table? It's on the floor. Biddy! Julia! Anna! move everything out of the room—table and all. Where are the tack-hammers?"

"Heavens, mamma—you are not going to take up the carpet?" screamed Julia.

"Here's the hammers, marm," said Biddy, advancing tremblingly.

"Hand them to me, then," cried my wife; for poor Biddy was, at long gun-distance, holding them out as if her mistress had the plague.

"Now, husband, do you take up that side of the carpet, and I will this." Down on her knees she then dropped, while I followed suit.

The carpet being removed, and the ear applied to the naked floor, not the slightest ticking could be heard.

"The table—after all, it is the table," cried my wife. "Biddy, bring it back."

"Oh no, marm, not I, please, marm," sobbed Biddy.

"Foolish creature!—Husband, do you bring it."

"My dear," said I, "we have plenty of other tables; why be so particular?"

"Where is that table?" cried my wife, contemptuously, regardless of my gentle remonstrance.

"In the wood-house, marm. I put it away as far as ever I could, marm," sobbed Biddy.

"Shall I go to the wood-house for it, or will you?" said my wife, addressing me in a frightful, business-like manner.

Immediately I darted out of the door, and found the little apple-tree table, upside down, in one of my chip-bins. I hurriedly returned with it, and once more my wife examined it attentively. Tick, tick, tick! Yes, it was the table.

"Please, marm," said Biddy, now entering the room, with hat and shawl—"please, marm, will you pay me my wages?"

"Take your hat and shawl off directly," said my wife; "set this table again."

"Set it," roared I, in a passion, "set it, or I'll go for the police."

"Heavens! heavens!" cried my daughters, in one breath. "What will become of us!—Spirits! Spirits!"

"Will you set the table?" cried I, advancing upon Biddy.

"I will, I will—yes, marm—yes, master—I will, I will. Spirits!—Holy Vargin!"

"Now, husband," said my wife, "I am convinced that, whatever it is that causes this ticking, neither the ticking nor the table can hurt us; for we are all good Christians, I hope. I am determined to find out the cause of it, too, which time and patience will bring to light. I shall breakfast on no other table but this, so long as we live in this house. So, sit down, now that all things are ready again, and let us quietly breakfast. My dears," turning to Julia and Anna, "go to your room, and return composed. Let me have no more of this childishness."

Upon occasion my wife was mistress in her house.

During the meal, in vain was conversation started again and again; in vain my wife said something brisk to infuse into others an animation akin to her own. Julia and Anna, with heads bowed over their tea-cups, were still listening for the tick. I confess, too, that their example was catching. But, for the time, nothing was heard. Either the ticking had died quite away, or else, slight as it was, the increasing uproar of the street, with the general hum of day, so contrasted with the repose of night and early morning, smothered the sound. At the lurking inquietude of her companions, my wife was indignant; the more so, as she seemed to glory in her own exemption from panic. When breakfast was cleared away she took my watch, and, placing it on the table, addressed the supposed spirits in it, with a jocosely defiant air: "There, tick away, let us see who can tick loudest!"

All that day, while abroad, I thought of the mysterious table. Could Cotton Mather speak true? Were there spirits? And would spirits haunt a tea-table? Would the Evil One dare show his cloven foot in the bosom of an innocent family? I shuddered when I thought that I myself, against the solemn warnings of my daughters, had willfully introduced the cloven foot there. Yea, three cloven feet. But, towards noon, this sort of feeling began to wear off. The continual rubbing against so many practical people in the street, brushed such chimeras away from me. I remembered that I had not acquitted myself very intrepidly either on the previous night or in the morning. I resolved to regain the good opinion of my wife.

To evince my hardihood the more signally, when tea was dismissed, and the three rubbers of whist had been played, and no ticking had been heard—which the more encouraged me—I took my pipe, and, saying that bed-time had arrived for the rest, drew my chair towards the fire, and, removing my slippers, placed my feet on the fender, looking as calm and composed as old Democritus in the tombs of Abdera, when one midnight the mischievous little boys of the town tried to frighten that sturdy philosopher with spurious ghosts.

And I thought to myself, that the worthy old gentleman had set a good example to all times in his conduct on that occasion. For, when at the dead hour, intent on his studies, he heard the strange sounds, he did not so much as move his eyes from his page, only simply said: "Boys, little boys, go home. This is no place for you. You will catch cold here." The philosophy of which words lies here: that they imply the foregone conclusion, that any possible investigation of any possible spiritual phenomena was absurd; that upon the first face of such things, the mind of a sane man instinctively affirmed them a humbug, unworthy the least attention; more especially if such phenomena appear in tombs, since tombs are peculiarly the place of silence, lifelessness, and solitude; for which cause, by the way, the old man, as upon the occasion in question, made the tombs of Abdera his place of study.

Presently I was alone, and all was hushed. I laid down my pipe, not feeling exactly tranquil enough now thoroughly to enjoy it. Taking up one of the newspapers, I began, in a nervous, hurried sort of way, to read by the light of a candle placed on a small stand drawn close to the fire. As for the apple-tree table, having lately concluded that it was rather too low for a reading-table, I thought best not to use it as such that night. But it stood not very distant in the middle of the room.

Try as I would, I could not succeed much at reading. Somehow I seemed all ear and no eye; a condition of intense auricular suspense. But ere long it was broken.

Tick! tick! tick!

Though it was not the first time I had heard that sound; nay, though I had made it my particular business on this occasion to wait for that sound, nevertheless, when it came, it seemed unexpected, as if a cannon had boomed through the window.

Tick! tick! tick!

I sat stock still for a time, thoroughly to master, if possible, my first discomposure. Then rising, I looked pretty steadily at the table; went up to it pretty steadily; took hold of it pretty steadily; but let it go pretty quickly; then paced up and down, stopping every moment or two, with ear pricked to listen. Meantime, within me, the contest between panic and philosophy remained not wholly decided.

Tick! tick! tick!

With appalling distinctness the ticking now rose on the night.

My pulse fluttered—my heart beat. I hardly know what might not have followed, had not Democritus just then come to the rescue. For shame, said I to myself, what is the use of so fine an example of philosophy, if it cannot be followed? Straightway I resolved to imitate it, even to the old sage's occupation and attitude.

Resuming my chair and paper, with back presented to the table, I remained thus for a time, as if buried in study; when, the ticking still continuing, I drawled out, in as indifferent and dryly jocose a way as I could; "Come, come, Tick, my boy, fun enough for to-night."

Tick! tick! tick!

There seemed a sort of jeering defiance in the ticking now. It seemed to exult over the poor affected part I was playing. But much as the taunt stung me, it only stung me into persistence. I resolved not to abate one whit in my mode of address.

"Come, come, you make more and more noise, Tick, my boy; too much of a joke—time to have done."

No sooner said than the ticking ceased. Never was responsive obedience more exact. For the life of me, I could not help turning round upon the table, as one would upon some reasonable being, when———could I believe my senses? I saw something moving, or wriggling, or squirming upon the slab of the table. It shone like a glow-worm. Unconsciously, I grasped the poker that stood at hand. But bethinking me how absurd to attack a glow-worm with a poker, I put it down. How long I sat spell-bound and staring there, with my body presented one way and my face another, I cannot say; but at length I rose, and, buttoning my coat up and down, made a sudden intrepid forced march full upon the table. And there, near the centre of the slab, as I live, I saw an irregular little hole, or, rather, short nibbled sort of crack, from which (like a butterfly escaping its chrysalis) the sparkling object, whatever it might be, was struggling. Its motion was the motion of life. I stood becharmed. Are there, indeed, spirits, thought I; and is this one? No; I must be dreaming. I turned my glance off to the red fire on the hearth, then back to the pale lustre on the table. What I saw was no optical illusion, but a real marvel. The tremor was increasing, when, once again, Democritus befriended me. Supernatural coruscation as it appeared, I strove to look at the strange object in a purely scientific way. Thus viewed, it appeared some new sort of small shining beetle or bug, and, I thought, not without something of a hum to it, too.

I still watched it, and with still increasing self-possession. Sparkling and wriggling, it still continued its throes. In another moment it was just on the point of escaping its prison. A thought struck me. Running for a tumbler, I clapped it over the insect just in time to secure it.

After watching it a while longer under the tumbler, I left all as it was, and, tolerably composed, retired.

Now, for the soul of me, I could not, at that time, comprehend the phenomenon. A live bug come out of a dead table? A fire-fly bug come out of a piece of ancient lumber, for one knows not how many years stored away in an old garret? Was ever such a thing heard of, or even dreamed of? How got the bug there? Never mind. I bethought me of Democritus, and resolved to keep cool. At all events, the mystery of the ticking was explained. It was simply the sound of the gnawing and filing, and tapping of the bug, in eating its way out. It was satisfactory to think, that there was an end forever to the ticking. I resolved not to let the occasion pass without reaping some credit from it.

"Wife," said I, next morning, "you will not be troubled with any more ticking in our table. I have put a stop to all that."

"Indeed, husband," said she, with some incredulity.

"Yes, wife," returned I, perhaps a little vain-gloriously. "I have put a quietus upon that ticking. Depend upon it, the ticking will trouble you no more."

In vain she besought me to explain myself. I would not gratify her; being willing to balance any previous trepidation I might have betrayed, by leaving room now for the imputation of some heroic feat whereby I had silenced the ticking. It was a sort of innocent deceit by implication, quite harmless, and, I thought, of utility.

But when I went to breakfast, I saw my wife kneeling at the table again, and my girls looking ten times more frightened than ever.

"Why did you tell me that boastful tale," said my wife, indignantly. "You might have known how easily it would be found out. See this crack, too; and here is the ticking again, plainer than ever."

"Impossible," I exclaimed; but upon applying my ear, sure enough, tick! tick! tick! The ticking was there.

Recovering myself the best way I might, I demanded the bug.

"Bug?" screamed Julia. "Good heavens, papa!"

"I hope, sir, you have been bringing no bugs into this house," said my wife, severely.

"The bug, the bug!" I cried; "the bug under the tumbler."

"Bugs in tumblers!" cried the girls; "not *our* tumblers, papa? You have not been putting bugs into our tumblers? Oh, what does—what *does* it all mean?"

"Do you see this hole, this crack here?" said I, putting my finger on the spot.

"That I do," said my wife, with high displeasure. "And how did it come there? What have you been doing to the table?"

"Do you see this crack?" repeated I, intensely.

"Yes, yes," said Julia; "that was what frightened me so; it looks so like witch-work."

"Spirits! spirits!" cried Anna.

"Silence!" said my wife. "Go on, sir, and tell us what you know of the crack."

"Wife and daughters," said I, solemnly, "out of that crack, or hole, while I was sitting all alone here last night, a wonderful———"

Here, involuntarily, I paused, fascinated by the expectant attitudes and bursting eyes of Julia and Anna.

"What, what?" cried Julia.

"A bug, Julia."

"A bug?" cried my wife. "A bug come out of this table? And what did you do with it?"

"Clapped it under a tumbler."

"Biddy! Biddy!" cried my wife, going to the door. "Did you see a tumbler here on this table when you swept the room?"

"Sure I did, marm, and a 'bomnable bug under it."

"And what did you do with it?" demanded I.

"Put the bug in the fire, sir, and rinsed out the tumbler ever so many times, marm."

"Where is that tumbler?" cried Anna. "I hope you scratched it—marked it some way. I'll never drink out of that tumbler; never put it before me, Biddy. A bug—a bug! Oh, Julia! oh, mamma! I feel it crawling all over me, even now. Haunted table!"

"Spirits! spirits!" cried Julia.

"My daughters," said their mother, with authority in her eyes, "go to your chamber till you can behave more like reasonable creatures. Is it a bug—a bug that can frighten you out of what little wits you ever had. Leave the room. I am astonished. I am pained by such childish conduct."

"Now tell me," said she, addressing me, as soon as they had withdrawn, "now tell me truly, did a bug really come out of this crack in the table?"

"Wife, it is even so."

"Did you see it come out?"

"I did."

She looked earnestly at the crack, leaning over it.

"Are you sure?" said she, looking up, but still bent over.

"Sure, sure."

She was silent. I began to think that the mystery of the thing began to tell even upon her. Yes, thought I, I shall presently see my wife shaking and shuddering, and, who knows, calling in some old dominie to exorcise the table, and drive out the spirits.

"I'll tell you what we'll do," said she suddenly, and not without excitement.

"What, wife?" said I, all eagerness, expecting some mystical proposition; "what, wife?"

"We will rub this table all over with that celebrated 'roach powder' I've heard of."

"Good gracious! Then you don't think it's spirits?"

"Spirits?"

The emphasis of scornful incredulity was worthy of Democritus himself.

"But this ticking—this ticking?" said I.

"I'll whip that out of it."

"Come, come wife," said I, "you are going too far the other way, now. Neither roach powder nor whipping will cure this table. It's a queer table, wife; there's no blinking it."

"I'll have it rubbed, though," she replied, "well rubbed;" and calling Biddy, she bade her get wax and brush, and give the table a vigorous manipulation. That done, the cloth was again laid, and we sat down to our morning meal; but my daughters did not make their appearance. Julia and Anna took no breakfast that day.

When the cloth was removed, in a business-like way, my wife went to work with a dark colored cement, and hermetically closed the little hole in the table.

My daughters looking pale, I insisted upon taking them out for a walk that morning, when the following conversation ensued:

"My worst presentiments about that table are being verified, papa," said Julia; "not for nothing was that intimation of the cloven foot on my shoulder."

"Nonsense," said I. "Let us go into Mrs. Brown's, and have an ice-cream."

The spirit of Democritus was stronger on me now. By a curious coincidence, it strengthened with the strength of the sunlight.

"But is it not miraculous," said Anna, "how a bug should come out of a table?"

"Not at all, my daughter. It is a very common thing for bugs to come out of wood. You yourself must have seen them coming out of the ends of the billets on the hearth."

"Ah, but that wood is almost fresh from the woodland. But the table is at least a hundred years old."

"What of that?" said I, gayly. "Have not live toads been found in the hearts of dead rocks, as old as creation?"

"Say what you will, papa, I feel it is spirits," said Julia. "Do, do now, my dear papa, have that haunted table removed from the house."

"Nonsense," said I.

By another curious coincidence, the more they felt frightened, the more I felt brave.

Evening came.

"This ticking," said my wife; "do you think that another bug will come of this continued ticking?"

Curiously enough, that had not occurred to me before. I had not thought of there being twins of bugs. But now, who knew; there might be even triplets.

I resolved to take precautions, and, if there was to be a second bug, infallibly secure it. During the evening, the ticking was again heard. About ten o'clock I clapped a tumbler over the spot, as near as I could judge of it by my ear. Then we all retired, and locking the door of the cedar-parlor, I put the key in my pocket.

In the morning, nothing was to be seen, but the ticking was heard. The trepidation of my daughters returned. They wanted to call in the neighbors. But to this my wife was vigorously opposed. We should be the laughing-stock of the whole town. So it was agreed that nothing should be disclosed. Biddy received strict charges; and, to make sure, was not allowed that week to go to confession, lest she should tell the priest.

I stayed home all that day, every hour or two bending over the table, both eye and ear. Towards night, I thought the ticking grew more distinct, and seemed divided from my ear by a thinner and thinner partition of the wood. I thought, too, that I perceived a faint heaving up, or bulging of the wood, in the place where I had placed the tumbler. To put an end to the suspense, my wife proposed taking a knife and cutting into the wood there; but I had a less impatient plan; namely, that she and I should sit up with the table that night, as, from present symptoms, the bug would probably make its appearance before morning. For myself, I was curious to see the first advent of the thing—the first dazzle of the chick as it chipped the shell.

The idea struck my wife not unfavorably. She insisted that both Julia and Anna should be of the party, in order that the evidence of their senses should disabuse their minds of all nursery nonsense. For that spirits should tick, and that spirits should take unto themselves the form of bugs, was, to my wife, the most foolish of all foolish imaginations. True, she could not account for the thing; but she had all confidence that it could be, and would yet be, somehow explained, and that to her entire satisfaction. Without knowing it herself, my wife was a female Democritus. For my own part, my present feelings were of a mixed sort. In a strange and not unpleasing way, I gently oscillated between Democritus and Cotton Mather. But to my wife and daughters I assumed to be pure Democritus—a jeerer at all tea-table spirits whatever.

So, laying in a good supply of candles and crackers, all four of us sat up with the table, and at the same time sat round it. For a while my wife and I carried on an animated conversation. But my daughters were silent. Then my wife and I would have had a rubber of whist, but my daughters could not be prevailed upon to join. So we played whist with two dummies, literally; my wife won the rubber, and, fatigued with victory, put away the cards.

Half past eleven o'clock. No sign of the bug. The candles began to burn dim. My wife was just in the act of snuffing them, when a sudden, violent, hollow, resounding, rumbling, thumping was heard.

Julia and Anna sprang to their feet.

"All well!" cried a voice from the street. It was the watchman, first ringing down his club on the pavement, and then following it up with this highly satisfactory verbal announcement.

"All well! Do you hear that, my girls?" said I, gayly.

Indeed it was astonishing how brave as Bruce I felt in company with three women, and two of them half frightened out of their wits.

I rose for my pipe, and took a philosophic smoke.

Democritus forever, thought I.

In profound silence, I sat smoking, when lo!—pop! pop! pop!—right under the table, a terrible popping.

This time we all four sprang up, and my pipe was broken.

"Good heavens! what's that?"

"Spirits! spirits!" cried Julia.

"Oh, oh, oh!" cried Anna.

"Shame," said my wife, "it's that new bottled cider, in the cellar, going off. I told Biddy to wire the bottles to-day."

I shall here transcribe from memoranda, kept during part of the night.

"One o'clock. No sign of the bug. Ticking continues. Wife getting sleepy.

"Two o'clock. No sign of the bug. Ticking intermittent. Wife fast asleep.

"Three o'clock. No sign of the bug. Ticking pretty steady. Julia and Anna getting sleepy.

"Four o'clock. No sign of the bug. Ticking regular, but not spirited. Wife, Julia, and Anna, all fast asleep in their chairs.

"Five o'clock. No sign of the bug. Ticking faint. Myself feeling drowsy. The rest still asleep."

So far the journal.

—Rap! rap! rap!

A terrific, portentous rapping against a door.

Startled from our dreams, we started to our feet.

Rap! rap! rap!

Julia and Anna shricked.

I cowered in the corner.

"You fools!" cried my wife, "it's the baker with the bread."

Six o'clock.

She went to throw back the shutters, but ere it was done, a cry came from Julia. There, half in and half out its crack, there wriggled the bug, flashing in the room's general dimness, like a fiery opal.

Had this bug had a tiny sword by its side—a Damascus sword—and a tiny necklace round its neck—a diamond necklace—and a tiny gun in its claw—a brass gun—and a tiny manuscript in his mouth—a Chaldee manuscript—Julia and Anna could not have stood more charmed.

In truth, it was a beautiful bug—a Jew jeweler's bug—a bug like a sparkle of a glorious sunset.

Julia and Anna had never dreamed of such a bug. To them, bug had been a word synonymous with hideousness. But this was a seraphical bug; or, rather, all it had of the bug was the B, for it was beautiful as a butterfly.

Julia and Anna gazed and gazed. They were no more alarmed. They were delighted.

"But how got this strange, pretty creature into the table?" cried Julia.

"Spirits can get anywhere," replied Anna.

"Pshaw!" said my wife.

"Do you hear any more ticking?" said I.

They all applied their ears, but heard nothing.

"Well, then, wife and daughters, now that it is all over, this very morning I will go and make inquiries about it."

"Oh, do, papa," cried Julia, "do go and consult Madame Pazzi, the conjuress."

"Better go and consult Professor Johnson, the naturalist," said my wife.

"Bravo, Mrs. Democritus!" said I, "Professor Johnson is the man."

By good fortune I found the professor in. Informing him briefly of the incident, he manifested a cool, collected sort of interest, and gravely accompanied me home. The table was produced, the two openings pointed out, the bug displayed, and the details of the affair set forth; my wife and daughters being present.

"And now, Professor," said I, "what do you think of it?"

Putting on his spectacles, the learned professor looked hard at the table, and gently scraped with his pen-knife into the holes, but said nothing.

"Is it not an unusual thing, this?" anxiously asked Anna.

"Very unusual, Miss."

At which Julia and Anna exchanged significant glances.

"But is it not wonderful, very wonderful?" demanded Julia.

"Very wonderful, Miss."

My daughters exchanged still more significant glances, and Julia, emboldened, again spoke.

"And must you not admit, sir, that it is the work of—of—of sp———?"

"Spirits? No," was the crusty rejoinder.

"My daughters," said I, mildly, "you should remember that this is not Madame Pazzi, the conjuress, you put your questions to, but the eminent naturalist, Professor Johnson. And now, professor," I added, "be pleased to explain. Enlighten our ignorance."

Without repeating all that the learned gentleman said—for, indeed, though lucid, he was a little prosy—let the following summary of his explication suffice.

The incident was not wholly without example. The wood of the table was apple-tree, a sort of tree much fancied by various insects. The bugs had come from eggs laid inside the bark of the living tree in the orchard. By careful examination of the position of the hole from which the last bug had emerged, in relation to the cortical layers of the slab, and then allowing for the inch and a half along the grain, ere the bug had eaten its way entirely out, and then computing the whole number of cortical layers in the slab, with a reasonable conjecture for the number cut off from the outside, it appeared that the egg must have been laid in the tree some ninety years, more or less, before the tree could have been felled. But between the felling of the tree and the present time, how long might that be? It was a very old-fashioned table. Allow eighty years for the age of the table, which would make one hundred and fifty years that the bug had laid in the egg. Such, at least, was Professor Johnson's computation.

"Now, Julia," said I, "after that scientific statement of the case (though, I confess, I don't exactly understand it), where are your spirits? It is very wonderful as it is, but where are your spirits?"

"Where, indeed?" said my wife.

"Why, now, she did not *really* associate this purely natural phenomenon with any crude, spiritual hypothesis, did she?" observed the learned professor, with a slight sneer.

"Say what you will," said Julia, holding up, in the covered tumbler, the glorious, lustrous, flashing, live opal, "say what you will, if this beauteous creature be not a spirit, it yet teaches a spiritual lesson. For if, after one hundred and fifty years' entombment, a mere insect comes forth at last into light, itself an effulgence, shall there be no glorified resurrection for the spirit of man? Spirits! spirits!" she exclaimed, with rapture, "I still believe in spirits, only now I believe in them with delight, when before I but thought of them with terror."

The mysterious insect did not long enjoy its radiant life; it expired the next day. But my girls have preserved it. Embalmed in a silver vinaigrette, it lies on the little apple-tree table in the pier of the cedar-parlor.

And whatever lady doubts this story, my daughters will be happy to show her both the bug and the table, and point out to her, in the repaired slab of the latter, the two sealing-wax drops designating the exact place of the two holes made by the two bugs, something in the same way in which are marked the spots where the cannon balls struck Brattle street church.

RECONSTRUCTED LECTURES

Statues in Rome

IT MIGHT BE SUPPOSED that the only proper judge of statues would be a sculptor, but it may be believed that others than the artist can appreciate and see the beauty of the marble art of Rome. If what is best in nature and knowledge cannot be claimed for the privileged profession of any order of men, it would be a wonder if, in that region called Art, there were, as to what is best there, any essential exclusiveness. True, the dilettante may employ his technical terms; but ignorance of these prevents not due feeling for Art, in any mind naturally alive to beauty or grandeur. Just as the productions of nature may be both appreciated by those who know nothing of Botany, or who have no inclination for it, so the creations of Art may be, by those ignorant of its critical science, or indifferent to it. Art strikes a chord in the lowest as well as in the highest; the rude and uncultivated feel its influence as well as the polite and polished. It is a spirit that pervades all classes. Nay, as it is doubtful whether to the scientific Linnaeus flowers yielded so much satisfaction as to the unscientific Burns, or struck so deep a chord in his bosom; so may it be a question whether the terms of Art may not inspire in artistic but still susceptible minds, thoughts, or emotions, not lower than those raised in the most accomplished of critics.

Yet, we find that many thus naturally susceptible to such impressions refrain from their utterance, out of fear lest in their ignorance of technicalities their unaffected terms might betray them, and that after all, feel as they may, they know little or nothing, and hence keep silence, not wishing to become presumptuous. There are many examples on record to show this, and not only this, but that the uneducated are very often more susceptible to this influence than the learned. May it not possibly be, that as Burns perhaps understood flowers as well as Linnaeus, and the Scotch peasant's poetical description of the daisy, "wee, modest, crimson-tipped flower," is rightly set above the technical definition of the Swedish professor, so in Art, just as in nature, it may not be the accredited wise man alone who, in all respects, is qualified to comprehend or describe.

With this explanation, I, who am neither critic nor connoisseur, thought fit to introduce some familiar remarks upon the sculptures in Rome, a subject which otherwise might be thought to lie peculiarly within the province of persons of a kind of cultivation to which I make no pretension. The topic is one of great extent, as Rome contains more objects of interest than perhaps any other place in the world. I shall speak of the impressions produced upon my mind as one who looks upon a work of art as he would upon a violet or a cloud, and admires or condemns as he finds an answering sentiment awakened in his soul. My object is to paint the appearance of Roman statuary objectively and afterward to speculate upon the emotions and pleasure that appearance is apt to excite in the human breast.

As you pass through the gate of St. John, on the approach to Rome from Naples, the first object of attraction is the group of colossal figures in stone surmounting, like storks, the lofty pediment of the church of St. John Lateran. Standing in every grand or animated attitude, they seem not only to attest that this is the Eternal City, but likewise, at its portal, to offer greeting in the name of that great company of statues which, amid the fluctuations of the human census, abides the true and undying population of Rome. It is, indeed, among these mute citizens that the stranger forms his most pleasing and cherished associations, to be remembered when other things in the Imperial City are forgotten.

On entering Rome itself, the visitor is greeted by thousands of statues, who, as representatives of the mighty past, hold out their hands to the present, and make the connecting link of centuries. Wherever you go in Rome, in streets, dwellings, churches, its gardens, its walks, its public squares, or its private grounds, on every hand statues abound, but by far the greatest assemblage of them is to be found in the Vatican. In that grand hall you will not only make new acquaintances, but will likewise revive many long before introduced by the historian. These are all well known by repute; they have been often described in the traveler's record and on the historic page; but the knowledge thus gained, however perfect the description may be, is poor and meager when compared with that gained by personal acquaintance. Here are ancient personages, the worthies of the glorious old days of the Empire and Republic. Histories and memoirs tell us of their achievements, whether on the field or in the forum, in public action or in the private walks of life; but here we find how they looked, and we learn them as we do living men. Here we find many deficiencies of the historian supplied by the sculptor, who has effected, in part, for the celebrities of old what the memoir writer of the present day does for modern ones; for to the sculptor belongs a task which was considered beneath the dignity of the historian.

In the expressive marble, Demosthenes, who is better known by statuary than by history, thus becomes a present existence. Standing face to face with the marble, one must say to himself, "This is he," so true has been the sculptor to his task. The strong arm, the muscular form, the large sinews, all bespeak the thunderer of Athens who hurled his powerful denunciations at Philip of Macedon; yet he resembles a modern advocate, face thin and haggard and his body lean. The arm that had gesticulated and swayed with its movement the souls of the Athenians has become small and shrunken. He looks as if a glorious course of idleness would be beneficial. Just so in the statue of Titus Vespasian, of whom we read a dim outline in Tacitus, stands mildly before us Titus himself. As the historian says, this Emperor was frank in his nature, and generous in his disposition. He has a short, thick figure and a round face, expressive of cheerfulness, good-humor, and joviality; and yet all know how different was his character from this outward seeming.

In the bust of Socrates is a kind of anomaly, for we see a countenance more like that of a bacchanal or the debauchee of a carnival than of a sober and decorous philosopher. At a first glance it reminds one much of the broad and rubicund phiz of an Irish comedian. It possesses in many respects the characteristics peculiar to the modern Hibernian. But a closer observer would see the simple-hearted, yet cool, sarcastic, ironical cast indicative of his true character.

The head of Julius Caesar fancy would paint as robust, grand, and noble; something that is elevated and commanding, typical of the warrior and statesman. But the statue gives a countenance of a businesslike cast that the present practical age would regard as a good representation of the President of the New York and Erie Railroad, or any other magnificent corporation. And such was the character of the man—practical, sound, grappling with the obstacles of the world like a giant.

In the bust of Seneca, whose philosophy would be Christianity itself save its authenticity, whose utterances so amazed one of the early fathers that he thought he must have corresponded with St. Paul, we see a face more like that of a disappointed pawnbroker, pinched and grieved. His semblance is just, according to the character of the *man*, though not of his *books*. For it was well known that he was avaricious and grasping, and dealt largely in mortgages and loans, and drove hard bargains even at that day. It is ironlike and inflexible, and would be no disgrace to a Wall Street broker.

Seeing the statue of Seneca's apostate pupil Nero at Naples, done in bronze, we can scarce realize that we are looking upon the face of the latter without finding something repulsive, half-demoniac in the expression. And yet the delicate features are only those of a genteelly dissipated youth, a fast and pleasant young man such as those we see in our own day, whom daily experience finds driving spanking teams and abounding on race-courses, with instincts and habits of his class, who would scarce be guilty of excessive cruelties.

The first view of Plato surprises one, being that of a Greek Grammont or Chesterfield. Engaged in the deep researches of philosophy as he was, we certainly should expect no fastidiousness in his appearance, neither a carefully adjusted toga or pomatumed hair. Yet such is the fact, for the long flowing locks of that aristocratic transcendentalist were as carefully parted as a modern belle's and his beard would have graced a Venetian exquisite. If this bust were true, he might have composed his works as if meditating on the destinies of the world under the hand of a hair-dresser or a modern *valet-de-chambre*, as Louis XIV mused over documents while he smelled his Cologne bottle.

Thus these statues confess and, as it were, prattle to us of much that does not appear in history and the written works of those they represent. This subject has been illustrated by instances taken from modern times with which we are all acquainted because in this way we best obtain a true knowledge of the appearance of the statues. They seem familiar and natural to us because the aspect of the human countenance is the same in all ages. If five thousand ancient Romans were mingled with a crowd of moderns in the Corso it would be difficult to distinguish the one from the other unless it were by a difference in dress. The same features—the same aspects—belong to us as belonged to them; the component parts of human character are the same now as then. And yet there was about all the Romans a heroic tone peculiar to ancient life. Their virtues were great and noble, and these virtues made them great and noble. They possessed a natural majesty that was not put on and taken off at pleasure, as was that of certain eastern monarchs when they put on or took off their garments of Tyrian dye. It is to be hoped that this is not wholly lost from the world, although the sense of earthly vanity inculcated by Christianity may have swallowed it up in humility.

Christianity has disenchanted many of the vague old rumors in reference to the ancients, so that we can now easily compare them with the moderns. The appearance of the statues, however, is often deceptive, and a true knowledge of their character is lost unless they are closely scrutinized. The arch dissembler Tiberius was handsome, refined, and even pensive in expression. "That Tiberius?" exclaimed a lady in our hearing. "He does not look so bad." Madam, thought I, if he had *looked* bad, he could not have been Tiberius. His statue has such a sad and musing air, so like Jerome in his cell, musing on the vanities of the world, that to some, not knowing for whom the statue was meant, it might convey the impression of a man broken by great afflictions, of so pathetic a cast is it. Yet a close analysis brings out all his sinister features, and a close study of the statue will develop the monster portrayed by the historian. For Tiberius was melancholy without pity, and sensitive without affection. He was, perhaps, the most wicked of men.

The statue which most of all in the Vatican excites the admiration of all visitors is the Apollo, the crowning glory, which stands alone in a little chapel, in the Belvidere court of the Vatican. Every visitor to Rome, immediately on his arrival, rushes to the chapel to behold the statue, and on his quitting the Eternal City, whether after a few weeks or many years, always makes a farewell visit to this same loadstone. Its very presence is overawing. Few speak, or even whisper, when they enter the cabinet where it stands. It is not a mere work of art that one gazes on, for there is a kind of divinity in it that lifts the imagination of the beholder above "things rank and gross in nature," and makes ordinary criticism impossible. If one were to try to convey some adequate notion, other than artistic, of a statue which so signally lifts the imaginations of men, he might hint that it gives a kind of visible response to that class of human aspirations of beauty and perfection that, according to Faith, cannot be truly gratified except in another world.

The statue seems to embody the attributes, physical and intellectual, which Milton bestowed on one of his angels, "Severe in youthful beauty." Milton's description of Zephon makes the angel an exact counterpart of the Apollo. He must have been inspired to a great degree by his recollections of this statue, once the idol of religion and now the idol of art; and the circumstance of his having passed a year in Italy might not be deemed unfortunate for England's great epic. In fact, the whole of that immortal poem, "Paradise Lost," is but a great Vatican done into verse. Milton must have gleaned from these representations of the great men or the gods of ancient Rome high ideas of the grand in form and bearing. Many of those ideas from heathen personages he afterwards appropriated to his celestials, just as the Pope's artist converted the old heathen Pantheon into a Christian church. Lucifer and his angels cast down from Heaven are thus taken from a group in a private palace at Padua, among the most wonderful works of statuary. This was sculptured out of a single solid block, five feet in height, by one of the later Italian artists. Three-score of the fallen lie wound together writhing and tortured, while, proud and sullen in the midst, is the nobler form of Satan, unbroken and defiant, his whole body breathing revenge and his attitude one never to submit or yield. The variety and power of the group cannot be surpassed.

Speaking of the Apollo reminds one of the Venus de Medici, although the one is at Rome and the other is at Florence. She is lovely, beautiful, but far less great than the Apollo, for her chief beauty is that of attitude. In the Venus the ideal and actual are blended, yet only representing nature in her perfection, a fair woman startled by some intrusion when leaving the bath. She is exceedingly refined, delicious in everything—no prude but a child of nature modest and unpretending. I have some authority for this statement, as one day from my mat in the Typee valley I saw a native maiden, in the precise attitude of the Venus, retreating with the grace of nature to a friendly covert. But still the Venus is of the earth, and the Apollo is divine. Should a match be made between them, the union would be like that of the sons of God with the daughters of men.

In a niche of the Vatican stands the Laocoön, the very semblance of a great and powerful man writhing with the inevitable destiny which he cannot throw off. Throes and pangs and struggles are given with a meaning that is not withheld. The hideous monsters embrace him in their mighty folds, and torture him with agonizing embraces. The Laocoön is grand and impressive, gaining half its significance from its symbolism—the fable that it represents; otherwise it would be no more than Paul Potter's "Bear Hunt" at Amsterdam. Thus the ideal statuary of Rome expresses the doubt and the dark groping of speculation in that age when the old mythology was passing away and men's minds had not yet reposed in the new faith. If the Apollo gives the perfect, and the Venus equally shows the beautiful, the Laocoön represents the tragic side of humanity and is the symbol of human misfortune.

Elsewhere in the Vatican is the Hall of Animals. In all the ancient statues representing animals there is a marked resemblance to those described in the book of Revelations. This class of Roman statuary and the pictures of the Apocalypse are nearly identical. But the ferocity in the appearance of some of these statues, such as the wolf and the slaughtered lamb, is compensated by the nature of others, like that of the goats at play around the sleeping shepherd. The quiet, gentle, and peaceful scenes of pastoral life are represented in some of the later of Roman statuary just as we find them described by that best of all pastoral poets, Wordsworth. The thought of many of these beautiful figures having been pleasing to the Romans at least persuades us that their violence as a conquering people did not engross them, and that the flame of kindness kindled in most men by nature was at no time in Roman breasts entirely stamped out. If we image the life that is in the statues and look at their more humane aspects, we shall not find that the old Roman, stern and hard-hearted as we generally imagine him, was entirely destitute of tenderness and compassion, for though the ancients were ignorant of the principles of Christianity there were in them the germs of its spirit.

Thus, when I stood in the Coliseum, its mountain-chains of ruins waving with foliage girdling me round, the solitude was great and vast like that of savage nature, just such as one experiences when shut up in some great green hollow of the Appenine range, hemmed in by towering cliffs on every side. But the imagination must rebuild it as it was of old; it must be repeopled with the terrific games of the gladiators, with the frantic leaps and dismal howls of the wild, bounding beasts, with the shrieks and cries of the excited spectators. Unless this is done, how can we appreciate the Gladiator? It was such a feeling of the artist that created it, and there must be such a feeling on the part of the visitor to view it and view it aright. And so, restoring the shattered arches and terraces, I repeopled them with all the statues from the Vatican, and in the turfy glen of the arena below I placed the Fighting Gladiator from the Louvre, confronting him with the dying one from the Capitol. And as in fancy I heard the ruffian huzzas for the first rebounded from the pitiless hiss for the last, I felt that more than one in that host I had evoked shared not its passions, and looked not coldly on the dying gladiator whose eyes gazed far away to

> "where his rude hut by the Danube lay,
> *There* were his young barbarians all at play."

Some hearts were there that felt the horror as keenly as any of us would have felt it. None but a gentle heart could have conceived the idea of the Dying Gladiator, and he was Christian in all but the name.

It is with varied feelings that one travels through the sepulchral vaults of the Vatican. The sculptured monuments of the early Christians show the change that had come over the Roman people with the joyous triumph of the new religion—quite unlike the somber mementoes of modern times. The statues are of various character: Hope faces Despair; Joy comes to the relief of Sorrow. The marbles alternate. On one side Rachel weeps for her children and will not be comforted while Job curses his maker; and then Rachel is seen drying her tears as Job rises above his afflictions and rejoices. But just as a guide hurries us through these scenes with his torch-light, bringing out one statue in bold relief while a hundred or more are hidden in the gloom, so must I do to keep within the limits of an hour.

In passing from the inside of the Vatican to the square in front, we find ourselves surrounded by the mighty colonnades with their statues, which overshadow the area like the wings of an army of Titans, and the great pile of confused architecture which is the outside of the Vatican. If one stands a hundred feet in front of St. Peter's and looks up, a vast and towering pile meets his view. High, high above are the beetling crags and precipices of masonry, and yet higher still above all this, up against the heaven, like a balloon, is the dome. The mind is carried away with the very vastness. But throughout the Vatican it is different. The mind, instead of being bewildered within itself, is drawn out by the symmetry and beauty of the forms it beholds.

But nearly the whole of Rome is itself a Vatican on a large scale—everywhere are fallen columns and sculptured fragments. These are of different and varied character. Remarkable, however, among all are the sculptured horses of Monte Cavallo, riderless and rearing, seeming like those of Elijah to soar to heaven. The most of these, it is true, were works of Greek artists, and yet the grand spirit of Roman life inspired them, for the marble horses seem to represent the fiery audaciousness of Roman power. The equestrian group of Castor and Pollux reining in their horses illustrates the expression of untamed docility, rather than conquered obedience, which ancient artists have given to the horse. From this can be deduced the enlarged humanity of that elder day, when man gave himself none of those upstart airs of superiority over the brute creation which he now assumes. A modern inscription attributes these famous animals to the chisels of Phidias and Praxiteles. There is no doubt that they are works of Grecian art, brought to Rome when the land in which they were sculptured had been conquered. The horse was idealized by the ancient artists as majestic next to man, and they loved to sculpture them as they did heroes and gods. To the Greeks nature had no brute. Everything was a being with a soul, and the horse idealized the second order of animals just as man did the first. This ideal and magnificent conception of the horse, which had raised that animal into a sort of divinity, is unrivaled in its sublime loftiness of attitude and force of execution. In truth, nothing even in the statues of gods could be more noble than the appearance of these horses. We see other instances of this same profound appreciation of the form of the horse in the sculpture on the frieze of the Parthenon, now in the British Museum.

Of other statues of large size much might be said. The Moses by Michelangelo appears like a stern, bullying genius of druidical superstition; that of Perseus at Florence would form a theme by itself. This statue, by Benvenuto Cellini, is another astonishing conception, conceived in the fiery brain of the intense artist and brought to perfection as a bronze cast in the midst of flames which had indeed overshot their aim. Another noble statue, conceived in a very different spirit, is the Farnese Hercules, leaning on his club, which in its simplicity and bovine good nature reminds us of cheerful and humane things and makes our hearts incline towards him. This statue is not of that quick, smart, energetic strength that we should suppose would appertain to the powerful Samson or the mighty Hercules; but rather of a character like that of the lazy ox, confident of his own strength but loth to use it. No trifles would call it forth; it is reserved only for great occasions. To rightfully appreciate this, or, in fact, any other statue, one must consider where they came from and under what circumstances they were formed. In other respects they reveal their own history.

Thus to understand the statues of the Vatican it is necessary to visit often the scenes where they once stood—the Coliseum, which throws its shade like a mighty thunder cloud, the gardens, the Forum, the aqueducts, the ruined temples—and remember all that has there taken place. I regret that the time will not allow me to speak more fully of these surroundings. But Roman statuary is by no means confined to the Vatican, or even to Rome itself. The villas around the city are filled with it, and, in those quiet retreats, we catch some of the last and best glimpses of the art. Here, where nature has been raised by culture and refinement into an almost human character, are found many of those trophies which have challenged the admiration of the world; here, where once exhaled sweets like the airs of Verona, now comes the deadly malaria, repelling from these ancient myrtles and orange groves. This reminds us that in a garden originated the dread sentence, Death—that it was amidst such perfumed grottoes, bowers, and walks that the guests of a Lucretia Borgia were welcomed to a feast, but received with a pall.

Many of these villas were built long years ago by men of the heathen school, for the express purpose of preserving these ancient works of art. The villas which were to shield and protect them have now crumbled, while most of the statues which were to be thus preserved still live on. Notable is the Villa Albani, built as it was by one who had made art and antiquity the study of his life, as a place to preserve the splendid works he had collected. Here are the remains of antiquity from Pompeii, and we might bring back the guests to the rooms where they sat at the feast on the eve of the fatal eruption of Vesuvius. It was not unusual for them at their feasts to talk upon the subject of death and other like mournful themes forbidden to modern ears at such scenes. Such topics were not considered irrelevant to the occasion, and instead of destroying the interest of the feast by their ill-timed intrusion, they rather added to it a temperate zest. One of the finest of the statues to be found in this villa is the Minerva, a creature as purely and serenely sublime as it is possible for human hands to form. Here also is to be found a medallion of Antinous with his eye reposing on a lotus of admirable design which he holds in his hand. In this villa is a bust of Æsop, the dwarfed and deformed, whose countenance is irradiated by a lambent gleam of irony such as plays round the pages of Goldsmith.

In conclusion, since we cannot mention all the different works, let us bring them together and speak of them as a whole. It will be noticed that statues, as a general thing, do not present the startling features and attitudes of men, but are rather of a tranquil, subdued air such as men have when under the influence of no passion. Not the least, perhaps, among those causes which make the Roman museums so impressive is this same air of tranquility. In chambers befitting stand the images of gods, while in the statues of men, even the vilest, what was corruptible in their originals here in pure marble puts on incorruption. They appeal to that portion of our being which is highest and noblest. To some they are a complete house of philosophy; to others they appeal only to the tenderer feelings and affections. All who behold the Apollo confess its glory; yet we know not to whom to attribute the glory of creating it. The chiseling them shows the genius of the creator—the preserving them shows the bounty of the good and the policy of the wise.

These marbles, the works of the dreamers and idealists of old, live on, leading and pointing to good. They are the works of visionaries and dreamers, but they are realizations of soul, the representations of the ideal. They are grand, beautiful, and true, and they speak with a voice that echoes through the ages. Governments have changed; empires have fallen; nations have passed away; but these mute marbles remain—the oracles of time, the perfection of art. They were formed by those who had yearnings for something better, and strove to attain it by embodiments in cold stone. We can ourselves judge with what success they have worked. How well in the Apollo is expressed the idea of the perfect man. Who could better it? Can art, not life, make the ideal?

Here, in statuary, was the Utopia of the ancients expressed. The Vatican itself is the index of the ancient world, just as the Washington Patent Office is of the modern. But how is it possible to compare the one with the other, when things that are so totally unlike cannot be brought together? What comparison could be instituted between a locomotive and the Apollo? Is it as grand an object as the Laocoön? To undervalue art is perhaps somewhat the custom now. The world has taken a practical turn, and we boast much of our progress, of our energy, of our scientific achievements—though science is beneath art, just as the instinct is beneath the reason. Do all our modern triumphs equal those of the heroes and divinities that stand there silent, the incarnation of grandeur and of beauty?

We moderns pride ourselves upon our superiority, but the claim can be questioned. We did invent the printing press, but from the ancients have we not all the best thought which it circulates, whether it be law, physics, or philosophy? As the Roman arch enters into and sustains our best architecture, does not the Roman spirit still animate and support whatever is soundest in societies and states? Or shall the scheme of Fourier supplant the code of Justinian? Only when the novels of Dickens shall silence the satires of Juvenal. The ancients of the ideal description, instead of trying to turn their impracticable chimeras, as does the modern dreamer, into social and political prodigies, deposited them in great works of art, which still live while states and constitutions have perished, bequeathing to posterity not shameful defects but triumphant successes. All the merchants in modern London have not enough in their coffers to reproduce the Apollo. If the Coliseum expresses the durability of Roman ideas, what does their Crystal Palace express? These buildings are exponents of the respective characters of ancients and moderns. But will the glass of the one bide the hail storms of eighteen centuries as well as the travertine of the other?

The deeds of the ancients were noble, and so are their arts; and as the one is kept alive in the memory of man by the glowing words of their own historians and poets, so should the memory of the other be kept green in the minds of men by the careful preservation of their noble statuary. The ancients live while these statues endure, and seem to breathe inspiration through the world, giving purpose, shape, and impetus to what was created high, or grand, or beautiful. Like the pillars of Rome itself, they are enduring illustrations of the perfection of ancient art.

> "While stands the Coliseum, Rome shall stand;
> When falls the Coliseum, Rome shall fall;
> And when Rome falls, the world."

The South Seas

THE SUBJECT OF OUR LECTURE this evening, "The South Seas," may be thought perhaps a theme if not ambitious, at least somewhat expansive, covering, according to the authorities, I am afraid to say how much of the earth's surface—in short, more than one-half. We have, therefore, a rather spacious field before us, and I hardly think we shall be able, in a thorough way, to go over the whole of it to-night.

And here (to do away with any erroneous anticipations as to our topic) I hope you do not expect me to repeat what has long been in print touching my own casual adventures in Polynesia. I propose to treat of matters of more general interest, and, in a random way, discuss the South Seas at large and under various aspects, introducing, as occasion may serve, any little incident, personal or other, fitted to illustrate the point in hand.

"South Seas" is simply an equivalent term for "Pacific Ocean." Then why not say "Pacific Ocean" at once?—Because one may have a lingering regard for certain old associations, linking the South Seas as a name with many pleasant and venerable books of voyages, full of well-remembered engravings.

To be sure those time-worn tomes are pretty nearly obsolete, but none the less are they, with the old name they enshrine, dear to the memory of their reader; in much the same way too that the old South Sea House in

London was dear to the heart of Charles Lamb.—Who that has read it can forget that quaint sketch, the introductory essay of Elia, where he speaks of the Balclutha-like desolation of those haunted old offices of the once famous South Sea Company—the old oaken wainscots hung with dusty maps of Mexico and soundings of the Bay of Panama—the vast cellarages under the whole pile where Mexican dollars and doubloons once lay heaped in huge bins for Mammon to solace his solitary heart withal?

But besides summoning up the memory of brave old books, Elia's fine sketch, and the great South Sea Bubble, originating in the institution there celebrated—the words "South Seas" are otherwise suggestive, yielding to the fancy an indefinable odor of sandalwood and cinnamon, more relishing of the old, antique exploring and buccaneering adventures of the fresh, imaginative days of voyaging in these waters. In the adventures of Captain Dampier (that eminent and excellent buccaneer) you read only of "South Seas." In Harris' old voyages, and many others, the title is the same, and even as late as 1803 we find that Admiral Burney prefers the old title to the new, "Pacific," which appellation has in the present century only become the popular one—notwithstanding which we occasionally find the good old name first bestowed still employed by writers of repute.

But since these famous waters lie on both sides of the Equator and wash the far northern shores of Kamchatka as well as the far southern ones of Tierra del Fuego, how did they ever come to be christened with such a misnomer as "*South* Seas"? The way it happened was this: The Isthmus of Darien runs not very far from east and west; if you stand upon its further shore the ocean will appear to the *south* of you, and were you ignorant of the general direction of the coastline you would infer that it rolled away wholly toward that quarter. Now Balboa, the first white man who laid eyes upon these waters, stood in just this position; drew just this inference and bestowed its name accordingly.

The circumstances of Balboa's discovery are not uninteresting. In the earliest days of the Spanish dominion on this continent, he commanded a petty post on the northern shore of the Isthmus, and hearing it rumored that there was a vast sea on the other side of the land—its beach not distant, but of difficult approach, owing to a range of steep mountain wall and other obstruction, he resolved to explore in that direction. His hardships may be imagined by recalling the narrative a few years since of the adventures of Lieut. Strain and party who in like manner with the Spaniard, undertook to cross from sea to sea, through the primeval wilderness. A party of buccaneers also likewise crossed the Isthmus under suffering, the utmost that nature is capable of sustaining. Balboa and the buccaneers, though not more courageous, were certainly more hardy or more fortunate than the American officer, since, after all they underwent, their efforts were at last successful.

The thronging Indians opposed Balboa's passage, demanding who he was, what he wanted, and whither he was going. The reply is a model of Spartan directness. "I am a Christian, my errand is to spread true religion and to seek gold, and I am going in search of the sea."

Coming at last to the foot of a mountain, he was told that from its summit he could see the object of his search. He ordered a halt, and, like Moses, the devout Spaniard "went up into the mountain alone." When he beheld the sea he fell upon his knees and thanked God for the sight. The next day with sword and target, wading up to his waist in its waters, he called upon his troop and the assembled Indians to bear witness that he took possession of that whole ocean with all the lands and kingdoms pertaining to it for his sovereign master the King of Castile and Leon. A large-minded gentleman, of great latitude of sentiment, was Vasco Nuñez de Balboa, commander of that petty post of Darien.

If we should take sail, and set out for Cape Horn, probably the longest voyage that can be made on this planet, we would encounter much foul weather, and be subjected to the cold water treatment in its fullest rigor. But having doubled the Cape and set sail for the North in the Pacific, we would be borne along by fair breezes that would send us skipping for joy, and in a short time would reach smooth seas and sunny skies, the air growing milder and more mild the further one goes north. The change during the run from Cape Horn to the Galapagos Islands is more telling than in going from New York to Cuba, where in one week you are whisked from icicles to oranges.

The European who first sailed upon those waters had this experience intensified. True, Magellan passed not round the yet undiscovered Horn, but through the straits which bear his name. But this only made the matter worse. For, in these straits, narrow, tortuous, and rockbound, dense fogs prevail and antarctic squalls, and the navigation is peculiarly dangerous. Magellan worked through, however, and when he beheld ahead a fine open ocean, by good fortune smooth and serene, in his excess of emotion he burst into tears, stout sailor as he was, and this was the man who gave to this sea its second name—Pacific.

Once, gliding through the tropics on the bosom of the Atlantic, the warm air and lulling calm made me say to myself, "Come, let us shut up the temple of Janus and dream"; and I thought that this ocean, rather than the South Seas, should have been named "Pacific." But the names were owing to first impressions, and the Pacific when introduced to the public happened to put its best foot foremost, being then in a happy humor. The great sea hence will forever be called Pacific, even by the sailor destined to perish in one of its terrible typhoons.

Although the Pacific covers half the surface of the planet, yet with all its dotted isles and people it remained almost unknown to even a recent period. Captain Cook's account of his visit to Tahiti could produce, as late as 1780, upon the English people almost the full thrill of novelty. Indeed, but little was known of the whole region till Cook's time. It was California that first brought the Pacific home to the great body of Anglo-Saxons. The discovery of gold in 1848, that memorable year, first opened the Pacific as a thoroughfare for American ships.

The world of waters here is so broad, covering, it is estimated, over a hundred millions of square miles, and its living races so various, that one is puzzled where to choose a topic from so vast a storehouse, upon which to expend the limited time of a single lecture. A haze of obscurity hangs over the Pacific even at the present day, and its geography is still but illy known. The ships which plough it for the most part go in established routes, and those vessels which leave these old roads continually run upon some island or cluster of islands unknown to the charts or to geographers. Even underwriters and shipping agents, if applied to about sailing to some of the islands in these seas, would not have a very distinct idea upon the subject. So with the student, also, and there is no full knowledge to be had of them anywhere. This, added to the immensity, makes one feel, in an attempt to speak of them, like embarking on a voyage to their far distant isles. But what is known, and well known, affords an abundant theme for a lecture.

We might tell of tribes of sharks that populate some parts of the Pacific as thickly as the celestials do the Chinese Empire, or we might introduce that gallant chevalier, the swordfish—a different fish from that of the same name found in our northern latitudes, being more daring, the Hector of the seas—and tell of his martial exploits; the tilts he runs at the great ships; the duels he fights with the whale—sometimes leaving his weapon in their ribs, or by withdrawing it, leaving an open wound in the mass of flesh or wood to the great peril of the craft and crew, as in the case of the English ship *Foxhound*.

We might tell of the devil-fish, over which a mystery hangs like that over the sea-serpent of North Atlantic waters. It is asserted by some mariners that he has horns and huge fins; and, sailors say, he dives to the profoundest abyss and comes up roaring with mouths as many and as wide open as the Mississippi. This I have not seen, but on one occasion, when off the coast of Patagonia early one evening, listening to a solemn ghost story from one of the crew of my vessel, we heard an awful roaring sound, something like a compromise between the snorting of a leviathan and the belching of a Vesuvius, and saw a bright train of light shoot along the water; the grizzled old boatswain, who was standing by, started and exclaimed, "There, that's a devil-fish!" On another occasion I saw, a few feet beneath the surface, a large, lazy, sleepy-looking object, and was told that that too was a devil-fish. I am surprised that Professor Agassiz, the great naturalist, does not pack his carpet-bag and betake himself to Nantucket, and from thence in a whaler to the South Seas, where he could find such a vast field for research!

We might speak particularly of the birds of those seas—the pelican, with his pouch stuffed with game like a sportsman's bag; the melancholy penguin standing on one spot all day with a fit of the blues; the man-of-war hawk, that fierce black bandit; and the storied albatross, with white and arching wing like an archangel's, his haughty beak curved like a scimeter. Yes, a whole hour might be spent in telling about either the fishes or the birds.

Furthermore, there are exceptional phenomena, such as the peculiar phosphoric aspect of the water sometimes. I have been in a whaleboat at midnight when, having lost the ship, we would keep steering through the lonely night for her, while the sea that weltered by us would present the pallid look of the face of a corpse, and lit by its spectral gleam we men in the boat showed to each other like so many weather-beaten ghosts. Then to mark Leviathan come wallowing along, dashing the pale sea into sparkling cascades of fire, showering it all over him till the monster would look like Milton's Satan, riding the flame billows of the infernal world. We might fill night after night with that fertile theme, the whaling voyage, and tell of the adventurous sailors, either on the blank face of the waters, where often for months together their ship floats lonely as the ark of Noah, or in their intercourse with the natives of coasts reached by few or none but themselves.

The islands, too, are an endless theme; thick as the stars in the Milky Way. No notion of their number can be gathered from a glance at the map, where the ink of one is run into that of another, blended together in a dark indistinctness. If not innumerable they are certainly unnumbered, as the name bestowed upon their swarming clusters—Polynesia—not inaptly hints. The most noted of these are the Sandwich and Society groups; the Friendly, Navigator, and Feejee clusters; the Pelew, Ladrone, Mulgrave, Kingsmills, and Radack chains—but there are more than Briareus could number on all his finger ends.

The popular notion, from the early vague accounts, imagines them to hold enameled plains, with groves of shadowing palms, watered by purling brooks and the country but little elevated. The reverse of this is true: bold rock-bound coasts—a beating surf—lofty and craggy cliffs, split here and there into deep inlets opening to the view deeper valleys parted by masses of emerald mountains sweeping seaward from an interior of lofty peaks.

But, would you get the best water view of a Polynesian island, select one with a natural breakwater of surf-beaten coral all around it, leaving within a smooth, circular canal, broad and deep, entrance to which is had through natural sea-gates. Lounging in a canoe, there is nothing more pleasant than to float along—especially where Boraborra and Tahaa, the glorious twins of the Society group, rear their lofty masses to the ever vernal heights, belted about by the same zone of reef—the reef itself being dotted with small islets perpetually thick and green with grass.

The virgin freshness of these unviolated wastes, the exemption of those far-off archipelagoes from the heat and dust of civilization, act sometimes as the last provocative to those jaded tourists to whom even Europe has become hackneyed, and who look upon the Parthenon and the Pyramids with a yawn.

Why don't the English yachters give up the prosy Mediterranean and sail out here? Any one who treats the natives fairly is just as safe as if he were on the Nile or Danube. But I am sorry to say we whites have a sad reputation among many of the Polynesians. The natives of these islands are naturally of a kindly and hospitable temper, but there has been implanted among them an almost instinctive hate of the white man. They esteem us, with rare exceptions, such as *some* of the missionaries, the most barbarous, treacherous, irreligious, and devilish creatures on the earth. This may of course be a mere prejudice of these unlettered savages, for have not our traders always treated them with brotherly affection? Who has ever heard of a vessel sustaining the honor of a Christian flag and the spirit of the Christian Gospel by opening its batteries in indiscriminate massacre upon some poor little village on the seaside—splattering the torn bamboo huts with blood and brains of women and children, defenseless and innocent?

New and strange islands are being continually discovered in the South Seas. And there are still others unknown and undiscovered, respecting which our charts are as guiltless as the maps of the world in Plato's time, when the Pillars of Hercules were the western verge of the orbit. There are many places where a man might make himself a sylvan retreat and for years, at least, live as much removed from the life of the great world as though its people dwelt upon another planet. This mantle of mystery long hid the Buccaneers, who plundered the Spanish commerce; and covered for years Christian, the mutineer of the *Bounty*, who, after a life of exile and immunity from European law, was found, bent with age, amid a thriving colony of half-breed children and grandchildren, whom his savage wives had reared for him amid ever-green woods, under ever-healthful skies, and through the plenty of perpetual harvests. Indeed, it is no difficult thing for a company of mutineers to bury themselves in the interior of one of these little worlds, and live undiscovered by navigators, who at most scarcely leave the beach if perchance they should land for fruit or water. Such colonies are sometimes found.

Then, too, there are some reformers who, despairing of civilizing Europe or America according to their rule, have projected establishments in the Pacific where they hope to find a fitting place for the good time coming. Shortly after the publication of "Typee," I myself was waited upon by a pale young man with poetic look, dulcet voice, and Armenian beard—a disciple of Fourier. He asked for information as to the prospects of a select party of seventy or eighty Fourierites emigrating to some of the South Sea islands, more particularly to the valley of Typee in the Marquesas. I replied that my old friends the Typees are undoubtedly good fellows, with strong points for admiration, and that their king is as faithful to his friend as to his bottle. These people have kind hearts and natural urbanity, and are gentlemen by nature; but they have their eccentricities, are quick to anger, and are eminently conservative—they would never tolerate any new-fangled notions of the social state. Sometimes they do not hesitate to put a human being out of the way without the benefit of a trial by jury. The kind way in which they treated my comrade and myself, I concluded, furnished little indication of how they would treat others, and hardly warranted the success of a larger expedition, who might be taken as invaders and possibly eaten.

A company of Free Lovers in Ohio has also proposed to go to the South Seas, and the Mormons of Salt Lake have likewise thought of these secluded islands upon which to increase and multiply—or this has been recommended to them, showing the drifting of imagination in that direction. So an acquaintance met in Italy, who had exhausted Jerusalem and Baalbec, and, like the man in the play, looked into Vesuvius and found "nothing in it," after an hour or two in conversation with me about the South Seas, started for an Italian port to sail for Rio en route to the Pacific; I hope that he has steered clear of the cannibals! The islands are admittedly good asylums—provided the natives do not object. But I can imagine the peril that a few ship-loads of Free Lovers would be in, on touching the Polynesian Isles. As for the plan suggested not long since, of making a home for the Mormons on some large island in Polynesia, where they could rear their pest houses and be at peace with their "institutions," the natives will resist their encroachments as did the Staten Islanders that of Quarantine. If sensible men wish to appropriate to themselves an uninhabited isle, that is all right, but I do not know of a populated island in the hundred millions of square miles embraced in the South Seas where these "fillibusterers" would not be imperatively and indignantly expelled by the natives.

While our visionaries have been looking to the South Seas as a sort of Elysium, the Polynesians themselves have not been without their dream, their ideal, their Utopia in the West. As Ponce de Leon hoped to find in Florida the fountain of perpetual youth, so the mystic Kamapiikai left the western shore of the island of Hawaii, where he suffered with his restless philosophy, hoping to find the joy-giving fountain and the people like to the gods. Thus he sailed after the sinking sun, and, like all who go to Paradise, has not yet returned to cheer mankind with his discoveries.

Another strange quest was that of Alvaro Mendaña, a bold Spanish captain, who stirred up such enthusiasm among the courtly Dons and Donnas of his time that many of them joined his expedition, in which he was sure he would find the Phoenician Ophir of King Hiram and bring from it more than the treasure stores with which Solomon had beautified his temple. After months and months of voyaging with hope deferred, the mines of Mammon were not found, and the poor Captain, dying, was buried in the solitude of an unfathomed sea. His followers returned to Peru, strongly impressed with the truth of those words of the Hebrew king, "Vanity of vanities; all is vanity." A group of the isles was called Solomon's in commemoration of the event.

There are two places in the world where men can most effectively disappear—the city of London and the South Seas. In cruising through the Pacific one frequently meets white men living as permanent residents, and others hope to return there some day. Many of the sailors who are supposed to be lost are thus really alive on islands of this ocean, though others, of course, lie in graves upon land or else have been eaten by the fish of the sea. It was my fortune on one occasion, after five months of weary navigation out of sight of land, to go ashore upon a secluded island in search of fruit. The pensive natives lay upon a bank, gazing listlessly, hardly turning on their mats at our landing, for they had seen white men before. And there, in that remote island, among its sixty or seventy lazy inhabitants, we found an American, settled down for life and to all appearances fully *naturalized*. He was scarcely imposing in his breech cloth and the scanty shreds of tappa which hung from his shoulders as signals of distress, which, it appeared to us, the assiduous dilligence of three wives—for the ill-clothed gentleman was blessed with that number—might have remedied. In conversation this virtuous exile from civilization manifested no ordinary intelligence. He stated that he had fulfilled the post of Professor of Moral Philosophy in some college in his own land whose name he wisely withheld; he was now, however, contented to lead a quiet and lazy life, apart from the walks of restless ambition.

The modes in which seamen disappear in the South Seas are various and singular. Some fall overboard, some are left on shore by unprincipled captains, some are killed in brawls, and so on. Some join that class of adventurers known as the "beachcombers," who infest the shores of the Pacific. This cognomen is derived from the fact that they hover upon the beaches and seem always upon the point of embarking or disembarking, being ready for anything—for a war in Peru, a whaling voyage, or to marry a Polynesian princess. They were among the first in California in the gold times, and afforded subjects for strange newspaper stories. They were also the occasion, as much as anything, of the Vigilance Committee there.

I have met many an old sailor in the South Seas not sufficiently educated to write who could tell tales about these regions stranger far than any that have ever yet been written. "Typee" and "Omoo" give scarcely a full idea of them except, perhaps, that part which tells of the long captivity in the valley of Typee. Had I time I should particularly like to repeat a traditional Polynesian legend, peculiarly adapted to the ladies of my audience, for it is a love legend of Kamekamehaha, Tahiti, and

Otaheite, that was told by a king of one of these islands, and which has much of the grace, strangeness, and audacity of the Grecian fables.

Some of these strange characters I have met exhibit sure vouchers of their stories in the shape of tattooing upon their persons. Many of them present such a horrid fright that they will never be caught showing their faces on Broadway! The custom of tattooing is prompted by religion, love of novelty, and various other causes. Many of the natives think it is necessary for their eternal welfare, and, unless a man submits to be tattooed, he is looked upon as damned. In their opinion I may now be in peril, for I stoutly resisted the importunities of the native artists to be naturalized by marks on my face as from a gridiron.

Different islanders have a different style of tattooing, so that one can often tell from this to what island a native belongs. The tattooing of the New Zealander and the Tahitian are thus as different as some styles of painting differ. A New Zealander presents a horrifying picture, but some of the Marquesan natives have a pleasant appearance. I have seen among them as graceful a young girl's foot and as delicately-turned ankle as those of the Grecian girls whose duplicate statues adorn the galleries of Europe. The men, too, have splendid figures, with symmetrical and columnar legs.

Tattooing is sometimes, like dress, an index of character, to be worn as an ornament which will never wear off, and which can not be pawned, lost, or stolen. Thus in the Georgian Isles the dandies wear stripes up and down their legs like pantaloons, and the dames have characters on their skins for jewelry—on their fingers, about their necks, and so on. Indeed, that style has many advantages for nuptial rings, since it can never be removed. Some of the robust islanders have tattooing of military insignia, others of eatables, and others of school-boy trinkets; and all reveal the character of the individual who wears them.

I would direct the gas to be turned down, and repeat in a whisper the mysterious rites of the "taboo," but the relation would so far transcend any of Mrs. Radcliffe's stories in the element of the horrible that I would not willingly afflict any one with its needless recital.

By contrast, the modern progress in some of these islands is seen in the publication there of newspapers; but on close inspection I have often found them to be conducted by Americans, English, or French. I have recently met with a Honolulu paper, the Honolulu "Advertiser," which is a mark of the prosperity of the Sandwich Islands, being almost a counterpart of the London "Times" with its advertisements, arrivals and departures of vessels, and so on—and that, too, where not long since the inhabitants were cannibals. But now Americans and other foreigners are there, and lately a suggestion has been reported to abolish the Hawaiian language in their schools and exclude those children who speak it. I threw down the paper on reading this, exclaiming, "Are they to give up all that binds them together as a nation or race—their language? Then are they indeed blotted out as a people." So the result of civilization, at the Sandwich Islands and elsewhere, is found productive to the civilizers, destructive to the civilizees. It is said to be compensation—a very philosophical word; but it appears to be very much on the principle of the old game, "You lose, I win": good philosophy for the winner.

The future prospects of Polynesia are uncertain and will only admit of fanciful speculation. Projects have recently been set on foot for annexing Hawaii and the Georgian Islands to the United States, and meanwhile the whalemen of Nantucket and the Westward ho! of California are every day getting them more and more annexed. I shall close with the earnest wish that adventurers from our soil and from the lands of Europe will abstain from those brutal and cruel vices which disgust even savages with our manners, while they turn an earthly paradise into a pandemonium. As a philanthropist in general, and a friend to the Polynesians in particular, I hope that these Edens of the South Seas, blessed with fertile soils and peopled with happy natives, many being yet uncontaminated by the contact of civilization, will long remain unspoiled in their simplicity, beauty, and purity. And as for annexation, I beg to offer up an earnest prayer—and I entreat all present and all Christians to join me in it—that the banns of that union should be forbidden until *we* have found for ourselves a civilization morally, mentally, and physically higher than one which has culminated in almshouses, prisons, and hospitals.

Traveling

Its Pleasures, Pains, and Profits

IN THE ISOLATED CLUSTER OF MOUNTAINS called Greylock, there lies a deep valley named The Hopper, which is a huge sort of verdant dungeon among the hills. Suppose a person should be born there, and know nothing of what lay beyond, and should after a time ascend the mountain, with what delight would he view the landscape from the summit! The novel objects spread out before him would bewilder and enchant him. Now it is in this very kind of experience that the prime pleasure of travel consists. Every man's home is in a certain sense a "Hopper," which however fair and sheltered, shuts him in from the outer world. Books of travel do not satisfy; they only stimulate the desire to see. To be a good traveler, and derive from travel real enjoyment, there are several requisites. One must be young, care-free, and gifted with geniality and imagination, for if without these last he may as well stay at home. Then, if from the North, his first landing should be on a fine day, in a tropical climate, with palm trees and gaily dressed natives in view, and he will have the full pleasure of novelty. If without the above qualities, and of a somewhat sour nature besides, he might be set down even in Paradise and have no enjoyment, for joy is for the joyous nature. To be a good lounger,—that is essential, for the traveler can derive pleasure and instruction from the long galleries of pictures, the magnificent squares, the cathedrals, and other places that require leisurely survey, only through this quality. The pleasure of leaving home, care-free, with no concern but to enjoy, has also as a pendant the pleasure of coming back to the old hearthstone, the home to which, however traveled, the heart still fondly turns, ignoring the burden of its anxieties and cares.

One must not anticipate unalloyed pleasure. Pleasure, pain, and profit are all to be received from travel. As Washington Irving has remarked, the sea-voyage, with its excitements, its discomforts, and its enforced self-discipline, is a good preparation for foreign travel. The minute discomforts, the afflictions of Egypt and Italy, in the shape of fleas and other insects, we will pass over lightly, though they by no means pass lightly over the traveler. A great grievance from first to last is the passport. You soon learn by official demands, what becomes to you an adage,—Open passport, open purse; and its endless crosses at the close of your travels remind you of the crosses it has cost you all the way through. The persecutions and extortions of guides, not only the rough and robber-like, but those who combine the most finished politeness with the most delicate knavery, are another serious drawback on your pleasure, though when we think of the thousand times worse extortions practised on the immigrants here, we acknowledge Europe does not hold all the rogues. There is one infallible method of escape from this annoyance: full pockets. Pay the rascals, laugh at them, and escape. Honest and humane men are also to be found, but not in an overwhelming majority.

For the profit of travel: in the first place, you get rid of a *few* prejudices. The native of Norway who goes to Naples finds the climate so delicious as almost to counterbalance the miseries of government. The Spanish matador, who devoutly believes in the proverb, "Cruel as a Turk," goes to Turkey, sees that people are kind to all animals; sees docile horses, never balky, gentle, obedient, exceedingly intelligent, yet *never beaten;* and comes home to his bull-fights with a very different impression of his own humanity. The stock-broker goes to Thessalonica and finds infidels more honest than Christians; the teetotaller finds a country in France where all drink and no one gets drunk; the prejudiced against color finds several hundred millions of people of all shades of color, and all degrees of intellect, rank, and social worth, generals, judges, priests, and kings, and learns to give up his foolish prejudice.

Travel liberalizes us also in minor points. Our notions of dress become much modified, and comfort is studied far more than formerly. The beard also, of late years, from our traveled experience, is admitted to its rightful degree of favor. In the adornment of our houses, frescoes have taken the place of dead white. God is liberal of color; so should man be.

Travel to a large and generous nature is as a new birth. Its legitimate tendency is to teach profound personal humility, while it enlarges the sphere of comprehensive benevolence till it includes the whole human race.

Among minor benefits is that of seeing for one's self all striking natural or artificial objects, for every individual sees differently according to his idiosyncrasies. One may perhaps acquire the justest of all views by reading and comparing all writers of travels. Great men do this, and yet yearn to travel. Richter longed to behold the sea. Schiller thought so earnestly of travel that it filled his dreams with sights of other lands. Dr. Johnson had the same longing, with exaggerated ideas of the distinction to be reflected from it. It is important to be something of a linguist to travel to advantage; at least to speak French fluently. In the Levant, where all nations congregate, unpretending people speak half a dozen languages, and a person who thought himself well educated at home is often abashed at his ignorance there.

It is proposed to have steam communication direct between New York and some Mediterranean port. Then the traveler would enter the old world by the main portal, instead of as now, through a side door.

England, France, the Mediterranean,—it is needless to dwell on their attractions. But as travel indicates change and novelty, and change and novelty are often essential to healthy life, let a narrower range not deter us. A trip to Florida will open a large field of pleasant and instructive enjoyment. Go even to Nahant, if you can go no farther—*that* is travel. To an invalid it is travel, that is, change, to go to other rooms in the house. The sight of novel objects, the acquirement of novel ideas, the breaking up of old prejudices, the enlargement of heart and mind,—are the proper fruit of rightly undertaken travel.

ATTRIBUTED PIECES

The Death Craft

A CALM PREVAILED over the waters. The ocean lay gently heaving in long, regular undulations like the bosom of Beauty in slumbers. Pouring forth a heat only known in torrid climes, the sun rode the firmament like some firey messenger of ill. No cloud disturbed the serenity of the heavens, which of the palest blue seemed withered of their brilliancy by the scorching influence of his rays. A silence, no where to be experienced but at sea, and which seemed preliminary to some horrible convulsion of nature, hushed the universal waste.

I stood upon our ship's forecastle. The heavy stillness lay upon my soul with the weight of death. I gazed aloft; the sails hung idly from the yards, ever and anon flapping their broad surfaces against the masts. Their snowy whiteness dazzled my eyes.

The heat grew more intense; drops of tar fell heavily from the rigging, the pitch oozed slowly forth from the seams of the ship, the stays relaxed, and the planks under my feet were like glowing bricks.

I cast my eyes over the deck: it was deserted. The officers had retired into the cuddy, and the crew worn out with the busy watches of the preceding night were slumbering below.

* * * * *

My senses ached; a sharp ringing sound was in my ears—my eyes felt as though coals of fire were in their sockets—vivid lightnings seemed darting through my veins—a feeling of unutterable misery was upon me. I lifted up my hand, and prayed the God of the Winds to send them over the bosom of the deep. Vain prayer! The sound of my voice pierced my brain, and reeling for a moment in agony I sank upon the deck.

I recovered; and rising with difficulty, tottered towards the cabin; as I passed under the helm my eyes fell upon the helmsman lying athwartships abaft the wheel.—The glazed eye, the distended jaw, the clammy hand were not enough to assure my stupified senses. I stooped over the body—Oh God! It exhaled the odour of the dead—and there, banqueting on the putrifying corpse, were the crawling denizens of the tomb! I watched their loathsome motions; the spell was upon me—I could not shut out the horrid vision: I saw them devour, Oh God! how greedily! their human meal!

A heavy hand was laid upon my shoulder—a loud laugh rung in my ear, it was the Mate. "See, see!"—"THE DEATH CRAFT!" He sprang away from me with one giant bound, and with a long, long shriek, that even now haunts me, wildly flung himself into the sea.

Great God! there she lay, covered with barnacles, the formation of years—her sails unbent—a blood-red flag streaming from her mast-head—at her jib-boom-end hanging suspended by its long, dark hair, a human head covered with congelated gore and firmly griping between its teeth a rusty cutlass! Her yards were painted black, and at each of their arms hung dangling a human skeleton, whiter than polished ivory and glistening in the fierce rays of the sun!

I shrieked aloud: "Blast—blast my vision, Oh God! Blast it ere I rave;" —I buried my face in my hands—I pressed them wildly against my eyes;—for a moment I was calm—I had been wandering—it was some awful dream. I looked up,—the ghastly appendage at the jib-boom seemed fixing its ghastly eye-balls on me—each chalky remnant of mortality seemed beckoning me toward it! I fancied them clutching me in their wild embrace—I saw them begin their infernal orgies;—the flesh crisped upon my fingers, my heart grew icy cold, and faint with terror and despair, I lay prostrate on the deck.

How long that trance endured, I know not; but at length I revived. The wind howled angrily around me; the thunder boomed over the surface of the deep; the rain fell in torrents, and the lightning, as it flashed along the sky, showed the full horrors of the storm. Wave after wave came thundering against the ship's counter over which I lay, and flung themselves in showering seas over our devoted barque. Sailors were continually hurrying by me; in vain I implored them to carry me below, they heard me not. Some were aloft taking in sail—four were on the main-top-gallant-yard-arm—a squall quick as lightning struck the vessel, took her all aback, whipping the canvass into ribbands, and with a loud crash sending overboard the mainmast. I heard the shrieks of those dying wretches, saw them clinging for a moment to the spar, then struggling for an instant with the waters, when an enormous wave bounding towards them, with its milk-white crest tossed high in the air, obscured them from my view. They were seen no more; they fed the finny tribes.

The ship with her hull high out of the water, her bowsprit almost perpendicular, and her taffrail wholly immersed in the sea, drove for a moment stern-foremost through the waters, when the wind shifting in an instant to the starboard quarter she made a tremendous lurch to port and lay trembling on her beam-ends. That moment decided our fate.

"Keep her before the wind!" thundered the Captain.

"Aye, aye, Sir!"

And docile as the managed steed she swerved aside, and once more sent the spray heaving from her bows! 'Twas an awful hour. Had the ship hesitated a second—aye, the fraction of one, in obeying her helm she would have gone to fill the rapacious maw of the deep. As it was, with her larboard side encumbered with the wreck of the mainmast, her coursers rent into a thousand tatters, her sheets and clew lines flying in the wind which ran whistling and roaring through her rigging, she seemed rushing forward to swift destruction.

I looked forward; in the chains were stationed men standing by to part the lanyards; while with axe uplifted stood an aged seaman prepared at an instant's warning to cut away the foremast.

"Cut away!" vociferated the skipper. The axe descended with the speed of thought—the shroud sprang violently up, till the lofty mast, yielding like some tall hemlock to the woodsman, fell heavily by the board.—The ship eased; still driving with fearful velocity before the wind. "Where's the Mate?" hoarsely inquired the Captain. No one answered, no one knew, but *me*. At that moment I lay clinging to one of the spare yards that were lashed around the deck. With a preternatural effort, I raised myself, and pointing to the foaming surface of the deep, I shrieked—"There—there!" The frightful apparition I had witnessed now flashed across my mind, and once more with the laugh of wild delirium I rolled upon the deck.

* * * * *

A gentle breeze lifted the locks from my brow; a delicious sensation thrilled through my veins; my eyes opened—the glorious main lay expanding before me, bright and beautiful and blue! I strove to speak: a rosy finger was laid upon my lips—a form as of an angel hovered over me. I yielded to the sweet injunction; a delightful languor stole over my senses; visions of heavenly beauty danced around me, and I peacefully slumbered.

* * * * *

Again I awoke; My God! did I dream? Was this my own fair room? Were these the scenes of my youth? No, no! They were far away across the bounding deep! The horrors I had witnessed had distracted my brain; I closed my eyes; I tried to regain my thoughts, to recollect myself. Once more the same sweet objects were before me—something flitted before me; two lovely eyes were upon me, and the fond young girl, whom twelve months ago, I had left a disconsolate bride lay weeping in my arms!

Harry the Reefer

On the Sea Serpent

I

PISCATORY SPORTS AT THE DOCKS.

Teg. Arrah! Looney, and is the Sae Sarpent slippery?
Looney. Faix, he is.
Teg. Then, be Jabers, I've cotched him!

2

$1,000 Reward

WE ARE HAPPY TO ANNOUNCE on behalf of the Postmaster General, that a reward of One thousand Dollars will be paid to any person who will procure him a private interview with the Sea-serpent, of Nahant notoriety. Mr. JOHNSON is convinced that an economical arrangement can be made with the Serpent, for the transmission of the European Mails from Boston to Halifax. He is the more anxious to effect this, from the universal satisfaction expressed at the advantageous conclusion of his negociation for the carriage of the mails between New York and Boston. The personage known to fame and to the Commercial Advertiser, as "the man who carries the long hose at fires" is supposed to be acquainted with the whereabouts of the Serpent, and his friends will confer a favor on the Department by calling his attention to this notice.

N. B.—A smart jockey of about twenty stone weight, wanted to superintend this line. One who can loan his employer between three and four thousand dollars without interest, to pay the balance of Mr. VANDERBILT's account, may hear of a permanent situation with a liberal salary. It is suggested, as no passenger will be carried by this line, and consequently no danger can result from explosions, that those who have had practice as engineers of steamboats and rail trains, will find it useless to apply for this situation.

On the Chinese Junk

I

Curious Exhibition

THE Chinese Junk, we understand, is to be exhibited this week at Barnum's Museum. After "indefatigable exertions," and at "an enormous expense," the enterprising manager of that laudable institution, has fitted up a large tank upon his premises, filled with water, on the surface of which the Junk will glide rapidly to and fro, its latteen sails filled full with the breeze of popular favor, while the Nahant Sea Serpent, engaged for this occasion only, will gracefully disport itself in a curious combination of circles, and at last, taking its tail in its mouth, conclude its performances by swallowing itself entirely, and disappearing to the eyes of the enraptured spectators.

N. B. The Chinese Junk is not, as has been currently reported, a junk of gingerbread.

2nd N. B. Yankee Doodle has consulted his lawyer and is now able to inform his readers, that although curiosities are bought and sold on board it, the vessel is not indictable, as has been supposed, as an unlicensed junk shop.

2

[*From* FIXED FACTS AND FACTS FIXED.

BEING THE CURRENT NEWS WITH YANKEE DOODLE'S COMMENTS.]

IN THE CHINESE SEAS the British have been spiking 870 guns in the forts of the Celestials, after which KEYING, the Chinese Commissioner—no relation to Keying the Chinese Junk now here—consented that an English church might be built wherein the outside barbarians might worship the Prince of Peace. YANKEE DOODLE suggests, that if the British should spike their own guns, the doctrines of Him who advocated Peace on Earth and good will to all men, would be much more likely to be effectually advanced.

3

THE CHINESE JUNK.

YANKEE DOODLE'S VISIT.

Yankee Doodle's Visit

Last Thursday, Yan-kee went with all his curious friends down to the Battery to see the famous far-fetched Junk, Key-ing. Yan-kee was much pleased to see the near approach of something Celestial to his countrymen, who like all mortal sinners, take so much pains to keep away from things heavenly, and in cordial good-heartedness greeted the great gathering. If there was any one thing more than another, that gave him particular pleasure, it was the affectionate entertainment of the swarthy pilgrims by his fair countrywomen, who hung over and thrust their arms and heads into, and felt about, the narrow closets where the Chinese kept their fleas, and pipes, and musty bedding, and their own oily, long tailed carcasses. It showed a warm and vigorous sympathy for the weary, toil-worn, home-sick stranger, that cannot be too highly commended. Yan-kee examined with much care and much interest the apparatus for navigating this curious craft. He clambered to the gallery across the bow, and surmounted the toppling poop-deck at the stern. He stumbled over slippery planks and useless cable, and curious dogs. He climbed up steps so short and close together that he was obliged to step on three or four at once. It is said this ship and appurtenances are just the same as those in use 2000 years since, and it is also said the Chinese have made no progress in civilization in that length of time. Query. If steps were two inches apart 2000 years ago, and are eight inches apart now, how long will it be before we can go *up stairs* without any? Yan-kee plunged into the cabins and bent his neck beneath some frightful beams, that crossed at intervals, elevated some three or four feet above the floor. He bruised his shins against sharp edges and angles of rough, carved, stone cushioned chairs. He caught his toe in the chain of an extremely slender monkey and flung himself on his face, prostrate, before the multi-armed idol, Ching-too. He periled his life in straggling through a crowd of needle-pointed, razor-edged rapiers and breechless carbines disporting themselves at the expense of numerous curious bipeds and bi-legs who suffered themselves to be horsed about by these death-dealing foreigners. When Yan-kee had become tired of these exciting "incidents of travel," he took a seat with the captain for a little conversation. Now the captain is as fine a fellow as ever walked; an Englishman, it is true, by birth, but a genuine cosmopolite, a universal spirit that finds a home and countrymen wherever man is found. Yan-kee could not help asking the captain why he had such a crooked mainmast?

"Oho!" said the captain, "they always make them so. They have a singular tradition about that. They say that after old KO-KA-POO, who built the first ship five thousand years ago, died, his spirit used to come every day at sundown and put his hat upon the top of the mainmast and sit there upon it till dark. He was a 'heavy dog,' and in time his weight made the mast crooked. In honor of KO-KA-POO they always get a crooked stick for the mainmast till this day."

YAN-KEE also wanted to know about the great man, CHANG-FOUE, or KE-SING, as he had heard some one call him.

"KE-SING," said the captain, "is a Mandarin at home. He is about as high in quality and rank as a Lord in England, or say as the President here."

"Ah, indeed!" said YAN-KEE, "but is not his highness sometimes troublesome? Does he not long for his country and its luxuries and make disturbance on ship board?"

"We easily settle that matter, good YAN-KEE. If he makes any noise or becomes impertinent, we just wring his nose a little or put his queue in a windlass and wind him up, and it's all right again very quick."

Just at this moment along came CHANG-FOUE himself. YAN-KEE motioned to him to take a seat with the captain and himself, and asked him what he thought of New York.

"Much watee—no good trees—plenty smokes," drawled out the Chinaman. Quoth YAN-KEE, "It's very warm here in this cabin."

"Ugh—iss—iss—" said the Celestial, "very warm—so muchee peoples—plenty Flun-kees come to junk."

YAN-KEE then desired to know how he liked this country so far.

"Um—um," whispered KE-SING from behind his fan. "Me like you Yan-kee!—me no like all these many Flun-kees," said the mandarin, looking anxiously around upon the crowd whose mingled breath rendered the air almost suffocating, "me no like Flun-kee."

While he was thus grumbling, a sun-burnt, bleached-haired, corpulent, quick-wit, from the State of Connecticut, with peacock plumes in his hand, bolted up to the Chinaman and shouted, "What's yer name?"—The Chinaman looked at him and muttered, "Flunk-kee—no like Flun-kee."

Jonathan not liking to be put off so, went at him again. "Are you a Chanyman?"

"Iss," said KE-SING.

"Where did you sail from?"

"London!" bellowed KE-SING, as loud as a Chinaman can roar, and covering his face with a fan, went out of the cabin.

"Humph," said Jonathan, "He a Chanyman!" and turned on his heel.

"Poor home-sick stranger!" said YAN-KEE as he left the Junk. "It is no wonder he don't like 'Flun-kees!' YAN-KEE DOODLE himself don't like Flun-kees."

4

THE CHINESE JUNK.

CHINESE METHOD OF HAULING UP THE STERN BOAT, ON THE ASSOCIATION PRINCIPLE OF COMBINED ACTION.

5

[*From* FIXED FACTS AND FACTS FIXED.

BEING THE CURRENT NEWS WITH YANKEE DOODLE'S COMMENTS.]

THE SEA WITCH has arrived in 81 days from China. No news of importance. The Junk Keying was 212 days. Although, we must allow the Chinese more of grace and beauty in their naval architecture, yet in a question of speed, it may not be presumptuous to claim a superiority for our own vessels.

"THE STRANGER'S GRAVE," BY GRATTAN, is still gaping wide for readers. It's an even bet now, whether the Grave or its readers gape the most.

A NEW COMET.—Another one of these very large sky rockets has lately been discovered from the Boston observatory—being the fifth, first seen from that position. Speeding hitherward from beyond, far beyond, the distant regions, amid which the planet Le Verrier in its immense orbit causes the far-off Georgian Sidus to oscillate with "a short, uneasy motion," it would be quite pleasant if the "long tailed stranger" would pass within hail, like the Chinamen, and answer a few questions—for instance, is Le Verrier a verity? and,

> What motive power is used in regions stellar,
> And what's thought there about the screw propeller?

6

[*From* FIXED FACTS AND FACTS FIXED.

BEING THE CURRENT NEWS WITH YANKEE DOODLE'S COMMENTS.]

A LATE FRENCH PAPER gives a list of articles most proper to be at the present time, exported to the Society Islands: in it are conspicuously inserted "Wines, Cordials, Absinthe, Beer, Cogniac; many colored calicoes and fashionable Parisian hats, with flowers and feathers," &c. We opine that in a few years these spirituous missionaries will have so civilized Tahiti and the neighboring isles, that there will be left no native heads to wear the hats, no aboriginal bodies to be covered with the calicoes.

"THE STRANGER'S GRAVE."—A correspondent says that "owing to our mention of this affair, he has had the curiosity to look into it; that it is really a pathetic thing, and that some passages made him feel very bad."

HE SING the Mandarin of the Chinese Junk has lately been proving that he *can* sing. He thus apostrophizes one of his wives,—

"O daughter of the great Chang Ching,
  Whose eyes with beauteous lustre glow;
Who took tea first, with your lord Hesing
  On the shady banks of the Hoang Ho!" &c.

7

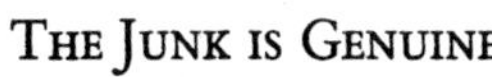

THE JUNK IS GENUINE

WANG TAOU, Emperor of the Celestials, and brother to the Constellation of the Great Bear, with the little star in his tail, to DOODLE, king of the Yankees; Greeting: light of twenty-nine stars and Uncle of Fun; this shall be presented to you by my faithful child, Hesing, of the famous Junk Keying, avouching that Keying is a genuine junk, and no fum, as we of the celestials say, neither is it a bam nor a hum, as you barbarians may call it. I could not order in time, the right moon for her to sail with therefore she will have a long voyage, perhaps two hundred days. But she is the genuine thing, my brother, and all the pig-tails are all that they look to be. I send you a little dog, without any hair, that you may know these things to be true: also a bowl of rat-tail soup, of the first water, to be handed to you by my faithful Hesing, Mandarin of the Red Button, (or as you would say, a true son of a gun.) Keying, take my word for it, is no flam.

*** In consequence of the many reports spread about as to the genuineness of the Junk, Keying, a careful search was instituted through the vessel for further documents and vouchers of her character, and just in the nick of time, as luck would have it, Mandarin Hesing, fished up yesterday, from the bottom of a chest, the foregoing authentic communication from the Emperor of China TAOU KWANG, which puts the character of the Junk at rest forever.

8

FAREWELL

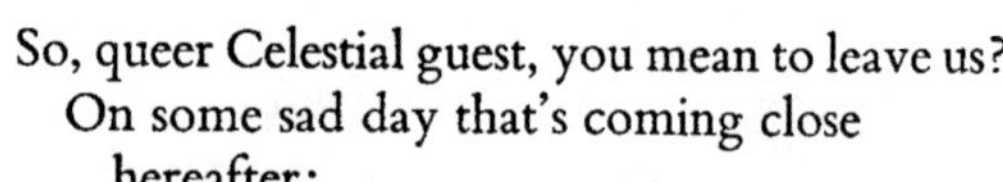

So, queer Celestial guest, you mean to leave us?
On some sad day that's coming close hereafter;
Ah me! *ami!* how can you thus bereave us
Of future chance to see so strange a craft, or
To wander thro' your decks, indulging wonder,
And prying deep with Yankiest curiosity,
Along your lockers, over, through and under,
O'er each antipodal Chinese monstrosity?
Or take away your multi-brachial Josh,
Which Yankees swear by, when they say "by gosh!"

How you contrived to get here, was a puzzle,
It *was*, I said, it *is*, and will be ever.
"Salt junk's" a tit-bit, in old Neptune's muzzle,
But I've been told, he tried to gorge you never;
Perhaps the reason was, he had no liking
To cats, rats, dogs, and so forth, in your cargo;
And when one thinks, there's nothing strange, nor striking,
That on your craft he puts a strong embargo!
He knew we Yankees in the humbug line,
Could swallow more than *forty* seas of brine.

For years and years, great actors, and great singers,
Great dancers on the rope, and other great jackasses,

Have thrust each day, their greedy foreign
fingers
Deep in the pockets, of our much gulled
masses.
But when, teak-timber'd, with your matted
sails on,
Thou, Junk! cam'st here with all thy curious
lumber,
And thy more curious crew, their heads with
tails on;
It was not strange that you increased the
number
Of Uncle Sam's bamboozled sons and
daughters,
Who like all things that come from cross the
waters.

9

Mr. Cave Johnson's New Method of Distributing the Mails

Cave Johnson has awakened to a sense of the inefficiency with which the operations of the Post Office department are conducted—and the inutility of the present contract-ed mode of carrying the mails. His late visit to this city, it is said was prompted by the desire to make an arrangement with the Magnetic Telegraph Co. to transmit the mails, the negotiation with the Chinese Junk having failed, from his not attending in person to urge its completion. The Telegraph Co. declined, we understand, on account of the weakness of their wires, but not until they had been assured by the worthy P. M. General, that at least one letter *per diem* from his pen would be added to the customary weight of each letter-bag. All his efforts to gratify the public and restore their confidence in the department having been thus signally unsuccessful, we are happy to announce that in a few days the P. M. General will introduce a novel plan for the transmission of the mails, by means whereof speed and promptness will be attained and the "big shooter" of Cap. Stockton made useful to the country, and practically worthy of its name "the peace maker."

10

The Opium War Revived

On Monday afternoon the great China war was re-opened at Castle Garden. The Chinese rose upon Capt. Killett (of the Junk) and made a ten-strike for wages. The pig-tails flew about with such activity that many people thought it was Cincinnati and not New-York; and it was the general opinion that the Chinamen had been indulging in rather strong opium that morning, for (with the co-operation of a number of MP's) it knocked them down all about the deck; and in consequence of their excessive indulgence these foreign gentlemen were unable to come to tea in the evening—having been carried as far as the Tombs, in the heat of the contest.

11

[*From* FIXED FACTS AND FACTS FIXED.

BEING THE CURRENT NEWS WITH YANKEE DOODLE'S COMMENTS.]

The Chinese Junk.—A gentleman on board the junk the other day, turning to his companion said, speaking of the Celestials, "I really do admire these strangers grave." Mr. Plunkett, who stood near, pressed his hand on his heart, bowed politely and said, "I am the author!"—"You their author! pardon me, their complexion—?" "Oh thereby hangs a tale."

"Yes, I see several of them—beautiful tails."

"You allude sir, I suppose, to the Stranger's Grave—a tale."

"No sir, I allude to those grave looking strangers with their tails."

"Excuse me, sir!"—exit Mr. P. in confusion.

12

Error Corrected

The people of the Chinese Junk, are not the same as the Junkers mentioned in Mrs. Hannah Adams' "History of Religious Sects." The Junkers at the Battery do not (as many suppose—who have seen them eying him with great attention) worship the little dog without hair: they only eat him, when he is well cooked. To a gentleman who dines constantly at Windust's and is curious in dishes, we cannot answer whether he is served with or without salt. Considering his playful turn during life, we suppose caper-sauce would not be far wrong.

13

YANKEE DOODLE PARTING WITH THE MANDARIN OF THE CHINESE JUNK.

Will You Go, Or Won't You?

In the fulfilment of our public functions, we bade a formal farewell to the Chinese Junk, week before last; in spite of which it still sticks close to Castle Garden; although every body thought it was off, a week ago, it has not yet even reached the offing. Yankee Doodle won't stand this kind of nonsense much longer. If you disregard this his last behest he will be compelled to adopt the most extreme measures; perhaps he may be obliged to cut off your pig-tails, and put you all on a full allowance of weak tea, from some of our retail groceries. How will you like that, ye slow-coach Junkers? A grave in this stranger land, distant from your native Ho-hang-ho! and all the glories of imperial Pe-kin. This you may count on, for the weak tea is pretty sure to be the death of you.

A Short Patent Sermon

According to Blair, the Rhetorician

NO. C.C.C.C.L.XXX.V.III

Text—"One wishy-washy, everlasting flood!"

Firstly, "*Introduction or Exordium.*" My hearers! allow me to introduce you to Dow Jr. of the Sunday Mercury; Dow Jr.! my hearers! Happy to make you acquainted!

Secondly, "*the Division of the Subject.*" The subject is divided into two parts. First—"wishy"; Second—"washy." The "everlasting flood" will not be considered, as it is a consequence of the "wishy-washy!"

Thirdly, "*Narration or Explication.*"

There was a man—his name was Dow—
  Who wrote a sermon rather clever!
'Twas liked! but vot's the consekwences now?
  He's going to write the like for ever!

Fourthly, "*The Reasoning or Arguments.*" A Sandwich Island lad who had been converted by the Missionaries of the A. B. O. C. O. F. M.—(the remainder of the alphabet is omitted, what is given means American Board of Commissioners for Foreign Missions,)—well! one day when this lad wrote a letter to his patrons, he ended each properly explained, opinional sentence, with the phrase "That idea's done!" A Sandwich Islander knows but little, but he does know when an idea is used up. But a Manhattan Islander doesn't know it—at least Dow Jr. doesn't—therefore it is clear that a native of Owyhee, (or Hawaii, as it is now-a-days spelt—*fonography* probably,) is a more clever man than the Manhattanese.

Fifthly, "The Pathetic part."

Dow's congregation always calmly sleeps,
  The tedious sermons of their preacher under,
  But after all, 'tis not a theme for wonder,
For, if a man such chronic pother keeps,
  It is not strange that folks get used to thunder!

Sixthly, "The Conclusion." Hence we conclude, with Hudibras, that when

"The pulpit-drum ecclesiastic
  Is beat with fist, instead of a stick"—

this, although the public may be a sheep, there will be a time, when even sheepskin is worn out, and can't bear "rapping on the head" any longer.

The New Planet

DEAR SIR:

I have observed, for several nights past, a strange light in the south-western quarter of the sky, inclining to the south. I find it laid down in none of the astronomical charts in my possession, nor am I able to fix it in any constellation or group. I recollect observing a similar appearance and pointing it out to Professor MITCHELL of the Cincinnati Observatory on his visit to this city last winter. He could make nothing of it. Perhaps you, who have the range of the sideral, as well as the terrestrial sphere, will be able to help me. Yours respectfully,

Prof. of Astronomy and Celestial Trigonometry,
Columbia College, N.Y.

To YANKEE DOODLE, Esq.

We have received communications of a similar tenor to the foregoing from several other quarters: among them, one from a distinguished scientific gentleman at Staten Island, who dwells upon the fluctuating and uncertain character of this light, "which," to use his own expressive language, "seems to be all up one minute and all down the next." A letter has, also, just come to hand from a farmer, living at Hackensack,

New Jersey, who describes a similar light, as flooding the neighborhood where he lives, shining, he says, from the direction of New York city, and bewildering, with its sudden and dazzling glare, the cattle in the fields. He speaks of having lost a fine heifer, engulphed in a morass, by attempting to follow its will-o'-the-wisp shiftings; also of the narrow escape of a neighbor's son, at Sekokus, who lost his foothold on a bridge, gaping at it. These communications all close with a request that YANKEE DOODLE will enlighten them as to the character of this new planet. In answer, YANKEE DOODLE suggests, it must be THE BARNUM which shines, at about S. S. E. from the City Hall, just over the American Museum. It is unquestionably a most potential planet, and has presided over the birth of a great many wonderful and curious creatures. It was under this star, we think, that Mrs. JOYCE HEATH attained her 104th birth-day and came to be the nurse of General WASHINGTON. This was the natal star, also, we believe, of the Feejee Mermaid. It ruled for a time the destinies of General TOM THUMB, and now culminates powerfully, according to popular belief, in the direction of the Chinese Junk. Its place was first fixed by a Mr. BARNUM, an enterprising citizen of this city, and it appropriately bears his name.

We have observed that every Monday evening, during the session of the City Council, it wheels about, as by some magical influence, and blazes in at the southern window of the Hall, with great power.

We have learned from a subordinate in the Mayor's office, just arrived, that this course of proceeding on the part of THE BARNUM saves the city about five shillings weekly in candles, and that the City Aldermen regard Mr. BARNUM as a great public benefactor.

View of the Barnum Property

AN *interior* view of the American Museum, can only be obtained by the payment of twenty-five cents, BARNUM currency: but our artist, who has a wonderful facility in stereotyping, on wood, the comicalities of our public places of amusement, having paid the required sum, we present above an exact likeness of this celebrated storehouse of grotesqueries at a much less price; thus out-Barnuming BARNUM, by giving for a sixpence what the father of TOM THUMBS would have charged a quarter for.

YANKEE DOODLE has come to one conclusion. If the whole world of animated nature—human or brute—at any time produces a monstrosity or a wonder, she has but one object in view—to benefit BARNUM. BARNUM, under the happy influence of a tallow candle in some corner or other of Yankee land, was born sole heir to all her lean men, fat women, dwarfs, two-headed cows, amphibious sea-maidens, large-eyed owls, small-eyed mice, rabbit-eating anacondas, bugs, monkies and mummies. His domain extends even to the forest, and he claims exclusive right to all wooden legs lost, as estrays on the field of battle, and, as a matter of course, to the boots in which they are encased. We give an interior view of the Barnum Property, embracing a life-sized exhibition of the great Santa-Anna Boot, which has been brought on—by the loops by two able-bodied young negroes—direct from the seat of war.

Report of the Committee on Agriculture

TO MORGAN LEWIS, Esq., President of the Berkshire Agricultural Society.

The Committee appointed to award Premiums on Crops have attended to the duty assigned them, and beg leave, before making a special report of their doings, to premise that, in the prosecution of their duties, they have observed with the highest satisfaction, the manifestations of the spirit of improvements exhibited throughout the county. Frequently has their attention been attracted by the many new and commodious dwellings—by the new and well-filled barns,—by plantations of thriving trees,—and by the numerous, extensive and well cultivated fields of Corn. The contrast between the present appearance of many parts of the County, and that which they exhibited but a few years ago, must strike with admiration, every beholder, who has a mind capable of estimating the value of useful improvement, and show to all, most conclusively, that the efforts of this Society have not been in vain.

Swamps and quagmires, in which the only vegetable productions were alders and ferns, with a few cat-tails interspersed among them as decorations, are now covered with a carpet of herds-grass and clover, and afford exuberant crops of hay. The Committee would be sorry that any words of theirs should give rise to suspicion that they are deficient in the milk of human kindness, and they profess to have as great an aversion to strife as the most enthusiastic members of the Peace Society; yet they cannot withhold their approbation of the determination manifested by the proprietors of these swamps, to exterminate the tribes of insects and reptiles, which, for ought that we know to the contrary, had a life estate thereof from generation to generation, since the day when Noah, with his numerous family, emerged from the Ark.

The evidences of a growing taste for the cultivation of the various kinds of fruits to which our soil and climate is adapted, and the success which has crowned the efforts to improve the qualities, and increase the quantity of that sort of food which nourished our great progenitors in the garden of Eden, were witnessed by the Committee with much delight. While they have seen with pleasure the growing disposition among their agricultural brethren, to cultivate the apple, pear, peach and plum, they have also had the satisfaction of observing the extensive embellishments of our road-sides with forest trees, and trust that at no distant day their successors may record the fact that these embellishments are continuous from one end of the County to the other,—that the shades that beautify our villages, extend over hills that are now bleak with the winter's wind, or arid with the summer's sun. But a few days' attention annually, by each landholder, would consummate this desirable object, and we believe, that the results of no part of their labor would be viewed with more satisfaction.

Another material improvement, which came under the notice of the committee, and to which they allude with pleasure and approbation, is the superior construction of barns, by which not only the comfort of domestic animals is much increased, but greater conveniences for their care, and for the accumulation of manure are attained.

A description of all that the committee noticed during their tour, would extend this report much beyond its proper limits, but they cannot omit this opportunity to impress upon the minds of all their agricultural brethren, the importance of saving every ingredient that can be made to enter into the composition of that substance which renovates exhausted lands, and returns to the earth those particles which have been drawn from it by successive crops; thereby enabling Nature to reinvest herself in her beautiful attire, and to present to her admirers her annual tribute of Flowers and Fruits. The greatest pleasure may be taken by the philosopher and naturalist, (and the farmer *should* be both.) in contemplating that benign process by which ingredients the most offensive to the human senses, are converted into articles that gratify the most delicate taste, and pamper the most luxurious appetite.

The number of entries demanding the attention of your Committee, was one hundred and thirty-one. The crops were generally good, with the exception of Potatoes, which are an entire failure; and many of them were possessed of merit so nearly equal, as to make it a matter of no little difficulty to decide who should become the successful competitor. We award as follows:

[*The list of awards is omitted in the present edition*]

Before closing this report, the Committee would advert to a circumstance with which they have been impressed by their examination of the corn crop, hoping that it may induce their brother farmers to enter upon a course of experiments, which they believe would be attended with interesting results. It has been customary among farmers to select their seed corn from stalks of considerable height and magnitude, and as a consequence, varieties bearing these characteristics have been produced; the natural result of which, is an enormous drain upon the land, together with the increased hazard of the crop being overtaken by frost before arriving to maturity. The examination of the corn crop has convinced the committee that a gigantic stalk is not pre-requisite for a large ear, but that on the contrary, a greater number of ears of a given size can be produced per acre, with equal, if not greater facility, upon stalks of much less dimensions, thereby materially diminishing the hazard of the crop and the exhaustion of the soil.

All of which is respectfully submitted,

ROBERT MELVILL, *Chairman.*

Editorial Appendix

HISTORICAL NOTE
By Merton M. Sealts, Jr.

GENERAL NOTE ON THE TEXT
By the Editors

NOTES ON INDIVIDUAL PROSE PIECES
By the Editors

RELATED DOCUMENTS
By the Editors

THE FIRST of the four parts of this APPENDIX is a note on the composition, publication, reception, and later critical history of The Piazza Tales and Melville's other prose pieces written between 1839 and 1860. The second is a general note on the textual history of these writings and on the editorial principles of this Edition. The third consists of notes on the individual prose pieces. The notes on Melville's three lectures of 1857–60 record variant passages of the extant newspaper reports on which the reconstructed texts of the lectures are based. Notes on the other writings specify the copy-text, discuss certain problematical readings, list emendations, and report line-end hyphenation; where applicable, these notes also list substantive variants between a given copy-text and other authoritative versions and record alterations in those manuscripts which have survived. The fourth part offers reproductions of (1) Elizabeth Shaw Melville's lists of her husband's contributions to magazines, 1853–56; (2) his own manuscript notebook of lecture engagements, 1857–60; and (3) Amasa Delano's Narrative, Melville's source for "Benito Cereno."

The three editors of The Writings of Herman Melville, Harrison Hayford, Hershel Parker, and G. Thomas Tanselle, are responsible for the planning and textual policy of all fifteen volumes of the Edition. For preparation of certain volumes, involving uncollected and manuscript writings, other editors assume responsibility as stated in those volumes.

In the protracted preparation of this volume, beginning in 1965 under a contract with the United States Department of Health, Education, and Welfare, Office of Education, several editors took part.

Preliminary planning, which included drafts of the GENERAL NOTE ON THE TEXT, of the NOTES ON INDIVIDUAL PROSE PIECES, and of the RELATED DOCUMENTS, and selection of the ATTRIBUTED PIECES, was done by Merton M. Sealts, Jr., during his association with the Northwestern-Newberry Edition, 1965–78. The reading texts of Melville's lectures of 1857–60 and the accompanying notes are his work, based on versions originally prepared for his Melville as Lecturer (© 1957 by the President and Fellows of Harvard College) and used with the permission of its publisher, Harvard University Press; all other texts and textual notes in their present form are the responsibility of the Northwestern-Newberry editors. The HISTORICAL NOTE (© 1980, 1981 by Merton M. Sealts, Jr.) was completed by Mr. Sealts during *research leaves underwritten by the Research Committee of the Graduate School, University of Wisconsin—Madison, and typed by Jane Renneberg and Cynthia Townsend of the Department of English, University of Wisconsin—Madison.*

Subsequently, from 1979 through to its publication, Harrison Hayford assumed primary editorial responsibility for all aspects of the completion of the volume; G. Thomas Tanselle assumed auxiliary responsibility. Hershel Parker joined them in decisions insuring execution of uniform editorial policy. Alma A. MacDougall, the Editorial Coordinator, worked closely with them in all aspects of its preparation for the press. Assistance was rendered by Richard Colles Johnson, Bibliographical Associate; by Brian Higgins, Lynn Horth, and R. D. Madison, Editorial Associates; and by Robert C. Ryan and Donald Yannella, Manuscript Associates. For historical and textual verification, extensive research was carried out by the Contributing Scholars, Mary K. Bercaw and Patricia L. Ward, as well as by David E. Schoonover. Other members of the Melville edition staff also assisted materially, particularly in collating and intensive proofreading: Ronald Alcock, Michelle Bobier, Ralph Hayford, Virginia Heiserman, William Holzberger, Kermit Moyer, Eugene Perchak, Karleen Redle, Peter Roode, Jeff Rytell, Justine Smith, and Harriet Zucker.

Authorization to edit manuscript materials and to publish items and reproductions from the collections indicated below has been granted (1) by these descendants of Herman Melville: Mrs. W. G. Ambrose, Mr. William Binnian, Mr. E. Barton Chapin, Mr. Melville Chapin, Mrs. John F. Howe, Mrs. J. Kobacher, Mr. David Metcalf, and Mr. Paul Metcalf; (2) by permission of The Houghton Library, Harvard University (Melville Collection, Harvard College Library); (3) by courtesy of The Newberry Library, Chicago (Melville Collection, The Newberry Library); (4) by permission of The New York Public Library, Astor, Lenox and Tilden Foundations (Duyckinck Collection and Melville Family Papers, Gansevoort-Lansing Collection, Rare Books and Manuscripts Division). Additional illustrations from the collections of The University of Chicago Library and The Newberry Library are used by permission. The editors have also made use of books, newspapers, and periodicals in the collections of The American Antiquarian Society, The Berkshire Athenaeum, The John Hay Library of Brown University, The Memorial Library of The University of Wisconsin—Madison, Northwestern University Library, the Troy, New York, Public Library, and the Woodstock Theological Center, and consulted autograph manuscripts in the collection of the Pierpont Morgan Library. They are indebted for assistance and information to Rev. Henry Bertels, S.J., William H. Bond, Herbert Cahoon, Carolyn Jakeman, Deborah B. Kelley, Frederick J. and Joyce Deveau Kennedy, Denis J. Lesieur, Jean R. McNiece, Robert Newman, Martha E. Shaw, the late Stuart C. Sherman, Faye Simkin, and Lola Szladits.

Historical Note

IN THIS VOLUME of the Northwestern–Newberry Edition Herman Melville appears not as the author of book-length works but as a writer of shorter fiction, a contributor of critical reviews to the New York *Literary World*, a staff member of a short-lived humorous weekly called *Yankee Doodle*, and as a lyceum lecturer. Although some of the varied prose pieces reprinted here are now regarded as classics of nineteenth-century American literature, ranking with the finest tales and critical writings of Hawthorne and Poe, during Melville's own lifetime the majority remained uncollected in the pages of newspapers and magazines for which they were originally written. The exceptions are his three lectures, which were unpublished, and five pieces from *Putnam's Monthly Magazine* brought together in 1856 as *The Piazza Tales*, Melville's ninth book, with which the present volume begins.

The Piazza Tales was published by the New York firm of Dix & Edwards, established in 1855 when Joshua A. Dix and Arthur T. Edwards bought *Putnam's Monthly* from its founder, George Palmer Putnam, and also began issuing a general list of books. Melville had been contributing to the magazine since 1853, its first year of publication, and Putnam had agreed before its sale to bring out Melville's *Israel Potter* in book form following its serialization there in 1854–1855. With this precedent in mind, Melville proposed to Dix & Edwards in December of 1855, after the third and final installment of his "Benito Cereno" had appeared, that the new proprietors publish, as "Benito Cereno and Other Sketches," a book comprising his contributions other than *Israel Potter* that the magazine had carried up to that time. The firm agreed, and by mid-February of 1856 he had prepared his copy, writing "The Piazza" as an introductory piece and rechristening the volume as *The Piazza Tales*.

When Dix first received Melville's proposal for the projected book he consulted George William Curtis, his private editorial adviser, who voiced some reservations in recommending its acceptance. Although Melville "is a good name upon your list," Curtis wrote Dix on January 2, 1856,[1] he has in recent years "lost his prestige,—& I don't believe the Putnam stories will bring it up. But I suppose you can't lose by it." Curtis knew that Melville's more recent works lacked the popular appeal of *Typee, Omoo,* and *White-Jacket,* and that the critical and financial failure of *Pierre,* his seventh book, in 1852 had halted the almost yearly publication of book-length works that Melville had begun in 1846. The hostile reception given *Pierre* apparently foreclosed the possibility of placing a new manuscript with his usual American publishers, Harper & Brothers, when he carried it to New York in the spring of 1853. Later in that same year Melville began sending shorter prose pieces both to *Harper's New Monthly Magazine,* which the Harpers had established in 1850, and its younger rival, *Putnam's Monthly*. Between November of 1853 and December of 1855, when he proposed collecting his contributions to *Putnam's,* eleven pieces in addition to *Israel Potter* had appeared in the two magazines, either anonymously or under a pseudonym; three more would follow in 1856.

When Melville turned professionally to short fiction in 1853 he had the benefit not only of his experience as the author of seven books but also of an even longer foreground as a dedicated writer, extending back to his school days. His earliest surviving compositions were published in 1839, his twentieth year, before he first went to sea. After his return from the Pacific and the publication of *Typee* he wrote occasionally for the New

1. See the section on "Sources" at the end of this NOTE, where the documentation is explained; for further details concerning Melville's career during the period covered by this volume, see the corresponding NOTES in other volumes of the Northwestern-Newberry Edition. Quotations from Melville's letters follow the Davis–Gilman transcription (1960), retaining Melville's erratic spelling. All other documents are likewise quoted *literatim*.

York *Literary World* and served for a time on the staff of *Yankee Doodle*, a humorous weekly; a series of comic articles on General Zachary Taylor (1847) and a major critical essay, "Hawthorne and His Mosses" (1850), were his principal contributions to these periodicals. Along with these works, there are scenes and episodes in Melville's earlier books that anticipate his magazine pieces of 1853–56. An excellent example is "The Town-Ho's Story" in *Moby-Dick* (Ch. 54), which the Harpers printed in their magazine for October of 1851 by way of advertising his forthcoming book. As the late Robert S. Forsythe remarked of "The Town-Ho's Story," it is a "sailor's yarn" that is "not closely woven into the fabric" of *Moby-Dick,* so that "there is no awkwardness in its publication as an independent work; it is complete in itself."[2] When Melville began writing directly for the magazines after *Pierre* he was already well prepared to compose short fiction, although at an earlier time its relative brevity might have seemed a drawback. "You must have plenty of sea-room to tell the Truth in," he had characteristically asserted in "Hawthorne and His Mosses," composed while *Moby-Dick* was taking form. But by 1853, after the disaster of *Pierre,* the briefer compass of the magazine story, which demanded a lesser investment of psychic energy and permitted him the luxury of anonymity, must have seemed to Melville a positive relief.

All of Melville's shorter prose pieces from 1839 to 1860 that are known to survive have been brought together in this volume, beginning with those in *The Piazza Tales* and then continuing with the uncollected pieces arranged chronologically: the juvenilia of 1839, the periodical pieces of 1847–50, his uncollected contributions of 1853–56 to *Harper's* and *Putnam's Monthly,* and reconstructed texts of his unpublished lectures of 1857–60. The lectures, delivered over three winter seasons following Melville's return from a Mediterranean trip in 1857, are the immediate sequels of the last two volumes of prose that he himself published, *The Piazza Tales* of 1856 and *The Confidence-Man* of 1857; they mark the close of his career of professional authorship. Other items ascribed to Melville over the years which have the strongest claims for consideration as possible work of his pen are also collected here in a final section of "Attributed Pieces." Although Melville's shorter prose works brought him little recognition or return in his own day, such compositions as "Hawthorne and His

2. Robert S. Forsythe, "Herman Melville's 'The Town-Ho's Story,'" *Notes and Queries,* CLXVIII (May 4, 1935), 314.

Mosses," "Bartleby," "Benito Cereno," and "The Encantadas" have since come into their own as major literary achievements. Here they can be studied in the context of Melville's development as seen in the entire canon of his shorter prose written over a period of more than twenty years, from 1839 to 1860.

Juvenilia

In October of 1845, while negotiations were in progress for the publication of Melville's first book, *Typee* (1846), his brother Gansevoort Melville assured the English publisher John Murray that Herman "has never before written either book or pamphlet, and to the best of my belief has not even contributed to a magazine or newspaper." But in seeking to make the point that *Typee* was the work of "a mere novice in the art" rather than "a practised writer," Gansevoort Melville was forgetful if not actually disingenuous, for there is evidence that his brother "had written many a fugitive thing," like the young title character of *Pierre*, before undertaking his initial book. One of Herman Melville's teachers at the Albany Classical School in 1835, Charles E. West, long remembered his student's "love of English composition" and "deftness" in writing, and Melville himself, while teaching school in 1837, remarked in a letter that during the "few intervals of time" his duties afforded him he was occupying himself with "occasional writting"—the spelling is characteristic.

None of Melville's school compositions or other pieces of these years have been found. His first identified appearance in print took place in 1838 when the Albany *Microscope* published three of his letters as part of a running controversy over affairs of a local debating group, the Philo Logos Society;[3] if he contributed additional letters or other materials to any of the Albany papers they remain unidentified. In May of 1839 the weekly *Democratic Press* of Lansingburgh, a small New York town near Albany where Melville was then living with his mother, printed over the pseudonym "L.A.V." two "Fragments from a Writing Desk" which constitute his earliest known imaginative writing. Although manuscripts have not survived, there are clippings of the two pieces among the Melville papers, inscribed "By Herman Melville" in the hand of his wife, and internal evidence supports her attribution.

3. See *Letters*, pp. 7–16.

While at first glance the "Fragments" resemble much of the sentimental prose to be found in American magazines and gift books of their day, material which local newspapers often reprinted, closer inspection reveals a number of elements that anticipate Melville's later writing, especially his characteristic habit of abundant literary allusion. The bookishness of these early pieces is related more to independent reading than to his formal education, which was repeatedly interrupted during the hard times of the 1830's. From October of 1830 until October of 1831 he was enrolled in the Albany Academy; in 1835 he attended the Albany Classical School; from September of 1836 until March of 1837 he was again at the Albany Academy; and in November of 1838 he began studying surveying and engineering for two quarters at the Lansingburgh Academy. At intervals during these same years he tried supporting himself by a variety of occupations as clerk, farmhand, and schoolmaster before going to sea in June of 1839.

Dr. West recalled the young Melville as "a favorite pupil, not distinguished in mathematics, but very much so in the writing of 'themes' or 'compositions,' and fond of doing it, while the great majority of pupils dreaded it as a task and would shirk it when they could." While in Albany he joined the local Young Men's Association, which possessed a well-stocked library and encouraged its members to write essays, and he was active in several debating societies, including the Philo Logos. Notwithstanding his interest in reading, writing, and speaking and his service as a teacher, the young Melville was by no means proficient in spelling and punctuation, as his early correspondence makes strikingly plain. The newspaper text of the two "Fragments" displays the same weaknesses, though whether the author, the compositor, or the proofreader should chiefly be blamed is of course problematical.

Both the material and the manner of these newspaper sketches show Melville's familiarity with the writings of Byron and Moore, the *Arabian Nights*, and the teachings of Lord Chesterfield, that favorite of his father, whose standards of polite manners provided models for the self-assertive narrator of the first "Fragment." This piece offers only a series of static characterizations, beginning with the narrator portraying himself and continuing with his praise of three contrasting village belles. The action of the second "Fragment" involves the narrator with a mysterious messenger whom he follows to a luxurious villa; there he meets a voluptuous beauty, but to his horror she is revealed as both dumb and deaf. The archetypal patterns of this second sketch are apparent to those who know Melville's later writing: the young man of sensibility telling his own story of extraordinary adventure; the movement through space; the building up of suspense; the quest for the exotic woman, a figure who anticipates the enigmatic Yillah and Hautia of Melville's *Mardi* (1849) and the ambiguous Isabel of *Pierre*. Commentators disagree, however, about its intended tone. Does the reversal of expectations at the end express Melville's early formulation of "the concept that pursuit of the ideal is foredoomed to disillusionment and defeat," as William H. Gilman suggested, or is it, in the words of Leon Howard, merely a "narrative hoax" illustrating the "crude humor" of its young author?[4] Perhaps Melville was simply avoiding the challenge, or embarrassment, of depicting a romantic fulfillment beyond the scope of his own experience or the power of his limited narrative skill.

It is worth pointing out that what comes between the protagonist and the mute lady of the second sketch is their inability to find a basis for mutual communication—a problem to which Melville would return in his short stories of the 1850's such as "Bartleby" (1853) and "Benito Cereno" (1855). Another mute was to make his appearance in the opening chapter of *The Confidence-Man*; and in Melville's final prose work, *Billy Budd, Sailor*, left unfinished in 1891, the young Billy resorts to a blow of the fist when speech fails him at a critical moment. Melville's deep concern with expression and communication evidently began early in his career. "What doth it avail a man," he asked in one of his newspaper letters of 1838, "though he possess all the knowledge of a Locke or a Newton, if he know not how to communicate that knowledge[?]" In later years, after becoming a professional writer, he was to complain to friends that authors dare not be frank with their readers; even Shakespeare, he asserted in "Hawthorne and His Mosses," was obliged to tell truth "covertly, and by snatches."

The fact that the two "Fragments" are numbered may suggest that Melville and the Lansingburgh editor were projecting an extended series of contributions to the *Democratic Press*. If so, the plan was abandoned once arrangements were made for Melville's Liverpool voyage, which took the young schoolmaster away from Lansingburgh from June to October of

4. William H. Gilman, *Melville's Early Life and* REDBURN (New York: New York University Press, 1951), p. 120; Leon Howard, *Herman Melville: A Biography* (Berkeley and Los Angeles: University of California Press, 1951), p. 15.

1839. If "L.A.V." wrote anything more for the paper, as he may have done before or after the "Fragments" were printed there, it was under some other pen name—perhaps that of "Harry the Reefer," the signature appended to "The Death Craft," a short tale of terror in the Gothic vein which appeared in the issue of November 16, 1839. The subject of a haunted ship, handled with Gothic touches, was familiar in American writing of the 1830's and 1840's, such as Poe's "MS. Found in a Bottle" (1833), John W. Gould's "The Haunted Brig," first published in 1834 and reprinted in 1839, or the title-piece of *The Haunted Barque and Other Poems* (1848) by E. Curtis Hine, a shipmate of Melville in 1843 and 1844 and the likely original of Lemsford the poet in *White-Jacket* (1850). Although Melville's conjectural authorship of "The Death Craft" struck Gilman as "possible but unlikely," other scholars including Howard, Jay Leyda, and Martin Leonard Pops have been inclined to accept the story as his.[5] There is no external evidence, it is true, to link it with Melville, but the subject matter would have been congenial to an amateur writer just returned from his first ocean voyage, and internal evidence, although not conclusive, is provocative enough to justify reprinting "The Death Craft" in this volume among other attributed but unauthenticated writings, and so making it readily available for further study.

1846–1850

Melville's next group of shorter prose pieces, his contributions to the *Literary World* and *Yankee Doodle*, were composed during his years in New York between 1847 and 1850—after the success of *Typee* had opened the possibility of a literary career and before his removal to Pittsfield in the course of writing *Moby-Dick*. Even earlier, while still living at his mother's home in Lansingburgh, he had drafted a projected newspaper article in defense of *Typee*, written in response to an "obnoxious" review of the book in the *Morning Courier and New-York Enquirer* of April 17, 1846. The article, apparently suggested to Melville by Alexander Bradford, a family friend, has not been located and may not have been published, but

5. Gilman, *Melville's Early Life and* REDBURN, p. 327, n. 84; Howard, *Herman Melville: A Biography*, p. 29; Jay Leyda, *The Melville Log*, I, 97–98; Martin Leonard Pops, *The Melville Archetype* (Kent, Ohio: Kent State University Press, 1970), pp. 264, n. 35, and 256–60.

Melville's letter of May 23 to Bradford indicates the spirit in which he approached it.

> I have endeavored to make it appear as if written by one who had read the book & beleived it—& morover—had been as much pleased with it as most people who read it profess to be. Perhaps, it may not be exactly the right sort of thing. The fact is, it was rather an awkward undertaking any way—for I have not sought to present my own view of the matter (which you may be sure is straitforward enough) but have only presented such considerations as would be apt to suggest themselves to a reader who was acquainted with, & felt freindly toward the author.—Indeed, I have moddled some of my remarks upon hints suggested by some reviews of the book.

In a postscript Melville went on to ask Bradford to "make any alterations you see fit in the accompanying document," since he himself was "wholly unused to this sort of work." For all Melville's disclaimer, he had apparently approached his task as though he were writing fiction, creating a persona and providing appropriate words for such a character, just as he would be doing more and more in *Mardi* and its successors.

By late November of 1846 Melville had finished *Omoo,* the immediate successor of *Typee,* and taken the manuscript to New York, where he showed it to his friend Evert A. Duyckinck before (as Duyckinck put it) "agitating the conscience of John Wiley," his first American publisher, "and tempting the pockets of the Harpers." Harper & Brothers accepted the book and brought it out in May of 1847 following its London publication; Melville stayed on in the city with his younger brother Allan, a New York lawyer. Although he intended, if *Omoo* sold well, to "follow it up by something else, immediately," as he told his London publisher in March, he was still not wholly committed to professional authorship, having taken a brief trip to Washington early in February in unsuccessful search of a government office. Meanwhile Duyckinck was making plans for a weekly journal, the *Literary World,* which he had agreed to edit during its first year for a salary of $500 and an allotment of "a thousand dollars for contributions," as he reported the terms to his brother George. In January Duyckinck sought authorization to print extracts from *Omoo* in advance of its publication, but at Melville's request he held off until the issue of April 24, just before the book's American appearance. On February 2, 1847, Melville accepted an invitation from Duyckinck to review a new work for the *Literary World,* J. Ross Browne's *Etchings of a Whaling Cruise,* saying that he had already secured a copy and anticipated "much pleasure in making it the basis of an article for your paper."

The entire review has considerable autobiographical flavor, for Melville's own experiences in the whale fishery had often paralleled Browne's, and in the passages on whaling he was able to speak out, in Howard Vincent's phrase, "not as a reviewer but as a witness."[6] Just at this time, moreover, he was thinking of incorporating his recollections in a projected third book. As Merrell Davis has remarked of Melville's original plans for *Mardi,* he "almost certainly expected to follow the general narrative pattern which he had used in *Typee* and *Omoo* and . . . praised in Browne's book, where the vicissitudes of the hardy whaleman's life were interwoven with a personal narrative that enlisted the reader's 'sympathies for the adventurous author himself.'"[7] The added paragraphs of the review on a second book, *Sailors' Life and Sailors' Yarns* by "Captain Ringbolt" (John Codman), express indignation against abuse of the common sailor like the feelings Melville had already voiced in *Omoo,* had shared with Browne in discussing *Etchings of a Whaling Cruise*, and was to direct even more tellingly in his own *White-Jacket* (1850).

The immediate sequel of Melville's review was a letter addressed to Duyckinck by Frederick Saunders of Harper & Brothers, Browne's publishers, relaying a request from Browne that "M^r. Melville . . . rectify an error, wh[ich]. he specified & copy of wh. I handed M^r. M's brother [Allan Melville] the other day." The journal published no correction, however, and nothing further is known of the supposed "error" in Melville's critique. In May of 1847 Duyckinck lost his editorship to Charles Fenno Hoffman, who continued the *Literary World* until October of 1848; Melville apparently wrote no more reviews until after the completion of *Mardi,* when Duyckinck was again in charge. No record has been found of payments to Melville for the review of Browne and Codman out of Duyckinck's allotment for contributions.

After the publication of *Omoo* in May of 1847 Melville left New York for Lansingburgh and went on to Boston. By mid-July he was back in New York, where Cornelius Mathews, another member of the Duyckinck

6. Howard P. Vincent, *The Trying-Out of* MOBY-DICK (Boston: Houghton Mifflin Company, 1949), p. 17.

7. Merrell R. Davis, *Melville's* MARDI: *A Chartless Voyage* (New Haven: Yale University Press, 1952), p. 50.

circle, had just taken over the editorship of *Yankee Doodle*. Melville was at once invited to join the staff of this humorous weekly, which had been established in the previous October as a would-be American *Punch.*[8] Writing for *Yankee Doodle* enabled him to develop the vein of satire that had emerged in *Omoo* and would become even more prominent in parts of *Mardi*, particularly the chapters on Vivenza that embody his comments on the contemporary scene in America. Among his anonymous contributions to the magazine was a series of so-called "Authentic Anecdotes of 'Old Zack.' Reported for Yankee Doodle by his special correspondent at the seat of War," articles supposedly dispatched from the battlefields of Mexico, which appeared in seven installments beginning with the issue of July 24. The military exploits of Major General Zachary Taylor, "Old Rough and Ready," were already raising talk of his possible presidential candidacy on the Whig ticket in the national election of 1848. Popular articles and books about Taylor's life and distinctive personal characteristics were being published on all sides; Melville's "anecdotes" burlesque these much-inflated accounts, and like them bear some relation to the tall tales and broad humor of the American frontier. As their repeated allusions to Phineas Barnum and his "American Museum" suggest, Melville was well aware how easily the American press and the American public alike could be manipulated by clever masters of publicity; in this sense the Old Zack pieces look forward to the less obvious satire of *The Confidence-Man* (1857), Melville's tenth book.

That the articles on Taylor attracted favorable attention from the contemporary New York press is probably due more to their explicit

8. There are four known documents in which contemporaries of Melville mention his association with *Yankee Doodle* between July 10, 1847, when Cornelius Mathews became its editor, and October 2, when the second year of its publication was completed. (1) On July 14/15 Evert Duyckinck, in a letter to his brother George, reported that "Mathews has taken hold of Yankee Doodle. . . . I wish you could have shared in the laugh last night we had here with Typee [i.e., Melville] over the wood cuts of No 41. . . . Herman Melville will probably in some shape or other take care of the sea serpent." (2) In the following September J. B. Auld, who also wrote for *Yankee Doodle*, observed in a letter to George Duyckinck that "Melville contributed some capital articles." (3) An entry in Evert Duyckinck's diary for October 5, 1847, refers to "Herman Melville's Old Zack Epistles in Yankee Doodle"; see p. 637 below. (4) On October 6, 1847, Evert Duyckinck wrote in a letter to George Duyckinck that *Yankee Doodle* "is in process of rapid evaporation. . . . After three months well applied labor Mathews gets nothing from Yankee Doodle, nor Melville, nor Bangs." All four documents are in the Duyckinck Collection, Rare Books and Manuscripts Division, The New York Public Library.

political overtones than to their slight intrinsic worth as humorous writing. Melville's party affiliations had remained nominally Democratic despite his failure to obtain office from the Polk administration, and his highly irreverent treatment of Taylor was obviously not calculated to enhance the General's presidential prospects. Along with his contemporaries, Melville clearly responded to the color and excitement of the war with Mexico, as passages in even his very late works reveal, but unlike his brother Gansevoort (who had died in London in May of 1846) he was not in sympathy with the expansionist policies of the current Democratic administration. Chapter 161 of *Mardi* pointedly observes that the "chieftain" of Vivenza "may not declare war of himself; nevertheless, has he done a still more imperial thing:—gone to war without declaring intentions. You yourselves were precipitated upon a neighboring nation, ere you knew your spears were in your hands." In the earlier "Old Zack" pieces the incumbent administration comes off no better than the General; in fact the incidental thrusts at William L. Marcy, Polk's Secretary of War, are more barbed than the comic handling of Taylor himself, and may reflect Melville's reactions to his unsuccessful office-seeking trip to Washington earlier in 1847. Marcy, a former governor of New York, was one of the party leaders to whom he had applied, but a bitter factional quarrel among the Democrats stood in the way of Melville's bureaucratic aspirations despite the strong letters of recommendation he had assembled and the acknowledged services of his late brother, to Marcy and to the national party, during the campaign of 1844.

Most of the "Old Zack" pieces must have been written in mid-July, while Melville was again in New York; later in the month he was once more visiting relatives upstate, returning briefly to the city before escorting his mother and sisters from Lansingburgh to Boston for his wedding on August 4 to Elizabeth Shaw. After a honeymoon trip to Canada the newlyweds stopped at Lansingburgh on August 27 and later proceeded to New York, where after Allan Melville's marriage in September the two couples commenced housekeeping together. Besides the "Authentic Anecdotes," which Duyckinck's diary identifies as Melville's, there is evidence suggesting his probable authorship of several other humorous squibs appearing in *Yankee Doodle* which are printed among the various attributed pieces collected in this volume. Melville, according to Duyckinck, might "take care of" another current topic, the "sea serpent" said to be frequenting Massachusetts Bay off Nahant. Allusions to the sea serpent occur in one of several paragraphs on a Chinese junk visiting

New York harbor, an appropriate subject for a sailor-author; some if not all of this and other related material is very probably from Melville's pen.[9] But *Yankee Doodle* had only a short life, and as the scarcity of surviving copies suggests, it left but little impression on the minds and manners of Americans of the 1840's. When it ceased publication in October of 1847 it had earned nothing for either Mathews or his contributors, Melville among them, as Duyckinck noted at the time. Mathews talked with Duyckinck and Melville of "a possible weekly newspaper" as its successor, but the project never materialized.

By the autumn of 1847, without further obligations to either the *Literary World* or *Yankee Doodle*, Melville was busy with *Mardi*, the longest work he had yet undertaken, which would continue to occupy him throughout 1848 and into the early weeks of 1849. The ambitious scale of *Mardi* and its new depth of insight match the wide range of Melville's reading during his residence in New York and the concurrent intellectual development that had been taking place since the writing of *Typee*. During his long struggle to complete his third book he had little time or inclination for occasional writing, though in November of 1848, when *Mardi* was at last virtually complete, he tentatively agreed to review Joseph C. Hart's *The Romance of Yachting* for the *Literary World*, of which Duyckinck and his brother George had recently become joint editors and proprietors. But after looking into Hart's work Melville returned the volume to Duyckinck on November 14 with a humorous though devastating letter about it that implicitly states his credo as a reviewer. "What has Mr. Hart done," he asked,

> that I should publicly devour him?—I bear that hapless man, no malice. Then why smite him?
>
> —And as for glossing over his book with a few commonplaces,—*that* I can not do.—The book deserves to be burnt in a fire of asafetida, & by the hand that wrote it.
>
> Seriously again, & on my conscience, the book is an abortion, the mere trunk of a book, minus head arm or leg.—Take it back, I beseech, & get some one to cart it back to the author.

His remarks did in a sense find their way into print, however, for on December 2 the *Literary World* carried a review—presumably by

9. For discussion of the Melville canon, see GENERAL NOTE ON THE TEXT, pp. 544–48 below. A number of items that may have been Melville's are reprinted from *Yankee Doodle*, pp. 428–48 above.

Duyckinck himself—which drew material from other parts of Melville's letter in pointing out the obvious weaknesses of Hart's volume.

1849 was a busy year for Melville, though it began leisurely. For most of its first four months, with *Mardi* behind him, he was at the home of his father-in-law in Boston, where on February 16 his wife gave birth to their first child. He now had time for significant reading, including his first close study of Shakespeare's plays, and for varied writing, particularly an unsigned review of Francis Parkman's *The California and Oregon Trail*, which as a story of adventures among savages the Duyckincks evidently thought appropriate for treatment by the author of *Typee* and critic of J. Ross Browne. Melville's article appeared under the title "Mr. Parkman's Tour" in the *Literary World* for March 31, just after *Mardi* had been published in England and was about to make its American debut. His treatment of Parkman's book begins with a one-sentence summary and praises the writing as entertaining, unpretentious, and truthful—in short, as another matter-of-fact personal narrative like *Etchings of a Whaling Cruise*, a form he himself had abandoned in composing *Mardi* but would reluctantly return to, with notable modifications, when writing *Redburn* and *White-Jacket* later in 1849. Two years before, in reviewing Browne, he had mentioned the tendency of authors to romanticize about the sea; here he agrees with Parkman that representations of Indian character in poetry and fiction are for the most part "mere creations of fancy," and in *White-Jacket* he was shortly to disclaim any intention of overpraising the character of seamen. Despite sharp disagreements with Parkman's choice of title, which in his view might be thought misleading, and especially with the book's unfavorable presentation of the Indian, which ran counter to his own fondness for uncivilized races, Melville scrupulously recognizes Parkman's announced intentions in gathering his material and acknowledges the handicap of illness which had forced him to compose entirely by dictation. The review gives a lively appreciative treatment of the book's narrative action, concluding in the usual fashion of the *Literary World* with a long representative extract.

As notices of *Mardi* began to come in, from England and at home, during April and May of 1849, it soon became plain to Melville that his experiment of writing an out-and-out romance was proving unsuccessful with the critics, Duyckinck and a few others excepted. Its failure, severely disappointing if not altogether unexpected, required immediate countermeasures; Melville not only needed money for his current expenses but was already overdrawn with his American publishers, and his only expedient now appeared to lie in writing something in the popular narrative vein of *Typee* and *Omoo* that would be readily saleable and might also offset the damaging effect of *Mardi* on his critics and the public generally. From May to September, driving himself at his desk, he turned out two such books in rapid succession: *Redburn* and *White-Jacket;* obviously he had no time during these months for further contributions to the *Literary World.* In October, having finished proofreading both of the new books, he sailed for England to place *White-Jacket* with a London publisher through direct negotiations, hoping to secure better terms than his agent had been able to make with Richard Bentley for publishing *Redburn.* The two hastily written books Melville described to his father-in-law as mere "*jobs,* which I have done for money—being forced to it, as other men are to sawing wood." They fared better than he expected—certainly better than *Mardi,* though he had learned a great deal from writing and publishing the earlier book, as he acknowledged to Duyckinck in a letter from London in December. In this same letter, taking account of how the reviewers had "stabbed *at* (I do not say *through*)" *Mardi,* he resolved never again to say "something 'critical' " about another man's work as he regretted having done with Parkman's *Oregon Trail:* "Hereafter I shall no more stab at a book (in print, I mean) than I would stab at a man."

Two of Melville's other articles for the *Literary World,* both dealing with his old favorite Fenimore Cooper, appear to reflect his sensitive reaction to criticism of *Mardi,* being noticeably shorter and less incisive than his earlier treatments of Browne and Parkman. The first, composed only a month after "Mr. Parkman's Tour" while the verdict on *Mardi* was beginning to come in, appeared in the issue of April 28, 1849, under the heading "Cooper's New Novel." It offers mainly a bare summary of *The Sea Lions,* praising its style as "singularly plain, downright and truthful" and concluding that "even those who more for fashion's sake than any thing else, have of late joined in decrying our National Novelist" will "perhaps recognize" the book as "one of his happiest." The subsequent article, published on March 16, 1850, following Melville's return from London and the continent, is appropriately entitled "A Thought on Book-Binding," being a brief notice of a new edition of *The Red Rover* that focuses on its physical appearance and says little about its content. Perhaps Melville's mind was on other matters as he composed the review, for by this time he was already at work on the book that became *Moby-Dick.* But when later invited to attend a memorial "demonstration" following

Cooper's death in 1851, he expressed his regard for that "great, robust-souled man" in a letter to Rufus Griswold. "I never had the honor of knowing, or even seeing, Mr Cooper," Melville told Griswold, but "his works are among the earliest I remember, as in my boyhood producing a vivid, and awakening power upon my mind."

During the summer of 1850, interrupting work on the new book he described as his "whaling voyage" in order to take his family to western Massachusetts for a holiday visit, Melville threw off the restraint with which he had treated Cooper's two books as he drafted his longest, most outspoken, and unquestionably his most important contribution to the *Literary World*, "Hawthorne and His Mosses." Presumably writing on his own initiative, he undertook to "review" a book already in print four years, *Mosses from an Old Manse*, composing an enthusiastic appreciation and lyrical interpretation of Hawthorne's achievement completely unlike the earlier notices of Browne, Codman, Parkman, and Cooper he had turned out at Duyckinck's invitation. Only in this almost rhapsodic article, which many modern readers have recognized as revealing even more about his own literary aspirations than it says of Hawthorne's actual accomplishment, does Melville exhibit anything approaching a developed rationale of the writer's art, reflecting both his accumulating experience as an author and his recent encounters with the essays of Romantic literary theorists such as Coleridge, Lamb, and Carlyle. "Hawthorne and His Mosses" transmits through its confident tone and eloquent expression his consciousness of awakening powers that distinguishes it markedly in style from the relatively matter-of-fact writing predominant in the earlier reviews. For by this time his imagination, taking fire from his voracious reading of the past years, disciplined by the failure of *Mardi*, and newly sensitive to creative possibilities of which he had only a dim awareness at the beginning of his career as a writer, was engaged in shaping a masterpiece.

The published version of "Hawthorne and His Mosses" opens informally as a personal essay by an unnamed "Virginian Spending July in Vermont," but the surviving fair-copy manuscript makes evident the fact that the assumed persona was an afterthought: all references to the "Virginian," beginning with that in the subtitle, are Melville's late insertions in his wife's transcription of his own earlier draft. The supposedly Southern author of the essay tells how he had been given a copy of *Mosses from an Old Manse* by a cousin "a day or two since" while visiting in the New England hills; in actuality, Melville himself received just such a volume from his "Aunt Mary" (probably Mrs. Thomas Melvill of Pittsfield) on Thursday, July 18, 1850, as his inscription in the book itself attests. On that same day he had set out on an excursion "to view the state of the crops" with her son Robert, chairman of the "Viewing Committee" of the Berkshire Agricultural Society. Melville probably did not begin reading the book until some undetermined time after his return on the following Saturday evening, July 20. On August 2 his New York friends Duyckinck and Mathews joined him in Pittsfield for a week's visit, and on Monday, August 5, when David D. Field of Stockbridge was host to a group of writers at a picnic on Monument Mountain and a later dinner, Melville met Hawthorne himself for the first time. Some of the essay may have been drafted before their momentous meeting; some parts at least were not written until after the dinner, as canceled phrasing in the manuscript strongly suggests.

Duyckinck published "Hawthorne and His Mosses" in two installments: in the *Literary World* for August 17 and August 24, 1850. Not until several weeks later, after the friendship of Melville and Hawthorne had begun to develop, did the Hawthornes learn that the anonymous "Virginian" was really Melville. As the persona had been made to say that he "never saw" Hawthorne and "perhaps never shall," so Melville was later to tell Mrs. Hawthorne that he himself "had no idea" in composing the essay that he would ever see her husband. These statements have been cited by those believing that he wrote, or at least began to write, "Hawthorne and His Mosses" before his introduction to Hawthorne himself on August 5. But Melville also acknowledged to Mrs. Hawthorne "that the Review was too carelessly written," explaining that he had "dashed it off in great haste & did not see the proof sheets," with the result that a "provoking mistake" appeared in the printing. To Duyckinck he had similarly complained of "ugly errors" when he received the first installment on August 16, suggesting that unless it proved inconvenient he should be sent proofs of the remainder. "Under the circumstances," however, as he wrote Duyckinck, he regarded the printing as "far more correct" than he expected—meaning, in all probability, that none of the article had been set in type until after Duyckinck's return to New York on Monday afternoon, August 12, only four days before. Duyckinck's projected visit of a week would have ended the previous Friday, the 9th, but in writing his wife on that day he remarked that "several circumstances" had intervened to delay his return. Although his letter gave no details, the principal reason was very likely to await the completion of Melville's essay and its copying by Mrs. Melville.

When Melville went over the fair copy before Duyckinck took it to New York he not only added the "Virginian" but made other changes as well, some of them in the interest of further concealing his own authorship. (So Shakespeare, he had written in the essay, "craftily says, or sometimes insinuates," through characters of his creation what would be "all but madness" even to hint "in his own proper character.") One prudent alteration was the removal of "Bostonian" from a revealing sentence that in manuscript had read: "Let us away with this Bostonian leaven of literary flunkeyism towards England" (248.15–16 above); otherwise, the phrasing might well have reminded those present at Fields's dinner on August 5 of Melville's vigorous attack on Oliver Wendell Holmes when the Boston doctor had repeatedly asserted the superiority of Englishmen over Americans. Certainly this passage at least must have been drafted only after the exchange between Holmes and Melville had actually taken place. An entire series of revisions was made to facilitate division of the essay into roughly equal installments before its publication. Duyckinck's hand appears on three successive leaves of the manuscript at this point, his changes serving not only to instruct the compositor but also to substitute a generalized statement where Melville himself had referred to eight American authors by name: Hawthorne, Emerson, Whittier, Irving, Bryant, Dana, Cooper, and Willis (247.6–8). Whether this group of alterations was made by Duyckinck alone or by Duyckinck in consultation with Melville before he left Pittsfield for his return to New York is impossible to determine, but in this significant instance the present edition restores the names as Melville himself inscribed them in revising the fair-copy manuscript.

In earlier pages of the essay, following the studied assertion that "It is July in the country" as its author, the purported "Virginian," reads and writes about the *Mosses*, there is a sketch of the master literary genius as suggested by the stories of Hawthorne. Contemplative humor, omnipresent love, and a great, deep intellect tranquil in its repose are alike indispensable to such a writer, who must above all be experienced in suffering, since for Melville "suffering, some time or other and in some shape or other,—this only can enable any man to depict it in others." With awareness of suffering comes consciousness of the fact of evil, expressed in the supposedly "harmless" Hawthorne through his pervasive "mystical blackness." And although this blackness, unperceived by his conventional readers and critics, may perhaps seem excessive in Hawthorne, it is nevertheless spiritually akin to "the infinite obscure of . . . that background, against which Shakespeare plays his grandest conceits." Its tremendous power as felt by the truly percipient reader lies in its "appeals to that Calvinistic sense of Innate Depravity and Original Sin" familiar at times and "in certain moods" to every "deeply thinking mind." But to the superficial understanding of the "mere critic" this richness of imaginative conception is baffling, since even keen intellectual understanding is insufficient because its comprehension of reality is too circumscribed. "For it is not the brain," Melville explains, that adequately tests a Hawthorne or a Shakespeare; "it is only the heart. You cannot come to know greatness by inspecting it; there is no glimpse to be caught of it, except by intuition."

Perhaps without fully realizing it, Melville here takes his stand squarely upon current Romantic theory, in company with the Transcendental school which he and his Knickerbocker contemporaries affected to disdain. And here too is a clue concerning his own dissatisfaction with "the unpleasantness of fault-finding" that seemed the principal business of the literary reviewers. In *Mardi* he had already declared that "true critics . . . are more rare than true poets"; here he finds "hardly five critics in America; and several of them are asleep." Not by a catalogue of errors or even by sheer intellectual analysis, in other words, can one capture the "intuitive Truth" of a Hawthorne or Shakespeare—or solve the "riddle" of *Mardi* which had eluded his own critics. Foreshadowings of this doctrine of the elusiveness of Truth and its difficult, even dangerous pursuit occur in Melville's earlier writings, such as the long chapter in *Mardi* on Lombardo the poet which can be read as a first draft of portions of the essay on Hawthorne. In the plays of Shakespeare, which he had studied intensively in 1849 under the tutelage of Romantic critics, he found "those short, quick probings at the very axis of reality" which in 1850 he was attempting himself in *Moby-Dick;* in the newly discovered achievement of Hawthorne was welcome confirmation that a "noble-souled aspirant" of the nineteenth century might go "as far as Shakespeare into the universe."

Like the doubloon in *Moby-Dick,* Hawthorne's book thus became a kind of subjective mirror, reflecting the very aims and ambitions that were infusing the mind of its enthusiastic beholder. Melville's reading the *Mosses* took place at a most auspicious stage in his career. Had he come upon the book at the time of its publication in 1846 he would not yet have been ready for his evidently empathic approach of 1850; as late as the summer of 1849 he had borrowed Hawthorne's *Twice-*

Told Tales from Duyckinck and read a few stories without the electrifying response of the following year. What seems to have made the difference, along with his growing consciousness of steady inward development, was his meeting with Hawthorne himself, and indeed the ripening of their friendship was to influence him even more in the months ahead than did his instructive acquaintance with Hawthorne's writings. Very possibly Melville did not look seriously into the *Mosses* until *after* the celebrated literary gathering on August 5. "A man will be given a book," he was to remark in *Pierre,*

> and when the donor's back is turned, will carelessly drop it in the first corner; he is not over-anxious to be bothered with the book. But now personally point out to him the author, and ten to one he goes back to the corner, picks up the book, dusts the cover, and very carefully reads that invaluable work. One does not vitally believe in a man till one's own two eyes have beheld him.
>
> (Book XXI.iii; NN 292.5–10)

Whatever the actual circumstances, the essay goes beyond recording Melville's response to Hawthorne's achievement, for its concluding sections make an eloquent appeal for due recognition of the general worth of American genius as expressed in its literature, work too long overlooked by those excessively preoccupied with the past or devoted solely to English authors. Here Melville was not merely refighting current literary wars on the side of Mathews and Duyckinck, champions of a native American literature, nor thinking primarily of the competent writing of Irving, Cooper, and Dana; he was feeling within himself "those grateful impulses . . . that may possibly prompt . . . to the full flower of some still greater achievement" in the eyes of his countrymen. Perhaps the manuscript of just such a work lay already under his hand.

The year that began in August of 1850, when Melville became thirty-one, is now recognized as the climax of his growth as a man and an artist. In September he bought the farm that he christened "Arrowhead," located south of Pittsfield and some six miles from Hawthorne's cottage at Lenox, and soon moved his family there from New York. Before settling into the routine of work that was necessary to complete *Moby-Dick* he may have written one more short article: a "Report of the Committee on Agriculture" ascribed to his cousin Robert Melvill which was printed in two Pittsfield newspapers, on October 9 and 10, 1850, and is included in this volume among other attributed pieces.[10] Otherwise there was to be no more occasional writing until 1853, when Melville first became a regular contributor to American monthly magazines. In the words of "Hawthorne and His Mosses," it was "not so much paucity, as superabundance of material" that confronted him in 1850. Conscious of his own growth and fecundity, he facetiously appealed to Duyckinck in December for the assistance of "about fifty fast-writing youths" to help in completing "about that number of future works" he purported to be planning. In the following June, close to completing *Moby-Dick*, when he looked back over his career in a long letter to Hawthorne, he disparaged not only the writing that had first brought him fame but the South Sea experiences on which he had initially capitalized. "My development," he asserted, "has been all within a few years past"—specifically, since 1844, when he returned home from the Pacific and began to compose *Typee*. "From my twenty-fifth year I date my life. Three weeks have scarcely passed, at any time between then and now, that I have not unfolded within myself. But I feel that I am now come to the inmost leaf of the bulb, and that shortly the flower must fall to the mould."

1851–1856

Between "Hawthorne and His Mosses" in 1850 and Melville's debut as a regular contributor to magazines in 1853 came the completion and publication of his sixth and seventh books, *Moby-Dick* in 1851 and *Pierre* in 1852. *Moby-Dick*, though it brought Hawthorne's approval in a "joy-giving and exultation-breeding letter" to Melville, was not the critical and popular success its author had hoped for, and *Pierre* proved nothing short of disastrous to his prospects as an author who was financially dependent on the sales of his books. In order to understand why Melville turned to magazine-writing after the failure of *Pierre* it is important to review his situation after the purchase of Arrowhead and his removal from New York City to Pittsfield. During the fall of 1850 and the ensuing winter, besides settling his family in the new residence and visiting occasionally with Hawthorne, he was engaged primarily in "shaping out the gigantic conception of his 'White Whale,'" to borrow Hawthorne's

10. Despite the prevalent belief that Melville may have contributed additional reviews to the *Literary World* there has been no convincing attribution to him of any articles besides those discussed here. See the General Note on the Text, pp. 547–48 below, concerning various reviews that have been nominated as Melville's.

words in *A Wonder-Book* (1852). According to Mrs. Melville, when she looked back on this period following Melville's death forty years later, he wrote *Moby-Dick* "under unfavorable circumstances" that gradually undermined his previously strong constitution. As she remembered, he "would sit at his desk all day not eating any thing till four or five o clock—then ride to the village after dark." A similar account of his working habits while he was composing *Pierre* was given by his Pittsfield neighbor Sarah Morewood. Writing to George Duyckinck in December of 1851, she reported that Melville regularly sat in his room "till quite dark in the evening—when he for the first time during the whole day partakes of solid food." In Mrs. Morewood's judgment "he must therefore write under a state of morbid excitement which will soon injure his health."

One reason for Melville's self-imposed isolation at Arrowhead was surely his need for undisturbed concentration while he was writing. His household in 1850 included not only his wife and child but his mother and sisters; in 1851 his second son was born, and in 1853 and 1855 two daughters were added to the family. The presence of so many mouths to feed meant increasing financial pressures throughout the decade of the 1850's. By the time the family settled at Pittsfield, where the Arrowhead property was encumbered by a mortgage of $1,500, Melville also owed $5,000 to his father-in-law. In May of 1851, needing more money for improvements, he borrowed an additional $2,050 from a friend just after Harper & Brothers had refused him a requested advance on his next book, *Moby-Dick*—partly because he was already in debt to the firm for nearly $700. All of these facts must have been in Melville's mind as he labored over the manuscript from which he expected so much. To Hawthorne in early June of 1851 he expressed discouragement about finishing his "Whale" as it deserved when he was forced to "work and slave" on later parts of it even as the earlier chapters were already being set in type.

> *That* is the only way I can finish it now,—I am so pulled hither and thither by circumstances. The calm, the coolness, the silent grass-growing mood in which a man *ought* always to compose,—that, I fear, can seldom be mine. Dollars damn me; and the malicious Devil is forever grinning in upon me, holding the door ajar. My dear Sir, a presentiment is on me,—I shall at last be worn out and perish, like an old nutmeg-grater, grated to pieces by the constant attrition of the wood, that is, the nutmeg. What I feel most moved to write, that is banned,—it will not pay. Yet, altogether, write the *other* way I cannot. So the product is a final hash, and all my books are botches.

What Melville meant by writing "the *other* way" can be illustrated from his correspondence of 1851. "Hawthorne and His Mosses" was his last article for the *Literary World* and for the Duyckincks, who also took over direction of *Holden's Dollar Magazine* with the issue of April, 1851; on February 12 of that year Melville declined their invitation to contribute to *Holden's.* "I can not write the thing you want," he told Evert Duyckinck in a letter. "I am in the humor to lend a hand to a friend, if I can;—but I am not in the humor to write the kind of thing you need—and I am not in the humor to write for Holden's Magazine." "The kind of thing" needed to sell a popular magazine was not the sort of writing *Moby-Dick* was demanding of Melville, and of course *Moby-Dick* had first priority. To his London publisher Richard Bentley, who offered less favorable terms for the new work than Melville had hoped for, he described at some length the current plight of American authors, then at great disadvantage in treating with publishers both at home and abroad because of the absence of an international copyright agreement. "In all reasonable probability," he wrote to Bentley on July 20, 1851,

> no International Copyright will ever be obtained—in our time, at least,—if you Englishmen wait at all for the first step to be taken in this country. Who have any motive in this country to bestir themselves in this thing? Only the authors.—Who are the authors?—A handful. And what influence have they to bring to bear upon any question whose settlement must necessarily assume a political form?—They can bring scarcely any influence whatever. This country & nearly all its affairs are governed by sturdy backwoodsmen—noble fellows enough, but not at all literary, & who care not a fig for any authors except those who write those most saleable of all books nowadays—i e—the newspapers, & magazines. And tho' the number of cultivated, catholic men, who may be supposed to feel an interest in a national literature, is large & every day growing larger; yet they are nothing in comparison with the overwhelming majority who care nothing about it. This country is at present engaged in furnishing material for future authors; not in encouraging its living ones.

Bentley's advance of £150 for *Moby-Dick* helped Melville through the summer and fall of 1851; American publication of the book in November substantially reduced the balance he owed the Harpers, which fell below $500 in that month and stood at less than $150 by February of 1852 when the contract for *Pierre* was signed. At that time the Harper firm was willing to pay him $500—roughly $200 from accumulated earnings and $300 as an advance against anticipated royalties. But it accepted *Pierre* on terms markedly different from those offered Melville for *Omoo*, *Mardi*, *Redburn*, *White-Jacket*, and *Moby-Dick*: under the previous contracts author and publisher shared equally in net profits; for *Pierre*, the new contract provided instead for a flat royalty to Melville of twenty cents per copy after expenses were paid, and it made no allowance for review copies except at the author's own expense.

The immediate reason for such a decided modification of customary terms may well have been an awareness on both sides of what the latest reviewers were saying about *Moby-Dick* in the January periodicals. Melville had sought to produce a book that would engage the common reader even as it exemplified "the great Art of Telling the Truth"—his own phrase in "Hawthorne and His Mosses"; on the evidence of these most recent reviews, among them some of the harshest he had ever received, the book failed to reach either objective. Melville, who was reportedly "very angry" at charges that the book was "Blasphemous," must have recalled his earlier words to Hawthorne: "What I feel most moved to write . . . will not pay"; though he declined to "write the *other* way" for *Holden's*, his enforced compromises in *Moby-Dick* had seemingly botched still another of his books. Its successor, *Pierre*, he planned as an experiment of a different order, in both subject matter and form. The book as he optimistically described it to Bentley was a work "very much more calculated for popularity than anything you have yet published of mine," being "a regular romance" treating "utterly new scenes & characters"; at the same time, he added, it would represent "a new & elevated aspect of American life." But the book Melville published is not the work he originally envisioned, and the changes he introduced early in 1852—among them the addition of what is now included in Books XVII and XVIII, "Young America in Literature" and "Pierre, as a Juvenile Author, Reconsidered"—are evidently another direct response to his situation of the moment as the reviewers denigrated *Moby-Dick* and the prudent Harper brothers, taking note, exacted different terms for its successor.[11]

11. "I do not know a better example of the sagacity with which the literary departments of our great publishing houses were managed, even a generation ago, than is presented by Melville's case." The words are those of Arthur Stedman, Melville's literary executor, in his "Melville of Marquesas" (1891). After studying Melville's publishing contracts, Stedman observed that Harper & Brothers had brought out his earlier works "on a half profit system;

The word from London in 1852 was even more discouraging. Bentley declined Melville's first offer of *Pierre*, pointing out that he had already lost £450 on four of Melville's earlier books; after seeing a set of corrected American proofs he bluntly refused to publish such a work on any terms unless alterations for an English audience were permitted. This condition Melville would not accept, and as a result he had no advance payments from abroad to expect in the summer of 1852; *Pierre* appeared in England only in the form of imported American sheets, so that any payments to Melville would necessarily have to be channeled through the Harpers. Bentley's apprehensions about public reaction to *Pierre* were only a foretaste of what Melville had to endure from his own countrymen during the summer and fall of 1852. The reviewers' harsh comments on *Pierre*, following upon the objections already made against *Moby-Dick*, gravely compromised his reputation as a writer. The universal distaste for the "ambiguities" of his new book is summed up in a long essay on Melville by Fitz-James O'Brien in *Putnam's Monthly Magazine* for February, 1853. "Let Mr. Melville stay his step in time," O'Brien warned. "He totters on the edge of a precipice, over which all his hard-earned fame may tumble with such another weight as Pierre attached to it."

Such pronouncements were not lost upon Melville's relatives, who were already concerned about his health and well aware of his financial problems. As a steady source of income and a relief from the demands of authorship they thought of a possible consular appointment abroad, and early in 1853 they began a letter-writing campaign to bring influence to bear in his behalf upon the new Democratic administration of Franklin Pierce. Whatever Melville himself may have felt after reading such articles as O'Brien's, he was noticeably reluctant to take an active part in the search for a consulship. "Herman dislikes asking favors from any one,"

---

but for 'Pierre' they offered a much more conventional arrangement, and for his other books, except 'Battle Pieces,' Melville had to seek new publishers. It must be remembered, in connection with their action, that Melville was at the zenith of his reputation in 1852. The wisdom of the firm's attitude was abundantly proved." The present discussion draws on two studies by Hershel Parker that modify assumptions previously made in the HISTORICAL NOTE to the Northwestern-Newberry Edition of *Pierre*: "Why *Pierre* Went Wrong," *Studies in the Novel*, VIII (Spring, 1976), 7–23; "Contract: *Pierre*, by Herman Melville," *Proof*, V (1977), 27–44. Other scholars, it should be noted, differ in some degree with Parker's interpretation of the evidence: e.g., Robert Milder, "Melville's 'Intentions' in *Pierre*," *Studies in the Novel*, VI (Summer, 1974), 186–99; Gerard W. Shepherd, "Pierre's Psyche and Melville's Art," *ESQ: A Journal of the American Renaissance*, XXX (2nd Quarter, 1984), 83–98.

his mother wrote on April 20, 1853. "He therefore postponed writing from time to time, until he became so completely absorbed by his new work, now nearly ready for the press, that he has not taken the proper, & necessary measures to procure this earnestly wished for office." His demanding "occupation as author," she explained, "is wearing Herman out," and a change of scene "would very materially renew, & strengthen both his body & mind."

What Melville's "new work" may have been is not specified in any surviving correspondence. During that same spring of 1853, when as his wife remembered "We all felt anxious about the strain on his health," he went to New York with a manuscript which—to quote his own later words to the Harpers—"I was prevented from printing at that time." In his letter just quoted, written on November 24, 1853, he says nothing about the nature of the manuscript or the considerations that had "prevented" its publication; the most likely inference is that the Harper firm, which had not been sanguine about *Pierre* in 1852, simply refused to bring out another work by Herman Melville in the following year to risk the renewed wrath of already hostile reviewers while his name lay under a cloud. Even before the attacks on *Pierre* he had been inclined to agree with Bentley that his books were "produced in too rapid succession," and in a postscript to Bentley on April 16, 1852, he toyed with the idea of publishing *Pierre* "anonymously, or under an assumed name"; in the book itself the title character regrets that he had not started his literary career under the "mask" of anonymity. A year later, it now appears, the possibility of anonymous publication had come up again in his dealings with the Harpers. According to Mrs. Melville's stepmother, Hope Savage Shaw, writing confidentially on July 27, 1853, to Samuel H. Savage, "the Harpers have persuaded Herman to write for him [i.e., them]; and he is admirably paid."[12] Since Harper & Brothers had recently declined Melville's "new work," she must have been referring to another kind of writing: stories for *Harper's New Monthly Magazine*, where his first contribution appeared anonymously in the following December. Internal evidence suggests that "Cock-A-Doodle-Doo!" was composed during the late spring or early summer of 1853, when Melville may also have written other stories for the magazine. His first story for Putnam, "Bartleby, the Scrivener," which was published, unsigned, in the Novem-

12. Quoted in Frederick J. Kennedy and Joyce Deveau Kennedy, "Additions to *The Melville Log*," *Extracts / An Occasional Newsletter* (The Melville Society), No. 31 (September, 1977), 8.

ber and December numbers of *Putnam's Monthly Magazine*, must also date from this same period.

As we know from Melville's disparaging remarks of 1851 to both Duyckinck and Bentley about American magazines and their readers, he had had no intention of writing fiction for periodicals, despite his persistent need for money, before finishing both *Moby-Dick* and *Pierre*. Having composed the two books in rapid succession, he then permitted himself a long holiday in the spring and summer of 1852: "For the last three months & more," he told Hawthorne in a letter of July 17, 1852, he had been away from his desk, "an utter idler and a savage—out of doors all the time." And though "often requested," as his mother reported, he had "not contributed one line" to a book on the Berkshires published in 1852, J. E. A. Smith's *Taghconic; or Letters and Legends about Our Summer Home*, by "Godfrey Greylock." In October of that year he received a circular letter from G. P. Putnam & Co. inviting him to write for *Putnam's Monthly*, which was to begin publication in the following January, and in December of 1852 Richard Bentley wrote Melville and other American authors about contributing to *Bentley's Miscellany*. But there is no evidence that he responded with an actual article before the spring or summer of 1853—after he had gone to New York with the unnamed manuscript he was "prevented from printing."

What had occupied Melville during the preceding winter was in all probability "the story of Agatha," as he called it, that he heard from a New Bedford lawyer while visiting Nantucket Island with his father-in-law in July of 1852. On the following August 13 he wrote to Hawthorne, then living in Concord, enclosing a memorandum the lawyer had sent him; "a regular story," he thought, might be based on the "striking incidents" it recounted, but such a tale seemed to him more in Hawthorne's vein than his own. The lawyer, he explained, had first told him of Agatha Hatch Robertson to illustrate "the great patience, & endurance, & resignedness of the women of the island in submitting so uncomplainingly to the long, long abscences of their sailor husbands"; the memorandum gives the details of her abandonment by an unfaithful mate who had left her with child and bigamously married two other women. In the facts of her situation, Melville felt, lay "a skeleton of actual reality to build about with fulness & veins & beauty. And if I thought I could do it as well as you, why, I should not let you have it." On October 25 he wrote again to offer another "little idea" for the story, in case his friend had "thought it worth while to write" about Agatha, but when he visited the Hawthornes at Concord early in December Hawthorne "expressed uncertainty" about undertaking the project and urged Melville himself to do so. Writing from Boston after their discussion, Melville reported his decision to "begin it immediately" upon returning to Pittsfield after the Christmas holidays and asked Hawthorne to forward the lawyer's memorandum to him with any further suggestions he might have for treating "so interesting a story of reality." Had he "come to this determination at Concord," he added, the two authors "might have more fully and closely talked over the story, and so struck out new light."[13]

This was Melville's last known contact with Hawthorne until their brief reunion in England four years later, when Melville was on his way to the Mediterranean and Hawthorne was American consul at Liverpool. If Melville wrote the story of Agatha during the winter months of 1853 "with Hawthorne's vein and style prominently in mind," as Henry A. Murray has suggested, the lost manuscript may well have constituted "a step or transition, one might say, toward the Hawthornesque symbolism of his later short stories." But "since no such story was ever published or found in manuscript form, the chances are it was destroyed, probably burnt by Melville himself in a moment of self-negating desperation" after his abortive trip to New York in the following spring.[14] Whatever the physical fate of the manuscript itself may have been, there are echoes of the "patience, & endurance, & resignedness" Melville associated with Agatha in much of the fiction he was to write over the next three years: one thinks immediately of such characters as Bartleby and Israel Potter, the Merrymusks in "Cock-A-Doodle-Doo!" and above all, Hunilla in the eighth sketch of "The Encantadas," published in April of 1854. The story of Hunilla, as Herbert F. Smith has observed, "is closely connected to the sensibility of an Agatha-character"; that of Bartleby, Smith conjectures, may even have been "abstracted from the philosophical and legal background of the problem of Agatha."[15]

13. See Harrison Hayford, "The Significance of Melville's 'Agatha' Letters," *ELH, A Journal of English Literary History*, XIII (December, 1946), 299–310, and *Letters*, pp. 153–63.

14. Quoted respectively from "the biographer" and "the second critic" in Henry A. Murray, "Bartleby and I," *Melville Annual 1965 / A Symposium: Bartleby the Scrivener*, ed. Howard P. Vincent (Kent, Ohio: Kent State University Press, 1966), pp. 22–23.

15. "Melville's Master in Chancery and His Recalcitrant Clerk," *American Quarterly*, XVII (Winter, 1965), 737. As Robert Sattelmeyer and James Barbour have shown, "the final link in a circumstantial chain" between the "Agatha" letters and the story of Hunilla is a newspaper account of a "Female Robinson Crusoe" that Melville read in November of 1853: see "The Sources and Genesis of Melville's 'Norfolk Isle and the Chola Widow,' " *American Literature*, L (November, 1978), 398–417.

Considerations such as these support the assumption that Melville began writing for the magazines only after his failure to place his book-length manuscript with Harper & Brothers in the spring of 1853. In early June he was in New York to see his uncle Peter Gansevoort off for Europe; during the summer his wife reported him as "very well," telling her father on August 10 that he had resumed his Berkshire excursions with friends by ascending Mt. Greylock on foot and exploring the Dome of Taconic. His new arrangements with the Harpers must have been concluded by late July, on the evidence of Mrs. Shaw's letter to Savage on July 27 saying that he was "admirably paid." What he received for "Cock-A-Doodle-Doo!" and when payment was made are not known, but by 1854 the firm was paying him for accepted manuscripts well in advance of their publication and independently of his account for books. From Putnam Melville received $85 for "Bartleby," paid in two installments in 1853 just after the story appeared in the November and December issues of *Putnam's Monthly*. Putnam's circular letter of the year before had offered potential contributors $3.00 per printed page; the Harpers were paying Melville's contemporaries such as J. Ross Browne a dollar more.[16] Since both firms considered Melville's work to be worth $5.00 per page, Mrs. Shaw was justified in thinking him well paid, at least in relation to other magazine-writers of the day. Successful magazines of the 1850's could afford to be generous to their ablest contributors, and whatever Melville's current standing as a writer of books, Putnam and the Harpers obviously regarded his magazine pieces as worth bidding for at a premium. *Harper's Monthly,* which had begun publication by levying heavily on English materials, needed to meet the challenge of its younger rival by introducing more American contributions, even though it continued to publish such articles anonymously. As for anonymity in the newer *Putnam's,* the *Literary World* for December 3, 1853, observed that its talented contributors "have defeated the anonymous system of the magazine" by writing such "clever" articles as "Mr. Melville's 'Bartleby, the Scrivener,' " which have made them "perfectly well known," and in the following February the New York *Evening Post* announced that in March *Putnam's* would begin publication of a new serial by Melville, "The Encantadas." Melville's pseudonym of "Salvator R[osa]. Tarnmoor" used with "The Encantadas" was thus as transparent a disguise as the "Ik Marvel" of Donald Grant

16. Eugene Exman, *The Brothers Harper* (New York: Harper & Row, Publishers, 1965), p. 316.

Mitchell; in after years Henry James, reminiscing about "the charming *Putnam*" of "the early fifties," recalled his "very young pleasure" in "the prose, as mild and easy as an Indian summer in the woods, of Herman Melville, of George William Curtis and 'Ik Marvel.' "[17]

Determining the dates of composition for Melville's magazine pieces is largely a matter of inference, since most of them are unmentioned in surviving correspondence between author and publisher and even those named were not necessarily published in the order of their writing and submission. "The Paradise of Bachelors and the Tartarus of Maids" is the first title named in Melville's known letters to Harper & Brothers during these years: on May 25, 1854, he acknowledged payment of "$100 on acct: of the 'Paradise of Batchelors &c.' " Since their magazine had already published "Cock-A-Doodle-Doo!" in the issue of December, 1853, and had presumably paid for it long since, the sum of $100 "on acct:" must have represented an advance payment for the entire group of Melville's later contributions that began to appear in the spring and summer of 1854: "Poor Man's Pudding and Rich Man's Crumbs" (June, 1854), "The Happy Failure" (July, 1854), "The Fiddler" (September, 1854), and—seven months later—the one item actually mentioned by name in his letter of acknowledgment, "The Paradise of Bachelors and the Tartarus of Maids" (April, 1855).

17. Henry James, "American Letters," in *Literature* (London), II (June 11, 1898), 676–77, as quoted in George Monteiro, "More on Herman Melville in the 1890's," *Melville Society Extracts,* No. 30 (May, 1977), 14. The identity of both Mitchell and Melville was evident to knowledgeable contemporary readers even when they published anonymously. Thus a writer for the *Home Journal* for April 7, 1855—probably N. P. Willis—in a notice of the current issue of *Harper's* attributed "Some Account of a Consulate" to Mitchell on the ground that it reflects "the consular experience at Venice, of 'Ik Marvel' " and also assigned "The Paradise of Bachelors and the Tartarus of Maids" to Melville, observing that "at all events, if he be not the author, it is written in his best vein." In the previous year the *Berkshire County Eagle* of Pittsfield, after reprinting the New York *Evening Post*'s announcement that Melville was contributing "The Encantadas" to *Putnam's,* had remarked on March 10 that in the new serial as in "other late articles in Harper and Putnam, Mr. Melville combines the excellencies of his early and later style"; when *Putnam's* began serializing *Israel Potter,* the *Eagle,* the Salem *Register,* and the *Morning Courier and New-York Enquirer* all attributed the story to Melville. The appearance of "Benito Cereno" in the following year led the New York *Dispatch* to write of it on November 25, 1855, as "a strange story, which we believe to be written by Herman Melville." Also in 1855 the Duyckincks' *Cyclopaedia of American Literature* noted that since the publication of *Pierre* Melville had been writing "chiefly for the magazines of Harper and Putnam"; the article on Melville specifically mentions "Cock-A-Doodle-Doo!" "Bartleby, the Scrivener," and *Israel Potter.*

The payment was evidently calculated on the basis of total wordage rather than by the printed page unless these pieces had actually been set in type by this time; in their printed form the four items ran to 19½ pages in all, worth roughly $100 at the rate of $5.00 per printed page that Melville evidently commanded.

When had Melville written and submitted these four compositions? Certainly well before May 25, 1854, since "Poor Man's Pudding and Rich Man's Crumbs" was scheduled for the June issue; from its inception *Harper's* had appeared "in all parts of the United States on the first day of every month" and was sent to press about the tenth day of the month preceding.[18] The four pieces must have been dispatched from Pittsfield to New York no later than the early spring of 1854; two of them, it would seem, were probably sent along with "Cock-A-Doodle-Doo!" on August 13, 1853, when Melville wrote to Harper & Brothers enclosing "three articles which perhaps may be found suitable for your Magazine." That these were his first submissions is suggested by his request that they be given "early attention" and that he be apprised "of the result."[19] The Harpers evidently returned a favorable answer concerning "Cock-A-Doodle-Doo!" which was used in the December number; if the other two pieces were "The Happy Failure" and "The Fiddler," which are shorter and less well developed than any of the other compositions named and may well have been Melville's first attempts in the new medium, they were held for later use—in July and September of the following year. Melville had also been in touch with G. P. Putnam & Co. about a possible contribution to *Putnam's Monthly*. By September of 1853 he had a first manuscript ready for *Putnam's* and either a fourth contribution for *Harper's* or a revision of one of the three manuscripts submitted in August, but apparently he erred in addressing his communications to the maga-

18. *Harper's New Monthly Magazine*, VIII (January, 1854), 145.

19. Davis and Gilman, *Letters*, p. 171, tentatively date the letter "13 August [1854?]". In attempting to identify the "three articles" they cite three pieces which subsequently appeared in *Harper's*: "The Paradise of Bachelors and the Tartarus of Maids" (April, 1855), "Jimmy Rose" (November, 1855), and "The 'Gees" (March, 1856). But the two-part article had already been paid for, as noted above, by May 25, 1854, and "Jimmy Rose" and "The 'Gees" appear to be the "brace of fowl—wild fowl" that Melville sent to Harper & Brothers "by Express" on September 18 [1854?] (*Letters*, p. 172). Thus the letter of August 13 clearly fits the circumstances of Melville's magazine writing of 1853 rather than his situation in the following year; moreover, as Davis and Gilman acknowledge in their textual notes, p. 354, the letter (No. 115) "is written on different paper [white] from that of the other letters to the Harpers" that they assign to 1854, which are on blue paper.

zines. On September 20 Charles F. Briggs, the editor of *Putnam's*, wrote to Harper & Brothers forwarding a "Ms. and note" intended for *Harper's* but "directed to *Putnam's Monthly*"; Briggs also inquired whether, "as something was expected from Mr Melville perhaps he may have misdirected it to you."[20] The manuscript Briggs was expecting must have been that of "Bartleby, the Scrivener," which subsequently reached *Putnam's* in time for publication in the November and December issues. During the summer of 1853 Melville had thus written at least three magazine pieces for *Harper's*, "Cock-A-Doodle-Doo!" and probably "The Happy Failure" and "The Fiddler," and another for *Putnam's*, "Bartleby." Between September and the following May he submitted four additional contributions: presumably "Poor Man's Pudding and Rich Man's Crumbs" and "The Paradise of Bachelors and the Tartarus of Maids" to *Harper's* and "The Encantadas" and "The Two Temples" to *Putnam's*.

Meanwhile, Melville had also projected another book, which he proposed to Harper & Brothers in a pivotal letter of November 24, 1853, that deserves quotation in full, since it bears not only upon the chronology of his writing in 1853 and 1854 but also upon his relations in these years with the Harpers.

> Gentlemen:—In addition to the work which I took to New York last Spring, but which I was prevented from printing at that time; I have now in hand, and pretty well on towards completion, another book—300 pages, say—partly of nautical adventure, and partly—or, rather, chiefly, of Tortoise Hunting Adventure. It will be ready for press some time in the coming January. Meanwhile, it would be convenient, to have advanced to me upon it $300.—My acct: with you, at present, can not be very far from square. For the abovenamed advance—if remitted me now—you

20. Briggs's letter (now in the Pierpont Morgan Library) is quoted in part by Davis and Gilman, *Letters*, p. 172, n. 3; their conjectural date is "Sept. 20 [1854?]" rather than 1853. Since Melville dispatched "a brace of fowl" to Harper & Brothers in September of 1854, according to his separate note of September 18 to the firm (note 19, above), it could be argued that he had misdirected that shipment to *Putnam's Magazine* and thus occasioned Briggs's letter to the Harpers. But Briggs mentions only one "Ms. and note" rather than the two pieces sent by Melville in September of 1854, and his further statement that "something was expected from Mr Melville" by his own magazine better fits the circumstances of September of 1853, when Melville, having already contributed to *Harper's*, must have been in communication with *Putnam's* concerning "Bartleby, the Scrivener."

will have security in my former works, as well as security prospective, in the one to come, (The Tortoise-Hunters) because if you accede to the aforesaid request, this letter shall be your voucher, that I am willing your house should publish it, on the old basis—half-profits.

Reply immediately, if you please,
And Beleive Me, Yours
Herman Melville

The opening sentence of this letter would seem to indicate that Melville had still "in hand" the unpublished work of the previous spring; if so, he had not at this point destroyed the manuscript. That he expected to finish by "some time in the coming January" another book of "300 pages, say" means that he had already been working on it during the fall of 1853—presumably after dispatching his first magazine pieces to *Harper's* and *Putnam's*. That he proposed his new book for publication by the firm "on the old basis—half-profits" attests to his assumption that by this point the Harpers might be less hesitant about bringing out another of Melville's works in the wake of *Pierre*. Their reply to his letter of November 24 has not survived, but an in-house report on the sales of Melville's books (filed with his letter to the firm) apparently justified their decision to send the requested advance on December 7. Three days later, on December 10, 1853, the firm suffered a disastrous fire at their New York establishment in Cliff Street which destroyed nearly 2,300 bound and unbound copies of Melville's books though not the plates; as Melville explained later to his father-in-law, this meant a loss to him of "about $1000" that would otherwise have come from his share of profits and royalties.

Melville's more immediate response to news of the loss may have been to open negotiations with G. P. Putnam & Co. for use of some or all of his account of "Tortoise Hunting Adventure" in *Putnam's Monthly*, perhaps in the belief that the Harper firm would be unable to publish the projected book because of the fire. All that is known is this: on February 6, 1854, he wrote a now-unlocated letter to Putnam on an unknown subject; on February 14 the New York *Post* announced that "The Encantadas" would begin in the March number of *Putnam's Monthly;* the March installment included an account of tortoise-hunting in Sketch Second. Meanwhile, Melville wrote to Harper & Brothers in late February about the book he had proposed two months before. When he "procured the advance of $300," his letter began, he

> intimated that the work would be ready for press some time in January. I have now to express my concern, that, owing to a variety of causes, the work, unavoidably, was not ready in that month, & still requires additional work to it, ere completion. But in no sense can you loose by the delay.
>
> I shall be in New York in the course of a few weeks; when I shall call upon you, & inform you when those proverbially slow "Tortoises" will be ready to crawl into market.

From recently discovered family correspondence (extracted in the forthcoming new edition of *The Melville Log*) it is known that Melville's trip to New York was delayed while his sister Augusta completed fair copies of his manuscripts—very likely "Poor Man's Pudding and Rich Man's Crumbs" and "The Paradise of Bachelors and the Tartarus of Maids" for the Harpers and possibly "The Two Temples," either for their magazine or for *Putnam's Monthly*. On March 30, 1854, writing to Frances Priscilla Melville, Augusta remarked that Herman had brought her

> another batch of copying which he was most anxious to have as soon as possible. . . . He is making preparations to go down to New York, that is he is getting his M.S. ready (not *the book*, for the Harpers owing to the two fires, are not in a situation to publish it now) but Magazine articles &c; & has written Allan [Melville] that he will probably leave here within a fortnight. . . .

Melville evidently arrived in the city in time for his brother Allan's birthday on April 7, when a work used in Chapter 23 of his *Israel Potter* was charged to his account with the Harpers. No written record is known concerning the delayed "book"—presumably the work on tortoises and tortoise-hunting—and its relation to "The Encantadas," which continued to appear in *Putnam's* for April and May. In any event, he repeatedly sought word from Harper & Brothers about "the 'Tortoises' extract," as he termed it in his letter of May 25, 1854, that he must have delivered to the firm by then, either during his March visit or later. He had received no reply by June 22, when he wrote again to inquire "whether it be worth while to prepare further Extracts":

> Though it would be difficult, if not impossible, for me to get the entire Tortoise Book ready for publication before Spring [i.e., of 1855],

> yet I can pick out & finish parts, here & there, for prior use. But even this is not unattended with labor; which labor, of course, I do not care to undergo while remaining in doubt as to its recompence.

Presumably the Harpers asked for additional extracts and Melville responded by writing on July 25 to say that he was sending by express "a parcel . . . containing M.S.S. for you"; the "M.S.S." must have been "parts, here & there," of the projected book rather than additional magazine pieces, since his last two contributions to *Harper's*, "Jimmy Rose" (November, 1855) and "The 'Gees" (March, 1856), were not ready for submission until September of 1854. Whatever the nature of these extracts, it seems evident that Melville wrote more about "Tortoise Hunting Adventure" for the Harpers than he had published in Sketch Second of "The Encantadas" in the March number of *Putnam's*. But there is no further information concerning the fate of the "Tortoise Book," which—like that of "the story of Agatha"—can only be conjectured.

When Melville wrote to the Harpers on May 25, 1854, acknowledging their payment for magazine articles and inquiring about their response to the extract he had sent, he also broached another subject: "When you write me concerning the 'Tortoises' extract, you may, if you choose, inform me at about what time you would be prepared to commence the publication of another Serial in your Magazine—supposing you had one, in prospect, that suited you." By this time he was obviously well along in composing *Israel Potter*, "the Revolutionary narrative of the beggar" he had thought of "serving up" more than four years before when he bought an old map of London for possible use in writing it. Evidently failing to interest Harper & Brothers in "another Serial," he addressed George Putnam on June 7, 1854, advising him of the shipment "by Express, to-day," of "some sixty and odd pages of MSS," part of "a story called 'Israel Potter.' " His proposal was for serial publication in *Putnam's Monthly* "at the rate of five dollars per printed page." Putnam agreed to all of Melville's several stipulations except one, that of a requested advance of $100 on acceptance of his proposal. A place was found for the first installment of this "Fourth of July Story" in the issue then in press, that of July, 1854; *Israel Potter* continued to appear through March of 1855, when Putnam issued the story in book form as Melville's eighth book. (Allan Melville had suggested in March of 1854 that his brother "ought to reserve to himself the right to publish his magazine matter in book form.") The nine installments ran to 84¼ pages, for which Melville received a total of $421.50 in the form of monthly payments. For his earlier contribution of "The Encantadas" he was paid $150, also in monthly payments, but still another story, "The Two Temples," was rejected in May of 1854 on the ground that "some of our church readers might be disturbed" by its *"point."*

Both Putnam and his editor, Charles F. Briggs, wrote Melville to apologize for their decision not to print "The Two Temples"; Putnam, in addition to asking Melville for "some more of your good things," also requested "some drawing or daguerreotype" to be used "as one of our series of portraits." Melville was unable to supply a likeness, he replied to Putnam on May 16, saying also that he had already written Briggs concerning "The Two Temples" and would soon "send down some other things, to which, I think, no objections will be made on the score of tender consciences of the public."[21] The opening portions of *Israel Potter* were to follow on June 7; "The Lightning-Rod Man," published in the August number, probably accompanied this or a later segment of the longer work. Putnam's prompt acceptance of *Israel Potter* and his apologetic letter about refusing "The Two Temples" both indicate his interest in having Melville as a contributor to his magazine. During the first six months in its existence *Putnam's Monthly* received 389 manuscripts, and 980 in all by the end of its first year;[22] clearly Putnam and Briggs singled out Melville's contributions for special handling as well as special payment.

From the evidence just reviewed of Melville's dealings with both Putnam and the Harpers it is possible to draw up a probable chronology of his magazine writing between the publication of *Pierre* in 1852 and the serialization of his eighth book, *Israel Potter*, in 1854 and 1855, though with one major reservation: there is no basis other than purely internal evidence for determining the sequence of individual compositions within certain groupings. From manuscripts by Melville on hand an editor may have selected a particular story because of its length, given the amount of space available in the next monthly issue of his magazine, rather than the period of time since its submission: was a long piece or a short one needed to fill out a number? "Cock-A-Doodle-Doo!" was the first story by Melville to appear in *Harper's*; it was not necessarily the first submitted or even the

21. See Catalogue 68 (1970), Paul C. Richards Autographs, Brookline, Massachusetts, Lot 1, for a full transcription of the letter and an accompanying facsimile reproduction. The letter itself is now in the personal collection of William Reese.

22. See the publisher's notes at the end of the first bound volume (I, January–June, 1853, unpaged) and the beginning of the second (II, July–December, 1853, [iii]).

first written, since Melville may previously have tried his hand at other pieces which are shorter and less complex, such as "The Happy Failure" and "The Fiddler." "The Two Temples," first mentioned in letters to Melville from Putnam and Briggs in May of 1854, has affiliations with Melville's other two-part pieces—"Poor Man's Pudding and Rich Man's Crumbs" and "The Paradise of Bachelors and the Tartarus of Maids," which were apparently paid for by *Harper's* in that same month. Does it follow, then, that all these pieces were written and submitted at about the same time? Or were one or more of them held for an extended period before they were acted upon? Answers to such questions must necessarily be conjectural at best.

Here is the probable chronology through the summer of 1854:

Winter of 1852–53: Work on "the story of Agatha," in all likelihood the manuscript that Melville submitted to Harper & Brothers in the spring of 1853 but was "prevented from printing."

Spring and summer of 1853: (1) Composition, copying, and submission to *Harper's New Monthly Magazine* (on August 13?) of "Cock-A-Doodle-Doo!" (published December, 1853) and two other pieces, probably "The Happy Failure" (published July, 1854) and "The Fiddler" (published September, 1854). (2) Either revision and resubmission of one of these pieces or submission to *Harper's* of a fourth contribution (before September 20), misdirected to *Putnam's Monthly Magazine.* (3) Composition, copying, and submission to *Putnam's* (after September 20?) of "Bartleby, the Scrivener" (published November, December, 1853).[23]

Autumn of 1853 and winter of 1853–54: (1) Work on the "Tortoise Book" proposed to Harper & Brothers on November 24 but apparently never finished. (2) Work on "The Encantadas" for *Putnam's* (possibly submitted, at least in part, on February 6; announced as forthcoming

23. "Bartleby" is printed here with the other stories Melville collected in *The Piazza Tales.* Since it is impossible to determine the order in which he composed these seven pieces, the other items are grouped arbitrarily as follows: (1) "The Happy Failure," "The Fiddler," and "Cock-A-Doodle-Doo!" as the stories probably first submitted to *Harper's* in 1853; (2) next the three two-part sketches—"Poor Man's Pudding and Rich Man's Crumbs," "The Two Temples," and "The Paradise of Bachelors and the Tartarus of Maids"—submitted to *Harper's* and *Putnam's* between September of 1853 and May of 1854. The sequence within each of the two groups is from the shorter and simpler pieces to the longer and more complex.

on February 14; published in March, April, May, 1854). (3) Work on "Poor Man's Pudding and Rich Man's Crumbs" (if not already submitted), "The Two Temples," and "The Paradise of Bachelors and the Tartarus of Maids."

Spring and early summer of 1854: (1) Acceptance by *Harper's* of "Poor Man's Pudding and Rich Man's Crumbs" (probably paid for in May, 1854; published in June, 1854) and "The Paradise of Bachelors and the Tartarus of Maids" (paid for in May, 1854; published in April, 1855). (2) Submission to *Putnam's* of "The Two Temples" (rejected on May 12, 1854). (3) Work on *Israel Potter* (proposed June? 7, 1854; serialized in *Putnam's*, July of 1854 through March of 1855; issued in book form in March, 1855). (4) Preparation of extracts from the proposed "Tortoise Book" (submitted to Harper & Brothers on July 25?). (5) Composition, copying, and submission to *Putnam's* of "The Lightning-Rod Man" (published August, 1854).

Between November of 1853 and March of 1855, when Putnam sold his magazine to Joshua Dix and Arthur Edwards, Melville earned \$674.50 from *Putnam's Monthly* alone, as shown by entries in a ledger (now lost) recording its payments to authors. During this same period he probably received an additional \$145 from *Harper's,* allowing for an estimated payment of \$45 for "Cock-A-Doodle-Doo!" (nine printed pages @ \$5.00 per page) in addition to the \$100 for other contributions that he acknowledged in May of 1854. There is no reason to suppose that he was paid for occasional reprintings in newspapers and magazines; for example, the *Western Literary Messenger* of Buffalo, which reprinted "Poor Man's Pudding and Rich Man's Crumbs" in August of 1854 and also copied two chapters of the serialized *Israel Potter,* was eclectic in a large degree and did not pay its authors.[24] For Melville's remaining contributions to *Harper's* and *Putnam's* in 1855 and 1856 there is only one known record of an individual payment, but if the magazines continued to pay at the same rate during these years the probable total was over \$400: approximately \$32.50 for two pieces in *Harper's,* "Jimmy Rose" and "The 'Gees" (total 6½ pages), and \$377.50 for five pieces in *Putnam's,* "The Lightning-Rod Man," "The

24. Frank Luther Mott, *A History of American Magazines,* 5 vols. (New York: D. Appleton and Co., 1930; Cambridge, Mass.: Harvard University Press and The Belknap Press of Harvard University Press, 1938–57), II, 20, 116. *The Melville Log,* II, 481ff., quotes entries from the now-lost Putnam ledger of payments to Melville by *Putnam's Monthly Magazine.*

Bell-Tower," "Benito Cereno," "I and My Chimney," and "The Apple-Tree Table" (total 75½ pages). The grand total of these several estimates is $1,329.50 for all of Melville's magazine writing of 1853–56, a larger sum than that formerly reckoned before it was known that his contributions commanded $5.00 per printed page.[25] In addition, he received at least one payment of royalties for *Israel Potter* in book form: $48.31 on October 8, 1855.

As this survey indicates, Melville sent more of his contributions to *Putnam's* than he did to *Harper's*; on the whole, his longer narratives went either to Putnam or Putnam's successors, Dix & Edwards, while his shorter pieces were awaiting action by Harper & Brothers. The fact that the Harpers held his manuscripts for such long periods, coupled with his difficulty in obtaining a decision concerning the projected "Tortoise Book," may have something to do with his apparent preference for dealing with *Putnam's Monthly*. If "Jimmy Rose" and "The 'Gees" constitute the "brace of fowl—wild fowl" mentioned in the letter headed "Sept: 18th" that Melville apparently wrote on that date in 1854, then it must be observed that "Jimmy Rose" remained unpublished for the next fourteen months and "The 'Gees" for eighteen—just at the time when Melville's contributions to *Putnam's* were appearing regularly. "Jimmy Rose" has affiliations with two other pieces sent to *Putnam's* rather than *Harper's*: "I and My Chimney" (published in March, 1856) and "The Apple-Tree Table" (May, 1856); since "I and My Chimney" is known to have been in the hands of Dix & Edwards by July of 1855, it appears that the three stories were written in sequence at some time between late summer in 1854 and the summer or fall of 1855. "The 'Gees" is like both "The Encantadas" (1854) and "Benito Cereno" (1855) in its association with Melville's knowledge of the sea, but it also looks forward to *The Confidence-Man* (1857), which Melville completed in 1856. That "The 'Gees" was written as late as 1856, when Melville was occupied with both *The Piazza Tales* and *The Confidence-Man*, seems unlikely, however, and indeed there is some internal evidence for placing its composition as early as July or August of 1854 on the ground that it is in part a response to an article that appeared in the July issue of *Putnam's*. In short, both "Jimmy

25. In 1943 William Charvat estimated that Melville received "a little over $725" in all for his magazine work of this period, or "an average of about $240 a year." See Charvat, "Melville's Income," *American Literature*, XV (November, 1943), 255; reprinted in *The Profession of Authorship in America, 1800–1870: The Papers of William Charvat*, ed. Matthew J. Bruccoli (Columbus: Ohio State University Press, 1968), p. 194.

Rose" and "The 'Gees" might well have been ready for submission by mid-September of that year.

Melville's correspondence with Dix & Edwards on August 7 and 10, 1855, concerning payment of $37.50 for "The Bell-Tower" (7½ printed pages) indicates that the new owners of *Putnam's Monthly* continued to pay him at the rate of $5.00 per page. He had evidently submitted the manuscript of "The Bell-Tower" by late May or early June of 1855, since it was included with other contributions that Joshua Dix forwarded to his editorial advisor, George William Curtis, in time for Curtis to comment on the story in his letters of June 18 and 19; the story was included in the August issue and paid for immediately upon publication. "Benito Cereno" was not handled so promptly. The longer work, probably composed during the winter of 1854–55, must have been submitted to *Putnam's* before mid-April of 1855, when it was discussed in correspondence between Dix and Curtis. Curtis thought the story as a whole to be "very striking & well done" and recommended its acceptance, although he disliked "the dreary documents at the end" and observed that Melville "does everything too hurriedly now." For some reason *Putnam's* did not begin serializing "Benito Cereno" until the October number, however, even though Curtis had urged Dix to use it in September, adding in his letter of July 31, 1855, that "You have paid for it."[26]

The first of Melville's two remaining stories for *Putnam's*, "I and My Chimney," was included in a batch of manuscript contributions that Dix forwarded to Curtis in July of 1855. Curtis held the manuscripts until September 7, when he singled out "I and My Chimney" for praise as "thoroughly magazinish," but Dix did not use the story until March of 1856—after the serialization of "Benito Cereno" in the October, Novem-

26. "Benito Cereno" appears to be the one story for which *Putnam's* paid Melville in advance of its publication. From this circumstance, and from Melville's own reference, in a letter to Dix & Edwards dated "April 1st 1855", to "proof" of an unnamed work (*Letters*, p. 173), it has been conjectured that the story had been submitted and set in type even before Dix & Edwards took over the magazine from Putnam. But Alma A. MacDougall has now demonstrated that Melville's letter was written on April 1, 185*6*, rather than 1855, and that its mention of "proof" must therefore refer not to "Benito Cereno" but rather to the volume then in press, *The Piazza Tales*. See (1) a study anticipating the present NOTE: Merton M. Sealts, Jr., "The Chronology of Melville's Short Fiction, 1853–1856," *Harvard Library Bulletin*, XXVIII (October, 1980), 401; (2) Alma A. MacDougall, "The Chronology of *The Confidence-Man* and 'Benito Cereno,' " *Melville Society Extracts*, No. 53 (February, 1983), 3–6.

ber, and December numbers and subsequent planning of the collection that became *The Piazza Tales.* "The Apple-Tree Table," unmentioned in Melville's surviving correspondence or that between Curtis and Dix, did not appear until May of 1856. As noted above, both of these stories have affiliations with "Jimmy Rose," published in *Harper's* for November, 1855, but apparently written as early as the summer of 1854. The narrator of "I and My Chimney" suffers from sciatica; Melville himself had an attack of "severe rheumatism" in February of 1855 and was treated for sciatica in the following June, when he may have been finishing work on his story. "The Apple-Tree Table" was probably written later in the year, either just before or just after the "severe illness" from which he was reported as recovering in mid-September. It was in December of 1855, after the final installment of "Benito Cereno" had appeared in *Putnam's,* that Melville proposed collecting those of his stories which had been published in the magazine up to that time, and in January or February of 1856 he composed "The Piazza" as a title piece for the volume. "About having the author's name on the title-page, you may do as you deem best," he told Dix & Edwards on January 19; "but any appending of titles of former works is hardly worth while."

The probable chronology of Melville's writing for the magazines can now be extended to summarize the remainder of this period.

Winter of 1854–55: Composition, copying, submission to *Putnam's* (by mid-April) of "Benito Cereno" (published October, November, and December, 1855, though paid for before July 31).

Spring of 1855: Composition, copying, and submission to *Putnam's* (by late May or early June) of "The Bell-Tower" (published August, 1855) and (by July) of "I and My Chimney" (published March, 1856).

Summer or fall of 1855: Composition, copying, and submission to *Putnam's* of "The Apple-Tree Table" (published May, 1856).

January–February, 1856: (1) Revision (by January 19) of the magazine pieces collected in *The Piazza Tales.* (2) Composition, copying, and submission to Dix & Edwards (on February 16) of "The Piazza."

On March 24, 1856, Melville returned the signed agreement for *The Piazza Tales* to Dix & Edwards along with unspecified "proofs"; these may well have been proofs of the five stories originally published in *Putnam's.* On February 16 he had also requested proof of his new title piece, "The Piazza"; this must have reached him between March 24 and April 1, when he wrote again, returning "the proof last sent" and requesting additional proofs of "the whole as made up in page form." Dix & Edwards published *The Piazza Tales* in May of 1856; there was an English issue in June.

Before writing "The Piazza" Melville was already well along with *The Confidence-Man,* his tenth book; there are several correspondences between its early chapters and "The Apple-Tree Table." Apparently he had first proposed *The Confidence-Man* to Dix as early as June of 1855, quite possibly for serialization in *Putnam's,* but Curtis had advised Dix at that time to "decline any novel from Melville that is not extremely good." Whether Melville may also have approached Harper & Brothers with his manuscript, either as a magazine serial or as a book, is not known.[27] Arrangements to publish it in book form were concluded with Dix & Edwards in October of 1856, before Melville sailed for Europe, and *The Confidence-Man* appeared in April of 1857 while he was still abroad.

Melville's primary objective in proposing to Dix & Edwards in December of 1855 the volume that became *The Piazza Tales* was to meet pressing obligations that his earnings from authorship were insufficient to cover. This is clear from two letters to his father-in-law, Lemuel Shaw, written during the month in which the book was published, that summarize his financial troubles. He had borrowed money from Shaw, first to pay for his share of the New York house he occupied with his brother Allan following his marriage in 1847; he had borrowed from Shaw again in 1850 when he purchased property at Pittsfield, increasing the debt to $5,000. At that same time he had also given a mortgage of $1,500 to Dr. John Brewster of Pittsfield, from whom he bought the Arrowhead property, and in 1851 he borrowed an additional $2,050 from Tertullus D. Stewart, an old friend from Lansingburgh, to pay for "building the new kitchen, wood-house, piazza, making alterations, painting" at Arrowhead, for "making up the deficiency in the sums received from the sale of the New York house," and for current expenses. But he had afterwards fallen behind in paying the interest due Stewart, which at nine percent came to $184.50 each year, and on May 1, 1856, the note itself matured. In this emergency he had already advertised all or part of his Pittsfield holdings for sale in order to pay both Stewart and Brewster. So Melville

27. "Don't have the Harpers," Melville was to tell his brother Allan four years later, on May 22, 1860, when he wrote a memorandum "concerning the publication of my verses."

informed Shaw on May 12, 1856. As of the previous March, moreover, he owed Harper & Brothers $348.51—"a balance which would not have been against me," he explained to Shaw on May 22, "but for my loss of about $1000 in their fire" in December of 1853. The account with the Harpers, he continued,

> will gradually be squared (as the original balance has already been lessened) by sales. Before the fire, the books (not including any new publication) were a nominal resource to me of some two or three hundred dollars a year; though less was realised, owing to my obtaining, from time to time, considerable advances, upon which interest had to be paid. After the present acct: is squared, the books will very likely be a moderate resource to me again. I have certain books in hand [evidently *The Piazza Tales* and *The Confidence-Man*] which may or may not fetch in money. My immediate resources are what I can get for articles sent to magazines.

In a postscript Melville added that he "should have mentioned above a book to be published this week," *The Piazza Tales*, "from which some returns will ere long be had. Likewise some further returns, not much, may be looked for from a book published about a year ago by Mr. Putnam," *Israel Potter* (1855). "The articles in Harpers Magazine are paid for without respect to my book acct: with them."[28]

Melville's expectation of "returns" from *The Piazza Tales* proved ill-founded, however. His publishing agreement with Dix & Edwards was similar to that concluded with Putnam for *Israel Potter*: the copyright would stand in Melville's name, and he would receive a royalty of 12½ percent per copy—but only after expenses of the volume were paid. The agreement, signed on March 17, 1856, provided that copy would be furnished by February 20, as had already been done, but set no date for publication. Advertisements subsequently published by Dix & Edwards announced the work as "in press" by April 5 and as scheduled to appear on May 15. It was May 20, however, before a copy was deposited for copyright, registered in the name of the author. It is a duodecimo volume printed by Miller & Holman, Printers and Stereotypers, of New York, with 431 pages of text followed by seven pages of advertisements for other publications of Dix & Edwards. The title page not only names Melville

28. Patricia Barber, "Two New Melville Letters," *American Literature*, XLIX (November, 1977), 418–21.

but goes on to do what he had considered "hardly worth while": it identifies him as "Author of 'Typee,' 'Omoo,' etc., etc., etc." The front and back covers, measuring 18.8 by 12 centimeters, are blind stamped with an ornamental border of rules and rosettes and with the centered initials "D & E" enclosed by a floral design. The spine is stamped in gold: at the top, "THE / PIAZZA / TALES / —— / MELVILLE" within a floral design; at the bottom, within rules, "DIX EDWARDS & Co.". The volume was issued in various colors of cloth (blue, violet, green, brown, and black among them). The book, priced at $1.00 per copy, was apparently not released to the public until the week of May 24–31, according to contemporary notices in the *American Publishers' Circular*; its first known review appeared in the New York *Atlas* for Sunday, May 25, 1856. More than thirty additional reviews appeared in American newspapers and magazines between May and September; on July 26 the London *Athenæum* reviewed its English publication by Sampson Low. Despite the generally favorable tone of these notices the book sold slowly, however. On August 25 Melville wrote Dix & Edwards requesting a report of sales; their reply of August 30 informed him that the book had "not yet paid expenses," which amounted to $1,048.62. Of 2,500 copies bound, 1,193 still remained on hand, 260 had been given free to editors, and 1,047 had been sold at sixty cents apiece, realizing only $628.20.[29] As events turned out, this discouraging report would be the last Melville received from Dix & Edwards.

On October 28, 1856, after Melville himself had sailed for Europe, his brother Allan signed an agreement on his behalf with Dix & Edwards for *The Confidence-Man,* which appeared in 1857 while he was still abroad. Like other American businesses in that critical year, the house experienced hard times, and on April 27, 1857, Dix & Edwards dissolved partnership, to be succeeded in turn by Miller & Company and then in June by Miller & Curtis. This firm too was soon in difficulty. In August, after selling the still-profitable *Putnam's Monthly* to *Emerson's United States Magazine*, Miller & Curtis failed. The absence of further statements of account from either Dix & Edwards or its successor firms suggests that Melville received not a penny of royalties from the American sales of either *The Piazza Tales* or *The Confidence-Man*, both of which had been published under similar

29. Merton M. Sealts, Jr., "The Publication of Melville's *Piazza Tales,*" *Modern Language Notes,* LIX (January, 1944), 56–59. Melville's publishing agreements with Dix & Edwards and the statement of account cited are now in the Melville Collection of the Harvard College Library (Houghton Library MS. Am 188, Nos. 451–55).

terms. As for sales abroad, Sampson Low, Son, & Co., the London publisher of *The Piazza Tales* (as of *Pierre* and *Israel Potter*), imported American printed sheets for English distribution, so that any purchases of sheets by Low should have been reflected in the American sales figures. Longmans, Brown & Green, the English publisher of *The Confidence-Man*, reported directly to Melville in June of 1857 and again a year later that sales of that work had not yet made expenses; here again the publishing contract provided that no payment would be made to the author until the work was yielding a profit.[30]

In September of 1857, following the failure of Miller & Curtis, the partners determined to sell their stock of books and stereotype plates at the annual auction sale conducted by the New York Book-Publishers' Association. Before the sale, pursuant to a clause in Melville's contract for *The Confidence-Man* with Dix & Edwards (and the firm's successors), George William Curtis wrote Melville offering him the opportunity to purchase the plates for that book and *The Piazza Tales* as well at 25 percent of their first cost, but Melville was obliged to reply on September 15 that he could not "conveniently make arrangements with regard to them." Four days later the plates went on sale at auction but were withdrawn after attracting no offers. Plates of other authors changed hands at the auction, though at phenomenally low prices, as Davis and Gilman remark, but "no one would risk a dollar on Melville."[31] It was Melville's own belief that "if held on to for a while," the plates might eventually be transferred to him "to the common advantage of all concerned," but on September 26, realizing that the partners were anxious to settle their affairs, he authorized Curtis to sell the plates for scrap—their probable fate, it would seem, since neither *The Confidence-Man* nor *The Piazza Tales* was again printed from them. The failure of Miller & Curtis reflects the times; the financial failure of both books and Melville's inability to raise even a nominal sum for buying in their plates reflect also the critical state of his professional career in 1857.

30. G. Thomas Tanselle, "The Sales of Melville's Books," *Harvard Library Bulletin*, XVII (April, 1969), 195–215; as Tanselle notes, p. 198, no Sampson Low account is present among the publishing documents now in the Melville Collection at Harvard.

31. *Letters*, p. 188, n. 9.

If Melville saw many of the contemporary reviews of *The Piazza Tales* he would have been entirely justified in expecting handsome "returns" from his new volume, which manifestly pleased his critics as no other work from his pen had done since the appearance of *Redburn* and *White-Jacket* in 1849 and 1850. Between May and September of 1856 at least thirty-seven notices appeared, ranging from two or three sentences of comment to full-length reviews with quotations from one or more of the stories.[32] The single English review that has been located appeared in the London *Athenæum* for July 26; it was one of five notices that can be classed as preponderantly unfavorable, although some of the other reviews praised the book with occasional reservations.

Like the *Athenæum*'s reviewer, those who either disliked the book or qualified their praise of it objected primarily to Melville's alleged eccentricities of literary style. The *Athenæum* quotes the opening paragraph of "The Bell-Tower" to support the reviewer's thesis: "Under the idea of being romantic and pictorial in style," Melville is "sometimes barely intelligible." Otherwise, he might belong with Irving, Poe, and Hawthorne among those Americans who "excel in short tales," but in this volume "he gives us merely indications, not fulfilment." Four American critics also took a generally negative position. Though the Boston *Monthly Religious Magazine and Independent Journal* liked "The Encantadas," calling them "pleasantly and attractively written" sketches, it objected to the other pieces as either "sentimental and silly" or "truculent and harrowing"; their "inverted and inflated style . . . should banish them from the favor of all who love the simple, straightforward Saxon." According to the Boston *Daily Evening Traveller*, Melville "is a very imaginative writer, and is so prone to travel into the mystic regions of fairy land, that it is very seldom he can be either appreciated or understood." The reviewer for *Godey's Lady's Book*, though aware of Melville's "numerous admirers," found his writing unsatisfying: "His style has an affectation of quaintness, which renders it, to us, very confused and wearisome. Nevertheless, those with whom he is a favorite will not think the worse of him" after reading *The Piazza Tales*. But the New York *Daily Times* held that the volume "will not augment his high reputation. . . . The author of 'Typee' should do something higher and better than Magazine articles."

32. A chronological listing of these reviews appears in the section on "Sources" at the end of this NOTE.

These unfavorable reviews, which object primarily to the supposed difficulties of understanding Melville, are more than outweighed by the thirty-two other notices, many of which have high praise for his "singularly graphic power" (Boston *Puritan Recorder*), "taking variety of style" (*The Churchman* of New York), "vivid imagination and wonderful faculty of description" (New York *Evening Post*), and "widely recognized power as a story teller" (*Morning Courier and New-York Enquirer*). He possesses "the art of conveying deep expression by simple touches," according to the New York *Sun*; each touch is "suggestive of a picture, the details of which appear on careful examination. His style is felicitously adapted to the subject." A Boston religious paper, the *Christian Freeman and Family Visiter*, found in Melville "two indispensable requirements for a successful romance writer—vivid imagination and remarkable descriptive powers." The *Hampshire and Franklin Express* of Amherst liked not only the "style of great beauty" and "graphic description," particularly of local scenery, in *The Piazza Tales* but the "life-like" characterizations and the "natural and beautiful" portraiture. According to the *United States Magazine and Democratic Review*, all of the tales "exhibit that peculiar richness of language, descriptive vitality, and splendidly sombre imagination which are the author's characteristics." They are written with Melville's "usual felicity of expression, and minuteness of detail," according to the *Knickerbocker* of New York, but the New York *Daily Tribune*, which granted that the stories "show something" of his customary "boldness of invention, brilliancy of imagination, and quaintness of expression," also saw in them "not a little" of his "apparent perversity and self-will, which serve as a foil to their various excellences." The Boston *Quarterly Journal of the American Unitarian Association* also recognized Melville's "own fresh and curt style." The tales "have an individuality peculiar to this writer, and one always readable, even when manner and sentiment may not be exactly to our taste."

It is evident that a number of these critics found *The Piazza Tales* more satisfying than *Mardi, Moby-Dick,* and *Pierre*. "This new work of our fellow citizen is decidedly the most readable which he has published since Omoo and Typee," according to the *Berkshire County Eagle* of Pittsfield on May 30, 1856. "Without so many striking passages as 'Moby Dick' and some others," the *Eagle* went on to say, *The Piazza Tales* "is more uniformly excellent and is more free from blemishes than any of Mr. Melville's later books." The local reviewer was presumably Melville's friend and later biographer J. E. A.

Smith.[33] In a subsequent article the *Eagle* of August 8 predicted that Melville, being "now in the prime of his life and in the freshness of his genius, . . . will yet write something much better than any of the works upon which his reputation now rests." The *Southern Literary Messenger,* remembering Melville's "unfortunate" appearance as the author of *Pierre,* found "much of his former freshness and vivacity" restored in *The Piazza Tales.* The *Churchman* placed the volume within "the just mean" between the two extremes of Melville's style, of which his *Typee* and *Moby-Dick* are "types." The New York *Evening Post* was reminded "agreeably" of Melville's "earliest and best works," and the Newark *Daily Advertiser* enthusiastically agreed:

> This book is in the real Typee and Omoo vein. One reads . . . with delight and with rejoicing that the author has laid his rhapsod[iz]ing aside, which savored too much of Swift, Rabelais and other such works, as suggest that they were the fruits of his reading rather than of his imagination. But this book evinces that he has neither "run out" or been overpraised, for the same freshness, geniality and beauty are as flourishing as of old.

A long notice in the New York *Daily News* is exceptional in taking issue with those readers and critics who wanted Melville to continue writing as "the author of *Typee*" and deplored both the subject matter and the style of his later works. "It is not long since we heard some pessimist lamenting the decline of Mr. Melville's brilliance as a writer," wrote the reviewer for the *News.*

> Now if the decay of which the said literary mourner complains be not in himself, we recommend him to purchase and peruse the delightful "Piazza Tales." They will effectually correct the acidity of his criticism.

33. The volume is described as comprising "several graphic tales, some of which have been before admired by us." During 1854 the *Eagle* of March 10 had commented on the first magazine installment of "The Encantadas" (note 17, above); on July 7 the *Eagle*'s notice of the July issue of *Putnam's* remarked that a "Berkshire story [*Israel Potter*], said—without doubt correctly,—to be written by Herman Melville, will be of especial interest in this quarter"; on August 25 the *Eagle* alluded to the "poetical thought and eccentric comment" afforded by the September installment of *Israel Potter.* Although Smith was not engaged as editor of the *Eagle* until the following December, he had been a contributor to Pittsfield newspapers "from about the year 1850," according to Edward Boltman, *The History of Pittsfield, Mass.* (Pittsfield, 1916), p. 315, and may therefore have written some or all of these notices.

> But we are inclined to think that the source of discontent is only the altered mood of the reader to which we have referred, as we can nowhere find in any of Mr. Melville's writings the slightest rational symptom of deterioration. They are, we admit, moulded in styles different from the peculiar setting of Typee, but that fact only proves the versatility of the pen which prepared them.

Enlarging on his point, the reviewer goes on not only to explain how and why *Typee* had captured popular interest but to argue that the public is unreasonable in expecting any creative talent repeatedly to surpass itself. If the artist does not do so,

> the world says he is declining, when a more philosophical examination of his efforts would prove the reverse. Intellect is not always revealed in a succession of surprises, but rather by its permanent and steady blaze. The human eye becomes at length tamely accustomed to the corruscations of the meteor which dazzled, at its first appearance—the common ear grows familiar at last with the crash of artillery, whose first detonation almost stunned it—yet the meteor is none the less bright; the ordnance not a whit fainter than before.

The reviewer for the *News* obviously took Melville's book more seriously than still others of his colleagues who praised *The Piazza Tales* as merely "a delightful companion for an afternoon lounge," to borrow the words of the New York *Sun*. "Scarcely a pleasanter book for summer reading could be recommended," said the *Churchman*, and the New York *Criterion* and *United States Magazine and Democratic Review* agreed. The Boston *Evening Transcript* expected it to be a favorite "at the watering places and in the rural districts this season," and the *North American and United States Gazette* of Philadelphia called it "a pleasant volume of sketches. . . . It has the author's characteristics, mannerisms and all, and is as desirable an afternoon book as one may meet." Most of these comments come from brief and almost cursory notices that are counterbalanced by several longer reviews. Here the critics evaluate one or more individual stories, sometimes providing illustrative extracts to support their pronouncements. The longest review, that in the *Churchman*, includes a dozen paragraphs from "The Piazza" and two more from "The Bell-Tower."

Several of the reviewers had especially kind words for "The Piazza," which was called "a very charming sketch" (Boston *Evening Transcript*), "one of the most charming . . . in our language" (New York *Daily*

News), "full of freshness and beauty" (New York *Daily Times*), and "one of the most graceful specimens of writing we have seen from an American pen. It is a poem—essentially a poem—lacking only rhythm and form" (Springfield *Republican*). An unusual comment on "The Piazza" was probably written by an old family friend of the Melvilles, William E. Cramer, editor of the Milwaukee *Daily Wisconsin*, whose paper described the sketch as

> a most happy reflection upon that fault-finding ideality which considers imaginary fancyings the true heaven of delights, and dwells upon reality as a useless institution. It is given in abrupt sentences, which shows a particular nervousness in the writer that makes it a rich literary treat, being so different from the old mule-team of authorship, that one feels new life in its perusal.

Apparently the reviewer regarded "The Piazza" as another of Melville's attacks on contemporary Transcendentalists. "Let it be read," he concluded, "for its influence will profit."

"Bartleby" drew praise from the New York *Daily Tribune* as "the most original story in the volume"; the Boston *Daily Evening Traveller* called it "a splendidly-told tale, which of itself renders the volume of value," and to the *Berkshire County Eagle* it seemed "one of the best bits of writing which ever came from the author's pen." "The first part of the story of the scrivener has a singular fascination," the *Morning Courier and New-York Enquirer* observed, but that fascination "was impossible, in the nature of things, to keep up."

The New York *Dispatch* thought "Benito Cereno" and "The Encantadas" to be "the best two tales" in the volume, but other papers had reservations; they are "fresh specimens of Mr. Melville's sea-romances," said the New York *Daily Tribune*, "but cannot be regarded as improvements on his former popular productions in that kind." "Benito Cereno" is "melodramatic, *not* effective," according to the New York *Daily Times*. In its descriptive passages the story "is unsurpassed by any thing which we ever read," said the *Christian Freeman and Family Visiter*, "and it keeps the reader's imagination constantly exercised." The New York *Sun* called "Benito Cereno" "a strangely conceived story"; the New York *Criterion*'s reviewer thought it "a thrilling, weird-like narrative, which, read at midnight, gives an uncomfortable feeling to a powerful imagination," and the *Knickerbocker* agreed: the tale "is most painfully interesting, and in reading it we became nervously anxious for the solution of the mystery it involves."

When "The Encantadas" first appeared in *Putnam's Monthly*, according to the New York *Dispatch*, "the chapters were universally considered among the most interesting papers of that popular Magazine, and each successive chapter was read with avidity by thousands." The New York *Daily Times*, which was disappointed by *The Piazza Tales* as a whole, thought "the sketches of the 'Encantadas'" to be "the best in the volume," and the *Southern Literary Messenger* also gave them "the preference," adding that here Melville again conducts his reader "into that 'wild, weird clime, out of space, out of time,' which is the scene of his earliest and most popular writings." The New York *Atlas*, which was also reminded of "the style of the author's first works," observed that "a more vivid picture of the fire-and-barren-curst Gallipagos we have never read," and quoted four sentences by way of illustration. The *Morning Courier and New-York Enquirer* found the sketches to be "more in the vein of the wondrous traveller's tales, the sober telling of which won Mr. MELVILLE his reputation," while the New York *Dispatch* thought them "a sort of mixture of 'Mardi' and 'Robinson Crusoe'—though far more interesting than the first named work." The New York *Daily News* compared these "beautifully written sketches" to a "gorgeous poem"; such compositions, said the *Christian Freeman and Family Visiter*, "could *not* have been written by a man of ordinary imagination."

"The Lightning-Rod Man," the fifth piece in the volume, also "excited great attention," according to the *United States Magazine and Democratic Review*, "when originally published in *Putnam's Monthly*," but the *Review* failed to enlarge on this observation. The New York *Daily News* noticed the "quaint, wild humor" of the story, which the New York *Daily Tribune* thought "ingenious," but two other comments were negative. According to the New York *Criterion*, it "shows that Mr. Melville can, if he so chooses, write a very indifferent paper," and for the *Southern Literary Messenger* the tale is "a very flat recital which we should never have suspected Melville of producing, had it not been put forth under the sanction of his name."

The prose style of "The Bell-Tower" which so offended the reviewer for the London *Athenæum* had also provoked some doubts about the story even before its original publication in *Putnam's Monthly*. George William Curtis, reading it in manuscript, first wrote Joshua Dix on June 18, 1855, to say that it had "*not* passed muster," but on the following day he reconsidered on the ground that "'The Bell Tower' is, after all, too good to lose," though "some erasures" would be necessary.

> To many the style will seem painfully artificial and pompously self-conscious. But it seems to me well suited to the theme.—The story has the touch of genius in it—and so—spite of the style—it should be accepted. . . .
>
> In reading "The Bell Tower" you must remember that the style is *consistently* picturesque. It isn't Addisonian nor is it Johnsonese.—Neither is Malmsey wine, Springwater.

When the reviewer for the New York *Criterion* first read "The Bell-Tower" "some time since" in *Putnam's*, the story, as he remembered, "rang in our mind for days after." The *Churchman* found in it "some of the weird conception of 'Frankenstein,'" but its "melodramatic effects" reminded the New York *Daily News* of "Poe in his strangest mood." The *United States Magazine and Democratic Review* detected "a broad tinge of German mysticism, not free from some resemblance to Poe," and the *Morning Courier and New-York Enquirer,* which also saw some resemblance to Poe's style, called the story "a happy emulation, though not an imitation," of Poe. The New York *Daily Tribune,* pairing "The Bell-Tower" with "The Lightning-Rod Man," characterized both as "ingenious rhapsodies," while the New York *Albion* considered "The Bell-Tower" as "a fine conception, rather bung[l]ingly worked out." Melville's friend J. E. A. Smith of Pittsfield evidently saw four illustrations of the story drawn by Henry G. Webber, who wrote to Melville on July 12, 1856, offering the drawings "at any price that you may set." Melville may have acquired the sketches, since the *Berkshire County Eagle* remarked on August 8 that " 'The Bell Tower' is a picturesque and arabesque tale well fitted to inspire an artist, as it did one in New York who has made four striking sketches from it, which we trust will be engraved."

"The Bell-Tower" was not the only story to remind readers of Poe. "Perhaps the admirers of Edgar Poe will see, or think they see, an imitation of his concentrated gloom in the wild, weird tale, called 'Bartleby,'" said the *United States Magazine and Democratic Review*; the New York *Dispatch* also found something of the "mysticism" of Poe's tales in "Benito Cereno." Although the London *Athenæum* compared Melville's stories unfavorably to those of Poe, Irving, and Hawthorne, the Springfield *Republican* wrote that *The Piazza Tales* generally are "not unlike, and seem to us not inferior, to the best things of Hawthorne," and two other American papers ranked Melville as a stylist with popular English contemporaries. The New York *Daily News* characterized Melville's prose, especially in "The Piazza" and "The Encantadas," as having poetic qualities reminiscent of Tennyson's verse, and the Boston *Daily Evening Traveller* held that "Bartleby" for its "originality of invention and grotesqueness of humor" is "equal to anything from the pen of Dickens, whose writings it closely resembles, both as to the character of the sketch and the peculiarity of the style." The most extended comparison of *The Piazza Tales* with the work of other American writers appeared in the New Bedford *Daily Mercury*. According to the New Bedford reviewer,[34] the volume offers

> stories of all descriptions, tales of the sea and of the city, some of which are told with due gravity, like that of "Benito Cereno,["] and others, such as "the Encantadas" with that copiousness of fancy and gentility of imagination, which resemble Melville more nearly to Charles Brockden Brown, the great nov[el]ist than to either of our other American story-tellers. Hawthorne is more dry, prosaic and detailed, Irving more elegant, careful and popular, but MELVILLE is a kind of wizard; he writes strange and mysterious things that belong to other worlds beyond this tame and everyday place we live in. Those who delight in romance should get the Piazza Tales, who love strong and picturesque sentences, and the though[t]-ful truths of a writer, who leaves some space for the *reader* to try his own ingenuity upon,—some rests and intervals in the literary voyage.

Most of the contemporary reviewers of *The Piazza Tales* noted that five of the component pieces had first appeared in *Putnam's Monthly Magazine*; according to the *American Publishers' Circular*, "they were, in no small degree, instrumental in raising that journal to its present proud position—the best of all American *Monthlies*." Melville's cousin Henry Sanford Gansevoort was much less generous, observing in a letter to his father, Peter Gansevoort of Albany, that except for "one or two capital pieces" the book was merely "a rehash of former dishes." What other

34. Probably William Ellery Channing II (as suggested by Hugh W. Hetherington, *Melville's Reviewers*, pp. 207, n. 35, and 249); according to Frederick T. McGill, Jr., *Channing of Concord: A Life of William Ellery Channing II* (New Brunswick: Rutgers University Press, 1967), p. 150, Channing, "appointed an assistant editor" of the *Mercury* in February of 1856, "wrote editorials and news articles, poems and reviews."

relatives may have thought of *The Piazza Tales* is not known, but when Lemuel Shaw, Jr., heard that Melville would soon be following it with another book-length publication he wrote to his brother in July of 1856 that "I have no great confidence in the success of his productions." A more responsive letter to Melville himself from an old shipmate, Richard Tobias Greene, the "Toby" of *Typee,* was prompted by Greene's reading of *The Piazza Tales*. Greene had been aboard the *Acushnet* with Melville when the ship visited the Galápagos Islands in search of tortoises; "The Encantadas" in particular, he told Melville, "called up reminiscences of days gone by." The reviewers too had frequently singled out "The Encantadas," and in 1857 Fitz-James O'Brien, writing a long essay on "Our Authors and Authorship: Melville and Curtis," for the April issue of *Putnam's*, chose the sketches to illustrate what he considered the best features of Melville's prose style, contrasting "the charm, and truth, and hazy golden atmosphere of 'Las Encantadas'" with what he called "the grotesque absurdity and incomprehensible verbiage of the 'Lightning-Rod Man.'" Other critics had also denigrated the latter story, although both compositions apparently attracted considerable notice on their first appearance in the pages of *Putnam's* and William E. Burton reprinted "The Lightning-Rod Man" in volume I of his *Cyclopædia of Wit and Humor* (New York: D. Appleton & Co., 1858). Following serialization of "The Encantadas" in 1854 Charles F. Briggs had told Melville of James Russell Lowell's admiration for the conclusion of the eighth sketch, the story of Hunilla; "The only complaint that I have heard about the Encantadas," Briggs added, "was that it might have been longer."

There is little to report concerning the contemporary reception of Melville's magazine pieces not collected in *The Piazza Tales*. When he submitted "I and My Chimney" to *Putnam's* in 1855 it was described by Curtis in a letter to Dix as "a capital, genial, humorous sketch" and "thoroughly magazinish." The same story puzzled Melville's brother Allan, who studded his copy with penciled question marks; Elizabeth Melville, who evidently identified the narrator of "I and My Chimney" with Melville himself, insisted in a later marginal note on another copy that the sharply etched portrait of the narrator's domineering wife applied not to herself but "to his mother—who was very vigorous and energetic—about the farm &c—". "The Apple-Tree Table" drew comment from the New-York *Dispatch* of May 4, 1856, as "an amusingly written chapter on Spiritual Manifestations," but there was no identification of the story as Melville's. Shortly after "Poor Man's Pudding and Rich Man's

Crumbs" appeared in *Harper's* it was twice reprinted without attribution: by the Salem, Massachusetts, *Register* and the *Western Literary Messenger* of Buffalo. In 1855 the Duyckincks' *Cyclopædia of American Literature* identified "Cock-A-Doodle-Doo!" as one of Melville's "most lively and animated productions"; in later years J. E. A. Smith of Pittsfield, in the biographical sketch he wrote after Melville's death in 1891, called "Cock-A-Doodle-Doo!" "a quaint piece of humor and thought" and "I and My Chimney" "a quaintly humorous essay." It was probably at this same time that Henry Mills Alden, editor of *Harper's* from 1869 until his death in 1919, told Arthur Stedman that "Cock-A-Doodle Doo!" was "about the best short story he ever read."

Stedman, who quoted Alden's remark and repeated Smith's phrasing about "Cock-A-Doodle-Doo!" "I and My Chimney," and the Berkshire setting of "The Piazza" in his own biographical articles, remarked in a notice of Melville for *Appleton's Annual Cyclopædia* in 1892 that *The Piazza Tales*, "while containing the powerful stories of 'Benito Cereno' and 'The Bell-Tower,' was published in an unattractive form." Stedman's regard for "The Bell-Tower" may have influenced selection of that story as the one prose piece by Melville to be included in volume VII (1889) of *A Library of American Literature*, edited by his father, Edmund Clarence Stedman, and Ellen M. Hutchinson (New York: Charles L. Webster & Co., 1887–90); the story had previously been reprinted by Rossiter Johnson in *Little Classics. Third Volume: Tragedy* (Boston: James R. Osgood and Co., 1875). In 1891 and 1892 Arthur Stedman, acting for Mrs. Melville, edited four of her late husband's longer works for republication: *Typee*, *Omoo*, *White-Jacket*, and *Moby-Dick*; he also agreed to "investigate" *Israel Potter* as a possible addition, but the publishers' bankruptcy prevented the publication of a fifth volume. Since Stedman had previously expressed slight regard for *Israel Potter*, it is intriguing to conjecture that he might have preferred a new edition of *The Piazza Tales* and perhaps other magazine pieces uncollected by Melville himself; if so, he would presumably have made use of the file of stories from *Harper's* and *Putnam's* that Mrs. Melville assembled and annotated.

It was not until the 1920's, when renewed interest in Melville brought publication of the first full-length biography and the first collected edition of his works, that the short fiction again received the attention of readers and critics. Melville's own contemporaries had thought of him as "the author of *Typee*"; in the early phases of the Melville revival his name was associated chiefly with *Moby-Dick*. But when, in the Constable edition of 1922, *The Piazza Tales* became available once again, Michael Sadleir made an appreciative comment that marked a turning-point in critical evaluation of the canon as a whole. "With no desire to denigrate *Moby-Dick,*" Sadleir wrote, "or to deny it the first place in *importance* among Melville's books,"

> I would venture that his genius is more perfectly and skilfully revealed in a volume of stories belonging to the so-called decadence. *The Piazza Tales* are liable to be dismissed by the critic of to-day with kindly condescension as "the best of the later work," a judgment as misleading as it is easily explained. In some degree the worship of *Moby Dick* and the comparative neglect of the other work are inevitable corollaries to the Melville boom at its present stage. . . . In years to come . . . it will be admitted that the book labours under a sad weight of intolerable prolixity. Nor is this prolixity implicit in the greatness of Melville's writing. This is proved by the two chief stories in *The Piazza Tales. Benito Cereno* and *The Enca[n]tadas* hold in the small compass of their beauty the essence of their author's supreme artistry.

In "the matter of technical control," Sadleir continued, they are an improvement on *Moby-Dick*, and if they "cannot as literary achievement compare with their vast and teeming predecessor," the stories nevertheless "mark the highest technical level of their author's work."[35]

In 1926 the Nonesuch Press published the earliest separate edition of any of Melville's short pieces, reprinting "Benito Cereno" from the 1856 text with illustrations by E. McKnight Kauffer, and in 1928 Edward J. O'Brien called "Benito Cereno" both "the greatest" and "the noblest" of American short stories.[36] In that same year Harold H. Scudder published the first scholarly article on the short fiction, a study of Melville's use of his major literary source for "Benito Cereno," and in 1931 and 1932 Leon Howard and Russell Thomas made similar studies of "The Encantadas."[37] Meanwhile, the bulk of Melville's previously uncollected magazine pieces had been identified and twice reprinted,

35. *Excursions in Victorian Bibliography* (London: Chaundry & Cox, 1922), pp. 220–21.

36. "The Fifteen Finest Short Stories," *Forum*, LXXIX (June, 1928), 909.

37. Harold H. Scudder, "Melville's *Benito Cereno* and Captain Delano's Voyages," *PMLA*, XLIII (June, 1928), 502–32; Leon Howard, "Melville and Spenser—A Note on Criticism," *Modern Language Notes*, XLVI (May, 1931), 291–92; Russell Thomas, "Melville's Use of Some Sources in *The Encantadas*," *American Literature*, III (January, 1932), 432–56.

first in 1922 by Princeton University Press and again in a volume added to the Constable edition of the *Works* in 1924. In 1940 E. H. Eby published a reading of "The Tartarus of Maids"[38] that led other admirers of Melville to begin examining the shorter fiction generally and to observe not only his use of source materials but his employment of imagery and symbol. These early studies and the published texts that made them possible inaugurated a flood of scholarly, interpretative, and critical writing that swelled to its crest in the 1960's and 1970's. During the 1960's Richard Harter Fogle wrote the first book dealing wholly with the magazine fiction and Howard P. Vincent edited the first book-length symposium on a single story, "Bartleby," that included a bibliography of 117 items published up to 1966 touching in some way upon it;[39] during the 1970's R. Bruce Bickley, Marvin Fisher, and William B. Dillingham each published a book on the short fiction.[40]

Of the pieces that Melville himself collected in *The Piazza Tales,* "Benito Cereno" and "The Encantadas" have steadily attracted the notice of scholars and critics over the years while "Bartleby" and "The Piazza" have drawn increasing attention since the 1920's. A number of recent studies have focused on "The Piazza," comparing its place in the Melville canon to that of "The Old Manse" in Hawthorne's writing and setting it against what Melville himself had written in "Hawthorne and His Mosses" to bring out changes in his thought and art between 1850 and 1856. Of the uncollected pieces, "The Paradise of Bachelors and the Tartarus of Maids" and "I and My Chimney" have generated the greatest amount of published discussion. Many of the earlier twentieth-century articles on the shorter fiction, reflecting current fashions of the time in literary study, emphasized what were taken to be autobiographical elements in such stories as "Bartleby" and "I and My Chimney"; other more recent studies have concentrated on their narrative techniques. Interpreters of the short fiction have moved

38. E. H. Eby, "Herman Melville's 'Tartarus of Maids,'" *Modern Language Quarterly,* I (March, 1940), 95–100.

39. Richard Harter Fogle, *Melville's Shorter Tales* (Norman: University of Oklahoma Press, 1960); *Melville Annual 1965 / A Symposium: Bartleby the Scrivener,* ed. Howard P. Vincent (Kent, Ohio: Kent State University Press, 1966).

40. R. Bruce Bickley, Jr., *The Method of Melville's Short Fiction* (Durham, N. C.: Duke University Press, 1975); Marvin Fisher, *Going Under: Melville's Short Fiction and the American 1850s* (Baton Rouge and London: Louisiana State University Press, 1977); William B. Dillingham, *Melville's Short Fiction, 1853–1856* (Athens: University of Georgia Press, 1977).

steadily from metaphysical to epistemological readings and from abstract ethical considerations to more immediate political and social implications—in "Benito Cereno," for example, read in relation to the controversy over slavery during the decade before the Civil War. Much of the commentary has been merely ephemeral, but other more substantial investigation of the magazine pieces has now established Melville's principal sources in his own observation of the contemporary scene (some of it recorded in his earlier journal-entries), his wide knowledge of general literature, and his reading of more specialized materials ranging from narratives of Pacific voyages to newspaper and magazine articles of the day that added both substance and topical interest to his writing.

The investigation of Melville's use of these varied source materials helps to explain what George William Curtis meant in 1855 when he applauded one of the stories as "thoroughly magazinish." Melville himself obviously read *Putnam's* and *Harper's* closely enough to see what kind of writing placed the two magazines among "those most saleable of all books nowadays," and in doing so he must have observed that a high proportion of that writing was in fact quality work—the kind of writing that led Thackeray to call *Putnam's* "much the best Mag. in the world," as Curtis reported in that same year.[41] In short, by contributing to such publications Melville did not have to prostitute himself by writing "the *other* way," as he had feared he must do were he to aim at such lesser periodicals as *Holden's*. In addressing his contemporaries who read *Harper's* and *Putnam's* he managed to work on more than one level, not alternately but simultaneously, so as to reach not only the "superficial skimmer of pages" but also the "eagle-eyed reader" he had distinguished in "Hawthorne and His Mosses," engaging his general audience through skillful use of setting, characterization, sheer good storytelling, and a beautifully modulated prose style while at the same time practicing "the great Art of Telling the Truth" for those capable of receiving it. The favorable contemporary notices of the shorter prose pieces testify to his success in reaching readers of his own day, however superficial their comprehension; the accumulating body of twentieth-century discussion is evidence of the impact his magazine fiction has made on more recent readers. What Sadleir wrote in 1922 about the

41. Curtis to Joshua Dix, September 7, 1855, as quoted in Laura Wood Roper, "'Mr. Law' and *Putnam's Monthly Magazine:* A Note on a Phase in the Career of Frederick Law Olmsted," *American Literature*, XXVI (March, 1954), 92.

high technical competence Melville displayed in the short stories has been repeatedly confirmed by other critics of stature during the past fifty years. In *The Example of Melville,* the best survey to date of Melville's development as a literary craftsman, Warner Berthoff has written that in these "later and mostly shorter writings" after *Pierre*

> we find Melville for the first time willingly confining his utterance within conventional forms, like the tale, the descriptive sketch, the familiar or fanciful essay; the forms, that is, favored by the magazine-public of the day. The work of these years is less "organic," less fused with private interrogation and self-consciousness, though it is not a bit less expressive of the consistent core of Melville's apprehension. And for the very reason that it is less revealing personally, it may actually be *more* instructive as art, more directly exemplary of the possibilities of imaginative composition. If Melville can serve as a practical model, it is likely to be in these performances.[42]

1857–1860

Melville's European tour, which was to last for approximately seven months, took him first to Glasgow and Edinburgh in Scotland and next to York and Liverpool in England. From Liverpool he wrote to his brother Allan that traveling had benefited his health, although in walking he still had "pretty often to rest." He looked up Hawthorne at the American consulate in Liverpool and spent three days with him at Southport before reembarking for Constantinople. Hawthorne left a celebrated account of the reunion in his English notebooks. Though Melville at first exhibited "his characteristic gravity and reserve of manner," Hawthorne noted, the two friends were soon "on pretty much our former terms of sociability and confidence." Melville's appearance was much the same, if "a little paler, and perhaps a little sadder"; his health, however, had declined in the four years since their last meeting, and he mentioned "neuralgic complaints in his head and limbs." To Hawthorne as to his own family he showed the effects of "too constant literary occupation, pursued without much success, latterly," and in Hawthorne's judgment "his writings, for a long while past, . . . indicated a morbid state of mind." Although the Atlantic

42. Warner Berthoff, *The Example of Melville* (Princeton: Princeton University Press, 1962), pp. 56–57.

voyage had already made him feel better, "the spirit of adventure is gone out of him," as Hawthorne put it, and he himself "did not anticipate much pleasure" in the traveling which lay ahead. When they talked on the sands at Southport, Melville began in his old way "to reason of Providence and futurity, and of everything that lies beyond human ken," leading Hawthorne to observe that religious doubt—particularly on the score of personal immortality—was troubling him deeply. "He can neither believe, nor be comfortable in his unbelief," Hawthorne wrote; "and he is too honest and courageous not to try to do one or the other. If he were a religious man, he would be one of the most truly religious and reverential; he has a very high and noble nature, and better worth immortality than most of us." Although other friends and relatives were to report frequently on Melville's health during the next few years there was no observer who penetrated more deeply than Hawthorne into Melville's state of mind in the mid-1850's.

From Liverpool Melville took a steamer for the Mediterranean, reaching Constantinople in December and spending the winter months of 1856–57 in traveling through Egypt, Palestine, Greece, and Italy. He had kept a detailed journal since leaving New York, at least partly to record material for possible literary use, as the tenor of some of the entries suggests. The accounts of persons and places are often impressionistic and fragmentary, punctuated by Melville's personal reactions to what he saw and heard; there are occasional hints of the religious doubts he had voiced to Hawthorne and scattered references to his physical ills—neuralgic pains in the head and body and recurrent trouble with his eyes. While at Rome in March he noted a week's abstinence from journal-writing "owing to state of my eyes and general incapacity"; but to Samuel Shaw, who saw him briefly there, it appeared that traveling had much improved his general health. Melville left Italy in April, proceeding northward through Switzerland, Germany, and Holland to England and taking time both to visit London, Oxford, and Stratford and to see Hawthorne once more before sailing for America in May. Arriving in New York on the 20th, he went at once to Boston, where his wife had been staying with her father. There he described himself as feeling better than at any time since his departure for Europe, though still not perfectly well.

While Melville was still abroad the Shaws and Gansevoorts had again been trying to secure a political appointment for him, this time in the customs service, in the belief that his uncertain health would not permit a return to his desk or continued farm work at Pittsfield. To these plans Melville himself was agreeable, telling the younger Lemuel Shaw in Boston that he "was not going to write any more at present" and that he hoped to "get a place" in the Custom House at New York. Following his return to Arrowhead, as the office-seeking in his behalf continued, he advertised the Pittsfield property for sale and arranged through his brother Allan to buy a house in Brooklyn, but in August Allan felt it necessary to obtain a release from the agreement to purchase: the appointment in New York had not materialized and the farm had not been sold.[43] In that same month, having been invited to contribute to a projected new magazine, the *Atlantic Monthly*, Melville replied favorably though he was merely keeping his future options open; he had nothing on hand to submit and was unable, as he said, to "name the day when I shall have any article ready." There was material enough in his European journal for a whole series of magazine pieces based on his travels, or even for a book, had he been willing to write, though to place a new book during the hard times of 1857 would have been difficult or impossible for him.

By the fall of 1857 Melville was considering a new expedient: like George William Curtis, also known to the public as a writer of travels, he would follow the current fashion and seek engagements as a lyceum lecturer. As early as February of 1854, when his brother-in-law John C. Hoadley had urged him to think of such a possibility, his mother had assured him it would bring "fame & fortune"; the subject had arisen again at a dinner party given for Melville in Boston shortly after his return from the Mediterranean, when his summer neighbor Dr. Holmes, as successful a platform speaker as he was a doctor, poet, and wit, had characterized a lecturer as "a literary strumpet" willing "for a greater than whore's fee to prostitute himself." Melville's own opinion of lecturers and lecturing had not been high, to judge from satirical jibes in *Pierre* and his earlier refusal to capitalize on the success of *Typee* by making lyceum appearances. But his situation in 1857 was far different, and itinerant lecturing might at least be preferable to the renewed drudgery of further magazine writing and perhaps just as profitable. By late September he had already accepted "two or three" invitations

43. See Patricia Barber, "Herman Melville's House in Brooklyn," *American Literature*, XLV (November, 1973), 433–34.

"prompted by" Curtis, and after the New York *Tribune* listed him in October among speakers available for the winter lecture season there were additional inquiries from cities as distant as Clarksville in Tennessee, Rockford in Illinois, and St. Louis. Not all of the possible engagements could be conveniently scheduled, but between November of 1857 and February of 1858 Melville lectured in sixteen cities and towns. Two of his appearances during this first season were without fee; elsewhere he received amounts ranging from $20.00 to $75.00. By his own reckoning, entered in the notebook of lecture engagements that is reproduced on pp. 801–7 below, his total receipts for the season were $645.00 and his traveling expenses $221.30, leaving a net gain of $423.70—a figure roughly comparable to the income from a winter of magazine writing.

Throughout his first season of lecturing Melville repeated a single offering that he himself referred to as "Statues in Rome," though it was advertised locally under a variety of titles such as "Sight-seeing in Rome" at Montreal and "The Remains of Ancient Art" at New Bedford. Although several newspaper reviews characterized the lecture as an admirable literary essay suitable for publication, Melville did not print "Statues in Rome" or either of his later lectures, and no manuscripts are known to survive. But from the thirty-two newspaper reports of 1857–58 that have been located it is possible not only to follow his somewhat mixed reception during this first season but also to study the content, organization, and even something of the style of "Statues in Rome" itself, since many of the papers carried long summaries of lectures that sometimes approached a full transcription of key passages.

Melville probably composed "Statues in Rome" in late September or early October of 1857. On September 15 he had written Curtis that he was "trying to scratch my brains for a Lecture. What is a good, earnest subject? *Daily progress of man towards a state of intellectual & moral perfection, as evidenced in history of 5th Avenue & 5 Points*"; he must soon have chosen a topic in order to announce it to local lecture committees, but none of the scattered letters of this year which have survived is specific on this point. In deciding to talk on Roman statuary Melville was not only making use of material from his journal but was also satisfying his desire to develop a philosophy of art and a theory of history. Since "Statues in Rome" considers ancient art in relation to other human activities, ranging from epistemology and religion to modern science and technology, the lecture also enabled him to address obliquely the issue of man's supposed "daily progress" mentioned ironically in his letter to Curtis. Much of the lecture grows directly out of observations recorded during his stay in Italy; its nucleus may well have been an idea occurring first in an entry on the Coliseum at Rome which is elaborated in notes at the end of the journal: to "restore" the Coliseum in imagination and "repeople it with all statues in Vatican." Descriptions of individual statues Melville had seen in the Vatican Museum constitute much of the first half of the lecture; an imagined gladiatorial contest in the Coliseum with the Vatican statues as spectators is the climactic set piece which follows, leading in turn to a panoramic view of Rome and a brief glimpse of the villas beyond its walls. Framing the lecture are an introductory passage on the relevance of art to men of all classes and a philosophical conclusion comparing art and science as indexes of ancient and modern civilization. Melville's own preference is clear: ancient civilization, creative and seminal, knew how to value its art and artists; nineteenth-century civilization, pragmatic and derivative, ignores art, preferring to exalt the ephemeral machines and buildings constructed by modern technicians.

Melville first delivered "Statues in Rome" on November 23, 1857, at Lawrence, Massachusetts—the home of John C. Hoadley, who had previously urged him to turn lecturer. Hoadley himself probably arranged this first engagement as a kind of practice session before Melville was due to appear in larger cities; he lectured there "gratuitously" in behalf of the poor, according to the Lawrence *Courier*. The *Courier*'s review praised the content and style of the lecture but offered two reservations, suggesting that the subject of Roman statuary was perhaps more suitable to "the scholar in the seclusion of his study" than to "jaded and listless auditors" at a lyceum lecture and remarking that the speaker's delivery was unfortunately "so low" that a large part of the audience could not hear it; similar criticisms were to be made in other cities throughout the season. From Lawrence Melville proceeded directly to Concord, New Hampshire, for his second November engagement, and during December he made further appearances in Boston, Montreal, Saratoga Springs, and New Haven. There was no coverage in the Concord and New Haven papers and only a brief but favorable notice in the *Daily Saratogian*, but the Boston and Montreal press carried extensive summaries of the lecture, reporting a large attendance in both cities.

In Boston, where Melville's appearance was considered "an 'event' ranging up to a 'sensation' point," according to the *Daily Bee*, he delivered

"Statues in Rome" to "a large and distinguished character-dotted audience." Although Henry Gansevoort, Melville's cousin, told his father privately that there was some difficulty in hearing the speaker at a distance, he added that the lecture was delivered "with animation and effect" and the newspaper critics observed that Melville was "at home in the lecture-room" and spoke "in a clear and distinct voice" and "with considerable enthusiasm." His presentation, though "interesting" and "quite able," lasted beyond the customary hour, as several reviewers noted; the audience listened throughout with "complimentary attention," said the *Bee*, but responded with "little applause." "The lecture was quite interesting to those of artistic tastes," the *Journal* concluded, "but we fancy the larger part of the audience would have preferred something more modern and personal."

In Montreal the lecture had been billed as a travelogue to be illustrated by a moving panorama entitled the "Mirror of Italy," but a railroad accident delayed Melville's arrival there and made it necessary to postpone his appearance for one night. Later newspaper reports do not indicate whether the panorama was actually displayed while Melville was speaking to his "numerous and respectable" audience, but there is evidence that some listeners were dissatisfied with his concentration on statuary, having expected him to deliver a popular travelogue on "Sight-seeing in Rome" as the advance billing had promised. There was applause at the conclusion, however, as the *Transcript* observed. The *Gazette*, though granting that some passages were "very fine," confessed "some feeling of disappointment" in the lecture as a whole, adding only that "The subject was too large to be condensed into a single lecture." No file of the Montreal *Herald* has been located; among other Montreal papers the *Witness*, an evangelical Protestant publication that recalled Melville's reputation as "an enemy to Christian Missions," held that such a speaker was "far from acceptable to a Christian audience," and the *True Witness and Catholic Chronicle* replied with a defense of Melville himself as "a scholar and a gentleman" whose lecture, though admittedly mistitled, "furnished a rich intellectual treat" to its listeners.

In January of 1858 Melville delivered "Statues in Rome" in Auburn and Ithaca, New York, at the beginning of a month's tour that took him west to Cleveland and Detroit, south to Clarksville, Tennessee, and north again to Cincinnati and Chillicothe, Ohio, before his return home in early February. Audiences were consistently good in the smaller cities, though competing attractions and bad weather affected attendance in Cleveland and Cincinnati, as the local reviewers observed. In Clarksville, where Melville's lecture was "one of the events of the season," the hall was "crowded with a large and fashionable audience," and both papers at Chillicothe described the audience there as large and appreciative. Newspaper coverage was generally extensive except in Detroit; only a single Detroit paper, the *Free Press,* reported the lecture, giving an unusually full summary but offering no critical comments. Most reviewers had high praise for "Statues in Rome" as a literary production, singling it out among other offerings as "by far the most chaste and classic of the season" in Auburn, superior "in point of style" to "nine-tenths of the lectures usually delivered" in Cleveland, and "by far the best" of the winter in Cincinnati. In Clarksville the *Jeffersonian* noted "general admiration" for "the finished and scholarly character of the composition," but felt obliged to say that the subject of Roman statuary was not one "to excite general interest or elicit much enthusiasm in any manner in which it could possibly be treated." The Auburn *American* judged the lecture worthy of Melville's "talents and reputation, but not a very popular one"; another paper, the *Advertiser,* agreed that it probably failed to "please twenty in the audience," but held that the same lecture "would have been considered brilliant and fascinating" had it been delivered by an accomplished elocutionist; the fault lay not in the subject but in Melville's "inexcusable blundering, sing song, monotonous delivery," which had "completely, absolutely spoiled" a "racy and rich descriptive lecture."

Other newspapers noted dissatisfaction with Melville's diction and delivery as he moved still further from the eastern seaboard into the West and South. At Cleveland the *Leader* remarked that Melville "speaks well, were it not for a slight indistinctness in articulation"; the *Herald* described his voice as "musical" and his delivery as "very correct" but held that his "subdued tone and general want of animation prevents his being a popular lecturer." In Tennessee the Clarksville *Chronicle* emphasized his "natural reserve" and "quiet manner," granting that some of his southern listeners had objected to his "subdued delivery." At Cincinnati, where Melville obviously spoke under the handicap of a cold, the *Commercial* reported that he "enunciates with only tolerable distinctness" and characterized his delivery as "earnest, though not sufficiently animated for a Western audience." The *Enquirer,* which wrote warmly of the lecture itself, described Melville's voice as "monotonous and often indistinct, but not devoid of impressiveness, which sometimes approached the ministerially solemn," and the *Gazette*, which agreed that Melville's manner was "too quiet, common-place and unobtrusive for a popular audience," distinguished his presentation from the more flamboyant performances of professional lecturers, holding that "he talks as he writes—without the pretension of those who make lecturing a business." The Chillicothe *Advertiser* offered a somewhat similar judgment. Though granting that among Melville's audience in Chillicothe "the general expression . . . was of high appreciation," the *Advertiser* considered the lecture "faulty" and its delivery hardly less so, but credited Melville himself with the courage and good taste "to reject the pretension to be what he is not, and stand forth to the world content to appear what he is."

After returning from Ohio Melville concluded his season with three additional lectures in February, speaking first at Charlestown, Massachusetts, and later at Rochester and New Bedford. The Charlestown *Advertiser* and the New Bedford *Mercury* agreed that "Statues in Rome" was "interesting and instructive," but other papers in all three cities had unfavorable reports of its popular reception. The New Bedford *Standard* held that Melville had offered "a well written and scholarly essay, which would doubtless be read with much pleasure, but was not calculated to interest as a lecture"; the *Bunker-Hill Aurora* of Charlestown caustically dismissed the lecture as "a monotonous description of . . . 'dead heads'" and blamed Melville for inflicting a "sell" on the holders of tickets. "No man," said this paper, "could reasonably hope to interest a common audience upon such a subject. Common people care but precious little about Italy or the statues therein." In Rochester the *Democrat and American*, though kinder to Melville and his "well written" discourse, reported that his subject had failed to interest listeners there: "The audience generally, were disappointed; and we think that the lecturer erred in his choice of a theme." But "Mr. MELVILLE is capable of doing better," the Rochester paper asserted, confident that he would not abandon the field "without further efforts to win laurels therein" as "a 'popular lecturer.'"

Melville's new venture into lecturing had thus brought him a sheaf of varying reports which commonly recognized the literary quality of "Statues in Rome" with occasional reservations about his voice and delivery—especially in the West and South—and more frequent complaints about his choice of topic. As Holmes or Curtis might have warned him at the outset, even the most dynamic orator with extensive professional experience would be courting audience resistance by offering the average lecture-goer of the 1850's a philosophical meditation on the ancient Romans and their statuary. Most of the newspaper reports of "Statues in Rome" display little concern with its intellectual and cultural implications, being content to summarize what Melville had said and to judge the lecture primarily as a public performance. In Boston, it is true, the *Traveller* noted that his proposition about the superiority of art to science had provoked discussion among homeward-bound listeners, and in other cities there were reviewers interested in art themselves, such as the writers for the Cleveland *Leader* and the Clarksville *Chronicle,* who admired the lecture and applauded Melville's ideas even as they recognized that other local listeners had found his discussion less than absorbing. The *Leader's* critic lamented that "we, Western people, have not got sufficiently beyond . . . the prevailing *practicality* of pioneer society" to achieve "a fine and general appreciation of Art," confident that such "cultivation of nature and taste" would serve to "liberate us from the iron slavery of railroad speculation, money panics, and the tyranny of the almighty dollar generally." But in other western cities, particularly Detroit and Cincinnati, the committees who planned lecture courses were receiving more and more complaints against the preponderance of "literary" lectures delivered by itinerant eastern writers, and during the next few years they attempted to respond by scheduling programs on more practical, or at least more popular, subjects. Even in New England, where the lyceum movement was still strongest, Henry Thoreau was complaining in 1858 that audiences no longer wish "to be stimulated and instructed, but entertained." If Melville's most successful engagement during his first season was in Boston, as a survey of newspaper reports of 1857–58 suggests, his most disparaging critic was clearly the reviewer for the nearby *Bunker-Hill Aurora,* and even in Boston itself the *Journal* had felt that most of his auditors would have preferred a topic "more modern and personal" than "Statues in Rome."

If Melville intended to continue for another season on the platform and win laurels as a popular speaker it was plain that the first requisite would be a popular subject—preferably one "with which his name is connected," as Henry Gansevoort had said after listening to Melville's performance in Boston: "'The South Seas,' 'Oceanica' or a thousand different subjects would have been preferable." Although Melville himself had been trying ever since *Mardi* to live down his early reputation, achieved with *Typee*, as the "man who lived among the cannibals," he was evidently willing to recognize that still more concessions to public taste must be made in order to establish himself with lecture-goers, and from the newspaper notices and reviews of his first season it was plain that he was still best remembered as the author of *Typee* and *Omoo*, not of *Moby-Dick, The Piazza Tales,* or *The Confidence-Man*. For the season of 1858–59 his announced subject was indeed "The South Seas" rather than a topic suggested by his more recent travels in the Mediterranean. Returning to the locale of his earlier adventures meant not only a concession on Melville's part but practical difficulties as well: having been away from the Pacific for more than a decade, he lacked new material and could not simply repeat from the platform what he had long since said in print. Instead of rehearsing his own "casual adventures in Polynesia," he therefore proposed "to treat of matters of more general interest," as he explained at the beginning of "The South Seas," and to illustrate his remarks with an occasional "little incident, personal or other," that might seem fitting.

The quoted phrases come from one of twenty-five known newspaper reports of "The South Seas"; Melville himself did not publish the lecture and no manuscript survives among his papers. From the newspaper résumés it is apparent that this was a less tightly structured and more informal composition than "Statues in Rome." After a preliminary survey of Pacific geography and exploration "The South Seas" touches briefly on the distinctive fishes and birds of the region, characterizes the countless islands and their inhabitants, native and white, with passing references to whalemen, buccaneers, and missionaries, and makes abbreviated comments on tattooing and taboo. The illustrative anecdotes come both from Melville's reading and from his own recollections, and some of the interspersed "yarns," as the New York *Evening Post* remarked, border "upon the 'Munchausen.'" The lecture concludes with an expression of hope that those "Edens of the South Seas" as yet "uncontaminated by the contact of civilization" might "long remain unspoiled in their simplicity, beauty, and purity." In this implied criticism of modern civilization and its corrupting influence Melville was extending the social commentary he had already offered in "Statues in Rome," but again his reviewers and probably most of his listeners responded to "The South Seas" as popular entertainment and took relatively little notice of the basic ideas underlying it.

During his first season as a lecturer Melville had cleared over $400 after appearing in sixteen cities; his second season, though it included fewer engagements, was considerably more rewarding financially. Between December of 1858 and the following March he delivered eleven lectures in ten cities, reading both "The South Seas" and "Statues in Rome" during his final engagement in Lynn, Massachusetts. He was able not only to command higher fees during this season, ranging from $23.50 at Quincy, Illinois, to a top payment of $100.00 at Baltimore, but to secure additional money for travel expenses, so that his clear income from fees was $518.50. Throughout the winter he continued to draw large audiences, but the reaction of both listeners and critics to "The South Seas" displayed an even greater difference in regional tastes than had been evident during the previous season. In general, eastern audiences liked the new lecture, but opinion in Illinois and Wisconsin was sharply divided, with several of the western reviewers roundly condemning both the lecture and the speaker in the harshest notices Melville received during his years as a lecturer.

The first engagement of 1858–59 was in December at Yonkers, New York, where the *Examiner* described the audience as "not only large, but very sympathetic" to Melville as "a humorist" and responding with "continuous merriment" to his "facetious tone." To the reviewer himself, however, the lecture was *"parvum in multo"*—a mere rehash of familiar information composed in Melville's "excessively florid style" and delivered in a peculiar cadence "anything but pleasant." The lecturer's "well-known" feelings about missionaries obviously irritated the Yonkers critic, and he took particular exception to Melville's defense of Polynesians against the further encroachments of Christian civilization. The article implies that the conclusion of the lecture also offended—or should have offended—other listeners, and that the audience consequently withheld its applause at the close. No such reaction was reported in other eastern cities. Melville's next engagement was at Pittsfield, where the single notice in the *Berkshire County Eagle* says nothing about the response of the lecturer's fellow townsmen. The reviewer himself, presumably J. E. A. Smith, found the lecture "pleasant and instructive," comparing its style with that of "Mr. Melville's best books." Eight papers covered Melville's next appearance at the end of January in Boston, giving most of their space to digests of what he had said rather than to critical commentary. "The lecture was quite interesting, and frequently elicited applause," said the *Atlas and Daily Bee*, and the *Advertiser* called it "a fine production" that "received the close attention of all who heard it." The *Traveller* wrote that the lecture "abounded with numerous anecdotes and facts of great interest"; Melville's performance "gave the most ample satisfaction," according to the *Journal,* "and was frequently applauded."

Perhaps Melville's most successful engagement during his second season was his appearance early in February before a congenial gathering at the New-York Historical Society that included "some of our most eminent *literati,*" as the New York *Express* reported. The *Express* considered the lecture "ably treated, full of rich, valuable information, and delivered with ease and grace"; the weekly *Century* found it "very interesting, . . . none the less so for its modest and unpretending composition and delivery," and other papers noted that the audience responded with interest and attention. Henry Gansevoort, who had thought "The South Seas" a better subject for his cousin than "Statues in Rome," was also present and wrote of the evening as "a treat long to be remembered." Melville had resumed his "true vein" and was now "emphatically himself," Gansevoort felt, speaking informally and even carelessly but carrying his listeners with him and winning their gratified applause. The lecture again went well on the following evening in Baltimore, according to two newspaper reports. The *American and Commercial Advertiser* gave over much of its front page to a detailed summary of what Melville had said in addressing a "fine audience"; the *Sun*'s briefer article praised "The South Seas" as abounding in "interesting personal narratives" and observed that it "held the interest of the audience to the close." Thus in his first five engagements of the new season Melville had earned favorable notices everywhere but in Yonkers, where the audience enjoyed the lecture more than the reviewer thought it deserved. He would have liked more engagements in or near New York—"or anywhere," he told George Duyckinck, who had helped to arrange for his appearance at the Historical Society. "If they will pay expences, & give a reasonable fee, I am ready to lecture in Labrador or on the Isle of Desolation off Patagonia."

While Melville was presenting "The South Seas" in eastern cities he was recognizably at ease with his audience and consequently spoke both naturally and effectively, creating and sustaining a rapport that had everything to do with his consistent success during these early appearances. But when he opened his western tour at Chicago in late February of 1859, addressing an audience described as "large and fashionable," the press reported that many listeners were unable to hear him. There had been objections to Melville's voice during his first season, especially west of the Hudson, where lecturers were expected to speak with more clarity, force, and animation than he and other visitors from the eastern seaboard were accustomed to demonstrate. The Chicago *Press and Tribune* in reviewing "The South Seas" took note that those sitting at a distance from the stage "lost a large share of the admirable entertainment," but in all other respects the lecture was "fully up to the standard of public expectation." The *Journal* strongly disagreed, in the first totally unfavorable notice Melville had received since his appearance in Charlestown a year before. The *Journal*'s reviewer declined to offer either a summary or specific criticism of "The South Seas," saying only that its failure might be due partially to Melville's "limited vocal powers, and particularly to an involuntary comparison between him and his immediate predecessors," or "wholly to the intrinsic defects of the lecture." As a further allusion makes clear, this writer was really saying that neither Melville nor "The South Seas" could bear comparison with Bayard Taylor and his travelogues. "The handsome Bayard," reigning lion among lecturers, had preceded Melville in Chicago and was scheduled to follow him in Milwaukee and again in Rockford, Illinois; critics in both cities made the same comparison and reached the same verdict as the *Journal*'s.

In Milwaukee Melville received a mixed response from the press and perhaps from his audience as well. A long and glowing report in the *Daily Wisconsin* resembles earlier comments about Melville's successful appearance in New York. According to this account, probably written by Melville's old friend William Cramer, "a very large and appreciative audience" in Milwaukee "seemed greatly to admire" his presentation, which was less "a stilted lecture" than "such a feast as one would like to sit down to in a club room, and with the blue smoke of a meerschaum gracefully curling and floating away, to listen . . . till the night wore away." The *Sentinel,* which carried a briefer résumé, found in Melville's lecture the same air of "romance" and "drowsy enchantment that makes his writings so fascinating," but it offered no assessment of popular response. The *Free Democrat,* however, reported that though Melville's auditors had listened attentively they gave him only "limited applause at the close," and "many, perhaps the most" were "disappointed in the lecturer and his discourse." Melville had offered them "a literary effort below mediocrity, and too bookish to please, unless he intended it as a reading." Instead of repeating "what the primary geographies told us in our school-days" Melville should have provided lively narration and illustrated his points with more frequent and more interesting personal anecdotes. What the reviewer had in mind is suggested by the concluding sentence of his article: "Next Thursday evening we are to have BAYARD TAYLOR."

The *Democrat*'s objections are echoed by two of Melville's three Rockford reviewers, both of them writing delayed reports composed after the ubiquitous Taylor had also performed there. An earlier article in the Rockford *Daily News* had reported favorably on Melville's appearance, but the *Register* had a different reaction: "He may have pleased the large audience who listened to him"—as the *News* had said, "but he certainly did not us. We think the *News* must have got an advance report of the gentleman's lecture." Like his colleague in Milwaukee, the *Register*'s critic had supposed that Melville would deliver a travelogue, probably because of the advertising which "preceded him on the posters" in Rockford. "But we were disappointed in this, and instead we received a record in *manuscript* of a few general, historical facts which could be gained by visiting almost any well selected library." On the next evening, by contrast, the reviewer had listened to a "widely different" presentation by Taylor, speaking in a larger but "densely packed" hall and delivering "the most interesting" lecture of the season. Taylor customarily performed without notes; Melville, as the reviewer pointed out, read from a manuscript—and in Rockford he obviously spoke without the élan he had displayed to his more sympathetic eastern audiences. "Lecturing is evidently not Mr. Melville's sphere," the *Register* concluded. "And no man has a right to set himself up as a lecturer at $50 per night, who cannot for one minute take his eyes from his manuscript." The Rockford *Republican*, which had also expected "a personal narrative," was even more devastating: "It has rarely been our lot to witness a more painful infliction upon an audience than was made by Mr. Herman Melville's lecture upon the South Seas. . . . He lacks depth, earnestness, consecutiveness and finish, without which qualities no man need hope of being a permanently successful lecturer. Lecturing is evidently not his forte, his style as well as the subject matter being intensely 'Polynesian' and calculated to 'Taboo' him from the lecture field in the future."

Melville probably did not see the reviews in the *Register* and *Republican*, published after he had gone to Quincy, Illinois, for another appearance; there are no clippings among his surviving papers as there are of reviews from other cities. A listener in Quincy found Melville "erratic but interesting," as he recorded in his diary, but the local newspapers did not report the lecture. One more appointment remained after Melville's return to Pittsfield early in March: his double engagement in Lynn, Massachusetts, where the *Weekly Reporter* printed only a short notice of "The South Seas," the first of his two readings, and nothing about "Statues in Rome." The first lecture was "tolerably well attended," according to this account, "but didn't touch the innermost, as did those of Emerson and Lowell. . . . It was good, though, of its kind, and went off very well." Perhaps a lecture about Pacific waters would naturally "go off" better in cities along the eastern seaboard than in Illinois or Wisconsin; perhaps Melville himself was more easily heard in Lynn than in Chicago, or was in better form than he appears to have been before his audience in Rockford. But if lecture committees making up their courses for 1859–60 examined the newspaper accounts of Melville's second season, as they customarily did through the exchanges circulating among editors and publishers, they surely would have hesitated to engage him, despite his acknowledged successes in the East, after reading the more recent reports from the West—particularly the two unfavorable reviews from Rockford, which seem deliberate efforts "to 'Taboo' him from the lecture field in the future."

Indeed Melville's career as a lecturer had nearly run its course with the close of his second winter on the platform, for his third season proved to be almost wholly abortive. Again he wrote a new lecture, "Traveling," which he first delivered at Flushing, New York, early in November of 1859, but either his illness later in the fall or a lack of invitations kept him from repeating it until the following February, when he spoke at South Danvers and Cambridgeport, Massachusetts. The three readings brought fees totalling $110.00. Lemuel Shaw was instrumental in arranging for at least one of these appearances and John C. Hoadley was also working in Melville's behalf, but there was no western tour for him in 1859–60 and no return engagements even along the eastern seaboard, where he had fared best with "Statues in Rome" and especially with "The South Seas." One local newspaper, the Cambridge *Chronicle*, carried a brief digest of "Traveling" which is reprinted here, but the lecture was otherwise unreported and the manuscript has not survived. From the abbreviated newspaper summary it is known that Melville spoke of travel as requiring a receptive and imaginative sensibility and a resistance to such irritations as insects, passports, and rascally guides; its rewards he specified as "the sight of novel objects, the acquirement of novel ideas, the breaking up of old prejudices, the enlargement of heart and mind." Presumably the lecture included more illustrative material than the newspaper report indicates, but it is impossible to say to what degree Melville responded to earlier criticism by offering "personal narrative" drawn from his own experience.

The engagement in Cambridgeport was Melville's final appearance as a lecturer. In May of 1860, with his health again a cause for concern, he was once more a traveler, this time as a passenger aboard the clipper ship *Meteor* under command of his younger brother Tom, bound for Cape Horn and the Pacific. San Francisco newspapers suggested that he be invited to lecture on his arrival there, but the three-year experiment of lecturing was over. For some time past his interest had been engaged by another new departure, the writing of verse, and when he accepted his brother's invitation to sail on the *Meteor* there were enough poems in manuscript to make up a volume if Allan Melville and Evert Duyckinck could interest a publisher in printing them. Melville's recurrent bodily ills had continued to trouble him throughout the later 1850's. The European trip had obviously been beneficial, and when Peter Gansevoort saw him in Albany during the close of his first lecture season he appeared to be "in excellent health & very fine spirits," but only a month later, in March of 1858, came "a severe attack of what he called crick in the back," and after this time, according to Mrs. Melville, "he never regained his former vigor & strength." Although he appeared "robust and fine looking" in the following summer, as George Duyckinck described him, his "affection of the spine" still troubled him, and both friends and neighbors spoke of him as "not well." Few of his own letters from these years are extant, and since no publisher was willing to undertake the projected volume of poetry there is little but the lectures and a few surviving poems to suggest the drift of his mind between *The Confidence-Man* and the eventual appearance of his Civil War verse, *Battle-Pieces*, in 1866.

What the lectures have to say about Melville's thought in the late 1850's is to be learned from the newspaper résumés rather than the relatively superficial comments of contemporary reviewers. Probably there were not many listeners who realized from what he said on the platform how radical was his rejection of the prevailing faith in progress towards "intellectual & moral perfection," though he had obliquely taken human progress as "a good, earnest subject" for all three of his lectures. "Traveling" is in large measure an appeal for the clear-sightedness, benevolence, and personal humility fostered by travel as against the narrow prejudices of those who never venture abroad. The earlier lectures are excursions in both space and time. The "social and political prodigies" of nineteenth-century reformers are targets in "Statues in Rome," where Melville celebrates the superiority of ancient art and civilization, and again in "The South Seas," where he looks back nostalgically to days when the islanders had not yet been corrupted in the name of progress and Christianity. Although newspapers occasionally recalled his earlier animadversions against the missionaries, it remained for one reviewer—the disapproving writer for the *Ohio Farmer* of Cleveland, a critic seemingly alone among his contemporaries—to recognize the depth and sincerity of what he called Melville's "affection for heathenism" and to detect even in "Statues in Rome" an undercurrent "of regret, or sorrow, or malice, at the introduction of christianity" into a world ennobled by its pagan virtues. When two students from Williams College sought Melville out at Arrowhead in April of 1859, not long after the close of his second lecture season, they were eager for talk of the South Seas, being sons of missionaries who had been born in the Hawaiian Islands; instead, Melville, "slightly flushed with whiskey drinking" and perhaps less guarded than usual, launched into a disquisition that paralleled exactly what he had been saying more discreetly on the platform. Expressing his disgust "with the civilized world and with our Christendom in general and in particular," Melville celebrated instead "the ancient dignity of Homeric times," which "afforded the only state of humanity, individual or social, to which he could turn with any complacency."

Skepticism about man's "progress," disgust with contemporary institutions, and preoccupation with ancient and primitive societies are persistent elements in at least two of the three lectures as in Melville's earlier and later writing. From the time of his Mediterranean voyage he had become increasingly interested in earlier civilizations, gradually turning away from the present for his subject matter as he was repeatedly to do in his later poetry—"The Age of the Antonines," *Clarel*, *John Marr*, and *Timoleon*—and in *Billy Budd*, where once again "a sort of upright barbarian" is defeated in an unsought contest with the corrupting forces of civilization. In theme as in chronology the lectures are a link between Melville's professional writing of the 1840's and the early 1850's and his later poetry and fiction composed not for the public but for himself.

SOURCES

REFERENCES TO DATES AND EVENTS in Melville's life, unless otherwise ascribed in footnotes, are based upon the following printed sources: *The Letters of Herman Melville*, ed. Merrell R. Davis and William H. Gilman (New Haven: Yale University Press, 1960); Jay Leyda, *The Melville Log* (New York: Harcourt, Brace, 1951; reprinted with a new supplementary chapter, New York: Gordian Press, 1969; a new and enlarged edition is forthcoming from Gordian Press); and Eleanor Melville Metcalf, *Herman Melville: Cycle and Epicycle* (Cambridge: Harvard University Press, 1953). Most references can be checked in the *Log*, which is arranged chronologically; some of the material quoted here has been generously supplied by Professor Leyda from his forthcoming new edition. The most detailed documentation of Melville's and his family's attitude toward his career—before his marriage in 1847, just after the publication of *Pierre* in 1852, and again following his return from abroad in 1857—is in Harrison Hayford and Merrell Davis, "Herman Melville as Office-Seeker," *Modern Language Quarterly*, X (June, 1949), 168–83, and (September, 1949), 377–88. Elizabeth Shaw Melville's private memoranda of her husband's life and writings and the published biographical sketches by J. E. A. Smith, Arthur Stedman, and other contemporaries who knew him are collected in Merton M. Sealts, Jr., *The Early Lives of Melville: Nineteenth-Century Biographical Sketches and Their Authors* (Madison and London: University of Wisconsin Press, 1974).

Excerpts from contemporary reviews of *The Piazza Tales* are assembled, with some differences in transcription, in Leyda's *Log*, in Hugh W. Hetherington, *Melville's Reviewers: British and American, 1846–1891* (Chapel Hill: University of North Carolina Press, 1961), in Hershel Parker, *The Recognition of Herman Melville* (Ann Arbor: University of Michigan Press, 1967), in Watson G. Branch, ed., *Melville: The Critical Heritage* (London and Boston: Routledge & Kegan Paul, 1974), and in Brian Higgins, *Herman Melville: An Annotated Bibliography*, Vol. I: 1846–1930 (Boston: G. K. Hall & Co., 1979). For reasons explained in Hershel Parker, "A Reexamination of *Melville's Reviewers*," *American Literature*, XLII (May, 1970), 226–32, all quotations from the reviews are drawn from the original magazine and newspaper printings. The known reviews of 1856, in chronological order, are as follows: New York *Atlas*, May 25; New York *Daily News*, May 26; *Berkshire County Eagle* (Pittsfield, Massachusetts), May 30; *American*

Publishers' Circular and Literary Gazette (New York), May 31; *The Criterion* (New York), May 31; *Southern Literary Messenger*, XXII (June, 1856), 480; Boston *Daily Evening Traveller*, June 3; Boston *Post*, June 4; New Bedford, Massachusetts, *Daily Mercury*, June 4; Boston *Puritan Recorder*, June 5; *The Churchman* (New York), June 5; New York *Evening Post*, June 5; Milwaukee *Daily Wisconsin*, June 5 (reprinted in the *Weekly Wisconsin*, June 11); *Morning Courier and New-York Enquirer*, June 6; Boston *Evening Transcript*, June 6; *North American and United States Gazette* (Philadelphia), June 7; New York *Dispatch*, June 8; New York *Sun*, June 9; *Christian Freeman and Family Visiter* (Boston), June 13; *Hampshire and Franklin Express* (Amherst, Massachusetts), June 13; Newark, New Jersey, *Daily Advertiser*, June 18; *Christian Advocate and Journal* (New York), June 19; New York *Daily Tribune*, June 23; Salem, Massachusetts, *Gazette*, June 24 (partly copied from the New York *Morning Courier* of June 6); Salem, Massachusetts, *Register*, June 26; New York *Daily Times*, June 27; *The Christian Examiner and Religious Miscellany* (Boston), LXI (July, 1856), 152; *Mrs. Stephens' Illustrated New Monthly* (New York), I (July, 1856), 54; Boston *Quarterly Journal of the American Unitarian Association*, III (July, 1856), 641; *The Albion* (New York), July 5; Springfield, Massachusetts, *Republican*, July 9; *The Athenæum* (London), July 26; *Putnam's Monthly Magazine*, VIII (August, 1856), 156 (as an incidental conclusion to an unsigned article, "The Islands of the Pacific"); *Godey's Lady's Book* (Philadelphia), LIII (September, 1856), 277; *The Knickerbocker* (New York), XLVIII (September, 1856), 330; Boston *Monthly Religious Magazine and Independent Journal*, XVI (September, 1856), 215–16; *United States Magazine and Democratic Review* (New York), N.S. VIII (September, 1856), 172.

All quotations from contemporary reviews of Melville's lecturing are also drawn from the original newspaper printings. Photocopies and transcriptions of the individual newspaper articles have been deposited both in the Melville Collection of the Harvard College Library, located in The Houghton Library, Harvard University, and in the Melville Collection of The Newberry Library. The known reviews of each lecture are listed in chronological order in the NOTES TO INDIVIDUAL PROSE PIECES: for "Statues in Rome," see pp. 723–24 below; for "The South Seas," pp. 753–54; for "Traveling," p. 780. Raymond Weaver offered a brief preliminary account of Melville's lecturing in the first book-length biography, *Herman Melville: Mariner and Mystic* (New York: George H. Doran, 1921), pp. 369–75, including excerpts from two of the newspaper reports as well as an inaccurate transcription of entries in Melville's notebook of lecture engagements; reproductions of the original pages appear below, pp. 801–7. Additional notices were subsequently located and reprinted by a number of scholars, particularly after an appeal from Newton Arvin in "Toward the Whole Evidence on Melville as a Lecturer," *American Notes and Queries*, II (May, 1942), 21–2. Merton M. Sealts, Jr., *Melville as Lecturer* (Cambridge: Harvard University Press, 1957), embodies a survey of all scholarly and critical work up to 1957 that deals with Melville's lecturing: Part I analyzes the lectures and their reception; Part II, based on the contemporary newspaper reports, prints composite texts of the three lectures. Accompanying notes and commentary quote the journal entries and other sources that Melville is known to have drawn upon for all three of his lectures and also cite comparable passages in his earlier fiction and later poetry.

Relevant scholarship on the lectures since 1957 includes the following: (1) Francis V. Lloyd, Jr., "A Further Note on Herman Melville, Lecturer," *Bulletin of the Missouri Historical Society*, XX (July, 1964), 310–12, which shows that the Mercantile Library Association of St. Louis offered an engagement that Melville was unable to fill; (2) G. Thomas Tanselle, "Melville Writes to the New Bedford Lyceum," *American Literature*, XXXIX (November, 1967), 391–92, which prints a letter of acceptance dated October 3, 1857; (3) Kenneth Walter Cameron, "A Melville Letter and Stray Books from His Library," *Emerson Society Quarterly*, No. 63 (Spring, 1971), 48, which reproduces Melville's letter of November 16, 1857, concerning a possible lecture at Rockford, Illinois; (4) Frederick James Kennedy, "Herman Melville's Lecture in Montreal," *New England Quarterly*, L (March, 1977), 125–37, which demonstrates that a railroad accident delayed Melville's arrival in Montreal and caused postponement of his lecture there from December 10, 1857, until the following evening; Kennedy quotes reactions to the lecture in private journals of Montreal residents and in previously unlocated newspaper accounts.

Both contemporary reviews and later scholarship and criticism dealing with *The Piazza Tales* and Melville's other miscellaneous prose pices are listed in Brian Higgins, *Herman Melville: An Annotated Bibliography, 1846–1976*, 3 vols. (Boston: G. K. Hall & Co., 1979–). In the present volume, those studies particularly concerned with textual considerations and with Melville's use of source materials are cited at relevant points in the GENERAL NOTE ON THE TEXT and the NOTES ON INDIVIDUAL PROSE PIECES.

General Note on the Text

THIS EDITION of *The Piazza Tales and Other Prose Pieces, 1839–1860* presents unmodernized critical texts of (1) the writings in *The Piazza Tales* (1856) and (2) all Melville's known uncollected contributions to newspapers and magazines up to 1860 and the one known surviving unpublished submission to a magazine. It also includes reconstructed texts of the three unpublished lectures he delivered on the lecture circuit between 1857 and 1860. Manuscripts for six of these items are known to survive: five pieces published in the New York *Literary World* between 1847 and 1850 under the editorship of Evert A. Duyckinck (now in the Duyckinck Collection, Rare Books and Manuscripts Division, The New York Public Library); and "The Two Temples," a tale submitted in 1854 to *Putnam's Monthly Magazine* but rejected and returned to Melville (now in the Melville Collection of The Houghton Library of Harvard University). For the remaining published pieces the only sources are the printed texts based on manuscripts Melville furnished; and in five instances there are two printed texts, since Melville revised five *Putnam's* pieces for inclusion (along with one new piece) in *The Piazza Tales*. The unpublished lectures are known only through contemporary newspaper reports based on his oral delivery.

THE TEXTS

SOURCES FOR A CRITICAL TEXT. The critical texts of *The Piazza Tales* and Melville's known contributions to newspapers and magazines have been established for this edition according to the theory of copy-text formulated by Sir Walter Greg.[1] Central to that theory is the distinction between substantives (the words of a text) and accidentals (spelling and punctuation). Persons involved in the printing and publishing of texts have often taken it upon themselves to alter accidentals; and authors, when examining or revising printed forms of their work, have often been relatively unconcerned with accidentals.[2] An author's failure to change certain accidentals altered by a copyist, publisher, or compositor does not amount to an endorsement of those accidentals. Because the aim of a critical edition is to establish a text that represents as nearly as possible the author's intentions, it follows that—in the absence of contrary evidence—the formal texture of the work will be most accurately reproduced by adopting as copy-text[3] either the fair-copy manuscript or the first printing based on it. The printed form is chosen if the manuscript does not exist or if the author worked in such a way that corrected proof became in effect the final form of the manuscript. This basic text may then be emended with any later authorial alterations (whether substantive or accidental) and with other necessary corrections. Following this procedure maximizes the probability of keeping authorial readings when evidence is inconclusive as to the source of an alteration. The resulting text is *critical* in that it does not correspond exactly to any one existing document; but it is closer to the author's intentions—insofar as they are recoverable—than any single documentary form of the text.

The surviving draft or fair-copy manuscripts have been adopted as copy-texts for "The Two Temples," unpublished in Melville's lifetime,

1. "The Rationale of Copy-Text," *Studies in Bibliography*, III (1950–51), 19–36; reprinted in his *Collected Papers*, ed. J. C. Maxwell (Oxford: Clarendon Press, 1966), pp. 374–91. For an application of this method to the period of Melville, see the Center for Editions of American Authors, *Statement of Editorial Principles and Procedures* (rev. ed.; New York: Modern Language Association of America, 1972) and the various discussions recorded in *The Center for Scholarly Editions: An Introductory Statement* (New York: Modern Language Association of America, 1977; also printed in *PMLA*, XCII [1977], 586–97).

2. Accidentals can affect the meaning (or substance) of a text, and Greg's distinction is not meant to suggest otherwise; rather, its purpose is to emphasize the fact that those involved in the transmission of texts have habitually behaved differently in regard to the two categories.

3. "Copy-text" is the text accepted as the basis for an edition.

and for his five pieces published between 1847 and 1850 in the *Literary World*. For each of these manuscripts a typed transcript to serve as printer's copy was made from a photocopy of the original and then read by different people against the manuscript itself at least five times to verify readings. These basic texts have been emended with necessary corrections. Collation of photocopies of the manuscripts with the *Literary World* printings reveals no authorial alterations in an intervening proof stage; indeed, there are significant substantive errors in the published texts. These considerations suggest that Melville usually did not correct proof for the *Literary World*.[4] A detailed description of each of the six known surviving manuscripts, a history of the text based on it, and related textual data appear below in the NOTES ON INDIVIDUAL PROSE PIECES.[5]

For each of the other prose pieces that Melville contributed to newspapers and magazines between 1839 and 1856 but did not himself collect or republish, in the absence of surviving manuscripts the periodical appearances have provided the copy-texts. Except in one instance, examination of each of the periodical texts in a number of copies has not disclosed textual differences or provided evidence of more than one printing.[6] Marked photocopies of these periodical printings served as printer's copy for this edition. For each piece, the NOTES ON INDIVIDUAL PROSE PIECES identify the copy-text, specify the document used as printer's copy, outline the history of the text, and provide textual data to complete the TEXTUAL RECORD.[7]

4. Hence, in the NOTES ON INDIVIDUAL PROSE PIECES below, information about *Literary World* readings is given for the historical record, not for any authority they carry. Although Melville requested proof of the second installment of "Hawthorne and His Mosses" (1850), there is no evidence he received it—see the discussion on pp. 654 and 661 below.

5. For "The Two Temples," see pp. 700–709; for the five pieces in the *Literary World*, see pp. 625–36 and 639–90.

6. The exception is "Fragments from a Writing Desk, No. 1," which appeared in another newspaper in the same setting of type—see p. 622 below. Whenever possible, copies of magazines in their original wrappers have been examined as well as copies in publishers' or library bindings. Volumes in publishers' bindings were often put together from sheets of the same printings as those used for the separate numbers, but it is conceivable that the sheets of certain numbers in such volumes might represent later impressions; any volume in a library binding could of course be either an assemblage of separately published numbers or a rebinding of a volume originally issued in a publisher's binding. (On "printing" or "impression," see footnote 13 below; on the examination of copies, footnote 17.)

7. For Melville's contribution to the *Democratic Press*, see pp. 622–25; for his contributions to *Yankee Doodle*, pp. 636–39; for attributed pieces, pp. 782–91; for uncollected pieces published in *Harper's* and *Putnam's*, pp. 690–99 and 709–22.

Five of the six pieces that Melville included in *The Piazza Tales,* published in 1856 by Dix & Edwards of New York, had originally appeared in *Putnam's Monthly Magazine,* "Benito Cereno" and "The Bell-Tower" having been submitted and printed after Dix & Edwards took over as publisher in March of 1855 from G. P. Putnam & Co. For the projected volume Melville supplied what he called "corrected magazine sheets" of these articles; later he supplied a fair-copy manuscript of "The Piazza" and requested proof of it. Neither the original manuscripts and magazine proofs nor the "corrected sheets" of any of the pieces are known to survive, but comparison of the texts of the five reprinted pieces in the 1856 book with their periodical texts shows that they differ substantively (in one or more words) at 262 points (there are many other differences in spelling and punctuation). A dozen or so of the 1856 variants are obviously the result of careless typesetting and proofreading,[8] but nearly two dozen are corrections of obvious substantive errors in the periodical texts.[9] Most of the variant readings, however, are neither obvious errors nor corrections of obvious errors. Of these variants, an important category consists of omissions and additions. The book text lacks some 280 words (at 68 points) that are present in the periodical versions—including two sentences in "Benito Cereno" (see the emendations at 58.14 and 116.35), one in "The Lightning-Rod Man" (124.21–22), and a 46-word epigraph and a 37-word footnote in "The Bell-Tower" (174.2–6, 187.4–6), along with many other scattered words and phrases, some of considerable significance.[10] Additions in the book text, on the other hand, amount to about 140 words (at 19 points), largely accounted for by a 93-word passage of six sentences in "Benito Cereno" (69.12–19) and a 27-word epigraph in "The Encantadas" (151.15–18), but also including such interesting insertions as the phrase "beside

8. Among such errors in the 1856 edition are "basket" for "baskets" (51.19), "had" for "hand" (77.32), "bowsmen" for "bowsman" (98.6–7), "discovering" for "his covering" (107.35), and "an an" for "an" (122.24). (These numbers refer to page and line of the Northwestern-Newberry Edition; numbers prefixed with PT refer to the 1856 edition of *The Piazza Tales;* see pp. 569–70 below for explanation of other symbols and abbreviations.)

9. For example, "one" is corrected to "out" (25.33), "the the" to "the" (53.18), "hatchets" to "hatches" (59.17), "I" to "It" (67.8), "Scaling-spears" to "Sealing-spears" (102.9; cf. 102.32), "which one" to "with one" (111.32), "masters" to "master" (112.11), "winged" to "ringed" (118.21), "Poles" to "Pole" (137.25), "no" to "on" (138.34), and "Emperors" to "Emperor" (167.15).

10. Such as the elimination of "and jumped upon him" (70.17), "and, as his enemies whispered, a pirate" (101.1–2), and "By Salvator R. Tarnmoor" (125.3).

thirty cases of hardware" in "Benito Cereno" (104.7). Of the remaining variants—that is, about half the total number—some are significant alterations that clearly seem to have been made by Melville, but many others appear to be routine compositorial substitutions or the work of a publishing-house editor, moving the text away from what Melville intended. Distinguishing between these categories is one of the central tasks an editor of these pieces must deal with.[11]

As for changes in accidentals, Melville complained to Dix & Edwards about a "surprising profusion of commas" when he returned proof for some or all of the volume. "I have struck them out pretty much," he wrote, "but hope that some one who understands punctuation better than I do, will give the final hand to it." In commenting on Melville's complaint the editors of his *Letters,* having counted commas in both the magazine and book versions of the stories, concluded "that not only was nothing done about giving a 'final hand' to the job but also that Melville's own deletions were ignored" when *The Piazza Tales* went to press in 1856.[12] The resultant textual situation provides a classic illustration of Greg's basic distinction between substantive variants (due to often identifiable authorial changes) and variants in accidentals (the source of which cannot be conclusively determined). Applying Greg's theory of copy-text to the five pieces originally appearing in *Putnam's,* an editor will adopt the magazine printings as copy-text, thereby minimizing that "profusion of commas" that

11. About two dozen variants involve the choice of nouns and verbs, such as PT's "measures" for P's "means" (31.12), "find" for "see" (34.16), "surtout" for "mantle" (46.14), "efficacy" for "efficiency" (77.5), "bower" for "tower" (154.28), "inspirited" for "inspired" (175.9), "conceded" for "concealed" (177.6), and "degree" for "amount" (183.40); and a slightly larger number involve adjectives and adverbs, such as "nice" for "spacious" (44.2), "piteously" for "pityingly" (44.17), "hapless" for "helpless" (59.30), and "further" for "farther" (158.9). A little more than a dozen have to do with tense or number: for example, "precede" for "preceded" (114.24), "is" for "are" (122.6), "office" for "offices" (155.16), or "would depart" for "had departed" (175.3). One special category consists of a score of instances in which proper names, especially Spanish names, and the word "Spanish" are eliminated from "Benito Cereno" (see the discussion at 53.31). Most of the remaining three dozen variants are revised expressions requiring the alteration of several words (notable examples are those at 69.35, 70.15–16, and 72.7–8). Analysis of the authority of certain classes of readings is made below, pp. 553–56, and comment on many individual readings will be found in the DISCUSSIONS sections of the NOTES ON INDIVIDUAL PROSE PIECES.

12. Merrell R. Davis and William H. Gilman, in *The Letters of Herman Melville* (New Haven: Yale University Press, 1960), p. 180, n. 7. It is not certain whether Melville's phrase "these proofs" refers to proofs of the entire book, as Davis and Gilman assume, or only to the proof of "The Piazza" that Melville had specifically requested.

provoked Melville's objections to the later printing, and will then emend this basic text with any later changes that Melville himself can be thought to be responsible for.

As the preceding HISTORICAL NOTE has shown, the only edition of *The Piazza Tales* published during Melville's lifetime was that of 1856. It was distributed in England by Sampson Low, Son & Co.; this firm's name was included, below that of Dix & Edwards, in the imprint of the American edition, and no separate issue of the book appeared in England. Machine collation of copies of this single impression[13] reveals ten points where individual letters, numbers, or marks of punctuation failed to print in some copies,[14] as well as some three dozen other points where in some copies individual characters are partly obscured. These variations obviously resulted from defective inking or plate damage, not from deliberate textual alteration, and there is no evidence to suggest that they are indicative of more than one impression.[15] Of the six pieces in *The Piazza Tales,* at least two reappeared in other books before Melville died in 1891: "The Lightning-Rod Man" in one new typesetting and "The Bell-Tower" in two. Collations have shown that all three printings were based on the 1856 text, without alterations that can be regarded as authorial.[16] In the light of these

13. Collations between *impressions* of the same edition (or copies of a single impression) are "machine collations"—so called because the Hinman Collator, by superimposing page images, enables the human collator to see differences, including minute changes not otherwise easily detected, such as resettings and type or plate damage. Collations between two *editions,* which (because they are printed from different settings of type) cannot be performed on that machine, are "sight collations." The terms *edition, impression (printing), issue,* and *state,* as used here, follow the definitions of Fredson Bowers in *Principles of Bibliographical Description* (Princeton: Princeton University Press, 1949), pp. 379–426, supplemented by G. Thomas Tanselle, "The Bibliographical Concepts of *Issue* and *State,*" *Papers of the Bibliographical Society of America,* LXIX (1975), 17–66.

14. Missing in some copies are commas after "there" at 67.20 (PT160.5), "Evidently" at 69.31 (PT165.21), "immediately" at 74.36 (PT178.14), and "Ah" at 88.16 (PT210.25); periods after "together" at 11.40 (PT26.19), "hatchway" at 75.35 (PT180.25), "eyes" at 97.33 (PT233.25), and "remain" at 181.3 (PT416.17); the "e" in "the" at 87.7 (PT208.1); and signature "14" (PT313).

15. Facts about the background and publication of this volume are given in the HISTORICAL NOTE; a precise physical description will appear in the full-scale bibliography to be published in conjunction with the Northwestern-Newberry Edition. The present discussion is not concerned with bibliographical details discovered in the process of collation unless they bear on textual questions.

16. For information on these later resettings, see the individual discussions below of "The Lightning-Rod Man," p. 599, and "The Bell-Tower," p. 619.

facts, and in the absence of both the manuscript and proofs of "The Piazza" and the original manuscripts, proofs, or "corrected magazine sheets" of the five other pieces, the copy-text of *The Piazza Tales* for the present edition comprises (1) the single 1856 printing of "The Piazza" (with the period present after "together" at 11.40 [PT26.19]) and (2) the original magazine printings, 1853–55, of the remaining pieces. Those magazine texts are then emended by authorial alterations—identified through multiple collations[17] with the 1856 printing—as well as by editorial correction of errors not caught in 1856. Routine procedures in the process of compiling, checking, and preparing the information for publication of this edition have resulted in further collations in addition to those reported in each case.[18]

TWENTIETH-CENTURY PRINTINGS. Since Melville's death in 1891 the whole of *The Piazza Tales* has been set in type as a separate volume at least three times, and most of the tales have appeared in a variety of collected volumes and anthologies.[19] None of these printings contains fresh textual authority, but they are of interest in illustrating the textual history of these pieces and in showing the few readings other editors have regarded as cruxes. The Constable edition of *The Piazza Tales*—in the collected *Works* (London, 1922; reprinted by Russell & Russell [New York, 1963] and Meicho Fukyukai Publishing Co. [Japan, 1983])—is significant because it was the first edition of the book after Melville's death and because it is part of the only complete set of his work that has been available in the past (and is therefore often cited as standard). Its text (reprinted in "Constable's Miscellany" in 1929) is based on that of the 1856 edition but departs from it in capitalization, punctuation, and spelling (especially through the substitu-

17. The number of collations which must be performed in order to detect all significant variations in a given text can never be prescribed with certainty, since chance determines, at least to some extent, the particular copies available for collation. Whether or not variant states of a first impression are detected, for example, depends largely on whether or not at least one copy of an earlier state is present in the collection of copies assembled for collation; regardless of the size of this collection, there is always a chance that an unknown earlier state is missing. To reduce somewhat the element of chance, the present editors have checked many points in every copy of both *The Piazza Tales* and the relevant numbers of *Putnam's Monthly Magazine* in the Melville Collection of The Newberry Library and have examined numerous copies in other collections. The particular copies used for these collations (and for those of the other printed pieces as well) are recorded in the NOTES ON INDIVIDUAL PROSE PIECES.

18. Proofreading provided the chief opportunity for making these additional collations.

19. Details of these editions will be included in the forthcoming descriptive bibliography. The Melville Collection of The Newberry Library contains these later editions.

tion of British forms).[20] The Elf edition (New York, 1929) is of no textual significance but is worth noting because it contains illustrations (showing, in their gratuitous suggestiveness, that Melville had become a cult figure among some homosexuals) and because it is the earliest instance of one of Melville's books supplying the text for a volume self-consciously designed as a "fine book." The first twentieth-century edition to offer an explanation of its editorial policy and an account of the textual history of *The Piazza Tales* is that edited by Egbert S. Oliver (New York: Hendricks House, Farrar Straus, 1948), which lists both the substantive changes Oliver believed Melville made as he prepared the magazine stories for book publication and also "the few corrections or emendations" made by Oliver himself (pp. 251–56). Another twentieth-century edition of *The Piazza Tales,* forming a volume with *Billy Budd,* is the Doubleday Dolphin Books edition of 1961.

Melville's "Hawthorne and His Mosses," written for the *Literary World* in 1850, and nine other previously uncollected prose pieces originally published in either *Putnam's Monthly Magazine* or *Harper's New Monthly Magazine* between 1853 and 1856 were first reprinted in *THE APPLE-TREE TABLE and Other Sketches by Herman Melville,* with an introductory note by Henry Chapin (Princeton: Princeton University Press, 1922). There was no textual apparatus either in this volume or in the next edition including some of Melville's uncollected prose: *BILLY BUDD and Other Prose Pieces,* edited by Raymond Weaver, which was added to the Constable *Works* in 1924. In their extensions of the canon to include items that Melville himself had published anonymously Chapin and Weaver were presumably guided by the printed copies (extracted from the original monthly numbers) that had been kept in the Melville family; these materials are now in the Melville Collection of The Houghton Library of Harvard University (see pp. 793–98 below). Weaver, in partially reprinting Melville's two "Fragments from a Writing Desk" (1839) from the *Democratic Press* of Lansingburgh, which he had already quoted extensively in his *Herman Melville: Mariner and Mystic* (New York: George H. Doran, 1921), based his text on clippings which Elizabeth Shaw Melville had annotated as "By Herman Melville" (see p.

20. This generalization is based on partial collations of the 1856 edition (M66–2471–59) and the *Putnam's* printing (Newberry Library A5.764) with the Constable edition (M66–2758) and the Russell & Russell reprint (M67–722–123) (see footnote 30 below). For some background relating to the Constable texts, see Philip Durham, "Prelude to the Constable Edition of Melville," *Huntington Library Quarterly,* XXI (1957–58), 285–89.

623 below). Further additions to the canon were reprinted for the first time during the 1930's by J. H. Birss, Willard Thorp, and Luther S. Mansfield. Birss and Thorp identified as Melville's the manuscripts of "Hawthorne and His Mosses" and four other contributions to the *Literary World* kept among Evert A. Duyckinck's papers, now in the Duyckinck Collection of The New York Public Library; Mansfield, also working with the Duyckinck papers, established Melville's authorship of the comic articles on Zachary Taylor originally published by *Yankee Doodle* in 1847.[21]

None of the collections of Melville's shorter prose can be regarded as complete, except the third volume of the Library of America's Melville series (New York: Literary Classics of the United States, 1984), which includes the Northwestern-Newberry texts of all the pieces in the present volume except the reconstructed lectures and attributed pieces. Among admittedly partial collections, a few may be mentioned for their special historical importance. *Shorter Novels of Herman Melville,* a volume in the Black and Gold Library with an introduction by Raymond Weaver (New York: Horace Liveright, 1928), was widely read during the first years of the modern revival of interest in Melville and has been kept in print through various later impressions. Along with Weaver's second version of *Billy Budd* it included three pieces from the 1850's: "Benito Cereno," "Bartleby the Scrivener," and "The Encantadas, or Enchanted Isles." *Selected Tales and Poems by Herman Melville,* edited with an introduction by Richard Chase, a popular and influential classroom text in the series of Rinehart Editions (New York, 1950), printed these same pieces plus six additional ones: "Jimmy Rose," "The Fiddler," "The Lightning-Rod Man," "I and My Chimney," "The Bell-Tower," and "The Paradise of Bachelors and the Tartarus of Maids." All of the shorter pieces of 1853–56 except "The 'Gees" were first collected by Jay Leyda in his carefully prepared edition of *The Complete Stories of Herman Melville* (New York: Random House, 1949; London: Eyre & Spottiswoode, 1951) and later reprinted without Leyda's name as part of *Selected Writings of Herman Melville,* a Modern Library Giant (New York, 1952). *Great Short Works of Herman Melville,* in the series of Perennial Classics, with an introduction by Jerry Allen (New York: Harper & Row, 1966), included all the *Putnam's* and *Harper's* pieces except "The 'Gees" and "The Town-Ho's Story" from *Moby-Dick* (first published

21. For citations, see the discussions below of "Fragments from a Writing Desk," pp. 622–25, Melville's several contributions to the *Literary World,* pp. 625–36 and 639–90, and "Authentic Anecdotes of 'Old Zack,' " pp. 636–39.

in *Harper's* in 1851), plus *Billy Budd*. What is described as a "second" Perennial Classics edition, with an introduction by Warner Berthoff (New York: Harper & Row, 1969), added "The 'Gees," "The Town-Ho's Story," six manuscript pieces of the 1870's and 1880's, and the Hayford-Sealts University of Chicago text of *Billy Budd, Sailor*. None of these collections provided any textual apparatus. Leyda used *The Piazza Tales* as copy-text, but emended both substantives and accidentals from the *Putnam's* magazine texts. His introduction to *The Complete Stories* discussed his general procedure in establishing these texts and those of a few of the other pieces but did not point out his own valuable silent emendations. With no acknowledgment, both the Harper Perennial Classics editions followed Leyda's texts (including his emendations).

Among many additional printings of the various prose pieces of 1839–56, some of them in anthologies prepared for classroom use, there are several which have made special contributions to textual study. William H. Gilman presented the first full twentieth-century printing of "Fragments from a Writing Desk, No. 2," in an annotated appendix of his *Melville's Early Life and* REDBURN (New York: New York University Press, 1951). Seymour L. Gross in *A* BENITO CERENO *Handbook* (Belmont, Calif.: Wadsworth, 1965), pp. 1–70, and John P. Runden, in *Melville's* BENITO CERENO*: A Textbook for Guided Research* (Boston: D. C. Heath, 1965), pp. 1–75, 189–93, provided edited texts of "Benito Cereno" and accompanying notes listing textual variants. Harrison Hayford and Hershel Parker, in their Norton Critical Edition of *Moby-Dick* (New York, 1967) included "slightly normalized reading texts," based on the manuscripts, of two of Melville's contributions to the *Literary World:* "Etchings of a Whaling Cruise" and "Hawthorne and His Mosses." *Shorter Works of Hawthorne and Melville,* edited by Hershel Parker (Columbus, Ohio: Charles E. Merrill, 1972), offered critical texts of "Authentic Anecdotes of 'Old Zack,' " "Hawthorne and His Mosses," "Bartleby, the Scrivener," "The Bell-Tower," "Benito Cereno," and "I and My Chimney," along with textual notes for each item.

ATTRIBUTED PROSE PIECES, 1834–56. For each of the compositions mentioned above solid objective evidence has authenticated Melville's authorship. In more recent years a number of scholars have attributed still other pieces to Melville, but in no case is their circumstantial or internal evidence beyond dispute. The most likely of these items are included as "Attributed Pieces" in the present volume. The earliest is "The Death Craft" (1839), which has provoked much discussion among Melville scholars. As the HIS-

TORICAL NOTE reports, this story of a haunted ship appeared in the *Democratic Press* within a month of Melville's return to Lansingburgh from his Liverpool voyage. Although William H. Gilman, in his *Melville's Early Life and REDBURN,* was skeptical, other commentators have been more inclined to accept the tale as Melville's. An excerpt from "The Death Craft" was given by Jay Leyda in *The Melville Log* (New York: Harcourt, Brace, 1951), I, 95; the full text was first reprinted in Martin Leonard Pops's *The Melville Archetype* (Kent, Ohio: Kent State University Press, 1970). Pops declared that Melville "undoubtedly" wrote the story "soon after returning from his voyage"; Pops's transcription regularizes spelling and punctuation—apart from what he calls "Melville's dramatic dashes and exclamation points" (p. 283). The other "Attributed Pieces," if less provocative than "The Death Craft," are also worth consideration. Evert A. Duyckinck's several allusions to Melville as one of the writers for *Yankee Doodle* in 1847 have led to speculation that more articles than the "Old Zack" series are his, but none have been identified with any certainty. Several of the most likely paragraphs from *Yankee Doodle* have been included here, on the basis of related comments by Duyckinck, under two supplied titles: "On the Chinese Junk" and "On the Sea Serpent." Another "which may have been Melville's," as Donald Yannella has suggested, is "A Short Patent Sermon. According to Blair, the Rhetorician," published on July 10, 1847, "a spoof in which Missionaries and a Sandwich Islander figure."[22] "The New Planet" and "View of the Barnum Property," which appeared in the numbers of July 24 and July 31, repeat topical allusions running through the "Old Zack" articles; they too may have come from Melville's pen.

Still another possibility dates from the autumn of 1850, when two Pittsfield newspapers carried a "Report of the Committee on Agriculture" of the Berkshire Agricultural Society over the signature of its chairman, Mel-

22. Donald Yannella, "Cornelius Mathews: Knickerbocker Satirist" (Ph.D. dissertation, Fordham University, 1971), p. 226. Yannella, pp. 226–27, also discusses a two-sentence "jab at Wiley and Putnam," the New York publishers, in the number of August 14, 1847, noting that John Wiley had called for the bowdlerization of Melville's *Typee* in the spring of 1846. But as Yannella acknowledges, Duyckinck and Mathews had even more cause to complain of Wiley, who as one of the publishers of the *Literary World* had dismissed Duyckinck from his editorship in May of 1847 for allowing Mathews to contribute. Moreover, the squib is directed not at Wiley but at his partner George P. Putnam, who had headed the London office of that firm, and Melville had continued on good terms with Putnam as bookseller and publisher after Putnam's partnership with Wiley dissolved.

ville's Pittsfield cousin Robert Melvill. In 1947 Jay Leyda partially reprinted the "delicately humorous" report, as he called it, attributing it to Melville acting as ghost-writer for his relative *(Town and Country,* CI [August, 1947], 68, 69, 114d, 116–18). Melville had known the region since his boyhood, when he had worked as a farmhand for Robert's father, and with his purchase of Arrowhead in September of 1850 he himself was planning to combine farming with authorship. During the previous July the cousins had made a three-day excursion "to view the state of the crops" in the southern part of Berkshire County, Melville keeping on the flyleaves of his copy of *A History of the County of Berkshire* (Pittsfield, 1829) a brief record (his account is quoted in *The Melville Log,* I, 379–80 and reprinted in the NN edition of the *Journals*). In the published report of the committee, along with the list of awards for the best wheat, rye, corn, oats, barley, peas, and carrots, are general observations on the Berkshire scene that have no parallel in Robert Melvill's surviving papers. Leyda's attribution of these comments to Herman Melville is plausible if not conclusive.

For each of these attributed pieces the first printing has served as copy-text in the absence of manuscripts. Printer's copy in the form of marked photocopies has been prepared from copies of the *Democratic Press* in the Troy Public Library and of *Yankee Doodle* in The Newberry Library and The University of Chicago Library. The "Report of the Committee on Agriculture" as first printed in the Pittsfield *Culturist and Gazette* has also been photocopied from the copy in The Berkshire Athenaeum at Pittsfield. In each case the Northwestern-Newberry text has been proofread against the original printing. Further details concerning all of these pieces, including textual data (and references not provided here), are given below in the NOTES ON INDIVIDUAL PROSE PIECES.

Other attributions to Melville deserve mention, although in no case does the evidence adduced appear to warrant their inclusion in this volume. Jeanne C. Howes, in "Melville's Sensitive Years," *Melville and Hawthorne in the Berkshires: A Symposium,* edited by Howard P. Vincent (Kent, Ohio: Kent State University Press, 1968; Melville Annual 1966), pp. 22–41, reports a search of the Pittsfield newspapers of 1833–38 for fugitive writings of Melville in both prose and verse. From the anonymous prose pieces carried by the Pittsfield *Sun* between 1834 and 1837 Howes singles out for discussion the story of a "Midshipman Wilson," which she finds reminiscent of "events in the life of ex-midshipman T. Wilson Melvill," a cousin of Herman Melville; a series called "The Philosopher," which "seems to reflect some of Melville's early thoughts on education"; "Dangerous Hoax," the story of a man on shipboard who masqueraded as a tattooed Indian chief; and "a column called 'Autumn' " published on September 25, 1834, which she thinks is "an earlier 'Sketch' of Major Thomas Melvill written by a devoted nephew," thus anticipating Melville's later account of his uncle contributed to J. E. A. Smith's *History of Pittsfield* (Springfield, 1876), pp. 38–39. In the absence of external evidence establishing a connection between Melville and the *Sun* these attributions remain conjectural.

In his unpublished doctoral dissertation, "Melville as a Magazinist" (Duke University, 1960), Norman E. Hoyle argues that Melville contributed more reviews to the *Literary World* than the five for which manuscripts survive in the Duyckinck Collection. Hoyle suggests (pp. 25–44) that Melville "may have been the principal author" of an extended series of reviews devoted to an outpouring of books about western travel and California gold-seeking: the series began with the number of February 24, 1849, while Melville was in Boston, included his own "Mr. Parkman's Tour" as the sixth review, and lasted in all for seven weeks. Hoyle's nominations for provisional inclusion in the Melville canon are a review of *A Tour of Duty in California* by Joseph Warren Rever (February 24); "The Western Trail," a review of *Oregon and California in 1848* by J. Quinn Thornton (March 3); "The Gold-Finders," a review of *Four Months among the Gold Finders in California* by J. Tyrwhitt Brooks (March 17); and—more tentatively—"Science of Gold Seeking," a review of *The Gold Seeker's Manual* by David T. Ansted and *The Miner's Guide* by J. W. Orton (March 24). Since Hoyle has located no manuscripts or references to the reviews among the Duyckinck papers, his argument for Melville's authorship necessarily involves circumstantial and internal evidence, as does his further nomination of "The New Edition of Cooper," a review of Putnam's revised edition of *The Spy* published in the *Literary World* for May 5, 1849 (pp. 48–51). Apart from the assumption that Duyckinck considered Melville "his Cooper specialist" (p. 46), Hoyle's evidence is entirely internal and would seem to point to Duyckinck's own manner rather than Melville's. Hoyle also calls attention to an article in the number of August 25, 1849, "Humors of Charles Lamb. Hitherto Unpublished. By One Who Knew Him," noting that on the surviving manuscript in the Duyckinck Collection an unidentified person has written that the hand may be Melville's (pp. 52–58). Melville of course did not know Lamb except through his writings, and the manuscript is not in Melville's hand.

Richard S. Moore, in "A New Review by Melville," *American Litera-*

ture, XLVII (May, 1975), 265–70, suggests still another contribution to the *Literary World* as Melville's: an unsigned review of *Southey's Commonplace Book* in the number for August 4, 1849. Moore's argument turns primarily on the prominence the reviewer gives to what Moore calls "Melville's favorite extract" from Thomas Fuller's *The Holy State and the Profane State,* together with further "stylistic evidence" for Melville's authorship. Like Hoyle, Moore lacks external documentation to clinch his case. "Stylistic evidence" is tenuous at best, and both the emphasis on Fuller and the possibility of Melville's having borrowed *The Holy State* from Duyckinck earlier in 1849, which Moore adduces, may point instead to Duyckinck himself not only as author of the review but as proponent of Fuller and his book to Melville.

Two supposed additions to the canon repeatedly mentioned in the last century by Melville's Pittsfield neighbor and early biographer J. E. A. Smith have been disproven by more recent investigators. Willard Thorp, in "Did Melville Review *The Scarlet Letter?" American Literature,* XIV (November, 1942), 302–5, shows that the article in question, which appeared in the *Literary World* for March 30, 1850, was in fact written by Duyckinck. Merton M. Sealts, Jr., in "Did Melville Write 'October Mountain'?" *American Literature,* XXII (May, 1950), 178–82, concludes, contrary to Smith, that Melville "never composed a story, sketch, or poem of that title." In "A Note on the Melville Canon," *Melville Society Newsletter,* V, no. 4 (December, 1949), p. [2], Sealts also demonstrates the unlikelihood that Melville wrote "Cruelty to Seamen," a five-paragraph piece of editorializing in a Melvillean vein that appeared anonymously in *Yankee Doodle* for August 21, 1847. Geoffrey Stone, in his *Melville* (New York: Sheed & Ward, 1949), p. 45, mistakenly took as Melville's the principal hand of a surviving manuscript in the Duyckinck Collection consisting of the three opening paragraphs of the article on Melville appearing in Duyckinck's *Cyclopædia of American Literature* (New York, 1855); in an illustrated appendix to *The Early Lives of Melville* (Madison: University of Wisconsin Press, 1974), pp. 189–93, Sealts identifies the hand as that of Melville's brother Allan.

THE LECTURES, 1847–60. In the absence both of surviving manuscripts and of authorized texts, the three lectures Melville presented on the circuit from 1857 to 1860, "Statues in Rome," "The South Seas," and "Traveling," are known only as they were reported in contemporary newspapers, sometimes briefly but occasionally in considerable detail. Beginning with Raymond Weaver in his pioneering biography of 1921, *Herman Melville:*

Mariner and Mystic, various Melville scholars have collected and reprinted surviving accounts. The most extended study is Merton M. Sealts, Jr.'s *Melville as Lecturer* (Cambridge: Harvard University Press, 1957), Part II of which includes the single newspaper report of "Traveling" and reconstructed texts of "Statues in Rome" and "The South Seas" conflated from the various known accounts of the two lectures. The present volume offers Sealts's revision, in the light of more recent scholarship, of the three texts he printed in *Melville as Lecturer.* Although these composite texts are critical in the sense that they involve editorial judgment in combining readings from different sources and contain further editorial emendations for accuracy and sense and—unlike the rest of the volume—for consistency and modernization (see p. 725), it must be emphasized that they cannot be considered critical reconstructions of Melville's fair-copy manuscripts. They simply represent the fullest possible reading, in those phrases which appear to be the most characteristic of Melville himself, that can be put together from the surviving newspaper reports.

TREATMENT OF SUBSTANTIVES

OF THE PIECES, other than the lectures, presented here in critical texts, four of Melville's contributions to the *Literary World* and probably the juvenile "Fragments from a Writing Desk" and all of his writing for *Yankee Doodle* in 1847 were set in type directly from his own manuscript drafts. But after his marriage in August of 1847, his wife and sisters, like Lucy in the later *Pierre,* began "mastering the chirographical incoherencies of his manuscripts, with a view to eventually copying them out in a legible hand for the printer" *(Pierre,* bk. 21; NN282.12–14). Elizabeth Shaw Melville is known to have "copied out" all or part of *Mardi* in 1848, Helen Melville worked on *Pierre* during the winter of 1851–52, and Augusta Melville copied all or part of *The Confidence-Man* in the summer of 1856. To judge from the fair copies of "Hawthorne and His Mosses," in Elizabeth's hand, and "The Two Temples," in Augusta's, Melville would correct and sometimes extensively revise these copies before sending them to the printer. The procedures of copying and correction have been deduced by Harrison Hayford and Hershel Parker from the manuscript of the essay on Hawthorne:

> Often enough his wife could not read his writing, and would either guess at a reading, or leave a blank space to fill in after consulting him or for him to

> fill in himself; sometimes, to complicate matters still more, he did not notice the misreadings or see that she had left a blank. Besides corrections, he would make final revisions on her fair copy before submitting it to the American publisher. When he did not notice errors, or when he simply forgot what he had first written and overlooked them in proofreading, his copyist's misreadings or omissions became part of the printed work.[23]

There is no evidence that Melville received proofs of his *Literary World* reviews, and the four manuscripts for them and the corrected fair copy of his Hawthorne essay are the only surviving evidence of his intended wording in these five articles.

Using these manuscripts as copy-text, the present edition therefore prints—for instance—"poesy" rather than the *Literary World*'s "poetry" (205.22), "divided" for "decided" (206.32), "buckling" for "truckling" (209.20), "stove" for "shore" (235.21), and "cosiest" for "easiest" (238.6). These examples of misreadings occur in articles set from Melville's holograph manuscripts, and his handwriting is so difficult to read that two words still remain conjectural (see the discussion at 210.26). But as other examples demonstrate, even the efforts of his family to prepare more legible copy for the printer did not insure a text free of substantive misreadings. In "Hawthorne and His Mosses," to cite the most notorious illustration, compositor Alexander mistook Elizabeth Shaw Melville's "sane madness" for "same madness" (244.26), an error that Melville himself deplored as "ugly" when he saw the first installment of his essay in print. Other manuscript readings restored in the present edition of the same essay include "like wine" for "likewise" (240.21), "mild" for "wild" (241.17), "my enthusiastic" for "my" (248.32–33), and "eagle-eyed" for "eager-eyed" (251.18).

The "Mosses" manuscript provides an editor with another problem. Normally when a fair-copy manuscript contains revisions in the hand of the author, those revisions would be accepted in a critical text as representing the author's intentions. A number of Melville's revisions here, however, appear to have been made under pressure from Evert A. Duyckinck as editor of the *Literary World*. Duyckinck was beginning to play down the

23. Norton Critical Edition of *Moby-Dick*, p. 472. The classic discussion of Melville's handwriting is provided by Davis and Gilman in their introduction to the *Letters*, pp. xxi–xxv; other relevant comment appears in Howard C. Horsford's introduction to Melville's *Journal of a Visit to Europe and the Levant* (Princeton: Princeton University Press, 1955), pp. 43–46. See also the Northwestern-Newberry Edition of *The Confidence-Man*, pp. 401–99.

cause of literary nationalism, and the "Mosses" manuscript shows that Melville toned down or made less explicit several of the vigorous statements he had originally made on this subject. Duyckinck was visiting Melville in Pittsfield at the time Melville was completing the essay, and one of the revisions in the manuscript is in his hand. The other similar revisions, even when they are in Melville's hand, could well have resulted from an editorial conference with Duyckinck or from Duyckinck's persuasion; indeed, it seems more likely that in these revisions Melville was following (or anticipating) instructions than that he had changed his opinion. In view of these circumstances, then, certain of Melville's substantive revisions in the manuscript are not adopted in the present edition, and his earlier wording stands in their place. (For a fuller discussion of this matter, see pp. 655–56.)

Of the pieces for which no manuscripts survive, those that present the principal challenge to an editor in deciding how to treat substantives are the five pieces in *The Piazza Tales* that were reprinted from *Putnam's*. For the other pieces there is only a single text, but for these five there are two, which differ substantively at 262 places; and the problem of determining which of the variants in the book text reflect Melville's intended revisions of the magazine text is complicated. Melville is known to have marked magazine sheets as copy for *The Piazza Tales* and then to have seen proofs for it. For this reason it has generally been thought that the substantive variants in the book text (except for those that are obvious oversights) must be authoritative. There are two kinds of evidence, however, suggesting that the book text may not carry the authority previously assigned to it and that an editor should therefore be cautious in admitting its substantive readings into the magazine copy-text.

The first kind of evidence consists of those variants that obviously do not reflect Melville's intention: they are largely compositorial errors, which thus reveal both a general lack of reliability in the typesetting for *The Piazza Tales* and a lack of care on Melville's part in proofreading. At one point in "Benito Cereno," for instance, the original reading "baskets" (51.19) becomes "basket", where clearly the plural is called for; and at another point "bowsman" (98.6–7) becomes "bowsmen", where it is equally obvious that the singular is required. Similarly, the book text of "The Encantadas" contains such erroneous variants from the magazine text as "Rotondo" for "Rodondo" (134.1) and "influences" for "influence" (139.13). Also in "The Encantadas" the large capital "E" used to represent the relation of two islands cannot be in the position Melville intended, for it faces downward rather than to the left (see the discussion at 140.3); perhaps it was not present in the book proofs when Melville saw them (as it had not been present earlier in the magazine text), but in any case it is another example of the unreliability of the book text. All these errors, and others like them, are obvious and can therefore be caught, but their cumulative effect makes one wonder how many other less obvious ones are present in *The Piazza Tales*. These patently nonauthorial changes should warn us, in other words, how risky it is to assume that Melville himself must have made, approved, or even known about more consequential changes in the book just because he prepared the printer's copy, making his own corrections and revisions, and then read proofs.

The second kind of evidence casting doubt on the authority of the book text comes from external documents which suggest the existence of editorial intervention on the part of the publisher. There is first of all Melville's complaint about the "profusion of commas" in the proofs for the book, demonstrating the presence of an editorial hand, one that could well have extended itself beyond matters of accidentals. Then there are references in letters directly linking the editors of and advisers to *Putnam's* with alterations in Melville's work for the magazine; while this evidence does not specifically relate to the book, it does show the climate of editorial control with which Melville had to deal (the book publisher was also the magazine publisher beginning in March, 1855). This control ranged from idiosyncratic spelling to avoidance of religious offense. Thus Charles F. Briggs, editor of the magazine until March, 1855, excised a few words near the end of Sketch Eighth of "The Encantadas," as he confessed in a letter to Melville; the context of Melville's passage suggests that Briggs's deletion may have been on religious grounds—and the same letter does contain his explicit rejection of "The Two Temples" for the reason that it might disturb "some of our church readers" (see the discussion of "The Encantadas" below, pp. 605–6). Frederick Law Olmsted, associate editor of the magazine after March, 1855, insisted on certain reformed spellings and was responsible for the spelling "hight" for "height", among others, in "Benito Cereno" (see footnote 28 below and the discussion at 46.14); what influence he may have had in matters other than spelling is not known. And George William Curtis, literary adviser to Dix & Edwards, recommended to Joshua A. Dix that some deletions be made in "The Bell-Tower"; he had first rejected the piece but then wrote to say, "making some erasures, we cannot afford to lose it" (see the discussion of "The Bell-Tower" below, p. 618). It is certainly possible, therefore, that some of the alterations in the *Piazza Tales* volume resulted from further pressure or direct intervention of this kind; if so, it would not have been the first time that Melville had experienced a publisher's demand for revisions in an already published work, for such was the case with the revised edition of *Typee.* That Melville had felt the pressure in writing some of the *Putnam's* pieces originally is clear from his reply to the letter of Briggs just mentioned, in which he promises to send some work that cannot be objected to "on the score of tender consciences of the public." Also his letter offering *Israel Potter* to George P. Putnam promises "nothing of any sort to shock the fastidious" *(Letters,* p. 170). Under these circumstances, any later changes that seem to tone down passages that might be thought offensive must be examined carefully, because they may stem from Melville's acquiescence to actual or assumed pressure rather than from his own altered views of his artistic intentions.

Given these two categories of evidence, an editor has no grounds for following a general rule of favoring the substantive variants in the book text, despite the knowledge that Melville made some changes in it; presumptive authority must still lie with the magazine text, and each substantive variant must prove itself if it is to be accepted into the critical text. Although such a procedure runs the risk of eliminating some revisions made by Melville and retaining instead his earlier wordings, the risk is justified in order to avoid incorporating into the text revisions that were imposed on Melville, directly or indirectly, or seeming revisions that are actually compositorial errors. This approach provides a means for analyzing the main classes of differences between the texts in *Putnam's* and in *The Piazza Tales:*

(1) The most immediately striking differences in the book text are a series of omissions of such prominent elements as a subtitle, a pseudonym, a triple epigraph, and a footnote. Thus, "Bartleby, the Scrivener / A Story of Wall-Street" becomes simply "Bartleby"; the pseudonym "Salvator R. Tarnmoor" is eliminated from "The Encantadas"; and the three epigraphs from "a Private MS.," as well as a concluding footnote, are omitted from "The Bell-Tower." In each case the omission could easily have resulted either from the compositorial carelessness apparent elsewhere in the volume or from a decision in the publisher's office; it is less easy for an editor to identify motives Melville himself could have had for eliminating elements that contribute to the meaning of the pieces involved. As a matter for editorial decisions the situation is doubtful enough that the conservative course is to keep the magazine readings. (See the discussions at 13.1–2, 125.3, 174.2–6, and 187.3.)

(2) Another important category consists of what may be called "softenings," revisions which tone down passages that might be thought offensive for one reason or another. In the magazine text of "Bartleby, the Scrivener," for example, the prison grub-man is named "Mr. Cutlets," and he extends Bartleby an invitation to dinner in "Mrs. Cutlets' private room"; in the book text the name "Cutlets" is eliminated, and the invitation becomes simply "What will you have for dinner to-day?" Because the revision (which was not, in fact, well carried out) may have been prompted by the possible interpretation of the original passage to refer to Mrs. Cutlets's sexual services (and in any case as a reflection on the management of the actual Tombs Prison—as "The Two Temples" was seen by Briggs to reflect recognizably on the actual Grace Church and its sexton, Brown), there is sufficient doubt as to whether the revision really reflects Melville's intention, so the conservative course is to retain what he first wrote (see the discussion at 44.4–5). Another kind of softening, this time of violence, occurs in "Benito Cereno": in the magazine text two blacks "flew out against" one of the sailors "with horrible curses", then "dashed him to the deck and jumped upon him"; in the book text the curses are gone, for the blacks merely "violently pushed him aside", and they do not jump upon him (70.15–17). These and other such softenings are rejected as a matter of policy by the present editors, for in them lurks the taint that quite possibly they (even if Melville's) were not prompted by his own better sense of his meaning but by his publisher's prudent attitudes if not actual intervention or suasion. Publishing-house pressure might work directly, as we happen to know Olmsted's, Curtis's, and Briggs's did, or it might work more subtly, as we also know it did through the inhibitory effect of *Putnam's* repeated editorial disapproval both of the general trend of Melville's work and of any sallies that might be offensive to readers. Moreover, there was the overhanging threat of the reviewers' excoriations (see pp. 468–70). For such reasons, the present editors believe that Melville's true intentions seem more likely to come across by preserving his forthright first phrasings than by adopting the softened versions, even if some of these (and how can one tell which?) may be his own considered preferences. Although one might conceivably argue that such revisions are part of a consistent movement in Melville's writing, increasing in later years, toward more ambiguous and less direct expression, the case for this point of view as applied to the revisions in *The Piazza Tales* seems less persuasive than the reasons for regarding them as the product of some form of pressure.

(3) A number of the variants in the book text seem relatively indiffer-

ent: it is difficult to see what motivation lies behind them. When no plausible reason can be adduced why they might result from publishing-house pressure or from the routine activity of a publisher's or printer's copy-editor (and when they do not seem likely compositors' errors), they are accepted into the critical text, on the grounds that no one other than the author would be likely to have seen reason to make them. There is a curious group of alterations in "Benito Cereno," for instance, in which proper names are eliminated—"Don Benito" becoming "his host" (as at 59.14, 65.9, and 70.34), "his captain" (80.11), or "the Spaniard" (80.17–18); and "Captain Delano" becoming "his guest" (63.34), "he" (65.10), or "the visitor" (79.31). It is hard to see how these changes can be regarded as softenings—as the elimination of the proper name "Cutlets" can be—and they are adopted in the present edition as more likely Melville's than not. Another characteristic, and often indifferent, kind of revision in the book text consists of brief shortenings or the omission of single words. One could perhaps argue that they represent a consistent effort on Melville's part to abbreviate his phrasing; however, the general lack of reliability of the book text makes unwise any policy of uncritical acceptance of small omissions—which could of course simply be the result of compositorial carelessness. Thus when the phrase "for the first time" in "Benito Cereno" becomes "for the first" (63.12–13), the latter idiom, though commonly used by Melville, could so easily have been caused by a compositor's oversight that it seems best to retain the original reading. Other small deletions are less indifferent, changing somewhat the stylistic effect or meaning, and when there is no strong reason to think of them as having been imposed on Melville from without, they can be accepted as his: one small group of this kind involves the skillful elimination of certain occurrences of "the", as in "the clenched jaw" (96.39) or "the air" (175.11). Here the likelihood of the omissions having been deliberate outweighs the possibility that they were mere slips. There are longer omissions, too, that may seem indifferent, as well as revisions not involving any shortening; and the same line of reasoning is applied to them. The awkward omission of "on that well-remembered morning, I saw" in "The Encantadas" (136.18–19), for example, can readily be explained by compositorial eye skip and cannot plausibly be attributed to the author, since the omitted words serve an important transitional function; they are therefore retained here. But when in "Bartleby" the book text changes "means" to "measures" (31.12), there is no reason not to go along with the change as Melville's; it makes less sense to think of the change as a copy-editor's revision or a compositor's slip than as the kind of slight shift in diction that an author might make. The procedure followed here, then, springs directly from the view that substantive differences in the book text cannot automatically be favored: each of these more or less indifferent alterations must be judged by weighing against one another the claims of editorial interference, compositorial error, and authorial revision.

(4) Finally there are those alterations which cannot reasonably be attributed to anyone other than the author and which show that Melville did indeed make revisions on the magazine sheets he furnished for the book. His presence can clearly be seen in the creation of a whole new paragraph for "Benito Cereno" (69.12–21). But his work can equally be recognized in various other insertions, revisions, and word changes. Thus the insertion of two references to "hardware" (55.15, 104.7), to account for the hatchets in "Benito Cereno," is obviously his, as is the insertion of the clause "which cometh by prostration" (174.14) in "The Bell-Tower." Revisions such as "hardly can I" for "I cannot adequately" (45.26) and the substitution of a ten-word phrase on "Don Benito's confessed ill opinion of his crew" for a twenty-four-word phrase that combines Delano's suspicions of the crew with Benito's ill opinion (72.7–8) must similarly be Melville's. And certain changes in diction, such as "surtout" for "mantle" (46.14), "idle" for "random" (69.31), "harboring" for "indulging" (97.2), "withdrawing" for "revoking" (97.16), "submersion" for "submission" (174.22), "inspirited" for "inspired" (175.9), "conceded" for "concealed" (177.6), and many others, occur at points where a copy-editor or publisher's reader would have no reason to question the word choice, and they often shift the meaning so appropriately but so subtly that no one except the author would have been motivated to think of them and incorporate them.

The remaining pieces, for which a single printed form is the only source of the text, are less complicated to deal with. Several substantive emendations have been made in them, but other errors probably exist in them, so far undetected, as well as others undetectable now for lack of evidence. Among the most error-ridden printings in the entire canon are those of the early "Fragments from a Writing Desk" in the Lansingburgh *Democratic Press,* whose compositor was neither skillful nor educated enough to decipher Melville's hand without error or to correct his erratic spelling and punctuation consistently. The present-day editor must introduce emendations where either a misprinting or a misreading is apparent, such as "Certes" for the clearly erroneous "Cerbes" (197.13), "actually" for "actual" (200.19), and "presentments" for "presentiments" (196.27); if

"The Death Craft" as printed in the same paper is also Melville's, "congelated" for "conjulated" (425.23) is still another example. From the surviving manuscripts of 1847–50 it is apparent that metropolitan compositors such as those for Melville's contributions to *Yankee Doodle* and his uncollected tales and sketches in *Harper's* and *Putnam's* were far more capable than their provincial colleague, but it is still possible to identify misreadings. Emended in the present edition are such likely compositorial (or scribal) errors as "short" (which should be "shirt") in "Authentic Anecdotes of 'Old Zack' " (215.21), "unobservantly" ("unobservedly") in "Poor Man's Pudding and Rich Man's Crumbs" (292.2), "elders" ("alders") in "Cock-A-Doodle-Doo!" (282.18), "Persian" ("Parisian") and "learning" ("leaning") in "Jimmy Rose" (342.3, 343.38), "shipper" ("skipper") in "The 'Gees" (349.36), and "Magnolia" ("Magnalia") in "The Apple-Tree Table" (380.37, 382.26). Other substantive errors made either by Melville or his copyist or compositor include "is" (which should be "are") at 351.13 in "The 'Gees" and the omission of "it" at 228.30 in "Authentic Anecdotes of 'Old Zack' " and "not" at 363.27 in "I and My Chimney." If manuscripts or corrected proofs of these works were available, it would no doubt be possible to identify still other errors, and given the practices of the *Putnam's* editors, discussed above, other nonauthorial readings are probably present.

The correction of detectable error is of course a category of emendations attempted throughout,[24] and one class of such emendations deserves special comment. When Melville quotes from other writers, as in the epigraphs to "The Encantadas," the possibility exists of locating errors by reference to the sources from which the quotations were drawn. Deviations from the sources in Melville's quotations are not automatically corrected, however, because the aim is fidelity to Melville's intention (or what he took to be the wording of a passage) rather than to the sources themselves. If the change of a word seems to serve no purpose and if the word in the source is one that in Melville's handwriting might have looked like the one that got printed, it seems proper to conclude that Melville intended no alteration and to emend the copy-text with the original reading. Thus,

24. Such changes are made only when the copy-text reading is unsatisfactory. The emendation must produce wording that Melville would have used in the context (judging from his literary practice); it must improve the sense and fit the tone of the context; and, if a substitution, it must be a word that in Melville's hand could have been misread as the word in the copy-text (or that Melville himself could mistakenly have written). Under these criteria, for example, "sails" is emended to "nails" (146.1).

among the quotations from Spenser prefaced to sketches of "The Encantadas," "secure" appears in both the magazine and book texts instead of Spenser's "recure" (125.16), "there" instead of "these" (130.14), and "fear" instead of "fears" (144.14); in cases of this kind the correct readings are restored here. In other situations, however, no emendation is made: "do a man" is allowed to remain for "did the knight" (130.8) and "these isles" for "the seas" (130.11), because they are obviously examples of intentional alteration to fit the quotation to Melville's purpose. Minor misquotations, when they do not seem likely misreadings of the original words, are similarly not emended, both because they could conceivably have been intended by Melville and because, given the custom in his time of approximate quotation, they would not have been considered inappropriate in what purports to be quoted material. The checking of sources, both for such quotations and for passages that paraphrase or loosely adapt the writings of others (see, for example, the discussions at 143.21, 172.33–34, and 173.9), can offer a clue—in the absence of Melville's manuscript—to the copy underlying the published text, so long as one keeps in mind the possibility that Melville's intention was to alter his source.[25]

TREATMENT OF ACCIDENTALS

WHEN ELIZABETH Shaw Melville was beginning her service as manuscript copyist for her husband, she once described, in a letter to her stepmother written on May 5, 1848, how she carried out her work. "I tore my sheet in two by mistake," she first explained, "thinking it was my copying (for we only write on one side of the page) and if there is no punctuation marks you must make them for yourself for when I copy I do not punctuate at all but leave it for a final revision for Herman. I have got so used to write without it I cannot always think of it." Her fair copy of "Hawthorne and His Mosses" shows that in 1850 (when she was probably copying as well the manuscript that became *Moby-Dick)* she was still leaving most of the punctuation for her husband to insert. But though Melville

25. For further discussion of this general problem, see G. Thomas Tanselle, "External Fact as an Editorial Problem," *Studies in Bibliography*, XXXII (1979), 1–47. Even when factual errors do not seem to be intentional—as when Melville, in his review of Cooper's *The Sea Lions*, calls Deacon Pratt the "father" (236.10) rather than the uncle of Mary—they cannot always be corrected, if Melville's ensuing discussion or understanding of a situation is based on the error. For other examples see the discussions at 169.32, 246.14, 317.3, and 338.34.

himself was evidently concerned about proper pointing, he had nevertheless come to depend on his editors and compositors—"some one who understands punctuation better than I do," as he put it to Dix & Edwards in 1856—to "give the final hand" to such matters. What sometimes happened with responsibility thus divided evidently baffled him, much as Pierre was afflicted by "minute, gnat-like torments" in his proofs. Melville, as we know, objected to the "profusion of commas" introduced in the 1856 typesetting of *The Piazza Tales;* the present edition, by adopting the earlier magazine printing as copy-text for the five pieces reprinted in that volume, is closer to Melville's original punctuation practice.

With *The Piazza Tales,* and also with those prose pieces whose first printing is the sole textual authority now available, a modern editor following Greg's theory of copy-text will emend only sparingly. Without a final manuscript, the degree to which the author was responsible for the accidentals—the spelling and punctuation—of a printed text is a matter impossible to settle conclusively. Even though changes in the spelling and punctuation of Melville's manuscripts were undoubtedly made by contemporary editors, publishers, and printers, the first printing is nevertheless the only source of the text in such cases (five of the *Piazza Tales* pieces of course excepted); and its accidentals, when they are not Melville's own, at least represent contemporary practice. Accordingly, the accidentals of the first printing have been retained in the present edition except in a few unusual instances, even when the spelling and punctuation may appear incorrect or inconsistent by late-twentieth-century standards. Some of the inconsistencies in spelling and punctuation may have been in the manuscripts, as the fair copy of "Hawthorne and His Mosses" demonstrates, and, although Melville may not have been aware of them, they constitute a suggestive part of his total expression, since patterns of accidentals do affect the texture of a literary work. On the other hand, some of the inconsistencies in accidentals may have resulted either from an imperfectly realized attempt to make the manuscript conform to a house style or from compositorial alterations. To regularize the punctuation and spelling would be to risk choosing nonauthorial forms and producing a consistency that was not necessarily regarded as desirable or important at the time.[26] Therefore no at-

26. Melville's habits in the extant manuscripts and letters are not definite enough to offer grounds to emend for consistency (and in any case the letters, not intended for publication, do not provide a parallel situation). Neither is contemporary house styling of the newspapers and periodicals to which he contributed consistent enough to be helpful in determining precisely what elements of the punctuation of his contributions resulted from it.

tempt has been made to impose general consistency on either spelling or punctuation.[27]

With those compositions for which either draft or fair-copy manuscripts are available to serve as copy-texts, one soon finds that Melville for the most part left to his editors and compositors the task of expanding his abbreviations, correcting his spelling, and dealing with his erratic punctuation, during which process the compositors at the *Literary World* sprinkled the printed text with commas. The present edition, using the manuscripts as copy-text, avoids the *Literary World*'s "profusion of commas" similar to those that offended Melville in *The Piazza Tales.* It transcribes words in standard spelling (see the discussion below) in those cases where Melville did not form all the letters distinctly (see, for example, "their", the fourth word in the second line reproduced on p. 630). Usually the word intended can be made out, sometimes only by the aid of the context; but an occasional simple word (or single letter determining number or tense) may offer alternative choices difficult to be sure about. Like the *Literary World,* the Northwestern-Newberry text expands abbreviations—"and" for the manuscript "&", "though" for "tho' ", and "through" for "thro' "—and corrects clear misspellings. Examples of words corrected are "viscicitudes" (205.27), "acheived" (205.28), "Brown" for "Browne" (206.14ff.), "beleive" (207.1), "benevolant" (207.5), "parlimentary" (207.35), and "gunwhale" (209.35).

These illustrations all come from Melville's manuscript of his review of J. Ross Browne's *Etchings of a Whaling Cruise;* other examples that might also be cited would lie on the borderline between definite misspellings and elided or imperfectly formed letters within individual words. To take a different case, that of "The Two Temples," Melville's sister Augusta prepared the fair-copy manuscript and Melville ostensibly corrected it, but the story went off to *Putnam's* in 1854 with as many inconsistencies as were in the manuscripts sent to the *Literary World.* Here again the present edition is not concerned with eliminating them, but it expands the manuscript "&" to "and" and corrects clear misspellings: "effulgance" (305.6), "alter" for "altar" (305.29), "beggers" (305.37), "apparal" (306.37, 310.21), "re-

27. For example, no emendations are made to secure consistency in the use (or nonuse) of apostrophes in contractions (such as "aint" or "dont"); or of italics or quotation marks (or both at once) for such items as foreign words, titles of poems and books, and names of ships; or of placement of punctuation within or outside of quotation marks (see also footnote 29 below and the discussion at 210.13).

sponce" (308.24), "secureing" (310.4), "vacillatations" (310.12), "Pandamonian" (311.3), "comparitive" (311.7), "turbulant" (311.19), and "consciencіously" (314.38).

In every case, whether a printing or a manuscript serves as copy-text, any changes in either spelling or punctuation have been made sparingly, according to the following guidelines:

SPELLING. The general rule adopted here is to retain any spellings (even when inconsistent) that were acceptable by the standards of the time, as well as any archaic forms that Melville may have been using intentionally; spellings are corrected only when they do not fall into these categories. One available guide for decisions about spelling is the 1847 revision of Webster's *American Dictionary of the English Language* (Springfield, Mass., 1848). Webster's was the dictionary used by Harper & Brothers at the time, for Melville remarked, in his letter to John Murray in London on January 28, 1849, that "my printers here 'go for' Webster." The Harper accounts show that Melville ordered at least three copies of Webster's (on April 10 and November 15, 1847, and on November 16, 1848), the third of which could have been the 1848 edition. In any case, the 1848 Webster's can be taken as a generally accepted standard in use when Melville was writing most of the work in this volume. In considering spellings that appear in *Putnam's*, one must also take into account the adoption of some of Webster's spelling reforms there.[28] Recourse to Webster's and to other contemporary dictionaries, such as Worcester's *A Universal and Critical Dictionary of the English Language* (Boston, 1847), to editions of American novels and other works published in the 1830's, 1840's, and 1850's, as well as to such sources for the historical study of spelling as the *Oxford English Dictionary* and the *Dictionary of American English*, has resulted in the retention of some anomalous-appearing copy-text forms. Any forms, in fact, that are supported by a tradition of use, whether or not they appear to have been

28. See Laura Wood Roper, " 'Mr. Law' and *Putnam's Monthly Magazine:* A Note on a Phase in the Career of Frederick Law Olmsted," *American Literature*, XXVI (March, 1954), 91: as a partner in the firm of Dix & Edwards and as of March, 1855, associate editor of *Putnam's*, Olmsted "introduced some of Webster's spelling innovations into the magazine." George William Curtis, the magazine's editorial adviser, after seeing proof for the October, 1855 number, which included the first installment of "Benito Cereno," protested in a letter to Joshua A. Dix about spelling in what he called "this hideous Websterian manner"—he specifically cited "molding," "luster," and "hight"; he had earlier complained about "penciling" and "subtile." "Mold" and various forms of "hight" appear in the P printings of "Benito Cereno" and "The Bell-Tower" (August, 1855), the two Melville pieces in which Olmsted had a hand (see the discussions at 46.14 and 50.13). As the spellings "mould" and "height" in *The Piazza Tales* suggest, Olmsted's practice was later abandoned.

employed in Melville's time, are retained; enough archaic forms are present to suggest that Melville was using them intentionally or was being influenced in his spelling by his reading of earlier literature—either of which justifies keeping them in this edition. Examples of anomalous-appearing forms that are retained are "prophecied" (88.2, 382.5), "secret" for "secrete" (167.21), "champaigne" for "champagne" (194.22), "passed" for "past" (199.23), "chord" for "cord" (201.13, 202.10), "prarie" for "prairie" (232.20,37, 249.3), "dreampt" (236.19), "morrocco" (237.9), "vail" for "veil" (333.36), and "negociation" (429.10). A few other forms, not found in relevant parallels, have been corrected: for example, "descryed" (200.38), "Chandeleres" (202.19), and "ottomon" (202.33). Foreign words, too, are sometimes spelled in the copy-text in an unacceptable way (e.g., "Excellenza" at 178.12ff.), and in these instances they are corrected. Consistency is not the object, and thus both "ascendency" (35.6) and "ascendancy" (35.5) are allowed to remain; two instances of British "-our" spellings ("neighbours" and "neighbourhood", 140.1, 2) are emended to "-or", not to produce consistency (which the change in fact does) but to conform with what is known to be Melville's own usage.

Proper names are treated in the same way, and in this volume many appear anomalous, particularly in "Benito Cereno." The aim here is to follow Melville's intention; alterations are not made, therefore, simply to bring a name into conformity with a more usual standard or with the spelling used in Melville's source (for "Benito Cereno," Amasa Delano's *Narrative),* nor are they made to produce consistent foreign-language forms. Thus among the copy-text forms retained are "Baldivia" (56.26), an acceptable variant of the "Valdivia" that appeared in Delano; "Bautista" (105.3), a correction (whether by Melville or someone at *Putnam's)* of the erroneous "Balltista" in Delano; "St. Maria" (46.4), a mixed-language form (the Spanish name with the English abbreviation) that occurs in Delano; and "Christopher Colon" (107.32), a mixed English and Spanish form introduced by Melville (for the name does not appear in Delano; on such mixed forms, see also the discussions at 49.16, 105.26, and 114.7, and cf. that at 104.18). However, a few corrections of obvious slips are made, whether the slip originated in Delano's account and was copied accurately by Melville ("Arruco" in Delano should be "Arauco", 106.14) or whether the slip first appeared in *Putnam's,* presumably as a result of Melville's miscopying from Delano or of someone's misreading his hand ("Nacta" is here corrected to "Natu", 104.25, for example, and "Mozairi" to "Morairi", 107.15). This treatment of proper names seeks to preserve both the wide latitude allowed in contemporary usage and Melville's evident casualness about such forms.

Punctuation. Emendations in punctuation are made only to correct obvious slips of the pen in manuscripts, typographical errors in first printings, and evidently incorrect pointing; no alterations are made in punctuation that is not manifestly wrong simply in an effort to bring it into conformity with some presumed standard. Therefore such inconsistencies as the use of both "fairy-land" and "fairy land" (see the discussion at 4.3), or of both "s' " and "s's" at the end of possessive proper nouns ending in "s" (146.20), are allowed to stand. And since contemporary practice did not demand accuracy in the use of accents on foreign words (indeed, contemporary dictionaries sometimes listed them without accents), such forms as "reênter" (308.14) and such words without accents as "protege" (191.13) and *"distingue"* (192.11) are retained as they appear in the copy-text. Several of the obvious errors, which have been emended, involve the absence of marks unquestionably needed, such as periods at the ends of sentences (e.g., after "sixty" at 15.8 and *"entrall"* at 130.11) or commas and semicolons essential to the sense (e.g., a missing comma after "servant" at 87.1), as well as the presence of misplaced marks (like the comma after "structures" at 175.30 or the one after "however" instead of "insignificant" at 177.18). One small group of errors concerns the terminal punctuation of questions and exclamations. When such sentences end with periods (as at 26.17; see also 385.29 and 390.26), no emendation is normally called for (exceptions are the periods after "ghost" at 38.24, after "forty" at 265.35, and after "Taylor's" at 267.5, because these questions are in series of parallel questions ending with question marks); but when a question mark or an exclamation point appears where the other is called for (probably as a result of an indistinctly formed mark in Melville's handwriting), emendation is required (a question mark is emended to an exclamation point after "too" at 89.7 and "failure" at 260.39, and the opposite change is made after "Sir" at 282.36). Perhaps the most interesting category involves the absence of quotation marks around certain obviously quoted words or statements, omissions which at first mislead the reader. Thus at 94.16, a closing quotation mark comes after "better" in the copy-text, though it is clear that the next two words, "Don Benito", should be a part of the quotation. Less immediately obvious, perhaps, but nevertheless unquestionable, is the fact that the sentence beginning "Here" at 172.33 is the quotation of the "inscription over a grave" just announced, and the absence of quotation marks in the copy-text, rectified here, makes it read instead as the narrator's comment. Similarly, twice in

"Cock-A-Doodle-Doo!" a quotation within direct discourse is not marked as such: the words "Said the Widow Wadman" (273.11–12), part of the narrator's quoted direct discourse, should be in single quotation marks to show that he is reading them; and the exclamation "Glory to God in the highest!" (286.10), part of a comment made by Merrymusk, should be in single quotation marks to make clearer that Merrymusk is attributing them to the cock. Emendations to add quotation marks at these points produce the readings clearly required by their contexts.[29]

EDITORIAL APPARATUS

FOLLOWING this General Note on the Text is a series of Notes on Individual Prose Pieces, arranged in the same sequence as the pieces to which they refer. For each piece, these notes begin with an introductory discussion, or headnote, about the composition and sources of the work. For all pieces except the lectures, each headnote also specifies the copy-text and identifies the printer's copy and the copies used for collation.[30] Headnotes for the three lectures include (1) a report of the localities where Melville appeared during the lecture season concerned, the date of each engagement, and the local newspapers which are known to have covered the lecture; and (2) for "Statues in Rome" and "The South Seas," the variant readings among the individual newspaper accounts on which the successive paragraphs of the reconstructed texts are based.

After each of these headnotes come lists of textual data (varying in number according to the nature of the surviving documents) relating to the same piece. They provide the basic evidence for textual decisions affecting

29. No attempt has been made to regularize the punctuation (and capitalization) of phrases or clauses that introduce or interrupt direct quotations (see the discussions at 207.35–36, 240.38, and 362.26). For NN positioning of indeterminately placed or missing punctuation with quotation marks in the manuscript pieces, see the discussion at 210.13. It is perhaps unnecessary to add that, in those instances in which a mark of punctuation in a printed copy-text has slipped out of position, the mark is placed properly in the present text, and any other errors in spacing are rectified (much of the punctuation in the *Democratic Press* is in fact above or below the line). Such alterations merely correct the typography of the copy-text but do not emend the text itself, and they are not recorded in the lists of emendations for the individual pieces. (A related category of defects in the copy-texts not reported in the lists of emendations consists of plate or type damage that creates no textual problems.)

30. The particular copies used for collation and (in photocopy form) for printer's copy are specified by identification number (for material in the Melville Collection of The Newberry Library) or by library name and call number (for material not in the Melville Collection).

the critical texts in the present volume and complete the TEXTUAL RECORD. The sections that can appear are as follows:

DISCUSSIONS. The discussions take up any reading (whether a copy-text reading or an emendation) adopted in the Northwestern-Newberry critical text which seems to require explanation beyond the general guidelines already stated. Certain instances of decisions not to emend, as well as many actual emendations, are commented upon.

EMENDATIONS. These lists record every change made from the copy-texts for the critical texts of this edition, accidentals as well as substantives. The first item in each entry is the Northwestern-Newberry reading,[31] the second the rejected copy-text reading. (Since the copy-texts vary from piece to piece, an abbreviation denoting the particular copy-text is provided for convenience in each instance. The abbreviations and symbols employed are identified below, pp. 569–70.) Items marked with asterisks are commented on in the DISCUSSIONS. No emendations of any sort have been made silently; using the list of EMENDATIONS and that of HYPHENATION, one can reconstruct the copy-text in every detail.[32]

HYPHENATION. Since some compound words are hyphenated at the ends of lines in the copy-text, the intended forms of these words become a matter for editorial decision. When such a word appears elsewhere in the copy-text for a particular piece in only one form, that form is followed; when its treatment is not consistent within that piece (and the inconsistency is an acceptable one, to be retained in the present text), the form that occurs more times in analogous situations is followed. If the word does not occur elsewhere in the copy-text for that piece, the form is determined by a survey of similar words, by the usage in the 1847 Worcester's and the

31. Calling these emendations "Northwestern-Newberry readings" signifies only that the readings do not occur in the copy-texts; it does not imply that no one has ever thought of them before. Indeed, in the case of the *Putnam's* pieces reprinted in *The Piazza Tales* (see the paragraph headed SUBSTANTIVE VARIANTS just below), Northwestern-Newberry emendations of the periodical copy-texts may of course follow the readings of the book text and in those instances are so identified.

32. That is, every *textual* detail: features of the styling or design of the copy-text documents—such as the length of lines, the form and content of captions in newspapers and magazines, the typography and punctuation of titles and headings, and the use of the phrases "Continued from . . . " and "To be continued" at the beginning and end of installments—are of course not recoverable from these lists. Also not recoverable is the end punctuation in titles, although internal punctuation follows the copy-text. This edition is styled with display capitals at the beginning of individual pieces (except where typographically awkward) and omits double quotation marks before them (see pp. 289 and 303).

1848 Webster's, and by any relevant evidence in a Melville manuscript. The first list in each report of HYPHENATION records these decisions, giving the adopted Northwestern-Newberry forms of compounds which are hyphenated at the ends of lines in the copy-text and which the editors had to decide whether to print as single-word compounds without hyphens or as hyphenated compounds. The second list is a guide to the established copy-text forms of compounds that are hyphenated at the ends of lines in the Northwestern-Newberry Edition; any word hyphenated at the end of a line in the present edition should be transcribed as one unhyphenated word unless it appears in this list. No editorial decisions are involved in this second list,[33] but the information recorded is essential for reconstructing the copy-text and making exact quotations from the present edition. A slash (/) in the first list indicates the line-end break in words which might possibly be hyphenated in more than one place.

SUBSTANTIVE VARIANTS. These lists record, for each case in which more than one text is involved (i.e., the five *Putnam's* pieces included in *The Piazza Tales,* the five *Literary World* pieces surviving in manuscript, and the "Report of the Committee on Agriculture"), all variant substantive readings between the two printed texts or between the final manuscript text and the printed version.[34] When the Northwestern-Newberry reading differs from the reading of either of these texts, it comes first in an entry, to provide a key to the present text; otherwise, whichever reading agrees with the present edition comes first, then the other one. Abbreviations used to signify these texts are identified below, pp. 569–70. Since Melville evidently did not see proofs of the *Literary World* pieces, the presence of the LW symbol in these lists merely records the fact that the reading appeared

33. Except in the cases of words coincidentally hyphenated between the same elements at line-ends in the copy-text as well. These words, which appear in both lists, are marked with daggers and are given in the forms which the present editors have adopted but which are obscured by hyphenation at the ends of lines in this edition.

34. Such variants as "can not"/"cannot", "Capt."/"Captain", "dyes"/"dies", and "20"/"twenty" are considered accidentals whenever the 1847 Worcester's, the 1848 Webster's, or other contemporary dictionaries indicate that they were interchangeable forms of the same word. A few variants are included in the lists of SUBSTANTIVE VARIANTS even though they could possibly function as forms of the same word: "secret"/"secrete" (167.21), "nought"/"naught" (186.17, 243.13), "harpooneer"/"harpooner" (209.29), and "round"/"around" (233.35). On file in the Melville Collection of The Newberry Library are complete lists of variants, including both substantives (reported here) and accidentals (reported in the EMENDATIONS lists only when they are adopted). (Also on file is the evidence for the decisions in the first of each pair of HYPHENATION lists.)

in that text and does not imply that the authority of the reading derives from its presence there. The same is true of the resettings of the "Report of the Committee" in the Pittsfield *Sun* (PS) and the *Massachusetts Eagle* (ME). (Features of the styling or design of the text from which a reading is adopted are not necessarily followed in the present edition, and such deviations are not reflected in the citations of readings here.)

MANUSCRIPT ALTERATIONS. Lists of alterations in the manuscripts appear in the notes on those six pieces in this volume for which there are surviving manuscripts.[35] The form in which these alterations are reported (using abbreviations and symbols listed below, pp. 569–70) is designed to show both the order in which a change in the initial inscription of the document was set down and the order in which Melville himself made later revisions. It also distinguishes among: (1) words first written down either by Melville himself or by his copyist (Elizabeth Shaw Melville in "Hawthorne and His Mosses," Augusta Melville in "The Two Temples"); (2) words which he or the copyist canceled at once and replaced by other words on the same line; and (3) words Melville or his copyist (or Evert A. Duyckinck in "Hawthorne and His Mosses") canceled at some later time and replaced by other words inserted above the line or added. In these lists only, all words in roman type are authorial; all words in italics are editorial. Vestigial punctuation, whether or not actually canceled, is reported as canceled along with its accompanying words.

In the notes on each individual work, readers will thus find grouped before them all the copy-text readings that have been emended in this critical text and any alterations in manuscripts or substantive variants in authorized printed texts. With these lists they can reconsider for themselves the textual decisions for the present edition and in the process see more clearly the relationship between either the manuscript or whatever printed text was available in Melville's lifetime and the text which is offered here as a more faithful representation of the author's intentions.

35. There are two lists of manuscript alterations for "Hawthorne and His Mosses," the second recording Melville's punctuation additions to Elizabeth Shaw Melville's initial inscription (except for those he made in the course of other revisions or which are impossible to list separately from her punctuation). See p. 686 below.

Notes on Individual Prose Pieces

IN THE NOTES that follow (explained in the GENERAL NOTE ON THE TEXT above, pp. 564–67), a number of abbreviations and symbols are used:

AM	Augusta Melville, sister of Herman Melville
CG	*Culturist and Gazette* (Pittsfield, Mass.)
DP	*Democratic Press* (Lansingburgh, N.Y.)
ED	Evert A. Duyckinck (editor of the New York *Literary World*)
EM	Elizabeth Shaw Melville, wife of Herman Melville
H	*Harper's New Monthly Magazine* (New York)
HM	Herman Melville
LW	*Literary World* (New York)
ME	*Massachusetts Eagle* (Pittsfield)
NN	Northwestern-Newberry Edition
P	*Putnam's Monthly Magazine* (New York)
PS	*Sun* (Pittsfield, Mass.)
PT	*The Piazza Tales* (1856)
WTA	*West Troy Advocate* (West Troy, N.Y.)
YD	*Yankee Doodle* (New York)

*	marks a reading for which a separate discussion is provided
~	stands for the word previously cited in the entry and signals that only a punctuation mark is changed
^	indicates the absence of a punctuation mark

[ ]	denotes the space where a letter or punctuation mark failed to print
†	calls attention to a word that is hyphenated at the end of the line in both the copy-text and the Northwestern-Newberry Edition
→ . . . →	revision enclosed between arrows was made immediately
[. . .]	revision enclosed in brackets was made after initial inscription of leaf
{ . . . }	revision enclosed in braces was made still later than revision enclosed in brackets
>	the word(s) following was inserted above, with caret
≯	the word(s) following was inserted above, without caret
add	the word(s) following was added, on same line
>>	the canceled word(s) following was restored (by underlining)
w.o.	the word(s) following was written over a previous word
<	the word(s) following was canceled (by lining out)
erase	the word(s) following was canceled (either by erasure or by wiping ink with finger)
xxxx	undeciphered letters (number of x's approximates number of letters involved)
?word	prefixed question mark indicates conjectural reading
/	end of line in manuscript or printed text

Full citations for works cited in the discussions by short titles or editors' or authors' names are given in the headnote above them or in the discussion of "Twentieth-Century Printings," pp. 541–44 above. *"Log"* refers to Jay Leyda, *The Melville Log* (New York: Harcourt, Brace, 1951; reprinted with supplement New York: Gordian Press, 1969), "Sealts" (followed by an entry number) to Merton M. Sealts, Jr., *Melville's Reading: A Check-List of Books Owned and Borrowed* (Madison: University of Wisconsin Press, 1966), and *"Letters"* to Merrell R. Davis and William H. Gilman, eds., *The Letters of Herman Melville* (New Haven: Yale University Press, 1960). References to dates, events, or documents that are not documented in these notes are based upon the printed sources listed on p. 531 of the Historical Note. All documents are quoted *literatim;* any variation between a document as transcribed in these sources and as printed in these notes is based on an examination of the original.

THE PIAZZA (pp. 1–12)

NN copy-text: the first printing, "The Piazza," in *The Piazza Tales* (New York: Dix & Edwards; London: Sampson Low, Son & Co., 1856), pp. 1–29 [PT]. No known manuscript, and no later printing in Melville's lifetime. NN emendations to PT (on principles stated on pp. 549–64): at five points. NN printer's copy: an emended photocopy of Northwestern University Library 813.3M531pi1856. Machine collations between copies of PT: M66–2471–60 *vs.* Gift M67–18, M66–2471–61, and Newberry Y255M515; M66–2471–61 *vs.* Newberry Y255M515.

Melville wrote "The Piazza" to come first in the collection of his *Putnam's Monthly Magazine* pieces which he had proposed to Dix & Edwards late in 1855. In that proposal he had volunteered to supply "some sort of prefatory matter, with a new title," but then he changed his mind and wrote to them on January 19, 1856, that the book would open with "Benito Cereno" and its title would be "Benito Cereno & Other Sketches." But Dix & Edwards seem to have suggested a different plan, for when Melville wrote again on February 16 he had composed "The Piazza" and re-christened his book *The Piazza Tales.* "I think, with you, that *'Bartleby'* had best come next," he conceded, with "Benito Cereno" third.

The reviewer (presumably J. E. A. Smith) in the *Berkshire County Eagle* of Pittsfield on May 30, 1856, noted, "The title is derived from the piazza on the north of the author's residence and the introduction will be especially interesting to Pittsfield readers for its description of familiar scenery." Several commentators have compared Melville's use of his Arrowhead residence and its environs in "The Piazza" to what Hawthorne had done in "The Old Manse," also written to stand first in a collection of already published pieces; Hyatt H. Waggoner, in "Hawthorne and Melville Acquaint the Reader with Their Abodes," *Studies in the Novel,* II (Winter, 1970), 420–24, proposes "The Old Manse" as the "inspiration" if not actual source of "The Piazza." As Egbert S. Oliver points out in his Hendricks House edition of *The Piazza Tales,* "The introduction of the girl Marianna whose life is weary with lonely waiting suggests Tennyson's two poems, 'Mariana' and 'Mariana in the South' " (p. 229). Both authors, Oliver adds, probably recalled Shakespeare's dejected "Mariana at the moated grange" in *Measure for Measure,* III.i. There are several other Shakespearean allusions, beginning with the epigraph from *Cymbeline* (see the discussion at 1.2–3) addressed to "Fidele" (the setting of *The Confidence-Man,* completed later in 1856, is a Mississippi steamboat named "Fidèle"). Melville reminds his reader also of *Hamlet,* I.v.59 (at 2.25),

Macbeth, V.i (at 4.35), and *A Midsummer Night's Dream* (at 5.32), makes numerous biblical and mythological references, and alludes to "old wars of Lucifer and Michael" in *Paradise Lost* (at 5.36), to Edmund Spenser and his *Faerie Queene* (6.20–21), and to Don Quixote (6.32)—he had bought a translation of *Don Quixote* in September of 1855 (Sealts 125).

For explanation of the following tabulations, see pp. 565–70.

DISCUSSIONS. 1.2–3 *"With . . . Fidele—"*] Accurately quoted from Melville's edition (Boston, 1837—Sealts 460) of *Cymbeline*, IV.ii.218–19.

4.3 fairy-land] NN follows the copy-text inconsistencies in hyphenation between "fairy-land" (at 4.3, 6.18[twice],19,21, 12.32) and "fairy land" or "Fairy land" (at 5.30, 7.27,32, 8.12,30). See p. 563.

6.3 farmers'] The singular possessive in PT is emended to the plural because "fathers" in the next line means they were children of more than one farmer. More obvious examples of such misplacement of the apostrophe are emended at 241.28, 243.7, 243.15, 247.21, and 362.13.

EMENDATIONS. 4.36 Adullam] NN; Adullum PT 5.32 Midsummer] NN; Midsummer's PT 5.32 Night's] NN; Night PT *6.3 farmers'] NN; farmer's PT 9.9 pleasant,"] NN; ~." PT

HYPHENATION. I. 2.9 picture-galleries 2.21 moss-padded 2.24 honey-suckle 3.2 red-barred 4.3 fairy-land 4.27 afternoon 4.32 far-off 4.39 northwestern 5.17 back-ground 6.18 fairy-land 7.14 namesake 7.19 flint-stone 8.3 low-storied 8.5 weather-stained 8.20 door-sill 11.13 mountain-window 12.6 hereabouts 12.28 cannot 12.33 box-royal

II. 1.4 old-fashioned 2.39 new-dropped 6.37 white-weed 7.13 Jacks-in-the-pulpit 8.16 farm-houses

BARTLEBY, THE SCRIVENER (pp. 13–45)

NN copy-text: the anonymous first printing, "Bartleby, the Scrivener. A Story of Wall-Street," in *Putnam's Monthly Magazine* [P], II, no. 11 (November, 1853), 546–57 [NN13.1–34.12], and no. 12 (December, 1853), 609–15 [NN34.13–45.37]. Emendations from *The Piazza Tales* (1856), pp. 31–107 [PT]: at ten points. NN emendations to P: at three points. (Principles for emendation are stated on pp. 549–64.) No known complete manuscript, and no later printing in Melville's lifetime. NN printer's copy: an emended photocopy of Newberry Library A5.765. Sight collations of P against PT: Northwestern 051P99 *vs.* M66–2471–58, M68–1922, and Northwestern 813.3M531pi (substantives only); Newberry A5.765 *vs.* M66–2471–59. Machine collations between copies of P: Newberry A5.765 *vs.* Northwestern 051P99, M72–3067, and M68–3078–9; M68–3078–9 *vs.* M68–3078–11. Machine collations between copies of PT: M66–2471–60 *vs.* Gift M67–18 and M66–2471–61; M66–2471–61 *vs.* Newberry Y255M515.

Melville probably wrote "Bartleby, the Scrivener" during the summer of 1853 (see p. 487 above). Only a single manuscript leaf, containing a brief passage in Augusta Melville's hand, is known to survive (see accompanying reproduction and transcription). After copying eleven lines for page 36 of an earlier version of what later became NN44.22–45.4, she discarded the leaf, perhaps because of the ink blot just before it breaks off; she later reused it, both recto and verso, to list addresses "For Cards". What part the marble headstone (finally replaced by the yard wall) played in this earlier version—whether Bartleby found and appropriated it in the prison yard or took it to prison with him (from the lawyer's office?) and then into his cell—must be conjectural. It may be suggestive that both "Cock-A-Doodle-Doo!" (written the same summer as "Bartleby") and "The Encantadas" (probably written that fall) end with a grave-monument that carries an epitaphic comment—in the latter written by a forecastle poet, like the ballad that ends *Billy Budd, Sailor.*

Melville submitted the completed story in September and received payment promptly upon publication, through his brother Allan, at the rate of $5.00 per printed page: $55 for the first installment of eleven pages on November 8, 1853, and $30 for the second, of six pages, on December 6. Evert and George Duyckinck's New York *Literary World* of December 3, observing that Putnam's "corps of contributors . . . have defeated the anonymous system of the magazine, by writing such clever articles that they have become perfectly well known," cited "Mr. Melville's 'Bartleby, the Scrivener' " as an example.

In 1856 the writer for the *Berkshire County Eagle* (presumably Melville's friend J. E. A. Smith) called the tale a "portrait from life," and the New York *Criterion* also said it was "based upon living characters," but neither paper named its supposed originals. Several twentieth-century commentators have named Melville himself as in part Bartleby's prototype, drawing parallels between his situation as a writer after the failure of *Pierre* in 1852 and Bartleby's plight: see Alexander Eliot, "Melville and Bartleby," *Furioso,* III (Fall, 1947), 11–21; Leo Marx, "Melville's Parable of the

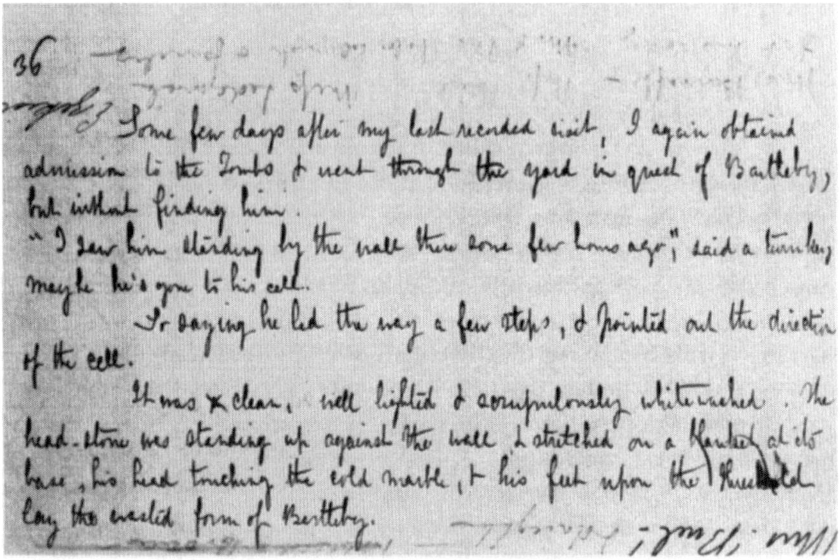

Surviving leaf 36 (reduced portion) of Augusta Melville's copy of an early version of "Bartleby, the Scrivener."

36

Some few days after my last recorded visit, I again obtained / admission to the Tombs, & went through the yard in quest of Bartleby, / but without finding him.

"I saw him standing by the wall there some few hours ago," said a turnkey / maybe he's gone to his cell.

So saying he led the way a few steps, & pointed out the direction / of the cell.

It was [a *canceled*] clean, well lighted & scrupulously whitewashed. The / head-stone was standing up against the wall, & stretched on a blanket at its / base, his head touching the cold marble, & his feet upon the threshold / lay the wasted form of Bartleby. [threshold *mended, blotted, then overscored with three long vertical strokes*]

Walls," *Sewanee Review*, LXI (Autumn, 1953), 602–27; and Henry A. Murray, "Bartleby and I," in *Bartleby the Scrivener: A Symposium*, ed. Howard P. Vincent (Kent, Ohio: Kent State University Press, 1966; Melville Annual 1965), pp. 3–24. Murray in the character of "biographer" specifies "three rough correspondences between Bartleby and the Melville of 1853: both at first prefer to copy [with Melville 'composing . . . pretty much as a copyist . . . of Hawthorne'], both prefer not to correct copy [in Melville's case, to correct *proof*], and both have lawyers trying to move them from their preferred location [with Allan Melville coordinating efforts to get Melville '*out* of the room in which he wrote at Arrowhead']. Furthermore, both prefer solitude, both are suspected of being mentally unbalanced, and both are inclined toward suicide." But Jay Leyda proposes as Bartleby's model Eli James Fly (1817–54), Melville's friend since their youth in Albany. After accompanying Melville to Illinois in 1840, Fly took "a situation with a Mr Edwards" in New York City, "where he has incessant writing from morning to Eve^{g}" (*Log*, I, 110). Later Fly had become "a confirmed invalid"; so Melville noted in a letter of March 26, 1851, to Evert A. Duyckinck, and, he added, "in some small things I act a little as his agent."

The original of Bartleby's employer has been sought among Melville's lawyer relatives: his uncle Peter Gansevoort in Albany, his father-in-law, Lemuel Shaw, in Boston, and his brothers Gansevoort and Allan, in New York, Allan's office being located at 10 Wall Street. Herbert F. Smith, in "Melville's Master in Chancery and His Recalcitrant Clerk," *American Quarterly*, XVII (Winter, 1965), 734–41, argues that the narrator's profession and office as Master in Chancery, involving an old distinction in Anglo-Saxon jurisprudence between chancery (or equity) and common law, are important to a full understanding of the story. Whether or not Melville intended to portray some individual attorney, he was obviously familiar with such legal distinctions and with the operations of a Wall Street law office.

Leon Howard, in *Herman Melville: A Biography* (Berkeley and Los Angeles: University of California Press, 1951), p. 208, noting that Bartleby's story "was supposedly based upon a certain amount of fact," speculates that "the fact may have been either some anecdote concerning a lawyer's clerk or the unfortunate condition of Melville's friend [George J.] Adler, who had developed such a severe case of agoraphobia that he was to be confined in the Bloomingdale Asylum. . . . Or it may have been simply the murder of Samuel Adams by John C. Colt, . . . to which allusion was made in the story" (36.6ff.)—a possibility explored at more length by T. H. Giddings in "Melville, the Colt-Adams Murder, and 'Bartleby,' " *Studies in American Fiction,* II (Autumn, 1974), 123–32. The "anecdote concerning a lawyer's clerk" that Howard postulates was perhaps the first chapter of James A. Maitland's *The Lawyer's Story,* which was printed as an advertisement for that forthcoming novel in both the New York *Tribune* and the New York *Times* for February 18, 1853; Johannes Dietrich Bergmann, in " 'Bartleby' and *The Lawyer's Story," American Literature,* XLVII (November, 1975), 432–36, shows that this single newspaper item may have suggested to Melville "a narrative structure he could use for 'Bartleby.' " The novel's opening sentence indicates its pertinence: "In the summer of 1843, having an extraordinary quantity of deeds to copy, I engaged, temporarily, an extra copying clerk, who interested me considerably, in consequence of his modest, quiet, gentlemanly demeanor, and his intense application to his duties." And as Bergmann, George Monteiro, and Hershel Parker have shown, the "rumor" that Bartleby had lost his place as "a subordinate clerk in the Dead Letter Office at Washington" (45.24) was probably taken by Melville from one or another of the recent sentimental accounts of the Dead Letter Office in various American newspapers; see Monteiro, "Melville, 'Timothy Quicksand,' and the Dead-Letter Office," *Studies in Short Fiction,* IX (Spring, 1972), 198–201; Parker, "Dead Letters and Melville's Bartleby," *Resources for American Literary Study,* IV (Spring, 1974), 90–99; and Parker, "The 'Sequel' in 'Bartleby'," in *Bartleby the Inscrutable: A Collection of Commentary,* ed. M. Thomas Inge (Hamden, Conn.: Archon Books, 1979), pp. 159–65.

The *Literary World* (cited above) called "Bartleby" "a Poeish tale," and other readers have compared it with writings of Charles Dickens, Charles Lamb, and Washington Irving. The most Dickensian touches are in the characterizations of Turkey, Nippers, and Ginger Nut. Bartleby himself, writes Joel O. Conarroe in "Melville's Bartleby and Charles Lamb," *Studies in Short Fiction,* V (Winter, 1968), 113–18, is a "superannuated son of Elia" who "would be a very different character, or possibly would not exist at all," had Melville not known Lamb's work. John Seelye, in "The Contemporary 'Bartleby,' " *American Transcendental Quarterly,* VII (Summer, 1970), 12–18, sees the story as a variation on Irving's "The Little Man in Black," which initiated a tradition of American stories about a mysterious stranger that Melville would return to in *The Confidence-Man* (1856). Recalling Egbert S. Oliver's "A Second Look at 'Bartleby,' " *Col-*

lege English, VI (May, 1945), 431–39, which traced "the germ of the character" to Thoreau's withdrawal from society, Seelye argues that Melville was satirizing Irving and the Whigs in the complacent attorney, and the New England Transcendentalists, as sketched in Emerson's essay "The Transcendentalist," in Bartleby himself. Support for Seelye's latter suggestion is offered by Christopher W. Sten in "Bartleby the Transcendentalist: Melville's Dead Letter to Emerson," *Modern Language Quarterly,* XXXV (March, 1974), 30–44.

A facsimile of the P text and an extensive checklist of criticism, with excerpts, by Donald M. Fiene, appears in the "Bartleby" symposium cited above, pp. 140-90. A later, newly annotated checklist, by Bruce Bebb with a supplement by Elizabeth Williamson, is included in the *Bartleby the Inscrutable* collection cited above, pp. 199-234. The results of a computer collation of the P and PT texts are presented in Appendix B of George R. Petty, Jr., and William M. Gibson, *Project Occult: The Ordered Computer Collation of Unprepared Literary Text* (New York: New York University Press, 1970), with some comment in Chapter 5 (pp. 41–50).

For explanation of the following tabulations, see pp. 565–70.

DISCUSSIONS. 13.1–2 *Bartleby . . . Wall-Street*] NN keeps this P title (converting it, of course, to italics) rather than adopting the shortened form "Bartleby" from PT, because the original form seems certainly Melville's, whereas one cannot be sure, given the nature of the variants as a whole, that the shortened form was his own, though he at least presumably saw it in the PT proofs. The sample title and contents page (listing "Bartleby") which Melville enclosed in his February 16, 1856 letter to Dix & Edwards is too casual to offer any proof of Melville's preference. This variant falls into the same class as several other doubtful omissions in PT of prominent elements of some significance for interpretation; none of these omissions is accepted in NN as unquestionably Melville's (see p. 553).

14.6 addresses . . . draws] NN does not emend these verbs to the plural because Melville took the singular emphasis of the sentence as governing them. Cf. the discussion at 360.39.

19.2–3 Of . . . was] Possibly the elliptical construction in P and PT was idiomatic; but possibly words were lost (e.g., "the worst" before "was").

26.17 unreasonableness.] Perhaps Melville overlooked supplying a question mark here in his fair-copy manuscript, but sentences interrogative in form yet declarative in tone, like this one, sometimes end with a period in Melville's and other nineteenth-century works. See p. 563 and examples at 32.4, 38.24, 89.7, 210.34, 240.8, and 249.1.

31.12 measures] NN accepts as Melville's the change in PT from the P reading "means" (which may have been a misreading of his original "measures"); the change seems deliberate (not a compositor's slip) but not of the sort an editor would have introduced, since "means" makes sense enough.

31.30 folding-doors] Since the plural form is used throughout the tale and since Melville's terminal "-s" is often indistinctly formed, NN assumes that the singular "folding-door" at this point in P and PT is an error.

32.4 yourself,] NN keeps the comma in P, although the form of Bartleby's sentence seems to call for a question mark. Possibly Melville overlooked supplying it in his fair-copy manuscript, and the one supplied by PT may have been his correction. Yet Melville may not have intended Bartleby's intonation to be interrogative in his "indifferent" but significant response (ironically, the lawyer does *not* see the reason—i.e., the wall), in which case omission of the question mark would mean that Bartleby does not seek an answer from the lawyer. Cf. the discussions at 26.17, 38.24, and 89.7.

34.13 arguing] This word in P and PT is conceivably a misreading for "auguring". One could say that the narrator is not "arguing"—that is, reasoning—about the probabilities *pro* and *con* but simply experiencing "veering" expectations (whereas at 35.22ff. he does "argue the matter" again with Bartleby). Cf. *Moby-Dick* (chap. 91; NN405.24), where "argued" in "Stubb argued well for his scheme" is emended in NN to "augured". The present case, however, seems too uncertain to justify emendation.

35.6 ascendency] The apparent error in the "-ency" spelling here, with "-ancy" in the same word earlier in the sentence, results from the NN policy of keeping variant spellings, acceptable at the time, that occur in the copy-text. See pp. 561–62.

36.21–22 "A . . . another."] Quoted exactly from John 13:34 in the King James Version, except for the inversion "give I" for "I give" and "that" for "That"; NN does not emend inexact quotations where, as here, Melville was evidently not aiming for accuracy. See pp. 557–58.

36.31 drown] Quite possibly Melville wrote "down", resuming the wrestling metaphor in the first sentence of the paragraph; NN keeps the P and PT reading because it makes sense and is idiomatic, even though it does not fit the passage as integrally as "down" and may be a misreading.

37.8 "Edwards . . . Necessity."] NN retains the P and PT forms, which include the authors' names within quotation marks, along with inexact short titles (for Jonathan Edwards, *A Careful and Strict Enquiry into the Modern Prevailing Notions, of . . . Freedom of Will* [Boston, 1754], and Joseph Priestley, *The Doctrine of Philosophical Necessity Illustrated* [London, 1777]). Melville was using a common citation formula of the time.

37.16 last] NN follows the change in PT from the P reading "least". The correction in PT was probably Melville's own, since "least" makes enough sense not to attract an editor's attention; but "last", once it is pointed out, seems clearly the intended word.

38.6 keep occupying] NN keeps the grammatically anomalous P and PT reading "keep" (and "outlive . . . claim" at 38.10–11) as Melville's own somewhat askew wording and not a simple grammatical slip emendable without rephrasing.

38.24 ghost?] NN emends as a slip the period in P and PT, since the clause is interrogative in form and moreover stands third in a series of parallel questions all punctuated with question marks. Cf. the discussions at 26.17, 32.4, 89.7, 265.35, and 267.5.

44.4–5 May . . . room?"] The excision in PT of the sentence inviting Bartleby to dinner "in Mrs. Cutlets' private room" (however related to other revisions in the passage, such as the removal of the name "Mr. Cutlets") may have been motivated by concern, on an editor's or even Melville's own part, about the innuendo that sexual services as well as food were available, as common in prisons. (For Melville's linking of a crude comic figure to sexual laxity in prisons, see the turnkey's remark while ushering Lucy and Isabel into Pierre's cell, "Thy wife and cousin—so they say;—hope they may be . . . " *Pierre,* bk. 26; NN360.24.) The revision is thus one of the instances of toning down that occur in PT and are rejected by NN, as explained on p. 554. In this case the likelihood that the revision was Melville's own is weakened by the awkwardness of the excision of the "Cutlets" name just above. When "Mr. Cutlets" was replaced by "a friend" at 43.39, the reviser failed to see that in the previous line the lawyer had asked the grub-man his name. Melville would have been less likely not to notice the absurdity of having the lawyer introduce the grub-man as "a friend" just after asking his name. (A similar awkwardness, however, was already present in the P text a few lines earlier: the parenthetical clause at 43.31, "for so they called him", referring to the grub-man, seems unnecessary because the grub-man had just said, at 43.26, "I am the grub-man".)

45.9 "With . . . counsellors,"] The phrase from Job 3:14 is quoted exactly from the King James Version (including the double "l" in "counsellors", which was changed to a single "l" in PT).

45.26 hardly can I] NN accepts as Melville's the change in PT from the P reading "I cannot adequately"; neither an editor's revision nor a compositor's memorial substitution seems at all likely to account for it.

EMENDATIONS. 13.21 *employés*] PT; *employées* P 15.8 sixty.] PT; ~[] P 24.14 exclaimed:] PT; exclaimed in an excited manner— P
24.15 "Bartleby a second time says,] PT; "He says, a second time, P
25.33 out] PT; one P *31.12 measures] PT; means P
*31.30 folding-doors] NN; folding-door P, PT 34.16 find] PT; see P
*37.16 last] PT; least P *38.24 ghost?] NN; ~. P, PT
43.35 seemed] NN; seem P, PT 44.2 nice] PT; —spacious P
*45.26 hardly can I] PT; I cannot adequately P

HYPHENATION. I. 13.12 law-copyists 14.8 title-deeds 16.10 tea-time 16.10 †afternoon 16.21 afternoon 16.26 afternoon 19.26 side-window 21.31 extraordinary 22.5 flute-like 22.27 ill-tempered 23.22 Ginger-nuts 25.38 point-blank 27.1 law-chambers 34.25 Broadway 37.4 dead-wall 37.12 all-wise 37.19 office-room 38.30 paper-weight 39.13 withdrawn 41.6 dry-goods 41.14 eyesight

II. 15.29 sand-box 21.5 plaster-of-paris 25.22 self-possessed 25.25 dinner-hour 28.4 not-unpleasing 42.1 Wall-street 44.14 genteel-like

SUBSTANTIVE VARIANTS. 13.1–2 *the . . . Wall-Street*] P; *[not present]* PT 13.21 *employés*] PT; *employées* P 15.36 easy] P; easily PT 18.26 boy, and] P; boy, PT 21.19 in hand] P; in his hand PT 22.21 with] P; in PT 24.14 exclaimed:] PT; exclaimed in an excited manner— P 24.15 "Bartleby . . . says] PT; "He says, a second time P 25.1 round] P; around PT 25.33 out] PT; one P 31.12 measures] PT; means P 31.25 *that's*] P; *that'*[ ] PT 34.16 find] PT; see P 37.16 last] PT; least P 37.36 was] P; *[not present]* PT 43.39 Mr. Cutlets] P; a friend PT 44.2 nice] PT; spacious P 44.3 sir] P; *[not present]* PT 44.4–5 May . . . room?] P; What will you have for dinner to-day? PT 44.17 pityingly] P; piteously PT 45.21 strange] P; *[not present]* PT 45.26 hardly can I] PT; I cannot adequately P

BENITO CERENO (pp. 46–117)

NN copy-text: the anonymous first printing, "Benito Cereno," in *Putnam's Monthly Magazine* [P], VI, no. 34 (October, 1855), 353–67 [NN46.1–70.7]; no. 35 (November, 1855), 459–73 [NN70.8–95.18]; and no. 36 (December, 1855), 633–44 [NN95.19–117.5]. Emendations from *The Piazza Tales* (1856), pp. 109–270 [PT]: at 121 points. NN emendations to P: at 26 points. (Principles for emendation are stated on pp. 549–64.) No known manuscript, and no later printing in Melville's lifetime. NN printer's copy: an emended photocopy of Newberry Library A5.765. Sight collations of P against PT: Northwestern 051P99 *vs.* M66–2471–59 and Northwestern 813.3M531pi (substantives only); Newberry A5.765 *vs.* M78–41457–20. Machine collations between copies of P: Newberry A5.765- *vs.* Northwestern 051P99 and M69–316–19; M69–316–19 *vs.* University of Chicago AP2P95. Machine collations between copies of PT: M66–2471–60 *vs.* Gift M67–18 and M66–2471–61; M66–2472–61 *vs.* Newberry Y255M515.

"Benito Cereno" was probably composed during the winter of 1854–55; the first reference we have to it is an April 17 letter to Joshua A. Dix (of Dix & Edwards, publishers of *Putnam's*) from George William Curtis, his editorial adviser: "I am anxious to see Melville's story, which is in his best style of subject." The "story" was evidently "Benito Cereno," which Dix then forwarded to Curtis after first showing it to another associate, Frederick Law Olmsted. On April 19 Curtis reported that "Melville's story is very good. It is a great pity he did not work it up as a connected tale instead of putting in the dreary documents at the end.—They should have made part of the substance of the story. It is a little spun out,—but it is very striking & well done: and I agree with Mr Law [i.e., Olmsted] that it ought not to be lost." The next day, on returning the manuscript to Dix, Curtis added that Melville "does everything too hurriedly now."

Curtis's next reference, in a letter to Dix of July 31, 1855, proposed beginning its serialization: "Why . . . don't you take up *Benito Cereno* of Melville. You have paid for it." Curtis still had reservations, however, about "all the dreadful statistics at the end. Oh! dear, why can't Americans write good stories. They tell good lies enough, & plenty of'em." Dix had decided by September to begin the story in the October number; on September 14, after mentioning it once more as "ghastly & interesting," Curtis asked him about how much space it would require. Near the end of 1855, probably after the final installment had appeared in the December number, Melville proposed reprinting "Benito Cereno" in a collection of his *Putnam's* pieces (G. P. Putnam had similarly reprinted *Israel Potter* in book form the previous March immediately after the final magazine installment).

When Melville prepared corrected magazine pages of the pieces as printer's copy for the new volume, then tentatively titled "Benito Cereno & Other Sketches," he appended "a M.S. note" to the title of "Benito Cereno"; but later, on February 16, 1856, he advised Dix & Edwards that "as the book is now to be published as a collection of '*Tales,*' that note is unsuitable & had better be omitted." Since the omitted note (not known to survive) was drafted to accompany "Benito Cereno" as a "sketch" but not as a "tale," a fair inference is that it touched somehow on the relation between the actual Captain Amasa Delano's own real-life account in his *Narrative* (see below) and Melville's reworking of it in his "sketch," a kind of relationship to factuality he thought better left unrevealed in a "tale."

Chapter 18 of Delano's *A Narrative of Voyages and Travels in the Northern and Southern Hemispheres* (Boston, 1817), pp. 318–53, is reproduced in this volume as a RELATED DOCUMENT, pp. 809–47, with marginal NN page and line numbers to indicate corresponding passages. This source was first identified and reprinted by Harold H. Scudder, as cited in the HISTORICAL NOTE, p. 511, n. 37. Chapter 18 is also reprinted by Seymour L. Gross in *A BENITO CERENO Handbook* (Belmont, Calif.: Wadsworth, 1965), pp. 71–98, and by John P. Runden in *Melville's BENITO CERENO: A Text for Guided Research* (Boston: D. C. Heath, 1965), pp. 76–104. Melville probably owned a copy of Delano's *Narrative,* though it has not been located; in "The Encantadas" (1854) he had already drawn on Chapter 20, and he must have written "Benito Cereno" with Chapter 18 constantly open before him.

No other important source has been established. Although H. Bruce Franklin argued at length that William Stirling's *Cloister Life of the Emperor Charles the Fifth* (London, 1853) was "a source of more ultimate significance" than Delano's *Narrative,* Hershel Parker concluded that no cautious scholar can be convinced that Melville knew and used Stirling's book or can believe in an interpretation of "Benito Cereno" built on the similarities between Melville's work and Stirling's. (Franklin, " 'Apparent Symbol of Despotic Command': Melville's *Benito Cereno,*" *New England Quarterly,* XXXIV [December, 1961], 462–77; Parker, " 'Benito Cereno' and *Cloister-Life:* A Re-Scrutiny of a 'Source,' " *Studies in Short Fiction,* IX [Summer, 1972], 221–32, with citations of extensions and reprintings of Franklin's argument.) Joshua Leslie and Sterling Stuckey, in "The Death of Benito Cereno: A Reading of Herman Melville on Slavery," *Journal of Negro History,* LXVII (Winter, 1982), 287–301, speculate on Melville's indebtedness to Mungo Park's *Travels in the Interior Districts of Africa* (1799) and on Melville's knowledge of African customs. In two further articles they offer background about the actual historical event, based on original Spanish documents concerning the trial of the Negroes and its aftermath: "Avoiding the Tragedy of Benito Cereno: The Official Response to Babo's Revolt," *Criminal Justice History,* III (Fall, 1982), 125–32; "Aftermath: Captain Delano's Claim against Benito Cereno," forthcoming in *Modern Philology.*

For explanation of the following tabulations, see pp. 565–70.

DISCUSSIONS. 46.1 *Benito Cereno*] In his own account Delano spells the first name "Bonito" repeatedly (pp. 324ff.) and spells the second "Sereno" the only time it occurs (p. 329), whereas his "officially translated" Documents (pp. 332ff.) consistently use "Benito Cereno".

46.4 St. Maria] NN here (and at 86.36–37 and 103.13) keeps the anomalous combination (in both P and PT) of the English abbreviation "St." with the Spanish form "Maria"; Melville found it in Delano's own account (pp. 318ff.)—though "Santa Maria" occurs repeatedly in Delano's Documents (pp. 333ff.). Melville, inconsistently, followed the latter form at 106.4,10 and 108.39. Imprecise or inconsistent foreign-language usage of this kind is characteristic of Melville's works and his times; cf. p. 562 and the discussions at 49.16, 105.26, 107.32, and 114.7.

46.14 mould] Here and at 174.8 and 175.36 in "The Bell-Tower" NN emends the P reading "mold" to "mould" (as did PT) because it is not Melville's regular spelling (as seen in his letters and journals) and because it was being imposed on P by Frederick Law Olmsted. See p. 561, n. 28 and the discussion of "hight" at 50.13.

49.16 SAN DOMINICK] Since this ship's name (in Delano's account "the Spanish ship Tryal", p. 318 and *passim)* was Melville's literary invention, NN retains as unemendable his archaic anglicized spelling "Dominick" in P and PT, even though the context and quotation marks would properly call for the correct Spanish "Santo Domingo". (Cf. the correct "Bouton de Rose" in a similar context in *Moby-Dick,* chap. 91, NN404.1.) On inconsistent foreign-language forms, see the discussion at 46.4 and the references listed there.

49.37 the] The PT omission of this word seems more likely to be another example of the carelessness of the PT compositors than Melville's effort to suggest a parallelism between "all eager tongues" and "all faces". Note that PT also omitted "the" before "hardships" at 52.4.

50.13 heightened] Here, at 57.18, 82.29, 85.7, and in related words at 51.33 and 95.6 in "Benito Cereno" and 176.37 in "The Bell-Tower," NN emends the P reading "hightened" to the "ei" form (as did PT) because it is not Melville's regular spelling and because it was being imposed on P by Frederick Law Olmsted. See p. 561, n. 28, and the discussion at 46.14.

51.19 baskets] The earlier statement that Delano "put several baskets of the fish, for presents, into his boat" (47.39) exposes the PT reading "basket" here as one of the irksome substantive compositorial errors PT introduced along with Melville's own changes—in this case, fortunately, one that betrays itself as not his.

53.31 here] The substitution in PT of "here" for "in Don Benito" (the P reading) is the first of a series of revisions in PT that eliminate proper names (often Spanish) as well as the word "Spanish." The reason for these changes is not clear, but since they do not appear to fall into any of the classes of alterations that the publisher was concerned to make, they are accepted in NN as probably Melville's own. For other examples, see the emendations at 59.14, 63.34, 65.9,10, 70.34, 79.31, 80.11,17–18,24, 98.25, 99.18, 114.32,38, 116.7,12. (Note, however, that one or two changes move in the opposite direction, as at 98.17 where "Don Benito" is substituted for "the Spaniard".)

55.15 hardware] See the discussion at 104.7.

56.26 Baldivia] NN keeps this P and PT reading for the Spanish "Valdivia" (in Delano, p. 348) as an instance of the then-common English "b" rendering of Spanish "v". (No misreading of Melville's hand or any "error" is involved, though both Leyda, *Complete Stories,* p. 269, and Gross, *Handbook,* p. 11, emend apparently on that assumption.)

57.23 utility than ornament] Possibly Melville meant the opposite of what this phrase in P and PT says, as Hershel Parker's emendation to "ornament than utility" assumes from the context (*Shorter Works of Hawthorne and Melville,* p. 315). See 116.23–25 and the discussion at 107.37.

59.25 Bachelor's Delight] Melville made this unemendable literary change from the name of Delano's actual ship, "Perseverance" (*Narrative,* p. 318 and *passim);* he also changed the spelling of "Batchelors Delight", the name he borrowed from the ship navigated by William Cowley, whom he quotes in "The Encantadas" (142.7ff.).

63.12–13 first time] NN keeps the P reading, although the PT reading (omitting "time") is an idiom common in Melville's writings. Many of the substantive variants in PT involve such indifferent shortenings, but when they could easily have been produced by compositorial oversight they are not adopted by NN.

65.38 you] The omission in PT of "on board" following "you" is accepted as producing what Melville meant here: the question of how many men are on board comes three lines later.

69.4 been . . . by] NN adds the words "been" and "by" to change to the passive voice the phrase which in P and PT reads "Don Benito's story had corroborated . . . the wailing ejaculations"; the word "by" at 69.6 below confirms that the passive voice was intended.

70.15–16 flew . . . curses] NN keeps the P curses that were softened in PT here to "violently pushed him aside" and keeps P's more violent assault, "and jumped upon him" (70.17), that PT deleted. Whereas the P wording is certainly Melville's, the PT readings may or may not be his. Note the inconsistency caused by the deletion in PT when at 78.36 Delano recalls "the trampling of the sailor by the two negroes", and when the deposition mentions the incident of the Negroes who had "thrown [Bartholomew Barlo] down and jumped upon him" (114.10).

72.6 combined] The omission in PT of the P reading "to be" before "combined", along with the inversion at 72.8 and the omission at 72.9, might be regarded as further instances of oversights in PT were it not for the substantial revision, clearly Melville's, in this passage at 72.7–8. NN accepts the three small revisions from PT as well as the long one, since it is more likely that they result from Melville's attention to this passage than that they are compositorial errors.

73.30 Mungo Park] This P reading is changed in PT to "Ledyard", but neither name quite fits the sentence, since the famous African traveler Park (1771–1806) did not write the "noble account" while John Ledyard (1751–89) did write it but about women of Asia not of Africa, where he had not traveled beyond the coast. The explanation of this crux seems to be that when Melville first wrote the sentence he had in mind the passage in Park's *Travels in the Interior Districts of Africa* (1799)—perhaps in a reprint or excerpt—about his kind treatment by African women that quotes Ledyard's parallel "noble account"—an account which Melville mistook or misremembered as Park's own. Then, as Seymour Gross has suggested, when Ledyard's account was quoted in a *Putnam's* essay (December, 1855 [VI, 608]), either Melville or a *Putnam's* editor noticed the discrepancy and "corrected" to "Ledyard", overlooking the fact that Ledyard was speaking of Asian women. In *Moby-Dick* (chap. 5), Melville identifies the two travelers correctly. NN keeps the P reading "Mungo Park" because it is more certainly Melville's and because the factual error is unemendable—neither name is right. See Gross, *Handbook,* p. 27n., and his "Mungo Park and Ledyard in Melville's *Benito Cereno," English Language Notes,* III (December, 1965), 122–23.

76.32 old] The PT reading "odd" is apparently a compositorial misreading plausible enough to look like a possible authorial revision of the P reading "old". The expression "old tricks", however, is so well established (as the *OED* makes clear), and the parallelism with "old knotter" in the previous line is so effective, that the chances of "odd" being an intentional revision are small.

77.5 efficacy] This substitution in PT for the P reading "efficiency" seems more likely an authorial correction than a compositorial error: the two words are clearly differentiated in contemporary dictionaries, and the PT reading is more precise in this context.

78.13 minutes'] Earlier in this sentence the phrase "ten minutes' sailing" has the apostrophe in both P and PT. The later parallel phrase in P, "sixty minutes drifting", does not contain an apostrophe, and the comma after "minutes" in PT is evidently the result of an attempt to insert an apostrophe: the compositor either misread an apostrophe Melville (or an editor) had called for, or he picked up a comma by mistake, or an apostrophe slipped out of place after typesetting. (The situation at 25.2 is different, because nothing there indicates that an apostrophe was intended.)

88.30 on] The P reading "in" is evidently a misreading of Melville's "on", and PT makes the necessary correction: the "in" conflicts with the sense of the sentence (beginning "On their way") and of the larger context (for they do not enter the cabin until 89.24).

89.7 too!] NN emends the P and PT question mark as someone's slip in punctuation; clearly, what Delano utters is an exclamation, not a question. (Similar confusion of the two marks occurs elsewhere in pieces in the present volume, as at 282.36. Cf. 26.17, 32.4, and 38.24.)

89.13 a sort of] Since this P and PT reading is an idiom not uncommon in

Melville's writings and times, no emendation is needed, though Gross comments on it as an unemendable "misconstruction" while pointing out that Weaver (1928) substituted "rather" and Chase (1950) "somewhat" (*Handbook,* p. 41n.). For examples, see 304.3, 353.30, 366.25, 367.7, and *Moby-Dick:* "said he, looking a sort of diabolically funny" (chap. 3; NN15.6).

92.39 straight forward] NN follows this change in PT from the P reading "straightforward"; the intended sense is so obviously PT's "look directly ahead", not P's "assume a moral stance of directness" (as in "The Encantadas," 132.29) that an attentive editor (or even a compositor), not Melville himself, may have made the necessary change.

96.29 her] NN keeps this word, which PT omitted, because here (unlike the situation at 96.38) there is no clear stylistic reason for Melville to have made the alteration and because it could easily have been a compositorial slip (especially since "at anchor" is idiomatic).

96.38 as] The PT reading, accepted here, leaves out the "his" present in P between "as" and "charmed"; this revision is evidently one of a pair, the other one being the deletion of "the" before "clenched" in the next line. The two changes together are more likely Melville's stylistic revision than either an editor's alteration or a compositor's double oversight.

98.6–7 bowsman] The change from the singular "bowsman" in P to the plural "bowsmen" in PT—a flat error in view of the reference below to a single bowsman (99.6–7)—is only one of the small substantive changes in PT that Melville cannot have intended but that somehow got made by an editor or compositor. See pp. 551–52.

100.15 gun's] NN emends the P reading "guns' " to the singular "gun's" in PT as a necessary correction whether made by Melville himself or by an editor or compositor attentive enough to recall from just above (100.11–12) that but one gun has been fired: "only the aftermost one could be brought to bear" (the passage closely follows Delano's *Narrative,* pp. 319, 325).

101.2 pirate] NN keeps the P reading although the PT revision (eliminating the seven words after "privateer's-man") has to be Melville's own retrenchment (no such hint of piracy occurs in Delano, needless to say). Probably Melville had belated scruples about blackening the actual mate's reputation; though not named in "Benito Cereno," Rufus Low (*Narrative,* pp. 319, 326) was a man easily identifiable within Melville's own Massachusetts orbit, unlike the South American whites and African Negroes he had made as libelously free with. Given this "softening" motive, NN sticks with Melville's original strong sally, on the policy explained on p. 554 (cf. the discussion at 70.15–16). See Melville's similar fictional use in "I and My Chimney" of a rumor that Captain Julian Dacres had been "a Borneo pirate" (370.10)—though in this case, presumably, no actual person is referred to.

103.28 Bishopric] NN follows the P and PT reading. However, given Melville's famous pun on "archbishoprick" in *Moby-Dick* (chap. 95; NN420.15), and the archaic spelling "San Dominick" at 49.16, Bernard Mosher has questioned the NN editors whether it was by Melville that the archaic spelling "Bishoprick" in Delano's Documents (p. 332) was razeed of its "k" in P and PT—and, if so, in what humor; or whether that letter was not more likely excised by the same corrective operation that wittingly or unwittingly has removed the point of Melville's joke in so many later editions of *Moby-Dick*. The point raised is ponderable but emendation seems too cocksure. (See also the discussion at 273.11–12, concerning the joke about Uncle Toby and the Widow Wadman.)

103.31 negroes] NN emends the P reading "Senegal negroes" from PT, where the omission of the limiting word "Senegal" (present at this point in Delano's Documents, p. 332) must have been Melville's own correction to fit his fictional "facts." Only he, as author, was likely to catch the reason for leaving that word out: whereas Delano's Documents here and elsewhere name only Senegals, Melville in P had transformed six of the Senegals into Ashantees as Babo's "bravoes"—five with their Document names—and had cast two of these "Ashantees" in the role of Don Alexandro Aranda's murderers and mutilators who had converted his skeleton into the ship's figurehead. So it would not do for his fictional version of the deposition to start off announcing "criminal cause" just against "Senegal negroes"; Melville saw the problem he had earlier overlooked, and he could solve it either by inserting "and Ashantee" or by deleting "Senegal". He chose the latter.

104.1 received] NN follows PT here in eliminating the P phrase "before Don José de Abos and Padilla, Notary Public of the Holy Crusade". That Melville himself removed it to avoid repetition seems more likely than that a compositor skipped it (especially as Melville gave close attention to this passage—see the preceding and following discussions).

104.7 beside . . . hardware] NN adopts this phrase from PT here and the addition of "hardware" at 55.15 as Melville's changes to account for the cases of hatchets (not in Delano's Documents, p. 333), which from a single reference elsewhere in the *Narrative* to a hatchet-weapon (p. 340) were magically multiplied in Melville's imagination for a major dramatic motif (50.27 and *passim*). Along with the excision of "Senegal" just above and the three respellings of "Francisco" as "Francesco" below, this slight addition shows that in his "corrections" of P for the PT printer's copy Melville had a close eye on his story and saw some details that were askew.

104.9 Mendoza] NN keeps the P and PT "z" spelling here (and at 107.12), although in Delano's Documents this place name is spelled with the variant "s" then common in English spellings of such Spanish proper nouns. Whether Melville intended "s" or "z" here—or in such words elsewhere—is uncertain because his written "s" and "z" are often difficult or impossible to distinguish.

104.18 Francesco] Here and at two other points where the mulatto steward's name occurs in the fictional deposition (111.25, 111.30) PT changes its spelling to

"Francesco" from the "Francisco" of P and Delano's Documents (pp. 334, 340, 341). NN emends in the three instances because it must have been Melville himself who made these careful changes, to remove the inconsistency in P of thrice spelling the name with "i" in the fictional deposition after four times spelling it with "e" in the foregoing story (89.13,28,30 and 91.23); more general consistency was not the purpose, since the name "Francisco" for a different man (107.12,17 and 111.35) was left unchanged. (An alternative NN emendation would change the P "Francesco" at the earlier points to "Francisco", to respect the Spanish "i" form found consistently in Delano's Documents; but Melville's intentional use of "Francesco" seems to be established by its repeated use in the narrative and the revision to that form in the deposition in PT. Melville often disregarded linguistic purism—and may even have thought it appropriate that "Francesco" as the name of a mulatto was only quasi-Spanish: see 88.23–89.23.)

104.21 Dago] This name in P and PT, for the "Joaquin" of Delano's Documents (p. 334), in which "Dago" nowhere appears, seems not to be a slip but a change Melville made. Why is hard to see, unless to avoid confusion with the name of Don Joaquin Arambaolaza, a character he was romantically ennobling. Also he built up "the Ashantee Lecbe" by switching to him the Documents' characterization (p. 340) of "the negro Joaquin", as "one of the worst of them" because he had defended the ship "with a hatchet in one hand and a dagger in the other"—the graphic detail that inspired all of Melville's dramatic hatchet business and his fictional episode of Don Joaquin's being forced to seem to defend the ship "with a hatchet tied edge out and upright to his hand" (113.20ff.).

104.24 Mure] NN emends the P and PT reading "Muri" (the only occurrence of this man's name in Melville's story, where his actual central role in Delano's version is blended with that of his father, Babo); in Delano's Documents the spelling "Mure" occurs nine times (pp. 336 thrice; 337; 338 twice; 340 twice; 341) and the spelling "Muri" only once (p. 334), presumably by a slip since the same man is being named.

104.25 Natu] NN emends the P and PT form "Nacta" as being not Melville's intentional change but a corruption of the name "Natu" from this point in Delano's Documents (p. 334; also p. 340), possibly by confusion with "Nasca" (pp. 335, 337).

104.27 Yau] NN emends the P and PT form "Yan" in its five occurrences (here, at 111.40 three times, and at 112.2) as a slip by Melville or more likely by his copyist or the P compositor. In Delano's Documents it is consistently "Yau" (pp. 334ff.).

104.28 Akim] Possibly this name in P and PT is Melville's invention, not drawn from any corresponding name in Delano's Documents. "Dago" (104.21) and "Ghofan" (104.26) are the other two Negro names he uses that are not in the *Narrative*. Possibly, however, "Akim" is a misreading (whether by Melville, his copyist, or a compositor) for "Alazase"—because that is the name of one of the several Negroes who are named in Delano's Documents (pp. 334, 347, and elsewhere) but not in Melville's fictional version. "Alazase" could conceivably be misread as "Akim" in Melville's hand. But in this inconclusive situation, NN does not emend.

105.3 Juan Bautista] This name (in P and PT) appears in Delano's Documents (p. 334) as "Juan Balltista", changed by Melville (or, if he had passed it along to *Putnam's,* by someone there) to the common Spanish name (for John the Baptist). NN assumes that "Balltista" was a corruption.

105.26 Nicolas] NN emends the P and PT form "St. Nicholas" as an inadvertent departure from the mixed form "St. Nicolas" at this point in Delano's translated Documents (p. 335). Melville did not hesitate to retain mixed forms from the *Narrative* (cf. "St. Maria" at 46.4), and it is more likely that "Nicholas" resulted from the unconscious substitution of the familiar English form (whether by Melville, his copyist, or the P compositor) than from Melville's intentional alteration of his source. (On the other hand, his introduction of "St. Bartholomew's church" at 117.1 and of "Bartholomew Barlo" at 114.7 shows that he was not concerned about consistently choosing Spanish proper names.)

106.1 they] NN emends the P and PT reading "he saw" to that of Delano's Documents, "they saw" (p. 335), which is required to restore the sense and force of Don Benito's argument to Babo in the context—that "they", the Negroes themselves, "saw plainly" what the shore was like.

106.4 and victual] The omission in PT of "and victual" was not likely Melville's doing: those words are in Delano's Documents (p. 335), and Melville's foregoing story insists that "their provisions were low", not just "their water next to none" (49.33–34, 51.18–24,34–35, 56.8, 79.12–13, 80.21–22, 89.25–27).

106.14 Arauco] NN corrects the P and PT misspelling "Arruco", although Melville found it in Delano's Documents (p. 336), because the entire *Narrative* contains too many slips along with its ear spellings (e.g., "Bonito Sereno", p. 329) to establish the currency or acceptability of such forms as this one.

106.32 Don . . . rest] In his ensuing fictional version of Don Benito's deposition, Melville reshaped from Delano's Documents the roles of the whites about as freely as those of the Negroes but preserved the spelling of their names more faithfully, and only two names call for emendation, at 107.13,15,18. Names of some characters not found in the *Narrative* cannot be so verified and (whatever their sources) are taken in the forms found in P and PT as Melville's fictional inventions: the monk Infelez (104.1), Don Alonzo Sidonia (107.4), Ponce the servant (107.14,18), the boatswain's mate Roderigo Hurta (107.20), the old sailor Luys Galgo (112.34), and two vengeful sailors—Martinez Gola and Bartholomew Barlo (114.4,7). Others, from the *Narrative,* are purposefully modified by Melville: Don Hermenegildo is given the family name Gandix (107.15, 113.11–12,14,21); Don Joaquin Arambaolaza is made Marques and given the servant Ponce (107.13, 113.20); and a cabin boy's name, Raneds, is given to the mate (106.30 and *passim).*

106.39 Matiluqui] This man's name occurs first in Delano's Documents at this point (p. 334) as one of the Senegal Negroes, "Matiluqui"—the same spelling followed by P and PT at 104.27 (where he is one of the six Ashantees Melville grafted into the story and its fictional deposition, taking over five of the Senegal names). Next the same man's name occurs, evidently corrupted, as "Matinqui" (p. 336), and at the corresponding point in P and PT is further corrupted as "Martinqui" (106.39). Finally it appears again as "Matinqui" (pp. 341, 347), and again in P and PT as "Martinqui" (111.23). Since the same man is referred to throughout, only confusion would be served by keeping the Delano or P and PT corruptions, none of which Melville apparently noticed, much less intended; consequently, NN emends the P and PT reading "Martinqui" here and at 111.23 to conform to "Matiluqui" (104.27).

107.13 Arambaolaza] NN emends the P and PT "Aramboalaza" to agree with Delano's spelling, which Melville follows exactly at 113.20.

107.15 Morairi] NN emends the P and PT form "Mozairi", here and at 107.18, as a misreading (by Melville, his copyist, or a compositor) of "Morairi" (Delano's Documents, p. 341; his spelling at p. 347 is "Moraira").

107.19 Viscaya] This P and PT reading is presumably Melville's correction of "Viseaya", the form in which this common Spanish name (that of a province of Spain, in English "Biscay") appears in Delano's Documents (p. 336).

107.32 Christopher Colon] NN keeps as unemendable Melville's combination of the English and Spanish name forms, which does not occur in Delano's translated Documents. (Cf. the discussion at 46.4 and the references listed there.)

107.35 his covering] NN follows P; the PT reading "discovering" is not a change by Melville but another of its substantive errors that he overlooked in proofreading. (The gesture Melville establishes here is repeated below, where "each Spaniard", upon hearing Babo refer to the whiteness of Aranda's skeleton, similarly "covered his face", 107.38–41).

107.37 spirit, . . . body] This phrase in P and PT (with no counterpart in the *Narrative)* tempts emendation by reversal, to "in body, as now in spirit", which might make better sense. Melville's writings have many such possibly reversed phrases: see the discussion at 57.23; also, for example, *Pierre* (bk. 8), the discussion at NN148.1–2.

108.20 towing] This PT reading seems clearly to be the word Melville meant (instead of "lowering", the P reading)—whether the change was his own correction or someone's in the publishing office (whose attention may have been drawn to "lowering" by the occurrence of "lowered" in the next line).

108.20 had it] NN keeps the grammatically superfluous "it" (in both P and PT) as not uncharacteristic of Melville's sometimes loose syntax.

109.21 them;] P lacked the semicolon which NN follows PT in supplying here to mark the end of the clause which begins "that them he stationed" (109.19). The emendation thus construes the passage as "a given word [that] he told them; that . . . " rather than as "a given word; he told them that . . . " (a possible alternative emendation). Although both readings make sense, the former is adopted because (by beginning a clause with "that") it parallels the other "that" clauses in the whole passage.

110.5 *proceeds:]*] NN removes the line of six asterisks in P (nine in PT) between NN lines 5 and 6 as evidently wrongly used at this point. See the placing of such asterisks at 108.22 (with none between lines 25 and 26) and 111.3 (with none between lines 11 and 12).

111.17 midnights, he used] The P and PT reading "in the preceding midnight, he use to come" is emended by NN, as doubly corrupt, from the corresponding clause in Delano's Documents (p. 340): "in the preceding nights he used to come"; a change from "nights" to "midnights" seems to be Melville's intention, but "use" for "used" is somebody's slip.

114.7 Bartholomew Barlo] The anglicized Christian name in P and PT might be emended to its Spanish form, "Bartolomé," if its inappropriate form came from Delano in Melville's source passage (p. 328), especially since no other Christian names (except of saints and of "Christopher" Colon, 107.32) are anglicized in the translated Spanish Documents—and also if Melville's treatment of those Documents showed concern for such matters (see the discussion at 46.4 and the references listed there). But it was Melville who gave this sailor his English name when he invented him to take the dishonorable place of Benito Cereno himself, whom Delano (in phrases Melville borrowed) reports as the one he saw "in the act of stabbing one of the slaves" with "a dirk, which he had secreted at the time the negroes were massacreing the Spaniards". Melville chose this stand-in sailor's name with more care for its possible allusiveness (e.g., to the St. Bartholomew's Eve massacre? to the Saint's iconic knife? to the Barlow knife?) than for national appropriateness. Cf. his similar introduction of "St. Bartholomew's church" as Benito Cereno's final resting place (117.1).

114.23 have] The revision in PT to "Deposition have" from the P reading "deposition of Benito Cereno has" is unmistakably Melville's own. His changing the verb's mood from the plain indicative "has" to the dubiety-stirring subjunctive "have" is crucial for interpreting his view of the deposition just presented and of the events of his story that they represent in documentary form. For the subjunctive clause, "If the Deposition have served as the key . . . ," raises a doubt whether indeed such a legal document can serve as the key to "fit into the lock of the complications which precede it" in the way so unwarily "hoped" at the point of their introduction, at 103.9–13. Melville's slight but substantial change at this point thus signals his own awareness of perplexities in the human situation addressed.

116.35 Babo.] PT omits the sentence that follows in P (see the EMENDATIONS list below); evidently Melville made this cut to sharpen the focus on Babo by removing a sentence that shifted attention back to Don Benito's attitude (but only repeated what had already been said).

117.1 St. Bartholomew's] This altogether English form in P and PT has no counterpart in Delano's *Narrative* (since Cereno's withdrawal and death are Melville's invention); it shows Melville's unconcern with consistent handling of Spanish name forms. (See the discussion at 49.16.)

EMENDATIONS. *46.14 mould] PT; mold P 46.14 surtout] PT; mantle P 47.5 incentives] PT; excitement P 47.20–21 hemisphered] PT; crescented P *50.13 heightened] PT; hightened P 51.33 heighten] PT; highten P 53.12 faithful] PT; *[not present]* P 53.18 the] PT; the the P *53.31 here] PT; in Don Benito P *55.15 hardware,] PT; *[not present]* P 55.22 mate] NN; mata P, PT 56.21 remaining] PT; *[not present]* P 57.16 could] PT; conld P 57.18 heightened] PT; hightened P 58.14 gentility] PT; aristocracy P 58.14 united?] PT; united? Such was his democratic conclusion. P 59.14 his host] PT; Don Benito P 59.17 hatches] PT; hatchets P 59.23 Don] PT; *[not present]* P 59.30 hapless] PT; helpless P 63.26 sourly] PT; slowly P 63.34 his guest] PT; Captain Delano P 65.4 silky] PT; velvet P 65.9 his host] PT; Don Benito P 65.10 he] PT; Captain Delano P *65.38 you] PT; you on board P 67.8 It] PT; I P 67.8 moment] PT; momext P *69.4 been] NN; *[not present]* P, PT *69.4 by] NN; *[not present]* P, PT 69.11 his] PT; the Spanish captain's P 69.12–22 But . . . dismissed. ¶ At] PT; ¶ In short, scarce an uneasiness entered the honest sailor's mind but, by a subsequent spontaneous act of good sense, it was ejected. At P 69.22 his former] PT; these P 69.26 and almost] PT; and, in a human way, he almost began to laugh P 69.31 idle] PT; random P 69.33 him,] PT; ~[] P 69.35 not more convenient] PT; which would prove no wiser P 70.34 his host] PT; Don Benito P 71.15 one or two] PT; some P *72.6 combined] PT; to be combined P 72.7–8 then . . . crew,] PT; then, however illogically, uniting in his mind his own private suspicions of the crew with the confessed ill-opinion on the part of their Captain, P 72.8 insensibly he was] PT; he was insensibly P 72.9 invariably] PT; as invariably P 74.16 ribbon] PT; ribboned P 77.5 unforeseen] PT; unforseen P *77.5 efficacy] PT; efficiency P *78.13 minutes'] NN; ~∧ P; ~, PT 79.31 the visitor's] PT; Captain Delano's P 80.11 his captain] PT; Don Benito P 80.17 it] PT; fresh water P 80.17–18 the Spaniard] PT; Don Benito P 80.24 whites] PT; Spaniards P 80.40 come the wind] PT; should the wind come P 82.29 heightened] PT; hightened P 85.6 shuddered;] PT; ~, P 85.7 heightened] PT; hightened P 85.13 always] PT; *[not present]* P 87.1 servant,] PT; ~∧ P 87.1–2 at convenient times,] PT; now and then P 88.17 man.—] PT; ~∧— P 88.27 salaam] NN; saalam P,

PT *88.30 on] PT; in P *89.7 too!] NN; ~? P, PT
*92.39 straight forward] PT; straightforward P 93.1 The man assented] PT; "Sí, Señor," assented the man P 93.3 intently] PT; askance P
93.20 seated Spaniard,] PT; Spaniard, on the transom, P 93.26 brisk] PT; buoyant P 93.27 indefinite] PT; involuntary P 94.2 indeed] PT; denied P 94.6 Again conversation] PT; Conversation now P
94.16 better,^] NN; ~," P, PT 94.16 Benito,"] NN; ~,^ P, PT
95.6 height] PT; hight P 95.20 smaller] PT; practical P
96.29 unharmed] PT; unarmed P *96.38 as] PT; as his P
96.39 clenched] PT; the clenched P 97.2 harboring] PT; indulging P
97.16 withdrawing] PT; revoking P 98.11 sailors] PT; Spanish sailors P 98.16 Spaniard] PT; Benito Cereno P 98.17 Don Benito] PT; the Spaniard P 98.25 white] PT; Spanish P 99.6 sailors] PT; Spanish sailors P 99.18 his host's] PT; Benito Cereno's P
*100.15 gun's] PT; guns' P 100.17 moors] PT; expanse P
100.32 his] PT; twenty-five P 101.5 more than a] PT; upwards of ten P 102.9 Sealing-spears] PT; Scaling-spears P 102.32 sealing-spears] PT; scaling-spears P *103.31 negroes] PT; Senegal negroes P
*104.1 received] PT; received, before Don José de Abos and Padilla, Notary Public of the Holy Crusade, P *104.7 beside thirty cases of hardware] PT; *[not present]* P *104.18 Francesco] PT; Francisco P
*104.24 Mure] NN; Muri P, PT *104.25 Natu] NN; Nacta P, PT
*104.27 Yau] NN; Yan P, PT 104.36 ¶ *[The catalogue over, the deposition goes on:]]* PT; *[After the catalogue, the deposition goes on as follows:]* P
105.12 during] PT; in P 105.14 being quickly wounded] PT; having been wounded at the onset P 105.24 them,] PT; ~. P
*105.26 Nicolas] NN; Nicholas P, PT *106.1 they] NN; he P, PT
106.5 solitary] PT; desert P 106.11 on] PT; in P 106.11 near] PT; in P *106.14 Arauco] NN; Arruco P, PT *106.39 Matiluqui] NN; Martinqui P, PT *107.13 Arambaolaza] NN; Aramboalaza P, PT
*107.15 Morairi] NN; Mozairi P, PT 107.18 Morairi] NN; Mozairi P, PT 108.18 destroyed] PT; destoyed P 108.19 which] PT; whlch P
*108.20 towing] PT; lowering P *109.21 them;] PT; ~^ P
*110.5 *[no line of asterisks follows]]* NN; *[line of asterisks follows]* P, PT
*111.17 midnights] NN; midnight P, PT *111.17 used] NN; use P, PT 111.23 Matiluqui] NN; Martinqui P, PT 111.25 Francesco] PT; Francisco P 111.30 Francesco] PT; Francisco P 111.32 with one] PT; which one P 111.40 Yau . . . Yau . . . Yau] NN; Yan . . . Yan . . . Yan P, PT 112.2 Yau] NN; Yan P, PT 112.11 master] PT; masters P
113.7 some] PT; a certain unconscious hopeful P 113.7 a] PT; some P
113.31 for] PT; fer P 113.37 disposition] PT; decision P

114.18 but] PT; bnt P 114.23 Deposition] PT; deposition of Benito Cereno P *114.23 have] PT; has P 114.24 precede] PT; preceded P 114.32 the sufferer] PT; Don Benito P 114.38 friend] PT; Don Amasa P 115.13 have] PT; *[not present]* P 115.25 interferences] PT; interferences with the blacks P 115.33 monster] PT; villain P 115.36 man] PT; men P 116.1 "You] PT; "I think I understand you; you P 116.7 cheek,] PT; cheek, Don Benito, P 116.12 saved,] PT; saved, Don Benito, P *116.35 Babo.] PT; Babo. And yet the Spaniard would, upon occasion, verbally refer to the negro, as has been shown; but look on him he would not, or could not. P

HYPHENATION. I. 48.22 superannuated 48.32 war-like 49.19 hearse-like 49.26 outnumbering 49.32 †shipwreck 50.32 hatchet-polishers 52.4 hardships 52.5 overlooked 53.25 pilot-fish 54.37 misfortunes 55.5 seamen 57.4 Guinea-men 57.21 high-crowned 59.20 forbear 59.35 oakum-picker 60.10 oakum-pickers 61.27 grave-yard 63.20 lordship 65.12 ill-health 66.24 withdrew 69.24 †scissors-grinders 69.29 good-naturedly 71.28 off-handed 72.18 †sleepy-looking 73.39 Venetian-looking 74.9 state-balcony 75.18 withdrawing 75.35 cross-legged 76.7 back-handed-well-/knot 77.6 well-known 77.16 duck-satchel 78.18 stage-box 79.26 half-mirthful 79.31 oakum-pickers 79.36 oakum-pickers 80.36 watering-place 80.38 sunset 82.28 walking-stick 82.35 bulk-head 83.30 †hair-dressers 85.16 chair-arm 85.17 ground-colors 89.30 withdrew 91.35 stern-window 93.1 tiller-head 93.33 good-breeding 95.15 †whale-boat 95.34 †half-averted 97.29 gangway 98.20 hatchet-polishers 99.6 †bowsman 99.37 figure-head 101.1 privateer's-man 104.26 forty-five 105.6 hand-spikes 105.16 companion-way 107.12 german-cousin 107.19 boatswain's 107.22 boatswain 113.12 seamen 113.29 seaman 113.39 forewarned 116.23 silver-mounted

II. 47.24 *saya-y-manta* 49.1 sea-moss 50.26 cross-legged 57.34 blunt-thinking 58.12 hawse-hole 59.11 organ-grinders 60.5 oakum-pickers 66.9 shoe-buckle 69.24 †scissors-grinders 71.26 kings-at-arms 72.18 †sleepy-looking 74.17 sea-weed 75.14 port-hole 76.6 treble-crown-knot 79.10 oakum-pickers 82.26 shooting-jacket 82.39 arm-chair 83.30 †hair-dressers

85.17 blood-red 87.26 statue-head 89.1 usher-of-the-golden-rod 91.28 cabin-windows 95.15 †whale-boat 95.34 †half-averted 100.24 cabin-passenger 102.9 hand-spikes 102.31 long-edged 110.8 fore-mentioned

SUBSTANTIVE VARIANTS. 46.14 surtout] PT; mantle P 47.5 incentives] PT; excitement P 47.14 for . . . to] P; *[not present]* PT 47.20–21 hemisphered] PT; crescented P 49.31 a fever] P; the fever PT 49.37 the] P; *[not present]* PT 51.19 baskets] P; basket PT 52.4 the hardships] P; hardships PT 53.12 faithful] PT; *[not present]* P 53.18 the] PT; the the P 53.29 as] P; *[not present]* PT 53.31 here] PT; in Don Benito P 54.5 more] P; *[not present]* PT 55.15 hardware] PT; *[not present]* P 56.21 remaining] PT; *[not present]* P 56.23 beggar's] P; beggars' PT 56.26 southermost] P; southernmost PT 58.14 gentility] PT; aristocracy P 58.14 united?] PT; united? Such was his democratic conclusion. P 59.13 fidgeting] P; fidgety PT 59.14 his host] PT; Don Benito P 59.17 hatches] PT; hatchets P 59.23 Don] PT; *[not present]* P 59.30 hapless] PT; helpless P 60.25 not] P; none PT 63.13 time] P; *[not present]* PT 63.21 in] P; *[not present]* PT 63.26 sourly] PT; slowly P 63.34 his guest] PT; Captain Delano P 65.4 silky] PT; velvet P 65.9 his host] PT; Don Benito P 65.10 he] PT; Captain Delano P 65.38 you] PT; you on board P 67.8 It] PT; I P 67.36 the point of] P; *[not present]* PT 69.11 his] PT; the Spanish captain's P 69.12–22 But . . . dismissed. ¶ At] PT; ¶ In short, scarce an uneasiness entered the honest sailor's mind but, by a subsequent spontaneous act of good sense, it was ejected. At P 69.22 his former] PT; these P 69.26 and almost] PT; and, in a human way, he almost began to laugh P 69.31 idle] PT; random P 69.35 not more convenient] PT; which would prove no wiser P 70.15–16 flew . . . curses] P; violently pushed him aside PT 70.17 the two blacks] P; they PT 70.17 and jumped upon him] P; *[not present]* PT 70.32 thus] P; *[not present]* PT 70.34 his host] PT; Don Benito P 71.15 one or two] PT; some P 71.34 with] P; *[not present]* PT 72.6 combined] PT; to be combined P 72.7–8 then . . . crew,] PT; then, however illogically, uniting in his mind his own private suspicions of the crew with the confessed ill-opinion on the part of their Captain, P 72.8 insensibly he was] PT; he was insensibly P 72.9 invariably] PT; as invariably P 73.20 distance] P; a distance PT 73.30 Mungo Park] P; Ledyard PT 74.7 lid,] P; lid; and PT 74.16 ribbon] PT; ribboned P 74.31 probably] P; *[not present]* PT 75.19 some plot] P; his plot PT 76.4 or] P; nor PT

76.32 old] P; odd PT 77.5 efficacy] PT; efficiency P
77.32 hand] P; had PT 79.31 the visitor's] PT; Captain Delano's P
80.11 his captain] PT; Don Benito P 80.17 it] PT; fresh water P 80.17–18 the Spaniard] PT; Don Benito P 80.24 whites] PT; Spaniards P 80.25 on his part] P; *[not present]* PT 80.40 come the wind] PT; should the wind come P 82.5 somewhat] P; *[not present]* PT
82.37 friar's] P; friars' PT 83.1 crutch] P; crotch PT
83.2 middle-age] P; *[not present]* PT 83.27 it] P; *[not present]* PT
84.1 all] P; *[not present]* PT 85.13 always] PT; *[not present]* P
87.1–2 at convenient times] PT; now and then P 88.30 on] PT; in P
91.13 this] P; his PT 92.39 straight forward] PT; straightforward P
93.1 The man assented] PT; "Sí, Señor," assented the man P
93.3 intently] PT; askance P 93.11 his] P; the PT 93.20 seated Spaniard,] PT; Spaniard, on the transom, P 93.26 brisk] PT; buoyant P
93.27 indefinite] PT; involuntary P 94.2 indeed] PT; denied P
94.6 Again conversation] PT; Conversation now P 95.20 smaller] PT; practical P 96.29 unharmed] PT; unarmed P 96.29 her] P; *[not present]* PT 96.38 as] PT; as his P 96.39 clenched] PT; the clenched P
97.2 harboring] PT; indulging P 97.3 almost] P; *[not present]* PT
97.16 withdrawing] PT; revoking P 98.6–7 bowsman] P; bowsmen PT 98.11 sailors] PT; Spanish sailors P 98.16 Spaniard] PT; Benito Cereno P 98.17 Don Benito] PT; the Spaniard P 98.25 white] PT; Spanish P 99.6 sailors] PT; Spanish sailors P 99.18 his host's] PT; Benito Cereno's P 99.25 the] P; *[not present]* PT 100.15 gun's] PT; guns' P 100.17 moors] PT; expanse P 100.32 his] PT; twenty-five P 101.1–2 and, as . . . pirate] P; *[not present]* PT 101.4 as good] P; good PT 101.5 more than a] PT; upwards of ten P
102.9 Sealing-spears] PT; Scaling-spears P 102.25 a] P; *[not present]* PT
102.32 sealing-spears] PT; scaling-spears P 102.38 two ships] P; ships PT 103.31 negroes] PT; Senegal negroes P 104.1 received] PT; received, before Don José de Abos and Padilla, Notary Public of the Holy Crusade, P 104.7 beside thirty cases of hardware] PT; *[not present]* P
104.30 owners] P; owner PT 104.36 ¶ *[The catalogue . . . on:]]* PT; *[After the catalogue, the deposition goes on as follows:]* P 105.12 during] PT; in P
105.14 being quickly wounded] PT; having been wounded at the onset P
105.15 they] P; *[not present]* PT 105.33 him] P; *[not present]* PT
106.4 and victual] P; *[not present]* PT 106.5 solitary] PT; desert P
106.11 on] PT; in P 106.11 near] PT; in P 107.35 his covering] P; discovering PT 108.20 towing] PT; lowering P 110.4 *strange*] P; *[not present]* PT 111.32 with one] PT; which one P 112.11 master] PT; masters P 113.7 some] PT; a certain unconscious hopeful P 113.7 a]

PT; some P 113.14 through a] P; through PT 113.15 American] P; *[not present]* PT 113.15 ran] P; run PT 113.37 disposition] PT; decision P 114.23 Deposition] PT; deposition of Benito Cereno P 114.23 have] PT; has P 114.24 precede] PT; preceded P 114.32 the sufferer] PT; Don Benito P 114.38 friend] PT; Don Amasa P 115.13 have] PT; *[not present]* P 115.25 interferences] PT; interferences with the blacks P 115.26 that] P; *[not present]* PT 115.33 monster] PT; villain P 115.36 man] PT; men P 116.1 "You] PT; "I think I understand you; you P 116.7 cheek,] PT; cheek, Don Benito, P 116.12 saved,] PT; saved, Don Benito, P 116.35 Babo.] PT; Babo. And yet the Spaniard would, upon occasion, verbally refer to the negro, as has been shown; but look on him he would not, or could not. P

THE LIGHTNING-ROD MAN (pp. 118–24)

NN copy-text: the anonymous first printing, "The Lightning-Rod Man," in *Putnam's Monthly Magazine* [P], IV, no. 20 (August, 1854), 131–34. Emendations from *The Piazza Tales* (1856), pp. 271–85 [PT]: at nine points. No NN emendations. (Principles for emendation are stated on pp. 549–64.) No known manuscript, and no later authoritative printing (see below) in Melville's lifetime. NN printer's copy: an emended photocopy of Newberry Library A5.765. Sight collations of P against PT: M66–2471–58 *vs.* Northwestern 051P99 and M67–722–75; M66–3627 *vs.* M67–722–75. Machine collations between copies of P: Newberry A5.765 *vs.* Northwestern 051P99 and M67–722–75; M67–722–75 *vs.* M69–316–18. Machine collations between copies of PT: M66–2471–60 *vs.* Gift M67–18 and M66–2471–61; M66–2472–61 *vs.* Newberry Y255M515.

"The Lightning-Rod Man" must have been written either during the winter of 1853–54 or—more probably—the following spring. If drafted and copied during the winter it could have been submitted to *Putnam's* along with an installment of "The Encantadas," which appeared in the numbers for March, April, and May of 1854, but we have none of the correspondence about "The Encantadas." If "The Lightning-Rod Man" was submitted along with "The Two Temples," which the magazine rejected in May, some reference to it might be expected in the letters exchanged from May 12 to May 16 between Melville and the editor and publisher. The piece could have been copied and forwarded to New York between May 16 and June 7, evidently when Melville wrote George P. Putnam to propose *Israel Potter* for serialization; the "sixty and odd pages of MSS."

sent on that same day were all "part of" the longer work. Or it could have been submitted during late June or July of 1854 in time to be printed with the second installment of *Israel Potter* in the August number. No correspondence betweeen Putnam and Melville during this period is known, but a ledger (now lost) of G. P. Putnam & Co. shows payments to Melville in August of $18.00 for "The Lightning-Rod Man" (three printed pages) and $55.00 for the second installment of *Israel Potter* (11½ printed pages)—see *Log*, I, 491.

Various analogues to the story and its characters have been put forward. Ben D. Kimpel, in "Melville's 'The Lightning-Rod Man,' " *American Literature*, XVI (March, 1944), 30–32, first suggested that its concern is less with lightning rods than various religious creeds; Egbert S. Oliver in his Hendricks House edition of *The Piazza Tales*, pp. 238–39, proposes the Reverend John Todd, pastor of the First Church (Congregational) of Pittsfield from 1842 to 1873, as the original of the lightning-rod man. Jay Leyda offers a "probable history" of the composition of the piece in his introduction to *The Complete Stories*, pp. xxvi– xxvii:

> Helen Morewood, a great-niece, furnishes a clue in recalling that her father [Melville's nephew] told the story to her as an encounter that Melville had had with a real lightning-rod salesman, who chose times of storm to pursue his trade. In the fall of 1853 the Berkshires were enduring an intense lightning-rod sales campaign, with advertisements and warnings and editorials on the subject in all the Berkshire papers. This September, too, Melville made one of his rare visits to St. Stephen's, Pittsfield's Episcopal church, to attend the wedding of his sister Catherine to his friend, John C. Hoadley. We cannot know what the Reverend Parvin pronounced on this occasion, but Melville was ready and tuned for the final chord that would bring all levels together. Just at this time the Pittsfield Library Association listed among their new acquisitions, Cotton Mather's *Magnalia Christi Americana,* a troubling and frightening record of religion in its most fiercely bullying and bigoted aspect, and there was Melville's theme, waiting for Melville's art—in the Sixth Book, Chapter III, "Ceraunius. Relating remarkables done by thunder." Among the Reverend Mather's listed admonitions is:
> IV. A fourth voice of the glorious God in the thunder, is *make your peace with* God *immediately, lest by the stroke of his thunder he take you away in his wrath.*
> This is the very voice of the Lightning-Rod Salesman who "still dwells in the land, still travels in storm-time, and drives a brave trade with the fears of man."

"Miss Margaret Morewood," Leyda adds, "recalls that there was also a copy of this work in the Arrowhead library." As Daniel G. Hoffman remarks in *Form and Fable in American Fiction* (New York: Oxford University Press, 1961; reprinted with corrections, 1965), p. 290, "a phrase in the very first sentence" of the story, "the Acroceraunian hills," "can allude only to . . . the title" of Mather's chapter. (Oliver, p. 238, had already noted that this section of ancient Greece was "famous for its frequent and violent thunder-storms.") The salesman, Hoffman goes on to suggest, "is a preliminary sketch" for the title character of *The Confidence-Man,* which Melville completed in 1856. Hershel Parker, in "Melville's Salesman Story," *Studies in Short Fiction,* I (Winter, 1964), 154–58, assigns the piece to that popular comic genre.

As Parker first pointed out, "The Lightning-Rod Man" was reset from *The Piazza Tales* (1856) in 1857; it appeared in Parts 9 and 10 (pp. 432–34) and that same year in the second collected volume (Division II, Parts 7–12) of William E. Burton's *Cyclopædia of Wit and Humor* (New York: Appleton); this work was frequently reissued under variant titles through 1898. Collation with the 1856 text (M68–1922 *vs.* M67–722–298) shows that the 1858 Burton printing has several misreadings but no authorial changes. The accompanying vignette (see the reproduction below) was the only original illustration published during Melville's lifetime for any of his

Vignette (2.5 by 3 in.) for "The Lightning-Rod Man" in William E. Burton's *Cyclopædia of Wit and Humor.*

signed works, though cartoons by "Read" (Donald F. or his brother James A. Read) accompanied some of his unsigned *Yankee Doodle* pieces (see pp. 216, 428, 431, 434, and 447 above). Evidently the artist for this unsigned vignette was Henry Louis Stephens (see Sinclair Hamilton, *Early American Book Illustrators and Wood Engravers, 1670–1870* [Princeton: 1968], I, 208, 432, and Harrison Hayford's pamphlet, *Henry Louis Stephens 1824–1882: Illustrator of Herman Melville?* [Evanston, 1984], with which an unpublished memorandum by M. Thomas Inge [1987] concurs).

Thus "The Lightning-Rod Man" was the one Melville tale regularly in print and available to the public throughout the remainder of his lifetime. No other reprinting has been located earlier than 1895, in *Capital Stories by American Authors* (New York: The Christian Herald, 1895), pp. 269–81.

For explanation of the following tabulations, see pp. 565–70.

DISCUSSION. 124.21–22 "Begone . . . worm."] The PT omission of these lines seems more likely an editorial effort to soften the passage or an "oversight," as Jay Leyda thought (*Complete Stories*, p. xxxiii), than Melville's revision.

EMENDATIONS. 118.21 ringed] PT; winged P 119.4 lengthwise] PT; lenghtwise P 119.16 Olympus] PT; old Greylock P
120.23 "My] PT; "How very dull you are. My P 122.6 is] PT; are P
122.12 room,^] PT; ~,, P 122.37 flashes] PT; fiashes P
122.37 surplus] PT; supplies P 123.28 conductor] PT; conducter P

HYPHENATION. I. 118.13 walking-stick 119.35 fire-place
120.24 specimen-rod 120.32 workman 120.36 finger-pointing
122.21 stand-point 124.14 sunshine 124.25 tri-forked
124.31 storm-time
II. 120.23 lightning-rods 122.1 bell-wire 123.13 thunder-storms

SUBSTANTIVE VARIANTS. 118.21 ringed] PT; winged P
119.16 Olympus] PT; old Greylock P 119.29 there's] P; there is PT
120.4 of] P; *[not present]* PT 120.23 "My] PT; "How very dull you are. My P 122.6 is] PT; are P 122.24 an] P; an an PT
122.37 surplus] PT; supplies P 124.21–22 "Begone . . . worm."] P; *[not present]* PT

THE ENCANTADAS, OR ENCHANTED ISLES (pp. 125–73)

NN copy-text: the first printing, "The Encantadas, or Enchanted Isles," over the pseudonym "Salvator R. Tarnmoor," in *Putnam's Monthly Maga-*

zine [P], III, no. 15 (March, 1854), 311–19 [NN125.1–142.25]; no. 16 (April, 1854), 345–55 [NN142.26–162.17]; and no. 17 (May, 1854), 460–66 [NN162.18–173.15]. Emendations from *The Piazza Tales* (1856), pp. 287–399 [PT]: at 48 points. NN emendations to P: at 27 points. (Principles for emendation are stated on pp. 549–64.) No known manuscript, and no later printing in Melville's lifetime. NN printer's copy: an emended photocopy of Newberry Library A5.765. Sight collations of P against PT: Newberry A5.765 *vs.* M66–3627; Northwestern 051P99 *vs.* M66–2471–58. Machine collations between copies of P: Newberry A5.765 *vs.* Northwestern 051P99 and M68–3078–15; M68–3078–15 *vs.* M67–722–293. Machine collations between copies of PT: M66–2471–61 *vs.* Newberry Y255M515 and M66–2471–60; M66–2472–60 *vs.* Gift M67–18.

We cannot now determine when "The Encantadas" was composed or how it was related to the projected book "partly of nautical adventure, and partly—or, rather, chiefly, of Tortoise Hunting Adventure" that Melville had proposed to Harper & Brothers on November 24, 1853. As the Historical Note shows (pp. 487–90), in December Melville received an advance for the book, which he promised for January, 1854; but in February he reported a delay and meanwhile must have submitted at least the first four sketches of "The Encantadas" to *Putnam's Monthly Magazine,* where they appeared in the March number.

The three installments carried the ascription "By Salvator R. Tarnmoor," but Melville's authorship was mentioned in the advance notice in the New York *Evening Post* of February 14, 1854, and in a comment in the *Berkshire County Eagle* of March 10 on his success with the first installment. In *The Piazza Tales* the ascription was dropped; whether by Melville's directive or by an editorial decision or printer's oversight is so uncertain that the NN editors have retained it (see the discussion at 125.3 below).

Melville received $50 for each of the three installments. Except in *The Piazza Tales,* none of the sketches was reprinted during his lifetime, but they have been often anthologized, complete or in excerpts, during the twentieth century. A limited edition (550 copies) of *The Encantadas* (Burlingame, Calif.: William P. Wreden, 1940), printed at the Grabhorn Press in San Francisco, has an introduction, critical epilogue, and bibliographical notes by Victor Wolfgang von Hagen and drawings by Mallette Dean; the text follows the 1923 Constable edition. Von Hagen, a naturalist, first read *The Piazza Tales* in 1935–36 on a scientific expedition to the Galápagos Islands, a volcanic archipelago lying along the equator six hundred miles off the coast of Ecuador; he visited "every part mentioned" in the sketches (p.

ix). As he notes (in commenting on what Russell Thomas had shown—see below—to be their literary sources), a chapter (20) of Amasa Delano's *Narrative* (1817) includes "a long summary of Captain Delano's various visits to the Galapagos" (p. 102). From this, von Hagen conjectures (going beyond Thomas), "Melville's lively memory recreated again the Encantadas' landscape" as he had seen it in the 1840's, and the first four sketches "are doubtless written out of Melville's own experience" (p. 102).

Although Melville, in von Hagen's words, "creates the impression that he visited several of the Galapagos Islands it is obvious to one who has checked this raconteur 'on the spot' that he never visited more than perhaps the northern tip of Albemarle Island . . . and he certainly sailed between the islands of Narborough and Albemarle and passed near, if he did not climb Rodondo Rock" (p. 101). While von Hagen concluded that Melville spent only "a very short time" at the islands (p. 110), it has since been established that his whaler, the *Acushnet,* cruised among them for some three weeks in the fall of 1841 and returned in early January of 1842. Her abstract log records the first sight of Albemarle on October 30, 1841, and an anchoring at Chatham Island on November 19; the captain evidently sent a boat's crew ashore at Albemarle for tortoises, as Melville remembers in Sketch Second, and the sailors must have fished off Rock Rodondo, as he writes in Sketch Third, in late October, just before several whale-ships spoke the *Acushnet.* Melville was again off the South American coast early in 1843 aboard the *Charles and Henry,* which was sighted on January 27 en route to the island of Más Afuera (Melville's "Massafuero"), and later in the same year aboard the frigate *United States,* which passed Más Afuera on November 19 and ran close in to Juan Fernández on the following morning; Sketch Fourth describes both islands as seen from passing ships. There is no record of a call at the Galápagos by either the *Charles and Henry* or the *United States,* but in Chapter 1 of *Mardi,* presumably remembering his cruise on the *Charles and Henry,* Melville mentions passing "Massafuero," alludes to "the Gallipagos, otherwise called the Enchanted Islands," and tells of an unsuccessful hunt for whales "a few leagues west" of the archipelago.

In "The Encantadas" Melville as usual supplemented his own memories with literary borrowings. Even in the first four sketches, where personal observation appears most prominent, he drew upon a number of other writers though naming only one—the "excellent Buccaneer" William Cowley, whose *Voyage Round the Globe,* collected in William Hacke's *A Collection of Original Voyages* (London, 1699), is quoted in Sketch Fourth (see the discussion at 142.7–11). The fifth sketch, which concerns the cruise of a ship "peculiarly associated with the Encantadas," the American frigate *Essex,* derives from Captain David Porter's *Journal of a Cruise Made to the Pacific Ocean* (Philadelphia, 1815; 2d ed., New York, 1822). This book, which Melville had repeatedly mined since *Typee,* provided ore for at least a dozen passages, among them the story of "Oberlus" (Patrick Watkins) in Sketch Ninth and the epitaph concluding Sketch Tenth. The "sentimental voyager" supposedly quoted in Sketch Sixth was Captain James Colnett, author of *A Voyage to the South Atlantic and Round Cape Horn into the Pacific Ocean* (London, 1798), whose brief description of James Island (p. 156), which Melville treated as about Barrington Isle, reads as follows:

> At every place where we landed on the Western side, we might have walked for miles, through long grass, and beneath groves of trees. It only wanted a stream to compose a very charming landscape. This isle appears to have been a favourite resort of the Buccaneers, as we not only found seats, which had been made by them of earth and stone, but a considerable number of broken jars scattered about, and some entirely whole, in which the Peruvian wine and liquors of that country are preserved. We also found some old daggers, nails and other implements. This place is, in every respect, calculated for refreshment or relief for crews after a long and tedious voyage, as it abounds with wood, and good anchorage, for any number of ships, and sheltered from all winds by Albemarle Isle. The watering-place of the Buccaneers was entirely dried up, and there was only a small rivulet between two hills running into the sea.

(Von Hagen, p. 105, points out that Melville misapplied this description; see the discussion at 144.38.)

Russell Thomas, in "Melville's Use of Some Sources in *The Encantadas,*" *American Literature,* III (January, 1932), 432–56, first documented Melville's borrowings from the three writers he names at the close of Sketch Fifth—Cowley, Colnett, and Porter—and from a fourth, James Burney, who is unmentioned in "The Encantadas." Probably Melville owned Burney's work, *A Chronological History of the Discoveries in the South Sea or Pacific Ocean* (London, 1803–17), since he used it even more heavily in 1858 for his lecture "The South Seas." Also unnamed among Melville's "authorities" is Charles Darwin, who studied the archipelago in 1835, six years before Melville was there. Charles R. Anderson, in *Melville in the South Seas* (New York: Columbia University Press, 1939), pp. 50–51, suggests the debt of Sketch First to Darwin's *Voyage of the Beagle,* which Melville bought in 1847 (Sealts 175). H. Bruce Franklin, in "The Island Worlds of Darwin and Melville," *Centennial Review,* XI (Summer, 1967), 353–70, argues that in citing Albemarle's population "statistics" in Sketch Fourth Melville both "challenges and parodies Darwin." Benjamin Lease's "Two Sides to a Tortoise: Darwin and Melville in the Pacific," *Personalist,* XLIX (Autumn, 1968), 531–39, and L. D. Gottlieb's "The Uses of Place: Darwin and Melville on the Galapagos," *BioScience,* XXV (March, 1975), 172–75, also consider their differing visions.

Two possible sources for Sketch Eighth are adduced by Robert Sattelmeyer and James Barbour in "The Sources and Genesis of Melville's 'Norfolk Isle and the Chola Widow,' " *American Literature,* L (November, 1978), 398–417. They argue that an article on "A Female Robinson Crusoe" in the Albany *Evening Journal* of November 3, 1853, later expanded in the Springfield, Massachusetts, *Sunday Republican* of November 22, supplied "details, tone, perspective, and even the gratuitous pieties of the story"; the article tells how a sea-otter hunter rescued an Indian woman abandoned for eighteen years on San Nicolas Island, off the California coast. They also see parallels—especially with Hunilla's white distress signal and the story's sense of despair—in the tale of five sailors left on an island to take sealskins and then abandoned there for three months which begins a chapter about the Galápagos in a book Melville owned (Sealts 372): Benjamin Morrell's *Narrative of Four Voyages to the South Seas . . .* (New York, 1832), pp. 118–19. Furthermore, they suggest, the description of Hunilla's hut derives from that of one surrounded by bones of land and sea tortoises in the same passage of Porter's *Journal* (I, 153) which Melville used in Sketch Tenth for the sailor who "killed two seals, and inflating their skins, made a float" (171.37–38). But they acknowledge that the newspaper story "is only the final link in a circumstantial chain" reaching back to the "story of Agatha," which he had worked on in 1852 (see the HISTORICAL NOTE, pp. 482–83). Reidar Ekner, in "*The Encantadas* and *Benito Cereno*—On Sources and Imagination in Melville," *Moderna Språk,* LX (1966), 258–73, and Charles N. Watson, Jr., in "Melville's Agatha and Hunilla: A Literary Reincarnation," *English Language Notes,* VI (December, 1968), 114–18, had already explored that relationship. Ekner also sees a resemblance to an actual 1852 event on Chatham Island.

No printed source is known for the "Dog-King" of Sketch Seventh, whom von Hagen identified as General José Villamil, a figure about whom Melville's misinformation (see the discussion at 146.37) probably came "from yarns that old sailors told to him. Like Defoe, Melville had to have actual evidence on which he could embroider" (p. 107).

The epigraphs to the sketches are from Edmund Spenser, Thomas Chatterton, and William Collins and from Beaumont and Fletcher's *Wit without Money:* see Leon Howard, "Melville and Spenser—A Note on Criticism," *Modern Language Notes,* XLVI (May, 1931), 291–92; Thomas's article of January, 1932; and D. Mathis Eddy, "Melville's Response to Beaumont and Fletcher: A New Source for *The Encantadas,*" *American Literature,* XL (November, 1968), 374–80. Penny L. Hirsch, in "Melville's Spenser Edition for *The Encantadas,*" *Melville Society Extracts,* No. 50 (May, 1982), 15–16, shows that Melville's text for the *Faerie Queene* epigraphs was one based on John Upton's edition (1758), with the reading "griesly" (rather than "griesie") at I.IX.xxxv.4 (162.23), and that all the epigraphs correspond more closely in wording, spelling, capitalization, and punctuation with the Upton-based Spenser texts in the compilation by Robert Anderson, *A Complete Edition of the Poets of Great Britain* (London, 1792–93), Volume II, than with those of any other edition listed in Frederic Ives Carpenter's *A Reference Guide to Spenser* (Chicago: University of Chicago Press, 1923). Melville's known set of Spenser (Sealts 483) is Child's edition, which was published (1855) and acquired (1861) too late for his use in "The Encantadas." So was one of his editions of Collins's *Poetical Works* (Sealts 156), but his other edition (Sealts 464; see the discussion at 151.15–18 below) was available. The old-spelling editions of Chatterton (Sealts 137) and Beaumont and Fletcher (see the discussion at 144.13–14) which Melville bought in London in 1849 were also available when he drew up the epigraphs. He gave away the Chatterton to his brother-in-law John C. Hoadley on January 6, 1854, which may suggest a terminal date for at least the eighth of the sketches (see the discussion at 151.8–14). Discussions below record the differences in wording between the copy-text (P) epigraphs and their sources (the texts just cited). NN emends P from these texts only when words in P make little or no sense and so cannot belong among Melville's intentional changes from his sources.

After "The Encantadas" appeared in print, the editor of *Putnam's,* Charles F. Briggs, wrote to Melville on May 12, 1854:

> I will take this opportunity to apologise to you for making a slight alteration in the Encantadas, in the last paragraph of the Chola Widow, which I thought would be improved by the omission of a few words. That I did not injure the idea, or mutilate the touching figure you introduced, by the slight

> excision I made, I received good evidence of, in a letter from James [Russell] Lowell, who said that the figure of the cross in the ass' neck, brought tears into his eyes, and he thought it the finest touch of genius he had seen in prose.

Jay Leyda (*Complete Stories,* p. 460) comments, "Apparently Melville agreed to the alteration, for he did not see fit to restore the 'few words' when this was reprinted in *The Piazza Tales.*" But an author's silence about editorial changes scarcely means consent, much less approval; and more likely by 1856 Melville simply overlooked the matter. As to Briggs's motive, Leyda suggests that he "may have been shielding the same 'religious sensibilities' that would have been offended by 'The Two Temples' (rejected for this reason in the same letter), for we find a hint as to what was excised, in *Clarel,* II.i":

> The ass, pearl-gray,
> Matched well the rider's garb in hue,
> And sorted with the ashy way;
> Upon her shoulders' jointed play
> The white cross gleamed, which the untrue
> Yet innocent fair legends say,
> Memorializes Christ our Lord
> When Him with palms the throngs adored
> Upon the foal.

Moreover, Melville scored the passage about a similar cross-marked and legended ass in Wordsworth's "Peter Bell" (lines 971ff.) in his copy of *The Complete Poetical Works* (Sealts 563a). See Thomas F. Heffernan, "Melville and Wordsworth," *American Literature,* XLIX (November, 1977), 340–51. Mary K. Bercaw, in "The Crux of the Ass in 'The Encantadas,' " *Melville Society Extracts,* No. 62 (May, 1985), 12, points out that the variety of ass actually marked by the legendary shoulder cross that both Melville and Wordsworth had in mind is common in South America, where Melville probably encountered it and the legend, as she did in the Galápagos.

For explanation of the following tabulations, see pp. 565–70.

DISCUSSIONS. 125.3 By . . . Tarnmoor] For two reasons NN keeps this pseudonym which P carried but PT omitted. First, its being on all three P installments was certainly Melville's own idea, but its omission from PT may have been editorial or compositorial. Second, the pseudonym has implications for criticism. These are raised in von Hagen's question (p. 116) and the statement by Lewis Mumford that he cites: "with the single exception of the *Encantadas,*" the PT pieces from

P had been published anonymously, "and no reason is given, by Melville at least, why he chose [in this instance] the pseudonym, Salvator R. Tarnmoor. Mr. Mumford states that his mood at the writing of these sketches was reflected 'in the very choice of his pseudonym,' but Mr. Mumford does not explain the reference. He may be referring to the Tarnmoor of Iceland which means 'small isolated mountainous lakes' and the image of desolation they would invoke." (Mumford, in *Herman Melville* [New York: Harcourt Brace, 1929], p. 239, and von Hagen here both probably take for granted that "Salvator R." is meant to evoke the picturesque paintings of Salvator Rosa.) For critical interpretation of "The Encantadas" the point is that this pseudonym may not have been added to P simply as an afterthought but may have entered into Melville's conception of the narrator (and hence, of the narrative and its genre), at least at some points, as did the persona of the pseudonymous "Virginian Spending July in Vermont" to whom Melville ascribed his essay on "Hawthorne and His Mosses" late in its composition (see the discussion at 239.2). NN keeps not only "Salvator R. Tarnmoor" but similarly the "Virginian" (239.2), "L. A. V." (196.34, 204.16), and the "special correspondent" of *Yankee Doodle* (212.3)—all personae arguably present within these pseudonymous works. It is common to preserve such authorial pseudonyms, recognizing the considerations just stated: Geoffrey Crayon and Mark Twain are examples. As the HISTORICAL NOTE shows (pp. 463–64, 483), Melville in the 1850's had various reasons for considering and using pseudonyms, and within the magazine pieces he created diverse narrative voices. In sum, the textual, critical, and biographical implications require the NN editors to retain this pseudonym.

125.6–126.6 —"*That . . . howl.*"] In P and PT the first of these epigraphs, made up of one whole stanza and part of the next from *The Faerie Queene* (II.XII.xi.1–9, II.XII.xii.7–9), differs in wording from Spenser in reading "For" for "But" at 125.13 and "secure" for "recure" at 125.16. For the Spenser text Melville was using, see above, p. 605. NN restores "recure", where a copyist or compositor probably misread Melville's looped "r" as "s" (a mistake that also occurred in the "Extracts" to *Moby-Dick,* in a different Spenser passage—see NNxix.24), but NN does not change "For", which may be Melville's intentional alteration. The second of the epigraphs, from I.IX.xxxiii.4–9, is accurate in wording. The quotation marks around each epigraph are Melville's, but he omitted (and NN does not supply) those designating what part of the first epigraph is spoken by the ferryman. Possibly the "e" spelling of "Wandering" at 125.12 (for "Wandring" in Anderson's text of Spenser) was not Melville's intention, since he followed the spelling without "e" for forms of the same word just below at 125.13,17, and 126.6.

129.33 "Memento ****"] Where P and PT have five superscript asterisks, separated by spaces from each other and from the closing quotation mark, NN emends to four asterisks grouped as a word with an unseparated closing quotation mark, because Melville presumably meant the asterisks not only to evoke the word "mori" but also to be printed as that four-letter word would be.

130.3–19 "*Most . . . lye.*"] These three epigraphs from *The Faerie Queene* (II.XII.xxiii.1–5, II.XII.xxv.6–9, II.XII.xxvi.1–3,6,8,9), as printed in P and PT, differ in wording from Spenser's text at seven points: "do a man" for "did the knight" at 130.8, "at home" for "on earth" at 130.9, "these isles" for "the seas" at 130.11, "not there" for "not these" at 130.14, "And" for "Tho" at 130.17, "Then" for "And" at 130.18, and "Zethy's" for "Tethys" at 130.19. NN restores the original letters in two of these instances—"these" and "Tethys"—where a scribe or compositor apparently misread Melville's "s" as "r" and "T" as "Z". ("Tethys", in Anderson's text of Spenser, has no apostrophe, but the erroneous "Zethy's" in P and PT suggests that Melville may have supplied one; NN places it correctly, after the "s"—Tethys, not Tethy, being the name of the wife of Ocean and the mother of sea gods and monsters.) NN leaves the other variants unchanged, as intentional alterations by Melville, and does not supply the missing quotation marks to designate the words spoken by the palmer (130.13–15).

131.32 three walled towns] NN emends the contextually senseless reading in P and PT, "three-walled towns" (as does Leyda, *Complete Stories,* p. 57); here each turtle in his calapee is thought of as a walled town and the three turtles as three such towns—above they are called "three Roman Coliseums."

133.6–27 "*Forthy . . . were.*"] In these lines from *The Faerie Queene* (II.XII.viii.1–6, II.XII.xxxiii.1–4,8–9, II.XII.xxxv.6–9, II.XII.xxxvi.1–2), P reads "For they" for "Forthy" at 133.6, "dreadful" for "detestable" at 133.7, "dreadful" for "wastfull" at 133.11, "vase" for "base" at 133.14, "Then" for "That" at 133.18, and "that" for "their" at 133.19. NN emends in two instances where Melville's hand was probably misread, restoring "Forthy" and "base" (the latter correction was also made in PT). The reading "For they" in P and PT makes ungrammatical nonsense of Spenser's "Forthy" or "For thy" (meaning "therefore"). The two-word misreading might be explained easily if Melville had had before him one of the Spenser texts with the two-word "For thy" rather than a text with the one-word reading "Forthy", such as Anderson's (and Upton's; see above, p. 605); since the texts of Melville's epigraphs are more like Anderson's Spenser text than any other, particularly any with "For thy", NN emends to Anderson's "Forthy"—which Melville himself may have misread as "For they" or, more likely, may have written correctly but in such a way that his copyist or compositor misread it.

136.18–19 on . . . saw] NN keeps this passage, omitted by PT, because PT's garbling of the preceding related phrase (from "The winged life clouding Rodondo" to "The winged, life-clouding Rodondo") makes the omission seem less likely Melville's cancellation than a compositorial eye skip (which would have been easy given how "Rodondo" and "had" stood in the lineation of P). Moreover, the way this sketch is structured around that morning's visit (134.11–24, 136.18–26,37ff.) shows that this paragraph (lines 8–17) needs the omitted words both to bring the reader back to that specific past occasion, reestablishing the advancing movement of that day, and to validate the abrupt shift of the paragraph into past tenses (beginning with "had"), which the omission in PT makes awkwardly unmotivated, if not senseless.

137.7–8 —*"That . . . show:"*——] In the first of these two separated lines from *The Faerie Queene* (I.X.liii.1, I.X.lv.1), "him" replaces the "them" of Anderson's Spenser, and so it may be Melville's deliberate change to agree with Spenser's "him" in the second quoted line, though in some other Spenser texts the reading here is "him". In the second line "whence", for Spenser's "thence", is also retained, as Melville's intentional change.

138.19 unimpaired . . . . .] NN keeps the anomalous five dots present in P and PT; possibly Melville meant them to suggest hesitation in finding the proper words, but possibly they were merely someone's error.

140.1 neighbors] The P (and not PT) "-our" spelling in "neighbours" and in "neighbourhood" in the next line occurs nowhere else in this work ("neighborhood" appears at 143.1); because it is not Melville's usage, NN emends to his customary "-or" spelling in both instances (as NN did throughout *Typee*—see NN323).

140.3 Ǝ] In P the space for this figure was left blank; in PT a downturned large capital "E" was supplied. Obviously, an "E" was needed for the "familiar diagram" and "letter" meant for the two-line blank space in P; von Hagen's conjecture (p. 117) seems right: "The typographer . . . neglected to insert the letter 'E' . . . thus rendering unintelligible two short paragraphs." Whoever supplied the downturned "E" in PT failed to make its position correspond to the island's westward opening as called for by Melville's description: "Albemarle opens his mouth towards the setting sun" and has north and south promontories (140.23ff.). (A glance at a Galápagos map confirms the westward opening of Albemarle; Thomas, pp. 453ff., points out that in two of Melville's sources, on both Porter's map and Colnett's, the "E" shape stands out, but not on Cowley's or other maps Thomas could find.) The southward opening of the downturned "E" in PT is so glaring a discrepancy that Melville himself (if he noticed the blank space in P and called for a large "E" in PT) cannot have intended the letter to be in that position. Consequently, NN (for the first time) corrects this lapse by supplying a reversed, westward-opening "Ǝ"—as not just the "letter" but the "diagram" called for by Melville's description and required to illustrate it. (See p. 619 for discussion of further possible printing-house lapses in PT; also Chapter 18 of *Moby-Dick* [NN89.15–19] for the unemendable discrepancy, probably of similar origin, between Ishmael's description of the "queer round figure" tattooed on Queequeg's arm and the cross printed to represent it.)

142.7–11 "My . . . city,"] As printed in P and PT this quotation from William Cowley's *Voyage Round the Globe* has three differences in wording (all retained in NN as Melville's intentional changes) from the passage (p. 10) in William

Hacke's *A Collection of Original Voyages* (London, 1699): the necessary "it" is provided after "call" (142.8), and "Isle" is substituted for *"Island"* (142.8) and "so" for "as" (142.9).

142.17 not] Although P and PT both lack this word, it is supplied by NN (as by Leyda in *Complete Stories,* p. 73) because it is required by Melville's obvious meaning that the "possibility" and "conceit" (142.14,17) suggested in the paragraph are warranted. Cf. the parallel speculation and expression ("Not very improbable") at 146.14 and the discussion at 363.27.

142.21 Wood's Isle] A probable, but unemendable, error Melville made in naming this island is suggested by Thomas (pp. 453–54), who could not find it on any map, although he found several references to the use of "Wood's" interchangeably with "Hood's"; but Melville includes "Hood's" as a separate island in this same list, and Thomas was unable to resolve the problem. Von Hagen does not notice it, and Wood's Isle is not on his map.

142.28–31 *"Looking . . . flight."*] The wording corresponds to the Anderson text of Spenser's "Visions of the World's Vanity" (ix.1–4).

143.21 northward] NN emends the P and PT reading "westward" from Melville's source: as Thomas (pp. 445–46) shows by parallel passages, he took the whole episode (142.34–143.25) from Porter's *Journal* (I, 208–10); he adapted it freely to his artistic purposes but adhered to the factual particulars so closely that the change from Porter's "northward" to the "westward" of P and PT seems better explained as a copyist's or compositor's misreading of "northward" in Melville's hand (or even as Melville's own slip) than as his intentional alteration.

143.36 but three] An unemendable because evidently intentional misstatement: as von Hagen (p. 102, quoted above on p. 602) points out, a chapter (20) of Captain Amasa Delano's *Voyages,* which Melville used, contains a long summary of his visits to the Galápagos. Possibly Melville avoided reference to a name and a source he had used so thoroughly without citation in "Benito Cereno." See also the comments above (pp. 603–4) on Melville's use of Burney and Darwin.

143.38 1793] NN emends the year 1798 in P and PT (as does Leyda, *Complete Stories,* p. 75) because it was the year of publication of Colnett's *Voyage,* not, as parallelism with the Cowley and Porter dates would imply, of his touching at the Isles.

144.2 BARRINGTON] Melville made an extended unemendable factual error when he assigned to this island the buccaneers discussed by Colnett. Von Hagen points out (p. 105) that "Colnett in his account was actually referring to James Island" and, quoting Colnett's statement that he named but did not land at Barrington, adds that his "lack of emphasis is what threw Melville on the wrong track." Probably so, but possibly Melville here deliberately moved Colnett's buccaneers and scenery from one island to another to suit his artistic purposes, just as elsewhere he fancifully elaborated a passage on the buccaneers and, putting it in quotation marks, attributed it not to Colnett but to "a sentimental voyager long ago" (145.7–8). See the passage from Colnett above, p. 603.

144.3–11 *"Let . . . any."*] In these eight lines from Spenser's "Prosopopoia: or Mother Hubberd's Tale" (lines 134–39, 168–69), NN emends two of the readings in P: "on" (before "hugger-mugger" at 144.8) to Spenser's idiomatic "in" (Melville's "in" was probably misread, as sometimes happened); and "Where—so" (144.11) to Spenser's "Where-so" (Anderson's text has the hyphen, but some other texts [and PT] have "Whereso"; on NN's use of Anderson, see above, p. 605). A third substantive variant from Spenser, "earth" for "world" (144.4), is retained as Melville's intentional alteration.

144.13–14 *"How . . . troubles!"*] These lines from the opening scene of Beaumont and Fletcher's *Wit without Money,* marked with a marginal check in Melville's copy of their *Fifty Comedies and Tragedies* (London, 1679; Sealts 53), p. 149, are worded accurately in P and PT except for the substitution of "we" for "I", "fear" for "fears", and "little" for "title-". NN corrects the second of these, restoring "fears", assuming that a copyist or compositor overlooked Melville's final "s", which is often indistinct. The other two may be Melville's deliberate changes, although, as Eddy points out ("Melville's Response to Beaumont and Fletcher," p. 376), "little" may be a compositorial error Melville missed in proofreading.

144.38 sheltered] This is a further unemendable error in P and PT due to Melville's misapplication of Colnett (see the discussion at 144.2). Von Hagen (pp. 104–5) comments, "If Melville had actually been to the island of Barrington, he would have instantly seen that that island is not sheltered, as he says 'from all winds by the high land of Albemarle,' for Barrington is almost out of sight of Albemarle and a good fifty miles from its eastern side."

145.7 a sentimental voyager] The textual accuracy of the whole passage in quotation marks cannot be verified because it is a pseudo-quotation Melville spun from a quite unsentimental passage by Colnett (see p. 603 above).

146.1 nails] NN corrects "sails" (the reading in P and PT) to "nails", as done in Elizabeth Shaw Melville's copy of *The Piazza Tales,* now in the John Hay Library of Brown University. The Colnett source passage cited in the discussion at 145.7 mentions "nails", which would have been used by "the ship's carpenter and cooper" and would not have rotted as sails would have. (Other corrections written by Mrs. Melville in that copy—corrections that would have to be made in any case—are "Rodondo" for "Rotondo" at 134.1 and "severed" for "served" at 185.29.)

146.19 SEVENTH] P numbered no sketch as seventh, and numbered as "EIGHTH", "NINTH", "TENTH", and "ELEVENTH" the sketches respectively renumbered by PT (and NN) as "SEVENTH", "EIGHTH", "NINTH", and "TENTH". (The large and small capitals are NN styling.)

146.20 CHARLES'] NN keeps the copy-text (P) form with "s' " in this word in eleven instances (here, and at 146.33, 147.9,10,26, 148.28, 149.19,31, 150.4,21, 151.19) because there is no way to tell whether the change in PT to "s's" (in all these instances) was made by Melville or by an editor or compositor. On the one hand, the fact that the change in this word in effect imposed an overall "s's" consistency on PT, where P had been inconsistent ("Charles's" appears in P at 142.24, 164.38, 170.3, 171.38; "James's" at 141.33, 142.2,20, 172.27; and "Oberlus's" at 162.34, 168.17,19), suggests a concern uncharacteristic of Melville. On the other hand, the prominence of the word "Charles' " in this sketch may have caught his attention and led him to make the change, especially if the "s' " form in P was not his own in the first place. Examples in his manuscript letters and journals occur both ways, but more often with "s' " (e.g., "St. Thomas' ", "Bacchus' ", "Hayes' ", "Keats' "), including "Charle's", where the misplaced apostrophe indicates a one-syllable pronunciation.

146.21–27 *So . . . warmd.*] NN keeps, as Melville's deliberate changes, the P and PT readings at two points of verbal difference from Spenser's text in these lines from *The Faerie Queene* (II.IX.xiii.1–7): "So" for "loe" at 146.21 (if Melville wrote "Lo", a copyist or compositor misread it as the more common word because his capital "L" and "S" were similar—Leyda, in *Complete Stories,* pp. xiv–xv, assumes this misreading, and "Sais" was misread "Lais" in Chapter 76 of *Moby-Dick);* and "him" for "them" at 146.22. This passage is otherwise accurate in wording, as is the next epigraph (146.29–32), from Spenser's "Prosopopoia" (lines 155–58). However, two P spellings in the first epigraph may not have been Melville's: "round" (146.22) for "rownd" in Anderson's Spenser (see the discussion at 162.20–31); and "warmd" (146.27), which follows Spenser's spelling, unlike the three rhyming words above, where P supplies the "e" (Melville perhaps intended consistency one way or the other).

146.37 Peru . . . Cuba] Several unemendable (because too likely intentional) factual errors occur here and in Melville's ensuing account of the "certain Creole adventurer", as von Hagen (pp. 106–7) reports: " . . . Peru, save in the days of the Spanish Viceroys, never had sovereignty over the Galapagos Islands. . . . I could easily identify the 'Dog-King' . . . , none other than General José Villamil who was, indeed, a creole although he was not born in Cuba, but in New Orleans, and who fought not for Peru, but for Ecuador in 1810 in its War of Independence."

147.2 itself] NN adopts, as Melville's, three PT alterations of P references to Peru as feminine: from "herself" to "itself" here, and from "she" to "Peru" and from "her" to "its" in the next sentence (147.4). Perhaps Melville's original equation in P of a feminine Peru with a "gentleman" struck him later as awkward; in *Omoo* (chap. 76; NN290.10) he apparently changed "whalemen" to "whalers" for a like reason.

151.3–7 *"At . . . evermore."*] This quotation accurately follows the wording of *The Faerie Queene* (II.XII.xxvii.5–9), except that "woman" is substituted for "maiden" (151.4). Possibly Melville intended to follow Spenser's spelling "lowd" at 151.7; see the discussion at 162.20–31.

151.8–14 *"Black . . . tree."*] As printed in P and PT, this passage from Thomas Chatterton's *Ælla* ("The Mynstrelles Songe" at I.82–83 in Melville's edition [Sealts 137]—the passage is unmarked) has been somewhat modernized; it also has these substitutions and mistranslations: "eye" for "cryne" (hair) and "midnight sky" for "wyntere nyghte" at 151.8; "neck" for "rode" (complexion) and "driven" for "sommer" at 151.9; "red" for "rodde" and "cheek" for "face" at 151.10; "cold" for "cale" and "ground" for "grave" at 151.11; and "cactus" for "wyllowe" at 151.14. NN accepts the modernization and all these P and PT readings as Melville's. At one point PT differs in wording from P, adding "ys" (with no word space) after "death-bed," at the end of the sixth line (151.13). NN rejects this addition because "ys" does not belong in Chatterton's line, upsets the meter with an added syllable, spoils the rhyme, alters the meaning pointlessly, and intrudes a single old spelling into the modernized text. Melville cannot have wanted to add "ys" to this line. Possibly, wanting to substitute "ys" for the modernized "is" of P in the preceding line, he wrote "ys" on his printer's copy and the PT compositor put it in the wrong line. (So Jay Leyda suggested, but mistakenly wrote "hys" for "ys," in *Complete Stories*, p. xv n.) If so, Melville (having by the time he revised P for PT given away his old-spelling edition of Chatterton—see p. 605) either remembered the "ys" spelling or had another old-spelling text at hand.

151.15–18 *"Each . . . dead."*] These lines, which accurately follow the wording of the last stanza of William Collins's "Dirge in Cymbeline," are not in P; clearly Melville added them to his printer's copy for PT. Melville owned the Cooke edition of *The Poetical Works of William Collins* (London, 1796), where the passage—unmarked—is on p. 16 (Sealts 464).

151.19 sequestered] Another unemendable (because presumably deliberate) factual error. Von Hagen (p. 108) comments: "Norfolk Island . . . instead of being 'sequestered from the rest,' is in the center of the archipelago, as a cursory glance at a Galapagos map will show. Melville in attempting to fit a story to each of the islands he has named in the last sentence of Sketch Fourth, has taken considerable geographical and chronological license, yet since the *Encantadas* is not a *Baedeker*, the matter is of no great importance." See also the discussions at 144.2 and 146.37.

151.27 on] P and PT read "turned her heel"; NN emends to the usual idiom, as at 161.32–33, assuming that the omission of "on" was a scribal or compositorial oversight.

152.34 Chola] NN emends the P and PT reading "Cholo" as a misreading because in each other instance (including the sketch's title) Melville uses the feminine "Chola" for Hunilla. Grammatically the word is a noun here in apposition to "woman" and "Hunilla".

154.19 bluely] NN adopts the PT adverbial form "bluely" (modifying "boundless") for P's adjectival "bluey" (modifying "sea") because the P reading is so likely a misreading of Melville's handwriting; in "The River," a rejected manuscript passage from *The Confidence-Man,* occurs the phrase "the bluffs sweep bluely away," where Melville's scrawled "bluely" could be misread as "bluey" (see the reproduction in the Northwestern-Newberry Edition, pp. 496–97, line 31).

160.32 tortoise] NN adopts the PT change to the singular, as presumably Melville's correction of the P plural, which had more than one tortoise being carried, contrary to his emphasis all along (e.g., just above, 159.38–160.3) on their great magnitude.

162.14–16 The . . . cross.] Somewhere in this sentence part of Melville's original wording was lost through "omission of a few words" (from either the fair-copy manuscript or the proofs) by Charles F. Briggs, the *Putnam's* editor, without consulting him; see above, pp. 605–6.

162.20–31 *"That . . . abouts."*] In this epigraph from *The Faerie Queene* (I.IX.xxxv.1–9, I.IX.xxxvi.1–3), NN emends two of the words in P and PT, changing "grouen" to "growen" (162.23) and "reads" (which makes no sense) to Spenser's "was" (162.30). As to "grouen", Melville would have no reason to substitute it for Spenser's spelling "growen": probably his copyist or compositor misread his "growen" as "grouen" because his medial "w" as usual lacked a distinct final ascending stroke and so looked like "u". (See the comments on "round"/"rownd" at 146.21–27 and "loud"/"lowd" at 151.3–7; in those two instances NN does not emend to Spenser's spelling because the modernization may have been Melville's.) NN retains, as Melville's deliberate changes, three further substantive variants in P and PT: "glen" for "cave" at 162.20; "the" for "his" at 162.28; and "garments" for "garment" at 162.29. The reading "griesly" (for "griesie") at 162.23 is chief among the substantive variants that identify the Spenser text Melville used as one based on Upton's (1758), such as Anderson's (see above, p. 605).

169.32 1st] NN emends the P and PT "2d" to correct the reference, as noted by Thomas, p. 433, n. 5.

170.10–13 *"And . . . been."*] In these lines from *The Faerie Queene* (I.IX.xxxiv.1–4), "knotty" (170.12) appears in P and PT for Spenser's "rocky". Although "rocky" in Melville's hand might be misread as "knotty", the latter makes sense enough to be a change he introduced. (In this same line, a PT compositorial error Melville overlooked omits Spenser's "the" before "ragged".)

171.1 ports, the] Melville's handwriting apparently led a copyist or compositor to capitalize "the" (and thus to put a period after "ports"), so that "ports. The" is the reading in P. But the resulting fragment is not characteristic of Melville, and, whoever made the change in PT to lowercase "the" (with a comma after "ports"), the PT reading is probably what Melville meant and is adopted here.

172.3 watering-place] NN accepts this alteration in PT of the P reading "watery place", which probably resulted from Melville's indistinct "ing" that could be misread as a "y". Accepting this PT change does not, however, necessitate accepting PT's elimination of "for" following "seeking" in the same sentence; "seeking for" is perfectly idiomatic, and "for" was more likely lost by the compositor's negligence than Melville's revision (given other such careless omissions in PT).

172.33–34 "Here . . . death."] Though neither P nor PT distinguishes this sentence typographically as the *verbatim* "inscription over a grave" that seems to be doubly introduced (by lines 25–26 and by the preceding clause in lines 31–33), Melville may have meant it to be so printed (like the concluding epitaph), since he adapted it from Porter's *Journal* (I, 221–22; see Thomas, pp. 446–47), where the lieutenant's death in a duel is told and the "inscription over his tomb" is so displayed. "Aged twenty-one" is part of Porter's phrasing, but the terse Melvillean phrase "attaining his majority in death" is substituted for the commonplace four-line tribute Porter records. Assuming that Melville meant the phrase, and the sentence, to be read as epitaphic rather than as an authorial comment, NN adds the quotation marks and changes the P and PT period after "grave" to a colon (as did Raymond Weaver, in *Shorter Novels of Herman Melville*, p. 225). (For other examples of missing quotation marks, see pp. 563–64.)

173.9 Chatham] A tempting emendation of "Chatham" to "Charles's" (or "Charles' ") is offered by the fact (noted by von Hagen, p. 112) that Melville's freely adapted direct source for the epitaph (see Thomas, p. 442) was Porter, whose *Journal* (I, 163–64) reports finding the epitaph on Charles Island, not Chatham. No use of the changed location is made by Melville that could not have been made of Charles, where the "bleak gorge" and sailor's grave might belong equally well. Furthermore, in Melville's handwriting "Charles's" (or "Charles' ") might be misread as "Chatham"—perhaps even more readily by Melville himself than by a copyist or compositor who might not have "Chatham" in mind. But not to emend seems best, given Melville's other free translocations (see the discussions at 142.21, 144.2, 146.37, and 151.19).

EMENDATIONS. *125.16 *recure*] NN; secure P, PT 126.19 unpleasurable] PT; unpleasureable P 127.5 *iguana*] NN; *aguano* P, PT 127.8 Atacama] NN; Aracama P, PT 127.36 ninety] PT; thirty P 128.38 wicked] PT; wrecked P *129.33 Memento ****"] NN; Memento * * * * * " P, PT 130.11 *entrall.*] NN; ~∧ P, PT *130.14 *not these*] NN; not there P, PT *130.19 *Tethys'*] NN; Zethy's P, PT *131.32 three∧walled] NN; ~-~ P, PT *133.6 *Forthy*] NN; For they P, PT *133.14 *base*] PT; vase P 134.27 uniform] PT; uni/form P 135.8 tree;] PT; tree· P 135.33 albatross] PT; albatros P 137.25 Pole] PT; Poles P 137.26 Equator.] PT; ~, P 138.34 on] PT; no P 139.10 Da] NN; De P, PT 139.14 circuitous] PT; dircuitous P 139.34 headland] PT; head-/lands P *140.1 neighbors] PT; neighbours P 140.2 neighborhood:] PT; neighbourhood. P *140.3 ∃] NN; *[not present]* P; ╓╖ PT 140.37 whilst] PT;

whilt P 140.38 broke] PT; looked P 141.33 spine] PT; spire P *142.17 not] NN; *[not present]* P, PT *143.21 northward] NN; westward P, PT 143.38 Colnett] NN; Colnet P, PT *143.38 1793] NN; 1798 P, PT *144.8 *hold in*] NN; hold on P, PT *144.11 *Where-so*] NN; Where—so P; Whereso PT *144.14 *fears*] NN; fear P, PT *146.1 nails] NN; sails P, PT *146.19 SEVENTH] PT; EIGHTH P *147.2 itself] PT; herself P 147.4 Peru] PT; she P 147.4 its] PT; her P 148.1 tortoises] PT; an inexhaustible tribe of tortoises, P 148.1 their] PT; the adventurer's P 149.1 Pretorians] PT; Pretorians of the Roman state P 149.1–2 Roman state] PT; commonwealth P 150.22 Mate] PT; mate P 151.1 EIGHTH] PT; NINTH P *151.15–18 *"Each . . . dead."*] PT; *[not present]* P *151.27 on] NN; *[not present]* P, PT *152.34 Chola] NN; Cholo P, PT 153.28–29 unstable] PT; unstabled P *154.19 bluely] PT; bluey P 154.28 bower] PT; tower P 154.31 how] PT; *[not present]* P 156.28 a sane] PT; one sane P 156.29 a hope] PT; another P 156.30 he reads] PT; he does read P 159.35 sandy] PT; Sandy P 160.8 landing.] PT; landing; memory keeps not in all things to the order of occurrence. P *160.32 tortoise] PT; tortoises P 160.39 peeled] PT; pealed P 161.10 rack] PT; rock P 162.18 NINTH] PT; TENTH P *162.23 *growen*] NN; grouen P, PT *162.30 *was*] NN; reads P, PT 165.28 commands] PT; demands P 167.15 Emperor] PT; Emperors, P 168.26 my] PT; *[not present]* P 169.32 1st] NN; 2d P, PT 170.8 TENTH] PT; ELEVENTH P *171.1 ports,] PT; ~. P *171.1 the] PT; The P *172.3 watering-place] PT; watery place P *172.33 grave:] NN; ~. P, PT *172.33 "Here] NN; ‸~ P, PT *172.34 death."] NN; ~.‸ P, PT

HYPHENATION. I. 128.6 whalemen 132.36 foreheads 135.2 red-robbin 136.7 seaman's 136.23 gold-fish 137.1 light-house 137.10 main-royal-/man 138.8 †overhanging 138.30 headlands 139.31 headland 141.7 foremast 141.22 glass-works 141.23 chimney-stacks 143.7 foam-lashed 143.33 tortoise-hunting 145.22 dwelling-houses 146.14 seat-builders 148.15 sportsman's 148.19 dog-regiment 150.7 shipwrecked 152.15 handkerchief 153.29 shipwreck 154.8 overset 154.23 smooth-flowing 155.9 withheld 155.24 †spell-bound 156.29 cat-like 159.23 hay-rick 159.27 night-skies 159.29 weather-stained 159.29 upright 160.21 daybreak 160.38 hour-glass 162.5 heart-strings 163.10 whalemen 168.25 ill-treated 169.22 sun-burnt 170.9 GRAVE-STONES 171.11 tortoise-hunting 171.24 outright 172.17 post-offices 172.17 †post-offices 172.34 twenty-one

II. 127.12 clinker-bound 134.4 sea-tower 135.1 terra-firma 136.20 honey-comb 139.38 chimney-stack 149.39 lurking-place 152.35 new-wedded 155.24 †spell-bound 156.40 self-same 157.37 whale-boats 161.2 cross-foot 163.20 night-wind 168.20 half-mildewed 172.17 †post-offices 173.5 good-natured

SUBSTANTIVE VARIANTS. 125.3 By . . . Tarnmoor] P; *[not present]* PT 127.36 ninety] PT; thirty P 128.38 wicked] PT; wrecked P 132.31 fungous] P; fungus PT 133.14 *base*] PT; vase P 136.18 winged∧ life∧clouding] P; ~, ~-~ PT 136.18–19 on . . . saw] P; *[not present]* PT 137.25 Pole] PT; Poles P 137.34 isles] P; isles of PT 138.21 unworthy] P; unworthy of PT 138.34 on] PT; no P 139.13 influence] P; influences PT 139.34 headland] PT; headlands P 140.3 ∃] NN; *[not present]* P; ⊓ PT 140.38 broke] PT; looked P 141.33 spine] PT; spire P 144.11 *Where-so*] NN; Where—so P; Whereso PT 146.19 SEVENTH] PT; EIGHTH P 147.2 itself] PT; herself P 147.4 Peru] PT; she P 147.4 its] PT; her P 148.1 tortoises] PT; an inexhaustible tribe of tortoises P 148.1 their] PT; the adventurer's P 149.1 Pretorians] PT; Pretorians of the Roman state P 149.1–2 Roman state] PT; commonwealth P 151.1 EIGHTH] PT; NINTH P 151.13 *death-bed,*] P; death-bed,ys PT 151.15–18 *"Each . . . dead."*] PT; *[not present]* P 151.22 strongest] P; strangest PT 153.28–29 unstable] PT; unstabled P 154.19 bluely] PT; bluey P 154.28 bower] PT; tower P 154.31 how] PT; *[not present]* P 155.7 our] P; her PT 155.16 offices] P; office PT 155.24 wandered] P; wandering PT 156.28 a sane] PT; one sane P 156.29 a hope] PT; another P 156.30 he reads] PT; he does read P 158.9 farther] P; further PT 160.8 landing.] PT; landing; memory keeps not in all things to the order of occurrence. P 160.32 tortoise] PT; tortoises P 160.39 peeled] PT; pealed P 161.10 rack] PT; rock P 162.18 NINTH] PT; TENTH P 163.15 a] P; *[not present]* PT 165.28 commands] PT; demands P 167.15 Emperor] PT; Emperors P 167.21 secret] P; secrete PT 168.26 my] PT; *[not present]* P 170.8 TENTH] PT; ELEVENTH P 170.12 *the*] P; *[not present]* PT 170.31 woods] P; wood PT 171.32 injecting] P; injected PT 172.2 for] P; *[not present]* PT 172.3 watering-place] PT; watery place P 172.4 hermit] P; a hermit PT 172.19 bottle] P; a bottle PT

THE BELL-TOWER (pp. 174–87)

NN copy-text: the anonymous first printing, "The Bell-Tower," in *Putnam's Monthly Magazine* [P], VI, no. 32 (August, 1855), 123–30. Emendations from *The Piazza Tales* (1856), pp. 401–31 [PT]: at 21 points. NN emendations to P: at 19 points. (Principles for emendation are stated on pp. 549–64.) No known manuscript, and no later authoritative printing (see p. 619 below) in Melville's lifetime. NN printer's copy: an emended photocopy of Newberry Library A5.765. Sight collations of P against PT: Newberry A5.765 *vs.* M66–2471–61; Northwestern 051P99 *vs.* M66–2471–58; M69–316–19 *vs.* M68–1397. Machine collations between copies of P: Newberry A5.765 *vs.* Northwestern 051P99 and M69–316–19; M69–316–19 *vs.* University of Chicago AP2P95. Machine collations between copies of PT: M66–2471–60 *vs.* Gift M67–18 and M66–2471–61; M66–2472–61 *vs.* Newberry Y255M515.

"The Bell-Tower" was probably composed during the early months of 1855. Melville must have submitted it to *Putnam's* by mid-June of that year, when Joshua A. Dix of Dix & Edwards forwarded it to George William Curtis, his manuscript adviser, for consideration along with other contributions. On June 18, Curtis wrote Dix that Melville's piece had "*not* passed muster," but the next day, after "looking again," he reported that he had become "converted" and recommended that, "making some erasures, we cannot afford to lose it": Dix should accept the piece in spite of its style, seemingly "artificial" and "self-conscious" but still "well-suited to the theme," since the story is "picturesque & of a profound morality," "rich in treatment," and with "the touch of genius in it." Dix & Edwards paid promptly upon publication, and Melville's letter of August 7, 1855, acknowledged receipt of $37.50 for his "article."

In "The Bell-Tower" Melville alludes both to classical mythology (the Titans, Vulcan, Prometheus) and to the Old Testament (Anak, Babel, Shinar, Shadrach, Haman, Deborah, Sisera, Shiloh, Jael, "the Six Days' Work"). Egbert S. Oliver, in the Hendricks House edition of *The Piazza Tales,* pp. 249–50, points out that Spenser's Una "is generally understood as representing truth" while Melville's has an "ambiguous, enigmatic smile" and observes that the Talus of *The Faerie Queene* (V.I.xii) is an "yron man"

> Who in his hand an yron blade did hould,
> With which he thresht out falshood, and did truth unfould.

Gerard M. Sweeney, in "Melville's Hawthornian Bell-Tower: A Fairy-Tale Source," *American Literature,* XLV (May, 1973), 279–85, adds Pierre Bayle's *Dictionary* (on Albertus and Agrippa), Mary Shelley's *Frankenstein,* and Ahab as man-maker in *Moby-Dick* as possible influences on Melville's conception of Talus and his creator. But he emphasizes the influence of

"Talus, the Man of Brass," an obstacle encountered by Theseus in Hawthorne's "The Minotaur" in his *Tanglewood Tales,* which Melville's son Malcolm received on January 1, 1854. Robert E. Morsberger, in "Melville's 'The Bell-Tower' and Benvenuto Cellini," *American Literature,* XLIV (November, 1972), 459–62, associates the casting of the bell by Bannadonna with two episodes in Cellini's *Life.*

Some differences in wording between the P and PT texts of "The Bell-Tower" are recognizable as Melville's own changes. But others are not, including the two most interesting ones—the omission of his three epigraphs and of his odd concluding footnote; while either or both may be his own excisions, they may be wounds ("erasures" in Curtis's chilling phrase quoted above) by an editorial hand. Or still a third possibility is that either or both of these passages were omitted by printing-house error, standing exposed as they did at the two ends of the tale (the P footnote unkeyed to the text above, and separated from it by the beginning of a new article), and both calling for a two-step compositorial handling separate from that of the main text—that is, first setting them in smaller type and then inserting them into the text, either of which steps would be easy to forget about (as the west-facing capital "E" was forgotten in making up the "Encantadas" in P—see the discussion at 140.3; cf. that at 125.3).

Two later printings of the piece during Melville's lifetime follow the 1856 text and show no evidence of further authorial changes: Rossiter Johnson, *Little Classics. Third Volume: Tragedy* (Boston: James R. Osgood and Co., 1875), pp. 122–48; and Edmund C. Stedman and Ellen M. Hutchinson, *A Library of American Literature from the Earliest Settlement to the Present Time* (11 vols.; New York: Charles L. Webster & Co., 1887–90), VII (1889), 464–76. Partial collations of the 1856 text against these printings have been made as follows: M68–1922 *vs.* Gift M66–78 (Johnson); M68–1922 *vs.* Newberry Y209.84 (Stedman and Hutchinson).

For explanation of the following tabulations, see pp. 565–70.

DISCUSSIONS. 174.2–6 *"Like . . . MS.*] These epigraphs, like the quotation in the "Extracts" in *Moby-Dick* similarly labeled *"From 'Something' unpublished",* are evidently by Melville himself, and therefore no external source exists with which to compare their texts. (On the omission of these epigraphs in PT, see the headnote above.)

174.8 mould] Here and at 175.36 NN follows PT rather than P ("mold"), for reasons offered in the discussion at 46.14 in "Benito Cereno."

175.11 air] Although the PT omission of "the" (the P reading is "in the air") may be a compositorial slip, it seems more likely to be Melville's revision for literary effect. (The phrase "in air" occurs again in the next paragraph, at 175.19.)

176.37 height] NN follows PT rather than P ("hight"), for reasons offered in the discussion at 50.13 in "Benito Cereno."

177.6 conceded] NN lets go the plausible P reading "concealed" and adopts the PT reading "conceded"—which makes so much better sense as to be among the two or three happiest examples of Melville's restoration in PT of words misread by his copyist or the P compositor. The adjective in P, "concealed", merely repeats the idea that Bannadonna was hiding behind "the . . . mysteries of his art"; whereas "conceded" in PT brings into play Melville's (otherwise lost) real point that Bannadonna was hiding behind mysteries that even such powerful patrons *conceded* to such an artist (his "trade secrets"), until he saw fit to unveil his product. For other good examples of Melville's restorative touch, see p. 556; two earlier instances in "The Bell-Tower" are "submersion" for "submission" (174.22) and "inspirited" for "inspired" (175.9).

179.10 first time] PT's omission of "time" is an indifferent change in the idiom, possibly Melville's, but possibly not; both forms occur in his writings. Cf. the discussion at 63.12–13.

179.12 Del Fonca] Melville is more likely inventing than garbling the painter and the painting—no such have been located.

179.30 then——.] The period (in both P and PT) after a dash indicating interruption is unusual enough to tempt emendation, but its use twice more below (180.11,37) shows that it is not a mere slip.

182.8 startled] PT substitutes a more common synonym ("started") for the P reading "startled", but Webster (1848) enters "startle" as an intransitive verb (citing Addison). The *OED*, while labeling its intransitive use obsolete or rare, cites examples from Lamb and Talfourd. Given Curtis's editorial comment (p. 618 above) on the tale's "seemingly artificial" and "self-conscious" style, an editor must hesitate to adopt as Melville's the reduction of such a fine old literary word to a commonplace one. (But cf. 8.39, 65.39, and 179.6.)

183.40 degree] This PT word achieves the sense inexactly stated by the P reading "amount"; while Curtis may have made this precisionist change (along with his "erasures"), Melville's own hand seems more likely at work in such instances, as his surviving manuscripts show, with their abundance of similar small revisions.

184.13 Magnus] NN corrects the reading "Magus" in P and PT because even if Melville himself, not a copyist or compositor, blundered into that error—and even though he overlooked it in his corrections for PT—he can scarcely have intended to misspell the well-known philosopher's Latin epithet.

185.29 severed] The PT reading "served" is an example of the gross compositorial substitution of a contextually almost senseless word for the author's precise one; compare the less palpable substitution in P (whoever did it) of "concealed" for "conceded" at 177.6. (See also the discussion at 146.1.)

187.3 fall.*] NN keeps the footnote omitted in PT (possibly by Melville, possibly by someone else) and supplies the asterisk P lacked to key the footnote to the text, after the last word being probably the most appropriate point. On the reason for keeping this and other such elements omitted by PT, see p. 619 above and p. 553.

EMENDATIONS. *174.8 mould] PT; mold P 174.14 which . . . prostration] PT; *[not present]* P 174.16 tree-top] PT; tree-top, when unabased P 174.22 submersion] PT; submission P 175.2 but] PT; but like P 175.2 rocket] PT; mountain rocket P 175.3 would depart] PT; had departed P 175.9 inspirited] PT; inspired P *175.11 air] PT; the air P 175.30 structures∧] PT; ~, P 175.31 dell'] NN; del∧ P, PT 175.31 ∧Orologio] NN; 'Orologio P, PT 175.36 mould] PT; mold P *176.37 height] PT; hight P 177.5 recompense] PT; compense P *177.6 conceded] PT; concealed P 177.18 however∧] PT; ~, P 177.18 insignificant,] PT; ~∧ P 178.12 Eccellenza] NN; Excellenza P, PT (The same correction is also made at 178.27, 179.21,31,35, 180.8,13,16,19,21,27,29.) 178.30 Una] PT; Unas P 178.30 Dua's] PT; Duas P 180.32 Signore] NN; Signor P, PT 180.38 Signore] NN; Signor P, PT 181.1 Signore] NN; Signor P, PT 182.4 soldiers] PT; solders P *183.40 degree] PT; amount P *184.13 Magnus] NN; Magus P, PT 185.24 figures] PT; figures,—Dua and Tra— P *187.3 fall.*] NN; ~.∧ P, PT

HYPHENATION. I. 174.7 once-frescoed 175.27 clock-work 176.39 blacksmith 177.13 withdrawn 177.33 workman's 178.31 To-morrow 184.33 vice-bench 186.6 upspringing 186.8 †post-mortem 186.16 bell-ringer 186.33 superstructure 186.37 overthrown

II. 177.13 cross-threads 177.15 lattice-work 178.8 hand-in-hand 182.17 dragon-beetle's 184.19 vain-glorious 185.19 four-and-twenty 185.26 four-and-twenty 186.8 †post-mortem

SUBSTANTIVE VARIANTS. 174.2–6 *"Like . . . MS.*] P; *[not present]* PT 174.14 which . . . prostration] PT; *[not present]* P 174.16 tree-top] PT; tree-top, when unabased P 174.22 submersion] PT; submission P 175.2 but] PT; but like P 175.2 rocket] PT; mountain rocket P 175.3 would depart] PT; had departed P 175.9 inspirited] PT; inspired P 175.11 air] PT; the air P 177.5 recompense] PT; compense P

177.6 conceded] PT; concealed P 178.30 Una] PT; Unas P 178.30 Dua's] PT; Duas P 179.10 time] P; *[not present]* PT 180.35 look] P; walk PT 182.8 startled] P; started PT 183.40 degree] PT; amount P 185.24 figures] PT; figures,—Dua and Tra— P 185.29 severed] P; served PT 187.2 that] P; the PT 187.4–6 *It . . . occur.] P; *[not present]* PT

FRAGMENTS FROM A WRITING DESK (pp. 191–204)

NN copy-text: the first printing, "Fragments from a Writing Desk," over the initials "L. A. V.", in the Lansingburgh, New York, *Democratic Press, and Lansingburgh Advertiser* [DP], II, no. 17 (May 4, 1839), p. 1, cols. 4–6, and no. 19 (May 18, 1839), pp. 1, cols. 3–6, and 2, col. 1. No known manuscript; one later printing in Melville's lifetime (see below). NN emendations to DP: at 75 points. Two emendations from the later printing. (Principles for emendation are stated on pp. 549–64.) NN printer's copy: an emended photocopy of DP in the Troy, New York, Public Library. Numerous independent sight collations between photocopies and the original cited newsprints of the sketches in the Troy, New York, Public Library and those in the Melville Collection of The Houghton Library of Harvard University (see below). No other copies of DP with these dates are listed in *American Newspapers 1821–1936,* ed. Winifred Gregory (New York, 1937), or are currently known.

On May 8, 1839, "Fragment No. 1" was printed in the West Troy, New York, *West Troy Advocate, and Watervliet Advertiser* [WTA], II, no. 31, p. 1, cols. 2–5, from the same setting of type but with the heading "For the West Troy Advocate", the "No. 1" dropped, and "Lansingburgh" (193.6) changed to "West Troy". Collations show that the WTA text (at the New York State Library) varies at several other points from the examined copies of DP: there is a comma after "Prophet" at 195.31, the word "comfortable" (192.8) is spelled correctly, the comma after "divinity" (195.36) is missing, and various line-end hyphens are different, either in printing clearly or failing to print. Copies of DP are known to vary among themselves (the first part of the quotation mark at 194.38 is missing in the Troy copy but present in the Harvard copies), and it is possible that all these non-substantive variants in the WTA text also appeared in some copies of DP. The correct spelling of "comfortable" would be supplied by NN in any case, and the comma at 195.31 is also adopted, on the grounds that it was more likely present in the DP standing type than supplied by a compositor for WTA.

The *Democratic Press* items at Harvard—a clipping of each "Fragment" and the first "Fragment" in a complete copy of the May 4 number—are all annotated in ink "By Herman Melville", by Elizabeth Shaw Melville. Along the inner fold of the complete May 4 number Melville wrote at some early date the following note in ink, probably addressed to his brother Gansevoort: "When I woke up this morning, what the Devel should I see but your cane along in bed with me / I shall keep it for you when you come up here again".

At least one of the "Fragments" was written before a notice from the *Democratic Press* editor, W. J. Lamb, appeared in the number for April 20, 1839 (p. 2, col. 1): "*To Correspondents.* The communication of 'L. A. V.' is received. An interview with the writer is requested." No other contributions after April 20 are signed "L. A. V."; on June 5 Melville sailed from New York for Liverpool and was not in Lansingburgh until the following October.

On twentieth-century printings and discussion of the "Fragments," see pp. 542–43 above. The *West Troy Advocate* printing of "Fragment No. 1" was discovered by Hershel Parker in September, 1986.

For explanation of the following tabulations, see pp. 565–70.

DISCUSSIONS. 192.33 "dazzled . . . upon."] Quotation unidentified.

193.19–28 "When . . . combined."] From Part II of Thomas Campbell's "The Pleasures of Hope," lines 73–82, perhaps taken from an edition owned by Melville's mother (Sealts 118): *The Pleasures of Hope and Other Poems* (New York: Longworth, 1811), p. 45. The only substantive variation ("in" for the source's "on" in line 75) is emended as more likely a misreading of Melville's handwriting than his intended change. Of the minor variations in accidentals, NN emends the DP "charmd" by adding the apostrophe that Melville would have had no reason to omit.

193.37 "my . . . Horatio,"] Quoted accurately from *Hamlet,* I.ii.185.

194.25 liveliest] Although in the context of the entire "Fragment" the expected reading would be "loveliest", NN keeps the copy-text reading because it also makes sense.

194.37–38 "Sail . . . bliss."] Quotation unidentified.

195.10 "dark-glancing daughters."] Quoted accurately from Byron, *Childe Harold's Pilgrimage,* I.lix.7.

195.34 "Lap . . . airs"] Quoted accurately from Milton's "L'Allegro," line 136.

196.6 "Effuse . . . beam;"] Quotation unidentified.

196.9–22 "Maid . . . ———."] This quotation from Coleridge's "Genevieve" is accurate in wording except for the omission of "Genevieve" in the first and last lines; there are minor variations in accidentals. For the punctuation missing in DP after the first line NN supplies the exclamation point present in most editions of the poem.

196.27 "counterfeit presentments,"] Cf. *Hamlet,* III.iv.54: "counterfeit presentment". NN corrects the DP misreading "presentiments".

197.13 Certes] "Cerbes" in DP is meaningless; Melville must have written "Certes" here, a word he used later in *Omoo* (chap. 43; NN166.12) and *Mardi* (chap. 67; NN203.11).

197.26 "The . . . over!"] Paraphrased from Edmund Burke's *Reflections on the Revolution in France,* or perhaps, as Gilman suggests *(Melville's Early Life,* p. 360, n. 4), from a reference to Burke in Byron's *Childe Harold's Pilgrimage.*

200.13 darkning] NN keeps this DP reading as Melville's likely poetic contraction of "darkening".

200.17 "my . . . going."] Paraphrased from Sheridan's *The Rivals,* V.iii.

200.19 actually] The DP "actual" may have resulted from Melville's frequent failure to form the terminal "-ly" clearly.

200.40–201.1 complacency . . . brooked] Although the subject of "brooked" would usually be a person, no emendation is made in this phrase because "complacency" as its subject is acceptable.

202.4 filled up] This DP reading makes such loose sense that the intended reading may have been "fitted up".

202.36–38 "See . . . cheek!"] From *Romeo and Juliet,* II.ii.23–25, with "kiss" substituted for "touch" and minor variations in accidentals.

203.22 single one] NN supplies "one", though possibly its omission in DP was then idiomatic.

EMENDATIONS. 191.10 huge-clasped] NN; hugh-/clasped DP 191.13 protege] NN; protage DP 191.18 *mauvaise*] NN; *mauvese* DP 191.20 appellations] NN; appelations DP 192.1 modeled] NN; moddeled DP 192.8 comfortable] WTA; cnmfortable DP 192.27 tapping] NN; taping DP 192.28 finally] NN; finaly DP 192.36 obeisance] NN; obesiance DP 193.3 unwittingly] NN; unwitingly DP 193.4 although∧] NN; ~, DP 193.6 this] NN; This DP 193.10 flitting] NN; fliting DP 193.11 embellishments] NN; embelishments DP *193.21 on] NN; in DP *193.22 charm'd] NN; charmd DP 193.29 Apelles] NN; Appeles DP 193.32 beau-ideal] NN; beau' idieal DP 193.39 sylvan] NN; sylvian DP 194.7 ruddy] NN; rudy DP 194.7 illumine] NN; ilumine DP 194.17 nevertheless] NN; neverthelcss DP 194.32 the least] NN; least DP 194.35 attribute] NN; atribute DP 194.36 which] NN; whieh DP 195.4 fancy.] NN; ~,

DP 195.5 Venus] NN; Uenus DP 195.15 la∧] NN; la' DP 195.15 Madonna] NN; Madona DP 195.19 noon] NN; noou DP 195.20 altars] NN; alters DP 195.25 splendid] NN; splended DP 195.31 Prophet,] WTA; ~∧ DP 195.31 roses] NN; roees DP 196.2 Cinderella's] NN; Cindrella's DP *196.9 sweet ——!] NN; ~——∧ DP 196.19 of] NN; ef DP *196.27 presentments] NN; presentiments DP 196.31 smiles] NN; smiies DP *197.13 Certes] NN; Cerbes DP 197.20 incontinently] NN; incentinently DP 197.25 thought] NN; thougnt DP 197.34 fugitive] NN; fugative DP 198.9 fatuus] NN; fatus DP 198.12 denouement] NN; denowment DP 198.19 precautions] NN; precations DP 198.20 periodical] NN; periodicel DP 198.22 courteous] NN; courtious DP 198.24 unperceived] NN; unperceiued DP 198.37 outgeneraled] NN; outgenerald DP 199.25 pursued] NN; persued DP 200.3 dusky] NN; duskey DP 200.9 Atlantean] NN; Atlantian DP 200.13 imaginings] NN; immagings DP *200.19 actually] NN; actual DP 200.20 movements] NN; movemements DP 200.22 adventure] NN; adveuture DP 200.28 appearance] NN; apperance DP 200.38 descried] NN; descryed DP 201.10 forbidding] NN; forbiding DP 201.13 thick] NN; thich DP 201.15 apparition] NN; apparation DP 201.25 nerves.] NN; ~[ ] DP 202.6 in] NN; iu DP 202.9 skill] NN; sklll DP 202.12 Psyche] NN; Physche DP 202.19 Chandeliers] NN; Chandeleres DP 202.28 superb] NN; supurb DP 202.28 profusion] NN; profusien DP 202.33 ottoman] NN; ottomon DP 202.36 "See] NN; '~ DP 203.4 transcendant] NN; t[ ]anscendant DP 203.13 fairy-like] NN; farey-like DP *203.22 one] NN; *[not present]* DP 203.31 the golden] NN; The golden DP 203.33 unutterable] NN; unuterable DP 204.7 "Speak] NN; '~ DP

HYPHENATION. I. 191.7 stiff-necked 191.10 huge-clasped 192.30 ill-suppressed 195.25 two-handed
II. 197.14 rose-coloured

ETCHINGS OF A WHALING CRUISE (pp. 205–11)

NN copy-text: Melville's untitled holograph printer's-copy manuscript [HM], now in the Duyckinck Collection, Rare Books and Manuscripts Division, The New York Public Library. First and only printing in Melville's

Leaf 1 (reduced) of Melville's holograph manuscript for "Etchings of a Whaling Cruise," with heading added by Evert A. Duyckinck.

lifetime: anonymous and untitled, in the New York *Literary World* [LW], I, no. 6 (March 6, 1847), 105–6. Collation of NN printer's copy against LW (Newberry Library A5.5292) reveals no authorial variants from HM (there is no evidence that Melville received LW proofs). NN emendations to HM (on principles stated on pp. 549–64): at 129 points. NN printer's copy: a typed transcript of HM thus emended (see p. 537). The title "Etchings of a Whaling Cruise" is supplied by NN. Machine collations between copies of LW: Northwestern L051L773 *vs.* University of Chicago AP2L7118 and Newberry A5.5292; Newberry A5.5292 *vs.* M67–722–108.

Sometime before the *Literary World* began weekly publication on February 6, 1847, its editor, Melville's friend Evert A. Duyckinck, asked him to review J. Ross Browne's *Etchings of a Whaling Cruise.* On February 2, Melville replied that he had "procured the book you spoke of from the Harpers—& shall find much pleasure in making it the basis of an article for your paper." Presumably he wrote the review after he came back to New York from a trip to Washington begun February 4. That he included John Codman's *Sailors' Life and Sailors' Yarns* only as an afterthought, his own or Duyckinck's, is suggested by his not referring to it in the first part of the review, by his ending that part with the formulaic advice to purchase, and by his beginning the second part on the separate Leaf 10 even though the lower third of Leaf 9 was available. Frederick Saunders of Harper & Brothers, Browne's publishers, wrote to Duyckinck on March 19 concerning an "error" in the review:

> Excuse I pray you my seeming interference with your Editorial prerogatives: but having rec^{d} an expostulatory letter from Mr Ross Browne touching your critique on his Whaling Cruise, he begs (Mr Melville)—the writer, to rectify an error, wh. he specified & copy of wh. I handed M^{r} M's brother [Allan Melville] the other day.

No correction was published and no more is known of Browne's objections; R. D. Madison, in "Melville's Review of Browne's *Etchings,*" *Melville Society Extracts,* No. 53 (February, 1983), 11–13, identifies several minor factual errors (the most noticeable Melville's naming as "H———" the man Browne refers to as "W———") and details Melville's "literary embellishments" of Browne's book. Lisa M. Franchetti similarly examines the Codman section of the review in "Exaggeration in Melville's Review of Codman," *Melville Society Extracts,* No. 56 (November, 1983), 4–6 (see the discussion at 236.10 in "Cooper's New Novel" for further evidence of Melville's hasty reading). Melville's note to Duyckinck (at one time fastened to Leaf 1 of the manuscript) and Saunders's letter are both in the Duyckinck Collection.

Willard Thorp first reprinted the review, untitled, in his *Herman Melville: Representative Selections* (New York: American Book Co., 1938), pp. 320–27. But although he had identified the manuscript in a file of unsigned *Literary World* contributions, his text "reproduces that of the first publication" with his comment:

> The copy which Melville furnished the printer was fairly "clean" so the errors are few. These have been corrected from the MS. No attempt has been made, however, to change the punctuation to accord with Melville's style. The usage of the *Literary World* required as many commas as a schoolmaster, but one is, at that, safer in following it than Melville's careless and inconsistent style. (p. 421)

Harrison Hayford and Hershel Parker in their Norton Critical Edition of *Moby-Dick* (New York, 1967), pp. 529–35, though using the manuscript as copy-text and calling attention "to points where we restore for the first time the manuscript reading," did not keep all its erratic punctuation but offered "a slightly normalized reading text." The NN text for the first time follows both the words and punctuation of the manuscript, normalizing only by expanding Melville's "&", "thro' ", and "tho' " (see also the discussion at 210.13).

Melville's initial inscription and all his revisions are in one ink on twelve 32-by-20-cm half-sheet leaves of uniform faintly ruled cream paper; along their left margins the first two are torn, the other ten irregularly scissored. The bibliographical heading at the top of Leaf 1 is in Duyckinck's hand in ink as are the recto notation "Save" and the verso endorsement "Brown's Whaling / Cruise &c / bgs" on Leaf 12. As Hayford and Parker remark (p. 529, n. 1), Melville made few revisions after his initial inscription, but as the MANUSCRIPT ALTERATIONS list below shows, he made numerous changes in wording within the lines as he was inscribing them—whether copying from an earlier draft (as Hayford and Parker suppose) or actually composing the manuscript as the first and final draft. (The latter is possible but unlikely; his surviving manuscripts show that he rarely composed straight off or copied without making such running revisions.) The same is true of the second part of the manuscript, though that is more likely a first draft, since in that part, as Hayford and Parker note, "Melville's handwriting has greatly deteriorated" (p. 535, n. 7).

For explanation of the following tabulations, see pp. 565–70. The LW readings are supplied here for the historical record, not for any authority they carry.

DISCUSSIONS. 205.2–8 *Etchings* . . . 12mo.] Duyckinck, as *Literary World* editor, added this heading, incompletely punctuated, to Melville's manuscript (see reproduction on p. 626, lines 1–7). In LW it was restyled, presumably by the compositor. For convenience NN follows LW.

205.21 Mr] Because this abbreviation (technically a suspension) was often used without a period in the nineteenth century (as it still is in Britain), NN does not supply one for Melville's "M^{r}", which appears throughout his manuscript pieces (but the superscript "r" is lowered as a nontextual matter of typography—see p. 565, n. 32). Cf. the discussion of "St" at 232.19.

205.25 vessels] NN (like LW) emends HM "vessel" to the plural; it seems unlikely that Melville was using a colloquial collective singular (which the *OED* labels obsolete with no example later than 1470).

207.35–36 "A . . . &c"] This quotation in HM is sparsely punctuated: it has no commas with the quotation marks where the speech is internally interrupted, no periods after the three "&c" abbreviations, no terminal period, and no closing quotation mark. Though this lack of punctuation may be due to Melville's carelessness, NN supplies only a closing quotation mark, after the third "&c". This punctuation best serves Melville's intention to suggest that the old gentleman's speech ran on interminably, its words equivalent to the "&c" marks, which thus belong inside the closing quotation mark, without a terminal period. Leaving the "&c" abbreviations with no periods serves the same intended effect. NN supplies no commas where the speech is internally interrupted because the same situation is left unpunctuated often enough in Melville's first printings to show that, unlike paired quotation marks, such commas were not yet established as automatic, even among editors and compositors. However, the LW compositor (or Duyckinck in proof) supplied commas at the interruption, ended the speech after "oppressed" with a comma and quotation mark—thus excluding the "&c"s from the quotation—and punctuated the "&c"s with commas and periods. See Thorp's comment on LW's schoolmasterish commas, p. 628 above; for NN treatment of punctuation around quotations, see p. 564, n.29.

210.12 "Sailors' . . . Sailors'] NN emends HM because Melville's placing the apostrophe before the "s" in the first word and supplying none in the second makes a substantively incorrect citation of the book—not treated by NN as a matter for authorial discretion. See also the emendations at 211.17–18 and p. 560, n.27.

210.13 question".] In accordance with its policy of not imposing consistency (see p. 560, n. 27), NN places punctuation marks inside or outside of closing quotation marks as they appear in the manuscripts. In some cases, however, the punctuation appears directly below the quotation mark. In such cases—and when necessary punctuation is missing, as here and at 240.17 below—NN places the punctuation outside the quotation, since this is the practice Melville used most often when punctuating the manuscript pieces in his own hand and when he added punctuation to Elizabeth Shaw Melville's fair copy of "Hawthorne and His Mosses." See also the discussion at 242.1–12.

210.19 the best] Between these words in the manuscript there is a three-letter word start ("ele" or "cle"), omitted by NN as not beginning any word that fits the context. It was not set by the LW compositor, who evidently took the stain which covers it as canceling it. (Similar stains, with fingerprints, appear in the right margin.)

210.26 esteemed citizen] Both words in the manuscript are poorly formed (see line 4 in the reproduction). For lack of a better, NN follows the conjectural LW reading "esteemed citizen". Apparently the first word begins with an "e", has two or more medial letters, and ends with "ted", but none of these letters is certain. For the second word, "citizen" is only a plausible reading. See the discussion at 211.11 below and p. 550.

Passage (reduced) containing conjectured words "esteemed citizen" in line 4 (NN 210.26)

210.28–29 disciplinarian",] Melville left out the needed comma (supplied in NN as in LW—for NN placement see the discussion at 210.13) probably by oversight when he made the running revision immediately following—see the MANUSCRIPT ALTERATIONS list below.

210.34 noticed?] Although this indirect question would normally end in a period, Melville's punctuation habits are idiosyncratic enough to justify retaining the HM question mark here, as possibly Melville's deliberate emphasis on the interrogative part of the sentence.

211.2 and] NN supplies "and" (where LW supplied a comma) to fill the gap left when Melville inadvertently canceled "&". See the MANUSCRIPT ALTERATIONS list below.

211.5 say—] NN assumes that the run-on conversational style of this passage, punctuated with dashes, justifies the HM omission of a terminal period, despite the following capitalized "Why", which may, but need not be, taken (as by LW, where a period was supplied) to signal a new sentence.

211.7 "quips . . . smiles"] NN keeps the manuscript reading, which adapts lines 27–28 of Milton's "L'Allegro": "Quips, and Cranks, and wanton Wiles, / Nods, and Becks, and wreathed Smiles", in Melville's copy of *The Poetical Works of John Milton* (Boston, 1836), II, 289. The LW correction "quips and cranks and wreathed smiles" was probably Duyckinck's intervention at the proof stage.

211.11 of . . . sympathy] Here the LW compositor gave up trying to decipher Melville's cryptic inscription and printed simply "of sympathy", as did Thorp (p. 327) and also Hayford and Parker, who noted the problem, misconjecturing, "In the manuscript there is a space between 'of' and 'sympathy' which is partly filled by what appears to be 'h n'; there is at least a chance that Melville meant to write 'of human sympathy' and simply did not notice that his pen did not work properly" (p. 535, n. 7). NN recovery (by Merton M. Sealts, Jr.) of the reading came from recognizing Melville's "k— or symty" as his abbreviation of his just-canceled quite legible words "kindness or sympathy" (see the MANUSCRIPT ALTERATIONS list below).

EMENDATIONS. 205.13 matter-of-fact] LW; ~-~∧~ HM 205.21 J.] LW; ~∧ HM *205.25 vessels] LW; vessel HM 205.26 what] LW; What HM 205.27 vicissitudes] LW; viscicitudes HM 205.28 achieved] LW; acheived HM 206.3 are] LW; are are HM 206.14 Browne] LW; Brown HM (the same correction is also made at 206.40, 207.11, 208.6,11,21,32, 210.9,13,15,20,31) 206.18 embrace∧] LW; ~, HM 206.19 essentially] LW; essentialy HM 207.1 believe] LW; beleive HM 207.5 benevolent] LW; benevolant HM 207.35 parliamentary] LW; parlimentary HM *207.36 &c"] NN; ~∧ HM 208.8 at the] LW; at [the] HM 208.11 he] LW; his HM 209.2 umbrellas,] LW; ~; HM 209.19 Marryat] NN; Marryatt HM 209.26 Believe] LW; Beleive HM 209.30 It] LW; Its HM 209.35 gunwale] LW; gunwhale HM *210.12 "Sailors'] NN; "Sailor's HM *210.12 Sailors'] NN; ~∧ HM 210.12 respect] LW; respects HM *210.13 question".] NN; ~"∧ HM 210.19 world∧] NN; ~. HM 210.23 too] LW; to HM 210.23 character∧] LW; ~. HM *210.28–29 disciplinarian",] NN; disiplinarian"∧ HM 210.29 mean] LW; means HM 210.30 than] LW; that HM *211.2 and] NN; *[not present]* HM *211.11 kindness] NN; k— HM *211.11 sympathy] NN; symty HM 211.13 Browne's] LW; Brown HM 211.15 Ringbolt's]

LW; Ringbolt HM 211.17 Sailors'] NN; Sailor HM 211.17 Rights] LW; rights HM 211.18 Sailors'] NN; sail HM 211.18 Wrongs] LW; wrgs HM 211.19 entertaining.] LW; ~, HM

NN also emends (as did LW) the "&" of HM to "and" at: 205.9,11,12,20,22,23, 206.4,9(second),19,23(twice),31,36,37, 207.6,18,20,23,26,27,30,31,32,34, 208.5,6(twice),12,15,18,19,20,24,26,31,32,35, 209.1,2,5,6,8,15,18,19,20,21,24,28,29,30,31,32,33,36,38, 210.2,5,6,12,15,20,28,31,32, 211.1,3,7(twice),13,18,19(twice); "tho' " or "tho" to "though" at 206.17, 209.39; and "thro' " to "through" at 208.21, 209.33.

HYPHENATION. II. 209.28 steering-oar

SUBSTANTIVE VARIANTS. 205.10 And] HM; *[not present]* LW 205.22 poesy] HM; poetry LW 205.25 vessels] LW; vessel HM 205.26 which] HM; which now LW 206.3 are] LW; are are HM 206.13 a matter] HM; or rather LW 206.17 though . . . place] HM; *[not present]* LW 206.32 divided] HM; decided LW 207.26 assuring] HM; assures LW 208.11 he] LW; his HM 208.23 Here] HM; There LW 208.36 bright] HM; light LW 209.8 way] HM; away LW 209.20 buckling] HM; truckling LW 209.29 harpooneer] HM; harpooner LW 209.30 It] LW; Its HM 210.22 mournfully] HM; manfully LW 210.23 too] LW; to HM 210.30 than] LW; that HM 211.7 wanton] HM; wreathed LW 211.11 kindness or sympathy] NN; k— or symty HM; sympathy LW 211.12 enough] HM; enough of LW 211.13 Browne's] LW; Brown HM 211.15 Ringbolt's] LW; Ringbolt HM 211.17–18 Sailors' . . . Wrongs] NN; Sailor rights & sail wrgs. HM; "Sailor's rights and Sailor's wrongs" LW

MANUSCRIPT ALTERATIONS. 205.2–8 *Etchings . . . 12mo.]* *inscription by* ED 205.10 when] men →<men >when→ 205.11 mermen;] mermen; ships, floating prodigies; [<ships, floating prodigies;] 205.12 the] the purely [<purely] 205.12 there] so many / plain, matter-of-fact →<so . . . matter-of-fact→ *add* there 205.16 the] the first [<first] 205.18 manipulating . . . wave] dabbling / in its bubbles [<dabbling . . . bubbles >manipulating the crest / of a wave] 205.21 impair] dissolve [<dissolve >impair] 205.23–24 facts; . . . unquestionably] & most disenchanting facts; & unquestionably [<& . . . disenchanting *and after* facts; & >with some f→<f→ *add* allowances for the general application of an individual example] 205.26 which] which now [<now] 205.26 their] their mighty [<mighty] 205.26 American] american *[alter to capital]* 205.26 Indeed, what] What [>Indeed *before* What *without changing* W *to* w *(emended)*] 206.1–3 commendation. . . . himself.] commendation. [>The personal . . . himself. *in left margin, with guideline to caret*] 206.3 presented are] described by the author are [<described >sketched {<sketched <by the author *without canceling* are *and* >presented are *(emended)*}] 206.3–4 graphicly . . . sketched,] graphic & truthful [*alter* graphic *to* graphicly *and* truthful *to* truthfully *then* >sketched,] 206.4 hence] hence in some cases [<in some cases] 206.6 true unreserved] true [>unreserved] 206.6 respect] way [<way >respect] 206.7 never dreamed] had no / idea [<had no idea >never dreamed] 206.8 anything] their aspects [<their aspects >anything] 206.8–9 his . . . pretty.] them pretty. →<pretty.→ *add* more attractive / and pretty. [<them >his sketches the] 206.11 When] The →<The→ *add* When 206.12 holds up] shows [<shows >holds up] 206.17 may] in →<in→ *add* may 206.17 though . . . place.] tho certainly out of place. [<certainly >it is rather {<tho it is rather out of place. >>tho it is rather out of place.}] 206.18 to embrace] to be, &, / in fact is, essentially, →<be >embrace,→ →<in fact is, *and add* is *after* essentially,→ *then alter* is *to* does→ *add* present [<& essentially . . . present *without canceling comma after* embrace *(emended)*] 206.19 essentially, possesses] in fact de →<in fact de→ *add* essentialy, *(emended)* deserves [<deserves >possesses] 206.20 curious] minor e →<minor e→ *add* curious 206.24 announcement . . . thing.] mention of such a / phenomenon. [<mention . . . phenomenon. >announcement of such a thing.] 206.28 leviathan,] monster, [<monster >leviathan] 206.31 the monster] the →<the→ *add* him [<him >the monster] 206.31 all] the →<the→ / all 206.33 —not by] by →<by→ *add* —not by 206.34 motion . . . water] motion [>in the water] 206.35 (descends) as] as →<as→ *add* (descends) as 206.36 usually] most →<most→ *add* usually 207.1 the shipping] the [>shipping] 207.1 in our] by the →<by the→ *add* in our 207.5–6 (one . . . author] (of whom M^{r} / Brown [>one of the shipping agents *before* of *and* <Mr Brown *adding in margins* our / author] 207.13 to send on to] into the →<into the→ *add* to send an / to [<an / *rewrite in left margin as* on] 207.14 without the office] without [>the office] 207.14 the anxious] the [>anxious] 207.14 few choice] few / [*add in margin* choice] 207.15–16 sail . . . long)—] sail— [>upon the most delightful voyages imaginable (only four years long) *before dash*] 207.19 a dark] a [>dark] 207.20 toils.] webs. →<webs.→ *add* toils. 207.21–22 notwithstanding . . . possibly] very possibly they may [<they may >notwithstanding their calling upon him, they may *before* very] 207.22 have heard] have heard / have heard [<*repeated* have heard] 207.24 any] so erron →<so erron→ *add* any 207.27 silken muscles] genteel / figures [<genteel figures >silken muscles] 207.27 those] his principals were not →<his . . . not→ *add* those 207.28–29 the . . . preferred] they

were in want / of [*alter* they *to* the <were in want / of >captains of whaling vessels *and add in left margin* preferred] 208.2 the unfortunate H———] [>the unfortunate] H——— 208.5 which,] which, →<which,→ *add* which 208.5 endangers] reduces him to →<reduces him to→ / endangers 208.8 at the] at the [*add brackets? around* the (*emended*)] 208.10 He never recovered] With →*erase* With *and before erasure add* He never→ *add* recovered 208.10 for . . . sequel] for [>in the sequel] 208.34 Hereafter] we →<we→ *add* Hereafter 208.35 "duck" trowsers] "duck" [>pants {<pants *add* trowsers}] 208.35–36 a bright blue] with an open / neck →<with . . . neck→ *add* a blue [>bright *before* blue] 208.39 survey] adres →<adres→ *add* survey 209.2 wet decks, and] wet [>decks, &] 209.3 all] the little anticipated [<the little anticipated >all] 209.3 will be] are [<are >will be] 209.4–5 which, . . . can,] which they must battle out the best way they can, month after month; [<month after month; *and, adding comma after* which >month after month,] 209.9 up with you, you] bare [bare *underlined*] you [<bare >you, {*add in margin* up with *before* you, you}] 209.11 sea-bludgeon] handspike [<handspike >sea-bludgeon] 209.14–15 (so . . . it)] so slend →<slend→ *add* slight that three men / may [*erase* may *w.o., beginning in margin* might] walk off with it upon their →<it upon their *and add parentheses around* so . . . with *then* >it *after* with→ 209.15 your] the →<the→ *add* your 209.18–19 excitement,] excitement, "Pull, Pull—break your →<"Pull, . . . your→ 209.20 oars] oars [*rewrite* oars] 209.22 palpitating] buoyant [<buoyant >palpitating] 209.23 My] Lord! My [<Lord!] 209.25 ripples . . . as if] about his vast head like →>ripples *before* about *and* <like→ / as if 209.30 we] / you [<you *add in right margin* we] 209.33 aside,] on her beam ends, / & so, starts off with it at a pace which / makes your hair bristle—to & fro, and →<on . . . and→ / aside, 209.33 madly,] foaming, [<foaming >madly] 209.36–37 tools . . . spades—] tools [>—lances, harpoons & spades—] 209.38 along] thro' [<thro' >along] 209.39 your person] your very persons [<your very *and alter* persons *to* person *then* >your *before* person] 210.1 But all] But [>all] 210.3 supply] fill →<fill→ *add* supply 210.4 between] in →<in→ *add* between 210.5 with it,] with [>it,] 210.5 bites it in] bits [*alter to* biets *for* bites] it [>in] 210.6 them.] the xx →*erase* xx *and alter* the *to* them.→ 210.7 the] a tyro what →<a tyro what→ / the 210.8 vocation] tour →<tour→ *add* vocation 210.8 further] in →*erase* in *w.o.* further→ 210.12 one . . . least] some respects [<some >one *without altering* respects *(emended) and after* respects *add in margin* at least] 210.15 Browne gives] Brown's has all →<'s *(emended)* has all→ *add* gives 210.16 and is not] Ringbolt →<Ringbolt→ *add* & is not 210.16 from] from those [<those] 210.17 Captain Ringbolt] Ringbolt [>Captain *before*

Ringbolt] 210.18 and . . . ins[…]inuates *[in left margin add* more than *before* insi[…]best] the ?ele →*erase?* ?ele→ *add* best *and* >not o[…]ws . . . maligned.] & most maligned fellov[…]ed → / but that they have been sorely maligne[…]d *(emended)* 210.21 presented] conveyed →<conveyed >give <give→ *add* presented 210.21 view] & xx →*erase* & xx *w.o.* view→ 210.21 the matter.] sea usages. [<sea usages ≯the matter] 210.21 And] he →*w.o.* And→ 210.23 character . . . aspersions.] character. [≯from unjust aspersions. *without canceling period after* character *(emended)*] 210.24 Now . . . class] Now [>as a class] 210.24 disposed partially to] disposed to [>partially *then cancel caret and insert new caret after* disposed] 210.25 the] these →*alter* these *to* the→ 210.26–27 the good . . . Boston—] Boston →<Boston→ *add* the good . . . Boston— 210.28 knowledge at least] knowledge [>at least] 210.28 Mr Dana's captain] the Captain →*alter* the *to* that→ →<that Captain→ / Mr Dana's captain 210.28 strict and harsh] strict [>& harsh] *210.29 which words so] which words from a s →<which . . . a s→ *add* which words →<words→ *add* words as →<as→ *add* so 210.29–30 the . . . question] he [<he >the man in question] 210.32 show] say that if there be any / factitious error →<factitious error *and add* th[in]g *to* any→ →<thg *and add* thing [thing *underlined*] / *and after canceled* error *add* out of the way→ →<say . . . way→ *add* show 210.33 regarded] held a scoundrel →<held a scoundrel→ *add* regarded 210.34–35 Now . . . contrary] Now [>for ought we know to the contrary] 210.35 Styx—] Styx—this same / may be a pretty →<this . . . pretty→ *add* this same petty tyrant / at sea, may →<this . . . may→ 210.36 tyrant] bully [<bully >tyrant] 210.36 quite] one of the →<one of the→ / a tolerably →<a tolerably→ *add* good natured →<good natured→ *add* quite 210.37 very] qu →*w.o.* very→ 210.37 the god Janus] Janus →<Janus→ *add* the god Janus *211.2–3 and relates] & tells a go →<& . . . go→ / relates *without replacing the canceled ampersand before* relates *(emended)* 211.3 adventures pleasantly] adventures [>pleasantly] 211.4 capital] glorious [<glorious >capital] 211.5 Why Sir,] Why, [>Sir *before comma (obscured by caret)*] 211.6–7 that when . . . smiles".] that His / Nautical Highness lost his →<lost his→ *add* left his →<his→ *add* all his / "quips & cranks & wanton smiles" beh →<beh→ *add* when he embarked / on the voyage. [<when . . . voyage *and after* that >when they embarked *and after* left ≯behind him] 211.7 Very far indeed] Alas! →<Alas!→ Bless you, xx how →<Bless . . . how→ / "My eyes", →<"My eyes",→ *add* Very far [>indeed] 211.8 his jokes] jo →<jo→ *add* his jokes *211.11 word . . . men.] word to / his [>men] of kindness or sympathy [<kindness or sympathy *and*

>*abbreviated, with canceled phrase underlined* of k— or symty *after* word *(emended)*] 211.11 True;] But the / truth is that sea captains →<But . . . captains→ *add* True; 211.11–12 in . . . still] all sea captains are alike in →<in >in this respect *before* all→ *add* but [>still] 211.13 nearly to] to →<to→ *add* nearly to 211.13 the general] all →<all→ *add* the general 211.14 to be drawn] drawn [>to be *before* drawn] 211.15 But] But "Sailor →<"Sailor→ 211.15 very far] / far [*add in left margin* very *before* far] 211.15 a mere] nothing more than a [<nothing . . . a ≯a mere] 211.16 the class . . . belongs.] / his tribe →<tribe→ *add* class. [<his *and add in left margin* the *then cancel period after* class *and* >to which he belongs.] 211.17 brief sketch] sketch [>brief *before* sketch] 211.17 under] in →<in→ *add* under 211.19 simply and pleasantly] pleasantly [>simply & *before* pleasantly] 211.19 entertaining.] entertaining.—We commend it to youth / in parti →<We . . . parti *and alter period after* entertaining *to comma*→ / & as such we commend it to youth. [<& . . . youth. *without altering punctuation after* entertaining *(emended)*]

AUTHENTIC ANECDOTES OF "OLD ZACK" (pp. 212–29)

NN copy-text: the anonymous first printing, "Authentic Anecdotes of 'Old Zack,' " in *Yankee Doodle* [YD], II (1847), in the following installments:

Anecdotes I and II	no. 42 (July 24), p. 152
Anecdote III	no. 43 (July 31), p. 167
"Gen. Taylor's Personal Appearance"	no. 44 (August 7), p. 172
Anecdote IV	no. 45 (August 14), p. 188
Anecdotes V and VI	no. 46 (August 21), p. 199
Anecdotes VII and VIII	no. 47 (August 28), p. 202
Anecdote IX	no. 49 (September 11), p. 229

No known manuscript, and no later authoritative printing in Melville's lifetime. NN emendations to YD (on principles stated on pp. 549–64): at 27 points. NN printer's copy: emended photocopies from bound files of Newberry Library A5.99 (first six installments) and University of Chicago AP101Y3 (seventh installment). Machine collations between copies of YD: Newberry A5.99 (first six installments) and University of Chicago AP101Y3 (photocopy) (seventh installment) *vs.* University of Vermont (photocopy); University of Vermont (photocopy) *vs.* Brooklyn Public 051Y23 (photocopy).

Melville's friend Cornelius Mathews, an intimate of Evert A. Duyckinck's literary coterie, was editor of *Yankee Doodle* from July 3, 1847, until publication ceased the following October. Melville's authorship of the "Old Zack" series was established by Luther S. Mansfield, in "Melville's Comic Articles on Zachary Taylor," *American Literature,* IX (January, 1938), 411–18, through an October 5, 1847 entry in Duyckinck's diary about a letter of George Washington's ordering a pair of pants, which "reminds one of Herman Melville's Old Zack epistles in Yankee Doodle." No other anecdote or series in *Yankee Doodle,* as Mansfield points out, has "Old Zack" in its title; Duyckinck's allusion is evidently to Anecdotes III and IX of Melville's series, both about General Taylor's pants. Melville later called Taylor "Old Zack" in a February 20, 1849 letter to his brother Allan: "When Old Zack heard of it [the birth of Melville's son Malcolm]—he is reported to have said 'Mark me: That boy will be President of the United States before he dies' "; and again in a March 3, 1849 letter to Duyckinck: "had not Old Zack's father begot him, Old Zack would never have been the hero of Palo Alto."

At least the first six installments must have been written in July of 1847, after Mathews became editor of *Yankee Doodle* but before Melville left New York for his wedding in Boston on August 4; the series continued to appear in successive numbers through August 28 even while Melville was on his honeymoon. Anecdote IX, published in the September 11 number after a week's interruption, may have been written somewhat later—possibly at his mother's home in Lansingburgh, where Melville and his bride arrived on August 27. Meanwhile the articles were noticed in at least one newspaper, the New York *Evening Post,* which on the first page (column 9) of the issue for Friday, July 23, hailed the opening of the "Old Zack" series: "Some clever hand has taken hold of the Zachary Taylor anecdote manufacturers, and, with a humorous introduction, gives the following authentic anecdotes of old Zack"—continuing with a full quotation of Anecdotes I and II. The same paper later reprinted Anecdote IV's "private letter" from Taylor to the Mexican general Santa Anna (Tuesday, August 17, p. 2, col. 5). When the bound volume of *Yankee Doodle* for 1847 was issued, a prefatory note on praiseworthy articles particularly mentioned "those delightful *'Authentic Anecdotes of Old Zack,'* copied everywhere, confided in and enjoyed heartily, even by the venerable old hero himself, (as we know from private advices from the Camp)" (II, iv).

No other printings of the "Authentic Anecdotes" have been located earlier than the quotations from them in Mansfield's 1938 article. The full texts appear in *Shorter Works of Hawthorne and Melville,* ed. Hershel Parker (Columbus, Ohio: Charles E. Merrill, 1972), pp. 205–20, and in a pamphlet, with an introduction by its bookseller-publisher Kenneth Starosciak, *Herman Melville's Authentic Anecdotes of Old Zack* (New Brighton, Minn., 1973).

The illustration reproduced here on p. 216 (accompanying the *Yankee Doodle* publication on p. [165]) is by Donald F. or his brother James A. Read, who also drew many of the cartoons which accompany the pieces attributed to Melville in *Yankee Doodle* (see pp. 428, 431, 434, and 447).

For explanation of the following tabulations, see pp. 565–70.

DISCUSSIONS. 214.10 ANECDOTE I] As a matter of styling NN alters YD's "Anecdote, No. I", "Anecdote, No. II", and "Anecdote, No. III" to the form followed in YD for the later ones. For NN policy on such nontextual matters, see p. 565, n. 32.

215.21 shirt] It is possible but unlikely that Melville was adding to his characterization of Old Zack as eccentric by portraying him rolling up "short" sleeves as in YD; NN assumes a compositorial or scribal error.

222.12 ANECDOTE IV] As at the beginning of "General Taylor's Personal Appearance," this installment was prefaced in YD with "By a Surgeon of the Army in Mexico". NN eliminates the ascription in this case because it was evidently not intended to accompany this anecdote, which, unlike the previous one, is supplied by the "correspondent."

228.30 sends it] NN inserts this pronoun to supply the object for "sends" lacking in YD; although it may have been colloquial to omit the object (cf. "contemplates" at 228.33), the presence of the pronoun with other transitive verbs in this sentence implies that Melville intended one here.

EMENDATIONS. *214.10 ANECDOTE I] NN; ANECDOTE, NO. I YD 214.20 supererogatory] NN; superogatory YD 215.15 ANECDOTE II] NN; ANECDOTE, NO. II YD *215.21 shirt] NN; short YD 217.5 ANECDOTE III] NN; ANECDOTE, NO. III YD 217.33–34 diabolical] NN; diabollcal YD 217.36 Mexican] NN; Mexicans YD 218.29 arrangement] NN; arrang[ ]ment YD 219.5 day.] NN; ~∧ YD 219.33 physiognomical] NN; physignomical YD 220.2 favor.] NN; ~∧ YD 220.2 developed] NN; devoped YD 220.4 *squashed*] NN; *squshed* YD 220.19 affects] NN; effects YD 220.35 ellipsis] NN; elipsis YD 221.12 included] NN; inclnded YD 222.2 the region] NN; region YD 222.10 Department] NN; Departmtent YD *222.12 ANECDOTE IV] NN; BY A SURGEON OF THE ARMY IN MEXICO. / ANECDOTE IV. YD 223.14 autograph] NN; autogragh

YD 223.15 indications,] NN; ~. YD 224.14 Monterey] NN; Montery YD 224.14 ZACK] NN; ~, YD 225.16 your] NN; you YD 226.22 His] NN; his YD 226.32 every time] NN; everytime YD *228.30 sends it] NN; sends YD

HYPHENATION. I. 214.35 polysyllables 219.30 †interlocked 223.34 †anything 227.25 misrepresenting

II. 218.12 straight-forwardness 225.15 Major-General 227.27 mal-information 229.7 coat-tail

MR PARKMAN'S TOUR (pp. 230–34)

NN copy-text: Melville's untitled holograph printer's-copy manuscript [HM], now in the Duyckinck Collection, Rare Books and Manuscripts Division, The New York Public Library. First and only printing in Melville's lifetime: anonymous, "Mr. Parkman's Tour," in the New York *Literary World* [LW], IV, no. 113 (March 31, 1849), 291–93. Collation of NN printer's copy against LW (Newberry Library A5.5292) reveals no authorial variants from HM (there is no evidence that Melville received LW proofs). NN emendations to HM (on principles stated on pp. 549–64): at 78 points. NN printer's copy: a typed transcript of HM thus emended (see p. 537). The title is supplied by NN, following the wording of LW. Machine collations between copies of LW: Northwestern L051L773 *vs.* University of Chicago AP2L7118 and Newberry A5.5292; Newberry A5.5292 *vs.* M67–722–108.

Melville obtained his review copy of *The California and Oregon Trail* during a business trip from his father-in-law's home in Boston, where he and Elizabeth were staying after the birth of their first child, back to New York soon after writing Evert A. Duyckinck, the *Literary World* editor, on March 3, 1849: see Hope Savage Shaw to Samuel H. Savage, Boston, March 7, 1849, as quoted by Frederick J. Kennedy and Joyce Deveau Kennedy, "Additions to *The Melville Log,*" *Melville Society Extracts,* No. 31 (September, 1977), 6. The book was advertised in the *Literary World* of March 10 among books "Just Published." Since the review (or book) is not mentioned in Melville's later Boston letters to Duyckinck, he probably read the book and wrote his review while still in New York, as the source of the manuscript paper suggests (see below). The review was apparently first listed as Melville's by Meade Minnigerode in *Some Personal Letters of Herman Melville and a Bibliography* (New York, 1922), p. 191.

The California and Oregon Trail: being sketches of Prairie and Rocky Mountain Life. By Francis Parkman Jr. with illustrations by Darley. Putnam.

Mr Parkman's book is the record of some months' adventures ever in the year 1846 among the Indian tribes scattered between the western boundary of Missouri and the Rocky Mountains. Though without literary pretension, it is a very entertaining work, straightforward & simple throughout, and obviously truthful.

The title ~~intended~~ will be apt to mislead. There is nothing about California or Oregon in the book; but though we like it the better for this, the title is not the less ill-chosen. And here we must remind all authors of a fact, which sometimes seems to slip their memory. The christening of books is very different from the christening of men. Among men, the object of a name is to individualize; hence, that object is gained whatever name you bestow, though it be wholly irrespective of the character of the person named. Not thus with books; where ~~names~~ names or titles are presumed to express the contents. And, although during this ~~California~~ present gold fever, Catholic fathers have a perfect right to christen their offspring "Sacramento," or "California"; we deny this privilege to authors, with respect to their books. For example, a work on Botany published to-day, should not be entitled "California, or Budded Flowers"; on the contrary, the "California" should be dropped.

Leaf 1 (reduced) of Melville's holograph manuscript for "Mr Parkman's Tour," with heading added by Evert A. Duyckinck.

Melville's initial inscription of the manuscript and all his revisions are in one ink on the versos of seven 32.5-by-21-cm identical legal forms, each torn at the left margin. The forms, intended for use in cases involving debts, are marked "Sold by Anstice, Law Stationer, 27 Nassau-street.", a New York City address, and could have come from the Wall Street office of his brother Allan. Added to the manuscript are the bibliographical heading on Leaf 1 in Duyckinck's hand and compositors' names and "takes" on Leaf 1 ("Alexander") at NN230.1, Leaf 3 ("Lyman 2") at NN231.20, and Leaf 5 ("3 Pary") at NN232.26.

For explanation of the following tabulations, see pp. 565–70. The LW readings are given here for the historical record, not for any authority they carry.

DISCUSSIONS. 230.1 *Mr Parkman's Tour*] NN follows the wording of LW in supplying this title, but omits the LW period after "Mr" to follow the form Melville used throughout these manuscript pieces (see the discussion at 205.21 and numerous examples in this piece).

230.2–4 *The* . . . Putnam.] NN follows the LW styling rather than that of Duyckinck's heading on the manuscript (see the reproduction on p. 640, lines 1–3).

232.19 St] Although Melville perhaps omitted a period here and at 232.20 by oversight, NN does not supply them because this abbreviation (like "Mr" technically a suspension—see the discussion at 205.21) was often used without a period in the nineteenth century (as it still is in Britain).

232.20 praries] See pp. 561–62; other examples occur at 232.37, 249.3, and *Moby-Dick*, chap. 42 (NN191.2).

234.8 following.] After this final word in the manuscript, Melville specified his selected extract from Parkman in these words (underlined): "(Beginning at the paragraph 'We had scarsely gone' etc on page 390 to the end of the chapter)." LW followed this directive. (Duyckinck made a slight revision of Melville's ending by canceling "have . . . for" and substituting "select".) Here is the Parkman extract, as printed in LW (with adjustment of the quotation marks):

> We had scarcely gone a mile when an imposing spectacle presented itself. From the river bank on the right, away over the swelling prairie on the left, and in front as far as we could see, extended one vast host of buffalo. The outskirts of the herd were within a quarter of a mile. In many parts they were crowded so densely together that in the distance their rounded backs presented a surface of uniform blackness; but elsewhere they were more scattered, and from amid the multitude rose little columns of dust where the buffalo were rolling on the ground. Here and there a great confusion was perceptible, where a battle was going forward among the bulls. We could distinctly see them rushing against each other, and hear the clattering of their horns and their hoarse bellowing. Shaw was riding at some distance in advance, with Henry

Chatillon: I saw him stop aud *[sic]* draw the leather covering from his gun. Indeed, with such a sight before us, but one thing could be thought of. That morning I had used pistols in the chase. I had now a mind to try the virtue of a gun. Delorier had one, and I rode up to the side of the cart; there he sat under the white covering, biting his pipe between his teeth and grinning with excitement.

"Lend me your gun, Delorier," said I.

"Oui, Monsieur, oui," said Delorier, tugging with might and main to stop the mule, which seemed obstinately bent on going forward. Then everything but his moccasins disappeared as he crawled into the cart and pulled at the gun to extricate it.

"Is it loaded?" I asked.

"Oui, bien chargé, you'll kill, mon bourgeois; yes, you'll kill—c'est un bon fusil."

I handed him my rifle and rode forward to Shaw.

"Are you ready?" he asked.

"Come on," said I.

"Keep down that hollow," said Henry, "and then they won't see you till you get close to them."

The hollow was a kind of ravine very wide and shallow; it ran obliquely towards the buffalo, and we rode at a canter along the bottom until it became too shallow; when we bent close to our horses' necks, and then finding that it could no longer conceal us, came out of it and rode directly towards the herd. It was within gunshot; before its outskirts, numerous grizzly old bulls were scattered, holding guard over their females. They glared at us in anger and astonishment, walked towards us a few yards, and then turning slowly round retreated at a trot which afterwards broke into a clumsy gallop. In an instant the main body caught the alarm. The buffalo began to crowd away from the point towards which we were approaching, and a gap was opened in the side of the herd. We entered it, still restraining our excited horses. Every instant the tumult was thickening. The buffalo, pressing together in large bodies, crowded away from us on every hand. In front and on either side we could see dark columns and masses, half hidden by clouds of dust, rushing along in terror and confusion, and hear the tramp and clattering of ten thousand hoofs. That countless multitude of powerful brutes, ignorant of their own strength, were flying in a panic from the approach of two feeble horsemen. To remain quiet longer was impossible.

"Take that band on the left," said Shaw; "I'll take these in front."

He sprang off, and I saw no more of him. A heavy Indian whip was fastened by a band to my wrist; I swung it into the air and lashed my horse's flank with all the strength of my arm. Away she darted, stretching close to the ground. I could see nothing but a cloud of dust before me, but I knew that it concealed a band of many hundreds of buffalo. In a moment I was in the midst of the cloud, half suffocated by the dust and stunned by the trampling of the flying herd; but I was drunk with the chase and cared for nothing but the buffalo. Very soon a long, dark mass became visible, looming through the dust; then I could distinguish each bulky carcase, the hoofs flying out beneath, the short tails held rigidly erect. In a moment I was so close that I could have touched them with my gun. Suddenly, to my utter amazement, the hoofs were jerked upwards, the tails flourished in the air, and amid a cloud of dust the buffalo seemed to sink into the earth before me. One vivid impression of that instant remains upon my mind. I remember looking down upon the backs of several buffalo dimly visible through the dust. We had run unawares upon a ravine. At that moment I was not the most accurate judge of depth and width, but when I passed it on my return, I found it about twelve feet deep, and not quite twice as wide at the bottom. It was impossible to stop; I would have done so gladly if I could; so, half sliding, half plunging, down went the little mare. I believe she came down on her knees in the loose sand at the bottom; I was pitched forward violently against her neck and nearly thrown over her head among the buffalo, who amid dust and confusion came tumbling in all around. The mare was on her feet in an instant, and scrambling like a cat up the opposite side. I thought for a moment that she would have fallen back and crushed me, but with a violent effort she clambered out and gained the hard prairie above. Glancing back I saw the huge head of a bull clinging as it were by the forefeet at the edge of the dusty gulf. At length I was fairly among the buffalo. They were less densely crowded than before, and I could see nothing but bulls, who always run at the rear of a herd. As I passed amid them they would lower their heads, and turning as they ran, attempt to gore my horse; but as they were already at full speed there was no force in their onset, and as Pauline ran faster than they, they were always thrown behind her in the effort. I soon began to distinguish cows amid the throng. One just in front of me seemed to my liking, and I pushed close to her side. Dropping the reins I fired, holding the muzzle of the gun within a foot of her shoulder. Quick as lightning she sprang at Pauline; the little mare dodged the attack, and I lost sight of the wounded animal amid the tumultuous crowd. Immediately after, I selected another, and urging forward Pauline, shot into her both pistols in succession. For awhile I kept her in view, but in attempting to load my gun, lost sight of her also in the confusion. Believing her to be mortally wounded, and unable to keep up with the herd, I checked my horse. The crowd rushed onward. The dust and tumult passed away, and on the prairie, far behind the rest, I saw a solitary buffalo galloping heavily. In a moment I and my victim were running side by side. My firearms were all empty, and I had in my pouch nothing but rifle bullets, too large for the pistols and too small for the gun. I loaded the latter, however, but as often as I levelled it to fire, the little bullets would roll out of the muzzle and the gun returned only a faint report like a squib, as the powder harmlessly exploded. I galloped in front of the buffalo and attempted to turn her back; but her eyes glared, her mane bristled, and lowering her head, she rushed at me with astonishing fierceness and activity. Again and again I rode before her, and again and again she repeated her furious charge. But little Pauline was in her element. She dodged her enemy at every rush, until at length the buffalo stood still, exhausted with her own efforts; she panted, and her tongue hung lolling from her jaws.

Riding to a little distance, I alighted, thinking to gather a handful of dry grass to serve the purpose of wadding, and load the gun at my leisure. No sooner were my feet on the ground than the buffalo came bounding in such a rage towards me that I jumped back again into the saddle with all possible dispatch. After waiting a few minutes more, I made an attempt to ride up and stab her with my knife; but the experiment proved such as no wise man would repeat. At length, bethinking me of the fringes at the seams of my buckskin pantaloons, I jerked off a few of them, and reloading the gun, forced them down the barrel to keep the bullet in its place; then approaching, I shot the wounded buffalo through the heart. Sinking on her knees, she rolled over lifeless on the prairie. To my astonishment, I found that instead of a fat cow I had been slaughtering a stout yearling bull. No longer wondering at the fierceness he had shown, I opened his throat, and cutting out his tongue, tied it at the back of my saddle. My mistake was one which a more experienced eye than mine might easily make in the dust and confusion of such a chase.

Then for the first time I had leisure to look at the scene around me. The prairie in front was darkened with the retreating multitude, and on the other hand the buffalo came filing up in endless unbroken columns from the low plains upon the river. The Arkansas was three or four miles distant. I turned and moved slowly towards it. A long time passed before, far down in the distance, I distinguished the white covering of the cart and the little black specks of horsemen before and behind it. Drawing near, I recognised Shaw's elegant tunic, the red flannel shirt conspicuous far off. I overtook the party, and asked him what success he had met with. He had assailed a fat cow, shot her with two bullets, and mortally wounded her. But neither of us were prepared for the chase that afternoon, and Shaw, like myself, had no spare bullets in his pouch; so he abandoned the disabled animal to Henry Chatillon, who followed, dispatched her with his rifle, and loaded his horse with her meat.

We encamped close to the river. The night was dark, and as we lay down, we could hear mingled with the howlings of wolves the hoarse bellowing of the buffalo, like the ocean beating upon a distant coast.

EMENDATIONS. 230.5 months'] LW; months∧ HM 230.19–20 Sacramento] LW; Sacremento HM 231.29 Eliot] NN; Elliot HM 232.18 A.] LW; ~∧ HM 232.26 Mississippi] LW; Missippi HM 232.35 Beelzebub] LW; Belzeebub HM 232.35 warrior] LW; warrier HM 233.11 warriors] LW; warriers HM 233.23 Esq.,] LW; ~∧, HM 233.30 A.] LW; ~∧ HM 233.32 cavalry] LW; calvary HM 233.34 fierce] NN; feirce HM 233.35 Siege] LW; Seige HM

NN also emends (as did LW) the "&" of HM to "and" at: 230.9(first),22, 231.4,9,12,13,23,27,29(first),36,37(twice), 232.5,16,17,20,22(twice),24,25(twice),26(twice),29,33,35,39(twice),40(thrice), 233.4(twice),5,9(twice),10(twice),12(twice),13,14(twice),15,16,17(twice), 21(twice),24(twice),25,26,28(twice),32,33,34,39, 234.1,4,7; "tho' " to "though" at 232.4; and "thro' " to "through" at 233.6,29.

HYPHENATION. I. 233.19 †war-parties
II. 233.19 †war-parties

SUBSTANTIVE VARIANTS. 231.38 reject] HM; regret LW 232.4 swing] HM; hung LW 232.18 Mr] HM; *[not present]* LW 232.20 praries] HM; Prairie LW 232.26 ascend] HM; ascended LW 232.30 over] HM; on LW 232.36 push] HM; pushed LW

233.32 cavalry] LW; calvary HM 233.34 fierce] NN; feirce HM; fancy LW 233.35 round] HM; around LW 234.7–8 have . . . for] HM; select LW

MANUSCRIPT ALTERATIONS. *230.2–4 *The* . . . Putnam.] *inscription by* ED 230.3–4 Jr. . . . Darley] ED Jr. [ED>with . . . Darley] 230.5 in] ?am →<?am→ *add* in 230.10 will] is calculated →<is calculated→ *add* will 230.11 but though] but [ED? >though] 230.12 all] the →<the >all→ 230.16 bestow, . . . be] bestow, / [*add in margins* though / it be] 230.17 names] names [<names] / names 230.18 present gold] California [<California / *add in margin* gold >present *before* gold] 231.7 be part of] be / [*add in margin* part of] 231.10 in a] in the [<the >a] 231.12 Parkman] Parkmans →<s→ 231.13 of the] of / [*add in margin* the] 231.19 much] an →<an→ *add* much 231.19 that to] that →>to→ 231.20 as] as →<as >as *rewritten*→ 231.23 soon] come →<come→ *add* soon 231.24 is almost] is [>almost] 231.25 wholly] wholly →<wholly *because of ink blot* >wholly→ 231.27 Pharisee] Pharsee [*insert* i *by error after* s] 231.27 in] we are →<we are→ *add* in 231.31 remember . . . so] rember [<rember >remember] / that in so →<in so→ *add* by so 231.33 the naked] the [>naked] 231.33 Rome] Rome for →<for→ 231.33 more] by the →<by the→ / more 231.36–37 are all . . . Indians—] are all / [*add in margins* of / us] —Anglo-Saxons & Dyaks— [<& *then add comma after* Anglo-Saxons *and* >& Indians *after* Dyaks] 232.1–2 savage; . . . more.] savage. [*alter period to semicolon and add* and the civilized being is born →<is born→ *add* but inherits his civilization, nothing more.] 232.3 it;] it; yea, [<yea,] 232.12 should,] wh →<wh→ *add* should, 232.18 Mr Quincy A.] M^{r} [>Quincy A *without period (emended)*] 232.19 that] whi→<whi→ / that 232.20 the praries] us→<us→ *add* the praries 232.20 At] The friends →<The friends→ *add* At 232.27 Here] Hence, / like sailors for sea, they put out on the broad prarie. →<Hence . . . prarie.→ *add* Here 232.32 soar with] dip into [<dip into >soar with] 232.32–33 with . . . other] with a pistol / in his hand →*after* with >his book in one hand, & / *and after* in <his hand→ *add* the other 232.37 praries] w →<w→ *add* praries 232.38 log-cabin] / [*add in margin* log-] cabin 232.39 cables, and set] cables & → *erase* &→ *add comma and* & set 233.2 near a] near the / ba →<the / ba→ *add* a 233.3 for] they →<they→ *add* for 233.4 eat] eate →<eate→ *add* eat 233.7 into . . . perilous] into [>all] the / [*add in margin* perilous] 233.8 out by night] out [>by night] 233.15 in] to →<to→ *add* in 233.17 birch] berch [*alter to* birch] 233.18–19 with the veritable] with [>the veritable] 233.20 Fe] fe →*erase* fe *w.o.* Fe→ 233.27 Scott.] Scott or Cooper →*erase* or <Cooper→ *add period after* Scott

233.30 Mr . . . Shaw] Q →*erase* Q→*w.o.* Mr Quincy a →*w.o.* A *without period (emended)*→ *add* Shaw 233.31 high-spirited] dashing →<dashing→ *add* high-spirited 233.34 bison] buffalo →<buffalo→ *add* bison
233.35 Byron's] the →*erase* the→ *add* Lord →*erase* Lord→ *add* Byron's
233.36 Returned] After →<After→ *add* Returned 233.40–234.2 it. . . . good.] it. [>*in margin with guideline to caret* It has two pictorial illustrations by the well-known / & talented artist Darley, one of which is exceedingly good.]
234.3–4 put together] composed / [<composed *add in left margin* put together] 234.4 the remote] the [>remote] 234.5 through] on the praries →<on the praries→ *add* thro ex →<ex→ 234.7–8 we . . . for] we have only room for [ED <have . . . for *and* ≯select]

COOPER'S NEW NOVEL (pp. 235–36)

NN copy-text: Melville's untitled holograph printer's-copy manuscript [HM], now in the Duyckinck Collection, Rare Books and Manuscripts Division, The New York Public Library. First and only printing in Melville's lifetime: anonymous, "Cooper's New Novel," in the New York *Literary World* [LW], IV, no. 117 (April 28, 1849), 370. Collation of NN printer's copy against LW (Newberry Library A5.5292) reveals no authorial variants from HM (there is no evidence that Melville received LW proofs). NN emendations to HM (on principles stated on pp. 549–64): at 30 points. NN printer's copy: a typed transcript of HM thus emended (see p. 537). The title is supplied by NN, following LW. Machine collations between copies of LW: Northwestern L051L773 *vs.* University of Chicago AP2L7118 and Newberry A5.5292; Newberry A5.5292 *vs.* M67–722–108.

This review of Cooper's *The Sea Lions* was evidently written at the request of Evert A. Duyckinck, the *Literary World* editor, after Melville's return to New York from Boston on April 11, 1849—probably after April 21, when *The Sea Lions* was advertised in the *Literary World* as "now ready." The review was apparently first listed as Melville's by Meade Minnigerode in *Some Personal Letters of Herman Melville and a Bibliography* (New York, 1922), p. 191.

Melville's initial inscription and all his revisions are in one ink on three 25.1-by-19.9-cm leaves of uniform unruled blue paper, each irregularly trimmed along the left margin. The leaves are now mounted on heavy paper with Melville's note of March 8, 1848, inviting Duyckinck to "come round and make up a rubber of whist." Added to the manuscript are the title and the bibliographical heading on the recto, and a notation "bgs /

Cooper's New Novel

The Sea Lions; or, the Lost Sealers: a Tale of the Antarctic Ocean. By J. Fenimore Cooper. 2 vols. 12mo. Burgess & Stringer.

The Sea Lions, or the Lost Sealers! An attractive title truly. Nor does this last of Cooper's novels disappoint the promise held forth on the title page.

The story opens on the sea coast of Suffolk County Long Island; & turns mainly upon the mysterious existence of certain islands within the Antarctic Circle, whose precise whereabouts is known but to a chosen few, & whose latitude & longitude even the author declares he is not at liberty to make known. For this region, impelled by adverse, if not hostile motives, the two vessels—the Sea Lions—in due time sail, under circumstances full of romance.

After encountering a violent gale described with a force peculiarly Cooper's, they at last reach the Antarctic seas, finding themselves walled in by "thrilling regions of thick-ribbed ice". Few descriptions of the lonely & the terrible, we imagine, can surpass the grandeur of many of the scenes here depicted. The reader is reminded of the appalling adventures of the United States Exploring Ships in the same part

Leaf 1 (reduced) of Melville's holograph manuscript for "Cooper's New Novel," with title and heading added by Evert A. Duyckinck.

(117)" on the verso of Leaf 1, all in Duyckinck's hand in ink; and compositors' names and "takes": "Pary" in brown crayon on Leaf 1 (NN235.1) and "Alexander" in pencil on Leaf 3 (NN236.15).

For explanation of the following tabulations, see pp. 565–70. The LW readings are supplied here for the historical record, not for any authority they carry.

DISCUSSIONS. 235.2–3 *The* . . . Townsend.] NN follows the styling of LW rather than of Duyckinck's heading on the manuscript (see the reproduction on p. 647). The one substantive change was probably introduced by Duyckinck at the proof stage: from "Burgess & Stringer" to "Stringer & Townsend."

235.6 County,] The omission of the comma in HM (supplied in LW) seems inadvertent; Cooper's first chapter names "Suffolk County, Long Island, New York".

235.15 rock-ribbed] NN keeps the HM misquotation of Shakespeare's *Measure for Measure,* III.i.122: "In thrilling regions of thick-ribbed ice"; the LW reading "thick-ribbed" was probably Duyckinck's correction at the proof stage. The last letter Melville received from his dying brother Gansevoort three years before enclosed Gansevoort's copied-out passage, with his title "Death," from Claudio's speech including this line (see the reproduction in *Log,* I, 209). Melville's memory of the passage with its contrast between warmth and "imprisonment" in "cold obstruction" seems to carry on into the imagery of his own ensuing passage.

235.19 Wilkes] Charles Wilkes, *Narrative of the U.S. Exploring Expedition . . . 1838–1842* (Philadelphia, 1845): this was a major source for Melville in *Omoo, Mardi,* and *Moby-Dick.* In his manuscript Melville wrote "Le" before "Wilkes", probably beginning (and misspelling) the word "Lieutenant", Wilkes's rank during the expedition, but then canceled it, perhaps because of uncertainty as to what rank to name—Wilkes had become Commander in 1843 (see the MANUSCRIPT ALTERATIONS list below).

235.19 Scoresby's] The "Greenland narrative" is William Scoresby's *An Account of the Arctic Regions* (Edinburgh, 1820), evidently like Wilkes's a work already so familiar to both Melville and his readers that he did not need to cite its title. It became a major source for *Moby-Dick* (Sealts 450).

235.21 stove] The true HM reading "Dutch stove", where the LW compositor plausibly read "Dutch shore", brings Melville's characteristic witty image into print for the first time—another instance of the continuing recovery of his intended words from his difficult handwriting (this one by Merton M. Sealts, Jr.). See the discussions at 210.26 and 211.11.

236.10 father] Melville nodded (or read too hastily). In Chapter 1 Cooper introduces Deacon Pratt as "childless . . . . He had only a niece"—Mary Pratt, "the only child of Israel Pratt, an elder brother of the deacon." The relationship is repeatedly mentioned. For the NN decision not to emend, see p. 558, n. 25.

236.15 Stimson] The HM reading "Stimpson" is Melville's nonce ear-spelling of the name of "Stimson, the oldest and best seaman in the schooner," whom he correctly describes. Other HM apparent ear-spellings in this manuscript are "Antartic" (235.14), "grandure" (235.16), and "nuptuals" (236.7)—all corrected by NN, as by LW. Also an ear-spelling is "dreampt" (236.19), which, however, was an acceptable variant (see pp. 561–62), and "soft-warfle", which reflects a dialect pronunciation (see the discussion at 336.9).

236.19 dreampt] See the preceding discussion and pp. 561–62.

236.26 The Sea Lions] NN does not supply italics or quotation marks for book titles or ship names (see 235.11 and 235.20) where HM lacks them (neither did Duyckinck, the LW compositor, or Cooper's book). See p. 560, n. 27.

EMENDATIONS. *235.6 County,] LW; ~∧ HM 235.7 existence] LW; existance HM 235.14 Antarctic] LW; Antartic HM 235.16 grandeur] LW; grandure HM 235.17 scenes] LW; scene HM 235.17 appalling] LW; apalling HM 236.4 fields] LW; feilds HM 236.7 nuptials] LW; nuptuals HM 236.12 scriptural] LW; scripitral HM *236.15 Stimson] NN; Stimpson HM 236.22 belief] LW; beleif HM 236.24 believers] LW; beleivers HM 236.26 recommend] LW; reccomend HM

NN also emends (as did LW) the "&" of HM to "and" at:
235.6,9(twice),16,19,21,23(twice), 236.2,3,5,7,8,9,11,15,22(first).

SUBSTANTIVE VARIANTS. 235.4 *The Sea . . . Sealers!*] HM; *[not present]* LW 235.15 rock-ribbed] HM; thick-ribbed LW 235.17 scenes] LW; scene HM 235.21 stove] HM; shore LW 236.2 their] HM; the LW 236.2 the] HM; a LW 236.2 are] HM; is LW

MANUSCRIPT ALTERATIONS. 235.1–3 *Cooper's* . . . Townsend.] *inscription by* ED 235.7 turns mainly] turns [>mainly] 235.10 at] a →<a >at→ 235.12 circumstances] circumstanc xx →<xx *w.o.* es→ *235.18–19 world . . . by] world →>as narrated→ *add* by Le →<Le→ 236.7 the hero] with →<with >the hero→ 236.15–16 Professor] xx →*w.o.* xx *with* Pr *in* Professor→ 236.16 wintering] whil →<whil→ *add* wintering 236.28 decrying] the →<the→ *add* decrying

A THOUGHT ON BOOK-BINDING (pp. 237–38)

NN copy-text: Melville's untitled holograph printer's-copy manuscript [HM], now in the Duyckinck Collection, Rare Books and Manuscripts Di-

A Thought on Book Binding 1

The Red Rover by J Fenimore Cooper. Revised edition. Putnam.

The sight of the far-famed Red Rover sailing under the sober broad muslin wherewith Mr Putnam equips his lighter sort of craft begat in us a fastidious feeling touching the propriety of such a binding for such a book. Not that we absolutely pretend to any elevated degree of artistic taste in this matter; — our remarks are but limited to our egotistical fancies. Egotistically, then, we would have preferred for the "Red Rover" a flaming suit of flame-colored morocco, as evanescently thin & gauze-like as possible, so that the binding might happily correspond with the sanguinary fugitive of the book. Still better, perhaps were it bound in jet black, with a red streak round the borders (pirate fashion) — or, upon third thoughts, omit the streak & substitute a square of blood-colored bunting on the back, imprinted with the title, so that the

Leaf 1 (reduced) of Melville's holograph manuscript for "A Thought on Book-Binding," with title and heading added by Evert A. Duyckinck.

vision, The New York Public Library. First and only printing in Melville's lifetime: anonymous, "A Thought on Book-Binding," in the New York *Literary World* [LW], VI, no. 163 (March 16, 1850), 276–77. Collation of NN printer's copy against LW (Newberry Library A5.5292) reveals no authorial variants from HM (there is no evidence that Melville received LW proofs). NN emendations to HM (on principles stated on pp. 549–64): at 17 points. NN printer's copy: a typed transcript of HM thus emended (see p. 537). The title is supplied by NN, following LW. Machine collations between copies of LW: Northwestern L051L773 *vs.* University of Chicago AP2L7118 and Newberry A5.5292; Newberry A5.5292 *vs.* M67–722–108.

This notice of a new edition of Cooper's *The Red Rover* was evidently written at the request of Evert A. Duyckinck, the *Literary World* editor, in late February or early March of 1850, the book having been reported as "now ready" and advertised in that journal (on February 23) as "recently published" by George Palmer Putnam. J. H. Birss identified the manuscript as Melville's and first reprinted the notice in "A Book Review by Herman Melville," *New England Quarterly*, V (April, 1932), 346–48. Melville's initial inscription and all his revisions are in one ink on the rectos of three leaves (each 21.8 by 12.3 cm) of uniform unruled white note paper torn from larger sheets, with irregular left margins and embossed "Bath" within an ornamented oval on the upper left corners. On the verso of Leaf 2 the notation "Wednesday Afternoon." appears in Melville's hand in blue ink. Added to the manuscript are the title and bibliographical heading in Duyckinck's hand in ink on Leaf 1; the only compositor's name ("Lyman") in another hand in pencil on Leaf 1; also in Duyckinck's hand "bgs Review" in pencil on the verso of Leaf 2 and "bgs Review / Thought on / Book Binding" in pencil on the verso of Leaf 3.

For explanation of the following tabulations, see pp. 565–70. The LW readings are supplied here for the historical record, not for any authority they carry.

DISCUSSIONS. 237.1–2 *A . . .* Putnam.] NN follows the LW styling rather than that of Duyckinck's heading on the manuscript (see reproduction opposite, lines 1–2).

237.4 Mr] See the discussion at 205.21.

237.9 flaming suit of flame-colored morrocco] The apparent redundancy of the HM readings "flaming" and "flame-colored" may indicate a miscarriage of Melville's intended wording, but the repetition is induced by his elliptically playing on his book/ship figure. At this point he punningly equates a ship's "flaming suit" of sails with a book's "suit" of "flame-colored morrocco"—that is, the goatskin binding leather usually dyed in strong colors. His rapid conversion of that leather into a "thin and gauze-like" cloth seems to stem from his recent reading of *Henry IV, Part 1,* with its references both to "leathern jerkins" and to "a fair, hot wench in flame-color'd taffeta." (He alludes to that play both in *White-Jacket,* written some months before this notice, and in *Moby-Dick,* which he was currently writing; he had bought a set of Shakespeare's plays in 1849 [Sealts 460].)

EMENDATIONS. 237.9–10 evanescently] LW; evannescently HM 237.21 relievo] LW; releivo HM 238.7 Chesterfield] LW; Chesterfeild HM 238.10 to] LW; too HM 238.10 appropriately] LW; appropriatly HM 238.10 apparelled] LW; apparalled HM 238.16 title] LW; titles HM

NN also emends (as did LW) the "&" of HM to "and" at: 237.10,13,16,17, 238.1,7,11,18(twice),19.

HYPHENATION. I. 237.9 flame-colored 238.3 bookbinders

SUBSTANTIVE VARIANTS. 238.6 cosiest] HM; easiest LW 238.16 title] LW; titles HM

MANUSCRIPT ALTERATIONS. *237.1–2 *A* . . . Putnam.] *inscription by* ED 237.11 title] xx →*w.o.* title→ 237.13 streak,] title [<title >streak,] 237.17 free and easy] free-a →*w.o. hyphen with ampersand and w.o.* a *with* e *in* easy→ 237.20 sea . . . pirates.] superstitions of the sea →>sea *before* superstitions *and* <the sea→ *add* pirates. 238.3–4 species of men,] species / [>*in margins* of / men,] 238.7 chat even] chat [>even]

HAWTHORNE AND HIS MOSSES (pp. 239–53)

NN copy-text: Elizabeth Shaw Melville's fair-copy manuscript, to which Melville added the title, most of the punctuation, and many revisions [EM/HM]; now in the Duyckinck Collection, Rare Books and Manuscripts Division, The New York Public Library. First and only printing in Melville's lifetime: anonymous, "Hawthorne and His Mosses," in the New York *Literary World* [LW], VII, no. 185 (August 17, 1850), 125–27 [NN239.1–246.21], and no. 186 (August 24, 1850), 145–47 [NN246.22–253.39]. Collation of NN printer's copy against LW (Newberry Library A5.5292) reveals no authorial variants from EM/HM (there is no evidence that Melville received LW proofs). NN emendations to EM/HM (on principles stated on pp. 549–64): at 114 points. NN printer's copy: a typed

Hawthorne & his Mosses,

By a Virginian spending July in Vermont.

A papered chamber in a fine old farm-house—a mile from any other dwelling, and dipped to the eaves in foliage—surrounded by mountains, old woods, and Indian ponds,—this, surely, is the place to write of Hawthorne. Some charm is in this northern air, for love and duty seem both impelling to the task. A man of a deep & noble nature has seized me in this seclusion. His wild, witch voice rings thro' me; or, in softer cadences, I seem to hear it in the songs of the hill-side birds, that sing in the larch trees at my window.

Would that all excellent books were foundlings, without father or mother, that so it might be, we could glorify them, without including their ostensible auth-rs. Nor would any true man take exception to this;—least of all, he who writes,—"When the Artist rises high enough to achieve the Beautiful, the symbol by which he makes it perceptible to mortal senses becomes of little value in his eyes, while his spirit possesses itself in the enjoyment of the reality." But more than this. I know not;

Leaf 1 (reduced) of Elizabeth Shaw Melville's fair-copy manuscript for "Hawthorne and His Mosses," with title and byline added by Melville.

transcript of EM/HM thus emended (see p. 537). Machine collations between copies of LW: Northwestern L051L773 *vs.* University of Chicago AP2L7118 and Newberry A5.5292; Newberry A5.5292 *vs.* M67–722–108.

Melville read *Mosses from an Old Manse,* drafted the essay, and revised the fair copy sometime between July 18 and August 12, 1850. Perhaps it was before he met Hawthorne, as the essay makes out; more likely soon after, as argued below. During this month Melville and his family were summer paying guests in the home (later called Broadhall) of his cousin Robert Melvill near Pittsfield, Massachusetts, in the Berkshires—the region and country mansion described in the opening of the essay. There on July 18, it seems, he was given the copy of *Mosses from an Old Manse* that is cited in the essay; this copy (two volumes in one; New York: Wiley & Putnam, 1846), with his annotations, but not exactly as fancifully described there, is now in the Melville Collection of The Houghton Library of Harvard University (Sealts 248); see the discussion at 240.34–36 below. Melville first met Hawthorne on August 5, during a visit from his New York friends Evert A. Duyckinck, editor of the *Literary World,* and Cornelius Mathews, formerly editor of *Yankee Doodle.* The occasion was the now-famous literary outing at nearby Stockbridge that included the Boston publisher James T. Fields and Boston poet and wit Dr. Oliver Wendell Holmes and that ended with a dinner-table debate in which Holmes ridiculed American literary nationalism while Melville vigorously advocated it, as in his essay. When Duyckinck returned to New York on August 12 he probably took with him the fair-copy manuscript of the essay. On August 16 Melville wrote Duyckinck that he had received the first *Literary World* installment and that "under the circumstances the printing is far more correct, that [than] I expected; but there are one or two ugly errors. However, no one sees them, I suppose, but myself.—Send me the other proof [i.e., of the second installment], if you can; but dont, if it will be the least inconvenience." In October Hawthorne's wife, Sophia, wrote to her sister: "We have discovered who wrote the review in the Literary World. It was no other than Herman Melville himself! He had no idea when he wrote it that he should ever see Mr. Hawthorne." Melville, she reported, had told her that "the Review was too carelessly written—that he dashed it off in great haste & did not see the proof sheets, & that there was one provoking mistake in it. Instead of 'the same madness of truth' it should be 'the *sane* madness of truth.' " The hasty composition mentioned in these letters suggests that, contrary to what the essay says, Melville did not write it until after he met Hawthorne on August 5—that is, during the ensuing seven days before Duyckinck left Pittsfield. (For the first installment's "ugly errors" and evidence that Melville did not get proofs for the second, see p. 661 below. For Sophia Hawthorne's letter, see Eleanor Melville Metcalf, *Herman Melville: Cycle and Epicycle* [Cambridge: Harvard University Press, 1953], pp. 91–92; also the forthcoming new edition of Jay Leyda's *Log*. For a further account of the composition of the essay, see the HISTORICAL NOTE, pp. 471–75.)

That Melville wrote the essay after, not before, he met Hawthorne, was argued in detail by Harrison Hayford in his unpublished 1945 Yale dissertation, "Melville and Hawthorne: A Biographical and Critical Study," pp. 40–91. His argument was accepted by Howard P. Vincent, in *The Trying-Out of MOBY-DICK* (Boston: Houghton Mifflin, 1949), p. 38, n. 9; by Jay Leyda, in *The Melville Log* (New York: Harcourt, Brace, 1951), I, 387; and by Leon Howard, in *Herman Melville: A Biography* (Berkeley and Los Angeles: University of California Press, 1951), pp. 158–60. However, Sophia Hawthorne's above-quoted letter (first published in 1953) is cause for reconsideration. Is she reporting that Melville himself told her he wrote the essay with no idea he would ever see Hawthorne, or simply repeating what "the Virginian" had asserted in it? And if the former, was Melville telling the truth or persisting in the fictional assertion? Hayford still holds to his original argument placing the composition after the August 5 meeting. Jay Leyda, in the 1969 reissue (II, 922) and the forthcoming new edition of his *Log*, backdates Melville's beginning the essay from August 11 to July, presumably on the evidence of Sophia Hawthorne's letter. The question, in sum, is still unsettled.

A question more relevant to the essay's textual problems concerns Duyckinck's editorial intervention in it. Just how much Duyckinck—who had arranged the publication of *Mosses* in Wiley & Putnam's Library of American Literature—had to do with getting Melville to write the essay and then to tone it down, must be inferential. So must Leon Howard's judgment that it was a last-minute Pittsfield editorial conference with Duyckinck and Mathews on Sunday, August 11, before their Monday return to New York, that led Melville to add the masking byline ascription and internal allusions to the "Virginian" and to remove both "his sneer at Boston and some of its anti-English nationalism while carefully disguising any other signs of its connection with a New York critic" *(Herman Melville,* p. 160). And so must Perry Miller's bold further reconstruction of the whole August literary jamboree from which he too concludes the essay emerged, in *The Raven and the Whale: The War of Words and Wits in the Era of Poe and*

Melville (New York: Harcourt, Brace, 1956), pp. 280ff. Miller embraced the Hayford-Vincent-Leyda-Howard earlier dating of the essay's composition after the meeting with Hawthorne, either overlooking or dismissing the implications of Sophia Hawthorne's newly revealed letter cited above, even while using other passages from it (p. 294). Howard's and Miller's agreement as to Duyckinck's editorial intervention has weighed heavily in NN textual decisions. Miller says:

> On Sunday [August 11] . . . Melville wrote all day; in the evening, evidently, he, Duyckinck, and Mathews held an editorial conference. . . . Most of the changes are merely verbal, but the major ones are all of a single tendency: they cut down or restrain the exuberant nationalism of the draft. Whether these alterations came out of the conference that Sunday evening, or whether they are Melville's own concessions to moderation, they are obvious efforts to accommodate Melville's rage to the new, conciliatory tone Duyckinck had imparted to the *Literary World*. (pp. 285–86)

Whereas Howard thinks Duyckinck's editorial motive was to conceal the New York critical bias of the essay by ascribing its authorship to a Virginian, Miller thinks it was to tone down the vehement literary nationalism in the essay to fit his own prudentially moderated editorial policy. For NN textual decisions Duyckinck's motives scarcely matter—granted that he persuaded Melville to soften what he had written and still meant. In light of Samuel Butler's apothegm "He that complies against his will / Is of the same opinion still," NN restores to the text words and passages that expressed Melville's own opinion as he first wrote it and rejects his revisions which are judged as "complying" with Duyckinck's persuasion. Accordingly, while NN accepts Melville's last-minute "Virginian" additions at six points as furthering his own authorial intentions (see the discussion at 239.2), NN rejects four of his revisions which are plainly prudential softenings of his actual literary opinions (see the discussions at 245.39, 246.26–30, 248.15, and 248.17–18; also p. 554). Several other revisions which qualify but do not eliminate strong statements are retained, though they are possibly (but not plainly) the result of Duyckinck's influence (see the discussions at 245.40–246.1, 247.5, 248.6, 248.23–24, and 249.19–20).

"Hawthorne and His Mosses" dropped from sight and was not printed again during Melville's lifetime; because neither Rose Hawthorne Lathrop, in *Memories of Hawthorne* (Boston, 1897), nor Julian Hawthorne, in *Nathaniel Hawthorne and His Wife* (Boston, 1884), knew anything about the essay, they garbled several unrecognized contemporary references to it (see Hayford, 1945, pp. 94–97). At the end of the century, long excerpts appeared in an illustrated article centering on Hawthorne, headed "Unveiling of a Great Genius. / Melville and Hawthorne," in the Springfield, Massachusetts, *Sunday Republican* for July 1, 1900, p. 14, cols. 3–7; the author, Harriette M. Plunkett, a Pittsfield friend of Melville's widow, had her assistance in preparing it (cited in Merton M. Sealts, Jr., *The Early Lives of Melville* [Madison: University of Wisconsin Press, 1974], pp. 78, 217, 248). The essay was first completely republished—its first book appearance—in 1922 in *THE APPLE-TREE TABLE and Other Prose Sketches by Herman Melville,* pp. 53–86, and was included in Volume XIII of the collected *Works, Billy Budd and Other Prose Pieces,* pp. 123–43. Both used the *Literary World* text. Willard Thorp identified the manuscript in a file of unsigned *Literary World* contributions and printed the essay in his *Herman Melville: Representative Selections* (New York: American Book Co., 1938), pp. 327–45. His text, however, "reproduced that of the first publication" (LW) but attempted to substitute manuscript readings "whenever the printer misread Melville's copy" (p. 422); nevertheless, some misreadings persisted, including "same madness." After 1938 the essay appeared often in anthologies of American literature. Edmund Wilson used the LW text in *The Shock of Recognition* (New York: Doubleday, 1943), pp. 187–204, taking a misinterpreted phrase from it for his title. Jay Leyda's carefully edited text in *The Portable Melville* (New York: Viking, 1952), pp. 400–21, was drawn from both the manuscript and LW; he restored Melville's "sane madness" (first pointed out by Hayford, 1945, p. 86, n. 60). The manuscript itself was not used as copy-text until Harrison Hayford and Hershel Parker's Norton Critical Edition of *Moby-Dick* (New York, 1967), pp. 535–51, in which they gave "a slightly normalized reading text." Their footnotes "report Mrs. Melville's scribal procedures and some of Melville's corrections and revisions" (p. 535n.). The NN text is the first to follow both the words and punctuation of the manuscript, normalizing only by expanding Melville's abbreviations (see also the discussion at 242.14–15).

The fair-copy manuscript is inscribed in ink on the rectos of twenty-seven leaves of gray-blue paper. The twenty-two leaves numbered 1–13 and 16–24 are whole ones (31.4 by 19 cm). Embossed on the upper left corner of Leaves 1, 2, 5, 6, 8, 11, and 17 is the stationer's mark "H & L" within an ornamented octagonal frame. The five leaves numbered 14, 14½, 15, 25, and 26 are not whole ones and may be separately described as follows:

Leaf 14 (18.4 by 19 cm) was scissored at the left and bottom edges from a larger sheet of a different paper stock from most of the leaves.

Matching tears and dabs of sealing wax on both leaves show that Leaf 14 was originally a revision patch which Melville attached as the upper segment of Leaf 14½ (then EM 14) to replace its cut-off original part (presumably because he had revised it heavily), and which Duyckinck later detached and replaced by the present upper-segment editorial patch (numbering it 14½) when he divided the manuscript here into the two LW installments. Except for Duyckinck's added words in ink "(to be concluded next week)" the writing on Leaf 14 is in Melville's hand, in ink.

Leaf 14½ is a composite one in two segments. The upper segment (10.4 by 19.5 cm), as just stated, is Duyckinck's editorial patch that replaced Melville's revision patch (now Leaf 14). It was irregularly scissored and torn from a different paper stock and fastened to the lower segment by dabs of sealing wax. (Later reinforcement tape has been placed along its top edge, verso.) The lower segment (28.2 by 19 cm) is of the same paper stock as most of the others; as just stated, it was EM Leaf 14, the top of which Melville replaced. At its top Duyckinck added in ink his page number "14½" and his doubly underlined heading "Hawthorne and His Mosses / By a Virginian Spending July in Vermont / (Concluded from the last number.)".

Leaf 15, from the same paper stock as most of the other leaves, was inscribed by Elizabeth Shaw Melville. Melville revised one passage so heavily that he needed to replace it with a fair-copy patch. Since this patch was longer (i.e., took more paper) than the original revised area, he scissored the leaf into two segments (both about 15.6 by 18.8 cm) but did not cut out the heavily revised passage. These two segments of the original leaf he then bridged with his fair-copy patch, irregularly scissored from paper of a different stock (7.8 by 19 cm), which he fastened to each of the two with sealing wax, so that it covered up the heavily revised passage. (This three-segment leaf was separated in February, 1945, by Robert W. Hill, Keeper of Manuscripts, at the request of Harrison Hayford, to permit recovery of the revised passage. See Hayford, 1945; also Hill's memo laid into the manuscript and his correspondence with Hayford, now in the Melville Collection of The Newberry Library.)

Leaf 25 is made up of two segments: the upper, inscribed by Elizabeth Shaw Melville, is the larger part of her Leaf 25; the lower, inscribed by Melville, is a fair-copy patch evidently replacing and expanding a nonextant revised passage on the corresponding part cut off the original leaf. The upper segment (23.5 by 20 cm) is embossed on its upper left corner with the stationer's mark "P S & CO" within an oval frame. The lower seg-

Leaf 15 (reduced) of the fair-copy manuscript for "Hawthorne and His Mosses."

them. But I am by no means desirous of the
glory of a prophet. I pray Heaven that Hawthorne may
yet prove me an impostor in this prediction.
Especially, as I somehow cling to the
strange fancy, that, in all men, hiddenly reside
certain wondrous, occult properties—as in some plants & minerals—
which by some happy but very rare accident (as bronze was
discovered by the melting of the iron & brass in the burning of Corinth)
may chance to be called forth here on earth; not entirely
waiting for their better discovery in the more congenial,
blessed atmosphere of heaven.
Once more—for it is hard to finite
upon an infinite subject, & all subjects are infinite.

Lower segment of Leaf 25 (reduced)

ment (11.3 by 19.4 cm) is on faintly ruled paper of a different stock, irregularly scissored at both its top and bottom edges and fastened to the upper segment with four dabs of sealing wax. Inscribed on what is now its verso (originally the recto) is Melville's holograph draft passage of material used in Chapter 38 of *Mardi* (reproduced in the Northwestern-Newberry Edition, p. 724).

Leaf 26 (25.2 by 20 cm) is shorter than the other full leaves; possibly it is a whole leaf of the same stock as the upper segment of Leaf 25, though without the stationer's embossed mark.

Elizabeth Shaw Melville inscribed the fair-copy manuscript in ink, and Melville revised it also in ink. In the left margin of the leaves is a series of small penciled "x" marks which Hayford and Parker (1967) explain as "Mrs. Melville's way of reminding herself that she was uncertain about what she had copied and that she would have to ask her husband for the correct reading. After she checked with him, she would erase the 'x'—but lightly enough so that most are still visible" (p. 539, n. 2). As reported in the GENERAL NOTE ON THE TEXT, on his instruction she did not include most punctuation in her fair copy, and he added it later along with his corrections and revisions (for convenience the MANUSCRIPT ALTERATIONS list below records his punctuation additions separately—see p. 686 below). For these and other of Elizabeth Shaw Melville's copying practices see the discussions and reproductions at 240.6, 241.1–12, and 242.14–15.

There are editorial additions in Duyckinck's hand on Leaves 14, 14½, and 15. Names of the three LW compositors are penciled in another hand assigning their respective "takes": on Leaf 1 "Lyman" (who set 239.1–240.40); on Leaf 4 "Alexander" (241.1–245.36); on Leaf 13 "Lyman" (245.36–246.21); on Leaf 14½ "M[c]Intyre" (246.22–249.30); and on Leaf 20 "Alexander" (249.30–253.39). On Leaf 21 "M'Intyre" is canceled. On the verso of the last leaf (26) is the penciled endorsement "Hawthor[n]e" in the same hand as the compositors' names. On Leaf 26 "(End)" is inscribed in ink—possibly by Melville—and canceled in pencil. On the verso of Leaf 13 (on which the first installment ends) are two ink endorsements in Duyckinck's hand: "Hawthorne / & his Mosses" and "bgs part 1" with two horizontal lines and circled "185"; and on Leaf 25 verso are his three ink endorsements: "Hawthorne / & his Mosses / "; "2 part"; and circled "186". The "takes" of the three compositors assigned on the manuscript itself offer an unusual chance to attribute misreadings (in LW) to individuals who made them as well as to study their differing treatments of its spelling and punctuation. Thus, Alexander, who set sixteen of the twenty-seven manuscript pages, made the LW misreadings "wild moonlight" for EM "mild moonlight" (241.17), "same madness" for EM "sane madness" (244.26), and "eager-eyed" for EM "eagle-eyed" (251.18). Lyman, who set five manuscript pages, made the LW misreading "likewise" for EM "like wine" (240.21); and McIntyre, who set six manuscript pages, made the LW misreadings "fully" for HM "freely" (248.23), "my" for HM "my enthusiastic" (248.32–33), and "one" for EM "our" (248.34). Incidentally, the presence of the last three misreadings (and others) in the second LW installment is mute evidence that Melville was not sent the proofs of it he requested of Duyckinck on August 17 after seeing the "ugly errors" in the first.

For explanation of the following tabulations, see pp. 565–70. The LW readings are supplied here for the historical record, not for any authority they carry.

DISCUSSIONS. 239.2 By a Virginian] NN retains the HM (and LW) pseudonymous byline, along with the five HM added passages (at 246.34–35, 247.14, 248.32–33, 249.13, and 250.27) that tie authorship to the "Virginian," on the ground that they are parts of Melville's evolving persona in the fictional narrative of his completed essay. (Likewise NN retains Melville's pseudonymous ascription for "The Encantadas"; see the discussion at 125.3.) These six retained "Virginian" passages and the four other late readings NN rejects are alike in being Melville's late changes (see the MANUSCRIPT ALTERATIONS list) in the EM fair copy that were motivated by his desire to mask its authorship and by extra-literary considerations all too probably urged upon him by Duyckinck as *Literary World* editor (see above, pp. 655–56). The NN distinction for keeping the "Virginian" passages but rejecting the others is that Melville in inventing the "Virginian" as author was not thereby compromising his literary freedom or modifying his views. By assuming that mask he was only extending the means he had already adopted in the essay (citing Shakespeare's example) for telling the truth by putting it into the mouth of a dramatized speaker. That is, he had already enabled himself to write the truth he wanted to tell about Hawthorne and his *Mosses* by means of a quasi-fictional setting and narrative voice that allowed him to speak, as if bewitched, of "Hawthorne in his writings" with an unguarded enthusiasm, if not "sane madness," less possible to a sober essayist writing in his own person, even if anonymously, about another actual, not fictional, person. In short, in his draft he had already given voice to the attitudes and views of a persona he could quite appropriately specify, in his final revisions, as a "Virginian"—a hot man in a cold climate. Evidence about Melville's creative methods, from "Fragments from a Writing Desk" on to *Billy Budd, Sailor,* shows him reaching toward technical means of "distancing" from his "proper self" truths he had written or wished to write. In the "Mosses" essay, and elsewhere, one way was to assign his already written words to an appropriate mouthpiece—as he does its authorship to the "Virginian" and an extreme sentiment in it to his "hot-headed Carolina cousin" (247.13–17, 248.32–34). See also the HISTORICAL NOTE, pp. 463–64, on his way of writing an anonymous review of *Typee.*

239.14–17 "When . . . reality."] Quoted from the last sentence of "The Artist of the Beautiful" in *Mosses,* II, 191, with "artist" capitalized and the four verbs changed from past to present tense. Melville thus converted Hawthorne's comment about the individual "artist" Owen Warland into a generalization about "the Artist." Adaptive quoting of this sort, common in the nineteenth century, calls for emendation only when it contains errors as distinguished from intentional changes (see pp. 557–58).

240.1 warranty] The EM misspelling "warrantry" (corrected by LW, compositor Lyman) probably reflects either Melville's or Elizabeth Shaw Melville's own misconception of the word, since the same misspelling occurs in *Moby-Dick* (chap. 28; NN122.21), for which she was a copyist.

240.6 visible frame] The irregular spatial placing of these words in Elizabeth Shaw Melville's hand shows one of her copying practices: when she could not decipher a word or phrase of Melville's she would leave a blank space for it in her fair-copy manuscript until she could make it out for herself or ask him what it was. The first of some two dozen such instances in the "Mosses" manuscript occurs here at Leaf 2, line 15, the second line in the excerpt reproduced below, where her later insertion of "visible frame" took more space than she had allowed, so that she began it to the left of her margin and crowded it right up to "betoken". See the MANUSCRIPT ALTERATIONS list below.

Excerpt from Leaf 2 (reduced)

240.8 glance.] NN retains the EM period where LW (compositor Lyman) substituted an exclamation point. Sentences interrogative in form sometimes end with a period in Melville's (and other nineteenth-century) writings (see the discussion at 249.1 and p. 563).

240.27 cheeks] NN (like LW, compositor Lyman) emends EM "cheek" to fit the sense and grammatical number ("those strawberry-beds her cheeks"); Elizabeth Shaw Melville as copyist probably failed to see Melville's often slight and turned-under terminal "s". Though Melville missed this instance he caught several others in proofing her fair copy and added the "s" to them: "edges" (243.39), "superstitions" (245.34), "parts" (246.6), and "writings" (249.12).

240.34–36 volume . . . fly-leaf] Melville (through his narrative persona) gives here a fanciful—but of course unemendable—description of the book and of where, how, and when he got it (in Vermont at breakfast from young "cousin Cherry"). Hence his account may also be fanciful, not factual, in saying he read it in July in the haymow and had not met Hawthorne before writing the essay. His book description is exposed as fanciful by several discrepancies between it and his copy of *Mosses* now at Harvard (see p. 654), his markings in which show it was the actual copy he read and had in hand when writing the essay (passages marked coincide with those quoted). (1) His notation on the front free endpaper (verso) is "H. Melville. / from Aunt Mary. Pittsfield. July 18, 1850". This means he was given the Harvard copy by an Aunt Mary not by "cousin Cherry"; presumably it means it was given to him that day in July, 1850, in Pittsfield. His most likely Aunt Mary was Mary Anna Augusta Melvill, the elderly widow of his uncle Thomas and mother of his cousin Robert, who was running the old family mansion as a summer boardinghouse, where Herman and his family were staying and where that Aunt Mary was present. An alternative Aunt Mary, however—if the noted date and place are not those of the gift but simply those of the notation itself—was his father's sister, then aged seventy-two, the wife of Captain John D'Wolf II, who in 1850 was living in Dorchester near Boston, as mentioned in *Moby-Dick* (chap. 45). That this less likely Aunt Mary was taken to be the book's donor by Eleanor Melville Metcalf, Melville's granddaughter who in 1937 gave it to Harvard, at least shows she knew of no contrary family tradition (letter to Harrison Hayford, August 30, 1942, now in the Melville Collection of The Newberry Library). (2) Pressed on a leaf attached by sealing wax to the front pastedown of the Harvard copy is something possibly corresponding to what the essay calls a "curious frontispiece" of moss. But Melville's subjoined ink notation raises further problems: "This moss was gathered in Salem, and therefore I place it here for a frontispiece. / P. S. It may be objected that this is sea-moss;—but then, it only went to sea—like many young mortals—in its youth, and to my certain knowledge has been ashore ever since." The later penciled date "August, 1850" to the right of this ink notation seems of no help in accounting for how and when this "moss" got there. Whereas in the essay "cousin Cherry's" gift volume already had a "curious frontispiece in green, . . . cunningly pressed to a fly-leaf," the Harvard volume's stringy "sea-moss" filaments are pressed not to a "fly-leaf" but, as just said, on a leaf attached to the front pastedown, and it is not green but red and pale yellow and in fact is not moss except by misnomer but one of the red marine algae. Pinholes in the actual "fly-leaf" do show that something now gone was once pinned (not "pressed") to its verso, whether or not the essay's green moss. (3) The copy of *Mosses* described in the essay is said to be "verdantly bound" and, though there were such first-edition copies, the Harvard one (now re-backed) was bound in dark blue cloth which has faded toward green. In sum, the essay's account of the book is shown by comparison with his actual copy to be so fanciful as to make biographically unreliable its report that he both read the book and wrote the essay in July before meeting Hawthorne (see Hayford, 1945). Passages throughout Melville's writings give similarly appropriate though fanciful bibliographical descriptions; see, for example, "A Thought on Book-Binding" (pp. 237–38); the dedication to *Israel Potter* (Northwestern-Newberry Edition, p. viii; also p. 284); and the metaphor of Love as a "gospel" in "a volume bound in rose-leaves, clasped with violets, and by the beaks of hummingbirds printed with peach juice on the leaves of lilies" *(Pierre,* bk. 2; NN34.3–5).

240.38 Manse' ".] For NN placement of the period missing in EM/HM after "Manse", see the discussion at 210.13. See also the emendations at 242.14, 243.6, and 253.36.

240.38 Yes" . . . Cherry] It is not NN policy to regularize (as did LW, compositor Lyman) by supplying commas before the quotation mark and after "Cherry", even though their absence from the manuscript may well be due to Melville's oversight. Interrupted quotations appear unpunctuated in Melville's works often enough to suggest that punctuation with them was not yet mandatory. Melville left the same situation unpunctuated at 240.39, though his wife supplied commas at 240.37. See also the discussion at 207.35–36.

240.38 flowery] The expected word would be "flowering"—in allusion to the flowering hawthorn. If Melville in fact wrote "flowering" in his draft, his wife could well have misread it as "flowery" since his "-ing" ending is often indistinct. While the EM word itself could be read as "flowering", it is probably "flowery" (so read by LW, compositor Lyman).

241.1–12 Stretched . . . Hill."] Hayford and Parker (p. 537, n. 1) point out that the opening lines of this passage, at Leaf 4, lines 2–20 of the manuscript, offer "clear proof" that in 1850 Elizabeth Shaw Melville as copyist not only of this essay but also of *Moby-Dick* "was still omitting punctuation" and Melville still supplying it later, as they had done in 1848 while preparing the fair copy of *Mardi*. But she included some punctuation, here the quotation marks—following old-fashioned

Stretched on that new mown clover,
~~with~~ the hill-side breeze blowing over me ~~from~~
thro' the wide barn door, and soothed by the hum of the
bees in the meadows around, how magically
stole over me this Mossy Man! And how amply,
how bountifully, did he redeem that delicious
promise to his' guests in the Old Manse, of whom
it is written—"Others could give them pleasure,
"~~and~~ amusement, or instruction—these could be
"picked up anywhere—but it was for me to
"give them rest. Rest, in a life of trouble! What
"better could be done for ~~those~~ weary and
"world-worn spirits? what better could be done
"for anybody, who came within our magic
"circle, than to throw the spell of a magic spirit
"over him?"—So all that day, half-buried in the
new clover ~~of the hay-mow~~, I watched this Hawthorne's
"Assyrian dawn, and Paphian sunset and moonrise, from the summit of our Eastern Hill."

Excerpt (reduced) from Leaf 4 (NN241.1–12)

practice by using them before each line (except two)—the dashes, exclamation points, question marks, and two of the commas (after "amusement" and "Rest"). The rest of the commas in this passage are Melville's, as are the substantive revisions; his contrasting hand and darker ink are usually clearly distinguishable from hers in the manuscript itself if not always in reproductions (see the accompanying reproduction and both MANUSCRIPT ALTERATIONS lists).

241.5–10 "Others . . . him?"] Quoted from "The Old Manse" *(Mosses,* I, 25–26), with "pleasure, or" for "pleasure and" and "weary" for "those weary", as well as the omission of some one hundred words (about three such world-worn spirits) between "spirits" and "what". Again, Melville generalized Hawthorne's specific references.

241.11–12 "Assyrian . . . Hill."] Adapted from "The Old Manse" *(Mosses,* I, 3): "It was here that Emerson wrote 'Nature;' for he was then an inhabitant of the Manse, and used to watch the Assyrian dawn and the Paphian sunset and moonrise, from the summit of our eastern hill." Melville apparently did not realize that the gorgeous images were not Hawthorne's own but his allusion to Emerson's *Nature* (chap. 3): "The dawn is my Assyria; the sun-set and moon-rise my Paphos . . . ."

241.15–16 "dismissed . . . him"] Adapted (with alteration of the pronouns) from "The Old Manse" *(Mosses,* I, 26; marked in Melville's copy with a marginal check): "we dismissed him, with but misty reminiscences, as if he had been dreaming of us."

241.24–26 "that . . . odd-fellows."] Quoted from "The Old Manse" *(Mosses,* I, 10; marked in Melville's copy with a marginal line), with "that" for "they" and the addition of a comma after "humorists" and a hyphen in "odd fellows".

241.29–31 "the thump . . . ripeness"] These words are taken exactly from "The Old Manse" *(Mosses,* I, 10), but their order is adapted: Hawthorne's sentence begins "In the stillest afternoon, if I listened, the thump of a great apple was audible, falling . . . " and continues to the end as Melville quotes it.

241.33–34 "Will . . . greenness?"] Quoted exactly from "Buds and Bird-Voices" *(Mosses,* I, 146), but with "Spring" for "spring"—and with uncapitalized "voices" in the cited title.

241.37–242.8 "Nor . . . man."] Quoted from "Fire-Worship" *(Mosses,* I, 130–31; marked in Melville's copy with a marginal line), with (1) the EM misspelling "offerred" (corrected by LW, compositor Alexander, and by NN at 241.39); (2) the change from a semicolon to a comma after "more" at 242.7; (3) the confused HM added punctuation "all; He" (followed by LW, compositor Alexander) for "all. He" (restored by NN at 242.7); and (4) the ending with a period at "man." where the sentence continues "man; and they pardoned his characteristic imperfections."

242.12–14 "subdued . . . age"] Quoted accurately from "The Old Apple-Dealer" *(Mosses,* II, 160). But in the EM citation of that title at 242.11 the hyphen is not present (supplied by LW, compositor Alexander).

242.14–15 Such . . . heart.] One of Elizabeth Shaw Melville's penciled "x" marks is visible in the margin of line 22 of Leaf 6 of the manuscript. Apparently she wished to check with her husband about the word she had copied as "tones", which she later canceled and replaced by "touches". However, not all EM corrections are accompanied by marginal "x" marks. In some cases she recognized her own transcriptional error and made an immediate correction, sometimes by erasing and rewriting, or sometimes by canceling what she had written and adding the correct reading at once right after it: for example, her misreading of "dimly" as "divinely", which she wrote, canceled, and immediately followed with "dimly" at 244.33; also, her memorial repetition then cancellation (after "felt") of "at some" at 245.30 (see the MANUSCRIPT ALTERATIONS list below). Other EM corrections, also without corresponding "x" marks, were made later, perhaps on her own, perhaps in a proofing session with her husband (if, unlike Bartleby, she consented to one). But the numerous HM corrections of her misreadings show Melville gave the manuscript a separate proofing while revising; he caught a dozen or more EM misreadings, but probably overlooked others still in the essay. NN emends as a substantive EM misreading only one word (see the discussion at 240.27).

242.32 height] NN (like LW, compositor Alexander) thus emends EM "heigth", though perhaps what Elizabeth Shaw Melville aimed at was "heighth" (the form retained by NN in "Fragments from a Writing Desk" at 194.28, 198.39, and 199.32; but cf. EM "height" at 250.21).

243.4–6 "Methinks . . . eyes".] The words of this passage (and of the two directly preceding quoted phrases) are taken exactly from the last paragraphs of "Monsieur du Miroir" *(Mosses,* I, 158), where "shape" was capitalized, the title was set in small capitals, and "power" was followed by a comma. For NN placement of the concluding period see the discussion at 210.13.

243.17 Serpent] Elizabeth Shaw Melville first wrote "friend" but later corrected it to "Serpent". Possibly it was her own memorial slip that turned one proverbial allusion ("bosom serpent") into another ("bosom friend"), but the same slip occurred in *Mosses* itself, in the "Contents of Part II", which lists the title as "Egotism; or the Bosom Friend", though not at the head of the story or in the running titles. Possibly Melville himself had taken the incorrect title from the table of contents without reading the tale (about which his remark is quite general). Later in the essay he confesses he had not read all the pieces when he wrote its first part—another token of his "great haste" when he "dashed it off" (see p. 654 above). An error in his review of Cooper's *The Sea Lions* suggests similar haste (see the discussion at 236.10).

244.15–16 "Off . . . Buckingham!"] This line (exactly as quoted) was interpolated by Colley Cibber into Shakespeare's *Richard III,* IV.iv, following Catesby's line (531) "My liege, the Duke of Buckingham is taken."

244.35 Shakspeare] Acceptable variant spellings are not regularized by NN (cf. "Spencer" at 252.7,8,12 and "Marlow" at 252.37). The spelling "Shakspeare" occurs five times in two Melville letters of 1849, along with "Shakesper" and "Shaksper" *(Letters,* pp. 77–80). It is used on the title page and throughout his edition of the *Dramatic Works* (Sealts 460), where it is remarked that either "Shakspeare or Shakspere" may be used, "for the floating orthography of the name is properly attached to the one or the other of these varieties" (I, v). It is Melville's own manuscript spelling here, even though "Shakespeare" is the consistent EM manuscript spelling, which he let stand twice in this passage and all through the essay, and "Shakespeare" is the spelling he himself used four times in revising the fair copy. Apparently he had no preferred spelling and did not notice the variants here. LW (all three compositors) in every instance regularized EM/HM "Shakespeare" to "Shakspeare".

245.24–25 "we . . . others"] Melville's exact source for this wording has not been found. In the 1706 London edition titled *Moral Reflections and Maxims* (p. 36) the "Moral Reflection" numbered CXCVIII reads, "We raise the Reputation of some, to pull down that of others . . . ."

245.39 that . . . born] NN rejects Melville's revision "that men not very much inferior to Shakespeare are being born" as a product of the toning down, too likely at Duyckinck's urging, by which he weakened a number of his original nationalistic extravagances. See the MANUSCRIPT ALTERATIONS list below.

245.40–246.1 say who] NN follows the unemphatic EM reading (sharpened by LW, compositor Lyman, to "say, Who") though its lack of the comma and capital obscures Melville's intended allusive reversal of Sydney Smith's famous question in 1820, "In the four quarters of the globe, who reads an American book?" In revising the EM fair copy Melville modified his original challenge "who reads a book by an Englishman?" by adding the restrictive phrase "that is a modern?" NN accepts this qualification as prompted not by Duyckinck's cautionary influence but by Melville's own genuine love and respect for the classic English writers.

246.14 Greene] NN emends Melville's naming "Chettle" here. As Willard Thorp pointed out, "Melville is unwittingly unfair to Chettle. It was Robert Greene who, in *A Groatsworth of Wit,* thus maligned Shakespeare" *(Herman Melville: Representative Selections,* p. 424, n. 6). Henry Chettle was the publisher of Greene's posthumous book in 1592. Melville may have either misread or misremembered the account of the affair which he marked with a marginal line in Charles Symmons's prefatory "The Life of William Shakspeare" in the *Dramatic Works,* I, xiv–xv (Sealts 460), where the parts played by both Greene and Chettle are told, or perhaps he was following John Payne Collier's suggestion, in his *Life of William Shakespeare* (London, 1842), that "possibly" Chettle was the real author of *A Groatsworth of Wit* (see S. Schoenbaum, *Shakespeare's Lives* [New York: Oxford University Press, 1970], p. 344). In any case, Thorp's statement remains correct, and NN emends the error in accordance with the policy stated on p. 558, n. 25.

246.15 other birds'] NN does not emend Melville's misquotation of Greene's epithet for Shakespeare, "an upstart crow, beautified with our feathers" (see the discussion just above) because nineteenth-century usage allowed quotation marks with such loose quotations. Melville's phrase "other birds' feathers" (NN—like LW—adds the apostrophe) seems to show he was aware that Greene was alluding to "the crow . . . taught to imitate its betters that derives ultimately from Aesop, Martial, and Macrobius . . . ," as S. Schoenbaum explains *(Shakespeare's Lives* [New York: Oxford University Press, 1970], p. 51).

246.22 I do not say] Since Melville's change of his categorical word "think" (in the EM fair copy) to the noncommittal word "say" strengthens his matching of Hawthorne with Shakespeare, it does not belong among the toning-down revisions which NN rejects as due to Duyckinck's influence.

246.26–30 equalled . . . none.] In this passage Melville made one of his most severe revisions, not followed by NN, toning down its enthusiastic nationalism, very likely at Duyckinck's instance, so that it read: " . . . if Shakespeare has not been equalled, give the world time, & he is sure to be surpassed, in one hemisphere or the other."

247.5 England . . . alien] Although it is possible that Duyckinck influenced Melville's addition here of "after all" and "in many things", NN follows his revision because the added words do not seriously weaken his original declaration. See the MANUSCRIPT ALTERATIONS list below.

247.6 bowels] Melville corrected the EM misreading "bonds"—an unconscious scribal conversion of a strong unexpected word to a weaker ordinary one. For further examples see the discussion at 177.6.

247.6–9 no Hawthorne . . . "Belfry Pigeon"] The original EM reading (from Leaf 15, lines 10–11—see the accompanying reproduction) was "no Hawthornes Emersons Whittiers Danas Coopers"; as Melville revised and expanded it, the reading became "no Hawthorne no Emerson no Whittier, no Irving, no Bryant, no Dana no Cooper no Willis (not the author of the 'Dashes', but the author of the 'Belfry Pigeon')." Later, probably in New York, Duyckinck lined out the individual names with heavy strokes in black ink and worded the passage in more general terms; his involvement is certain though its exact timing and degree are conjectural. See the MANUSCRIPT ALTERATIONS list. NN restores the HM revision. As it shows, Melville evidently thought less of Nathaniel Parker Willis (1806–57) as a prose writer (author of *Dashes at Life with a Free Pencil,* 1845) than as a poet (author of "The Belfry Pigeon," 1831). Perhaps Melville added Irving to this list because he is the "graceful writer" referred to below (247.34ff.).

247.10–18 praise . . . sound] NN adopts the HM revised version of this passage as inscribed on the patch (Leaf 15, lines 13–22) which he placed over the heavily revised EM lines 13–18 (see the last six lines in the accompanying reproduction and the MANUSCRIPT ALTERATIONS list). No taint is in question from the possible persuasion of Duyckinck, whose revision in the lines just above ("no Hawthorne . . . 'Belfry Pigeon' ") was made later, probably back in New York.

247.16 Pop Emmons] The jocular nickname for Richard Emmons, author of

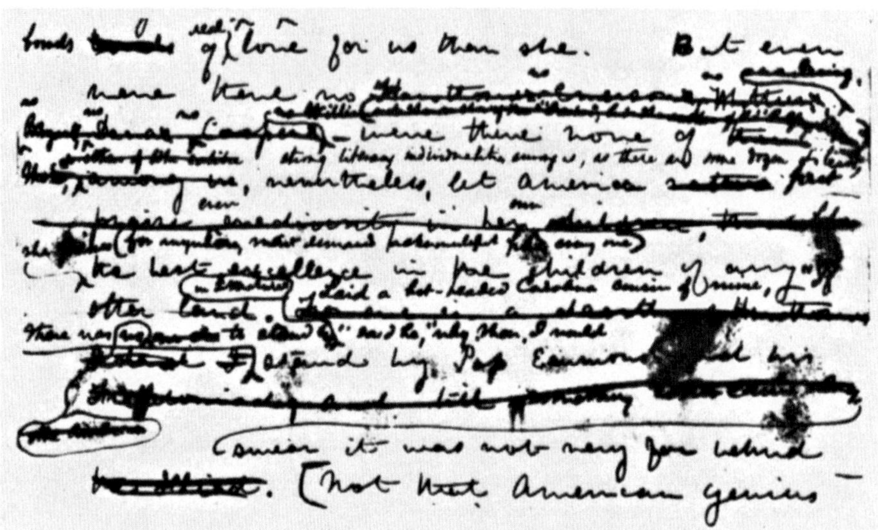

Leaf 15, lines 9–18 (NN247.6–19), as heavily revised by Melville (reduced).

the blatantly nationalistic and bathetic four-volume epic on the War of 1812, *The Fredoniad* (Boston, 1827), was current; Edgar Allan Poe used it twice in 1843 reviews and again in 1845, naming him for an extreme contrast to Homer as Melville does here.

248.6 Without . . . fact] Though the HM addition of this phrase somewhat softens the blow and may be the result of editorial pressure, NN keeps the revision since the strong statement remains.

248.10 Tompkins] Although the NN editors cannot satisfactorily explain the allusion, no textual error seems to be involved since the name is written clearly in Melville's hand (replacing EM "Milton") and went unquestioned by Duyckinck as editor.

248.15 Bostonian] NN restores this EM reading on the ground that the reason Melville canceled it was all too likely Duyckinck's moderating suasion rather than his own uninfluenced second thoughts.

248.17–18 And . . . it.] NN restores this prophetic sentence which Melville canceled, apparently under Duyckinck's influence.

248.23–24 while . . . everywhere,] This HM addition, though possibly resulting from Duyckinck's influence, is followed by NN because the main statement is not weakened.

249.1 Hawthorne.] NN (like LW, compositor McIntyre) keeps the period Melville added to the EM sentence, where a question mark would seem called for by the sentence form and sense (of which Melville may have lost track). See the discussion at 240.8.

249.2 beeches] Melville canceled the EM reading "birches" (evidently a misreading of "beeches" in his original draft) and careted in "beeches". In *Moby-Dick* (chap. 54), Melville failed to catch in either the American or English first editions the reverse misreading "beech canoes" for "birch canoes", emended by NN at 244.28. Cf. the discussion of "alders" at 282.18.

249.3 praries] For NN retention of this spelling, see pp. 561–62.

249.13 I never saw the man] This (still unverified) disclaimer is the first direct statement that the writer does not know Hawthorne the man; for some reason it comes near the end of the essay as it stood before the passage was added that is said to have been written twenty-four hours later (250.13). The purpose of the disclaimer is obscure, unless it is to conceal the fact that the writer does know Hawthorne and to emphasize the idea that he is personally disinterested, or to prevent his being identified as one of Duyckinck's Young America literary nationalist clique—and perhaps even as Melville, an easy identification for insiders, given his argument with Holmes at the August 5 dinner (see p. 654 above). Except for the word "plantation" the passage is all in Elizabeth Shaw Melville's hand, but it interrupts the sentence in a way that suggests it was inserted in the draft she was copying from, as a tactic of concealment earlier than the late invention of the "Virginian", which motivated Melville's insertion of "plantation" here at 249.13.

249.15 "Twice Told Tales"] How much of this collection Melville had read at this point is unclear: he had borrowed it from Duyckinck in the summer of 1849, and sometime inside the back cover of his *Mosses* he wrote, "I had formerly read his 'Twice Told Tales' "; but in a letter to Duyckinck on February 12, 1851, he said he had just recently read the tales and confessed, "I had not read but a few of them before" (see Sealts 259, 260).

249.19–20 displaced . . . authority.] Perhaps Melville cut his reference to "Oliver Goldsmith and many another brighter name than that" on Duyckinck's suggestion, but perhaps it was because he had already named Goldsmith twice (at 248.7,8).

250.4–11 "A . . . he."] Quoted exactly from "The Intelligence Office" (*Mosses,* II, 87; marked in Melville's copy with a marginal check), with the comma after instead of before the quotation mark following "Truth" at 250.11; NN adjusts the EM double quotation marks to single ones at 250.11.

250.16 Mosses] NN supplies the capital because EM "mosses" is more likely an oversight than an intended distinction from the same word three times capitalized in this passage—especially since Melville changed EM "mosses" to "Mosses" at 250.19, 250.23, and 250.39. Thus this word (and the others) is intended as a short title for the book itself, which, as common at the time, is not distinguished by quotation marks or italics (see also the discussion at 253.2).

251.25–26 "It . . . sin"] Adapted from "Young Goodman Brown" *(Mosses,* I, 82; marked in Melville's copy with a marginal line and underscoring): EM/HM reads "It is yours" for "It shall be yours," and ends the sentence after "sin" where Hawthorne's sentence continues.

251.28–30 " 'Faith! . . . wilderness."] In wording quoted exactly from "Young Goodman Brown" *(Mosses,* I, 77), but omitting a comma after "her" and placing the exclamation points outside the quotation marks (which NN puts back inside as an oversight on Melville's part as he added the quotation marks—see also the emendation at 240.31). NN also adjusts the EM double quotation marks around the first "Faith" and around the "Faith's" in the next line to single quotation marks and adds a double one before the first "Faith" to fulfill the intention made evident by the closing double quotation marks at the end of the passage (see also 250.4–11).

252.7 Spencer] Here and twice below (252.8,12) NN retains the EM spelling as a currently acceptable variant of "Spenser". See the discussion at 244.35.

252.16 sunset clouds] This phrase and the ensuing feast figure are drawn directly from the first paragraph of "A Select Party" *(Mosses,* I, 52, also 65).

252.21–22 "a . . . eminence"] From "A Select Party" *(Mosses,* I, 60; marked in Melville's copy with a marginal line): EM/HM reads "a young man of" for "a young man in"; Melville carelessly placed the opening quotation mark before "of" instead of "a" (emended by NN; see the MANUSCRIPT ALTERATIONS list below and cf. the emendation at 253.11).

252.27 at least] NN (like LW, compositor Alexander) omits the HM comma after "least"; its presence perverts the intended sense "at least in this one point".

252.37 Marlow] NN retains this EM spelling as a currently acceptable variant for "Marlowe". See the discussion at 244.35.

253.2 Specimens] As with the references to "Mosses" at 250.16ff., NN does not regularize by supplying quotation marks or italics for this short title of Lamb's *Specimens of English Dramatic Poets, Who Lived about the Time of Shakespeare* (for Melville's edition see Sealts 318).

253.7 illy] Changed to "ill" in LW (by compositor Alexander—or Duyckinck in proofs). As an adverbial form "illy" was becoming ill regarded: Worcester (1847) labeled it "rarely used by good writers," and Webster (1861) noted "sometimes used, though improperly, for Ill." The *OED,* nevertheless, cites Jefferson (1785), Southey (1795), Lowell (1848), and Irving (1849), and labels it "now *dial.*" Melville used both "ill" and "illy" but became uneasy about the latter, changing it to "ill" four times in a copy of *Israel Potter* (1855; see the Northwestern-Newberry Edition, p. 247).

253.9–10 "such . . . intellect."] Quoted from "A Select Party" *(Mosses,* I, 60; marked in Melville's copy with triple marginal lines), with a comma added after "light".

253.18 "The] NN follows EM (as did LW, compositor Alexander) in placing the quotation mark before "The", thus allowing loose citation of the title of the book under review.

253.20 prove] NN keeps this EM reading (with the sense "works which prove [to be] the culmination") whereas LW (compositor Alexander) emended to "proves" (giving the sense "sign which proves the culmination"). Since the copy-text reading makes satisfactory sense it is not emended by NN, though the other sense is arguably better, and it is possible that Elizabeth Shaw Melville missed Melville's terminal "s", as at 240.27. (The recurrence of "prove" just below does not seem to settle the point.)

EMENDATIONS. 239.2 Spending] NN; spending HM 239.7 task.] LW; ~∧ EM 240.1 receive] LW; recieve EM *240.1 warranty] LW; warrantry EM 240.7 nature∧] LW; ~. EM 240.20 perennial] LW; perrenial EM *240.27 cheeks] LW; cheek EM 240.31 Moss!"] NN; ~"! EM/HM *240.38 Manse' ".] NN; ~' "∧ EM/HM 240.39 Hawthorne."—] NN; ~."— — EM/HM 241.16 him".] NN; ~"∧ EM 241.28 Hawthorne's] LW; Hawthornes' EM *241.39 offered] LW; offerred EM *242.7 all.] NN; ~; EM/HM 242.11 Dealer"] LW; ~∧ EM 242.14 age".] NN; ~"∧ EM *242.32 height] LW; heigth EM 242.32 receive] LW; recieve EM 243.4 Miroir".] NN; ~".". EM/HM 243.6 eyes".] NN; ~"∧ EM 243.7 Earth's] LW; Earths' EM 243.15 men's] LW; mens' HM 243.28 blackness] LW; blackeness EM 244.6 gold.] LW; ~∧ EM 245.6 contemporaneous] LW; contemporanious HM 245.9 noiseless] LW; noisless EM 245.24 exemplify] LW; exemply EM 245.35 Forty.] LW; ~∧ EM/HM *245.39 Shakespeares] EM; men not very much inferior to Shakespeare, HM *246.14 Greene] NN; Chettle HM *246.15 birds'] LW; ~∧ HM 246.15 imitation] LW; immitation HM 246.20 sagacious] LW; sagatious HM *246.26 equalled,] EM; equalled, give the world time, and HM *246.27–28 and surpassed . . . born] EM; in one hemisphere or the other. HM *246.28 born.] LW; ~∧ EM *246.28–30 For . . . none.] EM; *[canceled]* HM 246.29 out-brag] NN; ~∧~ EM 246.29 world,] NN; ~∧ EM 246.29 say,] NN; ~∧ EM *247.6–9 Hawthorne . . . Pigeon")] EM/HM; *[canceled]* ED 247.7 Dana,] NN; ~∧ HM

247.7 Cooper,] NN; ~∧ HM *247.9 —were . . . us,] EM/HM; —were there none of *[uncanceled]* these . . . us, *[canceled]* strong literary individualities among us, as there are some dozen at least *[added]* ED 247.16 'Fredoniad,'] LW; "~," HM 247.17 Iliad] LW; Illiad HM 247.21 nation's] LW; nations' EM 247.25 received] LW; recieved EM 247.35 received] LW; recieved EM 248.1 greatness.] LW; ~∧ HM *248.15 Bostonian] EM; *[canceled]* HM *248.17–18 And . . . it.] EM; *[canceled]* HM 248.30 morning; and] LW; morning; And EM/HM 239.4 brethren] LW; bretheren EM *250.11 " 'I] NN; " "~ EM *250.11 Truth',] NN; ~", EM 250.15 gleaning] LW; geaning EM *250.16 Mosses] LW; mosses EM *251.28 " 'Faith!'] LW; "~'! EM/HM *251.29 'Faith!] LW; "~! EM/HM *251.29 Faith!'] LW; ~"! EM/HM *252.21 ∧of] NN; "of EM/HM *252.21 "a] NN; ∧a EM *252.27 least∧] NN; ~, HM 253.11 ∧—in] NN; "—~ EM/HM 253.11 "Select] NN; ∧~ EM 253.31 be] LW; *[not present]* HM 253.36 Literature".] NN; ~"∧ EM

NN also emends (as did LW) the "&" of EM/HM to "and" at: 239.1, 242.4,22,26,33, 243.9(twice),10,17,25,31,35, 244.8,26,30,32, 245.8,13, 246.13,21,31,36, 247.9,16(second),18,26,36,37, 248.25, 249.21,25(second),36, 250.5,14(second),16,22,38, 252.40, 253.25,27,31; "tho' " to "though" at: 242.24, 246.19, 249.37; and "thro' " to "through" at: 239.8, 241.2.

HYPHENATION. I. 240.26 strawberry-beds 241.12 moonrise 242.17 omnipresent 243.11 †all-engendering

II. 242.5 chimney-top 243.11 †all-engendering 253.37 five-thousand 253.38 hundred-thousand

SUBSTANTIVE VARIANTS. 240.21 like wine] EM; likewise LW 240.27 cheeks] LW; cheek EM 241.17 mild] EM; wild LW 243.7 Earth's] LW; Earths' EM 243.13 nought] EM; naught LW 243.15 men's] LW; mens' HM 244.26 sane] EM; same LW 245.14 utterances] EM/HM; utterance LW 246.14 hooted] EM; looked LW 247.6 bowels] HM; bonds LW 247.6–9 Hawthorne . . . Pigeon")] EM/HM; *[canceled]* ED, LW 247.9 —were . . . us,] EM/HM; —were there none of *[uncanceled]* these . . . us, *[canceled]* strong literary individualities among us, as there are some dozen at least, ED; strong literary individualities among us, as there are some dozens at least, LW 247.21 nation's] LW; nations' EM 248.23 freely] HM; fully LW 248.33 enthusiastic] HM; *[not present]* LW 248.34 our] EM; one LW 249.7 in] EM/HM; on LW 250.27 of] HM; in LW 251.18 eagle-eyed] EM; eager-eyed LW 252.10 the] EM; *[not present]* LW 252.15 this] EM; that LW 252.17 Belshazzar's] EM; Belshazzar LW 252.38 those] EM/HM; these LW 253.7 illy] EM; ill LW

253.20 prove] EM; proves LW 253.29 in] HM; at LW 253.31 be] LW; *[not present]* HM

MANUSCRIPT ALTERATIONS. I. 239.1–2 *Hawthorne* . . . Vermont] *inscription by* HM 239.13 their ostensible] their [HM >ostensible] 239.13 to] at →*erase* at *w.o.* to→ 239.18 know] kow [EM? *alter to* know] 239.20 of Junius,—] of [HM >Junius,—] 239.22 possesses] possesses all [HM <all] 240.1 from] by [HM <by >from] 240.5 that not] that [HM >not] 240.5 than] than [EM ≯mor *then* <mor] *240.6 his visible frame] his *followed by blank space* [EM *add in blank space* visible frame] 240.7 the nature within.] his [HM <his >the] nature. [HM >within. *without canceling period after* nature *(emended)*] 240.8 heaven] G →*w.o.* the→ God [HM <the God >heaven] 240.9 curious, how] very wonderful but [HM <very wonderful but >curious, how *with guideline to caret*] 240.9 travel] tra →*w.o.* travel→ 240.11 so] even so [HM <even] 240.11 way] way [EM *mend* way] 240.11 wide] wild →<wild→ *add* wide 240.11 beyond.] behind it. [HM <behind it. >beyond.] 240.12 has it] it [HM <it] has [HM >it] 240.13 this] the [HM *alter to* this] 240.14 a . . . since.] the / day before yesterday. [HM <the . . . yesterday. >a day or two since. *with guideline to caret*] 240.17 excellent",] ~"∧ [HM *add comma*] 240.20 It] But it [HM <But *and alter* it *to capital]* 240.20–21 be, however,] be [HM *add comma and with guideline to caret* >however,] 240.25 like the] ?the →*w.o.* like >the→ 240.25 pearls] pearles →*alter to* pearls→ 240.26 fairy-tale,] ~-~∧ [HM *add comma*] 240.28 hay-mow;] ~-~∧ [HM *add semicolon*] 240.29 'Dwight's . . . England'.] "~ . . . ~." [HM? *delete double and add single quotation marks and new period*] 240.31 —"Moss!"] "~∧" [HM *add dash before opening quotation mark and exclamation point after closing quotation mark (emended)*] 240.33 'Dwight' ".] ∧~∧"∧ [HM *add single quotation marks and period*] 240.34 With] With [HM *add bracket before* With *for new paragraph*] 240.34 me,] the table [HM *add comma then* <the table, >me,] 240.36 fly-leaf.—] ~-~∧∧ [HM *add period and dash*] 240.38 cousin Cherry] she [HM <she >cousin Cherry] 240.39 Hawthorne."—"Hawthorne] ~∧"∧ ¶"~ [HM *add period and dash after first* Hawthorne *and another dash before* "Hawthorne *then cancel EM paragraph break by guideline linking the successive sentences without canceling second dash (emended)*] 240.40 barn".] ~"∧ [HM *add period*] 241.1 clover,] clover / with [HM *add comma and* <with] 241.2 through] from [HM <from / *add in margin* thro'] 241.3 Mossy Man] mossy man [HM *alter to capitals*] 241.4 his] ?the →*w.o.* his→ 241.5 Old] old [HM *alter to capital*] 241.6 pleasure, or] pleasure, and [HM <and >or] 241.8 for] for those [HM <those] 241.11 half-buried] buried [HM *with guideline to caret* >half- *before* buried] 241.11 clover,] clover of the hay-mow [HM *add comma then*

<of the hay-mow] 241.19 No] no [HM *alter to capital*] 241.19 rollicking rudeness] rollicking *followed by blank space* [EM >rudeness] 241.21 relishable] reliable →*alter to* relishable <relishable→ *add* relishable 241.21 were hardly] would / hardly be [HM <would ≯were / <be] 241.21 It] it [HM *alter to capital*] 241.23 Old] old [HM *alter to capital*] 241.24 it] of →<of→ *add* it 241.26 humorists,] humor-/ous [HM <ous *and after* humor- >ists, *with guideline to caret*] 241.26 odd-fellows.] ~-~∧ [HM *add period*] 241.28 spell,] spirit [HM *add comma then* <spirit, >spell, *with guideline to caret*] 241.28 aptly] aptly →*mend* aptly→ [HM <aptly >aptly] 241.30 stillest] silent [HM <silent >stillest] 241.31 ripeness"!] ~"∧ [HM *add exclamation point*] 241.32 of the] of [HM >the] 241.33 "Buds] "Buds [HM *add then cancel dash before* "Buds *and add bracket before* "Buds *for new paragraph*] 241.34 greenness?"—] ~∧"∧ [HM *add question mark and dash*] 241.35 Fire-Worship".] ~-~"∧ [HM *add period*] 241.37 exquisite] excellent [HM <excellent >*with guideline to caret* exquisite] *242.7 all.] all∧ [HM *add semicolon (emended)*] 242.9 not] all not [HM <all] 242.11 sketch] Sketch →<Sketch→ / sketch 242.11 The] the [EM? *alter to capital*] 242.14 his] x →*w.o.* his→ *242.14 touches] tones [EM <tones >touches] 242.14 in] on [EM? *alter to* in] 242.16 all] it →*w.o.* all→ 242.18 his generation] his *followed by blank space* [EM *add in blank space* generation] [HM <his >his *and w.o.* tion] 242.19 Still] still [HM *alter to capital*] 242.19 more] m xx →<m xx→ *add* more 242.19 touches] words [EM <words >touches] 242.20 similar ones,] more [HM *add comma then* <more, >similar ones,] 242.21 where] whence [HM <whence >where] 242.22 suffering, . . . other,—] suffering at [HM *add comma after* at *then cancel comma and add new comma after* suffering] some time or other in himself [HM <at *and* <in himself >endured *after* other {<endured >*with guideline to caret* & in some shape or other,—}] 242.23–24 over . . . like] over Hawthorne's melancholy rests / like [HM *with guideline to caret* >upon him *before* like {<upon him >him, *after* over}] 242.24–26 Summer, . . . vale.] Summer [HM *add period then alter period to comma and add* which tho' bathing a whole country / in one softness, still reveals the distinctive features & hues of each towering hill / *continuing along right margin* or far-winding vale. *then alter* features & hues *to* feature & hue *then* <feature & <each >every *and before* far-winding <or >& each *circled with guideline to caret and add comma after* hill] 242.27 But] But [HM *add bracket before* But *to confirm EM new paragraph*] 242.28 deemed] recognized as [HM <recognized as >deemed] 242.30–31 would . . . meanings.] would be entirely [HM <entirely >all but] unlooked for [HM *add period then* <be . . . for. >*with guideline to caret* hardly be anticipated:—a man who means no meanings.] 242.31 in whom] in [EM >whom] 242.33 skies;—] skies in other words [HM *add semicolon and dash after* skies *and comma after* words {<in other words,}]

242.35 indispensable . . . these] indubitable *followed by blank space* / of this [EM <indubitable ⊁indispensable complement / <this ⊁these] 242.36 the] his [EM <his ⊁the] 242.36 plummet.] planet. [HM <planet. >*with guideline to caret* plummet.] 242.36 Or, love] Love [HM <Love >*with guideline to caret* Or, love] 243.1 Miroir";] ~"∧ [HM *add semicolon]*
243.1 a reader] a *followed by blank space* [EM *add in blank space* reader *then* <reader >reader] 243.1 of fully] of [HM >fully] 243.2–3 —Yes, . . . sits] ∧Yes∧ [HM *add dash and comma] followed by blank space* [EM *add in blank space* there he sits] 243.3 looks] look [HM *alter to* looks]
243.4 Miroir".] ~". [HM *add new quotation marks and period (emended)*]
243.4 —"Methinks] ∧"~ [HM *add dash*] 243.7 How] How [HM *add bracket before* How *for new paragraph*] 243.8 Holocaust";] ~"∧ [HM *add semicolon]*
243.8 where] when [HM *alter to* where] 243.8 affectations] affectation [HM *alter to* affectations] 243.9 all . . . forms,] all *followed by blank space* / [EM *add in blank space* vanities & lame theories] [HM <lame ⊁empty *and in margins add* & / forms,] 243.9–10 are, . . . comprehensiveness,] are [HM *add comma and with guideline to caret* >one after another, & by an admirably graduated comprehensiveness, {*after* graduated *add comma and* >growing}] 243.11 till, at length] till / gradually [HM *add comma after* till *and* >at length, / <gradually] 243.14 Of] of [HM *alter to capital and add bracket before* Of *for new paragraph*] 243.14 Office",] ~"∧ [HM *add comma*] 243.15 of the] of [HM >the] 243.15 men's souls] this world [HM *add period after* world {<this world. >*with guideline to caret* mens' *(emended)* souls.}] 243.15 There] There [HM <There >There, {<There, >>There}] 243.17 "The Christmas] "The Christmas [HM *add dash before* "The *then w.o. dash with bracket for new paragraph*] 243.17 Banquet", and] Banquet" [HM *add comma plus dash after* Banquet" *then w.o. dash with ampersand*] *243.17 Serpent"] friend" [EM <friend" >Serpent"] 243.18 fine subjects] excellent things [HM <excellent things >*with guideline to caret* fine subjects] 243.19 the Indian-summer] the [HM >*with guideline to caret* Indian-summer] 243.20 on] in [HM *alter to* on] 243.21–22 blackness, . . . black.] blackness *followed by blank space* [EM *add in blank space* ten times] darker [HM *add comma after* blackness *and* <darker ⊁dark {<dark >*with guideline to caret* black.}] 243.23 forever advances] forever *followed by blank space* [EM *add in blank space* advances] 243.23 and circumnavigates] and *followed by blank space* [EM *add in blank space* circumnavigates] 243.25 means to] means / for [HM <for >to]
243.29 Innate] innate [HM *alter to capital]*
243.31 For, in] In [HM <In >*with guideline to caret* For, in]
243.32 somehow . . . Sin] like original sin [HM <like >*with guideline to caret* somehow {>>like *and alter* original sin *to capitals*}] 243.33 writer] author [HM <author ⊁writer] 243.33–34 ever wielded] ever *followed by blank space* [EM *add in blank space* wielded] 243.34 greater terror] greater *followed by blank*

space [EM *add in blank space* terror] 243.35 black . . . him] black *followed by blank space* [EM *add in blank space* conceit pervades him] 243.38 his] these [HM <these >his] 243.38 bright] light [EM *alter* light *to* bright *then* <bright >bright] 243.38 gildings] gildings [EM *rewrite* gildings] 243.39 edges] edge [HM *alter to* edges] 243.39 thunder-clouds.] ~-~^ [HM *add period]* 244.2 misconception of him.] misconception [HM *add period then cancel period and, with guideline to caret* >of him.] 244.3 the brain] the *followed by blank space* [EM *add in blank space* brain] 244.4 inspecting it;] much pondering [HM *add semicolon then* <much pondering; >*with guideline to caret* inspecting it;] 244.5 you need not] you [HM >need not] 244.7 Now . . . blackness] Now this *followed by blank space* [EM >it is *before* this *and in blank space add* blackness] [HM <this ≯that] 244.8 be, nevertheless,] be however [HM *add commas then* <however, >*with guideline to caret* nevertheless,] 244.10 his] x →*w.o.* his→ 244.10 dark.] gloom [HM *add period then* <gloom. >dark.] 244.13 loftiest, . . . circumscribed] unmatched [HM <unmatched >*with guideline to caret* loftiest, but most circumscribed] 244.14 profoundest] deepest & subtlest [HM <deepest & subtlest >*with guideline to caret* profoundest] 244.14 adored] aclaimed [HM <aclaimed >adored] 244.16 interlined] introduced [HM <introduced >*with guideline to caret* interlined] 244.16 another] some other [HM <some *altering* other *to* another] 244.16 brings] bring [HM *alter to* brings] 244.17 a mere] a [HM >mere] 244.19 deep far-away] deep [HM >far-away] 244.20 at] of [HM <of >at] 244.22 mouths] issues [HM <issues >mouths] 244.23 says, . . . insinuates] says [HM *add comma and with guideline to caret* >or rather insinuates {<rather >sometimes}] 244.23 which] that [HM <that >which] 244.25 Tormented] Goaded [HM <Goaded >*with guideline to caret* Tormented] 244.26 King . . . and] King [HM >*with guideline to caret* tears off the mask, /&] 244.28 much . . . unbridled] all the / snobbish [HM <all the snobbish >*with guideline to caret* much of the blind, unbridled] 244.31 remembered, . . . perceived,] perceived [HM <perceived >*with guideline to caret* remembered {*add comma and* or even *and* >>perceived *adding comma*] 244.32 undeveloped, . . . undevelopable)] undeveloped [HM *add comma and with guideline to caret* >(& sometimes undevelopable)] 244.33 dimly-discernable] divinely →<divinely→ *add* dimly-discerned [HM *alter* discerned *to* discernable] 244.33 these immediate products] they [HM <they >*with guideline to caret* these immediate products] 244.35 Shakspeare] he [HM <he >Shakspeare] 244.36 did do,] did [HM *add comma then cancel comma and* >do,] 244.36 not do, . . . doing.] not do [HM *add comma and with guideline to caret* >or refrained from doing.] 244.37 forced] found [HM <found >forced] 244.39 masters] writers [HM <writers >masters] 244.39 Art] art [HM *alter to capital*] 245.1 But if] But [HM >if]

245.1 be] is [HM <is >be] 245.2–3 or, perhaps,] but [HM <but >*with guideline to caret* or, perhaps,] 245.3 stage, (which] ~∧ ∧~ [HM *add comma and dash after* stage *then cancel dash and add parenthesis before* which]
245.5 palate,] palate [HM *add comma and* ≯to *then* <to] 245.5 that] / a [HM <a *add in margin* that] 245.5–6 is, then,] is [HM *add comma and* >then,] 245.6 that . . . age,] / that [HM >a lesser man like *then* <a . . . like *and add in margin* in a day like this *then* <in . . . this *and in margin with guideline to caret* >in a contemporanious *(emended)* age,] 245.7 man, . . . almost] man [HM *add comma and with guideline to caret* >as yet, almost]
245.9 the noiseless] the *followed by blank space* [EM *add in blank space* noisless *(emended)*] 245.10–11 the contrary course] it [HM <it >*with guideline to caret* the contrary course] 245.11 Hawthorne (either] ~ ∧~ [HM *add comma after* Hawthorne *then cancel comma and add parenthesis before* either] 245.12 the popularizing] the [HM >popularizing] 245.12 noise] ?roar [HM <?roar ≯noise] 245.13 and] or [HM *w.o. ampersand*] 245.14 utterances] utterance [HM *alter to* utterances] 245.15 at] in [HM <in ≯at]
245.17 Nor] Nor [HM *add bracket before* Nor *for new paragraph*]
245.18 mostly,] only [HM <only ≯mostly,] 245.18 insinuated] intrusted [HM <intrusted >insinuated] 245.22 this small] this [HM >small]
245.25 others";—] ~"∧∧ [HM *add semicolon and dash*] 245.26 noble-souled aspirants] tyros [HM <tyros ≯me →<me→ *add with guideline to caret* noble-souled aspirants] 245.27 But] but [HM *alter to capital*]
245.27 Shakespeare has] he has [HM <he >*with guideline to caret* Shakespeare] 245.28 far] deep [HM <deep >far] 245.29 who,] that [HM <that ≯who,] 245.30 as great] at some →<at some→ / as great
245.30–31 not inferentially] not [HM >inferentially] 245.34 superstitions] superstition [HM *alter to* superstitions] 245.35 Thirty Nine] thirty nine [HM *alter to capitals*] 245.35 Forty] forty [HM *alter to capital*] 245.36 You] you [HM *alter to capital*] 245.36 Shakespeare's unapproachability,] Shakespeare [HM *alter to* Shakespeare's *and with guideline to caret* >unapproachability,] 245.38 progressiveness] progression [HM <ion >-iveness] 245.38 Literature] literature [HM *alter to capital*] 245.39 Life] life [HM *alter to capital*] 245.39 that Shakespeares] that Shakespeares [HM <s *and before* Shakespeare *with guideline to caret* >man →<man >*extending guideline* men→ *add* not very much inferior to *then add comma after* Shakespeare *(emended)*] 245.40 shall] shall [HM >perhaps <perhaps]
*246.1 Englishman . . . modern?] Englishman [HM *add question mark then cancel question mark and with guideline to caret* >that is a modern?] 246.2 forward to] forward for [HM <for >to] 246.3 great literary] great [HM >literary]
246.6 parts] part [HM *alter to* parts] 246.7 It] ¶It [HM *cancel new paragraph by adding guideline*] 246.7 piece] ?peice [HM *alter to* piece] 246.7 the] J →*w.o.* the→ 246.10 life-time,] ~-~∧ [HM *add comma*] 246.11–21 not

Shakespeare . . . there.] *inscription by* HM 246.12 the shrewd, thriving,] HM the [>*with guideline to caret* shrewd, thriving,] 246.13 courtly] HM gen →<gen→ *add* courtly 246.20 those] HM the →<the→ / those 246.21 there.] HM there. [ED *add on line below* (to be concluded next week)] 246.22 Now, I] I [HM *add bracket before* I *for new paragraph then cancel bracket and add preceding it a new bracket and* Now,] [ED *inscribe above this line at head of upper segment of leaf* 14½ / Hawthorne and his Mosses / By a Virginian Spending July in Vermont *doubly underlined* / (Concluded from the last number.)] *246.22 say that] think [HM <think >*with guideline to caret* say that] 246.24–25 were verily] were [HM >*with guideline to caret* verily] *246.26 equalled,] equalled [HM *add comma and* >in time {<in time *add with guideline to caret* give the world time, &} *(emended)*] *246.27–30 and . . . none.] and surpassed by an American born now or / yet to be born *without period (emended)* For it will never do for / us who in most other things out-do as well as / out brag *without hyphen (emended)* the world *without comma (emended)* it will not do for us / to fold our hands and say *without comma (emended)* In the highest / department advance there is none. [HM <and surpassed . . . none. >in one hemisphere or the other. *(emended)*] 246.30 it at] it [EM >at] 246.31 grey and grizzled] old [HM <old >aged {<aged >*with guideline to caret* grey & grizzled}] 246.34 this Vermont] the [HM *alter to* this *and with guideline to caret* >Vermont] 246.35 my] / our [HM <our *add in margin* my] 246.35 dew] was [HM <was >dew] 246.35 Adam's] Adam [HM *alter to* Adam's] 246.37 latter] later [HM *alter to* latter] 246.37–38 trillionth] brilliant [EM <brilliant >trillionth] 246.39 remains] was [HM <was >remains] 246.40 that . . . authors.] that incapacitates us [HM >seems to *after* that *and alter* incapacitates *to* incapacitate <us *add* modern authors.] 247.1 Let] Let [HM *add bracket before* Let *for new paragraph*] 247.1 prize] ?praise [HM <?praise >*with guideline to caret* prize] 247.1 writers;] authors [HM <authors >writers;] 247.2 good-will.] ~-~∧ [HM *add period]* 247.4 the household of] the / *followed by blank space* [EM *add in blank space* household of] *247.5 England, . . . things,] England is [HM *after* England *add comma and with guideline to caret* >after all, {<is *and after* all, >*with guideline to caret* is, in many things,}] *247.6 bowels] / bonds [HM <bonds *add in margin* bowels] 247.6 of real] of [HM >*with to caret* real] *247.6–9 Hawthorne, . . . us,] Hawthornes [HM *alter to* Hawthorne *and add comma*] Emersons [HM *alter to* Emerson *and add comma then* >no *before* Emerson] Whittiers [HM *alter to* Whittier *then* >no *before* Whittier *then add comma and with guideline to caret* >no Irving,] / [HM *add in margin* Bryant, *then* >no *before* Bryant] Danas [HM *alter to* Dana *then* >no *before* Dana *without adding comma (emended)*] Coopers [HM *alter to* Cooper *and add dash then* >no *before* Cooper *and with guideline to caret* >no Willis (not the author of the "Dashes", but the author of the "Belfry Pigeon") *between* Cooper *and dash without adding a comma after* Cooper *(emended)*] were there none of them [HM <them / *add in margin* these *then add comma and with guideline to caret* >& others of like calibre] among us [HM *add comma*] [ED <Hawthorne . . . Pigeon *and* these . . . us, *without canceling* were there none of *then* >strong literary individualities among us, as there are some dozen at least, *(emended)*] 247.10 first] rather [HM <rather *add in margin* first] *247.10–18 praise . . . sound.] praise [HM >even] mediocrity in her [HM >own] children [HM *add comma*] than [HM <than *add in margin* before] / [HM >she praises (for anywhere, merit demands acknowledgment from every one)] the best excellence in the children of any / other land [HM *add period*] For me in a dearth of Hawthornes / I said →EM *alter to* stand *then* <I stand→ I stand by Pop Emmons and his / "Freddoniad" [HM *alter to* "Fredoniad"*and add comma*] and till *followed by long blank space* [HM *add in blank space* something better came along, *with guideline to* swear] / swear it was not very far behind / the Illiad [HM *add period then* <For me . . . I ≯Said a hot-headed Carolina cousin of mine, "If / >there was no one else {HM <one else >*below, circled with guideline to caret* other American} to stand by" {HM >*above, circled with guideline to caret* in Literature" *without canceling quotation mark after* by} said he, "why, then, I would *continuing with* stand by . . . the Illiad.] [*Finally* HM *cancel* Fredoniad . . . along *and* praise . . . before *then rewrite entire passage on a patch fastening it with sealing wax and covering all of the foregoing except* the Illiad. *so as to read* praise mediocrity even, in her own children, before she / praises (for everywhere, merit demands acknowledgment from every one) / the best excellence in the children of any other land. Let / her own authors, I say, have the priority of appreciation. I / was much pleased with a hot-headed Carolina cousin of mine, / who once said,—"If there was {<was >were} no other American to stand / by, in Literature,—why, then, I would stand by Pop Emmons / and his "Fredoniad," *(emended to single quotation marks)* & till something →<something >a→ better epic came along, / swear it was not very far behind the Illiad." *(emended)* Take away / the words, & in spirit he was sound. *then cancel vestigial* the Illiad.] 247.19 Not] Not [HM *add bracket before* Not *for new paragraph*] 247.20 that explosive] that / [HM >explosive] 247.21 burst] burst [HM *mend* b *and* s] 247.22 increasing] developing [HM <developing >increasing] 247.23 For] Fow →<Fow >For→ 247.26 however loftily] however *followed by blank space* [EM *add in blank space* loftily] 247.26 given, . . . cases)] given [HM *add comma and with guideline to caret* >in some cases) {<some >certain}] 247.27 their] our [HM <our >their] 247.27–28 There . . . asleep.] and [HM *alter to capital then* <And >*in top margin, with guidelines to caret* There are hardly five critics in America; / and several of them are asleep.] 247.28 As] as [HM *alter to capital*] 247.31 more] a / [HM <a *add in margin* more] 247.31 always] alway [HM *alter to* always] 247.33 them] these [HM <these ≯them] 247.33 have evinced] have *followed by blank space* [EM *add in blank space* evinced] 247.33 that decided]

that *followed by blank space* [EM *add in blank space* decided] 247.34 writer] author →<author→ *add* writer 247.35 Americans] American authors [HM <authors *and alter* American *to* Americans] 247.35 received the] recieved *(emended)* [HM >the] 247.36 that . . . amiable] that / [HM >*with guideline to caret* very popular & amiable] 247.36–37 good, and self-reliant] good [HM *add comma and with guideline to caret* >& self-reliant] 247.37 reputation] excellence [HM <excellence >reputation] 247.38 a foreign] an English [HM *alter* an *to* a *and* <English ≯foreign] 247.39 smooth] smooth and / easy [HM <and easy] 247.40 succeed] excel [HM <excel >succeed] 247.40 He] And he [HM <And *and alter* he *to capital*] 247.40–248.1 failed somewhere,] failed [HM >somewhere,] 248.1 great. . . . greatness.] great [HM *add period and with guideline to caret* >Failure is the true test of greatness *without period (emended)*] 248.2 And if it] ¶ And it [EM *erase* And *w.o.* and if *so as to cancel new paragraph*] [HM *alter* and *to capital without adding period to preceding word (emended)*] 248.2 continual] critical [HM <critical >continual] 248.2 wisely] merely [HM <merely >wisely] 248.3 powers] ?power [HM *alter to* powers] 248.3 that, . . . case,] that [HM *add comma and with guideline to caret* >in that case,] 248.5 these] the [HM *alter to* these] 248.5 writers] writers of primers [HM <of primers] 248.5 powers.] places [HM <places >powers.] *248.6 Without . . . they] They [HM <They / >*with guideline to caret* Without malice, but to speak the plain fact, they] *248.10 Tompkins.] Milton [HM *add period then* <Milton. >*with guideline to caret* Tompkins.] 248.10 done;] done with it [HM *add semicolon then* <with it; *and add semicolon after* done] 248.11 say . . . him.] compliment him better [HM <compliment him better ≯say / a nobler thing of him.] 248.11 is not meant] is / *followed by blank space* [EM *add in blank space* the vilest thing {EM <the vilest thing >not meant}] 248.12 to nationality] to *followed by blank space* [EM *add in blank space* nationality] *248.15 Bostonian] Bostonian [HM <Bostonian *(emended)*] 248.15 of literary] of [HM >literary] 248.16 flunkey . . . thing,] flunkey [HM >in this thing,] *248.17–18 us. . . . While] us [HM *add period*] And / the time is not far off when circumstances / may enforce [EM *alter to* force *and after* force >her] to it [HM? *add period then* HM <And . . . it. *(emended)*] While [HM *add guideline linking* us. *to* While] 248.18 that political] that *followed by blank space* [EM *add in blank space* political] 248.18–19 among the] among [HM >the] 248.19 which prophetically] which *followed by blank space* [EM *add in blank space* prophetically] 248.19 awaits us at] awaits / [EM *add in margin* us at] 248.19 present] past [HM <past >present] 248.20 unprepared for it;] unprepared / [HM *add in margin* for it;] 248.23 this:] ~∧ [HM *add comma then erase comma and add colon*] *248.23–24 that, . . . everywhere,] that [HM *add comma and, circled, with guideline to caret* >while freely acknowledging all

excellence, everywhere,] 248.25 lauding] bespattering [HM <bespattering >lauding] 248.25 writers . . . time,] writers with our / praises [EM <praises >bravos] and [HM <with our bravos and *and add comma after* writers {*cancel comma and with guideline to caret* >&, at the same time,}]
248.25 recognize] rewarding [HM *add comma then* <rewarding, >*with guideline to caret* recognizing {*alter* recognizing *to* recognize}] 248.27 spirit of Christianity] spirit [HM *with guideline to caret* >of Christianity]
248.27 which] that [HM <that >which] 248.28 the practical] the [HM >practical] 248.28 this] the [HM *alter to* this] 248.28 at] led by us →<led by us→ *add* at 248.29 ourselves—us Americans.] us [HM *add period then* <us. >*with guideline to caret* ourselves—us Americans.] 248.30–31 foster all originality] foster *followed by blank spaces* [EM *add in blank spaces* all / originality] 248.31 though, at first,] though [HM *add comma and with guideline to caret* >at first,] 248.32–33 then, . . . let] let [HM *before* let >in the words of my Carolina cousin, {*with guideline to caret* >then, *before* in *and, circled, with guideline to caret* >enthusiastic *before* Carolina}] 248.34 that] ?then [HM *alter to* that] 248.35 this] the [HM *alter to* this] 248.37 say . . . ours.] call it ours [HM *add period then* <call it ours. / ≯say it will ever be ours.]
248.38 And] And [HM *add bracket before* And *to confirm EM new paragraph*]
248.39 unimitating] inimitating [HM *alter to* unimitating] 248.39 an inimitable] / inimitable [EM *before* inimitable *add in margin* an]
248.40 commend to] commend / [HM *add in margin* to] 249.1 and far] and [HM >far] 249.2 The] the [HM *alter to capital*] *249.2 beeches] birches [HM <birches >*with guideline to caret* beeches] 249.3 travel away] have far [HM >enough] sought [HM <have *and* <sought *and before* far >travel *then* <far enough >away] 249.7 impulses] impressions [HM <impressions >*with guideline to caret* impulses] 249.7 in] on [HM *alter to* in]
249.7 may possibly] may [EM >possibly] 249.8 some still] some [EM >still] 249.12 writings] writing [HM *alter to* writings] 249.13 quiet plantation] quiet [HM >plantation] 249.13 remote] rather remote [HM <rather] 249.14 treating] touching [HM <touching >treating]
249.14 of] of ?this [HM <?this] 249.15 Tales",] ~"‸ [HM *add comma*]
249.16 Letter".] ~"‸ [HM *add period*] 249.16 manifold, strange] manifold [HM *add comma and with guideline to caret* >strange] 249.17 diffusive] diffuse [EM? *alter to* diffusive] 249.17 would all but] would [HM >all but]
249.18 those] these [HM *alter to* those] *249.19–20 displaced . . . authority.] displaced *followed by blank space* [EM *add in blank space* Oliver Goldsmith] / and many another brighter name than that [HM <Oliver . . . that ≯many of the bright names we now revere on authority. *adding guideline from* displaced *to* many] 249.21–22 himself, . . . posterity;] himself [HM *add comma and with guideline to caret* > & to the infallible finding of posterity;]

249.23 served] raised [HM <raised >served] 249.25 of . . . this] of *followed by long blank space* [EM *add in blank space* a sincere and appreciative love & admiration towards / *and in left margin add* it] [HM *add comma and with guideline to caret* >this] 249.27–28 mouth; . . . others.] mouth [HM *add semicolon*] / [EM *between lines* ↣and it is an honorable thing to discern →<discern >speak out→ *add* what is honorable in others] [HM *add period and* <speak out *and, two lines above, circled, with guideline to caret* >confess to] 249.29 But] But [HM *add bracket before* But *to confirm EM new paragraph*] 249.32 the author] he [HM *alter to* the *and* >author] 249.33 somewhere] somehow [HM *alter to* somewhere] 249.34 verse),] ~)∧ [HM *add comma*] 249.35 who] will [EM <will >who] 249.36 sketched,] touched [HM <touched >*with guideline to caret* sketched,] 249.36 invariably] always [HM <always >*with guideline to caret* invariably] 249.36–38 own; . . . define.] own [HM *add semicolon and to end of paragraph add* & in all instances, they paint them / without any vanity, & with →<& with→ *add* tho', at times, with a lurking something, that would *continuing along right margin* take several pages to properly define.] 249.39 I] I [HM *add bracket before* I *to confirm EM new paragraph*] 250.17 me. And] me [HM *add period and with guideline to caret* >And] 250.19 Mosses] mosses [HM *alter to capital]* 250.20 sensible of] impregnated / with [HM <impregnated with >sensible of] 250.20 the] their [HM <their >the] 250.21 essence, . . . write] essence to stream forth [HM <to . . . forth *add comma after* essence *and with guideline to caret* >in them, as to write] 250.21 did.] did yesterday [HM <yesterday *and add period after* did] 250.23 Mosses] mosses [HM *alter to capital*] 250.23 their] the [HM *alter to* their] 250.27 the . . . soul.] me [HM *add period then* <me. >*with guideline to caret* my Southern soul. {*before* my *add, extending guideline* the hot soil of}] 250.28 By] By [HM *add bracket before* By *for new paragraph*] 250.28 "Table of Contents",] "~ ~ ~"∧ [EM? *delete quotation marks*] [HM *add new quotation marks and comma*] 250.29 but] and [HM <and >but] 250.31 Party",] ~"∧ [HM *add comma*] 250.31 Brown".] ~"∧ [HM *add period*] 250.31 Here,] Then [HM <Then >Here,] 250.34 or] and [HM <and >or] 250.37 and costliest] and *followed by blank space* [EM *add in blank space* costliest] 250.37 Falernian] Falernian [HM *w.o.* F *to emphasize capital*] 250.37 "Cider",] "~"∧ [HM *add comma*] 250.38 wine".] ~"∧ [HM *add period*] 250.39 Man] man [HM *alter to capital*] 250.39 Mosses] mosses [HM *alter to capital*] 251.2 be generally] be [HM >generally] 251.2 author;] author by the world [HM <by the world *and add semicolon after* author] 251.4 most] ?b →*w.o.* most→ 251.4 is, to] is to / say [HM <to say *adding comma after* is *and in left margin* to] 251.11 matter] matter →<matter→ *add* matter 251.12 charge] charge [HM >of braying, {<of braying,}] 251.21 thunder",] ~"∧ [HM *add comma*] 251.22 Brown"?]

~"∧ [HM *add question mark*] 251.24 Shoes".] ~"∧ [HM *add period*] 251.26 sin".] ~"∧ [HM *add period*] 251.26 Young] young [HM *alter to capital*] *251.28 " 'Faith!'] ~! [HM *add opening double quotation marks (emended) and bracket before* Faith *for new paragraph and add closing double quotation marks (emended) between* Faith *and exclamation point (emended)*] *251.29 'Faith! Faith!'] ~! ~! [HM *add opening double quotation marks (emended) before first* Faith *and closing double quotation marks (emended) between second* Faith *and exclamation point (emended)*] 251.31 Now] Now [HM *add bracket before* Now *for new paragraph*] 251.31 Young] young [EM *alter to capital*] 251.31 Brown",] ~"∧ [HM *add comma*] 251.34 mere occasional] mere [HM >occasional] 251.36 Brown",] ~"∧ [HM *add comma*] 252.3 The] The [HM *add bracket before* The *for new paragraph*] 252.3 Party",] ~"∧ [HM *add comma*] 252.6 chowder party] Chowder Party [HM? *alter to lowercase*] 252.6 Peedee!] Greece [HM *add exclamation mark then* <Greece! >Peedee!] 252.8 surpasses] equals [HM <equals >*with guideline to caret* surpasses] 252.8–9 it, . . . it.] it [HM *add comma and with guideline to caret* >perhaps, nothing that equals it.] 252.9 Queen",] ~"∧ [HM *add comma*] 252.10 Party",] ~"∧ [HM *add comma*] 252.10–11 most,— . . . judge.] most [HM *add comma plus dash and with guideline to caret* >that is, if you are qualified to judge.] 252.13 accounted] esteemed [HM <esteemed >accounted] 252.19 my chief] my [EM >chief] 252.20 who under] who *followed by blank space* [EM *add in blank space* under] *252.21 of "a] a poor [HM <poor *and add* "of *before* a *(emended)*] 252.23 of the] of this / gorgeous [HM <this gorgeous *add in left margin* the] 252.24 Genius",] ~"∧ [HM *add comma*] 252.27 ideas] idea [HM *alter to* ideas] *252.27 least∧] ~∧ [HM *add comma (emended)*] 252.27 point,] part [HM <part >point,] 252.28 man] ?calm person [HM <?calm person >*with guideline to caret* man] 252.30 Genius",] ~"∧ [HM *add comma*] 252.38 those] these [HM *alter to* those] 252.38 power?] genius. [HM <genius. >*with guideline to caret* power?] 253.3 Anaks of] now half forgotten [HM <now half forgotten >Anaks of] 253.11 —in the "Select] ∧∧~ ~ ~ [HM *add double quotation marks and dash before* in *(emended)*] 253.11 Party";] ~"∧ [HM *add semicolon*] 253.12 a coincident sentiment] a *followed by blank space* [EM *add in blank space* coincident sentiment] 253.12 ramblingly] feebly [HM <feebly >irre →<irre→ *add* ramblingly *with guideline to caret*] 253.14 Posterity] Posterity [HM *w.o.* P *to confirm capital*] 253.16 with] and [HM <and >with] 253.20–21 powers . . . however)] power [HM *alter to* powers *and with guideline to caret* >(only the developable ones, however)] 253.23 *yet*] yet [HM? *underline*] 253.23–32 Especially . . . infinite.] *original inscription unknown* / infinite subject [HM *add period then cut away original inscription* <infinite subject. *and substitute* ¶Especially . . . infinite. *on clip; then cancel indication of new paragraph*

by adding guideline linking Especially *to preceding paragraph*] 253.25 some plants and] HM some [HM >plants &] 253.32 subjects] HM things [HM <things >*with guideline to caret* subjects] 253.32 this] this →<this→ *add* this 253.32 scrawl of mine] dissertation [HM <dissertation >scrawl of mine] 253.35 parade forth] par *followed by blank space* [EM *add in blank space* ade forth] 253.35–36 this Portuguese diamond] this *followed by blank space* [EM *add in blank space* Portuguese diamond] 253.36 in our] in [HM *add in margin* our] / American [HM <American] 253.37–38 five-thousand,—] ~-~‸‸ [HM *add comma and dash*] 253.38 that] it [HM <it >that] 253.38 signify?—] amount to? [HM <amount to? >signify?—] 253.38–39 hundred-thousand;] ~-~‸ [HM *add semicolon*] 253.40 admiration] Admiration [EM *alter to lowercase*] 253.40 [HM? *add notation* (End) *later canceled in pencil*]

II. *All the punctuation in the following entries is judged (from the not always conclusive evidence of spacing and/or ink) as added by Melville to words his copyist had inscribed (other HM punctuation—added in conjunction with EM punctuation or along with his revisions—is included in the list above).* 239.3 —a 239.4 dwelling, foliage— 239.5 mountains, woods, ponds,— this, surely, 239.6 air, 239.8 seclusion. wild, me; 239.9 or, cadences, birds, 239.10 window. 239.11 foundlings, 239.12 mother, be, them, 239.13 authors. this; 239.15 Beautiful, 239.16 eyes, 239.17 reality. 239.18 this. 239.19 book, feel, 239.20 ones, 239.21 standing, do, mystical, Beauty, 239.22 genius. 240.1 appear, 240.2 fact, 240.3 reader. composed, 240.4 us? 240.5 spoken, man, 240.6 Saviour, 240.7 Else, 240.8 glance. 240.9 road, 240.10 grandest, prospects, hedge, 240.11 hedges, 240.13 Hawthorne, Mosses. 240.14 years, 240.15 —heard often— 240.16 friend, rare, book, 240.17 popular. 240.18 merit, things, 240.19 disregarded; 240.20 green. 240.21 while, book, wine, 240.22 body. rate, 240.23 result. day, girl, 240.24 mine, 240.25 raspberries,— which, 240.27 cheeks,— creature, me— 240.30 that,— hills. 240.31 raspberries, moss. 240.32 I.— Yes, you, 240.34 volume, 240.35 bound, green,— 240.36 less, 240.37 this, raspberries, 'Mosses 240.38 Manse' yes, 240.39 more: 240.40 morning: country: 241.2 door, 241.3 around, Man! 241.4 amply, bountifully, 241.5 Manse, written— 241.6 pleasure, 241.7 rest. trouble! 241.9 anybody, circle, 241.10 —So day, 241.11 dawn, 241.12 moonrise, Hill. 241.14 dreams,

closed, over, 241.15 reminiscences, 241.18 Manse!— heart.
241.19 rudeness, dinners, 241.20 wine,— gentle, high, deep,
241.21 relishable, angel. 241.22 mirth; that. 241.24 it. twisted,
trees, 241.25 branches, imagination, 241.26 then,
241.27 forms, 241.29 apple, 241.30 afternoon, wind,
241.32 Mosses. 241.33 —What that!— 241.34 decayed,
241.36 before? 241.37 volumes. this:— 242.3 long,
242.9 apples, ruddy, ripe;— 242.10 apples, tree, 242.11 past.
242.12 sadness; 242.13 prime, which, likewise, 242.15 heart.
242.16 tenderness, being, 242.17 love, say, 242.18 generation, —at
least, 242.19 things. more. these, —and many, 242.20 chapters—
clews, 242.21 intricate, originated. 242.22 see,
242.23 others. 242.27 admiration. 242.28 known, writer,
242.29 style,— sequestered, man, 242.31 man, love, peaks,
242.32 height, 242.34 genius; possessing, 242.35 these, great,
intellect, 242.37 eyes, world. 242.38 strength. What,
242.39 readers, 243.1 it, what, 243.2 time, 243.3 sits, me,—
"shape mystery", 243.4 now, 243.5 me, 243.7 profound,
appalling, 243.8 where— 243.9 world,— 243.11 fire,
243.12 man; unconsumed, 243.13 nought. 243.14 this,
243.15 sketches, 243.16 import. 243.18 analysis,
243.19 them. 243.20 soul, side— 243.21 sphere—
243.22 dawn, 243.23 it, world. 243.26 shades; him, himself,
243.27 gloom,— tell. is, 243.28 however, 243.29 Sin,
243.30 visitations, other, 243.31 free. moods, 243.32 world,
something, Sin, 243.33 balance. events, 243.35 Hawthorne. more:
him, 243.36 through. sunlight,— 243.37 you;— 243.38 beyond;
fringe, 243.39 word, 244.1 Hawthorne. 244.3 critic. man;
244.4 heart. 244.5 it, intuition; it, 244.6 it, 244.7 Hawthorne,
spoken, 244.8 me. 244.9 him. 244.10 be, 244.11 back-ground,—
back-ground, 244.12 conceits, 244.13 renown,
244.14 thinkers. 244.15 comedy.— head! 244.16 Buckingham! rant,
hand, 244.17 house,— souls, 244.18 humps, daggers.
244.19 him; flashings-forth 244.20 him; short, reality;—
244.21 Shakespeare, Shakespeare. 244.22 Hamlet, Timon, Lear, Iago,
244.23 things, 244.24 true, man, 244.25 character, utter, them.
244.25–26 desperation, 244.27 truth. But, said, 244.28 admiration.
so, 244.29 Shakespeare, 244.30 him. 244.32 great,
244.33 greatness, 244.34 indices. 244.35 wrote. Shakespeare,
244.37 lies, 244.38 woodlands; herself, 244.40 Truth,— covertly,
snatches. 245.2 readers, him, deeply, 245.3 made, 245.4 renown)—

time, 245.5 patience, genius;— 245.7 men. 245.8 there, town, 245.9 mountains, 245.10 is. Shakespeare, 245.11 circumstances, disinclination, 245.12 inaptitude) 245.13 farce, tragedy; still, 245.14 repose, 245.15 circulation, lungs, 245.16 heart. 245.17 him, not. Nor, 245.17–18 indeed, 245.18 it, is, 245.19 it, it; alike. 245.21 page. say, needed, 245.22 Hawthorne, yesterday. 245.23 not, willingly, those, who, 245.24 least, Rochefoucault, 245.25 some, who, 245.26 them, 245.27 unapproachable. 245.27–28 approached. 245.29 universe. man, other, 245.30 Hamlet. 245.31 man, 245.32 be. 245.33 make. Besides, 245.34 superstitions. 245.36 matter. 245.37 country. American, 245.38 Literature, 245.39 Life? me, friends, 245.40 Ohio. come, 246.2 be, 246.3 us, 246.4 day,— 246.5 history, Boccaccio. Whereas, 246.6 times; times; 246.7 coloring. Jews, 246.8 streets, 246.9 coming; chariot, 246.10 ass. forget, that, 246.23 Avon, great. 246.24 immeasurable. more, 246.25 William. 246.26 This, too, mean, 246.27 surpassed, 246.30 say, 246.31 now, 246.32 old, 246.33 be. so. 246.34 today, created; 246.35 feet, Adam's. 246.36 progenitors, 246.37 find. it. 246.38 said; said, 246.39 said. paucity, 247.1 yea, 247.2 them. number, 247.3 own, bosom, 247.4 alien. 247.5 us. 247.6 she. 247.10 nevertheless, 247.20 vice, 247.21 it, sake, 247.22 sake, 247.23 writers. shame, 247.24 her, pen. 247.25 now. 247.26 (however 247.27 Englishmen, countrymen. 247.28–29 patronage, 247.29 country, 247.30 him. 247.31 recognition, motives, 247.32 ones. 247.33 true, 247.34 praise. writer, 247.36 productions,— writer, 247.37 things, 247.38 model, 247.39 ones. 247.39–40 originality, 247.40 imitation. 248.2 said, 248.3 powers,— added, 248.4 small. it, then, all, 248.7 Goldsmith, authors. 248.8 Goldsmiths; nay, Miltons. 248.9 author, 248.10 American, 248.12 writings; this, 248.13 Englishman, Frenchman; 248.14 man, American. 248.16 England. it, 248.19 nations, 248.20 century; view, 248.21 Hitherto, 248.22 be; 248.23 matter, 248.26 own;— writers, 248.27 unshackled, things, 248.28 world, 248.29 imitation, 248.30 morning; 248.30–31 originality, 248.31 knots. 248.32 fail, fail, 248.33 shoulder, 248.34 round. is, 248.35 view, 248.36 us, bullies, lost, 248.37 us, 248.38 now, countrymen, author, 248.39 blood,— unimitating, and,

perhaps, way, man— 248.40 you, place, 249.1 Hawthorne. new,
249.2 writers. him; 249.3 soul; 249.4 nature, Niagara.
249.5 is. 249.6 self, generation; 249.7 him, 249.8 eyes.
249.9 him, others; brotherhood. 249.10 genius, world, hand,
249.11 round. 249.12 Hawthorne, (for 249.13 man; life,
249.14 haunts, shall) works, say, 249.16 excellent; 249.17 beauties,
me, 249.18 out. books, which, 249.19 ago, 249.22 him,
249.23 feel, doing, myself, him. 249.24 For, bottom, itself;
249.26 utterance; warm, 249.29 yet. author, 249.30 bones,
reads, 249.31 mind. 249.32 it, 249.33 picture.—
249.34 Nature, 249.35 pencil, portrait-painters, who, 249.39 it,
then, personally, 249.40 Hawthorne;— himself,
250.2 mind,— true, —a seeker, 250.3 yet:—
250.5 scholar. 250.6 beneath; 250.12 * * * * *
250.14 mow, 250.15 Hawthorne. 250.16 Mosses,
250.17 man, 250.18 others. (though, perhaps, foolish)
250.19 Mosses, 250.20 all; had, nevertheless, 250.22 borne,
250.23 Mosses, 250.24 being, that, tell. 250.25 soul.
250.26 down, him; further, further, 250.27 New-England
250.28 find, 250.29 sketches; wrote, 250.30 pieces,
250.31 attention,— 250.33 Mosses, 250.34 with, disappointed,
250.35 Sketches. instance, 250.36 piece. 250.37 Tokay, Perry,
250.38 be, 250.39 geniuses, 251.1 world,— least, himself.
Personally, not, 251.3 is, 251.4 judge— himself. Besides,
251.5 natures, Hawthorne, things, 251.7 them, 251.8 powers,
251.9 pastures. True, 251.10 enough, 251.11 matter; therefore,
251.12 originality. 251.13 motive, profound, 251.14 has,
certain, 251.15 deceive— deceive, 251.16 pages. more,
251.17 say, 251.18 myself; that, too, 251.19 man. 251.20 (as
neighborhood) 251.23 tale, 251.24 Whereas, Dante; it,
251.25 penetrate, 251.26 bosom, Goodman, too,
251.27 wife, anguish,— 251.31 piece, 251.32 yesterday; now,
251.33 is, itself, 251.33–34 Hawthorne, 251.34 it,
251.35 sketches. 252.1 conclusion, to, time, 252.3 to,
252.4 which, book, 252.5 Salem, 252.6 Cod. Whereas,
252.7 wrote. 252.8 Nay, 252.9 this: 252.11 this;
252.12 alive, 252.13 now,— man. 252.14 be, eyes,
252.15 sweetness,— his; 252.16 whom, clouds, 252.17 plate,
252.18 Babylon. 252.19 now, 252.20 piece, guest,
252.21 attire, 252.22 eminence", 252.23 Fancy, feast.
252.25 wrote, America, 252.26 coincidence; especially,

252.27 ideas, 252.28 me. 252.29 here, 252.30 Shiloh, him.
252.31 be, been, not, 252.32 be, man? it, indeed,
252.33 suppose, 252.34 be, be, genius? 252.35 Surely, record,
252.36 time; 252.37 Marlow, Webster, Ford, Beaumont, Jonson,
252.38 one, 252.39 day, 252.40 great. anyone,
253.1 authors, 253.2 thoroughly, them, 253.3 men,
253.4 fact, 253.5 merit,— though, merit, 253.6 none.
253.7 Nevertheless, 253.8 Hawthorne, man, already, 253.9 minds, light, earth, 253.10 intellect. 253.11 his, 253.12 own,
253.13 yesterday, himself. will, write, 253.14 proxy— 253.15 good, declare— American, day, 253.16 evinced, Literature, heart,
253.17 Hawthorne. Moreover, 253.18 write, 253.19 masterpiece. sure, 253.21 them. 253.22 prophet. 253.23 prediction.
253.32 people, 253.33 unnecessary, inasmuch, "as ago" (they say)
253.34 Hawthorne, 253.35 forth, 253.36 this; 253.37 it,
253.39 million; 253.40 admiration.

THE HAPPY FAILURE (pp. 254–61)

NN copy-text: the anonymous first printing, "The Happy Failure. A Story of the River Hudson," in *Harper's New Monthly Magazine* [H], IX, no. 50 (July, 1854), 196–99. No known manuscript, and no later printing in Melville's lifetime. NN emendations to H (on principles stated on pp. 549–64): at one point. NN printer's copy: an emended photocopy of Newberry Library A5.391. Machine collations between copies of H: Gift M69–114 *vs.* Newberry A5.391, Gift M78–3, and Northwestern L051H295 (copy 2); Northwestern L051H295 (copy 2) *vs.* University of Chicago AP2H3 (copy 2).

As the HISTORICAL NOTE shows, "The Happy Failure" was written probably during the summer of 1853, submitted on August 13, and paid for in May of 1854 in advance of its July publication.

Possible sources for some elements of the tale have been pointed out. The uncle and Yorpy resemble the treasure-hunting Legrand and his black servant Jupiter in Edgar Allan Poe's "The Gold-Bug," but they may have been drawn from life. Jay Leyda *(Complete Stories,* p. 467) likens the elderly uncle to Melville's "energetic and ingenious, but invariably disappointed and ineffectual uncle Thomas Melvill, Jr.," and compares Yorpy to "an old Negro named Tawney in Lansingburgh, whose name Melville had already attached to another Negro character, the admirable old sheet-anchor-man in *White-Jacket* (Chapter LXXIV)." Alice P. Kenney, in "Herman Melville and the Dutch Tradition," *Bulletin of the New York Public Library,* LXXIX (Summer, 1976), 386–99, maintains that "The Happy Failure" depicts Melville's maternal uncle Herman Gansevoort, "an old man broken by circumstances but serenely contemplating the evening of life," and also his homestead at Gansevoort, New York. Dorothee Metlitsky Finkelstein, in *Melville's Orienda* (New Haven: Yale University Press, 1961), p. 142, observes that "the unsuccessful invention in the tale is a 'Great Hydraulitic-Hydrostatic Apparatus' like Belzoni's hydraulic machine for the water of the Nile," a regulatory device for controlling its annual flooding; Melville, as she shows, shared the great contemporary interest in Giovanni Battista Belzoni, the Italian traveler, explorer, and showman. On January 4, 1852, Melville's Pittsfield neighbor Sarah Morewood had written to George L. Duyckinck with reference to Melville (then in New York) that the Housatonic River "has overflowed all the Marsh below his land—forming a Hudson as it were out of the Housatonic." The Roman emperor who "tried to drain the Pontine marsh, but failed" (256.19–20) is probably Augustus; in his poem "At the Hostelry" Melville later referred to modern efforts to drain the same marsh as a satiric example of "progress."

For explanation of the following tabulations, see pp. 656–70.

DISCUSSION. 260.39 failure!"] H has a question mark; for other examples of confusion between question marks and exclamation points, see p. 563.

EMENDATION. *260.39 failure!"] NN; ~?" H

HYPHENATION. I. 254.22 forlorn-looking 255.3 everlasting 257.10 wide-expanded 260.4 uprooted 260.32 tobacco-money

THE FIDDLER (pp. 262–67)

NN copy-text: the anonymous first printing, "The Fiddler," in *Harper's New Monthly Magazine* [H], IX, no. 52 (September, 1854), 536–39. No known manuscript, and no later printing in Melville's lifetime. NN emendations to H (on principles stated on pp. 549–64): at nine points. NN printer's copy: an emended photocopy of Newberry Library A5.391. Machine collations between copies of H: Gift M69–114 *vs.* Newberry A5.391 and Northwestern L051H295 (copy 2); Northwestern L051H295 (copy 2) *vs.* University of Chicago AP2H3 (copy 2).

An Index to Harper's New Monthly Magazine (New York: Harper & Brothers, 1870) lists "The Fiddler" not with the contributions of Melville

(p. 277) but of Fitz-James O'Brien (pp. 171, 183, 311), and that listing remains unchanged in the editions of 1875, 1880, and 1885. But Elizabeth Shaw Melville listed "The Fiddler" in her memoranda of her husband's periodical pieces and kept a copy of it in her collection of his magazine stories. See the RELATED DOCUMENTS, pp. 793–98 below, and Merton M. Sealts, Jr., "Did Melville Write 'The Fiddler'?" *Harvard Library Bulletin,* XXVI (January, 1978), 77–80. Sealts and the Northwestern-Newberry editors judge these documents more authoritative than the unsupported attribution to O'Brien in the *Index to Harper's.* As the HISTORICAL NOTE shows, "The Fiddler" was written probably during the summer of 1853, submitted on August 13, and paid for in May of 1854 in advance of its September publication.

The original of the title character may be Master Joseph Burke (1815–1902), a child violin prodigy in England and Ireland who eventually settled in Albany, where Melville at age fourteen may have heard his performance at Duffy's Theater on February 10, 1834; see William H. Gilman, *Melville's Early Life and* REDBURN (New York: New York University Press, 1951), pp. 76 and 316, n. 148. Master Betty, the "great English prodigy" of the piece, was William Henry West Betty (1791–1874), a child actor known as "the young Roscius," who went on the Belfast stage at eleven, then triumphed throughout the United Kingdom and amassed a fortune but retired before he was thirty-three, acknowledging "that the enthusiastic admirers of his boyhood had been mistaken" *(Dictionary of National Biography).* The narrator's visit to the circus reflects Melville's knowledge of contemporary New York City. An article on "Places of Public Amusement" in *Putnam's,* III (February, 1854), 141–52, notes that circuses, like the one staged in the New York Hippodrome on Fifth Avenue, are "still the most popular of public amusements, . . . conducted on a magnificent scale as a regular business speculation by enterprising citizens." "Taylor's" is "Taylor's Saloon," at the corner of Broadway and Franklin Street in New York City, described in *Putnam's,* I (April, 1853), 362–63, as "the largest and most elegant restaurant in the world."

The literary allusions in "The Fiddler" are both Shakespearean and classical. "Genius, like Cassius, is lank" (265.4–5) recalls the "lean and hungry look" of Cassius in *Julius Caesar,* I.ii.193. The "saying of the Athenian" (263.33) comes from Plutarch's "Life of Phocion"; as a Greek rather than a Roman, Phocian would scarcely have been "applauded in the forum." Melville alluded to the Orpheus myth (266.35) as early as *Redburn* (chap. 56) and returned to it as late as *Billy Budd, Sailor.* The reference to Cicero

(267.29–31) is inexact—it was his friend Sulpicius Rufus "traveling in the East" who wrote to Cicero with such sympathetic solace upon the death of his daughter Tullia: Melville could have found the letter quoted in Laurence Sterne's *Tristram Shandy* (bk. V, chap. 3).

For explanation of the following tabulations, see pp. 565–70.

DISCUSSION. 265.35 forty?"] For NN treatment of reversed exclamation points and question marks, as here and at 267.5, see p. 563.

EMENDATIONS. 264.16 acknowledged] NN; ac-/knowled H
264.30 existence."] NN; ~.∧ H 264.33 now.] NN; ~, H
265.21 crowd."] NN; ~.∧ H *265.35 forty?"] NN; ~." H
267.5 Taylor's?] NN; ~. H 267.22 ever."] NN; ~.∧ H
267.23 name?"] NN; ~?∧ H 267.24 ear."] NN; ~.∧ H

HYPHENATION. I. 262.5 †side-street 263.1 extraordinary
263.21 all-applauding 266.8 by-blow 267.15 Broadway
II. 262.5 †side-street

COCK-A-DOODLE-DOO! (pp. 268–88)

NN copy-text: the anonymous first printing, "Cock-A-Doodle-Doo! Or, The Crowing of the Noble Cock Beneventano," in *Harper's New Monthly Magazine* [H], VIII, no. 43 (December, 1853), 77–86. No known manuscript, and no later printing in Melville's lifetime. NN emendations to H (on principles stated on pp. 549–64): at 12 points. NN printer's copy: an emended photocopy of Newberry Library A5.391. Machine collations between copies of H: Gift M69–114 *vs.* Newberry A5.391, Gift M78–3, and Northwestern L051H295 (copy 2); Northwestern L051H295 (copy 2) *vs.* University of Chicago AP2H3 (copy 2).

Although "Cock-A-Doodle-Doo!" is not named in Melville's surviving correspondence with Harper & Brothers, it was evidently composed during the spring and summer of 1853 and sent to New York from Pittsfield on August 13 along with two other pieces—probably "The Happy Failure" and "The Fiddler" (see the HISTORICAL NOTE, pp. 486–87). It refers to events of that year both at home and abroad. The spring months had been a time of unrest in Latin America, southern Europe, and China, with "many high-spirited revolts from rascally despotisms" (268.3–4) commanding attention in the American press. Within the United States "many dreadful casualties, by locomotive and steamer" (268.4–5), had caused even more concern. "Our papers are filled with accidents—Railroad & Steamboat carelessness is alarming," wrote Hope Savage Shaw, Elizabeth Melville's stepmother, to her husband on August 26, 1853; the Pittsfield *Sun* for August 18, p. 2, under the heading "Railroad Murders," had cited from the New York *Herald* a table showing that since the first of the year 176 persons had been killed and 333 injured in a total of 65 accidents. The June number of *Harper's* (to which Melville had subscribed since 1851) singled out four disasters of "uncommon magnitude": in February of 1853, 129 persons had been lost at sea off the coast of Lower California; in April, about 20 were killed and many more injured in a railroad collision near Chicago, "the result of the most inexcusable negligence," and approximately 30 lost in a steamer fire on Lake Ontario; in May, more than 50 were killed at Norwalk, Connecticut, when a train passed through an open drawbridge (VII, 124).

The narrator's "densely-wooded mountain . . . (which I call October Mountain, on account of its bannered aspect in that month)" is a mountain southeast of Pittsfield which was so named by Melville himself, according to his widow's biographical memoranda—see Merton M. Sealts, Jr., *The Early Lives of Melville* (Madison: University of Wisconsin Press, 1974), p. 174. The Springfield, Massachusetts, *Sunday Republican* for December 6, 1853, in a notice of the current *Harper's,* detected a further local allusion: " 'Cock-a-doodle-doo' is good, and the Ex-Postmaster's neighbors will recognize in the hero of the story a near relative of the 'great departed.' " Readers familiar with the New York operatic stage would have identified another contemporary figure, the "certain Signor Beneventano" the narrator had seen "at a performance of the Italian Opera"; on Christmas Eve of 1847 Melville himself had seen Donizetti's *Lucia di Lammermoor* at the Astor Place Opera House with Ferdinando Beneventano singing the role of Lord Henry Ashton. The "Editorial Notes" in the July *Putnam's* may have reminded Melville of the occasion by a brief history of the Astor Place Opera House that mentioned "Beneventano, the burly baritone" (II, 113); the singer was again performing in New York during the summer of 1853 (II, 571). And in the Pittsfield *Culturist and Gazette* for February 23, 1853, Melville may have also seen an article on "The Shanghai Chickens," reprinted from the *Knickerbocker Magazine,* which like "Cock-A-Doodle-Doo!" itself comments unfavorably on the Shanghai's crow, carriage, and general appearance.

The narrator's frequent literary allusions reflect Melville's own reading tastes. He mentions figures from ancient mythology and history, such as

Charon, Jove, Xerxes, Socrates, and Hector, and refers to biblical names and places including Moloch, Samson, Goliath, Solomon, Babylon, and Joshua in the vale of Ajalon. He enjoys Laurence Sterne's *Tristram Shandy* and Robert Burton's *Anatomy of Melancholy;* he parodies stanza vii of William Wordsworth's "Resolution and Independence"; he echoes the phrasing of *Hamlet* and *Paradise Lost.*

For explanation of the following tabulations, see pp. 565–70.

DISCUSSIONS. 271.13 *"Glory . . . highest!"*] Quoted from Luke 2:14, with the word "be" added by Melville (from other renderings) for the fifth syllable needed to make the four syllables of the scriptural "Glory to God" fit the five-syllable pattern of "cock-a-doodle-doo," as the four of "in the highest" fit the four "oo" syllables of the rest of the cock's phrase (see 288.25)—as heard by both the narrator and Merrymusk. That Melville intended this biblical allusion to associate the cock's crow with the Latin doxology "Gloria in Excelsis Deo" (based on the angelic hymn in Luke) is clear from the pervasive ecclesiastical terms linking it with the Gloria as well as with the Jubilate based on the Hundredth Psalm's opening word (translated in the King James Version as "Make a joyful noise . . . ").

272.7–10 "Of . . . madness."] As Jay Leyda *(Complete Stories,* p. xxiv) indicates, Melville's lines are "an obvious parody . . . [of] a revelatory stanza [vii] . . . in Wordsworth's 'Resolution and Independence' . . . ": "We Poets in our Youth begin in gladness; / But thereof come in the end despondency and madness." Melville penciled a marginal line beside both stanzas vi and vii in his copy (Sealts 563a) of *The Complete Poetical Works,* ed. Henry Reed (Philadelphia, 1839).

272.38 Tristram] NN emends the H misspelling "Tristam", which was probably Melville's own, as in the entry for December 16, 1849, in his manuscript London journal and also in the *Putnam's* publication of *Israel Potter* (chap. 13; NN82.36).

273.11–12 'Said the Widow Wadman—'] H lacks the needed single quotation marks NN supplies to make clear that the narrator is reading the enclosed words from *Tristram Shandy.* The purportedly quoted phrase, exactly as worded, does not occur in the book, and NN does not emend to make it an exact quotation of the only closely so-worded phrase (among many repetitions of the similar tags, "quoth Mrs. Wadman" and "said Mrs. Wadman") that both comes near the end of a chapter (cf. 273.4) and introduces what could be called "a fine joke about my Uncle Toby and the Widow Wadman"—that is, the phrase " . . . said widow Wadman, . . . " (VIII.28) followed by a "joke" about her nagging concern that her prospective husband, Uncle Toby, "will not enjoy his health, with the monstrous wound upon his groin—". No emendation is needed, since Melville was not trying to quote a specific passage accurately; he was "quoting"—as relevant to "Cock-A-Doodle-Doo!"—from his memory of the whole comic courtship that ends *in medias res* (VIII.33) with a "COCK and a BULL" story.

275.34 master] The H reading "number" makes no sense as a word for what the cock is asked to "tell" in answer to the narrator's five-times-repeated question "where?" The word NN adopts, "master"—used at 271.27—makes such sense (and could be misread as "number" in Melville's hand) since the cock's telling who his master is would also tell where he himself is. Indeed, the narrator seeks his answer to "where?" by looking for the answer to the linked question "Whose cock is that?" (271.37). First, he expects the owner to be some opulent gentleman (276.1, 277.13–278.6), and then one of "various owners of fowls" (278.8); after asking the poor wood-sawyer Merrymusk if he knows "any gentleman hereabouts who owns an extraordinary cock" (281.23–27), he discovers that the owner is the poor man himself, who is rich as the owner of the cock (286.15–19) and as the master at whose command it crows (284.15,36, 285.1,15,31, 286.19, 287.5).

277.34 crow] NN keeps the singular form as idiomatic at the time.

282.9 cock-crow] The H reading "cock crow" lacks the hyphen NN supplies to obviate the misreading its absence induces (whereby "cock" becomes a subject and "crow" a verb); at 286.24,32–33, the absence of a hyphen creates no confusion.

282.18 alders] NN emends the H reading "thicket of elders" as a misreading, because alders not elders commonly grow in such a "thicketed swamp" (281.37). See also 354.33 and 449.18–19.

282.36 Sir?] NN emends the exclamation point in H as clearly an error, since Merrymusk's initial response—shown by "his honest stare" (283.1)—is not indignant recoil (as it is at 283.30,32,34, and the dunning farmer's is at 273.10) but puzzled incomprehension (as again in his "Sir?" at 283.26), and since he repeatedly responds to the narrator's own obtuse questions with either an arresting interrogative or a decisive yes or no—both of which serve to bring the narrator to a better understanding of Merrymusk's attitude. For further examples of confusion between question marks and exclamation points see p. 563.

285.19 Ajalon] NN emends the H reading "Askalon" because Melville's intended allusion here (as in *Clarel,* IV.xxi.37–38) is to Joshua 10:12: "Sun, stand thou still upon Gibeon; and thou, Moon, in the valley of Ajalon."

286.10 'Glory . . . highest!'] As at 273.11–12 (see the discussion) NN supplies the single quotation marks, lacking in H, that are needed to make clear that Merrymusk is quoting these words he hears in the cock-crow, just as the narrator did at 271.13,19, where H uses quotation marks.

288.19–20 Oh! . . . Oh!] NN does not emend these H readings for "O" (without exclamation points) in each line of the epitaph taken otherwise accurately from I Corinthians 15:55, since in all likelihood the slight changes were Melville's.

EMENDATIONS. 270.28–29 here's a] NN; here'a H
*272.38 Tristram] NN; Tristam H *273.11 'Said] NN; ∧~ H
*273.12 Wadman—'] NN; ~—∧ H *275.34 master] NN; number H

*282.9 cock-crow] NN; ~∧~ H *282.18 alders] NN; elders H
*282.36 Sir?] NN; ~! H *285.19 Ajalon] NN; Askalon H
*286.10 'Glory] NN; ∧~ H *286.10 highest!'] NN; ~!∧ H
287.38 pallor] NN; palor H

Hyphenation. I. 269.25 thick-headed 270.21 prayer-book 271.8 hair-trunks 271.13 thanksgiving 272.20 beef-steak 272.30 brown-stout 273.32 blue-nosed 274.7 sunlight 274.30 steamboat 275.5 sturgeon-nose 276.24 rail-fences 277.2 cock-crow 278.7 farm-house 278.34 bar-room 279.5 civil-process 280.13 bare-headed 281.25 wood-sawyer's 281.35 densely-wooded 284.20 †overhead

II. 271.3 miserable-looking 271.23 two-year-old 273.1 arm-chair 274.16 self-possessed 276.19 rail-fence 277.36 fowl-yard 278.2 carrot-colored 278.5 gallows-bird

POOR MAN'S PUDDING AND RICH MAN'S CRUMBS (pp. 289–302)

NN copy-text: the anonymous first printing, "Poor Man's Pudding and Rich Man's Crumbs," in *Harper's New Monthly Magazine* [H], IX, no. 49 (June, 1854), 95–101. No known manuscript, and no later authoritative printing (see below) in Melville's lifetime. NN emendations to H (on principles stated on pp. 549–64): at two points. NN printer's copy: an emended photocopy of Newberry Library A5.391. Machine collations between copies of H: Gift M69–114 *vs.* Newberry A5.391, Gift M78–3, and Northwestern L051H295 (copy 2); Northwestern L051H295 (copy 2) *vs.* University of Chicago AP2H3 (copy 2).

The structural device of paired sketches or episodes, one set in America and the other in England, is employed in three of Melville's tales: "Poor Man's Pudding and Rich Man's Crumbs," "The Two Temples," and "The Paradise of Bachelors and the Tartarus of Maids." As the Historical Note shows, they were evidently composed between the late summer of 1853 and the following spring. "Poor Man's Pudding and Rich Man's Crumbs," as the least developed of the three, was perhaps the first to be written; if so, it may have been submitted as early as September of 1853, when Melville misdirected to *Putnam's* an unidentified manuscript intended for *Harper's*. But it was not until May 25, 1854, that he acknowledged advance payment from *Harper's* for a group of contributions—"the 'Paradise of Batchelors &c.' "—that must have included "Poor Man's Pudding and Rich Man's Crumbs," which appeared in the June number. It was reprinted shortly afterwards in the Salem, Massachusetts, *Register* for June 19, 1854, p. 1, cols. 4–7, and in the Buffalo *Western Literary Messenger,* XXII, no. 6 (August, 1854), 260–64; collations of the Harvard College Library copies of these resettings against the *Harper's* printing (Gift M69–114) show that they were based on the *Harper's* text and contain no variants which appear to be authorial. (See the comments on the *Messenger* printing of a section of *Israel Potter,* NN243–44, n. 19.)

The Berkshire setting of the opening pages of "Poor Man's Pudding" is reminiscent of "Cock-A-Doodle-Doo!" (1853) and the first chapters of *Israel Potter,* which Melville dispatched to *Putnam's* evidently on June 7, 1854; the poverty and misery of the Coulters are not unlike the misfortunes of Potter, the Merrymusks in the earlier tale, and the Millthorpes in *Pierre* (1852). In "Rich Man's Crumbs" as again in "Temple Second" and "The Paradise of Bachelors" Melville drew directly on entries in his 1849 London journal. On Friday, November 9, he "went into Cheapside to see the 'Lord Mayor's Show' it being the day of the great civic feast & festivities. A most bloated pomp, to be sure." On the following day first he visited the Inns of Court and then, under the guidance of "an officer of the Fire Department," he was shown Richard Whittington's "birthplace" and made his way

> thro cellars & anti-lanes into the rear of Guildhall, with a crowd of beggars who were going to receive the broken meats & pies from yesterday's grand banquet (Lord Mayor's Day).—Within the hall, the scene was comical. Under the flaming banners & devices, were old broken tables set out with heaps of fowls hams &c &c pastry in profusion—cut in all directions—I could tell who had cut into this duck, or that goose. Some of the legs were gone—some of the wings, &c. (A good thing might be made of this) Read the account of the banquet—the foreign ministers & many of the nobility were present.

Working up these rough notes for the finished sketch, Melville set back the date of the "banquet" from 1849 to 1814. The narrator mentions the Battle of Waterloo as having already "closed" the Napoleonic Wars when in fact the battle did not take place until June of 1815. Beryl Rowland, in "Melville's Waterloo in *'Rich Man's Crumbs,'* " *Nineteenth-Century Fiction,* XXV (September, 1970), 216–21, points out that the Guildhall banquet described in the tale was held on June 18, 1814, to celebrate the Treaty of Paris; the guide mentions the same figures for expenditures that appear in Charles Knight's *London,* a work Melville had bought while in England

(Sealts 312). She notes further that the Guildhall charity and the London fire that the narrator mentions took place not on June 18 in 1814, a year before the Battle of Waterloo, but on November 10 and 11 (the charity following a much less extravagant banquet than the one described); also, the statues of Gog and Magog were not placed at the end of the hall until 1815. In "Sitting Up with a Corpse: Malthus according to Melville in 'Poor Man's Pudding and Rich Man's Crumbs,' " *Journal of American Studies,* VI (April, 1972), 69–83, Rowland sees Melville's anachronisms as intended to draw the reader's attention to events of 1814 and 1815: the year after Malthus published his *Observations on the Effects of the Corn Laws* in 1814, Parliament passed a new Corn Law "which set the conditions of extreme poverty for the labouring classes for many years to come." Ann Douglas, in *The Feminization of American Culture* (New York: Alfred A. Knopf, 1977), p. 300, holds that the tale is "a bitter parody" of Catharine Maria Sedgwick's *The Poor Rich Man and the Rich Poor Man* (1836), which takes the position that wealth has nothing to do with happiness and genuine success.

For explanation of the following tabulations, see pp. 565–70.

DISCUSSIONS. 291.31 found himself] The now obsolete idiom means that Coulter is to "find" or provide his own equipment for wood-chopping, just as in *Moby-Dick* (chap. 13) whaling ships "find their own harpoons" and in "Bartleby" (19.7 above) Turkey "finds" the lawyer in stationery.

292.2 unobservedly] NN emends the H reading "unobservantly" as a copyist's or compositor's error because it contradicts the narrator's "glancing . . . about the room".

301.1 crash] Possibly a misreading for "crush" since the ensuing passage emphasizes not so much a sharp collision with the mob as its pressure, in "wedge" (301.17) and "jam" (301.19).

EMENDATIONS. *292.2 unobservedly] NN; unobservantly H
292.15 affairs.∧] NN; ~." H

HYPHENATION. I. 289.11 husbandman 289.21 twenty-acre
290.2 spring-snow 290.10 snow-fleece 291.38 washing-day
292.28 ax-helve 294.16 good-enough 296.12 grind-stone
297.15 Cheapside 298.4 blind-walled 300.17 †golden-hued
301.10 half-sacked

II. 291.39 old-fashioned 294.13 time-piece 296.29 well-housed
299.2 field-marshals 300.17 †golden-hued 300.23 prince-regents

THE TWO TEMPLES (pp. 303–15)

NN copy-text: the fair-copy manuscript, inscribed by Augusta Melville, corrected and revised by Melville [AM/HM]; now in the Melville Collection of The Houghton Library of Harvard University (Ms Am 188, No. 389). Not printed in Melville's lifetime. NN emendations to AM/HM (on principles stated on pp. 549–64): at 170 points. NN printer's copy: a typed emended transcript of AM/HM (see p. 537).

As the HISTORICAL NOTE shows, "The Two Temples" and Melville's other two-part tales—"Poor Man's Pudding and Rich Man's Crumbs" and "The Paradise of Bachelors and the Tartarus of Maids"—were written between the late summer of 1853 and the spring of 1854. Unless "The Two Temples" accompanied a now-unlocated letter of February 6, 1854, from Melville to George Palmer Putnam, the manuscript was probably submitted shortly before May 12, when the *Putnam's* editor, Charles F. Briggs, wrote Melville that he was "very loth to reject" it. In a note next day Putnam himself suggested that disturbance of "some of our church readers" by "the *point* of your sketch" might be "avoided" through revision, but no surviving letters show whether Melville agreed to such a revision and nothing in the manuscript suggests that it has undergone one. On May 16, he acknowledged Putnam's note, saying that "in reply to a line from M[r] Briggs" he had also written him a letter (nonextant) "concerning the article" but giving no details. "Ere long I will send down some other things," he told Putnam, to which "no objections will be made on the score of tender consciences of the public." (See p. 491 above, n. 21.) These must have included the opening chapters of *Israel Potter.* On June 7 he evidently forwarded "some sixty and odd pages" of it, engaging that it "shall contain nothing of any sort to shock the fastidious"—another allusion to the fears of Putnam and Briggs about disturbing readers. On November 3, 1854, he wrote Putnam to acknowledge "the returned M.S." and a "note accompanying it, in which you allude to I[srael]. Potter"; perhaps the "returned M.S." was "The Two Temples," as Merrell R. Davis and William H. Gilman suggest *(Letters,* pp. 172–73, n. 5), but possibly some other work. The tale was first printed in Volume XIII of the Standard, or Constable, edition of Melville's *Works* (London, 1924), pp. 173–91.

The setting of "Temple First" reflects Melville's acquaintance with the opulently fashionable new Grace Church in New York City and its well-known sexton, Isaac Brown, a near neighbor at 107 Fourth Avenue during Melville's residence at No. 103 between 1847 and 1850. Briggs recognized the targets of Melville's "pungent satire," and warned in his letter that "the

The Two Temples
(dedicated to
Sheridan Knowles.)

Temple First

"This is too bad," said I, "here have I tramped this blessed Sunday morning, all the way from the Battery, three long miles, for this express purpose, prayer-book under arm; here I am, I say, &, after all, I can't get in.

"Too bad. And how disdainful the great, fat-paunched, beadle-faced man looked, when in answer to my humble petition, he said they had no galleries. Just the same as if he'd said, they didn't entertain poor folks. But I'll wager something that had my new coat been done last night, as the false tailor promised, & had I, arrayed therein this bright morning, tickled the fat-paunched, beadle-faced man's palm with a bank-note; then, gallery or no gallery, I would have had a fine seat in this marble-buttressed, stained-glassed, spic-&-span new temple.

"Well, here I am in the porch, very politely bowed out of the nave. I suppose I'm excommunicated; excluded, anyway.— That's a noble string of flashing carriages drawn up along the curb; those champing horses too have a haughty curve to their foam-flaked necks. Property of those "miserable sinners" inside, I presume. I dont a bit wonder they unreservedly confess to such misery as that.— See the gold hat-bands too, & other gorgeous trimmings, on those glossy groups of low-voiced gossippers near by. If I were in England

Leaf 1 (reduced) of Augusta Melville's fair-copy manuscript for "The Two Temples."

moral of the Two Temples would sway against us the whole power of the pulpit; to say nothing of Brown, and the congregation of Grace Church." Melville's interest in the church is attested to by an undated letter from his mother to his sisters Augusta and Fanny (February 13, 1863), in which she hopes "that New York will continue to amuse him & that he went to Grace Church to witness the queer couple that were so splendidly attended, & so peculiar in all respects." A possible literary analogue is one situation in "The Fanatic: A Tale of the Netherlands," the initial story in a gift book (Sealts 157) that Melville had presented on August 1, 1851, to Nathaniel Hawthorne and his wife—*The Continental Annual, and Romantic Cabinet, for 1832* (London, 1832): a Protestant leader dreams that he has hidden from a court of Inquisitors in the organ-loft of Antwerp Cathedral, where, like the narrator in "Temple First," he hears from below many voices, a preacher's "solemn and powerful tones," the peal of the organ, and the swell of a powerful hymn (pp. 6–8).

Melville's narrator goes up into the steeple, not the organ-loft; on January 28, 1848, Melville himself climbed "to the top of Trinity church steeple" in New York and "had a very fine view" of the city, according to his brother-in-law Lemuel Shaw, Jr., who accompanied him. As Beryl Rowland shows in "Grace Church and Melville's Story of 'The Two Temples,' " *Nineteenth-Century Fiction,* XXVIII (December, 1973), 339–46, some of the details are drawn from Trinity Church rather than from Grace. She also notes that pictures and discussion of both churches were included in an article on "New-York Church Architecture," *Putnam's,* II (September, 1853), 233–48; the article criticized the design of both buildings and perhaps "disturbed" church readers into responses that explain the fears of Briggs and Putnam about disturbing them further by "The Two Temples." The third sketch of "The Encantadas," which Melville may have been writing about the time the article appeared, begins: "To go up into a high stone tower is not only a very fine thing in itself, but the very best mode of gaining a comprehensive view of the region round about" (133.28–30 above).

In "Temple Second" the narrator's plight as a "stranger" in London was probably suggested by that of Melville's companion during his 1849–50 European trip, as Jay Leyda points out in *Complete Stories,* p. 463. Dr. Franklin Taylor, a cousin of Bayard Taylor, arrived there "on his last legs" financially, as noted in Melville's journal, November 14, 1849; the young doctor's "designs upon the two ladies" that Melville also noted may have been an attempt like the later narrator's to secure a position as "private Esculapius" (310.7) to a "Cleopatra" and "Charmian" (310.1–2). But whereas Taylor sailed for Jerusalem with the sickly son of a rich merchant, the narrator remains in London and there enters the gallery of a theater. So Melville himself had gone into the gallery of the Royal Lyceum Theater, Strand, on the evening of November 7, 1849, and seen a "fellow going round with a coffee pot & mugs—crying 'Porter, gents, porter!' "—the original of the lad in the tale with his "coffee-pot" and pewter mug of "humming ale." Later, on November 19, he saw Macready at the Haymarket Theater playing not Richelieu but Othello.

The manuscript of "The Two Temples" is inscribed on eighteen (so numbered) 32.5-by-20-cm leaves of blue laid paper with chain lines 2.7 cm apart and faint horizontal rules in dark blue .8 cm apart. Each leaf was torn from a larger sheet: Leaves 1–11, 16, 17 (all three segments), and 18 along the left margin, Leaves 12–15 along the right margin. Several of the edges are worn and the leaves vary somewhat in color from leaf to leaf, due at least partly to soiling. In Leaf 18 there are two small holes caused by burns. The initial fair-copy ink inscription is by Augusta Melville as copyist. The additional ink inscription is by Melville himself and includes (1) words he supplied where Augusta, evidently unable to read those in the draft she was copying, had left blank spaces (for examples see 303.20–21 and 310.21 in the MANUSCRIPT ALTERATIONS list below); (2) his interlinear or marginal corrections of her misreadings (such as "glanced" for "glared" at 312.25 and "rosy" for "very" at 315.5); (3) his interlinear or marginal revisions of single words or phrases; and (4) his rewriting of an entire paragraph on the three-segment composite Leaf 17 (see accompanying reproduction). He cut off the original Leaf 17 just below the canceled paragraph to form segment A (about 15.8 by 20 cm); he inscribed a substitute paragraph on similar paper to form segment B (about 19.1 by 20 cm), which he then fastened to A with four dabs of sealing wax. Finally, he fastened segment C (about 16.5 by 20 cm) to B with four dabs of sealing wax. Segment C, inscribed by Augusta, was the lower portion of the original Leaf 17: the parts of six letters of a word or words that appear along the top margin of C exactly match those on the bottom line of A. The verso of each leaf has a Harvard College identification number. On the verso of Leaf 1, in an unidentified hand, "1421 / Two Temples [underlined]" is inscribed in ink.

For explanation of the following tabulations, see pp. 565–70.

sovereign outlook, & imperial downlook, the whole theatre, with the expanded stage directly opposite, though some hundred feet below. As at the tower, peeping into the transatlantic temple, so stood I here, at the very mast-head of all the interior edifice.

Such was the decorum of this special theatre, that nothing objectionable was admitted within its walls. With an unlost eye of perfect love, I sat serenely in the gallery, gazing upon the blessing scene, around me & below. Neither does it abate from my pleased satisfaction, to remember, that Mr Macready, the chief actor of the night, was an amiable gentleman, combining the finest qualities of social and Christian respectability, with the highest excellence in his particular profession; for which last he has conscientiously done much, in many ways, to refine, elevate & chasten.

But now the curtain rises, & the robed Cardinal advances. How marvellous this personal resemblance! He looks every inch to be the selfsame, stately priest I saw irradiated by the glow-worm dies of the pictured windows from my high tower-pew. And shining as he does, in the rosy reflexes of these stained walls & gorgeous galleries, the mimic priest down there, he too seems lit by Gothic blazonings.—Hark! the same measured, courtly, noble tone. See! the same imposing attitude. Excellent actor is this Richelieu!

He disappears behind the scenes. He slips, no doubt, into the Green Room. He reappears somewhat changed in his habiliments. Do I dream, or is it genuine memory that recalls some similar thing seen through the woven wires?

The Curtain falls. Starting to their feet the enraptured thousands sound their responses, deafeningly; unmistakably sincere. Right-from the

Leaf 17 (reduced) of Augusta Melville's fair-copy manuscript for "The Two Temples," with paragraph inserted in Melville's hand.

DISCUSSIONS. 305.13 Domine] NN emends the AM "Domino" as an error probably caused by Melville's indistinct final "e" (although it is possible that Melville himself had written the wrong form of the word).

309.19 gentlemany] Possibly an error for "gentlemanly", but NN does not emend since there are examples of "gentlemany" as late as 1719 in the *OED* (labeled obsolete), and Melville deliberately used archaic forms in many of the pieces in this volume (see pp. 561–62).

309.35 fraternal] NN emends the AM reading "paternal" as an error probably caused by Melville's similar initial "fr" and "p". The intended reading here—unlike the correct "paternal" at 312.33—is obviously "fraternal", as a reference to Philadelphia as the "city of brotherly [not fatherly] love." Cf. the same emendation in *The Confidence-Man* (chap. 5; NN27.15).

312.29 Shall] NN omits the quotation mark Melville added before this word, since he did not also add its mate after the question mark or a pair around the narrator's continued musings at 312.29–313.1. An alternative emendation, adding quotation marks at these three points, is rejected because at other points in this piece no quotation marks are used for unspoken thoughts introduced with "mused" or "thought"—see 314.17–18.

313.6 far other] NN omits the AM hyphen; "far" is obviously intended to modify "side", not "other". There may have been some confusion with "far-under aisles and altar" at 305.28–29.

314.34 Mr] See the discussion at 205.21.

EMENDATIONS. 303.2 Dedicated] NN; dedicated AM 303.20 'miserable] NN; "~ AM 303.20 sinners'] NN; ~" AM 304.11 orchestra] NN; orchestre AM 305.6 effulgence] NN; effulgance AM *305.13 Domine] NN; Domino AM 305.29 altar] NN; alter HM 305.37 beggars] NN; beggers AM 306.37 apparel] NN; apparal AM 308.24 response] NN; responce HM 308.24 roundabout] NN; rounabout AM 309.17 violator] NN; violater AM *309.35 fraternal] NN; paternal AM 310.4 securing] NN; secureing AM 310.12 vacillations] NN; vacillatations AM 310.21 apparel] NN; apparal AM 311.3 Pandemonian] NN; Pandamonian AM 311.7 comparative] NN; comparitive AM 311.19 turbulent] NN; turbulant AM 312.20 and] NN; And AM *312.29 ∧Shall] NN; "~ AM/HM 312.29 It's] NN; Its AM *313.6 far∧other] NN; far-other AM 314.22 gallery,] NN; ~,, AM/HM 314.27 imperial] NN; imperiel HM 314.38 conscientiously] NN; consciencioulsy HM

NN also emends the "&" of AM/HM to "and" at: 303.7,12,15,22, 304.7,11,12,17,26(twice),27(twice),30,35,39, 305.2,8,10,15,16,18,19,28,29,32,35,38, 306.3,8,13(twice),25,26,27,34,36,38(twice), 307.1,4,12,15,21,23,24,25,28,31,33,34,35,38, 308.1,3,5,7,15,22,24,

309.8,13,17,22,23,27,31,34,35,36, 310.7,25(twice),26(twice),27(twice),36,39, 311.2,4,5(twice),6,14,17,19,24,28,32,33,36,37,39, 312.1,3,6,10,15,16(twice),17,19,21,33,34,37(twice),39, 313.2,3,4(thrice),7,10,12,20,21,23(twice),24,25,27,30,34(twice),37,38,40, 314.2,10,15,16,26(twice),33,38,39, 315.17,18,19,20(twice),21.

HYPHENATION. I. 303.19 foam-flaked 303.22 low-voiced 304.10 new-fashioned 305.9 magic-lantern 305.31 fine-woven 305.35 blacksmith's 308.29 beadle-faced 310.39 pew-opener 312.12 towards 313.27 deep-/sea-leads

II. 304.21 stair-way 305.28 far-under 306.15 window-stains 307.6 low-inclining 308.25 dwelling-houses 308.27 bell-rope 313.3 inferior-looking 313.5 ill-lit 315.1 self-same

MANUSCRIPT ALTERATIONS. 303.4 have I] have / [HM *add in left margin* I] 303.9 said] ~, [AM *cancel comma*] 303.20–21 they unreservedly] they *followed by blank space* [HM *add in blank space* unreservedly] 303.23 those chaps] them [HM <them >those chaps] 304.3 aristocratic] aristacratic [HM *alter to* aristocratic] 304.4 idly] patiently [HM <patiently >idly] 304.8 seem . . . way.] go through it. [HM <go through it. >seem to go that way.] 304.8 leads] goes [HM <goes >leads] 304.21 Ascending] Assending [HM *alter to* Ascending] 304.24 I] I [HM *add bracket before* I *for new paragraph*] 305.1 ladder] laddar [HM *alter to* ladder] 305.9 huge] high [HM <high >huge] 305.16 ladder] laddar [HM *alter to* ladder] 305.21 the tower attached] it [HM <it >the tower] attached 305.29 aisles and altar.] altar-rail [HM <altar-rail >aisles & alter. *(emended)*] 305.31 gauzy] gausy [AM *alter to* gauzy] 306.7 remain] stand [HM <stand >remain] 306.12 burst] broke [HM <broke >burst] 306.13 invoking] lauding [HM <lauding >invoking] 306.28 sumptuous] sumptious [AM *alter to* sumptuous] 306.31 sly] mysterious [HM <mysterious >sly] 306.37 black.] dark →<dark→ *add* black. 307.3 so] / as [<as *add in margin* so {<so *add in margin* so}] 307.3 him now] him [>now] 307.3–4 —repeated . . . quoted,—] ∧~ . . . ~,∧ [HM *add dashes*] 307.6–7 low-inclining] low-circling [AM *alter* circling *to* inclining] 307.7 foreheads] heads [HM >fore *before* heads] 307.9 Resurrection] resurrection [HM *alter to capital*] 307.10–11 like . . . drum-beat] —~ . . . ~-~— [HM *cancel dashes*] 307.11 enrapturing,] evoking, [HM <evoking, >enrapturing,] 307.12 brooks] / congregation [HM <congregation *add in margin* tide {<tide >brooks}] 307.15 imposing] inspiring [HM <inspiring >imposing] 307.16 do just now,] do [HM >just now,] 307.25 see] sees [HM? <s] 307.25 me—] ~, [HM *w.o. comma with dash*]

307.38 them] / those [HM <those *add in margin* them] 308.1 glasses;] ~∧ [HM *add semicolon*] 308.2 A Puseyitish] A [HM >Puseyitish] 308.3 child] her child [HM <her] 308.4 painted] mild [HM <mild >x →<x→ *add* painted] 308.14 temple,] church, [AM <church, >temple,] 308.20 I know,] I know, I know [AM? <*second* I know] 308.22 an] an [AM *mend second letter*] 308.24 no response.] it has / not been opened to me. [HM <it . . . me. >no responce. *(emended)*] 308.26 a stranger's] stranger [AM >a *before* stranger *and add* 's *to* stranger] 308.27 caller;] ~. [AM *alter period to semicolon*] 308.28 an appointment] a ?severe appointment [AM ≯*question mark in pencil above* ?severe {HM <?severe *erase question mark and alter* a *to* an}] 308.30 well knows] will know [HM *alter* will *to* well *and add* s *to* know] 308.30 bell] church / bell [AM? HM? <church] 308.38 Horrors!] ~∧ [HM *w.o.* rs *and add exclamation point*] 308.39 served] seemed [HM <seemed >served] 309.2 thrice . . . axis,] revolved . . . axis, at least three times, [HM >thrice *before* revolved *and* <at . . . times,] 309.10 turned] turned [AM *mend second letter*] 309.17 lawless] lawless sacreligious [HM <sacreligious] 309.20 judge.] Justice. [HM <Justice. >judge.] 310.1–2 the duenna lovely] / lovely [HM >*in margin* the duenna *before* lovely] 310.4 passage, the two] passage [HM *add comma and* >the pa →<the pa→ >*circled, with guideline to caret* the two] 310.7 knightly] masculine [HM <masculine >knightly] 310.9 European] Eurapean [AM *alter to* European] 310.9 tour, to follow.] tour. [HM *alter period to comma / add* to follow.] 310.10 Enough] Enough [HM *add bracket before* Enough *to confirm AM new paragraph*] 310.10 came] came [AM *mend last letter*] 310.10 man. We sailed.] man. [AM >We sailed.] 310.11 agonized] agonised [AM *alter to* agonized] 310.12 vacillations] vasillatations [AM *alter to* vacillatations *and w.o. third* a *(emended)*] 310.17 a sad] rapid [HM <rapid >a sad] 310.21 more slaughterous] more *followed by blank space* [HM *add in blank space* slaughterous] 310.24 indescribable] inde *followed by blank space* [HM *add in blank space* scribable] 310.25 bye-veins] bye-ways *followed by blank space* [HM <bye-ways *and add in blank space* bye-veins] 310.29 equally . . . own,] so hungry as was I, [HM <so >equally *and* <as was I, >with my own,] 310.29 as through] through [AM >as *before* through] 310.32 billows] bittows [AM *mend inadvertently crossed ells*] 310.37 pitiable] most pitiable [HM <most] 310.38 now] night now [HM <night] 310.39 chapel,] church, [HM <church, >chapel,] 311.3 Disentangling] Disentangle xx →<xx *w.o.* Disentangling→ 311.6 Strand] strand [HM *alter to capital*] 311.6–7 a crosswise] a *followed by blank space* [HM *add in blank space* crosswise] 311.8 surrounding] sxx →<xx *w.o.* surrounding→ 311.16 best] best in the town [HM <the {<in town}] 311.31 celebrated part] celebrated *followed by blank space* [HM *add in blank space* part]

311.33 Craven] / Wellington [HM <Wellington *add in margin* Craven]
311.34 muddy Phlegethon] muddy *followed by blank space* [HM *add in blank space*
Phlegethon] 311.35 cheer;] char; [HM <char; >cheer;]
311.38 multitude] multitu *followed by blank space* [HM? AM? *add in blank space*
de] 311.38 such assemblies] churches [HM <churches >such
assemblies] 311.39 accessible] accessable [HM *alter to* accessible]
312.2 tabernacles] churches [HM <churches >tabernacles] 312.5 last;] last
[HM *add semicolon*] 312.8 from this] from the *followed by blank space* / of this
[HM *leaving blank space* <the <of] 312.12 towards] to / [AM *add in margins*
= / =wards] 312.13 in;] ~, [HM *alter comma to semicolon*]
312.20 stranger; and] stranger. And [HM *alter period to semicolon without altering*
And *to lowercase (emended)*] 312.20 very maw] very *followed by blank space*
[HM *add in blank space* maw] 312.23 people,] men, [HM <men,
>people,] 312.23 one;] ~, [HM *alter comma to semicolon*]
312.25 glanced] glared [HM <glared >glanced] 312.29 Shall] Shall [HM
add opening quotation marks before Shall *(emended)*] 313.8 the countenance] it
[HM <it >the countenance] 313.14 gauzy] gausy [AM *alter to* gauzy]
313.31 crowds] the crowds [HM <the] 314.1 arrested . . .
wanderings,] brought back to common-/sense, [HM?AM? *in
pencil* ≯from its wanderings *above* back to common-] [HM <brought . . .
common-/sense *and erase* from its wanderings >*with guideline to caret* arrested in
its wanderings,] 314.3 ragged, but] ragged boy →<boy→ *add* but *and
comma after* ragged 314.10 humming ale] ale [HM >humming *before*
ale] 314.21 boy!] ~. [HM *alter period to exclamation point*]
314.22 gallery,] ~, [HM *add another comma (emended)*] 314.23 was,] ~∧
[HM *add comma*] 314.23 anything,] ~∧ [HM *add comma*]
314.24 contracted,] ~∧ [HM *add comma*] 314.25 limited] small / [HM?AM?
in pencil add in right margin limited? {<small *and (erased)* limited? >*in left margin*
limited}] 314.29 here] hear [AM *alter to* here] 314.29 main-mast-head]
~∧~∧~ [HM *add hyphens*] 314.31–38 Such . . . chasten.] ¶
Immense spiked screens cut off the gallery on either hand from all bordering
parts. Whether aught objectionable was behind those screens, or no, I cannot say.
I saw nothing wrong. It might have been, nay, I deem it probable, that,
considering the known decorum of this special theatre, nought objectionable was
willingly admitted within its walls. And therefore with no foul word, or horrible
titter of the painted corpse to trouble me, I sat serenely in the gallery, & looked
with an eye of perfect love on all the scene around me & below. Upward I could
not look, being already in the domineering gallery. [HM <Immense . . .
domineering gallery. *with two intersecting diagonal lines and on patch inscribe* ¶
Such . . . gazing upon the bright {HM <bright >pleasing} scene, . . . my pleased
{HM <pleased} satisfaction, . . . conscienciously *(emended)* . . . chasten.]
315.3 rosy] very [HM <very >rosy] 315.5 down] over [HM <over

>down] 315.8 slips] goes [HM <goes >slips] 315.13 deafeningly;] ~, [HM *alter comma to semicolon*] 315.21 one;] ~, [HM *alter comma to semicolon*]

THE PARADISE OF BACHELORS AND THE TARTARUS OF MAIDS (pp. 316–35)

NN copy-text: the anonymous first printing, "The Paradise of Bachelors and the Tartarus of Maids," in *Harper's New Monthly Magazine* [H], X, no. 59 (April, 1855), 670–78. No known manuscript, and no later printing in Melville's lifetime. NN emendations to H (on principles stated on pp. 549–64): at two points. NN printer's copy: an emended photocopy of Newberry Library A5.391. Machine collations between copies of H: Gift M69–114 *vs.* Newberry A5.391, Gift M78–3, and Northwestern L051H295 (copy 2); Northwestern L051H295 (copy 2) *vs.* University of Chicago AP2H3 (copy 2).

Along with "Poor Man's Pudding and Rich Man's Crumbs" and "The Two Temples," this tale was composed between the late summer of 1853 and the following spring. Melville's letter of May 25, 1854, to Harper & Brothers acknowledged receiving "$100 on acct: of the 'Paradise of Batchelors &c.' ", but for some reason its publication was delayed nearly a year. As in the other two-part tales, he drew on personal experiences both at home and abroad, but here setting the first rather than the second part in London. At six o'clock on Wednesday, December 19, 1849, he had dined in Elm Court, Temple, with the "R. F. C." of "The Paradise of Bachelors" (318.36): Robert Francis Cooke, a cousin of John Murray, Melville's first London publisher. According to his journal entry next day, he

> had a glorious time till noon of night. A set of fine fellows indeed. It recalled poor Lamb's "Old Benchers". Cunningham the author of Murray's London guide was there & was very friendly. A comical Mr Rainbow also, & a grandson of Woodfall the printer of Junius, and a brother-in-law of Leslie the painter. Leslie was prevented from coming. Up in the 5th story we dined. The Paradise of Batchelors. Home & to bed at 12.

The next evening Melville dined at the Erechtheum Club, St. James's, with William Henry Cooke, brother of Robert Francis. There were nine at table, including Rainbow and a Mr. Cleaves. On the morning of December 21 Melville

> called on Mr Cleaves at his rooms in the Temple, & we visited the Library—Hall of the Benchers—Kitchen—rooms—Dessert room & *table*. Portraits of the Benchers. In the Library saw some fine old M.S.S—of the Kings & Queens & Chancellors hundreds of years ago. Thence to Lincoln's Inn, & visited the New Hall, Kitchen, Library &c—Very fine. Sublime Kitchen—*chimney place*. Also visited the courts in the Inn—2 Vice Chancellors Courts,—and the Lord High Chancellor Cottenham—and *[sic]* old fellow, nearly asleep on the bench. Thence to the Court of the Master of the Rolls—Rolls' Court—a very handsome man—Lord Something, I forget what—Strange story about him.

He dined again at the Erechtheum Club on the twenty-second in a party of eight.

In the spring of 1853, when his uncle Peter Gansevoort was planning a trip abroad, Melville wrote to Robert Cooke, who invited Gansevoort to Elm Court, where he dined on July 4. Melville also prepared a list of sight-seeing suggestions for him: see *Journal of a Visit to London and the Continent,* ed. Eleanor Melville Metcalf (Cambridge: Harvard University Press, 1948), p. 175. Among them was a visit to the Temple, including the Church on Sunday, a glimpse of the Templars' tombs, the dining halls, the dessert room, and the kitchens—as well as those at Lincoln's Inn. These notes and the journal entries supply much material for "The Paradise of Bachelors"; as Jay Leyda suggests *(Complete Stories,* p. 466), Melville's uncle's later report on the bachelor circle may have added "a few appetizing details."

For the account of papermaking in "The Tartarus of Maids," Melville turned to the Berkshire paper industry and recalled his visit to a mill at Dalton, Massachusetts, in the winter of 1851: Robert S. Forsythe, in "Taghconic," *Saturday Review of Literature,* VIII (September 19, 1931), 140, first suggested Dalton and its paper mills as "perhaps the setting," and Harrison Elliott, in "A Century Ago: An Eminent Author Looked upon Paper and Papermaking," *Paper Maker,* XXI (September, 1952), 55–58, identified "the Defiance Mill built by David Carson in 1823" as the one "which Melville patronized in the 1850's." Writing to Evert A. Duyckinck from Pittsfield on February 12, 1851, Melville annotated the "Carson's Dalton MS" trademark on his writing paper: the mill, he explained, is "about 5 miles from here, North East. I went there & got a sleigh-load of this paper. A great neighborhood for authors, you see, is Pittsfield." Here is the basis for the "seedsman's" sleigh journey to get envelopes, as recounted in the tale. That the trip is "some sixty miles" with an overnight stop suggests another setting more distant from Arrowhead than Dalton: Mount Greylock, about twenty miles north, is clearly the tale's "Woedolor Mountain" with its "Mad Maid's Bellows'-pipe," "Black Notch," and "hopper-shaped hollow." Duyckinck's letter of August 13, 1851, about an ascent of Greylock with Melville gives details similar to the opening of the tale:

> Ascending you get to a passage, with Saddleback or Saddleball or Greylock as they call him for its southerly side which they cant easily deface. It is the "Bellows Pipe" or "Notch" pass to South Adams, the Eastern summit of which . . . turns very beautifully to the eye. Here you are in the midst of closely fitting mountains—a grand neighborhood. A part of these descending form the "Hopper" a deep valley with clean descending mountain sides in the shape of that household implement. (Quoted in Luther S. Mansfield, "Glimpses of Herman Melville's Life in Pittsfield, 1850–1851," *American Literature,* IX [March, 1937], 44.)

In 1852 Melville dedicated *Pierre* "To Greylock's Most Excellent Majesty" and climbed it again in the summer of 1853.

For explanation of the following tabulations, see pp. 565–70.

DISCUSSIONS. 317.3 Guilbert] NN emends the H reading "Gilbert" to the correct spelling of the name of this character in Scott's *Ivanhoe.*

333.39 wandering] Possibly an error for "wondering".

EMENDATIONS. *317.3 Guilbert] NN; Gilbert H 322.14 the] NN; the the H

HYPHENATION. I. 317.13 outskill 317.21 roast-mutton 318.28 patent-leather 318.30 banquet-halls 319.17 time-honored 320.26 raw-hides 320.28 snow-white 320.33 chicken-pie 321.18 well-being 322.14 field-marshal 322.24 fire-side 323.5 whereupon 324.15 lowlands 324.19 black-mossed 324.31 seedsman's 327.8 wood-pile 327.28 well-wrapped 329.9 dark-complexioned 329.19 Indiaman 329.21 water-wheel 330.2 sun-beams 331.33 air-bridge 332.36 sad-looking 334.32 Fast-days

II. 317.18 Knights-Templars 317.31 Knights-Templars 318.11 bomb-shells 320.32 aids-de-camp 324.19 spike-knotted 326.9 boarding-houses 333.21 evolvement-power 334.12 folding-room 335.14 Temple-Bar

JIMMY ROSE (pp. 336–45)

NN copy-text: the anonymous first printing, "Jimmy Rose," in *Harper's New Monthly Magazine* [H], XI, no. 66 (November, 1855), 803–7. No known manuscript, and no later printing in Melville's lifetime. NN emendations to H (on principles stated on pp. 549–64): at four points. NN printer's copy: an emended photocopy of Newberry Library A5.391. Machine collations between copies of H: Gift M69–114 *vs.* Newberry A5.391, Gift M78–3, and Northwestern L051H295 (copy 2); Northwestern L051H295 (copy 2) *vs.* University of Chicago AP2H3 (copy 2).

As the Historical Note shows, "Jimmy Rose" and "The 'Gees" were probably the "brace of fowl—wild fowl" that Melville dispatched to Harper & Brothers on September 18, 1854; both were published well after a year later. Internal evidence suggests composition during the summer of 1854. The expression "Poor Man's Plaster" (at 344.38–39) recalls Blandmour's phrasemaking in "Poor Man's Pudding," which had appeared that June, and the allusion to Templar tombs (337.14–15) is reminiscent of "The Paradise of Bachelors," then awaiting publication. Like "The Fiddler" and "Temple First," "Jimmy Rose" evokes contemporary New York, contrasting its ways with Jimmy's old-fashioned manner: thus there are knowing references to Broadway and the Bowling Green, Trinity Church and the Park Theater, and the "oyster saloon" of Alexander Cato, which flourished at 566 Broadway. Other elements anticipate two tales written in 1855, "I and My Chimney" and "The Apple-Tree Table." In all three the narrator, here called "William Ford," mentions his wife, his daughters, and "Biddy the girl," but in this one the women do not enter the action and are less developed than in the later tales, which are more concerned with his domestic affairs.

The setting of "Jimmy Rose" seems to involve several old houses familiar to Melville. According to Jay Leyda,

> The second house in New York City occupied by the Melville family after Herman's birth should have been the earliest one remembered by him, for he was five years old when they moved from it. This house, at 55 Courtlandt Street, may have been Jimmy Rose's former home, "in C—— Street,"—"a great old house in a narrow street of one of the lower wards, once the haunt of style and fashion, full of gay parlors and bridal chambers; but now [in the '50s?] for the most part, transformed into counting-rooms and warehouses." *(Complete Stories,* p. 468)

Interior details, however, are unmistakably drawn from the Pittsfield house formerly occupied by Melville's uncle Thomas Melvill, Jr., which in the 1850's was purchased by J. R. Morewood and christened "Broadhall." Merton M. Sealts, Jr., in "The Ghost of Major Melvill," *New England Quarterly,* XXX (September, 1957), 291–306, quotes similar phrasing from a passage describing the house in Melville's memoir of his uncle in *The History of Pittsfield* (1870): it is "somewhat changed, and partly modernized externally. It is of goodly proportions, with ample hall and staircase, carved wood-work and solid oaken timbers, hewn in Stockbridge. These timbers as viewed from the cellar, remind one of the massive gun deck beams of a line-of-battle ship." William B. Dillingham, in *Melville's Short Fiction, 1853–1856* (Athens: University of Georgia Press, 1977), p. 303, suggests still a third house as a model: that of the senior Major Thomas Melvill, Melville's grandfather, in Green Street, Boston, where he had also visited as a boy.

As Dillingham also suggests, Jimmy Rose himself "resembles at least three members of Melville's family. He is both a bankrupt and a man whom time has passed by." Both Melville's father and his Uncle Thomas suffered financial reverses that he remembered vividly, and there are strong resemblances between Thomas Melvill, Jr., and characters in his later writing, from Jimmy Rose to Jack Gentian and John Marr, as pointed out in Sealts's "The Ghost of Major Melvill." But Dillingham adds that in making Jimmy a "quaint anachronism" Melville "was almost certainly writing with his paternal grandfather in mind," the same old-fashioned figure who had inspired Oliver Wendell Holmes's "The Last Leaf" in 1831; in both tale and poem, the title character's cheek is "like a rose / In the snow," and Holmes's lines may well have supplied Melville not only Jimmy's last name but also the tale's chief symbol, which anticipates the pervasive rose imagery of his later writings.

For explanation of the following tabulations, see pp. 565–70.

DISCUSSIONS. 336.9 soft-warfle] NN keeps the variant H spelling "-warfle" as a currently acceptable ear-spelling. Another variant spelling—"warfields"—is reported by the *Dictionary of Americanisms* from a humorous dialect passage in John Pendleton Kennedy's *Quodlibet* (1840). Elizabeth Shaw Melville corrected the spelling to "-waffle" in the copy of "Jimmy Rose" she kept in a group of "Magazine Stories by Herman Melville" (see the RELATED DOCUMENTS, pp. 793–98). On ear-spellings, see the discussion at 236.15.

338.34 Cosmo the Magnificent] This H reading involves an apparent, but unemendable, confusion on Melville's part between Cosimo or Cosmo de' Medici (1389–1464), known as "Cosimo the Elder," and Lorenzo de' Medici (1449–92), known as "Lorenzo the Magnificent."

342.3 Parisian] NN emends the "Persian" of H as a misreading: note the earlier description of the "genuine Versailles paper" (337.28), with its "Parisian-looking birds" (337.34) in "the old parlor of the peacocks or room of roses" (338.18–19).

343.38 leaning] The H reading "learning" does not fit the context, as the obvious NN emendation does, and is clearly a mistake by the copyist or compositor.

EMENDATIONS. 336.15 despoiled] NN; dispoiled H *342.3 Parisian] NN; Persian H *343.38 leaning] NN; learning H 345.1 Rose!^] NN; ~!" H

HYPHENATION. I. 337.21 heavy-moulded 338.36 party-giving 344.38 gentleman's

II. 337.6 sounding-board 337.24 drawing-room 339.29 well-remembered 339.38 snow-storm

THE 'GEES (pp. 346–51)

NN copy-text: the anonymous first printing, "The 'Gees," in *Harper's New Monthly Magazine* [H], XII, no. 70 (March, 1856), 507–9. No known manuscript, and no later printing in Melville's lifetime. NN emendations to H (on principles stated on pp. 549–64): at four points. NN printer's copy: an emended photocopy of Newberry Library A5.391. Machine collations between copies of H: Newberry A5.391 *vs.* Gift M69–114 and Northwestern L051H295 (copy 2); Gift M69–114 *vs.* Gift M78–3; University of Chicago AP2H3 (copy 2) *vs.* Northwestern L051H295 (copy 2).

As the HISTORICAL NOTE shows, "The 'Gees" and "Jimmy Rose" were probably the "brace of fowl—wild fowl" that Melville dispatched to Harper & Brothers on September 18, 1854; "The 'Gees" remained unpublished even longer than "Jimmy Rose." Carolyn L. Karcher discusses its genesis and composition in "Melville's 'The 'Gees': A Forgotten Satire on Scientific Racism," *American Quarterly*, XXVII (October, 1975), 421–42, later expanded in her *Shadow over the Promised Land* (Baton Rouge: Louisiana State University Press, 1980), pp. 160–85. Her article argues that Melville was reacting to a review, "Is Man One or Many?" in *Putnam's*, IV (July, 1854), 1–14, of *Types of Mankind* (Philadelphia, 1854), by Josiah C. Nott and George R. Gliddon. The anonymous reviewer, in Karcher's words, "concluded that the 'scientific' evidence ethnologists presented pointed irresistibly toward 'fixed and primordial distinctions among the races.' He also assented readily to the principle of a biological hierarchy where the Negro occupied the lowest human rung"; she thinks Melville responded in "The 'Gees" with a "reductio ad absurdum of racist ethnology."

"The 'Gees" anticipates some aspects of *The Confidence-Man* (1857), which Melville probably began in the summer of 1855 and finished late in 1856. In Chapter 22, Pitch hires and works his boys on much the same principles as did Captain Hosea Kean, the experienced "'Gee jockey" of "The 'Gees." And Chapters 25–28, about "Indian-hating," also take up the subject of racial attitudes.

For explanation of the following tabulations, see pp. 565–70.

DISCUSSION. 347.14 Ge-e-e-e-e!] Even though all other occurrences of this word are preceded by an apostrophe in H (except at 349.11, emended by NN), NN does not add one here because in this case the reference is to the "monosyllable" not the people.

EMENDATIONS. 349.11 of 'Gees] NN; ~ ∧~ H 349.36 skipper] NN; shipper H 350.33 the monkey-jacket] NN; monkey-jacket H 351.13 are] NN; is H

HYPHENATION. I. 347.17 broadcast 350.35 monkey-jacket
II. 347.21 ship-biscuit 347.32 thin-skinned 350.5 man-of-war's-man's 350.8 trowser-legs 351.4 well-attested

I AND MY CHIMNEY (pp. 352–77)

NN copy-text: the anonymous first printing, "I and My Chimney," in *Putnam's Monthly Magazine* [P], VII, no. 39 (March, 1856), pp. 269–83. No known manuscript, and no later printing in Melville's lifetime. NN emendations to P (on principles stated on pp. 549–64): at ten points. NN printer's copy: an emended photocopy of Newberry Library A5.765. Machine collations between copies of P: Newberry A5.765 *vs.* Northwestern 051P99 and M67–722–207 (twice); M67–722–295 *vs.* M67–722–207 and M69–316–20.

As the HISTORICAL NOTE shows, "I and My Chimney" was probably composed during the spring and copied in the late spring or early summer of 1855. The fair-copy manuscript was submitted to *Putnam's* in time for inclusion with a batch of contributions forwarded in July to the editorial adviser, George William Curtis, that he acknowledged in a letter of July 31 to Joshua A. Dix of Dix & Edwards. The tale's narrator resembles Melville in 1855 in being sometimes "crippled up as any old apple tree" with sciatica (360.28); according to Elizabeth Shaw Melville, her husband had suffered "his first attack of severe rheumatism in his back—so that he was helpless—" in February of 1855 "and in the following June an attack of Sciatica—Our neighbor in Pittsfield Dr O. W. Holmes attended & prescribed for him" (quoted in Merton M. Sealts, Jr., *The Early Lives of Melville* [Madison: University of Wisconsin Press, 1974], p. 169). On September 7, 1855, when Curtis returned "all the *Mss.*" to Dix & Edwards, he singled out "I and My Chimney" for praise as "a capital, genial, humorous sketch . . . , thoroughly magazinish." But the story remained unpublished until the following March, perhaps because "Benito Cereno" was slated for the October, November, and December numbers.

Like "Jimmy Rose," written probably the year before, "I and My Chimney" has a first-person narrator with a wife and daughters and a housemaid called Biddy, but there are differences as well: the earlier tale's narrator, William Ford, is an old man who has "removed from the country to the city, having become unexpected heir to a great old house"; here the unnamed old narrator and his beloved chimney "reside in the country." The rural setting is evidently like that of Pittsfield; the huge central chimney is like the one at Melville's Arrowhead residence, "Ogg Mountain" (355.22) is presumably based on nearby Mt. Greylock, and "the Great Oak" (355.22), as Elizabeth Shaw Melville observed in a marginal notation, based on the celebrated "Pittsfield Elm." Her words appear on p. 270 of a copy of "I and My Chimney" now in the Melville Collection of The Houghton Library of Harvard University (see the RELATED DOCUMENTS, pp. 793–98); her further note three pages later suggests that she identified the narrator (at least at this point) with Melville himself. Where the narrator describes "this enterprising wife of mine" (360.24) she (with infirm pronoun reference) wrote: "All this about his wife applies to his mother—who was very vigorous and energetic—about the farm &c—. The proposed removal of the chimney is purely mythical." After Melville's brother Allan bought Arrowhead in 1863 he decorated the "old kitchen" fireplace with inscriptions from "I and My Chimney." A copy of the March, 1856 *Putnam's,* inscribed "Allan Melville. Arrowhead— / Pittsfield / Mass: / (I and my chimney)" and now in The

Berkshire Athenaeum at Pittsfield, bears penciled question marks in the margins of the story at NN352.1–3, 356.18–19, 357.19–20, 366.39–367.2, 377.19–20, and a check mark at 371.14–15. The "proposed removal" of the tale's central chimney may indeed be "purely mythical" in reference to the Arrowhead one, but a chimney at nearby Broadhall, once the home of Melville's uncle Thomas Melvill, Jr., was actually taken down in 1851 by the new owner, J. R. Morewood (see the possible allusion in *Moby-Dick,* chap. 3; NN13.31–33).

While the narrator may bear some relation to Melville and his state of health in the 1850's, he has other affiliations as well. George William Curtis's warm response on reading the manuscript is perhaps explained by Ann Douglas's observation in *The Feminization of American Culture* (New York: Alfred A. Knopf, 1977), p. 317, that the narrator is "closest in character to the narrator in Curtis's *Prue and I,* recently serialized in *Harper's.*" But the narrator, his ever-present pipe, and his "enterprising wife" may also be indebted to Melville's reading in a set of Washington Irving's works he had been given in June of 1853 (Sealts 292a). According to Irving's burlesque *History of New York* (bk. IV, chap. 8), the pipe was "the great organ of reflection and deliberation of the New Netherlander. It was his constant companion and solace: was he gay, he smoked; was he sad, he smoked; his pipe was never out of his mouth; it was a part of his physiognomy; without it his best friends would not know him. Take away his pipe? You might as well take away his nose!"

The old narrator's wife, with her "infatuate juvenility," is like such female Irving characters as Rip Van Winkle's wife; in the *History* (III, 4) Diedrich Knickerbocker calls women "those arch innovators upon the tranquillity, the honesty, and gray-beard customs of society." In her hostility to the chimney, which is repeatedly likened to a pyramid, and her desire to penetrate its mysteries through the operations of Scribe, the master mason, she may also reflect Melville's reading of "Legend of the Arabian Astrologer" in *The Alhambra*—a work that had supplied him imagery for *Pierre.* Irving's astrologer studied in Egypt, where a priest told him of "a wondrous book of knowledge containing all the secrets of magic and art," given to Adam after the Fall and handed down to Solomon the Wise. Later it was buried in a chamber of the central pyramid with the mummy of the high priest its builder. The astrologer pierces "the solid mass of the pyramid," comes upon a hidden passage, and finally penetrates "the very heart" of the structure, where he finds the book within the mummy's wrappings; in

Pierre Melville had written: "By vast pains we mine into the pyramid; by horrible gropings we come to the central room; with joy we espy the sarcophagus; but we lift the lid—and no body is there!—appallingly vacant as vast is the soul of a man!" (bk. 21; NN285.6–9).

Both Irving and Melville knew of the Egyptian explorations of Giovanni Battista Belzoni (1778–1823); as Dorothee Metlitsky Finkelstein demonstrates in *Melville's Orienda* (New Haven: Yale University Press, 1961), pp. 141–43, Melville in this tale maintains an analogy between exploration of the chimney and Belzoni's operations in Egypt, and Scribe's measurements for a possible secret closet within the chimney "may have been inspired by Belzoni's measurements and computations to determine the entrance into the Khefren pyramid." Had the wife's project been accomplished, the narrator wryly observes, "some Belzoni or other" might eventually penetrate the masonry of the chimney and emerge "into the dining-room" (363.26–28). Jay Leyda, in *Complete Stories,* p. xxv, had cited a journal entry on Belzoni by Benjamin Robert Haydon, the painter, given in a book Melville bought in April, 1854 (Sealts 262); Finkelstein, quoting the passage at more length, holds that Melville "fully agreed" with Haydon's high estimate of Belzoni "and probably applied it to himself." See also p. 691 above.

Another book that may have influenced both "I and My Chimney" and "The Apple-Tree Table" is Hawthorne's *Mosses from an Old Manse,* which Melville had first read in 1850 (see p. 654) and perhaps again in 1855 before writing these pieces and "The Piazza." Edward H. Rosenberry, in "Melville and His *Mosses," American Transcendental Quarterly,* VII (Summer, 1970), 47–51, explores this possibility, particularly Hawthorne and Melville's emphasis on the fireside as an altar and their narrators' conservatism. During Melville's 1849 London visit, it may be added, he had been struck by the "sublime Kitchen" and *"chimney place"* at Lincoln's Inn (journal entry, December 21, 1849). And in "The Lightning-Rod Man" (1854) the narrator describes himself as "standing on my hearthstone . . . at ease in the hands of my God" (118.2–3, 124.15).

Merton M. Sealts, Jr., in "Melville's Chimney, Reexamined," in *Themes and Directions in American Literature: Essays in Honor of Leon Howard,* ed. Ray B. Browne and Donald Pizer (Lafayette, Ind.: Purdue University Studies, 1969), pp. 80–102, surveys contrasting biographical, social, and political approaches to the tale.

For explanation of the following tabulations, see pp. 565–70.

DISCUSSIONS. 358.19–20 a council of ten flues] NN emends the P reading "a council-of-ten flues" by removing the hyphens (though possibly Melville's) that create a double grammatical impasse: that is, the singular article "a" modifies the plural noun "flues", and "ten" is asked to do impossible double duty (1) within the tied prepositional phrase "-of-ten" (modifying "council") and (2) as a separate ordinal adjective (modifying "flues"). The only solution, adopted by NN, is to remove the hyphens to clarify Melville's intended meaning, "a council [consisting] of ten flues". The allusion to the Florentine Council of Ten (cf. *Mardi,* chap. 181; NN604.10) is preserved without capitalization, which would reinstate the grammatical impasse.

360.39 dote] Since the P reading "dote" assumes "me" (not "dreamer") as the antecedent of "who", its first-person form is correct; still, it sounds a bit awkward because "dreamer" exerts a strong attraction as a third-person antecedent requiring "dotes". That Melville, however, had "me who dote" in mind is confirmed by "my" at 361.1. Cf. the discussion at 14.6.

361.20 moral . . . ruffle] The intended sense is so elusive that one suspects some verbal corruption has crept in: is "moral" the intended word? (Incidentally, the construction of the whole context would be clarified by emending the comma after "come" to a dash or colon.)

362.26 (she . . . man)] As commonly in Melville's time and works, P uses parentheses here, rather than the brackets now conventional, to enclose an interrupting element within a quotation. See 25.2 and p. 564, n. 29.

363.27 might not] NN supplies "not" (as does Hershel Parker in *Shorter Works,* p. 380), which P lacks but which the sense intended by Melville requires. Possibly the word was overlooked by the copyist or compositor, but Melville himself sometimes lost track of the positive/negative force of an involved sentence such as this. See, for example, the discussion at 142.17 and *Moby-Dick,* chap. 44 (NN210.24), where in the copy-text a rhetorical question requiring a "no" answer gets "yes" instead (emended by NN).

366.15 aint] See p. 560, n. 27.

371.30 "I . . . Chimney."] NN departs from P in indenting this line to fit the pattern set by the above two lines (and by the closing of Scribe's letter at 369.27–30); the P placing of the line at the same indention as "Very" (line 28) seems determined by the lack of space needed at the end of the line for the progressive pattern, rather than by Melville's, or even the compositor's, desired pattern.

EMENDATIONS. *358.19 council∧of∧ten] NN; ~-~-~ P
360.4 Indies] NN; Indias P 360.15 truth∧] NN; ~, P
362.13 granddaughters'] NN; granddaughter's P 363.12 you] NN; ysu P
*363.27 not] NN; *[not present]* P 368.13 assault.] NN; ~, P
373.12 mantel."] NN; ~.∧ P 373.20 out-of-the-way] NN;
~-~-~∧~ P 374.39 money.] NN; ~, P

HYPHENATION. I. 352.14 first-fruits 352.17 preëminence 353.34 chimney-top 353.39 honeycombed 354.32 misconception 355.5 church-spire 356.3 woodmen 356.13 neck-wringings 357.1 aforesaid 357.12 squint-eyed 358.31 fire-places 359.38 light-house 360.14 superstructure 361.23 ginger-beer 361.36 window-sill 362.11 hard-hack 362.20 club-footed 364.1 fire-place 364.24 gentleman 367.23 death-warrant 368.11 breakfast 368.20 long-suffering 373.33 crestfallen 377.1 portfolio

II. 361.33 claw-footed 363.1 happy-go-lucky 368.11 half-reproachful 374.16 fire-places 375.10 dining-room

THE APPLE-TREE TABLE (pp. 378–97)

NN copy-text: the anonymous first printing, "The Apple-Tree Table; Or, Original Spiritual Manifestations," in *Putnam's Monthly Magazine* [P], VII, no. 41 (May, 1856), 465–75. No known manuscript, and no later printing in Melville's lifetime. NN emendations to P (on principles stated on pp. 549–64): at 11 points. NN printer's copy: an emended photocopy of Newberry Library A5.765. Machine collations between copies of P: Newberry A5.765 *vs.* Northwestern 051P99 and M67–722–207; M67–722–295 *vs.* M67–722–207 and M69–316–20.

As the HISTORICAL NOTE shows, "The Apple-Tree Table" was evidently written after both "Jimmy Rose" and "I and My Chimney"—probably in the summer or fall of 1855; it is not mentioned in Melville's known correspondence with Dix & Edwards, then publishers of *Putnam's,* or that of Joshua A. Dix with his editorial adviser, George William Curtis. In each of the three tales the household includes the narrator, his wife and two daughters, and a servant named Biddy; here the narrator individualizes the other characters most fully, his daughter Julia in particular. All three tales also concern old houses, two of them in cities—in "Jimmy Rose" obviously New York; in this tale "in an old-fashioned quarter of one of the oldest towns in America." Melville may have been thinking of his paternal grandfather's Boston house, but also as in much of his writing during the 1850's the former Pittsfield home of his uncle Thomas Melvill, Jr. An old desk of his uncle's which he dragged from a corn-loft there (see his letter of August 16, 1850, to Evert A. Duyckinck) is probably the original of the tale's "old escritoir" (380.23–24), and its recovery may have suggested that of the old table in this tale; its pigeonholes and secret drawers reappear in the second chapter of *The Confidence-Man,* which he was probably writing at about the same time as this tale.

Melville's reading of Washington Irving may have given him a hint for "The Apple-Tree Table." Ichabod Crane loves to "con over old Mather's direful tales" and leaves behind at Sleepy Hollow his copy of what Irving calls "Cotton Mather's *History of New England Witchcraft.*" Melville's narrator brings down from the garret, along with the cloven-footed table, a "mouldy old book," Cotton Mather's *Magnalia Christi Americana.* Chapter 9 of *The Confidence-Man* contains a comparable reference to "old books" found "up in garrets." Melville had used a chapter of the *Magnalia* in writing "The Lightning-Rod Man" (1854); a copy was available from the Pittsfield Library Association, and perhaps there was already a copy at his Arrowhead residence (see p. 598 above). The *Magnalia* records forms of religion and superstition in colonial New England; Melville's narrator, like Melville himself, also knows Dr. Johnson's varied opinions about ghosts (see Melville's journals, November 10, 1849, and January 3, 1857; *Moby-Dick,* chap. 69 [NN309.15–17]; and *The Confidence-Man,* chap. 17 [NN85.25]) and the philosopher Democritus (see the "Lover of Lies" by Lucian, an author mentioned in *Pierre,* bk. 26 [NN356.20]; *Israel Potter,* chap. 13 [NN82.35]; and *The Confidence-Man,* chap. 5 [NN27.6]).

The narrator alludes to familiar superstitions of Melville's own day: "the 'Fox girls' " (382.15) were two sisters in upper New York state who were associated with widely reported instances of "spirit-rappings" in 1846–50. Melville could have read about them in the *Literary World,* VI, no. 163 (March 16, 1850), 256—on the same page as his "A Thought on Book-Binding"—and in *Putnam's,* I (January, 1853), 59–64, as well as in the local *Culturist and Gazette* in March and April of 1854; a more recent *Putnam's* article (IV [August, 1854], 158–72) had observed that "Spiritualism numbers its advocates by the hundred thousand; . . . there are some thirty thousand in the immediate vicinity" of New York. It specifically attacked Spiritualist doctrines as set forth in the writings of Judge John W. Edmonds, whom Melville himself mentioned to Evert A. Duyckinck in 1856 *(Log,* II, 523). The wife in "I and My Chimney" has "an itch after . . . Swedenborgianism, and the Spirit Rapping philosophy" (362.5–7); the wife in "The Apple-Tree Table" is obviously more skeptical.

For the action of the tale, a remark by Henry David Thoreau in the last chapter of *Walden* (1854) may be pertinent: "Every one has heard the story which has gone the rounds of New England, of a strong and beautiful bug which came out of the dry leaf of an old table of apple-tree wood . . . . Who does not feel his faith in a resurrection and immortality strengthened by this?" Whether or not he was reacting to Thoreau's response, Melville had access to two other versions of the story, both in books associated, like the old desk, with his stay at the old Melvill house in 1850. One of them, Timothy Dwight's *Travels in New England and New York,* 2 vols. (New Haven, 1821), is mentioned in "Hawthorne and His Mosses" (240.29); the other Melville had acquired at Pittsfield on July 16, 1850 (Sealts 216): *A History of the County of Berkshire, Massachusetts . . . By Gentlemen in the County, Clergymen and Laymen,* edited by D. D. Field (Pittsfield, 1829). This copy of the *History,* now in The Berkshire Athenaeum, was unknown to Douglas Sackman when he printed relevant extracts from both books in "The Original of Melville's Apple-Tree Table," *American Literature,* XI (January, 1940), 448–51; in fact it contains Melville's annotations and markings of passages used both in "The Apple-Tree Table" and in *Israel Potter* and his note (among others) on the back flyleaf: "Table-Bug—Block *[sic]* bug [—] 39" (the table-and-bug story appears on pp. 39–40 of the *History).* The fact that these annotations were made between July of 1850 and June of 1854, when Melville proposed *Israel Potter* to George Palmer Putnam, suggests that the germ of the tale was in his mind well before he wrote it in 1855.

For explanation of the following tabulations, see pp. 565–70.

EMENDATIONS. 380.37 Magnalia] NN; Magnolia P 382.25 first∧] NN; ~, P 382.26 Magnalia] NN; Magnolia P 385.31 things."] NN; ~.∧ P 385.35 energy.] NN; ~; P 386.31 directly] NN; di-/rctly P 387.28 rubbing] NN; rnbbing P 391.28 spirits!"] NN; ~!' " P 391.28 Julia.] NN; ~, P 394.19 dummies,] NN; ~; P 394.20 literally;] NN; ~, P

HYPHENATION. I. 378.14 old-fashioned 379.1 over-anxious 379.3 stair-door 379.32 cobwebs 379.34 cobwebs 380.5 †withdraw 380.7 padlock 380.26 broken-down 381.13 reading-table 381.26 whereupon 382.8 †reading-table 382.16 †cedar-parlor 382.27 hard-working 384.27 punch-drinking 384.38 midnight 386.8 gun-distance 386.26 upside 387.24 tea-table 388.18 reading-table 389.18 glow-worm 389.20 glow-worm 392.34 †ice-cream 393.27 laughing-stock

II. 379.6 above-mentioned 381.19 cedar-parlor 381.32 cloven-footed 382.8 †reading-table 382.16 †cedar-parlor 389.20 spell-bound 392.34 †ice-cream

STATUES IN ROME (pp. 398–409)

During his first season as a lecturer, beginning in Lawrence, Massachusetts, on November 23, 1857, and concluding in New Bedford, Massachusetts, on February 23, 1858, Melville discussed the subject of Roman statuary in sixteen cities and towns east of the Mississippi River. He did not publish his lecture in a magazine or book, and no manuscript is known to survive, but contemporary newspapers gave fairly full accounts of the content and even of the organization and style of the lecture. At least thirty-two papers carried reports of his local appearances, ranging in length from brief notices of a single paragraph to long articles that provided detailed résumés and assessments both of Melville's performance and of his listeners' reactions. There may have been still other reviews, since files of the newspapers of some of the towns where Melville spoke are either incomplete or no longer extant. A few editors did not report lectures; others reprinted, with or without acknowledgment, what had already been said of Melville's engagements earlier in the season by other newspapers. The following table lists the sixteen localities where Melville appeared during his first lecture season, the date of each engagement, and the newspapers of each locality that are known to have reported his lecture. [He also presented this lecture in Lynn, Massachusetts, during his second lecture season, but it was not reviewed; see p. 755 below.] The newspapers are listed alphabetically by date and numbered sequentially for convenient reference.

Lawrence, Massachusetts, November 23, 1857

1A. *Courier,* November 25, 1857: an original report

1B. *American,* November 28, 1857: a reprinting of #1A

Concord, New Hampshire, November 24, 1857

No report

Boston, Massachusetts, December 2, 1857

2. *Daily Courier,* December 3, 1857

3. *Daily Evening Bee,* December 3, 1857

4. *Evening Transcript,* December 3, 1857

5. *Evening Traveller,* December 3, 1857

6. *Journal,* December 3, 1857

7. *Post,* December 3, 1857

Montreal, Quebec, December 11, 1857

8. *Daily Transcript and Commercial Advertiser,* December 16, 1857

9. *Gazette,* December 14, 1857

10. *True Witness and Catholic Chronicle,* December 25, 1857

Saratoga Springs, New York, December 21, 1857

11. *Daily Saratogian,* December 24, 1857

New Haven, Connecticut, December 30, 1857

No report

Auburn, New York, January 5, 1858

12. *Daily Advertiser,* January 6, 1858

13. *Daily American,* January 6, 1858

Ithaca, New York, January 7, 1858

14. *Journal and Advertiser,* January 13, 1858

Cleveland, Ohio, January 11, 1858

15. *Evening Herald,* January 12, 1858

16. *Morning Leader,* January 12, 1858

17. *Ohio Farmer,* January 23, 1858

18. *Plain Dealer,* January 12, 1858

Detroit, Michigan, January 12, 1858

19. *Daily Free Press,* January 14, 1858

Clarksville, Tennessee, January 22, 1858

20. *Chronicle,* January 29, 1858

21. *Jeffersonian,* January 27, 1858

Cincinnati, Ohio, February 2, 1858

22. *Daily Commercial,* February 3, 1858

23. *Daily Gazette,* February 3, 1858

24. *Enquirer,* February 3, 1858

Chillicothe, Ohio, February 3, 1858

25A. *Advertiser,* February 5, 1858: an original report

25B. *Advertiser,* February 5, 1858: a reprinting of #22

26. *Scioto Gazette,* February 9, 1858

Charlestown, Massachusetts, February 10, 1858

27. *Advertiser,* February 10, 1858

28. *Bunker-Hill Aurora and Boston Mirror,* February 13, 1858

Rochester, New York, February 18, 1858

29. *Democrat and American,* February 20, 1858

New Bedford, Massachusetts, February 23, 1858

30. *Daily Evening Standard,* February 24, 1858

31. *Daily Mercury,* February 24, 1858

Photocopies and transcriptions of the individual articles, arranged and numbered as above, have been deposited in the Melville Collections of The Houghton Library of Harvard University and The Newberry Library; in the absence of a manuscript or printed text for the lecture they constitute the basis for the composite text printed in this volume.

Some ten variants occur in newspaper references to the title of Melville's first lecture, the following being most frequent: "Statues [*or* The Statues] in [*or* of] Rome", "Statuary [*or* The Statuary] in [*or* of] Rome [*or* Italy]", and "Roman Statuary"; there is disagreement not only among newspapers within the same city but even between the advance notices and the later review appearing in the same publication. Since all of the variants derive ultimately from Melville's own wording, either in his correspondence with local lecture committees or in his delivery of the lecture itself, the inference is that he was not consistent in his usage. His latest known reference to the lecture is in a letter of February 12, 1859, written to W. H. Barry of Lynn, Massachusetts, during Melville's second season on the platform, in which he listed the titles of his "two lectures" as "The South Seas," his staple offering of 1858–59, and "Statues in Rome." This volume employs these same titles.

The most detailed résumé of the content of "Statues in Rome" is that appearing in the Detroit *Daily Free Press*—#19 in the list above. Essential agreement in organization and even in phrasing between this report and the reviews carried by other newspapers indicates that Melville made few if any changes in his manuscript during his first lecture season. In an effort to recover as much as possible of the material of that manuscript, the author of *Melville as Lecturer* (Cambridge: Harvard University Press, 1957) prepared a composite text of "Statues in Rome," based primarily on the *Free Press* report but drawing also on other contemporary accounts to replace or supplement its wording wherever in his judgment "these other acounts offer a fuller or more accurate approximation of Melville's own language." The quotation is from the headnote to the reconstructed text (pp. 127–28), which explains that editorial decisions were "determined by collation of the several newspaper versions and by detailed comparison of their phrasing with that of similar passages of Melville's Mediterranean journal or in his published works." Notes and commentary accompanying the text of 1957 record many of these correspondences. The 1957 text itself retains the phraseology of the several newspaper reports except for minor emendations, as in the voice and tense of verbs, and for standardization and modernization of spelling and punctuation.

The present volume reprints on pp. 398–409, as a reading text, a revision of the composite reconstruction of 1957, which is used here with the authorization of Harvard University Press. This composite reading text does not constitute a critical reconstruction of Melville's manuscript; it simply represents the fullest wording, in those phrases which in the editor's judgment appear to be most characteristic of Melville himself, that can be put together from the surviving reports. The following changes have been made in the 1957 text to reflect the subsequent discovery of three newspaper reviews of Melville's appearance in Montreal (#8, #9, #10) and a new collation of the composite reconstruction with all of the newspaper reports. After the Northwestern-Newberry page and line number comes the NN reading, followed by the 1957 reading.

398.9 employ] enjoy 399.15–16 The topic . . . world.] *[not present]* 399.28 greeting] greetings 400.25–26 As . . . disposition.] *[not present]* 400.30 Socrates . . . for] Socrates 400.38–39 commanding, . . . statesman.] commanding. 401.9–10 just, . . . *books*. For] just, for 401.24 certainly should] should certainly 401.28 If . . . he] He 401.34 has been] was 401.36 appearance of the] *[not present]* 402.27–28 in . . . Vatican.] in the Belvedere chapel. 402.37 imaginations] imagination 403.1–2 The statue . . . beauty."] *[not present]* 403.6 circumstance] circumstances 403.15–16 block, . . . height,] block 404.25 girdling] girding 405.9–16 The sculptured . . . rejoices.] The statues there are of various characters: Hope faces Despair; Joy comes to the relief of Sorrow; Rachel weeps for her children and will not be comforted; Job rises above his afflictions and rejoices. The marbles alternate; some are of a joyous nature, followed by those that are of a sad and somber character. The sculptured monuments of the early Christians in these vaults show the joyous triumph of the new religion—quite unlike the somber mementoes of modern times. 405.21–23 colonnades . . . pile] colonnade with its statues, from whence we see the balloon-like dome of St. Peter's and the great pile 405.26–27 this, . . . dome.] this is the dome. 406.1 reining in their horses] *[not present]* 406.3 to] *[not present]* 406.4 elder] older 406.5 those] the 406.6–9 A modern . . . conquered.] *[not present]* 406.10 loved] longed 406.15–17 In truth, . . . horses.] *[not present]* 406.18 on] of 406.18–19 Parthenon, . . . Museum.] Parthenon. 406.27 leaning on his club,] *[not present]* 406.27 bovine] *[not present]* 406.28–29 things . . . him.] things. 406.31 lazy] large 407.13 with] *[not present]* 407.26 temperate] temporary 407.29–31 found . . . Æsop] found a bust of Aesop, 407.32–33 irony . . . Goldsmith.] irony like that we see in Goldsmith's. 408.4 in pure marble] *[not present]* 408.5 being] beings 408.36 sustains] supports

The notes which follow record the variant readings among the individual newspaper reports on which successive paragraphs of the composite text are based. The reports are quoted exactly as originally printed except for the silent correction of broken or reversed type and of errors in spacing between words; other editorial corrections and explanations have been made within square brackets—for example, when a single letter has been supplied or altered, as in "a[n]d" for "aad"—and editorial omissions have been indicated by spaced periods (. . .). Each variant is identified by the number assigned in the list above to the newspaper report from which it is extracted. Also included in the notes, immediately following extracts from the Boston newspapers, are relevant passages from a letter of December 9, 1857, in which Melville's cousin Henry Sanford Gansevoort, writing to his father, Peter Gansevoort, summarized "Statues in Rome" as he had heard it in Boston a week earlier; the letter, identified here by the abbreviation "HSG", is in the Gansevoort-Lansing Collection, Rare Books and Manuscripts Division, The New York Public Library. As collation reveals, Gansevoort refreshed his memory by referring to newspaper reports in the Boston *Daily Courier* and *Evening Traveller* (#2 and #5), borrowing phrases for his own synopsis. The Boston *Daily Evening Bee* (#3) and the Cincinnati *Daily Commercial* (#22) also reprinted, without acknowledgment, some or all of the *Courier*'s account of the lecture, and the Chillicothe *Advertiser* (#25B) in turn reproduced, with due credit, the full report given in the Cincinnati paper. At the close of the season the New Bedford *Daily Evening Standard* (#30) drew for its review on the earlier notice in the Boston *Evening Traveller* (#5).

PARAGRAPHS 1–3. 398.3–399.22 It might be . . . the human breast.]

5: After a brief introduction, he proceeded directly to his subject.

6: He began by suggesting that in the realm of art there was no exclusiveness. Dilletanti might accumulate their technical terms, but that did not interfere with the substantial enjoyment of those who did not understand them. As the beauties of nature could be appreciated without a knowledge of botany, so art could be enjoyed without the artist's skill. With this principle in view, he, claiming to be neither critic nor artist, would make some plain remarks on the statuary of Rome.

7: The lecturer commenced with remarking on the understanding of objects of nature and art by different classes, and said that thoughts and emotions were inspired in ordinary as well as in the minds of the most accomplished by nature's works; and in art as in nature it was not the accredited wise man who was always competent to pronounce an opinion.

HSG: He [*i.e.* His] object was to paint to his audience the appearance of Roman Statuary objectively and afterward to speculate upon the emotions and pleasure that appearance is apt to excite in the human breast. . . . He said that it was a mooted question as to whether objects of art sway with greater power the minds of the educated or uneducated, that a certain something was implanted by heaven in the breast of man which is naturally alive to the beautiful—

8: Mr. Melville began his lecture by stating that his subject was one of great extent, as Rome contained more objects of interest than perhaps any other place in the world.

9: Mr. Melville commenced by some observations upon the different emotions inspired in different classes of minds, by the works of nature and art.

12: The lecturer commenced by observing that it was not necessary to possess a nice and discriminating technical knowledge of the qualities of the flower to be enamoured of its beauties and appreciate the fragrance of its perfume.—Burns, in his Daisey, showed that the "nursling of the sky" had as much beauty for him as it had for the German Professor, who could minutely dissect its every part. And so, said the lecturer, do I, who am neither artist or critic, come before you to give my own views upon the Statues in a non-professional manner.

14: His subject, "Ancient Statuary," must, from the necessity of the case, be an unattractive one to the masses, who claim, with the lecturer himself, not to be students of art and connoisseurs of beauty in its difficult departments.

16: In opening his lecture, Mr. Melville took occasion to allude to the fact he that [*i.e.* that he] should speak of the impressions produced upon his mind by the Roman marbles, not as a professional critic or connoisseur, but as one who looks upon a work of Art as he would upon a violet or a cloud, and admires or condemns, as he finds an answering sentiment awakened in his soul. It might be, he thought, a question whether the professed critics and connoisseurs were after all, most deeply impressed with the beautiful in Art or Nature. The knowledge attained by the latter class of a beautiful object was akin to that of Linnæus, the scientific botanist; and yet it was Burns, the unscientific and uncultivated poet, whose soul had felt and immortalized the daisy.

19: Mr. Melville said that among the higher emotions is a feeling for art, and this exists wherever there is beauty or grandeur. This feeling appeals to all men. Art strikes a chord in the lowest as well as in the highest; the rude and uncultivated feel its influence as well as the polite and polished. It is a spirit that pervades all classes; but the uncultivated never express the emotions which they feel, from the fear that they may use terms that shall be unscientific and unprofessional. There are many examples on record to show this, and not only this, but that the uneducated are very often more susceptible to this influence than the learned. There can be no doubt that Burns saw more poetry in a single daisy than Linnæus in all the flora of which he treated. The speaker remarked that this must be his excuse; he pretended to be no critic or connoisseur in thus attempting to speak of the statuary at Rome, and he would relate merely his own impressions in reference to it.

22: If what is best in nature and knowledge cannot be claimed for the privileged profession of any order of men, it would be a wonder if, in that region called

Art, there were, as to what is best there, any essential exclusiveness. True, the dilletanti may employ his technical terms; but ignorance of these prevents not due feeling for Art, in any mind naturally alive to beauty or grandeur, just as the productions of nature may be both appreciated by those who know nothing of Botany, or who have no inclination for it, so the creations of Art may be, by those ignorant of its critical science, or, indifferent to it. Nay, as it is doubtful whether to the Scientific Linnaeus flowers yielded so much satisfaction as to the unscientific Burns, or struck so deep a chord in his bosom; so may it be a question whether the terms of Art may not inspire in unartistic but still susceptible minds, thoughts, or emotions, not lower than those raised in the most accomplished of critics. Yet, we find that many thus naturally susceptible to such impressions, refrain from their utterance, out of fear, lest in their ignorance of technicalities their unaffected terms might betray them, and that after all, feel as they may, they know little or nothing, and hence keep silence, not wishing to become presumptuous. * * * * May it not possibly be, that as Burns perhaps understood flowers as well as Linnaeus, and the Scotch peasant's poetical description of the daisy, "wee, modest, crimson tipped flower," is rightly set above the technical definition of the Swedish professor, so in Art, just as in nature, it may not be the accredited wise man alone, who, in all respects, is qualified to comprehend or describe. ¶ With this explanation, I, who am neither critic nor connoisseur, thought fit to introduce some familiar remarks upon the Sculptures in Rome, a subject which otherwise might be thought to lie peculiarly within the province of persons, of a kind of cultivation, to which I make no pretension.

23: He commenced with a very finely expressed introduction, and then branched into the subject of his lecture—"The Statues of Rome."

24: Mr. M. remarked, at the outset, that it might be supposed the only proper judge of statues would be a sculptor; but he believed others than the artist could appreciate and see the beauty of the marble art of Rome. All men admired and were drawn to flowers, though utterly destitute of a knowledge of botany. Burns' description of the daisy was far superior to that of Linnæus; the world had given its verdict in favor of the poet.

25B: [*reprints 22 with these variations:* . . . —True, . . . ignora[n]t . . . utterence . . . u[n]affected . . . professor in Art, . . .]

27: He commenced by saying that most persons were constituted by Nature to appreciate the beautiful—that the uneducated could, perhaps, take as much delight in art as the cultivated—the difference was, they were unacquainted with the technical terms, by means of which, the connoisseur in art makes others a sharer in his own delight—hence, all might enjoy a little talk about art.

28: . . . a monotonous description . . . by one neither a 'Professor' nor 'Artiste' by his own confession . . .

30: The lecturer remarked at the outset that it was not necessary to be acquainted with the technicalities of art, nor to be an exact critic in order to appreciate its productions, but we could feel their beauties, as we did those of nature, without being acquainted with the classifications of scientific men.

PARAGRAPH 4. 399.23–32 As you pass . . . are forgotten.]

2: Passing through the gate of St. John, on the approach to Rome by Naples, the first object of attraction is the group of colossal figures in stone, surmounting, like storks, the lofty pediment of St. John Lateran. Standing in every grand or animated attitude, they seem not only to attest that this [is] the Eternal City, but likewise, at its portal, to offer greeting in the name of that great company of statues which, amid the fluctuations of the human census, abides the true and undying population of Rome. It is, indeed, among these mute citizens, and mostly in the Vatican Museum, that the stranger forms his most pleasing and cherished associations.

3: He began by a description of the gate of St. John and its colossal figures.

5: The statues in Rome, he believed, were peculiarly attractive to strangers, and the denizens of the city with whom they became best acquainted. They were scattered everywhere, . . .

6: As you approach that city from Naples, you are first struck by the statues of the Church St. John Lateran. Here you have the sculptured biographies of ancient celebrities.

7: He then went on to describe the journey of the traveller from Naples to Rome and the objects that meet his eye. It was among the statues that the stranger made his first acquaintance, and wherever he went those mute citizens did the silent honors of the eternal city.

HSG: After alluding to the statues of the country he spoke of the gigantic figures which surmounted like storks the pediment of St. John Lantern as a meet company to welcome one to the eternal city— These with their thousand companions in other places in the city abide & mock the human census, the true and abiding population of Rome[.]

8: The approach to Rome from Naples was by the gate of St. John, and passing through this, what first struck the attention of the traveller was the group of collosal images of stone surmounting the church of St. John Lateren.

9: He described the entrance to Rome by the Naples road, and the effect produced upon the mind of the traveller, by the objects that first meet the eye.

12: The lecturer then proceeded to describe various statues and busts in Rome, and how their beauty and force struck him.

14: Mr. Melville gave a very highly finished as well as critical description of the statues at Rome, Florence, etc.

15: He mentioned some of the principal statues of Rome, . . .

19: As you enter Rome, upon its very threshold you meet with statuary. Here are the mute citizens who will be remembered when other things in the Imperial City are forgotten.

22: The approach to Rome from Naples is by the gate of St. John, passing through which the first object *[thereafter reprints 2]* . . . cherished associations. [*There are two variations:* . . . this is the . . . likewise at . . .]

23: —He described the approach to that city from Naples through the gate of St. John, as guarded by a group of colossal figures, in stone, which attest at the entrance that it is the "Eternal City," and at the same time, greet and welcome the traveler.

25A: He began with the collosal statues before the gate of St. John on the Naples road.

25B: [*reprints 22 with these variations:* . . . group af [*i.e.* of] . . . Museu[m] . . .]

27: The speaker led his audience into the Imperial city of Rome, . . .

30: The statues were the first and best acquaintances we made in Rome.

PARAGRAPH 5. 399.33–400.14 On entering Rome . . . of the historian.]

2: In that grand hall [the Vatican Museum] he will not only make new acquaintances, but will likewise revive many long before introduced to him by the historian. And he will find many deficiencies of the historian supplied by the sculptor, who has effected, in part, for the celebrities of old what the memoir-writer of the present day does for modern ones. In viewing the statues and busts of Demosthenes, Titus, Socrates, Cæsar, Seneca, Nero, and others, we feel a sense of reality not to be given by history; . . .

3: From this he proceeded to describe the most celebrated statuary in the Eternal City. In viewing, said he, the statues *[thereafter reprints 2]* . . . given by history; . . .

5: . . . and they [the statues] gave to the present a better idea of the reality of the men of elder days.

7: The statues of those long since passed from the scene of life imparted impressions not to be produced by history, and to the sculptor belonged the task which was considered beneath the dignity of the historian.

HSG: In the Vatican Museum one meets old acquaintences which the historian has introduced to him in times past.

8: It was chiefly in the museum of the Vatican, however, that the most famous statues of Rome were placed, and these stone representations of the great of past ages impressed the mind with an idea of the illustrious ancients they held up to view more than the most eloquent passages of the historians who narrated their deeds.

9: His first acquaintance was with statues, and among those mute citizens, rather than among the living ones, would he dwell during his stay in Rome. They did to him the honors of the Eternal City. Impressions not to be produced by the page of the historian, were imparted by the work of the sculpter. To those shadowy imaginings of historical personages, which alone are obtained from the pages of history, the sculptor gives life and reality. The lecturer went on to review the statues and busts of some of the most eminent personages of antiquity. Those of Demosthenes, Socrates, Julius Cæsar, Seneca, Nero and Plato, were spoken of at some length.

12: He gave a very brilliant and masterly description of the Vatican; . . .

17: . . . witnessing this skillful and appreciative master of ceremonies taking the robes from the pictured pages of Tacitus and putting them upon the lifeless marbles of the Vatican, and there breathing into them the breath of life, till Rome became living Rome again; . . .

19: Wherever you go in Rome, in its gardens, its walks, its public squares or its private grounds, statues are seen. They abound on every side, but by far the greatest assemblage of them is to be found in the Vatican. These are all well known by repute; they have been often described in the traveler's record and on the historic page; but the knowledge thus gained, however perfect the description may be, is poor and meagre when compared with that gained by personal acquaintance. Here are ancient personages, the worthies of the glorious old days of the Empire and Republic. Histories and memoirs tell us of their achievements, whether on the field or in the forum, in public action or in the private walks of life; but here we find how they looked, and we learn them as we do living men.

22: [*reprints 2 with these variations:* . . . introduced by . . . effected in . . . memoir writer . . . statues and basis [*i.e.* busts] . . . givea [*i.e.* given] by history; . . .]

23: As the observer progressed within its walls, he would meet every where, in street, squares, dwellings, churches, on every hand, statues which would form his chief acquaintances—that bid the observer a silent welcome, and yet imparted a sense of reality that could [not] be realized by a perusal of history alone.

24: On entering Rome, the visitor was greeted by thousands of statues, who, as representatives o[f] the mighty past, held out their hands to the present, and made the connecting link of centuries. The lecturer would not linger among the numerous statues of the Seven-hilled City, but hasten to the Vatican.

25B: [*reprints 22 with these variations:* . . . make acquaintances . . . Demonsthenes, . . . given . . .]

27: . . . into the Vatican, amidst the statues of the "great of old," representing the audience gazing at the real marble, and, by portraying the appearance of each statue, gave a very succinct idea of the character of each as it was when they figured among the haunts of men.

28: . . . a monotonous description of such 'dead heads' as Demosthenes, Julius Caesar, Seneca, Plato, Tiberius and Apollo, . . .

30: They were scattered all over the city. But the greatest collection was in the Vatican. ¶ The first works commented on were the busts of the Roman emperors and ancient philosophers. Among these were mentioned those of Tiberius, Titus, Socrates, Julius Cæsar, Seneca and Nero.

31: He took the statues of the Vatican, more especially, beginning with some of the portraits in the collection, and speaking especially of those of Demosthenes, Socrates, Seneca, Nero, Titus, Tiberius, Julius Cæsar and other celebrated ancients, . . .

PARAGRAPH 6. 400.15–29 In the expressive . . . outward seeming.]

5: In the expressive marble, Demosthenes became a present existence; so in the statue of Titus, of whom we read a dim outline in Tacitus, stood mildly before us Titus himself, with his lineaments and strength of form.

6: The speaker then vividly described the statues of Demosthenes, Titus Vespasian, . . .

7: The statue of Demosthenes was the first one the lecturer reviewed, and in speaking of this he said that standing face to face with the marble one must say to himself "this is he," so true had been the sculptor to his task.

8: The statue of Titus, the son of Vespasian was indeed a remarkable one, and gazing at its outlines one would coincide with what the historian says, that this Emperor was frank in his nature, and generous in his disposition.

19: Demosthenes is better known by statuary than by history. The strong arm, the muscular form, the large sinews, all bespeak the thunderer of Athens who hurled his powerful denunciations at Philip of Macedon. Just so it is with the chiseled Titus; his short neck, broad shoulders and thick-set person make him known and appreciated.

23: These statues, the speaker remarked, convey to the looker-on an impression of the original, and impressed upon the mind a reality which could not be effaced. The statue of Demosthenes of Titus, that flits across the page of Tacitus, embodied in the marble the idea of the living man, . . .

24: There was Demosthenes, who resembled a modern advocate, face thin and haggard, and his body lean. The arm that had gesticulated and swayed with its movement the souls of the Athenians, was small and shrunken. He looked as if a glorious course of idleness would be beneficial. Titus had a short, thick figure, and a round face, expressive of cheerfulness, good-humor and jovial[i]ty; and yet all knew how different was his character from this outward seeming.

25A: . . . many [listeners], learned, perhaps for the first time, that Demosthenes was emaciated by the intense activity of the mind which bequeathed to us . . . those immortal orations which are and have always been the models of the loftiest eloquence, . . .

30: [*reprints 5 in part:* In the statue of Titus . . . strength of form.]

PARAGRAPH 7. 400.30–36 In the bust of Socrates . . . true character.]

5: In Socrates' face we saw a countenance like a comic masque.

6: . . . Socrates, looking like an Irish comedian, . . .

7: The busts of Socrates, of Julius Cæsar, Seneca, Nero, and Plato were spoken of at much length, and the characters of those ancient celebrities fully discussed.

HSG: Socrates [presents the appearance] of a comic masque.

8: The bust of Socrates was a kind of anomaly, for instead of the calm, decorous face of the philosopher, the observer beheld a countenance which seemed to wear a carnival mask.

9: The face of Socrates had none of the gravity we imagined in a philosopher. It was full of mirth.

19: In the bust of Socrates we see a countenance more like that of a bacchanal or the debauchee of a carnival than of a sober and decorous philosopher. It reminds one much of the broad and rubicund phiz of an Irish comedian. It possesses in many respects the characteristics peculiar to the modern Hibernian.

23: . . . while the bust of Socrates, at a first glance, scarce gave one an idea of his character. At a first glance it reminded one of the head of an Irish comedian, but a closer observer would see the simple-hearted, yet cool, sarcastic, ironical cast, indicative of his true character.

24: Socrates reminded one of an Irish comedian.

30: *[reprints 5]*

PARAGRAPH 8. 400.37–401.4 The head of Julius Caesar . . . a giant.]

5: In Julius Cæsar's statue we beheld a practical, business-like expression.

6: . . . Julius Caesar, so sensible and business-like of aspect that it might be taken for the bust of a railroad president, . . .

HSG: Caesar [presents the appearance] of a practical business man—

8: The bust of Cæsar might be supposed to be typical of the warrior and statesman; but, on the contrary, it had a very business like air, which seemed to imply that Cæsar would have made some such man as the President of the Erie Railway.

9: Julius Cæsar looked as if he might be president of a New York railroad.

19: The head of Julius Cesar fancy would paint as robust, grand and noble; something that is elevated and commanding. But the statue gives a countenance of a business like cast that would well befit the president of the Erie Railroad.

23: Julius Cæsar looked like a man that the present practical age would regard as a good representation of the President of the New York and Erie Railroad, or any other magnificent corporation. And such was the character of the man—practical, sound, grappling with the obstacles of the world like a giant. And yet the appearance of these statues of the mighty dead, whom history made great in their day, disappointed the observer. We all looked for something wonderful—something beyond present experience, and were disappointed.

24: Julius Cæsar's bust indicated a practical, business-like turn of mind, and gave one the idea that he would make an excellent financier or President of the New York and Erie Railroad.

30: [*reprints 5 with one variation:* . . . business like . . .]

PARAGRAPH 9. 401.5–13 In the bust of Seneca . . . Wall Street broker.]

5: In that of Seneca, whose utterances so amazed one of the early fathers that he thought he must have corresponded with St. Paul, we saw a face more like that of a disappointed pawnbroker, pinched and grieved.

6: . . . Seneca, with the visage of a pawnbroker, . . .

HSG: Seneca presents the appearance of a disappointed pawnbroker.

8: The bust of Seneca was unlike that of an enthusiastic philosopher, and seemed to partake of the air of a man anxious for the interest on his money, or the appearance of a distracted pawnbroker.

9: Seneca pale, care-worn, miserly, an expression according to the character of the *man,* though not of his *books.*

19: Just such a one has Seneca, whose philosophy would be christianity itself save its authenticity. It is iron-like and inflexible, and would be no disgrace to a Wall street broker.

23: The same remark was true of Seneca . . .

24: Seneca wore a pinched and weazened appearance; would have made a good pawnbroker, and his semblance was just; but it was well known that he was avaricious and grasping, and dealt largely in mortgages and loans, and drove hard bargains even at that day.

25A: . . . and that Seneca was the prototype of the hungry, cunning and heartless Jew, who advances money upon the pledge of useless jewels, or gripes the threadbare cloak of the widow in exchange for the food which keeps the wolf starvation from her orphan children.

30: [*reprints 5 with one variation:* . . . face like . . .]

PARAGRAPH 10. 401.14–21 Seeing . . . excessive cruelties.]

5: In Nero's statue, at Naples, we saw only a fast and pleasant young man, such as those we saw in our day.

6: . . . Nero, the fast young man, . . .

7: To look at the statue of Nero one might fancy him to be a genteelly dissipated youth—a fast young man; . . .

HSG: Nero a fast young man[.]

8: In the bust of Nero was the face of a dissipated youth—a fast young man.

9: Nero looked like a fast young man of the present day, a genteelly dissipated youth.

19: That of Seneca's pupil, Nero, at Naples, done in bronze, resembles that of one of our fast young men who drive spanking teams and abound on race-courses.

23: . . . and his apostate pupil, Nero, and we could scarce realize that we looked upon the face of the latter without finding something repulsive, half-demoniac in the expression. And yet, the features were those of a fast young man of the present day, whom daily experience finds upon the race course—with instincts and habits of his class, who would scarce be guilty of excessive cruelties.
24: Nero was delicate in feature, and resembled a dissipated and fast young man—such as one meets on race-courses.
25A: . . . that Nero was the pale and sickly debauchee, livid with the wearing vigil of his own wicked spirit, . . .
30: *[reprints 5]*

PARAGRAPH 11. 401.22–31 The first . . . Cologne bottle.]
5: In Plato, that aristocratic transcendentalist, we beheld a smoothness and neatness in the hair, and a beard such as would have graeed [*i.e.* graced] a Venitian exquisite.
6: . . . Plato, with the locks and air of an exquisite.
7: . . . and Plato, with his long locks parted like those of a lady, supposed meditating on the destinies of the world while under the hands of his hair dresser.
HSG: Plato the aristocratic transendentalist [presents the appearance] of a Venetian exquisite.
8: The reputed bust of Plato represented him as possessing locks, as scrupulously parted as a lady's, and with a beard like that of a Venetian exquisite. If this bust were true, it would seem that this enthusiastic transcendentalist mused over his contemplations while under the hands of his hair-dresser—something like a modern personage of note, Louis the XIV.,—who perused his state documents while they lay on the stand which contained his Eau de Cologne.
9: Plato had his locks parted like a lady's, and his whole appearance betokened scrupulous care of his personal appearance. The lecturer was disposed to be satirical upon this. We thought of Kingsley's "Frank Leigh," and "that delicate instinct of self-respect, which would keep some men spruce and spotless from one year's end to another, upon a desert island."
19: The first view of Plato surprises one. Engaged in the deep researches of philosophy as he was, we certainly should expect no fastidiousness in his appearance, neither a carefully adjusted toga or pomatumed hair. Yet such is the fact, and this great transcendentalist has the sleek and smooth appearance of a modern Brummel.
23: To look at the statue of Plato, one would not think that *he* would pomade his hair and beard, and discuss grave subjects while making his toilet. But his long flowing locks, nicely dressed, looked as though, like Louis IV., he could muse over documents while he smelled his Cologne bottle.
24: Plato was a Greek Grammont or Chesterfield: his hair was oiled and

pomatumed, and carefully parted as a modern belle's. He might have composed his works under the hand of the barber, or a modern *valet-de-chambre.*
30: [*reprints 5 with these variations:* . . . hair and beard . . . graced a Venetian . . .]

PARAGRAPH 12. 401.32–402.10 Thus these statues . . . in humility.]
2: . . . and although we are at first startled by some of them from our preconceived opinions, yet we seldom, on reflection, fail to concede the general likeness to that which the historian has furnished us. The analysis of the marble coincides with the historian's analysis of the man.
3: [*reprints 2*]
5: Yet in all these we saw but the men of to-day, so that we might believe that if a hundred men of that age should be transplanted to this, we would perceive that humanity was the same to-day as ever,—in what went to make up the basis of human character.
6: Thus these statues confessed, and, as it were, prattled to us of much that does not appear in history and the written works of those they represent. They seem familiar and natural to us—and yet there is about them all a heroic tone peculiar to the ancient life. It is to be hoped that this is not wholly lost from the world, although the sense of earthly vanity inculcated by Christianity may have swallowed it up in humility.
HSG: The statues at first startle our preconceived opinions. . . . On closer examination however we perceive our former ideas to be correct. The analysis of the marble corresponds with that of the man—The component parts of character, are the same now as then.
15: . . . and showed that the marble image in most cases vividly represented the character and sentiments attributed by history to the original.
17: He speaks of the heathenism of Rome as if the world were little indebted to christianity; indeed, as if it had introduced in the place of the old Roman heroism, a sort of trusting pusillanimity.
19: This subject was illustrated by instances taken from modern times with which we are all acquainted because in this way we best obtain a true knowledge of the appearance of the statue. The aspect of the human countenance is the same in all ages. If five thousand ancient Romans were mingled with a crowd of moderns, it would be difficult to distinguish the one from the other unless it were by a difference in dress. The same features—the same aspects—belong to us as belonged to them. Their virtues were great and noble, and these virtues made them great and noble. They possessed a natural majesty that was not put on and taken off at pleasure, as was that of certain eastern monarchs when they put on or took off their garments of Tyrian dye.
20: Unbiassed by the prepossessions of fancy, he traced in the marble features

of those great warriors, philosophers, statesmen, and poets, whose names are now almost deified, the same lineaments of passion, and frailty, that blend in the noblest faces of our own day; and though thus stripping them of their divinity, made them dearer to us as men.

22: *[reprints 2]*

24: The lecturer stated that five thousand Romans, habited in the costume of the present day, would not, if placed in the Corso, be recognized from our own countrymen.

25B: *[reprints 22]*

30: In the lineaments of each of these we could perceive, although we might be disappointed at first, those traits which mark the characters of these men as handed down to us by history. . . . And we could not help being convinced that human nature and character was the same in those remote periods that it is today.

31: . . . whose faces as depicted in their busts not infrequently conveyed a very different impression from that we gain from their historic presentation.

PARAGRAPH 13. 402.11–25 Christianity has disenchanted . . . wicked of men.]

1A: "That Tiberius?" exclaimed a lady in our hearing, "He does not look so bad." Madam, thought I, if he had *looked* bad, he could [not] have been Tiberius." This is an illustration in point.

1B: "*That* Tiberius?" exclaimed a lady in our hearing, "He does not look so bad.["] Madame, thought I, if he had *looked* bad, he could not have been Tiberius. This is an illustration in point.

5: We might learn that then, as now, appearances were deceptive. "That Tiberias," said a lady, "it does not look bad." If he did, he would not be Tiberias. That arch dissembler wore a sad, intellectual look, in which only deep attention perceived the sinister lines. It was beautiful in its features. But all these things told us how true was the statue to the description of the man and his character.

7: Nothing so deceptive as appearance. Of Tiberius it had been remarked, he does not look so bad; for he seemed, like Jerome in his cell, musing on the vanities of the world, and if it were not known for whom the statue was meant, it might be taken for that of a man subdued by afflictions.

HSG: Although the arch dissembler Tiberius wears a sad intellectual countenance still deep attention recalls its sinister lines.

8: The statue of Tiberius gave no idea of the man, as they found him in the historian. The lecturer once heard a lady exclaim, while gazing at it, "This don't look so bad," to which he made reply, "Had it been bad it would not be Tiberius."

9: Tiberius seemed like Jerome in his cell, engrossed in melancholy musing on the vanities of the world, and at the first glance, one would say with a lady whom the lecturer heard, "that Tiberius! he does not look so bad after all." But examine the face more closely and the bad lines came out one by one, and the truth of the artist's portraiture is acknowledged.

19: —Christianity has disenchanted many of the vague old rumors in reference to the ancients. We can now easily compare them with the moderns. The appearance of the statues, however, is often deceptive, and a true knowledge of their character is lost unless they are closely scrutinized. A lady remarked in the lecturer's presence that the statue of Tiberius did not look so bad as he was represented; it has more of a sad and musing air. To some it would convey the impression of a man broken by great afflictions, of so pathetic a cast is it. Yet a close analysis brings out all his sinister features, and a close study of the statue will develop the monster portrayed by the historian.

24: Tiberius was handsome, was refined, and even pensive in expression. A lady had remarked in the lecturer's hearing: "Why, he does not look so bad." Had he looked badly, he would not have been Tiberius. He was melancholy without pity, and sensitive without affection. He was, perhaps, the most wicked of men.

28: Excepting for his conversation with the lady about the head of Tiberius, one would hardly have guessed that he had ever been in Italy at all.

30: In Tiberius we read profound dissimulation mingled with a melancholy and intellectual expression.

PARAGRAPHS 14–16. 402.26–403.32 The statue which most . . . daughters of men.]

2: The statue which most of all in the Vatican excites the admiration of all visitors, is the Apollo. Few speak, or even whisper, when they enter the cabinet where it stands. If one were to try to convey some adequate notion, other than artistic, of a statue which so signally lifts the imaginations of men, he might hint that it gives a kind of visible response to that class of human aspirations which, according to Faith, cannot be truly gratified, except in another world. It is infinitely grander than the Venus di Medici, in Florence, for while she is lovely, he is divine.

3: *[reprints 2]*

5: The Apollo, often drew the last glance of departing strangers, when bidding farewell to Rome, bearing as it did the appearance almost of divinity. It was a model for poets, and even Milton must have gleaned from these representations of the great men or the gods of ancient Rome high ideas of the grand in form and bearing. The Venus, in Florence, was beautiful, but it seemed, should a match be made between them, as if the divine was wedding one of the fair dauhgters of Eve. In the Venus the ideal and actual were blended, yet only representing nature in her perfection, a fair woman startled by some intrusion when leaving the bath.

6: The lecturer next turned to the celebrated Apollo Belvidere. This stands alone by itself, and the impression made upon all beholders is such as to subdue the feelings with wonder and awe. The speaker gave a very eloquent description of the attitude and spirit of the Apollo. The elevating effect of such statues was exhibited in the influence they exerted upon the mind of Milton during his visit to Italy. ¶ Among the most wonderful works of statuary is that of Lucifer and his associates cast down from heaven. This is at Padua, and contains threescore figures cut out of a solid block. The variety and power of the group cannot be surpassed. The Venus de Medici, as compared with the Apollo, was lovely and not divine. Perfect naturalness was its characteristic. Mr. Melville said he once surprised a native maiden in the precise attitude of the Venus.

7: Milton must have been inspired to a great degree by his recollections of the statue of Apollo, once the idol of religion, and now the idol of art; and the circumstance of his having passed a year in Italy might not be deemed unfortunate for England's great epic. The group of Lucifer and his fallen angels, the Venus, . . . were beautiful[l]y described, . . .

HSG: The Apollo, the masterpiece of the place [the Vatican] seems to respond to those aspirations of beauty and perfection that we only can hope to fully enjoy in another world. It seems to breathe divinity. It awes to silence. The Venus de Medici is lovely but the Apollo is divine. The Venus seemed to blend the actual & ideal[.] He had authority for the assertion as one day from his mat in the Typee valley he saw a maiden suprised in the bath retreating with the grace of nature to a friendly covert.

8: But the statue of Apollo, once the idol of religion, now the idol of art, stood alone in a little chapel, in the Belvidere court of the Vatican, and people came here as if to pray. A statue like this, so full of beauty, so grand in its outlines and truthful in its developements, was not to be found anywhere. It seemed to embody the attributes, physical and intellectual, which Milton bestowed on one of his angels,—

"So spake the cherub, and his grave rebuke
Severe in youthful beauty."

It seemed highly probable that Milton had seen this famous statue, for he had been two years in Italy, and as many months in Rome; his great poem, however, was a Vatican done into verse. There was another statue or series of statues combined in one, well worthy of attention—a piece of sculpture representing Lucifer and his company cast down from heaven, cut out of a block of marble, five feet in height; here were cut the figures of three score of angels, and Lucifer the noblest, with Michael standing above the whole—this constituted the wonderful specimen of sculpture of which he had told the audience. There was a famous female statue, the Venus di Medici, which was in Florence however, and ought to be classed with the Apollo, though far inferior to him in sculpture, beauty, or expression of countenance; the beauty of the Venus di Medici was far less in her face than in her attitude.

9: The lecturer spoke next of the Appollo Belvidere and the Venus. Milton's Cherub was an exact description of the former. Indeed, we may find many traces in Paradise Lost of Milton's year in Rome. While the Appollo had in it something of the grandeur of the immortal, the Venus was but a perfect mortal, true to nature, but not above nature.

12: His conceptions of the Adonis [*i.e.* Apollo] were refined and elevating, and his description of the Venus exhibited a finely cultivated and highly appreciative mind.

14: He eulogized the "Apollo Belvidere," and the "Venus de Medici," as all do who view them; . . .

15: The "Apollo Belvidere" he considered the perfection of statuary, remarking that the visitor to Rome, immediately on his arrival, rushes to see the Apollo in the Vatican, and on his quitting the Eternal City, whether after a few weeks or many years, always makes a farewell visit to the same statue the last thing to be done ere leaving. It is not a mere work of art that we gaze on, there is a kind of divinity in it that lifts the imagination of the beholder above "things rank and gross in nature," and makes ordinary criticism impossible. The lecturer's description of the statue reminded us of the passage in the poet Campbell's letters, where he says that the first sight of the Apollo struck him dumb, and that he shed tears of joy copiously at the contemplation of such sublime beauty.

17: It seemed to us as if the writer had never forgotten his imprisonment among the Pacific cannibals, and half regretted his extradition from that physical paradise. We would venture a bet that Mr. Melville, with all his admiration for the Medicean Venus, thinks Fayaway worth a score of cold unhabited marbles.

19: The lecturer next spoke of the Apollo, the crowning glory of all, which stands alone in the Belvidere chapel of the Vatican. Every visitor hurries to the chapel to behold the statue, and, when he departs, his last glance is turned toward this loadstone. Its very presence is overawing. Milton's description of Zephon makes the angel an exact counterpart of the Apollo.—In fact, the whole of that immortal poem, Paradise Lost, is but a great Vatican. Milton, when young, spent a year at Rome, and here he got many of those ideas from heathen personages which he afterwards appropriated to his celestials, just as the Pope's artist converted the old heathen Parthenon [*i.e.* Pantheon] into a Christian church. Lucifer and his angels cast down are taken from a group in a private palace at Ardua [Padua]. This was sculptured out of one block by one of the later Italian artists. Three-score of the fallen lie wound together writhing and tortured, while, proud and sullen in the midst, is the nobler form of Satan. ¶ Speaking of the Apollo reminds one of the Venus Medici, although the one is at Rome and the other at Florence. She is no prude, but a child of nature, modest and unpretending. She is pictured at the moment when, returning from the bath, she is surprised by an intrusion.

20: The description of the ideal statuary of Rome, held us breathless by its wonderful nicety of appreciation, and subtlety of expression. Of all the tributes of genius to the Apollo, and Venus de Medici, those statues that "enchant the world," we never read one more worthy of their divine beauty.

22: *[reprints 2]*

23: . . . and referred to the description of Milton as "a Vatican done into verse;" gave a vivid picture of a marble group representing Lucifer and his companions cast down from Heaven, cut out of a single block of marble, amidst which appeared the unbroken, defiant form of Satan, his whole body breathing revenge, and his attitude one never to submit or yield. He described the statue of the Venus de Medicis, as contrasted with the Appollo, . . .

24: The Apollo was so wonderful a creation that it was impossible to give any idea of its sublimity; all admired, all were attracted to it; it was almost worshipped by every one who came within its presence. Visitors looked at it in silence and in awe. There seemed to be in the Apollo something that answered the divine longings of our nature, and which Faith told us could not be gratified on earth. The Venus—which was at Florence—was lovely, beautiful, but far less great than the Apollo. She was exceedingly refined, delicious in everything; but she was of the earth and Apollo was divine.

25A: . . . eulogized the Oppolo, . . .

25B: [*reprints 22 with these variations:* . . . in the Apollo . . . artistic, for statue . . . signalally . . . Faith; . . .]

30: The lecturer then gave an account of some of the more ideal works, such as the Apollo Belvidere, which was a model for poets, and from which Milton must have obtained some of his grand conceptions of dignity and grace. This statue was contrasted with that of the Venus de Medici, whose chief beauty was that of attitude. If the two were wedded, the union would be like that of the sons of God with the daughters of men.

31: The lecturer next passed to that crowning ornament of the Vatican the Apollo, which represented the perfect humanity, while the Laocoon gave the tragic side and was the symbol of human misfortune. If the Apollo gave the perfect, the Venus equally showed the beautiful.

PARAGRAPHS 17–18. 403.33–404.23 In a niche . . . of its spirit.]

2: The thought of many of these beautiful figures having been pleasing to the Romans, at least persuades us that their violence as a conquering race did not engross them, and that the flame of kindness kindled in most men by nature was at no time in Roman breasts wholly stamped out.

5: The Laocoon, and its kindred class of horrible conceptions, formed the next subject of discussion, and after them, in contrast, the gentle and pastoral statues. The existence of the latter proved that the Roman people were not entirely destitute of the gentler feelings.

6: He then passed in rapid review the Laocoon and other celebrated sculptures, to show the human feeling and genius of the ancient artists.

7: . . . the wolf and the slaughtered lamb, the goats at play around the sleeping shepherd were beautiful[l]y described, and they went to show, said the lecturer, that conquest did not wholly engross the people of ancient Rome, and though ignorant of the principles of Christianity there were in them the germs of its spirit.

HSG: These beautiful figures he contended showed that the violence of the Romans as a conquering race did not engross them wholly. *[Discussion of the Gladiators follows.]* ¶ The Laocoon and its kindred class of horrible conceptions and in contrast the pastoral statues was his next topic—

8: Another most remarkable group in the Belvidere court was the Laocoon, representing three figures struggling helplessly in the pangs of death, and in vain trying to disentangle the folds of a serpent. All these sculptures, while they showed in a more or less degree the peculiar ideal belief of the ancients, and told of their stern[n]ess too, proclaimed at the same time that gentleness was not altogether quenched in the heathens.

9: Other statuary were described by him; that of the Dying Gladiator and the Goats at play round the Sleeping Shepherd, were proofs that conquest and the fiercer passions did no[t] altogether engross the Ancient Romans, and that there were some hearts among them, that possessed the spirit, if they were ignorant of the doctrines of Christianity.

19: In a niche of the Vatican stands the Laocoon, the very semblance of a great and powerful man writhing with the inevitable destiny which he cannot throw off. Throes, and pangs, and struggles are given with a meaning that is not withheld. The hideous monsters embrace him in their mighty folds, and torture him with agonizing embraces. In all the ancient statues representing animals there is a marked resemblance with those described in the Book of Revelations. This class of Roman statuary and the pictures of the Apocalypse are nearly identical. But the ferocity in the appearance of this statuary is compensated by the pastoral nature of others. The quiet, gentle, and peaceful scenes of pastoral life are represented in some of the later of Roman statuary just as we find them described by that best of all pastoral poets, Wordsworth.

20: The expression of doubt, and dark groping of human speculation, in the ideal statuary of that age, when the old mythology was passing away, and men's minds had not yet reposed in the new faith, was finely portrayed.

22: [*reprints 2 with these variations:* . . . violence, . . . race, . . . and the flame kindled . . .]

24: The Laocoon was grand and impressive, and gained half its significance from its symbolism—the fable that it represented—humanity struggling with destiny. Otherwise it would be no more that [*i.e.* than] Paul Potter's "Boar Hunt" at Amsterdam.

25A: . . . the Lecturer did not confine himself to those statues which immortalize the "Eternal City," but telegraphed his audience to Naples and Florence, and to Amsterdam with little regard for their convenience, and did not even take the trouble to render the travelling easy.
25B: [*reprints 22 with one variation:* . . . brea[s]ts . . .]
30: The Laocoon, Castor and Pollux, and the Hercules Farnese, with other statues, were also described. Some of these works proved that the old Roman, stern and hard hearted, as we generally imagined him, was not entirely destitute of tenderness and compassion.
31: —If we imaged the life that was in the statues, and looked at their more humane aspects, we should not find that the ancients were devoid of generous principles, . . .

PARAGRAPH 19. 404.24–405.7 Thus, when I . . . but the name.]
2: When I stood in the Colosseum, its mountain-chains of ruins waving with foliage girdling me round, as in some great green hollow in the Appenine range, the solitude was like that of savage nature; but restoring the shattered arches and terraces, I re-peopled them with all the statues from the Vatican, and in the turfy glen of the arena below, I placed the Fighting Gladiator from the Louvre, confronting him with the dying one from the Capitol. And as in fancy I heard the ruffian huzzas for the first, rebounded from the pitiless hiss for the last, I felt that more than one in that host I had evoked, shared not in its passions; that some hearts were there that felt the horror keenly as any of us would have felt it.
5: When he stood in the Coliseum, with its walls rising round him like a mountain range, the lecturer had felt as solitary as if in some deep green valley in the Appenines. Imagination restored the arches, and then taking the statue of the triumphant gladiator from the Louvre, and that of the dying gladiator from the Capitol, as a centre piece, there sprang up around him again the mighty crowds which once peopled that vast temple. And he had felt, from the knowledge of the gentler statues which existed, a belief that there were some among that gladiatorial people who beheld with horror and sadness the cruel scenes which the Coliseum had beheld.
6: None but a gentle heart could have conceived the idea of the Dying Gladiator.
7: He who chisselled the statue of the Dying Gladiator could not have possessed an unfeeling heart, and he was Christian in all but the name.
HSG: When he stood in the Colliseum its mountain hights of ruins waving foliage & girdling him around as some vast green hollow in the Appenine range, the solitude was that of savage nature, but restoring its shattered terraces and arches he repeopled them with the statues from the Vatican and in the arenas turfy glen he fancy free confronted the fighting Gladiator from the Louvre with the dying one from the Capitol. Again he heard the ruffian huzzah for the first mingle with the

pitiless hiss for the last and felt that more than one in the host around, shared not in the passions of the hour but some hearts felt the horror then as keenly as we would now[.]

12: . . . and the strife of the Gladiators, with the applause for the conqueror rebounding from the hiss for the conquered, was a rich scene of word painting.

19: When standing within the Coliseum the solitude is great and vast, just such as one experiences when shut up in a vale of the Apennines, hemmed in by towering cliffs on every side.—But the imagination must build it as it was of old; it must be repeopled with the terrific games of the gladiators, with the frantic leaps and dismal howls of the wild, bounding beasts, with the shrieks and cries of the excited spectators. Unless this is done, how can we appreciate the Gladiator? It was such a feeling of the artist that created it, and there must be such a feeling on the part of the visitor to view it and view it aright.

20: We do not remember in all our reading to have met with a more beautiful passage, than that in which Mr. Melville described his musings in the Coliseum, and the recurrence of his imagination far back to the day when its mighty walls enclosed such countless throngs to witness the gladitorial combats, and the eye of fancy saw many in the vast assemblage who looked not coldly on the dying gladiator whose eyes looked far away to

——where his rude hut by the Danube lay,
There were his young barbarians all at play.

22: [*reprints 2 with these variations:* . . . Colisseum . . . girding . . . repeopled . . . fighting . . . my fancy . . . rebound . . .]

25A: Thence by no very easy transitions wound among the streets and bye places of the city, cast a furtive glance at the Colosium, and the miracles of art gathered there, measured the statues by the Yankee method, . . .

25B: [*reprints 22 with these variations:* . . . terraces; . . . statue[s] . . . th[e] turfy geln [*i.e.* glen] . . .]

30: The dying Gladiator showed that some heart had looked with pity on the cruel and bloody scenes that the Coliseum had witnessed.

31: . . . and standing in the Coliseum and re-peopling its gigantic arches with the living crowd who had once sat upon the seats, we should not find that there were lacking hearts who sympathized with the last struggles of the "Dying Gladiator."

PARAGRAPH 20. 405.8–19 It is with . . . of an hour.]

6: The sepulchral monuments of the early Christians, in the vaults of the Vatican, show the joyous triumph of the new religion—quite unlike the sombre mementoes of modern times.

8: The sculptured monuments of the Vatican showed the change that had come over the Roman people. On one side might be seen Rachel weeping for her children—on another Job cursing his maker—and then Rachel drying her tears, and again Job sitting comforted.

19: It is with varied feelings that one travels through the sepulchral vaults of the Vatican.—The statues are of various character: Hope faces Despair; Joy comes to the relief of Sorrow; Rachel weeps for her children and will not be comforted—Job rises above his afflictions and rejoices. The marbles alternate; some are of a joyous nature, followed by those that are of a sad and sombre character. ¶ Just as a guide hurries one on through these scenes with his torch light, bringing out one statue in bold relief while a hundred or more are hidden in the gloom, so did the lecturer say it was necessary for him to do to keep within the limits of an hour.

PARAGRAPH 21. 405.20–30 In passing . . . forms it beholds.]

5: The great square of the Vatican was next briefly described; . . .

6: The lecturer then eloquently sketched the exterior of the Vatican.

8: Standing something more than five hundred feet from the front of St. Peter's Church, the spectator saw himself, surrounded by immense colonnades, which overshadowed the area like the wings of an army of Titans; and up against the heaven, like a balloon, would be seen the dome of St. Peter's, one of the most magnificent religious buildings in the world.

19: If one stands a hundred feet in front of St. Peter's and looks up, a vast and towering pile meets his view,—High, high above are the beetling crags and precipices of masonry, and yet higher still above all this is the dome. The mind is carried away with the very vastness. But throughout the Vatican it is different. The mind, instead of being bewildered within itself, is drawn out by the symmetry and beauty of the forms it beholds. These are of different and varied character.

25A: . . . carried his audience into the court yard and treated them to an extended view of the Palace, . . .

31: In passing from the inside of the Vatican to the square in front, we find ourselves surrounded by the mighty colonnade with its statues, from whence we see the balloon-like dome of St. Peter's and the great pile of confused architecture which is the outside of the Vatican.

PARAGRAPH 22. 405.31–406.19 But nearly . . . British Museum.]

5: . . . then followed a vivid description of the statues on Mount Cavallo, in Rome, where the marble horses seemed to represent the fiery audaciousness of Roman power.

6: But nearly the whole of Rome was a Vatican—everywhere were fallen columns and sculptured fragments. Most of them, it is true, were the works of Greek artists, and yet the grand spirit of Roman life inspired them.

HSG: The horses of Mt Cavallo, . . .

8: —On Monte Cavallo stood the statues of Castor and Pollux, reining in their horses; and how beautiful and gigantic were those horses! A modern inscription attributed these famous animals to the chisels of Phidias and Praxiteles—there was no doubt, however, that they were works of Grecian art, and brought to Rome when the land in which they were sculptured had been conquered. In truth, nothing even in the statues of gods could be more noble than the appearance of these horses; and the freize of the Pantheon [*i.e.* Parthenon] now in the British Museum, shewed how ideal were the conceptions of the ancients in regard to horses. The ancients did as much for the equine as they did for the human form.

19: Remarkable, however, among all are the sculptured horses, riderless and rearing, seeming, like those of Elijah, to soar to heaven. The most of these were sculptured by the Greeks.—The horse was idealized by the ancient artist as majestic next to man, and they loved to sculpture them as they did heroes and gods. To the Greeks nature had no brute. Everything was a being with a soul, and the horse idealized the second order of animals just as man did the first.

20: A most striking and beautiful thought was introduced, when speaking of the equestrian statues of Rome, and the expression of untamed docility, rather than conquered obedience which their artists have given to the horse, the lecturer deduced the enlarged humanity of that elder day, when man gave himself none of those upstart airs of superiority over the brute creation which he now assumes.

27: From individual statues, he passed to the consideration of groups—then going over a very general and extensive field in art, not aiming at anything in particular, but during which he said many beautiful things; . . .

31: Rome was also itself a Vatican on a large scale. . . . ¶ The lecturer dwelt at some length upon the equestrian group of Castor and Pollux, which stands on the Monte Cavallo, and was discovered amid the vast ruins of the Baths of Caracalla. This ideal and magnificent conception of the horse had raised that animal, into a sort of divinity and was as a conception of Greek art, unrivalled in its sublime loftiness of attitude and force of conception. We saw other instances of this profound appreciation of the form of the horse in the sculpture on the frieze of the Parthernon.

PARAGRAPH 23. 406.20–36 Of other statues . . . their own history.]

5: The Moses, by Michael Angelo, appearing like a stern, bullying genius of druidical superstition; the Hercules rescued from the ruins of the baths of Caracalla—formed further subjects of comment.

6: Passing from these ancient sculptures, tribute was paid to the colossal works of Benevenuto, Cellini and Michael Angelo.

HSG: . . . the Moses of Angelo and the Hercules of the Baths of Caracalla were also commented upon[.]

8: Conspicuous amongst these images was the figure of Hercules, leaning on his club, with that bovine good nature, which made one's heart incline towards him as to a pleasant ox.

19: Of the statues of large size much might be said, and that of Perseus at Florence would form a theme by itself. Prominent among the colossals, however, is that of Hercules. This statue is not of that quick, smart, energetic strength that we should suppose would appertain to the powerful Samson or the mighty Hercules; but rather of a character like that of the lazy ox, confident of his own strength, but loth to use it. No trifles would call it forth; it is reserved only for great occasions. To rightfully appreciate this, or, in fact, any other statue, one must consider where they came from and under what circumstances they were formed. In other respects they reveal their own history.

31: —Another noble statue, conceived in a very different spirit, was the Farnese Hercules, which in its simplicity and good nature reminded us of cheerful and humane things. The Perseus of Beuvenuto Cellini at Florence was another astonishing conception, conceived in the fiery brain of the intense artist, and brought to perfection as a bronze cast in the midst of the flames which had indeed overshot their aim.

PARAGRAPHS 24–25. 406.37–407.33 Thus to understand . . . of Goldsmith.]

5: To understand the statues of the Vatican, it was necessary to visit often the scenes where they had stood, the Coliseum, which threw its shade like a mighty thunder cloud, the forum, the ruined temples, and remember all that had there taken place. ¶ After extended allusions to all the statues and structures which we have enumerated thus far, the lecturer considered the Roman villas in a very pleasing way, and spoke also of the statues to be found in connection with them.

6: He regretted that the time would not allow him to speak of the scenery and surroundings of the Roman sculptures—the old Colliseum, the gardens, the Forum, and the villas in the environs. He specified some of the most memorable of the latter, and the best works they contain.

7: The lecturer next described the appearance of Rome, standing at a distance from the city; the impressions produced on the mind by its history, and the works of art contained in its public buildings; the ruins of the Coliseum, the Aqueducts, the villas of Rome, and their sculptured treasures, producing to the mind of the reader a beautiful and classic picture, . . .

HSG: The Roman villas, their statues and style was well treated.

8: The lecturer next passed in brief review the Collisium, the Forum, and the Aqueducts of Rome, and drew attention to the Villa Albania, as one amongst many, containing some exquisite remains of art—first of which was a full length statue of Minerva, of beautiful workmanship; and next a medallion of Antonius, which was also of charming make, representing a female of crystalline countenance with her eye reposing on a lotus of admirable design, which she held in her hand. In this Villa also, was the bust of Esop, with the hump on his back; he was represented with finely formed features, lit up by an eye of lambent irony, such as plays round the pages of Goldsmith.

9: The lecturer proceeded to describe the appearance of Rome, the ruins of the Coliseum, the Aqueducts, its Villas with their treasures of art.

15: In alluding to the statues of Pompeii, the lecturer drew a vivid picture of the feastings in that devoted city on the night previous to its terrible entombment.

19: But Roman statuary is by no means confined to the Vatican, or even to Rome itself. The villas around are filled with it, and, in these quiet retreats, we catch some of the last and best glimpses of the art. Here are found many of those trophies which have challenged the admiration of the world; here, where once exhaled sweets like the airs of Verona, now comes the deadly malaria, repelling from those ancient myrtles and orange groves, like Lucretia Borgia who invites to a feast and then destroys. One of the finest of the statues to be found in these villas is the Minerva, a creature as purely and serenely sublime as it is possible for human hands to form. Here, also, is found a bust of Æsop, the dwarfed and deformed, whose countenance is irradiated by a lambent gleam of irony like that we see in Goldsmith's. Many of these villas were built long years ago by men of the heathen school, for the express purpose of preserving these ancient works of art. The villas which were to shield and protect them have now crumbled, while most of the statues which were to be thus preserved still live on. ¶ Here the lecturer entered upon a discussion of the festive habits of the ancients. It was not unusual for them at their feasts to talk upon the subject of death and other like mournful themes. Such topics were not considered irrelevant to the occasion, and, instead of destroying the interest of the feast by their ill timed intrusion, they rather added to it a temperate zest.

23: The lecturer described the various statues and groups of the Vatican, the streets, churches and private palaces of Rome, . . . and the figures of the various heathen subjects which history so elaborately describes in words which convey but a faint conception as compared with the impression upon the mind, made by the marble representatives in the "Eternal City." ¶ The lecturer closed by a very beautiful description of the villas and private gardens of Rome, in which every breath of air that stirs is perfumed, and which reminded us that in a garden originated the dread sentence, DEATH—that it was amidst such perfumed grottoes, bowers and walks, the guests of a Lucretia Borgia were welcomed to a feast, but received with a pall.

25A: . . . shipped out to Villa Albanico, . . .

30: The lecturer referred also to the Roman villas and the works of art they contained, . . .

31: After enumerating other salient points in the Roman antique, and dwelling upon the vast ruins of the Coliseum and the Baths, the lecturer passed to the villas of Rome, which were the essence of the best collections of the finest objects in art, and where nature had been raised by culture and refinement into an almost human character. He more especially alluded to the Villa Albani, built as that was by one who had made art and antiquity the study of his life, as a place to preserve the splendid works he had collected. Here, were the remains of antiquity from Pompeii, and we might bring back the guests to the rooms where they sat at the feast on the eve of the fatal eruption of Vesuvius. They spoke of topics which were forbidden to modern ears at such scenes, and dared to allude to their mortality, even while at the banquet. Yet the gardens around the villas were the abodes of malaria, and the laurel and the myrtle in their beauty concealed the seeds of death.

PARAGRAPHS 26–30. 407.34–409.22 In conclusion . . . the world."]

2: Not the least, perhaps, among those causes which make the Roman museums so impressive, is their tranquil air. In chambers befitting stand the images of gods, while in the statues of men, even the vilest, what was corruptible in their originals, here in pure marble puts on incorruption. In the Roman Vatican and the Washington Patent Office the respective characteristics of the ancients and moderns stand contrasted. But is the locomotive as grand an object as the Laocoon? Does it attest this hurried intelligence? We moderns did invent the printing press, but from the ancients have we not the best thoughts that it circulates? As the Roman arch enters into and sustains our best architecture, does not her spirit still animate and support whatever is soundest in societies and States? Or shall the scheme of Fourier supplant the code of Justinian, only when the novels of Dickens silence the satires of Juvenal? If the Colliseum express the durability of Roman ideas, what does the Crystal Palace express? Will the glass of the one bide the hail storms of eighteen centuries as well as the travertine of the other?

——When falls the Colliseum, Rome shall fall;
And when Rome falls, the world!

3: [*reprints 2 with these variations:* . . . ¶ But is . . . we have the best . . . circulate? . . .]

5: In conclusion, some comprehensive ideas in reference to statuary, and to the influence exercised by the marble forms created by the sculptor, were advanced, and in this connection the lecturer said that as instinct is below reason, so is science below art—a proposition which caused some little discussion in several groups of homeward-bound listeners, after the lecture was closed.

6: He concluded by summing up the obvious teachings of these deathless marbles.

7: . . . and said that while states and constitutions perished the silent marble lived, bequeathing to posterity, not shameful defects, but triumphant successes; and concluded with a tribute to the ancients for the great debt due them for law, literature and art.

HSG: He compared the elements of Roman greatness wh[ich]. are incorporated into our system of government and present civilization. The Locomotive and the Laocoon. Our printing press circulating thoughts which they begot and their example which is the basis of our *idea*. The Roman arch entering into & sustaining our architecture and the Roman spirit still animating & supporting Societies and states. The Colliseum and the Crystal Palace as exponents of our respective characters. Will the glass of the former equal in durability the travertine of the other—

"When falls the Colliseum, Rome shall fall
And when Rome falls, the World—["]

8: The lecturer concluded—the statues of the Vatican seem not alone to be abstracted from earth but from time, but still the atmosphere of history is around them; and we can read sermons in these mute stones of Rome, aside from the sense of gratification which their beauty imparts. These mute marbles are immortal, however, through nothing but their beauty; and though Rome might be bought, all the coffers in Christendom could not make another Apollo. Rome stands amongst the fragment[s] of temples, but while these statues remain her name can never pass away. When the Colliseum falls Rome shall fall; and when Rome falls so shall the world. [Applause.]

9: He closed with an eloquent tribute to the successes of art. While states and constitutions had perished, those silent marbles had lived on. Artists alone had succeeded in realizing their ideal, while every one else had mournfully failed. He added: to Rome was the world indebted for nearly all that was best in law, literature and art, and when Rome fell, the world would fall with her.

19: In conclusion, said Mr. Melville, since we cannot mention all the different works, let us bring them together and speak of them as a whole. It will be noticed that statues, as a general thing, do not present the startling features and attitudes of men, but are rather of a tranquil, subdued air such as men have when under the influence of no passion. They appeal to that portion of our being which is highest and noblest. To some they are a complete house of philosophy; to others they appeal only to the tenderer feelings and affections. All who behold the Apollo confess its glory; yet we know not to whom to attribute the glory of creating it. The chiseling them shows the genius of the creator—the preserving them shows the bounty of the good and the policy of the wise. ¶ These marbles, the works of the dreamers and idealists of old, live on, leading and pointing to good. They were formed by those who had yearnings for something better, and strove to attain it by embodiments in cold stone. We can ourselves judge with what success they have worked. How well in the Apollo is expressed the idea of the perfect man. Who could better it? Can art, not life, make the ideal? Here, in statuary, was the Utopia of the ancients expressed. The Vatican itself is the index of the ancient world, just as the Washington Patent Office is of the modern. But how is it possible to compare the one with the other, when things that are so totally unlike cannot be brought together? What comparison could be instituted between a locomotive and the Apollo? The moderns pride themselves upon their superiority, but the claim can be questioned. They did, indeed, invent the printing press, but all the best thoughts that it sends forth are from the ancients, whether it be law, physics or philosophy.

The deeds of the ancients are noble, and so are their arts; and as the one is kept alive in the memory of man by the glowing words of their own historians and poets, so should the memory of the other be kept green in the minds of men by the careful preservation of their noble statuary.

"When the Coliseum falls, Rome shall fall,
And when Rome, the world[.]"

20: But we hung entranced upon the closing remarks of the lecturer, which vindicated these spiritual productions of the ancient mind from their alleged inferiority to the utilitarian inventions of the present age. Never before was the superiority of art over science, so triumphantly and eloquently sustained.

22: [*reprints 2 with these variations:* . . . impressive is . . . originals here . . . Locomotive . . . thoughts which . . . Colliseum expresses . . . "When falls . . . Coliseum . . . fall," . . . world."]

24: The lecturer spoke in fervid and eloquent terms of the influence of the statues of Rome; of the delight they inspired and the instruction they furnished. They were the works of visionaries and dreamers, but they were realizations of soul, the representations of the ideal. They were grand, beautiful and true, and they spoke with a voice that echoed through the ages. Governments had changed; empires had fallen; nations had passed away; but these mute marbles remained—the oracles of time, the perfection of art. ¶ We boasted much of our progress, of our energy, of our achievements; but did all our triumphs equal those of the heroes and divinities that stood there silent, the incarnations of grandeur and of beauty? The ancients lived while those statues endured, and seemed to breathe inspiration through the world, giving purpose, shape and impetus to what was created high, or grand, or beautiful. While the Colosseum stands, will Rome; and when Rome falls, the world.

25A: . . . closed with remarks applicable to statues in general.

25B: [*reprints 22 with these variations:* . . . ancient[s] . . . supports . . . Justinian only . . . novel[s] . . . traver[t]ine . . . Coliesum . . .]

27: . . . finally coming back to the consideration of the pillars of Rome, which aimed, like those of greater antiquity, to be enduring illustrations of the perfection of art of their time, he concluded with an elegant panegyric on art generally.

30: . . . and concluded with some comprehensive ideas in reference to statuary, and to the influence exercised by the marble forms created by the sculptor.

31: It was perhaps somewhat the custom now to undervalue art. The world had taken a practical turn. We boasted our scientific achievements. Yet science was beneath art, as the instinct is beneath the reason.—Modern times gave themselves airs, and the Crystal Palace possibly contemplated an equal resistance to the hailstorms of eighteen centuries, with the travertine of which the roof of the Pantheon was constructed.—Yet the ancients of the ideal description, instead of trying to turn their impracticable chimeras as the modern dreamer into social and political prodigies, deposited them in the great works of Art, which still lived. All the merchants in London had not enough in their coffers to re-produce the Apollo. And Rome was yet an evidence of its own ever lasting durability.

"While stands the Coliseum, Rome shall stand;
When falls the Coliseum, Rome shall fall;
And when Rome falls, the world."

DISCUSSION. 407.29 a medallion of Antinous] In a journal entry of February 28, 1857, describing his first visit to the Villa Albani, Melville had written as follows of this celebrated bas-relief: "Antinous—head like moss-rose with curls & buds—rest all simplicity—end of fillet on shoulder—drapery, shoulder in the mantle—hand full of flowers & eyeing them—the profile &c." The one newspaper report of "Statues in Rome" to mention this work is obviously garbled: the "medallion of Antonius," according to the Montreal *Daily Transcript and Commercial Advertiser* (#8), represents "a female of crystalline countenance with her eye reposing on a lotus of admirable design, which she holds in her hand." NN emends this phrasing to read ". . . Antinous with his eye . . . he holds . . . his hand."

HYPHENATION. II. 409.6 re-produce

THE SOUTH SEAS (pp. 410–20)

During his second lecture season, beginning in Yonkers, New York, on December 6, 1858, and concluding in Lynn, Massachusetts, on March 19, 1859, Melville appeared in ten cities and towns, presenting a new lecture, "The South Seas," in each locality and also repeating "Statues in Rome" at Lynn, where he was engaged for two lectures. Twenty-five local newspapers carried reports of his appearances. The following table lists the places and dates of each engagement and the newspapers which reported his lecture, the newspapers being listed alphabetically by date and numbered sequentially.

Yonkers, New York, December 6, 1858
 1. *Examiner,* December 9, 1858
Pittsfield, Massachusetts, December 14, 1858
 2. *Berkshire County Eagle,* December 17, 1858
Boston, Massachusetts, January 31, 1859
 3. *Atlas and Daily Bee,* February 1, 1859
 4. *Daily Advertiser,* February 1, 1859
 5. *Daily Courier,* February 1, 1859
 6. *Daily Evening Traveller,* February 1, 1859

7. *Evening Transcript,* February 1, 1859
8. *Herald,* February 1, 1859
9. *Journal,* February 1, 1859
10. *Post,* February 1, 1859

New York, New York, February 7, 1859

11. *Daily Tribune,* February 8, 1859
12. *Evening Express,* February 8, 1859
13. *Evening Post,* February 8, 1859
14. *Weekly Century,* February 12, 1859

Baltimore, Maryland, February 8, 1859

15. *American and Commercial Advertiser,* February 9, 1859
16. *The Sun,* February 9, 1859

Chicago, Illinois, February 24, 1859

17. *Daily Journal,* February 25, 1859
18. *Daily Press and Tribune,* February 25, 1859

Milwaukee, Wisconsin, February 25, 1859

19. *Daily Free Democrat,* February 26, 1859
20. *Daily Sentinel,* February 26, 1859
21. *Daily Wisconsin,* February 26, 1859

Rockford, Illinois, February 28, 1859

22. *Daily News,* March 1, 1859
23. *Republican,* March 3, 1859
24. *Register,* March 5, 1859

Quincy, Illinois, March 2, 1859

No report

Lynn, Massachusetts, March 16, 1859

25. *Weekly Reporter,* March 19, 1859

Photocopies and transcriptions of the individual articles, arranged and numbered as above, have been deposited in the Melville Collections of The Houghton Library of Harvard University and The Newberry Library; in the absence of a manuscript or printed text of the lecture they constitute the basis for the composite text printed in this volume.

Although Melville himself gave the title of his lecture as "The South Seas" (p. 725 above), there are several variants in newspaper references: "Adventures in the South Seas" (#3), "South Sea Adventures" (#5, #8), "South [*or* The South] Sea" (#7, #10, #13, #14), and "South Sea Islands" (#19). The most detailed résumé of the content is the report appearing in the Baltimore *American and Commercial Advertiser* (#15), which offered what must have been a shorthand transcription of the opening paragraphs of the lecture as Melville delivered it, followed by a combination of transcription and summary of the remaining passages. Essential agreement in organization and even in phrasing between this report and the reviews carried by other newspapers indicates that Melville made few if any changes in his manuscript during the season.

The present volume reprints on pp. 410–20, as a reading text, the composite reconstructed text of "The South Seas" prepared for *Melville as Lecturer* (1957), which is included here with the authorization of Harvard University Press. The editorial principles and procedures set forth on p. 725 above with respect to "Statues in Rome" were also followed in preparing the composite text of "The South Seas." This composite reading text, like that of "Statues in Rome," does not constitute a critical reconstruction of Melville's manuscript; it simply represents the fullest wording, in those phrases which in the editor's judgment appear to be most characteristic of Melville himself, that can be put together from the surviving reports. The following changes have been made in the 1957 text following a new collation with the newspaper reports from which it derives; after the Northwestern-Newberry page and line reference comes the NN reading, followed by the 1957 reading:

411.5 dusty] the dusty   415.24 act] acts   415.32–33 implanted] planted

The notes which follow record the variant readings among the individual newspaper reports on which successive paragraphs of the composite text are based. Each variant is identified by the number assigned in the list above to the newspaper report from which it is extracted. As collation reveals, the Rockford *Daily News* (#22) drew most of its review, without acknowledgment, from an earlier article in the Chicago *Daily Press and Tribune* (#18); the rival Rockford *Register* (#24), which took issue with the favorable account given by the *News,* observed that Melville "may have pleased the large audience who listened to him, but he certainly did not us," adding shrewdly that "the *News* must have got an advance report of the gentleman's lecture." The Lynn *Weekly Reporter* (#25) carried only a two-sentence reference to Melville's "first lecture" in Lynn, which was evidently "The South Seas" since its material was said to be "of the water, aqueous"; the *Reporter* did not review the second lecture, "Statues in Rome."

PARAGRAPHS 1–2. 410.2–14 The subject . . . in hand.]

1: As Mr. Melville said, the South Sea is a vast subject.—We are happy to be able to state that it was not entirely exhausted by this lecture.

3: He announced his subject as "Adventures in the South Seas." The subject, he remarked, was somewhat extensive, and might appear to some as ambitious. He should not, however, attempt to cover the whole field, but only give here and there some personal adventures, narratives, descriptions, &c.

4: The subject, the lecturer said, was very comprehensive and he hardly knew what parts to present, to his hearers.

5: He said that the multitude and variety of objects which might be treated upon with satisfaction, connected with the almost illimitable region of the South Seas, rendered it peculiarly difficult for him to select a theme.

9: On being introduced to the audience, Mr. Melville said that the field of his subject was large, and he should not be expected to go over it all; nor should he be expected to read again what had long been in print, touching his own incidental adventures in Polynesia. But he proposed to view the subject in a general manner, in a random way, with here and there an incident by way of illustration.

12: In prefacing his remarks, Mr. Melville stated that the subject was one which could be only partially treated in a single lecture, and that he should leave out of consideration any great notice of his personal adventures in the South seas.

14: Mr. Melville, of course, finds it impossible to tell us everything of a region literally half the globe, in the small portion of an evening allowed him. But he tells us a great deal.

15: The subject of our lecture this evening, "the South Seas," may be thought perhaps a theme if not ambitious at least somewhat expansive, covering according to the authorities, I am afraid to say how much of the earth's surface—in short, more than one-half. We have, therefore, a rather spacious field before us, and I hardly think we shall be able, in a thorough way, to go over the whole of it to-night. ¶ And here (to do away with any erroneous anticipations as to our topic) I hope you do not expect me to repeat what has long been in print touching my own casual adventures in Polynesia. I propose to treat of matters of more general interest, and, in a random way, discuss the South Seas at large and under various aspects, introducing, as occasion may serve, any little incident, personal or other, fitted to illustrate the point in hand.

16: His subject, the lecturer said, was literally an expansive one, and embraced an arena he would not dare say how much. He would not repeat old sayings, or summon back the memories of old voyagers, bu[t] would paddle along among its aspects at large, whether personal or otherwise.

19: He spoke of his subject generally, as he said he would at the outset, and so general were his remarks that they failed to create much interest in the minds of his hearers. He commenced by stating that he should not detail any of his own personal adventures, which, to our notion, was a great mistake, . . .

20: He introduced his subject by glancing at the title under which it had been published, . . .

21: He referred to the vastness of the subject of the *South Seas,* covering as it does an expanse of many millions of square miles. He said he meant to treat of the subject more generally than he had in the books which he had written, and to recount experiences which were not there to be found.

23: The first twenty minutes were devoted to discanting upon the magnitude of the subject, without any direct reference to the plan of the lecture.

24: The first portion of his lecture was devoted to an exposition of the greatness and vastness of his theme.

PARAGRAPHS 3–5. 410.15–411.21 "South Seas" . . . of repute.]

1: After giving his reasons for calling the ocean that extends to Bhering's Straits, the *South* Sea, which consisted merely in following a precedent set by old authors, . . .

3: The term "South Seas" was first defined, in connection with which he glanced briefly at their history.

4: After stating the location and extent of the South Sea or Pacific Ocean, and remarking the propriety of the names, Mr. Melville proceeded to describe its most striking peculiarities.

6: He announced as his subject "The South Seas," and commenced by giving an extended account of the origin of the name, South Seas, which was but another name for the Pacific.

9: He first referred to the title of the lecture, and the origin and date of the name "South Seas," which was older than the name "Pacific," to which preference is generally given now.

10: In commencing the lecturer enlarged on the origin of the name South Sea, . . .

12: The name South Seas was but a term for the Pacific Ocean, to be found in old books of voyages and travels, and full of many pleasant associations.

14: He adopts "The South Seas" as a title for his lecture in preference to "The Pacific;" he finds it more relishing of the old, antique exploring and buccaneering adventures of the fresh, imaginative days of voyaging in those waters; . . .

15: South Seas is simply an equivalent term for Pacific Ocean. Then why not say Pacific Ocean at once?—Because one may have a lingering regard for certain old associations, linking the South Seas as a name with many pleasant and venerable books of voyages, full of well remembered engravings. ¶ To be sure those time-worn tomes are pretty nearly obsolete, but none the less are they, with the old names they enshrine, dear to the memory of their reader; in much they same way too that the old South Sea House in London was dear to the heart of Charles Lamb.—Who that has read it can forget that quaint sketch, the introductory essay of Elia, where he speaks of the Balc[l]utha-like desolation of those haunted old offices of the once famous South Sea Company—the old oaken wainscot hung with dusty maps of Mexico and soundings of the Bay of Panama—the vast cellarages under the whole pile where Mexican dollars and doubloons once lay heaped in huge bins for [M]ammon to solace his solitary heart withal? ¶ But besides summoning up the memory of brave old books, Elia['s] fine sketch and the great South Sea Bubble, originating in the institution there celebrated—the words South Seas are otherwise suggestive, yielding to the fancy an indefinable odor of sandal wood and cinnamon. In the adventures of Captain Dampier (that eminent and excellent buccaneer) you read only of South Seas. In Harris' old voyages, and many others, the title is the same, and even as late as 1803 we find that Admiral Burney prefers the old title to the new, Pacific, which appellation has in the present century only become the popular one—notwithstanding which we occasion[al]ly find the good old name first bestowed still employed by writers of repute.

16: The name South Seas generally applied to this body of water, is synonymous with Pacific ocean, which was afterwards applied to it because of the tranquility of its waters.

18: The lecturer commenced by defining the South Seas. They are simply the great Pacific Ocean, . . .

21: The South Seas is another name for the Pacific Ocean, and they are associated with many a romance or history. He alluded to an instance of the ancient South Sea House in London, so admirably spoken of in "Elia," by the gifted Charles Lamb, and so dear to him. He mentioned how the subject was otherwise suggestive, in the adventures of ancient Captains and explorers. ¶ The name of South Seas is used to some extent even in modern times.

22: *[reprints 18]*

PARAGRAPHS 6–9. 411.22–412.20 But since . . . of Darien.]

1: . . . Mr. Melville proceeded to mention the early explorations in that region, which mention we can confirm as correct, for we remember reading of them in our school-days.

9: The voyages of early navigators into the South Seas, and especially of Bilboa, commander of the petty post at Darien, from whence he had taken formal possession of all the South Seas, and all lands and kingdoms therein, in behalf of his master, the King of Castile and Leon, were noticed by the lecturer.

10: . . . and sketched the adventures of its discoverer, Vasco Nunez de Balboa.

12: Balboa, the first discoverer of the Ocean, gave it this name. Lt. Strain and others, parties of buccaneers, hardy, ambitious men, had from time to time explored these seas.

13: He first gave an account of the adventures of its discoverer, Vasco Nunez de Balboa.

14: . . . and he, probably from old experience, has a lurking distrust of the pacific qualities of that great ocean. It got its name up at a favorable moment, and in spite of pouting, storms, tempests and hurricanes, has lain abed upon it ever since. When the Spanish discoverers first saw this vast expanse of waters, it was from the Isthmus of Panama, which, running east and west, placed the ocean to the south of their view. Hence the name.

15: But since these famous waters lie on both sides of the Equator and wash the far northern shores of Kamskatka as well as the far southern ones of Terra del Fuego, how did they ever come to be christened with such a misnomer as *South* Seas? The way it happened was this: The Isthmus of Darien runs not very far from East and West; if you stand upon its further shore the ocean will appear to the *South* of you, and were you ignorant of the general direction of the coast line you would infer that it rolled away wholly toward that quarter. Now Balboa, the first white man who laid eyes upon these waters, stood in just this position; drew just this inference and bestowed its name accordingly. ¶ The circumstances of Balboa's discovery are not uninteresting. In the earliest days of the Spanish dominion on this continent, he commanded a petty post on the Northern shore of the Isthmus, and hearing it rumored that there was a vast sea on the other side of the land—its beach not distant, but of difficult approach, owing to a range of steep mountain wall and other obstruction, he resolved to explore in that direction. His hardships may be imagined by reca[l]ling the narrative a few years since of the adventures of Lieut. Strain and party who in like manner with the Spaniard, undertook to cross from sea to sea, through the primeval wilderness. A party of buccaneers also likewise crossed the Isthmus under suffering, the utmost that nature is capable of sustainining. Balboa and the buccaneers, though not more courageous, were certainly more hardy or more fortunate than the American officer, since, after all they underwent, their efforts were at last successful. ¶ The thronging Indians opposed Balboa's passage, demanding who he was, what he wanted and whither he was going. The reply is a model of Spartan directness. "I am a Christian, my errand is to spread true religion and to seek gold, and I am going in search of the sea." ¶ Coming at last to the foot of a mountain, he was told that from its summit he could see the object of his search. He ordered a halt, and, like Moses, the devout Spaniard "went up into the mountain alone." When he beheld the sea he fell upon his knees and thanked God for the sight. The next day with sword and target, wading up to his waist in its waters, he called upon his troop and the assembled Indians to bear witness that he took possession of that whole ocean with [a]ll the lands and Kingdoms pertaining to it for his sovereign master the King of Castile and Leon. A large minded gentleman, of great latitude of sentiment, was Vasco Nunez de Balboa, commander of that petty post of Darien.

18: . . . of which Balboa first took possession in the name of his royal master the King of Castile and Leon.

21: He spoke of ancient explorers in the South Seas, how it became christened so, how the whole Western ocean was taken possession of by Capt. Bilboa, for his master, King Charles, of Castile of Leon.

22: *[reprints 18]*

PARAGRAPH 10. 412.21–30 If we . . . to oranges.]

10: He said that in sailing to Cape Horn, probably the longest voyage that could be made on this planet, we should encounter much rough weather, but after rounding Cape Horn we should in a short time reach smooth seas and sunny skies, and probably the change would be greater than in going from New York to Cuba, where in one week we go from icicles to oranges.

15: The tempests off Cape Horn were here described by the lecturer, with allusion to the rapid run often made up the west coast of South America, sometimes leaving but a few days between the latitudes of icebergs and oranges.

20: . . . and giving a succinct account of the early voyagers who sailed to the South Seas, touched upon some of the incidents in Captain COOK's and MAGELLAN's explorations, and described in his own inimitable way the beauties of a run through the Tropics. ¶ If you should take sail, he said, and set out for Cape Horn, you would perhaps encounter foul weather, and be subjected to could water treatment in its fullest rigor, but past the Cape the breeze would send you skipping for joy, the weather grow milder and milder: the run from Cape Horn to the Islands is more telling than from New York to Cuba, where you are whisked from icicles to oranges.

21: Gave a graphic description of a sail around Cape Horn, and of the foul weather encountered there, and having doubled the Cape and set sail for the North in the Pacific, you are borne along by fair breezes and have a pleasant voyage, the air growing milder and more mild the farther you go North. Compared this speedy change to that from New York to the South, where in a few hours, as it were, you are transported from icicles to oranges.

PARAGRAPHS 11–12. 412.31–413.8 The European . . . terrible typhoons.]

3: From this he proceeded to portray ship-board life on the Pacific, portions of which were represented as halcyon-like as the Mediterranean.

5: He commenced by giving a brief history of the progress of discovery in the Pacific Ocean, from the time Magellan first entered its quiet waters to the present day.

9: Magellan was the man who, after the first hazardous and tortuous passage through the straits which now bear his name, gave the peaceful ocean to which he came out the name of "Pacific[.]"

12: Magellan being ignorant of an outside passage round Cape Horn, discovered the Straits of Magellan, hardly less dangerous in navigation than the Cape, but made his way at last to the outer sea, and himself called it Pacific, from its tranquil stillness. But the Pacific must have put its best foot foremost when so discovered[.]

15: The European who first sailed upon those waters had this experience intensified. True, Magellan passed not round the yet undiscovered Horn, but through the straits which bear his name. But this only made the matter worse. For, in these straits, narrow, tortuous and rock bound, dense fogs prevail and antarctic squalls, and the navigation is peculiarly dangerous. Magellan worked through, however, and when he beheld ahead a fine open ocean, by good fortune smooth and serene, in his excess of emotion he burst into tears, stout sailor as he was, and this was the man who gave to this sea its second name—Pacific. The great sea then was in a happy humor, and hence received a name which will forever be called Pacific, even by the sailor destined to perish in one of its terrible typhoons.

20: And the first European who sailed through these Southern waters, had the same experience, only more intensified. Magellan instead of going round the Horn, went through the straits, and emerging from the mists saw the sun lighting up the placid fields beyond, he blessed God and called it Pacific. ¶ The Speaker questioned the propriety of the name, and said he had glided through the tropics on the bosom of the Atlantic when the warm air and lulling calm had made him say to himself "come, let us shut up the the temple of Janus and dream." The Pacific when introduced to the public happened to put its best foot foremost, and ever will be called Pacific, even by the sailor who perishes in one of its mighty Typhoons.

21: Dwelt on Magellan's expedition through the Straits of Darien, and how perilous a time he had, in the wilderness and the poisonous miasms of that country. Having reached the Western shores, and being elated with the vision, he burst into transports of joy, and called the ocean Pacific, because it was truly so at the time, the Pacific happening at that time to put her best foot foremost. He here drew a beautiful picture of a sight he once had of the Atlantic, from the deck rail of a steamship, and he thought that it should rather have been named the Pacific. But the names were owing to first impressions, and the Pacific will always be called by that name, even by the sailors who perish in her dreadful typhoons.

PARAGRAPH 13. 413.9–16 Although the Pacific . . . American ships.]

5: It is only since 1848—since the discovery of gold in California—that the civilized world has been brought to a sensible knowledge of this vast expanse of waters.

9: It was California, said the lecturer, which first made the Pacific shores the home of the Anglo-Saxons.

12: In 1780 the accounts of Tahiti, as found in the books of Capt. Cook, were a novelty, and not until the California discovery was made did we possess any special knowledge of the South Seas.

15: Although the Pacific covers half the surface of the planet, yet with all its dotted isles and people it remained almost unknown to even a recent period. Captain Cooke's account of his visit to Tahiti could produce, as late as 1780, upon the English people almost the full thrill of novelty. Indeed, but little was known of the whole region till Cooke's time. It was California that first brought the Pacific home to the great body of Anglo-Saxons.

16: Little was known of the "South Seas" by Americans until 1848.—The discovery of gold in California, in that memorable year, first opened the Pacific and made its waters a thoroughfare for American ships.

18: Comparatively nothing was known of the South Seas up to Cook's expedition, and from that date up to the gold discoveries of California in 1848, little progress had been made in the knowledge of their boundless extent and diversity. California first brought the South Seas into general notice.

21: Little was known of these seas till Captain Cook's time. In 1848 they became more generally known than ever before, through the wonderful exodus that then sailed for California.—But even now there is great ignorance on the subject.

22: [*reprints 18 with one variation:* . . . expedition, aad . . .]

PARAGRAPH 14. 413.17–30 The world . . . a lecture.]

5: Even now its geography is but illy known. The ships which plough it for the most part go in established routes, and those vessels who leave these old roads continually run upon some island or cluster of islands unknown to the charts or to geographers.

6: He felt, in lecturing upon the South Seas, like one embarking on an exploring expedition. . . . He then went on to speak of the vast extent of the Pacific, covering, it was estimated, over a hundred millions of square miles, and said that the modern explorations had not dispelled the mystery which had hung about it.

9: Even now, there were many places in this wide waste of waters which were not found upon the charts. But what was known, and well known, afforded an abundant theme for a lecture.

10: A haze hangs over the remote waters of the Pacific even at the present day, and the number of islands they contain are comparatively but little known.

12: A haze of obscurity seemed to have hung over the whole of these waste of waters.

14: Glancing at the immense extent and number of islands unknown to any chart, . . .

15: The world of water here is so broad and its living races so various, that one is puzzled where to choose his matter for a lecture.

16: The South Seas, or Pacific Ocean, is reckoned to embrace one-half of the earth's surface, or an expanse of one hundred millions of square miles. Explorations have failed to rend away the veil of its mysteries, and every expedition thither has brought discoveries of new islands until on our maps the ink of one is run into another.

18: It is not easy, said the speaker, to decide what topic to select from so vast a storehouse, upon which to expend the limited time of a single leture.

20: He said it was not easy to decide what topic to select from so vast a storehouse upon which to expend the limited time of a single lecture. A haze of obscurity hangs over those waters and this added to the immensity makes one feel in an attempt to speak of them like embarking on a voyage to their far distant isles.

21: He mentioned several groups of islands that are not down on the maps, and said that even underwriters and shipping merchants, if applied to about sailing to some of the islands in those seas, would not have a very distinct idea upon the subject. So with the student, also, and there is no full knowledge to be had of them anywhere. And to him, who had sailed far and wide among them, there is ignorance and mystery with regard to them.

22: *[reprints 18]*

PARAGRAPHS 15–16. 413.31–414.16 We might tell of tribes . . . for research!]

1: He then gave a vivid description of the sword-fish, pelican, and whale, which, upon referring to Buffon, we find to be eminently truthful. . . . and spoke of the "Devil fish," which he did not see.

3: Allusion was made to the atmosphere and waters of this region, the wonderful fishes that populate them—the sharks, sword-fish, devil-fish, &c. He was surprised that Prof. Agassiz did not take his carpet-bag and go to Nantucket, thence to these regions where there was so much to be learned and studied.

4: Its natural phenomena, its fishes and birds were dwelt upon at some length.

6: He might confine his lecture to the fish of those seas—the sword-fish, unlike the fish of that name in our waters, after stabbing vessels and leaving his sword broken off in the ship, or at other times withdrawing it, leaving an open wound, to the infinite terror of the seamen—the devil-fish—or he might occupy whole hours about the birds, or the whaling voyages of those seas or the Polynesian Islands.

9: The fish found in those waters, he said, would furnish an abundant subject, of which he named the sword fish, a different fish from that of the same name found in our northern latitudes—and the devil-fish, over which a mystery hung, like that over the sea-serpent in northern waters. The birds, also, of those latitudes might occupy a full hour. The lecturer said he wondered that the renowned Agassiz did not pack his carpet bag and betake himself to Nantucket, and from thence to the South Seas, than which he could find no richer field.

10: The lecturer spoke of different kinds of fish which are common in certain latitudes; among the number was the devil-fish, over which a degree of obscurity hangs like that of our sea-serpent. It is asserted by some mariners that these devil-fish have horns and mouths like those in the Mississippi. When off the coast of Patagonia, on one occasion, early in the evening, the lecturer heard a strange, roaring noise, and saw a bright train of light shoot along the water; the old boatswain, who was standing by, declared it was a devil-fish. On another occasion the lecturer saw, a few feet beneath the surface, a large, lazy, sleepy-looking object, and was told that that too was a devil-fish. He was surprised that Agassiz did not pack his carpet bag and ship for the South Sea where he could find such a vast field for research.

11: . . . with some notice of the curious and rare fishes which inhabit those waters, . . .

12: The natural phenomena of the water and air; the finny tribes which inhabited the ocean, particularly the vast body of sharks, devil-fish (which might well afford room for the researches of an Agassiz); . . .

13: His descriptions of the phenomena observed in this region—of the curious fish and monsters that sport in its waters . . .

14: . . . with a glimpse of the world of wonders in Ichthyology, and a recommendation to Agassiz to embark at Nantucket, in a whaler, for a tour of observation, Mr. Melville ran lightly over some of the more recent topics suggested by the islands.

15: We might tell of tribes of sharks that populate some parts of the Pacific as thickly as the celestials do the Chinese Empire, or we might introduce that gallant chevalier, the swordfish—the Hector of the seas—and tell of his martial exploits; the tilts he runs at the great ships; the duels he fights with them—sometimes leaving his weapon in their ribs, or by withdrawing it, leaving an open wound, to the great peril of the craft and crew, as in the case of the English ship Foxhound. We might tell of the devil fish, which sailors say, dives to the profoundest abyss and comes up roaring with mouths as many and as wide open as the Mississippi.

16: Much might be said of the finny inhabitants of this waste of waters—of the sword-fish, and the tilts he runs with ships; of the devil-fish, and the weird yarns of the sailors concerning him. The lecturer only wondered the great naturalist, Agazzis, did not pack his carpet bag and betake him to Nantucket, and from thence to the South Seas—the argosy of wonders.

18: We might dwell upon the fish which people those unmeasured depths—the "south sea shark" as populous in those waters as the Chinese in China, the sword fish that Hector of the ocean with his daring til[t]s at great ships and his duels with the whale, the devil fish as strange a monster as the sea-serpent of Atlantic navigators.

20: He might dwell upon the fish which people those unmeasured depths—the south Sea sharks, as populous in those waters as the Chinese in China; the sword fish, that Hector of the deep, with his daring tilts at great ships and his duels with the whale oftentime returning from the combat leaving his sword in the mass of flesh or wood.

21: He spoke of the natural phenomena of the water and air of those seas; of the fish, the sharks, the sword-fish, differing from those north. Those in the

South Seas are more daring, and fight their duels, and run tilts with their companions of the sea, making terrible havoc with one another. Then there is the devil-fish, of which he drew a most fearfully unfavorable picture for his Satanic fishship. Some say he has horns, huge fins, cloven hoofs &c., said the speaker, but of that he could not say. He did remember, however, that once when off Patagonia, he and his shipmates were upon the deck of the vessel listening to a solemn ghost story from one of the crew, when he heard an awful roaring sound, something like a compromise between the snorting of a leviathan and the belching of a Vesuvius, and the grizzly boatswain started and exclaimed, "There, that's a devil-fish!" He also mentioned other incidents to the detriment of the devil-fish. He was surprised that Agassiz, the great naturalist, did not go to the South Seas to add to his vast stores of knowledge.

22: [*reprints 18 with these variations:* . . . shark," . . . fish, . . . ocean, . . . tilts . . .]

23: The next twenty minutes were occupied in telling what *might* be said if there were time to say it in during the evening, which, happy for the audience, there was not, . . .

24: The middle portion was made up of a few *inklings* of what he saw, and what he *might* have said on what he saw, *if he had time!* Here we noticed an inconsistency. He was constantly telling that he must omit much that he would like to say, but never for once did an omission in his speech make an advance in his manuscript. The omissions were not put in.

PARAGRAPHS 17–18. 414.17–37 We might speak . . . but themselves.]

3: Then, too, the birds, so rare and beautiful: the philosophic phenomena: the adventures of the whalers, . . .

9: Full of interest, also, were the fisheries of the South Sea, and the life of the whaling crews, on the broad waters, or visiting lands, seldom, if ever, touched by any but themselves, was covered over with a charm of novelty.

10: The birds, too, were peculiar[.] Sometimes strange phosphoric phenomena are seen on these waters in certain latitudes. The lecturer was once in a whaleboat, at midnight, when for a time having lost the ship, a light burst upon the boat's crew with a sudden gleam and the men in the boat presented a pallid appearance, looking like so many corpses.

11: . . . and the many beautiful, as well as strange, birds which are so numerous in those islands.

12: . . . the birds, in their endless variety, the exceptional phenomena, . . .

13: —of the mysterious phosphoric lights that mingle with its waves—of the rare birds that flit above its surface, were replete with interest.

15: The Pelican, with his pouch stuffed with game like a sportsman's bag; the melancholy penguin standing on one spot all day with a fit of the blues; the man-of-war hawk, that fierce black bandit; and the storied Albatross, with white and arching wing like an Archangel's, his haughty beak curved like a scimeter. Yes, a whole hour might be spent in telling about either the fishes or the birds. Furthermore, there are exceptional phenomena, such as the peculiar phosphoric aspect of the water sometimes. I have been in a whale-boat at midnight when, having lost the ship we would keep steering through the lonely night for her, while the sea that weltered by us would pres[e]nt the pallid look of the face of a corpse, and lit by its spectral gleam we men on the boat showed to each other like so many weather-beaten ghosts. Then to mark Leviathan come wallowing along, dashing the pale sea into sparkling cascades of fire, showering it all over him till the monster would look like Milton's Satan, riding the flame billows of the infernal world. We might fill night after night with that fertile theme, the whaling voyage. The adventurous sailors, either on the blank face of the waters, where often for months together their ship floats lonely as the ark of Noah, or in their intercou[r]se with the natives of coasts reached by few or none but themselves.

16: The birds, also, in their variety and strange plumage—birds never seen elsewhere—were a study.

18: We might speak particularly of the birds—the pelican with his leather gamebag, the cape-pigeons, the war-hawk black pirate of the feathered races, or the white winged albatross of the "Ancient Mariner." Or again, the time might be given to tales of the waters themselves,—the phosphoric depths whose color most nearly resembled the face of a corpse, the leagues of ocean impregnated with bitumen of inky blackness. Or tales might be told by the hour of the adventures of whalemen in those wondrous latitudes.

20: He might speak of the birds, or again the time might be given to tales of the waters themselves, the phosphorescent depths whose ghastly flash lights up the whalers in the boat at night with a spectral glare, and the ship like a leviathan comes plashing through cascades of light, or he might tell tales by the hour of the whalemen, in those wondrous latitudes.

21: He next mentioned the birds of those seas—the pelican, the penguin, the man-of-war hawk, the albatross, with her white wing and snowy plumage, and many others, and so he could mention them by the hour. He then spoke of the phosphoric phenomena of the Seas, giving a spirited and brilliant description of a whaling adventure in the night, and said that he might spend an evening or two recounting similar adventures.

22: [*reprints 18 with these variations:* . . . war-hawk, . . . themselves— . . . wondrous waters.]

PARAGRAPHS 19–21. 414.38–415.22 The islands . . . with grass.]

3: . . . the countless islands in their vast clusters—each of which would afford entertainment for a whole evening. Some of the Polynesian groups were decided as among the most beautiful in the world.

4: The islands, however, constituted its most remarkable feature, and presented, he said, some of the most sublime specimens of natural beauty to be found on the globe.

5: It is an erroneous idea to picture the islands of the Pacific as low tracts, barely rising above the surface, and reposing as it were in quiet beauty upon its bosom. There are a few coral islands of this character; but for the most part they present a bold shore of rocky cliffs, here and there breaking away and receding into beautiful ravines, further inland rising into lofty mountain summits, which stand as gigantic chimney stacks to give vent to internal fires of the earth, to whose force they owe their existence.

6: The lecturer dwelt at some length upon the great beauty of these, in many respects, superior to any yet discovered in the world.

9: Again, the islands were an interesting study.

10: In speaking of the Islands, the lecturer said that the Polynesian Archipelago was the most striking in the world.

11: These islands, occupying so large a space in the Pacific waters, offer rare attractions to the traveler seeking after unknown and untried scenes of interest. New beauties present themselves continually, and nature seems to hav[e] decorated their hills and valleys with a most lavish hand.

12: . . . the countless number of islands which dot its surface, all these might afford subjects of studious investigation. A map gave no idea of the extent of the islands. Polynesia, hinted in its very name, at the immensity of their number.

15: The islands, too, are an endless theme; thick as the stars in the milky way. The name bestowed upon their swarming clusters—Polynesia, not inaptly hints at their numberlessness. ¶ The most noted of these are the Sandwich and Society groups; the Friendly, Navigator and Feejee clusters; the Pelew, Ladrone, Mulgrave, Kingsmills and Radack chains—but there are more than Briareus could number on all his finger ends. ¶ The popular notion, from the early vague accounts, imagines them to hold enamelled plains, with groves of shadowing palms, watered by purling brooks and the country but little elevated. The reverse of this is true: bold rock-bound coasts—a beating surf—lofty and craggy cliffs, split here and there into deep inlets opening to the view deeper vallies parted by masses of emerald mountains sweeping seaward from an interior of lofty peaks. ¶ But, would you get the best water view of a Polynesian Island, select one with a natural breakwater of surf-beaten coral all around it, leaving within a smooth, circular canal, broad and deep, entrance to which is had through natural sea-gates. Lounging in a canoe, there is nothing more pleasant than to float along—especially where Boraborra, and Tahar [Otaha], the glorious twins of the Society group, rear their lofty masses to the ever vernal heights, belted about by the same zone of reef—the reef itself being dotted with small islets perpetually thick and green with grass.

16: . . . the Archipelagoes and the Polynesian isles that lie scattered through that ocean, like stars in the heavens.

18: No notion of the number of islands in the South Seas can be gathered from a glance at the map. If not innumerable, they are certainly unnumbered. The chief groups are the Sandwich, the Society, the Georgian, the Phillipian, the Ladrone, the Marquesas, the Caroline, and the Friendly Isles. The man who called them *Polynesia* gave them a proper designation. We are apt, in our imaginings of those distant shores, to picture enameled caves and pearly brooks, and valleys of sylvan sweetness. Yet their distinctive features are lofty broken coasts, and deep and abrupt valleys. Sublimity, rather than graceful beauty, is their marked natural characteristic.

20: One gets no idea by the map, of the immense multitude of these islands. They are blended together in a dark indistinctness.—No one would attempt to count them on his fingers, even were he Briarius, with a hundred hands. ¶ He spoke of the scenery as more sublime than beautiful, of the islands with natural breakwaters of coral, along whose side one might lounge in a canoe and in vain try to fancy anything more pleasant.

21: The islands of the South Seas are like the stars in the milky way, and could not be counted by the fingers, even were he Briareus, with a hundred hands. He mentioned the names of many of them, and said we were apt to draw high colors of them in our fancy flights, and to imagine them low, smooth beds of verdure, just elevated above the level of the sea.—Though this might be true, in some respects, of the coral isles, yet the most of them have bold coasts, towering mountains, lofty cliffs with deep inlets, and similar features. The group comprising the Polynesian Archipelago are the most striking in the world.

22: [*reprints 18 with two variations:* . . . Friendly Isles, . . . apt in . . .]

PARAGRAPHS 22–23. 415.23–416.3 The virgin . . . and innocent?]

1: Of course, he could not forbear making a splenetic al[l]usion to the missionaries, concerning whom his feelings are well-known, and are too bitter to be impersonal. He spoke indirectly of the destruction of Malolo by the U. S. Squadron, in 1840, placing it in the light of an atrocity rather than a just punishment. We would remind our readers that the *slight* offence of the natives consisted in killing two officers of the Squadron, in an outrageous manner. Nor was this the first crime; for a long time murder after murder had been committed and passed unnoticed, till affairs were at such a crisis as to render it unsafe for ships and crews. The prevention of further evil was one avowed object of the Expedition. However severe the punishment may have been, the benefit is now being reaped in the totally different state of things.

3: The lecturer asked why some of those Englishmen who owned large yachts, and went up the Mediterranean, did not go among these islands? But, he continued, the whites are in extremely bad favor among these islands. Christians, so called, were regarded instinctively with abhorrence.

6: He wondered why Englishmen, who went yachting in various waters in Europe, did not sail among the Polynesian islands of the South Seas.

9: Why, asked the lecturer, do not those Englishmen, who own large yachts with which they sail up the Mediterranean, why don't they go yachting in the South Seas? The white race have a very bad reputation among the [P]olynesians. With few exceptions they were considered the most blood-thirsty, atrocious and diabolical race in the world. But there was no danger to voyagers if they treated the natives with common kindness.

10: The Polynesians, however, deem the whites the most barbarous, diabolical and dangerous characters on the face of the earth.

15: The virgin freshness of these unviolated wastes—the exemption of those far-off archipelago[e]s from the heat and dust of civilization, act sometimes as the last provocative to those jaded tourists to whom even Europe has become hackneyed, and who look upon the Parthenon and the Pyramids with a yawn. ¶ Why don't the English yachters give up the prosy Mediterranean and sail out here? Any one who treats the natives fairly is just as safe here as if he were on the Nile or Danube. But I am sorry to say we whites have a sad reputation among many of the Polynesians. They esteem us, with rare exceptions, such as *some* of the missionaries, the most barbarous, treacherous, irreligious and devilish creatures on the earth. It may be a mere prejudice of these unlettered savages, for have not our traders always treated them with brotherly affection? Who has ever heard of a vessel sustaining the honor of a Christian flag and the spirit of the Christian Gospel by opening its batteries in indiscriminate massacre upon some poor little village on the seaside,—splattering the torn bamboo huts with blood and brains of women and children, defenceless and innocent?

18: The natives of these islands are naturally of a kindly and hospitable temper, but there has been implanted among them an almost instinctive hate of the white race. The vengeance not infrequently taken on whole villages for some private injury or crime, is remembered from generation to generation, and the resentment provoked by the bombardment or sacking of an inoffensive town, where bamboo huts have been sprinkled with the blood and brains of women and children, stands ready to be wreaked upon the first unfortunate pale face cast upon their shores.

21: He wondered that the English, who go on great yacht voyages, do not make trips to the South Seas. As long as we treat the natives with kindness, it would be safe. But they have many wrongs to remember at the hands of the whites. Many of the Polynesians think us the most barbarous, villainous, and diabolical race of people on the globe. In many cases this feeling seems like instinct, but in most of course it is prejudice.

22: *[reprints 18]*

PARAGRAPH 24. 416.4–20 New and strange . . . sometimes found.]

5: It was upon one of the many islands of the South Seas, that Christian, one of the famous mutineers of the Bounty, desired to found a little State, and to live shut out from the rest of the world. Indeed it is no difficult thing for a company of mutineers to bury themselves in the interior of one of these little worlds, and live undiscovered by navigators, who at most, scarcely leave the beach, if perchance they should land for fruit or water. Such colonies are sometimes found.

9: In the Pacif[i]c there were yet many unknown and unvisited isles. There were many places where a man might make himself a sylvan retreat and for years, at least, live as much removed from Christendom as if in another world.

12: After a brief description of the appearance of these islands, of their excellent natural facilities, the lecturer glanced at the character and habits of the inhabitants, their progress in civilization, &c. In 1824 several buccaneers first cherished the idea of creating a home in the South Sea Islands and emigration thither had since rapidly increased.

15: We have not space to follow the speaker fully in the remainder of his lecture, in which he graphically described the boundless expanse of the Pacific and its myriad islands as a hiding place as far removed from the life of the great world as though its people dwelt upon another planet. This mantle of mystery long hid the Buccaneers, who plundered the Spanish commerce; and covered for years Christian, the mutineer of the Bounty, who, after a life of exile and immunity from European law, was found, bent with age, amid a thriving colony of half-breed children and grandchildren, whom his savage wives had reared for him amid ever-green woods, under ever-healthful skies, and through the plenty of perpetual harvests.

16: A lone inhabitant on one of these islands would be as effectually separated from his fellow man as the inhabitant of another world.

18: New and strange islands are being continually discovered in the South Seas—as secluded and secure as though planted in another world. And there are still others unknown and undiscovered, respecting which our charts are as guiltless as the maps of the world in Plato's time, when the pillars of Hercules were the western verge of the orbit.

22: *[reprints 18]*

PARAGRAPHS 25–26. 416.21–417.20 Then, too . . . the natives.]

1: Mr. Me[l]ville mentioned, with a feeling that did him credit, his friend the King of the Cannibal Islands, or Marquesas, we are not sure which, and the King's great dislike to Fourinism *[i.e.* Fourierism] and Polygamy. We had supposed that his majesty and subjects were rather practically fond of both these institutions, but we may be mistaken.

3: The virgin freshness of those vast regions were pictured in glowing terms, the only drawback in visiting it being the danger of becoming subjects of the insatiable cannibals. The Tyees were described as a virtuous and gentlemanly people, when they took a notion to be, but somewhat fickle and uncertain.

5: It has been suggested that these islands would make good homes for thriving colonies of Free-Lovers, or Mormons, who could there show forth to the world the benefits of their peculiar religious views.

9: The lecturer described an interview he had with a poetical young man who called upon him to get his opinion upon what would be the prospects of a number, say five score, of disciples of Fourier to settle in the valley of Typee. He had not encouraged the scheme, having too much regard for his old friends, the Polynesians. The Mormons had also had such a scheme in view—to discover a large island in the Pacific, upon which they could increase and multiply.

10: The lecturer was once visited by a youthful poet, dulcet voiced and of mystic appearance, who wished to ascertain what the chances would be for a select company of seventy or eighty Fourierites on some of the South Pacific Islands, more particularly in the Valley of the Typee. The lecturer took occasion to advance his views on the subject, and to discourage the rash young man from contemplating any such scheme.

12: Parties of Fourierites had looked to Typhee as their future paradise, but the natives would never tolerate any new fangled notions of the social state; they would reject all "fillibusters," and resist their encroachments as did the Staten Islanders that of Quarantine.

14: He appeared a little disposed to dash the imaginative views of the socialistic philosophers who look upon these spots as future elysian havens for the race. He had been waited upon, shortly after the publication of "Typee," by a pale, bearded philosopher, a disciple of Fourier, who asked for more particular information as to the prospects of a party emigrating to the Marquesas. He replied that his old friends, the Typees, were undoubtedly good fellows, with strong points for admiration; that their king was as faithful to his friend as to his bottle, but that the treatment he and his crony received at their hands hardly warranted the success of a larger expedition, who might be taken as invaders and possibly eaten. The Free Lovers of the West and the Mormons had thought of these secluded islands, or they had been recommended to them—showing the drifting of imagination in that direction. An acquaintance whom he met in Italy, who had exhausted Jerusalem and Baalbec, and, like the man in the play, looked into Vesuvius and found "nothing in it," had, after an hour or two in conversation with him, started from an Italian port for Rio en route to the Pacific. The lecturer charitably hoped he had steered clear of the cannibals.

15: The Lecturer then spoke of the projects of some Reformers who, despairing of civilising Europe or America according to their rule, projected establishments in the Pacific where they hoped to find a fitting place for the good time coming.

16: They would be good asylums, the lecturer said, for the free lovers and Mormons to rear their pest houses in—provided the natives, degraded as they are, did not object.

18: The speaker referred to the plan suggested, not long since, of making a home for the Mormons on some island in Polynesia, where they could carry their pest houses and be at peace with their "institutions." But he did not know of an island in the 100,000,000 of square miles embraced in the South Seas, where they would not be imperatively and indignantly expelled by the natives.

19: . . . such bombast as his asserted reply to the young Fourierite.

20: After alluding to the proposition, a young man, with poetic look, a dulcet voice and Armenian beard, once made him to establish a Fourier sect in Polynesia.

21: —He took off, admirably, the vagueness that exists in the minds of almost every one, about those seas, but said that was fast wearing away. Mentioned several instances of young men about to rush with enthusiasm to the South Seas, with the fanciful idea that they would there find a Paradise. Those who had gone he hoped had not fallen among the cannibals. ¶ He said he was in confidence with the king of Typee, and that he was a man of much merit. Those people have kind hearts, natural urbanity, and are gentlemen by nature. But they have their eccentricities, are quick to anger, and are eminently conservative, and sometimes do not hesitate to put a human being out of the way without the benefit of a trial by jury. The kind way in which they treated my comrade and myself, furnishes little indication of how they would treat others. A company of Free Lovers in Ohio had proposed to go there, and so had the Mormons of Salt Lake. He could imagine the peril that a few ship loads of Free Lovers would be in, on touching the Polynesian Isles. If sensible men wish to appropriate to themselves an uninhabited isle, it is all right, but they have no right to all the Pacific.

22: [*reprints 18 with one variation:* . . . miles in . . .]

23: . . . and the last twenty minutes were filled up with old historical incidents, as before mentioned, coupled with gratuitous advice to Reformers not to think of locating in any of the Islands of the South Seas, which in general were inhabited by a very sensible people, particularly the Typee's, the confidence of whose government—incautiously let out as a diplomatic secret—the lecturer fully enjoyed.

24: . . . and generous advice to Mormons, Free Lovers, and other Reformers, as to the impracticability of their attempting to locate thereon.

PARAGRAPH 27. 417.21–28 While our . . . his discoveries.]

9: The Polynesians themselves have ideas of the same nature. Every one has heard of the voyage of Ponce de Leon to Florida to find the fountain of perpetual youth. Equally poetical, and more unfamiliar, was the adventure of Cama Pecai [*i.e.* Kamapiikai], who set sail alone from Hawaii to find the fount of eternal joy, which was supposed to spring up in some distant island where the people lived in continual joy and youth. Like all who go to Paradise, he was never heard from again.

12: While our visionaries had been looking to the South Seas as a sort of Elysium, the Polynesians also had their Utopia in the West.
15: The Polynesians themselves, he said, were not without their dream, their ideal, their Utopia. As Ponce de Leon hoped to find in Florida the fountain of perpetual youth, so the mystic Kamapuhai [*i.e.* Kamapiikai] left the western shore of the island where he suffered with his restless philosophy and hoping to find the joy-giving fountain and the people like to the Gods, sailed after the sinking sun, and has not yet returned to cheer mankind with his discoveries.
16: The lecturer spoke of several adventurers who went in search of mystical spots, said to be embosomed somewhere in these seas. They were like those who went to Paradise—they probably found the good they sought, for they never returned more.
21: He adverted to a Polynesian Ponce de Leon, a certain Prince of the Sandwich Islands, who like Ponce de Leon of old, went wandering among the isles of the seas, in search of a joy-giving fount in which he could renew his youth. Whether he found it or not he did not know, for he was never heard of again; but this did not preclude the probability that he found it, for those who go to Paradise, are heard of no more.

PARAGRAPH 28. 417.29–39 Another strange . . . the event.]
12: Two hundred years ago Albano [*i.e.* Alvaro] Mendana embarked from a port in Peru for the seas in search of the material which Solomon employed in his temple; but Mendanus sickened and died, and his followers returned to Peru strongly impressed with the truth of the Scripture "Vanity of vanities, all is vanity." A group of the isles was called Solomon's in commemoration of the event.
15: Another strange quest was that of Alvaro, a bold Spanish Captain, who stirred up such enthusiasm among the courtly Dons and Donnas of his time that many of them joined his expedition, in which he was sure he would find the Phœnician Ophir of King Hiram and bring from it more than the treasure stores with which Solomon had beautified his temple. After months and months of voyaging with hope deferred, the mines of Mammon were not found, and the poor Captain dying, was buried in the solitude of an unfathomed sea.
21: So an adventurer of Peru once embarked for the waters of the South Seas, to find the Scriptural Ophir, and many went with him to make their fortunes in solid ingot of gold. But their leader perished after a while, and the remainder got back to Peru, to think of the Hebrew King, as the author of the proverb, "Vanity, vanity, all is vanity."

PARAGRAPH 29. 418.1–21 There are . . . restless ambition.]
3: There were two places where men might effectively disappear—the city of London and the Pacific Ocean. Among these islands were often found white men.

While on a voyage, the lecturer went ashore to a distant island, occupied by a pensive race of some 60 persons—a pensive race, who do nothing, and looked as though they would like to get rid of doing that. And yet here they found a white man settled down for life, having three wives, and living in luxurious ease.

5: In cruising around in these seas one frequently meets with a sort of inexplicable class of people. It was the lecturer's fortune on one occasion to fall in with a person, whose wardrobe three wives should have kept in better repair, who manifested no ordinary intelligence. He stated that he had formerly resided in the more civilized portions of the world, and had fulfilled the post of professor of moral philosophy in some college whose name he wisely withheld; he was, however, contented to lead a quiet and lazy life, apart from the walks of restless ambition.

9: A tranquil scene from the South Sea Islands was remembered by the lecturer. In a ship from a port of the Pacific coast he had sailed five months, and come upon an island where the natives lived in a state of total laziness. Here they found a white man who was a permanent inhabitant, and comfortably settled with three wives, who, however, failed to keep his wardrobe in good order.

12: There were two places where men disappeared, London and the Pacific Ocean. Men every year were lost to home, who had scattered themselves about the isles. The lecturer in a recent tour around one of them, found, dwelling alone among the savages, a white man, to all appearances fully *naturalized,* clothed in rags, which might have been "signs of distress." This fellow was a Professor of Moral Philosophy, whose name had been suppressed.

14: There were two places in the world, said Mr. Melville, where a man might lie concealed—in London and the South Seas. Various and extraordinary were the waifs and strays of humanity which turned up in traversing those waters. He remembered once, after five months weary navigation out of sight of land, turning to a secluded island in search of fruit. The pensive natives lay upon the bank, gazing listlessly, hardly turning on their mats at their landing, for they had seen white men before. There, in that remote island, among its sixty or seventy lazy inhabitants, he found an American, not imposing in his breech cloth and the scanty shreds of tappa which hung from his shoulders as signals of distress, which, it appeared to the traveller, the assiduous diligence of three wives—for the ill-clothed gentleman was blessed with that number—might have remedied. On conversation it came to light that this virtuous exile from civilization had been Professor of Moral Philosophy in a college in his own land; though, for the credit of the country, he did not mention the name of the institution.

15: There is no such hiding place on earth, said the lecturer, except the solitude of London.

16: There were only two places where adventurers can most effectually disappear, and they are London and the South Seas.

21: He said there were two places where men often disappear, and are never again heard of; that is in London and the Pacific ocean. Many of the seamen who are supposed to be lost, are on the islands of this ocean, while many are in graves upon land, or have been eaten by the fish of the sea. Many are living there as permanent residents, while some hope to return some day. He spoke of a white man he once found upon an island in the Pacific, who said he had been a Professor of Moral Philosophy in some Eastern Institution of learning. He was almost naked, and had three wives, who should have seen better to his wardrobe, said the lecturer. To all appearance he was quite cultivated.

PARAGRAPH 30. 418.22–32 The modes . . . Committee there.]

9: The manners of death in the South Seas were various and singular. That class of men were spoken of which we hear occasionally, and seldom in any good connection—the beech-combers of the Pacific, who were adventurers of the most unprincipled character.

16: The lecturer spoke of the "beach hovers," a class of adventurers, or those cast by accident or chance upon the Polynesian Isles. This cognomen was derived from the fact that they always hovered upon the shores, and seemed every moment on the point of embarking or disembarking.

21: The modes in which seamen disappear in the Pacific are various. ¶ Some fall overboard, some are left by unprincipled captains, some are killed in brawls, &c. He alluded to the class known as Beech-combers, who infest the shores of the Pacific, who are ready for anything, for a war in Peru, a whaling voyage, or to marry a Polynesian princess. They were among the first in California in the gold times, and afforded subjects for strange newspaper stories. They were also the occasion, as much as anything, of the Vigilance Committee in California.

PARAGRAPHS 31–32. 418.33–419.11 I have . . . a gridiron.]

1: . . . Mr. Melville's Polynesi[a]n friends consider tattooing necessary for admission to Paradise, and wished him to be tattooed, as, we presume, his last chance, but Mr. Melville preferred trying his luck without it. . . . Mr. Melville also mentioned a love story, peculiarly adapted to ladies, which he would not tell, . . .

6: Various matters connected with his own experience in those waters were given, . . .

9: Wonderful tales were told of adventures in the South Sea, and the lecturer said he believed that the books "Typee" and "Omee" gave scarcely a full idea of them except, perhaps, that part which tells of the long captivity in the valley of Typee. He had seen many of these story tellers of adventures in the South Seas with good vouchers of their tales in the shape of tattooing. . . . The lecturer had successfully combated all attempts to naturalize him by marks as from a gridiron, on his face, for which he thanked God.

10: In speaking of the strange stories that are told of Islands in the Pacific, the lecturer said he had met many an old sailor, who was not sufficiently educated to write, but who could tell stories stranger than any that have ever yet been written.
12: His countenance was so disfigured that as a tattoed citizen he would never have shown his face on Broadway. This custom of tattoeing was prompted by a concern for a man's spiritual state. If a man died without being tattoed he would most surely be damned.
13: . . . and related some "yarns" that bordered upon the "Munchausen," though they were undoubtedly true. Mr. Melville said that many old sailors could tell tales about these regions stranger than any that had yet been written.
16: He also alluded to the natives and their modes of tattooing. Unless a man submits to be tattooed, he is looked upon as damned, which was the case with the speaker, as he frequently resisted the importunities of the native artists to sit.
18: Mr. Melville made some allusions to his own experiences as detailed in "Typee," not abating anything from the marvels there narrated, but declaring on the contrary that he had found adventures in the South Seas far surpassing anything ever appearing in print, in strangeness and incredibility—and not only himself but many others he had met, who had passed months or years in those balmy lands.
21: Spoke of the many strange characters he had met, whose experiences if written out, would form volumes of weird, wild and fanciful interest. Spoke of a manuscript tradition he had [s]een that was told by a King of one of those Islands. It had much of the grace, strangeness and audacity of the Grecian Fables. Some of these strange characters whom he had met, exhibited sure vouchers of their stories, in the tattooing upon their persons. Many of them present such a horrid fright, that they will never be caught showing their faces—well at the table of the Newhall House. ¶ Their disfigurements are sometimes prompted by religion, love of novelty, and various causes. Many of them think it is necessary for their eternal welfare, and in their opinion I may now be in peril, for I stoutly resisted everything of the kind.
22: [*reprints 18 with one variation:* . . . experience . . .]

PARAGRAPHS 33–34. 419.12–29 Different islanders . . . wears them.]
1: His account of tattooing was fine, and corroborated in every particular by Lieut. Wilkes in his Narrative of the U. S. Exploring Expedition. Thus we learn that some of the natives wear a regimental stripe on their flesh tights; that others have representations of nuts and figs painted on their chests, which denote that they are very fond of figs and nuts; . . .
3: Some of the religious systems of the Polynesians were mentioned, and their peculiarities alluded to. Among the signs of religion was the tattooing process, which indicated the different degrees of piety. The relation of tattooing and character were amusingly referred to.
4: He also gave a graphic and humorous description of the natives and their

habits and customs. The various processes of tattooing peculiar to these islands, were also noted and explained.

9: A full and interesting description of the process of tattooing with its various styles was given. Tattooing was sometimes, like dress, an index of character, and worn as an ornament which would never wear off, and could not be pawned, lost or stolen.

11: Mr. Melville also gave a slight sketch of the manners, customs and religious belief of the inhabitants of the different groups of islands, relating many interesting incidents concerning them.

12: Each island was distinguished by its tattoeing, and the character was indexed by it. A brief notice was made of the styles and uses of tattoeing.

13: The lecturer also gave an account of the manners, customs and religion of the various islands of the South Sea, . . .

15: —Graphic descriptions were given of the graceful forms of the Polynesian women, and the splendid figures of the men, with their symmetrical and columnar legs.

16: The tattooing, like the uniform of a soldier, is here symbolical of the Isle, or class to which the person belongs.

18: He also gave an amusing sketch of the tattooing propensities of the various tribes—islands being often distinctively known by their tattoos.

20: He narrated some of the peculiarities of the tribes in the South Seas, . . .

21: Different islanders have a different style of tattooing. So that you can often tell by this to what island one belongs.—The tattooing of the New Zealander and the Tahitian are as different as some paintings differ. A New Zealander presents a horrifying picture, but some of the Marquesan natives have a pleasant appearance. He has seen among them as graceful a young girl's foot and as delicately-turned ankle as those of the Grecian girls whose duplicate statues adorn the galleries of Europe. ¶ Some of the tattooing is grotesque. In the Georgian Isles the dandies have stripes up and down their legs like pantaloons. The dames have characters on their skin for jewelry, on their fingers, about their necks, &c., and he thought that style of rings had many advantages for a nuptial ring, since it could never be removed. Some of the robust islanders have military characters, others of eatables, others of school-boy trinkets—all reveal the character of each one they are on.

22: *[reprints 18]*

24: The latter portion of the lecture was made up of the announcement that the inhabitants of the different South Sea Islands were different in their manners and customs, and had many traditions, not one of which did he give us, . . .

PARAGRAPH 35. 419.30–33 I would . . . needless recital.]

1: He alluded to some legends he had plucked from the native lore, which would cause excellent Mrs. Radcliffe to shake in her stockings, and, told by the dim gas light, would force even the bravest heart to

"Quake
And tremble like a leaf of aspen green."

18: He said he would direct the gas to be turned down, and repeat to his audience in a whisper the mysterious rites of the "taboo," but the relation would so far transcend any of Mrs. Ratcliffe's stories in the element of the horrible, that he would not willingly afflict any one with its needless recital.
20: . . . and mysteriously hinted about the awful ceremony of taboo.
21: He would pass over the dread taboo.
22: [*reprints 18 with one variation:* . . . myster[i]ous . . .]

PARAGRAPHS 36–37. 419.34–420.28 By contrast . . . and hospitals.]
1: Mr. Melville closed his lecture by desiring all good people to join in the prayer, that those Islands of the South Sea, which were yet in their natural condition should ever so remain, that their innocence and repose should be neither destroyed nor disturbed, that they might be preserved from the misery of enlightenment. The good people did not say "Amen."
3: The progress in some of these islands was seen in the publication of newspapers; but on close inspection the lecturer often found these were conducted by Americans, English or French. The lecturer, in concluding, hoped that these islands, many of which were yet uncultivated by the contact of civilization, would long remain in their simplicity, beauty and purity.
4: In conclusion, the lecturer spoke of the projects recently set on foot for annexing the Sandwich Islands and others to the United States. As a philanthropist in general, and a friend to the Polynesians in particular, he hoped, that these Edens of the South Seas, blessed with fertile soils and peopled with happy natives, would long be preserved from the contaminating influence of foreign powers.
9: A brief notice was made of the Islands of the Pacific, where the Anglo-Saxons had settled, and civilized the people, and the lecturer had been disgusted, and thrown down a paper published in the Sandwich Islands, which suggested the propriety of not having the *native language* taught in the common schools! ¶ In conclusion, the lecturer spoke of the desire of the natives of Georges Island to be annexed to the United States. He was sorry to see it, and, as a friend of humanity, and especially, as a friend of the South Sea Islanders, he should pray, and call upon all Christians to pray with him, that the Polynesians might be delivered from all foreign and contaminating influences.
12: In conclusion Mr. Melville considered the present condition and future prospect of the Island[s]. A Honolulu paper was a mark of the nation's prosperity, but he was pained to see an advertisement in it for the exclusion of children from the public schools who spoke the Hawaiian language. Should the language be done away with, the future obliteration of the r[a]ce would be sure. The future prospects of Polynesia were uncertain and would only admit of fanciful speculation. Projects

had been made to annex Hawaii and the Georgian islands to the United States, but the speaker pra[y]ed that the Edens of the South Sea might never be entangled with any foreign alliance, or other demoralizing association.

14: The results of civilization, at the Sandwich Islands and elsewhere, Mr. Melville found productive to the civilizers, destructive to the civilizees. It was said to be compensation—a very philosophical word; but to the lecturer it appeared very much on the principle of the old game, "You lose, I win;" good philosophy for the winner. With a humorous and well wrought out exhibition of the various fashions and stripes of tattooing in the different islands, Mr. Melville concluded . . .

15: The rapid advance, in the externals only, of civilized life was then spoken of, and the prospect of annexing the Sandwich Islands to the American Union commented on, with the remark that the whalemen of Nantucket and the Westward ho! of California were every day getting them more and more annexed. ¶ The lecturer closed with an earnest wish that adventurers from our soil and from the lands of Europe would abstain from those brutal and cruel vices which disgust even savages with our manners, while they turn an earthly paradise into a pandemonium. And as for annexation he begged, as a general philanthropist, to offer up an earnest prayer, and he entreated all present to join him in it, that the banns of that union should be forbidden until *we* had found for ourselves a civilization moral, mental and physical, higher than one which has culminated in almshouses, prisons and hospitals.

21: Recently he had met with a Honolulu paper, the Honolulu Advertiser, which looked like a city paper, and was almost a counterpart of the London Times, with its advertisements, arrivals and departures of vessels &c., and that, too, where not long since the inhabitants were cannibals. ¶ But now Americans and other foreigners are there, and lately a proposition had been made to abolish the Hawaian language in their schools. He threw down the paper in reading this, exclaiming, "are they to give up all that binds them together as a nation or race, their language? Then they are indeed blotted out as a people." A proposition had been made to annex the Hawaian group to the United States. As a philanthropist and a friend of the Polynesians, he prayed that those islands, with their balmy climes and beautiful landscapes, might be kept free from the demoralizing associations of modern civilization.

DISCUSSIONS. 418.37–419.2 Had I time . . . Grecian fables.] The wording and placement of this sentence are conjectural. The Milwaukee *Daily Wisconsin* (#21), whose long account of the lecture appears to involve little rearrangement of the material, includes the following sentence at this point: "Spoke of a manuscript tradition he had [s]een that was told by a King of one of those Islands. It had much of the grace, strangeness and audacity of the Grecian Fables." But the Yonkers *Examiner* (#1) had previously noted that among Melville's topics was "a love story, peculiarly adapted to ladies, which he would not tell," and had also printed a letter signed "Herr Honeytown" complaining about Melville's lecture that mentioned a "legend so interesting to the 'ladies of my audience, for it is a love legend of Kamekamehaha, Tahiti, and Otaheite' " ("A 'South Sea' View of the Monday Night Lecture," December 9, 1858, p. 2, col. 2). In the absence of other evidence it has been assumed that all three references are to the same allusion, and that it occurred at this point in the lecture. (The Milwaukee writer, it might be added, was not referring to the legend of Kamapiikai mentioned at 417.24 above, for he had already devoted two sentences to that subject in an earlier paragraph.)

419.6 on Broadway] Here Melville apparently introduced varying local allusions. When in Milwaukee, according to the *Daily Wisconsin*, his phrase was "at the table of the Newhall House"—a fashionable local hotel where his friend William Cramer, the *Wisconsin*'s editor, long maintained an apartment.

HYPHENATION. II. 410.5 one-half 410.7 to-night 413.14 Anglo-Saxons 414.19 man-of-war

TRAVELING (pp. 421–23)

During his third season as a lecturer, when he spoke on the general topic of traveling, Melville was able to secure no more than three engagements, only one of which was reported by a local newspaper. His appearances were as follows:

Flushing, Long Island, New York, November 7, 1859
No report
Danvers, Massachusetts, February 14, 1860
No report
Cambridgeport, Massachusetts, February 21, 1860
1. Cambridge, Massachusetts, *Chronicle*, February 25, 1860

Melville did not publish the lecture, and there is no reference to his manuscript in surviving correspondence of the Melville family later than a letter of January 4, 1860, from his sister Augusta to Catherine Gansevoort ("I read it in M S. . . . "). A clipping of the relatively brief report in the Cambridge *Chronicle* is in the Melville Collection of The Houghton Library of Harvard University; a photocopy and transcription have been deposited there and in the Melville Collection of The Newberry Library. Like "Statues in Rome" and "The South Seas," the third lecture was presumably written to serve for the customary hour of oral delivery; the newspaper summary obviously represents only a portion of the full lecture. The *Chronicle*'s report is the basis for the present text, which is reprinted here from *Melville as Lecturer* (1957) with the authorization of Harvard University Press.

There is some indication that Melville himself used a longer title than either "Travel," which occurs in the heading of the *Chronicle*'s report, or "Traveling." The lecture was advertised in Flushing under the full title "Traveling: Its Pleasures, Pains, and Profits"; the phrasing "Travel, its pains, pleasures and profits" was used by Melville's brother-in-law John C. Hoadley in a letter of November 30, 1859, when he sought the aid of a business associate in attempting to secure lecture engagements for Melville. There was no newspaper publicity concerning the engagement at Danvers.

The present reading text retains the phraseology of the newspaper report except for minor emendations and for standardization and modernization of spelling and punctuation, all changes being recorded below. This reading text does not constitute a critical reconstruction of Melville's manuscript; it simply represents the fullest wording provided by a single incomplete report.

For explanation of the abbreviations and symbols used below, see pp. 569–70.

EMENDATIONS. 421.11 "Hopper,"] NN; '~,' 1860 421.13 traveler] NN; traveller 1860 421.17 trees^] NN; ~, 1860 421.21 traveler] NN; traveller 1860 422.1 squares] NN; Squares 1860 422.1 cathedrals] NN; Cathedrals 1860 422.4 which,] NN; ~^ 1860 422.4 traveled] NN; travelled 1860 422.6 pain,] NN; ~^ 1860 422.10 fleas^] NN; ~, 1860 422.12 traveler] NN; traveller 1860 422.12 passport. You] NN; passport, and you 1860 422.14 travels^] NN; ~, 1860 422.18 pleasure, though] NN; pleasure. Though 1860 422.19 immigrants] NN; emigrants 1860 422.25 Naples^] NN; ~, 1860 422.27 matador] NN; Matador 1860 422.27 a] NN; *[not present]* 1860 422.28 are] NN; *[not present]* 1860 422.29 *beaten;]* NN; ~, 1860 422.31 infidels] NN; Infidels 1860 422.35 rank,] NN; ~^ 1860 422.35 priests,] NN; ~^ 1860 422.39 traveled] NN; travelled 1860 423.10 idiosyncrasies] NN; idyosyncracies 1860 423.10 views^] NN; ~, 1860 423.13 travel that] NN; travel, 1860 423.16 Levant,] NN; ~^1860 423.18 home^] NN; ~, 1860 423.21 traveler] NN; traveller 1860 423.28 that is,] NN; ~ ~^ 1860

HYPHENATION. II. 422.8 self-discipline

THE DEATH CRAFT (pp. 424–27)

NN copy-text: the first printing, "The Death Craft," signed "Harry the Reefer," in the Lansingburgh, New York, *Democratic Press* [DP], II, no. 45 (November 16, 1839), p. 1, cols. 3–4. No known manuscript, and no known later printing in Melville's lifetime. NN emendations to DP (on principles stated on pp. 549–64): at 15 points. NN printer's copy: an emended photocopy of DP in the Troy, New York, Public Library. No other 1839 copies of DP are listed in *American Newspapers 1821–1936,* ed. Winifred Gregory (New York, 1937).

The date of publication suggests composition in October or November of 1839. The newspaper text is captioned "For the Democratic Press" (as are Melville's earlier "Fragments from a Writing Desk") and signed "Harry the Reefer"—that is, "midshipman"; the author was evidently interested in the sea and may well have drawn on firsthand experience. Melville himself had returned to his mother's home in Lansingburgh early in October from his first sea voyage aboard a Liverpool packet. Although there is no objective evidence to establish his authorship of "The Death Craft," the technique and style of the narrative are somewhat reminiscent of the "Fragments." All three pieces, moreover, differ markedly from other stories and sketches appearing in the *Democratic Press,* most of which were taken from magazines and gift books of the day and credited accordingly.

The case for attributing "The Death Craft" to Melville must necessarily rest chiefly on parallels in theme and especially in phraseology with the earlier "Fragments" and also with later works such as *Mardi* (1849), *Redburn* (1849), and "Benito Cereno" (1855). The opening and closing passages resemble Melville's descriptions of the three "seraphic visions" in the first "Fragment" and his later presentation of Yillah in *Mardi*. Here and in other descriptive passages, such as those treating the heavens, the sun, and the stars, the phrasing is similar to that of his known works. The "devoted" ship (426.2) is like King Piko's "devoted" empire in *Mardi* (chap. 138; NN440.1); Webster in 1806 had defined "devoted" in such a context to mean "given up" or "cursed." The narrator's thoughts and feelings pass through him like "vivid lightnings" (425.2); "like lightning" is a characteristic phrase in *Mardi* and other later works. The appearance of the helmsman's dead body is comparable to that of "A Living Corpse" in Chapter 48 of *Redburn,* which is based in part on Melville's Liverpool voyage of 1839; in Chapter 22 of that book Redburn tells us how the *Highlander* passes a wrecked ship not unlike that in the story: a frayed signal flies from the stump of her mainmast and the bodies of three sailors are lashed to the taffrail; Redburn's shipmate Jackson calls the wreck "a sailor's coffin" and asks how Redburn would "like to sail with them 'ere dead men." Perhaps Melville himself had seen such a vessel during the summer of 1839 and would recall it once again in "Bartleby" (1853), where the forlorn clerk is likened to a "bit of wreck in the mid Atlantic" (32.35 above). There are no skeletons in *Redburn* as there are in "The Death Craft," but in "Benito Cereno" the "piratical revolt" of the *San Dominick*'s crew is recounted in a passage concluding with revelation of "death for the figure-head, in a human skeleton" (99.37–38 above), a Gothic touch similar in its effect to that of the severed head and dangling white skeletons of the earlier tale. Finally, the affectation of experienced maturity in the narrator's concluding paragraph, as he recalls "scenes of my youth" and particularly the "fond young girl" left "twelve months ago . . . a disconsolate bride," contrasts abruptly with what has gone before, like the reversal marking the end of Melville's second "Fragment."

On treatment of "The Death Craft" in Melville scholarship and its reprinting as Melville's by Martin Leonard Pops, see pp. 544–45 above. Further work on the attribution of "The Death Craft" to Melville has been done by Warren F. Broderick, in *Hudson Valley Regional Review,* III (March, 1986), 91–105.

For explanation of the following tabulations, see pp. 565–70.

DISCUSSION. 425.23 congelated] The DP reading "conjulated"—not found in Webster—presumably resulted from a misreading of the manuscript. NN emends on the analogy of "congelation" in "The Paradise of Bachelors and the Tartarus of Maids," 325.13 above.

EMENDATIONS. 424.7 serenity] NN; serenety DP 424.15 dazzled] NN; dazled DP 425.5 deep.] NN; ~; DP 425.7 tottered] NN; totered DP 425.8 fell] NN; feel DP 425.9 clammy] NN; clamy DP 425.13 the] NN; The DP *425.23 congelated] NN; conjulated DP 425.23 griping∧] NN; ~, DP 425.27 vision,] NN; ~∧ DP 426.6 whipping] NN; whiping DP 426.15 stern-foremost] NN; stern-foremast DP 426.26 rigging,] NN; ~∧ DP 426.31 away!"] NN; ~∧∧ DP 426.39 apparition] NN; apparation DP

HYPHENATION. I. 425.8 helmsman 426.4 †main-top-/gallant-yard-arm 426.7 mainmast

II. 425.8 athwart-ships 426.4 †main-top-gallant-yard-arm

ON THE SEA SERPENT (pp. 428–29)

NN copy-text: the anonymous first printing, "Piscatory Sports at the Docks" and "$1,000 Reward," in *Yankee Doodle* [YD], II, no. 37 (June 19, 1847), 101, and no. 49 (September 11, 1847), 223. No known manuscript, and no later printing in Melville's lifetime. No NN emendations. The title "On the Sea Serpent" is supplied by NN. NN printer's copy: photocopies of Newberry Library A5.99 (item 1) and University of Chicago AP101Y3 (item 2). Machine collations between copies of YD: Newberry A5.99 (item 1) and University of Chicago AP101Y3 (photocopy) (item 2) *vs.* Brooklyn Public 051Y23 (photocopy) and Yale A95Y18 (photocopy).

Although the cartoon reproduced as item 1 here is not Melville's, it shows that the Nahant sea serpent was already a subject of *Yankee Doodle*'s fun before Melville became a contributor in July of 1847. The second item can reasonably be attributed to Melville on the basis of Evert A. Duyckinck's remark of July 14 of that year, in a letter to his brother George, that Melville "will probably in some shape or other take care of the sea serpent" (see p. 466, n. 8 above). There is also a reference to "the Nahant Sea Serpent" in another piece Melville may have written in July of 1847: one of *Yankee Doodle*'s series of squibs concerning the Chinese junk then visiting New York harbor; see 430.9–10 above, from the issue of July 17 (no. 41, p. 148). Although the subject received no further exploitation in *Yankee Doodle,* there are several allusions to it in Melville's later works. "The sea-serpent is not a fable," declares the narrator of *Mardi* (1849) in Chapter 13 (NN39.13); in Chapter 66 he describes the prows of canoes as "thrown back like trunks of elephants; a dark, snaky length behind, like the sea-serpent's train" (NN199.11). In "The South Seas" (1858) Melville mentions the "mystery" hanging over "the sea-serpent of North Atlantic waters" (414.1–2 above).

DISCUSSION. 429.10 negociation] For NN retention of this spelling, see pp. 561–62.

ON THE CHINESE JUNK (pp. 430–42)

NN copy-text: the first printings of thirteen anonymous items in *Yankee Doodle,* II (1847) [YD], as follows: item 1: no. 41 (July 17), p. 148; item 2: no. 42 (July 24), p. 153; item 3: no. 42 (July 24), p. 154; item 4: no. 43 (July 31), p. 164; item 5: no. 43 (July 31), p. 168; item 6: no. 46 (August 21), p. 194; item 7: no. 46 (August 21), p. 199; items 8-10: no. 48 (September 4), p. 218; item 11: no. 49 (September 11), p. 223; item 12: no. 50 (September 18), p. 232; item 13: no. 50 (September 18), p. 240. No known manuscript, and no later printing in Melville's lifetime. NN emendations to YD (on principles stated on pp. 549–64): at 15 points. The title "On the Chinese Junk" is supplied by NN. NN printer's copy: emended photocopies of Newberry Library A5.99 (all except item 11); University of Chicago AP101Y3 (item 11). Machine collations between copies of YD: Newberry A5.99 (all except item 11) and University of Chicago AP101Y3 (photocopy) (item 11) *vs.* University of Vermont (photocopy); University of Vermont (photocopy) *vs.* Brooklyn Public 051Y23 (photocopy).

Melville became a regular contributor to *Yankee Doodle* in July of 1847 and began his series of "Old Zack" articles in the number of July 24; as noted above, p. 466, n. 8, Evert A. Duyckinck also expected him to "take care of" the current subject of the Nahant sea serpent. Although no full series on that subject (beyond the two items reproduced and reprinted above) appeared in *Yankee Doodle,* there is a passing reference to the serpent in the initial piece on the Chinese junk, published on July 17, and the junk in turn figures in Anecdote VI of Melville's "Old Zack" series, which appeared on August 21. Perhaps the staff of *Yankee Doodle* found the visiting Chinese ship even more attractive as a topic for comment than the rumored sea serpent. Certainly Melville himself was aware of the junk's presence in New York harbor; as a former sailor he may well have been one of the "curious friends" who went "down to the Battery" to inspect it, as recounted in *Yankee Doodle* on July 24. The report of their visit in item 3 is probably his writing. This and the other materials assembled here, which include woodcuts and their captions and the shorter squibs printed during Melville's absence from New York on his honeymoon in August (see pp. 467–68 above), represent the range of *Yankee Doodle*'s coverage of the junk and associated topics--including the Nahant sea serpent, Barnum's Museum, Cave Johnson (Postmaster General from 1845 to 1849), who also figures in "On the Sea Serpent" (p. 429 above), and Henry Plunkett Grattan's "The Stranger's Grave: A Tale of the Seventeenth Century," the subject of the punning in item 11. Plunkett (or Grattan) was the target of satirical squibs in *Yankee Doodle* in the late summer through early fall of 1849. Some but not all of this writing is very likely Melville's.

For explanation of the following tabulations, see pp. 565–70.

EMENDATIONS. 432.5 countrymen,] NN; ~. YD 432.19 and] NN; aud YD 432.29 Ching-too.] NN; ~-~∧ YD 432.35 Englishman,]

NN; ~. YD 433.5 'heavy] NN; "~ YD 433.5 dog,'] NN; ~." YD 433.6 Ko-ka-poo] NN; Ko-ke-poo YD 433.27 "Um—] NN; '~— YD 437.19 word∧] NN; ~, YD 437.19 it,] NN; ~∧ YD 438.15 *was,]* NN; ~∧ YD 440.6 Cincinnati] NN; Cincinnatti YD 440.20 pardon] NN; pordon YD 440.20 complexion—?"] NN; ~—?∧ YD 441.4 Adams'] NN; ~∧ YD

Hyphenation. I. 432.29 Ching-too 442.2 farewell II. 432.28 multi-armed 437.5 Yan-kees

A SHORT PATENT SERMON (pp. 443–44)

NN copy-text: the anonymous first printing, "A Short Patent Sermon. According to Blair, the Rhetorician," in *Yankee Doodle* [YD], II, no. 40 (July 10, 1847), 131. No known manuscript, and no later printing in Melville's lifetime. NN emendations to YD (on principles stated on pp. 549–64): at seven points. NN printer's copy: an emended photocopy of University of Chicago Library AP101Y3. Machine collations between copies of YD: University of Chicago AP101Y3 (photocopy) *vs.* Boston Public 5240.20 (photocopy) and American Antiquarian Society PRQ Yankee (photocopy).

"Dow Jr. of the Sunday Mercury," the butt of *Yankee Doodle*'s satire, was Elbridge G. Paige, then part owner of the New York *Sunday Mercury* and author of the Dow, Jr., "Short Patent Sermons," which were well known in the nineteenth century. Melville's authorship of this mock sermon (in the first number of the magazine edited by Cornelius Mathews) is suggested by Donald Yannella in "Cornelius Mathews: Knickerbocker Satirist" (Ph.D. dissertation, Fordham University, 1971), p. 226, on the basis of the references to missionaries and a Sandwich Islander. There are other parallels as well. The composition purportedly follows the precepts of Hugh Blair's *Lectures on Rhetoric* (1783); in *White-Jacket* (1850) Melville alludes to "Blair's Lectures, University Edition—a fine treatise on rhetoric" (NN168.2), and in *Moby-Dick* (1851), besides the rhetorical set-piece of Father Mapple's sermon in Chapter 9, there is the mock sermon in Chapter 64, Fleece preaching to the sharks. With his friend Evert A. Duyckinck, a staunch Episcopalian, Melville shared an interest in sermons and a liking for Samuel Butler's *Hudibras*. In 1850 he gave Duyckinck a copy of *Hudibras* he had bought in London; another edition kept in his own library is not known to survive (Sealts 104, 105). The "Sermon" draws on *Hudibras,* The First Part, Canto I, lines 11–12, which in the text of 1678 reads:

And Pulpit, Drum Ecclesiastick,
Was beat with fist, instead of a stick.

For explanation of the following tabulations, see pp. 565–70.

EMENDATIONS. 443.17 A. B. O.] NN; A. B. O∧ YD
444.1 Hawaii,] NN; ~,, YD 444.3 "*The*] NN; ∧~ YD
444.3 *part.*"] NN; ~.∧ YD 444.9 "*The*] NN; ∧~ YD
444.9 *Conclusion.*"] NN; ~.∧ YD 444.9 Hudibras] NN; Hudribras YD

HYPHENATION. I. 443.10 wishy-washy 443.23 †therefore

THE NEW PLANET (pp. 445–46)

NN copy-text: the anonymous first printing, "The New Planet," in *Yankee Doodle* [YD], II, no. 42 (July 24, 1847), 153. No known manuscript, and no later printing in Melville's lifetime. NN emendations to YD (on principles stated on pp. 549–64): at one point. NN printer's copy: an emended photocopy of Newberry Library A5.99. Machine collations between copies of YD: Newberry A5.99 *vs.* University of Vermont (photocopy); University of Vermont (photocopy) *vs.* Brooklyn Public 051Y23 (photocopy).

If Melville wrote some or all of *Yankee Doodle*'s various articles on the Chinese junk and Phineas T. Barnum's American Museum, he may also have written "The New Planet," which mentions the junk and makes similar references to Barnum's exhibits; moreover, the allusion in Anecdote VI of Melville's "Old Zack" series to "the venerable nurse of our beloved Washington and the illustrious General Tom Thumb" (225.24–25 above) seems to echo this earlier composition. The astronomical language anticipates the imagery of Melville's later work, beginning with *Mardi* (1849); he was to meet Professor William Mitchell, the astronomer, and his astronomer daughter Maria at Nantucket Island in July of 1852.

For explanation of the following tabulations, see pp. 565–70.

DISCUSSION. 445.9 sideral] Possibly an error for "sidereal," but since "sideral" was an acceptable adjectival form at the time, it is not emended.

EMENDATION. 445.3–4 south-western] NN; south[ ]/western YD

HYPHENATION. I. 445.3 †south-western
II. 445.3 †south-western

VIEW OF THE BARNUM PROPERTY (pp. 447–48)

NN copy-text: the anonymous first printing, "View of the Barnum Property," in *Yankee Doodle* [YD], II, no. 43 (July 31, 1847), 168. No known manuscript, and no later printing in Melville's lifetime. No NN emendations. NN printer's copy: a photocopy of Newberry Library A5.99. Machine collations between copies of YD: Newberry A5.99 *vs.* University of Vermont (photocopy); University of Vermont (photocopy) *vs.* Brooklyn Public 051Y23 (photocopy).

The case for Melville's possible authorship of this squib on Phineas T. Barnum rests on certain parallels in subject matter and phrasing between its paragraphs and his "Old Zack" articles also published by *Yankee Doodle* in the summer of 1847. There are repeated allusions to Barnum in installments of the "Old Zack" series appearing on July 24 (Barnum's desire to exhibit a Mexican shell supposedly defused by General Taylor), July 31 (a placard offered Barnum for his museum), August 21 (a letter "on behalf" of Barnum that incidentally mentions the visiting Chinese junk), and September 11 (Barnum's plans to exhibit "one of the General's old roundabouts"). Both "View of the Barnum Property" and the "Old Zack" series use the phrases "seat of war" (212.4,18; 448.21) and "animated nature" (220.18; 448.10); both mention the Mexican General Antonio López de Santa Anna (223.12, 225.32; 448.20).

Melville may also have contributed other comments on persons and events of the day to the column of "Fixed Facts and Facts Fixed" appearing on the same page of *Yankee Doodle* for July 31 as "View of the Barnum Property": see "On the Chinese Junk," item 5, p. 435 above. In the number for July 24, moreover, *Yankee Doodle* had stated that both the Chinese junk and the Nahant sea serpent would be "exhibited this week at Barnum's Museum" (430.4–5 above). All these topics were within the orbit of Melville's current interests.

For explanation of the following tabulation, see pp. 565–70.

HYPHENATION. I. 448.19 life-sized

REPORT OF THE COMMITTEE ON AGRICULTURE (pp. 449–51)

NN copy-text: the first printing, "Report of the Committee on Agriculture," over the signature of Melville's cousin Robert Melvill, in the Pittsfield, Massachusetts, *Culturist and Gazette* [CG], III, no. 41 (October 9, 1850), p. 1, cols. 3–5. No known manuscript; two later printings (see below) in Melville's lifetime. NN emendations to CG (on principles stated on pp. 549–64): at four points. The extensive listing of individual awards for various crops is omitted here. NN printer's copy: an emended photocopy of CG in The Berkshire Athenaeum at Pittsfield. No other 1850 copies of CG are listed in *American Newspapers 1821–1936,* ed. Winifred Gregory (New York, 1837).

Essentially this same material appeared in a new setting of type on the following day, with the caption "Report on Agriculture.", in the Pittsfield *Sun* [PS], LI, no. 2612 (October 10, 1850), p. 2, cols. 1–2, as part of the *Sun*'s coverage of the fortieth anniversary celebration of the Berkshire Agriculture Society, headed "The Farmers' Festival." But the committee report signed by Robert Melvill was quoted only in part in later coverage of the event by the *Massachusetts Eagle* [ME] of Pittsfield, XXII, no. 11 (October 18, 1850), p. 1, cols. 4–5, headed "CATTLE SHOW AND FAIR, / OF THE BERKSHIRE AGRICULTURAL SOCIETY: / October 2d and 3d, 1850." The opening portion of the *Eagle*'s account, captioned "THE SECRETARY'S REPORT.", corresponds in wording to the opening portion of the earlier "Farmers' Festival" article in the *Sun,* but in dealing with the reports of the various Awarding Committees the *Eagle* abbreviates that of Robert Melvill's group by omitting the initial paragraphs as carried in both the *Sun* and the *Culturist and Gazette,* beginning instead with the lists of individual awards. The full text of the "Report of the Committee on Agriculture" in the *Culturist and Gazette* has been collated with the versions carried by these other Pittsfield papers, using the file of the *Sun* in The Berkshire Athenaeum and that of the *Eagle* in the American Antiquarian Society at Worcester, Massachusetts; there are no variants which appear to be authorial.

Attribution of the "Report" to Herman Melville was first proposed by Jay Leyda, who partially reprinted it in his "White Elephant vs. White Whale," *Town and Country,* CI (August, 1947), 68, 69, 114d, and 116–18, and later quoted it in *The Melville Log,* I, 398. No subsequent reprinting is known. In the absence of a manuscript and other documentation, the case for Herman Melville's authorship of at least a part of the "Report" rests on a combination of circumstantial and internal evidence. Melville had accompanied his cousin at the beginning of Robert Melvill's tour of the county "to view the state of the crops" during the previous July, keeping notes on the trip in his copy (Sealts 216) of *A History of the County of Berkshire* (quoted in *Log,* I, 379–80). Faced with the obligation of composing a committee report, Robert Melvill "appealed to his 'writing' cousin," Leyda conjectures, "and Herman could not resist the opportunity to write an agricultural report to end all agricultural reports" ("White Elephant vs. White Whale," p. 114d).

The expression "strike with admiration . . . capable of estimating" (449.14–15) is like the conclusion of Melville's "Hawthorne and His Mosses," also written in the summer of 1850: "admired by every one . . . capable of admiration" (253.39–40 above). The Shakespearean phrase "milk of human kindness" (450.2) and biblical allusions to "our great progenitors in . . . Eden" (450.12–13) and to Noah and the Ark (450.7–8) are characteristic of Melville. The extended discussion of the virtues of barnyard manure and the art of converting it from foul to fair has several parallels in Melville's writings, such as Ishmael's treatment of the virtues of foul-smelling ambergris in *Moby-Dick* (chaps. 91–92). In the present volume, "Poor Man's Pudding" (1854) opens with a somewhat similar disquisition on the value of "farm-yard enrichments" (289.15), and in "Statues in Rome" (1857) Melville returns to the Pauline theme of the corruptible putting on incorruption (408.3–4).

The "Report" as printed in the *Culturist and Gazette,* which Leyda interprets as a "satirical triumph," provoked a response in kind that appeared in the same paper on October 23, 1850 (III, no. 43, p. 1, col. 1). Purportedly written by "Z. W. Factminus," identified as "Chairman of the Committee on Crops" of the "Bunkum Agricultural Society," this further "Report" opens as follows:

> Your Committee have examined a very large number of crops, many of which were extremely fine, and have become fully satisfied that our County can produce excellent crops, but since we have learned but very little ourselves how they can be produced, you will expect from us nothing farther than to hold out to you encouragement from the fact that such is the fact. . . .

There follows a burlesque report of the "Plowing Match" by "Storrow G. Keepdark, Chairman of the Committee." The obvious target of these two squibs is the opening of the "Report of the Committee on Agriculture" signed by Robert Melvill—those paragraphs omitted by the *Eagle* that may have come from Herman Melville's pen.

For explanation of the following tabulations, see pp. 565–70. The PS and ME readings are given here since they possibly have authority (i.e., the three Pittsfield newspapers may have used the same manuscript, or even have had separate manuscripts).

EMENDATIONS. 450.16 satisfaction] PS; satifaction CG 450.39 farmer] NN; former CG, PS 451.4 number] PS; numbers CG 451.24 diminishing] PS, ME; dimininishing CG

HYPHENATION. I. 449.20 herds-grass

SUBSTANTIVE VARIANTS. 449.9 improvements] CG; improvement PS 450.1 suspicion] CG; a suspicion PS 450.6 ought] CG; aught PS 450.6 that] CG; *[not present]* PS 450.6 had] CG; had held PS 450.8 numerous] CG; *[not present]* PS 450.18 embellishments] CG; embellishment PS 451.4 number] PS; numbers CG 451.5 thirty-one] CG; twenty-one PS 451.8 competitor] CG; competitors PS 451.11 this] CG; their PS, ME 451.19 frost] CG; the frost PS, ME 451.20 to] CG; at PS, ME 451.21 not] CG; not a PS, ME 451.24 diminishing] PS, ME; dimininishing CG

Elizabeth Shaw Melville's Lists of the Magazine Stories

THE most authoritative contemporary listing of Melville's *Putnam's* and *Harper's* stories appears among Elizabeth Shaw Melville's collection of these stories and her notes about his works now in the Melville Collection of The Houghton Library at Harvard University. Copies of all of Melville's published contributions of 1853–56 to these magazines are laid into a cover of cloth over boards, made in Pittsfield and formerly kept in the Melville family, stamped "Magazine Stories by Herman Melville" in gold on the front (AC885M4977LZ999). Each piece was taken from a wrappered number (not a bound volume) of one of the magazines, as evidenced by various physical details. Elizabeth Shaw Melville wrote "Herman Melville" on each piece except "Bartleby" and made additional notations on some of them (see p. 716 and the discussion at 336.9 above).

Also laid into the cover are her notes in ink concerning nine of the stories, reproduced here as Items A and B. Item A is a single part-leaf (13.4 by 10.2 cm) on the recto of which Mrs. Melville listed four stories first published in *Harper's New Monthly Magazine*. The copies of the four stories referred to are "fastened together", and this part-leaf was at one time pinned to them. Item B is a single 21.4-by-14 cm leaf on the recto of which she listed the five stories first published in *Putnam's Monthly Maga-*

zine and collected in *The Piazza Tales.* At one time Item B may also have been pinned to the fastened together copies of these stories. The added pencil notation, "except . . . Tales' ", is Raymond Weaver's.

Reproduced here as Items C and D are the fourth and fifth pages of Mrs. Melville's unnumbered six-page listing in ink of "Herman Melville's books", also at The Houghton Library (bMS Am 188, No. 329). Item C, the last page (20.5 by 12.7 cm) of four created by folding a sheet, lists all of Melville's "Magazine Stories" except "The Encantadas," including the eight installments of *Israel Potter* that were "afterwards published in book form", as she noted, in 1855. "The Encantadas" is, however, listed on the third page of the conjoint leaf, as well as on Item D, the fifth page of the six-page listing, on the recto of a separate leaf measuring 20.5 by 12.6 cm. On this page Mrs. Melville lists the contents of *The Piazza Tales,* then re-lists them (omitting "The Piazza") with their earlier dates of publication in *Putnam's*; she also gives the dates and places of both printings of *Israel Potter.*

Worthy of special mention is the fact that Mrs. Melville included "The Fiddler" in two of her lists and wrote "Herman Melville" on the copy of it from *Harper's.* Melville's authorship of this story has sometimes been questioned because it was credited not to him but to Fitz-James O'Brien in *An Index to Harper's New Monthly Magazine* (1870, 1875, 1880, 1885), but that unsupported attribution lacks the authority of the family documents cited here. (See pp. 691–92.)

Items A, B, C, and D can probably be dated as early as 1891–92 and possibly as late as 1901. When Mrs. Melville made these lists, she was evidently sorting her husband's papers and setting down the dates of his principal publications. (1) During the months following Melville's death on September 28, 1891, Arthur Stedman as his joint literary executor published five articles about him and his writings and also prepared new editions of four selected works—*Typee, Omoo, White-Jacket,* and *Moby-Dick*—that appeared in 1892. At this time Mrs. Melville gave Stedman access to Melville's papers and provided him with biographical and bibliographical information. (2) During the summer or early fall of 1901 she responded to an inquiry in the *New York Times Saturday Review* of July 6, 1901, p. 490, col. 2, reading: "Can you give an admirer of Herman Melville a list of his books, and tell me if any of them are still in print." The *Review* of October 5, 1901, pp. 706, col. 2, and 707, col. 1, reported in an article headed "Herman Melville's Works" that the inquiry had "elicited a communication from Mrs. Melville," who "very kindly corrected and annotated" a tentative list provided by the *Times;* the list and her comments conclude the article.

These leaves fastened
together are
"Poor Man's Pudding and
Rich Man's Crumbs"
"The Happy Failure"
"The Fiddler"
"The Paradise of Bachelors
and the Tartarus of Maids"
all from Harpers
Monthly Magazine

A. Elizabeth Shaw Melville's list of four *Harper's* stories.

From these
Magazine Stories by
Herman Melville
"Bartleby the Scrivener"
"Benito Cereno"
"The Lightning Rod Man"
"The Encantadas" and
"The Bell Tower"
were published in one
volume — "The Piazza Tales"
(None others are published)

except for "The Piazza",
which appeared first in "The Tales"

B. Elizabeth Shaw Melville's list of five *Putnam's* stories collected in *The Piazza Tales* (reduced).

"The Bell Tower" Aug. 18[55]
The Lightning Rod Man Aug. 1854

Magazine Stories

From Putnam's Monthly Mag–
Don Benito Cereno Oct to Dec 1855
I and My Chimney – March 1856
"Apple Tree Table" May 1856
"Israel Potter" or Fifty Years Exile
July. Aug. Sept. Oct. Nov. Dec. – 1854 &
Jan. & Feb. 1855 – afterwards published
in book form by G. P. Putnam – N. Y.
Bartleby – the Scrivener – Nov & Dec. 1853

From Harper's Monthly Magazines

"Cock-a-doodle-doo" Dec 1853
"Poor Man's Pudding and Rich Man's Crumbs" (June 1854
"Happy Failure" July 1854
"The Fiddler" Sept 1854
"Paradise of Bachelors & Tartarus of Maids" (April 18[55]
"Jimmy Rose" – Nov. 1855 –
"The 'Gees" – March – 1856

C. Elizabeth Shaw Melville's list of Melville's "Magazine Stories" (reduced).

(29)

Dix & Edwards N.Y. and
Sampson Low — London
Piazza Tales. 1856

"The Piazza" – "Bartleby the
Scrivener" – "Don Benito Cereno"
"Lightning Rod Man"
"Encantadas" or Enchanted Islands
"The Bell Tower" Reprinted &
published from Putnams Monthly
Magazines – as named below.

Bartleby the Scrivener Nov–Dec 1853
Lightning-Rod Man Aug. 1854
Encantadas or Enchanted Islands
March–April–May – 1854
Don Benito Cereno – Oct. Nov. Dec 1855
*Israel Potter or fifty years exile
July–Aug–Sept. Oct. Nov. Dec. 1854
Jan. Feb. March. 1855
"The Bell Tower. – Aug. 1855

*Issued in book form in 1855 by
G. P. Putnam & Co. New York.

D. Elizabeth Shaw Melville's list of *Putnam's* pieces collected in *The Piazza Tales* and *Israel Potter* (reduced).

Melville's Notebook of Lecture Engagements

MELVILLE'S LECTURE ENGAGEMENTS and fees are recorded in a small notebook, 18.4 by 12.3 cm, which is now in the Melville Collection of The Houghton Library of Harvard University (Ms Am 188, No. 376). On the front cover of the notebook, which is bound in blue cardboard, is a paper label bearing the notation "Lecture Engagements / 1857–8–9–60". Inside the front cover are two brief penciled memoranda in Melville's hand: "Herald stops Jan 7th 1854." and "Brown owes me 75 cts." Seven of the eight pages of the notebook are reproduced here (reduced), the eighth being without entries.

PAGE 1: The items for 1851 and 1850 are in Melville's hand; the subsequent notations, in Elizabeth Shaw Melville's hand, refer to the lecture season of 1857–58. "T. D. S." is T. D. Stewart of Lansingburgh, New York, from whom Melville borrowed $2050 on May 1, 1851, to make improvements at Arrowhead; see Melville's letters to Lemuel Shaw, May 12 and 22, 1856, in Patricia Barber, "Two New Melville Letters," *American Literature,* XLIX (November, 1977), 418–21. "Brewster" is evidently Dr. John Brewster of Pittsfield, from whom Melville had bought the Arrowhead property on September 14, 1850.

PAGES 2 and 3: The initial inscription is in Melville's hand, with additions by Mrs. Melville. The entries record tentative lecture engagements for 1857–58.

PAGE 4: The inscription is in Mrs. Melville's hand. The first address is that of Richard Tobias Greene, the "Toby" of Melville's *Typee*. Melville's relation to Archibald T. Cochran of Louisville has not been established.

PAGE 5: The inscription is in Mrs. Melville's hand. Melville probably planned to call on Charles Wells because Wells's late wife was the sister of Melville's brother-in-law John C. Hoadley (see letter of Allan Melville to Augusta Melville, March 30, 1855, in The New York Public Library).

PAGE 6: The inscription is in Mrs. Melville's hand. The entries record Melville's lecture engagements and fees, 1857–58. There are several errors: Melville gave his lectures in Montreal on December 11, not December 10; in Saratoga December 21, not December 30; and in Rochester February 18, not February 23. Omitted are the dates for his lectures in Chillicothe (February 3) and Cincinnati (February 2).

PAGE 7: Also in Mrs. Melville's hand, accurately recording Melville's lecture engagements and fees, 1858–59, 1859–60.

Lectures 1857-8-9. 1859-60

~~R. R. S. $2050. May 1st 1857. For five years. 9 per cent.~~

Brigham's (?) Note (1500) is dated Sept. 1st 1858.

at Boston after Charlestown (?) lec	15.00
few days after	9.00
Before going to Montreal	19.00
at N. H. on leaving	19.00

100
50
90
240

8 × Cleveland — Middle of January. Jan 11th [illegible] Fixed

× 9 Detroit — Early part of January. [illegible] Jan 12th Fixed

6 × Auburn First week in Jan. (Fixed) Jany 5th

~~Washington~~ ~~[illegible]~~

1858 × 7 Ithaca ~~Syracuse~~ First week in January Jany 7th (Fixed)

11 × Rochester — Feb 18th (Fixed) a Fixed

~~Detroit~~

~~Rockford~~ ~~About middle of Jan~~ [illegible]

Jan 22d ?

Clarksville — Tenn. Middle or latter part of January.

3 Boston Mercantile Library — Wednesday before or after
X Thanksgiving. — Wednesday after Dec. 2d (Times)
5 New Haven Young Men's Institute — Middle or latter part of December. Dec. 30th Fixed
~~[illegible] before Beginning of January.~~

12
X New Bedford — first of February to be sent.
~~of Dec. or after?~~
1858 Feby 23d Fixed ~~[illegible]~~

10
X Charlestown — ~~After Thanksgiving~~ or late in the season Feb 10th
Fixed

2
X Concord (N. H.) November ~~[illegible]~~ 24th
Fixed

1
X Lawrence November 23d ~~[illegible]~~
Fixed

4 Montreal Dec. 10th

6 Malden ~~Dec 28th~~?

Call on A. D. Lamson 70 State St.
after 1st Jan — see note

4 Toby's address—

166 Water St—Sandusky—Ohio—
"Cosmopolitan Art Association"
his brother-in-laws connected
with it named Derby (C. L.)

Archibald T. Cochran
Jefferson St—between 7th & 8th
streets—south side.—~~Cincinnati~~
Louisville, Ky.

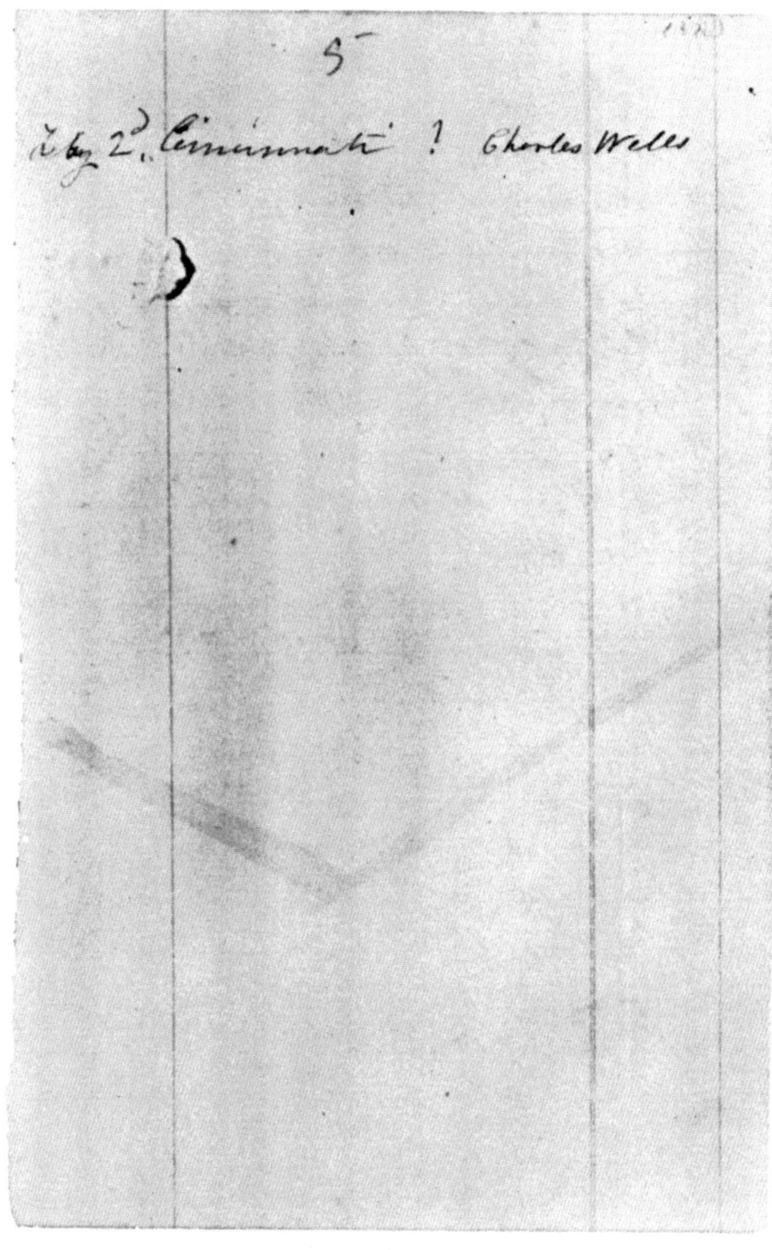

5

Feby 2d. Cincinnati ? Charles Wells

Lectures 1858-&9

6

Nov 23d	Lawrence —	—	
" 24th	Concord	30.00	
Decr 2d	Boston	40.00	
" 10th	Montreal	50.00	
" 30th	Saratoga	——	
30th	New Haven	50.00	
Jan 5th	Auburn	40.00	1859
" 7th	Ithaca	50.00	
" 11th	Cleveland	50.00	
12th	Detroit	50.00	
22d	Clarksville	75.00	1858
	~~Chillicothe~~ ~~Louisville~~	40.00	
	Cincinnati	50.00	
Feby 10	Charlestown	20.00	
Feby 23	Rochester	50.00	
" 23d	New Bedford	50.00	
	~~Malden~~	645.00	
Travelling Expenses —		221.30	
		423.70	

Lectures 1858-9 7

Decr 6th	Yonkers N.Y.	30 00
14th	Pittsfield Mass	50.00
Jany 31st	Boston 1859	50.00
Feby 7th	New York	55.00
8th	Baltimore Md	100.00
24th	Chicago	50.00
25th	Milwaukee	50 00
28th	Rockford Ill	50.00
March 2d	Quincy Ill	23.50
March 16	Lynn Mass - 2 Lec.	60.00
		518.50

1859-60

Nov 7th	Flushing L.I.	30.00
Feby 14th	Danvers-Mass	25.00
21st	Cambridgeport Mass	55.00

Melville's Source for "Benito Cereno"

ALTHOUGH MELVILLE did not cite or acknowledge his debt to Captain Amasa Delano's *A Narrative of Voyages and Travels,* he based "Benito Cereno" on Chapter 18 of that work, imaginatively refashioning it much as he used source works for *Israel Potter* and Chapters 26 and 27 of *The Confidence-Man.* (See p. 582). Nothing in "Benito Cereno" indicates whether the copy of Delano's book that Melville used was from the first printing, dated 1817 (Boston: Printed by E. G. House, for the Author), or from the second printing, dated 1818 (with "Second Edition" on the title page and the same imprint). Delano's Chapter 18 is reproduced below from an 1817 copy in The Newberry Library (Ayer 119.1D6.1817). Accompanying the reproduced text are marginal page and line numbers to indicate the corresponding passages of "Benito Cereno" in the present edition.

Capt. Amasa Delano.

A

NARRATIVE

OF

VOYAGES AND TRAVELS,

IN THE

NORTHERN AND SOUTHERN HEMISPHERES:

COMPRISING

THREE VOYAGES ROUND THE WORLD;

TOGETHER WITH A

VOYAGE OF SURVEY AND DISCOVERY,

IN THE

PACIFIC OCEAN AND ORIENTAL ISLANDS.

BY AMASA DELANO.

BOSTON:

PRINTED BY E. G. HOUSE, FOR THE AUTHOR.

1817.

CHAPTER XVIII.

Particulars of the Capture of the Spanish Ship Tryal, at the island of St. Maria; with the Documents relating to that affair.

IN introducing the account of the capture of the Spanish ship Tryal, I shall first give an extract from the journal of the ship Perseverance, taken on board that ship at the time, by the officer who had the care of the log book.

46.4,8 "Wednesday, February 20th, commenced with light airs from the north east, and thick foggy weather. At six A. M. observed a sail opening round the south head of St. Maria, coming into the bay. It proved to be a ship. The captain took the whale boat and crew, and went on board her. As the wind was very light, so that a vessel would not have much more than steerage way at the time; observed that the ship acted very awkwardly. At ten A. M. the boat returned. Mr. Luther informed that Captain Delano had remained on board her, and that she was a Spaniard from Buenos Ayres, four months and twenty six days out of port, with slaves on board; and tha the ship was in great want of water, had buried many white men and slaves on her passage, and that captain Delano had sent for a large boat load of water, some fresh fish, sugar, bread, pumpkins, and bottled cider, all of which articles were immediately sent. At twelve o'clock (Meridian) calm. At two P. M. the large boat returned from the Spaniards, had left our water casks on board her. At four P. M. a breeze sprung up from the southern quarter, which brought the Spanish ship into the roads. She anchored about two cables length to the south east of our ship. Immediately after she anchored, our captain with his boat was shoving off from along side the Spanish ship; when to his great surprise the Spanish captain leaped into the boat, and called out in Spanish, that the slaves on board had risen and murdered many of the people; and that he did not then command her; on which manœuvre, several of the Spaniards who remained on board jumped overboard, and swam for our boat, and were picked up by our people. The Spaniards, who remained on board, hurried up the rigging, as high aloft as they could possibly get, and called out repeatedly for help—that they should be murdered by the slaves. Our captain came immediately on board, and brought the Spanish captain and the men who were picked up in the water; but before the boat arrived, we observed that the slaves had cut the Spanish ship adrift. On learning this, our captain hailed, and ordered the ports to be got up, and the guns cleared; but unfortunately, we could not bring but one of our guns to bear on the ship. We fired five or six shot with it, but could not bring her too. We soon observed her making sail, and standing directly out of the bay. We dispatched two boats well manned, and well armed after her, who, after much trouble, boarded the ship and retook her. But unfortunately in the business, Mr. Rufus Low, our chief officer, who commanded the party, was desperately wounded in the breast, by being stabbed with a pike, by one of the slaves. We likewise had one man badly wounded and two or three slightly. To continue the misfortune, the chief officer of the Spanish ship, who was compelled by the slaves to steer her out of the bay, received two very bad wounds, one in the side, and one through the thigh, both from musket balls. One Spaniard, a gentleman passenger on board, was likewise killed by a musket ball. We have not rightly ascertained what number of slaves were killed; but we believe seven, and a great number wounded. Our people brought the ship in, and came to nearly where she first anchored, at about two o'clock in the morning of the 21st. At six A. M. the two captains went on board the Spanish ship; took with them irons from our ship, and doubled ironed all the remaining men of the slaves who were living. Left Mr. Brown, our second officer, in charge of the ship, the gunner with him as mate, and eight other hands; together with the survivors of the Spanish crew. The captain, and chief officer, were removed to our ship, the latter for the benefit of having his wounds better attended to with us, than he could have had them on board his own ship. At nine A. M. the two captains returned, having put every thing aright, as they supposed, on board the Spanish ship.

The Spanish captain then informed us that he was compelled by the slaves to say, that he was from Buenos Ayres, bound to Lima; that he was not from Buenos Ayres, but sailed on the 20th of December last from Valparaiso for Lima, with upwards of seventy slaves on board; that on the 26th of December, the slaves rose upon the ship, and took possession of her, and put to death eighteen white men, and threw overboard at different periods after, seven more; that the slaves had commanded him to go to Senegal; that he had kept to sea until his water was expended, and had made this port to get it; and also with a view to save his own and the remainder of his people's lives if possible, by runing away from his ship with his boat."

I shall here add some remarks of my own, to what is stated above from the ship's journal, with a view of giving the reader a correct understanding of the peculiar situation under which we were placed at the time this affair happened. We were in a worse situation to effect any important enterprize than I had been in during the voyage. We had been from home a year and a half, and had not made enough to amount to twenty dollars for each of my people, who were all on shares, and our future prospects were not very flattering. To make our situation worse, I had found after leaving New Holland, on mustering my people, that I had seventeen men, most of whom had been convicts at Botany bay. They had secreted themselves on board without my knowledge. This was a larger number than had been inveigled away from me at the same place, by people who had been convicts, and were then employed at places that we visited. The men whom we lost were all of them extraordinarily good men. This exchange materially altered the quality of the crew. Three of the Botany-bay-men were outlawed convicts; they had been shot at many times, and several times wounded. After making this bad exchange, my crew were refractory; the convicts were ever unfaithful, and took all the advantage that opportunity gave them. But sometimes exercising very strict discipline, and giving them good wholesome floggings; and at other times treating them with the best I had, or could get, according as their deeds deserved, I managed them without much difficulty during the passage across the South Pacific Ocean; and all the time I had been on the coast of Chili. I had lately been at the islands of St. Ambrose and St. Felix, and left there fifteen of my best men, with the view of procuring seals; and left that place in company with my consort the Pilgrim. We appointed Massa Fuero as our place of rendezvous, and if we did not meet there, again to rendezvous at St. Maria. I proceeded to the first place appointed; the Pilgrim had not arrived. I then determined to take a look at Juan Fernandez, and see if we could find any seals, as some persons had informed me they were to be found on some part of the island. I accordingly visited that place, as has been stated; from thence I proceeded to St. Maria; and arrived the 13th of February at that place, where we commonly find visitors. We found the ship Mars of Nantucket, commanded by captain Jonathan Barney. The day we arrived, three of my Botany bay men run from the boat when on shore. The next day, (the 14th) I was informed by Captain Barney, that some of my convict men had planned to run away with one of my boats, and go over to the main. This information he obtained through the medium of his people. I examined into the affair, and was satisfied as to the truth of it; set five more of the above description of men on shore, making eight in all I had gotten clear of in two days. Captain Barney sailed about the 17th, and left me quite alone. I continued in that unpleasant situation till the 20th, never at any time after my arrival at this place, daring to let my whale boat be in the water fifteen minutes unless I was in her myself, from a fear that some of my people would run away with her. I always hoisted her in on deck the moment I came along side, by which means I had the advantage of them; for should they run away with any other boat belonging to the ship, I could overtake them with the whale boat, which they very well knew. They were also well satisfied of the reasons why that boat was always kept on board, except when in my immediate use. During this time, I had no fear from them, except of their running away. Under these disadvantages the Spanish ship Tryal made her appearance on the morning of the 20th, as has been stated; and I had in the course of the day the satisfaction of seeing the great utility of good discipline. In every part of the business of the Tryal, not one disaffected word was spoken by the men, but all flew to obey the commands they received; and to their credit it should be recorded, that no men ever behaved

41

better than they, under such circumstances. When it is considered that we had but two boats, one a whale boat, and the other
built by ourselves, while on the coast of New Holland, which was
very little larger than the whale boat; both of them were clinker
built, one of cedar, and the other not much stouter; with only
twenty men to board and carry a ship, containing so many slaves,
made desperate by their situation; for they were certain, if taken,
to suffer death; and when arriving along side of the ship, they
might have staved the bottom of the boats, by heaving into them a
ballast stone or log of wood of twenty pounds: when all these
things are taken into view, the reader may conceive of the hazardous nature of the enterprise, and the skill and the intrepidity which
were requisite to carry it into execution.

On the afternoon of the 19th, before night, I sent the boatswain
with the large boat and seine to try if he could catch some fish;
he returned at night with but few, observing that the morning
would be better, if he went early. I then wished him to go as
early as he thought proper, and he accordingly went at four o'clock.
46.7 At sunrise, or about that time, the officer who commanded the
deck, came down to me while I was in my cot, with information
that a sail was just opening round the south point, or head of the
island. I immediately rose, went on deck, and observed that she
47.14 was too near the land, on account of a reef that lay off the head;
and at the same time remarked to my people, that she must be a
47.15,29 stranger, and I did not well understand what she was about. Some
of them observed that they did not know who she was, or what
she was doing; but that they were accustomed to see vessels
46.20 shew their colours, when coming into a port. I ordered the
47.33 whale boat to be hoisted out and manned, which was accordingly
47.38 done. Presuming the vessel was from sea, and had been many
47.39 days out, without perhaps fresh provisions, we put the fish which
had been caught the night before into the boat, to be presented if
necessary. Every thing being soon ready, as I thought the strange
ship was in danger, we made all the haste in our power to get on
48.1 board, that we might prevent her getting on the reefs; but before
48.4 we came near her, the wind headed her off, and she was doing well.
48.18 I went along side, and saw the decks were filled with slaves. As
49.25 soon as I got on deck, the captain, mate, people and slaves, crowded
49.28 around me to relate their stories, and to make known their griev-

ances; which could not but impress me with feelings of pity for 49.29,34
their sufferings. They told me they had no water, as is related in
their different accounts and depositions. After promising to relieve 51.19
all the wants they had mentioned, I ordered the fish to be put on
board, and sent the whale boat to our ship, with orders that the
large boat, as soon as she returned from fishing, should take a set
of gang casks to the watering place, fill them, and bring it for their
relief as soon as possible. I also ordered the small boat to take, 51.23
what fish the large one had caught, and what soft bread they had
baked, some pumpkins, some sugar, and bottled cider, and return to
me without delay. The boat left me on board the Spanish ship,
went to our own, and executed the orders; and returned to me
again about eleven o'clock. At noon the large boat came with 79.16
the water, which I was obliged to serve out to them myself, to
keep them from drinking so much as to do themselves injury. I
gave them at first one gill each, an hour after, half a pint, and the
third hour, a pint. Afterward, I permited them to drink as they
pleased. They all looked up to me as a benefactor; and as I was
deceived in them, I did them every possible kindness. Had it been
otherwise there is no doubt I should have fallen a victim to their
power. It was to my great advantage, that, on this occasion, the 115.21
temperament of my mind was unusually pleasant. The apparent
sufferings of those about me had softened my feelings into sympathy; or, doubtless my interference with some of their transactions 115.28
would have cost me my life. The Spanish captain had evidently lost 51.37
much of his authority over the slaves, whom he appeared to fear,
and whom he was unwilling in any case to oppose. An instance of 59.16
this occured in the conduct of the four cabin boys, spoken of by
the captain. They were eating with the slave boys on the main
deck, when, (as I was afterwards informed) the Spanish boys, feel- 112.40
ing some hopes of release, and not having prudence sufficient to
keep silent, some words dropped respecting their expectations, which
were understood by the slave boys. One of them gave a stroke 113.3
with a knife on the head of one of the Spanish boys, which penetrated to the bone, in a cut four inches in length. I saw this and 59.22
inquired what it meant. The captain replied, that it was merely
the sport of the boys, who had fallen out. I told him it appeared
to me to be rather serious sport, as the wound had caused the
boy to lose about a quart of blood. Several similar instances of

unruly conduct, which, agreeably to my manner of thinking, demanded immediate resistance and punishment, were thus easily
winked at, and passed over. I felt willing however to make some
51.35 allowance even for conduct so gross, when I considered them to
have been broken down with fatigue and long suffering.

The act of the negro, who kept constantly at the elbows of Don
Bonito and myself, I should, at any other time, have immediately
resented; and although it excited my wonder, that his commander
should allow this extraordinary liberty, I did not remonstrate against
it, until it became troublesome to myself. I wished to have some
private conversation with the captain alone, and the negro as usual
following us into the cabin, I requested the captain to send him on
deck, as the business about which we were to talk could not be
conveniently communicated in presence of a third person. I spoke
90.35 in Spanish, and the negro understood me. The captain assured
me, that his remaining with us would be of no disservice; that he
had made him his confidant and companion since he had lost so
90.37 many of his officers and men. He had introduced him to me before, as captain of the slaves, and told me he kept them in good
order. I was alone with them, or rather on board by myself, for
three or four hours, during the absence of my boat, at which time
the ship drifted out with the current three leagues from my own,
when the breeze sprung up from the south east. It was nearly
four o'clock in the afternoon. We ran the ship as near to the
Perseverance as we could without either ship's swinging afoul the
94.22 other. After the Spanish ship was anchored, I invited the captain
to go on board my ship and take tea or coffee with me. His answer was short and seemingly reserved; and his air very different
95.9 from that with which he had received my assistance. As I was at
a loss to account for this change in his demeanour, and knew he
had seen nothing in my conduct to justify it, and as I felt certain
that he treated me with intentional neglect; in return I became
less sociable, and said little to him. After I had ordered my boat
97.21 to be hauled up and manned, and as I was going to the side of the
vessel, in order to get into her, Don Bonito came to me, gave my
hand a hearty squeeze, and, as I thought, seemed to feel the weight
97.25 of the cool treatment with which I had retaliated. I had committed
a mistake in attributing his apparent coldness to neglect; and as
soon as the discovery was made, I was happy to rectify it, by a

prompt renewal of friendly intercourse. He continued to hold my 97.36
hand fast till I stepped off the gunwale down the side, when he let 98.5
it go, and stood making me compliments. When I had seated myself in the boat, and ordered her to be shoved off, the people
having their oars up on end, she fell off at a sufficient distance to
leave room for the oars to drop. After they were down, the Spanish captain, to my great astonishment, leaped from the gunwale of
the ship into the middle of our boat. As soon as he had recovered 98.10
a little, he called out in so alarming a manner, that I could not understand him; and the Spanish sailors were then seen jumping
overboard and making for our boat. These proceedings excited
the wonder of us all. The officer whom I had with me anxiously
inquired into their meaning. I smiled and told him, that I neither 98.16
knew, nor cared; but it seemed the captain was trying to impress
his people with a belief that we intended to run away with 99.8
him. At this moment one of my Portuguese sailors in the boat,
spoke to me, and gave me to understand what Don Bonito
said. I desired the captain to come aft and sit down by my side,
and in a calm deliberate manner relate the whole affair In the
mean time the boat was employed in picking up the men who had
jumped from the ship. They had picked up three, (leaving one in
the water till after the boat had put the Spanish captain and myself 99.34
on board my ship,) when my officer observed the cable was cut,
and the ship was swinging. I hailed the Perseverance, ordering
the ports got up, and the guns run out as soon as possible. We 100.9
pulled as fast as we could on board; and then despatched the boat
for the man who was left in the water, whom we succeeded to
save alive. 100.10

We soon had our guns ready; but the Spanish ship had dropped 100.12
so far astern of the Perseverance, that we could bring but one gun
to bear on her, which was the after one. This was fired six times,
without any other effect than cutting away the fore top-mast stay,
and some other small ropes which were no hindrance to her going 100.15
away. She was soon out of reach of our shot, steering out of the
bay. We then had some other calculations to make. Our ship
was moored with two bower anchors, which were all the cables or 100.19
anchors of that description we had. To slip and leave them would
be to break our policy of insurance by a deviation, against which
I would here caution the masters of all vessels. It should always

326 VOYAGES AND TRAVELS. [CHAP. XVIII.

be borne in mind, that to do any thing which will destroy the guaranty of their policies, how great soever may be the inducement, and how generous soever the motive, is not justifiable; for should any accident subsequently occur, whereby a loss might accrue to the underwriters, they will be found ready enough, and sometimes too ready, to avail themselves of the opportunity to be released from responsibility; and the damage must necessarily be sustained by the owners. This is perfectly right. The law has wisely restrained the powers of the insured, that the insurer should not be subject to imposition, or abuse. All bad consequences may be avoided by one who has a knowledge of his duty, and is disposed faithfully to obey its dictates.

100.20 At length, without much loss of time, I came to a determination
to pursue, and take the ship with my two boats. On inquiring of
the captain what fire arms they had on board the Tryal, he an-
100.25 swered, they had none which they could use; that he had put the
few they had out of order, so that they could make no defence
with them; and furthermore, that they did not understand their
use, if they were in order. He observed at the same time, that
100.28 if I attempted to take her with boats we should all be killed; for
the negros were such bravos and so desperate, that there would be
no such thing as conquering them. I saw the man in the situation
that I have seen others, frightened at his own shadow. This was
probably owing to his having been effectually conquered and his
100.32 spirits broken.

After the boats were armed, I ordered the men to get into them;
and they obeyed with cheerfulness. I was going myself, but Don
Bonito took hold of my hand and forbade me, saying, you have
100.36 saved my life, and now you are going to throw away your own.
Some of my confidential officers asked me if it would be prudent
for me to go, and leave the Perseverance in such an unguarded
state; and also, if any thing should happen to me, what would be
the consequence to the voyage. Every man on board, they observ-
100.38 ed, would willingly go, if it were my pleasure. I gave their remonstrances a moment's consideration, and felt their weight. I
101.2 then ordered into the boats my chief officer, Mr. Low, who commanded the party; and under him, Mr. Brown, my second officer;
my brother William, Mr. George Russell, son to major Benjamin
Russell of Boston, and Mr. Nathaniel Luther, midshipmen; William

1801.] COAST OF CHILI. 327

Clark, boatswain; Charles Spence, gunner; and thirteen seamen. 101.2
By way of encouragement, I told them that Don Bonito considered
the ship and what was in her as lost; that the value was more 101.5
than one hundred thousand dollars; that if we would take her, it
should be all our own; and that if we should afterwards be disposed to give him up one half, it would be considered as a present.
I likewise reminded them of the suffering condition of the poor
Spaniards remaining on board, whom I then saw with my spy-glass
as high aloft as they could get on the top-gallant-masts, and knowing that death must be their fate if they came down. I told them,
never to see my face again, if they did not take her; and these
were all of them pretty powerful stimulants. I wished God to
prosper them in the discharge of their arduous duty, and they 101.8
shoved off. They pulled after and came up with the Tryal, took 101.10
their station upon each quarter, and commenced a brisk fire of mus- 101.28
ketry, directing it as much at the man at the helm as they could,
as that was likewise a place of resort for the negroes. At length
they drove the chief mate from it, who had been compelled to steer 113.15
the ship. He ran up the mizen rigging as high as the cross jack
yard, and called out in Spanish, "Don't board." This induced our 113.18
people to believe that he favoured the cause of the negroes; they
fired at him, and two balls took effect; one of them went through
his side, but did not go deep enough to be mortal; and the other
went through one of his thighs. This brought him down on deck
again. They found the ship made such head way, that the boats
could hardly keep up with her, as the breeze was growing stronger. 101.34
They then called to the Spaniards, who were still as high aloft as
they could get, to come down on the yards, and cut away the
robings and earings of the topsails, and let them fall from the
yards, so that they might not hold any wind. They accordingly 101.39
did so. About the same time, the Spaniard who was steering the
ship, was killed; (he is sometimes called *passenger*, and sometimes
clerk, in the different depositions,) so that both these circumstances 102.2
combined, rendered her unmanageable by such people as were left
on board. She came round to the wind, and both boats boarded, 102.8
one on each bow, when she was carried by hard fighting. The
negroes defended themselves with desperate courage; and after 102.22
our people had boarded them, they found they had barricadoed
the deck by making a breast work of the water casks which we

328 VOYAGES AND TRAVELS. [CHAP. XVIII.

102.22 had left on board, and sacks of matta, abreast the mainmast, from
one side of the ship to the other, to the height of six feet; behind
102.25 which they defended themselves with all the means in their power
to the last; and our people had to force their way over this breast
work before they could compel them to surrender. The other
parts of the transaction have some of them been, and the remainder will be hereafter stated.

On going on board the next morning with hand-cuffs, leg-irons,
and shackled bolts, to secure the hands and feet of the negroes, the
sight which presented itself to our view was truly horrid. They
114.1 had got all the men who were living made fast, hands and feet, to
102.31 the ring bolts in the deck; some of them had part of their bowels
hanging out, and some with half their backs and thighs shaved off.
This was done with our boarding lances, which were always kept
114.3 exceedingly sharp, and as bright as a gentleman's sword. Whilst
putting them in irons, I had to exercise as much authority over the
Spanish captain and his crew, as I had to use over my own men on any
other occasion, to prevent them from cutting to pieces and killing
114.4 these poor unfortunate beings. I observed one of the Spanish sailors
had found a razor in the pocket of an old jacket of his, which one of the
114.6 slaves had on; he opened it, and made a cut upon the negro's head.
He seemed to aim at his throat, and it bled shockingly. Seeing several more about to engage in the same kind of barbarity, I commanded them not to hurt another one of them, on pain of being
114.7 brought to the gang-way and flogged. The captain also, I noticed,
had a dirk, which he had secreted at the time the negroes were massacreing the Spaniards. I did not observe, however, that he intended
to use it, until one of my people gave me a twitch by the elbow, to
114.9 draw my attention to what was passing, when I saw him in the act
of stabbing one of the slaves. I immediately caught hold of him,
took away his dirk, and threatened him with the consequences of
my displeasure, if he attempted to hurt one of them. Thus I was
obliged to be continually vigilant, to prevent them from using
violence towards these wretched creatures.

After we had put every thing in order on board the Spanish ship,
102.38 and swept for and obtained her anchors, which the negroes had cut
her from, we sailed on the 23d, both ships in company, for Conception, where we anchored on the 26th. After the common forms
were passed, we delivered the ship, and all that was on board her,

to the captain, whom we had befriended. We delivered him also a
bag of doubloons, containing, I presume, nearly a thousand; several
bags of dollars, containing a like number; and several baskets of
watches, some gold, and some silver: all of which had been
brought on board the Perseverance for safe keeping. We detained
no part of this treasure to reward us for the services we had rendered:—all that we received was faithfully returned.

After our arrival at Conception, I was mortified and very much
hurt at the treatment which I received from Don Bonito Sereno;
but had this been the only time that I ever was treated with ingratitude, injustice, or want of compassion, I would not complain. I will
only name one act of his towards me at this place. He went to
the prison and took the depositions of five of my Botany bay convicts, who had left us at St. Maria, and were now in prison here.
This was done by him with a view to injure my character, so that
he might not be obliged to make us any compensation for what we
had done for him. I never made any demand of, nor claimed in any
way whatever, more than that they should give me justice; and did
not ask to be my own judge, but to refer it to government. Amongst
those who swore against me were the three outlawed convicts,
who have been before mentioned. I had been the means, undoubtedly, of saving every one of their lives, and had supplied them
with clothes. They swore every thing against me they could to
effect my ruin. Amongst other atrocities, they swore I was a
pirate, and made several statements that would operate equally to
my disadvantage had they been believed; all of which were
brought before the viceroy of Lima against me. When we met at 102.39
that place, the viceroy was too great and too good a man to be
misled by these false representations. He told Don Bonito, that
my conduct towards him proved the injustice of these depositions,
taking his own official declaration at Conception for the proof of it;
that he had been informed by Don Jose Calminaries, who was com-
mandant of the marine, and was at that time, and after the affair of
the Tryal, on the coast of Chili; that Calminaries had informed
him how both Don Bonito and myself had conducted, and he was
satisfied that no man had behaved better, under all circumstances,
than the American captain had done to Don Bonito, and that he
never had seen or heard of any man treating another with so
much dishonesty and ingratitude as he had treated the American.

The viceroy had previously issued an order, on his own authority, to Don Bonito, to deliver to me eight thousand dollars as part payment for services rendered him. This order was not given till his Excellency had consulted all the tribunals holding jurisdiction over similar cases, except the twelve royal judges. These judges exercise a supreme authority over all the courts in Peru, and reserve to themselves the right of giving a final decision in all questions of law. Whenever either party is dissatisfied with the decision of the inferior courts in this kingdom, they have a right of appeal to the twelve judges. Don Bonito had attempted an appeal from the viceroy's order to the royal judges. The viceroy sent for me, and acquainted me of Don Bonito's attempt; at the same time recommending to me to accede to it, as the royal judges well understood the nature of the business, and would do much better for me than his order would. He observed at the same time, that they were men of too great characters to be biassed or swayed from doing justice by any party; they holding their appointments immediately from his majesty. He said, if I requested it, Don Bonito should be holden to his order. I then represented, that I had been in Lima nearly two months, waiting for different tribunals, to satisfy his Excellency what was safe for him, and best to be done for me, short of a course of law, which I was neither able nor willing to enter into; that I had then nearly thirty men on different islands, and on board my tender, which was then somewhere amongst the islands on the coast of Chili; that they had no method that I knew of to help themselves, or receive succour, except from me; and that if I was to defer the time any longer it amounted to a certainty, that they must suffer. I therefore must pray that his Excellency's order might be put in force.

Don Bonito, who was owner of the ship and part of the cargo, had been quibbling and using all his endeavours to delay the time of payment, provided the appeal was not allowed, when his Excellency told him to get out of his sight, that he would pay the money himself, and put him (Don Bonito) into a dungeon, where he should not see sun, moon, or stars; and was about giving the order, when a very respectable company of merchants waited on him and pleaded for Don Bonito; praying that his Excellency would favour him on account of his family, who were very rich and respectable. The viceroy remarked that Don Bonito's character had been such as to disgrace any family, that had any pretensions to respectability; but that he should grant their prayer, provided there was no more reason for complaint. The last transaction brought me the money in two hours; by which time I was extremely distressed, enough, I believe, to have punished me for a great many of my bad deeds.

When I take a retrospective view of my life, I cannot find in my soul, that I ever have done any thing to deserve such misery and ingratitude as I have suffered at different periods, and in general, from the very persons to whom I have rendered the greatest services.

103.9

The following Documents were officially translated, and are inserted without alteration, from the original papers. This I thought to be the most correct course, as it would give the reader a better view of the subject than any other method that could be adopted. My deposition and that of Mr. Luther, were communicated through a bad linguist, who could not speak the English language so well
as I could the Spanish, Mr. Luther not having any knowledge of 103.17
the Spanish language. The Spanish captain's deposition, together with Mr. Luther's and my own, were translated into English again, as now inserted; having thus undergone two translations. These circumstances, will, we hope, be a sufficient apology for any thing which may appear to the reader not to be perfectly consistent, one declaration with another; and for any impropriety of expression.

OFFICIAL DOCUMENTS.

A FAITHFUL TRANSLATION OF THE DEPOSITIONS OF DON BENITO CERENO, OF DON AMASA DELANO, AND OF DON NATHANIEL LUTHER, TOGETHER WITH THE DOCUMENTS OF THE COMMENCEMENT OF THE PRO-
103.26 CESS, UNDER THE KING'S SEAL.

I DON JOSE DE ABOS, and Padilla, his Majesty's Notary for the
103.29 Royal Revenue, and Register of this Province, and Notary Public of the Holy Crusade of this Bishoprick, &c.

Do certify and declare, as much as requisite in law, that, in the criminal cause, which by an order of the Royal Justice, Doctor DON JUAN MARTINEZ DE ROZAS, deputy assessor general of this province, conducted against the Senegal Negroes, that the ship Tryal was carrying from the port of Valparaiso, to that of Callao of Lima, in the month of December last. There is at the beginning of the prosecution, a decree in continuation of the declaration of her captain, Don Benito Cereno, and on the back of the twenty-sixth leaf, that of the captain of the American ship, the Perseverance, Amasa Delano; and that of the supercargo of this ship, Nathaniel Luther, midshipman, of the United States, on the thirtieth leaf; as also the Sentence of the aforesaid cause, on the back of the 72d leaf; and the confirmation of the Royal Audience, of this District, on the 78th and 79th leaves; and an official order of the Tribunal with which the cause and every thing else therein continued, is remitted back; which proceedings with a representation made by the said American captain, Amasa Delano, to this Intendency, against the Spanish captain of the ship Tryal, Don Benito Cereno, and answers thereto—are in the following manner—

103.30 *Decree of the Commencement of the Process.*

103.34 In the port of Talcahuane, the twenty-fourth of the month of February, one thousand eight hundred and five, Doctor Don Juan Martinez de Rozas, Counsellor of the Royal Audience of this Kingdom, Deputy Assessor, and learned in the law, of this Intendency,

having the deputation thereof on account of the absence of his
Lordship, the Governor Intendent—Said, that whereas the ship
Tryal, has just cast anchor in the road of this port, and her cap- 104.5
tain, Don Benito Cereno, has made the declaration of the twentieth
of December, he sailed from the port of Valparaiso, bound to 104.7
that of Callao; having his ship loaded with produce and merchan-
dize of the country, with sixty-three negroes of all sexes and ages,
and besides nine sucking infants; that the twenty-sixth, in the night,
revolted, killed eighteen of his men, and made themselves master
of the ship—that afterwards they killed seven men more, and
obliged him to carry them to the coast of Africa, at Senegal, of
which they were natives; that Tuesday the nineteenth, he put
into the island of Santa Maria, for the purpose of taking in water,
and he found in its harbour the American ship, the Perseverance,
commanded by captain Amasa Delano, who being informed of the
revolt of the negroes on board the ship Tryal, killed five or six of
them in the engagement, and finally overcame them; that the ship
being recovered, he supplied him with hands, and brought him to
this port.—Wherefore, for examining the truth of these facts, and
inflict on the guilty of such heinous crimes, the penalties provided
by law. He therefore orders that this decree commencing the
process, should be extended, that agreeably to its tenor, the witnesses, that should be able to give an account of them, be examined—
thus ordered by his honour, which I attest.—Doctor ROZAS.

Before me, Jose de Abos, and Padilla, his Majesty's Notary of
Royal Revenue and Registers.

103.33

Declaration of first Witness, Don Benito Cereno.

The same day and month and year, his Honour ordered the
captain of the ship Tryal, Don Benito Cereno, to appear, of whom 104.1
he received before me, the oath, which he took by God, our Lord,
and a Sign of the Cross, under which he promised to tell the truth
of whatever he should know and should be asked—and being in- 104.4
terrogated agreeably to the tenor of the act, commencing the process, he said, that the twentieth of December last, he set sail with
his ship from the port of Valparaiso, bound to that of Callao; load- 104.8
ed with the produce of the country, and seventy-two negroes of
both sexes, and of all ages, belonging to Don Alexandro Aranda,

104.10

inhabitant of the city of Mendosa; that the crew of the ship consisted of thirty-six men, besides the persons who went passengers;
104.15 that the negroes were of the following ages,—twenty from twelve
to sixteen years, one from about eighteen to nineteen years, named
Jose, and this was the man that waited upon his master Don Alexandro, who speaks well the Spanish, having had him four or five
104.20 years; a mulatto, named Francisco, native of the province of Buenos Ayres, aged about thirty-five years; a smart negro, named
Joaquin, who had been for many years among the Spaniards, aged
twenty six years, and a caulker by trade; twelve full grown negroes, aged from twenty-five to fifty years, all raw and born on the
104.24 coast of Senegal—whose names are as follow,—the first was named Babo, and he was killed,—the second who is his son, is named
104.29 Muri,—the third, Matiluqui,—the fourth, Yola,—the fifth, Yau,—the
sixth Atufal, who was killed,—the seventh, Diamelo, also killed,—
104.32 the eighth, Lecbe, likewise killed,—the ninth, Natu, in the same
manner killed, and that he does not recollect the names of the
104.35 others; but that he will take due account of them all, and remit to
104.37 the court; and twenty-eight women of all ages;—that all the negroes slept upon deck, as is customary in this navigation; and none
104.39 wore fetters, because the owner, Aranda told him that they were
105.1 all tractable; that the twenty-seventh of December, at three
o'clock in the morning, all the Spaniards being asleep except the
two officers on the watch, who were the boatswain Juan Robles,
and the carpenter Juan Balltista Gayete, and the helmsman and
105.5 his boy; the negroes revolted suddenly, wounded dangerously the
boatswain and the carpenter, and successively killed eighteen men
of those who were sleeping upon deck,—some with sticks and daggers, and others by throwing them alive overboard, after tying them;
that of the Spaniards who were upon deck, they left about seven,
105.9 as he thinks, alive and tied, to manœuvre the ship; and three or
four more who hid themselves, remained also alive, although in
the act of revolt, they made themselves masters of the hatchway,
six or seven wounded, went through it to the cock-pit without any
hindrance on their part; that in the act of revolt, the mate and
another person, whose name he does not recollect, attempted to
105.15 come up through the hatchway, but having been wounded at the
onset, they were obliged to return to the cabin; that the deponent resolved at break of day to come up the companion-way,

where the negro Babo was, being the ring leader, and another who 105.16
assisted him, and having spoken to them, exhorted them to cease
committing such atrocities—asking them at the same time what
they wanted and intended to do—offering himself to obey their 105.20
commands; that notwithstanding this, they threw, in his presence,
three men, alive and tied, overboard; that they told the deponent
to come up, and that they would not kill him—which having done,
they asked him whether there were in these seas any negro countries, where they might be carried, and he answered them, no; 105.25
that they afterwards told him to carry them to *Senegal*, or to the
neighbouring islands of St. Nicolas—and he answered them, that
this was imposible, on account of the great distance, the bad condition of the vessel, the want of provisions, sails and water; that 105.30
they replied to him, he must carry them in any way; that they
would do and conform themselves to every thing the deponent
should require as to eating and drinking, that after a long conference, being absolutely compelled to please them, for they threatened him to kill them all, if they were not at all events carried to 105.34
Senegal. He told them that what was most wanting for the voyage
was water; that they would go near the coast to take it, and thence
they would proceed on their course—that the negroes agreed to it;
and the deponent steered towards the intermediate ports, hoping
to meet some Spanish or foreign vessel that would save them; that
within ten or eleven days they saw the land, and continued their 105.40
course by it in the vicinity of Nasca; that the deponent observed
that the negroes were now restless, and mutinous, because he did
not effect the taking in of water, they having required with threats 106.1
that it should be done, without fail the following day; he told them
they saw plainly that the coast was steep, and the rivers designated
in the maps were not to be found, with other reasons suitable to
the circumstances; that the best way would be to go to the island
of Santa Maria, where they might water and victual easily, it being 106.5
a desert island, as the foreigners did; that the deponent did not go
to Pisco, that was near, nor make any other port of the coast, because the negroes had intimated to him several times, that they
would kill them all the very moment they should perceive any city,
town, or settlement, on the shores to which they should be carried; 106.10
that having determined to go to the island of Santa Maria, as the
deponent had planned, for the purpose of trying whether in the

106.11 336 VOYAGES AND TRAVELS. [CHAP. XVIII.
passage or in the island itself, they could find any vessel that should
favour them, or whether he could escape from it in a boat to the
106.15 neighbouring coast of Arruco. To adopt the necessary means he
immediately changed his course, steering for the island; that the
negroes held daily conferences, in which they discussed what was
necessary for their design of returning to Senegal, whether they
were to kill all the Spaniards, and particularly the deponent; that
106.19 eight days after parting from the coast of Nasca, the deponent
being on the watch a little after day-break, and soon after the
negroes had their meeting, the negro Mure came to the place
where the deponent was, and told him, that his comrades had de-
106.23 termined to kill his master, Don Alexandro Aranda, because they
said they could not otherwise obtain their liberty, and that he
106.31 should call the mate, who was sleeping, before they executed it,
for fear, as he understood, that he should not be killed with the
rest; that the deponent prayed and told him all that was necessary
106.34 in such a circumstance to dissuade him from his design, but all was
useless, for the negro Mure answered him, that the thing could not
be prevented, and that they should all run the risk of being killed
106.38 if they should attempt to dissuade or obstruct them in the act; that
in this conflict the deponent called the mate, and immediately the
106.40 negro Mure ordered the negro Matinqui, and another named Leche,
who died in the island of Santa Maria, to go and commit this murder; that the two negroes went down to the birth of Don Alexandro,
and stabbed him in his bed; that yet half alive and agonizing, they
dragged him on deck and threw him overboard; that the clerk,
Don Lorenzo Bargas, was sleeping in the opposite birth, and
awaking at the cries of Aranda, surprised by them, and at the sight
of the negroes, who had bloody daggers in their hands, he threw
107.10 himself into the sea through a window which was near him, and
was miserably drowned, without being in the power of the deponent to assist, or take him up, though he immediately put
out his boat; that a short time after killing Aranda, they got
107.15 upon deck his german-cousin, Don Francisco Masa, and his other
clerk, called Don Hermenegildo, a native of Spain, and a relation of the said Aranda, besides the boatswain, Juan Robles, the
boatswain's mate, Manuel Viscaya, and two or three others of
107.21 the sailors, all of whom were wounded, and having stabbed them
again, they threw them alive into the sea, although they made

no resistance, nor begged for any thing else but mercy; that 107.21
the boatswain, Juan Robles, who knew how to swim, kept himself
the longest above water, making acts of contrition, and in the last 107.24
words he uttered, charged this deponent to cause mass to be said
for his soul, to our Lady of Succour; that having finished this 108.2
slaughter, the negro Mure told him that they had now done all,
and that he might pursue his destination, warning him that they 108.5
would kill all the Spaniards, if they saw them speak, or plot any
thing against them—a threat which they repeated almost every
day; that before this occurrence last mentioned, they had tied
the cook to throw him overboard for I know not what thing they
heard him speak, and finally they spared his life at the request of 108.9
the deponent; that a few days after, the deponent endeavoured
not to omit any means to preserve their lives—spoke to them
peace and tranquillity, and agreed to draw up a paper, signed by
the deponent, and the sailors who could write, as also by the ne.
groes, Babo and Atufal, who could do it in their language, though 108.14
they were new, in which he obliged himself to carry them to
Senegal, and they not to kill any more, and to return to them the
ship with the cargo, with which they were for that satisfied and 108.32
quieted; that omitting other events which daily happened, and
which can only serve to recal their past misfortunes and conflicts, 108.34
after forty-two days navigation, reckoned from the time they sailed
from Nasca, during which they navigated under a scanty allowance
of water, they at last arrived at the island of Santa Maria, on
Tuesday the nineteenth instant, at about five o'clock in the afternoon, at which hour they cast anchor very near the American ship
Perseverance, which lay in the same port, commanded by the 108.40
generous captain Amasa Delano, but at seven o'clock in the morning 109.1
they had already descried the port, and the negroes became uneasy
as soon as they saw the ship, and the deponent, to appease and 109.8
quiet them, proposed to them to say and do all that he will declare to have said to the American captain, with which they were 109.10
tranquilized, warning him that if he varied in the least, or uttered
any word that should give the least intimation of the past occur- 109.12
rences, they would instantly kill him and all his companions; that 109.35
about eight o'clock in the morning, captain Amasa Delano came in
his boat, on board the Tryal, and all gladly received him; that 109.38
the deponent, acting then the part of an owner and a free captain

43

109.39

109.42 of the ship, told them that he came from Buenos Ayres, bound to
Lima, with that parcel of negroes; that at the cape many had
died, that also, all the sea officers and the greatest part of the crew
had died, there remained to him no other sailors than these few
who were in sight, and that for want of them the sails had been
torn to pieces; that the heavy storms off the cape had obliged them
to throw overboard the greatest part of the cargo, and the water
pipes; that consequently he had no more water; that he had
thought of putting into the port of Conception, but that the north
wind had prevented him, as also the want of water, for he had only
enough for that day, concluded by asking of him supplies;—that
the *generous captain Amasa Delano* immediately offered them sails,
pipes, and whatever he wanted, to pursue his voyage to Lima,
without entering any other port, leaving it to his pleasure to re-
fund him for these supplies at Callao, or pay him for them if he
thought best; that he immediately ordered his boat for the pur-
110.6 pose of bringing him water, sugar, and bread, as they did; that
Amasa Delano remained on board the Tryal all the day, till he left
the ship anchored at five o'clock in the afternoon, deponent speaking to him always of his pretended misfortunes, under the fore-
110.10 mentioned principles, without having had it in his power to tell a
single word, nor giving him the least hint, that he might know the
truth, and state of things; because the negro Mure, who is a man
of capacity and talents, performing the office of an officious servant,
with all the appearance of submission of the humble slave, did not
110.14 leave the deponent one moment, in order to observe his actions
and words; for he understands well the Spanish, and besides there
were thereabout some others who were constantly on the watch
and understood it also; that a moment in which Amasa Delano left
the deponent, Mure asked him, how do we come on? and the deponent answered them, well; he gives us all the supplies we want;
but he asked him afterwards how many men he had, and the deponent told him that he had thirty men; but that twenty of them
were on the island, and there were in the vessel only those whom
110.28 he saw there in the two boats; and then the negro told him, well,
110.36 you will be the captain of this ship to night and his also, for three
negroes are sufficient to take it; that as soon as they had cast anchor, at five of the clock, as has been stated, the American captain
took leave, to return to his vessel, and the deponent accompanied

1801.] COAST OF CHILI 339
110.41
him as far as the gunwale, where he staid under pretence of taking 111.1
leave, until he should have got into his boat; but on shoving off,
the deponent jumped from the gunwale into the boat and fell into
it, without knowing how, and without sustaining, fortunately, any
harm; but he immediately hallooed to the Spaniards in the ship,
"Overboard, those that can swim, the rest to the rigging." That
he instantly told the captain, by means of the Portuguese interpreter, that they were revolted negroes, who had killed all his
people; that the said captain soon understood the affair, and recovered from his surprise, which the leap of the deponent occasioned, and told him, "Be not afraid, be not afraid, set down and 99.33
be easy," and ordered his sailors to row towards his ship, and be- 100.12
fore coming up to her, he hailed, to get a cannon ready and run it 100.9
out of the port hole, which they did very quick, and fired with it a
few shots at the negroes; that in the mean while the boat was sent
to pick up two men who had thrown themselves overboard, which 99.34
they effected; that the negroes cut the cables, and endeavoured
to sail away; that Amasa Delano, seeing them sailing away, and
the cannon could not subdue them, ordered his people to get muskets, pikes, and sabres ready, and all his men offered themselves
willingly to board them with the boats; that captain Amasa Delano
wanted to go in person, and was going to embark the first, but the
deponent prevented him, and after many entreaties he finally remained, saying, though that circumstance would procure him much
honour, he would stay to please him, and keep him company in his
affliction, and would send a brother of his, on whom he said he
placed as much reliance as on himself; his brother, the mates,
and eighteen men, whom he had in his vessel, embarked in the two
boats, and made their way towards the Tryal, which was already
under sail; that they rowed considerably in pursuing the ship,
and kept up a musketry fire; but that they could not overtake 101.34
them, until they hallooed to the sailors on the rigging, to unbend
or take away the sails, which they accordingly did, letting them
fall on the deck; that they were then able to lay themselves along-
side, keeping up constantly a musketry fire, whilst some got up 102.9
the sides on deck, with pikes and sabres, and the others remained
in the stern of the boat, keeping up also a fire, until they got up
finally by the same side, and engaged the negroes, who defended
themselves to the last with their weapons, rushing upon the points

102.30 340 VOYAGES AND TRAVELS. [CHAP. XVIII.

of the pikes with an extraordinary fury; that the Americans killed
five or six negroes, and these were Babo, Atufal, Dick, Natu, Qiamolo,
molo, and does not recollect any other; that they wounded several
others, and at last conquered and made them prisoners; that at ten
o'clock at night, the first mate with three men, came to inform the
captain that the ship had been taken, and came also for the purpose of being cured of a dangerous wound, made by a point of a
102.34 dagger, which he had received in his breast; that two other Ameri-
102.38 can had been slightly wounded; the captain left nine men to take
care of the ship as far as this port; he accompanied her with his
own until both ships, the Tryal and Perseverance, cast anchor between nine and eleven o'clock in the forenoon of this day; that
the deponent has not seen the twenty negroes, from twelve to sixteen years of age, have any share in the execution of the mur-
111.12 ders; nor does he believe they have had, on account of their
age, although all were knowing to the insurrection; that the negro
Jose, eighteen years old, and in the service of Don Alexandro, was
111.15 the one who communicated the information to the negro Mure
and his comrades, of the state of things before the revolt; and
this is known, because in the preceding nights he used to come to
111.19 sleep from below, where they were, and had secret conversations
with Mure, in which he was seen several times by the mate; and
one night he drove him away twice; that this same negro Jose,
111.27 was the one who advised the other negroes to kill his master, Don
Alexandro; and that this is known, because the negroes have said
it; that on the first revolt, the negro Jose was upon deck with the
111.24 other revolted negroes, but it is not known whether he materially
participated in the murders; that the mulatto Francisco was of the
band of revolters, and one of their number; that the negro Joaquin
was also one of the worst of them, for that on the day the ship was
taken, he assisted in the defence of her with a hatchet in one hand
111.34 and a dagger in the other, as the sailors told him; that in sight of
the deponent, he stabbed Don Francisco Masa, when he was carrying him to throw him overboard alive, he being the one who
held him fast; that the twelve or thirteen negroes, from twenty-
five to fifty years of age, were with the former, the principal revolters, and committed the murders and atrocities before related;
that five or six of them were killed, as has been said, in the attack
on the ship, and the following remained alive and are prisoners,—

1801.] COAST OF CHILI 341

to wit—Mure, who acted as captain and commander of them, and
on all the insurrections and posterior events, Matinqui, Alathano,
Yau, Luis, Mapenda, Yola, Yambaio, being eight in number, and
with Jose, Joaquin, and Francisco, who are also alive, making the 112.9
number of eleven of the remaining insurgents; that the negresses
of age, were knowing to the revolt, and influenced the death of 112.14
their master; who also used their influence to kill the deponent;
that in the act of murder, and before that of the engagement of the
ship, they began to sing, and were singing a very melancholy song
during the action, to excite the courage of the negroes; that the
statement he has just given of the negroes who are alive, has been 112.21
made by the officers of the ship; that of the thirty-six men of the
crew and passengers, which the deponent had knowledge of, twelve 112.23
only including the mate remained alive, besides four cabin boys,
who were not included in that number; that they broke an arm of 112.25
one of those cabin boys, named Francisco Raneds, and gave him
three or four stabs, which are already healed; that in the engage- 113.14
ment of the ship, the second clerk, Don Josi Morairi, was killed
by a musket ball fired at him through accident, for having incautiously presented himself on the gunwale; that at the time of the 113.20
attack of the ship, Don Joaquin Arambaolaza was on one of the
yards flying from the negroes, and at the approach of the boats, he
hallooed by order of the negroes, not to board, on which account 113.18
the Americans thought he was also one of the revolters, and fired
two balls at him, one passed through one of his thighs, and the
other in the chest of his body, of which he is now confined, though
the American captain, who has him on board, says he will recover;
that in order to be able to proceed from the coast of Nasca, to the
island of Santa Maria, he saw himself obliged to lighten the ship,
by throwing more than one third of the cargo overboard, for he 114.12
could not have made that voyage otherwise; that what he has said
is the most substantial of what occurs to him on this unfortunate
event, and the truth, under the oath that he has taken;—which 114.14
declaration he affirmed and ratified, after hearing it read to him. 114.16
He said that he was twenty-nine years of age;—and signed with
his honour—which I certify. 114.21

BENITO CERENO.

Doctor ROZAS.

Before me.—Padilla.

RATIFICATION.

In the port of Talcahuano, the first day of the month of March, in the year one thousand eight hundred and five,—the same Honourable Judge of this cause caused to appear in his presence the captain of the ship Tryal, Don Benito Cereno, of whom he received an oath, before me, which he took conformably to law, under which he promised to tell the truth of what he should know, and of what he should be asked, and having read to him the foregoing declaration, and being asked if it is the same he has given and whether he has to add or to take off any thing,—he said, that it is the same he has given, that he affirms and ratifies it; and has only to add, that the new negroes were thirteen, and the females comprehended twenty-seven, without including the infants, and that one of them died from hunger or thirst, and two young negroes of those from twelve to sixteen, together with an infant. And he signed it with his honour—which I certify.

BENITO CERENO.

DOCTOR ROZAS.

Before me.—PADILLA.

Declaration of DON AMASA DELANO.

The same day, month and year, his Honour, ordered the captain of the American ship Perseverance to appear, whose oath his Honour received, which he took by placing his right hand on the Evangelists, under which he promised to tell the truth of what he should know and be asked—and being interrogated according to the decree, beginning this process, through the medium of the interpreter Carlos Elli, who likewise swore to exercise well and lawfully his office, that the nineteenth or twentieth of the month, as he believes, agreeably to the calculation he keeps from the eastward, being at the island of Santa Maria, at anchor, he descried at seven o'clock in the morning, a ship coming round the point;

1801.] COAST OF CHILI. 343

that he asked his crew what ship that was; they replied that they did not know her; that taking his spy-glass he perceived she bore no colours; that he took his barge, and his net for fishing, and went on board of her, that when he got on deck he embraced the Spanish captain, who told him that he had been four months and twenty six days from Buenoes Ayres; that many of his people had died of the scurvy, and that he was in great want of supplies—particularly pipes for water, duck for sails, and refreshment for his crew; that the deponent offered to give and supply him with every thing he asked and wanted; that the Spanish captain did nothing else, because the ringleader of the negroes was constantly at their elbows, observing what was said. That immediately he sent his barge to his own ship to bring, (as they accordingly did) water, peas, bread, sugar, and fish. That he also sent for his long boat to bring a load of water, and having brought it, he returned to his own ship; that in parting he asked the Spanish captain to come on board his ship to take coffee, tea, and other refreshments; but he answered him with coldness and indifference; that he could not go then, but that he would in two or three days. That at the same time he visited him, the ship Tryal cast anchor in the port, about four o'clock in the afternoon,—that he told his people belonging to his boat to embark in order to return to his ship, that the deponent also left the deck to get into his barge,—that on getting into the barge, the Spanish captain took him by the hand and immediately gave a jump on board his boat,—that he then told him that the negroes of the Tryal had taken her, and had murdered twenty-five men, which the deponent was informed of through the medium of an interpreter, who was with him, and a Portuguese; that two or three other Spaniards threw themselves into the water, who were picked up by his boats; that he immediately went to his ship, and before reaching her, called to the mate to prepare and load the guns; that having got on board, he fired at them with his cannon, and this same deponent pointed six shots at the time the negroes of the Tryal were cutting away the cables and setting sail; that the Spanish captain told him that the ship was already going away, and that she could not be taken; that the deponent replied that he would take her; then the Spanish captain told him that if he took her, one half of her value would be his, and the other half would remain to the real owners; that thereupon he ordered the people 46.19

belonging to his crew, to embark in the two boats, armed with knives, pistols, sabres, and pikes, to pursue her, and board her; that the two boats were firing at her near an hour with musketry, and at the end boarded and captured her; and that before sending his boats, he told his crew, in order to encourage them, that the Spanish captain offered to give them the half of the value of the Tryal if they took her. That having taken the ship, they came to anchor at about two o'clock in the morning very near the deponent's, leaving in her about twenty of his men; that his first mate received a very dangerous wound in his breast made with a pike, of which he lies very ill; that three other sailors were also wounded with clubs, though not dangerously; that five or six of the negroes were killed in boarding; that at six o'clock in the morning, he went with the Spanish captain on board the Tryal, to carry manacles and fetters from his ship, ordering them to be put on the negroes who remained alive, he dressed the wounded, and accompained the Tryal to the anchoring ground; and in it he delivered her up manned from his csew; for until that moment he remained in possession of her; that what he has said is what he knows, and the truth, under the oath he has taken, which he affirmed and ratified after the said declaration had been read to him,—saying he was forty-two years of age,—the interpreter did not sign it because he said he did not know how—the captain signed it with his honour—which I certify.

AMASA DELANO.

DOCTOR ROZAS.

Before me.—PADILLA.

RATIFICATION.

The said day, month and year, his Honour ordered the captain of the American ship, Don Amasa Delano to appear, of whom his Honour received an oath, which he took by placing his hand on the Evangelists, under which he promised to tell the truth of what he should know, and he asked, and having read to him the foregoing declaration, through the medium of the interpreter, Ambrosio Fernandez, who likewise took an oath to exercise well and faithfully his office,—he said that he affirms and ratifies the same; that he has nothing to add or diminish, and he signed it, with his Honour, and likewise the Interpreter.

AMASA DELANO.

AMBROSIO FERNANDEZ.

DOCTOR ROZAS.

Before me.—PADILLA.

Declaration of DON NATHANIEL LUTHER, *Midshipman.*

The same day, month and year, his Honour ordered Don Nathaniel Luther, first midshipman of the American ship Perseverance, and acting as clerk to the captain, to appear, of whom he received an oath, and which he took by placing his right hand on the Evangelists, under which he promised to tell the truth of what he should know and be asked, and being interrogated agreeably to the decree commencing this process, through the medium of the Interpreter Carlos Elli, he said that the deponent himself was one that boarded, and helped to take the ship Tryal in the boats; that he knows that his captain, Amasa Delano, has deposed on every thing that happened in this affair; that in order to avoid delay he requests that his declaration should be read to him, and he will tell whether it is comformable to the happening of the events; that if any thing should be omitted he will observe it, and add to it, doing the same if he erred in any part thereof; and his Honour having acquiesced in this proposal, the Declaration made this day by captain Amasa Delano, was read to him through the medium of the Interpreter, and said, that the deponent went with his captain, Amasa Delano, to the ship Tryal, as soon as she appeared at the point of the island, which was about seven o'clock in the morning, and remained with him on board of her, until she cast anchor; that the deponent was one of those who boarded the ship Tryal in the boats, and by this he knows that the narration which the captain has made in the deposition which has been read to him, is certain and exact in all its parts; and he has only three things to add: the first, that whilst his captain remained on board the Tryal, a negro stood constantly at his elbow, and by the side of the deponent, the second, that the deponent was in the boat, when the Spanish captain jumped into it, and when the Portuguese declared that the negroes had revolted; the third, that the number of killed was six, five negroes and a Spanish sailor; that what he has said is the truth, under the oath which he has taken; which he affirmed and ratified, after his Declaration had been read to him; he said he was twenty one years of age, and signed it with his Honour, but the Interpreter did not sign it, because he said he did not know how—which I certify,

NATHANIEL LUTHER

DOCTOR ROZAS.

Before me.—PADILLA.

RATIFICATION.

The aforesaid day, month and year, his Honour, ordered Don Nathaniel Luther, first midshipman of the American ship Perseverance, and acting as clerk to the captain, to whom he administred an oath, which he took by placing his hand on the Evangelists, under the sanctity of which he promised to tell the truth of what he should know and be asked; and the foregoing Declaration having been read to him, which he thoroughly understood, through the medium of the Interpreter, Ambrosio Fernandez, to whom an oath was likewise administred, to exercise well and faithfully his office, he says that he affirms and ratifies the same, that he has nothing to add or diminish, and he signed it with his Honour, and the Interpreter, which I certify.

NATHANIEL LUTHER.

AMBROSIO FERNANDEZ.

DOCTOR ROZAS.

Before me.—PADILLA.

SENTENCE.

In this city of Conception, the second day of the month of
March, of one thousand eight hundred and five, his Honour Doctor Don Juan Martinez de Rozas, Deputy Assessor and learned in
the law, of this intendency, having the execution thereof on account of the absence of his Honour, the principal having seen the
proceedings, which he has conducted officially against the negroes
of the ship Tryal, in consequence of the insurrection and atrocities which they have committed on board of her.—He declared,
that the insurrection and revolt of said negroes, being sufficiently
substantiated, with premeditated intent, the twenty seventh of
December last, at three o'clock in the morning; that taking by
surprise the sleeping crew, they killed eighteen men, some with
sticks, and daggers, and others by throwing them alive overboard;
that a few days afterward with the same deliberate intent, they
stabbed their master Don Alexandro Aranda, and threw Don Fran-
ciso Masa, his german cousin, Hermenegildo, his relation, and the
other wounded persons who were confined in the births, overboard
alive; that in the island of Santa Maria, they defended themselves
with arms, against the Americans, who attempted to subdue them,
causing the death of Don Jose Moraira the second clerk, as they
had done that of the first, Don Lorenzo Bargas; the whole being
considered, and the consequent guilts resulting from those henious
and atrocious actions as an example to others, he ought and did
condemn the negroes, Mure, Matinqui, Alazase, Yola, Joaquin,
Luis, Yau, Mapenda, and Yambaio, to the common penalty of death,
which shall be executed, by taking them out and dragging them 116.36
from the prison, at the tail of a beast of burden, as far as the gil-
bet, where they shall be hung until they are dead, and to the for-
feiture of all their property, if they should have any, to be applied to the Royal Treasury; that the heads of the five first be cut 116.38
off after they are dead, and be fixed on a pole, in the square of 116.37
the port of Talcahuano, and the corpses of all be burnt to ashes.
The negresses and young negroes of the same gang shall be present at the execution, if they should be in that city at the time
thereof; that he ought and did condemn likewise, the negro Jose,
servant to said Don Alexandro, and Yambaio, Francisco, Rodriguez,

to ten years confinement in the place of Valdivia, to work chained, on allowance and without pay, in the work of the King, and also to attend the execution of the other criminals; and judging definitively by this sentence thus pronounced and ordered by his Honour, and that the same should be executed notwithstanding the appeal, for which he declared there was no cause, but that an account of it should be previously sent to the Royal Audience of this district, for the execution thereof with the costs.

DOCTOR ROZAS.

Before me.—JOSE' DE ABOS PADILLA.

His Majesty's Notary of the Royal Revenue and Registers.

CONFIRMATION OF THE SENTENCE.

SANTIAGO, *March the twenty first, of one thousand eight hundred and five.*

Having duly considered the whole, we suppose the sentence pronounced by the Deputy Assessor of the City of Conception, to whom we remit the same for its execution and fulfilment, with the official resolution, taking first an authenticated copy of the proceedings, to give an account thereof to his Majesty: and in regard to the request of the acting Notary, to the process upon the pay of his charges, he will exercise his right when and where he shall judge best.—

There are four flourishes.

Their Honours, the President, Regent, and Auditors of his Royal Audience passed the foregoing decree, and those on the Margin set their flourishes, the day of this date, the twenty first of March, one thousand eight hundred and five;—which I certify,

ROMAN.

NOTIFICATION.

The twenty third of said mouth, I acquainted his Honour, the King's Attorney of the foregoing decree,—which I certify,

ROMAN.

OFFICIAL RESOLUTION.

The Tribunal has resolved to manifest by this official resolve and pleasure for the exactitude, zeal and promptness which you have discovered in the cause against the revolted negroes of the ship Tryal, which process it remits to you, with the approbation of the sentence for the execution thereof, forewarning you that before its completion, you may agree with the most Illustrious Bishop, on the subject of furnishing the spiritual aids to those miserable beings, affording the same to them with all possible dispatch.—At the same time this Royal Audience has thought fit in case you should have an opportunity of speaking with the Bostonian captain, Amasa Delano, to charge you to inform him, that they will give an account to his Majesty, of the generous and benevolent conduct which he displayed in the punctual assistance that he afforded the Spanish captain of the aforesaid ship, for the suitable manifestation, publication and noticety of such a memorable event. God preserve you many years.

SANTIAGO, *March the twenty second, of one thousand eight hundred and five.*

JOSE' DE SANTIAGO CONCHA.

DOCTOR DON JUAN MARTINEZ DE ROZAS,

Deputy assessor, and learned in the Law, of the Intendency of Conception.

I the undesigned, sworn Interpreter of languages, do certify that the foregoing translation from the Spanish original, is true.

FRANCIS SALES.

Boston, April 15th, 1808.

N. B. It is proper here to state, that the difference of two days, in the dates of the process at Talquahauno, that of the Spaniards being the 24th of February and ours the 26th, was because they dated theirs the day we anchored in the lower harbour, which was one day before we got up abreast of the port, at which time we dated ours; and our coming by the way of the Cape of Good Hope, made our reckoning of time one day different from theirs.

It is also necessary to remark, that the statement in page 332, respecting Mr. Luther being supercargo, and United States midshipman, is a mistake of the linguist. He was with me, the same as Mr. George Russell, and my brother William, midshipmen of the ship Perseverance.

On my return to America in 1807, I was gratified in receiving a polite letter from the Marquis De Case Yruso, through the medium of Juan Stoughton Esq. expressing the satisfaction of his majesty, the king of Spain, on account of our conduct in capturing the Spanish ship Tryal at the island St. Maria, accompanied with a gold medal, having his majesty's likeness on one side, and on the other the inscription, Reward of Merit. The correspondence relating to that subject, I shall insert for the satisfaction of the reader. I had been assured by the president of Chili, when I was in that country, and likewise by the viceroy of Lima, that all my conduct, and the treatment I had received, should be faithfully represented to his majesty Charles IV, who most probably would do something more for me. I had reason to expect, through the medium of so many powerful friends as I had procured at different times and places, and on different occasions, that I should most likely have received something essentially to my advantage. This probably would have been the case had it not been for the unhappy catastrophe which soon after took place in Spain, by the dethronement of Charles IV, and the distracted state of the Spanish government, which followed that event.

Philadelphia, 8th September, 1806.

Sir,

His Catholic Majesty the king of Spain, my master, having been informed by the audience of Chili of your noble and generous conduct in rescuing, off the island St. Maria, the Spanish merchant ship Tryal, captain Don Benito Cereno, with the cargo of slaves, who had mutinized, and cruelly massacred the greater part of the Spaniards on board; and by humanely supplying them afterwards with water and provisions, which they were in need of, has desired me to express to you, sir, the high sense he entertains of the spirited, humane, and successful effort of yourself and the brave crew of the Perseverance, under your command, in saving the lives of his subjects thus exposed, and in token whereof, his majesty has directed me to present to you the golden medal, with his likeness, which will be handed to you by his consul in Boston. At the same time permit me, sir, to assure you I feel particular satisfaction in being the organ of the grateful sentiments of my sovereign, on an occurrence which reflects so much honour on your character.

I have the honour to be, sir,

Your obedient servant,

(Signed) Marquis De CASE YRUSO.

Captain Amasa Delano, *of the American Ship Perseverance, Boston.*

Boston, August, 1807.

SIR,

WITH sentiments of gratitude I acknowledge the receipt of your Excellency's much esteemed favour of September 8th, conveying to me the pleasing information of his Catholic Majesty having been informed of the conduct of myself and the crew of the Perseverance under my command. It is peculiarly gratifying to me, to receive such honours from your Excellency's sovereign, as entertaining a sense of my spirit and honour, and successful efforts of myself and crew in saving the lives of his subjects; and still more so by receiving the token of his royal favour in the present of the golden medal bearing his likeness. The services rendered off the island St. Maria were from pure motives of humanity. They shall ever be rendered his Catholic Majesty's subjects when wanted, and it is in my power to grant. Permit me, sir, to thank your Excellency for the satisfaction that you feel in being the organ of the grateful sentiments of your sovereign on this occasion, and believe me, it shall ever be my duty publicly to acknowledge the receipt of such high considerations from such a source.

I have the honour to be

Your Excellency's most obedient,

And devoted humble servant,

(Signed) AMASA DELANO.

His Excellency the Marquis DE CASE YRUSO.

Consular Office, 30*th July*, 1807.

SIR,

UNDER date of September last, was forwarded me the enclosed letter from his Excellency the Marquis DE CASE YRUSO, his Catholic Majesty's minister plenipotentiary to the United States of America, which explains to you the purport of the commission with which I was then charged, and until now have anxiously waited for the pleasing opportunity of carrying into effect his Excellency's orders, to present to you at the same time the gold medal therein mentioned.

It will be a pleasing circumstance to that gentleman, to be informed of your safe arrival, and my punctuality in the discharge of that duty so justly owed to the best of sovereigns, under whose benignity and patronage I have the honour to subscribe myself, with great consideration, and much respect, sir,

Your obedient humble servant,

(Signed) JUAN STOUGHTON,

Consul of his Catholic majesty,
Residing at Boston.

Amasa Delano, *Esq.*

Boston, August 8th, 1807.

Sir,

I feel particular satisfaction in acknowledging the receipt of your esteemed favour, bearing date the 30th ult. covering a letter from the Marquis De Case Yruso, his Catholic Majesty's minister plenipotentiary to the United States of America, together with the gold medal bearing his Catholic Majesty's likeness.

Permit me, sir, to return my most sincere thanks for the honours I have received through your medium, as well as for the generous, friendly treatment you have shown on the occasion. I shall ever consider it one of the first honours publicly to acknowledge them as long as I live.

These services rendered his Catholic Majesty's subjects off the island St. Maria, with the men under my command, were from pure motives of humanity. The like services we will ever render, if wanted, should it be in our power.

With due respect, permit me, sir, to subscribe myself,

Your most obedient, and

Very humble servant,

(Signed) AMASA DELANO.

To Don Juan Stoughton *Esq. his Catholic Majesty's Consul, residing in Boston.*

COLOPHON

THE TEXT *of the Northwestern-Newberry Edition of* THE WRITINGS OF HERMAN MELVILLE *is set in eleven-point Monophoto Bembo, two points leaded. This exceptionally handsome type face is a modern rendering of designs made by Francesco Griffo for the office of Aldus Manatius in Venice and first used for the printing, in 1495, of the tract* De Aetna *by Cardinal Pietro Bembo. The display face is Bruce Rogers's Centaur, a twentieth-century design based on and reflective of the late-fifteenth-century Venetian models of Nicolas Jenson.*

This volume was composed by William Clowes & Sons, Ltd., of Beccles, Suffolk, England. It was printed and bound by Bookcrafters, Inc., of Chelsea, Michigan. The typography and binding design of the edition are by Paul Randall Mize.